A New Collection of
Three Complete Novels

JANELLE TAYLOR

A New Collection of
Three Complete Novels

JANELLE TAYLOR

Bittersweet Ecstasy

Forever Ecstasy

Savage Conquest

WINGS BOOKS

NEW YORK • AVENEL, NEW JERSEY

This omnibus was originally published in separate volumes under the titles:

Bittersweet Ecstasy, copyright © 1987 by Janelle Taylor.
Forever Ecstasy, copyright © 1991 by Janelle Taylor.
Savage Conquest, copyright © 1985 by Janelle Taylor.

This 1994 edition is published by Wings Books,
distributed by Random House Value Publishing, Inc.,
40 Engelhard Avenue, Avenel, New Jersey 07001,
by arrangement with Zebra Books, an imprint of Kensington Publishing Corp.

Random House
New York • Toronto • London • Sydney • Auckland

Printed and bound in the United States of America

Library of Congress Cataloging-in-Publication Data

Taylor, Janelle.
    [Novels. Selections]
    A new collection of three complete novels / Janelle Taylor.
      p.   cm.
    Contents: Bittersweet ecstasy—Forever ecstasy—Savage conquest.
    ISBN 0-517-12205-7
    1. Indians of North America—Great Plains—Fiction. 2. Man-woman relationships—
Great Plains—Fiction. 3. Historical fiction, American. 4. Love stories, American. I. Title.
PS3570.A934A6   1994
813'.54—dc20   94-26087
                                                                                CIP

8 7 6 5 4 3 2 1

Contents

BITTERSWEET ECSTASY
1

FOREVER ECSTASY
257

SAVAGE CONQUEST
553

Bittersweet Ecstasy

"To every thing there is a season,

And a time to every purpose under heaven:
A time to be born, and a time to die; . . .
A time to kill, and a time to heal; a time to destroy;
* a time to rebuild;*
A time to cry; and a time to laugh; a time to
* grieve, and a time to dance; . . .*
A time to get; and a time to lose; a time to keep,
* and a time to cast away;*
* . . . a time to be quiet; and a time to speak up;*
A time to love; and a time to hate; a time for war,
* and a time for peace . . . "*

—Ecclesiastes 3:1-8

And *bittersweet* are those times in which Fate intercedes, when all we seek is the blissful *ecstasy* of love and peace.

Prologue

In 1776, while the conflict between the whites and Indians was raging into a bitter war which would last for over one hundred years, a wagon train, led by Joe Kenny, brought nineteen-year-old Alisha Williams to the vast Dakota Territory. She was thrown into the perilous life of Gray Eagle, a Lakota Sioux warrior who fiercely defended his lands and people against the white invasion. For weeks, the English beauty doubted her survival and sanity at the hands of the legendary warrior who took her captive, but theirs became a love and passion too powerful and consuming to resist.

Tragically and greedily, the whites refused to leave the Indians in peace or to honor their treaties with them. Months after her capture, Alisha was *rescued* by the cavalry, then forced to endure more anguish and perils from soldiers and settlers who felt it was better for a white woman to be tortured and slain rather than to survive Indian captivity. At the fort, Alisha met Lieutenant Jeffery Gordon and a half-breed scout named Powchutu: who desired her, who soon lost her to their mutual foe Gray Eagle, and who nearly destroyed her in their quests for revenge.

Kind fate and a bold Indian bluff returned Alisha to the Oglala chief's son. Disregarding his people's resistance and dismay, especially the feelings of his promised one, Chela, who tried to slay the white girl who was stealing her place and love, Gray Eagle claimed Alisha as his own. After Alisha was alleged to be Shalee, the daughter of a white captive and a Blackfeet chief who had been kidnapped by whites and had been missing since age two, she was taken away from her captor and told to marry Black Cloud's adopted son, Brave Bear. Given a path to honorable possession when his love was proclaimed Shalee, Gray Eagle fought a death challenge to obtain her return and hand in marriage. Having won, she was forced to "join" Gray Eagle in a marriage which entwined their destinies and sealed her false identity as Princess Shalee, a mistaken identity which she allowed to stand for many reasons. To prevent trouble in the Oglala camp, Gray Eagle gave Chela to Brave Bear as his wife, never imagining how many times and ways their paths and bloodlines would cross.

Shalee doubted Gray Eagle's sudden claim of love; she was bewildered by his marriage to her; and she mistrusted his incredible acceptance of her as Black

Cloud's long-lost daughter, for he knew she was not the real Shalee. Confused and frightened, she was misled by her friend Powchutu, who had become as a brother to her during her tormenting sojourn at the fort. Powchutu tricked her into fleeing her new husband and into returning to St. Louis, where he hoped to win her for himself. Powchutu never told her that he had shot Gray Eagle in order for them to escape the Dakota Territory in the fall of 1776; she had departed believing Gray Eagle did not love her and that he wanted her dead, a mistake which cost the life of their unborn child and once again thrust her into the lives of Joe Kenny and Jeffery Gordon.

After she recovered from her miscarriage in Kenny's cabin, Shalee and Powchutu reached St. Louis, to find their old enemy Jeffery Gordon lying in wait for them. In a flurry of events, Powchutu, living as her brother "Paul Williams," was reported slain: she was told his head had been crushed beyond recognition and he had been identified by his clothes. Penniless, alone, and defenseless, she was forced to marry Jeffery Gordon. Soon, Jeffery's evil resulted in his death at the hands of Gray Eagle. Once more, Shalee was reunited with her true love and destiny.

It had required more than love and passion for them to accept each other, to find peace, and to win the approval of his people for their mixed union; it had required months, many hardships, and sufferings. They had challenged all they knew and felt to win the other's heart and commitment; they had defied their people, laws, and ways to fuse their Life-circles into one. Time and fate had been good to them and had allowed them, in a maze of hatred and perils, to find each other and to experience unique love.

In February of 1778, their son Bright Arrow was born, and five years of peace ruled their lives before more greedy whites and cruel soldiers entered the Dakota Territory in 1782, along with a female named Leah Winston. The white captive, a gift to Chief Running Wolf from Gray Eagle's lifelong friend White Arrow, took insidious advantage of Shalee's disappearance and amnesia. Using guile and her resemblance to Alisha Williams, Leah attempted to steal Shalee's existence and possessions. After many sufferings, Leah failed, a defeat which resulted in the wounding and near death of Running Wolf.

During his delirium, Running Wolf exposed a painful secret to Shalee— Powchutu was a full-blooded Indian, his first-born son by a lost love—a secret which nearly resulted in brother slaying brother, for they had become bitter enemies and fierce rivals. Running Wolf had never revealed his secret because the mother of Powchutu was a Crow—the Crow were fierce enemies of the Sioux— and she had married a French trapper while carrying their love child, then had raised their son as a despised half-breed who hated and battled the Sioux. Knowing that to expose Running Wolf's secret would bring anguish and shame to those she loved, Shalee kept it to herself for many years.

When Running Wolf died in 1783 and Gray Eagle became the Oglala chief, his rank and responsibility bred fear in her each time the Indian/white conflict increased in hostility and bloodshed. However, years of peace finally wafted over their lands, due to the friendship and efforts of a soldier named Derek Sturgis, who had been assigned back East in 1795, and whose replacement was a cold and cruel white leader who was determined to crush the Indians.

In 1796, Bright Arrow, son of Shalee and Gray Eagle, also captured and enslaved a white girl, an incident which inspired new perils and pains for all involved. Shalee and Gray Eagle wanted to spare their son the torment of forbidden love, but the bond between Bright Arrow and his white captive was too strong to break or to battle. Bright Arrow fell in love with the white girl who was revealed to be the daughter of Joe Kenny and a mute woman named Mary O'Hara, friends whose paths had crossed theirs many times. Despite everything, the Oglalas would not accept Rebecca Kenny as the wife of their future chief Bright Arrow, not even after she challenged all dangers to rescue him when he was a prisoner of the whites, an action which thrust Rebecca into the grasp of Lieutenant Timothy Moore and almost cost her her life. When the son of Gray Eagle and Shalee refused to give up his white love, he was stripped of everything and banished into the wilderness, to live as a trapper called Clay Rivera. Six years passed before Bright Arrow admitted to his self-destructive emotions and behavior and battled all forces to be reunited with his tribe.

In 1804, Bright Arrow and Rebecca won the right to marry and to return to his people, along with their two daughters, Little Feet and Tashina. While "Clay Rivera" was on the Lewis & Clark Expedition, Rebecca had worked valiantly in the Cheyenne camp to battle the dreaded disease of smallpox which took the life of their third daughter and the lives of two children belonging to Bright Arrow's closest friend, Windrider. Since that day, Tashina and Soul-of-Thunder, the surviving child of Windrider, had been the best of friends, as both had been close friends of Sun Cloud.

Sun Cloud, the second son of Gray Eagle and Shalee, had been born in 1797 and had been accepted as Gray Eagle's heir to the Oglala chief's bonnet and rank, until the unexpected return of Bright Arrow and his rapid gathering of numerous *coups*—deeds of immense valor or generosity. Upon his return, Bright Arrow was reminded of his father's past vision which said, "The seed of Gray Eagle will not pass through our first son; the greatness of the Oglala will live within Sun Cloud and his children," and he had accepted his lesser rank. Yet, as years passed and Bright Arrow's legend increased, many, including Bright Arrow, gradually forgot the vision of Gray Eagle, forgot Bright Arrow's past weakness and banishment . . .

Rebecca's problems had not ended with the Oglalas' acceptance of her. As when Chela had tried to slay Shalee for taking Gray Eagle from her, Windrider's first wife Kajihah had been slain while trying to kill Rebecca for bringing Bonnie Thorne into Windrider's life, a white girl whom the Cheyenne warrior loved and took as his third wife. After that bitter incident, love and happiness had ruled the lives of Rebecca Kenny and Bright Arrow.

Over the years, Windrider and Bonnie "Sky Eyes" Thorne had found great happiness and had given birth to four children. Windrider remained Bright Arrow's close friend, and they often hunted or raided together. His son by Kajihah, Soul-of-Thunder, had become a great warrior, a close friend of Sun Cloud, and the secret desire of Tashina's heart. Windrider had become the Cheyenne war chief and he led his warriors valiantly.

So much had happened in the span of forty-four years, since the arrival of Alisha Williams in the Eagle's domain. After the return of Bright Arrow from his exile, Shalee had revealed the truth about Powchutu to Gray Eagle. The half brothers had been similar in looks and in character, but had led such different lives, different because of their father's tragic secret and misguided pride. Gray Eagle had comprehended the truth and accepted it, delighting and touching his wife with his forgiving heart and generosity. At last, he had understood why Powchutu's path had continually crossed with theirs and why Powchutu's restless spirit had been drawn time and time again toward his Indian blood and heritage. Gray Eagle had confessed to wishing Powchutu were still alive so he could make peace with him . . .

During the past forty-two years, Bright Arrow had gone through many changes in his life and in his appearance. Up until the age of twenty, he had looked Indian like his father, after which his looks began to reveal his mixed blood by favoring his white mother more and more. His once-ebony hair now captured a slight fiery underglow beneath the sun or near blazing firelight, his brown eyes exposed a detectable hazel tinge, and his skin was not as dark as an Indian's. The whites often mistook him for a man of Spanish heritage, which allowed him to play "Clay Rivera" when necessary.

In the last twenty-three years, Shalee had watched her second son grow to manhood, following closely in his father's legendary footsteps and becoming a noted warrior in his own right. Sun Cloud was his father's image: hair like midnight, eyes like polished jet, and skin of bronze. Although desired and pursued by many females, he was not ready or willing to settle down yet. He was fearless, clever, energetic, and strong; he considered himself the protector and provider for his aging parents. He had given his parents joy, pride, and peace. He had been trained to take his father's place, and he looked forward to that moment with a mixture of excitement and sadness, as a son usually took over at his father's death.

Both sons had kept the names which had been selected for them by the Great Spirit before their births, for a male's name usually changed during his vision-quest. Both sons rode at their father's side or at each other's side during hunts and during raids, as another vision of Gray Eagle's had revealed long ago: "Long before we join the Great Spirit, our sons will ride against the white man together. Both will be great leaders." Gray Eagle's sons had been guided and instructed by White Arrow, best friend and lifelong companion to Gray Eagle, and second father to the boys, as was the Indian custom.

Shalee had met White Arrow, when she had been captured by Gray Eagle, and they had become fast friends. In 1782, with Shalee's assistance, White Arrow had married Wandering Doe, a lovely and gentle female who had died in the previous year, 1819. Wandering Doe had left three children to carry on her bloodline and love. One son, Flaming Star, was a close friend to Bright Arrow; while another, Thunder Spirit, was the best friend of Sun Cloud. When Wandering Doe's strength and health failed in 1805, White Arrow had taken a second wife, Pretty Woman, who had given him two more children. Shalee was glad White Arrow had someone special to help him survive Wandering Doe's loss.

Indian and white foes recognized the prowess and power of Gray Eagle and his Oglalas, whom the whites called Sioux. At sixty-nine, Gray Eagle remained a leader to be feared, respected, and obeyed. There had been a time when no warrior was stronger, faster, braver, or craftier; but his foes were increasing in numbers and powers, and age and responsibilities were taking their toll on the chief. Many realized it would soon be time for Gray Eagle to yield his rank to his son. That realization and action would be difficult for everyone, as Gray Eagle epitomized the spirit and heart of the Oglalas, of the Lakotas, of all Indian tribes in the Dakota Nation; he was their mouth, their courage, their bond; he was the scourge of the soldiers, and the reason why his people had not been vanquished. Friend and foe knew what the loss of Gray Eagle would mean to the "Sioux" and to the Indian/white conflict . . .

Times had changed; people had changed. Shalee had come to realize her husband was not invincible, not immortal, as many had believed or feared. Yet, he could still warm her heart and body with his smiles and nearness. He had never ceased to be a passionate lover, and she thrived in his strong arms and exciting Life-circle. Even with its hardships, life had been good and happy for them. Shalee knew time and health were slipping away from them, but she was not filled with resentment or dread. When their time came to walk with the Great Spirit, she could die peacefully, knowing she had shared a full and happy life with those she loved, knowing that their way of life and peace were vanishing forever. She knew the white man's evil and greed were mounting again, and she knew there would be no end to this madness and bloodshed, no answers which could bring lasting peace, not until the Indians surrendered all they had and were, and they could not and would not . . .

Times and peoples had changed in the nearby Blackfeet camp, too. Long ago, Brave Bear had been slain in valiant battle and Chela had died in childbirth with Singing Wind, leaving their four children in the care of others: Redbird and Deer Eyes, the oldest girls, had been raised by the shaman; Silver Hawk had been raised by the war chief; and Singing Wind, their youngest, had been reared by the tribe's head chief, Medicine Bear.

Gossip said that Redbird had lived with the medicine man, as his mistress the whites would say, until he was shamed into asking her to become his third wife, but she astonishingly had refused. Deer Eyes, a girl loved by all who met her, had chosen to remain as the shaman's helper, not wanting anyone's pity for her physical disabilities. Silver Hawk, who at twenty-seven found himself joined to the barren Cheyenne maiden Shining Feather, was rumored to be seeking a second wife, and further rumors whispered that Tashina had captured his eye. Shalee hoped that gossip was not true, for Silver Hawk was nothing like his father Brave Bear; but then, she admitted to herself, the boy had been only five when his father was slain and he had been denied Brave Bear's influence and guidance. Shalee supposed it was natural for a man to be bitter over the loss of his heritage and rank, as Silver Hawk was, even though he concealed his feelings.

Shalee hoped that Chela's blood did not run too swiftly and turbulently in Singing Wind, who as a child of nine had tended Rebecca's needs after her miscarriage in the Blackfeet camp. Singing Wind was beautiful and tempting, full of life and energy. She could turn most men's heads, and many warriors were pursuing her. But Singing Wind did not appear ready or willing to settle down yet. Clearly she loved her freedom and wanted to be a female warrior. Raised in a tepee of males, she had learned to ride, shoot, fight, and hunt. She was like a wild creature, one who was sensual and earthy. Shalee had realized that Sun Cloud could not keep his eyes and thoughts off that particular vixen. Often, Shalee had wondered if she should encourage that match and union, or if she should wait until those two settled down a little more. There was no doubt in Shalee's mind that they were well suited for each other, just as there was no doubt that both were resisting their attraction.

Since Shalee's—Alisha Williams had lived as Shalee for over forty years and would die as Shalee—arrival in this forbidden land, many friends and family members had been slain and many villages had been destroyed. The threat of the whites was growing rapidly like a fatal disease that seemed determined to consume all Indians in its path. For the whites to obtain a quick or final victory, they had to defeat the "Sioux"; and to defeat the "Sioux," they had to defeat Gray Eagle and the Oglalas. Only one white leader had obtained a real treaty with the Indians, and many now prayed for the return and help of Derek Sturgis.

Many also prayed for the return of Rebecca Kenny, who had disappeared without a trace last spring. Bright Arrow and his friends had searched for his wife until no hope remained for her rescue and return, yet Bright Arrow and Shalee had been unable to accept Rebecca as dead. Somehow, both felt that the Great Spirit would return Rebecca, who had been given the Indian name Wahea, which meant Red Flower, because of her fiery curls. In the lonely tepee of Bright Arrow, his seventeen-year-old daughter Tashina looked after his chores and cared for him, but Tashina was beautiful and many suitors hungered for her, unaware her heart was lost to a Cheyenne warrior, the son of her father's best friend. Bright Arrow's twenty-two-year-old daughter, Little Feet, had married a Sisseton chief years ago; she lived in another village with her husband and two sons, but a warrior in the Oglala camp still remembered, loved, and desired her . . .

In the Dakota Territory, it was April of 1820. Forty-four years had passed since the lives and hearts of Alisha Williams and Gray Eagle had become entwined. Many new perils and adventures awaited the aging lovers and their two sons . . .

Chapter One

Miles from the Oglala camp, the youngest son of Gray Eagle and Shalee eyed tracks which brought a mischievous grin to his handsome face. The warrior's midnight eyes sparkled with anticipation as he stealthily followed the unconcealed trail which snaked through the forest along the riverbank. Sun Cloud had been told only to discover where the white trappers had made camp to steal the Great Spirit's creatures from their lands, then return to camp to report their location without endangering his life by attacking them alone. He had obeyed his father's orders, as he had promised when they had come upon the fresh tracks during their hunting trip, until a new set of prints had urged him to close the distance between him and his foes. A keen hunter, he could read the signs which had been made by someone light of body and wearing Blackfeet moccasins, for each tribe's leather shoes made a different design upon the face of Mother Earth. At last, he had sighted the person who also had found the white men's tracks and was furtively following them: Singing Wind, adopted daughter of the Blackfeet chief!

Sun Cloud's dark eyes narrowed in annoyance and apprehension as he watched the Indian girl slip from tree to bush to tree as she daringly moved closer to the two trappers. Having observed and heard of her skills, he knew she could hunt, shoot, fight, and ride as well as most braves, but her actions on this day were foolish and perilous. He wondered what she was doing this deep in the forest alone and what had possessed her to behave so impetuously. She might not only endanger her own life, but his as well. If he was forced to protect her, he would be compelled to challenge death to save her.

His vexation and begrudging respect increased as he secretly watched her cunning and daring. He kept mentally commanding her to give up her reckless pursuit, but she did not. When the trappers reached their camp and joined a third white man, she concealed herself nearby and seemed to be listening to their words; for, like himself and his family, she too knew the white man's tongue.

Sun Cloud thought of signaling her with a special bird call, but decided that one of the trappers might recognize it, for many had been taught by traitorous white-loving Indians how to detect a foe's nearness and plans. He dared not toss a rock or pine cone her way, for she could jump or squeal and alert the men to her presence, and he could imagine what those rough males would do to a beautiful and helpless Indian maiden. The same was true if he sneaked up on her and startled her. For now, it was unwise for him to move any closer or to take any action, so all he could do was watch and wait, and mutely scold Singing Wind for placing them in this predicament.

As he sat there hidden from his self-proclaimed foes, he knew he could not attack, even if he was one of the chosen bow carriers for his Sacred Bow Cult. The bow carriers were selected and rewarded for being the four highest-ranking warriors of their tribe, along with four staff carriers and two club bearers. The sacred bows were revered by all Dakota tribes, collectively called Sioux by the whites, and were kept in the ceremonial lodge when not in use. All the Dakota believed the bow ceremony was powerful medicine for war and peace, and the choosing and present-ing of a sacred bow was done carefully under strict rules. The ten men who were selected for these honors held their ranks until death or relinquishment, for death usually came quickly for them because of their duties. Each of the ten were re-quired to be leaders in battle, to display enormous courage, and to slay at least one enemy during every battle. After a member had acquired numerous *coups*, he could return his bow, staff, or club with honor. The Sacred Bow Ceremony was nearly as difficult and revered as the Sun Dance, and was done frequently for the same reason: to show loyalty, to fulfill a vow, to seek protection and guidance, and to honor the Great Spirit.

Time passed, and his patience was tested sorely. He failed to realize it was the fetching view of the Indian beauty, not their precarious positions, which teased at his susceptible flesh and mind, and caused him to grow tense and clammy. She was slim and shapely, a female who tempted a man to seize her and to toss her to his mats, to seduce her with gentleness, leisure, and skill after he had taken her with consuming passion and swiftness to cool the fire in his blood.

Several times his near-black eyes walked over her body from shiny midnight mane to leather-clad feet. Surely by now he had memorized every visible inch of her face and body, for he had done such a study many times before. Her hair fell in silky strands to her waist and was usually tucked behind her ears, making her appear younger and displaying her face more fully. Her dark brown eyes always sparkled with some powerful emotion, as she seemed incapable of feeling anything halfway. Her skin was as smooth as the surface of a tranquil pond and was colored like the underbelly of an otter. If there was a mark or flaw upon her body, it did not show, for no one could consider the tiny dark circle upon her throat as anything but eye catching. Each time he noticed it, he wanted to touch it with his lips, then let his tongue play over it before deciding whether to move up or down her body . . .

Sun Cloud recalled past days when they had tangled with mischievous words, for he had known her since childhood. She had always been bold of speech and manner, and as a boy in warrior training, it had often angered or challenged him to have a girl question or trail him and try to join in on such events. From what he could tell, Singing Wind had never wished she were a man, but she wanted to be able to do whatever pleased her or whatever needed to be done, even if only men did such things. It had angered her to be told she could not join their games and practices because she was "only a girl." She had never seemed to accept her place as a female, to the irritation of many and to the disappointment of others. To

Singing Wind, anyone with the right skills should be allowed to help or to protect her people. To be fair, perhaps he should not blame her for her untamed character and masculine behavior, for her parents had left her, a baby, in the care of others when they had walked the ghost trail.

Sun Cloud wished her father, Chief Brave Bear, and mother, Chela, had lived long enough for him to know them, for they had played such vital roles in his parents' pasts. Singing Wind was twenty-three, a few months older than he was, but she had not known her parents either. Chela had died giving birth to her, and he wondered if that troubled the audacious girl or if that was the reason why she wanted to capture and savor excitement before she risked her own life having children. It had to be frightening and tormenting to know your mother had died giving you life, and that you could die bearing a child. Perhaps this explained why she had rejected all men who had pursued her and did all she could to repel new chases. Her father, Brave Bear, had been slain in battle. Perhaps, no surely, she would be different if she had been raised by her parents instead of Chief Medicine Bear and his sons. Still, one day she had to destroy her wildness and conquer her fears.

Sun Cloud watched as her hand eased down her leg to brush away an insect, and he wished he could do that simple task for her. The way she was sitting behind the clump of bushes, her buckskin dress was hiked far above her knees, displaying an ample view of lovely thighs. He admired their sleekness and tone. Surely not an ounce of fat lived on that enticing figure, and he grinned and wet his lips.

As his responsive maleness alerted him to his carnal line of thought, he frowned in vexation. He should not allow his attention to stray when he was so close to an enemy's camp. Sun Cloud asked himself if he could excuse or deny what others considered flaws in her character, or if it even mattered what other people thought about the girl who caused uncommon stirrings within him. He wondered if she was as spoiled and willful as many alleged, for that was not how he viewed her love of life and adventure or her spirited nature. Many claimed she would never be satisfied to be a mate and mother, that she would distract and harass the strongest of men with her unwomanly antics. A chief, for he would become chief one day, must marry a woman he could be proud to call his own, a woman who would not embarrass him before others, a woman whose purpose in life was to make him happy and to care for their home and family. Many accused Singing Wind of wanting more than her rightful share from life and vowed that she would make herself and her mate miserable! Sun Cloud did not want to believe such words, for he could not deny she was the most desirable creature he had seen and she caused him to think of more than taking her swiftly and casually to ease his manly needs. Surely such a strong woman would make a good wife for a chief, if she could prove the tales about her were untrue or exaggerated. As children of chiefs and members of allied tribes, if she would . . .

Sun Cloud stiffened as he watched her pull the knife from its sheath at her slim waist. Her body was on full alert. He thought she was planning to attack the man who had been left to guard the camp while the other two went to check their traps before nightfall, just as he felt they were not far away and their absence would be short. He mused, If she was so clever and skilled, why did she not realize the rashness of such an attack? If she tasted defeat, she could get them both killed, as he could not remain where he was and do nothing.

Sun Cloud drew his knife and grasped it securely between his teeth. He flattened himself against the ground to crawl to her side, to stop her attack or to defend her, whichever became necessary within the next few minutes. Suddenly he was halted when one of the men returned to camp. He strained to hear the man's words.

"We need help, Big Jim. Those traps are full and we have to empty them afore dark. Our camp ain't in no danger. We didn't see any Indians or signs of them all day."

Sun Cloud was relieved when both men gathered a few items and disappeared into the trees. He was glad Singing Wind was smart enough to know she could not attack two men whose combined sizes would make nearly four of hers. Surely, he reasoned, she would not hang around until they went to sleep to make another attempt to . . . To what? he asked himself. Did she only want to steal some possession for *coup*? Get a *coup* scalp? Prove something to herself or others? No, Singing Wind could not be that foolish.

The Indian girl looked his way as he inched toward her, making enough noise for her ears alone. Surprise and pleasure crossed her lovely features first, then she quickly concealed her curious reaction. After replacing his knife, he carelessly frowned at her, bringing a look of annoyance to her face. "Why do you trail three large enemies alone in the forest when night is upon you? Go quickly while it is safe," he whispered between clenched teeth to reveal his displeasure. He hoped she did not read the anxiety in his eyes or hear it in his voice, for a warrior should never expose such weaknesses. Before making his feelings towards her known, he had to make certain she was a unique woman.

Singing Wind eyed the handsome male, and misread his behavior. Sun Cloud could always get beneath her flesh and her control with a look or a word; that admission worried her, for it was unwise to chase a man who appeared to have little or no interest in her as a woman. For years he had caused a strange warmth and tingle in her with his presence. They were no longer children, but she did not know how to be a woman around him. She had done so many foolish and rash things while finding herself, or by trying to be all she could be. She feared that he believed all those silly tales about her being defiant. Unlike his brother, he was tall and lean, his body appearing all muscle and strength. He had the darkest and most expressive eyes she had ever seen. He always wore his long ebony hair loose, and usually wore only one eagle feather dangling from the back of his head, even though he had earned countless *coup* feathers. His features were sized and arranged in such a manner as to forcefully and appreciatively draw a woman's eyes to them. Yes, Sun Cloud set her skin tingling and heart racing, and countless females desired and chased him. Yet he had pursued no female, and certainly not her! Over the years, he spent too much time scolding and shaming and making fun of her to notice she had become a woman! How she wished that he would forget her rebellious years and take a new look at her. How she wished he could understand her. Catching her loss of attention and poise at his close proximity, she defensively sought to dispel his powerful pull. Noticing his seeming displeasure with her, she unwittingly accused, "Why do you trail Singing Wind and seek to prevent a victory over these foes? We cannot sneak away as cowards. You are a Sacred Bow carrier; together, we could defeat them."

Sun Cloud's eyes narrowed in warning at her unintentional affront, which made it appear as if she was always picking and poking at him, as if they were still children. He concluded that this little wildcat could have anything and anyone she wanted, including him, if she would sheathe her claws and open her eyes. He unwisely reproached her, "Singing Wind is a fool if she believes she can defeat three men who are as grizzlies to a tiny fawn. Sacred Bow carriers know when to attack and when to wisely retreat. Return home and forget the impossible."

"I will return home when I have taken their scalplocks, weapons, and horses," she rashly informed him, knowing she had been doing nothing more than spying on them to report their actions and location to her people. She had drawn her knife to be prepared to battle any peril which threatened her retreat. She was angered by this particular warrior's low opinion of her intelligence. What did it matter who discovered and observed their mutual foes? she scoffed mentally. She felt as if he had cornered her and insulted her; now, she must prove her mettle and skills, or slip away as a coward.

Sun Cloud felt there was no time to argue with this headstrong girl. Without warning, he skillfully delivered a noninjuring blow to her jaw which rendered her unconscious. After replacing her knife in its sheath, he scanned the area for movement from the trappers. Detecting none, he gathered Singing Wind into his arms and vanished along the riverbank. He put a lengthy distance between them before stopping to rest and to revive Singing Wind. He grinned as he dribbled cool water over her face and caused her to awaken with a start, then chuckled as she gathered her wits and glared up at him.

"How dare you attack me and treat me like a child!" She verbally assailed him as she came to a sitting position before him.

Sun Cloud decided a soft tongue and mellow mood might have more effect on her than a strong hand and scolding. "Your fiery words are untrue, Singing Wind. I saved your life. Be satisfied you live to take warning words home to your people. I could not allow you to place our lives in danger for a wild dream."

"Singing Wind did not endanger the life of Sun Cloud," she refuted, believing that misconception was the reason for his anger and action.

"What warrior of honor and courage would allow a woman to be captured, raped, and killed by white foes?" he reasoned, his tone calm and almost caressing. "You speak of your warrior skills, yet you prove you have few or none when you attempt such a futile deed, then risk another's life to rescue yours." He told her how he had trailed her and observed her, and had reacted only when she'd appeared to be in peril.

As he warmed and enlivened her with his presence, she scoffed softly, "If your skills and instincts are as large as you think and claim, Sun Cloud, you would have seen I was not preparing to attack their camp; I was preparing myself to flee at the right moment. You think badly of me. I am no fool. To enter a battle which is lost before it begins is to beg for defeat and death. I desire and tempt neither."

His face exposed an expression of enlightment and respect. He smiled and nodded that he stood corrected. "Knowing of Singing Wind's rebellious and bold nature, my mistake was logical," he teased.

"You know nothing of Singing Wind, but for mean rantings and wild charges. I behave only as others allow me to do without losing my honor. I am the daughter of a great chief, and I have duties to my people as you have to yours. If I had not followed the tracks and they had been those of scouts for a white attack, then I would be a fool and my people or yours could be dead before a new sun. I knew the danger of my tracking and I took no risks. You know this to be true."

"Yes, your words . . . and actions were true and wise," he concurred. "I feared for your life, and spoke too quickly. I am glad the daughter of Brave Bear has wisdom and courage. Come, I will take you to your camp and return home. Soon, the sun will sleep."

Singing Wind was baffled by the warrior's mood and behavior. She nodded and stood, then straightened her garment. She was surprised when he grasped her hand and led her away from the river. It felt good not to argue and fight, so she willingly let him take control. Perhaps, if she tried hard, she could convince him she was not the untamed creature which so many called her. Perhaps he would come to respect and to admire her, if he realized she was not a bad person.

Suddenly he whirled and seized her and pressed her against a tree, warning with a whisper, "Be still and silent, pretty one, something moves beyond us." Sun Cloud knew what was ahead of them, two foraging deer, but he had yielded to the temptation to feel her within his arms and to see how she would react to his touch as a man to a woman. When the full lengths of their bodies made enticing contact, he pretended to peer around the tree to study the direction in which they had been heading, causing him to press more closely and tightly against her. When she trembled slightly, he bent his head forward and murmured in her ear, "Do not be afraid, little princess, I will guard you."

Afraid, Singing Wind's mind echoed; the only thing which panicked her was her possibly noticeable response to the man imprisoning her against the tree and breathing warm air into her ear each time he spoke in a voice which teased sensitively over her nerves. As she lifted her head to question their peril, he looked down at her, their actions fusing their gazes and mingling their respirations.

Their gazes roved the other's face, and some potent force seemed to transport them to a private world where only they existed. Enrapt, all they could do was absorb the nuances of the other and submit to this irresistible attraction between them, an attraction which had been mounting within them for several years.

Sun Cloud's left hand slipped upward into her hair and admired its silky texture. He looked at the strands resting over his fingers and noticed how they shone like dark blue night beneath a rising moon. With ensnaring leisure and the determination of a conqueror, his right hand moved up her arm. Along its journey, his strong and gentle fingers stroked her supple surface, then drifted over her face as they mapped each feature. Very slowly and sensuously his fingers moved back and forth over her lips as if they were extracting some magical potion from them. Finally they wandered round and round her dainty chin which no longer jutted out with defiance. Her eyes were entrancing him as they visually explored his face and torso. He could feel the heat between their bodies, and their mutual quiverings. He wanted her here and now.

Singing Wind's senses were reeling from mounting desire and his tantalizing touch. His manly scent wafted into her nose and enflamed her blood. His body was smooth and hard and enticing. She could not resist tracing her fingers over his arms, shoulders, and chest, or lightly fingering the tiny battle scars on them which did not mar his appeal. As she marveled at the evidence of his courage and stamina at such a young age, his dark gaze ignited her passion like black coals in a fire. She hungered to taste those full lips, a craving which increased when he seductively moistened them.

Sun Cloud bent forward and did as he had dreamed many times; his lips and tongue teased at the flat mole which rested over the throbbing pulse of her throat. He heard her inhale sharply and stiffen briefly at that stimulating contact. Then his lips roamed to her left ear and he nibbled at its lobe, causing both of them to shudder with rising needs. Finally his lips tentatively sought hers, touching, nipping, brushing, probing, but without fully kissing her. When he leaned backward to see how she was looking and responding, her hands gently seized the hair on either side of his face and pulled his mouth to hers.

Their lips meshed fiercely and urgently, and they hugged tightly. Pent-up emotions burst free and raced rampantly. He captured her face between his hands and his tongue greedily invaded her mouth. She responded in like force and yearning, her hands wandering up and down his back and adoring the movements of his muscles as he embraced or caressed her. They were lost in a beautiful dream world until . . .

"Do you not see and feel it is better for you to behave like a woman instead of a man? Come, my pretty wildcat, and let Sun Cloud remove your claws and tame you. Halt your defiance and forget your rash dreams. Let Sun Cloud give you great pleasure."

Fury surged through Singing Wind's mind and cooled her passion. She roughly shoved the enticing warrior away. She mistakenly assumed he was only having fun with her, or trying to use her to sate his loins' hunger. She was embarrassed and wounded, and she struck out in her pain. She laughed and taunted, "It will take more than an eagle's fledgling to tame Singing Wind or to give her such sweet pleasures. I only wished to show thanks for what you believed was my rescue. Become a full man, then return to see if you can enflame me."

"The only thing which flames within you is temper and rebellion. It is you who needs training, Singing Wind, for you know not of the danger of teasing a man when his body burns with the mating fever. There was no need to thank me falsely; I would save any woman or helpless creature in danger. Come, we must go before our words become harsher and we behave as spiteful children."

Sun Cloud guided the silent girl to where he had left his horse. He mounted and pulled her up behind him, then rode swiftly for the edge of her camp, and left her there, without speaking or looking at her. If he rode swiftly, he could reach his own camp before the moon was sitting overhead. Perhaps the night air would cool his head and loins, and a rapid pace would lessen his tension.

Singing Wind watched Sun Cloud's retreat until shadows surrounded him. She lowered her head in shame and remorse, knowing she had overreacted and been hateful. Perhaps his words had only been impassioned endearments, not jokes or insults; she had been frightened by the powerful emotions they had unleashed and panicked by her weakness for him. Doubtless he would never come near her again, and she could not blame him. Unless she proved to him that he was mistaken about her and her feelings . . .

In the Oglala camp of Gray Eagle, Sun Cloud's mother was resting near the edge of camp following a lengthy walk to release her own edginess which had been inspired by an overwhelming sense of foreboding. Shalee slid off the rock upon which she had been sitting for a short time while reminiscing. She straightened her buckskin dress as she admired its artistic beadwork which had been done for her by Tashina. She was glad she had such a loving and giving granddaughter, a child who helped her on those days when her hands and bones troubled her with their advancing age. Trailing her fingers over the lines on her face, she wondered if they distracted from her looks. She captured one of her braids and held it before her eyes, femininely delighted to find only a few gray hairs were mixed with the auburn ones. She was no longer young and vital, but time had been good to her.

Shalee closed her eyes and inhaled the mingled smells of nature's awakening. It was nearing time to prepare the evening meal, but her husband and sons had not returned to camp from their afternoon hunt. Keeping her eyes shut, she lifted her face to the lowering sun and absorbed its tension-relieving warmth. When Gray Eagle . . .

"You're as beautiful as ever, Alisha," a masculine voice murmured softly and affectionately to her right.

Despite the radiant sun's glow, Shalee trembled and paled as she slowly turned, recognizing that voice from the distant past. Her wide gaze perused the man standing before her, smiling, and looking more like her husband than he had years ago. His thick hair was more gray than black and it loosely fell just below his broad shoulders. His Indian heritage was abundantly visible in his coloring, bone structure, and features. His dark brown gaze seemed to entreat, *please, tell me it was not a mistake to come here.*

Shalee opened her mouth to speak, but no words came forth. Her heart began to thud forcefully and rapidly. It was impossible; he was dead . . . "Powchutu?" she whispered, then swooned as he nodded.

Chapter Two

*P*owchutu bounded forward and caught Shalee before she collapsed to the ground. He carried her to the shade of a tree and gently placed her on the grass. Comprehending her reaction to his abrupt return from the grave, he gazed into her ashen face and prayed his decision had been a wise one. Perhaps his return was dangerous and selfish, but he was seventy-one and had to see her one last time; he had to beg her forgiveness for his harmful intrusion on her life. *Great Spirit, help me make amends, for I almost destroyed her, and damned myself. Open her heart and mind to me. Do not allow others to interrupt us before I have told her all things.*

Shalee stirred as Powchutu tenderly stroked her cheek. Her green eyes fluttered, then opened to stare disbelievingly at him. He smiled and coaxed, "Don't be afraid, Alisha. I'm very much alive. I'm getting old and I had to see you before the Great Spirit calls my name. I have a lot to say if there's any hope of earning your forgiveness."

Shalee pushed herself to a sitting position and continued to gape at the man on his knees before her. As with the first time they had met, she stared at him as if she were seeing a mild reflection of her husband Gray Eagle. Except for his grayer hair and white man's clothes, today he favored his half brother more than he had over forty years ago. "Mary told me Jeffery murdered you and Celeste, and made your deaths appear an accident. I saw you buried in St. Louis, and I grieved over your loss as if you had truly been my brother. You never sent word or visited me all these years. I do not understand."

Powchutu was also recalling their first meeting at Fort Pierre. He had believed she had been sent to him to fill the loneliness and hunger in his heart; he had believed with all his being that she had been meant to be a part of his Life-circle and without her his existence would not be complete. A fierce and greedy flame of love and desire had ignited in his heart, mind, and body that day when he had first looked upon her, scarred and terrified of the man who was now her husband. He had seen her and accepted her as *the* girl to fulfill his dreams, a girl worth fighting the entire world to possess. He had challenged everyone and everything to win her, and he had lost. In trying to make his dream come true, he had blinded himself to all else, even to her sufferings and especially to her love for another man. She had given him so much of herself, but he had demanded her soul. He asked himself if she could ever forgive all the wrongs he had done her.

He wondered how Mary O'Hara, a mute girl, had uncovered the truth of his "murder" and "told" Alisha of it. All these years he had thought she had accepted the news that he had died accidentally. She must have suffered greatly from undeserved remorse. "Where do I begin, Alisha? I brought nothing but anguish and peril into your life. I am not worthy to stand in your shadow or to hear your voice, but I could not die with such black stains upon my soul."

"Begin with how you survived and why you kept it a secret," she commanded softly, her gaze unable to leave his. "All these years I suffered, believing I was responsible for your death. Why did you do this to me?"

Powchutu inhaled deeply and sat beside her. The journey from New Orleans had been arduous for a man of his age, a man alone. "This story is long and it takes much energy. Be patient, for I am no longer a young man." Inherently he had slipped into the Indian speech pattern.

Shalee held silent while he gathered his thoughts and settled himself near her. She could see him, touch him, hear him, and smell him; yet, his reality and presence were hard to accept. His age and fatigue were noticeable, but he was still very appealing and robust. Had it actually been over forty years since they had last seen each other? she wondered, for it did not seem that way with him sitting here beside her and talking so calmly. How could she be angry when he was alive and had returned home?

Powchutu explained how Jeffery Gordon had tricked him into a meeting that bitter day in January of 1777, and had beaten him senseless. "I knew I was going to die that day, but I prayed to the Great Spirit to help me seek revenge, to help me find a way to protect you from Gordon. My head was in agony and I couldn't move or speak. Evidently I didn't appear to be breathing, because Gordon believed he had murdered me. It seemed like from far away I heard him giving his men orders on how to get rid of my body. When his men realized I was alive, they substituted the body of a trapper they had robbed and killed earlier that day. Lucky for me, that dead man had my size and coloring, and his men were greedy and dishonest. They exchanged our clothes, stuffed me in a crate to be sent downriver, then dropped that tree on him and Gordon's ex-whore several times. Since his face was crushed beyond recognition and he had on my clothes and belongings, everyone was fooled. The Great Spirit protected me that day."

As Powchutu halted for a breath of air, Shalee recalled Moses' words that awful day: "Both they heads was crushed flat!" She had never viewed the body; she had been told he was dead and had been handed his possessions, then had never seen or heard from him again. She asked, "But why did Jeffery let you live? What happened to you afterward? Why did you keep your survival a secret?"

"Gordon never knew his men betrayed him. They saw a way to make some extra money by selling me to a ship's captain. I was shanghaied. White slavery, it's called. They were working with a man named Frenchy behind Gordon's back. Just about every time they robbed some man, they sneaked him downriver to be sold like a slave instead of killing him like Gordon ordered. I was hurt bad, hardly alive, so I don't know why they even fooled with me, unless they didn't realize how bad off I was. They took me to a doctor's house near New Orleans to be tended until the next Spanish ship arrived. When I came to, I didn't even recall my name until fourteen months later. You can't imagine my shock when my past—my identity—thundered back inside my head one night. I still can't believe the awful things I did during those empty-headed months. As soon as my memory returned, I hurried to St. Louis as fast as I could, terrified for you all the way. After I frantically tracked you back to Gray Eagle's camp and tepee, I was forced to accept the truth about you two. You had a son and looked happy, so I didn't intrude. I thought it was best for you, and especially for Gray Eagle, to believe I was dead, so I returned to New Orleans to make a new life there. I never knew you had learned the truth about Gordon's treachery. If Gordon hadn't been dead by the time I got back, I would have cut him into a thousand pieces. I'm sorry I put you through all that anguish." His dark eyes lowered in guilt and shame. They were moist when they lifted and locked with hers again.

His voice quavered when he continued. "By the time I recovered my memory, all of our lives were different. I realized Gray Eagle had survived my evil, had tracked us, slain Gordon, and recaptured you. I could tell things had worked out between you and Gray Eagle. You were safe and happy, and that was all I needed to know. I didn't want to stir up the past and start new trouble with Gray Eagle by suddenly returning. I probably shouldn't be here now, but I had to settle our past before I die. Everything I did, Alisha, I did because I loved you and because I was blinded by hatred and jealousy. At that time, I honestly believed you were in danger from Gray Eagle. I wanted to help you escape all the torment you had faced here. I didn't want you ever to experience pain, humiliation, and fear again. I was determined to break his hold over you. I couldn't allow Gray Eagle to use you or deceive you or harm you again. I wanted you to find happiness and freedom and honor once more, and to find them with me as my wife. I needed you and wanted you. I was wrong, Alisha. Your love was good and true; you two were meant for each other. How can you bear to look upon me?"

Shalee gazed at him, witnessing his anguish and remorse and sincerity. Over the years, time and her secret knowledge of his tragic life, and all they had been to each other, had softened or removed her bitterness; and she must not allow it to return to plague her or to punish him. She had learned the heavy burden and price of revenge and hatred; if allowed to live or breed, they took their tolls, more on the innocent or misguided than on the guilty. "It is in the past, Powchutu, and we have all learned from our mistakes. Everything worked out for each of us, as the Good Book promises." A sad smile crossed his lined face, still handsome and full of character. As with Gray Eagle, his once ebony hair was almost gray, and time had stolen part of his stamina and body tone. His eyes were a deep brown, but not as dark as Gray Eagle's, which were shaded like polished jet. There was a new kind of sadness, loneliness, and emptiness within them, and it tugged at her heart. Perhaps he had suffered more than anyone over the years, suffered for a lie which she must dispel as soon as she found the right words.

Powchutu shook his head as if refusing to allow her to accept even a small portion of the blame. "You know the evils I committed. Gray Eagle did not leave you to die that day. He knew you would be safe during his absence: the fort had been destroyed, and the Indians had a truce or were busy celebrating their mutual victory. After I shot Gray Eagle, I wished a thousand times I could bring him back to life. I mourned his death and could not savor such a bitter victory. I was tempted to sing the Death Chant for him, but couldn't find the courage. It had been easy to plan my treachery, but so hard to carry it out. I had sworn he would never lay eyes or hands on you again as long as I lived, and Gordon almost made that vow come true. I was the one who should have died for my wickedness. I had no right to inflict such savage wounds upon your trusting heart or to make you suffer for two days in the desert. While we were staying with Joe Kenny, I saw you return to the girl you had been before your capture, the girl Gray Eagle had viewed and desired at the fortress. It was then I realized his love and desire for you were real, but it was too late, or so I believed. If only I had known he still lived, I would have returned you to his side and sacrificed my life to make peace between you two. What I did to you and to others was cruel and unforgivable, but I've changed. I'm not that same man you met so long ago."

Shalee reached out and caressed his leathered and wrinkled face. She smiled and softly debated, "We were as much at fault as you were. There were so many secrets and obstacles between us. We were all wrong, and we all suffered. You only did what you truly felt was right. You must forgive yourself as we have forgiven you. You must forget all bitterness and hostility as we have done over the years."

A look of curiosity and surprise roamed his features. He had not anticipated her attitude and behavior. She was still so generous and trusting. "We?" he repeated the intriguing word.

Shalee smiled once more and nodded. "Gray Eagle understands what you did and why. There is no reason to be rushed or afraid. I speak the truth and from my heart; he does not hate you or wish you dead. The war between you two was a terrible mistake. Many times he has said he wished you still lived so all could be made right between you two. I am so happy you are alive and you have returned. There is so much to tell you, and so much for you to tell us. You are family."

Confusion filled his dark eyes and creased his brow. "How can such words and feelings be true?" he inquired skeptically, and hopefully.

"How can they not be, my friend and brother? You honestly do not know who or what you are, do you?" she asked mysteriously, eyeing him closely and intently. He was alive, and he was here. Prayers had been answered; wrongs could be righted, and peace could be forged. At last, the son of Running Wolf and brother of Gray Eagle could take his rightful place in life. At last, evil could be conquered. Looking at him, speaking with him, and being with him brought back memories of good times and good feelings. It seemed like yesterday or only last year when they were so close. The years of doubts and torments seemed to ebb like gently vanishing waves.

"I am the son of a Crow woman named Tamarra and a French trapper named Pierre Gaston. Since I recovered my memory, I have been living under the name my father gave me, Tanner Gaston," he responded, yet he sensed this was not the response she was evoking. "I was born a despised half-breed, but I have been living as half-French/half-Spanish."

"You are wrong, Powchutu. Yes, your mother was Tamarra, but your father was Running Wolf. You are Gray Eagle's half brother. That is why you two favor one another. That is why you kept being pulled back to the Indian world. That is why the Great Spirit never allowed you two to kill each other. That is why you have been drawn home this sun. That is why Gray Eagle does not hate you. He mourned your death. Listen to your heart, Powchutu; can you not hear and feel this bond to us? They were mistaken when they believed and claimed I was Black Cloud's Shalee, but this is no mistake or lie. You are the son of Tamarra and Running Wolf; this I swear on my life and honor." She waited for his reaction, almost holding her breath.

Even as Powchutu recalled how many people—Joe Kenny, Alisha Williams, Jeffery Gordon, and others—had voiced their awareness of his similarity in looks and character to Gray Eagle, his head began to move from side to side in mandatory denial of her shocking words. He recalled two meetings with Chief Running Wolf of the Oglala. He recalled his confrontations with Gray Eagle. He recalled certain words his mother had said . . . She had told him many times never to become the enemy or betrayer of Running Wolf, but she had never explained why a Crow woman should speak such words about a Sioux foe. In a fever, at her death, she had told him, "Leave the white man's world and evil, my son. Go to Running Wolf. Tell him you are the son of Tamarra. Accept him and be happy." He remembered the day the mirror had told him why Alisha had been susceptible to him and to his treachery: his heavy resemblance to Gray Eagle! Was it possible . . . ?

Powchutu wondered if this revelation explained why he did not favor the short, blue-eyed, blond Pierre Gaston in the slightest. True, he did not look like a half-breed; he looked Indian, and had passed for Spanish with his dark skin, hair, and eyes, especially without braids and dressed in white garments and speaking the white tongue. Yet, as he refuted her words, he somehow knew them to be true. "How can this be? If it were true, why did my mother never tell me? Why did Running Wolf or Gray Eagle say nothing? Why would they let me live in agony and shame? Why would they make me their enemy? How did a Crow maiden gather the seeds of a Sioux warrior?"

Shalee sighed heavily, wondering how she could explain such an injustice, an injustice which had done so much damage to so many innocent people. She certainly could not excuse either Tamarra's or Running Wolf's action. She remembered what it felt like to be deceived, especially by those you loved and trusted. "Gray Eagle did not know the truth until fifteen years ago, and we both believed you were long dead. I do not know why your mother never told you, and I cannot forgive Running Wolf for not doing so, especially after he saw you in Black Cloud's camp and realized what that secret had done to you and your life. All I can say in his defense is he did not learn of your existence until shortly before I arrived in these lands in '76. You were a grown man, a scout for his white enemies, and your mother had married one of them while carrying you. When your mother became ill and knew she was dying, she sent word about you to Running Wolf. He tried to doubt her claims, to deny them and you. He was a proud and stubborn man, Powchutu. How could he claim a son by an Indian enemy who was now working for his white foes, by a woman who, to him, had betrayed his love and commitment by joining another? How could he accept a son who did all in his power to help wipe out his tribe and others? A son who was filled with hatred and contempt for him and his people? A son whose mother wed a white man and slept with him while carrying you? A son he had been denied all of the boy's life? A son he felt it was too late to claim? Times were so bad then, Powchutu; he felt he could not tarnish his name and rank by claiming you. He did not know you or understand the man you were. He was confused and embittered. And I also believe he feared you would hold him to blame for your mother's secret and your misery, that you would reject him and shame him before his tribe and others. I think he feared the rivalry and hostility between you and Gray Eagle. You do recall how it was between you two in those terrible days?" Shalee hinted pointedly.

Then she continued. "I believe Running Wolf thought it was less harmful for all concerned to let the lie stand. When he died in 1783, he was a sad and guilt-riddled man who was burdened by his costly and painful secret. My heart ached for him, and for you. I do not think he ever got over what their lie had done to you and had caused you to do to others. He did love you and want you, Powchutu; this much I do know and believe," she vowed earnestly.

Powchutu sank into pensive silence, permitting this news and its effect on his life to consume his thoughts. He could not forget the things he had done out of pride, jealousy, greed, selfishness, honor, helplessness, anger, and love. Who was he to judge his mother or father? Yes, he believed it was true. His heart and thoughts had always been Indian. There had been times when he had dreamed of Running Wolf as his father and Gray Eagle as his brother. He had always felt this strange attraction to them, some curious bond, some intangible clue. Perhaps he should have guessed it long ago and challenged Running Wolf to deny him and his birthright. That day when he had stared into Gray Eagle's eyes before shooting him, he had felt . . . Felt what? he asked himself, and was unable to reply. It all made sense. Yet, there was a puzzle here . . .

He looked into Shalee's entreating eyes and questioned, "How did you learn such things? If Running Wolf died many years ago, how did Gray Eagle learn them only a few years past? I am confused."

"Now," she advised, "you are the one who must be patient, for the telling of this story is long and painful." Shalee related the 1782 episode involving her amnesia, the violent intrusion on their lives by Leah Winston, and the near-fatal wounding of Running Wolf. "While I tended him during his delirium, he revealed how you were his first-born son, a full-blooded Indian; he cried out for you and begged for your understanding and forgiveness. He talked of how he had secretly loved your mother and wanted to marry her, but their tribes were fierce enemies and their fathers would not make truce. He told of how Tamarra was traded to a French trapper and was lost to him, until she appeared at the fort to work there. He was stunned to learn you were his son, but he believed it. He suffered greatly knowing you had been condemned to the life of a half-breed. He wanted to acknowledge you, Powchutu, but he said he was too cowardly to take that risk."

Shalee added, "He was glad Gray Eagle had spared your life at the fort and in Black Cloud's camp. You recall how he came to visit you while White Arrow held you captive after my escape?" She prompted that particular memory. "He wanted to tell you then, but could not. He saw how much trouble there was between his two sons, and he feared what his confession would inspire. After all, you were all Indian and you were his first-born son. If others accepted his claim on you, that would have placed you above Gray Eagle. How could he allow his two sons to battle over the chief's bonnet or cause dissension during such perilous times? He thought in time things would work out for all of you, but when you tried to slay Gray Eagle in the desert, he realized how deep your hatred and rivalry were. Even so, he loved you; he understood your actions and motives, and he mourned your loss till his death."

Shalee inhaled deeply, then confessed, "I never told Running Wolf about his confession. He died believing no one knew his dark secret. There had been so much anguish and trouble because of our connection that I thought it was best to allow your ghost to remain buried, so I kept silent to my husband for many years. I did not want Gray Eagle to know his worst enemy was his own brother. I thought you were dead, and it would have served no good or logical purpose to stir up tormenting memories."

She fused her gaze to his and then finished. "Until we thought you had been reborn in a child by Mary." She told him about her son Bright Arrow and Joe Kenny's daughter Rebecca. She could tell he was stunned to learn of Mary's pregnancy and of the loss of their child, and he was saddened visibly by the news of Mary's sufferings after his alleged murder and of her death from cholera. She exposed the facts of Bright Arrow's exile and his battle to return home. "After our son's return to us in the winter of 1804, I knew the past must be resolved for all time; that is when I told Gray Eagle about you."

Powchutu had gone by Kenny's cabin while tracking Alisha after his memory returned, but it had been uninhabited and locked. He had been standing near his first child's grave, ignorant of its existence. He must think about and pray for his lost child and Mary later. His path had led where the Great Spirit willed; this he knew for certain. Just as he knew the woman sitting before him had prepared his heart to accept his rightful destiny. After departing these lands, he had been happy and successful; he had been rewarded for his many losses and sacrifices. His love and life had not been here, but his return to and death in his people's sacred lands would complete his Life-circle. "News of our matching bloods birthed Gray Eagle's forgiveness?"

Auburn braids teased at her breasts as she nodded. Natural skepticism filled his eyes. It would take awhile for him to accept such a staggering revelation and its effects on him. "I am sorry you never had the chance to really get to know him, Powchutu. He is strong, but gentle. He is a kind and giving man. He is understanding and wise. His people love and admire him and follow his lead. I worry so about him these days. He has done all he can for peace, and wars only when necessary. We have so many white foes. To capture and destroy Gray Eagle and his legend, the soldiers would bargain with the Devil. He is the essence of the Indian: their spirit, their mouth, their image, their courage. Without him, all would have been lost long ago. But like you, he is getting weary and his body tells him daily he is no longer a young warrior. I am glad you have returned at this time. You can tell him all you have learned about the whites and give him advice. You can make peace and, for once, brothers can battle enemies, not each other."

"You do not know how happy you have made me, Alisha. I must speak with Gray Eagle; there is much to say between us."

"He hunts with our sons and his band. Come, we will return to our tepee and await him. All will be good and safe; you will see."

Since the others were resting or working inside their conical homes, no one saw them as they walked to and entered the large and brightly decorated tepee of Chief Gray Eagle. After Shalee served Powchutu buffalo-berry wine and dried fruit pones, she pressed him anxiously. "Tell me where you have been and what you have been doing all these years."

"First, you must complete your story," he coaxed, eager to hear how she had spent these many years with his half brother. "Start from your first day in these lands, and leave nothing untold."

Shalee laughed and teased. "You are as impatient as a child of two." But she waxed serious as she confessed, "It is strange that you return from the grave on a day when I was reliving my past within my head. Fears and apprehensions fill the spaces in my heart and mind where joy does not reach. I command myself not to worry or be afraid, but the greed and evil of the white man are spreading so rapidly." She lowered her gaze to prevent him from reading the remaining truth which was surely written there: his return seemed to signal Fate's callings for those whom his Life-circle had touched or interlocked . . .

To distract herself from her tension and doubts, she did as he asked. He was amused and astonished when she revealed how years ago she had traveled to Williamsburg to lay claim on Jeffery Gordon's estate as his legal widow and heir. She had sold everything and then returned home, using the money to purchase guns and supplies for her adopted people. She talked about her family and friends, those dead and alive. Anger and bitterness crept into her tone as she related incidents similar to those he had witnessed or participated in when he had been a fort scout. "The soldiers attack camps when they are vulnerable or the warriors are away. They seek to destroy the warriors' homes, families, and supplies. They burn and slay all within their evil path. Then they scorn us and attack again for our retaliation. They cannot even be content with trampling some tribes to the earth; they crave the annihilation of all Indians. I fear for the lives of my family and friends; I fear for the survival of our people. You come at a good time and a bad time, my brother, for the whites are massing men and supplies for what they hope is a final attack on the Oglalas. You have lived as white, but you carry Oglala blood; now you must choose your fate. If you side with us, you will probably die before winter returns to our lands."

Powchutu knew he could leave the Black Hills and Dakota Territory this very day and return to a life awaiting him in New Orleans, just as he knew, if he did not, her warning would come true. He had known that the moment he had decided to come here. "Even if it costs my life to face Gray Eagle once more, I had to come before I left Mother Earth. I have no time or energy left to share with guilt and bitterness. The past is gone forever as each sun's crossing of the sky. Here, I will live out my remaining days in peace, honor, and love. If my brother and his people will allow it, I will fight at his side and he will be my chief. Soon, my Life-circle will be complete; this I knew when I left the white lands to return home."

A voice which had not lost its strength and tone over the years replied from the tepee entrance, "Your words are true and wise, my brother. Before my second son was born, a vision came to me from the Great Spirit. I saw our father dying upon his mat when a warrior stepped from the nearby shadows. It was Gray Eagle; yet, it was not. I wondered, who but my son could reflect my face? When I learned of your existence as my brother, I understood and accepted that vision. My heart is full of joy and confusion at your return. Speak of such a victory over death and our past enemy," Gray Eagle encouraged as he came forward and sat down near them. His gaze roamed Powchutu's face and body, and he needed no white man's shiny glass to tell him how much they resembled each other. He was surprised and pleased that no hidden resentment and hatred surfaced against this man who had been his fiercest enemy and rival.

The two men's gazes locked and spoke, then both smiled, as if amused by some private joke. Gray Eagle remarked, "If we had ridden and lived as brothers long ago, our white foes would number less in our lands. You are cunning and powerful, my brother, for you escaped the Bird of Death. During these many past winters, our people could have used your skills."

Powchutu grinned and responded, "If I had known the truth of our bloods and your forgiveness, I would have returned long ago. My heart fills with excitement and pride to call you brother and chief. I could die this sun a happy man. I will speak of my survival and of life far away."

Powchutu repeated the account of how he had survived Jeffery Gordon's murder attempt, which left him with amnesia for over a year. "For six weeks I was tended by Dr. Thomas Devane and his widowed daughter Sarah Anne Sims. They were good people, but I was too hurt and confused to think much about them at that time. When I was strong enough to travel, the man named Frenchy sold me to a Spanish sea captain, but my enslavement didn't last long. Two weeks out of port we were attacked by pirates and I was given the choice of sinking with the ship or joining up with them. Since I didn't remember my past, I became a pirate. You don't know how strange and scary it is to have no memory." Gray Eagle and Shalee exchanged looks which said they were acquainted with that fear because of her bout with amnesia in 1782. Powchutu went on to explain ships, voyages, and pirates to the Indian chief.

"I sailed with them for six months, robbing and killing innocent people, always fighting and watching my back. Finally I reached a point where I couldn't stomach that life anymore. I jumped ship near an American port that September. The only people and place I could remember were New Orleans and the Devanes. I made my way there, hoping they could help me find myself and peace. Tom's daughter was very special, with gentle hands and ways and soft brown eyes and hair. Plenty of men wanted her, but she took a liking to me, thank goodness. She had married the man her father chose, Matthew Sims, and he'd died three months after their marriage, killed by a thief for a cheap watch and a few coins."

Powchutu's voice and expression softened visibly as he reflected on this area of his past. "Sarah Anne had made him a good wife, but she hadn't loved him and they didn't have any children. She had been a widow for two years when I first met her. We got real close, real fast, and I guess that scared me. Since I didn't know who or what I was, but surely knew what I had been for months, I felt I had nothing to offer her and I was afraid of hurting her. I took off to sea again just before Christmas. I didn't know I left her carrying my child. Seems that wasn't the first time I made that cruel mistake," he scoffed remorsefully as he thought of Mary O'Hara and their dead child.

Shalee noticed the bittersweet love and sadness which mingled in the man's eyes and voice as he spoke of Sarah Anne Devane Sims. She knew there was more to this part of his story, but she also knew not to press him. She passed Powchutu some water to wet his dry throat and lips. He thanked her, then continued his enlightening tale.

"Just before we reached port on our return voyage that spring, a terrible storm struck and I was thrown against the ship's hull. My head was bleeding and throbbing like crazy. One of the sailors made his way to me and asked, 'You hurt, Williams?' I just stared at him as he kept calling me Paul Williams, and everything in my past started coming back as fast and furious as those waves were crashing over the ship. I realized that damned Frenchy who had shanghaied and sold me had known who I was, or who he believed I was, Alisha Williams' brother. Lordy, some men are devils! I would have slit his miserable throat if someone hadn't done it before I could get to him, just like you did to Gordon."

Gray Eagle nodded as he recalled that momentous trip to kill the man who had set a bounty on his head, a man who had bought and sold bloody Indian *souvenirs*, as he called scalps, and possessions from brutally butchered warriors. He glanced at his wife and smiled, knowing that confrontation had resulted in them being reunited. She was still as beautiful and desirable as she had been at their first meeting. It did not matter that they were in their sixties, they still made passionate love upon their sleeping mat. He could not imagine life without her; she was his air, his heart, his joy, food for his soul.

Powchutu observed the look and felt the bond which was between them. His heart warmed, and he knew each of them had found the right destiny. If only his cherished wife still lived . . .

"After we weathered the storm and reached port, I went to see Sarah Anne to tell her I had regained my memory and I had to go rescue my sister Alisha. My gut was crawling with fear; I dared not imagine what Gordon had done to you. When I realized Sarah Anne was carrying our child, I married her, left her my money, asked Tom to watch over her, then headed out after you. With a little snooping around, I realized what had happened. I sneaked to your camp and watched you two for a few days. I could see you were happy and safe, so I returned to New Orleans and my new family. Our daughter was born in late August; we named her Alisha Gaston, since I was using the name my father gave me, Tanner Gaston. By then, I had told Sarah Anne all there was to know about me."

A hearty laugh came forth as Powchutu remarked, "She knew every mean and bad thing I had done, but loved me anyway. She really changed me over the years, for the better. I had a family to take care of, so I went back to sea to earn a living. It was the only thing I could do in that area. I sailed ten months and stayed home two months of each year, until my son Stede was born in '86. My family was the most important thing to me, so I found work in port. I ran a shipping firm until I earned enough to buy it. Stede owns it now," he divulged proudly.

Powchutu's eyes became dreamy for a while as he thought about his family, a family he knew he would never see again. "We were real happy and doing good with our business. By 1803, America was annoyed because the Spanish wouldn't let her ships use their ports; she solved her problem by buying the entire area, called it the Louisiana Purchase. That's what sent those explorers into this area, the ones you said Bright Arrow traveled with and earned his way home." That land sale was intriguing to Shalee and Gray Eagle, so Powchutu explained its meaning. "I sailed with the Spanish to help America fight the British in '79. But

America wasn't finished with her old enemy. My son Stede went back to war in '12 when America and Britain fought for three more years." Powchutu then explained, at Shalee's request, the War of 1812 with her motherland before returning to his personal history.

"I was a lucky man to have found Sarah Anne. Stede is thirty-four, but his ship's his first love. I was hoping he would be settled down by now, but he's too adventurous and hot-blooded like I was. My girl Alisha is married to Wesley Clarion. They live in New Orleans and Wes runs the firm for Stede. They have four children, from thirteen to twenty-two, two boys and two twin girls. Their oldest boy Allan is Stede's first mate. My Sarah Anne died two years ago, and I've been lonely and restless ever since she was taken from me. My children know all about me, or we thought they did, so they know why I had to come here. Like me, they know we've been together for the last time. I surely do miss being young and strong and happy," he confessed.

Shalee looked at Gray Eagle as he looked at Powchutu. Both men were the son of a chief. Both had lost their first child. Both had loved and wanted her. Both had found happiness, love, and peace, despite their losses and perils. Both had found what they had been denied at their births, to meet and to get to know each other. Both had changed and matured.

"There is another reason why I had to return to these lands," Powchutu revealed a new mystery. "After the birth of my son, I knew for certain the Great Spirit was guiding my steps. While I was helping Sarah Anne into a fresh night-gown, I saw something I had not noticed on her body before that night, the *akito* of Black Cloud. The Great Spirit had guided me to the real Shalee and joined our Life-circles. It was shocking to realize Alisha was living as Shalee when I was married to the real Shalee. I wish you two could have known her. Tom and Clara did a good job raising Black Cloud's daughter. I told her the truth about herself; I felt she should know who she really was. We both decided it was best if we didn't return here and cause new problems or dangers for anyone, but Shalee died wishing she had seen her father again. I brought her body home to rest near Black Cloud's on the land where she was born. Now all is right and they are at peace. I'm not angry about Running Wolf's silence. If he had claimed me, look what I would have missed in life. Every event, good or bad, pushed me toward my true destiny."

"It is so, my brother, many times our lives or the lives of those we love have crossed each other. It is good the Great Spirit mated the son of Running Wolf to the daughter of Black Cloud. It is good her spirit now roams the ghost trail with her father's. But we must keep such news hidden in our hearts. Times are bad, and it might cause trouble if my people learn we deceived them about my wife for these many winters. This is a perilous time when I must have their complete trust and confidence. Until we cease to breathe, Alisha Williams must live as Shalee, for this claim harms no one."

Powchutu agreed. "I will do all you say, my brother. My heart is no longer bitter and my mind no longer dark. Our war has ended for all time."

Gray Eagle focused his attention on the major problem at hand. "Many will see how our faces try to reflect each other's, but few, if any, will recall you as the scout who battled me so many winters past. Those who saw you as a half-breed foe no longer walk Mother Earth, nor will others remember when or where our paths crossed. We must not stain the honor and memory of our father by revealing his black deed against you. We must speak only as many true words as are safe. You will live here as the son of Running Wolf and Tamarra, but she will be a Cheyenne love, lost to him through trading before he could claim her as his wife. From this day forward, you will be claimed half-Oglala and half-Cheyenne. No one must be told of your Crow blood, for we battle them as fiercely as we battle the whites. You will be named Eagle's Arm, and you will live and ride with me. We will say your mother told you the secret of your birth when she died and you have returned to our people. We will say you have lived far to the south of our lands, which is true. We will not speak the name of Powchutu again, for you are no longer that half-breed scout. Only that truth which can hurt or destroy will be left unspoken. We will tell no one of such secrets except White Arrow and my sons. You are home, my brother, and Running Wolf's spirit can rest."

Powchutu concurred with his half brother's decisions. He would live as Eagle's Arm, half brother to Chief Gray Eagle. He would tell no one of his deceased wife Shalee, who had been born half-white and half-Blackfeet. But with the discovery of his true identity, a reality had filled his mind: his children were three-fourths Indian. It did not matter to Powchutu, but the truth was his son Stede carried more Indian blood and a higher birthright rank than either of Gray Eagle's sons. He must find a way to send a letter to Stede and Alisha to let them know he was safe and well, and to, perhaps, tell them of their true heritage. He was not embittered by the fact Gray Eagle was living, and had lived, in his rightful place; yet, he could not help but wonder what his life would have been like if he had been raised as Running Wolf's first-born son and Gray Eagle's brother.

"Come," Gray Eagle suggested, "we must speak with White Arrow before my sons return and your story must be told again."

Shalee watched the two men enter White Arrow's tepee, and she could imagine the scene taking place. An hour later, she was heading for the stream to fetch water when the Cheyenne war chief Windrider and his eldest son Soul-of-Thunder galloped into the Oglala camp, with her son Bright Arrow riding between them. She smiled as she envisioned her granddaughter Tashina's reaction to her father's visitors, one in particular.

The moment Shalee returned from the stream, Tashina rushed inside Gray Eagle's tepee and nervously disclosed, "Grandmother, Father brought Windrider and Soul-of-Thunder to visit and I have no fruit pones and berry wine to offer them. Father is too generous at times, for he has given away most of our winter supplies. I am glad spring is here and I can soon collect more food for us and our guests. What must I do and say?" she asked anxiously, for hospitality was important in the Indian culture, just as charity was. But presently, all Tashina could think about was that she had no refreshments to serve their company.

Even as her seventeen-year-old granddaughter softly scolded her kindhearted father, Shalee knew the girl loved and respected Bright Arrow deeply and would never complain within his hearing. She was aware that her son's hand opened freely to those in need, and that quality warmed her heart. Yet, she knew that Bright Arrow must learn it was not his duty to care for all those in need. As his father aged, Bright Arrow had taken on certain responsibilities of a good chief to lighten Gray Eagle's load. The same was true of Sun Cloud, who often hunted all day to provide game for those who had no husband or son or father. She was proud of her two sons and of their sensitivity.

Shalee realized the young girl knew these facts and was flustered only because of one particular visitor. "Do not fret, Granddaughter. I will give you all the fruit pones your men can stuff into their mouths and all the berry wine they can drink. You must calm yourself, little one, or they will wonder why Tashina's cheeks glow like the evening sun and why her hands shake and her voice quivers when she speaks."

Tashina laughed and teased, "You have more eyes than two, Grandmother, and you see all things. I do not understand why he causes my heart to race so wildly and my face to burn so brightly when he is near, and I try to halt such silly behavior. I do not want him to think badly of me for running out of supplies before the new growing season appears. Father worries more about the mouths of others than of those in his tepee. Perhaps I should hide our new supplies from his giving hands next season," she hinted mirthfully, knowing she would not.

"Perhaps you will not live and work in your father's tepee next season," Shalee retorted mischievously as she embraced Tashina.

Tashina's smile faded. "He fills my heart with worry, Grandmother. He will not face the truth of mother's death. He must look for another mate to fill his heart and life. I would risk all perils to return Mother to his side, but the Great Spirit has taken her from us. If Mother still lived, she would have returned to us by now or she would have found a way to send a message of her survival and location. I do not wish Father to join another, but he needs peace and help before I leave his side. He must face the truth; Mother is lost to us forever."

Shalee advised solemnly, "Do not burden your heart and shoulders caring for your father, little one. When he is ready, he will cast his eyes upon another. Do not live your life as his. You are beautiful and your time for choosing a mate draws near. Perhaps your father would make his choice sooner if he did not have you to help him." The moment Shalee said those words, she regretted them. She felt she must be honest, so she revealed, "I understand why he hesitates, little one; he does not believe Wahea is dead and lost to him forever, as I do not believe this to be true. No one has seen her or heard words about her since she vanished from our forest as Mother Earth renewed her face before this past winter. I do not understand why she was lost to us, but I pray for her safety and return. She is strong and brave; she will battle this defeat to be reunited with her loved ones. If only she had taken others with her to gather the medicine herbs so far from camp, then we would know what enemy captured her and we would know where to seek her, but we do not. It is as if Mother Earth opened her mouth and swallowed Wahea, for no trace or clue was found. A full span of seasons has passed since she was lost, but do not give up hope. Perhaps she will return as mysteriously as she vanished. Let Bright Arrow wait for your mother a while longer, but do not lose your dreams while he sleeps restlessly."

"I am glad you spoke such brave words, Grandmother. The words in Tashina's mouth do not agree with those in her heart. I fear if I chase my new life, Father will lose hope in a tepee alone and he will also pursue a new one for himself. I must not fail Mother and Father during this time of separation. Some braves and warriors have come to me to seek a joining, but none who stir my heart and body to accept."

"What of the son of Windrider? Is he not the one who brings that sparkle to your eyes? He is a good man like his father, and it is unwise to lead a rare man on a chase too long. Does his heart race and his eyes glow when he looks at Tashina?" the older woman asked seriously.

Tashina flushed and lowered her lashes. "I do not know, Grandmother. Is it wrong to say, I hope your words are true?"

Shalee's green eyes softened with understanding and affection. "No, little one, that is how it should be between two special people. Go, serve them berry wine and fruit pones, then return and we will prepare the evening meal together. First, send your father to me. There is something I must tell him."

A look of worry filled the young girl's eyes. "Is there danger in the wind, Grandmother?" she asked as she watched Shalee intently.

Shalee smiled encouragingly. "No, little one. I have happy news which must be shared with my son before others. Stay with your guests until he returns to his tepee. I will tell you all while we cook."

Tashina accepted the bag of wine and pouch of fruit pones, smiled, and left her grandmother's tepee. Shalee sat down and waited for her eldest son. News of the man who had once almost ruined his life should come from her. How she wished Rebecca were here to meet this man whom her mother had loved so long ago, whose child she could have been. Again, she prayed for Rebecca's safe and speedy return. If only this dark mystery did not surround Rebecca's disappearance last spring . . . if only there were clues to inspire hope or to lead them to her . . . Bright Arrow needed his lost love, and Tashina needed her mother's guidance during this period in her life. Things were changing so rapidly these days, and Shalee could not imagine what the new sun would bring.

During the evening meal in the tepee of Gray Eagle, Powchutu was introduced as his half brother Eagle's Arm. The men talked while Shalee and Tashina served the meal they had prepared, the five men eating first as was the Indian custom. Gray Eagle told them, "On the new sun, we will feast my brother's return and we will make plans to break winter camp. Stay, my friends, and share this happy time."

Soul-of-Thunder and Tashina exchanged smiles at the thought of having more time together, but only Shalee noticed. She sighed happily, for she could think of no one more suited to her granddaughter than the son of Windrider, best friend to her son Bright Arrow. Their union would forge a bond between friends and allied tribes. She was glad her son understood about Powchutu and accepted him as part of their family. She knew the same would be true of Sun Cloud when he was enlightened.

The meal passed leisurely, and the men lit their pipes and slipped into genial conversation. When the talk shifted to news or concerns over the soldiers' actions, Shalee innocently and slyly asked Tashina if she would fetch water, and if Soul-of-Thunder would go along to protect her in the darkness. The two rose quietly and left. She was not overly concerned with Sun Cloud's absence, as Gray Eagle had explained his mission, and she knew her son always obeyed his father's orders.

At the stream, Tashina filled the water skins. Moonlight danced off her dark brown hair which had an auburn cast in the sunlight and was always wildly disobedient when wet or when the air was filled with moisture before a rain. She turned to find Soul-of-Thunder watching her.

Tashina straightened and returned his probing gaze. For a time, they seemed spellbound, as if content to do nothing more than look at each other, or more so as if that was all they could do. Her golden brown eyes softened, as did his darker

brown ones. Lips parted, but neither spoke. A sensual heaviness seemed to surround them. It was as if each was waiting for the other to say or to do something.

Moonlight filtered through the trees, casting shadows upon their faces and
bodies, creating an aura of sensuality and mystery. Sweet smells of wildflowers and
heady pine filled the air around them. It suddenly seemed warm and peaceful near
the stream. Their breathing heightened, and still they did nothing more than stare
at each other, as if each was afraid that moving or speaking would break the
romantic spell which encased them in a private world, or as if each was the only
one caught up in the magic of this moment.

Soul-of-Thunder wanted to reach out and snatch Tashina into his arms, to
cover her lips with kisses. He wondered if this was the time to make his manly
desires known. They had been friends for so many years, but she was consumed by
her father's life these days. They had met when he was three and she was less than
two, and they had shared many childhood adventures because their fathers were
best friends. But since her mother had vanished last year, she had seemed to think
of nothing and no one except her father and his pain. Perhaps he should give her
more time to accept the loss of her mother, more time to give her hints of his
feelings for her as a man. If only her father would find another mate and would
release her from her sense of duty to him, he could approach her and reveal his
love. They had had so little time together during the last year, and he wondered if
she had missed him as he had missed her. So many braves and warriors from her
tribe, and others, desired her, for Bright Arrow had told Windrider of the many
offers he had received for her. Why, Soul-of-Thunder worried, would she select a
nineteen-year-old warrior who had not yet submitted himself to the Sun Dance,
and who carried the careless scar from an enemy's knife across his right shoulder,
over famed and seasoned warriors who had much to offer for her and to her? If she
felt only friendship and sisterly affection for him, it could spoil their relationship if
he exposed deeper feelings and desires for her. Every time they held hands or
embraced, his body burst into fiery need for a union with hers. He could not seem
to look at her or be with her enough. He asked himself what she would do if he
covered her mouth with his.

Tashina watched Soul-of-Thunder as he watched her. She wondered if he
realized how much his gaze and nearness affected her, for her body was trembling
and tingling. This last year had demanded a great deal from both of them; her with
her father, him with their white foes. So many maidens hungered for him and
trailed him like she-wolves with the mating fever! His father had trained him to be
a superior hunter and fighter, and any female would be honored and overjoyed to
call him her mate. They had spent so much time together while reaching these
ages, but a strangeness had fallen over their relationship during the past two
winters. They spoke less and seemed to be secretive. They watched each other slyly
and curiously. Maybe he was confused and alarmed by her new behavior toward
him. She tried to comprehend why he seemed so nervous and reserved around her
each time they were alone. She fretted apprehensively. Did he fear she would
throw herself at him or try to entrap him with girlish wiles?

Tashina could not help but think of her white blood, enemy blood. Even if
she wanted to deny it existed, it was impossible, for her colorings and features
made it known. She hated the word "half-breed," but she had been called that
many times in secret by other children. To her, all that mattered was she was

Indian, Oglala, in heart and life. Her sister Little Feet was lucky, for she passed as Indian and she had won the heart of Races-the-Buffalo, chief of the Sisseton tribe.

Many braves and warriors had asked for her hand in joining, but why? Because she was a chief's granddaughter? Or because she was Tashina? Besides, the only man she wanted was standing before her, and she dreaded how her white blood and looks might affect his feelings. He was willing and eager to be her friend, but would he become more? If only he would view her in the same light in which she viewed him. If only she dared to make her feelings known, but that meant risking their closeness . . .

Soul-of-Thunder and Tashina simultaneously took a few steps toward each other, but each was only aware of his or her advance. Just as they reached for each other, a rider noisily approached the stream. Both reacted as if caught doing something naughty and moved away from each other. They watched Sun Cloud dismount and let his horse drink after the long ride. They could tell he was distracted, for it was a few minutes before he looked at them and spoke.

Sun Cloud was not so self-engrossed that he failed to realize he had interrupted a romantic scene between his brother's daughter and the son of her father's best friend. He wondered if Bright Arrow knew about their relationship and if he thought it was wise to throw them together so frequently, and often alone, for they were still young, and young blood often raced too hotly and rapidly in the body. He and Soul-of-Thunder were friends, but Soul-of-Thunder had not exposed such intense feelings for Tashina to him. Perhaps he should discuss this matter with his friend later.

The two warriors spoke as Tashina's eyes went from one to the other. At nineteen and twenty-three, both were handsome and strong, and both were males to enslave a woman's senses. She wished her young uncle had not intruded at this particular time, and she wondered what he had witnessed and might tell her father. Reminding herself how close in age she was to Sun Cloud and knowing of his alleged conquests with women, she asked herself if she should entreat Sun Cloud to explain men and their feelings to her. Perhaps her uncle could tell her how to win Soul-of-Thunder's attention and heart.

Just before telling Sun Cloud his uncle Eagle's Arm had arrived, she decided it was best for her grandparents to share that news with him. She did inform him of her father's guests and said she had come to fetch water for her grandmother. "I will tell Grandmother and Grandfather you have returned to camp. We saved food for you."

Sun Cloud smiled at his niece, and knew something was brewing inside her lovely head. If they were not related, she would make a perfect choice as his mate; she was beautiful, intelligent, giving, strong, and gentle. Tashina knew she was a woman, and she was proud and happy to be one. She did her chores with skill and without complaint. He was very proud and fond of her.

"Tell Mother I will be there shortly. I must tend my horse and refresh my body. Guard her well, Soul-of-Thunder," he remarked genially to the warrior at her side, "for she is beyond price and words."

"You are too kind, Uncle, but your words and feelings please me. It is good you are home safe. Grandfather has a surprise for you," she helplessly hinted, then boldly winked at the man she loved.

The Cheyenne warrior grinned and nodded agreement. He was moved by her control, for most females would have blurted out news of an uncle's unexpected arrival. More and more he realized how special she was. He followed her into camp, wishing Sun Cloud had arrived later.

Sun Cloud dropped to the ground while his horse drank his fill of water. All the way home he had thought of nothing but Singing Wind and of what had, or almost had, transpired between them in the forest. He had been stupid not to comprehend her abrupt change of heart and her rejection. He realized he had been blind and foolish. He had spoiled everything with innocent words. It was exasperating to have to guard one's tongue at a time like that. He had offended her and challenged her, without meaning to do so. Soon, he must correct her mistaken impression and appease his growing hunger for her . . .

Chapter Three

*E*arly the following morning, Windrider and his son left the Oglala camp to return home. Tashina and Soul-of-Thunder had been given no time alone after their brief encounter at the river, nor the privacy for either to speak the feelings in their hearts. After the men left camp to hunt game for the impending feast to celebrate the arrival of Gray Eagle's half brother, Tashina went to visit with her grandmother.

As the two women carried out their morning tasks, Tashina told Shalee what did, and did not, take place last night. "I fear I was too bold, Grandmother. I was about to approach him and confess all when Sun Cloud returned. Perhaps his intrusion was for the best. Perhaps my move to him was coming too swiftly and rashly. If only I could read his feelings as he reads tracks upon the face of Mother Earth."

"Do not worry so, little one. If the Great Spirit wills the joining of Tashina and Soul-of-Thunder, no power can defeat it. Many times I have told you of the forces which tried to keep me from Gray Eagle's life and side, but the Great Spirit destroyed them and we became as one. You must have patience and faith," the older woman encouraged.

"It is hard to wait, Grandmother, for other maidens desire and chase him. He does not know I think of him as a man. If he chose another, I could not bear it. Soon we will leave our winter camp and the distance between us will be greater. As troubles with the whites grow larger, his time for visits grow smaller. He has just left my side, and I miss him as if it has been a whole season."

"Does your father know of such feelings for the son of his friend?"

She glanced away guiltily as she confessed, "I have not revealed such things for I feared he would see danger in leaving us alone. And I did not think it wise to speak such words if Soul-of-Thunder does not feel as I do. If Father approached Windrider and his son with my secret, it could spoil things between them if Soul-of-Thunder rejected me. We have been friends for many winters, and I do not wish to cause trouble."

"You are wise and kind, Granddaughter, for the pride of a man is often too large and blind where his family is concerned. You must seek the truth from your love before you reveal it to others."

"But how do I seek this truth?" Tashina inquired seriously.

"Time will answer your questions. If his feelings match yours, he will be unable to conceal them for many more moons. Watch his eyes and listen to his voice, for the secret will be exposed there first."

"What if my father accepts trade for me before that moon?"

Shalee laughed affectionately. "My son would never accept trade for his daughter without her approval and knowing. If your father comes to you to speak of such matters, you must speak from your heart. He knows the powers of love, and he knows only one special person can claim a heart. Even if your victory seems dark or distant at times, you must not lose hope, as Gray Eagle and Shalee did not, and Bright Arrow and Wahea did not. If Soul-of-Thunder does not make such feelings known before the Sun Dance, we will find a way to ensnare him."

"You would help me win my heart?" the eager girl probed.

"When we reach our summer camp, I will find a way to open your love's eyes, to show him only Tashina is the mate for him. It has been a long time since I was a young girl trying to steal a man's eyes and heart. I will think hard and remember how it is done. If we are clever like the raccoon, you will capture your prize."

Tashina hugged her grandmother tightly. "My heart nearly bursts with love and pride for you, Grandmother. I will do all you say."

In the Blackfeet camp, Singing Wind was arguing with her brother Silver Hawk. "I owe no words to you, brother. I come and go as I wish."

The twenty-seven-year-old warrior glared at his audacious sister. He inhaled deeply and straightened, trying to make his body look taller than its five feet eleven inches. He possessed eyes which could send forth messages of fire and ice or conceal forbidden emotions. The knife scar which ran from above his left brow to beneath his cheekbone was startlingly white against his dark skin. He was lucky the knife wound had not blinded him as it had sliced through his eyebrow, leaving a tiny section where no hairs grew. Even so, the mark had not disfigured him, for he had inherited his father's looks and features, and few men had been as handsome and manly as Brave Bear.

Silver Hawk warned, "If you do not learn to hold your tongue in respect, sister, you might find it missing. Three Feathers revealed your boldness on the last sun. Why did you not come to me with news of the whites? I could have counted many *coup* on them."

Singing Wind knew it was too late for her brother to go after the trappers, for the son of Chief Medicine Bear had informed him of the war party which had left upon her return home with her information. She knew her brother was furious with her, but she did not care. She had gone to live in the tepee of Medicine Bear at two winters, but Silver Hawk had been adopted by the war chief when he was five. Only blood said they were from the same parents, for feelings and actions did not. He had always been mean and spiteful to her, jealous of her place in the chief's tepee. She knew he was bitter and cruel, traits which were frowned upon in their culture, but he wisely concealed them from most members of their tribe. Four winters past, he had married Shining Feather, daughter to a Cheyenne chief, only to find she could not bear children. "I did not choose which warriors to send from camp, only the chief can do so. It would be wrong to sneak to your tepee and allow you to ride out before the band chosen by our chief. Many times your heart and mind are not Blackfeet. The sun must come when you enter the sweat lodge and purify yourself of such wickedness."

"And will you sit beside me, sister, and purify yourself of your defiance and evil? I am not the child of Brave Bear who brings dishonor to his name and camp. You make a fool of Singing Wind each sun. When you have cast away your darkness, then speak to me of mine. Why did Sun Cloud not count *coup* on our enemies?" he asked, changing the subject. "I am told no fear lives in his body, or within yours. Surely you two could have defeated them," he scoffed.

"We could have defeated the whites, but he did not wish the help of a woman, and the odds were too many for one warrior to challenge," she informed Silver Hawk coldly, still angry with Sun Cloud, and not wanting her brother to think her a coward or a weakling.

To vex his sister, the warrior teased, "Sun Cloud makes no secret of his thoughts of you. He laughs and scorns Singing Wind, and makes jokes with others when you look the other way," he lied. "How can you allow him to shame you and use you for fun? Many will soon follow his lead and Singing Wind will have no warrior seeking her hand in joining. Sun Cloud should watch and hear his brother Bright Arrow to learn of wisdom and kindness. It is wrong to shame a chief's daughter even when she is bad, as you are many times. Bright Arrow is strong and true; he will make a good chief. If you wish to claim great honor and to prove Sun Cloud's words of you are false, seek to join with Bright Arrow. It will be good for a chief's daughter to join a chief's son and to unite our tribes with such a bond."

Singing Wind's eyes enlarged as she listened to her brother's suggestion. "Open your eyes and see how I have changed, Silver Hawk. I try to be as all expect me to be, but it is hard. I only wish to help our people. Is this so wrong? What you say is strange, for Bright Arrow does not know I live as more than the child of his mother's brother. He mourns for Wahea and looks for no other mate."

"He cannot mourn for another season. He is a man, and a man must have a woman for many reasons. He is a great warrior and women find his face and body desirable. It is long past the time for Singing Wind to choose a mate. Who better to join than a future chief?" he reasoned, delighting in the thought of getting her out of his life and camp. Besides, she had too many eyes and could ruin his plans . . .

"Is it not true Sun Cloud is to follow his father as chief? Bright Arrow gave up his right as first-born when he joined a white woman and left his tribe. I am destined to join a chief," she reminded him.

"That was long ago, and times have changed. When Gray Eagle rides the ghost trail, Bright Arrow will become chief. He is older and wiser, and he is no longer joined to a white woman. It is his right and duty to become chief. Others would look more favorably on his choice if he is wed to the daughter and grand-daughter of chiefs."

Singing Wind stared at Silver Hawk in disbelief. "You wish me to join Bright

Arrow to help him become chief?" she hinted. "All know of Gray Eagle's vision which says his first son will never be chief. It is wrong to battle the will of Grandfather."

"Bright Arrow is my friend, and I must do all to help him obtain his rightful place. If your heart is good and true, you will do the same. Think of how your joining to Bright Arrow will prick Sun Cloud as buffalo berry thorns. As the wife of Bright Arrow, never would he laugh at you or scorn you again. You must think and decide quickly, sister, for Bright Arrow will soon take another mate."

"How do you know such things?" she asked skeptically, as if such an event truly affected her life and feelings, which it did not. She had decided that Sun Cloud was the man for her, and somehow she must win him. From now on, it was her task in life to obtain her love. She would seek ways to prove she was a worthy mate for him.

"Bright Arrow will need a mate to take the place of his daughter, for I soon go to bargain for her hand in joining. Tashina comes from a line of chiefs and is worthy to become my second wife. I have need of children which Shining Feather cannot bear. It will be as I desire."

"You desire a woman of our bloodline as your mate?" she probed.

Silver Hawk debated cunningly, "She is not close to me by blood. Our father was adopted by Chief Black Cloud and was not the true brother of Shalee. We are not related by blood or seed, just as you are not related to Bright Arrow. When he comes to visit our camp, make your desire for him known, sister. It must be this way."

"What if Bright Arrow does not find Singing Wind desirable?"

"You are not blind, sister. Who is more beautiful or desirable than Singing Wind? Only Tashina, and she is his child. If you make your willingness known to him, he will look at no other; this I know."

Singing Wind mentally debated, *If I make my willingness known to him, he will tell Sun Cloud, then Sun Cloud will be angry and . . .*

A mischievous smile tugged at her pretty mouth. Perhaps it would make Sun Cloud jealous and anxious! "I will think on your words, brother, for they sound of cleverness and truth," she replied, deciding it would be unwise to move too fast and without caution. It was hard to judge how a man would react to any situation, especially when provoked or cornered. Besides, Silver Hawk might be using her to obtain Bright Arrow's daughter. No matter, everything was dependent on both brother's feelings for her. If she did not win Sun Cloud, it would not be from a lack of love or trying . . .

The Oglala warriors returned from a successful hunt. While the women prepared for the feast at dusk, the council, which consisted of members of the Big Belly Society, met in the ceremonial lodge. Big Bellies were a group of older men who had proven their prowess throughout the years and who had held ranks of honor: chiefs of every degree, shamans, and renowned warriors, most of whom had seen the last of their fighting days and were now called upon for their wisdom. These men were responsible for the tribe's leadership and for making the crucial decisions for the tribe's benefit. Working with and for them was a group of ten warriors, known as "shirt wearers," who carried out the instructions of the council. When selected for this important honor and rank, a man was given a painted shirt which was fringed with scalplocks and which he guarded with his life if necessary, as it was a big *coup* for an enemy to steal such a sacred shirt. Many shirts were half-blue and half-yellow, others were half-red and half-green, and others were all yellow or striped with black. The colors were to remind the warrior of his responsibility to the Great Spirit, and the scalplocks were to remind him of his duty to his people. These prized shirts, one of which belonged to Bright Arrow, were worn only during special ceremonies and during all battles.

Gray Eagle introduced Powchutu to the other fourteen council members, the "shirt wearers," and Sacred Bow members who were present; and all seemed pleased by his arrival. The ex-scout was voted into the tribe; but, like all Indian braves, he would be required to prove himself before becoming a member of the *O-zu-ye Wicasta*, the Warrior Society, to which all proven warriors belonged.

Gray Eagle looked around the circle of men as he told how his half brother would accomplish this task. "My brother speaks the white tongue as easily as the whites. Many times he has dressed white and moved among them without suspicion. On the new sun, he will ride to the fort and enter it. He will say he wishes to send messages on the white man's paper to his children far away in the white lands. While he is there, he will study the soldiers' strength and plans. Our scouts have warned us the bluecoats are gathering men and weapons to attack us during our journey to the Plains. The bluecoats know we are vulnerable during this season while Mother Earth renews her face. We must prepare weapons and make plans before we begin our journey in five moons. We must find ways to hunt the buffalo and guard our new camps at the same time. The bluecoats are known for their attacks while warriors and hunters are away from camp. We must trick them this season. We must learn their size, skills, and thinking. When my brother has learned such things, he will return to us, and he will become a member of our council and Warrior Society. Is there one among you who says no?"

Many of the "shirt wearers"—Bright Arrow, Flaming Star, Deer Stalker, and Star Gazer—and of the Sacred Bow carriers—Sun Cloud, Night Rider, Rising Elk, and Thunder Spirit—observed while the council talked and voted. Unless a warrior fiercely disagreed with the council, he did not speak out in a lodge meeting. Members, who were the wisest and bravest of warriors, made the decisions for the tribe, which the head chief was duty bound to carry out, with the help of the "shirt wearers." But when it came to crucial matters, such as intertribal war or allied war with the whites, each man spoke his mind and gave his vote, and the majority always ruled. Today, the business was simple, so only the council members talked and voted.

White Arrow, best friend to Gray Eagle and father of Flaming Star and Thunder Spirit, spoke up in a strong voice which belied his sixty-nine years, "I say we send Eagle's Arm to the fort to spy on our foes. I say we accept him into council when he returns."

Big Elk, the war chief of forty-three years of age, concurred. "I say we must know the secrets of our foes to defeat them. They have become many and strong since we left the Plains. They seek to destroy all Lakotas and their allies. We must plan our defenses and attacks cunningly. Eagle's Arm can be our eyes and ears inside the fort."

Talking Rock, Plenty Coups, Walks Tall, Black Buffalo, and the other councilmen all nodded agreement. All had spoken and/or voted except the shaman

Mind-who-Roams. All eyes focused on the medicine chief and holy man of fifty-six as he carefully chose and weighed his words before speaking.

"The visions which come to me these moons bring sadness to my heart. I see evil shadows over our lands. I see the blood of many Oglalas spilled. I see many mourning for the losses of those we love. There is danger and trouble ahead for us, my brothers. We must be brave and strong, for the Great Spirit will lead us from our perils and darkness into the light and safety. We must prepare ourselves, for the demands we shall soon face are great and painful. There are those who sit in this council who will not live to see the Sun Dance. We must not lose hope and faith, my brothers, for the greatness of the Oglala lives beyond us. We will destroy our enemies and know great victory before winter returns to our lands, but our lands must first taste the blood of those we love. The Great Spirit wills Eagle's Arm to ride to the fort, but he did not ride alone in my vision."

"I will become a white man once more and join my father's brother on his quest. Once more I will look and speak as Clay Rivera," Bright Arrow announced, as if the shaman had named him as Powchutu's partner. "I know the white man's tongue and ways. I will cut my hair, dress as white, and play the white man for two suns."

Walks Tall argued. "It is wrong to cut your hair; it is your honor."

"Hair can grow again, Walks Tall, dead brothers cannot. If two lost braids save only one warrior, it is worth my sacrifice. Pray each hair cut saves the life of an Oglala. What is the honor of one man over the survival of his tribe? I do this with love for my people."

Mind-who-Roams raised his hand to silence Walks Tall's next remark. "The son of our chief follows the will of *Wakantanka,* do not speak against it, my brother. They will return safely, for I have seen them riding upon the Plains."

Sun Cloud remembered how Bright Arrow had ridden into a Crow camp, duped them, and rescued him when he was seven years old. He had seen his brother's prowess in battle, and he knew Bright Arrow would be victorious. He beamed with pride and pleasure. No man could have a brother who walked taller or stronger than his did. Perhaps this stirring trip would enliven his brother's heart, for he had not been himself since the loss of his wife. If only they knew what had happened to Rebecca "Wahea" Kenny after she mysteriously vanished last spring while gathering herbs in the forest, but this was not the time to dwell on that incident. Bright Arrow would travel as Clay Rivera, the name he had used during his banishment from their tribe. This time, the Spanish name would protect his identity as it had done long ago.

When there was nothing more to say and all had agreed, the council meeting ended. Some of the men separated into small groups to converse or to exchange tales of past days as they drifted outside for fresh air to await the feast. Gray Eagle left to speak with Shalee, to reveal their plans and the departure of Powchutu and Bright Arrow. Sun Cloud vanished with his friend Thunder Spirit, and Flaming Star went to see his wife Morning Light and their three children.

White Arrow approached Powchutu after the lodge was empty of all except them and Bright Arrow, who had not left his sitting mat and seemed to be ensnared by deep thought. "What you do is a good and generous thing, my new brother. Your journey will be hard and dangerous. My heart rejoices at your return and help."

Powchutu, who was now called Eagle's Arm, smiled at the man he had met when Gray Eagle had come to him to plead with him to explain Chief Black Cloud's claim over Alisha Williams, in those days before Alisha had discovered Gray Eagle could speak English. He had traveled with White Arrow and Gray Eagle to the Blackfeet camp, and had carried out blind treachery there. Along the way, he had come to know White Arrow as an honorable man, a tried and trusted friend of Gray Eagle's. As it had been with him, White Arrow had loved Alisha from the first; he had been kind and gentle with her, and they had become friends. Indeed, Powchutu had White Arrow to thank for making Alisha's life easier and happier in the Eagle's domain before love and peace had come between his half brother and his first love.

White Arrow noticed Powchutu's smile and faraway gaze. He remarked genially, "Each season my mind drifts into the past more and more, as yours does now. It has been many winters since I held you captive for Alisha to become Shalee and to find my brother's heart."

Powchutu chuckled and nodded. "We are lucky, for our lives have known more good than bad. If things had been different long ago, she could be your wife or mine this day. She touched both our lives and hearts, and we are better men for having known and loved her. It is strange how the Great Spirit works his will, and sometimes it is hard to accept and to understand. The sufferings I caused others trouble me deeply, but they led us to the paths of our true destinies. It is good to find peace in my heart and acceptance in my people's lands."

Bright Arrow stood to join them. "Your words are true, my uncle, for the Great Spirit works in mysterious and often painful ways. I have been my own prisoner since spring last touched our lands. Sometimes it is easier to die than to live as dead without your heart. Tell me, how did you slay the pain of your mate's loss and become a whole man again?" he asked both men, for Powchutu had lost Sarah Anne—the real Shalee—and White Arrow had lost his Wandering Doe, whose loss had also saddened Bright Arrow because White Arrow and Wandering Doe were his second parents, as was the Indian way.

White Arrow and Powchutu exchanged looks, neither knowing how to respond. Finally, Powchutu replied in a strained voice, "I miss her each day and night, Bright Arrow. She took a part of me when she left my side. The pain is less, but it still lives. Each sun I long for her and force myself not to weep openly for her absence. Some days, it is as if she still lives and I might see her soon. But she was very ill, and it was best she did not linger and suffer. She lives in our children and in my heart. She lives in the land and in the wind. She can never die, for my mind keeps her alive. It is different with you, Bright Arrow; you are young and have much of your life ahead of you. You should seek another mate to take away your loneliness and pain. Let her smile and arms bring you comfort and new life. You are too young and vital to be alone, to be without spirit and heart."

"Eagle's Arm speaks wisely and kindly, my son. My life with Wandering Doe was long, and I have many good memories. Yours with Wahea was short and troubled, and only a new love and life can heal your wounds. I would be as a walking dead man if I did not have Pretty Woman to send laughter into our tepee and to pull me from my dark moods. I do not love her as I loved Wandering Doe, but she fills an emptiness and longing within my heart and life. She has given me two fine children, Crow Stalker and Prairie Flower. If I had not joined with her, I would not have them, and I would be forced to live with my other children. It should not be so, for Flaming Star and Medicine Girl have tepees and families of their own, and soon Thunder Spirit will begin his new life with a chosen mate. He is like your brother Sun Cloud; he thinks I am too old to hunt and thinks he must protect me and provide for me and my second family. Thunder Spirit is like you, Bright Arrow; he lost the woman he loved, but to another man. Who is to say which loss is harder to accept? His eyes were for Little Feet alone," the older man murmured without thinking.

Bright Arrow looked surprised. "Why did he not come to me and ask for my first daughter in joining? She accepted Chief Races-the-Buffalo's offer because she feared no other would ask for her. I had placed the marks of the white man and evil upon her face and body." He blamed himself, alluding to her auburn hair and hazel eyes, and the scars on her face and body from the smallpox attack in the Cheyenne camp when she was six and nearly died as her sister Moon Eyes had.

"But she is beautiful and all love her," White Arrow protested.

"She panicked when all her friends were joined except her. She believed it was the white man's evil touches upon her body which turned warriors' eyes away. She is a good wife to her mate and a good mother to her two sons, but she does not love her husband. When I visit her, I see a sadness and loneliness which matches mine for Wahea."

"Thunder Spirit was away for many full moons. If he had been here, he would have challenged for her hand. Such a loss is sad."

Powchutu remarked, "Men have often lost the women of their hearts or dreams because they held silent. Sometimes it is hard to know when it is the 'time to be quiet; the time to speak up.'"

Bright Arrow knew this was a "time to be quiet," for he recalled hearing Little Feet crying and confessing her love for Thunder Spirit to her mother Rebecca "Wahea" Kenny. Knowing now that love was returned, he wished he had gone to his second father as he had been tempted to do and had asked him to speak with his son about Little Feet; he had been too proud to risk rejection. Now, each must walk the path he chose when he did not wait for *Wakantanka* to work His will.

White Arrow advised his friend's son. "When you find another who captures your eye and passion, speak for her quickly before she is lost to another. Come, we must rest before the feast. I am no longer a young man, and the suns grow longer for me between the moons."

"When we have moved our camp, I will obey your words, Father and Uncle; I will seek another mate who causes my heart and body to reach for her. A man should not be alone." Bright Arrow watched the two older men depart, then turned to pray. *Forgive me, Rebecca, my love, for someone must ease this pain of your loss. I must feel joy and life again. If you lived, you would have been returned to me.*

He had set the pattern for his life when he was eighteen, and he had captured Rebecca Kenny and had slain two warriors to keep her. Many things, bad and good, had happened to him, and to others, because of that action. He had lived in torment until *Wakantanka* had guided his steps home. Yet, if he had that part of his life to live over again, he would make the same decisions. Surely there was a purpose to his losing Rebecca . . . If only *Wakantanka* would reveal it to him, he could move on with his life. Perhaps the Great Spirit had allowed him time to enjoy his willful mistake before correcting it. Perhaps he and Rebecca had been returned to their destined paths. But if she had to be removed from his Life-circle, why were his love and desire for her not removed? he questioned in renewed anguish.

They had endured many dangers and hardships to be together, but they had shared a special love and closeness which few lovers ever knew. He should not be bitter, but happy for those many seasons. Perhaps it was time to turn his eyes from the past and to look to his future, for this year without her had been long and self-destructive. Years ago, he had promised himself and others never to harm himself or others again, and to pine for what could never return kept him from thinking clearly and reacting wisely. Perils were ahead for him and his people, and he needed his concentration and spirit to battle them.

When Rebecca had been lost to him during her capture at the fort and during her capture by an evil white man, he had known she was alive somewhere and waiting for his rescue; this time, could he go on hoping the same was true? Before, there had been signs and messages to guide him to her; this time, there were none. This time, it was as if she had never existed, but he knew she had. "If you are alive, my heart, find some way to return to me. If you watch me from the side of the Great Spirit, you know what is in my heart and life."

The drums began to summon the Oglalas to the feast for one who had returned from the dead. Did that not, he asked himself, tell him and others it could be true for his love? One morning she was walking at his side; then the next, she was gone, and he did not know where or how. "Do not dream the dreams of the foolish, Bright Arrow," he warned hoarsely, "for she has been lost too long for a woman alone to survive." He dried the moisture from his eyes, inhaled deeply, squared his broad shoulders, and headed to join his parents and tribe.

A large fire had been built in the center of their camp and the elders sat on buffalo mats a short distance from it. Since this was a celebration, the women and children did not have to stand or sit behind the warriors and braves as was done during ceremonies. A tall pole displaying a sacred medicine wheel, which represented all influences and forces, was positioned a few feet from the campfire. The buffalo skull in its center signified *Lakol wicoh'an*, the traditional way of life, and *Pte Oyate*, the spiritual life. There was a great significance to the four directions upon its face: south, the innocence of mind and body at birth; east, enlightenment; north, wisdom gained during life; and west, meditation for self-examination and understanding. All spokes radiated toward the center: the heart and meaning of life itself, which was total harmony with one's self and with nature. The skull was old and weathered, and painted white to express purity. From a male buffalo, it depicted the wisdom and generosity of the Great Spirit, who had sent the buffalo to feed, clothe, and shelter His people.

The Oglala believed that the eagle, exhibited by four feathers which dangled from the wheel's bottom, had a special place among the animals and birds. The sacred hoop portrayed the four virtues in the Lakota culture: wisdom, courage, constancy, and generosity. The four feathers and four intersecting bars of the medicine wheel related the significance of the number four in their religion. The four bars pointed in separate directions which represented danger from the west, life from the north, knowledge from the east, and introspection from the south. The four points crossed in the center of the medicine wheel to speak of harmony and peace when all things came together as they should. The hoop alleged the never-ending circle of life which started with birth, to maturity, to old age, to death for rebirth in the spirit world; it was the symbol of the continuity of Indian life.

The same was true of the sacred pipe which was being smoked and shared by all warriors who cared to partake of it. After it was lifted skyward as an offering to the Great Spirit *Wakantanka* and downward to the Mother Earth *Makakin* for all they provided, each of the four directions was acknowledged: to the east to summon enlightenment and peace, to the south where warmth was born, to the west which brought rain, and to the north which offered fortitude. It was accepted as the mingling of one's breath with the Great Spirit's, and to share it had deep meaning to each man.

Pipe smoking was done on many occasions—in prayer rituals, friendship parley, and council or society meetings. A man's personal prayer pipe was sacred and was never to be touched by women or foes. To steal a warrior's sacred pipe was a high *coup*. When members of tribes, friends or foes, met, they smoked the pipe of friendship or truce. When tribes joined to declare war together, they smoked the same pipe to show oneness in will and spirit. The smoke of the pipe was said to be the sharing of the breath of the Great Spirit, to instill courage and knowledge or to make truce between those who shared it.

Food and drink were served, and the mood was happy and light. As they finished eating, many conversed with those nearby; others entered the wide circle, one or more at a time, to enact tales of past adventures and events; while some were content to observe and quietly enjoy this stirring occasion. Prayers and chants were given by the shaman. Music began to fill the air: kettle drums, around which sat eight men with sticks, for the Indian never touched the surface of the drum with his hands; eagle-bone whistles and flutes; and a variety of different-size gourds, which were used as rattles. Some began to dance; others swayed or clapped to the music and revelry. It was a celebration of *Wakantanka's* generosity, of the joy of living, of Mother Earth's renewal; it was the continuation of their Life-circles.

Shalee sat between her husband and oldest son. Feeling Bright Arrow and Powchutu could carry out their deception, she experienced no guilt in looking forward to their absence. Soon they would be breaking camp for a long journey which would allow no privacy, so time alone was short and precious. Then, upon their arrival at their summer camp, the buffalo hunt and trouble with the whites would claim their time and energies, and perhaps even more . . .

When her smile vanished and she lowered her head, Gray Eagle asked quietly, "What troubles you this happy day, little one?"

Her gaze met his, and her love glowed in its green depths. She did not want to burden him with her feelings of foreboding, so she smiled and caressed his cheek. "It has been a long and busy day for an aging woman. Perhaps we should seek you a second wife to help with our chores as White Arrow did."

Gray Eagle grinned and his eyes brightened with amusement and love. "Since when has Gray Eagle needed more than one female in his tepee? You do not grow old and weak, my love; you simply change with the seasons. Do you worry over our son's departure?"

Shalee glanced at Bright Arrow to find him in conversation with Plenty Coups. She leaned toward her husband and murmured softly, "I know the Great Spirit will guard him, and it is good he has a mission to distract him from his sadness and to fill him with excitement. I was thinking of our journey and new camp; they will take much of our days and strength. Perhaps we will have none left to be together."

Gray Eagle chuckled and his eyes sparkled with understanding and warmth. "Our brother has been with us for only one moon, and you feel denied of my touch," he teased. "When we reach our summer camp, we must find him a new mate and tepee so my wife will not starve for me," he hinted as his caressing gaze roamed her lovely face and slender body. "We do not feed as often as in past days, but each feast is better and richer than the last. Never will we grow too old or weak to ride love's stallion together. I will prove this to my doubting wife on the new sun when we are alone."

Shalee laughed softly and stroked his arm. "No man has ever matched or will match the prowess of Gray Eagle upon the Plains or upon the sleeping mats. Your promise and your look cause me to quiver with longing and suspense. If you forget and leave with the hunters, I will come after you and drag you home to *rest* with me."

Their eyes fused and spoke of undying love and powerful passion, emotions greater than time or distance or measure. He grasped her hand, pulled it into his lap, covered it with his other one, and held it interlocked while their attention returned to the feast.

Bright Arrow glanced at his friend Flaming Star who was talking with his two sons, aged thirteen and eleven. He assumed his friend's five-year-old daughter was with his wife Morning Light. Unbidden envy surged through Bright Arrow, and he wished he had a son or sons to teach and train. His children were all girls and he loved them dearly, but he had missed the closeness and bond between father and son.

His father had sons; his best friend Windrider had sons; his close friend Flaming Star had sons. A man needed sons to help provide for and protect the family and tribe if anything happened to the father. Soon, he would be alone, for Tashina was of joining age and many men desired her and made offers for her. Yet, he wanted to wait until she came to him to speak of one special man, a man she could love and share a life with as he had done with Rebecca. Perhaps if he found another mate, she could bear him a son. He was still young and virile; and many men had children at ages longer than his, like White Arrow, who had given his seeds to Pretty Woman when he was fifty-four and fifty-six winters old. Surely a man of forty-two winters could plant his seeds in a fertile maiden, seeds to grow a son who would one day follow him as chief as he would follow his father.

Bright Arrow looked around the ever-widening circles and studied the females among them. Desert Flower smiled at him, a smile which implied she would leave her husband if he reached out for her. That insight did not come as a surprise to him, for she had chased him since they were young. After he had taken Rebecca captive, Desert Flower had been cruel and spiteful to his secret love. From the way she was enticing him, she had changed little over the years.

The same was true of Little Tears, her cohort in those brutal games with Rebecca. His gaze sought and found the other female, who had lost her mate only a few months past and had not as yet accepted a new one. She, too, was watching him and inviting him to take her bait.

Bright Arrow knew he could lure either female to his mat to appease his manly needs, but that would inspire them to dog him; and neither appealed to him as a mate, certainly not after Rebecca. Besides, they were his age, and perhaps their womanhoods were no longer fertile. Only a son could remove this void left by his lost love. If he must find another mate, she must be young and pretty and special. Perhaps the best thing to do was to visit the Cheyenne and Blackfeet camps to study their young maidens. Windrider and Silver Hawk could assist his search. Yes, after they set up summer camp, he would do that.

Thunder Spirit nudged Sun Cloud and remarked, "Your brother looks at women again. Perhaps we should capture him another white girl to fill his needs until he selects a new mate," he playfully suggested, careful to conceal his lingering resentment of Bright Arrow for allowing a warrior of another tribe to take his love before he could speak for her. At seventeen, Little Feet had been too young and innocent to be sent far away with strangers. One day, the brother of his close friend would pay for that mistake. Perhaps he should take Tashina in Little Feet's place and leave Bright Arrow alone in his empty tepee.

"No one can replace Wahea. He still longs for her return. It is hard to lose the woman you love as your own life. One day, my friend and brother, we will know such feelings."

Thunder Spirit pulled his probing gaze from Bright Arrow. "Yes, my friend and brother, such words are true. When do you ride to the camp of the Blackfeet again to tame a pretty wildcat?" he asked, recalling what Sun Cloud had shared about his time with Singing Wind.

"I will wait many moons to let her remember and crave the prowess of Sun Cloud. When next we see each other, she will be eager for my forgiveness and touch. She is strong and brave, and times are bad. A chief has need of a woman with courage and stamina, a woman who knows how to defend herself and her people when warriors are away. Perhaps in these troubled days it is not bad for a woman to be as she is. But she must be taught to conquer her tongue and ways when necessary. She must learn when and how much of her skills to use. She must learn that pride and honor are important, and must not be endangered. She must learn such things before Sun Cloud can approach her."

"Then you must find ways to teach her such things, my brother."

"The thinking or saying is easy, my friend, but the doing is not. In fifteen moons we will reach our summer camp, then I will begin my attack on Singing Wind's defiance. When it is conquered, I will lay claim to her," Sun Cloud boldly announced as the decision was made.

"What if you are defeated in this heady mission?" Thunder Spirit inquired, smothering his laughter.

"What woman of any intelligence and pride would refuse to be mellowed and claimed by the future chief of the awesome Oglala? But," he added mirthfully, "tell no one of my quest, in case I fail."

"You can trust no one more than your friend and brother," the warrior vowed honestly. "Be patient and have faith, and you will claim your love and destiny." As *I will somehow reclaim mine* . . .

Later, Sun Cloud slipped away to be alone. He could not forget his hunger for Singing Wind, or her stinging rebuff. This was a busy season for his tribe, but he needed and wanted to find time to win the heart and hand of the female whom he could not get out of his mind. With the move to their summer camp approaching and probable battles with the whites rapidly closing in on them, it would be difficult, if not impossible, to visit with Singing Wind. As the son of Gray Eagle and the future Oglala chief, his first duty was to his people. Sometimes he wished that Bright Arrow had not lost the right to become chief, for Bright Arrow had lost that rank through their father's vision and through his brother's love and choice of a white girl over his duty and tribe. Being a chief was a heavy responsibility, one with many sacrifices and demands. Yet, obviously the Great Spirit had chosen him as the future chief, and he could never refuse that honor and duty.

Sun Cloud strolled in the edge of the forest, deep in thought. Suddenly his keen senses detected another's presence. He turned cautiously and found Singing Wind leaning against a tree nearby. At first, he was annoyed with himself for allowing anyone to sneak up on him; then he smiled in delight and headed toward her.

"We are having a great feast tonight. Why do you not join us? Mother will be happy to see you," he remarked in a mellow tone. His sensual gaze noticeably and caressingly admired her from head to foot.

Singing Wind felt a tingle race over her body, and she was glad she had followed her impulse. She laughed softly as she sat down. "I watched for a long time, but I did not think it proper to interrupt a special ceremony. I was riding and thinking, and found myself nearby. There is something I must tell you, Sun Cloud," she hinted evocatively.

"Speak," he encouraged eagerly and sat down beside her. He was enlivened by the way she was looking at him. She smelled like a fresh day, and she sparkled with radiant life. When she spoke, her voice was like warm honey flowing over every sensitive area of his body.

"I do not wish you to think badly of me. In past moons we have teased each other without mercy, but those days must end. We are no longer children. I spoke in anger when we last talked. It was silly, and I ask your forgiveness. I thought you had insulted me and made me feel unworthy. I wanted to hurt you as you hurt me; this was childish and wrong. Sometimes I do not understand why I behave this way. Such warring thoughts and feelings often fill my head and heart, and it is hard to conquer them. I must learn to tame my wild tongue and temper. Is this not true?" she inquired, grinning mischievously.

He was thrilled by her arrival and mood. Not wanting to offend her again, he chose his words carefully. "It is true for everyone, Singing Wind. We have known each other since we were children, and it is hard to change the way we behave to each other. Often I tease you and anger you when I do not mean to do so. I wish us to be friends."

Singing Wind beamed with pleasure and relief. "I also wish us to be friends, Sun Cloud. I will try to be worthy of such a rank."

Grasping her hand, he replied tenderly, "There is no need to seek a rank which you already possess. You are a strong female, a special one. Let no one change you with their silly talk and envy. Come, join our feast," he invited, then explained the reason for it.

"The night grows darker and I must return home or my family will worry. If I am to prove the wicked tales about me are false, I must work to destroy one each sun," Singing Wind replied. "We will speak again soon. I only wished you to know I spoke rashly and hastily in the forest, and I wished to thank you for your help." She smiled and arose gracefully, hoping he would insist that she remain in his camp for the night.

Sun Cloud did not want her to leave, but he decided it was best for her to make that decision. If he pressed her too swiftly, she might dart away like a frightened doe, for she seemed nervous. He felt that this new relationship between them must be given time to grow before he pressed her for more than friendship. He stood, then walked with her to her waiting horse. When she turned to him before mounting, he leaned forward and kissed her lightly upon the lips. He was surprised and pleased when her lips clung to his for a greedy and lengthy kiss.

Abruptly she pulled away, lowered her gaze as if embarrassed, quickly mounted, then kneed her horse to carry her away rapidly. Sun Cloud observed her retreat and was tempted to race after her. This was a bad time, as vital events were taking place within his camp.

"Soon, my love, you will be mine," he vowed, then smiled happily.

Chapter Four

*E*arly the next morning, Shalee took a sharp knife and cut Bright Arrow's hair until it rested slightly above his shoulders and shortened gradually as it moved toward his jawline and up the sides of his face. She showed him how to "rag wave" the top and edges to make it appear more in a white man's style. Then she watched him adjust the garments which had been provided by Powchutu, dark pants and a deep green shirt. The color of the shirt brought out the hazel in his eyes, as the bright light enhanced the dark auburn of his hair. She eyed him from head to foot, then smiled at their success. Yes, he could pass for white.

Her gaze traveled to Powchutu, who was wearing a dark Eastern suit and off-white shirt. His hair had been trimmed earlier and its nearly gray color, along with the effects of advancing age and his lack of exposure to the Plains sun, took away from the darkness of his skin and eyes. Hopefully no one would guess his heritage or identity. It was done, and they were packed and ready to begin their journey.

Powchutu checked his pocket to make certain he had the letters he was to mail to New Orleans to Stede Gaston and Alisha Clarion. He was relieved that there was a way to contact his children one last time. He looked at Shalee and smiled. "Do not worry; we will be careful."

"Do what must be done and return to us safely," she replied. She hugged her son and gazed into his eyes for a moment, expressing her love and prayers. She knew Gray Eagle would not mind if she did the same with Powchutu, who seemed touched by her gesture.

Gray Eagle clasped forearms with his half brother and wished him victory and safety. "It is good you returned when your people and family need you." He embraced his son and smiled, knowing no words were necessary between them, but saying, "*Wakantanka* go with you and guide you, my son. Your courage and sacrifices are large this day. I am proud to be the father of Bright Arrow."

"As I am proud to be the son of Gray Eagle and Shalee," he replied.

Sun Cloud stepped forward and clasped forearms with Powchutu, then bear-hugged Bright Arrow. "You bring much honor to our tepee, my brother, and to yourself. You will know victory," he declared confidently. "Before I hunt, I will ride a way with you, for my heart beats with excitement and envy."

Bright Arrow grinned and gave Sun Cloud another bear hug. "We have ridden together many times, my brother and friend. If your face did not reflect that of our father, you could ride with me this sun. Guard our parents and people, my brother, for the whites are sly and eager. See to Tashina if trouble overtakes us," he entreated pointedly.

As they mounted, others came forward to speak their well-wishes. They rode away to the sound of the shaman's prayer. Gray Eagle and Shalee stood before their tepee, arm in arm, until they vanished.

All morning as the hunting party moved through the forest and meadows, Sun Cloud found himself straining for a sight or sound of Singing Wind. Twice he spooked deer while his concentration was low. He chided himself for his reckless lapses, for it easily could have been white or Indian foes he had flushed from hiding. Perhaps he should ride to the Cheyenne camp to visit with his friend Soul-of-Thunder. No, that was not wise with his brother gone and no one to see to their parents if there was a problem. Despite how strong and vital they appeared, Sun Cloud knew they were not. He had seen both grimace and battle the aches which chewed at aging bones. He had seen them tire more quickly and easily than the winter before this one. He knew that his parents sometimes forgot things and could no longer see with keen eyes. Living with them, he witnessed and grasped these changes more often than Bright Arrow who had his own tepee. It tugged at his heart to know their days on Mother Earth were numbered, but it gave him peace to know their perils and pains would end when they joined the Great Spirit. Perhaps he should find ways to do more of the hunting and the making of weapons, and perhaps he should capture a slave to help his mother with her chores. Yes, he must find ways to ease the burdens of daily existence upon his cherished parents.

The hunting party returned to camp during the rest period. Sun Cloud found the tepee flap closed, which indicated "do not disturb." A smile traveled across his handsome face as he wondered if his parents needed more than rest during this short time of privacy. He had never ceased to be amazed by their great passion for each other and for the sharing of a mat together. He saw the way they still looked at and touched each other. Their love was powerful and endless; their union had taught him what true love and fiery passion were, and it had caused him to long for the same with a woman. If he confessed the truth, perhaps he unwisely and un-fairly judged females by his mother's pattern and found them lacking her mixture of strength and gentleness, of pride and humility, of giving and taking.

He scowled at the thought of a major flaw in his character and thinking. Then he headed for Bright Arrow's tepee to see if Tashina was awake. If so, they could work on their gifts for Gray Eagle and Shalee: a new quiver for his arrows and new moccasins for her. Tashina was skilled with her sewing and beading. It gave him great pleasure to give her pictorial suggestions, to collect special items to include, and to mark the patterns upon the leather for her; for he was talented with his hands and paints, and had done most of the colorful designs and depic-tions of *coups* on his father's tepee. He was also responsible for the paintings on the buffalo robe which revealed the pictographic history of their family. When time allowed, he must include the description of the return and existence of his father's brother. As instructed, he would record Powchutu as Eagle's Arm, half-Oglala and half-Cheyenne son of Running Wolf and Tamarra. Sun Cloud realized, for a tribe and chief who were alleged to reject all foes, the Oglalas and Gray Eagle had accepted two whites and a half-Crow into their tribe. Of course, few Oglalas were aware of the enemy bloods that lived in their camp.

Sun Cloud found Tashina beading in her tepee with the flap tossed aside, so he ducked and joined her for the afternoon.

In the tepee of Gray Eagle, the chief was lying upon his mat with his wife. His lips and hands had been teasing over her flesh with appreciation and stimulation. He smiled into her eyes as his mouth covered hers. She clasped him to her naked body and ran her fingers over his shoulders and back as she savored their contact and impending union. She knew his desire matched hers, for his manhood had grown larger as he tantalized her to quivering anticipation.

As her lips teased over his face, she murmured, "How is it possible to love you more and more each day when my heart has been filled with love for you for so many winters? I shall love you forever."

He looked down into her face, treasuring her expression and words. "No matter how full a heart, there is always space for more love. No power or man has existed who could take you from my side. You have been my air, my water, the force of my heart. Without your possession, I would not have been complete. If I had lost you, I could not have lived without you. I have even challenged the Bird of Death to keep you. You are mine forever, even beyond Mother Earth. I never grow weary of having you in my life or upon my mat. You captured my heart and inflamed my body the moment I saw you long ago. No matter how many times my lips and body claim yours, each new time is sweeter than the one before. I love you with all I am and will ever be."

Tears of joy dampened her lashes. "Only a man of great strength and honor can confess to such feelings, my love. I am what I am for knowing you. Make our bodies one as our hearts are one."

Gray Eagle gently lay upon her and sealed their lips as he entered her. Slowly he carried her to sensual heights in the Eagle's domain. They soared in the magic wonder of their never-ending passion. Soon, they clung tightly as they were rewarded blissfully for their mutual efforts. Then leisurely their spirits descended to reality, and they lay nestled together as sleep overtook them.

It was midmorning of the following day when Powchutu and Bright Arrow arrived at the fort. Neither was surprised to find the gates open, for the soldiers were cocky this time of year, knowing the Indians were busy obtaining supplies, making weapons, and preparing for their moves to their summer encampments. The guard eyed them nonchalantly as they rode inside and dismounted near the sutler's post.

The sutler was a husky man in his early forties, eager to meet new faces, especially those who needed supplies. "What can I do for you, fellers?" he inquired genially.

"Me and my friend's son need a few supplies. We're camping over there on Chucker's Creek. We'll be heading farther west as soon as we take a few days to catch our breaths. It's been a long journey from St. Louis. We heard it's good trapping a week's ride upriver," Powchutu chatted amiably as he collected an item here and there.

Bright Arrow had lazed against a wooden support post, having reminded himself not to stand straight and alert. Last night, he had wet his hair and secured rags around the edges to make it wave slightly as his mother had shown him. A flintlock musket was thrown over his shoulder and a bag of cartridges hung from his belt, as did a hunting knife. He seemed content to let his friend make their purchases.

Powchutu was also carrying a breechloader which used a cartridge containing powder and ball that fired from the impact of the hammer on a percussion cap which was held by a nipple. He wished he had brought along the "Brown Bess" flintlock musket he had gotten in England. Although it required twelve steps to prime and load the awkward weapon, a trained man could fire five balls a minute, which favorably compared to the number of arrows a hostile Indian could fire, and certainly could beat the skills and speed of the common American soldier.

"You two chose a bad time to take up in this area. I suppose you've never heard of them Sioux who still think this whole goldarn area is theirs. Now that we own her, the Army should stop taking their crap and kick their asses as far west as possible, right into that ocean Clark and Lewis found."

Powchutu smiled, then asked jokingly, "Sure we've heard of the Sioux, and Cheyenne, and Crow. I guess nobody asked them if they cared if we bought all this land from the French. From what we've been told, they didn't recognize Spanish or French ownership, so why should they think the Americans could buy what wasn't the French's to sell? I think we'll be plenty safe with so many forts and soldiers out here. We're thinking about setting up a permanent camp along the Missouri, and it's best to get the jump on other trappers before the new season starts. From the hides and pelts we've seen from this area, hunting and trapping's got to be mighty rewarding."

"Yep, it's that alright. What's your name, stranger?"

"I'm Tanner Gaston, and that there is Clay Rivera. Me and his pa's been partners for nigh unto forty years."

The man extended his hand and responded, "Good to meet you. I'm Edward Jackson, but most call me Jacks."

"Who's in command here, Jacks?" Powchutu inquired.

"Right now, Major Gerald Butler, but we're expecting a big general next month, Phillip Cooper. Won't be none too soon if you asked me," he remarked, then glanced around to make sure they were alone before confiding, "When the colonel took sick and died, Butler only outranked Major Ames by two months, and Bill thinks he's better qualified than Gerald. They been fussing for months over how to whip those Sioux into line before General Cooper arrives. The other officers are split down the middle on loyalty. Wouldn't surprise me none if Major Ames met with an accident, if you know what I mean. If it's up to Captain Smith and Captain Rochelle, he won't live to meet General Cooper to complain. If I was Major William Ames, I would watch my back real careful like. Which is what you fellers better do when Butler goes charging after them Sioux and stirrin' 'em up again."

"Why doesn't Major Butler wait for this General Cooper's arrival to see how he wants to handle the problem, if there is one? We haven't noticed any trouble since we got here."

"That's because they just got spring stirrings in their guts. They'll be heading out of them hills soon, then you'll know they're around, mark my words. Once that Gray Eagle riles 'em up, you won't see no peace around these parts till next winter."

"I thought Gray Eagle was only a legend. Is he for real?"

"For real?" the man echoed incredulously. "Are you joshing? There ain't a man, red or white, who wouldn't turn tail and run from him. He's a real devil, and them Indians would follow him through the flames of hell and back. If we could get rid of him, we could tame the rest of 'em. Lordy, Tanner, you and Clay don't want to tangle with him."

"Seems to me like you have plenty of men and supplies here. I doubt those redskins will give the U.S. Army much hassle. We saw so many soldiers, the fort can't hold them all; they're camped all around this place. And we passed lots of supply wagons on our way here."

"You're right about us having more men and supplies than we've had since we got here, but I won't feel good until General Cooper arrives with his troops and wagons. Once they get here, every Injun in this territory could ride against us and it won't make no never mind."

Two men entered the sutler's post. "What'll it be Capt'n Smith?" Edward Jackson inquired, alerting his guests to the man's identity and hoping they would hold his previous comments a secret. It wouldn't do to get thrown out of this fort! He warned himself it was best to learn to keep his mouth shut, especially around strangers.

Clarence Smith studied the two unknown men as he responded, "Give me a plug of your best chew. Haven't seen you two around before," he remarked evocatively.

Bright Arrow could feel the keen eyes of the Crow scout Red Band on him. He remained loose and calm, as if nothing and no one troubled him on this lovely day. He smiled and nodded affably when Captain Smith glanced his way.

Powchutu introduced them and repeated his tale; this time, he added, "I was about to ask Mr. Jackson if there is a place on the fort where I can post some letters home to my children."

"Where's home?" Smith asked boldly.

"New Orleans for my family, but me and my partner, Clay's pa, travel a lot looking for new trapping grounds and setting them up for our men. I'm getting too old for this kind of work and worry. This'll be my last year in the wilds. I plan to settle down and play with my grandchildren."

"If I was you two, I would head that way at sunrise. This area ain't gonna be safe for anyone come next month."

"What do you mean?" Powchutu questioned in mock surprise, as if Jackson had told him nothing. "You expecting trouble?"

"Yep, big trouble, with them Sioux," Smith stated; then he sneered.

"America bought this land fair and square, Captain Smith. Why shouldn't we be safe? The Army is here to protect us, isn't it?"

"The only place you would be safe is inside this fort, Gaston, and it's brimming with men and horses now."

"We were told the Army has a treaty with the Indians."

"Injuns can't read and they don't honor treaties. They're stupid savages who don't know nothing but fighting and killing."

Without even looking his way, Bright Arrow knew the scout's gaze had not left his face since their arrival. Surely the despicable Crow could not recognize him . . . Surely he could not "smell a foe a meadow away" as the Crow boasted? Bright Arrow knew Red Band was trying to use the force of his stare to compel his attention, but he simply kept watching and listening to the others. He was careful to keep an interested look on his face and to hold his body lax. He had noticed that Captain Clarence Smith had not introduced the scout.

"That's probably true, Captain Smith, but a man is still just as dead from their arrows. We'll keep guards posted at our camp."

"You do that, Gaston," Smith scoffed, then turned to leave. To Bright Arrow he advised, "If I were you, Rivera, I would get your old friend out of this area so he'll live to play with those grandchildren."

Bright Arrow sent the surly man a lopsided smile and then replied, "My pa hasn't been able to talk any sense into Tanner's head for forty years, Captain Smith, so I doubt he'll be able to at this age. He's a feisty old coot, tougher than he looks and talks. We'll be real careful."

"Be a shame for this good ole' coot to lose his hair. How long you two staying around?" the captain asked a final question.

"Soon as we get our supplies, we'll be returning to camp. Course, we would like to meet the commanding officer if that's possible."

"Afraid it ain't. He's out scouting the area and making plans to surprise them Sioux." A cold, evil burst of laughter came from the man as he reflected on the "surprise" in store for Gray Eagle's band. "Come on, Red Band, let's get moving. We've got something to handle."

Powchutu and Bright Arrow glanced at the scout for the first time. He was wearing a bright yellow bandana around his head which had been rolled into a two-inch headband, a faded cavalry jacket—beneath which he wore the top to a pair of red Longjohns from which the arms had been removed to battle the heat—buckskin pants, and knee-high moccasins. The scout's expression was stoic, but his eyes were cold and shiny like dark icicles. There were numerous lines around his eyes from squinting in the harsh sunlight and from studying his surroundings. On his head, he placed a black felt hat from which dangled several scalplocks, no doubt Sioux. He stared at both men as they studied him. His eyes narrowed as he took one last look at each, then he left.

"That fort scout isn't talkative or friendly, is he?" Powchutu joked.

"Red Band don't like nobody, but he's a damn good scout, the best. He can smell a Sioux a mile away. Hates 'em. Crow and Sioux been enemies longer than whites been in this area. You said you wanted to send some letters out?" the sutler reminded Powchutu.

"Can you handle it for me?"

"No trouble at all. I handle all the mail for regular folk in this area. My man will take it to St. Louis, then it'll be put on a riverboat to New Orleans. Cost you a dollar to send mail that far."

"It's worth it for my family not to worry about me. They think I've been too old for traveling for years." He pulled the two letters from his pocket, then handed the man two dollars.

Edward Jackson looked at the names and addresses. He smiled and said, "I can tie 'em together and charge you only one dollar since they're going to the same place."

"It might be best if you leave them separated, just in case one gets lost," Powchutu suggested.

The man smiled and nodded. "Ain't lost a letter yet, but it's bound to happen one day."

"We'd best be on our way before dark, Clay. Been nice meeting you and doing business with you, Jacks. Maybe we'll see you again soon."

"Been my pleasure, Tanner, Clay. You fellers take care."

Bright Arrow and Powchutu gathered their purchases and left, to find the Crow scout Red Band near their horses. Bright Arrow dared not glance around to see if any soldiers were approaching or watching them, for that would give away his feeling of suspicion and alarm. Without appearing to do so, he called his body and mind to full alert. He saw Powchutu's hand tighten ever so slightly on the cotton sack he was holding, which revealed that his uncle also sensed danger and was preparing himself, unnoticeably, to confront it.

They looked at the Crow Indian, but did not smile or speak, as scouts were considered beneath whites and treated as invisible unless there was a reason for acknowledging them or their presence. Powchutu tied his bundle to his horse, as did Bright Arrow. Both secured their muskets in place. Before they could mount, the Indian spoke.

"Your horses not shod. They strong and alert."

Powchutu halted his movements and turned. He looked at the scout indignantly and asked, "Are you addressing me?" It was not a good sign that the scout felt confident enough to approach them.

"I speak to you. Your horses wear no shoes. They Indian trained."

"What business is it of yours, scout?" Powchutu asked angrily.

"Horses are Indian; they Sioux," the scout persisted boldly.

"You have a problem here, Red Band?" an officer inquired.

The scout repeated his words, then the officer looked from Bright Arrow to Powchutu as he reasoned out the scout's insinuation. Before he could ask for an explanation, the sutler joined them and asked, "You got a problem, Tanner? 'Morning, Major."

The officer inquired, "You know these men, Jackson?"

The sutler smiled and replied, "That's Tanner Gaston and Clay Rivera. They been visiting me this afternoon and picking up some goods."

The officer looked at the two men and announced pleasantly, "I'm Major William Ames. Pleased to meet you. How'd you rile our scout?"

"He demanded to know why our horses aren't shod. Can't say it's any of his affair, but we traded them off some friendly Indians, about fifty or sixty miles southeast of here, best I recollect. They've been damn good mounts, real strong and fast and alert. We came this way by boat and needed them. Can't get around this area on foot. It isn't against the law to trade for Indian horses, is it?"

As with Captain Smith, this officer was duped by Powchutu's easy command of the English language, his appearance, and manner. "Nope, especially not from Indians in that area. They're about as peace-loving and gentle as Indians come. They do a lot of trading with whites. Made a real impression on Lewis and Clark when they traveled through that area. We ain't had no trouble with them, and don't expect to. If I can get President Monroe to listen to me about creating an Indian bureau and sending some specialized agents out here, we could solve some problems before there's more bloodshed. We can't keep pushing these Indians around and out; there's too many of them, and they got rights. It's all a lack of trust and communication. I suppose you two disagree?"

"Whenever and wherever it's possible, Major Ames, we work and pray for peace. Seems to me if some giving and sharing and understanding were done, there wouldn't be so much taking and killing and dying. Like you said, Major, we need some serious talk and trust."

"I wish you would take those thoughts and feelings to the President, Mr. Gaston; I can't seem to catch his ear."

"I just might do that after I return home to New Orleans. I can't ask men to hunt and trap for my company in a land that isn't safe. We should be riding along, Major Ames; it still gets dark early. Is this the only fort in this area? I'm sure we'll need supplies again."

"There's a fort in every direction from us, two to five days' ride. Next time you're here, drop in to see me," Ames invited.

"I'll do that, sir. It's refreshing to meet a soldier who thinks with his head and heart instead of his saber and musket. If I see Monroe, I'll tell him to be certain to heed all letters from you."

Powchutu and Bright Arrow mounted, waved, and rode toward the gate. The scout looked at Major William Ames and remarked, "They bad enemies of whites. Do not trust them. They Indian, Sioux."

Major Ames laughed heartily. "You've been riding with Major Butler and listening to him too long, Red Band. Those gentlemen aren't any threat to us. They're about as Sioux as I am. You should be careful who you insult," he warned. "Where's Captain Smith? I thought you two were riding out this morning."

The scout replied, "Captain in quarters. We leave after sun pass overhead." Red Band would never tell this officer that Captain Clarence Smith had joined one of the "laundresses" in his bunk for an hour. "I get things ready; captain join; we ride."

"Just be careful where you two ride," Ames cautioned. "We don't need any trouble before General Cooper arrives. We'll let him handle the situation, if one arises." Ames knew those two loved to bait and fight Sioux, especially when they were low on supplies and busy with their spring trek, or out hunting in small parties.

"We follow Major Butler's orders. We scout and plan."

"Like I said, Red Band, only scout and plan," Ames stressed. "And I want a full report when you return," Ames told him, hoping it would be before Butler's return, as that glory-seeking bastard was always countermanding his orders and pulling dangerous stunts.

Red Band looked at the major as the officer strolled away. He disliked and mistrusted this man who was becoming an Indian-lover, and Major Ames obviously felt contempt for him. He had to be careful in his siding with Butler and Smith because he needed the cavalry to help wipe out his tribe's enemies, the Sioux. When that was accomplished, his people could claim this area. He would not report to Major Ames; he and Smith would report to Major Butler as ordered. Butler and Smith were right, he decided; Ames was a threat to all of their plans, and should be slain soon. He knew his instincts had never failed him, and he felt challenged to prove Ames wrong. He glanced at the gate, then headed to the corral for his horse to track the two men. He had enough time to check out his suspicions before Smith was ready to ride. Before he could leave, another white man rode up and dismounted. Red Band eyed his buckskins and curly hair.

"You know all trappers?" the scout asked.

"You could say I know most of them, and those I ain't met, I know about," the man replied, his curiosity seized.

"You know man called Tanner Gaston?" Red Band questioned. The tall white man gave the name some thought, then shook his head. "You know man called Clay Rivera?"

"Sure do," Murray Murdock replied with a sly grin.

"When you last see?" the scout asked, eyeing Murray strangely.

"What's in your craw, Red Band?"

"Man called Clay Rivera here today. Red Band no trust, no like."

Murray laughed. "You two tangle?" he teased, but the scout shook his head. "I met Clay Rivera years ago. He had a cabin about fifty miles from here. Every so often, we saw each other hunting or at the old trading post. We were guides and hunters for that Lewis and Clark expedition. Never met a braver man or better guide. Saved my hide and I saved his a time or two. He returned to his cabin and family after we finished. He's got a wife and three girls, probably grown by now. Haven't seen him since. Is he living and trapping in this area now?" Murray asked innocently. He wondered why Bright Arrow would come to this fort, then decided it was to check out the rumors of the Army's preparation to begin a full assault on the Sioux next month. He had been good friends with Gray Eagle's son, as Clay Rivera, and knew him to be a fair and honest man. He had not learned of his true identity until they were parting for the last time. The Sioux had wanted to know what Lewis and Clark were up to, and Bright Arrow had joined the group, found they were no threat, and had left them alone. He could not find fault in the Sioux's wanting to know what they're up against, so they could protect their families and homes.

Murray knew that trappers, often called mountain men, usually were considered kindred spirits by most Indians because these restless white men rarely staked claims on Indian land, and they often married Indian women and sometimes became tribal members—if they earned that right. Most Indians realized that mountain men were similar to them, lovers and protectors of nature, men who wanted to get away from other whites and their evils. Most lived and trapped alone or with a squaw and gave the Indians no trouble or problems. Yet, as hundreds of trappers had followed the path of Lewis and Clark, along with soldiers, forts had been built and they had encouraged the coming of trading posts and fur companies. With these had come the white man's evils: whiskey, illnesses, weapons, and the items which had made many Indians into dependent creatures who now lived near forts where they could obtain trade goods. The same items—kettles, blankets, guns, knives, hatchets, and such—which had made the Indian's life easier also took away from his self-sufficiency and pride. Murray knew "Clay Rivera" was not a trapper, just as he knew and understood why he and his tribe were concerned and provoked by the white man's selfish intentions and abuses of their sacred lands and people.

Murray's replies to Red Band were true, so the scout could not read deception in his expression or tone. "He no look white."

"That's because he isn't. I was told Clay Rivera is Spanish."

"You trust this man?" the scout probed.

"Haven't been given any reason not to. Where are they camped?"

"Chucker's Creek, they say," Red Band replied skeptically.

"I'll be riding that way in a few days. I'll stop by and visit with him. How's things going here? General Cooper arrived yet?"

"Major Butler say talk to no man not soldier. Plans secret."

Murray shrugged and grinned. "That sounds like you don't trust anyone, Red Band. Suit yourself. I ain't got no quarrel with the Indians, so they leave me alone. If I were you and Major Butler, I'd be real careful who I antagonize. If you think you can squash those Sioux, you best talk with some of the old-timers before you find out you're *dead* wrong to challenge them." Murray headed for the sutler's post, whistling and grinning.

Captain Clarence Smith joined the scout, strapping on his holster and scowling. He grumbled, "I wish one of them traveling sutlers would come this way with some women who know how to please a man. Them Injun washwomen don't do nothing but lay there or grunt like pigs. What were you and Murray jawing about, Red Band?"

The scout related all that had taken place since they had parted earlier. "I say, track them. Red Band have bad feelings."

Excitement charged through Clarence Smith. "I ain't had me a good fight in ages, Red Band. Let's go."

Miles from the fort, Bright Arrow caught up with Powchutu. He chuckled as he told his half-uncle, "When that Crow dog comes after us, he will find nothing but dirt and wind. The day will not come when a Crow dog can track Bright Arrow. We ride home, Eagle's Arm," he stated in high spirits. He was eager to reach camp the next day to report their findings.

Silver Hawk rode into the Oglala camp with several warriors. They dismounted and headed for Gray Eagle's tepee, to be greeted by Shalee. Silver Hawk looked at the woman who should have been his mother. He knew of the stories which told of how his mother Chela had been disobedient, willful, and overly bold, of how she had tried to kill Shalee who had been living as Gray Eagle's white captive in those terrible days before it was revealed that she was the long-missing daughter of Black Cloud. If Shalee had joined to his father Brave Bear, he and his sisters would have different lives, better ones. And doubtlessly his father would still be chief, still be alive to leave the chief's bonnet to him, a rank which he had lost because he had been only five when his father had died, too young to become chief. Gray Eagle was to blame for stealing the daughter of Black Cloud from her people and from her place in his life. She was what a mother and wife should be, and he envied her loss to the Oglala. Even though Shalee had lived over sixty winters, she was beautiful and desirable. If others would not think him mad, he would steal her as his own, for he loved her and often dreamed of possessing her in all ways.

As was common in the Indian culture, he embraced her and addressed her as mother. "I come to see my other family, Mother. The lands and animals grow restless during their rebirths, as do warriors who are eager to hunt and to raid. We come to learn when our Oglala brothers leave the sacred hills to hunt the buffalo."

Shalee halted her task to smile at Silver Hawk and to welcome him to their camp and tepee. There was something about Silver Hawk which troubled her, but she concealed her curious feelings. She knew that the Blackfeet warrior was very fond of her, but she wondered how he would feel if he knew she was not Shalee and was all white. On occasion he would visit his "cousins" Bright Arrow and Sun Cloud, and was considered a good friend to her oldest son. Yet, she always sensed he was after something and was not thinking the same way he spoke.

"We travel in three moons, Silver Hawk. We await the return of Bright Arrow and Eagle's Arm from the white man's fort. Speak the news of your wife and sisters," she entreated politely.

He responded hurriedly, then returned to the statement which had caught his ear. "All is good with them, Mother. Why did Bright Arrow ride to the white man's fort? Who is the man at his side?"

Shalee patiently related the public story about Powchutu, then revealed their mission at the fort. She witnessed Silver Hawk's annoyance and disappointment, and was not surprised by his next words.

"I should be at the side of Bright Arrow in this great *coup.*"

Shalee smiled indulgently. "You cannot look white, my son, and would endanger your life and his. Will you stay to hear his words?" she invited cordially, hoping he would not accept, but knowing he would. She scolded herself for feeling intimidated around Silver Hawk and for having such wild speculations about his conduct and feelings, but he touched her frequently and strangely and he observed her intensely: looks and touches of a man who was wooing a woman or a man who desired a woman. If she did not know better . . . She pushed such foolish charges from her mind, telling herself she was mistaken.

Silver Hawk questioned, "When does Bright Arrow return?"

"Before the sun sleeps on the new day, if all goes as planned."

"We will remain to hear his words," Silver Hawk replied without conferring with his three warriors. "Where is Gray Eagle and Sun Cloud? We will share news and words with them."

"Gray Eagle sits near the river with others. They make plans and weapons for the buffalo hunt. Sun Cloud is away hunting." She pointed out the direction and watched them leave. Then she went to find Tashina, to ask her help with preparing a large meal for their guests.

Sun Cloud was irritated to discover that Silver Hawk was visiting the Oglala camp and had probably taken Singing Wind with him. He had ridden swiftly to the Blackfeet camp with hopes of spending a short time with the adopted daughter of Chief Medicine Bear before having to return home from "his hunt." He wanted to show Singing Wind that he was very interested in her by promptly returning her recent visit. Soon, their summer camps would place a lengthy distance between them, and spring tasks would consume most of their time and energies.

As casually as possible, Sun Cloud questioned the chief about Singing Wind. As no one knew of her whereabouts, Medicine Bear said that he suspected she had left with Silver Hawk to visit Gray Eagle and Shalee and had forgotten to tell anyone. Medicine Bear told Sun Cloud that Singing Wind often went riding, even hunting, just to be alone. He revealed how the girl had been observed practicing her skills with the bow, lance, and knife in the depths of the nearby forest. He spoke of how Singing Wind would track and slay animals, then give their meat and hides to those in need. He said it was no secret that Singing Wind had become an expert rider, and she often challenged boastful warriors to races, but none would compete, to her vexation.

Medicine Bear explained how Singing Wind was changing rapidly these days, and she no longer wanted to be teased or scolded. "It is hard for one with such a brave heart and bold spirit to live as a woman. It is as if the Great Spirit mistakenly placed a warrior in the body of a female. Sometimes I forget she is a girl and I treat her like a son. I wish it could be different for Singing Wind, but it cannot. She is a woman, and she must live and die as one."

Sun Cloud listened to the impressive tales about the female who was sounding more and more like his mother in character and appeal. He never doubted Singing Wind's skills and courage, but he wondered how long she could continue battling everyone who thought she was wrong to behave in the manner described by Medicine Bear. "Perhaps when your daughter finds love and accepts a mate, she will become more like a female. Her spirit is restless and wild, as her mother's was. Some warrior will conquer her and tame her as Brave Bear did to Chela. It will be a mighty battle of wills, Medicine Bear. The man who accepts her challenge must be brave and blind," he joked, not wanting the chief to suspect his feelings and motives yet.

The older man laughed heartily and agreed. "It is so, Sun Cloud. I must seek a warrior with the heart and strength of a bear, the cunning of the wolf, and the patience of a beaver to defeat my daughter."

"Do you think such a strong man exists?" Sun Cloud inquired, attempting to extract the name of any male who might be after her.

"I pray there is at least one such man, and that he finds her and wins her soon. Few women live in their father's tepee at her number of winters. If she remains with me for her twenty-fourth winter, others will wonder what is wrong with her. I love her, and I worry about her. I wish her to be happy, to accept herself and rank."

"I will help you find a mate for Singing Wind. Her mother was Oglala, so there is a place for her in our camp. The sun moves closer to the breast of Mother Earth; I must return to my camp."

"May the Great Spirit go with you and guide you, Sun Cloud. If we do not meet again before we leave the sacred hills, I will see you at the joint buffalo hunt and Sun Dance."

"It will be good to ride and to feast with Medicine Bear and the Blackfeet once more." He wanted to hurry home, envisioning Singing Wind sitting in his tepee this very moment.

Sun Cloud was mounted and ready to leave when Medicine Bear exclaimed, "There she is! Singing Wind, come to us," he called to the girl not far away. "We did not know where you were."

"I have been riding and hunting," she informed them. "Why were you seeking me?" she asked, her gaze remaining on the chief. She had overheard enough of Sun Cloud's playful words to be perturbed. She had hoped that he no longer teased her or joked about her. Why did everyone think she had to be conquered and tamed? She was not an animal. What was she doing that was so terribly wrong? Sun Cloud had offered her friendship and had made romantic overtures toward her; then, behind her back, he made fun of her! Obviously he had not changed his bad opinion of her, but he would one day!

"Sun Cloud came to visit Silver Hawk and Singing Wind, but your brother is visiting the Oglalas. When we could not find you, we thought you had forgot to tell me you had ridden away with Silver Hawk."

"I would never leave camp without telling you, my second father. I would not wish to worry you. I did not know of Silver Hawk's visit."

"If you wish to visit my father and mother, you can ride to our camp with me," Sun Cloud offered, trying to control his eagerness as he grinned enticingly at her.

Singing Wind shook her head. "When my brother is away, I hunt for Shining Feather and guard her for Silver Hawk. I will visit them another sun. If you do not hurry, darkness will surround you."

Sun Cloud gazed at her oddly, for it seemed as if she was trying to get rid of him quickly. She looked and sounded as if she was angry with him, and he could not imagine why. After their last meeting, he assumed things would be different, better, between them. Obviously he had misread her behavior, or she had been playing with him. He nodded acceptance of her refusal, then rode away.

Singing Wind followed Medicine Bear to their tepee, hoping he would say more about Sun Cloud and his visit, and the chief did.

He handed her a lovely white hide and told her, "Sun Cloud left this gift for you. It is very beautiful and special. You were cold to him."

Singing Wind fingered the exquisite hide which would make a prized cape for the next winter. She was surprised by the gift, and questioned its meaning. Immediately she grasped her new error where the appealing warrior was concerned. She sighed in annoyance, knowing she could not go chasing after him to apologize again. To do so would only prove to him that she had been mean intentionally. If she let it pass, perhaps, hopefully, he would think she had been fatigued or distracted. She berated herself for losing the chance to be alone with him on the trail. She promised herself she would never act this foolish way again.

It was late when the men in Gray Eagle's tepee finished eating and talking. Shalee told the Blackfeet warriors where to place their bedrolls for the night. No one had questioned Sun Cloud's absence from the meal, but all had noticed it. When Tashina arose to return to her tepee, Silver Hawk smiled broadly and asked to escort her there, to share some words from Singing Wind.

Silver Hawk left the tepee with Tashina close behind him. He was glad Sun Cloud was late in returning to camp, for it allowed him time to be alone with this female who resembled Shalee and carried her blood. "We will walk and take fresh air before we sleep."

"I am weary, Silver Hawk. The day has been long and busy," Shalee's granddaughter softly rejected his suggestion.

He caught her hand in his and coaxed as he pulled her past Bright Arrow's tepee. "Come, the air will calm your mind and body." He would not take a polite "no" for an answer, and knew she would not offend him by blatantly refusing to be friendly. He walked along the stream bank, remaining silent and continuing to hold her hand.

Tashina felt nervous and timid, for Silver Hawk had been watching her strangely during his last few visits and especially during this one. "What words did Singing Wind send to me?" she finally asked.

He grinned and confessed, "She sent no words. I wished to be alone with you. You are beautiful, Tashina, and you make Silver Hawk feel good and happy."

Tashina did not know how to respond to his words and warm tone. When he halted and lifted her chin to look into her eyes, she trembled.

"Have you chosen a mate for joining?" he asked unexpectedly.

Confusion filled her gaze. "I have not," she replied.

"It is time to think on such matters, Tashina. Does no warrior stand above others in your eyes and heart?"

"My father needs me to care for him. I cannot think of such things when there is much work to be done. We leave this place soon."

"I must think of such things. Shining Feather can bear no children. I have need of a second wife to give me sons. Tashina is strong and good, the granddaughter of a great chief. She would make a good wife for Silver Hawk," he concluded aloud, to her astonishment.

She used the only argument to come to mind. "We are of the same family, Silver Hawk. You must cast your eyes on another."

"There is no bloodline between us, Tashina. It will be good for the son of Brave Bear to join with the daughter of his friend Bright Arrow and the granddaughter of Shalee. Do you find Silver Hawk ugly?" he inquired, motioning to his facial scar.

"I do not," she quickly replied. "Silver Hawk is a great warrior, and the scar takes nothing from his looks. I am not ready to think of joining or ready to leave my father alone."

Silver Hawk clasped her face between his hands and looked deeply into her eyes. "You are a woman, Tashina, and I desire you." His mouth covered hers and his arms quickly captured her body against his.

Taken off guard, she could not react. He kissed her skillfully and hungrily until her wits cleared and she pushed away from him. "You are joined to another and should not speak so and do such things."

His gaze and voice were seductive as he huskily protested. "It is our way to have more than one wife when a mate cannot care for all of her husband's needs. I have need of children. I wish you to be the mother of my sons and to give me pleasure on my sleeping mat. As I will give you pleasure, Tashina. Do not fear me or fear joining. You are brave and must face becoming a full woman. I will protect you and provide all you need. I will make you my number one wife, and Shining Feather will do your bidding."

"It is wrong to put another in her place because she cannot bear children. She will be sad. She might return to her people," Tashina warned, for a Cheyenne wife was permitted to leave her mate if she chose.

"If Tashina enters my life and tepee, I will need no other woman. You bring fires to my heart and body as no woman has before. I have waited many full moons before coming to you and your father. I knew of your sadness over Wahea's loss. It is time for life to begin anew for Bright Arrow and Tashina. I will give you all a woman desires." His hands were stroking up and down her arms and he was enslaving her gaze. "I will be all you need in a man and husband. Join me, Tashina," he urged, sealing their lips once more.

Tashina was flattered by Silver Hawk's proposal and confession of desire. His kisses and touches were pleasing, but she did not want him to fill her life and heart. She must not spurn him cruelly. "I am honored you wish Tashina as your mate, but

I do not love you, Silver Hawk. Your words and feelings surprise me. I cannot say yes to a man who does not fill my heart as I fill his," she told him softly. Tashina wondered what would happen to her if Soul-of-Thunder took another woman. He had made no advances to her, and might never do so. She thought of the sufferings her father had endured since her mother's loss. It was terrible to experience such anguish, such loneliness. Could she love and desire another man? she asked herself. This man? She had to admit that Silver Hawk was wickedly handsome and stimulating. How, she wondered, did a woman know her feelings for a man until she tested them? Silver Hawk was tempting and appealing, and he desired her greatly. No man had kissed her this way or revealed such a potent hunger for her. If Soul-of-Thunder had such feelings, surely he could not hide them. The responses Silver Hawk created with his words and actions were exciting, and his heady ache for her caused tingling sensations to travel her body, and mischief to tease her mind.

Silver Hawk knew he had taken her unaware; yet, he knew he must not be pushy and frightening. A woman liked to be first in a man's life, as he liked to be first in hers. He would chase her slowly and gently, for a while. He would find a way to possess her, with or without her agreement. He had felt her tremble at his touch, and presumed she desired him. She was too caught up in her father's life and problems. If Bright Arrow would take another mate, Tashina would feel it was time to leave the tepee of new lovers. He would watch her closely on the new sun to see if any male brightened her eyes.

Silver Hawk smiled and caressed her cheek. He vowed slyly, "I will give Tashina time to match Silver Hawk's feelings. Think on me and my words. I will speak them again another moon. Come, it is late and you are weary. I wish you to be happy, Tashina, and it will be so with me. I love you and desire you, and I will not give up on you. You are more special than any other woman. If you had not been a child when it was time for me to take a wife, I would have claimed you four winters ago. Each time I see you or hear your voice, my heart races like the wild stallion. I will not be complete without you."

"You are kind and gentle, Silver Hawk. But know, I can join only the man who stands above all others to me alone. Have you spoken of your feelings to my father?" she asked suddenly.

"It is not right to speak of a mate trade to your father before you know of my thoughts and plans. Many take mates against their wishes; I do not want it this way between Silver Hawk and Tashina." His hands clasped her face between them again and his thumbs stroked the area beneath her eyes as he said, "When you look at me, I wish you to see and think of no other. When my lips claim yours, I wish you to hunger only for my taste," he murmured as his mouth brushed over hers and his tongue teased at her parted lips. "When my hands reach for you, I wish your body to respond only to their loving touch," he whispered into her ear as his palms lightly and sensuously rubbed over her brown peaks which came to life beneath her garment.

"When I take you to my sleeping mat, I wish you to desire only my body locked with yours." He pressed her tenderly to the tree behind her, brushing his aroused maleness against her womanhood as his mouth seared over hers in a blaze of rising passion. As his lips drifted over her face, he vowed, "I want no woman but you, Tashina, and I wish you to desire no man but me. It will be so one day," he stated in confidence, for her taut breasts and lack of resistance had misled him. "We must return to camp before your magic enslaves me and I cannot control my cravings for you. I should fear your powerful hold over me, Tashina, but I am too weakened and inflamed by you to be careful or wise. I will suffer larger than the mountains if I do not win you."

"I will think on you and your words," she promised, slightly breathless and quivering. If she could not have Soul-of-Thunder . . .

Sun Cloud reached his tepee before Silver Hawk's return. He told his parents that, since they had guests and the tepee was full, he would sleep in Bright Arrow's tepee. He left quickly, wanting to avoid Silver Hawk, and not wanting to explain why he had been late. Too, there was the matter of an unpredictable Singing Wind to study.

Chapter Five

The council and warriors were delighted with Powchutu's and Bright Arrow's success and safe return. But the news and facts which they delivered home were distressing, for they alluded to more harassment and bloodshed by confirming their scouts' findings and suspicions. The two had reported how the soldiers were practicing with guns and sabers and were honing their hand-to-hand fighting skills.

"We must send warnings to our brothers and allies. All must be prepared to confront this new threat. Big Elk," Gray Eagle addressed the war chief, "choose two warriors to take word to each tribe. They must go and return swiftly. We will change our path to the Plains this season so the soldiers cannot ambush us. They are too eager for the blood of Gray Eagle and the Oglalas. Soon, we must send scouts to track the new white leader and we must destroy his warriors and wagons. We must not allow the whites to become stronger than the Oglalas and our brothers. Their forts have grown many during the winter. When we reach our summer camp, we must send Bright Arrow and Eagle's Arm to check their strengths and weaknesses, or they will conquer us."

From the rear of the crowd of warriors observing the council meeting, Silver Hawk listened intently . . .

Gray Eagle continued, "When all tribes have made their summer camps, we must hold a war council before we ride after the buffalo. This is a time when all tribes must think and work as one, or the whites will destroy us by burning our camps and killing our families, as they have tried to do many times in past seasons.

We must be alert when the sun glows overhead, and when the moon chases at shadows."

Mind-who-Roams, the shaman, lifted his eyes skyward and said, "Evil will soon blanket our land as darkness covers it after each sun. The destinies of many are at hand, and we must yield to them."

"Do you say we will be defeated?" Walks Tall asked anxiously.

"There will be defeat amidst great victory," the shaman replied, anguish tugging unmercifully at his heart.

"Your words confuse us, Wise One," remarked Plenty Coups. "When and how does victory and defeat walk hand in hand?"

"I can speak only of those things shown to me by the Great Spirit. He does not reveal all to me yet. He sends warnings of great peril."

"Does He say how we must confront this evil and peril?" Black Buffalo added his thoughts to the grave discussion.

"He says we must follow our chief and obey his words."

Talking Rock vowed, "We do this each day, Wise One. All tribes look to our chief for leadership. It has been, and will be, this way."

The chief smiled and his heart warmed as he heard and witnessed his people's confidence and pride in his prowess and wisdom. He silently prayed to *Wakantanka* to be worthy of such love, respect, and loyalty.

With keen perception, Gray Eagle's best friend White Arrow asked worriedly, "Does He show more than you tell us, Wise One?"

The shaman glanced at the alert man and grimaced. "Yes, my brother. He showed me a hill covered with death scaffolds, and the grass was green beneath them. Soon, many we love will be taken from us." He lowered his head for fear of looking at those involved, and for once regretted his undeniable gift of foresight.

Gray Eagle said comfortingly, "We will not ask their names, Wise One. It is not good to know the time of your death, for it is a part of each man's Life-circle. All warriors face this reality each day. Those who are called by *Wakantanka* must join him in honor and courage."

"Our chief speaks wisely, and so it must be," Black Buffalo said.

Powchutu revealed the error of the Santee Sioux, who had sold most of their lands for the establishment of military forts for a mere two thousand dollars and had agreed to what was being called the first treaty between the Sioux and the American government.

"First treaty?" scoffed the war chief Big Elk. "They have offered us many and they have signed words on paper which burn easily when they wish to break them. They are not men of truth and honor."

"We have many tribes and bands, and no chief or band can speak or sign for another as the White Chief can do for all whites and their lands. When the sun rises after two moons, we will leave this place."

The war chief Big Elk announced, "It is time for our brother Eagle's Arm to join our warrior society and council. He has proven himself worthy of both. We need his wisdom and courage. What say you?"

Not a vote was cast against Powchutu, and he and Bright Arrow were honored for tricking their enemy. The ceremonial chief handed each a specially notched eagle feather which told of their daring *coup*. All warriors agreed to the schedule and plans, and the meeting ended. They left the lodge to join their families for the evening meal.

Sun Cloud furtively observed Silver Hawk as he talked with Bright Arrow. The Blackfeet warriors had rejected the invitation to stay another night in the Oglala camp. He had watched Silver Hawk all morning, and was dismayed by his interest in Tashina. He did not like the way Silver Hawk's eyes stripped away Tashina's garments, or the wicked look on the warrior's face when he mentally mated with his brother's child. He did not trust or like Silver Hawk, and wondered how his brother could be friends with this particular man. To his relief, Tashina displayed no interest in the offensive warrior.

Sun Cloud was right. Tashina could not believe what she had thought and how she had behaved last night. She did not know what had come over her. She had been in a dangerously inquisitive mood, and she had felt an enormous need to be comforted and desired. She had wanted to study a man's words and behavior, masculine emotions where a woman was concerned. She had wanted to learn how, and if, another man affected her. Such conduct was a perilous sport, a wicked use of another person. She loved Soul-of-Thunder. She could never take Silver Hawk or any warrior in his place. She must find a way to discourage Silver Hawk and to win Soul-of-Thunder. She prayed no one had observed her wanton behavior last night, which would not be repeated. She was glad Silver Hawk was leaving this very minute, for his stares in the bright sunlight did not have the same effect as they had in the soft moonlight; they made her nervous and panicky.

When Tashina heard that her father was to ride as the messenger to the Cheyenne, her heart leapt with joy and suspense. If she could see her love, she could reveal the truth to him and discover his feelings. Perhaps he would play the flute for her, which was said to convey a lover's desire for his chosen one. It was known that flute music was used as signals between lovers: certain songs spoke of love, others of caution, and others still of secret meetings to be shared.

How wonderful it would be if Soul-of-Thunder lived in her camp and could romance her each night. Most men were so timid when it came to revealing their affections. She had seen many an ardent young brave seek ways to meet *accidentally* with his beloved while she fetched wood or water. How Tashina wished she could share blanket meetings with her love. As privacy was hard to find, in her village and others, when a young brave came to call, the girl would stand before her family's tepee and cover them with a blanket so they could whisper, and sometimes steal a kiss. As was the custom, everyone would pretend they did not see them. Sometimes, if a girl was highly desired, braves might stand in line to share a blanket with her while she decided which one to select for romancing. So far, Tashina had refused to share a blanket.

Among her people, a young girl's purity was guarded carefully by her family and herself, and she was taught she must not give away her future husband's treasure. Females were reared to become wives and mothers, and usually did so as soon as they came of age around seventeen. Even a girl's toys were designed to educate her to her role in life: small tepees, travois, dolls, and wooden horses. Joinings were normally arranged by a girl's father, but usually he tried to respect her wishes and choice. As with the white culture, it was up to the man or his family to broach the joining subject first, so a girl had to let a certain male know of her interest immediately, and hope he felt the same. Even when a proposed union did not suit the girl, she tried to accept her father's choice and obey his wishes. If the choice was truly bad in the girl's eyes, she eloped with her true love; they could spend several weeks in hiding, then return and join publicly, and eventually everyone forgave them and accepted their wishes. It was rare for a warrior to pursue a female who made her dislike for him known publicly, just as it was practically unknown for a man to hold on to a wife who wished to leave him for any reason. In some tribes, all a woman had to do for her freedom was to pack her belongings and leave her mate or toss his belongings out of the tepee which was her property. No man with any pride would return to her or beg her to return to him.

Yet, there were many unfair practices in marriage. A man could seek out another woman or take one to his mats or on the forest ground and it was acceptable; but if a married woman did the same, she was beaten and banished for her wicked behavior! A man could take many women or mates; a woman was allowed only one! A man could take a white or enemy slave to his mat, but a woman could not! For a woman, nothing was worse than giving your body and love to a foe.

The whites did not understand the Indian courting process. Many thought the man purchased the woman. True, the man did give the female's family gifts, usually horses or furs or weapons, but he was not paying for her. The kinds of gifts and their amounts revealed the man's depth of love and desire for a particular female, and proved he had the prowess to be a good protector and provider for her.

As for multiple wives, Tashina felt as her grandmother, father, and the whites: a man should have only one wife. Yes, life on the Plains was dangerous, and there were more females than males for many reasons, and the Indian female's life was hard, and there was a need for a warrior to have as many children as possible; but not where she was concerned. She wanted her husband all to herself. If she needed help, her husband could buy or capture her a slave or two.

In most tribes, as well as her own, a girl became a woman when she had her first monthly flow, which was usually at age fifteen or sixteen. It was an occasion for a feast and special ceremony, certainly if she was a chief's or a high-ranking warrior's daughter. Despite a girl's modesty, everyone was told of the wonderful news of her arrival at the flap to womanhood. Yet, men feared and were awed by a female during her monthly; some tribes treated or viewed her as if she became an evil spirit once a month. In many, a bleeding female was forced to remain in a separate tepee during this time, to prevent the spread of her evil and to prevent her from touching anything that belonged to a warrior and thereby allowing her evil spirit to steal his power and magic. During this brief exile, a young girl spent time with her mother, grandmother, or an older female being educated on female tasks, responsibilities, and such.

At her feast following her first menstrual period, she was told of her duties and destiny by the shaman and was given a fluffy white eagle breath-feather to reveal her new status. The shaman prayed for her to be blessed by *Whope'*, the sacred White Buffalo Calf Woman, whose touch, Indian legend and religion said, possessed the power to heal and whose sharp eyes could pierce the shadows which concealed the future. It was said that *Whope'* was involved in the creation of the Lakota people and she was the divine spirit who had birthed the sacred pipe ritual. During this part of a girl's ceremony into womanhood, to honor *Whope'* a beautiful white shield was used, one with a white buffalo head on a white hoop which bore white designs and displayed eight white eagle feathers: white, for the purity of the soul and body involved, which told a young girl how important chastity was.

Tashina had earned her eagle plume last summer, and braves had quickly taken notice of her marriageable status. She had pretended not to notice them or her rank, but when she was near Soul-of-Thunder, she forgot the importance placed on virtue. He stirred feelings to life within her which she knew must be a mating fever. She wanted him to hold her tightly, to kiss her feverishly, to fuse their bodies as one. Perhaps it was wicked of her to think and to feel—and especially to encourage—such behavior and emotions, but she could not help herself, and she could not believe such beautiful feelings were evil or wrong.

Bright Arrow returned to their tepee to gather a few belongings for his hasty trip. Tashina eagerly asked to go with him.

"I ride swiftly, daughter. You must prepare to break camp." He did not want to frighten her with what he had learned at the fort, but he knew terrible times were ahead for them. He could not risk placing her life in peril for a visit to her Blackfeet friends. If there was trouble along the way, she could endanger him and Flaming Star.

She coaxed, "It will be many suns before I can visit again. Please, Father, take me with you. All is done but dismantling the tepee."

"Remain and help your grandmother. Her hands and body do not work as they used to. There is no time to ride slowly for a female."

She knew it was useless and rude to plead or protest. "Will you take this to Soul-of-Thunder? The beading came loose and I repaired it."

Bright Arrow accepted the knife sheath and smiled. "You are kind to your friends and your fingers are skilled. I cannot see where it was damaged or repaired. Windrider's son will be pleased."

Tashina felt guilty about lying to her father. That was a new flaw in her character, one perhaps born from the mating of love and desperation. She had asked Soul-of-Thunder if she could keep his sheath for a while to learn to make one for her father. She had fulfilled her intention, which was to bead it with his symbol: the ghostly shape of a man in white, clasping black thunderbolts in his hands and holding them above his head to reveal his power and magic. She was proud of her work and hoped he liked it and guessed the love with which it had been done.

Yet, when her father returned to camp, she learned that her love had sent only a polite thank you for her gift! It was their custom for a special gift to be given in return, but her love had ignored it. She had been hoping he would send her one of his colorfully etched armbands with which she could make a wristlet to wear with pride and joy. She helplessly wondered if his action was meant to tell her something, something which she did not wish to admit to herself.

Two days later, it was time to break camp. Early that morning, Shalee saddled her horse and used his strength to pull out the two largest tepee support poles to construct her travois. Two feet from the top ends, she crossed the poles above the animal's withers and lashed them together, being careful not to catch the animal's mane in her tight knots, as it could be yanked out during movement. Positioning the lower ends five feet apart, she secured them in place with wide strips of rawhide which ran from pole to pole beneath and over the horse, just behind his forelegs and before his hindlegs. The strips which encircled the helpful beast were lined with fur to prevent chaffing and discomfort when the weight of the travois pulled on the makeshift straps. As with the warriors, the women took the best of care with their horses, for their work load and survival depended upon the loyal beasts.

Next, Shalee fashioned a shelf with widths of rawhide and sturdy saplings to carry their home and belongings. Blankets had been placed over the animal's back and flanks to prevent the poles from rubbing against his hide, and two thick buffalo skins were tossed over the poles for Shalee's comfort while riding him. Items which she needed to reach quickly or to use during the day were placed inside a large double-sided parfleche and tossed over the horse's croup like saddlebags. As if the first step in dismantling the chief's tepee had been taken as a sign, all others had begun the same task on their conical abodes.

Shalee worked skillfully and diligently, having performed this task twice yearly since meeting Gray Eagle. The tepee lining was taken down, folded, and set outside near the travois. The buffalo skin beddings were rolled and bound tightly, and placed with it, as were all other possessions until the tepee was empty. Wooden pins which held together the one unstitched seam were removed to allow the *tipi* to slide down the remaining poles to the ground, where it could be folded and secured first to the travois. Two backrests were lashed to the makeshift cart, along with Shalee's sewing pouch and assorted parfleches which contained the family's possessions and their provisions for the impending journey. As with the other males, Gray Eagle and Sun Cloud strapped their weapons and sacred belongings in place; women were not supposed to handle them, and guards, hunters, and scouts could not be encumbered while carrying out their vital assignments during the trek.

Within a short time, all tepees were down, the horses and travois were loaded, and everyone was ready to leave the winter encampment. As nothing was wasted, the remaining poles were stacked aside to be used for firewood another day. Children were loaded last. Each family was given an assigned place for the long trek, and was expected to keep to it each day so a man could locate his family easily when they halted for a rest or for the night.

Sun Cloud helped his mother to mount her horse. In tepees where there was more than one wife, one guided the horse, either by hand or by riding him, and the other or others took turns walking beside or riding upon the travois, unless it was filled with small children. Sometimes women carried babies in cradleboards or in their arms. If or when necessary, others gave help to the ill or injured or overburdened or widowed so the trip would not be slowed.

The man packed nothing except his weapons and sacred items; for the division of labor was strict, and men were never to do anything which was, or appeared, menial or feminine. Men were appointed to one of several groups during the trek: hunter, guard, or scout. Guards rode before, beside, and behind the long line of women and children to protect them from perils and to make certain nothing and no one delayed their progress; they could halt the long procession if a need—such as childbirth or illness or injury—arose or to prevent stragglers from being left behind. Others hunted for game which was shared amongst all the families. Others scouted ahead of the main group for dangers, campsites, and fresh game. Loyalty and duty were vital for the safety and survival of the tribe, and each man was expected to do his part, willingly and efficiently.

As the large group headed toward the Plains, Shalee remembered how many times she had performed this task. She recalled the first time, when she had not known what to do or how to do it. She recalled the year of 1782 when Leah Winston was in their lives, and she had been plagued with amnesia. Yet, with Turtle Woman's help and kindness, she had dismantled Gray Eagle's tepee and packed their belongings. What joy and excitement she had experienced that day when her labors had been so richly rewarded. That was one time when Bright Arrow and Gray Eagle had helped her with the chores, and had ignored the prohibition against men doing demeaning "woman's work."

Five days passed swiftly and wearily, and uneventfully. The group moved more slowly than they did during the fall trek, for bodies were still sluggish from the winter's rest. Too, they realized how busy they would be as soon as their summer camp was set up and the buffalo hunt was in progress. For the women, there was wood and fresh water to be fetched each day; wild vegetables, fruits, and berries to be gathered; food to be cooked for daily consumption; meat to be dried and preserved for winter rations; children to be tended and educated according to sex; hides to be tanned; garments to be made; beading to be done; and mates to be enjoyed. For the men, there was hunting each day; there were raiding parties; there were meetings with other tribes; there were weapons, shields, and sacred items to be made or repaired; there were ceremonies to perform; there were boys to train as hunters and warriors; there was painting to be done on tepees and shields; there were friends and tepees to be guarded; there were tales to be told, lest they be forgotten by the young; there were games and contests which made and kept warriors strong and alert; and there was strategy to be planned against their enemies.

Spring, summer, and fall were busy seasons; the white man knew this and chose his assault times cunningly. Shalee dreaded this approaching summer, for not in years had the white man been so determined to defeat the Indians. Each time they approached an area where foes could hide and attack, the column was halted while warriors made certain it was safe to proceed. It was infuriating and depressing to live one's life in constant peril and doubt. Again, Shalee was reminded of the peace they had enjoyed before Colonel Derek Sturgis had been reassigned back east, before the Lewis and Clark Expedition and the ending of the War of 1812 had inspired more men to move westward, and before the whites felt they owned this land through the Louisiana Purchase.

"What troubles your mind, Mother?" Sun Cloud asked as he rode up beside Shalee, as it was his turn to be a guard that day.

She smiled at her younger son and confessed ruefully, "I was remembering how it was in seasons past when our lands knew peace. I wish you could know such times, my son, but they are gone forever. When I think of what is before you and our people, my heart is heavy with sadness and grief. So much will be asked and expected of you," she murmured as moisture dampened her lashes.

"You must not worry, Mother. Sun Cloud will protect you and father and our people," he spoke confidently to reassure her.

Shalee gazed at him, seeing how much he favored Gray Eagle in looks and character. "You are like your father was long ago when we first met—strong and bold and confident and cocky." She halted to explain the English word "cocky" and watched her son laugh in amusement. "Long ago, he also thought nothing and no one could defeat him or conquer his lands. He was forced to learn a bitter lesson. My beloved son, if only you knew what perils stand before you. I know of the white man's numbers and weapons; I know of his greed and power. I dread the day when you must learn of such evil and its demands. You were born to become chief of the Oglalas, my son, and you will do so very soon. You will be feared and respected and loved and hated, as your father is. You must be strong, Sun Cloud, for many dark days are ahead. You must allow nothing and no one to sway you from your destiny. You must allow your head to rule over your heart. Being a chief is difficult and painful, but your father has trained you well. When you take his place, remember all he has taught you," she advised.

"We will defeat the whites, Mother. Peace will rule our lands."

"No, my son, lasting peace is gone forever. You must defend your people; you must guide them wisely. You must seek truce if the whites will allow it; only through truce can the Oglalas survive. You must learn to share our lands, or the whites will take them by force. You must learn to accept them, or they will destroy all you know and love. They are powerful, my son, know and accept this fact, or you will battle for a victory which can never be won. Seek peace with honor, even if you must taste it as a bitter defeat."

"The whites do not wish peace, Mother; they desire all we have in lands and lives," he argued softly, not wanting to upset or hurt her.

"I know, my son; that is why you must work hard and long to capture any measure of peace. Do not allow your pride to destroy your people forever. Some white leaders and peoples are not evil; it is those you must seek out and work with. The whites cannot be kept out of our lands forever. If you do not strive for peace or truce, the Oglalas will vanish from the face of Mother Earth. Hear me, my son, these are not the words of a silly woman. I lived with the whites, and I know them. Truce, however bitter, is better than Mother Earth with no Oglalas. One day, the white man will realize his evil and he will halt it. Until that day, you must make certain the Oglalas survive. Do not allow false pride to blind you, to say you can defeat this enemy. They are not Crow or Arikara, my son; they are countless and strong. Promise me you will remember my words and heed them if the time for truce approaches you. Your father is a legend in these lands, and legends live as challenges to enemies. Seek to be a wise chief more than a powerful one. Seek to be a leader, my precious son, not a legend, for few legends live on more than pages of history."

"All listen to and follow my father. Is it wrong to be a great chief?"

"No, Sun Cloud, but the day has come when a great chief must lead his people into peace, not war, unless peace is impossible."

"The whites make it impossible, Mother," he stressed.

"Then you must find a way to make it possible, my son."

"How so?" he inquired gravely. "It is the duty of a Sacred Bow carrier to protect his people and lands, to make war on their enemies."

"It is also the carrier's duty to seek and to find peace for his people, my son. Keep your eyes and mind open, and the Great Spirit will guide you to the path for survival for His people."

Sun Cloud eyed his mother intently, wondering how much she truly knew and understood about this conflict. She had lived as white for many winters and carried white blood; perhaps she was still plagued by the war between her two peoples and perhaps she only dreamed of peace, a peace which he knew was impossible. "I will think upon your words, Mother, for you have lived many seasons and witnessed many things. We will speak later. I must return to my duty."

Shalee watched him ride away and felt the tuggings at her heart, for she knew he had no accurate idea of what he was confronting. Like Gray Eagle of years past, he believed he and his people were invincible. Anguish swept over her, knowing the arduous road he would travel. Sun Cloud was so young and full of life, and he had no idea of the toll constant war could have on a chief and his family and his people. If only he could have a little span of peace and happiness before his illusions were shattered brutally by the hatred between the Indians and the whites. She dreaded to think of the bitterness and hatred which would consume and alter him once he lost loved ones and witnessed the dark evil of her people. It would be a long time, if ever, before peace was obtained.

Time came to make camp for the night. Shalee spread the sleeping rolls as she waited for their evening meal to be ready. Then Gray Eagle joined her, kissing her cheek and embracing her tenderly. When she told him about her talk with Sun Cloud, he smiled sadly and remarked, "As with your husband, he must learn such things for himself. You must also face the truth, my wife; peace died long ago in our lands. There is nothing more to be done except to survive as best we can until the Great Spirit calls our names. I am weary of fighting, but we must continue our battle with the whites, for they will claim all if we weaken or yield. Oglalas were not born to live on reservations or to live beside forts near the soldiers' evil. We must do all necessary to keep our honor and freedom. We must pray for strength and guidance."

"I do this each day, my love, but it grows harder."

Gray Eagle lovingly stroked her cheek and looked deeply into her green eyes. "No matter the troubles, we have lived a long and good life."

She nestled against his chest and murmured, "I am grateful for all we have shared, but I wish our sons to know a little peace and joy."

"They will, my love, for the Great Spirit has promised this to me."

Tashina returned with their food, for she had been helping a group of women to cook a joint meal, as was their custom on the trail. She looked at her grandparents and their closeness warmed her heart. How she longed to know a love as powerful and passionate as theirs, and she would if she could win Soul-of-Thunder's heart. She glanced around as Eagle's Arm, Bright Arrow, and Sun Cloud joined them to eat and to sleep. But this was not to be a peaceful night in their camp; she knew this when Silver Hawk and two Blackfeet warriors galloped to the spot where they were preparing to spend the night.

Shalee asked the warriors if she could fetch food for them, but they were too anxious to eat. She realized that Gray Eagle sensed the news was bad when he asked the warriors to walk with him while they spoke. She noticed how Silver Hawk's ravenous gaze feasted greedily on the delectable Tashina before he turned to join her husband and sons and Powchutu. Apprehension charged through her like the terror of a runaway horse. Suddenly she scolded herself for her silly fears, for Tashina had lost her heart to another, and her oldest son would never force his precious daughter to wed any man. Perhaps she should speak with Bright Arrow and Gray Eagle about this man who caused such alarming stirrings within her, even if men did not like women to meddle in their affairs and friendships.

Sitting on large rocks not far from the camp, Silver Hawk explained his abrupt visit. "We captured three soldiers and a Crow scout who have been trailing us for many suns. One was weak in body and courage and we forced him to speak of others who are trailing our brothers. They count the number of warriors in each band and tribe and they mark which paths we take. The white-dogs said we must free them or all would be chased and slain; we silenced their foolish words with death. Chief Medicine Bear said we must ride to warn our brothers as they warned us. The white-dogs are seeking the path of Gray Eagle and the Oglalas. They believe Gray Eagle and the Oglalas are the evil power in our lands, and they offer peace to any tribe who refuses to band with them. They offer many trade goods to any warrior or band who will sneak into your camp and slay you. They believe they can win their war against all Indians when you are dead."

Sun Cloud held silent as he observed Silver Hawk's expression and listened carefully to the man's tone. He did not like what his keen senses were telling him, for he perceived an undercurrent within this man which was dangerous and too far below the surface for the others to notice in their states of anger and resentment. Warnings throbbed within his head as he comprehended the jealousy toward his father which this warrior was experiencing and attempting to conceal. Yet, he had nothing more than his gut feeling that this man was a threat to Gray Eagle, and it was not enough with which to challenge a famed warrior. For now, he must keep quiet, and alert.

Bright Arrow stated coldly, "I will slay all bluecoats, and I will slay any or all warriors who are tempted by their devious offer. It is a trick. They know all will lose hope and courage if my father is slain. They seek to turn his allies and brothers against him, to destroy the power and magic of the Indian, to destroy our unity. It will not be so, for his blood also runs within Bright Arrow and Sun Cloud. Even if they found a way to slay him, we would ride in his place."

Sun Cloud added, "Yes, we will defend our father's life with our own. No man will live who becomes a threat to him or our people."

Powchutu watched the scene. From past experience, he knew how frightened of Gray Eagle the soldiers and whites were, and he knew what his half brother's death could mean for the whites in their war against the Indians. It was a clever plot to place a sort of bounty on Gray Eagle's head. Jeffery Gordon had tried that ploy once, and had died for his recklessness. Over the years, many had tried to eviscerate the heart of the Dakotas, and all had failed. But it was the nature of men to be greedy and rash, and some might be blinded by this lucrative offer of goods and truce. From now on, Gray Eagle and those who loved him must guard his back. He must speak with his nephews about this Blackfeet warrior, for he did not trust the shiny brittleness in the man's eyes or the tightness in his voice; there was some guarded emotion here to be watched carefully.

The aging chief gave his orders. "Sun Cloud, go to Big Elk and reveal these things to him. Bright Arrow, take warriors and scout the area for white wolves who sneak around in the shadows. Eagle's Arm, guard my wife and granddaughter. I will call the council and speak with them. Silver Hawk, will you rest this night with us?"

"We will take refreshments, then ride to our camp, my second father. Other white-dogs might lurk near the shadows of our camp."

"If there is more news or trouble, send word to us. Did Medicine Bear send messages to the other bands?" Bright Arrow inquired.

"Yes, my friend and brother. Soon, we will ride together against these white foes who sneak around while *Wi* sleeps."

Bright Arrow smiled and clasped arms with Silver Hawk. "We will claim many *coups* when we ride to victory over the whites, my friend. Come, I will take you to our camp, then obey my father's command."

Silver Hawk and Bright Arrow walked away together, talking excitedly about past and future battles. Gray Eagle headed for the area where White Arrow was camped for the night. Powchutu and Sun Cloud turned and found that they both had been watching Silver Hawk.

Their intuitive gazes met and they smiled knowingly. "He is a man to watch, Sun Cloud," the older man advised the young warrior who could have been his son if he had not lingered one day too long at Fort Pierre years ago. Powchutu decided that Sun Cloud was like his father; he was strong and brave, and true to his calling. Shalee, as he had learned to think of and to call Alisha Williams, had told him of the past which would make this warrior chief after Gray Eagle, and he realized it was meant to be. "You have learned well, Sun Cloud. You will become a great chief like your father. Your brother does not see the evil in his friend, and he will suffer for his blindness. Many times a leader must stand alone when he stands above others. Your brother is a good warrior, but he does not have your strength and insight. I see why the Great Spirit chose you to walk after your father. Does your brother truly understand and accept his destiny?"

"Yes, Eagle's Arm, he chose his path long ago with knowing. Father told us about his vision which said I was to become the next Oglala chief. When Bright Arrow returned home after his banishment, he agreed to follow me as chief when that moon arrived. He knows that he lost his right to be a chief when he chose his love over his rank. Father said the Great Spirit was kind to give him his white love since he could never be chief. I wish I did not have to be the one who takes what would be his if things were different. As the oldest son, it will be hard for him to see his younger brother lead his people. We do not know why Grandfather replaced Bright Arrow with me, but my brother is not bitter over his loss. Perhaps we will understand this one day. He will obey the will of *Wakantanka*. Watch Silver Hawk when he is near Tashina," he suggested meaningfully before they parted.

Silver Hawk was annoyed when Powchutu seemingly clung to Tashina as a badger to its kill, preventing even one private word with her. He tried everything he could to obtain a moment alone with her, but the older man prevented it. He was even more annoyed when Tashina seemed cool and distant with him, refusing to look at him or to catch his clues for a few stolen minutes. Soon, no one would keep him from her. Soon, Bright Arrow would owe him whatever he chose in payment, and his demand would be Tashina. After she had given him children, if she continued to behave as if she were so repulsed by him, he would get rid of her, for children belonged to their father or to his people.

His anger simmering, Silver Hawk bid them farewell and rode away with his warriors, vowing to have all he desired very soon . . .

It was during the night when Sun Cloud was besieged by dreams of Singing Wind. He saw them running through the forest, laughing and playing, but this time not as children. He curled to his side on his sleeping mat and enjoyed the heady dream:

"You run as swiftly and agilely as a doe, Singing Wind," he murmured into her ear as he captured her hand and pulled her into his arms. His mouth covered hers and they sank to a soft bed of wildflowers, sharing numerous kisses and caresses which heightened their passions.

Singing Wind was lying beneath him and gazing up into his face. His eyes roamed her exquisite features and he smiled at the way her sleek hair was spread upon the ground. His fingers wandered over her supple flesh, and he suddenly realized that they were naked and their bodies were pressed snugly together. "I have craved this moment and waited for it too long, my love. You must be mine, Singing Wind."

Stroking his cheek, she replied, "I have craved you and waited longer to win you than you have done for me, Sun Cloud, for you forced me to chase you many years before you noticed I had become a woman. I wish to be yours forever." She pulled his head downward and sealed their lips in a pervasive kiss.

Sun Cloud could feel her hands caressing his body and increasing his great hunger for hers. He ached to possess her. As he tossed upon his sleeping mat in rising need, he was awakened. His respiration was rapid and sweat glistened on his face and chest beneath the moon. He knew he had to end this bittersweet yearning for her, and there was only one way: win her and take her.

In the Blackfeet camp, a similar incident was occurring with Singing Wind, as if their subconscious minds were drawing them together. She watched as Sun Cloud rode up to her, swept her into his arms, and raced away with her. They galloped for a long time, allowing the sun and wind to tease over their susceptible bodies and free their spirits.

She did not halt Sun Cloud or feel embarrassed when he removed their garments; then they were lying on a fuzzy buffalo mat beneath sensuously swaying trees. The heady scents of nature filled their nostrils, and they laughed joyfully. She became breathless and fiery as Sun Cloud stimulated them to blazing desire. She could not kiss him or caress him enough to appease her hunger for him. It had taken so long for her to win him, but at last he was hers.

She ran her fingers through his sleek mane and admired the way it fell loose and shiny around his strong shoulders. His eyes glowed with emotions which matched her own. She could wait no longer to join their lives and bodies. "Take me, Sun Cloud, or I will die of need," she whispered boldly and bravely, for she had never been a coward. She knew he was the man she wanted above all others, the only man she wanted. At last, they could become as one.

Yet, Sun Cloud continued to stimulate her until she was thrashing upon the mat and begging him to halt this bittersweet torment. Her flesh itched and burned, she could hardly breathe, and still he did not take her fully. She jerked to wakefulness and grasped her surroundings. She was dismayed to find it was only a dream. She wiped the moisture from her face and sighed heavily. Whatever she had to do to win him, she must do it quickly before enduring more nights of suffering.

Chapter Six

Two more days passed on the trail. Then the Cheyenne war chief Windrider and two of his warriors rode into their evening camp, as the tribes and bands had been asked to keep in touch with each other during this hazardous time and each had been told which path the others were taking. When Tashina saw her father's best friend, the father of her love, her pulse raced madly as she eagerly glanced around for Soul-of-Thunder. He was nowhere in sight, and she wanted to rush over to ask about him. Deciding her excitement might reveal her inner emotions to Windrider and others, she did not. She continued her chores until she calmed herself and completed them. Since he had not sent her a return gift, she waited to see if there was a message from him, but Windrider did not mention one. Even when she politely inquired about his family, he smiled and said they were all fine and safe.

Tashina's suspense was nearly unbearable and her grandmother astutely came to her aid. Shalee asked, "It has been many moons since we saw you and your son, Windrider. Did he ride with you to our camp? Is he visiting others and will he join us for the evening meal?"

Not wishing to worry his mother, Bright Arrow had asked Windrider not to mention the trouble in the other Indian camps, so the Cheyenne warrior laughed and joked. "It is the time when Mother Earth renews her face and causes young bucks to think of young does too frequently. Soon, my son will seek a tepee of his own, and he casts his eyes about in search of the right mate, so he did not wish to ride from camp at this time. Perhaps on our next visit he will bring along a giggling mate to meet his other family," he said with a grin and a chuckle which led the listening Tashina to form the wrong conclusion.

Her heart ached at this tormenting discovery, and she fled to a private distance to deal with her anguish, believing he was lost to her. Her grandmother had told her to wait for the truth, for a sign from him about his feelings, and now she had it. She begged and commanded herself not to weep, but her eyes refused to obey. She angrily pushed her tangled hair from her moist face, wishing she had braided it, for its unruly waves and hint of auburn declared her white blood. Perhaps that was the obstacle between her and her love, she painfully mused. Suddenly, agony thundered through her head and everything went blacker than the night which surrounded her.

The Army scout quickly scanned each direction, aware of where the Oglala guards were posted. He realized how difficult escape would be with the girl, but knew he could obtain needed information from her, by force if necessary. Since she was white, she should be grateful for his rescue and be willing and eager to help the Army punish the Sioux who had captured and enslaved her. Presently, he had to sneak away from this area as stealthily as he had arrived. Later, he could question the girl and report to Major Butler. He tossed her over his shoulder, covered them with a dark blanket, then gingerly returned to his horse, a mile away.

No one realized the danger Tashina was in, for each person assumed she was visiting and sleeping in a friend's camp. With guards posted and with Tashina's responsible nature, no one imagined she would leave the lighted area or that a Crow scout could get near their camp. It was morning when her absence was discovered, and the Crow's tracks were found. As time and safety were essential for the tribe, Gray Eagle ordered them to continue their journey. He placed Shalee in Powchutu's care while his two sons went to rescue his granddaughter and to slay the scout before he could report his findings. No guard was reprimanded, but all knew they had been careless and lax.

Tashina had awakened shortly before dawn to find herself in the arms of a Crow who was dressed as a white man. Instantly the Indian had halted and lowered her feet to the ground, then agilely dismounted. She rubbed her head as she cleared her wits and took in her peril, for the Crow had always been fierce enemies of the Oglalas. She had no weapon and the man looked strong and mean. She trembled, then berated her recklessness last night, but within moments she realized he was a fort scout and her family and people were in greater danger than she was. She had to find a way to trick this man and escape to warn them.

"I take you to fort. First, you tell Sly Fox all he asks or he will slay you. You captive, squaw, or half-breed?" he questioned coldly as he seized her wrist and squeezed it painfully to intimidate her.

"Who are you? What do you want with me?" she replied in her best English to stall for time and to dupe him.

"Sly Fox asks questions; you answer or be hurt," he warned.

"I'm a captive," she declared bravely and tried to pull free.

"You no captive; you free to come and go around camp. You lie," he accused as he twisted her arm behind her. He yanked her forward, bringing their bodies into snug contact, close enough so that she could feel his respiration upon her face. His dark gaze bored into her frantic one. "Speak truth or Sly Fox cut out tongue."

She shrieked, "You're breaking my arm, Sly Fox! My head is pounding where you struck me last night and I'm confused by all this. I'll tell you the truth; I have nothing to hide. Me and my mother were taken captive when I was ten. She died this past winter. Take me to the fort and they can return me to my father Clay Rivera. He's a trapper and many of the soldiers know him. I can't let the Indians catch me again. Me and my mother tried to escape before, but they punished us horribly. They know I was too scared to try it again, so they don't watch me anymore. They treat me like a slave, and one of the warriors is trying to bargain for me. That's why I was standing in the dark and crying, because I was too cowardly to run away and I knew my owner was going to trade me to him. Please help me. My father will pay you. I know he wouldn't leave this area without me."

"That Gray Eagle's camp?" he probed, as if unmoved by her tale.

Tashina realized the man was testing her, for he had to know whose camp he had discovered. She had to play along with him, or he would kill her. "He's the chief. They're heading for their summer grounds. We should get out of here. Surely they know I'm gone by now. They're probably tracking us this very minute. If they catch us, they'll kill us both." She had to hope he would let her mount behind him, then she could grab his knife and . . . slay him.

"Who holds you captive?" he demanded, wishing there was time to appease the gnawing which her beauty and close proximity were creating in his manhood. Auburn highlights gleamed in the morning sun and her large eyes looked golden brown, implying she was indeed white or mostly white. Her long hair settled wildly around her face and shoulders, and her full lips were innocently inviting. Although she was slender, he could feel a rounded bosom pressed against his hard chest. She was most tempting, for she had an aura of gentleness and purity. He knew that once they were back at the fort, one of the white officers would claim her for his personal use, but he dared not throw her upon the ground and waste valuable time enjoying her. He needed to carry his information and captive to the fort where he could prove to the soldiers and to Red Band that he was the better scout!

Tashina had not responded, for she had been observing her enemy as he obviously deliberated her fate and words. She had seen that same glint in a man's eyes before, in Silver Hawk's, and now she could put a name to it—lust, not desire —which caused her to fear rape more than death.

The Crow scout shook her and asked his question again. She shouted, "Walks Tall, but Night Rider wants to buy me. If we don't get out of here, Sly Fox, he'll have his captive back and your life."

The sullen man leaned back and glared at her as if insulted, releasing his grasp on her. He eyed her up and down with a scowl. "No dirty Sioux can defeat Sly Fox. See how easy I find Gray Eagle's camp and take captive between guards. You need bath; you smell like Sioux. Speak no more till Sly Fox tells you. We ri—"

As Tashina seemingly stared into his eyes while he spoke, her hand had moved forward slowly to snatch his knife. Detecting her movement and guessing her intention, the Crow scout used his palm against her face to shove her backward to the ground. She landed roughly on her seat and was shaken by the fall, but heard him threaten, "Sly Fox leave your body to feed coyotes and sky birds when he finish with it. I not kill you, half-breed; I leave you too weak and hurt to get away or survive. You be sorry you tried to attack and trick Sly Fox."

Her head spinning with dizziness and terror, Tashina inched backward on her hands and seat, pushing frantically with moccasins which kept slipping on the loose dirt. Her eyes widened in panic as his hand grazed the handle of his knife.

He grinned wickedly as he stalked toward her and yanked her to her feet, increasing her dizziness. "I cut off dress, then I take you with much hunger and anger." He glared at her, then laughed coldly. The terrified girl struggled frantically with him, until the Crow scout landed a stunning blow across her jaw and flung her to the ground, rendering her unconscious.

An arrow thudded forcefully into Sly Fox's left eye, bringing forth a scream of agony and causing him to stagger backward a few steps. Blood streamed between his fingers and rushed down his arm and face as he clasped his hand over his wound. He shuddered and moaned in torment, and tried to draw his knife with his right hand. Silver Hawk flung himself at the Crow scout and knocked him to the ground. The Blackfeet warrior straddled the man, pinned his arms to his sides, then gripped the slender shaft and drove the arrowhead into the man's brain, killing him instantly. The Crow scout went limp. Then Silver Hawk yanked the arrow free, lifted it above his head, and sent forth a cry of victory and pleasure.

When Tashina aroused, she found herself enclosed in Silver Hawk's embrace. She tried to sit up, but he told her to remain still while her sense cleared. She reluctantly obeyed as he revealed how he had arrived and slain the Crow scout, whose body she refused to view.

"My heart has never known such fear, my lovely flower. We have been tracking you for hours and waiting for the moment to strike at the Crow dog who stole you from us. How did he capture you?"

Tashina frowned as she related, "I was walking near camp last night and strayed too far. He was spying on our camp. He sneaked up on me and struck me senseless. I have not been awake for long." She glanced around, to find they were alone, and she became nervous. "How did you find me? Where are the others you spoke of?"

"I sent them ahead to your camp to tell your family I have rescued you. Silver Hawk and his warriors have been riding each moon to catch the enemy scouts who trail us. We saw his tracks leading to your camp and we followed. The Crow dog passed near our hiding place and I saw your face. I feared you were injured. I dared not attack until I knew you would be safe. He is dead and cannot harm you or your people."

Tashina realized this warrior was taking all the credit for her rescue, as if his men had done nothing. She was grateful to him for saving her life and for preventing the scout from taking his report to the fort, but she resented it was Silver Hawk who had performed this deed. Now, he would feel she should be indebted to him, and she already knew what reward he desired. She angrily concluded that her love was partly responsible for her predicaments with the Crow scout and with Silver Hawk. If Soul-of-Thunder had visited her with his father or sent her a message, she would not be here now!

"I thank you for saving me and my people, Silver Hawk. You will earn a large *coup* for this brave deed. I must return home quickly to prove I am safe," she murmured, as his gaze increased her tension.

He shook his head and smiled strangely. "You must rest a short time. I will guard you. When we return to your camp, I will speak to your father about us. I have proven I can protect you and provide for you. I have proven my love for you. We will join, then ride to my camp and celebrate."

Tashina removed herself from his arms and told him, "It is too soon to speak of such matters, Silver Hawk. My grandmother and father need me; these days are busy and dangerous for my family and people. Grandmother is old and will need my help setting up in her new camp, and Father has no one to help him. I have not decided to join you," she confessed as pleasantly as possible. "Do not be angry or impatient; joining is an important decision and time for a woman."

"Is there another who has asked for you?" he inquired oddly.

"Several braves and warriors have asked for me, but I do not consider taking any of them," she replied truthfully. "I cannot think of such serious matters until my thoughts and the lives of my loved ones are settled. It is wrong to join a man without love or from gratitude. Is this not so?" she queried, feeling he must agree.

The warrior argued gently and firmly. "There is no better man for Tashina than Silver Hawk. I will make you happy, and you will come to love and desire me as I love and desire you. Do you care nothing for me, for my feelings, for what I have done for you and your people?" he reasoned slyly to appeal to her conscience.

"I did not know love was a lesson to be learned, Silver Hawk. One person cannot make another happy. Such feelings must come from within the heart of each person. We have known each other for many winters, and I have thought of you as a brother, not a future mate. It is not easy to change such thoughts or feelings so quickly. I do not wish to hurt you or to reject you, but I must think of my feelings too. For me, love must come before joining."

"If there is no other to challenge or to battle for you, then I will seek more patience and understanding. Help my friend and mother, then I will speak to you again on this matter. I have lived twenty-seven winters and I have no son to follow me. I pray you will give me your love and a son before another winter is added to my body."

"I promise I will think seriously on you and your words, Silver Hawk," she vowed, aware of what those thoughts would be and intentionally leading him to misunderstand her. She had to get away from him. She had to find a way to let Soul-of-Thunder know of her love; that could make a difference in his coming decision. Perhaps her love did not realize the girl who had lived as a sister to him loved him and desired to become his mate. Perhaps the thought of taking her as his wife had never entered his mind or he was afraid to approach her. She had to plant her seed in his head before it was too late. She was expecting him to know of her feelings, and to be purposely rejecting her, when that might not be true. If she did not take action to alert him to her love, she had only herself to blame for losing him to another.

"Your eyes say your mind runs in many directions at once, Tashina."

She lowered her lashes to conceal her deceit. "I was thinking what danger I placed myself and my people in with my foolishness. It must never happen again, for I love them above my own life."

"One sun, I hope you say and feel the same for Silver Hawk," he told her, then pulled her into his arms and sealed their lips.

Tashina wriggled free and softly scolded, "You must not do such things, Silver Hawk. Someone could see us and think badly of me."

The darkly tanned Indian chuckled. "If others know of my love and pursuit, it will discourage theirs," he teased. His fingers pushed straying curls from her face, then caressed her pinkened cheek. "When I am near you, my body and heart burn for yours. Come to me soon, and I will show you such love and passion as no other couple shares. I will make your body hunger for mine as if starving. I will make your lips thirst for mine. I will make you crave to join our bodies each moon. I will make you tremble with desire. Come to me soon, Tashina, and I will prove all I say is true. When I show you such things, you will regret this delay and doubt. You will wonder how I had the strength to allow you to keep me away. You will scold me for not going to your father and claiming you this very sun. But I will wait, and I will smile and tease you when you learn such things for yourself."

Tashina could not suppress a grin as she listened to a tongue which was as smooth as the surface of a tranquil pond. For certain, Silver Hawk was experienced and skilled in clever seduction. She could understand how women would be ensnared by his looks, mood, and words. "Come, we must go before I am left behind. We will speak later." She smiled as she hoped that talk would reveal her impending union with another man.

He stood, pulled her to her feet, then stole a quick kiss. He nimbly mounted and reached downward to assist her up behind him. *I will let you escape me this sun, my pretty flower, but I will pluck you and enjoy you soon, enjoy you until you wither and die*. "Hold tightly, my pretty flower, and we will ride swiftly." He waited for her to band his waist with her arms and to interlock her fingers, and his lips lifted at one corner as he relished the feel of her warm body snuggled against his. He gently kneed his horse and off they galloped, causing her to cling to him and to rest her face on his back.

Within an hour, they met Sun Cloud, Bright Arrow, Windrider and his warriors, and two Blackfeet warriors. The grim tale was related by an almost boastful Silver Hawk, who savored the leisurely telling of every detail; then his friends added more color. Tashina sat quietly and respectfully until it was her turn to reveal her side. Looking ruefully at her father, she promised never to repeat her mistake. She thanked Silver Hawk once more, eager to leave, but Bright Arrow was not; he asked the warrior to repeat the tale once more to make certain he knew each part so he could relate it to his tribe.

When Silver Hawk finished, Bright Arrow thanked him and praised him, then withdrew one of his eagle feathers and presented it to the grinning warrior. "When our tribes meet for the Sun Dance, I will sing the *coups* of my friend Silver Hawk who has returned my heart to me. Soon, I will reward you greatly for this brave and special deed. No warrior has shown more courage and daring, or more love for his friend and brother. My life is yours if you need it."

Silver Hawk helped Tashina to dismount to join her father. He then said he and his warriors needed to return to their people, but would be on guard against more enemy scouts. The meaning and intensity of his parting smile to Tashina were lost to no one in the group.

Unaware of her feelings for Silver Hawk and Soul-of-Thunder, Bright Arrow's heart raced with happiness. He thought, *Who better to win my beloved Tashina than a great warrior who saved her life and who lives as my friend?* He mistakenly assumed that Tashina would be enchanted by a man of such appeal and prowess, and he looked forward to the day when Silver Hawk approached him for Tashina's hand in joining. As that would leave him alone, he should begin his search for a new mate. He had been selfish to demand so much from his daughter, and it was past time to release her from what she felt was her duty to him. In a few days, he would visit the Blackfeet camp to carry gifts and to acknowledge his friend's deed. Once he let Silver Hawk know he was seeking a new mate, that would allow his friend to speak up for his child.

They talked briefly with Windrider; then he and his warriors rode to join their people. There had been no way for Tashina to send a message to her love, not without being brazen before so many warriors. She was perturbed by her helplessness when time was slipping away from her. She had no way of knowing that Windrider would reveal the incident to his son, along with the way Silver Hawk had eyed her . . .

The Oglala band halted to welcome Tashina's safe return and to praise Silver Hawk's rescue. Gray Eagle embraced his granddaughter tightly for a few moments, allowing his fears and relief to settle.

Shalee did the same and, in doing so, sensed the curious trembling and anguish within her precious Tashina. She whispered in the girl's ear, "We will talk later when we are alone."

Tashina's gaze met her grandmother's and she smiled gratefully. Then Powchutu stepped forward to show how delighted he was with the return of Bright Arrow's child. After the adults had claimed Tashina's attention, her friends rushed forward and seemingly covered her with questions and comments. When calm was restored, the journey began anew.

Sun Cloud rode off with the son of White Arrow, to take his place as a hunter that day. Far away, he reined in to speak with his friend. "My head is filled with worries and doubts, Thunder Spirit. I fear my brother will be tricked into giving Tashina to Silver Hawk. He is trailing her as a wolf with mating fever. I know it is bad to speak evil of another warrior, one who saved her life and who killed the scout who would have betrayed us to the soldiers, but there is something in him which troubles me. You have not taken a mate and your time is near. If your eyes and heart belong to no woman yet, think on Tashina. I do not wish her to join with Silver Hawk, but I cannot stop it. My brother is blinded by his friendship and gratitude. When Silver Hawk comes to ask for Tashina, Bright Arrow will accept, and Tashina will obey her father's wishes, even though I read mistrust and fear in her eyes when Silver Hawk is near or his name is spoken."

Thunder Spirit looked off into the distance as his mind traveled far away to where his true love lived as the mate of a Sisseton chief. "Your words are true and wise, Sun Cloud; yet, they are not. I must tell you a secret; I have loved and desired only Little Feet since females entered my blood. I was a fool; I waited too long to tell her of my love and to ask for her in joining. She is lost to me. For many winters I have waited for her return, but that is foolish. I will think on your words, for Tashina is beautiful and precious and she would be a good mate. First, I must push Little Feet from my heart and mind, and it will be a hard task. If Silver Hawk comes to speak for Tashina, I will also speak for her. If she feels as you say, she will choose me over him. When we reach our summer camp, I will play the flute for her and ask her to share a blanket with me."

"You are a true friend, Thunder Spirit. One sun, my brother will thank you as I do this sun. As with a fawn's spots, Silver Hawk will lose his clever covering soon, then all will see the evil within him. I would challenge him before allowing Tashina to join with him."

"How will you make peace with Singing Wind if you declare a private war with her brother?" his friend asked gravely.

Laughing roguishly, Sun Cloud replied, "I will find a way, my friend, for she has stolen my heart and eye. Soon, I will stalk her as the lovely prey she is, and I will capture her and make her mine."

Thunder Spirit mused aloud, "Will it be different for us when we are both joined? Will we still ride and laugh and be playful?"

"Some things change between friends when they join and become fathers, but not all things. Look at our fathers and my brother: White Arrow and Gray Eagle are as close this sun as countless suns past, as is Bright Arrow and Windrider, and with your brother Flaming Star. The day will not come when Thunder Spirit and Sun Cloud do not ride, joke, and become as boys again together. I wish you could have the woman of your heart, but Tashina will be good to replace her sister."

"Perhaps things are as they were meant to be."

Sun Cloud parried, "If not, *Wakantanka* will change them."

The Oglalas halted near dusk to camp for the night. Shalee and Tashina busied themselves with the evening meal, and when no one was around, Tashina told her grandmother what had really happened the previous night.

"You have much to learn, little one. Men always tease about such things. A father is eager for his firstborn son to find a mate, to earn his own tepee, and to give him grandchildren. In doing so, his Life-circle and bloodline continue. Perhaps Windrider only spoke in jest or from wishful thinking, for his son is a warrior and a man. Too," she teased mirthfully, "Windrider's tepee is full with a wife and five children, and perhaps he misses his privacy with Sky Eyes. Love and desire are ageless, little one. It is so in every culture, Tashina; when spring arrives, all eyes and hearts think of love and mating; it is the way of nature to inspire hungers to renew old life and to birth new life. Warm and scented nights cause stirrings in young bodies. Such fevers are as old as *Wakantanka* and will continue forever."

"You know all things, Grandmother, and I love you."

Shalee stroked Tashina's hair and smiled. "Sometimes I wish I knew all things and other times I am glad I do not. To remove the bad surprises in life, such a gift would also remove the good ones. Yearning for love to be fulfilled is like suffering from bittersweet ecstasy. The love and desire are always present, but there are bitter days and sweet days to be confronted. Waste none of those days, Tashina, for each one is precious and it shapes you into the person you must be. Life is not easy, little one, and neither is love."

"What will I do when Silver Hawk comes to ask for me?"

"Do not worry, Granddaughter. If Soul-of-Thunder has not spoken for you by that sun, then I will speak to your father. I do not believe Silver Hawk will speak to your father before he approaches you once more. When he does so, come to me and I will tell your father to reject his desire."

"Silver Hawk is his friend, Grandmother, and this deed makes him larger in Father's eyes. What if he will not listen to you?"

Shalee wrapped her arms around Tashina and replied, "I promise you, while I live, Silver Hawk will not have you."

There was no more trouble on the trail, and they reached their chosen spot three days later. Everyone went to work immediately on their personal tasks, and soon the camp was in place by a small river, along whose banks grew trees and bushes here and there.

Soon, it would be time for the buffalo hunt, when small groups of women and men spent weeks on the open Plains hunting this vital game. The groups would trail the large beasts while skilled hunters picked off an ample supply from the rear of the herd. The women skinned and gutted the huge animals where they fell and sent the meat back to camp to be divided and prepared by each family. In the camp, wooden racks were constructed upon which to hang the strips of meat while they dried, becoming *pa-pa*, jerky to the whites. Some of the dried meat was packed in parfleches, to be eaten as was; other portions were pounded almost to powder, mixed with berries and hot fat, allowed to cool, then formed into rolls of *wakapanpi*, what the trappers called "pemmican," which would not spoil for years. It was a long, hard, sweaty, and bloody episode; and each family did its share of work. At Shalee's age, she was one of the women who would remain in camp and help with the meat as it was brought in on travois by young braves. When the hunt was over until fall, the tribes would get together to have a great feast and to observe the Sun Dance Ceremony.

The Sun Dance Ceremony began with a fast, prayer, and a visit to the sweat lodge for purification. It was not required, but most great warriors attempted it. If a man did not have stamina, he could die from the ordeal which he willingly endured. Sometimes it was done to show love and gratitude to the Great Spirit, as a man truly owned nothing but his body. Sometimes it was done to fulfill a warrior's vow when his prayer was answered a certain way by *Wakantanka*. Sometimes it was done to plead for help in a critical matter or to prove a man's worth and courage. Bright Arrow and Gray Eagle had conquered their Sun Dances, but Sun Cloud's time had not yet arrived.

Early the next morning while the men were hunting, the call went out for any available women to come and to help construct a tepee for a newly joined couple. Many women gathered and a lodge-maker was chosen, an older female who was skilled and well liked. Each female brought a spare hide, if she possessed one, and her sewing supplies. They formed a circle around the buffalo skins and began their mutual task. The young bride and her mother spent their time preparing food and serving the other women while they worked. It was a wonderful occasion when the women got together for this helpful chore; they laughed, talked, shared stories, gave advice, and sang funny songs. The work went swiftly and efficiently until, a few hours later, the tepee was completed, put up, and ready for use that night. The women who had helped handed their elkhorn fleshers to the lodge-maker, and she marked them with a blue dot.

The women were proud of their fleshers, which represented their deeds—female *coups*—by the color and number of dots. A girl was given her elkhorn flesher at her celebration into womanhood; then it was up to her to fill it with good deeds: deeds such as for hides tanned and robes made, for winning a beading or quilling contest, for helping others to construct their tepees, or for performing some charitable or brave deed. A man often asked to see a woman's flesher before he asked for her hand in joining to decide if she would make a good wife. To a woman, counting her dots was comparable to the counting of *coup* for a warrior. After refreshments were served a last time, the women returned to their own homes and chores.

Shalee blew on her new dot to dry it, then smiled as Tashina did the same. "You have earned many dots since your mother was taken from us, little one. Soon, it will have no room for new ones. You must show it to Soul-of-Thunder when he comes to visit us again."

That night, Sun Cloud nonchalantly announced he and Powchutu wanted to sleep near the river so they could get acquainted better. He claimed he was eager to hear the tales of the white man and his ways, and his uncle was eager to explain them. Gray Eagle grinned at his son and half brother, knowing this was only a ruse to allow him and his wife to have privacy. Hungering for it, he smiled and nodded.

Later, Gray Eagle and Shalee lay on their sleeping mat tantalizing each other with kisses and caresses. His tongue savored her peaks as his hands stroked her body to rising need for his. His kisses swept leisurely over her body as he called upon his sexual prowess to send flames of desire scorching through both of them. She nibbled on his ears, shoulder, and roamed his appealing frame with her lips and hands. The fire was ignited, carefully and enticingly fanned until it was a roaring blaze, then he entered her to douse it blissfully. When it was rapturously extinguished, they lay nestled together, warming themselves from the heat it had left behind. Neither talked, for words and voices would spoil the mood which surrounded them and which bound them together. Sleep overtook them, but they remained locked in each other's arms.

The Oglala council met the next morning; they voted to send messengers to the other camps to call for a joint meeting of all chiefs and leaders, at a point in the center of where each tribe or band was camped for the summer, to discuss and decide their impending course of action. Since this was a perilous time, only leaders would attend this crucial meeting while the warriors guarded the camps, for all knew how the soldiers loved to attack while the men were away.

Bright Arrow asked to go to the Blackfeet camp of Chief Medicine Bear and Silver Hawk, for he also had personal business there. Many donated gifts to be taken to Silver Hawk for his defense of Tashina and their camp. Sun Cloud and Thunder Spirit were told to ride to the Cheyenne camp of Windrider. Other warriors were assigned to take word to the remaining tribes and bands in the area. They were told to leave immediately, so they could return as soon as possible. While they were gone, warriors would guard the camp while braves hunted for game to supply the camp until the war council ended and the buffalo hunt, or the battle with the whites, could take place.

Shalee talked privately with her youngest son and asked him to speak of Tashina to Soul-of-Thunder. Sun Cloud looked surprised, but knew he should not be, for he had witnessed the strong attraction between the pair that night at the river in their winter camp. He realized he had spoken to the wrong man about claiming Tashina; he should have approached the Cheyenne warrior whom she loved, who loved her. He had learned a lesson today: Thunder Spirit had warned him about waiting too long to speak for the woman of your heart. Each always expected the other to grasp feelings which were kept hidden. Perhaps he should tell Tashina that Soul-of-Thunder loved and desired her, but that was not his place. He chuckled and said, "Do not worry, Mother; I will drop hints even one without eyes could see. It is good. I do not wish Silver Hawk to ask for her."

Shalee hugged him tightly and admitted, "I do not wish it so either. Be careful, my son, for our enemies abound everywhere."

"Worry not, Mother. When the war council votes and we attack the whites, they will lick their wounds all summer and leave us in peace for another season."

"I pray it is so, Sun Cloud, but I fear not. Seek the guidance and help of the Great Spirit, for often man cannot be trusted."

The moon was high overhead, but Tashina could not sleep. She looked toward the flap when someone crawled beneath it. The tepee was warm from the dying campfire, for she always kept the flap laced when her father was away. In the dim glow, she made out the face and body of the man coming toward her. Clutching the light blanket before her naked body, she pushed herself to a sitting position and stared at him in disbelief. Did he not realize how dangerous and forbidden this behavior was? she wondered.

He knelt beside her and simply stared at her for what seemed like a long time. Finally, he whispered, "Forgive me, Tashina, but I had to come, to see with my eyes you are safe. Father says Silver Hawk has cast his eyes on you, and makes no secret of it. I must hear from your lips you choose Silver Hawk because you desire only him, not to honor your father's wishes. We have been close since we were small children, but something has come between us and you no longer tell me the secrets of your heart. I could not come sooner, for there was trouble along the journey and near our camp, and I promised my father to guard his family. I wished him to bring you this gift in return for yours, but I was away from camp when he came to visit your father." He held out his favorite armband, his message clear. "I beg you, Tashina, do not join to Silver Hawk if you do not love him."

She chose and spoke her words carefully and softly. "I do not love or desire Silver Hawk as a man or as a mate, Soul-of-Thunder. If he approaches my father, I will speak the truth: my heart has been lost to another for many winters, longer than even I realized it." His expression and voice had exposed what she needed to know, as her grandmother had told her they would. Before she could reach for the armband, he dejectedly dropped his hands to the ground.

He lowered his head and confessed hoarsely, "Since the sun drifted below the trees, I have waited till my courage grew large enough to visit you. I know it is wrong to come when your father is away. Do I know this man who has stolen your heart? Is he worthy of you?"

Tashina's hand boldly lifted his chin and she smiled into his sad eyes. "You have known him all of your life. He is a great warrior and a good man. I love and desire only him, and I pray he feels the same for me. Can you love me as I love you, Soul-of-Thunder? If you give me time, I will prove I can be a good mate for you. If it is wrong of me to speak so boldly, forgive me, for I can bear this secret no longer in fear of losing you to another while I play the coward. If you only wish to be my friend, I will take that part of you, and I will not run to Silver Hawk in my pain. Am I unworthy of you because of my white blood? Is it impossible to win your love and acceptance as a mate?"

He gaped at her, then shook his head as if to clear dull wits. "Surely my mind sleeps and this is only a beautiful dream. Do not awaken me, Tashina, for it is all I desire. I have feared to speak to you of the feelings in my heart, for I could not bear your rejection. Can it be true? You love and desire me as I love and desire you?"

"With all my heart, Soul-of-Thunder. My grandmother said she would teach me how to snare you, but you are here and you are mine."

"Father told me of Silver Hawk's rescue and his desire for you. I feared your father would give you to him before I could race to your side and plead for you. You must be mine, Tashina, or my life is empty."

"As mine would be without you." She told him of her kidnapping and rescue, and of Silver Hawk's desire for her, and of her feelings.

"When the war council ends, I will come to your father and speak for you. We will join after the buffalo hunt, if you are willing."

"I am more than willing, Soul-of-Thunder. Father has given up hope of Mother's return and he casts his eyes around for a new mate. After the buffalo hunt, all will be settled and we can join. I love you."

The Cheyenne warrior gazed deeply into her eyes. His hand reached out to stroke her unbound hair. He wanted to kiss her and to hold her, but he was alarmed by the flames of passion which her nearness and love kindled within him. He slipped the armband over her wrist and smiled into her softened eyes, eyes which mirrored the emotions that surged inside his mind and body. As their gazes locked, they slowly leaned toward each other and sealed their lips. His arms encircled her body and hers slipped around his waist, unmindful of the blanket which fell free as they kissed and embraced.

His lips brushed over her entire face, then captured her mouth once more. His hands wandered up and down her bare back and savored its soft firmness. His fingers drifted into her hair and pressed her mouth more tightly against his own as he tasted the sweetness of her kisses.

Tashina was lost in the wonder and power of love. Her hands roved the muscles of his back and shoulders as she encouraged more kisses and caresses. Never had she felt anything so marvelous as she was experiencing, and she did not want it to end.

They sank to the sleeping mat and continued their discoveries of each other while they reveled in the joy of a mutual pleasure. Soul-of-Thunder's lips traveled down her throat and his hand moved over her quivering flesh. His mouth explored her shoulders and breasts, then captured one peak to lavish it with moisture.

Tashina's head moved from side to side as she was captivated by blissful sensations. She made no move to halt him as one hand lightly fingered his neck and the other stroked his silky hair. Suddenly he lifted his head and looked into her eyes. She could tell he did not want to halt this rapturous trek to sated passion, but knew they should.

Tashina tenderly caressed his cheek and locked her gaze with his, letting him know it was too late to retrace their steps to innocence. Each read the burning desire in the other's eyes. Right or wrong, dangerous or wise, this moment had to be fulfilled. When she smiled at him, it drove every doubt or restraint from his mind and body. There was no need for words, for her aura said it all to him. She knew she was sure about sharing herself with him, and he realized it.

His head came down to seal their lips once more, to fuse their destinies into one. Her arms went around his neck, and they drifted into a dreamy world which was shared only by lovers. He was thrilled and inflamed by her responses. He crushed her tightly within his arms, then relaxed his grip to hold her tenderly as his mouth sought hers time and time again. His gentle kisses became more ardent and possessive, as did his caresses. He knew this first union should not and could not be rushed, for it was special. His lips touched every inch of her face and throat, and his body surged with new life and joy. She was his and he was hers. Nothing and no one could halt their sensual union tonight or their marital union in the near future . . .

Never had Tashina known such excitement and happiness as here in his arms tonight, with her love returned. His warm breath caused tremors to sweep over her tingly flesh. As his tongue swirled about over her breasts, she quivered with delight and suspense. She did not feel embarrassed by her nakedness, nor when he removed his garments.

As it should be between lovers, there were no reservations, no inhibitions; it was right and natural between them. There was no modesty or shame, only pure love and its mate, untarnished desire. His hands were careful as they claimed her flesh, roaming her sensitive body as each area responded instantly to his contact. His touch was not as skilled and masterful as that of a man with more experience, but she did not notice. Soon there was no spot upon her that did not cry out for him to conquer it and to claim it as his own. Flames licked greedily at their bodies, enticing him to hasten his leisurely exploration.

When he bent forward and teased a compelling breast with his teeth, she groaned softly in pleasure. As his tongue circled the taut point, she watched with fascination, wondering how such an action caused her body to quiver and to warm. Wildly wonderful emotions played havoc with her thinking; it seemed she could do nothing but surrender to pure sensation. One hand slipped down her flat stomach to eagerly assail another peak, and he teased both simultaneously.

Her hand wandered up his powerful back into his ebony mane. Each time his mouth left one breast to feast upon the other, it would protest the loss of warmth and stimulation. His mouth drifted upward to fuse with hers. Between kisses, muffled moans escaped her lips, sounds which spoke of her rapidly mounting passion, if it could climb any higher or burn any brighter.

His own passion was straining to break free like a captured stallion. He moved over her to feel her warm moistness against his throbbing flesh. Assured she was prepared for his entrance, he cautiously pushed past the barrier which eagerly gave away to his loving intrusion. Her demanding womanhood surrounded his aching shaft with a mixture of exquisite bliss and sheer torment. He was so consumed by desire, by bittersweet ecstasy, that he nearly lost all control. He halted all movement to cool his fiery blood. Dazed by heady passion, he urged her to lie still until his mastery over his manhood returned.

Tashina could not lie still. She was feverish from blazing desire by now, caressing his body with hers. As he began to move within her once more, the contact was staggering and she would have cried her need aloud if his lips had not covered hers. He imprisoned her head between his hands as his mouth worked deftly on hers. His hips labored swiftly and urgently as he increased her great need. She heatedly yielded her body to his loving hands and lips, seeking the pleasure and contentment which she somehow knew only he could provide.

He dared not free her mouth as he felt her body tense and shudder with her release. He muffled her cry of victory which would have alerted anyone nearby or awake. A sense of intoxicating power surged through him just before his own stunning release came forth. He was so shaken by their potent joining and so enchanted by her magic that he almost shouted his own victory aloud. Instead, he moved rhythmically until the urgency had fled and they were holding each other tenderly.

He shifted to his side and continued to embrace her. When his respiration returned to normal, he turned his head to gaze over at her. Sensing his movement, she shifted her head and her eyes met his probing gaze. In the vanishing light, they exchanged smiles, then hugged and kissed joyfully. Theirs was an intense sharing of love and contentment. She laid her face on his wet chest and inhaled his manly odor, then she snuggled closer to him and smiled to herself.

He pressed kisses to her damp hair and held her possessively. It was not the time for speaking; it was the time for touching and feeling. An hour passed as they lay quietly in the tranquil aftermath of their first union. He longed to stay at her side, but he knew he must leave. He propped himself on an elbow and tried to pierce the darkness to view her lovely features. It was unnecessary, for he knew every inch of her face by heart. Soon, others would be stirring in the Oglala camp. He hoped he could sneak away without being seen, for he did not wish to darken her reputation, even if they were to join.

He whispered into her ear, "I must go, my love, before *Wi* awakes and reveals our night together. You are mine, Tashina, and I will return for you soon. I love you, and each sun and moon without you will be harder to endure now than before this union. My heart flows over with happiness and pride. Stay close to camp and guard your life well, for I would cease to be without you. I will sneak to the river and swim beneath its surface until I am beyond your camp."

"Do not allow *Unktehi* to seize you." She teased him about the mythical monster of deep waters.

"No power or person could take me from your life, my love."

They kissed deeply and longingly, only to find passions rekindled. They made love swiftly and urgently, for each knew their time was short. He quickly dressed and hugged her tightly. Tashina loosened the flap and peered outside. Sighting and hearing no one, she kissed him farewell and watched him vanish between the other tepees.

After sealing the flap, she returned to her sleeping mat and curled up on her side, smiling as she drifted off to sleep while thinking of her love.

Chapter Seven

In the Blackfeet camp, Bright Arrow was talking with Silver Hawk in his tepee while his wife Shining Feather was at the river doing her wash and her other chores. After Bright Arrow's arrival late yesterday, time and attention had been consumed by the revealing of his father's message about the impending war council and by gift-giving and *coup*-telling where Silver Hawk was concerned. Many had gathered to share in the excitement—eating, laughing, talking—and to celebrate the daring deeds of their past chief's son, along with his other recent *coup* of defeating the four foes who had been spying on their camp. It had been a glorious day for Silver Hawk, the kind of day which the insidious warrior intended to experience many more times in the near future.

Silver Hawk smiled with pleasure as he remarked smugly, "We have gathered many *coups* together, my friend and brother; and in the suns to come, we will gather many more. Our tribes would know such power and greatness as no others if Silver Hawk was chief of the Blackfeet and Bright Arrow was chief of the Oglalas." He lowered his tone as if to speak conspiratorially and leaned closer to the man on the sitting mat across from him. "It is strange how the Great Spirit chooses to work His will among His people. I am first-born son of a great chief and you are first-born son of a great chief, but our ranks were lost long ago. Medicine Bear makes many mistakes these suns and moons, and many grow dissatisfied with him. Times are bad, my brother, and our tribes need brave and cunning leaders."

Silver Hawk inhaled deeply before cautiously going on with his plan. "I do not speak bad of my other father Gray Eagle, but his time as chief nears an end. His spirit and heart are young and brave, but his body and mind grow older and weaker each sun. When I visit your tepee, my heart is full of pain when I see it hurt him to move and I see his once-keen eyes dulling and I hear the words and thoughts which he forgets. We face more peril soon than we have known before, my brother. I fear only a terrible defeat will prove to your father and people that Gray Eagle is no longer young and strong enough to lead the mighty Oglalas. I speak these words with a troubled heart, for I see the hatred and the determination of our white foes to conquer us this season; and I fear the Oglalas love and respect your father too much to ask him to step aside for a younger and stronger chief. I fear the war council will appoint him as leader for the joint battle, and I fear he is unable to carry it out safely. Most of all, my brother, I fear these fears, for fear does not belong in a warrior's mind, body, or heart."

As it was not their way to interrupt when another was talking and Bright Arrow could not honestly disagree with Silver Hawk's gentle words and seemingly sincere concern, Bright Arrow held silent. Lately, especially along the trail to their summer camp, Bright Arrow had noticed the very points which Silver Hawk was making—Gray Eagle's aged body, eyes, ears, and mind—and it tormented him deeply. Yet, he had forced himself to ignore those warning signs, for he hated to admit such a thing even to himself. He also knew that Silver Hawk was right on another matter; this new battle with the whites would be their worst and they needed a superior chief and war leader. No matter how much he loved and respected his father, his people and other tribes should not wishfully choose to ride, and to die, behind a legend. One lapse in thinking, planning, or fighting and all could be lost forever. He wished his father would grasp his limitations and gently refuse the honor which Bright Arrow knew would be placed upon his shoulders as a burden which could destroy them, but he knew his father would lead them and fight for them until his death. He asked himself if he should speak openly and honestly with his father on this grave and personal matter. It would do no good, he decided, recalling how many had talked with Bright Arrow long ago over a grave and personal matter—Rebecca Kenny—and how he had not listened to or heeded their words; and look what it had cost him. Perhaps his father was remaining chief only long enough for his chosen successor to get enough age, size, respect, *coups*, and experience to take over as chief. If he had not lost that right, he had enough of each to take his father's place this day. Anguish and anger filled him as he realized he no longer possessed the reason for his loss of rank, Rebecca Kenny. Now he had neither.

Silver Hawk had pretended to wet his throat with water while giving his words time to sink in and to work on Bright Arrow. Yes, Bright Arrow had been his friend and companion since childhood, but if he had to use him, or even destroy him, to get what was rightfully his, he would. If they could work together, they could continue as friends and allies, but work together without Bright Arrow's knowledge.

The devious Silver Hawk kept his tone controlled as he informed Bright Arrow, "Medicine Bear has lived sixty-two winters and he has no son worthy of becoming the Blackfeet chief, yet it is time for him to release the chief's bonnet. No warrior in my camp has *coups* or skills to match Silver Hawk's. Many whisper about voting me chief over Medicine Bear's sons, for it is my right and duty. Evil took my father, not the Great Spirit, so I still have a claim and right to the chief's bonnet. Because our tribes are linked through our mother Shalee, many know this bond will grow larger and stronger if I become chief. On my last visionquest, I saw myself standing on a hill, looking over our lands free of whites, and I was wearing the Blackfeet chief's bonnet."

Silver Hawk locked his gaze with Bright Arrow's as he added, "And my friend and brother Bright Arrow stood beside me, wearing the Oglala chief's bonnet. The time has come, my brother, when your rank must, and will, be returned to you.

The Great Spirit has made you a matchless warrior and He has removed all reasons to prevent your rightful destiny. You have but one need to prove your heart is all Indian; you must marry an Indian girl of high rank, one who can bind you to the bloodline of other great chiefs and prove your value."

Bright Arrow's gaze widened as he caught Silver Hawk's meaning. "You speak of your sister Singing Wind. What does she say of such things? And what of my father's words, Sun Cloud is to follow him?"

"Singing Wind has chosen no love or husband, for she waits for one worthy of her blood and rank. She is destined to become a great chief's wife; I know this and she knows this. She has much love and respect in her heart for Bright Arrow. If you approach Medicine Bear for her hand in joining, she will agree. Her head is strong and willful many times, but she is smarter than most females and she has much courage and daring. With the love and guidance of a strong hand and good husband, she will become all she is meant to be. Do you not see the truth, my brother? The Great Spirit did not make Brave Bear and Shalee of the same blood-line so this union could be possible. He gave you the white woman to fill your days to prevent you from joining another before Singing Wind was of age. He used the white woman to take you from your people so He could remove all weaknesses and flaws from your body, so He could test you and strengthen you and return you to your people to become a matchless warrior and chief. When the time came, He removed her from your life, for her work was done. Do not suffer over her loss, my brother, for I am sure the Great Spirit did not slay her; He has returned her to her rightful destiny. Long ago, He made us friends and blood brothers and He has chosen this season to return our ranks, to make us chiefs who will ride together and lead our peoples to survival and greatness."

"How can this be, Silver Hawk? When I returned to my people after I was banished, I agreed to follow Sun Cloud after my father."

Silver Hawk eyed the warrior across from him, his dark hair still short from his recent *coup*. He could tell that Bright Arrow was wavering, in doubt and in hope. "You agreed before you knew the truth, my brother. Sun Cloud is young and he is not ready to be your chief. He will know this to be true, and he will yield to your higher rank. Perhaps it is the will of the Great Spirit for Sun Cloud to follow you as chief, unless Singing Wind gives you a son," he added slyly, knowing how important a son was to a warrior, especially to a chief. He saw Bright Arrow's eyes gleam with anticipation at his last words.

Bright Arrow responded, "Sun Cloud will be chief one day, for my father saw it in his vision, but perhaps it is meant to be after me. If this is so, the Great Spirit will guide us to the right path."

"Perhaps your father had a dream, my brother, which he mistakes for a vision," the Blackfeet warrior suggested. "We must seek a vision together to see if the Great Spirit will give us answers. There are evil days ahead, and we must take the time to seek His will for us and our people. Will you come to the sweat lodge with me to begin our journey to the truth? We must find it, for the sun approaches when both our tribes will choose new chiefs. If it is our duty to lead our peoples, we must be ready and willing to face all who think otherwise, and perhaps battle any who go against the will of the Great Spirit."

"You speak wisely, Silver Hawk. If *Wakantanka* desires me to lead our people after my father, I must learn this quickly, so I can obey His call when the moment arrives."

"Come, speak with Singing Wind while I prepare things for us."

"I must seek *Wakantanka*'s will before I approach your sister. If she knows she is to join a chief, she will not consider me at this time."

"I do not mean you to ask for her hand in joining this visit, but you must make your interest in her known so she can be thinking of you, or dreaming of you," Silver Hawk teased with a mischievous grin. "Many women desire you, and she will feel honored you notice her. Spark an ember in her heart this sun, then when the time is right, kindle it into a raging flame of desire for you. Once when we spoke of you, she said you did not know she lived as a woman. She thinks you still mourn for Wahea and wish no woman to take her place. Her eyes danced with fire and light as she spoke of you. She can be yours, my brother."

As Singing Wind's image came to mind, Bright Arrow smiled. She was a beautiful and desirable female, and young enough to bear children. Too, she had spirit and strength, which many often confused with defiance. Perhaps Silver Hawk was right, he mused; perhaps his life was taking the path he was meant to walk . . .

While Silver Hawk went to see the ceremonial chief to ask his help with their joint visionquest, Bright Arrow walked around camp, as if visiting others while he secretly sought his friend's sister. He located her gathering firewood near the river. She halted and smiled genially when he approached her. "It is good to see you, Singing Wind. Your beauty increases with each season, and it brings joy to look upon it." He glanced around, then remarked, "I am surprised there is no line of warriors trying to share a blanket with you. Surely Blackfeet braves are not blind this season," he teased in a mellow voice.

Singing Wind laughed softly, for his expression and tone were sincere and flattering. She had always felt at ease with Bright Arrow, and they had laughed and talked countless times over the years. She jested in return, "Many think I am too wild and headstrong to please them. It is good to see your smile and to hear your laughter again; I have missed them since Wahea was taken from your side."

Bright Arrow inhaled deeply, then slowly released the spent air. He eyed the beauty of the land and the woman before him. "It is good to want to smile and laugh again. *Wakantanka* has renewed my heart and spirit as Mother Earth renews our lands. My life with Wahea is over, and I must seek a new one. But the available women of my tribe are as undesirable as the men of your tribe are blind. Perhaps we will both be lucky this season and find our rightful mates."

She eyed his robust frame which was so different from the sleek body of Sun Cloud. Her gaze took in his fire-tinged hair and leafy brown eyes, so unlike the midnight shades of his younger brother's. She liked how Sun Cloud wore his hair loose, whereas Bright Arrow wore his braided. As with his name, he wore a shiny arrow medallion around his thick neck, which was not as striking as the sun-cloud design of her love's. Yet, he was handsome and virile like Sun Cloud. "You do not need luck, Bright Arrow, for you are a warrior who causes women to chase after you. See, I still speak too boldly."

Between chuckles, he replied, "But the women who chase me do not appeal to me. I seek a special woman, one with strength and pride, one who is unafraid to speak her thoughts and to obey them. Let no one change you with their words, Singing Wind, for it is good to have strength and confidence, to be smart and brave. Other females only tease you because they are jealous and envious, for they wish they had the courage to be like you. And a man of real strength and honor has the courage and wisdom to realize and appreciate your value. Do not worry when others wonder why you remain unjoined, for the Great Spirit will choose a special man and send him to you."

"This I also know, Bright Arrow; this is why I wait patiently for him. Long ago, I told myself to stop listening to and being hurt by the jests of others. Sometimes it is difficult; sometimes it is not."

They laughed as she placed her wood in a sling and, together, they headed back to her tepee. "You have learned much about men from living in the tepee of Chief Medicine Bear."

"Perhaps too much," she stated with a playful grin. "I have seen them at their best and worst, and viewed their strengths and flaws, but I pray there are a few surprises left to learn, or life will be dull."

"There are, Singing Wind, there are," he told her confidently.

Silver Hawk joined them, delighting in the easy rapport which he had observed. Without knowing it, this man would help him obtain all of his desires: the Blackfeet chief's bonnet, his sister's absence, Sun Cloud's bring-down, Gray Eagle's death, and Tashina. Yet, Bright Arrow would be rewarded for his unknowing aid, for he would become the next Oglala chief and he would obtain a wife to give him sons.

"All is ready, my brother, and Jumping Rabbit waits for us," he announced happily, even sending his sister a warm smile.

"We seek a joint vision in these evil times; we need the Great Spirit's guidance," Bright Arrow told the girl at her look of bewilderment.

The two warriors went to the sweat lodge, which was constructed near the edge of camp and shaped like a bowl turned upside down. It was built of sturdy and flexible saplings, then covered snugly with hides to shut out light and air and to trap steam inside. This purification ceremony must be carried out before a man could seek a vision.

Silver Hawk and Bright Arrow entered, their eyes slowly adjusting to dimness. Each removed his breechcloth and moccasins, and handed them to the ceremonial chief, who placed them outside the lodge. Jumping Rabbit filled a hole in the ground with hot rocks from his fire outside the hut. He handed Silver Hawk a bag of water, then took his place near the entrance to continue his duty when necessary. He began to chant for the Great Spirit to aid the men's search for His will.

Silver Hawk poured some of the water over the rocks, which sizzled and popped and caused steam to rise from them. He continued this process until moist clouds surrounded them and covered their nude bodies. At a special signal, Jumping Rabbit entered quickly, added more hot rocks, then left swiftly to prevent the steam from escaping. He did this several times during the sweating process, which was done to release all impurities, evil spirits, and fear from warriors. It was to prepare their bodies to be worthy of accepting a message from the Great Spirit. The men sweated profusely as they rubbed sage over their wet flesh and chanted to *Wakantanka*. They inhaled the cloudy mist, believing it to be the cleansing breath of the Great Spirit. They swayed to and fro as they sang and prayed to be worthy of this rite.

Neither talked, for words could break the spell which was being created with this first step. As it was the end of April and they did not have the aid of the scorching summer sun to beat down upon the hut which made the sweating come easier, the ceremonial chief had to heat and add more rocks than usual for the heat and humidity inside the hut to do its task. Sweat mingled with steam soaked their bodies and ran down them like tiny rivers over hard ground. Their sitting mats were drenched in less than an hour. Their hair was wet, and it clung to their necks, and to Silver Hawk's back for his was long. As time passed, breathing became harsh and difficult, and faces grew red from their efforts to endure this ritual. Still, they sat cross-legged and chanting as if nothing were sapping their energy as they lost precious body fluids, a dangerous state for weaker men, especially when it followed a fast and preceded a Sun Dance rite.

When their required time elapsed, the ceremonial chief handed them more sage to rub over their bodies. He then removed hides from the far side of the hut and allowed cooler air to revive the men while they dressed, to head from camp to seek privacy for their visionquest.

Seeking a lofty place which put them in full view of the Great Spirit, as was their custom, the two warriors dismounted and followed the ceremonial chief to the place which he had chosen for them. As silence was commanded throughout the entire ritual, neither had spoken since just before entering the sweat lodge. The area in which they were to sit and wait was staked off, a small post representing each direction of the medicine wheel. A rawhide rope was strung from post to post; from which, Jumping Rabbit suspended bunches of sweet grass, sage, and sacred tokens. Two sitting mats were placed inside the square, and the men were instructed to take their places, facing eastward, from which enlightenment was said to come.

When they were seated, the ceremonial chief handed each man an eagle-bone whistle—used to summon the Great Spirit—and a peyote button from the mescal cactus—a powerful hallucinogen which induced sights and sounds and feelings for a "vision." Jumping Rabbit called on the Great Spirit to guide and protect the warriors along their mystical journeys, then told them to consume their *unkcekcena taspu*.

Both men placed the cactus buttons in their mouths, but Silver Hawk only pretended to chew and swallow his; instead, he placed it beneath his tongue. They nodded to Jumping Rabbit and he left them alone, to wait with the horses. Both closed their eyes, began to sway back and forth, and blew on their whistles. Silver Hawk had pushed his peyote button near his cheek, to await its removal when it was safe.

For a spring day, it grew hot beneath the sun, and more sweat glistened on their bodies and faces. No warrior, not even a foe, was allowed to disturb a man on a visionquest, for it was considered bad medicine, a curse from their god. But because of the constant threat from their white enemies these days, they were not required to spend four days and nights at the mercy of the elements before using their peyote buttons, which usually lasted for a couple of hours.

Soon, Bright Arrow succumbed to the powerful drug, for the peyote was strong and quick. Colorful lights and fuzzy images flickered in his mind, and strange music filled his ears, and curious sensations roamed his body. From the mental merging of deepest dreams, darkest desires, countless experiences, and varied thoughts . . . hallucinations began to form. First, he saw Rebecca Kenny standing before him, holding out her arms in beckoning, her eyes filled with sadness and accusation, as if she was mutely begging him to find her and charging him with the betrayal of their love and vows. Then, her voice seemed to fill his ears as she repeated words he had said to her long ago: "No matter what power says otherwise, you are mine. No matter where our bodies are, our hearts will beat as one. Whatever the future holds for us, my true heart, there can never be another love as powerful, as perfect, or as passionate as ours." Suddenly she vanished, as if called to another place by a force greater than him.

Silver Hawk buried his peyote button and looked at Bright Arrow, realizing he was deep in a trance. As in the sweat lodge, his thoughts were not on good or guidance; his thoughts were on obtaining his desires, in any way necessary. He did not fear the wrath of *Napi*, as the Blackfeet called the Great Spirit, for if *Napi* was as powerful and perfect as all claimed, his people would not be losing their battle to the whites and he would be chief. *Napi* had not rewarded him for his prowess and deeds; he had rewarded himself. Life in their territory was perilous, harsh, and often brief. If he wanted his days filled with the objects of his desires, it was up to him to obtain them. He would no longer wait for *Napi* to answer his prayers, to punish his foes, to return his rightful rank, and to help his people; he must handle those matters himself. Either *Napi* lacked the greater power or He had deserted his people. He was allowing them to suffer, to be defeated by their foes, to be replaced by the white-eyes. If *Napi* could punish him, He would have done so by now, for Silver Hawk had committed many evils. He was no longer afraid of *Napi*'s power or punishment, and he would only pretend to honor and to follow Him. He leaned slightly toward Bright Arrow and whispered words into his ear to control his "vision."

Bright Arrow witnessed a terrible battle with the soldiers. He saw his father lying upon a death scaffold, and he was vowing revenge, wearing the Oglala chief's bonnet. He saw Silver Hawk approach him, wearing the Blackfeet chief's bonnet, and he saw Tashina at his friend's side. He saw the flap to his tepee tossed aside, for the face of Singing Wind to greet him as he walked into her arms. He saw Singing Wind remove the blanket from their first child, a son. He saw his brother refuse to obey the Great Spirit's commands. He saw himself stand against his brother, for Sun Cloud fiercely battled the truth. He saw his brother try to take everything that was rightfully his. He saw victory and peace for his people under his leadership . . .

When Bright Arrow regained his senses, these "messages" filled his mind, both haunting and stimulating him. He glanced at Silver Hawk and believed he was still swaying and mumbling incoherently under the power of his peyote. Not once did he recall the time when Windrider had tricked him in a similar manner, or suspect that he was being duped today. He waited patiently until Silver Hawk was released by the Great Spirit. Then he smiled and told him, "All you said was true, my brother. Now, I must find the strength of mind and body to obey."

"Do not speak of your vision this sun, my brother, for the Great Spirit told me to reveal them to no one but our shamans or they would lose their power. When all has come to pass, we will reveal our visions to each other. We must refresh ourselves and return home."

"It will be so, my brother," Bright Arrow agreed. "I must ride swiftly, or others will worry over my delay. Soon, we will meet again, for the Great Spirit has locked our destinies together."

In the Blackfeet camp, Bright Arrow spoke privately with the chief. "My words are for your ears alone, Medicine Bear. Soon, I will seek a new wife, and I wish her to be Singing Wind. It is not the time to approach her, but if others speak to you for her hand, know I have spoken for it first. Our union will create a stronger bond between the Blackfeet and the Oglalas. I will bring you many gifts to prove my desire for her and my prowess. Say nothing to her or to others until I return. Is this agreeable with her second father?"

Medicine Bear smiled and nodded. "I will hold your words and desires in secret, Bright Arrow, and I will give you the hand of Singing Wind when you return and ask for it before my people."

"I must leave swiftly. It is a happy day in the life and heart of Bright Arrow. Medicine Bear is a wise and good chief. May your suns be many and happy." Bright Arrow clasped Medicine Bear's forearm and smiled.

Silver Hawk rode a short distance with Bright Arrow, then watched him continue his misguided journey. A wicked smile played over his features as he praised his courage and cunning. He headed his horse in another direction, to leave a message in the appointed place for Red Band to collect that night. When he met with his temporary ally on the morrow, his final plans would be put in motion . . .

In the Oglala camp, Sun Cloud could not stop thinking about Singing Wind. The days were so busy and filled with dangers, and he longed to see her again. A curious panic was plaguing him that day, as if some evil force was at work in his life and lands, other than the whites. He had given Windrider's Cheyenne band his father's message, but he had been unable to meet with Soul-of-Thunder. Sun Cloud had made it a point not to speak with Thunder Spirit again about Tashina, and would not do so unless the Cheyenne warrior's feelings did not match hers. He worried over his brother's late return, and wished Bright Arrow had not sent Flaming Star home when the Blackfeet camp was in sight.

He had noticed how weary his father and mother were, and he was concerned for them. Some days, they seemed filled with life and energy; on other days, they seemed tired and weak. When they returned from the war council, he was going to find a slave to help his mother. Too, he must find the right words and time to speak with his father, to implore him not to accept the leader's role in the upcoming battle. As difficult as it was for Sun Cloud to admit, he knew his father should follow, not lead, this time. His father had borne the weight of the white man's wars on his shoulders for many years. He had held the tribes together; he had given them hope, courage, and guidance. He had planned great defeats and he had ridden to great victories before united tribes. Gray Eagle had given much of himself to his people and to other tribes, but he must be persuaded not to do so again. Gray Eagle needed to conserve his strength and to enjoy his remaining days with Shalee. It was time for another to bear this heavy burden. Yet, Sun Cloud knew that his father would feel that others would lose hope and courage if they lost the one man who could hold them together, the one man whom the whites feared. He wondered, *If the Legend steps aside, what will it do to our mutual cause?*

Sunday, April twenty-third, was a beautiful day, but treachery abounded in the Dakota Territory. After meeting with Silver Hawk, Red Band reported to Major Gerald Butler.

"What a stroke of luck, Red Band. You've earned a month's extra pay. Before

Cooper arrives, our problems will be solved. You sure the area you've picked is perfect for our plans?" he asked.

"Gray Eagle must pass that way to reach war council."

Butler turned to Captain André Rochelle and asked, "You sure you can carry off your part, Rochelle? If you mess up, we've got hell to pay, and you know what I mean. Gray Eagle will eat us alive."

The Frenchman laughed arrogantly. "My great-grandfather belonged to King Louis' grenadiers, and he passed his knowledge and skills to his son, and my grandfather passed his secrets to my father, and my father gave them to me," he boasted accurately. Tapping the curved *sabre-briquet* which he always wore in a crossbelt strapped over his chest during battles, the forty-seven-year-old soldier told them again, "He was given this saber in 1770 for his talents and courage when he fought for your infant country against France's enemies."

"We know all that, Rochelle, but will it work?" Butler pressed.

"The grenades are ready. The smithy made them exactly as I instructed, and I have trained twenty men in how to light and throw them. But to make certain no one learned of our secret weapon, I did not allow them to practice with loaded ones. I will position them on both sides of the canyon. When I give the signal, the Indians will not know what hit them. Most will be killed, and others will be put afoot during the commotion; then your men can pick them off easily. As you ordered, we will aim for Gray Eagle first. He will not escape. If my little ones fail, I will give you my entire year's pay."

"Excellent," Major Butler remarked with a devilish grin, as he rubbed his hands together with anticipation. "By this time tomorrow, that bastard will be dead and those Injuns will scatter like a dandelion in a stiff breeze. By God, we've got the son-of-bitch this time."

"What about the others, Major?" Captain Smith asked eagerly.

"We'll send a regiment over to their meeting place and have them pick off as many leaders as possible, just in case one of them gets the bright idea of replacing Gray Eagle. But right now, my only concern is getting rid of their legend; that'll make 'em think twice about who's the most powerful and indestructible force around. Let's get all of this set up tonight. I don't want any horses in sight or sound of them Sioux when they head out in the morning. Red Band, you make sure all our tracks are covered before their scouts ride through."

"You want any camps attacked?" Smith asked his final question.

"Not this time. Let's make it look like we're only after the warriors. My guess is most of the bands will hightail it out of my area. The ones that don't, we'll run 'em out with a few more of Rochelle's babies. Any more questions or comments?"

The men exchanged glances and all shook their heads. Major Gerald Butler laughed coldly as he declared smugly, "Then let's go burn the Eagle's wings. If no other redskin is killed tomorrow, make sure he doesn't come out of that canyon alive. Make sure I get his body and possessions. Understand?" The men nodded, then were dismissed.

Outside, Captain Clarence Smith asked the Crow scout, "You sure you can trust Silver Hawk? He ain't setting a trap for us, is he?"

Red Band replied, "I promise him truce for his people and many trade goods. I promise he be new Blackfeet chief. He crazy; he believe. He hate Gray Eagle much as whites do."

"You're a sly and cold-hearted devil, Red Band," the captain teased.

"Silver Hawk is mine. I cut out traitorous tongue and heart before I kill. No warrior with honor betray own people. He must die."

"But you're helping us to destroy them," Smith reasoned.

"I help destroy enemies of Crow, not my people. You white, English white, but you kill each other. Same is true of Indian. We not alike. We ride, much to do before sun awakens."

Bright Arrow asked Powchutu and Sun Cloud to sleep in his tepee so Gray Eagle and Shalee could have this night alone before they rode out to the council. While Bright Arrow met with the shaman Mind-who-Roams, Powchutu and Sun Cloud talked with Tashina, who was delighted that her father had not mentioned Silver Hawk to her.

Mind-who-Roams observed Bright Arrow intently as he revealed his vision near the Blackfeet camp yesterday and his talk with Silver Hawk before it. When Bright Arrow finished, he looked at the shaman and stated honestly, "I do not understand, Wise One, for this is not what my father has told me, and it is not what he believes. Tell me what the vision means."

"There are many things which the Great Spirit has not revealed to me, Bright Arrow. But I saw a great battle in my vision. I saw a new chief leading the Oglalas, but his face was concealed. I saw two brothers fighting the enemy and each other. I saw the bodies of Gray Eagle and Shalee upon the death scaffolds. But I did not see which moon would bring these visions to pass. It is true, Sun Cloud is young to become our chief. He has not sat on the council and he has not endured the Sun Dance. He has not lived and trained under the Eagle's eye as long as you. It is true, the reason you were banished no longer exists. But it is also true, you once chose another path over your people and duty. I cannot say it was not a test or a means to remove your weaknesses and to make you stronger than before. Long ago, Gray Eagle told me of his visions, and I do not know why the Great Spirit gave you a different one, but I know you speak the truth. We must wait for Him to reveal more to me."

Bright Arrow returned to his tepee, and was glad the others were asleep. He did not feel like talking anymore that night. He glanced at the mat where his brother was slumbering peacefully and wondered what troubles lay ahead for them. Whatever happened, he had to obey the will of the Great Spirit. Never again must he let his people down.

In the tepee of Gray Eagle, the chief murmured, "You are restless this moon, little one. Do you worry over the days ahead?"

Shalee knew she had been tossing for some time and it was wrong to pretend to be sleeping. She did not want to confess her fears about this impending journey, not after his talk with Sun Cloud. Nor did she want to tell him of the pains which kept attacking her near her heart. She was so weary, but rest was eluding her. "Hold me in your arms, my love, for the night air is cool," she finally replied.

Gray Eagle pulled her against him and wrapped his arms around her. He was worried about her. She had been so pale and quiet that day. "Do not allow Sun Cloud's words to trouble you, little one. He made me face the truth; I cannot be band leader this time. I will do nothing more than speak of all I have learned and hope it helps others in battle. I know my son does not hunger for my place, but he is right; it is time for Gray Eagle to yield his chief's bonnet to one younger and stronger. I cannot allow pride to keep me from doing what is right."

Shalee hugged him tightly and kissed his lips, for she knew how hard those decisions were. "Do not fret, my love, for I will keep you busy in our tepee. We will enjoy our remaining days with each other, and with our sons and grandchildren. I love you even more for your courage and strength to take these difficult steps. There is nothing wrong with getting old; it is the way of nature."

"You have much wisdom, little one. There will be no more battles for Gray Eagle. He will be content to accept his age and new rank. I will ride to the war council one last time; then I will belong to you alone for the first time since we met so many winters past. No matter our troubles long ago, we have shared a good and long life. When the ever-moving line which draws my Life-circle closes, it will do so knowing I am complete for having captured Alisha Williams."

"If I could return to England and be seventeen, I would take this same path once more, if the Eagle awaited me again."

They embraced and kissed, then snuggled together to sleep.

Chapter Eight

Gray Eagle and Shalee kissed and embraced once more in the privacy of their tepee. Holding her in his arms with his cheek resting against her auburn head, he did not want to release her. He felt as if there was a curious force which was trying to keep them together today, yet another was trying to separate them. It was strange how he had awakened before dawn and lain there remembering the span of sixty-nine years which made up his current Life-circle. It had been as if every deed, word, feeling, and thought he had known since birth rapidly had visited his mind. He had reminisced about his mother Flower Face, a beautiful Sisseton female who had died at thirty-five winters from a fall in the sacred Black Hills while gathering herbs. He had been twenty; and he had refused for five winters to allow another woman that near his heart and life until the white, English girl had entered his territory. He had thought of his father Chief Running Wolf, who had known only two brief moments of weakness during his life-span— Leah Winston and Powchutu—yet both mistakes had damaged many lives and had caused Running Wolf and others much anguish.

Gray Eagle's hands began to caress his wife's back as he nestled her closer to his body. He did not know why his mind and heart were so troubled and reflective this morning. Life had been perilous and hard on the Plains, causing a man of his age to feel, and often to look, much older than his years. He had thought about his sons, and had tried to imagine their lives after he and Shalee were gone. He had wondered what would happen in and to his cherished lands and people. He had thought about friends he had lost, foes he had defeated, battles he had fought, truces he had achieved, and mistakes he had made. He had thought about the changes in his lands, but mostly those within him. He had thought about White Arrow, who had ridden at his side since childhood, who had stuck with him during right and wrong, during good and bad. Whatever he had needed or done, White Arrow had stood beside him to give love, help, encouragement, or guidance.

He had not set out to become a living legend, and had done nothing intentionally to increase it. Often, that honor had been as a curse which had compelled him to think of and to put others before himself and his family. His prowess and victories had been gifts from the Great Spirit, gifts which had carried heavy responsibilities and personal sacrifices, gifts which had made him the "scourge" of the white man and their Indian foes. Many times, weary of the endless war and tormented by the death and destruction around him, he had sought peace and/or truce with both enemies, but their foes had failed to remain honorable and truthful, and he had been chosen to unite the Lakota Tribes and to call upon their allies to join them to fight "only one more battle" to push their foes back forever. But there was always another skirmish. Now, all of that could be placed behind him. He could live out his remaining days with pride and satisfaction, knowing he had done his best for the Great Spirit and his people. Yes, he was a little sad and depressed, for it was hard for a warrior to hang up his bow and war shield, and for a man to admit his age and infirmities, something he had never been more aware of than this morning.

He was tired and achy this morning, and almost was tempted not to ride to the war council. But if the Eagle failed to appear, the meeting could go badly, for so many depended on him. Sun Cloud and Shalee were right; it was time for the united tribes to select another leader, another source of magic and legend. He was ready to finish his life as a Big Belly whose days of glory were in the past, whose duty to his people consisted only of sharing his wisdom and love.

Shalee's cheek rested near her husband's heart and her arms were wrapped around his waist. How she dearly loved and needed this man who had changed her and her life drastically long ago. She enjoyed touching him and having him touch her. Sometimes he inflamed her senses so brightly that she feared she would be consumed by the roaring blaze; he had always had that effect on her. His face did display many lines and a toughness from the elements, but they had not stolen his manly appeal and exceptionally good looks. His body was not as lean or hard or muscular as it had been once, but it still enticed her to admire it and to crave it. His hair had not turned fully gray; it was half ebony. His dark eyes had not lost their sparkle and vitality. One hand wandered to his chest, to finger the scars there: the musket wound from his half brother, the Sun Dance markings, the Crow's lance wound when Sun Cloud had been captured at age seven, and other tiny scars from so many battles. He had given so much of himself to his people and to allied tribes. It was time for him to rest and to be safe; he had earned those rights. She turned her head to place kisses on his chest, then lifted it to entreat his mouth to hers.

After which, his lips trailed over her features before he murmured, "You are as beautiful and desirable this day as on the one when I captured you. I have loved you and needed you each sun and moon since that day. I would defend you with my life and all my skills. I would never desert you or forget you in life . . . or in death, little one. You are as much a part of me as my body and my spirit. Our destinies were matched before we entered life, and they will remain locked even beyond this life. We are bound forever."

Her eyes tenderly caressed him. "This I know to be true, my love. If I join the Great Spirit before you, do not be sad. Watch over our sons and grandchildren until you join us." When he returned from his last war council, she would confess the troubles she was having, for she knew they revealed her days were short. She did not want to worry him or to spoil this final trek; she would wait awhile longer.

He lifted her chin and gazed into her green eyes. "Why do you speak of such things, little one? We will have many days together. I have chased the Bird of Death away from us many times."

She smiled and she refuted gently, "The Great Spirit did not allow the Bird of Death to enter Gray Eagle's tepee; but, one day, he must come for us. I am not afraid. Our lives have been full and long. It will be good to know lasting peace and safety. My thoughts have been on Wahea and Moon Eyes, and I miss Little Feet and her sons. When the war council ends and all is safe, Little Feet must bring Buffalo Boy and Spirit Sign to visit us. Soon, our sons and Tashina will marry, and their days will be busy with new families. Soon, there will be many lives to carry on the bloodline of Gray Eagle."

Gray Eagle did not want to admit he had been thinking about Rebecca Kenny and her daughter and his grandsons this morning. "I have missed Wahea and Little Feet, too, little one. I am glad the Great Spirit allowed our son many happy years with his love before she was taken from his side. I must ask Bright Arrow to send word to Races-the-Buffalo to allow his wife and sons to visit us. I wish all my family could live together in my camp, as I wish for Wahea's return."

"I also pray for her return; I do not believe she is dead. I believe she lives in sadness for she cannot get back to us. Say nothing yet, my love, but Tashina will leave us soon to join her love, for she has lost her heart to the son of Windrider."

Gray Eagle's eyes filled with concern. "I wish that was not so, little one. When Sun Cloud took the war council message to the Cheyenne three moons past, they were holding the Dog Men ritual. The son of Windrider was chosen as one of the four to wear the sash until next summer. With war upon us, he will be lucky to survive the first battle. Now, I understand why Sun Cloud asked me to keep his news within me until Soul-of-Thunder could reveal it to his friends."

At this perilous discovery, knowing what it would cost her beloved grand-daughter, Shalee's heart throbbed with new anguish, physical and emotional pain. Windrider's band belonged to the Dog Men Society, which was the largest group in and among the Cheyenne tribes. Most males became members at fifteen, as would Soul-of-Thunder's half brother Sky Warrior this season: a boy of mixed blood who had sky blue eyes, blond hair, dark skin, and Indian features. She knew what it meant for a member to be selected as a sash wearer.

The four Dog Men who had captured the most *coups* and displayed the most prowess in the past year were chosen to wear the "dog-ropes" for the next year. These four men were to defend the society and their people with their skills and lives. When selected, each was presented with a tanned sash which was ten feet long and six inches wide, with an exposed split at one end which went over the man's head, to rest on his right shoulder and under his left arm. These trailing sashes had a small wooden stake on the far end which, during a fierce battle, was driven into the ground as a challenge to his foes, as a decoy to cover the retreat of his war party, and he was to die defending his band's retreat rather than remove the peg and escape. Yet, his courage was usually honored and protected by the right of another warrior to allow his retreat by signaling him like a dog. If the "dog-rope" was stolen by a foe or lost during a battle, the sash wearer's mother or widow was required to make a new one to replace it.

Gray Eagle said, "The sun moves higher; I must go, little one."

"So much hatred and fighting, my love, so many dangers. How I long for the peace we knew long ago, but was too brief. Send our sons to me so I can give them my prayers and goodbyes."

Sun Cloud arrived first. He was anxious to know if his words had distressed his parents, and was relieved to hear his mother's response. "It is good my father is wise and brave, Mother."

She caressed his cheek and smiled into his shiny eyes. "Soon, you will become chief, my son, and you will know the burdens your father carries. I pray your rank will not make the same demands upon you and your loved ones as it made upon your father and me. Be a wise and good chief, Sun Cloud, but do not forget yourself. Life is often brief and hard, and you must feast on its rewards each day. When the Bird of Death comes for you, you will leave Mother Earth full and happy, as I and your father will. You have been a blessing to us, Sun Cloud, and you must never regret our journey to the Great Spirit's side. Find a true love, have children, and collect much joy in life. Do not allow the white man's hostilities to harden your heart and to delay your dreams. You have brought much pride and love and joy to me."

Sun Cloud warmed at her words and sunny smile. He grinned and teased, "I pray you will not be angry with me when I reveal the name of the woman who has stolen my eye and endangered my heart."

Shalee laughed and retorted, "Does Singing Wind feel the same?"

Sun Cloud looked surprised, then inquired, "How did you know?"

More laughter came from his mother as she explained, "I have seen the signs for a long time, my son."

"I did not know I was so careless," he stated humorously.

"Only a mother would guess your secret," she told him, to his relief. "I would say Sun Cloud has not known this secret very long?"

"You are right, Mother. I tried to resist her, but I could not."

"Such is the way of love, my son. Does she know and agree?"

"She has not witnessed the truth and confessed it, even to herself. But she finds me irresistible," he jested, then laughed heartily.

"What female would not find the reflection of Gray Eagle so?"

"We will speak of Singing Wind and the chief's bonnet when we return. Rest, Mother, for you appear tired and pale. I will find you a slave to care for your chores so you can enjoy these coming days with my father at your side."

"You are a good son, and I love you," she said, then hugged him.

Within minutes after he left, Bright Arrow arrived. He seemed pensive, and she wondered why. She knew he had spent a long time with the shaman yesterday; but she could not question his motive, for it was not their way. "Take care, my first son, for danger and evil are around us," she cautioned as she embraced him.

He looked deeply into her eyes, his troubled spirit exposed in his gaze. "When

I return, there is much I must say to you and father," he remarked mysteriously. "Tashina will help you until I buy you a slave."

Shalee smiled and teased, "What mischievous spirit plays within my sons to make the same promise on the same sun? But you are right," she confessed. "It is time for Shalee to have help from another. We will talk later. Go, and let the Great Spirit ride with you. He will tell you what you must do to find peace again. You were born of great love, Bright Arrow, and you must live with great love. Do not allow the demands of life to burden and embitter you. Seek the will of the Great Spirit, and He will fulfill your destiny and dreams."

"It will be as you say, Mother, but it will be hard."

"I know, my son; for there are hardships and sacrifices and perils in life, and only in death can we find true safety and peace. Take control of your life once more. If a part of it ends, you must seek a new beginning. But live your future suns so your past will not be burdened with pains and guilts. I love you, Bright Arrow."

Bright Arrow hugged her tightly, almost desperately. "As I love you, my mother . . . and my friend." He kissed her cheek and left.

Shalee walked outside and observed the group of twenty-six men who were preparing to leave: the council members, the four Sacred Bow carriers, the top four shirt wearers, and two warriors who would act as advance scouts. Her gaze slipped over her beloved husband, her two sons, her closest friends, and Powchutu. He had been with them for three weeks; some times, it seemed perfectly natural to see him there; other times, it still seemed strange and impossible.

Powchutu glanced her way and smiled, then came to speak with her. "When I return, Shalee, I will seek a new wife and tepee. Our last days must be lived with happiness. I have done as the Great Spirit commanded by returning here to make peace with those I wronged. Now I am content. It is good to spend my last days in my father's lands."

Shalee caught his hand and squeezed it affectionately. "How our lives have changed since that first day we met," she stated with a soft laugh. "Shalee is very proud of you," she remarked meaningfully.

Powchutu hugged her, and whispered in her ear, "Farewell, Alisha Williams. May the Great Spirit guide us all."

She watched the men mount and ride away, and trembled at how many times the words "when I return" or "when you return" had been spoken today and during the past few days. She glanced at the sky to determine the time of day, and decided it was around ten o'clock.

Captain Clarence Smith was leaning against a boulder as he cursed the midday sun and sipped water from his canteen. He removed his hat and used his right sleeve to wipe the sweat from his forehead and upper lip. Sometimes he hated this area with a passion; other times, he wished he owned a large chunk of it. Everything had been prepared for their surprise attack during the night. Red Band had removed all signs of their arrival, preparations, and presence. The soldiers were concealed at strategic points on both sides of the canyon through which Gray Eagle and his band had to pass some time today. All they could do was watch and wait, and pray for success.

The fifty-six-year-old man beside him was nervous and fidgety. "What's wrong, Clint? You sitting on an ant bed?"

"We all are, Capt'n," the corporal replied. "I'm a damn fool to keep reenlisting and staying around here, after what I've seen over the years. The next time my duty's up, I'm gone."

"Don't tell me you're scared of the almighty Eagle," Smith taunted.

"If you'd been in these parts as long as I have and seen what I've seen, you'd be shaking too," Corporal Clint Richards scoffed in return.

"Tell me, Clint, just what have you seen and done to make such a coward of a damn good soldier," Smith questioned in annoyance.

Clint settled himself cross-legged on the ground and sipped from his canteen. He stared Smith in the eye and said, "Enough to know Gray Eagle isn't a legend for nothing, and enough to know we're crazy to pull a stunt like this. We'll all be dead by nightfall. If we had any brains at all, we would get the hell out of his territory or make a real truce with him and those Sioux."

"You've got rocks in your head!" Smith nearly shouted at him.

"I was at Fort Henry in '82 when Major Hodges thought he could capture the Eagle, and darn near got us killed with his scheme. Oh, he lured Gray Eagle into his trap, but not for long. We had him trussed up like a chicken, standing in Hodges' office, and he tricked his way free. I should know, I was the guard holding a gun on him."

"Well, what happened?" Smith asked impatiently.

"Hodges was boasting to this Spaniard named Don Diego de Gardoqui, who was visiting us for his government. I won't ever forget that day. Hodges argued like a wild man when Diego insisted Gray Eagle be cut loose 'cause his wrists were bleeding all over the floor. Hodges kept spouting about Gray Eagle wasn't just any man and couldn't be trusted. Diego pulled rank on Hodges and he buckled. Afore we knew what hit us, Gray Eagle had snatched Hodges' knife and had it at Diego's throat and was demanding his freedom. Lordy, Hodges wanted to let Gray Eagle slit it for him, but he knew what trouble he would be in if he did. He let the Eagle fly away as pretty as you please."

"How the hell did you survive?"

"Gray Eagle made Hodges tie me up, then he walked right out of there, without killing a single man, except the one who betrayed him and got him caught. 'Course, his horse was the one who did Jed Hawkins in for him, but he ordered it and that steed obeyed, like everything else does as he says. But Hodges was real riled and set another trap for Gray Eagle. He had soldiers attack Running Wolf's camp; that was when the old man was still alive and chief. Major Sturgis over at Fort Meade tried to reason with Hodges and Collins, but they wouldn't listen. I must have some angel watching over me 'cause I was sick with dysentery and couldn't ride out with them. The Eagle fooled 'em and wiped 'em out. It wasn't long before Hodges vanished one day. Still don't know what happened to him, but I can guess."

This time, Smith did not interrupt when Clint caught a breather and sipped more water. "Somehow Sturgis wrangled a treaty with Gray Eagle and things settled down until he left in '95, then hell broke loose again, because the new commander in this area wouldn't honor Sturgis' treaty. He stirred things up so much that he got Fort Dakota nearly destroyed that following year. That time, it was Lieutenant Timothy Moore and the Eagle's son in the middle. I was at Fort Meade then, but we heard what happened from a few survivors."

Clint glanced at Smith again and was surprised to find the man listening intently, for Smith rarely held silent very long. "This tiny white girl who belonged to Bright Arrow arrived at the fort, enchanted Moore, then helped Bright Arrow escape. From what we were told, Moore was completely fooled by her and was planning to marry her. She must have been real clever and pretty to pull off a *coup* like that. While Moore was off trying to wipe out the chiefs and leaders at a war council—sound familiar, sir?" he hinted pointedly—"Gray Eagle attacked Fort Dakota and Moore's troops. I don't need to tell you, only a few men survived and the fort was plundered."

"You ain't got your facts straight, Clint," Smith debated. "Timothy Moore isn't dead. He's on his way here with General Cooper."

"Yep, as a major. After he lost his fort and men, he was demoted to a private. He's been working his way back up the ranks for years. I bet his desire for revenge is as red as his hair."

"You know Moore?"

"Yep. He was at Fort Meade for a while, then back at Fort Dakota after she was rebuilt. He was one of the men called back east in '12 to help fight those English devils. I bet he's been chomping at the bit to get back here and finish this matter with Gray Eagle and his son. Seems like some men don't learn from their mistakes."

"What happened to the white girl?" Smith asked suddenly.

"Rumor said she married the Eagle's son, then they got rid of her. Name was Rebecca Kenny. Sure would like to meet me a woman like that," Clint murmured dreamily. "Then I wouldn't be single long."

Smith sighed heavily and sank into deep thought, from which Clint withdrew him. "Right after them mappers, Lewis and Clark, came through, people started heading this way. More of 'em after the war ended in '15. The more which comes, the more the Sioux gets riled. If'n I was President Monroe, I would be real careful out here."

"Why should we? We own this damn land, paid enough for it."

Clint laughed and shook his head. "It weren't the French's to sell, and it ain't ours to claim. If'n we wanted to buy it, we should have dealt with the real owners, them Sioux. And we should have waited for General Cooper to arrive before we brought our asses here today."

"Major Butler ain't got no intention of waiting for Cooper to steal all the glory, and medals, and promotions. Hell, man, there's history to be made here!" Smith exclaimed excitedly.

"Yep, past history, ours," Clint Richards scoffed.

"Not with Rochelle's tricks to help us," Smith argued.

"You really think those exploding balls are going to work?"

"You will too when you watch Gray Eagle go *poof*." Smith clamped his hands over his mouth to prevent his raucous laughter from spilling forth into the quietness which surrounded them.

Clint eyed the wicked man and shook his head. He wished he was anywhere but here today. Gray Eagle had spared his life once, and that memory had never deserted him. Gray Eagle was a great leader, and a special man, and Clint hated to think he'd be killed in this cowardly and despicable manner. A soldier like the Eagle should die in battle; it turned Clint's stomach to envision this kind of death.

* * *

Gray Eagle rode between his sons on a ghostly white stallion, for his beloved Chula had been set free from old age years ago. It was a must for a warrior to have a mount who was fleet, responsive, agile, alert, strong, and smart. A warrior depended on his horse in battle and on the hunt for his success and survival. It was one of the highest *coups* to steal a foe's war horse, which, in battle, carried symbols of his and his master's prowess. Such a prized animal was kept near a warrior's tepee and was cared for lovingly, and only he could ride it.

At most times, a warrior rode bareback with only a leather thong in the animal's mouth for control and guidance. Sometimes, a light saddle which was made of a hide filled with grass or buffalo hair was used. The Indian horses could not be compared to the white man's mounts, for the Plains-bred animals far excelled those used by the Army.

During an Indian boy's training period, which covered many years, he was taught how to fight and ride simultaneously by using the animal as a shield. As with hand-to-hand fighting, lance throwing, arrow shooting, and hatchet tossing, a boy was drilled in battling on horseback with all weapons. He was also taught how to retrieve a wounded comrade by practicing with objects which grew larger and heavier as his size and skills improved. By the time he was a warrior, he could pick up a wounded or slain warrior and carry him away without breaking his speed. Agility for this necessary skill came from years of races, games, and sports which involved all of his senses working as one.

The four Sacred Bow carriers rode as the four points of the Medicine Wheel —one on each side, one in the front, and one in the back—as it was their duty to protect their people with their lives and skills, just as it was the responsibility of each man not to allow a sacred bow to fall into the hands of an enemy if a carrier was slain. The four "shirt wearers" rode amongst the council members, chatting genially, while the two scouts stayed ahead of the group, ever alert for any sign of danger.

The scouts had checked the first two canyons thoroughly and were approaching the third and next to last one before they reached open land. They had decided, if there was trouble, it would come at the last one, five miles beyond this point. One had ridden to the left and one to the right to scan behind the clusters of tall boulders; neither had sighted horses or men. They entered the canyon and studied it, finding no tracks and hearing no sound. They waved the party forward . . .

The four Sacred Bow carriers rotated their positions, placing Sun Cloud to the left of the group. Bright Arrow dropped back to speak with Flaming Star, son of White Arrow. Gray Eagle did the same to speak with the war chief, Big Elk. Powchutu was talking with Strong Heart and Snow Warrior as they entered the canyon at three o'clock.

Powchutu adjusted the shield he was carrying for his half brother. His eyes roamed its taut surface. The pattern represented the powers of the sky and its starburst design gave its owner protection. An ermine skin, for an ermine was said to deliver messages from the Great Spirit, was attached to its center, along with four eagle feathers from the warriors of the sky. Sacred and magical tokens, *coup* feathers, and scalplocks were fastened to its borders and at points on the painted star. It was a shield few men earned the right to make and to carry, and it thrilled him to know his bloodline possessed one.

"Which one is him?" Smith whispered to Clint as the unsuspecting Oglala band neared the center of the enclosed area.

Clint peered between the rocks and replied tonelessly, "The one near the front, with gray hair, carrying that Shooting Star shield."

Smith's eyes enlarged as he recognized the old man who had visited the fort under the name of Tanner Gaston. He was astounded to realize he had met and spoken with the Eagle himself! Surely Red Band had been half-accurate, and that second man had, indeed, been Bright Arrow, son of Gray Eagle. How those two Indians must have laughed at their stupidity. But soon, he vowed, he would have the final laugh.

The signal to attack came when the band reached the appointed place. Suddenly bursts of light and loud noises filled the air as grenades, designed by Captain André Rochelle, were tossed into the group. Smoke surrounded them; horses reared and whickered; and men and mounts went down. There was a desperate scramble for weapons and cover, but gunfire opened up on them; and more men and horses were slain.

Some made it to the rocks nearby, but they were trapped between their enemies. It looked impossible to get to the wounded and dead. Bright Arrow saw his father move slightly and his heart pounded fiercely. Amidst gunfire, he flung himself onto his horse. Hooking one heel over his mount's back and beneath the thong which surrounded his belly, he caught his rein in the bend of his elbow, slipped to the animal's side, and raced toward his father. Concealed by his horse's body, no soldier could recognize him as the man who had visited the fort as Clay Rivera. He moved so quickly and skillfully as he mounted and retrieved his father, that no musket fire struck them.

Having that same intention, Sun Cloud swept up Powchutu as his brother was rescuing his father. Both made it to the safety of cover and placed their precious burdens side by side. From his uncle, Sun Cloud took the shield which Powchutu had refused to release earlier, and placed it beside his wounded father.

The others were returning the gunfire with arrows when a target seemed in the clear, for it was foolish to waste shafts when they were pinned down. The two scouts lay dead near the front of their column. Sun Cloud checked for movement from any of the other fallen warriors, but saw none. His tormented gaze went to his father's face.

"Sun Cloud," Gray Eagle spoke weakly, "you must ride for help."

"I am needed here, Father," he protested, knowing the odds.

"You must go quickly before more bluecoats arrive and we all die."

Sun Cloud knew his father could not survive his wound long, and he hated to leave his side. "It is your duty, Sun Cloud," Gray Eagle said.

Sun Cloud's eyes sparkled with moisture as he embraced his father and vowed, "I will return and slay them all, Father. I love you."

"Remember all I told you and taught you, my son. Go quickly."

Sun Cloud mounted in the rescue fashion and galloped from the canyon. As Plenty Coups watched his dust lengthen, he told his dying chief, "He is away safe, my friend and brother."

Gray Eagle looked at Bright Arrow. "You must return to camp and warn our people, for the bluecoats may strike there next. Care for your mother, Bright Arrow, for she was my life."

As with Sun Cloud, Bright Arrow protested with damp eyes, "How can I leave you and the others unprotected, Father? They are many."

"Do you wish them to attack our camp by surprise? You are a shirt wearer and must do the bidding of the council and your chief. You must not die this day, for the Great Spirit has work for you. Your duty is to your people, Bright Arrow, not to yourself or to your family. I am old, and my life has been long and good; do not risk all for a dying man. The lives of many are more important than the life of one or those of a few. You must take all of my possessions with you; do not allow the bluecoats to have bloody souvenirs from Gray Eagle."

"But how can you fight without your bow, lance, and shield?"

"My fighting days are over, my son; you know this. The Great Spirit calls my name this sun, and I must answer. All is good with me."

Anguish seared through Bright Arrow as he watched his "vision" coming true. He removed Gray Eagle's *wanapin* from his neck and collected his other possessions. He raged at the gunfire which was filling the area around them. "I love you, Father, and I will return for you when my mission is done. I swear on my life and honor, no white man will touch you this day or any day."

Gray Eagle smiled faintly. "Remember all I have taught you, my son, and lead your people wisely and bravely," he remarked without meaning his words to sound as he and others nearby took them. "Go quickly, and tell your mother of my love for her."

Bright Arrow embraced his father as he fought back his tears. "The white man will curse this day, Father; this I swear." He did as his brother earlier, and cleared the canyon with only a slight wound.

Gray Eagle looked at Powchutu. "Our lives have been entwined since birth, my brother, and we will die together. It is good."

Powchutu smiled and replied, "It is good." Then he died.

Far away, on a ship, Stede Gaston caught the railing and inhaled sharply. When his nephew Allen Clarion asked what was wrong, Stede stared into the distance and replied, "My father is dead, and rests now."

Gray Eagle lifted his eyes skyward and prayed. *Bring victory and peace to my people, Great Spirit. Watch over my loved ones, my beloved Alisha. Guide and protect Sun Cloud as he receives the chief's bonnet, for the days ahead will be filled with dangers and pitfalls.*

Gray Eagle began to sing the Death Chant weakly for himself and Powchutu. When he was done, he said, "Your sons come to join you, Father. Meet us on the ghost trail and guide us to the Great Spirit. Together we will watch my son lead our people." He closed his eyes, envisioned Alisha "Shalee" Williams, then ceased to breathe forever.

The warriors around Gray Eagle began to sing the Death Chant together for their fallen chief and brothers, and the soldiers wondered what was taking place until a Crow scout explained. Then a cheer arose at four o'clock on April 24 of 1820 to alert the soldiers on the other side of the canyon of their victory. Clint turned away to retch, sick over his part in this tragic episode.

* * *

In the Oglala camp, Tashina was leaning over her grandmother and trying to discover the problem. "I will seek out the shaman's helper, and he will make you well again, Grandmother," she stated frantically.

"It is too late, Granddaughter. The Great Spirit calls to me. I go to join your grandfather," Shalee murmured as her strength failed her.

"But grandfather is away. He will return soon," the girl reasoned.

"No, little one, your grandfather is dead. I can see him waiting for me. Do not be sad, Tashina; it is the way of all things to complete their Life-circles. Care for your father, for he faces a great test. Seek out your love and be happy. I am coming, my love," she whispered, reaching out her arms to the warrior only she could see . . .

It was dusk when Bright Arrow charged into the camp and shouted a signal for the warriors to gather quickly about him. Failing to notice the items that Bright Arrow was carrying which told a gruesome tale, Tashina rushed forward to meet her father before another could reveal Shalee's death to him. She told him sadly, "Grandmother walks with the Great Spirit. She said grandfather summoned her."

Bright Arrow lifted his head, cried out in anguish, then drew his knife to slice across his right forearm and then his left to reveal his double sorrow. Holding up the possessions of Gray Eagle, he announced, "Our chief and many of our council are dead. We were attacked by the bluecoats, two canyons away. My father commanded me to warn our people to watch for an attack here. I must return to help them battle our foes. He sent his weapons and *wanapin* home so the bluecoats could not take them and count *coup* on Gray Eagle."

Many warriors surged forward and demanded to ride with him, but he repeated the partings words of his father. "I must return, for I have sworn vengeance, but you must guard our camp and people. I will take ten warriors with me." He yielded slightly, then selected them. He appointed the shaman's helper as the guardian of Gray Eagle's shield, medallion, and other belongings.

Tashina wept as she watched her father ride into danger once more. She wondered how love could be so powerful as to go beyond death, for her grandmother's last words kept racing through her mind.

Sun Cloud rode for hours with a heavy heart. In the distance, he saw dust rising from the hooves of numerous horses. His eyes widened and his heart thudded in dread, wondering if it was more soldiers heading for the canyon. If so, those remaining alive had no chance of survival or escape. If his father still lived, which he doubted, his body was in peril of theft. He was a Sacred Bow carrier and his duty was clear: he must try to slow them until help could arrive.

Chapter Nine

❧ *T*he large party from the war council approached Sun Cloud and halted. Sun Cloud explained the trouble and asked for their help, already knowing they would respond.

Before riding off, as their horses rested for a short time, a Sisseton chief Fire Brand revealed, "A band of soldiers tried to attack the camp of the war council. We killed many and drove the others away. When the Oglala band did not arrive, we suspected your peril."

Chief Flaming Bow of the Red Shield Band of the Cheyenne asked, "Do you think any still live? It has been a long time since the attack."

It was like driving a hot knife into Sun Cloud's body to reply, "In my heart, I know my father and his brother are dead. But others might breathe longer if we return swiftly and slay the bluecoats."

Fire Brand declared confidently, "We will defeat them as in the sun past when we rode against Fort Dakota and destroyed it." He recalled that episode in his life clearly. He had pretended to be a scout for the fort, while learning their secrets. He had met Bright Arrow's woman when she had come to aid his escape, and she had suffered at the hands of Lieutenant Moore for doing so. He had heard of her disappearance last spring, and had mourned for the valiant female. In the past, he had ridden many times with Gray Eagle and Bright Arrow; now, one great leader was dead, but another would replace him, for few warriors could match the prowess and *coups* of Bright Arrow.

Silver Hawk spoke coldly, "We must slay every bluecoat in our lands. Gray Eagle will be avenged; this I swear, for he was my second father." He was furious with Red Band for betraying him, and almost getting him killed. Red Band had given his word and the Army's word that only the Oglala band would be attacked! He decided it was perilous to trust or to depend on anyone but himself for his future moves.

"There is more, Sun Cloud," Fire Brand hinted. "Races-the-Buffalo was slain in our battle. His warriors take his body home."

Sun Cloud could not help but think of his friend and Sacred Bow carrier Thunder Spirit, who was pinned down in the canyon with his brother Flaming Star and their father White Arrow. It would be cruel if the Great Spirit allowed Little Feet's husband and true love both to die on the same day. Since the wounded and aged could not flee, the other warriors would remain with them, defending them, until death.

Flaming Bow said, "You are brave, Sun Cloud, for you were willing to stand against a large band to fulfill your duty. We must tell others of this great deed. Come, darkness is near; we will use it wisely, for the whites foolishly believe Indians do not ride or attack when the moon replaces the sun." Flaming Bow oddly reflected on the day when he had ridden into the Oglala camp twenty-four winters past to slay two warriors of his own tribe who had gone there to challenge Bright Arrow to the death for his white captive and to "avenge" the blood of Standing Bear who had committed that fatal error moons earlier. If not for Bright Arrow and Rebecca Kenny, the treachery of Standing Bear and White Elk might have remained concealed long enough to destroy his Cheyenne band. That season, he had taken Silver Star's place as chief, just as Bright Arrow would take Gray Eagle's. It was good that Bright Arrow had a brother worthy of riding beside him.

Windrider spoke with Sun Cloud for a moment, and told him he had sent his son back to camp to warn and to protect their people.

Then the Oglalas galloped toward the canyon from one direction, while the war party of united tribes approached from another, with Bright Arrow's band arriving first. Both groups reached the canyon within thirty minutes of each other, near two in the morning. They began to inch their way toward the hiding places of the soldiers and toward the Oglalas who were trapped between them. No signal was given which might alert the Crow scouts to their presence, for both groups had left their horses at a safe distance to approach stealthily on foot.

Captain Clarence Smith had left earlier, to report their victory to Major Gerald Butler, and to tell him the men would be along after sunrise, when they finished off the few remaining warriors and retrieved the body of Gray Eagle. He knew two warriors had escaped, but never imagined they would return with help before his troops could leave in the morning. Actually, he believed they had gone to warn and defend their camps and would probably think more soldiers were on the way. He wondered why Red Band had not recognized Gray Eagle at the fort and why the scout had denied the fallen man was the great Sioux leader, as others claimed. Red Band had suggested that Gray Eagle must have a brother who favored him, but no one had ever heard of such a brother. No matter, Smith assumed every Indian would be dead before dawn. He had taken Clint with him, for the man was violently ill and needed to see the doctor: they would become the only survivors of the grim raid which had slain one legend and would birth another . . .

By the time the sun gave light and warmth to the land once more, all the other soldiers were dead. Silver Hawk took sinister pleasure in removing a scalp-lock from the slain Crow scout Red Band. When the Oglala dead were laid in a row on blankets, Sun Cloud and Bright Arrow stood beside the grim sight: Gray Eagle, Powchutu, Strong Heart, Badger, River Snake, Snow Warrior, Calls Loud, Wolf's Head, and White Owl.

Several others were wounded, but they would recover. Many horses had been slain, so several warriors offered to ride double while their mounts transported the nine bodies home. Their task done, the war council separated to return to their camps, to reveal this new treachery and to stand guard against attacks on their villages.

Windrider and his warriors were the last to depart. He talked with Bright Arrow, feeling empathy for his best friend. He said he would come to visit when all was safe, then galloped away swiftly.

Sun Cloud looked at the cuts on his brother's arms and said, "Mother taught us the danger of such cuts, Bright Arrow. If you do not tend them, you will not live to avenge our father and people. When we reach our camp, let Mother tend them."

Bright Arrow stared at his brother for his soft scolding and curious words, then realized Sun Cloud did not know about Shalee's death. "It is our way, Sun Cloud. One is for Father, and one is for Mother." He revealed the heartrending news to his brother, who was shaken visibly.

The younger man's voice was hoarse as he responded, "I will place my cuts upon the bodies of those who killed my father, for two escaped. I will track them and make them suffer as we do, then I will return home to mourn our parents on their death scaffolds. When our parents and people have been avenged, I will take their bodies to the sacred hills where no enemy can find them and disturb them."

Bright Arrow nodded in agreement. "It will be as you say, for they must not be dishonored by those seeking treasures from our dead."

Sun Cloud walked away to speak with his friend Thunder Spirit, to reveal the news which concerned his mother and Little Feet. His heart was aching and he wished he could release his pain with tears and screams. He could not; he must be strong, for soon he would be voted chief and take his father's place. He was no longer a child who could reveal his emotions before others. His first thoughts and duties must be for his people, for his parent's deaths were in the past. How he wished his parents could have lived to see him become chief and to guide him during this adjustment period, but it was not to be. He must remember all they had taught him and told him, especially lately. It was shortly after dawn and, if he rode swiftly, he could avenge his people and return home sometime tomorrow.

Walks Tall and Talking Rock joined Bright Arrow. Talking Rock remarked, "It is not right for Sun Cloud to reject our way of sorrow."

Bright Arrow said, "My brother is young and is filled with pain. In time, he will learn his duty, as I have. I will see to our parents and people while he does what he must."

Talking Rock said, "You returned quickly and saved our lives, just as you saved the body of our chief. You have gained many *coups* this day, Bright Arrow. The vote will go easily for you."

Walks Tall remarked, "Chief Flaming Bow and Chief Fire Brand said they will attend the celebration when you are made chief. It is good we have a warrior of such prowess to lead us after Gray Eagle."

Bright Arrow smiled sadly as he recalled his "vision" for a time.

Sun Cloud left with Thunder Spirit, Star Gazer, and Night Rider. The three warriors trailed the two survivors, knowing the tracks were old, but hoping the soldiers would ride slowly with conceit or halt to rest before reaching the fort which would allow them to be overtaken.

The Oglala party reached their camp an hour after the sun passed overhead. The people were shocked and distressed over the white man's victory, but the shaman Mind-who-Roams had foreseen this grim event, and he had spoken of great victory afterward. For now, they must bury and mourn their dead. It required three hours for a selected band to cut, haul, and construct the ten burial scaffolds.

The slain warriors, their chief, and his beloved wife were prepared by washing them, dressing them in their finest garments, and then wrapping their bodies in thick buffalo hides; then, the bodies were placed atop their scaffolds which were built at a height to place them in view of the Great Spirit and out of the reach of animals. It was believed that the fallen one's spirit was claimed by the sun, wind, and rain elements and taken to the *Mahpiya Ocanku*, the Ghost Trail, where it could make its way to the Great Spirit and a happy afterlife. On the Ghost Trail, a soul walked in peace until received by *Wakantanka*. A warrior's weapons, and sometimes his slain horse's head, were placed on the scaffold to aid him on his journey to his new life. Once the warrior and his belongings were placed on the sacred scaffold, no one was to touch him or his possessions: it was the stealing of such "treasures" and the disturbing of these spirits by the white man which enraged the Indians.

Bright Arrow hung his father's bow, quiver with arrows, horse-dance stick, and shield on the four corners of his scaffold. Gray Eagle's lance was laid on one side of his body and his feathered tomahawk was placed on the other side. His sacred pipe rested over his heart, as did his medicine bundle, beneath the burial wrappings. The horse-dance stick had been made in honor of Chula, his beloved and loyal steed for numerous years. During special ceremonies, a warrior carried his horse-dance stick in remembrance of the animal who had served him well in life. Since his ghostly white horse had been slain yesterday during the battle, he could not accompany Gray Eagle on his long journey to the Great Spirit. The horse-dance stick was placed there to summon Chula from the spirit world to bear his master skyward. Gray Eagle's *wanapin*, an intricately carved eagle medallion, had been placed around his neck and he was wearing his best buckskins and moccasins, which had been beaded beautifully and with much love by his wife Shalee, who was resting beside him.

Shalee had been dressed by Tashina in a lovely white buckskin dress and moccasins. In her grandmother's lovingly brushed auburn hair, Tashina had placed Shalee's dainty Elk Dreamer's hoop with its white breath-feather and quilled design. Around Shalee's neck, she wore two items: her joining necklace and a carved white eagle on a thong with white and turquoise beads and rattlesnake rings: a charm given to her by Gray Eagle before they married, a symbol of his acceptance and of her first attempt to escape him in 1776, which had resulted in her beating and her rescue by Fort Pierre soldiers, allowing her to meet Powchutu, who rested on the other side of her.

Powchutu had been dressed in Gray Eagle's second finest set of garments and moccasins. His white man's garments and possessions had been burned, and he had been given weapons from other warriors to carry with him along his journey at his half brother's side.

White Arrow looked at the three scaffolds and could not halt the tears from flowing down his cheeks. He had known and loved Gray Eagle since birth, and he had ridden at his side since boyhood. They had trained together, raided and warred together, suffered and rejoiced together, and grown old together. His heart grieved at this second loss of a special loved one. His gaze went to Shalee's scaffold. He had known and loved her for forty-four years. They had shared a rare friendship, and almost a joining. They had laughed together, cried together, learned together, and worried together. Their lands would be darker without her sunny smile and bright presence. He had watched Gray Eagle and Alisha Williams meet, fall in love, battle their attraction, and then yield to it, to find powerful love and passion. It was good they had died on the same day, without knowing of the other's fate. It was good neither had been left behind to mourn for the other, for neither could be replaced in the life of the other.

Suddenly White Arrow felt very old and alone. The three people he had loved above all others were gone. Flaming Star approached his father and embraced him. "Do not torment yourself, Father. They have peace and safety now. Good memories must not pain you so deeply."

White Arrow turned. His gaze fell on his second wife Pretty Woman and their two children, Crow Stalker and Prairie Flower; somberly moved to his eldest son Flaming Star, his wife Morning Light, and their three children: Little Star, Stargazer, and Buckskin Girl. He thought of his other daughter, Medicine Girl and her husband Tall Tree and their four children. He thought of Thunder Spirit who was riding with Sun Cloud. He had many loved ones left and he needed them, as they loved and needed him. He smiled and went to join them, to await the burial ceremony.

Mind-who-Roams said, "It is sad the children of Eagle's Arm's do not know of their father's death."

Bright Arrow glanced at the tightly wrapped body of the man whose Life-circle had been entwined with his parent's Life-circles. How strange that all three should leave Mother Earth on the same day. "If it is possible, shaman, I will find a way to send a message to them."

The other seven bodies were placed on their scaffolds, and the tribe gathered around to mourn their deceased loved ones. Tears fell as an abundant rain, prayers of supplication lifted skyward, wails of grief rent the deathly still air, steady drumming matched painful heartbeats, and soulful chanting surrounded the anguish-filled group.

After the ceremony, guards were posted around the camp. The families returned to their tepees, but few felt like eating or talking, and each person was left to deal with his grief in his own way. Although they had been told of Sun Cloud's vengeance mission, many were dismayed that he was not here to mourn his parents and people . . .

Mind-who-Roams watched Bright Arrow leave the area of the death scaffolds. He placed his hand on his chief's body and wept. "Your spirit must guide me, my brother and friend, for the days ahead are dark and filled with conflict. Much of Bright Arrow's vision has come to pass, and I do not know how to accept the rest of it. If it is your will and the will of the Great Spirit for him to follow you as chief, give me sign before it is too late." The old man returned to his tepee, his shoulders slumped with sadness and his mind filled with confusion.

Bright Arrow went to the tepee of his parents and sat down upon his father's mat. His eyes slowly and painfully took in his empty surroundings. He could not believe his parents were out of his life forever, as was his true love. He had known this moment would come, but not this soon, and not in this way. The first assault of the white man had occurred, and he must be strong to lead his people against the next one, and those that followed it. The new council must be selected, then it would meet to vote in the new chief. As was their way, they would allow four days of mourning and soul-searching before that awesome event. To keep from hurting his brother, he would let the shaman reveal his vision during the council meeting. Once the talks and votes were taken, Sun Cloud would obey their words.

Tashina entered the tepee and came to kneel beside her father. They talked for a time about Gray Eagle and Shalee, and Moon Eyes, whom Tashina could not remember, as she had been only two when her sister died of smallpox in the Cheyenne camp, where she had first met her true love. How she wished he was here to comfort her. How she wished Little Feet was home, for she had been given the news of Races-the-Buffalo's death. Yet, she could not feel overly sad at that news, for she knew of her sister's love for White Arrow's son.

"When will you go to bring my sister home?" she asked, to pull her father from his painful thoughts.

"I will leave in two moons. I have sent word to her of my coming. I will take Flaming Star and Thunder Spirit with me."

"That is good, Father," she remarked softly, catching his hand. "Come, let me tend your wounds or they will grow inflamed."

Bright Arrow glanced at the two cuts, which he had hardly noticed in his anguish. He rose from the sitting mat and followed her outside, sealing Gray Eagle's flap until Sun Cloud's return.

As the Oglala party was reaching their camp shortly after one that afternoon, Sun Cloud, Thunder Spirit, and Night Rider neared the repaired Fort Dakota, but remained out of sight. The two soldiers had reached the fort safely, but Sun Cloud vowed to learn their names and to slay them. The warriors remained long enough to estimate the number of soldiers camped nearby and the number of supply wagons clustered near the gate. Added to those which they knew were inside the fort, the figures and their meaning were staggering. Behind the fort were several tepees where the Crow scouts and their families lived.

"We must track the bluecoats to where they attacked the war council. There is something I must know," Sun Cloud hinted mysteriously.

As he had suspected, the cavalry's trail led straight to the meeting place, a trail so bold that it was traced easily and quickly. As they rested for one hour before heading for their camp, Sun Cloud spoke aloud what each man was thinking. "We were betrayed, my brothers. No Crow scout discovered our plans and brought troops to attack us. The bluecoats knew where to ride and when to ride against us. We must keep this secret between us until we can learn the traitor's name."

Night Rider protested, "You speak as if we can trust none of our brothers or our council. This is a matter for all to know and settle."

"I do not speak evil of our brothers, Night Rider. But how do we tell others of this treachery without revealing our discovery to the guilty one? If he learns we suspect and seek him, he will mask his shame and walk with caution. If a man commits one such treachery, he will commit another. We must watch and wait, and catch him with his hands stained with dishonor."

Thunder Spirit concurred with his friend, "Sun Cloud speaks wisely and cunningly, Night Rider. To tell one of this dark deed, tells all. We are Sacred Bow carriers, and the protection of our people is our first duty. There is but one way to uncover the evil amongst us, to do as Sun Cloud says."

Night Rider looked from one warrior to the other. He did not like this secrecy which, to him, bordered on mistrust and deceit. He would tell Mind-who-Roams of this treachery, and allow the shaman to decide how it should be handled. "You are band leader, Sun Cloud, and I will follow you," he remarked, knowing that rank was over once they entered their camp, and he would be free to follow his conscience.

Sun Cloud looked at the sky and knew there were a few hours of daylight left. He also knew their camp was an all-night ride from this spot, which should place them home around dawn. He knew his parents had been laid upon their death scaffolds by now, just as he knew he had done what his father would have expected of him. "When we learn the name of the man who betrayed my father and our people, he is mine."

"You must cut his heart from his body and feed it to the sky birds, so his soul can never find peace or walk the Ghost Trail."

"This I will do, Night Rider, for it is my duty and right."

Three weary warriors rode into the quiet camp the next morning, to learn that many of the men had risen early to hunt game for the families of the Oglala who had not returned alive from the soldiers' ambush. Bright Arrow approached his brother and embraced him.

Sun Cloud informed him, "The two men who escaped our arrows reached the fort before we could overtake them. My blade will find their hearts another sun; this I swear as *watokicon*, an avenger."

"You are ready for Mother Earth to catch you, Sun Cloud. Rest and eat. We must be strong to face our enemies."

Sun Cloud revealed the sights at the fort. "They are many this season, Bright Arrow, but they will savor their large victory and think on their small defeat for a few suns. When they have licked their wounds and regained their false prides, they will strike again. While they talk and plan inside the fort, we must do the same. We must be ready to confront them and defeat them, as the shaman saw in his vision. It is time for the *wihpeyapi*." He reminded his brother of the practice of giving away the property of a family member after his death. As generosity and charity were two of the highest traits a man could possess and it was not good for a man to grow rich while others suffered without, a deceased man's belongings were shared with others.

Bright Arrow summoned the tribe's drummers to give the signal while Sun Cloud entered his parents' tepee and collected their things. Sun Cloud carried out the procedure quickly, as it pained him deeply. He handed Gray Eagle's items to White Arrow, Mind-who-Roams, Plenty Coups, Black Buffalo, Big Elk, and Star Gazer. Shalee's belongings were shared among Tashina, White Calf, Elk Woman, Pretty Flower, Moon Face, and others. No one ever questioned who received such prized gifts, and usually no envy was involved, for belongings were given to those closest to the one who died. "It is done, my brother."

Bright Arrow nodded, then called the hunting party together. "We will talk when I return," he said, then left with the others.

Sun Cloud walked to the area where the death scaffolds stood against a rich blue horizon, almost appearing artistic in their designs and decorations. He went to sit on the ground between his parents. For a long time, he remained there with head bowed and shoulders slumped as he called to mind his entire life with his mother and father: it was his way of saying farewell to them.

Mind-who-Roams wondered if the fatigued warrior had dropped off to sleep, for he had not moved in such a long time. When Sun Cloud straightened his body and lifted his head skyward to inhale deeply, the shaman joined him. "It is hard to say farewell to those we love."

Sun Cloud looked up into the older man's somber gaze and nodded. "Now I must do something even harder, Wise One. My father made me promise to collect his sacred belongings and give them to the *Peta Wanagi* to bring to him, and to prevent the white men from stealing them from his death scaffold and body."

Mind-who-Roams stared at the young man as he revealed his past chief's words about the Fire Spirits. He knew how many death scaffolds had been robbed and desecrated by their white foes, and he knew what the white men would give to own something which had belonged to the legendary Eagle. He knew they would want proof that Gray Eagle was dead. Anguish engulfed him at this necessity.

"I must obey, Wise One. And when it is safe to leave our camp, I must take their bodies to the sacred hills where the white man cannot dishonor them or steal them. Many fear he cannot die, and will not believe it is true until they possess his body and weapons. They will wish to destroy them so his spirit cannot return. They will wish to butcher his body to show his power and magic are gone forever. They would use his body to break the spirit and unity of our people and allies. My father knew this, and he asked me to prevent it."

"Your father was wise, my son, for his words are true. It is hard, but you must do as he commanded."

Sun Cloud collected his father's Shooting Star shield, his bow, his quiver of arrows, his tomahawk, his lance, his prayer pipe, and horse-dance stick. Together, they lowered Gray Eagle's body, cut the ties, and carefully unwrapped it. Sun Cloud removed his father's medallion, armbands, medicine bundle, moccasins, and garments, except for his breechcloth. With loving respect, they rewrapped and retied the precious body, then lifted it back onto the death scaffold. Sun Cloud retrieved only three items from his mother's body: her hair ornament, joining necklace, and eagle amulet. He placed these items in a pile, then fetched wood and glowing embers, and set the stack aflame.

When others headed their way from the camp after sighting the strange fire, Mind-who-Roams met them and halted them, and explained what Sun Cloud was doing. Many were shocked and dismayed, even if their beloved chief had ordered this tormenting action. Sun Cloud sat down before the fire with his back to the camp. He sang the Death Chant soulfully until the flames had consumed the items.

As if in a trance, Sun Cloud went to the camp and asked Tashina to dismantle Gray Eagle's tepee. The girl did so, but observed her uncle oddly at this request. He carried his personal possessions and the family's pictographic history skin to Bright Arrow's tepee and stored them there. When he returned, Sun Cloud gathered the beautifully painted hides which had formed his home, took them far from camp, and repeated his previous action, burning them until only ashes remained. Later when both fires cooled, he would lift the ashes and let the wind scatter them. It was done. Sun Cloud went to his brother's tepee and collapsed on a mat to fall into an exhausted slumber.

When the warriors returned from their successful hunt and were passing out the game, many related the startling behavior of Sun Cloud to Bright Arrow and the other hunters. Mind-who-Roams joined the group and explained the matter to them, but many were dismayed.

Bright Arrow went to his tepee and found his brother asleep. He stood over Sun Cloud, watching him and thinking. He wondered why his father had told Sun Cloud to carry out this difficult task, rather than him. Recalling the displeasure of many of their people, he decided that had been Gray Eagle's motive: to prevent the tribe from being angry with him. Even if this unusual request pained him and others deeply, he understood his father's command. Soon, when Gray Eagle's and Shalee's bodies were claimed by the elements, there would be nothing left of them. No, he quickly corrected himself, there would be the legends they had created and left behind; they would live forever.

It was late afternoon when Sun Cloud awakened. He found Bright Arrow sitting on his mat near his tepee entrance, working on his weapons. When he sighed heavily and stretched to loosen stiff muscles, Bright Arrow turned and gazed at him, and Sun Cloud noticed something in that look which bewildered him, something distant and secretive which had never been present in his brother's eyes before.

"They have told you of our father's wishes?" he hinted.

"You have done as our chief and father commanded, as it should be. They are not dead, Sun Cloud; their spirits live all around us and within us, and they will guide us in the troubled days ahead."

"It is true, my brother, but the doing was hard," he confessed.

"Father knew this, and he knew you would obey. It is good. I leave with the next sun to bring my daughter home. Watch over our people and protect them. Hunt for those in need."

"When you lost Wahea, how long did the pain and loneliness live within you?" Sun Cloud asked unexpectedly.

Bright Arrow's head lowered while he grieved anew for his lost love. Finally, he replied, "Such feelings have not given me release. Many tell me, they will pass after many moons. Many say, it takes new happiness to drive away the old pains."

"Then we must seek new happiness and peace."

"First, we must seek to avenge our father and people, and to destroy our white foes. We will make plans when the council meets after three moons. There is much to do before we ride against our foes."

"Yes, my brother, there is much to do," Sun Cloud concurred. He did not know the thoughts and feelings which were running through his brother's mind and body, for he assumed Bright Arrow had accepted their ranks long ago and would follow him as the new chief. It was sad to recall that his brother had sacrificed everything for a woman whom he no longer possessed, and he did not wish to refresh that shame.

Bright Arrow started to have a serious talk with his brother about the chief's bonnet, but decided this was not the time. Perhaps Sun Cloud still believed he would become the next chief, and he did not want to distress him further when he was consumed with grief. It was not good or easy to lose so much in such a short time span.

That next morning, Bright Arrow, Thunder Spirit, and Flaming Star rode out to bring Little Feet back to her family and people. Sun Cloud knew it would be late the next day before they reached home. It was good, he felt, that Bright Arrow had something to do to fill his thoughts and time. Determined to keep himself occupied, Sun Cloud gathered a small band and went hunting for fresh game.

When they returned, he found Singing Wind in the tepee of Bright Arrow. She looked up at him and waited for him to speak, for she knew how heavy his heart must be. Tashina had told her of the happenings in the camp since his parents' deaths. She had planned to spend the night with Tashina and Bright Arrow, but that was not wise with Sun Cloud living in their tepee.

"I came to mourn for my second mother and father. I did not know Bright Arrow would be away," she said for some inexplicable reason, just to make conversation in the quiet and suddenly small tepee.

"Where are the others?" Sun Cloud inquired, not wishing to see her brother today, but assuming he could not avoid it.

"I came alone," she responded softly.

Sun Cloud frowned. "I do not know which grows larger in you, Singing Wind, bravery or foolishness. Our foes have declared war again."

She had needed to see him, for it had been such a long time and she had been unable to forget their last encounter. She wanted to comfort him. Now that he was alone, surely he would be seeking a mate soon. She wanted to remind him she was alive and available!

"There is no danger, Sun Cloud. The soldiers will not attack while they recover from their stunning defeat."

"You are as clever and smart as you are brave and rash." Suddenly he had the overpowering urge to sweep her into his arms and forget all of his anguish. Her lips called out to him to kiss them. Her expression entreated him to seize her and to make passionate love to her. He wanted to reach out his hand and run his fingers through her silky black hair. He needed to kiss those arresting eyes closed so they would stop enchanting him. He yearned to feel her warm flesh pressed against his. He could not understand where he found the strength and will to remain at this short distance from her, for she made him feel as weak and trembly as a newborn. "I am glad you came, for your beauty brings sunshine to the darkness of my heart. But it was still foolish, for our enemies cannot be trusted to behave as we believe."

Singing Wind warmed at the sight of a tiny smile and at hearing his voice soften noticeably. "That is not a new trait for me, Sun Cloud, for you have scolded me for it for many seasons."

"Then why do you keep it?" he teased, moving a little closer.

Singing Wind laughed. "Because it annoys you and makes you notice me," she replied without thinking, for his nearness was destroying her poise and control. She had even forgotten about his parents, for their deaths did not seem real to her, nor to him yet.

He replied huskily, "You need no tricks to seize my eye, for you wickedly capture it each time you are near."

"As quickly as I capture your anger and annoyance?" she probed.

Before he could respond or move any closer, Tashina returned with their food, for several of the women had joined forces to cook meals to share with those in need. Reflecting on her grandmother, Tashina did not catch the currents which were passing between Singing Wind and Sun Cloud. She handed her uncle his food and placed the other container on the rocks which surrounded her campfire.

The food smelled delicious, and Sun Cloud realized his hunger. He devoured his meal as slowly as possible, but without delay so the women could eat. When he was finished, he thanked Tashina and left so the females could eat and talk privately, as women loved to do.

Singing Wind fretted over the way Sun Cloud had seemingly forgotten her presence after Tashina's arrival. She could not help but wonder if he had only been teasing her again. When he did not return for two hours, she had to leave to reach her camp before dark.

"You must not ride out alone, Singing Wind. Stay with us until the sun returns. Little Feet will desire to see her old friend, and so will her father," Tashina remarked with a secretive smile, as her father had mentioned this female too many times lately not to have an attraction for her. Besides, if she wanted to leave soon to join her love, she needed to help her father find a good mate, like Singing Wind.

Singing Wind's mind retorted, *Stay with us until Sun Cloud returns.* No, she could not linger and appear to be chasing him! She had made the first move; now, it was up to him to make the next one. "I will be home safely before the night arrives. I do not wish others to worry. I did not tell them I was riding here. I will return in a few suns to visit you and Little Feet. Tell her my heart feels sorrow over her loss."

Tashina related the news that Thunder Spirit had already spoken to her father for the hand of Little Feet in joining, and she revealed the secret love of each for the other.

Singing Wind felt a rush of envy. Her friend had just lost one man and now she was obtaining another, when she could not seem to catch just one. Perhaps it was because she was pursuing the wrong man! "Tell Bright Arrow I will be eager to see him again. I am glad the life has returned to him, and I pray this new sorrow does not destroy it once more," she told Tashina in a softened voice which vexed and drove away the man who had been about to join them again.

Sun Cloud paced unnaturally by the river, then returned to his brother's tepee. Singing Wind had left. "I will ride after her and take her home. She challenges danger too eagerly. I will speak with Medicine Bear, then return with the new day."

That suited Tashina just fine, for she rarely had privacy, and this was a time when she needed it.

It took Sun Cloud over two hours to catch the bedeviling maiden, for she was riding swiftly to feel the wind racing through her hair and over on her skin. When she saw him, she slowed her pace. He scowled at her again, but she taunted, "See, the trick works each time. You are angry with me, and I have done nothing wrong, as usual."

He eyed her tangled hair which made her appear a wild beauty. Her cheeks were flushed and her eyes were shiny with excitement. Her buckskin dress did not conceal her appealing figure, and he wanted to explore it, leisurely. He had to admit she was an expert rider, and she could defend herself against even odds. "You were wrong to leave before I could offer to ride with you."

She was aware of the stimulating way he was studying her, as he had done earlier. But a frown still lined his handsome face. "To hear you scold me all the way to my camp? Or to protect me?"

Sun Cloud narrowed his eyes in frustration. "My heart and head are not in the mood for battling words with you, Singing Wind. I wish only to see you reach home safely. I will remain in your camp till morning. I will not scold you again, if you behave."

"It will be difficult, Sun Cloud, for good behavior is unknown to me. Perhaps it is because I had no mother and father to—" She halted instantly as she caught her words and their effect on Sun Cloud. "Forgive me. I did not mean to cause you fresh pain. It was a silly joke."

Sun Cloud halted and dismounted, and she did the same. He walked to where thick grass grew in abundance beneath several trees which seemingly stood as guards near a lovely, but very small, pond and he leaned dejectedly against one. "I cannot believe they are gone, even though I have visited their death scaffolds. How can I be whole again until I have avenged their deaths? Tashina told me Mother died soon after Father, for Father's spirit called to her. Even in death they could not be parted. The bluecoats are responsible for both losses."

The Blackfeet princess came to stand beside him, where he was facing the water and staring at it. He seemed so vulnerable and human today, so reachable. "The bond between Gray Eagle and Princess Shalee was known to all. It is good she was not left to suffer without him, and it is good she is at his side in the afterlife. I do not remember my parents, but I have loved Gray Eagle and Shalee as much as I would have loved my mother and father if I had known them. I do not mean to annoy you when you are tormented by such losses. I will behave."

Sun Cloud turned, placing his back against the trunk, and gazed at her, and his heart rate increased steadily. He looked at how her nose came to a pretty, round point and how it seemed tempted to turn up slightly on the end. She was only seven inches below his six-foot-two height, making her a touch taller than most females. But those few inches gave her a longer and leaner middle, which he had viewed by accident while she was swimming, and legs as sleek as a matchless steed's. Unlike so many females after passing twenty winters, no fullness had been added to her body; it had remained slender and shapely. He recalled how firm her breasts were and how dark the fuzzy place was between her thighs. As she had risen from the water that day, he had been stunned motionless by her beauty, and he had wondered suddenly why he had been resisting her magic and allure.

Yet, Singing Wind had more than exceptional looks and a passion-stirring body; she had strength and courage, more than a physical supply. She had emotional courage and stamina, for she was willing to accept the jests of others to await her true destiny. Most females joined soon after entering their womanhood, to prove their value and appeal to themselves and to others, he decided, having overheard many girlish talks about men and love and unions. Many were too eager to rush into a joining, as if it magically settled all things for them. Many thought they would have more freedom once they left their parents' tepees. Many were eager to taste passion's forbidden fruits.

Sun Cloud had not taunted her or replied. It was as if he were content to watch her and study her. Singing Wind was acutely aware of their heady solitude and of Sun Cloud's intense scrutiny and warring emotions. She had witnessed enough bursts of desire to recognize the signs: rapid and deep respiration—which sometimes flared the nostrils like a winded stallion's after a swift race—glazed eyes, tensed body, parted lips—which many licked frequently, either for relieving moisture or bold enticement—perspiration above the mouth, and sometimes a flushing of the cheeks, as if the body were suddenly ablaze.

At this moment, she could tell that Sun Cloud was highly aware of her as a woman and was affected by it, but there was something different in his desire. His respiration was deep, but slower and quieter than in her past observations. His body was held in relaxed control, a quality of his warrior training and practice. His lips were slightly parted, but his teeth appeared to be lightly gripping the lower one near the left corner, and she could see those white teeth which were unstained and unbroken. But the most noticeable difference was in his gaze. It had a compelling power and tenderness which others had lacked. At last, she had discovered the difference between desire and lust.

Her hand reached out to graze his strong jawline, for she could not resist the impulse to touch his flesh. Her fingers trailed down his neck and across his chest, her senses consuming and admiring the soft hardness of his torso. He was leaner than most warriors, but he was strong and agile. His flat stomach was revealed by the way his rib cage ended prominently and sank in slightly. Except for where his muscles rose or tapered off, his skin was stretched snugly over his well-developed and well-toned frame, which was a rich and dark golden brown. His hair was the color of the darkest night, and he rarely wore it braided. His nose and lips were full, but not overly large. His brows were dark and well shaped, and his nearly black eyes were enslaving. He looked so much like his father; yet he was different.

Her touch and enchanting gaze were the undoing of Sun Cloud's control. His hands grasped her silky head between them and he lowered his mouth to claim hers in a series of kisses which became more feverish with each one shared. As he pulled her body against his, her arms went around him and he shuddered with an overwhelming need for her. He instinctively knew the moment for surrender was upon them.

Singing Wind could read the same strengths in his features and expression which were visible on his body. The muscles in his arms and torso rippled with his movements. His chest was smooth and inviting to her touch and contact. Only Sun Cloud had kissed and was kissing her in this utterly intoxicating manner, but she craved more from him, more from their closeness and this rare moment.

Sun Cloud worked skillfully and hungrily to arouse her higher, for he realized she wanted this irresistible union as much as he did, and she was not afraid or reluctant to take what she wanted and needed. His tongue swirled around her lips and within her mouth, then drifted across her face to tease at one earlobe. He felt his hot breath enliven her senses, and he continued down her throat to press his lips against the black mole upon her throbbing pulse. To make certain he was not mistaken about her passion and surrender, his hands eased beneath her buckskin top and gently fondled her breasts. He carefully kneaded the taut peaks and brought a moan of pleasure from beneath his kiss.

His fingers moved from under her top and unlaced its ties beneath her hair. He did not separate their lips until that was necessary in order to remove it. Instantly their lips fused once more and their bare chests pressed tightly together. His mouth traveled down her neck and over her collarbone, and fastened provocatively to one breast. With tantalizing leisure, he moistened it and caused it to grow tauter before shifting to the other one. Each time he left one to lavish attention on the other, his deft fingers would work upon it until his mouth returned.

Singing Wind had never experienced anything so wildly wonderful. The fingers of one hand wandered through his hair as the fingers of the other teased over his back. Her head was bending forward to brush her lips over his dark head. His skin felt so cool and sleek while hers felt fiery and tight. His smell was fresh and appealing, and manly. She closed her eyes to allow her senses to absorb the sensations which he was creating. Her respiration had become quick and shallow, her lips were suddenly dry, and her cheeks were hot. She felt she would explode from the force building rapidly within her body as bittersweet ecstasy assailed it.

Sun Cloud halted briefly to remove her fringed skirt, and allowed it to slide to the ground. As he kissed her greedily, his fingers untied the laces of her breech-cloth, allowing it to join her skirt at her feet. Now, his hands could freely roam and stimulate her entire body, which they did. His fingers fondled her buttocks, then eased over her shapely hip to search for a fuzzy forest which he entered to seek another tiny mound. Soon, he had it throbbing with need and pleasure.

Singing Wind derived exquisite delight from his actions and wanted them to continue. She could think of nothing and no one except him and this blissful episode. She felt as if she were drifting dreamily on the puffy clouds above them, and he was the sun which warmed her. She felt empty and tense when he stopped to remove his breechcloth and leggings, then a thrill of erotic desire as his naked body touched hers.

Sun Cloud guided them to the grassy earth, then resumed his titillating siege. His fingertips stroked her thighs and fuzzy covering before invading it once more, causing her to quiver with anticipation. He carefully gauged their journey to the land of rapture. At last, he moved atop her and tentatively pressed his fiery shaft against the barrier of her womanhood. It gave way easily and he slipped within her.

For Singing Wind, there was little discomfort, for she had led an active life and was eager and moist for his loving assault. She was clinging tightly and wildly to him. She arched her back to accept his full length and savored this heady and total contact. The feel of their joined bodies was overpowering. She yielded to instinct and followed his lead. Consumed by fiery passion, she returned his kisses and arches with savage delight. A curious bittersweet aching filled her body, despite the sheer bliss of their lovemaking. She wanted . . . What?

Sun Cloud was working frantically now, for he did not know how long he could master his demanding shaft. Perceiving her high state of arousal, he increased his pace and force. When he felt her arch and stiffen and a breathless sigh escaped her lips, he knew his control was no longer needed. He entered and withdrew quickly and sensuously, coaxing his own rapturous release to spill forth.

Together they savored the delectable experience until each drop of bliss was ingested or shared. Still they kissed and embraced. Soon, Sun Cloud felt the need to relax his body and to regain his normal breathing. He rolled onto his back, but pulled her against his side. They lay there until reality and contentment surrounded them. Each dozed lightly as they rested and recalled this blissful union.

Chapter Ten

Sun Cloud noticed the angle of the sun which indicated dusk was approaching, and he knew they had to leave this tranquil spot. He looked over at Singing Wind, his movement causing her to open her eyes and to meet his gaze. He smiled and hugged her possessively. "We must ride, dark eyes, or we will not make your camp before night."

Singing Wind rolled onto her stomach. She propped herself on her elbows and cupped her chin in her hands, gazed across the pond and lifted her eyes skyward. He was right; the sun would sink into Mother Earth soon. She glanced at him and smiled. "Why should I be afraid when I have a Sacred Bow carrier to protect me?" she playfully inquired.

Sun Cloud laughed, his gaze roaming to where the points of her breasts were grazing the earth and were nearly hidden by her long hair and folded arms. He had never seen this sultry, serene mood before; it enticed his loins to plead for another union with her. He shifted to his side. His fingers traced over her bare back, then stroked her firm rear before they pushed aside her hair so he could assail her earlobe.

Silver laughter came from her as she closed the distance between her head and shoulder, for his action tickled. More laughter came forth as his lips worked their way along her neck, then up to her mouth. She fell to her side as her arms moved to encircle his neck to hold his mouth against hers.

Their tender kisses waxed urgent and soon they were making love once more. This time, they did not move slowly and cautiously; this time, they came together swiftly and feverishly. When they had been rewarded richly for their efforts, their noses touched as they gazed into each other's eyes and comprehended their fierce attraction for each other. Yet, neither spoke nor confessed such powerful emotions. Each felt it was unnecessary to express in words what had been proven that day.

Sun Cloud arose, unmindful of his nakedness. "We must not waste this moment and place, dark eyes; a swim is what we need to cool our bloods." He dove into the cool water, splashing her.

Without modesty or humiliation, Singing Wind followed him. They laughed and played for a time, then left the water to dry and to dress.

Sun Cloud noticed her bundle for the first time and asked, "You did not plan to return home this sun?"

Singing Wind grinned and replied, "How could I sleep in the tepee of Bright Arrow when his brother lives there?"

"You feared my brother would see the flames which spark between us?" he teased, tugging mischievously at her soaked hair.

Singing Wind tossed the wet mane over her shoulder and retorted, "No, I feared you would see those which leap between me and him."

Sun Cloud chuckled. After kissing and caressing her, he asked wickedly, "Could my brother cause your body to burn as I can?"

The audacious girl replied, "Could other women cause your body to burn as I do? Can they lure you from your camp and take you boldly as I did? They are all cowards, for they demand a joining first."

"Perhaps all women should be tested in this manner before men become their property. If passions are not matched . . ."

Movement in the trees nearby seized his attention. He rapidly shoved the startled girl behind him and drew his knife. His keen eyes pierced the leafy foliage, then he laughed. "It grows late and the Great Spirit's creatures wish to drink. We must go, dark eyes."

They mounted and rode from the area which would remain green forever in their memories. The warm air whipping through Singing Wind's telltale hair dried it before they neared her camp. As they slowed their pace, they began to converse.

"When will the war against the whites begin?" she questioned, for she knew it would claim his attention and time.

In the emotional state which had been created by his parent's loss and by Singing Wind's unexpected surrender, Sun Cloud spoke unwittingly. "First, I must find the man who betrayed us to our foes. The ambush was not their stroke of luck. The bluecoats knew when and where to wait for the Oglala band, and they knew of the war council. An evil warrior walks among us. I must learn his tribe and name, and slay him."

To make matters worse, Sun Cloud looked at her with narrowed eyes and asked, "Does your brother Silver Hawk ride from camp alone? Does he stay gone for many hours before returning?"

Singing Wind was intelligent and astute, and she grasped his implication. Her brother was many wicked things, but a traitor! "Your words cut me deeply, Sun Cloud. They dishonor you and they shadow my brother. You have known Silver Hawk since birth. What madness enters your mind and causes you to make such cruel charges?"

Sun Cloud recognized his lapse and scolded himself for his error. "I make no accusations, Singing Wind. I must watch each warrior to learn the truth. There are three of us who know this secret, and we were not to reveal it to others until the black-hearted one is exposed."

Anger thundered through Singing Wind like a violent storm, for she could tell whom he felt was guilty. "Watch in another camp, for it is not Silver Hawk, or one of my people," she stated coldly, feeling protective of her family and tribe. "I will tell no one of your madness, for these suns are perilous for all tribes and you will soon be a chief and your people must trust you to ride behind you. I warn you, Sun Cloud, drive such shame from your body or it will harm you and others. Enter the sweat lodge and purify yourself of such evil and dishonor."

Abruptly a wild thought flashed through her mind, and she painfully wondered if that was the reason why he had pursued her and was riding home with her: to spy on Silver Hawk and/or others. After all, she had tempted him to seduce her along the way; it had not been his idea. She was tormented by the realization that this warrior might have betrayed her love and casually used her body. She glared at him and vowed impulsively and dishonestly, "I am shamed for giving myself to one so unworthy of me. I only desired to see what it was like to have the glorious Sun Cloud just once, but do not come near me again, for I was foolish and wrong. If you seek to harm my brother, I will see his honor avenged myself." She clicked her reins and raced away.

Sun Cloud followed her, but she reached the Blackfeet camp before he could catch her and explain. She dismounted and asked one of the young boys to care for her mount, and he gladly complied. Then she hurried to Chief Medicine Bear's tepee, determined not to be alone with Sun Cloud again until her temper cooled and her poise returned.

Silver Hawk joined him as he was dismounting. "Do you bring bad news, Sun Cloud?" he inquired, intrigued by his sister's behavior. He could tell she was vexed, and was eager to put distance between them.

"I rode to guard your sister. She is rash, Silver Hawk. She does not know she cannot ride when and where she chooses. She came to visit Tashina and Bright

Arrow. My brother is away returning Little Feet to her family and people, and Singing Wind would not stay with us until the new sun, for Sun Cloud lives in Bright Arrow's tepee these moons. She is willful, and troubles a man's anger and control," he declared irritably to relax and disarm the crafty and alert Silver Hawk.

Silver Hawk chuckled deceitfully. "Come, eat and sleep in my tepee. You can return to your camp on the new sun. One season, my sister will learn she cannot behave as a child or a man."

"That season comes too slowly, Silver Hawk; she is as a wahoo thorn in the flesh. I must care for my horse, then I will join you." He accepted; he was delighted by Silver Hawk's invitation, for it would allow him to study the man closely. After his horse was taken to water and grass, the Oglala warrior followed Silver Hawk to his tepee.

The warriors ate and talked, but Silver Hawk was careful to drop no clues about his feelings and actions. As Sun Cloud lay on his borrowed sleeping mat, he was disappointed by this unsuccessful visit, and what it had cost him. Somehow, he had to make Singing Wind understand and forgive him. If only she had not relaxed and enchanted him so deeply that it had loosened his lips and dazed his mind!

In the Oglala camp, Tashina hastily sealed the flap to her tepee and turned to slip into the entreating embrace of Soul-of-Thunder. Both knew the danger was greater for this second secret meeting than for their first. She related the news of her father's and uncle's departures, and all that had taken place in their camp.

As her face nestled against his hard chest, his arms banded her tightly. His torso was darkly tanned and smooth. His flesh felt as soft as a doe hide, but his muscles beneath were hard as stone. Like her uncle, he was lithe and strong, and he was lean, but not as tall as Sun Cloud. No mark of the Sun Dance marred his chest, but a knife wound had left a scar on his right shoulder. Although his nose had been broken during a training practice, the bump along its ridge gave it appeal. How she loved him, and wanted him again. She hated this waiting to reveal their love and to share each night.

The Cheyenne warrior did not want to release her, for he knew each day could be his last. His lips sought and found hers, and he kissed her with a desperation which she found bewildering. When she looked up into his eyes, he kissed them closed, for he feared she would read the emotions which warred within him. He had come to comfort her and to reveal his selection as a dog-rope warrior. Not wanting to spoil their brief time together so quickly, he kept silent.

Their kisses and caresses increased their great yearning for each other. Soon, they parted to remove their garments and to lie down together on her sleeping mat. They touched and enticed until they could no longer restrain their ardor, and they united their bodies to share a blazing passion. They climbed higher and higher until they soared in ecstasy's domain, releasing their tensions and claiming blissful pleasure. They gazed into each other's eyes and smiled.

"You are my love and without you I am incomplete," he murmured.

Tashina embraced him possessively and replied, "As I with you."

"There is something I must tell you," he began reluctantly. "I was chosen as a dog-rope wearer," he revealed just above a whisper.

Tashina paled and trembled. Her gaze sought his, but he would not look at her. She stared at him for a time, absorbing his perilous existence for the next year. "You must refuse it, my love," she urged.

"I cannot. I am a member of the Dog Men Society. I am a Cheyenne warrior. I am the son of war chief Windrider. I am a man. I must wear the sash until Mother Earth renews our lands once more."

Tears began to ease down her cheeks. "I cannot lose you."

His gaze finally met hers. "Until we join, I swear my second mother Sky Eyes will not make a new sash for my people and I swear, after we are joined, my wife Tashina will not. It is our way, my love, and I must follow my destiny."

"I am your destiny, as you are mine. I could not survive without you. You are my life and my true love."

"Do not weep, my love, and do not ask me to refuse my duty. If I must worry over you, I cannot guard my life, for my thoughts will be of you. Trust me, Tashina, and wait for me."

"Wait for you?" she echoed in confusion.

"We cannot join until my duty is done. If the Great Spirit calls me, I cannot leave my new wife Tashina and the child she might be carrying in the care of others. We are young and these days are filled with evils. We will join when we reach our summer campgrounds again. It is best this way. We must not unite our bodies again, for a child could come from such a union. Until the danger is past, we must return to how it was before we yielded to love."

"We cannot, Soul-of-Thunder. It is a long time until Mother Earth renews her face again, and much happiness will be lost. If the Great Spirit calls your name, I wish to have our child to carry our love forever. Is your love not as strong as mine? Can you be near me and not desire me? Can you remain in your camp and never come to me?"

"To do such things is harder than wearing the sash," he admitted.

"Then we must join quickly and seize all the happiness we can."

Soul-of-Thunder looked at her and could not bear the thought of another man joining her if he was slain, another man raising his child. Yet, he felt it would be harder for her to accept the death of a husband and the father of her child than it would be to accept the death of a twice lover. "I must think and do what is best for you, my love."

"What you demand is not best," she argued frantically.

"I will think again on this matter, for my head is not clear when I am with you. I do not think I could bear to see your face each time before I ride out to endanger my life in battle," he told her, knowing he must leave the battlefield last each time, and a great war was near.

"Do you think it will be easier for us if we are separated, if I must live in dread of each sun, not knowing if you are alive? How can your head be clear knowing I have such fears and worries?"

"It is an honor to be chosen, Tashina. It is only one span of seasons." He tenderly caressed her cheek, then hugged her against him.

"A span of one seasons and an honor which can take you from me forever, as my mother and grandparents were taken from me."

"Your heart is filled with pain and you do not think as I do."

"If we must sacrifice our life together for a span of seasons for you to fulfill your duty, then I will never think as you do. Why can you not become a member of our tribe after my father becomes chief? Then, we can join. We can be happy and safe, and share a mat each moon. Why must it be the female who leaves her people?"

"It is our way, my love. Have you forgotten, Sun Cloud is to become chief? My father told me this long ago."

"My father and many others say he will not be voted chief. Sun Cloud is too young and he does not have my father's prowess and wisdom."

"It will not be so, Tashina. Bright Arrow sacrificed his right to follow his father long ago when he married a white girl and was banished."

"I am worse than a white girl, Soul-of-Thunder; I am a half-breed. If we join, you will be banished and you will lose your right to be a sash wearer. If you love me, do this for us," she implored him.

"My people's laws and ways are not the same as those of the Oglalas. My father's third wife Sky Eyes is white, and my people love and respect her. They do not call their children half-breeds, for they are from the seeds of Windrider, a great Cheyenne warrior and leader, and they grew inside the white shaman who saved our tribe from certain death. I do not care if your blood is half-white or all white, I love you. But I am not Bright Arrow, and I cannot betray my duty and tribe."

Tashina was disturbed by his words. "My father did not betray his people and duty. His people turned against him and sent him away."

"No, my love," he debated softly. "Bright Arrow was given a choice, and he chose your mother over his rank, his duty, and his tribe."

"You would not risk all for your love, Soul-of-Thunder?"

He knew he was trapped by her words. "I love you with all my heart and I wish you to be a part of my Life-circle, but I could not become less than what I am to claim you and your love. It would destroy me, as it nearly destroyed your father. Have you forgotten?"

"I have not forgotten, for it is how we met. And I have not forgotten the reason he lost all, lives no more. He became a greater warrior for his troubles, and my people know this. He will be chief."

Soul-of-Thunder looked worried. He realized, if there was a conflict over the chief's bonnet, much pain and dissension would occur. Bright Arrow was a powerful warrior, but his friend Sun Cloud would make the best chief. For now, he would allow the matter to rest.

"It will be many days before I can return to see you, Tashina. We must not spend this short time fighting with words."

Tashina decided there was one way to show him how powerful their love was, so she replied, "No, we must spend it making love, and pray it will not be for the last time." She pulled his lips to hers, and soon drove all thoughts from his mind, except those of her.

Silver Hawk and Sun Cloud joined the group of men who were gathering around Chief Medicine Bear's tepee. The chief informed them of news which implied trouble and peril: two of his three sons—Magic Hail and Finds Water—had gone hunting yesterday, and they had not returned to camp. Early this morning, women gathering firewood had found their blood-spattered horses, roaming and grazing not far from camp. Alarmed, Medicine Bear was forming a party to look for them.

Something told Sun Cloud to accompany the band on its search. The horses' tracks were traced to where two bodies lay dead on the rocky bank near a wide stream which was four miles from camp. Magic Hail and Finds Water had been shot with arrows, which no longer protruded from their chests and throats, striking Sun Cloud as very odd. Adding to his suspicion was the discovery that no other track or clue could be found near the slain warriors. A killer had appeared, carried out his evil task, concealed his trail, and then vanished. The way the bodies had fallen, neither had defended himself, suggesting a surprise attack. Or, Sun Cloud reasoned skeptically, the approach of one who was not a stranger to them. The only clues which suggested this dark deed was done by a foe, instead of a traitor, were their missing scalplocks—a one-inch circle of hair and scalp which was taken skillfully and then displayed on the victor's clothing, possessions, or horse: a far different manner from what the white man called, and the way he practiced, scalping. Still, the missing scalplocks could be a trick to delude them, and they could have been discarded or buried nearby.

Chief Medicine Bear and his remaining son, Three Feathers, who was very ill and weak this morning, wailed in grief; they drew their knives and sliced mourning marks across their arms and stomachs. The crimson liquid looked dark as it seeped from the wounds and rolled down reddish brown flesh to soak into tanned buckskins.

Silver Hawk drew his knife and cut two lines across one arm. Then he lifted his bloody knife skyward and declared, "The next blood on our knives must be that of the killers of our brothers. Look again, my friends; surely there is a track or clue somewhere to follow."

Everyone searched again, but nothing could be found. Sun Cloud furtively watched Silver Hawk during this episode which put the clever warrior only two steps from the Blackfeet chief's bonnet. If anything happened to Three Feathers, Medicine Bear should guard his back well!

The somber group transported the bodies to camp. Before they reached it, Three Feathers was doubled over with agonizing pains in his stomach and was swaying precariously on his mount. He was helped down and into the chief's tepee. The shaman, Jumping Rabbit, was summoned. While War Chief Strikes Fire appointed another band to search the murder area again, the shaman tried to save the life of Three Feathers, and failed, removing another obstacle for Silver Hawk.

Chief Medicine Bear was filled with anguish at having lost his three sons within two days. Singing Wind, Redbird, Deer Eyes, and Silver Hawk tried to comfort him. "We are your children, our father. Do not be sad. We will care for you and love you," Deer Eyes told him.

Sun Cloud glanced at the woman with a twisted foot and partially paralyzed face. She had been the shaman's helper since age sixteen when her father Chief Brave Bear had been slain in battle. She was such a gentle and loving female, who seemed content in life to help others. He glanced at her older sister Redbird, who also lived with the shaman, and who had slept upon the shaman's mats without marriage or children since she was twenty-one. He did not know why Redbird refused to become the shaman's second wife or to join another warrior, for she was a pretty female, a smart and strong one. Redbird seemed satisfied to be the shaman's and his wife's helper, and they seemed delighted to allow the female's almost slavish assistance. From what he had heard, the shaman's wife did not even mind Redbird sharing her husband's mat. If tales could be trusted, the wife was overjoyed to have Redbird take that task from her body, as well as others.

Sun Cloud looked at Singing Wind, who was careful to keep away from him. As for Silver Hawk, the eye and ear could detect nothing suspicious in his manner, but Sun Cloud had a gut feeling that Medicine Bear's three sons were dead because of his love's brother. If only Brave Bear and Chela had lived, their four children would be different.

The small group went outside where most of the tribe was awaiting news of the chief's remaining heir. Medicine Bear clasped arms with Silver Hawk and announced sadly, "Three Feathers is dead, and I claim Silver Hawk as my new son. When Medicine Bear walks with the Great Spirit, it is my desire for the son of Brave Bear to become chief of the Blackfeet. Come, we must lay my sons to rest."

Just before entering Silver Hawk's tepee to retrieve his belongings to head home, Sun Cloud overheard a curious and intriguing statement from Jumping Rabbit: "It was the will of Napi for Medicine Bear to select you as his son and our future chief. Napi knew of this evil which would strike our chief and his sons, and He warned you. The visionquest you shared with Bright Arrow six moons ago is coming to pass. You will soon be a great chief, as will he."

Sun Cloud went to fetch his horse, then he would return to Silver Hawk's tepee for his things. He was puzzled by his brother's concealment of such a vision, and he was worried over Silver Hawk's helping it to come true. He must return home to hunt for those in need and to help Tashina complete the gifts for Gray Eagle and Shalee, to be given to White Arrow and his wife Pretty Woman. Too, he needed to do some serious thinking. Unable to locate Singing Wind to reason with her and to tell her goodbye, Sun Cloud mounted and rode from the camp.

Singing Wind leaned against the tree behind which she had been hiding from Sun Cloud. His slip of the tongue and his grim suspicions kept running through her mind, more so today with the sudden and mysterious deaths of all three of Medicine Bear's sons and her brother's selection as the next chief. Many times, Silver Hawk had implied his hatred and jealousy of Sun Cloud, and he wanted her to hate and mistrust her secret love. Lately, her brother had been pushing her rapidly and persistently toward Bright Arrow, saying the Oglala warrior would be chief soon, "when Gray Eagle rides the Ghost Trail," which had come to pass unexpectedly in a curious ambush which had Sun Cloud thinking wildly. She recalled parts of her quarrel with Silver Hawk not long ago: "I must do all to help him obtain his rightful place. Think how your joining to Bright Arrow will prick Sun Cloud. . . . You must think and decide quickly." She had noticed Sun Cloud furtively watching her brother that day, and she had tingled with alarm. She was angry with herself for allowing Sun Cloud's doubts and charges to linger in her mind and to torment her. She scolded herself for even imagining that her brother, or any Blackfeet, could be that evil and clever.

As Jumping Rabbit and her brother headed for the chief's tepee, the expression on Silver Hawk's face as he trailed the shaman seized her attention and curiosity. Most had already gone to the burial area, to await the ceremonial chief and tribal chief, but the two who had entered Medicine Bear's tepee did not appear an escort to the death scaffolds. Suddenly she realized she had been edging stealthily toward the chief's tepee. Making sure to take the side where the sun would not cast her revealing shadow on the skins, she listened as the shaman and Silver Hawk revealed the recent visionquest with Bright Arrow . . .

* * *

Bright Arrow told Thunder Spirit, "Take Little Feet and her sons to safety. We will halt to battle the Crows who follow us."

"Be careful, Father," Little Feet entreated, her hazel eyes filled with worry and her dark auburn hair blowing about her face in the wind.

Bright Arrow smiled encouragingly at his twenty-two-year-old child and his two grandsons: Buffalo Boy, age four who was riding with him, and Spirit Sign, age two who was riding with his mother. He handed the older boy to Thunder Spirit. "Go with White Arrow's son; he will protect you. We will join you very soon," he stated confidently.

The two horses galloped away while Bright Arrow and Flaming Star concealed themselves and their horses behind thick bushes. As the first two Crow warriors drew near, both men loosened arrows which found their marks. The other three Crow quickly leaped off their mounts and, with loud yells of fury, raced toward the men to attack while they still held the number advantage and were too close for arrow range.

Bright Arrow tossed his bow aside, deftly yanked his tomahawk from his waist, and forcefully buried its tapered edge in the center of one foe's head, killing him instantly. He whirled nimbly to meet the attack by a second foe. Each brandishing a shiny blade, the two men sized up each other as they circled and watched for an opening.

Flaming Star was battling hand to hand with the third foe, a tall and husky male. They sliced at each other, a few blows catching flesh and causing blood to come forth rapidly. Flaming Star tripped the man and dove for him, but the foe lifted his feet and they sent the Oglala warrior flying over his head to land roughly on the hard ground.

Bright Arrow side-stepped his foe's charge, seized his arm, and twisted it behind the man's back. Entangling the man's left leg, Bright Arrow caused his foe to stumble and fall. Swiftly Bright Arrow drove his knee into the middle of the man's back at his spine, bringing a scream of pain from the Crow. Bright Arrow grabbed the man's hair, yanked his head backward, then slid his knife across the man's throat.

Bright Arrow turned to see the last Crow warrior seize a handful of dirt and fling it into Flaming Star's eyes, temporarily blinding his friend. As the man was about to take his friend's life, Bright Arrow gave a shout and charged. The foe whirled too late, for Bright Arrow ducked and rammed into the man's stomach, shoving him to the ground beside Flaming Star, who flipped over and sent his knife into the Crow's heart, then came to his knees and wiped his grainy eyes.

Bright Arrow and Flaming Star exchanged looks, then began to laugh. "We fight good together, my brother. We must collect their possessions, horses, and scalplocks; and join the others."

When Thunder Spirit heard many horses behind them, he glanced over his shoulder and grinned broadly at the thrilling and relieving sight. He called to Little Feet to halt, and both reined their mounts. When his older brother and Bright Arrow reached them, Thunder Spirit remarked proudly, "You have earned many new *coups*, my brother and my friend. It is a good day. Tell us of the battle," he coaxed, a little disappointed in having missed it, but his love and family were safe.

Little Feet reached over to take her father's hand, to squeeze it as she had done so often in the past to relate her love and joy. Her greenish brown eyes glowed as she smiled at Bright Arrow. "I am glad you are safe, Father. It is a great victory." She did not feel guilty over her lack of sadness and mourning marks, for she was too happy to be going home after five years with another tribe and with a husband who was too rough and greedy on the sleeping mats. Her heart had leapt with happiness to see Thunder Spirit once more and to learn he had not taken a mate yet. She glanced timidly at him, her gaze exposing much to all three men. She mused wishfully, if only . . .

Bright Arrow looked at Thunder Spirit who was eyeing his daughter with the same look which burned within his child's gaze. He exchanged grins with Flaming Star, both recalling how Thunder Spirit had revealed his love and desire for Little Feet during their journey to fetch her, fearing he could lose her again if he did not speak up boldly and promptly. Bright Arrow told his astonished daughter, "If you agree, Little Feet, I have promised you in joining to Thunder Spirit."

Little Feet's enticing gaze settled on the grinning Thunder Spirit. Clearly his expression was entreating her to say yes. She could not believe her sudden luck. She smiled happily and nodded, having dreamed of this moment and this man countless times before and during her marriage, and after her mate's death five suns past.

"We will have the joining after the council meeting on the next sun," Bright Arrow decided, mentally planning a big feast where he would celebrate becoming the Oglala chief in the morning, celebrate Little Feet's joining in the afternoon, and celebrate Tashina's promise to Silver Hawk as his future mate. When they reached camp near dusk, he should send a message to his friend to ask Silver Hawk to visit them later tomorrow to join the feasting.

"When we return to our camp," Thunder Spirit said, interrupting Bright Arrow's dreamy thoughts, "I will bring you many horses and hides."

Bright Arrow smiled. "I know of Thunder Spirit's prowess and love for Little Feet; there is no need to prove them to me. I am honored to have my daughter joined to a Sacred Bow carrier. Keep the horses and hides; you will need them for your new family. You will soon have a wife and two sons. You will need a large tepee; others will help make and lift it skyward on the new sun. I will be proud to call you son, brother to my good friend and son to my second father and mother. It is good to join our bloodlines."

Flaming Star grinned and agreed, "Yes, it is good for the bloodlines of Gray Eagle and White Arrow to join."

Sun Cloud became concerned over the number of gifts and messages which were arriving in their camp for the new Oglala chief, Bright Arrow! The Dakota Nation, which the whites called Sioux, consisted of three divisions: Lakota/Teton, Nakota/Yankton, and Dakota/Santee. There were seven branches under the three divisions, called the Seven Council Fires of the Sioux, *Dakota Oceti Sakawin*: Teton, Yankton, Yanktonais, Mdewakanton, Wahpekute, Wahpeton, and Sisseton. The Lakota/Teton branch was divided into seven more tribes: Brule, Oglala, Hunkpapa, Minneconjou, Blackfeet, Two Kettle, and Sans Arc.

He wondered if the other chiefs and tribes merely assumed the oldest son would follow his father or if they had forgotten, or were ignorant of, the fact that Sun Cloud was Gray Eagle's heir. Yet, so many were mistaken: Flaming Bow of the Cheyenne Red Shield Band; Rapid Tongue of the Cheyenne Coyote Band;

Windrider of the Cheyenne Dog Men Band, who should know the truth; Fire Brand of a Sisseton band; Long Chin of another Sisseton band, who had taken Races-the-Buffalo's place at his recent death; Running Horse of a Blackfeet band; Medicine Bear of his mother's Blackfeet band, who should also know the truth; Whispering Pine of the Brules, Blue Moon and Quick Fox of other Oglala bands, Walking Pipe and Conquering Bull of two Hunkpapa bands, Summer Wind of the Minneconjou, and White Robe of the Lakota Sans Arc.

The words his mother had spoken along the trail to this place filled his mind. He wondered if she had known or felt something was in the wind. "So much will be asked and expected of you. You were born to become the chief of the Oglalas. . . . You must be strong, Sun Cloud, for many dark days are ahead. You must allow nothing and no one to sway you from your destiny . . . Seek the guidance and help of the Great Spirit, for often man cannot be trusted," she had told him.

Anguish and doubt chewed upon him, for he had never imagined the man who could not be trusted was his own brother, and his brother's friend Silver Hawk. It did not look as if what should be a simple task of voting on a new chief was going to be a quick or easy one after all. He would wait until the council meeting in the morning to see if he should be alarmed, or if he was worrying over nothing . . .

Bright Arrow's tepee was full and busy that night with Little Feet's arrival home with her sons. News of Bright Arrow's recent *coup* spread eagerly around the camp, and Sun Cloud realized its timing could not be worse. Yet, he was careful to say and do nothing to spoil Little Feet's return or the joy of her impending union with his good friend and fellow bow carrier. He was delighted for Thunder Spirit, but knew this development left Tashina in jeopardy if Silver Hawk came to ask for her. If only Windrider's son would make his love and claim known. If only Tashina would reveal her feelings to her father. He had too quickly forgotten his recent lesson about procrastination. As soon as the council meeting ended tomorrow, he must ride to the Blackfeet camp and place his claim on Singing Wind, whether she liked it or not!

Singing Wind was confused and panicked. If her brother's vision and the one he had shared with Bright Arrow were real and accurate, she was destined to marry Bright Arrow! She fretted, but what of her love and desire for Sun Cloud? What of her wanton and uncontrollable union with him? Had she spoken the truth to him, that she had only wanted and needed to possess him "just once"! If the Great Spirit willed her to join with Bright Arrow, how could she not obey? Yet, how could she, loving and desiring Sun Cloud, obey? There was a way to see if Silver Hawk's visions were honest: if Sun Cloud was not made chief on the next sun, she would know she must not go to him again.

Chapter Eleven

pril twenty-ninth was a refreshing spring day. Nothing unusual happened during the council meeting until after the legend of Gray Eagle and Shalee had been chanted and the new members—Beaver Hands, Blue Feather, Angry Eyes, Kills-in-the-woods, Crows-heart, Charging Dog, and Dull Knife—had been selected to join those who had survived the cavalry's ambush: Talking Rock, White Arrow, Plenty Coups, Black Buffalo, Big Elk, Walks Tall, and Mind-who-Roams.

The problem began when Big Elk suggested, "We must cast our votes for our new chief Bright Arrow, so we can make plans to avenge our old chief's death and decide how to battle our white foes." Many heads turned and eyes widened at the war chief's words.

Black Buffalo hastily protested, "Sun Cloud is to be the next chief. It was in the vision of Gray Eagle. Why do you speak so?"

Walks Tall argued, "Visions can change, or be misunderstood, or be fulfilled another sun. I say, Bright Arrow should lead the Oglalas. He is older and wiser and has more *coups*. Sun Cloud can follow him as chief; then Gray Eagle's vision will come to pass in its right season."

Bright Arrow and Sun Cloud did not look at each other as they stood in the outer circle of warriors who were observing this meeting. Neither was surprised by the debate in progress, nor halted it.

White Arrow softly injected, "This *is* the season for Sun Cloud." His two sons watched, and one disagreed. Flaming Star mutely took his friend Bright Arrow's side, while Thunder Spirit did the opposite. A shirt wearer and a Sacred Bow carrier like the two brothers involved in this discussion and crucial vote, they would hold their tongues and votes until later, for it would surely come to a tribal vote.

Angry Eyes, a new member and famed warrior, said, "I say Bright Arrow leads us during these perilous suns. Have you forgotten his many deeds and his daring *coup* on the last sun? He killed three Crows, saved Flaming Star's life, and took many rewards."

Plenty Coups reasoned, "But Sun Cloud has more *coups*. He is a Sacred Bow carrier. He was born to shine brightly before our people and to rain on our enemies. He draws power, strength, and cunning from the Thunderbirds. He is like our old chief in prowess and in looks, but the image of the whites is upon Bright

Arrow. Sun Cloud was chosen to be our chief before his birth, and he was raised to know this and trained to accept it. I vote for Sun Cloud."

His brother Walks Tall debated. "Bright Arrow's hair is short because he cut it to save his people when he went to the fort to spy with Eagle's Arm. He is first-born. He has lived more suns beneath the eyes and guidance of his father and the Great Spirit. He has proven himself worthy to be our chief. In his vision as a boy, he saw a large arrowhead which held great magic and power. It was said the arrow would protect our people, for it was straight and true; it was swift and accurate to slay our foes and to point the way to peace and survival for us. It was shiny to light his path, to show him the way."

Plenty Coups refuted. "But the vision did not say he was to become chief, just a great warrior and leader, which he is."

Talking Rock remarked biasedly, "Sun Cloud was not in our camp for his parents' burial. He burned the *tipi* and belongings of our chief and his wife. He refused to place mourning marks on his body, as his brother did, as is our way. He is not stronger than his brother."

Plenty Coups disputed. "Sun Cloud obeyed the will of his father and the Great Spirit; they did not wish his body and possessions to fall into the hands of evil whites. He brought help to us when the bluecoats had us pinned down in the canyon where Gray Eagle was slain. He went to track those who escaped our vengeance, as is our way and must be done quickly. Did you not see how it pained him to leave his dying father's side and to destroy all earthly signs of Gray Eagle?"

Talking Rock asserted, "It was Bright Arrow who rescued his father and returned first with help for us during the bluecoats' ambush. He saved our lives and protected the bodies of our fallen warriors."

Blue Feather remarked, "Bright Arrow is a shirt wearer and a great warrior. He helped to destroy Fort Dakota years past. Sun Cloud is young; he is not ready to become the Oglala chief."

Beaver Hands declared, "But Sun Cloud is the one who drove the whites from our lands to the south when they tried to clear them of Mother Earth's trees to build a new trading post where more whites would come and settle. He stole many horses from our enemies and shared them with those in need."

"There is nothing more important than generosity, and Bright Arrow has proven he is more charitable than his younger brother. Many times he has given away the last of his food and winter supplies. He has hunted for those in need, and shared blankets and garments with them," reported Crowsheart with deep feeling and pride.

"What of the winter when our people were starving and Sun Cloud pursued the game for many moons and brought many travois of meat to feed his hungry people?" Black Buffalo called this memory to mind.

Angry Eyes inquired, "But who rode at his side? Bright Arrow."

Big Elk, the war chief, asked, "Do you recall it was Bright Arrow and his brave followers who drove the gold seekers from our sacred hills? It was Bright Arrow and his father who punished those who stole souvenirs from the death scaffolds of our tribe."

Beaver Hands retorted, "But Sun Cloud has done the same, and more. Many times he has tracked and slain scaffold robbers and returned our fallen warriors' belongings to them. Two summers past, Sun Cloud recovered our sacred Medicine

Wheel when it was stolen by the Pawnee, and he rode alone during that great *coup*."

"Flaming Bow told us, before he knew who was approaching, Sun Cloud made a stand against their large group to defend those who were ambushed." White Arrow revealed this fact to those who did not know it. "Bright Arrow knows he cannot become chief. He walks the path he believes Grandfather has made for him. Cease this confusion."

A moment of silence passed, but Bright Arrow did not respond to the evocative implication, distressing the hearts and minds of many, especially Sun Cloud. It was clear to him that his older brother wanted the chief's rank and had forgotten his vow long ago to accept Sun Cloud as the next chief. It saddened Sun Cloud to suspect that his beloved brother was being ruled by blindness, greed, and loneliness.

Crowsheart asked, "Did Bright Arrow not ride in our chief's place when he was wounded? Did he not prove he was worthy and skilled to be chief himself? Did he not lead as Gray Eagle had or would? Sun Cloud is wild and undisciplined. He has no wife. He has not submitted to the Sun Dance. Bright Arrow will obey the vote of the council."

Only through years of training and practice and by fierce control did Sun Cloud keep his expression stoic and his body lax. More than he wished he was not being subjected to such insulting remarks, he wished these men did not feel or think them. He had not been aware that others saw such flaws or weaknesses in him, or that some of them actually existed. Later, he must work hard to correct such stains. He had to push aside his love and loyalty to his brother, and consider only what was best for their people. He hated this episode where brother must battle brother to do what each thought was right, for Bright Arrow had to believe he was right to do this grievous thing. It was also sad that others must take opposite sides: fathers, sons, brothers, and more. He must pray that each man would hold his temper.

Charging Dog took offense to one insinuation. "Sun Cloud is a Sacred Bow carrier. He has run the sacred race many times and fulfilled its purification rite. He has endured this test and won it three times. The Sacred Bow ceremony can kill or defeat as easily as the Sun Dance. He has already vowed to submit to the Sun Dance this coming season."

Blue Feather asserted, "Bright Arrow is above all Oglala warriors. He rescued many of our women when they were captured and enslaved by the Crow. He taught us the use of the white man's captured guns. He saved Sun Cloud's life when he was still a child, and he saved our people when our chief lay dying from Crow and Pawnee wounds."

Charging Dog reminded, "Long ago, our noble chief said, 'For a chief, the good of his people must come before his own desires and dreams; when Alisha Williams entered his life, Gray Eagle obeyed this law even when it was hard and painful; Bright Arrow did not when Joe Kenny's daughter entered his life. He chose a white woman over his rank and duty and people. Bright Arrow was warned by his friends and people when they refused to vote him band leader, teased him, ridiculed him, and avoided him during his blindness and rebellion. The council begged him to think of his rank and duty. I say, no stain of defiance and selfishness marks Sun Cloud as they do Bright Arrow."

Bright Arrow had known that point would surface during this council; now, he must see how it was handled. He wanted this new life which was looming before him. He wanted new love to fill his emptiness. He wanted to be complete once more. He wanted to lead his people, and truly believed it was his duty and right. If all went well with this vital point, he would be where he had been before Rebecca; he could start his life over again. A second chance . . .

Talking Rock said, "I was on the council when Bright Arrow left our people, and when he returned to them. I say there was a reason why the Great Spirit put the white girl in his life. He was proud and stubborn and reckless. The Great Spirit used her to take him away, to strike him low, to remove his weaknesses and flaws, and to raise him to walk taller and stronger than before. We prayed and worked to free him of the evil white spirit who had enslaved him and blinded him to his duty and destiny, but we were wrong. The council ordered him to seek that which he could not survive without and release all else forever. For a long time, he lived without honor, without his people, rank, and customs; without his spirit. We took his destiny and Life-circle. He learned, as we did, he could not live without these parts of him, but he has proven he can live without the white girl. When she vanished, he did not desert his people and duty to search endlessly for her. We blamed her for dishonoring and weakening him long ago, but it was not true; he was following the path of the Great Spirit."

Kills-in-the-woods replied, "It is true he made peace with himself and his tribe long ago. He regained his honor and became a greater warrior. But he accepted the fact that Sun Cloud would become the next Oglala chief, not him. All he wanted was to be a warrior again, to live with his family and people, and to have his white love. We allowed this because we felt it was the will of *Wakantanka*."

Talking Rock stated, "Many were not in council that day when Shalee came to speak with us before her son's return. I will repeat her words, for they are true and wise: 'Have you forgotten all my first son has done for his people? Have you forgotten his love for us? He risks his life to help us even after we turned our faces from him. Who among you can swear without a doubt that Rebecca was not chosen for Bright Arrow by the Great Spirit? And if this is so, can we resist Grandfather's wishes any longer? Why do you punish him for obeying Grandfather, for following His guidance? Was Rebecca not willing to live among us, to call us friends and family? Is it not time to halt the pain and sadness? Is it not time to open our hearts to forgiveness and understanding?' Our chief's wife told us of how the white girl Rebecca Kenny, known to us these winters as Wahea, helped our allies the Cheyenne to survive the white man's evil disease. Shalee said, 'Grandfather should decide whether or not she lives at Bright Arrow's side. Why do you punish your chief by denying him his son, his happiness? Why do you make him choose between his son and his people? This is wrong.' We agreed. We forgave him and accepted his return. We gave him back his rank. How can we hold forgiven charges against him? Besides, the white girl is no longer in his life. Grandfather left her at his side many winters, then removed her after her purpose was served. Do you not see His will working in this matter? We said we wished him to return, to ride with his father, to take his father's place."

"If our chief was slain before Sun Cloud became a warrior," White Arrow inserted softly, for he was concerned deeply over this conflict.

Walks Tall looked at Gray Eagle's best friend since childhood. "White Arrow, you are his second father. You were at Gray Eagle's side when he said, 'Remember all I have taught you, Bright Arrow, and lead your people wisely and bravely.' Why do you speak against him?"

White Arrow's eyes revealed great sadness and dismay. "I do not speak against my second son; I speak for Sun Cloud to become chief, as I know it is the will of Gray Eagle and the Great Spirit. You did not understand the dying words of our chief and my closest friend. We have spoken many times over these winters. His choice was Sun Cloud."

Although Bright Arrow knew that statement to be true, it still pained him deeply. He wished his father had settled this cloudy matter before his death. Somewhere there was a mistake . . .

"Bright Arrow is first-born, and most worthy," Crowsheart stated.

White Arrow shook his graying head and revealed, "He is not the first seed of Gray Eagle. There was another son before Bright Arrow, a son who died at the hands of evil whites when Shalee was stolen after their joining. Neither Gray Eagle's second nor third son is unworthy to become our chief, but it must be Sun Cloud. He was sent to his father when Bright Arrow left us; it was a sign in his favor. I have witnessed the life of Gray Eagle as closely as my own. When Bright Arrow returned home, Gray Eagle told him, 'You will ride at my side. Your people need you. I need you.' And Bright Arrow replied, 'I will accept my place here. I will follow you as chief, then my brother Sun Cloud.' I remember Rebecca Kenny, and I loved her as a daughter. She risked her life to rescue my second son from the fort. She was gentle and kind. She was obedient and respectful and had many skills. But she fulfilled Gray Eagle's vision about his two sons."

Big Elk returned to their former point. "In the council long ago, Mind-who-Roams told us, 'I say the matter is for Grandfather to settle. Bright Arrow's life and destiny are here with his people and family.' My brother Plenty Coups asked, 'What if he does not escape the Crow camp alive?' Cloud Chaser responded, 'If Bright Arrow escapes with Sun Cloud and returns to our camp, I say it is the sign for our brother's forgiveness and acceptance.' We all voted to agree with that sign, to allow Grandfather to decide Bright Arrow's destiny, and He did. When the council met again after Bright Arrow's return, we gave him back his past rank, rank of the first-born, rank of future chief, not the rank of a new warrior. We cannot hold against him past deeds which we forgave or decided were the will of Grandfather. The sun has come to follow our vote of long ago. Talking Rock and White Arrow reminded us of the words of Gray Eagle and Shalee, but there are more. Shalee asked, 'Does a man who rejects his people seek to save them from enemies? He has not rejected us; we sent him away because he could not deny his love and cast her aside.' Shalee said we must unblind our eyes and open our hearts to understanding and forgiveness, and we did. I say the past is dead, to be forgotten; it has no vote this sun."

"But Bright Arrow saw this truth and agreed to it," argued Charging Dog. "He did not protect the life of his middle child or his woman. How can he protect his people? I say, if a message came this sun of his lost white woman, he would rush to help her and leave us in danger."

"You are wrong, Charging Dog," chided his brother Angry Eyes. "His child died while he was away helping his people and other tribes. Bright Arrow agreed to this so-called truth because it was what he was told, before he knew the truth. He would never desert his people."

"What is this truth you speak of, Angry Eyes?" Dull Knife asked his first question, for he had been observing this situation intently.

The shaman Mind-who-Roams came to his feet, his action and presence silencing the group. "I must reveal the visions of Gray Eagle, Mind-who-Roams, Silver Hawk, and Bright Arrow. I cannot speak in favor of either son, for the face of our new chief has not been shown to me." The older man went on to repeat the vision of Gray Eagle from long ago: "Our people will know a greatness other nations will not. The white man will fear the power of the Dakota Nation. Our sons will ride against the white man together. Both will be great leaders. The seed of Gray Eagle will not pass through our first son; the greatness of the Oglala will live within Sun Cloud and his children. Sun Cloud will ride as chief. Sun Cloud will show a greatness few warriors ever know. His *coups* will outnumber even mine. Many winters after we join the Great Spirit, the line of Sun Cloud will rival the power of all white-eyes. A woman will enter Bright Arrow's life; he will choose her love over his duty. His destiny lies in the hands of *Wakantanka*. Perhaps He will find some way for Bright Arrow to have both. Perhaps it is only a warning, nothing more. She would not enter his life and heart if it is not the will of the Great Spirit."

Dull Knife pointed out, "The vision has come to pass; his seed will not survive through his first son, for White Arrow revealed that his first son was slain; that part of the vision was not about Bright Arrow as we believed, as our chief believed, for he had forgotten his past loss. It is also true that Bright Arrow has no son to pass along the seeds of his father; this could be the message and meaning of the Great Spirit. The greatness of our people can live through Sun Cloud and he can become chief, but the vision did not say when these events would take place. Perhaps they should be fulfilled this season, or another season far from this one. *Wakantanka* decided Bright Arrow's destiny and returned him to his family and people and made a great warrior of him, but was his becoming chief the Great Spirit's plan? I do not know which way to lean, for both are worthy leaders, and I would gladly follow either of Gray Eagle's sons. Tell us more, Wise One."

The Holy man went on to relate his past visions which had been revealed in earlier council meetings: dark and evil shadows had blanketed their lands, the blood of many Oglalas had been spilled, council members had been taken from them, and they had tasted bitter defeat. The shocking news came when he revealed the recent vision of Silver Hawk and the joint visionquest by Silver Hawk and Bright Arrow.

Many realized how much of those visions had come to pass: the terrible battle with the soldiers, Gray Eagle's death, Silver Hawk within one step of the Blackfeet chief's bonnet, many voting for Bright Arrow to accept the Oglala chief's bonnet, the Great Spirit's removal of Bright Arrow's one dark stain from his life, Medicine Bear's agreement to the union of Bright Arrow and Singing Wind, Bright Arrow's agreement to the joining of Silver Hawk and Tashina, and Bright Arrow having to take a stand against his brother.

"It is as it should be," Blue Feather asserted confidently. "The white girl is out of Bright Arrow's life and he will soon join with an Indian princess. One daughter was joined to a chief and will soon join a Sacred Bow carrier of our tribe. Another daughter will soon join the next chief of the Blackfeet. The Indian blood flows swift and powerful in the bloodline of Bright Arrow. He and his family have earned many *coups*. Sun Cloud is young and has no family. I say, he must become chief later when he has more winters on his body and his life is settled."

Kills-in-the-woods looked at Sun Cloud and inquired, "Have you chosen a woman to become your mate?"

Sun Cloud was consumed by anger and a sense of betrayal toward his brother and his love, which he struggled to keep hidden, and succeeded. He replied truthfully, "I have been watching one female for a long time, and I planned to join her before winter returns to our lands. I cannot speak her name, for I have not approached her or her father. Yes, I am young and wild, but my father and people have taught me well. I will not fail my people when I lead them."

Kills-in-the-woods asked Bright Arrow, "Does Singing Wind know of this joining you speak of? The white woman is dead to you?"

Bright Arrow looked around the circle of important men as he replied, "Wahea is gone from me forever, and I accept this as the will of *Wakantanka*. If news comes of her, I will not race off to search for her. If it is Grandfather's will for her to return to my life and tepee, He will send her home to us. I will never leave or be taken from my people again. Singing Wind knows of our joining; Medicine Bear, Silver Hawk, and their shaman Jumping Rabbit have spoken to her." Bright Arrow was glad he had sent word to Silver Hawk to reveal this news to Singing Wind, so he could speak the truth and have the matter settled. He never imagined the Indian princess might not obey.

Sun Cloud found himself wondering if he was about to lose all he loved and needed; his parents were gone, it looked as if he had lost Singing Wind, it appeared he might lose the chief's bonnet, and Tashina was to be given to that guileful Silver Hawk. He asked himself if Bright Arrow had revealed his plans to Tashina before announcing them, for the girl was in love with Soul-of-Thunder. Again, that procrastination lesson was sent home painfully. Perhaps Windrider could have gotten his friend to reconsider his choice for Tashina's mate. That was impossible now, for the announcement had been made, and no honorable male could battle a public claim on a woman by another man. A man lost all face if he whined after a lost love; it exposed great strength for a man to control his emotions and actions when he lost the woman he desired. It was said, only a foolish weakling would go to her and beg her to change her mind. But to make a fuss over a woman you had not revealed a public interest in previously would make you appear a troublemaker. It was their way, once a claim was made and accepted, that a proud and strong male ignored the female completely, and tried to forget her. Singing Wind was beyond his reach now, for to race after his brother's chosen one would be a shame too large to endure. Besides, Bright Arrow said she knew about the joining, and he would not lie to his tribe and brother.

"Other tribes and chiefs have shown their choice as Bright Arrow. Many gifts and messages have arrived for him," Crowsheart reminded them.

"Because they do not know the truth," Black Buffalo refuted.

As the council and warriors continued to refresh the *coups* of their chosen one, Sun Cloud was entrapped by pensive thought, even though the discussion appeared to hold his undivided attention. He called to mind the day he had made love to Singing Wind by the pond, and fretted over the fact she must have known about Bright Arrow's claim on her. If that was true, why had she yielded to him two moons past? Had she been testing her feelings for him and his brother, deciding which one she desired most? Clearly she had not made love to Bright Arrow before that day, and there had been no meeting between them after that day. What if Singing Wind had chosen him, not Bright Arrow? No, for she would not have allowed Bright Arrow to announce their joining today, and a messenger had arrived from the Blackfeet camp to speak privately with his brother just before the council began. It was true that Singing Wind was impulsive, defiant, and audacious; but she would never do this to spite or to punish him. No matter why she was marrying Bright Arrow, it was Sun Cloud she loved and desired!

Night Rider moved forward and stated, "It is my duty to speak out in council this sun." He slowly related what had occurred after the ambush while he rode with Sun Cloud and Thunder Spirit, exposing Sun Cloud's suspicions and secrecy, which did not sit well with many.

Sun Cloud silenced the soft rumblings in the meeting lodge by explaining the facts and his motives. "It is unwise and shameful to make wild charges without proof, but I am certain a traitor walks among one of the tribes. How could I tell those who should know about this matter without also alerting the guilty one that we suspect him?"

Even though war chief Big Elk was on Bright Arrow's side, he vowed, "Sun Cloud acted wisely and cunningly. This should have been kept secret, Night Rider. It must not go beyond this council until the guilty one is trapped and punished. This is Sun Cloud's duty and right."

At last, the shaman called for the vote: white sticks for Sun Cloud and black sticks for Bright Arrow; the majority would win and all must honor it. While the men cast their votes, Sun Cloud's gaze fused with Thunder Spirit's. With the return of Little Feet, his friend had been unable to contest Silver Hawk's claim on Tashina as they had agreed not long ago. Sun Cloud smiled and nodded, letting his friend know he understood and agreed. Just as Thunder Spirit's gaze expressed empathy for Sun Cloud's lost love.

The shaman announced, "I cannot vote, for I must obey the will of the Great Spirit and He has not revealed it to me. There are six votes for Sun Cloud and six votes for Bright Arrow. The decision is yours, Dull Knife."

All waited while the man gave more thought to his tie-breaking vote, for usually that honor or responsibility fell to their chief as the fifteenth member of the council. It was noticeable that most of the older, and supposedly wiser, members of the council had voted for Sun Cloud; while the younger members, except for Talking Rock, had sided with Bright Arrow. Dull Knife's age rested between those two groups. He could not get it out of his mind that Sun Cloud was Gray Eagle's choice, or that Bright Arrow had proven himself worthy.

Dull Knife said, "I cannot cast my vote this sun, for my mind and heart rage a fierce battle over who should become our chief. I say, let both brothers lead war parties and see which one the Great Spirit shines on more favorably. I believe Grandfather has kept our new chief's face hidden from the Wise One because he does not wish us to cast our votes this sun. I say, wait and watch for one full moon, then meet and vote. If none of you change your mind about either son of Gray Eagle, I will cast the deciding vote; this I swear."

The shaman concurred, "Dull Knife's plan is a good one. We will test the brothers, and we will wait for Grandfather to pick one for us. In one full moon, one brother will shine brighter than the other. Is it agreed? Both will ride as leaders of their bands until then?"

This time, the entire pile of voting sticks was white, which meant yes. The shaman smiled in relief and said, "It is good." The meeting ended with a call for a new war council in five days.

The council members drifted from the meeting lodge. As the younger warriors lingered to reveal whose side they were taking, two of the remaining three Sacred Bow carriers went to stand with Sun Cloud, as did several shirt wearers: including Star Gazer, Rising Elk, Deer Stalker—son of Talking Rock of Bright Arrow's side —and Thunder Spirit. Standing with Bright Arrow was one bow carrier, Night Rider, and many shirt wearers, among them Flaming Star—son of White Arrow and brother to Thunder Spirit of Sun Cloud's side—Good Tracker, and Touch-the-sky. Plenty Coups and his brother Walks Tall had taken opposite sides, as had Charging Dog and his brother Angry Eyes. The family of Windrider would also stand divided on this issue: Windrider for Bright Arrow and Soul-of-Thunder with Sun Cloud. Now that Bright Arrow had promised Tashina to Silver Hawk, it probably would not matter that her true love was siding against her father. But, it could make a difference between Thunder Spirit and Little Feet.

Bright Arrow left to speak with his two daughters, to reveal his actions and those of their loved ones. The two females looked at their father in disbelief, then exchanged probing glances with each other.

Tashina felt crushed by this heavy burden which her father had unknowingly placed upon her. If she defied her father by refusing to join with Silver Hawk, she would be forced to leave his tepee and camp forever, and she could not bear that thought. Far worse, if she failed to fulfill his words, that would make his vision look false or weak. By following her heart, she could be responsible for snatching the chief's bonnet from his head and for resisting the will of the Great Spirit for each of them. Was this the reason why Soul-of-Thunder had been forced to back away from her? she mused in anguish. She knew her love would side with his friend Sun Cloud, which would place a barrier between them. Perhaps there was a purpose and time for all things. Her sister had been compelled to marry another before she was claimed by her true love. Would it be the same for her? she fretted. She loved her father dearly and knew he would be a great chief, but she could ruin everything for him if she rejected Silver Hawk.

Little Feet's nervous fingers teased over several smallpox scars upon her face, tiny and faint scars which did not steal from her beauty and allure. If she joined with Thunder Spirit today, would it appear she was siding with her husband and Sun Cloud over her father? she worried anxiously. Would it look as if Bright Arrow's own family doubted him and this calling by the Great Spirit? Perhaps she could persuade her love to join her father, for he needed the support of another Sacred Bow carrier. If not, perhaps they should not join until this was over.

Sun Cloud arrived soon. He collected his belongings, then looked at his older brother. "I will stay in the tepee of Mind-who-Roams until I have my own tepee. I wish this conflict did not exist between us, for we both know our father's command. Soon, Bright Arrow, you must face the truth, and see this is wrong and selfish." Sun Cloud left after hugging Tashina and Little Feet.

Chapter Twelve

 ar away from the Dakota Territory, Rebecca Kenny was thinking of all she had lost and was wondering for the thousandth time how to get back to her love and family. Last spring, she had been wounded, almost critically, by fur trappers and taken captive to prevent trouble with the Sioux, to whom they had presumed she belonged because of her garments and location. She had traveled with them many days before she was strong enough to protest her abduction, which had been futile, for no one would return her home to her trapper husband "Clay Rivera" and she could not make the difficult and perilous journey alone. To survive until an opportunity for return was presented to her, she had been given no choice but to remain with the group of men.

Rebecca recalled all she had learned about this area from the men. Lewis and Clark had opened this route for countless trappers and rival companies to ply their trades. By this year, nearly a thousand men worked along routes through this opulent area where beaver and other animals with expensive hides and skins were located. Companies competed for this trade in any manner necessary, for it was very lucrative. With them, they had brought many evils to the Indians: disease, whiskey, greed, deceit, and white man's progress.

The American government had already taken advantage of these trappers, called Mountain Men, by making their leaders the forerunners of the Indian agent. During the War of 1812, a man called Manuel Lisa had been appointed by the government to hold the loyalty of the Sioux, while Robert Dickson served that same purpose for the British from his trading post on Lake Traverse. The success of Lisa established what eventually became the American-Canadian border.

The fur trade was based on several methods: trade with the Indians, private trappers, and company hired trappers. Reaching the backwoods areas, these trappers had labored diligently under the worst conditions, which honed them into tough and brave men who came to know this land and nature as well as the Indians and creatures present.

The surge into this beautiful and untamed land began with the Lewis and Clark Expedition. During its return east, it met two men following its lead: Forrest Hancock and Joseph Dickson, who pleaded and reasoned with the two explorers to lend them one of their best men: John Colter. A deal was struck: Colter could return west with them, but no other man was permitted to leave their group.

Colter became widely known by whites and Indians, and by the two largest fur trapping and trading companies: North West Company and the Hudson Bay

Company. Soon, other companies wanted their "piece" of this area and trade. Boldly and bravely, Colter and his men established many trails and routes in the expansive area, for he had learned its secrets and had adapted himself to them. He guided Dickson and Hancock to the Yellowstone valley and set up their camp there. But on his first trip back toward St. Louis, he met Manuel Lisa and was persuaded to work with and for him.

Manuel Lisa was a man of Spanish descent who had very few, if any, scruples and little conscience. He knew what he wanted and was willing to do anything to obtain it. His dark skin, eyes, and hair should have warned others of the "devils" which lurked within his body. Lisa, under the eye of John Colter, set up a post where the Yellowstone River was joined by the Bighorn River, in the future state of Montana, around forty-five miles from where the infamous Battle of the Little Bighorn would be fought in 1876. Quickly Lisa's holdings and profits multiplied, for he had learned how to dupe the Indians and the trappers who worked for him. He had the largest post in that area. Trappers had to bring their pelts and hides to it to be sent to St. Louis.

Oddly, Lisa was credited with keeping the peace between the whites and Indians in "his" wilderness. Although doing so necessitated a trip abounding with dangers and hardships, many men joined him and his Missouri Fur Company. By 1815 when the war was over, water routes and land trails were relatively easy to follow. By that time, few men could work for themselves, or other companies, and survive. Manuel Lisa also had a large post, called Fort Manuel, near what would one day become the border between North and South Dakota. By 1820, he had established other posts and he was said to run his company like an army. Working for Lisa was a man named Jeremy Comstock, who had been responsible for Rebecca's injury and abduction.

Jeremy Comstock entered his cabin and observed the flaming-haired beauty for a few minutes before inquiring, "What are you doing, Becca?"

She turned and focused liquid brown eyes on him, then replied casually, "I'm packing to go home, Jeremy. I heard the others say you and Mister Lisa are heading for Fort Manuel and then St. Louis in the morning. I'm going with you," she stated with determination. Her dainty chin and narrowed eyes revealed her resolve and courage.

The sandy-haired, blue-eyed male of thirty-nine, whose husky weight was spread evenly over his six-foot frame, shook his head. He eyed the woman he had known and wooed for the past year. She had refused to marry him, even though she had lived with him during that time. He stated flatly, "The journey is too hard and dangerous for you, woman. By now, your husband either thinks you're dead or permanently lost to him. It's been a year, Becca."

"But I'm not dead, Jeremy, and he would know I was alive and well if you had allowed me to send a message to him. Besides, I've made that same journey before; that's how I got in this predicament." She returned to her packing as she waited for him to debate her point.

Jeremy Comstock sighed heavily. He loved and needed this woman. She was brave and strong, and a vital part of his life. At forty-one, no woman could stand next to her and claim to possess more beauty or appeal. He had tried everything to get her to forget her past and to marry him. Each time, she had reminded him of the husband and children she had waiting for her in the Dakota Territory, facts which he resented. "I love you, Becca," he argued. "I want you to marry me. Don't you know he's probably taken another wife by now? You want to walk in from the dead and give him more problems and torment? Damnation, woman, he could be anywhere in this big country by now!"

She whirled and declared, "He's waiting there for me! You'll see. He would never take another wife until he was certain I was dead, and he would never believe that. I've worked for you for a year, Jeremy; you owe me this. Please," she added entreatingly, her whiskey-colored eyes dampening with unshed tears.

"Lordy, woman, do you know what you're asking of me? You want me to take the woman I love and need to search for a lost husband who's probably married to someone else. Lisa would never allow it."

Rebecca placed her hands on her hips and refuted his claim. "You're Lisa's top man; he would refuse you nothing. You don't have to tell him anything. Or tell him I'm going to St. Louis with you."

"Just how do you propose to look for your husband along the way?" he inquired skeptically, knowing he could not allow her to leave him.

She read his stubborn look as she told him, "When we reach the area where your men wounded me and took me prisoner, I'll slip away. I know where to find him; he always . . . works in the same area. You can't hold me captive forever."

"Damnation, woman! You aren't my captive," he protested.

"I might as well be," she retorted. To keep the other men away from her, she had been forced to live in this cabin with Jeremy Comstock. At times, she had doubted her reunion with her true love, her lost love. At times, she had feared he had married again, thinking her dead and wanting to ease his sufferings. But she loved Bright Arrow, and somehow she would return to him and her daughters. Long ago, Alisha had been taken from Gray Eagle's side, then miraculously returned to him. Surely the same could be true for her! Each passing day her loneliness, fears, and desperation mounted. She felt if she did not get back to him soon all would be lost between them.

Jeremy watched that faraway and sad look in her compelling eyes, and it tormented him. How could he say no to her? But if he said yes, he could lose her. Maybe he should let her return to look for Clay Rivera; maybe that would prove to her that he had gone on with his life. What man, after knowing and having Rebecca Kenny, could carry on without her, unless he replaced her with another female? An idea came to his keen mind. "If I let you go with me," he began, then scowled at the look of joy and excitement which flooded her lovely features. "If he's got another woman now, promise you won't intrude on his new life and promise you'll return here . . . and marry me."

"That's deceit, Jeremy," she accused softly.

"Those are my terms, Becca. I have to think about you and me. I know you'll keep your word, so make the promise, or you don't go."

Rebecca apprehensively paced the small cabin as she deliberated his "terms." In a way, he was right, and generous and kind. There was no way of imagining what she might find in the Oglala camp. If her life there was lost to her, could she turn to Jeremy Comstock?

"Well?" he hinted anxiously. "Do we have a bargain?"

Rebecca faced him and replied, "We do, Jeremy Comstock. How long will it take to reach the area where I was stolen?"

"A month or two, depending on how many stops Lisa wants to make and how long we stay at each one. Tell me, Becca, how will you explain this last year to him?"

"I'll tell him the truth, Jeremy," she responded with a shudder.

Singing Wind gaped at Medicine Bear as he revealed her brother's vision and the one he had shared recently with Bright Arrow, and his acceptance of both "messages" from the Great Spirit. She listened intently and incredulously as he related her destiny and theirs. But what stunned her the most was the fact that these matters had been announced publicly that morning. Her thoughts and worries flew to Sun Cloud, and she was troubled by what he must be thinking and feeling.

"Silver Hawk has gone to the Oglala camp to accept his claim on Tashina and to carry gifts to Bright Arrow to prove his worth and courage. He will join the feast for their new chief, his friend and brother, and plan his joining with Tashina. Soon, Bright Arrow will come to prove his claim and worth, to make plans for his joining with my daughter Singing Wind," he disclosed happily.

In a tone which held all of the respect and poise she could muster, the disquieted girl softly chided, "You are not my blood father, Medicine Bear; it was not your place to accept his joining offer before he approached me or you spoke with me. What if I love another? What if I do not wish to join with Bright Arrow? What if I have accepted the offer of another warrior? What if I refuse?" she questioned anxiously.

Medicine Bear stared at her in consternation. He challenged hoarsely, "You would not refuse this high honor. If you love another, you would be joined this sun, for Singing Wind would not be calm or satisfied until she possessed her desire. All know you have rejected any warrior who approached you, and you cast eyes on no man. I have given my word as your chief and as your father since Brave Bear was slain. It was my right and duty to follow the will of *Napi* and to do what is good for my daughter and her people. It will unite our two tribes once more, for the daughter of Black Cloud and sister of Brave Bear has left Mother Earth. It is good to have a blood bond to our Oglala brothers, for they are powerful; they are feared by whites and Indians. We need this bond, Singing Wind, for our band is not large or powerful and this is an evil season. You must not shame me, your people, or yourself. It is decided. The words have been spoken. Only Bright Arrow can break them. Or Singing Wind must be banished forever."

That mild threat did not sit well with the agitated female, but she wisely, though resentfully, prevented a harsh reply. "A joining should be a happy time, Medicine Bear. I feel I am a sacrifice to help my people. What of me, my father? I do not love Bright Arrow."

"There is no higher honor or *coup* than to help your family and people survive, daughter. You must not be selfish or stubborn. Love will come after you are joined. He is a great warrior, a chief. Many females desire this high rank you have been given," he reasoned.

Singing Wind placed her back to him. Her mind echoed his words. *Selfish?* Why was it selfish to capture her own dreams, instead of being forced to fulfill those of others? *Love will come . . .* Love was not someting to be learned, or something which came to you in time like age or gray hair! *Many females desire this high rank* . . . Then, let one of them have it, she decided peevishly. *Given?* She was not being *given* anything! Since the joining had been spoken aloud before the Oglalas, it was accept her new fate or betray her people's laws and faith in her. Yet, to go along with this unwanted union, she must betray herself and Sun Cloud. *Napi* help her, for she had been tossed into a pit which she feared she could not escape.

Her mind roamed sadly to the Oglala camp, envisioning the feast in progress. She could not imagine Sun Cloud's feelings and thoughts, for he had lost so much recently. Even if he did not feel the same as she did, he had lost his parents and his destiny. And surely he had lost his brother, for how could any man accept such a betrayal? Where would he live now, for he had burned his father's tepee? He could not stay with Bright Arrow, not after his brother's treachery; stealing the chief's bonnet and his destiny was treachery in the highest. She wondered if Bright Arrow knew he had also claimed the woman his brother had taken first by a lovely pond. She brooded over Sun Cloud's reaction to the news of their joining and over what he must view as another betrayal; this time, on her part.

Singing Wind dropped heavily to her sitting mat. As she squinted her eyes in pensive thought, lines creased her forehead and teased at the corners of her expressive eyes. She absently nibbled on the inside of her lower lip, and she breathed erratically. She could not reveal the truth to either brother, for it would do harm in both situations. She was Blackfeet first, a person and a woman second. She had to fulfill her duty; she had to honor their laws and customs; she had to ignore her own desires. After the way Bright Arrow had treated her during their last meeting, he would not break his word or remove his offer for her. She fumed over the fact that he had not even hinted at his intentions, but his mood and tone should have spoken loudly to her. If only Sun Cloud had not angered her with his grim accusations against her brother and if he had declared his, or any, strong feelings for her after they made love . . . There was no denying he was attracted to her, but did he love her? Did he want her as his mate? Did he realize such things himself? No matter, it was too late for them.

Medicine Bear looked down at the apprehensive female. "Will you obey our law, daughter?" he asked simply as his wrinkled hands quivered.

She inhaled deeply and met his imploring gaze. "I am a Blackfeet, daughter of two chiefs and granddaughter of another. I will do my duty."

The feast continued with singing, chanting, dancing, talking, and eating. Most seemed in high spirits, and the rival brothers put on skilled fronts to conceal their emotions and concerns. It was a pleasant truce between those who had sided openly with different choices, for all felt this matter would be resolved peacefully in the best interests of Grandfather's children.

Little Feet sat with Thunder Spirit and his family, but there was a slight strain between the reunited lovers. She had been unable to convince him to switch his selection and loyalty to her father, and he had pleaded for her understanding, then softly scolded her for intruding on his decision and duty. He had not been pleased when she had postponed their joining for a few days, telling him they could not share a happy first night together at this time. When she had suggested a new joining date in four moons, he had replied sadly, "If you change our joining sun again, Little Feet, we should think more on your feelings. If a warrior cannot do what he feels his duty without his love turning her face from him, something is wrong."

Little Feet was vexed with herself for causing this rift between them. They had waited so long to be together. She wished she was sitting beside her new husband tonight, eagerly looking forward to sharing his mat later. She had been foolish, and wrong. Thunder Spirit was more than Sun Cloud's friend, he was a superior warrior and he had to obey his conscience. It was too late today to change her mind again, for his mood and disappointment would spoil their first union.

Little Feet locked her gaze on Thunder Spirit's handsome profile, causing him to sense her attention and look at her. She placed her quivering hand on his arm and whispered, "I am sorry, my love; I spoke unwisely and selfishly and falsely. If you did not follow your head and heart, you would not be the man I have loved since I was a child. We will join in four moons, for I want you above all things."

Thunder Spirit observed her contrite expression and tone. He smiled tenderly. "It is good, Little Feet, for I would not give you up without a fierce battle," he teased. "I have waited many winters for your return, but these next four moons will seem longer than them."

She squeezed his arm and smiled radiantly. "It has seemed forever since we parted long ago. But it is good we have four moons to prepare for our new life together. I must make a tepee for us, to be alone. Our fathers' tepees are full," she hinted provocatively.

He laughed and agreed, "It is good, but hard."

Silver Hawk sat between Bright Arrow and Tashina. His grin was smug to the girl beside him. She prayed they would not be left alone that night, for she could not bear the thought of him touching her again. How ever would she endure a life with him? she wondered frantically. She looked at her sister who was beaming with happiness, and she was glad Little Feet and Thunder Spirit had overcome their brief conflict, which their smiles and closeness revealed to her. *Duty*, she fumed the offensive word. Her dreams would be destroyed if she did not find a way to save them, and she did not know how.

Sun Cloud furtively observed his family and friends. He knew one of Bright Arrow's daughters was happy and one was miserable. He was delighted by his friend Thunder Spirit's joy and victory. It did not trouble Sun Cloud that Little Feet and Tashina were loyal to their father; that was expected and natural. He loved them like sisters and he understood their emotions and behaviors. For Tashina's and Soul-of-Thunder's sakes, he must speak privately with his brother about their feelings. Silver Hawk had a wife, and Tashina loved another. Since Bright Arrow was a friend to Soul-of-Thunder's father and to Silver Hawk, perhaps he could solve this predicament.

Watching Silver Hawk, Sun Cloud admitted the Blackfeet warrior would never reinquish that beautiful treasure, and it pained him. He had been close to Tashina since her arrival at two winters; he hated to see her lose her hopes and dreams, and go to that wicked man. Only by exposing Silver Hawk's treachery could he free her, and that would be difficult, if not impossible.

Soul-of-Thunder could not challenge for Tashina, for the Cheyenne warrior had not spoken for her in the past. Long ago, Gray Eagle had challenged Silver Hawk's father Chief Brave Bear for Shalee's hand in joining, but only because Gray Eagle had already mated with her while she had lived as his white captive, which had given his father the right to call for *ki-ci-e-conape*, the death challenge.

If his father had not spared Brave Bear's life after his victory, Silver Hawk would not exist! But neither would Singing Wind and her two sisters.

A flurry of cold thoughts fell over Sun Cloud's mind, forcing him to shove the frigid ideas from his path. He could use that same challenge to fight for his lost love, but the other man would be his own brother. He could not commit such a shameful offense, not even to obtain Singing Wind, especially when his brother was unaware of the bond he had severed. Too, others would learn of their passionate mating by the pond, and a female's purity was her highest *coup*. Singing Wind's face would be stained, and he could not allow that disgrace. He was as tightly ensnared as a helpless animal in the white man's steel traps!

The following morning, Sun Cloud and several men went to hunt fresh game for their families and for those in need, including his brother's family, as Bright Arrow and a small band of warriors were leaving camp for a few days to scout for cavalry details on the move and to spy on the fort once more, to see if the new white commander had arrived with his soldiers and wagons, for that would signal the beginning of the next conflict. When Sun Cloud's band returned, it was to guard the women while they gathered wild vegetables in the area which surrounded their camp, then keep guards posted.

Sun Cloud had thought of going to visit Singing Wind to try to resolve their personal dilemma. He ruled against that impulse, for he was needed at home, and following it would change nothing. He worked hard on not appearing overly quiet that morning, but only half succeeded.

Thunder Spirit hated to see his friend so low and so on guard with his words and behavior. As they tracked game, he remarked, "I wish it did not have to be this way, my friend. Be patient and do not lose hope. Grandfather will make things right soon, as He did for me."

A haunted look made Sun Cloud's eyes a shade darker. "It was five winters before Grandfather answered your prayers, my friend. I cannot wait that long to be happy again. Tashina is caught in the same trap as Sun Cloud, but we must both do our duties," he stated bitterly.

"It will be as your father saw it in his vision, Sun Cloud. The same evil which shadows our lands shadows our camp and your brother's heart. Grandfather will remove them when the season is right. You did not tell Bright Arrow of your love for Singing Wind or Tashina's love for Soul-of-Thunder?" his friend inquired knowingly.

"I will not speak to him of my feelings, but I must reveal his daughter's to him. He did not know of Little Feet's love and he gave her to another to suffer for many years. The same must not happen to Tashina; she is very special to me. Grandfather has a large plan for her life, but only at the side of Soul-of-Thunder."

"Then, it will be," Thunder Spirit reasoned.

"Evil also lives and breeds on the face of Mother Earth, my friend. Sometimes evil is stronger and defeats good. If this was not true, our war with the evil whites would have been won long ago, and my parents would not be dead. Grandfather tries to work His will, but sometimes He cannot," Sun Cloud replied dejectedly.

Thunder Spirit encouraged, "Do not lose all heart and spirit."

"I have already lost my heart, and my spirit is battling to survive. I fear for the evil of Silver Hawk, for others are blind to it. Tashina cannot escape his snare unless I defeat him, and I cannot defeat him with instincts alone. She cannot even run away to the tall grass and return as Soul-of-Thunder's mate, for Windrider's son would never break the bond between his people and mine by taking another chief's promised."

"But Silver Hawk is not chief yet," his friend reasoned.

"He will be chief soon, Thunder Spirit; he will make certain. I fear for Medicine Bear's life, but I can do nothing to save him. To approach him with such a warning would defeat all I work and live for. My father told me many times, 'The lives of many are more important than the life of one or a few.' Medicine Bear is a walking dead man, and I curse my helplessness." Before his friend could respond, Sun Cloud lifted his hand to signal for silence as a large buck appeared.

During the afternoon trouble struck. Sun Cloud was too restless to remain inside Mind-who-Roams' and White Calf's tepee. When movement caught his attention, he was sitting near the edge of the forest and leaning his back against a tree, almost concealed by leafy bushes. His gaze widened, then narrowed and chilled as he observed two Crow warriors sneaking toward the burial scaffolds on their stomachs. He knew what they wanted, and rage consumed him.

He stealthily made his way to the ceremonial lodge and seized his sacred bow from its resting staff; there was no time to seek help from others. He slipped into the forest once more and moved as closely as possible to the scaffold ground, which was located in a cleared area. He laid two arrows beside him and placed the third's nock against his bowstring, then drew it taut, and aimed carefully. As the first Crow reached Gray Eagle's scaffold and stood up beside it, on the side away from their camp, Sun Cloud released his fatal arrow.

The foe screamed in pain and was thrown backward, falling against his mother's scaffold and causing it to shake precariously. The other foe made a wild dash for the forest to his left, but Sun Cloud was swift and accurate and lethal. He knew it was the Crow's way to leave a scout with their horses, so he had a third enemy to find and slay.

War chief Big Elk had heard the commotion and witnessed part of Sun Cloud's new *coup.* He saw the younger warrior sneaking into the woods to seek the last Crow. He quickly summoned others to help and to warn the guards, for there could be more than one Crow remaining.

Big Elk was accurate; two Crow warriors were awaiting their daring comrades. When Sun Cloud had them in view, his heart began to drum heavily; Little Feet and her oldest son had been captured, along with Elk Woman, wife to Crowsheart. Before he was sighted, Sun Cloud loosened his last arrow and killed the warrior who was trying to load a bound Buffalo Boy on his horse. The boy fell to the ground, but was uninjured. The fourth Crow seized Little Feet's hair, yanked her before him as a shield, and placed a blade at her throat. The Crow warned Buffalo Boy and Elk Woman to remain still and silent or he would slit Little Feet's throat, then slay them.

Sun Cloud daringly approached them and scoffed, "Crow are cowards; they hide behind women and children. I spit on you, white man's dung," he shouted, then spat on the ground as if removing a foul taste from his mouth. "You are so weak, I will fight you without a weapon to make us even." With that, he drew his knife and flung it forcefully into the earth, the blade sticking deeply and the handle vibrating wildly.

"You think Crows are fools," the man retorted sullenly. "She is my shield.

Others will come soon, and it is foolish to remain to prove I am a better warrior with both hands bound than you with two free."

The Oglala warrior laughed insultingly. "You fear the son of Gray Eagle this much, white man's dung? You are no match for Sun Cloud."

That bittersweet disclosure was the other man's undoing. In his astonishment, his grip loosened; Little Feet rammed the back of her head into his nose and jerked free. Sun Cloud surged forward to place himself between the Crow and Oglala hostages to prevent his foe from grabbing and using one or all again. A lopsided grin teased over Sun Cloud's face and brightened his eyes. He glanced at the knife in his foe's grasp and taunted, "White man's dung, were you taught how to defend your life when you have no female shield?"

"I will slay you, son of a fallen eagle," the man vowed smugly, gripping his knife securely to attack and ignoring his bloody nose.

Sun Cloud agilely dove for his own blade and retrieved it as the man stumbled past him. He knew others had approached and were watching suspensefully, but his attention never strayed from his foe. The two men circled each other, looking for an attack point. The Crow lunged at him, but Sun Cloud first delivered a stunning chop to the man's wrist and then to his throat. Almost in the same movement, his other hand sent his blade into the man's left kidney area. His foe staggered, one hand covering the gushing wound. Sun Cloud had the urge to play with his foe, but that was not his way. He swiftly shoved the injured man backward, straddled him, and drove his blade home. He stood, then stared at the dead man for a moment.

He turned to Big Elk and said, "The four scalplocks are yours. Wear them when we ride into battle with our white foes." To others, he gave the Crows' weapons, horses, and belongings, except for the *wanapin* of the man who had tried to kidnap Buffalo Boy, to whom he presented a skillfully carved buffalo's head. He told Little Feet's son, "Wear it always to remind you of my love and the power of your people."

Crowsheart rushed forward to cut his wife's bonds and to embrace her with love and relief. He looked up at Sun Cloud and worriedly said, "This new *coup* is large, and it is special to me, but I cannot change my council vote because of it. Do you accept my gratitude and understand my problem?"

Sun Cloud smiled encouragingly. "Do not worry, Crowsheart. You must follow the words Grandfather puts in your head and heart. It would be wrong for this deed to sway you. You owe me nothing. If those who voted against me were in danger, I would still risk my life to save them, as they would risk their lives to save me. It is our way."

Big Elk immediately summoned all warriors in camp to a meeting where he admonished some for their carelessness and cautioned all others to be more alert. Holding the scalplocks above his head and shaking them, he stated, "This is why Sun Cloud was ordered to burn his father's possessions. If Grandfather had not made his spirit restless this sun and if he had not obeyed his father's command, our chief's sacred belongings would be stolen and his body dishonored and those of his bloodline would be slaves to our hated foes, as with others of our fallen warriors. If it had been a Crow war party, our camp would be under attack and many could have been wounded or slain. We ask Sun Cloud forgiveness for our anger at his actions that sad day. He has shown his many skills and courage this sun; it is good he is Oglala, not a Crow, or we would fear him greatly. I give you this eagle feather with great pride," the war chief announced, placing it in Sun Cloud's hair: a special *coup* feather with four markings to reveal he had slain four foes, and other markings to show he had captured enemy horses and possessions and saved three Oglala lives.

"This will not be the last time someone tries to rob the scaffolds of our chief and his slain people. Other Crow and Pawnee crave the weapons, medicine bundle, and *wanapin* of Gray Eagle, for they know of their great power and magic. All Oglalas are known for their prowess and powers. We must also place a guard near our death scaffolds," Sun Cloud suggested, and all agreed. "When we have defeated the whites, I will take their bodies to the sacred hills for safety."

"It will be as you say," Big Elk replied, a new glimmer of respect for this young warrior in his eye. He grasped how cunning Sun Cloud was, for only Sun Cloud had realized there was a traitor among them. Perhaps Sun Cloud's mind and body were not as young as his age.

Crowsheart tried not to allow this deed to sway his thinking, but it did, especially Sun Cloud's words and kindness afterward. Sun Cloud was not wild and undisciplined, as he had stated in the meeting. Nor was Bright Arrow, the first-born, more generous, as he had believed.

Sun Cloud went to make certain Little Feet and Buffalo Boy were all right. "Why were you in the forest during the rest time?" he asked.

Little Feet looked him in the eye and replied, "To give Sun Cloud another *coup* in his battle for the chief's bonnet, as it should be."

Sun Cloud embraced her affectionately and whispered in her ear, "It is good to have you home, Little Feet. My heart is filled with joy to know my friend has reclaimed his lost love. But do not speak such words aloud, for they will cause pain in your father's tepee. When Grandfather reveals his choice for chief, all will accept it."

Little Feet did not explain that she and her son had been restless too, and had gone to swim in the river. Her unexpected words had not been spoken from gratitude, but from her heart and mind, for she truly felt that Sun Cloud should become chief; and she prayed her father would come to know and accept that reality soon.

Tashina hugged Sun Cloud and thanked him for rescuing her sister and Little Feet's child. Sun Cloud caught her beautiful face between his hands and fused their gazes as he murmured softly, "Do not fear or worry, Tashina, for I will never allow Silver Hawk to take you. You belong to Soul-of-Thunder, and I will not allow evil to change your rightful destiny. This I swear on my life and honor."

Sun Cloud kissed the tearful and ecstatic girl on the lips, then smiled. "When it is possible, I will get word to your love and tell him not to worry or to react rashly at this offensive news."

"You have returned my heart and spirit, Sun Cloud. You have lived as a brother and friend to me, and I love you. I know of your prowess and truth, so I know my dreams are not lost. I believed my father should become chief; but now, I do not know for sure."

Sun Cloud tugged playfully on a lengthy braid. "I do not seek to win over my brother's children to my side. Know only that Sun Cloud will help you and protect you from evil, and Silver Hawk is evil. The sun will rise one morning and reveal his evil to your father, my brother. If it is Grandfather's will for Bright Arrow to become chief, I will accept it and I will ride with him into battle."

* * *

Bright Arrow and his band rode swiftly, taking only a few stops to rest and to water their horses. The night was half gone before they arrived in the forest which halted at the edge of the enormous clearing where Fort Dakota sat upon their lands. "We will camp here. Remain alert and ready to ride at the first sign of danger. I will take Night Rider and Flaming Star and we will sneak near the campfires of the bluecoats and listen to their words," he plotted, choosing the two men who could understand and speak English.

"You must rest first; our ride has been long and hard," Good Tracker reasoned.

"We need the cover of darkness, my friend. We must go now," Bright Arrow told him, genially clasping the man's forearm.

The others watched as the three warriors removed any item which might make noise or show movement. Then, gingerly and stealthily, the three sneaked toward the numerous tents which nearly surrounded the fort.

Chapter Thirteen

Flaming Star cautiously inched near one tent which had been erected near several wagons. He listened to the conversation in progress:

One soldier declared moodily, "I agree with Major Ames; we were *loco* to bushwack those Sioux. What's Major Butler gonna tell General Cooper when he arrives in two days?"

"Probably a pack of lies, like them Sioux provoked us."

"You know Ames is gonna call him a liar."

"Not if he ain't alive. Ames better watch his step; he's made bad enemies in Butler and his sidekick Smith. I hear 'em arguing all the time, and I seen the death look Butler and Smith put in Ames's back."

"Yeh, but Butler's lost some of his best allies; the Sioux got Rochelle and Red Band. That Smith's damn lucky to be one of the two survivors of that crazy plan. I heard tell, Clint was so repulsed by the slaughter that he got sick and ain't been the same since."

"Ever'body's heard Clint's wild tales about Gray Eagle being captured by Major Hodges when his brat was five or six and the Eagle traded himself for the kid, then walked out of the fort like he was on a Sunday stroll. Why, they're practically friends, to hear Clint talk."

"Can't blame 'im. Not many Injuns spare your life when you're helpless and they've tricked you. Looks like Clint will be getting out of the Army and leaving with that detail to Fort Meade next week."

"Probably for the best if he ain't got the guts to kill Injuns no more, 'cause we're sure as fire gonna kill plenty after Cooper gets here with all those men and supplies. For once, we'll have more than them."

"Smith says he hasta finish his duty on his feet, not on his butt in the infirmary. Smith's gonna send him on every patrol he can, the bastard. You know some of them wild tales Clint throws around, happened right here. If'n you ask me, this place is bad luck. Them Injuns done rifled it once. What's to stop 'em from trying again?"

"Us and General Cooper. You know they're sending him here to finish off those Sioux for keeps. I say, get rid of all Injuns. I bet Major Butler grabs all the glory he can before Cooper arrives and takes over. He'll have Smith sending us out to harry them ever'day."

"If I was Smith, I'd quit wearing that red bandana instead of the regulation yellow one. Makes him stand out like snow in July, and I'm sure there's lots of Sioux who'd like to get their hands on 'im."

"Red Band gave it to 'im, said it was an Apache good-luck charm."

On another side of the fort, Night Rider was carrying out his duty.

"I ain't afraid to admit it; I'm scared shitless. I sure hope Colonel Sturgis gets here afore General Cooper and his bloodthirsty pack. Them Sioux must be real mad about now; maybe he can calm 'em down a mite."

"Sturgis ain't in the Army no more, and he's an old man, sixty-eight, I heard tell, so he can't interfere in Army affairs."

"He's coming straight from the President, and the Army won't go against the President's man. Maybe he can make a truce with them Sioux; he did once before, with the Eagle himself. Met him face to face, and got him to settle down for years. Lordy, he scares me."

"The Eagle is dead, boy, so stop shaking like it's winter and you got icicles in your britches. Smith saw him hit the dirt, dead. He was just like you and me and ever other man, bones and flesh and blood. Weren't nobody thought he could be defeated, but he was. I bet that'll shock the fool outta Injuns and whites."

"We don't know he's really dead. Smith didn't bring back his body or none of his gear. Hellfire, man, we can't get cocky or lax! He could still be alive or just wounded. I say he don't die that easy."

"Them Crow scouts said he was dead, said them Sioux sung that Death Chant for 'em. You ain't scared of his ghost, are you boy?"

"What do them Crow know about anything except screwing their own kind. My papa always taught me, don't trust no man who betrays his family or people. And you can bet, if any man can lick death or come back from Hell's gates, it's Gray Eagle. So don't laugh at me. You can bet there's certain men they'll be coming after, like Smith."

"Shame Captain Rochelle was done in. He's the only one who knowed how to make them grenades, or whatever he called 'em. Those exploding balls he flung at them Injuns did some real damage."

"Not enough; it didn't kill all of them."

Near another area, Bright Arrow was eavesdropping intently, and caught two very familiar names . . .

"I think the Army should'a hung James Murdock!"

"They can't prove Murray knows who Bright Arrow is just 'cause Red Band claimed Clay Rivera was Bright Arrow, and Clay and Murray were supposed to be good friends. I saw those two men that day, so did Major Ames. They didn't look or talk like savages to me."

"Smith and some men rode over to where that Clay Rivera and his friend were supposed to be camping. Weren't hide nor hair of anybody in that area. And Red Band said they covered their tracks after they left here. They just vanished. Something's up, if you asked me. If Red Band was right, them Injuns know all we got."

"Don't make no never mind. We're covered until Cooper arrives, then we'll have more than enough to finish 'em off. Besides, them other Crow scouts told us Bright Arrow was banished, but we know that ain't right. He's been riding at his papa's side for years."

"Red Band said that's because they let him come back. If Red Band was right, he was living as Clay Rivera after he was kicked out for getting hung up on that white whore. Anyway, he's a half-breed; so how do we know he can't look and pass for white like his mama? Leastwise the Eagle and his brood got good taste in women; they prefer white ones. If they keep snatching white women and bedding 'em, won't be no Injun blood left in 'em. Maybe they'll get civilized."

Bright Arrow fumed at the insults about his lost wife, himself, and his family; but he kept still and silent. He realized he could never use his "Clay Rivera" identity again. He waited for the men to sneak swallows of whiskey before continuing with their potvaliant chatter.

"I still say they should haul Murdock in and beat the truth from him. Lordy, man, he might know all about the Eagle and the Sioux."

"If Bright Arrow was playing Clay Rivera, Murray might not know it's him. Murray's a good man, and he's white. We need his help. Nobody knows this area better than a trapper who's been here long as he has."

"Murdock won't work with us; that should tell you something."

"Yep, he wants to stay neutral to keep his hair and hides, but he's agreed to meet with General Cooper when he gets here."

"Yep, probably to spy for his Injun friends. Red Band—"

"Shut your trap about that stupid Injun! If'n he was so smart, why's he dead like all the others Smith left behind out there?"

"I was gonna say, if he's alive, he could recognize Clay Rivera."

"We don't need Murray or Red Band to point out Bright Arrow to us. Major Timothy Moore is heading this way with General Cooper and, the way I hear it, Moore's got a debt to settle with Gray Eagle's son. Yep, Moore knows exactly what the baby Eagle looks like. We'll see if it's the same man who visited our fort."

The men laughed and talked a while about Timothy Moore, and Bright Arrow's capture, that time when Rebecca Kenny had enchanted the lieutenant and helped her Indian lover to escape Moore's grasp.

"Besides, it ain't Bright Arrow we got to worry about; it's his brother Sun Cloud. Lordy, boy, he's just like his father. Sun Cloud would never capture no white woman and marry her. He would die before he weakened his Injun bloodline. I shore hope he don't get chief."

"But the Crow scouts said the oldest son took a father's place."

"I shorely hope this is one time them scouts know what they're talking about, but I can't see them Sioux picking Bright Arrow over Sun Cloud, unless they're all dumb and reckless. Bright Arrow ain't got what his father had or his brother has. We'll be damn lucky if Sun Cloud don't make chief, 'cause we can whip Bright Arrow easier."

"Yep, that papoose's gonna be a legend like his pa, if we let him live long enough. A real shame to kill such a great fighter."

"He's already lived long enough to make a name for himself, boy. Ain't no Injun in this area who can match Sun Cloud, including that other little eagle with ten more warriors added to 'em; and there ain't no soldier or white who don't know and fear Sun Cloud like his papa. If Gray Eagle really is dead, all we gotta do is kill off his baby, and this war's over for good. I need to get rid of some of this whiskey and turn in. We gotta ride out on patrol right after dawn."

Bright Arrow quickly and silently crept from their area to make his way back to the waiting warriors. No alert had been given yet, so his friends should be safe. He tried not to think about the white man's opinion of his brother, or their opinion about him.

When the soldier returned to his friend after relieving himself, he was chuckling. "What's so funny?" the other man asked.

"Oh, I was just thinking about Red Band and how he got himself killed in that ambush. I wonder how he knew where to strike at 'em."

"Beats me, but Smith's gonna miss his Injun scout."

"That's 'cause Red Band was always making them Injuns' squaws spend time in Smith's quarters for free, if you know what I mean."

"Smith best watch himself. One of them squaws might stick a knife in his gullet one night. His tongue and his ways ain't nice to 'em. You think Smith's right about them Sioux being out there watching us and waiting to pick us off when we ride out?"

"Don't matter what they're doing or planning. But if they try to retaliate with an ambush, Smith's trap will work. If'n anybody follows us tomorrow, we'll have 'em trapped between us. Course, I'd rather be riding behind them Sioux with Smith instead of before 'em."

By the time Bright Arrow reached his band, the others had returned. The warriors exchanged information. Although he did not want to repeat what the men had said about him and his brother, Bright Arrow felt he should reveal every word, in case there was a helpful clue hidden amongst them. He was relieved when none of his men agreed.

"We will watch the fort and trail those who leave when *Wi* lights our lands. It is not wise or safe to attack their camp now; there are too many in one place. It is better to pick them off in smaller groups."

"What about the supply wagons?" one warrior inquired.

"They are empty, so there is no need to burn them. It would only alert them to our presence. It is best to nibble cautiously and slowly at our prey, not devour it rashly and swiftly; it could choke us in our rush, or it could be bait to lure us into peril, or it could be tainted to kill us. We will slay those who leave soon, then we will seek this new leader they speak of. We must learn of his size and power."

"What of the man who captured you long ago?" Night Rider asked.

"He is mine," Bright Arrow declared coldly.

"How will we know him?" Night Rider asked.

"His hair is like flames of a fire and his eyes are as blue as the best summer sky we have seen. I will point him out to you."

"What of the other men whose names you know?" Good Tracker inquired, recalling what they had been told about those white men.

"We must slay them all," Touch-the-sky declared. "As with the Sacred Bow carriers and Cheyenne dog-rope wearers, we must never surrender to our foes. We must fight till death, or honorably retreat to battle them another day. We must slay all whites," he stressed.

"No, we must try to spare the lives of our white friends, for they are few and could help us another sun. Surrender is sometimes necessary, Touch-the-sky, to survive to find a chance to escape, to seek victory and vengeance another day. Guards must be posted while others sleep," Bright Arrow told them, ending the conversation.

The sentry continually scanned the area from which the signal would come if there was trouble. Suddenly a flash of light caught his eye. "Major Ames and his men just passed the lookout, sir," he called down to the waiting officers, then watched that area intently.

Smith said, "If any Sioux start following them, we'll get another signal, then Ames will be alerted. He's to keep riding for ten minutes while we get into position, then his detail is to turn and fight."

Butler laughed wickedly and whispered, "I bet that order stuck in his craw, and he hopes we're wrong. I can't wait to see his red face when we have to rescue him from Sioux. You sure you told Sims to warn him? Shame if he got killed before we could reach him."

Smith chuckled with his commanding officer and good friend. "Afraid so. Too many men out there with him. Wouldn't look good on me to lose another troop. We'll get Ames another day, real soon."

"I'm depending on you, Clarence. Your neck's in this noose too if Ames tattles on us. Best knock off Daniels too; they're real close."

"Red Band was going to handle them for us, and the fool went and got himself and my men killed. Must have been sleeping to let them Sioux sneak up on him. We still got us an Ace or two," he hinted.

"You mean that two-faced brave?" Butler probed. "What will he do for us? We've already double-crossed him. We weren't suppose to attack that war council, and I bet he's boiling mad, if he's still alive."

Smith grinned and replied smugly, "Don't you worry none; I'll have him eating out of my hand in a week or so. We know each other and how to get in touch. He'll get rid of Ames and Daniels for us, and Cooper too. I'll even let him get rid of Bright Arrow and Sun Cloud for us before we do him and his Blackfeet in. He's real greedy and crazy, and the fool thinks he needs us."

"You didn't tell any of the men about Gray Eagle's visit, did you?"

"No way. They'd be wetting their pants if they learned who strolled in and out of here with that so-called Clay Rivera."

The sentry stared through his field glasses, then saw it again. He called down, "Major Butler, there she is; they're being followed by Sioux like Captain Smith said. Message was, they're hanging back right now, probably waiting until they're out of our hearing range to attack."

"They'll reach that box canyon in about fifteen minutes. Mount up," he shouted to the men who were waiting beside their horses.

"How do you plan to get that brave's help again?" Butler asked skeptically as his company prepared to leave to spring their trap.

To make certain no one heard him, Smith leaned toward Butler. "Make him two offers he can't refuse: silence and rewards. I'll have him convinced the attack on the war camp was a mistake, on Ames's part naturally. I'll persuade him you can make him the most powerful chief in this area. 'Course, for my help, I'll let him give me that chief's daughter Red Band pointed out to me. Singing Wind . . . Yep, she'll have me singing happily real soon," he murmured satanically. "I might even share her with you, old friend."

"You mean if there's anything left after two days in your quarters. Let's ride, men," Butler shouted to his troops. "We got to make sure they follow Ames into that canyon and we don't let them out again."

Flaming Star had turned to speak to Night Rider when he saw the flash of light from a hill behind them. He realized the soldiers before them had been riding slowly, as if going nowhere. As they neared the entrance to the canyon, he realized where they were heading, or being led. He reined in sharply and yelled, "Stop! It is a trap! I saw their signal. This is the only path to and from this place." He related his observations and suspicions, and the others concluded he could be right.

The warriors concealed themselves to check out this suspicion before pursuing the men ahead of them, which soon proved to be a wise decision when a large troop passed, led by the man wearing a red bandana. It was obvious another clever trap was in progress. As there were too many soldiers to challenge, the Oglala band had no choice but to slip away carefully, which galled Bright Arrow, who had recognized Clarence Smith—his father's slayer—among them.

"Good Tracker, take the duty and *coup* for slaying the white-eyes who sent the shiny signals; it will be our warning, to show them they cannot trick us. Slay him and join us as we ride. We will seek out this General Cooper to see if he is all they claim," Gray Eagle's oldest son scoffed irritably, for he was fatigued from his exertions and lack of sleep and from his minor defeat, and he was perturbed by the evil soldier who seemed to know their moves and thoughts.

The band rode in the direction from which Cooper and his regiment were said to be approaching. Once that joined the one at Fort Dakota, it would be difficult to battle such a combined force. The warriors rested little all day. By the time they sighted the large regiment, which had just halted for the night, it was after six o'clock. The soldiers looked tired, as if they had been pressed onward at a murderous pace. It appeared that they were setting up camp for more than one night in this spot. The Oglalas concealed themselves in the woods to wait for dark to arrive, resting and sleeping and eating as they did so. Good Tracker arrived, grinning in pleasure and victory.

"They will be slow to seek to trap us again," Bright Arrow praised his friend's success, then focused on the task at hand. "We will sneak to their camp as we did the fort and hear their plans," he suggested, as the quarter moon put out little light to expose their approach.

Night Rider argued, "There are many of them; they camp in the open, and there are guards everywhere. This leader is careful and cunning. I say it is too dangerous to sneak to their tepees, and few are awake to talk," he remarked on the exhausted camp.

"If you do not wish to help us, Night Rider, Flaming Star and Bright Arrow will go alone," Bright Arrow informed him peevishly. "How can we defeat men and plans which we do not know?"

Touch-the-sky protested, "Do not endanger your life to seek the man with flaming hair and sky eyes. You can slay him another sun or moon. Night Rider's words are true and wise; it is too risky."

"On the last moon, did you not say it is better to die than to surrender? Allowing this chance to learn about our worst and newest foe to slip from our grasp is a defeat we cannot accept. If we must risk our lives for our poeple's safety and survival, so it must be. I will not try to find and slay my former foe; I will only seek information to help our people in this new war. I wish to study this new leader before he is hidden behind the fort walls," Bright Arrow debated, duping the others and himself, for he truly did not realize how much he had to prove to himself if Timothy Moore was in that camp nearby.

Good Tracker remarked, "If I could speak or understand the white man's tongue, I would go with you, my friend and future chief."

"You are brave and cunning, my friend Good Tracker. There is little light from *Hunwi's* face, so we will be hidden in the darkness. Many do sleep, so our task is easier. We will seek those who are restless in mind and body, and learn why."

Flaming Star eyed his friend intently, and worried. He, too, was against this action, but he would follow the band leader's orders. He could tell that Night Rider and Touch-the-sky were annoyed with Bright Arrow, but the others appeared pleased with his words and deeds.

It was hours before Bright Arrow rejoined them, holding a blue and yellow uniform in his hand. All eyes widened as they viewed his newly cut hair, which was resting far above his shoulders, and listened to his recent behavior: he had slain a soldier, stolen a uniform, cut his hair shorter, and visited the center of the camp in his disguise!

"I will save this, for I may need it again," the overly confident warrior announced. "It is a good trick. Perhaps we should steal many uniforms and fool them during a raid."

"We cannot pass for white as you can," Night Rider reminded him.

"That does not matter. We need only to fool them until we can get within striking distance," Bright Arrow reasoned wishfully.

"That would work only at night, and only if we also stole their horses and gear," Touch-the-sky debated his confidence and reckless idea.

"We will decide that matter another time. What did you learn?" Flaming Star asked eagerly.

"He is there," Bright Arrow carelessly revealed. "I could not get to him, for two soldiers guard his tepee. Another sun, and he will die."

"Why did you not slay his guards? To kill their leader would bring disunity and confusion," Night Rider inquired in dissatisfaction.

"Their leader?" Bright Arrow echoed, exposing the warrior's mistaken impression before he could halt his words. "I could not get near his tepee," he quickly explained, "for many guards are posted around it. I see he fears the Oglalas before he confronts us. It is good. I did hear two white-eyes talking who are angry with him, as are most. He has forced them to march all day and half the night for weeks, for he is eager to get to Fort Dakota to take control. They said he is heartless; they do not like or respect him; this is good. They did not wish to come to our lands and battle us; they are afraid. They do not know my father is dead; this news has been kept from them."

"We must use this fear," Night Rider suggested.

"Yes, we must use this fear of the Oglalas and Gray Eagle," he agreed. Unaware Cooper had altered his plans without informing his troops, Bright Arrow reported what he had overheard, "The leader, General Cooper, plans to leave half of his men and supplies here to fool us, for he thinks we may be watching the fort and he does not wish us to know how strong they are. We must seek help from other tribes to attack here and destroy half of them while they are divided."

"Will the one with flaming hair be left behind?" Night Rider asked.

Bright Arrow turned and eyed him strangely. "Yes," he replied.

"It would take many warriors to destroy this camp. That would leave our camp and others vulnerable to this new leader."

"More vulnerable than after they unite and ride against us, Touch-the-sky? We must strike swiftly and lethally while we are strongest."

"What of the war council in three moons? It will take nearly two suns to get home and to ride to where it will meet. How long will these bluecoats camp here? Is there time to warn others and collect warriors to help us? It will not look good if you are not present at the council."

"Your words are wise and true, Night Rider, but which is more important: losing this chance to even the odds once more or attending a council where men will talk until the sun rises before they decide to do what is best for all? We must strike before they know we have discovered this camp and their plans."

"They will know as soon as they find the soldier's body."

Flaming Star suggested, "Why not take it with us? It will look as if he has run away during the night, if we hide our tracks."

"It is good, my friend," Bright Arrow concurred, smiling.

Night Rider, a Sacred Bow carrier, and Touch-the-sky, a shirt wearer, both eyed Bright Arrow closely and curiously, and both decided they should watch him and his deeds even closer in the future, before the next vote for chief . . .

The Oglala band rode for hours, with two warriors trailing them and covering their tracks. Flaming Star noticed how often Bright Arrow grimaced in discomfort and gingerly rubbed his left forearm. When they halted to rest, he demanded to look at it, and discovered one of Bright Arrow's "mourning cuts" had become infected.

"See how it festers and flames? We must build a fire to clean it and burn it, or it will poison your body and mind," his friend warned.

"No, we must ride home quickly," Bright Arrow protested.

"If we do not tend this injury, you will not live to battle your foe again," his friend retorted almost angrily, aware that Bright Arrow's actions were not sitting well with some of his band, nor with him.

Their gazes met, and Flaming Star frowned. "You must clear your head of revenge, my brother, for it worries others and causes them to doubt your motives," he whispered in deep concern. "You must know when to ride and when to halt. These past suns have been hard on each of us. Remember the bluecoats' words against their leader who pushes them too hard and long," he hinted meaningfully.

Bright Arrow stole a glance around his camp, and realized his friend was right. "Do what must be done, Flaming Star."

The eldest son of White Arrow built a fire, heated his knife, and prepared a potion from his own *pezuta wopahte,* medicine bundle. He lanced the injury, drained it, sealed it with his white-hot blade, placed a mixture of healing herbs on it, then wrapped it with a stolen cloth. He looked at Bright Arrow, whose pallor, glazed eyes, beads of sweat, and quiverings exposed his sorry condition.

"We must go," Bright Arrow said, wincing with pain as he tried to rise. When his friend firmly pressed him to the sleeping mat, he asked, "What if a foe saw our fire? If we are attacked and I cannot ride, you must leave me and save yourselves." He felt weak and shaky, for it had taken all of his strength and courage to hold still and quiet while Flaming Star tended his throbbing arm. He wished his brother's words about the danger of such cuts would leave his troubled mind.

"No. The fire is out and we will set a guard. The horses must rest and graze, and we must eat and sleep," Flaming Star refuted. "Take this," he offered, pushing a piece of a medicinal root into his friend's mouth to ease his pain and to help him sleep.

Miles apart, many things took place on the second of May. General Philip Cooper disguised himself as a captain, took only a few of his men, and left his camp to complete his arduous journey to Fort Dakota, where he would claim to be an advance unit sent to "let the commander and soldiers there know that General Cooper would be arriving in three or four days," but actually his devious plan was to check out the men without their knowledge. Major Timothy Moore was left behind to take charge of this secret camp and to arrive at Fort Dakota on the morning of the fifth with half of the troops, while the other half were to arrive on the seventh, unless Cooper changed those orders.

Near the fort, Captain Clarence Smith left a message for Silver Hawk in the usual manner and place, asking for a meeting the day after the war council on Friday, which his Indian scouts had discovered.

Far away, Bright Arrow and his band rode swiftly toward their camp. Singing Wind and Silver Hawk made separate plans to visit the Oglala camp. Little Feet and Thunder Spirit prepared for their joining the next morning; Tashina helped her sister and fretted over her own impending fate; and Sun Cloud did whatever was needed by his people.

On the morning of May third, Little Feet and Thunder Spirit were joined by the ceremonial chief. As they raced happily into their new tepee, Tashina and Sun Cloud took charge of her two small sons. Tashina had no way of knowing that far away, her true love had just learned of her claim by Silver Hawk and of Bright Arrow's shocking acceptance . . .

Nearing the midday meal before the afternoon rest period, two guests arrived at the Oglala camp: Silver Hawk and Singing Wind. When Sun Cloud was told by Deer Stalker of their arrival and presence in Bright Arrow's tepee, he could not imagine staying there as promised to help care for Little Feet's sons. Sleep near his lost love . . . Four moons had passed since Bright Arrow had announced their imminent joining, and she had not come to explain it or to deny it. He had to remember his pride and rank; he must not reveal any anguish or desire where she was concerned. He hated to leave Tashina with Silver Hawk, but they would not be alone.

He realized he could not stall returning to camp any longer; the boys were getting hungry and sleepy after the long walk to fatigue them for Tashina so they would nap peacefully while he was gone hunting and their mother was enjoying her new husband. As they headed back, he encountered Little Flower, Dull Knife's daughter. The girl boldly sent him an enticing smile and swayed her hips seductively as she caught his eyes upon her. She moistened her lips in a wickedly suggestive manner and headed toward him. Sun Cloud decided there was no better way to prove his disinterest in one female than by showing interest in another one, and he could not allow Silver Hawk or anyone to notice his hunger for Singing Wind, or hers for him. He sent the girl a sensual smile and asked her to walk with them, making sure they laughed and chatted merrily all the way to Bright Arrow's tepee.

By the time they reached it, Little Flower had asked Sun Cloud to join her family for the coming meal; he had thrilled, and duped, her by accepting eagerly. Responding to his seemingly receptive mood, the enchanted girl flirted openly and sultrily with him, and he pretended to enjoy it and return it. Fortunately, there were no Oglalas close enough during the mealtime to observe this curious sight.

From where the two Blackfeet were standing, they glimpsed the couple and children who were approaching the tepee. Tashina had left earlier to fetch fresh water and firewood. Silver Hawk commented, "I hear he has stolen many girls' treasures, but all fear to reveal it and dishonor themselves. See how he works his magic on her. After he lures her to his mats, he will go chasing another fringed skirt. I hear he has a stick which he notches with each conquest and it is nearly full. A female is a fool to give him her best treasure before he gives her a joining necklace, for Sun Cloud will join only the female he cannot have without it. It is good you will join his brother instead of him, as even you would have trouble keeping him faithful. No doubt he will need many wives to cool his fiery blood and to feed his greedy appetite. Many say he is more skilled on the sleeping mat than battleground."

Little Feet's boys, Sun Cloud, and Little Flower entered the tepee to find a male guest there, for Singing Wind, backed against the covering near the open flap, went unnoticed for a time, by all except Sun Cloud who sensed her presence nearby. In the excitement, the boys rushed forward to seize the fruit pones which Tashina had made for them, and the others exchanged amiable greetings.

"Silver Hawk, it is good to see you, my friend and brother," Sun Cloud said, smiling and clasping the man's arm, his mood implying he was relaxed and happy. "Where is your mate to be?" he asked casually. "You are lucky to have captured the most beautiful and rarest flower around."

After Silver Hawk replied, Sun Cloud smiled and said, "Buffalo Boy and Spirit Sign are to eat and sleep here with Tashina, for Little Feet and Thunder Spirit were joined this sun and wish to be alone," he disclosed with a lewdly mischievous grin. "I go to eat with Little Flower in the tepee of her father Dull Knife. If Tashina has not prepared enough food for guests, tell her to send for me and I will seek a rabbit to roast before I eat with my"—he glanced at Little Flower, his eyes roving her suggestively before he finished in a sensuous tone which belied his simple word—"friends." He inquired, "Do you need me to remain here to watch them until Tashina returns? Little Flower can go to her tepee and tell her family I will be there soon."

"There is no need to wait; the boys can stay with us until Tashina returns,"

Singing Wind said as she stepped forward to join them, and seized everyone's attention with her voice and beauty. "She has prepared plenty of food for all. She will make my brother a good wife."

"And Silver Hawk will make Tashina a good husband," Sun Cloud replied smoothly as he nodded a casual greeting to her. He added in a deceptively calm and genial tone, "As Bright Arrow will make Singing Wind a good mate. It is good our tribes will be twice bound through our families. I am sure Tashina told you her father is away, but he was to return this sun or the next, if you wish to wait for him. Do not worry over your love; he is safe. I have not seen my brother this happy since before Wahea was lost. It is good you returned the glow to his eyes and face. When he revealed your joining plans, his eyes and voice exposed his great love and desire for Singing Wind."

A compelling smile was sent to her as Sun Cloud said, "If you feel as he does, you will be happy with him. Soon, you will be my sister, and I will be a good brother to you. If you have needs while he is away, speak them to me. When he is gone, I protect his family for him and provide for them. I will do the same for my brother's new mate."

Singing Wind could not tell if Sun Cloud was speaking words with dual meanings, for his expression and tone imported only friendliness and joy. Today, he was like a casual acquaintance or a stranger. She could not believe how easily he was accepting this situation, and it troubled her deeply to think her impending union with another man did not bother him in the slightest. He behaved and sounded as if he was delighted she was going to join his brother, as if there had been nothing special between them. He even talked as if Bright Arrow were actually in love with her and that fact pleased him! She was tormented and bewildered. She had come seeking the truth, not to visit Bright Arrow. If only she could speak privately with Sun Cloud, but that was impossible. Jealousy chewed viciously at her as Little Flower cuddled against him and he sent the girl a smile which could melt her flesh. Perhaps, she angrily decided, Silver Hawk was right; Sun Cloud only sought and enjoyed daring conquests, and she was no longer a temptation.

Holding herself under rigid control, Singing Wind replied just as nonchalantly, "You are very generous, Sun Cloud. You will make a good brother, and I am sure I will need you many times. You do not mind if your brother replaces Wahea with me?" she probed craftily.

"No, a man must push aside his painful past and go on with his life. Do not worry; you mean more to your love than any woman ever has. I have been told of the visions of Silver Hawk, Bright Arrow, and Singing Wind; your union with the Oglala chief is the will of the Great Spirit, and must not be resisted." Sun Cloud chuckled playfully and teased, "This news surprised me when I heard it in council, for you and my brother kept your love and plans a secret from all."

As his words and their laws settled in on her, Singing Wind experienced a surge of pleasure and suspense. Maybe . . . She must be careful about hints before her brother, so she held back the reply she wanted to make: *So was I, when I was told all and commanded to obey!* Instead, she laughed mirthfully and said, "Sometimes it is best to keep secrets until the right time to reveal them. I would have told you, but I have not seen you since it was decided. We will wait for Bright Arrow's return, if there is space and you do not mind."

"There is space, for Sun Cloud lives in the tepee of Mind-who-Roams until his gets a new tepee," he informed her. He glanced at Silver Hawk and ventured devilishly, "I am sure my Blackfeet brother also wishes to spend time with his love and future mate."

Silver Hawk laughed heartily and nodded, for he assumed he had finally succeeded in disarming and deceiving Sun Cloud. The timing was perfect when Little Flower left to tell her family about their meal guest and Singing Wind dropped to her knees to pour the boys some water, for Silver Hawk asked, "When will you seek your own tepee?"

Sun Cloud lowered his voice as if the two men were speaking privately, but he knew Singing Wind could hear them and was listening. "When I find a female who is special in the light and in the dark, I will claim her quickly before another steals her. If I find her and win her, I will build a new tepee and join her that same sun. If it is not so before winter, I will build a new tepee, then find a slave to care for me until I can seek her again." Singing Wind was behind Sun Cloud after he placed his weapons nearby. As he continued, one hand rested over his buttocks and his fingers irresistibly stroked her hair. "You must tell me your secrets, Silver Hawk; you will soon have two mates, and I have none. What do I do wrong? When Tashina, Little Feet, and Bright Arrow are joined, I will be alone. Perhaps I should look and work harder on this matter."

"What of Little Flower? She is pretty and has fires burning for you."

Sun Cloud shook his head. "She chatters like a busy squirrel. I have seen no female in our camp who stands beyond the others."

"Why do you not come to my camp and look among our females?"

Sun Cloud's breath caught in his throat as he felt Singing Wind's tongue tease the palm of his hand. He defensively shifted it to his hip, for the sensation and its meaning inflamed his mind and body. This was crazy, to fool around with his brother's promised, in his brother's tepee, with his worst foe standing nearby! "We must ride to the war council on the new sun. Soon, we will be battling our foes. There is little time for such personal matters."

"You must take the time, my brother and friend. If you are slain, you must not carry your bloodline with you. That is why I came to speak with Bright Arrow. I must join with Tashina before this new season of battles, for Shining Feather can give me no sons."

Sun Cloud asked himself whatever was he thinking and doing to send out wanton enticements with words and actions toward his brother's promised. And what was Singing Wind doing and thinking to behave this way toward him after promising herself to his brother? Was it a joke or a test? Or did she want him, only him? Or did she desire both of Gray Eagle's sons? "I will do as you say, Silver Hawk. We will speak after the war council. Soon, you could be chief, and you will have need of sons. I must go, for the family of Dull Knife waits for me." He turned to Singing Wind who was kneeling with her back to them and said, "If I do not see you again before the joining ceremony, be safe and happy. It is good for the son of Gray Eagle to win the daughter of Brave Bear. Our lives have touched many times for many seasons."

Singing Wind stood and faced him. "Guard your life, my brother. Perhaps the Great Spirit will send you a new mate soon."

"It will be good; I have remained to myself too long." He knew remaining near her any longer was perilous, so he left.

Silver Hawk remarked, "Sun Cloud has changed since his parents' deaths and the discovery of his people's choice of his brother as chief."

Singing Wind did not want to quarrel with him, so she replied, "It is good for a man to lose all extra pride and boldness. His hardness and coldness have lessened, and that is good too. He did not tease me or insult me this sun, and I am glad, since we are to be a family soon."

"You have changed too, sister. You are mellow and obedient."

"My life has changed, so I must change with it. I cannot do my duty if I remain as I was. I pray you will feel and do the same."

"I am restless. I will go for a long ride. Tell Tashina I will return before dark." Yes, he should check the message place one last time, to make certain nothing was left there to implicate him.

"But what of eating?" she inquired.

"I am not hungry. Perhaps I will hunt awhile. Tashina will be busy with Little Feet's sons and will have no time to talk until later. I will scout around and see if Bright Arrow is nearing camp."

Singing Wind watched her brother depart, and wondered why he was leaving when the boys would be asleep for hours soon. She was tempted to follow him, but could not leave the children alone. She fed them and placed them on their sleeping mats, wondering why it was taking Tashina so long to return.

Singing Wind stood in the opening, to catch the refreshing breeze and to observe the tepee of Dull Knife. She had to learn if Little Flower left during the rest period to follow Sun Cloud into the forest. She scolded herself for her behavior earlier. She loved and desired Sun Cloud, but she was promised to another. They had to forget what had happened between them near the pond. They had to forget and to ignore each other. They had to resist each other's temptation. She had to stop searching for double meanings in his words and looks.

Yet, if she did not expose the truth to Sun Cloud, there was no telling what he would think or feel about her, after the pond incident, after her sudden claim by his brother, and after her behavior earlier. She had to know if she had meant anything special to him.

When one of the boys whimpered, Singing Wind went to check on him, then returned to the entrance after deciding it had been nothing more than a tiny bad dream which was gone now. During her absence, Sun Cloud had left Dull Knife's tepee and gone hunting, unaware that Silver Hawk was gone and Tashina had not returned, leaving his love alone.

Finally, Tashina returned. "I am sorry, Singing Wind. Pretty Red Fox gave birth to a son in the forest while we were gathering wood. It happened so quickly there was no time to seek help until it was over. I have seen very few babies come so swiftly and without warning. Where are the others?" she asked.

"Sun Cloud eats and talks with Dull Knife. Silver Hawk went riding. He will return before dark. He was restless being near his chosen one and being unable to share private words and touches."

Tashina blushed. "Did he say such things?" she asked worriedly.

Singing Wind caught Tashina's undercurrents of fear and dread. "You do not love my brother or wish to join with him, do you?"

Tashina knew her face and voice had given away her feelings, so there was no reason to lie to her friend, and she desperately needed to discuss this matter with another female. "No, it was decided for me and I was ordered to do my duty to my father and people. I am trapped, for I love and desire another. Do you hate me and think badly of me because I cannot bear the thought of joining your brother?"

"How can I, Tashina? I am trapped by my duty and orders, but I feel as you do. I do not love or desire your father," she revealed.

Chapter Fourteen

right Arrow and his band returned shortly after the rest period and called for the council to be summoned for their report. When he learned of his guests, he hurried to his tepee, to find only Singing Wind there preparing wild vegetables for the stew for their evening meal.

"It is good to see you, Singing Wind," he murmured joyfully. "I am glad you came. We have much to decide. I am honored you accepted my joining claim, but I do not know why it took me so long to ask for you. There is no other female in our lands who stirs my heart and body as you do. I promise I will make you a good husband and lover. At last, I can be happy and whole again. Where are the others?"

Singing Wind was touched, and distressed, by his words and mood. She wished he did not want her. She wished he would release her from his claim so she could go to his brother. How could she make him a good wife when she was the mate of another in her heart, and in her body? Why had he not come to her before Sun Cloud had revealed his desire, before she had learned what it was to have his brother, and hopefully his brother's love? Bright Arrow was good and kind and virile and handsome; but he was not Sun Cloud. Yet, how could she hurt this man or refuse her duty? Agony without end, for she could not.

"Tashina is preparing the meal for Pretty Red Fox; she had her child when the sun was overhead. Tashina helped him into the world while they were gathering wood, and they named him Comes Quickly. My brother rides to scout and hunt, and will return soon. Sun Cloud also hunts for those in need." Fearing to hesitate on that soul-stirring name, she hurriedly went on, "Your grandsons have returned to their mother in her new tepee. Little Feet is very happy with her new mate. You know they were joined after the sun returned?" she hinted.

Bright Arrow unthinkingly revealed, "It is good they have joined, for they have been much in love for many winters. It was not good they were separated through their own foolishness. New lovers need time alone; I will visit them later. The call has gone out for council."

"Your arm is hurt," she remarked, noticing the soiled cloth on it. "I must tend it and change your binding."

Bright Arrow allowed her to mix a potion, to remove the dressing, clean the injury, and treat it. He enjoyed her gentle touch and nearness, her fresh smell, soft skin, and abundant appeal. She was the most beautiful Indian maiden he had seen. It had been a year since he had touched a female, and his body was responding rapidly to her. He wished she was Rebecca Kenny, but that life and love were gone forever. He had to reach out to this female who would be his wife soon. In time, he might come to love her, for it was easy to desire her.

"You must have it tended each sun, Bright Arrow, for it is red with anger and gathering poison. It might cause your arm to grow weak with pain and your head cloudy with fever. Why must men always be stubborn and careless with such things?" she softly scolded him. "A man of much wisdom and strength knows when he must yield to his body's weakness and needs. To deny them is foolish."

He lifted her hands and kissed each fingertip. "I will obey you, for you are wise and enchanting. Your touch is very gentle and warming, little heartfire." As he pressed a kiss to each knuckle and palm, he teased huskily, "No wonder my arm flames with fire, my whole body burns at your nearness and attention. See how I quiver with eagerness? I have taken no woman but Wahea to a mat since I met my wife over twenty winters past. I will be as true to you, Singing Wind, for my heart has room for only one love and woman, as I give all of myself to her and our union." His fingers brushed over her lips and he gazed into her golden brown eyes as he vowed, "If you need help, we will find you a slave, for I desire only you as my mate. We must join soon, for I grow wild to have you near me at all times. You fill my head and heart."

He captured her chin and pulled her face to his, sealing their lips. His fingers wandered into her silky hair and his mouth greedily explored hers, for she could not decide if or how she should resist him.

Sun Cloud peeked inside the tepee and his heart ached at the scene which he viewed, for he had arrived as his brother was kissing each fingertip and making his sultry confession. As Singing Wind was not resisting Bright Arrow, he assumed she was responding, and was agreeable to the union which was set between them. He could not let them know he had witnessed this tormenting sight, so he left quickly.

It was Tashina who interrupted them with her return. She was baffled by what she observed, for she had believed both were in love with others. Too, the flap was not closed to indicate privacy. "I have returned, Singing Wind," she called out to catch their attention as she ducked to enter, pretending she saw nothing.

"It is good to see you, Father," Tashina added as she looked at him and smiled. "How was your journey? You are injured?"

"It is good to see you, daughter. It is a small injury from my mourning cut. Do not worry; Singing Wind has tended it for me. All went good on our mission. When the council meeting is over, we will talk of our joinings. Perhaps they can be on the same moon."

Neither female replied as he grinned and left. "What will we do?" Tashina asked in dread. "What if they set the joining date for soon? Have you changed your mind about my father?"

Singing Wind gave it some thought and answered, "We will use our woman's ways to stall it as long as possible. All is resting upon their visions; we must find a way to prove they are wrong."

"What if we cannot?" the younger female questioned in panic.

"Then you must join Silver Hawk and I must join Bright Arrow."

* * *

The Oglala council met and a full report was given, even the parts which Bright Arrow wished he could hold secret. His arm was aching again, and he wanted the council over so he could chew the special root which removed his pain, but also his consciousness. He was tense and irritable, impatient and uneasy. He hated going through all of this again, and it showed. It did not help when Night Rider and Touch-the-sky gave their reports and impressions, for neither gave Bright Arrow credit for their success, but did for their minor defeats.

Matters grew worse for Bright Arrow when war chief Big Elk was the one to relate Sun Cloud's newest *coups*. It was clear to everyone that Sun Cloud's deeds far outweighed Bright Arrow's information. It was also clear that several council members and high-ranking warriors were being drawn toward Sun Cloud.

Sun Cloud was dismayed by what he was perceiving. He said, "My brother is injured and feverish. He needs to rest before we ride to the war council on the new sun. He has gathered many important facts for us, and we must think carefully on them. His plan to attack small bands is a clever one, and we must use it. If there is no more to discuss, we all need food and rest, for our journey is upon us."

Bright Arrow glanced at his brother and frowned, for Sun Cloud's words seemingly pointed out his weakness and tension. "I am fine, my brother. There is no need to end the council early for me."

Big Elk said, "There is nothing more to say until after the war council. We must plan how to use the whites' fears and rivalries against them, but we must not attack their new camp until we have help from our allies. Do not worry over the whites' words, for they do not know our ways. If all goes well, you can be the one to slay Flaming Hair. I am pleased you did not fall into the bluecoat's trap. You were wise to save the bluecoat's garment; we may have need of it. Return to your future mate and share time with her before the sun sleeps."

Bright Arrow snipped, "No sun has gone to sleep on a day when a woman is more important than missions or a council meeting."

Mind-who-Roams ventured, "You are weary and injured, Bright Arrow. You must make yourself strong to ride for your people again. Return to your tepee; I will send a special herb to you to ease your pain."

Flaming Star squeezed Bright Arrow's arm to caution him against speaking sharply again, and Bright Arrow, suddenly realizing how foolish he was being, said, "Forgive me, for I am weary and injured. I will do as my council says, for they are wise and kind. Many good and brave men rode with me; at the next council, I must tell of their *coups*. No men could do more to help than Flaming Star, Good Tracker, Night Rider, and Touch-the-sky. When I was about to make errors in my eagerness and illness, they halted me or corrected me. I thank them and honor them. I will think and plan while I rest."

If any two women could be grateful for the bad luck of others, Tashina and Singing Wind were that night. Pretty Red Fox was weak and sick, and asked Tashina if she would sleep in her tepee to help her care for her new child and husband, for she was an only wife. Tashina explained the problem to her father, then left quickly. As she fetched water, Sun Cloud approached her and they talked.

She confided her new fears and doubts to him, then asked, "Are you certain you can prevent my joining to Silver Hawk?"

"I will do all I can, Tashina. Pray I find victory soon, for your fate is tied to mine and to our people's," he responded sadly.

"And to Singing Wind's, for she is trapped too," she murmured absently. "I wish we could both be free of our duty and pain."

Sun Cloud looked at her and asked, "What do you mean?"

"I do not wish my father to be hurt by the loss of another woman he loves, but Singing Wind does not wish to join him. She loves another. As with me, she is being forced to join him. Father announced it in council before she was told. As with you, she says our fates depend on the truth of the visions, and she waits to have them proven wrong."

"Who is this man she loves?" he asked, his heart drumming wildly.

"I do not know; she said it was wrong to think or to speak of him while she is promised to another."

Sun Cloud questioned hoarsely, "Why has she kept this love a secret? Why did she agree to join my brother?"

"She could not speak of him to others until he made his claim on her. There was no time after she learned of their love, for her joining to my father had been accepted by Medicine Bear and spoken aloud by Father. He has not challenged for her or gone to her in love or anger, so she fears he does not love her as she loves him. What does it matter? Our laws and duties must come first with us and with our loves. Yet, I would rather die than accept Silver Hawk in my love's place."

Sun Cloud hugged her affectionately and coaxed, "You will join Soul-of-Thunder, I promise you, so do not worry this pretty head." As he watched her return to camp, he wished Singing Wind was not trapped in the tepee with Silver Hawk and Bright Arrow. Right or wrong, there was something he had to do very soon . . .

Bright Arrow had taken the medicine herb which the shaman had brought to him, so he was drowsy when Silver Hawk returned. It was a battle for him to stay awake long enough to relate his recent deeds. Singing Wind served her brother's meal, aware of his annoyance at the event which had taken Tashina from his grasp, but ignorant of his vexation toward the devious bluecoat who had left a message for him. Soon, Bright Arrow was asleep, taking her from his eager grasp. Silver Hawk left to speak with Sun Cloud, to see what he could learn about the council meeting, preventing her from going to her love secretly.

When Silver Hawk returned, he could not sleep. He tossed and turned until he was irritable. Singing Wind saw him as he sneaked the remaining medicine root and devoured it to help him sleep. Soon, both men were deep in peaceful slumber. Singing Wind was edgy too, for she was so close to her love, but unable to seek him in another's tepee. She decided to go for a swim, even if the camp was asleep and it was rash. She slipped from the tepee and made her way to the river. She walked down its bank for a ways, then stripped, and dove into the water.

When she surfaced and wiped her face of moisture, she found herself looking into the grinning face of Sun Cloud. She glanced around in alarm, then whispered, "What are you doing here? This is forbidden. Your brother could slay you for this offense."

Sun Cloud stepped toward her. She defensively tried to back away, her eyes wide with panic, but he gently seized her shoulders and pulled her against his nude body. His face came close to hers as he vowed confidently, "I do not believe you love and desire my brother or will be happy with him, for I own your heart and body. I cannot push our past aside and go on without you. No woman has touched me as you have. I believe it is the will of the Great Spirit for you to join the Oglala chief; that will be me after the vote is taken. I was coming to tell you of my love and to ask for your hand in joining from Medicine Bear after our council, but Bright Arrow announced his joining to you. I could not challenge him before I learned the truth from your lips, not without staining your life by revealing our stolen passion. If evil has separated us, we must destroy it to be joined. If it is the will of the Great Spirit for Bright Arrow to be chief and to win you, then I must tell you of my love, and I must have you one last time. And know, no other woman will ever take your place in my heart."

Singing Wind was stunned by his confession and suggestion. "If you love me and want me as you vow, how can you allow me to join your brother, or any other man? You have the right to me by first possession and can challenge for me."

"Challenge my own brother to the death? I cannot. He did not know about us when he asked for you and made a public claim on you. If I had known of his desires and plans for you, I would have spoken to him and halted this matter which rips out my heart. He has been misguided, but soon he will be enlightened; then he will release you to me. If I challenged and lost, all would know of your dishonor; I cannot do this evil thing to you, for I love you, Singing Wind, and wish no harm to come to you, from me or from others."

"It is no dishonor to love you," she protested his choice of words.

"To us, it is not; but to others, we both know it is viewed that way. I cannot slay my own brother. If he was not my brother, I would forget the shame we would endure and challenge for you this sun. There is another reason; to challenge for you when our love has been kept secret would make it appear I only seek to hurt him and to snatch the chief's bonnet for myself. Others do not know his vision is not from the Great Spirit. I must be chief, as is my duty to my people and to my father. We must be patient until Grandfather reveals this evil."

"Are you sure it is me you desire, or only the chief's bonnet?"

Anguish flooded his eyes. "If you must ask such a question, you do not know me or trust me. It is wrong to battle for our union."

"You are right. It is only that such fear lives within me. I have waited for you since I was born; now, I might lose you to evil. It clouds my mind and controls my tongue. I love and desire only you. Why must our laws bind us more to them than to each other?"

"We are bound by men's interpretation of them, but that changes nothing. We will win this battle, my love."

"Will we, Sun Cloud? Will we?" she asked frantically.

"If the vision is true, you are to join the Oglala chief. Do not agree to join Bright Arrow until he is chief, for it will not come to pass." His eyes roamed her face; then he smiled into her worried gaze. His hands left her shoulders to push her hair aside and to stroke it, relishing its texture. Unable to halt himself, he pulled her into his arms. He sighed happily when she cuddled against him, knowing she was there with eagerness and trust. He had longed for this moment since their meeting by the pond. He could feel her heart beating rapidly and he could feel her tremors, or were they his? This was perilous before everything was straightened out, but he could not help himself.

With Sun Cloud touching her and declaring his love for her, she could think of nothing except how much she loved him and wanted him. She knew how much they were risking, being together like this, but she could not resist this stolen moment. His smell tantalized her nose, and her hands wandered over his dark and sleek torso. He was so unique, so splendid, so perfect, so intoxicating.

He lifted her and carried her into the concealment of the trees and laid her upon the damp grass. Hungering to feel her flesh beneath his starving hands, he claimed her body, caressing here and there. He nibbled at her ears and shoulders, and teased his tongue over his favorite spot on her throat. His mouth took hers possessively, exploring and heightening their desires. His hands grew bolder as his passions burned brighter. His hot breath made her quiver and cling to him as his lips traveled down her neck and to her breasts.

Singing Wind dreamily trailed her fingers over his hairless frame. Her respiration had quickened with his movements, and she was tense with anticipation as she recalled their last and first union. Her entire body seemed to glow with the heat of his actions. He was enticing; he was stimulating; he was hers. No man could compare to him in looks or appeal. He was more important to her than her own life and honor. She was more alive in his arms than anywhere. He could take full control of her being, for she did not care and she yielded her all eagerly. Her body reacted to each touch, to each kiss, and seemingly pleaded for more and more. That day by the pond had been marvelous; but tonight, their contact was sheer ecstasy.

Sun Cloud's hand drifted down her taut stomach and across her sleek thighs, covered the dark domain which it located there. He could feel the heat radiating from it like a roaring fire. Bittersweet ecstasy filled him, for he wanted her instantly and urgently, but leisurely and gently. He called on all he knew and had heard to bring her to an almost unbearable height of arousal. His fingers invaded her secret domain and claimed it blissfully, causing her to moan and writhe as his mouth added further rapturous torment to her breasts and lips. He wished they had forever to make love, but they did not. The longer they lingered here in passion's fiery embrace, the more likely they were to be discovered. He worked swiftly and greedily to prepare her to accept his entrance, but she had been ready for him long ago.

Singing Wind's body and mind were ensnared by the delightful sensations which he was creating and stimulating. She wanted to relax and enjoy them, but she was too tense and ravenous to stall her feeding much longer. Each action brought bliss and sated one need, while tormenting her and inspiring a deeper need which demanded appeasement. She could lie there forever, allowing him to have his way with her.

Sun Cloud moved between her parted thighs and very slowly entered her, staggering both of them with the heady contact. As he set his pattern, she joined him. Their bodies moved to and fro in a magical dance of love. When he began to tease her sensuously by nearly withdrawing between each stroke, she wrapped her legs around him and captured him tightly against her womanhood. Their mouths fused feverishly as they performed their own magical dance of love. Soon, neither could contain their hunger and they demanded to feast on delectable passion. Their bodies worked in unison as they sought the ultimate peak of pleasure, and found it together.

He murmured over and over in her ear, "I love you, I love you, I love you, Singing Wind. You are mine forever and beyond as with my mother and father. One day our love and passion will rival theirs."

Singing Wind kissed him and hugged him fiercely while the stunning release to her tension struck her forcefully, as did his words. "I love you, Sun Cloud. I will never give myself to another, for I am yours," she vowed as she began her downward spiral into a tranquil state.

Still, they kissed and pressed close together, knowing how long it would be until they were together this way again. Their hearts drummed heavily and they were wet with love's laborious perspiration. It was difficult to breathe after their passionate task and between kisses, but they did not mind.

Sun Cloud finally leaned away from her and gazed into her lovely face. Moonlight played over her naked and damp flesh with its rosy glow. Sated passion caused her eyes to darken and soften. She was a mixture of innocence and earthy sensuality. His hands caressed her cheeks and teased over her glistening skin. She was powerful magic; she was irresistible allure; she was heady enchantment; she was his.

Her fingertips lovingly and appreciatively grazed his jawline and traced over his shadowed features. "If this is the last time you have me, you will never be able to forget me or to replace me," she teased provocatively, then mischievously seized his hair to pull his mouth back to hers. Her mouth meshed with his and tasted his response.

When their lips parted, his teeth playfully grasped her lower lip and tugged on it. His eyes were filled with devilish mirth, but she could barely read it, for he was still above her in the shadows, and still within her body. He did not move aside or withdraw, for his manhood was growing large and hot with renewed desire. As he began to move seductively, he saw her smile knowingly, then lift her arms to encircle his neck. He heard her moan in rising desire and felt her arch to meet him. Soon, they were making love again.

Later, he lifted her as before, this time returning her to the water. He sat in the chest high section and placed her on his lap. As his lips worked upon hers, his hands sensuously bathed her.

When he lingered too long and too enticingly in her private domain, she laughed against his lips and murmured, "Do you have such hunger and stamina that you can make love three times each night?"

His merry gaze met hers as he replied, "I have never done so before, but you inspire me and arouse me as no woman ever has before. I cannot seem to have my fill of you, even though each feeding seems matchless. I am like the earth in the hottest summer; each time you rain love on me, I savor it, only to dry quickly and demand more of love's refreshing and enlivening liquid. If you are near, I crave you." He nuzzled her ear as he added, "When you are not, I pain for you."

"Then quickly prove our brother's visions are false or wrong, so we will not suffer apart. My body needs love's rain each sun and moon."

"Love's rain? Or mine?" he taunted, nibbling at her earlobe.

Her gaze locked with his as she vowed, "Only yours, my love, only yours." Their lips sealed in another blazing kiss.

It was difficult, but he pulled her arms from his neck. "We must go, my love, for we tempt danger by remaining here too long."

"It is so hard to leave you, to return to our pretenses."

"I know, my love. Swear you will not be angry at my next words."

She stiffened slightly and gazed at him as if to mutely say, please do not spoil this time together. "I swear," she hesitantly replied.

He suggested in a strained voice, "Watch over Medicine Bear. With his sons dead and Silver Hawk standing one step from the Blackfeet chief's bonnet, I fear for his life. If your brother's vision is true, your chief and father must die for it to come to pass."

Singing Wind shifted her position from his lap to between his legs, her knees sinking in the soft mud on the river bottom. She gazed into his entreating eyes and placed her hands upon his shoulders. "You are still suspicious of him, are you not?" she probed.

He did not want to reply, at least not honestly, but did. "Yes."

She smiled and caressed his cheek, for he had trusted her and their love enough to be honest. "He left camp while you were eating with Dull Knife and did not return until it was eating time again. He was tense and angry, at more than Tashina's absence," she confessed painfully. "I do not wish to accept it or to speak it, but there is a bad spirit in him, one I have viewed and denied too long. He causes stirrings of doubt and fear within me, and your words tell me why. Perhaps it is wrong, but I will watch over Medicine Bear, and I will watch my brother. I do not believe his vision is true, but I cannot explain Bright Arrow's, for he is not like Silver Hawk and would not lie about the Great Spirit's message. Silver Hawk desires Tashina and the chief's bonnet, and I fear he will do anything to win them." She related her past talks with her brother, especially those involving him and her and Bright Arrow. "You trick him, for you are not his friend."

"I am sorry he is your brother and the son of Brave Bear, but I must not allow him to join his evil and greed to those of the white man. If he is wrong, I must do all I can to expose him and punish him. Will you still love me and join me if I must . . . destroy him for his evil?"

She realized how confident he was about their relationship to speak so openly. "You must do what is best for our people. If he is bad, you must punish him. If he is evil, you must . . . destroy him. I beg you, my love, be sure you are right before you take either action against him, for others might be as blind as I was and may side with him."

He hugged her so fiercely that she could hardly breathe. Love and gratitude shone brightly in his eyes. "I was right to choose you, Singing Wind, for you stand above all other women, as my mother did. No other woman could have won my heart. One day our love and passion will rival those of Gray Eagle and Shalee. You have her same mixture of strength and gentleness. You have her same courage and cunning. You have her same wisdom and pride. You take much and you give much, as it should be. You are mine forever and beyond."

As she had done earlier, Singing Wind's fingertips traced his proud chin and full lips, then trailed over his nose and across his forehead. She wanted to know, to touch, to admire, to kiss every inch of him. As before, she playfully seized his hair on either side of his arresting face and pulled his mouth to hers, fusing their lips as she straddled his lap and brought their private domains into intimate contact. She spread kisses over his face, then the top of his wet head as his mouth searched for and found her taut breasts and lavished attention on them.

He gazed into her serene eyes and revealed, "Shalee knew of my love and desire for you, and they pleased her. When I tried to speak of you to her, she laughed and said she had seen the signs for a long time. She guessed I had not discovered this truth long before I spoke to her. I told her of how I had tried to resist you, but could not. She said, 'Such is the way of love, my son.' She asked if you felt the same about me, and I joked about you resisting my magic as I had resisted yours. She said no female could resist me for I was my father's image in looks and ways. Their love is powerful and endless; even death cannot destroy it, as it will be with us. She said we would speak of you and of my taking the chief's bonnet after the war council, and my father agreed, for he knew he was no longer a top warrior and it was time for me to take his place. They did not live to see that sun."

His hands grasped her face and pulled it close to his. "I must have you and the chief's bonnet, my love; it is my destiny and my duty."

"With all my heart, I know your words and feelings are true. We will expose my brother's evil. We will prove his vision is false, and we will be free to join each other. I will stick to him as a feather to a greased hand. He will do and see nothing which I do not."

He cautioned worriedly, "Take no risks, Singing Wind. Do not return to your stubborn and daring ways. He is your brother, but he is dangerous. He would not hesitate to slay you or me to get his desires. Watch him, but do nothing more. Do not follow him or ask him questions. He will become suspicious; then all is lost. Promise to obey me, for I could not bear to see you harmed or to lose you forever. Please," he urged her, showing his inner emotions to her.

"You are right again. I would risk my life to expose such evil, but I will not risk yours, my love. We will wait and watch, for surely Grandfather will expose such evil. When can we be together again?"

"I do not know, my love. We must be careful until this mistake is corrected. I will try to find a time and place which are safe."

"If we tell Tashina, she could help us meet when her father is away."

"Tashina is young and in love. She is afraid. If trouble arises, she could tell all to free herself from her own trap. No one must know."

"I am still impulsive and selfish, for my mind is cloudy."

"Return to camp, and I will remain here for a time. Make sure you avoid me, or the truth will be as clear as spring water."

"I can sleep now, and calm my fears, for you will be mine," she stated confidently. "Be sure to avoid other women as you avoid me."

"Who could even stand in your shadow, Singing Wind? No one."

"As no one can stand in yours, Sun Cloud, no one." She kissed him and, after pulling on her garments, returned to camp.

In the Cheyenne camp, Soul-of-Thunder lay awake for hours as he deliberated his impending course of action. Finally, he slipped from his father's tepee and walked a short distance from camp, then sat on the ground with his legs crossed and his gaze on the partial moon.

"What troubles you so deeply, my son?" Windrider asked, which did not startle Soul-of-Thunder who had sensed his father's approach.

The younger Cheyenne warrior shifted his gaze to the older one. "As with my name, my spirit trembles as the earth when it thunders. I do not know if my father and my people will understand what I must do in two moons, for this is a bad time to do it," he murmured mysteriously. "But I have searched my heart and my head, and I must follow them, for they worked together. My life rests in the Great Spirit's hands."

"Speak of what troubles them," Windrider coaxed earnestly, taking a matching position close to his oldest son, whom he had tried not to love and favor over his other children, but it was difficult. This child was so much like him, and had brought great pride and joy to his heart. As a Dog Man and war chief, he was thrilled by his son's new rank; as a father, he was tormented by the numerous perils in it.

Soul-of-Thunder was proud of his father, their war chief and a survivor of the dog-rope season. He loved and respected his father above all men. His father was a great warrior, and a good man. Even Windrider's joining to a white woman named Bonnie Thorne, now called Sky Eyes, had changed no one's opinion of him. The somber male revealed, "After the war council on the next sun, I must ride to the Oglala camp to speak with your friend Bright Arrow . . . to challenge for Tashina in joining. After my words are spoken, I will return home to await the sun of my battle when Bright Arrow sends for me." He finished his unexpected confession by adding, "She is my love and my destiny, and Silver Hawk cannot have her. She loves and desires only me."

"Do you know what words you speak, my son? A death challenge. Silver Hawk is to be a chief. You are a dog-rope wearer. This is bad. We are at war with the white man. This will cause trouble for our tribes."

"It must be, Father, for I cannot live to see her bound to another. Our lives have been as one since you brought her to our camp long ago. We have waited until we were old enough to seek a tepee and union together. Silver Hawk cannot step between us. She was not approached about this joining, and she does not wish it. It is wrong to force her to join another when she loves me, when I love her. How can Bright Arrow say such a wicked thing is her duty to him and their people? Silver Hawk craves my love and his chief's bonnet, and he speaks falsely to get them. I say his vision is false, if there was a vision. If his words and claims are true, he will win our challenge. If they are not, I will return home with Tashina as my wife. It must be, Father."

"My son, my son," Windrider murmured worriedly, "you have no right to call for the death challenge. You know our laws and theirs."

"I am sorry to change your thoughts and feelings for me, Father, but I do have the right to challenge for her," he refuted pointedly.

"How can this be?" Windrider questioned in amazement. "You have taken the daughter of my friend to a sleeping mat?"

"We are in love and we plan to join. Our bodies burned so fiercely with the power of our love that we could not control our actions. Twice we have come together upon the sleeping mat, but we promised never to unite our bodies again until after we were joined, after my year as a Dog-rope wearer, if I survived it. She did not want to wait, but I refused to share a tepee with her until my danger was past. I was wrong not to announce my claim and to make her mine in joining. Now, she is trapped by Silver Hawk's and her father's dreams of glory."

"Do not speak badly of great warriors," his father warned. "Love and defeat steal your tongue and senses. Why did she not tell her father of your love and unions before he accepted Silver Hawk's claim?"

Soul-of-Thunder responded bitterly, "She was not asked her feelings or told of Silver Hawk's offer until it had been revealed to all in council. She was given to him as if a lifeless possession; this was wrong. She loves her father and feared to make his vision appear false by running away to me, for it would steal the chief's bonnet from his head. She feared it would cause Silver Hawk to death-challenge me for her. She is confused by what she feels and fears, and by what she is ordered to do. If her union with Silver Hawk was the will of Grandfather, He would not have placed love in our hearts for each other, and He would have prevented us from uniting our bodies. Grandfather does not halt all from doing mischief or evil, but He prevents it when it interferes with His will. Your friend was wrong and blind to give away his child before speaking to her. Would you give Heart Flower to Black Moon before asking her if she loved or desired another? No, you would not."

Soul-of-Thunder had made his point by using Windrider's lovely daughter and the worst warrior he could think of as his example. He reasoned urgently, "What if she carries my son, your first grandson, the bloodline of Windrider? How can I allow another man to take what is mine? I love her, Father. I need her. Do you recall how it was when Sky Eyes entered your life and land? You took her to your sleeping mat before you were joined, not because she was your slave, but because your heart and body burned for hers. That is how it was and is between me and Tashina. Help me win her, Father. Help me," he implored, in anguish which seized Windrider's heart and soul.

"Say nothing at the war council, my son. When it is over, I will ride with you to the Oglala camp to speak with my friend Bright Arrow. I will try to settle this matter without bloodshed. And without dishonoring Tashina. If this can be done quickly and easily, all will soon forget it, for our lives are surrounded by darker matters."

Soul-of-Thunder felt as if a burden were lifted from his body. He smiled and embraced his father. "All is good now, for Windrider will be at my side. You have been his friend longer and closer than Silver Hawk; he will listen to you. This is Grandfather's will; I am sure of it."

Windrider watched his son head for the river to enjoy an enlivening swim, for he would be able to sleep after his worry sweat was removed from his body. Windrider sighed heavily. Long ago he had nearly won the heart and hand of Rebecca Kenny, Tashina's mother. It had not been meant to be. Now, his son was after the heart and hand of Rebecca's daughter, and perhaps that was not meant to be . . .

Chapter Fifteen

The joint war council, which took place in another spot and nearer to the Oglala camp this time, went smoothly and rapidly, for all involved in the impending strategy were eager to return to their tribes to prepare for it. All scouting reports were given, and recent war *coups* were related. It was decided that

that day and on the morrow numerous small bands would harry the Army patrols and distract the fort from the Indians' real target: Cooper's secret camp, late tomorrow night. It was agreed that the other tribes would honor the Oglalas' choice of chief, between Gray Eagle's sons. It was also decided that Sun Cloud would paint his face as his father had, ride a white horse, carry weapons and a shield which matched Gray Eagle's, and wear the chief's bonnet to strike terror and doubt into the hearts of the soldiers and other whites, who would believe he was the spirit of Gray Eagle. Each time Sun Cloud rode as his father's ghost, he was to leave a Bluejay with an eagle feather piercing its heart as a warning sign. Surely the bluecoats' fears would mount quickly, considering the words Bright Arrow and his band had overheard in both white camps. The warriors and chiefs went their separate ways five hours before dusk.

When the Oglala band reached their camp, Silver Hawk took his sister and went home, leaving Sun Cloud no chance to speak with her. Silver Hawk had talked briefly and privately with Tashina, who looked rather pale and shaky afterward, and Sun Cloud knew he must check on this curious matter before leaving camp that afternoon.

The Oglala warriors met to select which bands would try to locate and harass the whites and which ones would hunt for their people and guard their camp. Although his arm still pained him, Bright Arrow insisted on seeking their foes and destroying as many as possible. Sun Cloud agreed to take charge of their tribe's safety and food supply.

Sun Cloud approached Bright Arrow while he was preparing his horse and weapons. He cautioned, "You must worry more over what is best for our people rather than competing with me for voting *coups*. Do not risk your life or those of your band by doing as you did when you rashly sought Flaming Hair. You are injured, my brother, and do not have full strength at this time. Forget him, Bright Arrow, until Grandfather places him before you for destruction, not because of your hunger for revenge, but for the good of our people and lands."

Bright Arrow stared at Sun Cloud. He refused to see the demands, sacrifices, and dangers of obtaining his dreams. He was blinded by the false vision which Silver Hawk had given to him, and had helped bring to life with his unknown treachery. "I will be chief, Sun Cloud."

Sun Cloud eyed his brother, anguish and disappointment vividly exposed in his expression. "If it is the will of the Great Spirit, so be it, my brother, but we must not make this a personal rivalry between us; and you must not force Tashina to be a part of your dreams," he added shockingly. "It is not her duty or destiny to join to Silver Hawk. She loves the son of Windrider and suffers over his loss. If you had spoken to her before announcing your selfish decision, she would have told you the truth and halted this cruel command. While you are gone, my brother, think on what you desire and see if it matches the will of Grandfather. Before you give your precious child to Silver Hawk, consider what is best for Tashina, not for you. She has the right to enjoy the same happiness, love, and passion which you shared with Wahea, which Silver Hawk will deny her. Soul-of-Thunder is her destiny and love; do not alter them to make your vision come true."

"A man does not make his vision come true; the Great Spirit does," Bright Arrow protested. "Why has she not spoken of this to me?"

Sun Cloud explained her reasons. "Are you sure this vision came from Grandfather, or from the depths of your own mind and desires?"

"Next, you will tell me Singing Wind should not be mine," Bright Arrow scoffed, as a curious feeling washed over him and he denied it.

"I believe it is her destiny to marry the Oglala chief," Sun Cloud stated carefully.

Bright Arrow glared at him. "She is mine and the chief's bonnet is mine," he replied to his brother's shocking insinuation. "Such things were revealed in two visions, and two visions cannot be wrong."

Sun Cloud knew it was best not to argue at this time, so he said, "Go and do what is best for our people, but think on my words."

"I will forget them, for they come from a jealous heart and tongue. Long ago, I lost all because of my mistakes; I will make no more." He relented slightly. "But I will speak to Tashina when I return."

"That is all I ask, my brother, for I love you and know these times are difficult for you. Watch over your life and arm. Ride with Grandfather and let Him guide and protect you."

Bright Arrow had been about to send forth another sharp comment, but could not after witnessing his brother's sincerity. "These days are hard for all, Sun Cloud. I will remember we are brothers and sons of Gray Eagle and Shalee, as you must." Bright Arrow mounted and left.

Sun Cloud went to speak with Tashina before he left to hunt. "What words did Silver Hawk say to bring such fear and panic to your face?" he asked her the moment they were alone.

"He says he will insist on our joining after the victory on the next moon. I told him I was in my woman's way and we must wait, but he knew I lied. He refused. He said he had saved my life and I was promised to him and he would wait no longer to claim what is his. There was a coldness and cruelty in his eyes and tone, Sun Cloud."

"I spoke to my brother of your love for Windrider's son. I told him it is wrong to force you to make his vision come true. He said he will speak to you when he returns. I sent a message to your love. There was no time for us to speak at the war council, but I saw the look in his eyes. Soul-of-Thunder will not lose you; he loves you."

"But I am trapped unless . . ." She halted and blushed.

"Speak, Tashina, for time to save you is short," Sun Cloud urged.

Without meeting his probing gaze, she confessed, "Unless he fights the death challenge for me, as is his right by first possession."

Sun Cloud frowned in dismay, then began to smile. "It is good; it is Grandfather's answer to our prayers."

Her head jerked upward and she stared at him. "I do not care if I am shamed for loving him, but I cannot let him challenge death."

"He would win, Tashina, if it came to a battle for you. But I do not think it will. If you confess all to your father, he will speak privately with Silver Hawk and they will agree to sever his claim on you. Silver Hawk would choose to reject you rather than have this information revealed, for he still could not have you afterward. No man of honor would fight for a woman who desires another man, who has given herself to this other man, who will show her choice of the other man during the battle. A man of wisdom would not risk his life to battle for a prize already lost, to risk jokes and taunts."

"But Silver Hawk is not a man of wisdom or honor," she asserted.

"Whatever happens, you must take this last chance. Agreed?"

Tashina thought for only a moment, then said, "Agreed."

General Phillip Cooper, under the guise of "Captain Paul Willis," had been observing the men and conditions at the fort since Tuesday night. Friday morning, tomorrow, half of his men would arrive and he would expose his identity and take charge. He had learned a great deal about the situation and soldiers soon to be under his command.

He knew that Major Gerald Butler had not followed the orders which had been sent to him: keep the peace and stay out of trouble. He knew about the ambush on Gray Eagle and the Sioux, which alleged the infamous leader was dead. He knew how many soldiers had been slain because of that stupid blunder by a glory-seeking officer who was not fit to wear his uniform. He knew about the foiled trap earlier this week, and the death of the signalman. He had heard the rumors about the rivalry between Butler and Ames, who appeared to be a good man. Butler, he concluded, had been a fool to give the Indians such a superior martyr, if indeed Gray Eagle was dead. Butler had not stolen or reduced their spirit; he had given it new blood and purpose! Butler had been here a long time, but he had failed to assess his foe wisely or accurately. As with that idiotic trap, didn't Butler know the Indians could hear him coming for miles with the fast and noisy riding his men had done to catch up to close the ridiculous trap? Did the man know nothing about strategy and surprise? Cooper decided his first act would be to reprimand and demote Butler and Smith. His second would be to defeat all Indians, once he taught the men their fears were groundless.

Cooper realized the men were a mixture of cowardice and cockiness, and both flaws had to be corrected instantly. By the time the other half of his men arrived, the Indians would not stand a chance against them. He hoped the notorious Gray Eagle was not dead, for he wanted to capture him and study him; any great leader could teach another great leader many things. There was no denying that Gray Eagle had that special ability to band men together and to lead them into countless dangers and victories. But Gray Eagle's day was past, and he would prove it. He did not want the American government to weaken before the Indians by offering them a truce; he wanted to prove the whites were superior and could defeat any foe.

If necessary, he would drive these weaklings into the ground if that was what he had to do to whip them into proper soldiers. He had displayed his skills in the last war, and he would do so again in this one. America and the U.S. Army would not back down before savages! He would teach Butler how to set a real trap and spring it . . .

Early the next morning, Captain Clarence Smith took a small detail to cut wood. While a few of his men stood guard over the cutters, he took a walk, he claimed to relieve himself. Knowing Silver Hawk could speak English, he did not take a scout with him to interpret. He reached the area where Red Band always met with the traitorous Blackfeet warrior and waited for the man's arrival. Just as he was about to give up, assuming either Silver Hawk had not found his message or was not coming, the Indian joined him.

"You are a fool to come alone, white-dog," Silver Hawk scoffed.

"You have things all wrong, Silver Hawk. Me and Butler didn't have anything to do with the attack on your war camp. That was Major Ames's doing. He's been trying to outshine Butler before our new commander arrives. He knew our ambush would work and we'd be ranked higher than him. Don't worry, Butler won't let Ames leave the fort again, not until we find a way to get rid of him. How about we set up a trap for him? He's trouble. We all need to be rid of him, and his friend Daniels. Hell, we hope you can trap Cooper when he arrives and get rid of him too. We'll make it worth your while."

"How so? I do not need your help. I will be chief soon."

"Not if your people and the other tribes find out you've been helping us defeat them," Smith boldly refuted.

"If I slay you, no one can learn the truth," the warrior parried.

"You're wrong. I'm not the only one who knows about you. If I don't return safely, Butler will order the scouts to expose your deeds."

"Who would believe you?" Silver Hawk debated coldly.

"Come on. You know that ambush smells of treachery. With a little help, they'll figure it out. Besides, we don't need to be threatening each other. We need each other."

"How so?" the Indian asked skeptically.

"We need you to get rid of our enemies for us, and you need us to give you supplies and protection for your people. What good is it to become chief if we harass you so much you can't do your buffalo hunt or make weapons or defend your camp? We can make sure you have all of those things, Silver Hawk. Once we're rid of the troublemakers, Indian and white, we'll form a truce with your tribe. You can come and go as you please. Isn't that what you want?"

"How can Silver Hawk trust you again?"

"The same way we can trust you. You're forgetting, you know the truth about us. If we fail, we all go down together."

Silver Hawk eyed the soldier wearing the red bandana and knew he could not trust this man, that the bluecoat was only trying to use him to get what he wanted. Yet, that was exactly what he was doing to them. Perhaps he could use them a while longer . . . "I will trust you until you prove false once more. Give me your weapon. I wish to use it to slay Medicine Bear to make it appear the doing of a white man."

"I'll trade you the gun for a girl in your camp," Smith countered.

"Which girl?" Silver Hawk inquired quickly.

"The one called Singing Wind. I want her."

"Do you know who this girl is?" Silver Hawk demanded.

"Red Band said she's the daughter of Medicine Bear. You won't need her around after you become chief."

"She is the sister of Silver Hawk," he informed the soldier.

"Your sister?" Smith echoed incredulously.

"But you can have her later. I do not like the way she watches me. The next time we meet, I will bring her to you. She is wild, so you must tame her," he said with a chilling laugh.

Smith licked his lips in anticipation, rubbed his hands together eagerly, and chuckled. "Good. Here," he offered, handing Silver Hawk his gun. "You know how to use it?"

"I know. We will meet here again in four moons, and she will be yours." Knowing Smith and Butler might be angry with him after the impending attack on the soldiers' camp far away, he slyly warned, "Your leader has angered the others and they will be nipping at your heels for the next few suns. This will not be my doing, but I cannot stop them. Watch your life and men closely for surprise attacks. When we meet again, you will tell me of the trap planned for your enemies."

"I will, Silver Hawk. You're a smart man."

"That is how I have stayed alive so long. Do not trick me again."

"You've got my word. I'd best get back before they come looking for me. Here, in four days." Smith left the grinning man standing there.

"You are a fool. I will use you, then destroy you," he vowed before slipping away as secretly as he had arrived. As he rode, intrigue filled his mind: "Trap Cooper *when he arrives* . . ."

Silver Hawk would not learn until much later that Smith and his detail never made it back to the fort. Flaming Bow, chief of a Cheyenne band, attacked and killed all but one man. As Smith had shouted in panic, "Throw me your gun, Clint," the chief had realized who the other man was, the one mentioned at the war council.

As planned, if possible, Flaming Bow spared Clint's life and gave him a message, "We let you live, bluecoat, for you battle a war which is not of your making. Your name and deeds are known to us. The sons of Gray Eagle say you are to live. Take these words to the bluecoat called Ames: his life is in danger; the one called Butler wishes to slay him secretly so he cannot speak the words of truth to the new white leader. Tell the one called Butler he is a walking dead man, for the spirit of Gray Eagle is seeking his life. Go, and leave these lands before you are slain without our knowing."

Clint could not believe this second stroke of luck, and he promised to relay the two messages. He looked at Flaming Bow for a moment before saying, "Be careful; the new white leader is not a good man. But another white man is coming soon, called Sturgis, a friend of Gray Eagle's and all Indians. If peace can be made, Sturgis will do it. Tell your people and the other tribes to make sure he lives long enough."

"We know of this man and wait for his coming. It is good."

Flaming Bow removed the red bandana and scalplock of Clarence Smith to give to the Oglalas; Gray Eagle was avenged at last.

Bright Arrow's band returned as the rest period was beginning to prepare for the attack on Moore's camp tonight. Soul-of-Thunder and Windrider had arrived an hour ago and were waiting for him with Tashina; they had discussed the predicament and decided how to handle it, based on Sun Cloud's advice to Tashina. All looked at Bright Arrow as he entered his tepee and halted to gaze at them, one at a time.

Before she lost her courage, Tashina hurriedly confessed, "Father, it is past time for the truth. I cannot join Silver Hawk. I belong to Soul-of-Thunder in all ways. If you cannot convince Silver Hawk to release me, my love must issue the death challenge for me." If necessary, Tashina was prepared to claim she was pregnant.

"It has gone this far between you?" Bright Arrow inquired.

"Yes," Tashina and Soul-of-Thunder replied simultaneously, holding hands tightly to give each other support and encouragement.

Bright Arrow looked at Windrider and said, "I cannot believe my tepee faces dishonor through the family of my best friend. My heart suffers from this pain and betrayal. I did not know your son was weak and cruel. I should not have trusted him alone with my daughter. Did you know of their secret love and shame, Windrider?"

A surge of protective loyalty and vexation charged through the Cheyenne war chief. "My son told me of their love and trouble two moons past. I asked him to wait until the war council ended and we could come to speak with my friend." Windrider carefully related what he knew and how he believed the problem should be solved.

"You know of the visions, my friend. How can this be right? Does Evil seek to harm me through the son of my best friend?"

Windrider replied softly, "Silver Hawk said he saw Tashina standing at his side; he did not say they were joined. Is this not true?"

Bright Arrow recalled Silver Hawk's words and nodded. Windrider suggested, "Explain this matter to him, and give him another female of high rank. Surely he will agree when he knows all. It will spare your daughter and my son of shame before their tribes."

Bright Arrow glared at Windrider's son. "If you love her, why did you do this to her?" he accused with fatherly instinct. "A man does not dishonor his true love; he does not take her before a joining."

"As Windrider did not take Sky Eyes before their joining; as Gray Eagle did not take Shalee before their joining; as you did not take my mother before your joining," Tashina reminded him, her eyes misty and her heart aching. "Love is not dishonor; love is impatient when times are filled with evil and dangers, when your love could be dead that sun or the next. I am to blame, Father, for I enticed him beyond his strength to resist me and our desires."

"No," Soul-of-Thunder interjected. "I am to blame. She is young and innocent of mind. I swayed her thoughts and feelings."

"But what will others say and think of this flaw in my vision?" Bright Arrow argued. "To cast doubts on one part may cast doubts on others, and on me. How can I resist the vision's commands?"

Windrider pulled him aside and asked, "Do you recall how I once blinded you to the truth when we shared a vision over Rebecca? Men can be misguided by their greed or desires, and trick others."

Bright Arrow looked at his friend and remembered that day long ago when Windrider had controlled his vision and tried to steal his love, but with good intentions. He remembered Sun Cloud's words about a traitor in one of the camps. He remembered how suspicious the deaths of Medicine Bear's sons were. He thought of everything that had taken place recently. He recalled his past. Was it possible that Silver Hawk had duped him? Was this Grandfather's way of revealing the truth to him? No, it could not be, for that would make him a fool! And all was going as the vision had said! No, all was not going that way . . .

"Your son is a sash wearer and goes into battle this night. If it is the will of Grandfather for him to survive and return, I will accept it and they will join before another moon passes. If he is slain, she will join Silver Hawk as the vision commands. I will tell Silver Hawk the truth, and I will give him another mate. We must prepare for battle."

Tashina rushed forward to hug her father, but he held her away and warned, "You must obey the will of Grandfather. Do you agree?"

She glanced at her true love and said, "I will obey, Father."

Before they could depart, Silver Hawk arrived, to accompany them to the meeting place. Bright Arrow called his friend into his tepee and related this turn in events to the astonished warrior. A quick thinker, Silver Hawk deliberated, "Perhaps I allowed my desire for her to mislead me. Perhaps she only stood at my side as a friend and family. If she loves Soul-of-Thunder, she must join to him. Perhaps it is good, for another seizes my eyes and loins each time I visit you, Little Flower, the daughter of Dull Knife. Will she join to me?"

"What if the son of Windrider is slain this night?"

"Then I will join both, for I will need two wives. Shining Feather desires to return to her tribe and family. She is shamed by her lack of children and does not wish to live in the tepee with those of another woman. I will have the female I desire, and I can spare Tashina of all shame and help her find new happiness and love if he dies this moon. It is good, my friend and brother," he lied cheerfully, artfully.

Bright Arrow quickly sent for Little Flower who was soothing her anger at Sun Cloud for spurning her. When she was told of Silver Hawk's desire and offer, she impetuously accepted it; for he was handsome, virile, and would soon be a chief. Dull Knife was summoned and he agreed, after he heard that Silver Hawk desired his daughter more than Tashina and Tashina desired another over the Blackfoot warrior. Dull Knife was anxious to get his daughter joined, for he was becoming aware of her fiery blood which would soon need appeasing.

The men laughed and the joining gifts were agreed upon, to be delivered after the coming battle, when the Indian marriage would take place. Dull Knife and Bright Arrow left to relate this news to the others involved, as the tribe would be informed tomorrow of their misinterpretation of this vision point.

Silver Hawk lowered the flap for a few moments of privacy with Little Flower. He guessed why the hot-blooded girl had accepted, but he did not care. All he wanted from her was her helpless body and children. He would make everyone think he preferred her over Tashina. Later, he would deal with Tashina and Soul-of-Thunder! This girl was as ripe as a buffalo berry and he would pluck her from beneath Sun Cloud's nose! One day, he would have Tashina too; she would pay for her betrayal with the death of her love and under his cruel hands.

"I am happy and honored you will become my mate on the new sun, Little Flower. Each time I see you my heart races with excitement and my body burns with desire. I could not join Tashina when you are the woman who causes me to ache with hunger. I did not wish to hurt my friend or Tashina by refusing her, but you are the one I want and need. When I said I would take you both as mates, Windrider's son took her off my hands. It is good. When a man has a woman of such beauty and fire, he only wishes to sleep upon her mat."

As he spoke seductively, Silver Hawk caressed her cheek and began to nibble at her ear, causing her to tremble and flush. He sealed their mouths and drove her wild with his skills. His hands boldly wandered under her top and teased her taut peaks between his fingers. Soon, his hand lifted her skirt and eased beneath her breechcloth to tantalize the throbbing peak there. He kissed her and fondled her feverishly. Laughing inside at her weakness for him and these sensations, he raised her top and suckled erotically at her breasts as his hand continued to stimulate her until she shuddered with a release.

He kissed her once more, then said, "This pleasure is nothing compared to what you will enjoy on my mat on the next moon. Sleep while the sun is high, for we will work the moon away passionately."

Little Flower breathlessly replied, "I am happy and honored. I will be ready and eager for you, Silver Hawk. My treasure is yours."

Silver Hawk left her standing there, quivering and dreaming of tomorrow night, when he would show her what it was to have a man take a woman with savage pleasure. He vowed she would regret the many times she had offered her "treasure" to Sun Cloud and other men!

It was nearing one o'clock in the morning when the united tribes began to creep toward the sleeping camp. The guards were quickly and silently slain, then the sleeping soldiers were attacked without warning, for the Indians' plan was clever and their skills were superior.

Silver Hawk sneaked to where Medicine Bear was waiting with the horses, for the Blackfeet chief wanted to view this stunning defeat, but was too old to participate in a sneak raid of such importance. The chief's mind was distracted by the talk he had had with Singing Wind earlier that day, when she had confessed her love for Sun Cloud. He had reminded her of her duty and of Bright Arrow's claim on her. Then she had warned him that evil was in their camp and to watch his life carefully. He envisioned a terrible rivalry between the two Oglala brothers, for the chief's bonnet and the same woman. He decided it was best to end this matter quickly, perhaps by giving Singing Wind to another man.

A warrior sneaked over to join him, and he smiled at Silver Hawk. Then, he saw the white man's gun in the young warrior's hand, pointing at him. He read the evil intent in Silver Hawk's eyes, but it was too late to defend himself or to call for help. Guns were firing as the soldiers scrambled for their weapons, so Silver Hawk's attack went unnoticed. He shoved the barrel against the old man's heart and fired. Medicine Bear sank to the ground, dead. Silver Hawk grinned wickedly, then flung the gun into the concealing bushes. He cleverly did not drag a soldier's body over and try to claim he had slain the bluecoat after the foe had slain their chief. Instead, he stealthily returned to the battlefield and made his presence known with a vengeance. He fought with sheer ecstasy, knowing he would become chief before dawn.

The assault finally ended, and no soldier was left alive. Their bodies were loaded on horses, to be dumped near the fort as a warning and a taunt. The weapons and supplies were stolen so they could not be retrieved and used against them another day. Soon, the signal was given, and all learned of Medicine Bear's fatal wound. The Blackfeet warriors gathered around Silver Hawk and declared him chief on the spot.

Bright Arrow had been annoyed to find more than half of the soldiers were gone, but it had assured their victory. He checked each dead man to make certain Moore was not among them, and was pleased to make this discovery, for he wanted Moore to himself. As he watched Silver Hawk's vision come to pass, he smiled in relief, deciding there must be truth to it, for Silver Hawk was not responsible for this great victory which Mind-who-Roams had foretold or for the death which made him chief as they had both foreseen. He went to congratulate his friend.

Sun Cloud looked at Soul-of-Thunder whom he had guarded that night and murmured, "It is good you put your claim on Tashina before this event. I do not know how he did this thing, but he killed Medicine Bear; I am sure of it. Join her quickly and guard both your lives well."

That next morning at the fort, a grim sight was exposed by the morning light. The Indians had traveled like a wildfire to display their victory as soon as possible, to terrify the soldiers, and to hold them still for a time while they hunted and prepared for the next battle.

General Cooper stared at the antagonistic sight, gritting his teeth and narrowing his eyes as his rage mounted. This was more than a bloody challenge to him. He vowed he would slay ten Indians for every soldier who lay dead outside the fort. He turned to the man beside him and accused, "This is your doing, Butler. You were told not to rile them. I promise you, you'll be in the front line when we ride against them. I hope they cut out your heart and feed it to you. You aren't worth even one of those dead men."

"I told you they were provoking us, General," Butler debated. He did not know what to do now that Smith and Rochelle were dead and he was standing alone against this formidable foe in blue and yellow.

"Provoking you, my ass," Cooper sneered frostily. "This is the work of Gray Eagle; he can't be dead. Nobody else could band these redskins together and pull off a clever attack like this."

"Sun Cloud could, and probably did," Butler refuted as respectfully as possible. "What are we going to do now?" he asked.

"We?" Cooper echoed sarcastically. "I'm going to kill the bastards."

"What about Colonel Sturgis? Maybe he could settle them down?"

"There won't be any savages left by the time he gets here. Send a detail after that James Murdock. I have a plan in mind."

"He's done said he won't help us, sir."

"He won't have a choice; it's help us or lose his damn hide!" Cooper stared at the figure in the distance. "What the hell is that?"

The men were gathering around and gaping at the lone rider who was poised on a small knoll within sight, but not gun range, of the fort.

Butler felt damp and trembly. He called to the sentry to toss down his field glasses. He stared through them and inhaled sharply. "Lord, help us, it's the Eagle himself," he spouted nervously.

Cooper yanked the field glasses from Butler's shaky hands and looked through them. The rider's face was masked with yellow warpaint, in sunny dots and strips. He was wearing a Sioux chief's bonnet. The shield in his grasp displayed the Shooting Star design, which had to be earned. He was sitting astride a cloud white horse. An eagle amulet was around his neck. The warrior dropped something to the ground, then vanished from sight into the forest. The brave who was flattened against the ground and brushing away their tracks could not be seen due to the lay of the land. "Fetch that message, Butler."

"Are you crazy?" Butler shouted in panic. "It's a trap!"

"I don't give a damn, you glory-seeking snake!" Cooper snapped. For a moment, Cooper worried that the wildness of this land and of these "uncivilized" people was bringing out the "savage" within him, for he was known for his poise and self-control, known for his easy domination over his soldiers, known for his clever strategy and numerous victories. He did not like having soldiers—especially officers—talk back to him or doubt his capabilities, didn't like being edgy and short-tempered, or displaying such silly and authority-threatening traits before his command. Maybe this land and its people were bringing out the worst in him, for it was said that every man had a dark side. Maybe it was the loss of nearly half of his regiment, a stunning blow to any leader, for he had believed his strategy was so clever.

That maybe sent Cooper's mind to racing with questions and vexation. Who could have imagined that those infernal savages would *dare* to attack his camp! Who would have imagined they could succeed so grimly, so thoroughly? How had they known about him and his camp? Why weren't they off hunting buffalo like they were supposed to be? Because that damned Butler had riled them, he concluded, new fury blazing through him. He ordered himself to calm down, for a man could not think clearly or act soundly in an agitated state. Besides, more than this unforgivable defeat was troubling him.

Maybe it was the soldiers and conditions he had been sent to shape up and to lead, for he had never seen worse, and this was not how he wanted to spend his time and energies. Maybe he was just tired from the grueling pace he had set for himself and his men, only to get here too late to prevent Butler's lethal recklessness. Maybe it was the Indians' total lack of respect and fear for the U.S. Army and America, which he would remedy very soon. Maybe it was his hip throbbing from a past wound. Maybe it was from leaving, not his proper wife, but his splendid mistress behind; a powerful man had plenty of frustrations and energies to get rid of, and there was no better way to release them than with fighting or loving. Maybe there was something strange in the air here, but not Gray Eagle's ghost! Whatever was eating at him and changing him had to be comprehended and changed pronto!

Butler had no choice but to retrieve the object, which turned out to be a Bluejay with an eagle's feather piercing its heart. When he and the scout returned to the fort, the news spread rapidly, news of the implied message and of no tracks . . .

"Dinna ye worry, sir. I hae ae feelin' tis tha work o' them Sioux tae scear us or fool us. Dinna fall fur their tricks. They be sneaky, sly divils. Gie me ae week, an' I'll hae 'em runnin' sceared. I owe 'em death 'n destruction, sir. They made ae fool o' me, an' destroyed my men 'n command. I was outnumbered an' had tae hide in tha bushes tae survive. Fur wha'? Tae be dishonored an' stripped o' me rank. I know 'em an' their tricks. Gie me ae detail tae send 'em runnin'. Wha' sae ye, sir?" the flaming-haired, blue-eyed officer subtly pleaded.

General Phillip Cooper studied Major Timothy Moore with keen interest. No man had worked harder to regain his lost honor and rank. Moore had been with him for several years, and they seemingly knew each other well. Looking no more than forty, despite his fifty-three years, Moore was strong and alert, and he was familiar with this land and its people. "Timothy, let's me and you do some serious talking and planning," Cooper suggested, smiling and placing his arm around the man's broad shoulders. They headed for Cooper's quarters, as Butler glared at their backs.

*   *   *

Singing Wind watched her brother with dread as he donned the Blackfeet chief's bonnet and grinned maliciously at her. They were in his tepee alone, for he had ordered Shining Feather to leave so they could speak privately. He was preparing to ride to the Oglala camp to join with Little Flower, and he had commanded that she go along.

"You can carry your things and join to Bright Arrow after I have taken my new mate. There is no need to linger over this matter. It is settled. As your chief, I command it."

"No," she refused bravely. "I will not marry him until he is voted chief. Let the vision be proven first; let me make certain he will become chief and not his brother."

Silver Hawk laughed coldly and tauntingly. "It will be Bright Arrow, you will see. If you crave Sun Cloud, you are foolish, sister. I have snatched his new conquest from his grasp. He probably seeks another to chase this very moon. He does not desire a defiant wildcat like you. Until you join Bright Arrow, you will remain in Medicine Bear's tepee and you will move it to the last circle while I am gone. I want no reminder each sun in the center of my camp of their old chief. I will paint my new *coups* upon my tepee and make it more beautiful than Medicine Bear's. If you are afraid in the outer circle, go to join and to live with your new mate. Be grateful Bright Arrow will accept you. If you dare to reject him and dishonor both of us, I will sell you as no more than a slave. I warn you, do not cast your eyes upon Sun Cloud," he stated in a tone which was intimidating and chilling.

"You bring a new wife home this moon. Do you wish Shining Feather to sleep in my tepee to give you privacy?" she asked, to change the subject and to release their tension.

He laughed strangely, satanically, and shook his head. "There is no need. A husband does not send one wife out into the darkness or cold each time he mates with another. They must share me, and see how it is with the other; it helps them to learn and it causes them to compete for my attention by seeing which can give me more pleasure."

Singing Wind's cheeks went scarlet, causing him to laugh harder. "That is cruel and wicked, my brother. Little Flower should not have another watching and listening on the first time she is taken."

"You talk foolish again, sister. We will leave the Oglala camp when the joining ceremony is over. We will find a private place in the forest, and I will take her this first time before we reach camp."

She lowered her lashes to conceal her modesty and to hide her curious feelings, for there was something about her brother's mood and gaze which worried her where Little Flower was concerned. "It is good."

Again that malicious laughter came forth when Silver Hawk said, "Yes, it will be very good for me."

Singing Wind observed her brother's departure with several warriors and with many gift horses for Dull Knife. She longed to go with them on the chance of seeing and speaking with her love, but it was too perilous, for Silver Hawk might try to force the issue of her joining to Bright Arrow that day; this was too early for a confrontation.

* * *

The Oglala war party returned to camp at midmorning and related their great victory. Bright Arrow announced the change in plans for Silver Hawk's and Tashina's joinings, and of how they had "mistakenly translated" this message in their visions. When the facts of Silver Hawk's "love" for Little Flower and of Tashina's love for Soul-of-Thunder were revealed, the people accepted it and were pleased by it, as they were already in an elated mood. Those who were still on Bright Arrow's side saw this change as a favorable sign—to have his friend and fellow vision sharer join the daughter of Dull Knife, the council member who supposedly controlled the deciding vote for chief.

Neither brother comprehended how many councilmen and warriors were being swayed in Sun Cloud's direction. As each member of the Warrior Society keenly observed them, many realized how mistaken they had been in their thoughts and charges. Several misconceptions had come to light, as well as the vast difference in the two sons of Gray Eagle. Some of the men were beginning to whisper amongst themselves, but most were holding their opinions secret for now.

Tashina and Soul-of-Thunder were joined before the midday meal so, they claimed, they could leave promptly and take advantage of the daylight, which would allow them to reach the Cheyenne camp by the time the moon was overhead. Tashina was ecstatic and she wished Sun Cloud were there to share this hard-won moment with her, but he had ridden to the fort to carry out a special mission and might not return until dawn. She could not wait for him, for Silver Hawk would arrive soon, and she wanted to be far away when that occurred.

Little Feet and Tashina hugged and kissed, wishing they were not being separated so soon after Little Feet's return home. Both were married now, to the men they loved; and both looked forward to happy lives with their mates and children. Thunder Spirit and Soul-of-Thunder promised the sisters they would arrange visits between them later.

Tashina embraced White Arrow, Pretty Woman, Flaming Star, Morning Light, and other close friends. Many gave them gifts and wished them joy and safety. Tashina approached her weary father last. She gazed into his eyes, then hugged him tightly. "I love you, Father, and I will miss you. Little Feet will see to your needs until your mate joins you. Be happy, Father, and always remember me."

Bright Arrow embraced Tashina affectionately. He could see how happy she was, and knew this union was for the best. "You be happy, my little one. I will come to visit soon. Go with the Great Spirit and let Him guide you and protect you. I love you, my precious little one."

Windrider and Bright Arrow clasped forearms and exchanged smiles. "It is good and wise, my friend and brother," the Cheyenne remarked.

Bright Arrow glanced at the blissful couple and nodded. As he watched them ride away, he was aware of how his life had changed in the last year. Loneliness attacked him fiercely, and he prayed that Singing Wind would arrive with Silver Hawk. If she did, he would convince her to join him this day and ease his sufferings this night.

Silver Hawk reached the Oglala camp during the evening meal, after everyone had rested and eaten. He presented his many gifts to Dull Knife, making quite an impression with his generosity which was supposed to indicate his feelings about his impending mate and union. He watched Little Flower's eyes sparkle with pleasure and conceit, and it made him eager to tame her wild spirit and to destroy her arrogance.

The joining ceremony was a little longer than most, for he was a chief. Afterward, fruit wine and fruit-speckled pones were served by the families of Bright Arrow, Dull Knife, and several others. There was singing, dancing, and other forms of merrymaking. There was much to celebrate this day, and all delighted in the happy occasion. Yet, Bright Arrow worried over Singing Wind's absence.

The moon was climbing above the treetops and glowing brightly when Silver Hawk said it was time to leave. Bright Arrow tried to encourage him to spend the night in his tepee, but Silver Hawk smiled and declined, for himself. He encouraged his warriors to remain to indulge themselves during this special feast, and they eagerly agreed. After gathering his things and his new wife, Silver Hawk bid everyone farewell and departed. They rode for two hours in silence, until they reached a spot which he had chosen earlier for his wicked intention.

Little Flower did not suspect a thing as he helped her to dismount. He placed a sleeping mat on the ground between several trees and then told the girl to remove her garments and to lie upon it. Recalling yesterday in Bright Arrow's tepee, Little Flower quickly and joyfully obeyed.

But Silver Hawk did not join her as she expected and desired. He smiled as he bound her wrists, then secured the rope to the tree beyond her head, pulling the rope just tight enough to stretch her arms above her and to prevent their interference later. When she questioned his actions, he smiled again and told her it was a special part of the ritual for a first union. He teased her about protecting himself while driving her wild with so much pleasure that this was to make certain she did not claw him to pieces during her excitement and mindless state.

Little Flower's desire and anticipation increased as she waited tensely for him to begin. He took a strip of rawhide and gagged her, telling her it was to prevent her from crying aloud with delight and perhaps causing someone to think there was danger and interrupt them. She watched Silver Hawk as he stood and stripped off his garments, exposing a manhood which evinced his hunger. She saw him position himself between her legs and let his eyes rove over her body.

By now, the reality of her misjudgment of Silver Hawk and her impending peril consumed Little Flower; she realized he was not going to stimulate her, or slake her desires, or be gentle with her. His eyes were like black ice and his hands were rough. She had watched his protective covering slip away before her wide eyes . . .

Singing Wind drew her knife to defend herself against the intruder who had unlaced her tepee flap and was sneaking inside. When the moonlight washed over him, she sighed happily and rushed forward . . .

Chapter Sixteen

After the flap was secured for total privacy, they embraced and kissed with deep emotion, for this was not a time for words. They held each other tightly, almost desperately, as they savored this blissful and stolen contact. His lips pressed kisses on each feature of her face as her hands stroked his coppery flesh with admiration and delight. Greedily their mouths fused once more and they clung to each other.

When they had taken enough lover's sustenance to survive apart for a short time, he questioned hoarsely, "Why are you here alone?"

Singing Wind explained her trying dilemma, and he embraced her gratefully. "I am glad you did not go to our camp," he murmured into her ear, then told her of his mission today as the "ghost" of Gray Eagle, and of his overwhelming need to see her and hold her, and of his hope he would find her here.

"When Medicine Bear's tepee was gone, I feared you were sleeping with Shining Feather, but I could see only one body there. I prayed you had not gone to my camp when my brother's mind is on joinings. You must stand firm against them, my love, until this bitter problem is solved. I was sneaking back into the forest when I saw Medicine Bear's tepee and came to check out my suspicion. Silver Hawk will pay for this black deed. He knows the outer tepees are the first ones to suffer attack from foes and he knows tepee placement indicates rank and honor. It is wicked of him to put the daughter of a chief and future mate of a chief in the last circle. He grows too bold."

She caressed his cheek and coaxed, "Do not worry, my love; it is a trick to frighten me into joining Bright Arrow quickly."

He took a lock of her silky ebony hair and rubbed it between his fingers as he stated, "But it is dangerous, my love. We have challenged the whites by attacking and defeating them. The others will be on the warpath soon. You must find someone to stay with until it is safe."

She smiled mischievously and retorted, "Then, you could not sneak into my tepee to . . . visit me, and the vote to make you chief is far away. I cannot wait so long to have you again; I crave you more and more with each breath I take. This is meant to be." She pulled his mouth to hers and fused them, ravenously feasting on his.

Sun Cloud became breathless and weak, and his body shuddered with rising need. It seemed he could not be near her like this without craving her wildly and completely. As if mesmerized, he watched her back away gracefully to halt in the large shaft of moonlight which came from the ventilation flap at the pinnacle of the tepee, which was spread to its fullest opening to encourage fresh air and soft light to enter. He was enthralled as she enticingly removed her garments and dropped them to the dirt floor. The silvery glow from overhead bathed her in an enchanting mixture of pale light and dim shadows. She remained there a time, allowing him to visually admire her captivating beauty and shape; then she stepped forward and boldly removed his garments. She grasped his hand, led him to her sleeping mat, and lay down, drawing him along with her. "We waste precious moments with talk which changes nothing. Make love to me," she urged huskily.

His mouth closed over hers in a tantalizing and yearning kiss. He relished the thrill of her utter abandonment, her sweetness, her eagerness. He caused each inch of her face to tingle from his ardent kisses. He began a new trek toward mutual bliss when his mouth roamed down her throat to capture a passion-firm breast and to drive its peak to tautness with his stimulating action. His moist tongue delightfully circled and teased each brown point until she was writhing upon the fuzzy mat. He sucked upon each in turn as if drawing life-giving liquid from them, without which he would die quickly and painfully.

Singing Wind could not imagine how long he feasted upon her breasts before his lips sought hers once more. His kisses were urgent and intense, but he did not fuse their bodies too rapidly. Her fingers played wildly in his hair, for he always wore it loose. There was a heady scent about him which teased at her smelling sense and filled her head with sensually masculine images. Her stomach tensed, then relaxed, as his hand wandered very slowly over it and into her private domain. She shifted her thighs to make room for his loving labor, which he deftly performed with a pervasive effect. As if a highly trained warrior tracking his clever prey in a private forest with slow deliberation and enjoyment, he explored each area—lush mounds, a tiny peak, silky valleys, hidden crevices, and a dark and damp cave. She was nearly mindless with hunger, but still he whet her appetite.

Sun Cloud savored the way she was responding to his skills and rapturous torments. Their bodies and wills were pliant, and he artfully molded them to grant them the most pleasure. He inhaled sharply when her hand closed around his throbbing manhood and began to fondle it, creating exquisite sensations over his body, sensations perilous to his control over it. He was enslaved by her tantalizing caresses and her obvious delight with her ability to arouse him to a greater desire for her. After a short time, he gently and defensively pushed her hand aside to enter her, pausing to master his urge to take her swiftly. She sorely tested his restraint again as she arched to meet him and wrapped her legs around his and matched his rhythm perfectly.

The heights of their desires and her provocative enticements urged him to slake passion's demands fiercely. His slow and gentle strokes became stronger and swifter as their hungers mounted with each one given and returned. They rode urgently toward the land of rapture until there was no holding back or stopping their brazen ecstasies from spilling forth and mingling rapturously. Still they labored lovingly and savagely as if there were no beginning or ending to their potent releases. When every spasm had ceased, they were drained and breathless, but still they clung to each other, kissing tenderly and sharing endearments.

They remained locked together, absorbing the emotions and touches which were vital to such a union. Their hearts surged with love and contentment as their sated passions responded to their closeness and this peaceful aftermath. They treasured what they had shared, and knew they would share forever. Their caresses and kisses were light as their bodies cooled and relaxed.

"I wish I did not have to take everything from my brother," he murmured sadly into her ear. "Soon, he will lose you and the chief's bonnet. He has been unhappy and incomplete for too long."

"It is not our doing, my love," she told him tenderly. "He blindly seeks what is not meant to be his. Grandfather is generous and kind; He will find other things to fill Bright Arrow's life and heart."

"I pray it is soon, my love, for it is hard to see him so empty and miserable. If I could give you to him to soften his heart and to help him, I would step aside, but I love you and need you too much."

"In time, your sacrifices would not matter, for it is his true love that he longs for," she whispered to comfort Sun Cloud.

"If only Wahea was alive and I could find her for him . . ."

At Fort Manuel the next morning, Rebecca Kenny packed her belongings to continue her exciting and intimidating trek home. They had traveled swiftly, for Manuel Lisa was not feeling well and was anxious to reach St. Louis; none realized how serious his illness was, nor that he would be dead soon after reaching his destination. As best she could judge, they were one hundred and fifty miles from her love's territory, but the trip by boat on the Missouri River should pass rapidly. Her only problem was locating Gray Eagle's summer camp, for it often changed locations as the buffalo did, and she could not risk asking suspicious questions about the Sioux. But she would worry about that predicament when she reached Fort Dakota, the nearest place to her love's domain, a point from which she could solve this mystery and begin her final leg homeward.

She brushed her long auburn hair and let it fall loosely down her back. Her whiskey-colored eyes were bright and her cheeks were flushed with anticipation. Each mile covered caused her heart to race more forcefully and swiftly with mounting excitement and suspense. She hated to reveal her eagerness, which was nearly impossible, for she realized how difficult this momentous journey was for Jeremy Comstock, for he knew that her success meant his defeat where she was concerned. *Defeat*, her mind echoed painfully. What if the defeat was hers? What would she do if Bright Arrow had a new life, and a new love?

If only their separation had not been so long. If only he knew she was still alive and on her way back to him. What if he did not understand about Jeremy Comstock, for he hated and battled whites? Yes, she had been forced to live with Jeremy for over a year, but she had never slept with him, no matter what others believed or what Jeremy had wanted. She frowned as she wondered if Bright Arrow had been as faithful to her during her lengthy absence. She would admit, at times, it had been hard to refuse the attentions of this gentle and ruggedly handsome male who loved her and desired her, and made those facts known as often as possible. And yes, at times, her denied and susceptible body had burned from unrequited passions and physical need. She had been tempted on a few occasions to yield to him, but she had not. Still, she knew it was different for men; men could enjoy and accept sex without love. She feared that in his loneliness and despair he had turned to another woman. Could she accept that situation? Sex, yes, she decided wisely, but not love. If he was married again, could she disrupt his new life? Perhaps it would be wiser to seek the truth and vital information from his best friend Windrider . . .

The detail to Fort Meade was ready to leave at dawn, a day earlier than planned, but General Cooper changed his mind. He decided it might be best if the detail traveled at night, for surely those sly Indians were waiting nearby to slaughter more of his soldiers and had perhaps learned of this mission as they had learned about his secret camp. Until he could figure out how they were getting their information, he must be extra careful and cunning. If the detail left during the night when the Indians were sleeping, they should reach the next fort safely. From there, he planned to send messages to the other forts in this territory. He would use one of Gray Eagle's tricks; he would band the soldiers together and attack each camp in massive numbers and without warning, by making certain no clues were leaked to them. The more Indians they killed, the fewer were left to reunite to battle them. He knew his conflict was with the aggressive warriors and, at this point in his thoughts and command, he hated the idea of destroying camps filled with women and children and old folks; but it was necessary to end this bloody clash, and he was determined to do so and quickly. The warriors were to blame, for they were leaving him no choice . . .

The Oglalas enthusiastically gathered in the center of camp and waited for the Sacred Bow ritual/race to begin, for it was believed to yield powerful medicine for war and for peace. The sweat lodge had been prepared, and those involved had entered it earlier to purify themselves. Four posts, one representing each direction of the Medicine Wheel, were set in place beyond the circle of tepees and decorated with sacred symbols. The runners, including Sun Cloud, left the sweat lodge and allowed the shaman's helpers to paint their bodies with the Medicine Bow colors and designs; then they gathered around the starting point which faced west. When the ceremonial chief gave the signal, the sacred race would be underway. Each man was to run to each post, seize an object from it, then race for the next one. The winner would be the man who returned to the ceremonial chief first and handed him the four tokens which he had collected. If a camp was large, as was the Oglala, the lengthy race called upon all of a man's stamina and strength to run it, and especially to win it.

The ceremonial chief raised his hands, as did the participants, to evoke the spirits and powers which were a part of this ritual. Those of the lightning, wind, thunder, and hail were summoned. Those of the snake and bear, representing striking speed and strength, were summoned. The spirits of the air were summoned. Prayers were chanted.

The runners began to perform a special dance, dressed only in breechcloths. Their bodies were painted with designs which sent forth a message to the spirits and powers and depicted their purpose to those who observed this ceremony. The four sacred bows, four staffs, and four clubs were placed near the ceremonial chief, to be reclaimed by those who proved during this ritual that they deserved their ranks.

The ceremonial chief signaled for the race to begin. All tribe members fell silent, as this was a religious rite, not a sport or contest to be cheered. The runners raced westward, then back to touch the center pole, then raced eastward and back to the center pole, then southward and northward to complete this seasonal challenge. Sun Cloud handed the ceremonial chief his collected tokens first, then Night Rider and Thunder Spirit finished their race almost simultaneously, with Rising Elk and the other eight men following suit, one at a time. The twelve runners entered the sweat lodge once more to complete the last part of this ceremony with a final purification rite, rubbing their sweaty bodies with sweet and sage grasses afterward.

Although the Sun Dance was normally held after the buffalo hunt and when other bands joined them to perform this ceremony together, Mind-who-Roams had called for it to be carried out today, for his vision two days ago had commanded it in order to give the Oglalas special powers and guidance before they faced the bluecoats once more, and Indians always obeyed such divine commands.

Usually it was a twelve-day ritual which was divided into three periods of four-day events. The first four days were a time for feasting, to celebrate their recent and hopefully successful buffalo hunt, to show their unity, and to meet and talk with friends and family who had joined them for this special occasion. During this time, the shaman selected and instructed his helpers for the upcoming ritual, which included several high-ranking women to carry out the honored task of chopping down the sacred cottonwood tree for the Sun Dance pole.

During the next four days, the ceremonial dancers were chosen and instructed. All warriors knew these dances, but only those selected by the shaman could perform them during this ritual. The dancers met every day in the sacred lodge to practice each movement to make certain no errors were made and to be assigned the particular designs to be painted upon their bodies when their part in this ritual arrived.

The final four days were the most important, as the preparations for the Sun Dance would be completed. On day one, a warrior was chosen to locate a sturdy and straight cottonwood tree around thirty feet tall and with a fork at its top, which he marked with the appropriate symbol. Upon his return to camp, the Buffalo Dance was done. Any warrior could participate, using a buffalo bull's skull which was painted in a special pattern with its openings stuffed with buffalo grass. The symbols, chosen and painted by the shaman, all dealt with the powers and forces of the sky: rain, hail, lightning, and wind.

On day two of this period, the female assistants located the tree which had been marked by the warrior yesterday, then summoned the tribe to watch them chop it down and carry it back to camp. On day three, the sacred cottonwood tree was prepared; its bark was stripped, and sacred symbols were painted and carved upon it. When it was placed in the center of camp, the warriors danced around it.

On day four, the chosen dancers were painted and prepared, for they were to dance and blow eagle-bone whistles throughout the Sun Dance, a feat which required and used much energy and stamina.

The men who had chosen to endure this ceremony gathered in the sweat lodge and purified themselves. There were several degrees of participation which a man could choose from, depending upon what he needed to say or accomplish with his action. Some men worked their way up to the final feat of sacrifice, and some chose the highest degree of difficulty and danger from the start. The lowest task was for men who only danced and chanted around the sacred pole for as long as they could move and speak. Others allowed tiny pieces of their flesh to be

removed and placed at the base of the sacred pole. Others allowed their bodies to
be pierced on their chest muscles and secured by thongs to the sacred pole, from
which they were required to pull free. The Sun Dance did not end until all
participants either pulled free, died trying, or had to yield defeat.

For those who chose the piercing, there were two ways to accomplish their
tasks: they could stand on the ground, stretch the attached thongs tight, then sway
to and fro while blowing on eagle-bone whistles and trying to pull free; or they
could be lifted into the air to hang suspended until their flesh gave away and
released them. This last method was the most difficult and painful, and was rarely
chosen; the last man who had attempted it and succeeded was Gray Eagle in 1805
when, at fifty-four, he had sought to prove he was still worthy to lead his people
after his recovery from the Crow wound which had returned Bright Arrow to his
people after his six-year exile.

Those who participated in the Sun Dance did so for themselves and for their
people, for it summoned the blessings and guidance and protection of the Great
Spirit and it declared their gratitude for all He had given to them and done for
them.

This Sun Dance was different. The pole had been located and prepared, but
the other parts of the ceremony would not be carried out this time. The men who
had decided to participate had met in the sweat lodge to purify themselves and to
choose which part of the ritual they would endure today. Those who had been
dancers before were quickly reinstructed and painted, and they went to perform
their task.

The tribe gathered around as the warriors left the sweat lodge and approached
the shaman, each one revealing what part he would attempt. One by one, Mind-
who-Roams prepared the men. Only three warriors chose to submit to the piercing,
but standing on the ground. The last man stepped forward, selecting the lifted
position: Sun Cloud.

Mind-who-Roams and his friends worriedly reminded him of the strenuous
task which he had just completed an hour ago, including two draining purification
rites in the sweat lodge, which had caused most of the red and blue water-based
body paints to wash away. The yellow oil-based designs on his face which represented stars and lightning bolts had smudged slightly, but were still noticeable.

Touched by their concern, Sun Cloud smiled at his friends and said, "It is the
will of Grandfather; it is my season to obey. As my father did fifteen winters past, I
must be lifted up in sacrifice."

"But you are tired and weak from your race and purifications," Thunder Spirit
protested, for he knew how fatigued he was and he knew how difficult and perilous
the Sun Dance was, especially this part.

Sun Cloud clasped his friend's arm and said, "It must be. I am ready," he
announced to the shaman and faced him, placing his hands behind his body and
sticking his chest forward as he gazed at the sun.

The shaman took the sacred knife and made two slices half an inch apart on
Sun Cloud's left breast, causing blood to seep forth and ease down his bronzed
abdomen. Using an eagle's clawed foot, he forced one of the sharp talons through
the sensitive underflesh, then pulled on it to lift the severed section from the
warrior's chest to allow a ten-inch thong to follow its path. He repeated the
procedure on Sun Cloud's right breast, and was pleased when the young warrior
never grimaced or flinched. He gave Sun Cloud a peyote button to be eaten later

to seek his vision, but after most of his ordeal. The holy man tied the two thongs to rawhide ropes which were hanging from the fork of the sacred pole, then called three men forward to raise Sun Cloud into the air and to secure the rope ends tightly to the base of the pole.

As the men lifted him, the thongs yanked upon his tender flesh and sent radiating pain through his chest and neck and arms. As he was pulled higher, the men's movements sent agony charging through his body and mind and he felt as if he were being torn apart. At last, the jarring ordeal was complete and he was suspended three feet from the ground by his protesting flesh. He had never imagined pain could be this enormous, but it was. He could not understand how, with his heavy weight pulling on them, the severed sections of flesh held fast to his chest and he hoped they would tear free soon, though he was aware this excruciating ritual could take hours or all day. In fierce resolve to hold silent and to grasp victory, Sun Cloud recalled his instructions and his father's Sun Dance. Ignoring his agony, he arched his back and left his arms hang loosely at his sides. He stared at the sun and blew on his whistle, each inhalation and exhalation increasing his torment.

There was no turning back; the sacrificial ritual was underway, so it was onward to victory or defeat or truce. The steady beat of the kettle drums was heard, along with prayers and chanting. The other participants blew on their whistles as all involved began their bittersweet tasks as they mentally searched for savage ecstasy.

Hours passed and the men's agonies increased. Many were consumed by a fear of defeat, and prayed for the determination to endure and succeed. Some could not help but cry out as flesh was ripped apart or staggering pain shot through them as they attempted to pull free to end this self-inflicted torment. Blood ran down stomachs and soaked breechcloths, their only garments. The movements of bare feet caused dust to rise and swirl about in the wind created by them. Some would slacken the ropes to rest a moment before straining upon them once more. Even after one side of a man's torso was freed, the other seemingly resisted freedom more than the first. Clearly all of the men were becoming exhausted; some had fainted from pain or fatigue, some to regain consciousness and begin the ordeal once more.

Bright Arrow watched his brother submit to what he knew from experience was excruciating pain; yet, Sun Cloud's expression and behavior did not expose what he was suffering. A new sense of respect and awe filled Bright Arrow as he observed his brother's courage and stamina. At first, he had been angry with Sun Cloud for attempting two perils and challenges on the same day, then jealous at how his brother was succeeding with them. Slowly those forbidden emotions lessened and vanished, for he knew Sun Cloud was obeying Grandfather. His gaze went to the red bandana which Sun Cloud had tied around his neck, the one which had belonged to the slayer of their father. The air seemed charged with a strange force, and Bright Arrow felt it.

The heat and humidity made May seventh an unusually oppressive day, and the men's bodies glistened with moisture. The ritual dancers halted one by one and took their seats. The men who had been pierced all freed themselves, collapsed to the ground, and were helped to their mats to be tended and refreshed.

Only Sun Cloud remained at the Sun Dance pole. Everything and everyone was silent, but for the kettle drums and Sun Cloud's whistle. It did not appear as if his taut flesh had yielded in the least. Yet, blood slipped around his sides to saturate the back of his breechcloth. He hung limply as if he would either die or fail at this awesome task. When he wiped the beads of moisture from the humidity and his profuse sweating from his face, it caused the yellow markings to alter their shapes, to form dots and strips which could not be seen by those beneath his suspended body due to the backward angle of his head.

Suddenly his tongue shoved the whistle from his mouth and he lifted his arms skyward, calling out, "Hear me, Grandfather; Sun Cloud and his people need your help and guidance. Speak to us. Send us a sign." He placed the peyote button in his mouth and consumed it, for he had endured this ordeal long enough to prove he was not fleeing it.

No one had noticed the dark clouds moving their way, until the wind picked up and carried them overhead, blocking the sun from view. It was almost as if dusk had settled over them. Bright flashes of lightning charged across the heavens and rumbling thunder followed it, rapidly moving closer and closer and louder and louder. Sun Cloud implored, "I call on you, spirits of thunder, lightning, rain, and wind, to bring us a message; tell us how to defeat our white foes."

The ground seemingly trembled as the power of nature increased and boldly displayed itself. Rain began to pour upon everyone, but no one moved, for they felt as if the Great Spirit was communicating with them through Sun Cloud, as if the valiant warrior was the one calling down these powers to compel a message from them.

The sky grew darker and darker. Rain poured heavier and faster, soaking everyone and washing away all traces of blood and sweat. Lightning zigzagged constantly and fiercely across the heaven above. The thunder seemingly had no beginning or ending to his loud voice. Brisk winds yanked at tepees and clothing, and wet hair was whipped into eyes and faces. The storm raged in a powerful frenzy. It was raining so hard it was difficult for the people to keep their eyes open and heads upward to witness this stirring event. The sounds of pouring rain, booming thunder, and wild winds combined to almost painfully assail everyone's ears. The Sun Dance pole appeared to sway eerily, and Sun Cloud's body twirled slowly, tangling the rawhide ropes.

The shaman jumped up to chant and dance around the pole as the storm's fury mounted and Sun Cloud prayed for a vision. He closed his eyes and allowed himself to travel with the force which was flowing within and around him. He was no longer aware of the agony in his chest, nor of his violent surroundings. Colorful images danced inside his head, changing shapes and sizes every few minutes. Far away he could hear something beating steadily, perhaps it was his heart or his life-force leaving his body to communicate with the Great Spirit.

He saw himself standing on a lofty hill, overlooking his lands. He saw units of bluecoats coming from every direction to band together to attack his people and other tribes. He saw his people using the Apache war skills to attack each band and destroy them. He saw a white man whose face was hazy approach him and shake hands with the warrior at his side; turning, he saw his father standing there. He watched the two make and accept the signs for peace, and heard his father call the man *kola* and Colonel Derek Sturgis, then Gray Eagle placed Sturgis' hand in Sun Cloud's and smiled meaningfully. His mother joined the two men and whispered, "Peace, my son, it is the only path to survival for the Dakota Nation, and it must survive."

He saw a warrior whose hands were covered in blood, Indian blood, and his face was that of Silver Hawk's. He saw himself walk forward and slay this wicked traitor, then hold out his hands in beckoning to the man's sister, Singing Wind, and he saw her running eagerly toward him with love in her gaze. He heard someone call his name over and over and he looked around to answer. He could find no one, but he recognized the voice from far away: Rebecca Kenny's. He saw himself standing with his brother; he was wearing the tribal chief's bonnet and Bright Arrow was adorned as the war chief.

Sun Cloud lifted his arms skyward once more and said, "It will be done as you command, Grandfather. Free me so I can obey."

A strong gust of wind surged through the center of camp and, as if untied by its mystical fingers, the soppy bandana around Sun Cloud's neck loosened and plunged to the ground. A dazzling bolt of lightning nearly sheared through the Sun Dance pole three feet upward from its mud-spattered base, sending forth a loud boom and an ominous cracking sound. Bright sparks shot in all directions and puffs of smoke swirled into the air, but the sacred pole did not catch fire. It swayed to one side, gradually splintered and eased to the drenched ground, lowering Sun Cloud without injuring him or ripping the thongs from his chest.

People squealed and scattered rapidly, but the pole landed between tepees as if intentionally avoiding all life and property. All eyes looked above and around them as the rain, wind, thunder, and lightning ceased almost instantly and simultaneously. A strange aura hung over the camp and its people. The storm rapidly moved off into the distance, leaving a colorful rainbow stretched across the horizon and fluffy white clouds leisurely drifting overhead. Gradually the sky lightened; the hazy mist cleared; the rainbow faded; and the sun climbed from behind what resembled a pile of clouds. The radiant ball peered over them, as if creating the same image as upon Sun Cloud's possessions and his *wanapin*—which had been exposed to their eyes after the red bandana had fallen off. While catching his breath and summoning his lagging strength, he edged to the remaining base of the sacred pole and leaned his back against it. His long hair was soaked and nearly all of his body paint had been washed away, all except for the yellow strips and dots on his face, which formed the pattern belonging to Gray Eagle.

Sun Cloud gazed at the fiery ball which was shining brightly on his weary, but tranquilly victorious, face and reflecting off of his sun-and-clouds medallion. It was strange; his chest was sore and uncomfortable, but the searing agony had vanished. In fact, a numbing sensation seemed to engulf his injuries. His body was exhausted; yet he felt wonderful inside, where his spirit was soaring.

The shaman came forward with the sacred knife, dropped to one knee in the mud, cut the thongs which were still secured to the young warrior's chest, and carefully removed them. His hands cupped Sun Cloud's shoulders and he smiled. To him, it was almost like gazing into the face of Gray Eagle many years ago! "Grandfather honored and freed Sun Cloud, so we must do the same. Grandfather revealed a powerful vision with strong medicine to Sun Cloud. When we hear it, we must obey. Come, my son, you need care and rest."

Forcing himself to ignore his weakness, Sun Cloud stood and looked around him. All who had observed this ceremony knew it was powerful medicine, and the warriors were eager to hear of his sacred vision. As with the shaman, others felt as if they were in the presence of Gray Eagle reborn and they could not help but stare at Sun Cloud.

"I must eat, drink, and rest for a time, then we will meet in the ceremonial lodge. There is much to tell." Sun Cloud glanced at his father's lifetime friend White Arrow and smiled, love and respect filling both men's eyes as they seemed to talk without words. His gaze drifted around the front circle of council members and high-ranking warriors, wondering if any of their eyes and hearts had been opened to the truth; he smiled and nodded to each. His gaze lingered a time on his observant brother before he left with the shaman to have his chest tended and to discuss the meaning of his vision with the wise one.

As he doctored the young warrior's chest—cleansing and then covering the wounds with potent healing herbs, pressing the flesh back into its proper place, and binding his chest snugly—Mind-who-Roams listened intently and reverently as Sun Cloud related his vision. He gave the young warrior nourishing food to eat and chokecherry wine to drink. The wine was laced liberally with a variety of medicinal herbs to promote healing, to prevent shock and fever, and to lessen pain.

The shaman remarked, "It is as I believed; you must become chief." The older man smiled and stated, "You will become chief. You are much like your father. It is as if he has returned to us in you."

Sun Cloud smiled gratefully and replied, "This is not the time to seize my advantage. Our warriors must stand and ride and fight as one, not battle over helping friends to win votes. I must see my brother before the council; there are special messages for him."

Chapter Seventeen

Sun Cloud revealed his vision to Bright Arrow, except for the part about Silver Hawk, wickedness which he felt his brother must uncover on his own, for only then would Bright Arrow believe that his friend Silver Hawk was capable of such evil and treachery.

Bright Arrow and Sun Cloud were alone, so they could talk openly and honestly. Bright Arrow studied his younger brother and wondered how much, if any, of these stunning words he should, or could, believe. To accept Sun Cloud's contradictory vision weakened or destroyed his own vision, denied him his dreams and desires. If Sun Cloud's vision was placed above his own in power and meaning, he, Bright Arrow, first-born of Gray Eagle and Shalee, would appear a fool or an evil-heart, a greedy misguider and deceiver, to his tribe and to others. His troubled spirit asked how could he lose everything again? How could he return to being an empty shell which did nothing more than fight, hunt, and exist? And all alone? He fretted mentally, why was Sun Cloud doing this to him? Why was Grandfather allowing it? "You say the bonnet I was wearing in my vision was that of the war chief?" When Sun Cloud nodded, Bright Arrow asked, "What of Big Elk? He is only forty-three winters old, too young to die."

"Not in battle, my brother, but we must hold this sad news between us, for a man should not know when the Bird of Death is flying over his head. You are to be our war chief, my brother; this is the will of the Great Spirit and our father," he stated gently, kindly.

"Is it the will of our people and our allies?" Bright Arrow scoffed.

"When the time comes, it will be so," Sun Cloud responded softly.

"Do you tell me Rebecca still lives only to steal Singing Wind from my side? Do you crave her so much, my brother, that you would lie about a sacred vision? You did not share my vision; you do not know what I was told and shown. You tell me my headdress was that of the war chief's in your vision; it was not so in mine. I cannot speak for the truth or power of your vision, only mine, and I must obey it. My vision said you would try to take *all* things from me, and though I doubted such bitter words, they have come to pass, as all things in it will come to pass. You must face what we both know to be true: Rebecca is dead; Singing Wind and the chief's bonnet will be mine," he vowed confidently, but his emotions were at war within him, for the man who had left the Sun Dance pole had done so with his father's image, and he felt as if he were being tricked. He argued, "It was not a sacred vision which came to you this day, Sun Cloud; you were only dreaming from your pain and desires. You called upon your name and Sacred Bow spirits to help you; they should not have answered as you begged them and misguided our people. Cast aside their mischief or wickedness, my brother; it creates a cover of evil over our camp."

Sun Cloud wearily shook his dark head and inhaled deeply. His somber eyes scrutinized his brother closely, gravely, regrettably. He was suddenly very tired and discouraged, as if he were being drained rapidly of life, hope, joy, and confidence. Even as a child, he had never wanted to weep more than at this moment. He was consumed by frustration and disquiet, for he realized that Bright Arrow truly believed every word he was speaking. In a tone which was low and heavy with emotion, he refuted, "You are the one who is misguided, Bright Arrow. How I wish Grandfather would open your eyes and heal your wounded heart quickly, for this conflict between us is painful and destructive, and we must not allow it to cause dissension and rivalries amongst our friends and people . . . or we could all perish. Your vision was a dream of desires, not mine. Can you not see that Silver Hawk has misled you and deceived you? Can you not see how he tries to place your feet on my destined path? When Big Elk is slain and Rebecca returns, you will know I speak the truth. Make certain it is not too late to leave my path to return to your own," he advised gravely. "When our foes have been defeated and our camp is safe, before the buffalo hunt, we must share the sweat lodge and a vision-quest. Only then can we learn the truth, can we find and accept our true destinies."

Bright Arrow watched Sun Cloud conquer his fatigue and weakness to stand. "What will you tell the council?" he inquired.

Sun Cloud met his gaze and answered, "I will not speak of Rebecca or Singing Wind. I will not speak of Big Elk's death. I will not speak of the chief's bonnet. I will not speak of you and your friend. I will speak only of war and peace, for only they matter at this time. Agreed?"

Bright Arrow was surprised and pleased by that news. Witnessing his brother's concern and love for their people, he wished he had not made such cold and mean accusations, for Sun Cloud could be honestly mistaken, and he wanted to seek the truth through a joint visionquest. He and his brother loved each other, and they loved their people. They could not endanger their lands and tribe with a rash quarrel. The final decision belonged to Grandfather, so it was cruel and ruinous to clash with each other. He smiled contritely and nodded. "Do you wish the council to meet when the sun returns? The Sacred Bow race and Sun Dance take much from a man. You have honored yourself and our family with your two victories. No other warrior has claimed both in one day. You are much like our father, for he too chose the hanging rite." He had noticed how shaky and pale his brother was, and it tugged at his heart and mind, for they had been close for years.

Joy and relief surged through Sun Cloud; he had not seen that look of mingled pride, love, and worry on his brother's face in weeks. Gingerly touching his injured chest, he grinned and teased, "You did not warn me of what it was to endure the Sun Dance. I do not see how you yielded to it twice. Much courage and strength run in your blood and body, my brother. I remember the first time I looked upon you in the Crow camp when I was seven winters old and they had captured me, for I was a baby when you left our tribe and you were as a stranger. No man stood taller or braver in my eyes. You tricked and defeated our enemies, and you must do so again. In my medicine bundle, I still carry the Crow *wanapin* you gave me when you saved my life and rescued me. We share the blood of Gray Eagle and Shalee, and our spirits can never be parted. How I wish I could say, you are the oldest son and must become chief, but I cannot. Forgive me and understand, my brother, but I must obey Grandfather, no matter how great my love and pride for you or the torment we must endure."

With his eyes sparkling from unshed moisture, Bright Arrow clasped his brother's shoulder gently and replied, "I know of your sadness and suffering, for it is the same with me. I wish Grandfather could swiftly reveal who is to walk upon the one path which is stretched before us and concealed by shadows, for only one can travel it safely and happily, but we must wait for our joint vision to seek and learn the truth. Come, we will have the meeting quickly so you can rest and heal."

Together, the brothers headed for the ceremonial lodge as the summons was sent forth, *"Omniciye iyohi"*: "Come to council."

As Sun Cloud slept deeply in the tepee of the Oglala shaman, a detachment of soldiers left Fort Dakota for Fort Meade. General Phillip Cooper watched the anxious group, led by Corporal Gerald Butler, leave as a decoy to any Indians who might be spying on the fort. He was not worried about the safety of Butler's detail, for it was large and well armed and had the power of night for defense. He had a gut feeling that the Indians were not watching them at this time; no doubt, he vexingly concluded, they were home celebrating their recent victories and plotting new attacks. Too, unlike them, the Indians had to hunt fresh game daily and construct new arrows. And, there was worry over that so-called vital buffalo hunt upon which their survival depended; the longer it was stalled, the greater the advantage over the Indians.

Cooper knew Butler was still seething over his four-step demotion from major to corporal, but he knew the man would watch himself and his people carefully.

Except for being a glory-seeking and reckless fool at times, Butler appeared to be a good soldier. The man was smarter and braver than he had realized, for Butler's accusations and observations about these hostiles had proven to be lethally accurate. Butler seemed to know a great deal about this wild territory and these uncivilized heathens, and how to battle them with cunning and success, as with that ingenious grenade attack. Maybe, Cooper deliberated, he had been too hasty and harsh with Butler's reprimand and demotion. Maybe he could use Butler to win a quicker and easier victory out here.

After giving Butler's detachment time to lure away any Indian scouts or cocky warriors, Cooper ordered his three two-man units to head for forts James, Henry, and White, which were all located within three to five days of steady travel from Fort Dakota: Meade was north of them, Henry was west, James was east, and White was south to southeast. When his men returned in a week or less with four large regiments to add to his, then he could fiercely attack each Indian camp and end this ridiculous and humiliating conflict.

By two o'clock Monday afternoon, Cooper was grinning broadly and praising his crafty intelligence. Since nothing had happened by now, such as having more blue-clad bodies dumped before the fort, he correctly assumed that his men had gotten away safely and secretly. He called his officers in for a meeting.

"I want this fort stocked with plenty of meat, wood, and water while those red pigs are wallowing in their bloody *coups* and fatal plans. My instincts tell me they'll be feeling smug enough to attack this fort real soon, and we want to be ready to defeat the bloodsuckers. All we have to do is hold them at bay but keep them hanging around like a hungry hound after a juicy bone until our reinforcements get here, no more than a week. Once those red bastards are trapped between this fort and four tough regiments of U.S. soldiers, we'll mash them into the same dirt which holds the blood of my men," he stated coldly.

Major William Ames worriedly looked at his new commander and asked, "Sir, don't you think it might be wise to wait for President Monroe's special agent to arrive before we declare all-out war? Maybe Colonel Sturgis can work out a truce and sign a treaty with them. You know Ma— Corporal Butler's actions are the reason they took to the warpath again. Maybe Colonel Sturgis can straighten out this mess. Seems to me like a peaceful solution is the best course of action."

Cooper eyed Ames for a long time, then allowed his keen gaze to sweep the other officers in the room. "It seems to me, Major Ames, that you're at the wrong post if you don't like fighting Indians," he replied rather sarcastically. "Now that I've been given a chance to learn more about this area and these savages, it seems I was wrong about the situation when I arrived, and I'm man enough to admit that error. I realize, Butler has these heathens and conditions pegged right, and I plan to reinstate his rank when he returns from this current mission. And I plan to give him a medal for ambushing their infamous leader Gray Eagle. To offer them a truce after what they've done lately would be nothing short of cowardice and stupidity. I know Mr. Sturgis is an Indian lover too, and I don't plan to await his arrival so he can interfere with military affairs. I'm in charge. Is that clear?"

Major Ames felt trepidation wash over his entire body, making his flesh clammy. He knew better than to argue with a commander whose mind was set differently, but he violently disagreed. All he could do was pray that Derek Sturgis arrived swiftly and safely. Cooper had lost numerous lives to the Indians, and that was not sitting well with this tough general. It looked as if Butler's coldness and ruthlessness were rubbing off on Cooper, and that was tragic for both sides.

"Tell me, Major Ames," Cooper inquired mockingly, "how long does it take you to decide if you're going to obey your commanding officer and if you're going to give him a reply? Surely you aren't weighing your rank and loyalty against those Indians' lives? Surely you aren't trying to plot against me in favor of Mr. Sturgis' foolish plans? Just how many could you save by defying my orders and committing treason? How many red lives would make it worth such a sacrifice? If you have any objections to me or my orders, I can have you transferred today. If your Indian friends let you make it to the next fort alive . . ."

Ames's cheeks burned brightly with embarrassment and outrage. "I did not realize you were asking me a question, sir; I thought it was merely a statement of fact. If you'll check my record, sir, you'll see my obedience and loyalty have never been in question. For the record, sir, I must object to your insults in the presence of other officers. As this supposedly is a meeting, I presumed you called us here to voice our honest opinions and suggestions, which I gave and which I still believe offer the best route to peace for the Army and the white civilians in this area."

"Rest assured, Major Ames, every word you have spoken will be placed on the record," Cooper stated, making it sound like a threat. "Anyone else got any *honest opinions and suggestions?*" he queried.

When no one spoke up, Cooper smiled and said, "I'm putting Colonel Moore in charge of preparations. Congratulations, sir," he remarked humorously to Timothy Moore, whom he had just decided to promote to give Timothy more power and rank than Major Ames. "Ames, see that news of Major Butler's and Colonel Moore's promotions are posted immediately and called to every man's attention."

"Yes, sir." Ames astutely acknowledged the perilous order.

Timothy Moore grinned in pleasure and surprise. The last time he had been at this fort, he had been her commander, and he had been a lieutenant—and he had suffered an awesome defeat: personally and professionally. With luck, he had escaped the Indians' death traps twice, years ago and one a few days ago. Soon, he would help slaughter every warrior in this territory, and he would savor every minute of their pain and defeat and every drop of their spilled blood. There were three savages in particular to whom he owed severe punishment: Bright Arrow, Fire Brand, and Rebecca Kenny. With a little more luck, they were all still alive and nearby . . .

Earlier that morning, the Oglalas sent word to their friends and allies to request another intertribal war council, for they needed to strike again at their foes while the soldiers were weak and afraid. Once the bluecoats were intimidated sufficiently, the Indians could carry out their buffalo hunt and sacred ceremonies. The hotter the weather got, the farther northward the buffalo roamed, which drew the hunters too far from their camps and lands. The hunt needed to begin soon, for it was already the second week of May, and a good hunt required six to eight weeks or longer. The war council was planned for the next day at dusk, and Oglala warriors had left to deliver the message to all tribes.

Bright Arrow wanted to see his daughter Tashina and his friend Windrider, so he chose to deliver the message to their Cheyenne band. He was anxious to see and to speak with Silver Hawk and Singing Wind, but oddly did not want to face either of them at this time. He rode from camp with his good friend, White Arrow's son Flaming Star.

Deer Stalker and Night Rider were assigned to ride to the Blackfeet camp of Silver Hawk, while Sun Cloud and Thunder Spirit were assigned to the Sisseton tribe of Chief Fire Brand. All seemed to work out perfectly when Deer Stalker secretly asked Sun Cloud if they could swap destinations so he could see the female he was to join soon. Sun Cloud, hungry to see his love once more, eagerly switched.

When Thunder Spirit learned of this change, he grinned playfully at his friend and speculated mischievously, "Perhaps I could ride ahead of you after we give Silver Hawk our message. I could camp alone to think and rest, then you could join me to ride home together when the sun returns to brighten our lands and lives. No one would know we had become separated for the night."

"You would sacrifice one of your precious nights with Little Feet to help me? You would take this risk for me, my friend and brother?"

"You would do the same for me. We are as real brothers and our friendship could be no closer or stronger. Soon, we go to war once more, and each sun could be our last. You must have this time with your true love, not be denied it as I was. There is no shame or evil in this deed, for she will become the mate of Sun Cloud soon."

When they reached the Blackfeet camp just before the evening meal, they discovered that Silver Hawk was not there. It was said their chief had taken a few of his warriors and gone riding and scouting and would not return until the next afternoon. Sun Cloud was relieved that Silver Hawk did not know of the new war council, just in case he was secretly meeting with his white friends to plan more treachery; now he would learn about the meeting too late to endanger it.

Sun Cloud and Thunder Spirit gave their message to the Blackfeet war chief Strikes Fire and the Blackfeet shaman Jumping Rabbit. They alleged they must return to their camp and could not spend the night with the Blackfeet, but they would accept the invitation to partake of the evening meal in the tepee of Chief Silver Hawk. Catching a moment in passing with Singing Wind, Sun Cloud asked her to meet him by the pond later that night, and she happily agreed.

Sun Cloud paced near the tranquil pond, yearning for Singing Wind to join him quickly. As he waited, his thoughts returned to the Blackfeet camp and Little Flower. Silver Hawk's Oglala wife did not look happy or calm for a new mate, and that concerned him. When she had served his food, he had noticed marks on her wrists, which she had attempted to conceal with wide, beaded wristlets, and she had refused to meet his gaze or to converse genially. Having seen such marks before on prisoners or on friends who had escaped captivity, he recognized the signs of tight rawhide bindings which had been strained against fiercely. Another fact which piqued his curiosity was her beaded moccasins which came to her knees, as such fancy moccasins were only for special occasions. He wondered what they were concealing, and how she had been injured so oddly. She had been shaky, pale, and withdrawn, which was unlike the vivacious girl who had left his camp. As surely as death followed an arrow through the heart, she was terrified. Most intriguingly, the girl had appeared too intimidated to ask for help.

Sun Cloud advised himself to ask for Singing Wind's assistance with this curious and distressing matter. If Little Flower was as miserable and scared as he believed, something should be done to help her. A man should not abuse his wife or children, and that was how it looked to him. Perhaps Little Flower or Shining Feather would enlighten Singing Wind, who could relate the truth to him, then . . .

"You are too deep in thought, my love, and a foe could pounce upon you," Singing Wind teased as she wrapped her arms around him.

Sun Cloud sent her an engulfing glance before he swept her off her feet and swung her around, their laughter spilling forth to mingle with the sounds of the night creatures, for near darkness surrounded them. He held her tightly as his mouth captured hers and invaded it. His tongue danced wildly with hers as he seemed to draw her closer and closer to him when no space seemed left between them.

His lips brushed over her face, delighting in her taste and surface. He nuzzled his neck and face against hers, thrilling to the contact between them and the sheer joy of being with her and touching her. "You make me feel so strange, Singing Wind, as if I would cease to exist if you were taken from me. You are like my air and food, my water and my spirit. You cause me to feel weak and rash when I am not with you, and weak and bold when I am near you. You are a fierce desire burning within me, and I must have you in my Life-circle forever or perish. But I want you more than on my sleeping mat; I want to see your smile and hear your laughter each sun. I want to walk with you and speak with you. I want to see our child grow within your body, then sleep within your arms. I want to feel your hand in mine and see you at my side. I want to share all things with you."

It was as if nature's beautiful tepee surrounded them and protected them from all eyes and harms. Her body was a contradictory blend of tension and serenity. Her head seemed to spin dizzily at his nearness, touch, and stirring words. She was enchanted by him and the romantic aura which encompassed them. She gazed into his glowing eyes and said, "It is the same with me, my love. I suffer each moment we are apart. My mind spins from trying to plot clever ways for us to meet and to destroy this shield between us. Sometimes I foolishly and rashly care nothing for our duties or the thoughts of our peoples, only for us. All I desire is to be at your side each sun and moon. I have lost all patience, all modesty, all wisdom, all restraint."

Needing to have nothing between them, Sun Cloud removed her garments, then his own. As her admiring gaze leisurely roamed his flesh, his did the same with hers. There was such pleasure and excitement in merely looking at each other while yearnings increased, while fingers grew itchy to reach out and explore the other's body, while mouths became dry and in need of quenching kisses, while arms begged to embrace the other, while loving spirits mingled and communicated, while tenderness and emotions could mount and radiate to the other. It was a time for feeling with eyes and minds and hearts, before passions blazed and took control of actions and bodies.

Sun Cloud reached for her hand and raised it to his lips, and she followed his guide. He kissed her fingertips, her knuckles, the back of her hand, her wrist, and her palm. He quivered as her matching actions sent tingles over his entire body. His lips began a snailish trek up her right arm, and she began one up his. His mouth rounded her shoulder, crossed the span to her neck, drifted up her throat—

halting briefly to tease at her pulse mole and earlobe—and sensuously wandered over her cheek to capture her mouth as it completed its journey.

Sun Cloud leaned away slightly to lose himself in her enthralling gaze for a brief time. It was as if each were being drawn into potent black depths which surrounded them like very warm liquid and flowed over their sensitive flesh, sensuously massaging and enflaming them from head to toe. His head came downward as his hands cupped her face between them and his mouth melted with hers to work very gently and tantalizingly. Singing Wind's arms slipped beneath his and her palms flattened against his back to feel his muscles as they responded to his stimulating task. His body was so strong, so sleek, so beautiful.

They fused their lips many times, and each kiss increased in pressure and urgency until both were a little breathless and trembly. Their mouths began to lock feverishly and their hands began to roam. There seemed no spot of flesh on either which did not mutely call out to be caressed and noticed, and both obeyed this loving summons.

From his own dreamy haze, Sun Cloud witnessed the height of the passion which enslaved her, the love which she felt for him, the commitment which she shared with him, and these overwhelming realities sent charges of powerful love and tenderness through him. All he could think about was wanting to give her everything he could and was.

Singing Wind's back was pressed against a tree as Sun Cloud's mouth roved to her breasts, to enflame the brown peaks with a greater need to be taken eagerly and constantly. When his lips left one taut nub, his fingers would tantalize it until their return from a journey to the other one. Her head leaned against the tree behind it and she closed her eyes to absorb every exquisite sensation which he was creating. The moisture on her breasts seemed to cool them as his lips began to trail down her abdomen, to tease ticklishly at her navel before continuing its titillating journey over the area between it and her private domain. His hands grasped her buttocks and pulled her hips forward as he spread his kisses along her hip bones. A soft laugh came forth for his actions tingled and enchanted her simultaneously.

Sun Cloud sank to his knees on the supple grass. His adept hands stroked her sleek thighs, then one invaded the dark forest near his chin as he teased her flesh with his tongue. He felt her stiffen and heard her catch her breath as his fingers made contact with the bud of her womanhood. As he labored deftly upon it, causing it to become hotter and harder beneath his masterful touch, he felt her relax and heard her sigh in pleasure. He knew this task should be done slowly and carefully at first, for this tiny mound was very sensitive; later, when her passions were at their peak, he could increase his pace and pressure.

Sun Cloud nuzzled his cheek against the downy covering which concealed the heart of her sensual being. When his fingers cleared a path in her forest, his lips lavished kisses upon the straining bud. Her body and passions responded instantly to this enticing stimulation, and he thrilled to her enjoyment. His teeth playfully and exquisitely nibbled upon the tender mound and caused her to shudder with delight and a loss of control. Her thrashings, quiverings, and moanings encouraged him to continue his delectable task and to become bolder with it. Sometimes slowly and sometimes swiftly, his tongue circled the peak before he gently attacked it or engulfed it hungrily with his mouth. As he feasted upon it, one finger eased into the moist and dark canyon near it and began to travel its distance back and forth at a steady pace.

Singing Wind felt as if her flesh were burning and itching all over, and her legs felt weak and shaky, as if they would soon give way beneath her. This new pleasure was mind staggering; she felt in a fiery trance, from which she did not want to ever awaken. Her body felt as taut as a bow string, but as limp as a freshly skinned pelt. It felt wonderful and satisfying; yet it caused her to hunger for more, for a total contact with his body. It made her feel daring and wild, and she wanted to try this new pleasure upon him. She felt a strange tension building rapidly within her and she instinctively knew something different and rapturous was awaiting her. The tiny mound and its cave both throbbed and blazed with desire. She tried to relax to allow the flow of this powerful river of passion to carry her wherever it willed. Suddenly it happened, and she was stunned by the force of her release. Her hands buried themselves in his hair and she arched forward to offer all of herself to him as he drove her to mindless bliss. When the spasms ceased, she was trembling uncontrollably and breathing erratically.

Before these sensations and her hot glow could vanish, she pushed him to the ground by his shoulders and, without warning or hesitation, her mouth rapaciously covered his tasty shaft and she seemingly feasted wildly and enthusiastically upon it. He was surprised and elated by her bravery and ardor. As her fingers skillfully caressed and stroked every inch of his manly loins, her lips and tongue fervidly lavished his manhood with kisses and swirls, and her mouth gently encased it fully time and time again. Her head moved up and down as she delighted in the bliss which she knew she was giving him in return, as he was now the one who was squirming and quivering and moaning in the throes of bittersweet ecstasy, for that was exactly what it was: a blend of torment and rapture which ravished the very soul with its demands and pleasures.

Ensnared by feverish intoxication, Sun Cloud battled to keep his control over his demanding flesh. She was driving him wild, dangerously near the point of no return. He had to stop this maddening bliss or it would be too late. He called upon all of his strength and will and grasped her shoulders to force her to her back. His flaming manhood entered her receptive womanhood, which was fiery and pleading and did nothing to help him retain his mastery over the perilously quivering shaft. He felt it pulse and twitch threateningly, and he concentrated fiercely to prevent it from spilling forth its release too quickly. He murmured precautions into her ear, but she seemed too entrapped by hunger to hear them or to heed them.

Singing Wind pressed her body against his and shifted to take all of his manhood within her greedy body. She wiggled seductively beneath him and ravenously sought his mouth. Her hands roughly fondled his back and shoulders and tried to pull him more tightly to her.

Sun Cloud realized how aroused she was and was amazed by her intense craving for him. As he felt her body working with his to obtain a mutual victory, he cut his tight leash and raced for passion's peak. He felt her match his pace and quickly increase it. They rode freely and happily as they covered the short distance to their destination. As they seized their victory together, they kissed and hugged joyously.

Later, they snuggled together on his sleeping roll as their fingers lightly and lovingly grazed the flesh of the other. A refreshing breeze played over their sated bodies which were cooled and relaxed now. Shafts of moonlight filtered through the trees to dance mischievously on their naked skin and to display it to the other. The fragrance of wildflowers and the heady odor of pine and spruce mingled and teased at their noses. Tree frogs and crickets sang merrily at the pond. Owls and bobwhites persistently called to their mates. For a time, all else was pushed aside and they existed only in a world of peace and love.

As Singing Wind's fingers trailed up his stomach to his chest, they abruptly halted as she recalled what he had endured so recently. She felt the snug band of rawhide which the shaman had wrapped around his torso to hold his severed flesh in place until it reunited and healed, then leaned her head back and looked into his handsome face. "I am very proud of you, my love, but this could have taken you from me. I am glad I did not know of it before you faced such a dangerous task, and too soon after the Sacred Bow race. The hanging ritual can take a man's life. Can you speak of them to me?" she inquired.

Sun Cloud smiled and hugged her against him. "I can speak of all things to you, my love. But why do you wish to hear it all again; you sat near as Thunder Spirit told Strikes Fire and Jumping Rabbit how I challenged the Sacred Bow race and Sun Dance on the same sun? I had to do these things to prove myself to Grandfather, to my people, to my brother, and to Sun Cloud." Yet, he patiently and proudly related his experiences—physical, mental, and emotional—to her.

Singing Wind listened carefully as he spoke of his meetings with Mind-who-Roams, Bright Arrow, and the Oglala Council. "Soon, my love, all will be as Grandfather revealed to you. When you leave the war council on the coming sun, return to my side for one more touching of hearts and bodies before this new battle begins," she entreated.

"The war council will be held as Wi sinks into the body of Mother Earth on this coming sun. The talk will be long; then we will share food and sleep. If I meet you here and linger for a time, the others will reach camp long before me and will wonder where I am. It is dangerous to arouse suspicions and angers against us at this critical time." As he watched the sadness and disappointment cross her features and he imagined it could be their last meeting for a long time or on Mother Earth, he relented slightly, "I will try to sneak away before the others break camp. If I do not come before Wi sits overhead, return to your camp and safety. If Silver Hawk returns from council and notices you are gone and remembers I left early . . ."

There was no need to complete his intimidating statement. Sun Cloud inhaled deeply and frowned as he realized that his enemy could grasp this secret and ruin his life. They were too close to victory to take such risks. "I will come only if it is truly safe and wise. There is another matter which worries me: Little Flower," he hinted, then explained his meaning and requested her help in investigating the problem.

Singing Wind was embarrassed by her brother's apparent new evil. Yet, she asked herself, had she not already suspected this wickedness? She had known the flirtatious and lively Little Flower for many years, and this was not the same female who had arrived with Silver Hawk. It was not newly joined nerves or modesty which had changed her. Even Shining Feather had appeared distant and afraid for many moons; Singing Wind scolded herself for ignoring such warning signs and for thinking only of herself lately. Something had to be done about her mean and selfish brother, for his heart was growing blacker each sun. "I fear you are right, my love. I will see to it. I will come here when the sun sits there," she told him, pointing to a height which made it ten o'clock in the morning. "I will wait for you until it sits over me, then I will return to camp if you have not come. Promise you will come to me as often as you can; your council's vote was set for one full moon and only half of it has passed. It was not easy to wait for you, and after having you completely, it is impossible."

He covered her face with kisses and embraced her. "It is the same with me, my love. The more I have you and come to know you, the more I crave of each. This powerful bond and secrecy between us make it harder, not easier, to wait. I grow careless and rash. I should not have asked you to meet me here this moon. What if others find you gone? My heart clouds my head when I am near you."

She caressed his cheek. "I closed the flap on my tepee, so it is forbidden for another to enter or to call out to me. I will return while others are busy with chores; no one will see me or know I was gone. It will be the same on the coming sun. I will be careful and cunning. Where is Thunder Spirit?" she asked, suddenly remembering him.

Sun Cloud laughed mirthfully as he related his friend's suggestion and help, astonishing and pleasing her. "It is good to have such a special friend, and more so to have such a rare woman."

She smiled and concurred. "Yes, it is very good to find and to capture such a unique man. You alone can fill my heart and life."

They made love once more before they slept in each other's arms, to awaken at dawn to part reluctantly. Glancing backward as her horse weaved through the trees, Singing Wind seized every sight of him as she headed for her camp.

Sun Cloud watched her departure until she vanished from view, then joined Thunder Spirit to head home. It would be only a few hours before it was time to ride to the war council; then their crafty plans would be put in motion. He could not help but wonder where Silver Hawk had gone and what was taking place within that warrior's head.

Silver Hawk knew he could not linger near the fort much longer or it would look suspicious. He was vexed with Smith for not leaving him a message since the soldier obviously could not meet him this morning. He scoffed, what did it matter? He did not need the white man's help; he was only playing with the bluecoat for amusement.

As Silver Hawk and his band rode toward their camp, they encountered Chief Flaming Bow of the Cheyenne Red Shields Band. They halted to speak. The Blackfeet chief remarked, "We were seeking fort scouts or work parties. No bluecoat showed his face beyond their camp around the wooden tepee. I wished to slay the one who wears a red cloth around his neck; he is the one who killed my second father Gray Eagle and I seek vengeance upon him," he lied convincingly.

Flaming Bow smiled and informed him, "He is dead. I killed him four moons past and gave the red cloth to Sun Cloud when we jointly attacked the bluecoat camp far away. He wore it during his Sacred Bow race and Sun Dance two moons past, and he seized great victories in both. He chose the hanging position and the heavens cried out at his pain and sacrifice. Word came to us this past sun of a new war council; that is where we ride. Have you not heard of it?"

"We have not been in our camp. We will ride with you and your warriors. Tell me all of Sun Cloud's challenges and victories," Silver Hawk coaxed with feigned pride and pleasure, but anger and envy surged madly within him, as the last things he wanted to hear about were Sun Cloud's enormous prowess and Smith's death. For a long time, he had looked forward to slaying both, very slowly and painfully. He had to find a way to make Bright Arrow chief swiftly . . .

Chapter Eighteen

As Sun Cloud figured, the war council was a very long meeting, for the tribal leaders wanted to hear all the details of Sun Cloud's rituals and the reports from every band who had scouted or encountered the white enemy since their last meeting, before this one continued.

Mind-who-Roams and White Arrow delighted in relating the prowess of Gray Eagle's youngest son. All agreed the Sacred Bow race and Sun Dance vision were powerful medicine; and all were amazed by Sun Cloud's twofold stamina, bravery, and success. It was decided that Grandfather had blessed him and used him, and would do so again.

The joining of Silver Hawk to the daughter of Dull Knife was announced, and many congratulated the young chief, whose mind seemed to be on other matters and places today. The death of Medicine Bear was mentioned again, and his passing was mourned with a few moments of silence for he was well-liked and respected.

The joining of Tashina and Soul-of-Thunder was announced. Many congratulated him as he stood proudly between his father, Windrider, and Tashina's father, Bright Arrow. He smiled happily and thanked them.

Mild skirmishes with hay gatherers, woodcutters, and hunters from the fort were revealed and discussed. Flaming Bow's band related the discovery of the tracks of the detachment to Fort Meade and the trails of three small units to the other forts.

Sun Cloud stated factually, "Their tracks are now two days old; they are out of our reach. They go to seek help to replace the men and supplies lost to them in our attack. They work as swiftly and eagerly as the beaver before a storm." He pointedly questioned, "Why do they seek to make their home stronger and to store food? Do they prepare against being swept away by a flood of Indians, or seek to hold out against us until others come and they are strongest once more? We must not allow it. Our time is short and our moves crucial. We must strike swiftly and cunningly before more whites and weapons arrive."

Big Elk stood and suggested, "Flaming Bow, Windrider, and Fire Brand can surround the fort and cut it off from supplies and help. We can defeat them by biting off a few at a time and chewing them carefully. Your warriors can sneak close to the fort in the darkness and slay as many as possible, and they can steal or destroy all supplies and weapons. Each man slain or supply ruined must have a bluebird and eagle feather painted or placed upon it; they will fear Gray Eagle has returned from the dead to avenge himself. His spirit strikes terror and trembling in them, and we must play upon those fears and doubts. You must nip at the bluecoats each moon until they are driven inside the fort. You must not allow them to fetch wood, water, or fresh game. They will be cramped tightly and will soon grow edgy. When *Wi* dries all things, you can pile brush around the fort. The smoke and fire will drive terror into their hearts. If you can burn the wooden shield around them, they can be attacked. Even if you do not slay them all, they will flee our lands in fear and dread of our power."

This idea was praised and accepted. Big Elk smiled gratefully at Sun Cloud, for his vision plan was a clever one. The Oglala war chief continued, "There are five forts in our sacred lands. The one nearby will be cut off from the others. Three bands of warriors must prevent the others from sending more men and supplies to Fort Dakota. They dared to build it upon the face of Mother Earth, then call it by our sacred name! Once Fire Brand nearly destroyed it, but they returned and made it strong again. Silver Hawk and his warriors must ride to the west to lay in wait for the soldiers from Fort Henry. Bright Arrow and his band must ride south toward Fort White. Sun Cloud will attack the bluecoats from Fort James. Those from Fort Meade to our north who return with those from Fort Dakota will be attacked nearby; we will let the ones inside witness our power and cunning. They will tremble and leave. If they do not, we will outwait them and slay them."

"Do you say you will allow them to ride away if they ask it?" Silver Hawk inquired, as if he disapproved of this show of mercy.

Sun Cloud replied, "We must not appear 'blood-thirsty savages' as they call us. We must seek to prove we have the power to destroy each white man, but do not because we are men of honor and control. We must teach them this is our land and we will defend it with our lives, but we slay no man without reason. We must prove we are higher beings than they are. If we slay them all, they will only send more bluecoats and weapons. If we show mercy and truce, they might linger a while to think of their greed and its demands. They might realize we only want to live in peace on our lands. They might realize we are strong, yet gentle. We are firm, but our hearts are good. We must reveal the value of peace. We cannot survive if we are constantly at war; we must have time to hunt, to hold our ceremonies, to make weapons, to join in love, to train our children, to care for our old ones, to feel joy racing through our hearts, and to do many other things. Long ago, our father's father's fathers or beyond pushed others from these lands, now the whites seek to do the same with us. They are many and powerful. My father and others of you have battled them for countless winters; each time they are driven out, more take their places. Their forts are destroyed, but more are built. Even their weapons grow more powerful and dangerous with each passing season. We cannot hold them back forever. We must show signs which give them hopes of peace, or they will seek to destroy all of us."

Silver Hawk saw these statements as a way to humiliate Sun Cloud and to make him appear flawed. He jumped to his feet and shouted incredulously, "You speak of weakness and cowardice! We must not yield! We must destroy them! How can you show such prowess and courage at the Sun Dance pole, then speak of yielding to our foes? Do you wish your people to live as the white man's slaves? To hang around the forts as the Crow and live off white goods? Do you wish to see your braves take white mates or bluecoats take Indian mates and weaken the Indian bloodlines? Do you wish to hear your people insulted, and see them abused? Do you wish the white man's whiskey to dull Indian heads, and their diseases to plague Indian bodies? They cannot live in our lands! Perhaps your white blood sways your thinking and your feelings; perhaps it does not wish to war against the whites," he accused coldly, his insults barely cloaked.

Although it was a fierce struggle, Sun Cloud leashed his fury and kept it under control. He asked in a calm tone, "Must all suffer and cease to exist to prove we are braver and stronger, more honorable, than our white foes? Must a truce and peace be viewed as a defeat or weakness? Have we not made truce with Indian foes? Is a white foe any different because of his skin color? Must we fear him more? Must we make special choices for him? A foe is a foe, Silver Hawk, if he be Indian or white. Must we all die because we remain blind to the truth, the truth that we cannot war against them forever?"

Silver Hawk almost committed a terrible offense by interrupting Sun Cloud, but Sun Cloud steadily continued his reasoning. "It is not the same as warring endlessly with the Crow and Pawnee: the whites do not count *coup*; they do not touch a man with a weapon or take his possessions; they kill and destroy. Indians, even foes, do not take another's life easily or quickly, for we know the need and value of a warrior to his people and his family; we seek to defeat him in other ways, without death. Our Indian foes do not war each sun; they give time for the buffalo hunt and our other needs, which match theirs. They do not attack during sacred ceremonies, or attack like sneaky wolves who only wish to kill, not to count *coup*. The whites have no such feelings or honor."

Sun Cloud knew he was being a little contradictory, but he needed to make these leaders think, think about this bitter war and think about peace. "How long can we keep destroying them and watching them destroy us? Surely they also grow weary of war and death. We must teach them how to live and feel and think as we do, or fight them forever. Which takes and reveals more courage, wisdom, cunning, honor, and patience: teaching and surviving, or warring and dying? From birth until death, must our lives be nothing more than one endless battle? I desire more for my people, more for myself. Is it not our way to retreat honorably when the odds are against us? My mother and my father went to the white lands and they saw the power and greed of our foes; that is why my father sought peace when it was good, and battled when it was not, as we must do."

To get his points across, Sun Cloud used what the ex-scout Powchutu had related to him. "Eagle's Arm, my father's brother, visited the white lands and lived there many winters to study them; he told us the white lands are large and the whites are many and their weapons are terrible. Eagle's Arm said the white-eyes had battled larger and stronger foes than all tribes banded together, and they had won those two battles in less than eleven winters. This space of time is nothing when compared to how many winters they have battled us, and they are not at full strength. Eagle's Arm said, now that these white foes were conquered, more whites would enter our lands, and the white warriors who won those victories will be sent here to protect them. My father's brother said they believe they purchased all Indian lands from those who came as trappers long ago and called themselves French and Spanish. Their people are many; they need and desire more lands, these lands. They will fight us for them, for they believe these lands are theirs," he stressed to open their eyes and minds.

"To rush foolishly into battle accomplishes nothing but the deaths of many good warriors. We must teach them they are mistaken and greedy. We must teach them of counting *coup*, of how we battle; we must show them we do not slay good warriors unless they force us to defend our lives and lands. We must teach them the value of life, and the honor of a true warrior. I was born Oglala; I have lived as Oglala; and I will die as Oglala. I would never allow my people to be crushed beneath the bluecoats' boots, but peace is survival. We must battle the whites until we can seek it with honor. What little white blood I carry from my mother's mother does not enter or sway my thoughts."

Big Elk stated, "Sun Cloud has proven himself to Grandfather and to his people, so your fiery words shot as wounding arrows must be withdrawn from his body. He does not fear to battle the whites; each plan we have made and accepted came from his sacred vision and cunning mind. You heard the vision, Silver Hawk; it spoke of war, but also of peace. Sun Cloud was commanded by Grandfather to seek it to save all tribes from total destruction. Even as you insulted him, he held a tight rein on his anger. Such control and wisdom are great *coups*."

Silver Hawk recognized his error and quickly sought to correct it to keep from drawing unnecessary or suspicious attention to himself. "Your words are true and wise, Big Elk. I spoke too swiftly from the fires of my hatred which burn within my head and heart for the whites. I still suffer from the losses of Chief Medicine Bear and his sons at the hands of our white foes. I still suffer from the evil slaying of my second father Gray Eagle, which caused the death of my beloved second mother Shalee. It is hard to consider truce when a hunger for revenge and righting wrongs chews viciously at me. I was trained as a warrior, to defend my people, even with my life. Wisdom comes with age and experience, as with those of you who sit on tribal councils. That is why we need your guidance and knowing. Many evils of the whites trouble my mind these moons, for I know more of my people will die before we settle this new conflict. I forget I am not a chief, and we are no longer boys who can quarrel when we disagree. The taste of a truce with the whites is bitter in my mouth, but perhaps Sun Cloud speaks wisely. We must think of survival for our peoples and lands. I ask my brother Sun Cloud's understanding and forgiveness."

Sun Cloud knew Silver Hawk was lying, but he was doing it so artfully that others did not see through him. Sun Cloud smiled and said, "Many heads are hot against our foes this sun. Soon, we will cool them with victory and peace. Grandfather has spoken. I promise you, Silver Hawk; I will do all in my power to destroy all enemies of our peoples, white or Indian." He smiled again and took his seat.

Sun Cloud sat around a small campfire with his friends Thunder Spirit and Soul-of-Thunder. He was thinking perhaps the Thunder beings, who controlled their names and influenced their Life-circles, had drawn them together and made them fast friends. To forget his worries, he coaxed eagerly, "Tell me of Tashina and your family."

The Cheyenne warrior beamed with happiness as he began talking about his new wife, the sister of Thunder Spirit's new wife. Sun Cloud could see how much love and joy his two friends were experiencing and he could not help but envy them. He had not dared tell the Cheyenne warrior of his misconduct with the promised mate of his wife's father, and he continued to hold his defensive silence. Sun Cloud was closer to the son of White Arrow and knew he could trust him completely.

Sun Cloud smiled as he received news of Windrider's wife, Bonnie "Sky Eyes" Thorne, who had been a close friend of Rebecca "Wahea" Kenny. He listened to tales about the children of Windrider and Sky Eyes: Three Son, Little Turtle, Heart Flower, and Sky Warrior. He wondered if the fifteen-year-old blue-eyed blond named Sky Warrior would remain with the Cheyenne; often life was difficult for a half-breed, and Sky Warrior's looks loudly proclaimed him as half-blooded.

It was strange how the Life-circles and bloodlines of Running Wolf, father of Gray Eagle; Windrider, best friend to Bright Arrow; Black Cloud, father of the real Shalee who had married Powchutu who was the half brother to Gray Eagle and friend to Alisha who was wife to Gray Eagle and the alleged Shalee; and Brave Bear, adopted son of Black Cloud and father of Singing Wind and Silver Hawk, had crossed or mingled many times in the past and present.

Singing Wind . . . Her name warmed his very soul as it drifted across his mind. Thunder Spirit had agreed to leave early to allow him another meeting with her, if they could slip away safely at dawn. This had to be their last encounter before their joining, for it was dangerous to his rank and to her life to continue with them. If others learned he had been slipping around with his brother's promised mate, they would doubt his words and motives. Too, his love had to remain in camp where she would be safe from the whites once they were riled.

His assignment included returning to the Oglala camp to summon and to prepare his band of warriors to intercept the soldiers from Fort James, which was eastward of Fort Dakota and farthest away. He had related his vision messages and his ideas to Big Elk, who had chosen which band would attack which group of bluecoats. He knew Big Elk was not sending him far away so that Bright Arrow could quickly complete his task and earn more *coups* to help him obtain more Oglala votes for chief. Big Elk had said to him, "As you return, you will pass the area which your brother must defend. Make certain all goes well with his band. This victory is vital to us." Sun Cloud had grasped the underlying meaning of the war chief's words, just as he realized who would receive Big Elk's next vote for chief, if he lived long enough to cast it, which Sun Cloud sadly doubted. That secret worried him, for Big Elk was to ride with Bright Arrow's band . . .

Bright Arrow lay on his sleeping mat near his friend Windrider. He was glad Silver Hawk had been too busy to approach him to talk. He was angry with Silver Hawk for trying to shame his brother before the war council and to cast doubts upon Sun Cloud's powerful vision. Twinges of alarm pulled at Bright Arrow. He had been watching Silver Hawk closely, furtively. He was concerned over what certain looks and words of the Blackfeet chief had revealed. He did not want to think he had been duped, but . . .

Bright Arrow was haunted by memories of his father's visions and by his past vow to accept Sun Cloud as chief. He had witnessed his brother's courage, daring, wisdom, control, and cunning. Gray Eagle had trained Sun Cloud to take his place, and Sun Cloud was both worthy and prepared, despite his younger age of twenty-three. Sun Cloud had never failed to obey their father or the Great Spirit; nor had Sun Cloud failed or weakened in his duty and loyalty to their people, as he had done long ago in order to possess a white "foe" as his wife. His white mother and his white wife had weakened Gray Eagle's bloodline in him. Sun Cloud would marry an Indian girl, and his bloodline would remain strong. He had no sons, but his brother might have a son. Perhaps it was true that the Life-circles, powers, and bloodlines of Running Wolf and Gray Eagle must pass through Sun Cloud. He wondered, was it such a terrible thing to be only a famed Oglala warrior? Being chief was a heavy responsibility. Was he as worthy and prepared as Sun Cloud?

Bright Arrow was plagued by the memory of how Windrider, from his love and concern, had once created a false vision for him; so he knew such a thing was possible. Tonight, he had grasped Silver Hawk's hatred and envy of Sun Cloud. He knew there was something to Sun Cloud's suspicions about a traitor, just as the deaths of Medicine Bear and his sons were very strange. His entire life kept wandering before his mind's eye, and doubts were nagging at him constantly.

White Arrow placed his wrinkled hand on Bright Arrow's brow and stroked it as if he were a small boy who needed comforting. The older man smiled and advised, "The truth fights fiercely within you, my son. Accept it and be troubled no more. It is time to cast aside foolish dreams and to do what must be done."

Bright Arrow felt as if he had been given much-needed permission to relent to his conscience. He returned the smile and nodded. "You are right, my second father, but it is hard. My friends and people trusted me. I will lose all face at this second defeat."

In a voice of wisdom and gentleness, White Arrow refuted, "No, my son, it was meant to be this way. There is evil to battle, and Sun Cloud cannot do it as chief. You must be proud, for you are Grandfather's weapon. Say nothing until the time is right."

"How will I know when the time is right?" Bright Arrow asked, ready to end this heart-rending matter at once.

"When all things in Sun Cloud's vision come to pass, it will be the right time. You will know it, for there are secret messages which he has told only you. Be at peace, my son; all he told you is true."

Bright Arrow's heart raced as he echoed, "All, my second father?"

White Arrow smiled and, although unaware of the secrets of Sun Cloud's vision, but knowing it to be true and powerful, replied, "All."

Bright Arrow watched his father's lifelong friend and companion return to his sleeping mat. His mind called up Rebecca's image and the pain of her loss knifed him brutally. No, he could not allow himself such a foolish dream. Sun Cloud was wrong; White Arrow was wrong; Rebecca had to be dead or lost permanently to him by now.

Rebecca stood at the edge of their camp along the Missouri River. She was extremely restless that night; she could not shake the intimidating feeling that something horrible was going to happen soon. In a few more days, she would be home again, after a year's absence. She wondered what had taken place during that long and difficult period, and what was taking place in her love's lands this year. The news she had received from that area was old, and situations changed rapidly, especially during the spring and summer.

Rebecca's troubled mind asked why she was trembling so violently and why this aura of evil and peril seemed to permeate her entire body and even the air which surrounded her? Was she in danger or facing defeat? Was Bright Arrow in danger? Were her beloved girls in danger? She had lost one daughter at age four and one unborn child, and she could bear to lose no more children. She yearned to see Tashina and Little Feet; she had missed them terribly and worried about them each day. She was eager to see Shalee and Gray Eagle, for their days were numbered. She had missed her friends White Arrow, Windrider, and Bonnie. No, she corrected herself, Sky Eyes.

But most of all, she longed and pined for Bright Arrow. She closed her eyes and called his image to mind. He was so handsome and virile. They had been happy for years, ever since the Oglalas had allowed them to return to their camp and to join under their laws. Bright Arrow had been reborn; no, he had become more than he had been when she had met him. Her heart quivered with suspense and her body ached with need. She remembered how it felt to be locked in his arms, how it felt to be kissed and caressed by him, how it felt to feverishly share the fires of passion, and how it felt to rest serenely near him afterward. He was such a skilled and generous lover, and her flesh burned to have him cool her flames of desire.

Special times and places and ways they had made love drifted through her susceptible and dreamy mind. Her imagination was so vivid and her desires so immense that she could almost see him, taste him, feel him, smell him, and hear his voice. Leisurely nights of lovemaking and urgent bouts of mating in the daytime filtered through her thoughts.

The peaks of her breasts strained against her dress and they thrilled to his light touch as his fingertips circled and caressed them. When he began to nibble at her earlobe, she sighed in rising need. But when he found her aching and pleading peak below and massaged it, she moaned and reached for him, to urgently fuse their mouths. Despite her passions and hungers, she knew something was wrong; his face was rough with stubble, and Bright Arrow had none.

Rebecca pushed against the man who was nearly mindless with lust and who had taken advantage of her dreamy state. She did not want to scream or to cause an embarrassing scene for either of them, but she would if he did not release her. "Stop it, Jeremy," she ordered.

His voice was hoarse and muffled as he vowed, "I love you, Becca. I need you. You've been driving me crazy for over a year. If I'm gonna lose you, at least let me have you once. Please, you owe me that much since you won't love me or marry me. Lordy, woman, you can't convince me you don't want this too. Your body's like a poker that's been left in the fire too long. You were enjoying it, and I can make it feel even better. You want to burn up from denial?"

"No, Jeremy, this is wrong. I'm married to another man, and I love him," she reasoned frantically, for his desire was making him strong and rough, and he had always been gentle and understanding.

Waves of sandy hair fell over his forehead and teased the bottom of his collar. His blue eyes exposed such deep and warring emotions. "I love you and need you, Becca. I'm begging you," he entreated. "Your husband won't ever know. Think what you're denying us. I can make you happy, love, if you give me the chance."

He was an appealing man in looks and virility, but he was not the one who had enflamed her body; dreams of Bright Arrow had. To slake her passions with another was wrong. She apologized softly. "I'm sorry if I aroused you, Jeremy. I honestly did not mean to. I was nearly asleep on my feet. I must be faithful to my husband."

"I doubt he's been faithful to you," he scoffed in pain and need.

"Perhaps, but he probably thinks I'm dead," she refuted.

"Does that change anything? How are you gonna feel when you get home and find another woman sleeping in your bed with your man?"

"If that problem arises, I'll deal with it then," she retorted. Jeremy was tall and husky, but she realized he would not force himself on her. She could empathize with him, for they had been together over a year and, at most times, that year had been a good one, especially under the circumstances. She reasoned, "Would you feel the same if the husband I was forced to leave behind was you? You know how I feel about you, Jeremy. Why do you make this harder on us?"

Jeremy realized she was not going to yield to him or relent to her own desires. His had cooled slightly during their debate. He asked, "Will you make me one promise?" He did not wait for her response before continuing, "Will you marry me and return home with me if you can't locate him, or if his life's changed, or if he don't want you back?"

Rebecca did not want to consider any of those possibilities, but she had to, in case one of them was true. "If you promise to stop tempting me until I can learn the truth, yes, Jeremy; I will marry you." Why not? she asked herself. If her past was lost forever, she had to go somewhere and live somehow. She knew the fates of women who lost husbands and were left alone in this wilderness, and she could not endure such a despicable life. Besides, she was very fond of Jeremy; he was a good man, and he truly loved her.

Jeremy beamed with happiness and relief, for he could not imagine any man remaining alone after having and losing a woman like this. Too, this territory was dangerous and demanding on a trapper. If Clay Rivera was smart and lonely, he had made his fortune and left! One thing that gave him hope was the fact none of the other trappers, company or private, had heard of his rival. There was only one more trading post, then Fort Dakota. If nobody knew him or had seen him during this past year, Rebecca would be his. Six more days, and this tormenting wait would be over, then St. Louis and marriage . . .

The Oglala camp was busy the next day with warrior selections and preparations for the departure of the two war parties, headed by Sun Cloud and Bright Arrow. Plans were made for the hunters and guards for their camp. Families spoke words which could be their last ones. An aura of apprehension and excitement filled the air.

Little Feet hated to release the man in her arms, for she had waited years to have him. Her hazel eyes attempted to memorize each line and feature on his face, as if she did not already know them by heart. Her arms tightened around his waist and she rested her auburn head against his drumming heart. She could tell how much he hated to leave her side too, for his embrace was almost painful and he could not speak. "I love you, Thunder Spirit; I have always loved you, and I will always love you, only you," she murmured, then spread kisses over his chest and neck, then sealed her mouth to his.

The warrior's arms crushed her against his hard body and his mouth urgently feasted on hers. When the kissing bout ended, his left hand buried itself in her hair and pressed her head snugly near his pounding heart. He was glad that he and Sun Cloud had not been able to sneak from the war camp this morning, for it would have denied him these precious hours with his love. Pretty Woman, his father's second wife, had kept Little Feet's two sons so they could be alone. They had made love as if it were the only chance they would be given in an entire life span; yet he was consumed by desire for her again, though there was no time left to enjoy it or appease it. It would be days before he returned home, and this parting was difficult.

"My father and others will protect you and care for your needs until I return. Do not let fear live in your heart; I will be safe. No man would dare take me from my love, not even Grandfather," he teased. "Soon, we will have peace in our lands once more; Grandfather has revealed this to Sun Cloud. I love you and I will miss you."

"Take no risks, my love, even if you are a Sacred Bow carrier."

"I will be careful, for I have sons to teach and train, and a wife to enjoy." He kissed her and smiled, then went to join Sun Cloud.

Bright Arrow and Sun Cloud looked at each other, then embraced. "Guard your life, my brother, for our people need you."

Sun Cloud smiled and replied, "As they need you, my brother and my friend. Watch all directions and be safe. My love goes with you."

Sun Cloud's band rode eastward and Bright Arrow's rode southward. As they traveled, each pushed distracting thoughts aside and planned his strategy. Victory or defeat was now in the Great Spirit's hands.

In the Cheyenne camp, Windrider was saying farewell to his wife and children. The war chief's gaze scanned his love's silvery blond hair and sky-blue eyes. He had never been sorry for taking a white woman to his heart and mat, and he was glad his people and others had never protested; as Bonnie Thorne, his captive, she had saved his tribe from total destruction from smallpox and had prevented the spread of the white man's dreaded disease to other tribes.

Most called Sky Eyes his second wife, but she had been his third. His first wife, Kajihah, Soul-of-Thunder's mother and the mother of the two daughters lost to smallpox, had been weak and evil, and she had died from such wickedness. His second wife, Sucoora, had been released to marry White Antelope, after Windrider had found and fallen in love with Bonnie Thorne. But all of that had happened long ago.

Windrider joined his oldest son outside and observed the love which passed between his son and his new wife, Tashina. It was good they had joined; it was good to have his best friend's daughter as his own now.

Tashina's heart was filled with panic and dread, for her husband was a dog-rope wearer and they were heading into fierce battle. "If you do not return to me, I shall die, Soul-of-Thunder. I love you."

She looked at Windrider and pleaded, "Guard him closely, my father, and be prepared to give the barking signal if all goes bad, for he cannot retreat without it. Bring him home safely to me, and I will serve you as a slave forever."

Windrider embraced her fondly, for he had known her since her birth and she was special to him. "He will return to you; I swear it."

Despite the many onlookers, Tashina and Soul-of-Thunder hugged and kissed, then he mounted. Their gazes locked and they spoke mutely and tenderly. As she watched him ride away, tears dampened her lashes and she scolded her weakness.

Bonnie "Sky Eyes" Thorne put her arm around Tashina and said, "Come, we will work and talk to ease our worries."

* * *

In the Blackfeet camp, Shining Feather did her chores slowly near the river, for Silver Hawk had ordered her to stay out of their tepee until he left camp. Her love for him had vanished, for he had become cruel during this past winter and had not touched her gently since then, if he touched her at all. She was glad he no longer desired her, but she was not glad it was because of his evil and because of Little Flower. She longed to return home to her Cheyenne people, but she and her parents would be dishonored if she left a chief, and who would believe such black evil of him? How she wished she knew what vile mischief he was committing. She would expose him.

Shining Feather scrubbed her clothes roughly as she expended energy to appease her anger. She wondered why Singing Wind had been asking her such curious questions about her life with Silver Hawk and about their life with Little Flower. She had not dared to relate her brother's wickedness, for the malevolent male would surely kill both of them! She had seen Little Flower speaking with Singing Wind on the past moon, and she fretted over what the foolish girl might have revealed, for this second wife knew little about their husband's flaws and cruelty, or how he had others fooled by his false face. No, that was not true, Shining Feather refuted her own words. Little Flower's mood and expressions said she had been introduced to their husband's malicious ways. She hated to imagine what Little Flower was enduring at this moment, but she could not help her. They were both trapped. All she could do was pray for Silver Hawk's death, and sweet freedom.

In the tepee of Silver Hawk, he was glaring at the bound and gagged female upon his sleeping mat. He had spoken with his sister, and Singing Wind had questioned him boldly and persistently about his treatment of his wives. He had threatened to send her away if she did not marry Bright Arrow when they returned to camp. He had been furious when his sister had refused and shouted "Never!" at him. In her anger, she had exposed Little Flower's careless words about her fears of him and her desire to return home.

In her anger, Singing Wind had ridden from camp; no doubt, he decided, to cool her temper and to quake in fear of his threat and punishment! He had entered his tepee and ordered Shining Feather to vanish until his departure. He knew his first wife was too weak and scared to disobey him or to speak against him, but Little Flower . . . His Oglala wife was different. She carried a weakness of another kind, a rash weakness. Shining Feather was too proud to expose her shame and strong enough to bear it silently. Little Flower believed others would help her escape him and she cared nothing about others' thoughts of her. He would teach her a lesson which would silence her!

He scoffed with a sneer, "You are a fool, Little Flower. I should cut your tongue from your careless mouth. If you speak to my sister or others about me again, I will do so. You cannot harm me or leave me, for I am a chief. Others will think you mad if you make such rash charges against me. I would be forced to whip you at the post to cure you. No one will believe you or help you. If you speak to your father, I will tell him and all others that I beat you because you had given your treasure to Sun Cloud before you joined to me. I will say you cried and begged for my forgiveness. All will praise me for punishing you and for being kind enough to keep a stained woman so your father and people would not suffer from your shame. My charges against you could have you beaten, dishonored, and banished."

He laughed coldly and madly. "Who would doubt my words? Who would challenge me to save you? Not Sun Cloud. Not any warrior. Keep silent, or I will punish you every sun and moon," he warned.

After Silver Hawk's departure, Shining Feather entered the tepee to find Little Flower weeping and injured. Her anger and hatred mounted. As she tended and comforted the girl, she vowed, "When he returns, Little Flower, we must slay him in his sleep. We will say an enemy sneaked into our tepee and killed him. We will burn his weapons and say they were stolen. I will bind you and strike myself upon the head. We will say something frightened the foe and he left swiftly before harming or capturing us. We must be free of him."

Between sniffles, Little Flower weakly protested, "But he is a chief, a warrior. Grandfather will expose us and we will be punished. It is wrong to kill. He is our husband."

"He is cruel and evil. He must die. Grandfather wishes us to slay him, for He has finally given me the courage to do it. Hear me, Little Flower, this is a mild punishment. He can do worse, and he will. Do you wish to live this way, or be free and happy again? We cannot be free of him until he is dead. You must help me."

Little Flower recalled what Silver Hawk had done to her on their joining night in the forest and what he had done to her today. He had no right to abuse her, to humiliate her, to hurt her. She had done nothing wrong by desiring him! "Yes, I will help you slay him."

Chapter Nineteen

By Wednesday night, everything was in progress. The three war parties were enroute to carry out their interceptive assignments on the trails to the other forts, and the joint Cheyenne and Sisseton bands were initiating their strategy of terror and entrapment at Fort Dakota.

While many soldiers were being slain and valuable supplies were being stolen or destroyed, no enlightening shout or warning shot pierced the peaceful aura of the encampment, as warriors were masters of the art of hand-killing without a sound. As silently and effortlessly as a feather drifts on a breeze, the Indians sneaked into the area, skillfully performed their lethal or plunderous duties, and stealthily retreated. Over each soldier's missing scalplock, they laid two plumes—

large tail feathers from a bluejay and an eagle—which were bound with a blade of bunch grass and held in place by sticky blood. On the men's possessions or tents or ruined goods, the same warning sign was painted, or scratched with a blade, whenever there was time. All but one Crow scout were gone; he was slain, and the Crow females and children were taken captive.

The three tribes of skilled warriors took turns working all night to achieve the largest victory possible by the next morning. When it arrived, not a warrior had been seen, much less injured or captured. The world seemed so peaceful on this lovely day, until the grim discovery of the Indians' brazen deed; then the alarm was issued loudly.

The men were placed on constant alert, but ordered to hold their positions outside the fort walls. "If those red bastards think they'll frighten me, they're fools!" Cooper shrieked in outrage. He walked around the fort and surveyed the awesome damage, mainly the men's fears. "That Gray Eagle, if he's still alive, is damned clever. He knows these pea-brained men who call themselves soldiers are scared stiff of him. Hellfire, they think his ghost is after them!"

Cooper knew better than to send out patrols into the "waiting arms of those savages," and he was provoked by his helplessness and defeat. He had never tangled with this type of enemy and situation before, and he was baffled by how to conquer them. Although he refused to admit it, he was scared and worried, and had nightmares about his first defeat. He and his sentries could not detect any movement nearby, but he sensed the Indians' presence, a presence which infuriatingly caused his entire body to itch with alarm. He was eager for the arrival of his reinforcements so he could teach them a brutal lesson. As he made his rounds to each company which was camped outside the fort, he tried to reason, then shame, the men out of their fears, but he failed; maybe because he was not totally successful with concealing his own trepidation, and he despised the Indians for those feelings. His fury mounted as he realized the men seemed more afraid of Gray Eagle than of him or the Army. When many of the men pleaded or demanded to be allowed inside the fort's walls, Cooper's face went red with rage and his body was assailed by tremors and heat. The veins near his temples were pulsing noticeably as he vented his fury on the troops.

"You infernal cowards! If you're so scared out here, me and my officers will camp out with you tonight! Every man that leaves his post will lose two months' pay. And if any of you try to desert, I hope those Injuns get you and cut out your lily-livers. I've fought in many battles with odds greater than these, but my men have never had yellow streaks down their backs. You know we've got reinforcements coming, so settle down. If those red bastards had caught our scouts, they would have dumped their bodies on us last night to make us think we're cut off from help. They didn't; so that means our men got through, or will in a day or two. When they get back, we'll show those Injuns how real men fight. I expect every man to kill at least ten savages for every friend or soldier we've lost. And another thing," he shouted to them, "Gray Eagle is dead. Butler's men killed him. This," he sneered as he crumpled the two bound feathers in his hand, then flung them to the dirt to grind them beneath his booth, "is nothing more than a clever scare tactic. I bet those Injuns are watching you right now and laughing their heads off at the way you're all quaking in your boots and pissing in your pants. Are you men or babies?"

"How can we defend ourselves against braves who move like shadows? We didn't see or hear nothing all night, sir," one soldier protested the slur on his courage and honor.

As if utterly insentient, Cooper scoffed, "Then make sure each tent keeps a guard posted tonight. If you let them sneak in here and slay you or your friends or fellow soldiers, you deserve to die. Damn it, man! They're soldiers; we're soldiers; we're at war. It's kill or be killed. The choice is yours. You're not saying those heathen savages are smarter and braver than American soldiers, are you?"

"Course not, sir. But I was—"

Cooper interrupted him harshly, "No buts, soldier. It's yes or no. It's live or die. I haven't lost a battle yet, and I don't aim to let these uncivilized wretches do me in. I'll confess they caught me with my pants down last week, but they're up now and buckled tight. I recognize those savages for the devils they are, and we're gonna send them back to Hell. Stick with me, and I'll make sure you live."

"Listen tae General Cooper an' ye won't be sorry," Colonel Timothy Moore advised. "Nae better leader kin be found. These redskins hope tae win by makin' ye run in fear. Stand ye ground, lads. Timothy Moore hae faced 'em many ae time; they kin be whipped. We're brave an' strong lads, an' soon we'll outnumber 'em. I'll gie each o' ye ae dollar fur ever' one ye slay. Ye want tae hae plenty o' money fur lassies an' whiskey? Then earn ye bonus with Injun blood and scalps."

Cooper was surprised by Moore's offer and impressed by the man's cleverness, for it got the men's attention and interest. Suddenly, many were laughing and talking about how they planned to earn it and spend it. The bold reward had relaxed the men, and instilled false courage. Cooper whispered, "That was a rash statement, Tim, but you'll have to stand by it. How do you plan to pay off such a large debt?"

Moore stared him straight in the eye and replied quietly, "Ye hae best pray I'll make ae large debt tae settle with my savin's. Ye still underestimate these savages, Phillip. Ye're right; they be from tha divil an' they got 'is luck an' pow'r an' evil. This is nothin' more 'an ae taunt. Ye hae better hope ye reinforcements arrive, fur ye kin bet they hae war parties on their tails. We canna sit 'ere an' do nothin'. When they dump those bodies in our laps, it'll be tae late tae work an' worry. We got tae think of somethin' real clever an' very soon, an' we will," he asserted confidently, then coldly eyed the forest.

Cooper studied the blue-eyed flaming-haired man and asked, "You aren't teasing, are you? Those damn bastards are trying to wipe out all of us! You had a spy in your fort, that Sisseton scout Fire Brand; you think they've got a spy here, or we've got a traitor?"

"Nae, it's tha work o' tha Eagle's son. He taught 'em well. Not tae worry, sir; this time, those babe birds are mine. Tha bes' we kin do is let 'em play ae while, an' ignore 'em."

"Ignore them?" Cooper echoed skeptically. "Look at this mess."

"We were lax, sir. We bes' make sure it dinna happen ag'in. They're waitin' fur their war parties tae wipe out our reinforcements an' return 'ere tae attack us. It canna work, sir. Four bands defeated? Nae, sir, never. Relax. We'll win this time," he vowed sardonically.

"I hope to hell you're right, Tim, because I have this powerful urge to massacre every one of them, including their breeders and brats. The only way to rid ourselves of this problem is to squash it into the ground, then prevent it from reoccurring. What do you think?"

Timothy Moore grinned wickedly and replied, "Ye be right an' clever, sir. Nae women, nae babies; nae babies, nae warriors; nae warriors, nae war. Nothin' could be simpler, sir, nothin'."

"You think the men will go for total annihilation?"

"After this?" Moore hinted, nodding to their bloody surroundings. "An' their next attack? Ye kin bet on it, sir," he declared with a merry laugh. "I sac we dinna leave ae single one alive an' kickin'."

"I say, you're right," Cooper agreed, then joined Moore's chuckles. "Let's get some crafty plans to brewing," he suggested eagerly.

Thursday night, in spite of every precaution, more soldiers were killed and more supplies lost. This time, however, two warriors were slain. As promised, Cooper and his officers had camped outside with the men, but had made certain they had heavy and competent guards.

Moore stopped Cooper from humiliating the nervous men again, warning him that many men were close to the panic edge, which could cause trouble. He cautioned him about how important it was to retain the men's loyalty and confidence, and how rash it could be to provoke them with insults. A terrified man was an unpredictable man, and an undependable one. Moore concluded that the Indians did not want to attack during the night, so he wondered just how many were hiding in the forest nearby. Perhaps only a small band of elite warriors, he mused. Moore advised Cooper to allow the anxious men to enter the fort at dark and to sleep inside, or their terror could mount and get the best of them. The man with fiery hair hung the lifeless warriors' bodies from the supporting post over the fort gate. Taking his sword, he malevolently hacked at them, laughing and dancing about playfully as if it were some game or sport. Moore knew he was being observed by dark eyes in the forest, and he knew nothing pained or riled an Indian more than having a friend's body chopped up like firewood.

Cooper would not allow any soldier or officer to interfere, even though Major Ames loudly protested the barbaric behavior. "Have you taken a look at your men, Major? They were butchered in their sleep. And while you're answering, tell me who and what provoked them for the past two nights? The slaughter of half of my troops amply paid for the lives of Gray Eagle and his party of Sioux. These last two attacks weren't for revenge or justice or their so-called honor; this was a damn declaration of war, one I aim to accept."

"We're supposed to be soldiers, sir, men of honor and intelligence. We're supposed to be civilized and level headed. This conduct is outra—"

"Silence, Major Ames!" Cooper ordered, his eyes appearing to glitter with wildness. "Those Injuns made the damn rules, not me. This display is to teach them a lesson, to throw a little fear and hesitation in them. I want those red bastards to think hard and long before attacking us again. I want to repay them in like kind: vengeance seems to be the only thing they understand. If this doesn't provoke them into an open fight where we can defend ourselves, then it will let them know we won't take their savagery lying down. When they see we aren't scared and we'll retaliate, they'll attack or retreat. I'll settle for either. You should learn to hold your tongue, sir, because you're forgetting who I am and who you are."

Ames responded bravely. "I think the problem is, sir, that you've forgotten who you are and what you stand for. A man of your rank and reputation and intelligence should never allow something like this. I'm sorry you lost half of your regiment on arrival and I'm sorry you weren't adequately informed and prepared for this assignment because it has done something terrible to you, sir. May I respectfully request, sir, that you return to your quarters and give this matter deep study?"

Cooper glared at Ames, then stated tersely, "Request denied. You're the one who's blind and foolish where those savages are concerned. Take a detail and bury those soldiers. And if I were you, Major Ames, I would place plenty of guards around; you wouldn't want your Injun friends out there killing you by mistake and making a liar of you."

As William Ames was walking away, Cooper halted him to add, "When the next detail heads for another fort, I want you to go with them, and remain there. You prepare your transfer papers and I'll fill in the date and place as soon as I can. I don't want you around this fort much longer, Ames; misguided men and dreamy-eyed fools like you are dangerous in a situation like this one."

Ames did not protest Cooper's intention or insult. He realized it was futile to argue with a man who had lost his honor, reason, and perspective. The only person who could get through to Cooper was Derek Sturgis, President Monroe's personal agent, and Sturgis was intimidatingly late. Lord, help the whites and the Indians if anything had happened to the only man who could lessen or solve this crisis . . .

The burial detail had no problems with the Indians, to Ames's relief. But when he tried to cut down the Indians' bodies to bury them, Moore refused to allow it. Ames snapped, "My heavens, man! This isn't ancient Rome and those aren't Christians we're fighting! There isn't any need to hang their mutilated bodies along the roads or tack their heads over our gates as warnings."

Moore's blue eyes narrowed and frosted. "Ye been fightin' 'em ye way fur years, an' look wha' happens, Major; now, we try it my way. I dinna plan tae lose another lad tae them divils."

"Don't you think you should keep your personal feelings out of this situation, sir? I know all about what happened to you at this very fort years ago. If you've returned to avenge yourself and your men, you could be dead wrong, and you can get all of us killed. Don't you realize those Indians believe they are only protecting their lives and lands from a white invasion? They've been here forever and they don't recognize the Louisiana Purchase. Don't you understand that we have to make peace with them? Lord knows they're probably just as eager and ready for peace as we are. How many lives are you willing to sacrifice before you come to your senses? Why don't you stop filling Cooper's head with these crazy ideas?"

"We should hae sent ye tae Fort Meade instead o' Major Butler. When he returns with our troops, ye Injun friends will be dead."

"You really hate them, don't you, and you're willing to do anything to punish them?" Ames probed knowingly.

"They butchered my men an' destroyed my command. They tried tae kill me. I kin never rest till I slay those who tricked me."

"You mean Fire Brand, Bright Arrow, and Rebecca Kenny?"

"All those red bastards, Ames, but especially those three," Moore admitted freely. "Go do ye duty an' leave tha savages tae me."

Several intrepid warriors who could speak English, and who had concealed themselves inside empty crates near the fort to observe the soldiers closely during the day, intending to escape when darkness covered the land once more and to report their findings to the others, listened carefully to the words each man spoke and memorized each's face.

One of the hidden braves, Soul-of-Thunder, knew he must recover the slashed bodies of their fallen warriors before his retreat that night . . .

The Crow scout returned to where Gerald Butler was camped with his men, and with those from Fort Meade, to report the shocking situation at Fort Dakota. Butler listened carefully, then grinned at Cooper's predicament which, he felt, the commander deserved for not heeding his warnings! Butler thought for a time, then said, "Since we can't get in right now, I think we should go raiding. If we attack a few camps and they send for help, that should pull that war party off the fort."

Butler looked around and concluded that he had plenty of men and supplies to "hit those Injuns where it hurts, in their camps and at their families." He looked at the Crow scout and ordered, "Find us some camps that don't have many warriors around." To the men, he said, "Mount up, boys; we're going Injun hunting."

One soldier asked, "You sure we should do this, sir?"

Butler laughed satanically and replied, "How else are we going to lure those savages away from Fort Dakota? General Cooper is there, and he put me in charge. Mount up and let's ride. We got us some red hides to skin."

To the west of Fort Dakota on the trail to Fort Henry, Silver Hawk and his band were camping and waiting for the soldiers to head into their impending trap. The Blackfeet chief kept wondering if he should find a way to alert the soldiers to their imminent peril, in case he needed their help or truce later.

There was no need, for the Crow scout discovered the warriors' camp and warned the soldiers to skirt that area. The detachment headed northeastward, hoping to join up with the one from Fort Meade.

That night at Fort Dakota, warriors bravely and furtively piled brush against the back wall of the fort and set it ablaze. Remaining out of gun range and trying to draw the soldiers' attention while the concealed warriors escaped, Sisseton warriors sent forth blood curdling yells and Cheyenne Dog Men yelped wildly.

Before seeking safety, Soul-of-Thunder and one other warrior cut the bodies of their fallen comrades free and returned them to their people. Their courage and daring was praised highly, and Windrider smiled proudly at his valiant son. The Indians knew how the fire and the missing bodies would affect the soldiers, and they were right.

Before Cooper and Moore realized what the Indians were attempting it was too late. The fire was doused, but the bodies were gone. It was clear to them that they had to be more careful and alert. The men were ordered to remain inside the fort until the reinforcements arrived, for Moore suspected that the Indians' daring would increase after tonight's victory, to include daylight attacks.

* * *

Saturday afternoon, Sun Cloud's band cunningly and successfully ambushed the detachment from Fort James by imitating the Apache attack skills. The soldiers and Crow scouts had been fooled completely by the artfully camouflaged warriors, warriors who had used gravelike holes, bushes, rocks, landscape, animal hides, and body paint to conceal their presence until it was too late for defense. Once the soldiers had ridden into the midst of the warriors, they were too close to use rifles or to flee. There was nothing left for them to do but fight hand to hand, at which the Indians were masters.

When the soldiers were all wounded or slain or pinned down, their leader offered surrender, hoping to save his remaining men. When he shouted, "This is Lieutenant Thomas Daniels of the U.S. Army; I want to speak truce with your leader," Sun Cloud ordered the battle to halt.

Sun Cloud shouted to the man, "Come forward, man called Daniels, and speak with Sun Cloud, son of Gray Eagle."

Without hesitation, Thomas Daniels obeyed. "You've proven your point, Sun Cloud; why kill helpless men? We don't want to battle you."

Sun Cloud replied smoothly and astonishingly, "We do not wish to battle with you, Daniels, friend to Ames. We know this war is not of your making, but you follow the orders of your evil leader. Return to the fort and tell the man called Cooper, the Indians will never leave these lands. He must stop the killing and attacking, or all whites will die. We left the fort and the white settlements in peace, but your men have not left us in peace. Stay where you have settled, but do not attempt to take more land or to push us aside. We tolerate your presence, but we will never allow your evil and greed to harm our people and our lands. We did not begin this new conflict; the one named Butler did so, and the one named Cooper does so. This cannot be. Return to your fort and warn your people of our anger and revenge if they continue this war against us. Warn them to heed the words of Ames and Sturgis. Warn them to reject those of Butler, Cooper, and Moore; they are enemies of all Indians. Go, Daniels, for you are known to us as a good man, and Indians do not slay good men."

"What about my men, Sun Cloud?" Thomas Daniels inquired.

"If you order them to remain here or to return to their fort on the James River, they will be spared. If they refuse, they must die."

Daniels smiled and nodded. "You're a good and fair man like your father, Sun Cloud. We'll do what you say, and thanks. I pray Cooper will listen to me, or that Sturgis arrives soon. He's late. Ames and me hope he gets here safely, and real soon. Most of the men don't want to fight your people, but we have our orders. I promise you, if those orders could come from Sturgis and the President, they would be different. Please, make sure he gets through," Daniels urged gravely.

"We know of the man called Sturgis and we trust him. We will speak to him of truce when he reaches our lands. Do not fear, he will not be harmed. He is as important to us as he is to you. We do not wish war, but your people force it upon us. Sturgis can help both sides."

Daniels said sincerely, "If your father is dead, Sun Cloud, I'm sorry. Gray Eagle is, or was, a great man. I want you to know, Major Ames didn't have anything to do with that bloody ambush."

"We know this, that is why we sent the warning to him to guard his back against the one called Butler, who wishes Ames and Daniels dead to continue his evil. We know the hearts of those at Fort Dakota. We do not wish to kill good and honorable men. When they side with those who are evil, we have no choice."

"I'll carry your message to General Cooper and I hope he'll listen. If not, me and Bill, Ames," he clarified, "will see if we can get in touch with Sturgis or the President before things get out of control here."

Sun Cloud warned solemnly, "You must work fast, man called Daniels, for control is vanishing swiftly and evil is growing rapidly."

After Daniels rode off, Sun Cloud's party left the wounded men to tend themselves and to return to Fort James as promised. "We ride toward my brother and Fort White, Oglalas, for my heart is troubled."

Sun Cloud had reason to worry, for the battle between Bright Arrow and the Fort White troops was not going well. Bright Arrow had attempted a cunning plan of his father's: lure the foe into an ambush by using a small band of warriors who retreat under fire and entice the boastful foes to follow them, placing the enemy band between two hidden groups of warriors, who can attack triangularly once the soldiers are in the middle of all three bands. The Crow scout had recognized this ploy and warned the others about it.

Bright Arrow had divided his band into three parts and had hoped to entrap the white unit between them, but he had not planned on the cunning and intelligence of the white leader, who had divided his troops and sent them right and left to close in on and surround the fleeing band.

Outnumbered and outmaneuvered, Bright Arrow and his band realized they had to turn and attack boldly and rashly to protect the other two unsuspecting bands from their clever foes. Bright Arrow heroically charged toward the approaching soldiers, hoping to seize their attention, and that of his other bands.

As hoped and expected, the military detachment reunited to accept Bright Arrow's bold challenge . . .

The Blackfeet camp was attacked without mercy by Gerald Butler's troops, and the beautiful girl in the Chief Medicine Bear's colorful tepee was taken hostage. As with the other camps nearby, Butler allowed several young braves to escape, to warn and to summon the Indians who had Fort Dakota surrounded. He shouted to his men, "Let's ride, men. Those warriors should be returning with help before dawn. By the time we reach Fort Dakota, they'll be gone. This pretty thing will be our protection," he remarked of Sun Cloud's secret love.

Singing Wind fought Butler valiantly and rashly, until he struck her forcefully across her jaw and rendered her unconscious. As he rested her limp body before him, he realized why Smith had asked for her as a reward from Silver Hawk; she was beautiful, ravishing. Many braves had died trying to prevent her capture, and he smiled wickedly. As long as they had her, they were safe, he decided.

Around three o'clock on Sunday morning, the tribes at the fort received the dire news of the attacks on their camps, and all raced from the fort to defend them, leaving several scouts and spies behind.

At dawn, Butler and his troops, along with those from Fort Meade, arrived and revealed their actions of the past two days, which had resulted in this reprieve. Singing Wind was placed under guard in the blockhouse. Then Butler told of how they had hidden along the trail until the Indians passed them on their frantic return to their camps. He was astonished and pleased to learn of his reinstated rank and exoneration of all past guilt, especially since these had occurred before his heroic and daring escapades.

A few hours later, the troops from Fort Henry arrived, bringing along several civilians whom they had encountered on the trail and taken into their protective custody. They reported on the ambush, which they had avoided, and hinted at the peril that the others must be facing.

Cooper's gaze scanned the number of soldiers, and he remarked aloud, "Even if they don't get through, we have plenty of men and supplies to repel any Injun attack. When they realize two detachments arrived safely, they'll get nervous. After they get over their fury at Butler's clever foray. You men get rested, then we'll handle them good."

Just as Jeremy Comstock informed General Cooper of his reason for coming to this area, Timothy Moore approached from behind him and stated, "Dinna worry, lad; I'll take guid care o' Mrs. *Clay Rivera*. She is jus' tha weapon wha' we've been needin'. Guid tae see ye ag'in, Rebecca. How is ye husband Clay, er should I sae, Bright Arr'r?"

Rebecca whirled and stared at him, for that was a voice which she would never forget, a voice which she believed had been silenced forever. "Timothy Moore?" she murmured in disbelief, then fainted as she comprehended the meaning of his reality and presence.

Jeremy caught Rebecca before she could hit the hard ground. His curious gaze engulfed the soldier who had brought on her condition, the flaming-haired man who seemed to know his love. Hastily he asked questions and demanded answers. The men talked and argued.

Timothy Moore laughed and scoffed, "Tha filthy bitch lied tae ye, Mr. Comstock. She be tha whore an' squaw o' Bright Arr'r, son o' Gray Eagle. I hae tae take her prisoner. She be ae criminal an' foe."

Jeremy Comstock could not believe the words which the officer spoke against his love, for he had known Rebecca Kenny for over a year. Yet the commander in charge swore that his officer was speaking the truth, and ordered Jeremy's beloved to be imprisoned. Things looked and sounded bad for Rebecca, but Jeremy vowed to remain at the fort until this crazy matter was clarified.

The unconscious Rebecca was tossed into the blockhouse with Singing Wind, who was stunned and overjoyed by the flaming-haired woman's return. The Indian princess listened as the white men talked freely and carelessly outside her prison . . .

Bright Arrow's Oglala band watched in mounting dread and fury as their captive leader was lashed shamefully with the soldier's belt after responding to a deceitful truce flag. The wounded warrior never cried aloud, but he uncontrollably winced at each agonizing blow and cursed his stupidity. Their war chief, Big Elk, was dead, as Sun Cloud had foretold. The Oglala trap had failed, and Bright Arrow had sought to dupe the soldiers with a truce, but the trick had been on him. As they tortured him to force his warriors to surrender, he knew his braves would not, for it was forbidden, even unto death. He could not help but wonder if this was his punishment for intruding on Sun Cloud's fate. He told himself he was wrong, for he had decided to step aside, so his removal by death was unnecessary. His thoughts were of his family and people as he yielded to the blackness which was filling his head.

Slowly Bright Arrow aroused and found himself looking into the worry-lined but smiling face of his brother. He was confused, and exhausted. His body trembled and ached. He tried to sit and talk.

Sun Cloud prevented it and entreated, "Do not worry, my brother, for our enemies have yielded. We will take you home to heal and to rest."

From his blur of pain and bewilderment, Bright Arrow murmured weakly, "I am . . . ashamed, my brother. I . . . tried to take the chief's bonnet and Singing Wind . . . from you. I was blind and foolish. You must forgive me. I have dis . . . honored myself and our people."

Sun Cloud stroked Bright Arrow's sweaty brow and refuted, "No, my brother, you have done as Grandfather wished. You will become war chief, for Big Elk is dead. Rest, and we will speak later."

"I do not deserve to live. I let my foes trick me with a truce flag and many of my warriors died over my foolishness."

"No, my brother," Sun Cloud protested firmly. "We were told to seek peace where we could find it. It is not your fault it was not here, for you obeyed in the face of great danger. You were very brave and all will honor you." His dark eyes roamed his brother's numerous injuries and darkened ominously as they reached the wales from the soldier's leather belt. That treatment was humiliating and unforgivable, and the soldier had paid for his action with his life. Sun Cloud gently tended his brother's wounds as he related his own battle.

Sun Cloud announced to the group, "We will take our brave warriors home; then we will join those at the fort. Our victory is near."

Travois were constructed to carry the wounded and dead home, which would slow their return. This time, there was only one survivor, a young soldier whom Sun Cloud had chosen as his warning messenger to Fort Dakota. The two bands realized, if Silver Hawk had been as successful as Sun Cloud had, the hostile fort would soon be helpless . . .

"Wahea?" Singing Wind gently shook Rebecca's shoulder as she called her name to arouse her. She watched Rebecca stir and moan, and was eager to hear how the woman had survived and returned.

Rebecca gazed into the Indian maiden's face, then smiled. "Singing Wind, what are you doing here? What happened? What's going on?" she probed, then frowned worriedly as reality swiftly engulfed her.

Singing Wind hurriedly explained the attack on the Blackfeet camp and her capture. She related the current events and dire situation to the stunned woman whose return would fulfill her dreams and destiny.

"Dead?" Rebecca murmured sadly at the news about Gray Eagle and Shalee. "How is Bright Arrow? Are my children safe?"

Singing Wind tried to bring Rebecca up to date gradually, not wishing to overwhelm the woman with so many distressing facts at once. She could tell that Rebecca was happy for her daughters and was eager to see them. But Rebecca was distressed over the other episodes. She thought it was best to keep silent for now about the brothers' rivalry over the Oglala chief's bonnet and her. "Tell me of your trouble."

Before Rebecca responded, first, there was something she had to know. "He hasn't given me up for dead yet? He hasn't . . . joined to another?" the auburn-haired beauty inquired anxiously.

"No, but he has suffered greatly over your loss. Where have you been? What happened to you?" Singing Wind asked apprehensively.

Rebecca told the woman whom she had known since childhood the details of her stunning trek away from and back to this land and her love. She talked about Timothy Moore and the peril he represented.

"It is bad, Wahea," Singing Wind concurred. "My brother was a fool to fail in his duty. His heart and deeds have been wicked for many winters, but they darkened during this past season. We will speak of Silver Hawk later," she hinted, knowing that to expose her brother's evil would also expose the false visions and their effects on many lives, including theirs. "I pray the other bands are safe and victorious. We must find a way to escape and to warn our tribes. It is clear the bluecoats see us as weapons against our peoples. We must not allow this, even if we must die. Grandfather will help us return to our loves and destinies. All is good, for He has brought you home."

"I pray it wasn't to get this close, to die before . . ."

As Rebecca began to weep softly and fearfully, Singing Wind comforted her, "Do not say or think such things, Wahea. All is not lost."

Rebecca looked into the Indian beauty's eyes and argued, "But you do not know of his evil and hatred. Timothy wants me hurt and dead."

The women were given food and water that night, and Timothy Moore came to visit. He stood at the door and gazed through the bars at the woman he had loved and wanted to marry long ago, the woman who had duped and betrayed him, the woman who had taken nearly everything from him. He was consumed by the desire to see her suffer, and to see Bright Arrow suffer through her pain and loss, more than the warrior had suffered during her mysterious absence. He had ordered Jeremy to stay away from Rebecca, and the trapper was compelled to obey. Presently, Jeremy was getting drunk at the sutler's place.

"Ye are like ae little red bird in ae cage, Rebecca Kenny," he taunted her. "I plan tae wrap my hands around ye neck an' squeeze tha life from ye traitorous body, when I hae nae more use for ye."

Rebecca stared at the spiteful male, but did not reply. She knew it was useless to debate his hatred, his past actions, and his current ones. He would merely derive sadistic pleasure from her displays of fear and protest. Silence and courage would serve her and suit her better.

"My little bird hae nae song tae sing tonight?" he jested mirthfully. "Ye will be singin' plenty soon, singin' o' ye pain an' for ye betrayal."

Rebecca clenched her teeth to hold back her retorts. She shifted sideways on the bunk to place her back to him. No cunning plan came to mind, for it was perilous to try to dupe Timothy again, and it probably would not work. Escape seemed impossible, for this fort would be guarded like a bank filled with gold!

Timothy laughed maliciously, then strolled away to his quarters.

Singing Wind went to sit beside Rebecca. Their gazes met and they embraced each other for comfort and encouragement.

It was around midnight when Singing Wind and Rebecca were aroused from their restless sleep by the door opening to their prison. The nervous guard entered with Timothy Moore, who reeked and swayed from whiskey. The two women sat up on their bunks and Moore glared from one to the other in the eerie glow which was cast by his lantern.

"Sir, I don't think we should be in here," the guard advised, for he perceived that the man was up to no good. He would be discharged soon, and he did not want any more trouble than they already had.

Moore faced him and sneered. "I be ae colonel an' ye be ae corporal, so stay out o' my affair. I want tae question this Injun whore."

Singing Wind rose quickly and took Rebecca's side protectively as the drunken man started toward the auburn-haired woman. Moore's agitation increased, and he charged forward to deliver a stunning blow across the Indian woman's jaw. When Singing Wind collapsed to the ground, Moore kicked her in the ribs, nearly breaking one.

The guard rushed forward and seized Moore's arm to keep the officer from kicking the unconscious female again. "Sir, what are you doing? These are helpless women. They're valuable captives. General Cooper won't like this," he reasoned anxiously.

"Git ye ass outside, Corporal," Moore commanded harshly. "An' dinna ye enter ag'in before I leave. An' cover tha window on ye way out."

The guard was alarmed and repulsed, but figured he should obey the uncontrollable man who was a higher-ranking officer and a friend of his commander's. He took a blanket and covered the window over the door, the only one in the small blockhouse, then left reluctantly.

Moore glanced at their private surroundings and grinned satanically. He grabbed Rebecca as she tried to flee past him to the door, either to escape or to cry for help. He clamped his large hand over her mouth and nose, then shook her roughly. "There be nae escape for ye this time, Rebecca. I should hae done this long ago. When I finish with ye, nae man will want ye or will look at ye," he threatened.

He backed her to the bunk and shoved her upon it. Pinning her down with his weight and strength, he yanked off his yellow bandana and gagged her with it. When she continued to struggle with him, he slapped her several times to stun her. Then, withdrawing his belt, he bound her hands securely behind her back before he slowly and intimidatingly removed his boots and shirt and tossed them aside. When Singing Wind moaned and moved, it seized his attention. Taking his knife, he cut strips from a thin blanket, then bound the Indian girl's wrists and ankles and gagged her. As he pulled off his pants, he chuckled and said, "If I hae time an' energy left, little savage, I'll take ye too."

Rebecca's dazed senses gradually cleared and she recognized her perilous fate. Her wide eyes gaped at the naked man who was standing beside her. A muffled cry and more vain struggles came forth as Timothy seized her dress and ripped open the front of it. One hand roughly fondled a soft breast as the other moved up her thigh and halted as it made contact with her womanly region. "I see ye be hot an' eager for me. I bet ye ain't slept with tha trapper, so I bet ye be real hungry tonight. I been waitin' o'er twenty years for this moment."

"And it won't come tonight either, Colonel Moore," Major Ames declared from the doorway as he entered to halt this despicable cruelty. The guard had rushed to his quarters, awakened him, and warned him of this vindictive and outrageous situation.

Moore whirled at the intrusion and, unmindful of his nudity, scoffed, "Ye bes' git out o' here, Major Ames, or ye be ae dead man."

Ames did not waver or retreat. "Not this time, Colonel. I'll fight you and kill you before I let you rape these two women."

Timothy Moore chuckled and invited, "Why dinna ye take tha pretty Injun girl for yeself? This one be mine. Rebecca owes me plenty, an' it's time tae collect."

"She doesn't owe you anything, you vile bastard. You brought your troubles on yourself. Don't go putting the blame for your mistakes and cruelties on her. Now, get out of here and sober up."

"I see, ye wants her too. Dinna worry, lad; ye kin take her after I finish. She's got enough treats tae feed this whole fort. Tha's ae guid idea," he stated crudely and wildly. "Let all tha men hae her; tha' will punish them divils. Bright Arr'r will die o' grief an' pain."

"You're crazy, Moore," Ames charged as he observed the man.

"Aye," Moore nonchalantly agreed. "But she will cure me real soon."

Ames approached to subdue the officer, but Moore attacked him. They scuffled frantically, for Moore had grabbed his knife and was trying to kill Ames to cease the man's interference.

Singing Wind had recovered her senses, and both females were trying futilely to free themselves. As the enraged Moore pinned Ames to the ground and raised his knife to plunge it into Ames's heart, the guard clobbered Moore with the butt of his rifle. Moore fell aside, and Ames scrambled to his feet.

Ames tried to slow his rapid respiration before saying, "Thanks, Corporal Richards. Lordy, what a mess we got here," he mumbled, not knowing what to do next.

Corporal Clint Richards scratched his graying head and hinted, "This ain't the end of it, sir. I wouldn't be surprised if he talks General Cooper into letting him have this girl. Cooper's been *loco* ever since he got here, and Moore's got him under his control."

"You're right, but I can't go against them. Unless . . ." he murmured thoughtfully, then eyed the two women. "Bind and gag Moore while I free these women. It seems to me like there's gonna be an escape tonight. I doubt Moore will contradict us once he sobers up."

While Clint obeyed Ames's order, which he found most agreeable, Ames freed Rebecca and Singing Wind and explained the shocking plan to them. The two women listened carefully and gratefully. As he bound and gagged Clint, he said, "This won't seem impossible. You know about the secret gates. I wish I could get you some horses and supplies, but that ain't smart. Just get out of here and as far away as possible. Find a place to hide until those warriors return and find you."

The women thanked Major William Ames and followed his clever plan. Getting out of the fort was easier than they had expected, for the cell and concealed gates were blocked from the sentry's view by another structure and the troops were camped on the far side of the wall. After they vanished into the darkness, Ames completed his daring scheme. All he could do was pray that the escape was not discovered for a long time, time enough for the two women to hide themselves. If Moore reported the truth, it would be his word against theirs, for they would swear that Moore had attacked Clint to keep the guard from protecting the women or from summoning help. They would deny that Clint had sought Ames's help and received it. They would swear that the women had overpowered the wicked Moore and escaped.

Ames smiled at Clint and said, "Let's just hope nobody saw us." The gagged Clint nodded, then Ames stealthily retraced his earlier steps after leaving the guardhouse door cracked.

Crawling gingerly on their stomachs until they were a safe distance from the fort, Singing Wind and Rebecca snailishly reached a cover of tall grass and bushes. From there, they cautiously made their way to the forest. Well-trained and highly skilled, Singing Wind concealed their tracks from the Crow scouts who were certain to pursue them soon.

Rebecca whispered, "I hope they fall for Major Ames's tale, or he's in big trouble. And we are too if we don't find a perfect place to hide. We can't get far on foot and without supplies. Do you think anyone will return in time to rescue us?"

Singing Wind halted her task briefly and replied, "I do not know, Wahea. All camps are busy with raids and defense. These new whites are evil and clever. We must get home to warn them of this new treachery. If we . . ." The Indian female went silent to check their shadowy surroundings with her keen ears, eyes, and nose. *Someone comes*, she warned with sign language, and the women prepared themselves to confront this new peril.

Chapter Twenty

As the scouts who had been left behind surrounded the two women, Soul-of-Thunder stared at Rebecca Kenny in disbelief. "It *is* you, Wahea," he stated incredulously, then hugged her tightly and joyfully.

Rebecca knew from Singing Wind's words that this young man had married her daughter Tashina recently. She hugged him affectionately, for she had known the son of her husband's best friend since he was a baby. "I am home at last, and I have heard the wonderful news about you and my daughter. I am proud to have you as my son, and I am eager to see my family. We need help. What are you doing here?" she suddenly asked, as if just realizing they had been rescued.

Soul-of-Thunder hurriedly explained their presence and their observations earlier that day. "We were told of Singing Wind's capture and the attack on the Blackfeet camp and other camps. Silver Hawk was not with us; he was band leader for one of the war parties. We sent word to him along the trail to Fort Henry. When I saw the flaming-haired woman enter the fort with bluecoats, I shivered and rubbed my eyes, then told myself I had not seen what I believed I had. How can this be? All feared you dead or lost to enemies."

As quickly as she could, for she knew time was short, Rebecca related the highlights of her disappearance and return. "They will discover our escape soon. We must all flee, for many will pursue us. It is not safe here." She reported the Army's size and strength, and revealed the evil of its leaders. "We must all leave. If we are to know victory and peace, all tribes must battle this foe as one."

"That is what we do, Wahea, my new mother; all tribes ride and attack as one to be stronger than our foe. We must leave before they search for you and capture all of us. They are too many for only four scouts to battle. It is good you have returned before Bright Arrow and Singing Wind could join. Little Feet has returned to your camp and joined to White Arrow's son, Thunder Spirit. Chief Races-the-Buffalo was slain while you were lost," he rapidly explained at her look of confusion. But Rebecca's bewilderment had come from his previous statement, and she turned to gaze probingly at the Indian girl.

Singing Wind smiled contritely and entreated, "Do not worry, Wahea; we do not love each other and we will not join. I will explain this matter to you later when we are away and safe, for it requires much talk. My heart belongs to Sun Cloud and I wish to join him. Bright Arrow desires only your return and your love."

"Why did you not tell me about you and my husband?" she asked.

"It was not the time or place to burden you with news which means nothing. All will be settled soon, you will see."

Rebecca scoffed. "Means nothing? My husband was going to marry you soon, and you say that means nothing? Tell me everything."

Soul-of-Thunder comprehended the problem and Rebecca's reaction to it. He had not thought before speaking of Bright Arrow's impending mating, but Singing Wind's words surprised and intrigued him. He wondered if they were true, or if the girl was only trying to comfort and relax Rebecca. It was clear that Singing Wind had not related this news, and it had shocked and disturbed the mother of his beloved wife.

Soul-of-Thunder said, "Singing Wind is right, Wahea; we must flee quickly and talk later. You have returned; Bright Arrow will not take another in your place; he has suffered greatly over your loss. He only wished to end his torment and to begin a new life. Bright Arrow and Singing Wind were told it was the will of Grandfather for them to join; that is why they agreed." He spoke with the other scouts and they made plans. Two Sisseton warriors agreed to loan him one of their horses and to ride double to their camp so Rebecca and Singing Wind could ride together. The other Cheyenne warrior would return to his tribe while Soul-of-Thunder escorted the women to the Oglala camp. When the other warriors reached home, they were to send messages to all other tribes, to report their observations and escape.

Soul-of-Thunder warned the women, "The journey is long and hard and dangerous. We must work together, or all is lost. Obey me swiftly when I speak. The others will trail us for a time and conceal our tracks."

Rebecca mounted behind Singing Wind and placed her arms around the female's waist. Singing Wind whispered before they galloped away, "I promise, Wahea, all will be as you remember it and wish it."

The women's escape was not discovered until the changing of the guards at dawn because Clint had slammed his forehead against the wall to create a bloody wound to use as a pretense of a dazing blow, but the too-forceful blow had stunned him for hours. What Clint and Ames did not realize was that Clint's blow to Moore's right temple had killed him . . .

When Clint was questioned in the infirmary, he was distressed to learn of the murder he had committed accidentally, but he stuck to his story about Moore being responsible for his injury and bonds. He told them Moore had been trying to rape Rebecca Kenny and he had tried to prevent it, even after he was bound; he alleged that Moore had whirled on him in a drunken rage when he had threatened to shout for help and had shoved him into the wall, where he had struck his head and lost consciousness and could only assume what had happened afterward: the women must have overpowered Moore and escaped.

Ames speculated cleverly, "Evidently the women didn't know they had killed him or they wouldn't have bound and gagged him. You can't blame them for trying to defend themselves against his brutal attack."

Butler glanced at Cooper before he argued, "There's only one problem with your story, Corporal Richards: the Crow scout says a fierce fight went on in there, a fight between men wearing boots. Yep, he says there are three sets of boot tracks in the blockhouse: Corporal Richards', Colonel Moore's, and . . . I wonder who that third set belongs to? Comstock wears moccasins and he was drunk on his butt before ten last night, so it wasn't him who helped her escape. Too bad those outside got mussed or we could see where they lead. He also says the two women were bound at one point and were cut free. Tell me, how did they get free to attack Colonel Moore? We all know how you feel about them Injuns, so think hard before you answer."

Clint glanced at Ames as if to ask, what's going on here?

Ames asked, "Just what are you hinting at, Major Butler? The other tracks probably belong to the guard who locked them up or to the man who brought their food and water. I don't like your tone, sir."

"Neither of those men entered the blockhouse, Major Ames. There should only be two sets of female tracks and two sets of boot tracks, Moore's and Richards'. I find it odd there are three sets of boot tracks. We have an officer dead, Major Ames, so I want all the facts. Savvy?"

Clint found his wits and suggested, "Maybe somebody came in after I was knocked out. Maybe those extra tracks belong to the morning guard. Maybe Moore freed one of the women and she got the drop on him. I told you, sir; he said he was going to rape both of them. He was crazy with whiskey and hatred, and stronger than a bull. Maybe that white girl tricked him; they knew each other from way back."

"And maybe we got us a traitor in camp," Butler murmured.

Clint protested, "You ain't got no right to make such a charge!"

"Settle down, Corporal Richards, I wasn't talking about you. I think you're right; I think somebody came in after you were knocked out and helped those little savages escape. Yep, this incident bears a little more investigation and study. Don't you agree, Major Ames?"

Ames smiled and replied, "Give it up, Butler. I know you want to be rid of me, but you aren't going to hang this absurd charge on me."

"We'll see, won't we?" Butler scoffed. "I think you should return to your duties, Major Ames. We're expecting a little trouble soon, and we need to have the men and supplies ready. You do recall that I outrank you?" Butler hinted tauntingly.

"How could I forget it? You remind me at least once a day. Take it easy, Clint; that's a nasty bump on your head. I'll check on you later."

"Thanks, Major. I'll be fine," Clint replied, then smiled, for he realized he had done the only thing he could last night. He would be out of the Army soon, and he could hardly wait to return to Georgia.

Outside the infirmary, Butler said to Cooper, "Those two need watching, sir. I got me a feeling they both know what really happened in that blockhouse last night."

"Timothy was a fool, Major; he let his loins burn with more revenge than his head. I saw how he looked at that girl after her arrival; I should have warned him to stay clear of her, or to have a guard stand watch while he settled the past on her."

"You mean, you would have let him have her?" Butler inquired.

"Damn right! She owed him, and how else can a beautiful woman pay off such a large debt? I wouldn't have minded having a taste of her myself. Damn him," Cooper muttered in irritation. "That isn't any way for a good officer to die, or to be found and remembered. I want those two savages back, then we can finish what Timothy started; we'll punish them real good. Right, Major Butler?"

Butler's eyes sparkled with anticipation and he grinned broadly. "Right, General Cooper. I'll take the patrol out myself. We'll have those two bitches back in custody before nightfall."

"When we aren't on duty or around the other men, call me Phillip, Gerald," Cooper encouraged, deciding this man would replace his deceased friend Timothy Moore, for he needed somebody he could trust and depend on fully out here. Besides, he needed a woman real bad, and he wanted a white woman, even if she was an Indian's mate. He realized how valuable and useful Bright Arrow's wife could be . . .

Butler whispered lewdly, "You get ready to question her real good, Phillip, because I'll have her back for you pronto. She couldn't have gotten far on foot, and I doubt she's been gone more than a few hours."

It was late afternoon when the two combined Oglala bands reached their camp. The tribe was thrilled by their victories, but saddened by the deaths of many warriors, including shirt wearers Good Tracker and Touch-the-Sky and their war chief, Big Elk. The two bands were informed promptly of the astonishing attacks on several Indian villages, particularly the Blackfeet camp from which Singing Wind had been captured. The bands learned of how the tribes had been lured from their joint assault on the fort and of how they were awaiting the return of the war parties to hold a new war council.

Sun Cloud was angered and alarmed by the capture of his love, and he swore to himself he would rescue her. He carried Bright Arrow to his tepee and had the shaman come to tend his wounds. After the shaman left, Sun Cloud confessed his love for Singing Wind to his brother.

"I should not have kept silent about the truth this long, Bright Arrow. I love her and she loves me. We mated before your vision, but you claimed her in council before I knew of your plans. I tried to back away from her until this matter between us was solved, but I could not. She is mine in body and heart, as I am hers. I had taken her first and by right she was mine, but I could not death-challenge my own brother for her, and I could not free her to join you. It was wrong to continue meeting her secretly when all believed and accepted your claim on her, but I could not stop myself. I endured the Sacred Bow ritual and Sun Dance ceremony so Grandfather could send me a message, so He could tell me what to do. Forgive me for taking her and the chief's bonnet from you, but they are my destiny, and a man cannot reject his fate."

"They were never mine to take from you, Sun Cloud. I was blind and foolish, and greedy. I know it is meant for you to have both, and I accept this truth. Grandfather opened my eyes before the war council, but White Arrow advised me to hold silent until your vision proved your claims. Big Elk is dead. Do you still wish me to take his place after you are voted chief? The vote must not wait; the time is now."

"Yes, you will be our war chief. But the vote for chief must wait until I have rescued Singing Wind and our foes are defeated, and your love is returned to you. Grandfather seeks to remove all reasons why others voted against me, and He seeks to fulfill my vision so all will know I spoke the truth. Once I have proven myself and my vision, the vote will go easier for all concerned. It must be this way for all to have confidence in me. My heart sings with joy to hear your eyes have seen the truth and you accept it. It is good, my brother."

Bright Arrow and Sun Cloud locked hands and exchanged smiles. Bright Arrow replied, "It is more than good, my brother. I will remove my claim on Singing Wind. Save her and join her, as it should be. I thank you for saving my sacred shirt."

"Rest and heal, Bright Arrow. I will ride to the war council on the new sun. I cannot get into the white man's fort, so I must find another way to retrieve what is mine. They will not harm her; they will seek to use her against us. She is brave and smart; she will be safe for a time. Grandfather will help us," he vowed confidently.

"I wish I could ride with you into battle, Sun Cloud, but I can feel my weakness. I would only endanger the lives and safety of others if I did not remain here to become strong and well once more. It is hard, but I must yield to it. I will join you in a few suns."

Late the following day, four important events took place. The joint war council met and made new plans; Derek Sturgis and James Murdock arrived at Fort Dakota; Singing Wind, Rebecca, and Soul-of-Thunder evaded Butler's patrol and came to within a few hours ride of the Oglala camp; and General Cooper decided to use all of his men to, one by one, attack and destroy all Indian camps in the region.

The sixty-eight-year-old Derek Sturgis, ex-colonel of Fort Meade and current special agent for President James Monroe, absorbed the shocking reports of each officer at the meeting. He was more than vexed to hear the details of the grim happenings in this area and wondered if he had arrived too late to halt them and to prevent more. He was staggered by the rumored death of Gray Eagle, and prayed it was not true, for he deeply respected the Oglala chief and needed his help to form a workable treaty. He listened intensely and observed the men around the table, especially General Cooper and Major Ames.

Sturgis ordered firmly, "I want all hostilities to cease immediately, General Cooper. We'll let tempers and bloods cool for a few days, then I'll try to arrange a meeting with Gray Eagle or his son. The President wants a truce, and he sent me here to make sure he gets one."

"Are you crazy, Sturgis? Those Injuns have been slaughtering my men left and right. This is Army business, so keep your nose out of it. In a few days, we won't need a treaty with those savages, 'cause there won't be any left to sign one."

"The President gave me full authority to handle this matter any way I choose, General Cooper, which means you will do exactly as I say. With a lot of luck and work, we might save the rest of our men. You have no idea what you've done, and I can't allow you to do more damage. I fully intend to bring charges against this Major Butler, if he returns. And I'll bring them against you, too, if you force my hand. You can't beat these Indians, especially the Sioux. But if you keep challenging and provoking them, you'll get a lot of good men killed. I know Gray Eagle, and I know this uprising wasn't his doing."

Derek Sturgis looked at Major William Ames and asked, "Would you mind telling me everything you know about this situation?"

Ames glanced at Cooper as he replied, "No, sir. In fact, it's about time somebody sets the record straight."

"Major Ames, I'm ordering you to silence," Cooper warned.

Sturgis caught the bad currents between the two men and decided to speak privately with Ames. "This meeting is over, gentlemen. Major Ames, you stay behind and have coffee and a chat with me. We'll have another meeting around noon tomorrow. See you gentlemen then."

Cooper said, "I have a patrol out there with one of my best men. I plan to take another one out to look for them in the morning. I'm afraid the safety of my command comes before your silly meeting."

Sturgis settled back in his chair. "That's fine, General. Go look for your men, just make certain you don't intentionally engage the enemy. I'm here to make peace, not war."

When Ames and Sturgis were alone, Sturgis sent for James Murdock. "Murray, I want you to hear this too; then you can tell Major Ames what you've learned. I need to know every detail, Major Ames, every detail, no matter who it hurts. If we can't get this conflict settled soon, this entire area will be bloodwashed."

William Ames eyed the two men and decided he could trust them completely. He took a deep breath and confessed all he knew.

* * *

General Cooper went to the cookhouse after he had visited the infirmary. He ordered the man on duty to prepare a large pot of coffee for "Mr. Sturgis and his guests." When it was ready, he sent the man to fetch some sweet rolls left over from the evening meal. While the man was retrieving them and placing them on a platter, Cooper poured sleeping powder into the coffee, milk, and sugar—to make certain each of the three men ingested plenty, enough to keep them knocked out until noon tomorrow. To cover the bitter taste, he placed a bottle of Irish whiskey on the tray, hoping the men would lace their coffee with it, then drink plenty to keep them awake to talk.

Cooper watched the cook head to Sturgis' room with the drugged items and smiled evilly. By the time his foolish rival awoke, it would be too late. He and his men would ride out at dawn, and they would not return until every camp was destroyed and every Indian was dead. After all, Sturgis had not shown him any official credentials or orders, so he was still in command for a while, and he was not about to allow Sturgis or the Indians to make him look like a coward or a weakling. By noon tomorrow, it would be too late for Sturgis to interfere . . .

In the war camp, it was decided that an all-out attack on the fort would take place the next afternoon, as soon as all tribes could reach the meeting point and band together. First, they would try to lure the inhabitants out by using Sun Cloud dressed as Gray Eagle as bait. If that failed, they would lay siege to the fort, and refuse to pull out until the bluecoats surrendered.

"I will miss my friend Bright Arrow in the battle. Will you return to your camp to lead your warriors?" Fire Brand asked Sun Cloud.

"Thunder Spirit will summon them for me. I ride to the fort to study it for weaknesses and to watch it. I will wait for you there."

When they were alone, Thunder Spirit asked Sun Cloud, "Are you sure it is safe to go alone? The soldiers will be watching for scouts."

Sun Cloud looked at his friend and said, "I must go. Her life is as important to me as my own. If I can locate the secret gate which Bright Arrow told me about, perhaps I can rescue her before our attack. I must go quickly, for I need the cover of darkness to help me."

At their last rest stop before reaching the Oglala camp, Singing Wind finally completed her explanation to Rebecca. "When we reach camp, if he is there, you will hear the truth from his lips. I am happy you have returned to us. Do not let foolish pride ruin this moon."

Rebecca realized the Indian girl was telling the truth, and was giving her good advice, advice which she could follow. "I must see him alone, Singing Wind. Can you stay with another?"

Singing Wind smiled knowingly. "We will sleep in the tepee of Little Feet. I must wait in your camp until Sun Cloud returns."

"You do love him very much, don't you?"

"Yes, very, very much," she replied happily. "I pray he is in camp so I can see him. If he knows of my capture, he will worry."

"It seems both of our men are in for big surprises in a few hours."

Soul-of-Thunder joined the two laughing women. "All is good now?" he asked, for he had allowed them time to talk.

"We must get home quickly, my son, so you can return to your wife. I do not wish her to worry about us. When our land is at peace, bring her to visit me."

They mounted and continued their journey, to arrive at the camp shortly after midnight. They were confronted by guards, who allowed them to pass once they were recognized. Singing Wind and Soul-of-Thunder headed for Little Feet's tepee, to reveal her mother's survival and return, and to spend the night with her.

Rebecca laced the flap to the tepee and made her way forward. She was glad there was a small fire which cast a dim glow inside. She visually scanned the tepee, delighted and warmed to find that her surroundings had changed little during her year's absence.

On trembly legs, she went and knelt beside Bright Arrow's sleeping mat. Her eyes filled with tears of joy and dismay. Her frantic gaze examined the injuries on his broad chest—they were smeared with a healing salve made from special herbs and roots—and the two bound wounds, one on his left forearm and one on his right bicep. Her gaze hurriedly and anxiously checked the bruises and marks on his handsome face, concluding that he had not fared well during this last battle. From the looks of them and from Singing Wind's words, they must be a few days old. She realized how close she had come to losing him before she could reach home. She hated to awaken him, for he appeared to need this healing rest, but she had to see his eyes and hear his voice and feel his touch. They were alive, and they were together again.

Rebecca's quivering hand reached out and gently stroked his brow, then she leaned forward to allow her lips to press kisses there. She sat down near his waist and allowed her starving senses to absorb him greedily. As if his hunter's instincts caught her presence, she saw his eyes flutter, then slowly open. He smiled at her as if it were a reflexive action. She nuzzled his left hand when it reached up to caress her cheek. When he pulled her downward to seal their lips, she was careful not to put her weight upon his injuries.

Bright Arrow kissed her hungrily, then tried to draw her to him. The pain which charged through his right arm and torso aroused him fully. Suddenly his eyes widened and he shook his head to test this incredulous illusion, for he was touching her and she was touching him, and she felt real. Tears dampened his eyes, then slipped from the corners to roll into his dark hair. "Please be alive and real, my love. Please don't be another cruel dream," he beseeched hoarsely.

Rebecca grasped his hand and pressed it near her thudding heart so he could feel its beat and her respiration. "I am real, my love. I have been returned to you. How I have missed you and loved you."

Bright Arrow stared longingly at her as her voice and touch sent a warming glow over his body and a thrill to his heart. He tried to sit, to be closer to her. His disabled body refused to support him. His left hand slid behind her neck and drew her down to him once more.

They kissed, and caressing fingers evinced deep emotions. They kept gazing into each other's eyes, as if speaking without words. Each visually mapped and explored the other's face, taking in the toll of their tormenting separation. Their breaths mingled and their mouths joined. It was as if they had been together forever, yet apart forever.

Bright Arrow and Rebecca wanted to snuggle tightly together; but, if they did, they could not see enough of each other. Both were keenly aware of his many injuries, which prevented him from seizing her and crushing her beneath or against him. Both were aware of the craving to fuse their bodies as one, but of the obstacle between him.

Her palms flattened on the mat on either side of his neck and she gingerly leaned forward to shorten the distance between them, a distance more unbearable than his physical pain. His left arm lifted so his hand could wander through her hair. Closing her eyes and cuddling to it as a contented cat, she let her feelings rove freely and wildly. His hand moved over her face, stroking and admiring each feature.

He uncontrollably pulled her to the mat and rolled to his left side, grimacing as the injuries on his chest and back protested loudly. He endured the pain, and rested his wounded arm across her body, for he desperately needed this contact. The problem was, he was lying on his best side and his least injured arm was under her head, so he could do nothing more than gaze at her and stroke her hair.

Rebecca's arm carefully slipped over his waist and touched his back, making contact with the sticky salve and numerous injuries there. "What happened to you, my love?" she asked in alarm, as she struggled to keep her wits so she would not roll against him and hurt him.

Bright Arrow related how the "mourning cut" on his left forearm had become infected and was being tended. He told her how he had been shot in the right arm by a soldier. He revealed how he had been tricked by a false truce flag, captured, then beaten and lashed to compel his war party to surrender. He explained how Sun Cloud had rescued him, brought him home, then left him here to heal while the others returned to battle. Unable to shoot a bow or use a knife or war lance or to safely endure the arduous ride or to keep from endangering others, he had accepted his brother's command to remain in camp. He smiled and murmured, "I am glad I was here when you returned, even if it took many wounds to hold me down. If I had learned of your return while I was away, I might have deserted my band to rush to your side. Where have you been, my love?"

Rebecca kept her gaze fused to his as she enlightened him. When she reached the episode in the blockhouse, fury caused his jawline to grow taut and his dark eyes to narrow. "Do not worry, my love, I was not harmed in body, only in pride. The Great Spirit will punish him; that is why he has returned to our lands after these many winters: he has returned to pay for his evil deeds with his life. The soldier called Ames is a good man; I hope your people will spare his life."

"It will be so, if possible," he replied, then related what they knew and felt about this white man and others.

For a time, they talked about their family and discussed the events which had occurred during their lengthy separation. Finally, Bright Arrow asked, "What of Jeremy Comstock?"

A look of dismay crossed her face. "He was a good man and I could not have survived or returned without his help and protection. I did not see him again after Timothy Moore revealed the truth about me and arrested me. He probably thinks I lied to him and used him, and betrayed him. Perhaps that is best, Bright Arrow, for it will make it easier for him to forget me if he hates me. I never went to his sleeping mat, my love, nor any man's but yours."

He smiled and said, "There is no need to tell me such things, for I know them. Now, there is something more I must tell you," he hinted, then related the facts about him and Singing Wind and Silver Hawk and the false vision. "It seems I have been tricked many times. Why does Grandfather allow me to make such a fool of myself? I do not love her, Wahea; I only needed someone to remove the pain and emptiness of your loss. I did not give up on you until father and mother were slain and Silver Hawk entrapped me with his dark dreams and desires. Before Sun Cloud rode from camp, I confessed the truth of my blindness. He told me of his love for Singing Wind and of hers for him. It is good, and it is right, and it will be this way."

He smiled as he told her about Sun Cloud's victories in the Sacred Bow race and Sun Dance ceremony. "He said you were alive and you were calling to me. He said you would return, but I feared to believe it. Sun Cloud knows he must be chief and have Singing Wind; I know this, and soon all will know it and accept it. I have loved no woman in heart or body since I met you. As with my father Gray Eagle and my mother Shalee, we are as one and will live and die as one."

Rebecca thought for a moment about Powchutu, the man who could have been her father, who was once believed to be her father. How she wished she could have returned sooner so she could have met him. He had been her mother's first love and the reason why Joe Kenny had married her pregnant mother. Tomorrow, she would visit his death scaffold and pray for him, and for her parents. So many circles had closed during this last year, and so many mysteries had been solved.

"What troubles your mind, my love?" he asked tenderly.

"I was thinking about Powchutu. I wish I could have met him. He must have been very special for our mothers to love him and for your father to forgive him and to accept him as his brother. It is good he returned to settle their stormy pasts before . . . Tell me all you learned about him," she coaxed, wanting to keep her mind off of the hungers which were gnawing at her ravenous flesh from head to foot.

Bright Arrow grinned as he recognized her ploy, and he complied. When he finished, he teased, "If the shaman was awake, I would force him to smear numbing salve over my body so I could seize you." He rolled carefully onto his back to ease the tension on his chest.

Rebecca smiled provocatively and whispered, "I have not forgotten how to ride a wild stallion. If you lie very still, would it hurt you for me to mount him and to carry our spirits away on the wind?"

Bright Arrow grinned once more and his eyes seemingly sparkled. "If you do not, soon he will ache more than my wounds. I must warn you, he is weak and has little control this moon."

"Then our feelings match, my love, for I have been lingering on the edge of passion's cliff since I entered our tepee." She lifted his knife to sever the cloth strip which held her dress together in the front. When she noted his probing look, she said, "He tried to rip off my clothes. Ames tied it for me before we escaped."

Rebecca removed her clothes, then his breechcloth. She leaned forward and kissed him, gently at first, then urgently. She felt his hand fondle her breasts; then he asked her to shift forward so he could taste them. She eagerly obliged him, her stomach and womanhood tensing as his mouth feasted on one, then the other. His left hand roamed her bare flesh and slipped between her parted thighs. She moaned with exquisite pleasure as he skillfully stroked the hardened bud. She wished she could reach his manhood to caress it, but she had to use her arms to prop herself where he could reach her easily and painlessly. When she glanced at it, she realized it needed no enticement to become fully aroused, and its eagerness and beauty enflamed her.

The firelight was nearly gone, and soon their sights of each other would be too. She wanted to watch his face and for him to watch hers as they shared this first reuniting of bodies. She reluctantly pulled herself from his lips and hand, and gingerly straddled his hips. Taking his shaft in her grasp, she held it in position while her receptive body closed over it. There was instant pleasure from their action. Their gazes locked and remained so as she lovingly and skillfully labored to slake the passions which blissfully tormented their senses.

Bittersweet ecstasy teased over their joined bodies and promised to reward them quickly by rapturously appeasing their mutual needs. Spirits soared and passions mounted until they were feverishly attacked and conquered. Still, she rocked upon him to extract every drop of love's nectar from their fused bodies. When their spasms ceased, they smiled tenderly into each other's eyes.

He reached for her and drew her down beside him once more. He kissed her and vowed, "I love you with all my heart, Wahea."

"As I love you, Bright Arrow. You must rest and sleep. We will talk later." She cuddled next to him, and both were slumbering within a few minutes, their Life-circles entwined once more.

Hours later, Sun Cloud watched the large regiment of soldiers leave the fort and head westward. He deliberated his next move; for he could not attack such an enormous band alone, and he would be visible to their scouts if he trailed them too soon. He had no choice but to remain hidden in the forest near the fort for a time. He had dressed and painted himself to match his father's image, to lure the soldiers into their trap this morning. He wished he had his war horse, instead of the ghostly white one which could be mistaken for Gray Eagle's, for they were not completely accustomed to each other and the stallion did not respond to his commands as rapidly or as agilely as his loyal and intelligent beast.

He realized the regiment, if it did not change directions, was heading toward the area where their trap had been planned and was being prepared at this very moment. Yet, there was no way he could get in front of the soldiers and entice them to the right spot. He could only hope that the Great Spirit would perform his duty for him today, and end this madness for a time. He was not worried about the soldiers attacking the united bands by surprise, for their scouts would see them approaching, and the bands would carry out their strategy even if he was not luring them into their cunning snare.

He glanced at the fort and wondered how many soldiers were left inside, and whether he could enter secretly to rescue his love. No, the light and his looks would expose him. As much as he loved Singing Wind, it was foolish to risk everything to rescue her. Once the soldiers were conquered, the survivors could be forced to return her to him. He would linger here for a short time, then follow the regiment.

* * *

Derek Sturgis cleared his cloudy wits and looked at the two men who were sleeping in the chairs with their heads resting on the small table: James Murdock and Bill Ames. The loud noises of the departing regiment had aroused Sturgis, but for a time he'd failed to grasp what had disturbed him. He glanced at the tray, then comprehended Cooper's brazen deceit. He hurriedly awakened the two men and enlightened them as to his suspicions and their possibly grim situation. Fortunately, none of them used milk or sugar in coffee, so they had not consumed as much of the sleeping powder as Cooper had hoped.

"That bloody fool!" Sturgis declared in disbelief. "Bill, go see if my worries are real ones. Murray, you get us some horses and supplies ready, because I'm certain they are. I'll join you two in a moment."

Outside, Sturgis joined three men and discovered the extent of Cooper's crazed behavior and intentions. Lieutenant Thomas Daniels had been arrested that morning for refusing to obey Cooper's orders, but Ames had demanded his release from the blockhouse. However, Ames had left Jeremy Comstock imprisoned, for the trapper insisted on leaving to search for Rebecca Kenny, and that action could endanger everyone and everything, including Jeremy.

Sturgis learned that the reckless Cooper had left only one company of men to defend the fort, but he had been gone less than thirty minutes. Sturgis shouted to the cook, telling the man to get rid of everything on the tray in his office because it was drugged. He put Major Ames in charge and told him to remain on full alert. Sturgis made certain he had his papers from the President, as he knew he would be forced to use them to halt Cooper's madness. "Let's ride. If we don't catch him and stop him . . . Lord, help us all."

Sun Cloud was ready to trail the regiment when he saw three men race from the fort, heading after the soldiers and carrying a military standard which flew a white truce flag instead of the Army pennon. He eyed the two "civilians;" one was a trapper by his garments and the other was wearing clothes similar to those Powchutu had worn when he had arrived from the white lands far away. The other man was a soldier, the man whose life he had spared recently. The white men looked upset and were in a big hurry. This was very strange, he reasoned.

Sun Cloud decided it was safe and smart for him to check out this mystery. He mounted the white horse and rode toward the men at an intersecting angle. He cautiously slowed when he had their attention.

The men reined up sharply and stared at the incredible sight before them. Sturgis murmured, "It's Gray Eagle himself, and alone. So, Butler's men didn't kill him after all," he stated happily, then waved.

Sun Cloud had watched the oldest man's reactions and instinctively guessed his identity. He prodded his horse forward, halting only four feet from the men, just enough room to defend himself if there was trouble or deceit, which he doubted.

Sturgis' smile faded and he said, "You aren't Gray Eagle. I would know him anywhere. I hope to God this doesn't mean what I think it does. Is he—"

Daniels spoke up. "This is Sun Cloud, Gray Eagle's son. You can trust him, Mr. Sturgis."

"I'm James Murdock, Murray to my friends. I know your brother."

Sun Cloud's gaze went from one man to the next, until he had studied each twice. "My father spoke of the man called Sturgis many times, and he called you friend. My brother spoke of the man called Murray, and called him friend. Sun Cloud knows the man called Daniels, and calls him friend. Four days past, Bright Arrow honored such a flag, but he was deceived and captured; your soldiers beat him and tried to slay him. Less than a full moon past, your soldiers ambushed the Oglala Council and took the life of Gray Eagle. I ride in his place. Speak your words to me. Why does a large band of soldiers leave your fort? Why do you bolt like a chased deer and carry a truce flag?"

Sturgis said, "I'm sorry about your father, Sun Cloud; no greater man than Gray Eagle ever lived. These lands will be less without him. I was hoping and praying they had lied about his death. I needed his help to end this bloody conflict. The soldiers who started this new trouble are not obeying the orders of our Great White Leader, our President. I was sent here to stop them, to make peace, to sign a treaty with all Indians in this area. General Cooper hasn't been himself since he arrived; some of the evil leaders at the fort misguided him. He left while we were asleep. I have to catch him and prevent him from attacking any camps; he wants to destroy every one before I can halt him." He held up the papers which he had withdrawn from his pocket. "I have letters, a message, from our highest chief, commanding him to obey me. His men do not know I am the President's agent. When they do, they will obey me, not him. I can promise you, hardly a one of those soldiers wants to harm your people. They want this war over as quickly and badly as we do. Help me," he pleaded.

Daniels said, "He's telling the truth, Sun Cloud. If we don't work together to stop Cooper, this war will go on and on. Smith's been killed; he's the one who ambushed your father. Butler's patrol hasn't returned to the fort; he's the one who gave the order to attack your father, and he's the one who's been inciting Cooper against all Indians. He's probably dead. Cooper's best officer, Timothy Moore, was killed, so that only leaves General Cooper to get under control."

"You hold the woman I am to marry captive. Will you return to the fort and release her?" Sun Cloud asked unexpectedly.

"That Indian girl that Butler captured in the Blackfeet camp is your sweetheart?" Daniels asked. When Sun Cloud nodded, Daniels revealed her escape two days ago. "I suppose she made it home, because Butler went after her and hasn't returned. She escaped with a white girl named Rebecca Kenny; they say she's your brother's wife."

Sun Cloud could not conceal his astonishment, even though he had anticipated this news very soon. "Both got away?"

Daniels quickly related what they knew about the incident, to Sun Cloud's pleasure and relief. "My brother's wife has been missing since last winter. It is good she has returned to us safely. If the man called Butler has recaptured or harmed them, I must slay him."

"The man you need to slay is called Silver Hawk," Sturgis revealed. "He's the one who's been helping Butler defeat your people." Sturgis related what Ames and Daniels had discovered about the Indian traitor.

Daniels added, "We got real suspicious of Butler and Smith, so we started spying on them. Bill overheard Butler telling Cooper all about this Silver Hawk, so we told Mr. Sturgis all we knew."

At last, he had the proof to back his and Powchutu's suspicions about Silver
Hawk; soon the Blackfeet warrior's evil would die. "I also suspected Silver Hawk,
but I could prove nothing against him. Come, we must ride swiftly. All tribes have
banded together to battle Cooper, and he rides toward their trap. We will speak
with both sides, and we will make truce, as my father would do."

Chapter Twenty-One

Cooper's regiment traveled along the large coulee which ran for miles in
this deserted area, attempting to hide their approach and presence
from their enemies. They had ridden hard and fast to reach this concealing area.
Knowing they were only ten miles from the first Indian encampment, they had
now slowed their pace to prevent any alerting dust and noise. The coulee was
around twelve feet deep and sixteen feet wide, and the men rode bunched together
to disallow any stragglers.

The Indians had been observing the regiment for a long time, and many
wondered where Sun Cloud was, for he should be racing before them and luring
them into this clever snare which he had planned. Still, all was going as expected,
so they waited patiently to spring their trap.

They had used the Apache camouflage tricks which Sun Cloud had explained
to them. Even though the surrounding area looked safe and empty, countless
Indians were hidden amidst the landscape, their horses having been taken to a
distance by other braves. Once the soldiers reached a certain point, they were to
block both paths of escape, then close in on the coulee from both sides. The
soldiers would be helpless.

Cooper was in the lead when trouble struck. Suddenly burning brush blocked
the trail before him. Grasping their peril, he shouted a warning to retreat, but it
was too late; brush had been shoved into the coulee to their rear and set ablaze.
Indian war whoops filled the air as blazing brush was kicked into the coulee. The
frightened horses reared and whinnied, throwing several men to the hard ground.
Panic seized the soldiers and they did not know what to do. Even if the Indians
had not suddenly appeared on both sides and begun firing upon them, the embank-
ments were too steep for horses to climb.

Soldiers quickly dismounted and pressed against the banks, using their horses
as shields against the numerous arrows which came from both directions. Their
guns were useless, for they could not locate their targets and they were fighting to

control their frantic mounts. Each man who released his reins lost his cover and was struck quickly with several arrows. Horses that yanked free raced into other horses and men, then pranced and pawed in their terror. The soldiers could do little except pray this onslaught would end quickly.

Sun Cloud had planned this trap perfectly, for there was no place for the soldiers to hide or to flee. All his warriors had to do was pick them off or wait for them to surrender. At first, the Indians savored their victory and were in no rush to end it swiftly, even though they could.

Cooper shouted, "Use the dead men as shields! Draw your guns and shoot at anything that moves. Damn it, men! If they can see us, we can see them! You going to sit here like stupid targets and let them fill you with arrows! Kill the bastards!"

The Indians were quick and agile. They would jump up, fire, and drop out of sight before the men could take aim on them; and few soldiers were real marksmen. They shoved more burning bush into the coulee, and killed the men who moved to dodge the flaming weapons. Soon, it became too easy to kill the entrapped soldiers, and the Indians lost their feelings of challenge and excitement during this one-sided battle. Even the few brave men who tried to clear an escape path through the burning brush were slain without any trouble.

The soldiers forced Cooper to realize they could not escape and they would all die if he did not surrender. At least alive, the men stood a chance of survival and escape, or so they believed. One man took his white handkerchief, tied it to his gun barrel, then lifted it and waved it. The other soldiers sighed with relief, for dead men surrounded all of them. The arrows ceased immediately and silence fell over the area, as even the horses calmed. For a time, nothing . . .

A shout went up from the victorious Indians when Sun Cloud was spotted riding swiftly toward them. He arrived with three white men, carrying a flag of truce. He hurriedly dismounted and was given the details of their successful attack, which he related to the white men with him. He explained who the white men were and why they were here. The leaders of each tribe were summoned, and a council ensued.

Singing Wind bravely and insistently rode at Soul-of-Thunder's side as he followed the trail of the soldiers toward the area where the Indian ambush was to take place. She felt she had to reach Sun Cloud to let him know she was safe, to let him know about Rebecca, for she feared he would try something rash to rescue her.

As they traveled, she thought about the meeting between Rebecca and Little Feet that morning, and of the joyous reunion the two women had shared. She and Soul-of-Thunder had asked Little Feet not to disturb her parents last night, and the elated female had understood that Bright Arrow and Rebecca needed their first night alone.

This morning, Bright Arrow had looked stronger, and certainly happier, but he'd been in no condition to join the war party. They had looked so perfectly matched and contented, standing arm-in-arm and smiling at each other like young lovers. When she had left his camp, the Oglalas had been celebrating Rebecca's return and Bright Arrow had been telling his people that Sun Cloud should be chief and that Sun Cloud and Singing Wind would join. That news had pleased his people as much as it had pleased her. *Soon, my love,* she vowed dreamily.

When the council meeting was over and it was voted to give Derek Sturgis a chance to make acceptable and honorable peace for both sides, Sun Cloud announced, "I must go after Silver Hawk and slay him for his betrayals," for the Blackfeet chief must have suspected his exposure when he arrived with the three white men and had sneaked off during the excitement. Sun Cloud revealed Silver Hawk's treachery to them.

The council had voted to spare the lives of the soldiers trapped in the coulee, even General Cooper's, if he was punished as Sturgis promised. It had been revealed that Butler and his troop had been defeated yesterday while tracking the escaped women, and all were dead. The council had been told of Rebecca's return and of Sun Cloud's claim on Singing Wind. The Oglala leaders had tried to proclaim Sun Cloud chief on the spot, but he had smiled and asked them to vote in council at home. When all was decided and accepted, Derek Sturgis walked to the coulee and informed the men of the truce, and of his authority by order of President James Monroe, and of Cooper's arrest.

Cooper went wild, jumped up, and shouted, "I'll never surrender, you coward!" He drew his pistol and tried to shoot Sturgis.

Since no man was close enough to seize him, two soldiers grabbed their rifles and fired, killing the crazed officer.

As the Indians watched the curious sight, Sturgis' words were translated, "He is at peace now. I don't know what happened to him; long ago, he was a good man and a superior leader. They're all dead now, so we can have peace between our peoples once more. You honor yourselves, your tribes, and the memory of Gray Eagle. He touched my heart and mind long ago, and I shall never forget him."

Sun Cloud clasped arms with Derek Sturgis and smiled. "As long as there are white men like you, my friend, there will be peace."

Tears misted Sturgis' eyes. "You look and sound like your father, Sun Cloud. I'm as proud to know you as I was to know him. As long as the blood of Gray Eagle flows within his sons and his sons' sons, Dakotas will rule these lands, whether in peace or in war. Come to the fort after your marriage and visit me. We'll sign the treaty and I'll personally take it to the President for his signature. You're a brave man, a wise one, for you realize the old days are gone and peace now carries a high price and lots of work."

"No matter what price or how much work, peace is brief, my friend. As long as greed and evil fill some men's hearts, white or Indian, lasting peace is impossible. But for a time, we can enjoy life."

Sturgis observed Sun Cloud as he gathered a few supplies, then mounted to track his enemy Silver Hawk. He looked at the medallion which Sun Cloud had removed and had pressed into his hand, although it was only a replica of Gray Eagle's *wanapin*. He closed his eyes and mourned his friend's loss. He watched the others build a large fire and burn the replicas of Gray Eagle's weapons, and he almost felt as if Gray Eagle was witnessing this occasion and was smiling.

*   *   *

Hours passed as the wounded men were tended and preparations were made to return to camps or to the fort. Soul-of-Thunder arrived with Singing Wind, and they were told of the victory and truce, and of Sun Cloud's journey after the traitorous Silver Hawk. It would be dark in several hours, so many camped for the night in this spot.

Singing Wind decided she would track Sun Cloud, and nothing anyone said could change her mind. She was given supplies and weapons, and she galloped off in the direction which Sun Cloud had taken.

Sturgis smiled secretly as he watched the Indian girl ride away eagerly and bravely, for he was reminded of another woman of such love and valor and intelligence: Alisha "Shalee" Williams. He recalled the night he had sneaked into Gray Eagle's tepee years ago to warn his wife of the danger of attack. She had been so beautiful and so smart and so courageous that he had never forgotten her and had always envied Gray Eagle such a unique woman. Now, it appeared his son had found himself a rare woman to share his life, and that was perfect, for a good woman inspired and molded an equally good man.

All night and all the next day, Sun Cloud tracked the rapidly fleeing Silver Hawk, wondering where the warrior thought he could go to escape his vengeance. He had rested little, as had the warrior who had been chief of the Blackfeet tribe for only a short time and only through his evil actions. He knew Silver Hawk could not keep up this pace much longer; then they would meet face to face and settle this matter between them. At last, others knew that his suspicions were accurate and they expected him to seek justice for them.

Even when Silver Hawk took the precious time to attempt to cover his trail, it failed, for Sun Cloud knew every trick there was and did not fall for them. He kept pressing onward, toward the sacred Black Hills, in pursuit, knowing he could not halt until his duty was done.

Nights were the slowest for Sun Cloud, for Silver Hawk was hurrying but he was tracking. After two had passed, he reached the *Paha Sapas*, and realized Silver Hawk had chosen the sacred hills to make his last stand. Sun Cloud ordered himself to full alert, for he knew that Silver Hawk would know that he would never give up his pursuit until they fought to the death. It seemed as if both had known it would come to this one day, and it had.

When Sun Cloud approached Silver Hawk, the warrior was standing on a rock which overlooked the immense lands beyond the sacred hills. His foe turned and smiled. The two warriors gazed at each other, each recalling their entwined pasts as they mentally prepared to do battle.

Silver Hawk spoke first. He said, "I knew you would come, Sun Cloud; it is our destiny. Long ago, some evil and powerful force exchanged them when your father stole the woman who should have been my mother and he put a wicked Oglala in my Life-circle as the wife of my father. I was destined to be the son of Shalee, not you, as she was destined to be the wife of Brave Bear. Gray Eagle stole my life and fate, and I punished him for his evil."

Silver Hawk drew his knife and lovingly stroked its sharp blade. "As with your father, you take all from me. You turned Tashina against me, and you have stolen the chief's bonnet from my head. I tried to take Little Flower from you, but she was weak and foolish, and I realized you could not have desired a woman like

her. I should have killed her after I raped her. Each time I took her viciously, I told
her it was your fault and she hates you now, as I hate you."

Sun Cloud remained motionless and silent, for he wanted to learn why this
man hated him and had tried to destroy him, if there was a logical reason. He
wondered if Silver Hawk was merely crazy, or if something had happened to mis-
guide him. He listened intensely.

"If Shalee had joined my father, he would not have been slain and I would
not have lost my rank. The blood of Chela stained the hearts and lives of my
sisters, not so with Shalee as their mother. I was forced to slay Medicine Bear and
his sons to reclaim my rank, and I was forced to take Little Flower to save face
when your brother's child sought to dishonor me with her rejection and betrayal.

"Your father used the white men for his gain; but, when I tried, they tried to
deceive me and use me. The fools are all dead. My people still speak of how Gray
Eagle defeated my father in the death challenge for Shalee, then generously spared
his life," he sneered coldly. "All my life, all I have heard is Gray Eagle, Gray Eagle
and his sons! Your father stole my bloodline. Brave Bear was not of the blood of
Black Cloud. I needed Shalee, daughter of Black Cloud, to give me power and
protection; these were stolen from me!" he shouted.

When he did not speak again, Sun Cloud said, "Brave Bear was a good man,
Silver Hawk, and a good chief. It did not matter if he was not the blood son of
Black Cloud. He died bravely for his people. You shame him with your evil and
greed. It was only right for my father to win Shalee, for they loved each other and
had belonged to each other before your father knew her and wanted her. My father
was a great man, the heart and spirit of all Indians. To destroy him nearly destroyed
all. You betrayed your people; you betrayed all Indians. There is no place to run,
Silver Hawk, for all know of your evil."

"You will never be chief, Sun Cloud," he asserted confidently.

"I am already chief, Silver Hawk. My brother's wife has returned, and all
know your vision was false, a lie. Bright Arrow has confessed his blindness and
mistake, and he has voted me chief. I will join to Singing Wind and reunite the
bloodlines of Brave Bear and Gray Eagle and the tribes of the Oglala and Blackfeet. It is Grandfather's will; it is my destiny, and you cannot change it."

Sun Cloud revealed his recent vision and the new treaty between the Indians
and the whites, and vowed, "We will have peace, Silver Hawk, if only for a short
time."

"You will have nothing, Sun Cloud, for I will slay you!" he shouted, then
started to charge the other warrior. His foot tangled in a strong vine, causing him
to stumble. Unable to recover his balance, he fell, screaming, from the lofty rocks
to his death.

Sun Cloud looked over the edge and realized he could not reach the body,
which would be located and consumed by vultures, fulfilling his vision about birds
eating Silver Hawk's heart and preventing him from finding eternal peace. His eyes
lifted skyward and he murmured, "It is done, Great Spirit; it is over, Father."

It was late afternoon and Sun Cloud was exhausted. He decided to make
camp at the edge of the sacred hills, then head home in the morning. He longed to
see his love, but he needed to refresh his mind and body before he began his
journey home. He shot a rabbit, and while it was roasting, he stripped and entered
the large creek beside his camp for the night. He sat down and splashed water on
his face and over his sweaty body. He was so weary after traveling without sleep for

two days, which came atop his nocturnal vigil at the fort. He rested his face in his wet hands. When he lifted it, Singing Wind was standing before him, naked and grinning.

"You must be very tired, my love, to allow a mere woman to sneak up on you," she teased, dropping to her knees between his. Her gaze scanned his body for injuries and she was delighted to find none.

His hands gently seized her upper arms and drew her close to him. "What are you doing here, woman? How did you find me?"

"I have been trailing you since you left the others. You moved too swiftly for me to catch up. Soul-of-Thunder found us after we escaped the fort and took us to your camp. I tried to wait there, but I could not. There are many things to tell you. Wahea has returned."

"I know," he murmured, happiness and excitement glowing in his dark eyes. "We will join when we return to my camp. All is good once more, my love, but Silver Hawk is dead," he stated gravely.

"I know," she replied, wishing she could feel more deeply for the death of her brother. "He was evil; it was his destiny. I saw his body. Was the battle terrible?" she reluctantly inquired.

Sun Cloud related the episode, then said, "I am glad he did not have to die by my hand. I cannot recover his body to place it upon a death scaffold. He must face the Grandfather as he lived, violently."

"He was wrong to hate you and to crave your Life-circle. If father had lived . . ." She went silent.

"Silver Hawk would have shamed him and broken his heart, for a man's destiny cannot be changed. When we reach my camp, I will send a message to your people and tell them all things."

"Bright Arrow told your people we will join and you will become chief. He and Wahea looked so happy together." She told him about his brother and Rebecca, and about the things which Rebecca had explained to her.

"All is as it should be. Bright Arrow's heart and destiny have been returned to him. Soon we will join and I will be chief. Evil has been conquered and destroyed. For a time, our lands will know peace and happiness once more. Now my father's spirit can rest."

His hand brushed aside her long hair and he gazed into her eyes. "I searched for a way to rescue you from the fort, but my senses could find none. I planned to force the survivors of our attack to release you to me. When I met with Sturgis, he told me of your escape and of Wahea's return. You were brave and cunning, my love. I knew you would be safe until I could claim you once more."

Singing Wind related the truth about the incident in the blockhouse; and Sun Cloud smiled with pleasure, for he recognized the names of the two white men who had helped his love and his brother's wife. After she told him what she had learned about Little Flower, a look of distress crossed his face; then he revealed what Silver Hawk had said before his death.

"Little Flower and Shining Feather are free of his evil; they can seek new mates and new happiness," she remarked with relief. "And my people can find a new chief, one who is good."

"After we join, I must ride to the fort to meet with Sturgis; then all will be settled. Our people can hunt the buffalo and enjoy a big feast." He inhaled deeply and closed his eyes briefly.

Singing Wind's gaze walked over his face and body, and she realized he was as exhausted as she was, and as elated. He was so strong and compelling, and she wanted to lose herself in his arms.

"How is my brother?" he asked, opening his sandy eyes.

"Bright Arrow's wounds heal good. But we can speak of such things later," she hinted, then began to lift water in her hands and to pour it over his shoulders as she rubbed them gently and lovingly.

Sun Cloud began to do the same with her, until the washings became caresses and their breathing grew shallow and swift. His fingertips moved back and forth over her parted lips, and she did the same. Their gazes were locked, and they leaned forward until their mouths did the same. As their kisses waxed urgent, her hands played as wildly in his hair as his did in hers.

He broke their contact to scoop her up in his arms and to carry her to his sleeping mat, which had been unrolled nearby. Their wet bodies stretched out on it and they clung passionately, knowing they were safe from all eyes and all foes. Their hands feverishly roamed and caressed, as if making certain the other was real.

Desires mounted rapidly and fatigue was forgotten, as was the slowly roasting rabbit. She lay on her back with one hand behind his neck to hold his mouth to hers while the other traveled up and down his muscular back. His hand cupped a breast and softly kneaded it before allowing his fingers to massage the taut peak.

Snailishly his lips left hers and trailed sensuously down her neck to engulf the tiny bud and to pleasure it. As he shifted his body to permit room to tantalize the other one, she closed her eyes and sighed dreamily, her body alive and eager for the union which awaited them.

Sun Cloud's right hand drifted over her sides, stroking her feather-soft skin. His hand entered the dark triangle between her thighs and he located the peak there which was taut and ready for his deft labors. He worked pervasively on her body until it was squirming with delight and hunger, and he was more than willing to comply when she urged him to enter her womanhood. He knelt between her legs, lifted them, and guided his shaft into the entreating darkness.

Their gazes fused once more as he entered and withdrew, this position allowing him to look at her tempting flesh and radiant face as he created blissful sensations at this contact and view. Their gazes drifted to where their bodies were united and both watched the beauty of it for a time. When she reached for him, needing to feel their flesh and lips against each other, he released her legs and gently came forward to lie upon her.

Singing Wind's legs overlapped his and she matched his thrusting pattern. They kissed greedily and sought release from this rapturously tormenting siege upon their senses. Even though they craved this intoxicating attack and could allow it to continue forever, a victory was needed and desired. Their respirations increased and they joined swiftly. As if a flower bursting instantly and magically into full bloom, their releases came in glorious splendor. They plucked each petal and savored its beauty, continuing until love's blossom was bare and they seemingly lay on a soft and tranquil bed of its discarded petals.

They savored each other's kisses and caresses until their trembling bodies and erratic breathing calmed. Sun Cloud leaned away and looked down into her dreamy gaze and flushed face, which exposed her contentment. His gaze shifted to her lips, which revealed how urgently she had worked for this moment of sweet ecstasy. Her body was relaxed and her once-taut breasts were soft. She was so irresistible, but hadn't he known that for years? He had been foolish to wait so long before admitting this truth and claiming it. But all things had their seasons, and this one belonged to them. She was his now, completely his, and forever. Such happiness loomed before them, and he was eager to capture it and to savor it. *"Micante petanl,"* he whispered as his mouth covered hers once more, for she was the fire in his heart.

Suddenly she sniffed the air and jerked her head toward the fire. She laughed merrily and retorted, "What you smell, my love, is the fire eating our rabbit."

Sun Cloud glanced at the meat which was burned to a crisp. They had been so consumed with each other that they had lost all reality of their surroundings, even control of their keen senses. He began to chuckle. Their gazes met and they shared more laughter.

Sun Cloud went to remove the ruined meal from the holder which he had constructed from supple branches, as green wood was hard to set aflame. He tossed it away, scolding himself for such a waste of the Great Spirit's creature.

He returned to kneel beside her and said, "I must hunt us more food, my love. We must eat and rest; our journey is long."

Singing Wind sat up and snuggled against his still-damp chest. She murmured provocatively, "You are all the food I need this sun and moon. We can feast upon each other, then rest before our journey home." Still nestled against his chest, she tilted her head to look up at him, to send him a seductive smile.

Sun Cloud's heart seemed to catch in his throat as his senses engulfed her. He replied huskily, "You are the perfect match for me, Singing Wind. I am glad you chased me and captured me," he teased.

"Since you are my prey, lie down so I can feed this hunger for you which never seems appeased for more than a short time."

Laughing, he lifted her in his strong arms and carried her back to the creek. "First, we must wash our food; then, I will prepare it with the blaze which now burns within my body and my heart. I love you, Singing Wind; you belong in my Life-circle forever."

"As you belong in mine. I told you I was destined to join the Oglala chief. Until all ceases, we shall live together as one. I love you, Sun Cloud; I love you."

Their lips fused as they realized this was no longer stolen ecstasy, for it truly belonged to them, and always would.

Their journey home took several days, for they halted many times to play like happy children or to make love passionately. They did not want to worry others with a lengthy absence, but they needed to savor every moment of this special time together, for much work awaited them after they reached home.

Rebecca stood within the circle of Bright Arrow's embrace as they looked at the large and colorfully decorated tepee in the center of camp, the one which all women had gathered about joyfully to construct for their new chief and his wife. The Oglala chief's feathered standard was placed in the ground beside the open flap, and many skilled warriors had painted the *coups* of Sun Cloud on the hides which formed his new tepee. Everyone was pleased with the results of his tasks and was eager for their new chief to see it, for the council had met yesterday and voted.

Members of the tribe and of other tribes had placed countless gifts inside the tepee, to reveal their joy at the impending union of the son of Gray Eagle and Shalee with the daughter of Brave Bear and Chela. A big feast was planned to celebrate the selection of their new chief and his joining. Food was being gathered and prepared. The music and dancing were planned. Berry wine was ready. The camp was clean, and the people waiting. It seemed as if everyone, no matter the age or sex, performed a task for these two happy occasions.

Rebecca shifted in her husband's arms to meet his gaze. It had been over a week since his wound and injuries, and they were healing nicely and quickly. For days they had talked and laughed and made love. She had learned of Jeremy Comstock's departure for St. Louis, along with James Murdock; she hoped Jeremy understood her feelings and forgave her for deceiving him. When she had visited Powchutu's death scaffold, a curious glow had filled her, for she knew he had found lasting peace. The news had spread quickly about Sun Cloud's successful strategy and the truce following it, yet she knew how deeply her love was disturbed by his misplaced trust in Silver Hawk.

"You must stop worrying about Sun Cloud. He will capture Silver Hawk and punish him. You did not see his evil, my love, but you were not alone. All trusted Silver Hawk and believed him. You must not be so hard on yourself. It was all a part of Grandfather's plan."

He smiled at her and nodded. "That is why I can finally accept it. He is dead, for I can feel his evil missing. I have not known such peace and joy since before you were lost to me. So much has happened since the last full moon, but all is as it should be. I have my love; my lands are at peace; my father has been avenged; and I have my chief's bonnet. See, I was not totally mistaken," he jested.

"Our lives have followed many thorny paths and many lovely ones. It is so good to be home again," she whispered and snuggled against him, careful of his healing body.

He put his arm around her shoulder and guided her toward their tepee. "It is the rest period, my love. Come and lie with me."

Rebecca laughed as he laced the flap and walked toward her, a walk which said his confidence was restored and his strength was returning rapidly. She removed her garments and waited for him to reach her. He dropped his breechcloth along the way, so their naked bodies touched intimately as they embraced and kissed.

They made love leisurely and blissfully, then slept for a short time. After bathing in the river, they dressed and returned to camp, just in time to receive guests.

As tears flowed down her cheeks, Tashina raced forward to hug her mother tightly. The waiting to come home, after she had learned of her mother's survival and return, had been tormenting. Although she knew the whole story from her husband, Soul-of-Thunder, she coaxed her mother to repeat it once more, just in case something had been omitted. Rebecca urged her youngest daughter to tell her all about her romance and marriage to the handsome male at Tashina's side.

After the women had embraced several times and exuberantly exchanged tales, Windrider and Bonnie "Sky Eyes" Thorne came forward to reveal their elation at Rebecca's return. Between joyful tears, Rebecca embraced both affectionately, then hugged each of their children, immediately noticing how muscular and handsome and virile Sky Warrior had become during the past year. She was glad her daughter had married the son of Windrider, for both were unique males.

When Little Feet and Thunder Spirit joined the laughing group, she and her sister hugged and whispered about their new lives and this happy occasion. As Rebecca placed her arm around Bright Arrow, he drew her close to his side, as if he could not endure her absence very long. Little Feet and Tashina went to stand at either side of their reunited parents, clasping their hands before and behind them to form a circle of shared love. After releasing each other's hands, the two women joined their husbands and nestled close to them.

The merriment seemed contagious, for White Arrow and Pretty Woman strolled over to where the smiling couples were standing and talking. His aging gaze walked slowly over the group and he smiled. He watched his son Thunder Spirit and was glad to observe his happiness and peace, for he and Little Feet were well suited and it suited him to have his son joined to the granddaughter of his best friends Gray Eagle and Shalee. He would miss those two terribly, but he would watch over their sons and grandchildren for them.

Flaming Star returned from his hunt and came to see what was going on in the center of camp. He grinned at Rebecca, then clasped forearms with Bright Arrow. Suddenly, giggling children surrounded Flaming Star and he leaned forward to scoop up Buckskin Girl and to ruffle the dark heads of his two sons. Soon, the little girl wiggled to get down, for she wanted to race off to play with White Arrow's second set of children. Flaming Star glanced at his father and smiled, for they were very close.

Everyone was in a good mood, ready to celebrate the joys of living and loving. Bright Arrow's gaze scanned the group around him and his heart surged with deep emotion. All of them had been touched and loved and influenced by Gray Eagle and Shalee, and they would never be forgotten. He had vowed to send word through Sturgis to Powchutu's son, Stede Gaston, to let Stede know all about his father's life and death, and to let Stede know about his true heritage. His gaze met White Arrow's, and he realized how closely their thoughts and feelings matched. Now that his father was gone, White Arrow would be the one to give him guidance. They smiled and nodded in understanding.

A hunter galloped into camp to send up the signal that Sun Cloud and Singing Wind were approaching, and the Oglalas quickly dropped their tasks and rushed forward to greet their new chief and his future mate. They cheered loudly and merrily as Sun Cloud dismounted agilely. Then Thunder Spirit stepped forward and helped Singing Wind from her horse's back, and they exchanged grins.

Sun Cloud eyed the lovely and smiling Rebecca, then hugged her tightly. "It is good to have you home again, my sister."

Sun Cloud embraced his brother and queried him about his health. When Bright Arrow told him he was fine, and ecstatically happy, Sun Cloud greeted his friends and people. Grasping Singing Wind's hand and pulling her to his side, he announced, "I wish to join the daughter of Brave Bear this moon. Do my people accept her?"

A cheer arose and all shouted, *"Han, han.* Yes, yes."

Bright Arrow revealed the news of the vote making Sun Cloud chief, then placed the bonnet made from his many *coup* feathers upon his head, and was glad

Mind-who-Roams had completed it and had handed it to him to carry out this thrilling duty. He asked everyone to make a path so Sun Cloud and Singing Wind could see the generous gift from their people: the beautiful tepee with the Oglala chief's markings. "All is prepared for your joining and our feast. It is good to have you home safely, my brother, and my chief."

Sun Cloud looked around at all of his friends, loved ones, and people. His eyes were misty and his voice was choked with deep emotion as he said, "My people are generous and kind. I pray I will be a worthy chief like my father Gray Eagle and his father Running Wolf. This is a good day for living and for joining. My heart swells with joy and pride, and I fear it will burst from fullness."

Bright Arrow suggested, "Come, let the ceremonial chief join you to your chosen one, then our celebration can begin."

Sun Cloud squeezed Singing Wind's hand and pulled her forward. "It is time, my love," he whispered near her ear. "Are you ready?"

Singing Wind looked up at him and smiled. "More than ready, my love," she replied, for the bitter demands on all of their lives were over, and only sweet ecstasy loomed before them. She entwined her fingers with Sun Cloud's and they approached the area where their lives would be joined as one, just as their hearts were bound as one.

Forever Ecstasy

FOR:

the family of Hiram Owen, in loving memory of my
dear Dakota friend, translator, and adviser
who passed away 8/31/88.
Wakantanka nici un.

Eileen Wilson, who loves Gray Eagle
and his heirs as much as I do.

Debbie Keffer, for her kindnesses.
and,
my many friends and readers at Sinte Geleska College
and St. Francis Indian Mission.

ACKNOWLEDGMENTS AND SPECIAL THANKS TO:

Marvene Riis, Archivist, Cultural Heritage
Center in Pierre,
Lawrence Blazek, Mayor of Marcus,
Gary LeFebre of Lodgepole,
The Pierre Chamber of Commerce,
Ken Wetz, Mayor of Newell,
The staff of Bear Butte State Park,
Spearfish and Sturgis Chambers of Commerce,
and
many historical societies and staffs of historical sites
in the friendly and generous state of South Dakota.

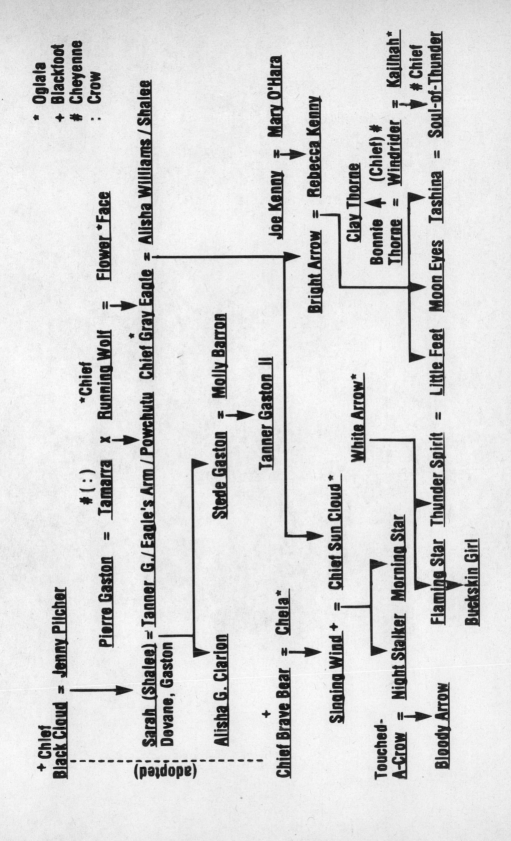

* Oglala
+ Blackfoot
# Cheyenne
: Crow

(:)

*Chief

+ Chief
Black Cloud = Jenny Pilcher

Pierre Gaston = Tamarra x Running Wolf = Flower *Face

Sarah (Shalee) = Tanner G./Eagle's Arm/Powchutu Chief Gray Eagle = Alisha Williams/Shalee
Devane, Gaston

Alisha G. Clarion

Stele Gaston = Molly Barron

Tanner Gaston II

Joe Kenny = Mary O'Hara

Bright Arrow = Rebecca Kenny

Clay Thorne

(Chief) #
Bonnie   Windrider = Kajihah*
Thorne =

Moon Eyes Tashina = Soul-of-Thunder

Chief

Little Feet

Chief Brave Bear = Chela*

Singing Wind + = Chief Sun Cloud*

White Arrow*

Touched-
A-Crow = Night Stalker Morning Star

Bloody Arrow

Flaming Star Thunder Spirit = Little Feet

Buckskin Girl

(adopted)

Prologue

"As the sun last slept, Grandfather gave me a vision," Standing Tree told the men gathered in the meeting lodge at their winter camp in the Black Hills. "Before I speak it, let us prepare ourselves."

The Oglala shaman lifted the sacred catlinite pipe and fingered the smooth red bowl on a four-foot stem that had ceremonial beads and feathers attached at the joining point. His wrinkled fingers packed tobacco inside it, then took a burning stick from the fire and lit the fragrant contents. Standing Tree raised the pipe upward to honor Wakantanka—the Great Spirit—and downward to honor Makakin—Mother Earth. Next, he saluted each of the four directions: the east to summon enlightenment and peace, the south where warmth was born, the west which brought rain, and the north which offered fortitude. "As I share your breath, Grandfather, open my heart and mind to receive and accept your sacred message," he invoked. He drew the smoke deep into his lungs, held it there for a moment, then exhaled curls of smoke that went heavenward. He passed the pipe to the man at his right, the Oglala chief, Sun Cloud.

Strong hands accepted the sacred item. The supplication to the Great Spirit was repeated. Then the pipe was passed to the next man, to continue around the group until all participants had done the ritual four times. During this reverent ceremony, no one talked and all meditated.

Sun Cloud gazed at the buffalo skull, weathered and bleached by Wi—the sun —and Makajou—the rain, that was lying on the mat before the shaman in a place of honor. It was painted with the colors and symbols of nature, and was stuffed with a mixture of sweet grasses. The buffalo was viewed by Plains Indians as the most powerful animal of the Great Spirit's creation—a generous and clever gift to His children to provide them with food, shelter, clothing, tools, and medicine.

Sun Cloud shifted his gaze to the Medicine Wheel that was mounted on a tall cottonwood post, the same tree chosen for the Sun Dance ritual. The wheel's surface was divided by four bars which represented the four directions: west for danger, north for life, east for knowledge, and south for quiet: the influences and forces of life. Made of brain-tanned hide stretched taut over a willow hoop, its roundness told of their belief in the Circle of Life: *Canhdeska Wakan*. Hair, heart-beads, fur, and feathers decorated it. Another buffalo skull was attached to its center to signify *Lakol wicho'an*, the traditional way of life, and *Pte Oyate*, the spiritual life. All spokes radiated toward the center—the heart and meaning of life, which was total harmony with one's self and with nature. That skull was painted white to express purity. A Hoop of Life hung beneath the Medicine Wheel.

The Hoop of Life symbolized all stages of man's existence: the never-ending circle of life from birth, to maturity, to old age, to death, then rebirth in the Spirit World. Four bars and four feathers were displayed on its surface for the four virtues of wisdom, courage, constancy, and generosity. The four directions to which it pointed were the same as those of the Medicine Wheel. Here, too, the four points radiated toward the center for total harmony. The chief repeated the pipe ritual a fourth time.

A fire glowed in the center of the large tepee. Its undulating flames created shadows against the buffalo-hide wall which seemed to breathe with a spiritual life of their own. A flap was opened at the top to allow smoke to escape, but it did not release the fire's heat. It was cold outside the meeting lodge on the moonless night. The floor was the earth upon which the Indians lived. The men sat on buffalo mats, huddled in several circles around the blaze, their bodies also giving warmth to each other.

The only sounds heard were the soft breathing of the men, the invocation words, and the crackling of burning wood. No wind howled around the tepee. No dog barked. No child cried. No horse neighed. It was as if all creatures and forces of nature sensed and honored the gravity of this moment.

Many smells filled the air: the sweetness of cherrywood sticks and special grasses in the fire, the animal-skin mats upon which they sat and the hide walls which surrounded them, the fragrant tobacco in the pipe, the dirt beneath them, and the grease—human and animal—upon their bodies for protection against winter's chill. No man seemed to feel the stinging of smoke in his eyes or mind the familiar odors. All were too ensnared by suspense and a feeling of oneness.

The Oglala chief, council members, and high-ranking warriors were eager for their shaman to reveal his vision. Standing Tree commanded their respect, awe, and loyalty. He was a man of wisdom, mystical insight, healing skills, and "powerful magic." All remained still and silent as the spiritual leader of their tribe rose to enlighten them.

"Grandfather spoke to me in a sacred vision while I slept," he began. "We have been at peace with the white-eyes for many winters, a peace that came from the loss of our great leader, Gray Eagle, father of Chief Sun Cloud. But Grandfather warned that a season of bitter conflicts and greed will destroy that peace. The Great Mystery showed me two men. One's face was hidden from my eyes, but Grandfather said he carries Oglala blood. A chief's bonnet lay at his feet, torn from his head by evil. In the winters to come, Grandfather will make his heart grow restless. He will call the lost warrior back to the land of his people to share our destiny." The shaman was quiet.

Chief Sun Cloud pondered the holy man's words. Bright Arrow—his brother —had been driven away by evil, but had returned. Powchutu—his father's brother —had been driven away by evil, too, but had returned. Both were dead now. "Your words confuse me, Wise One," he said. "If he is of our blood and tribe, why do we not know of him? What evil drove him from our people? When was the past moon that witnessed such a black deed?"

"I do not know," the sixty-year-old man answered. "His face and markings were not clear. We will know his words are true when he speaks them to us. When white trappers and traders came to our land, we met them as friends. We let them trap our streams and hunt in our forests. We made truce and trade with them. What they have seen and done here calls other white-eyes to our lands; many of them will be evil and dangerous. A dark moon in the winters to come will flood our land with white-eyes, and war will thunder as a violent storm across it."

"Why would the soldiers attack?" the chief reasoned. "Since my Grandfather's time, we let the whites roam our lands and draw maps of our hills and valleys, our forests, plains, and rivers. We let trappers and traders build posts to sell goods to whites and to Indians. We let soldiers cut trees and build forts so we could observe them and learn their ways. When battles came between our two peoples, it was the whites' doings. They asked for treaties, and we gave them. Eleven winters past we made a new truce with them. The one called Derek Sturgis took the paper I signed to their Great White Chief Monroe. The fort was abandoned, and the soldiers left our territory. As promised, they have not returned to threaten us. When Colonel Leavenworth came with troops eight winters past to seek our help to defeat the Arikaras, we gave it; they thanked us, presented us with gifts, and rode away." Sun Cloud kept his probing gaze on the older man.

"Such good things will not halt what is to come, my chief. Trouble will be reborn, but its life will be cut short by the warrior Grandfather sends to us. A long peace will follow—"

Smiles, nods, and murmurs of relief took place before Standing Tree could finish his sentence. They ceased when he continued. "But more white-eyes will journey here in great numbers. Their hungers will bring even darker and bloodier suns. They will crave all Grandfather has given to us: our lands, our animals, our rocks and trees, our grasses, our lives, our honors, and our freedom. They can have none of those sacred gifts unless they destroy us. Many seasons after I begin my walk at Grandfather's side, they will try to do so, and my people will resist. The white-eyes will come to fear and do battle with the Dakota Nation as they do with no other. The Tetons will lead all tribes of the Seven Council Fires and our allies in the last battle for survival. Grandfather did not reveal the final victor to me."

Sun Cloud was angered by this news. "We trusted the White Chief, and we kept our word. Why can he not honor his? Must we drive all whites from our land and stop others from coming? Will not their number and strength grow faster and stronger than the grasses upon our plains?"

"We cannot keep them away until time is no more. Feed upon the seasons of peace ahead, for many of starving will come. The first trouble will bring the two men that Grandfather revealed to me in my sacred vision."

"How can this be?" Sun Cloud asked. "My brother was slain in battle with the Crow this summer past. Bright Arrow has no sons to challenge me. He has no grandsons who match your words. My memory knows of no man who lost the chief's bonnet and was driven away. If it was long ago, how can a distant evil hold such power? Who seeks my rank?"

"My vision did not say he wants to take the chief's bonnet from Sun Cloud. It said he was denied his rank, land, and people and that Grandfather will draw him to us for help in a time of great danger."

Sun Cloud's heart pounded inside the bronzed flesh of his broad chest, scarred by the Sun Dance ritual. "My son is ten winters old. Do you speak of him? Will he be taken from us, but returned one moon?"

"I do not know. His face was kept hidden from me. When the moon comes, Grandfather will reveal all to me. I will speak His words to you."

"What of the other man, Wise One?" a council member asked.

"He is a white-eye who will come to help us defeat our enemies. He is unlike other white-eyes. He will prove himself worthy to become our blood brother. His words and ways will be hard to accept and obey, but we must do so to survive. The white-eyes will not honor the treaty we signed. After many snows have covered Mother Earth with their white blankets, our land will be darkened by dangers. The blood of many, Indian and white, will soak into Mother Earth. Peace lies within the grasp of the white-eye whose hair blazes as the sun and in whose eyes the blue of sky lives. His heart will side with us. Many foes, Indian and white, will try to defeat him. An Oglala maiden will be chosen to ride with him, and she will become a skilled warrior at his side. She will guard his life and help defeat foes."

"Why does Grandfather use a white man?" another elder asked.

"I do not know. But I do know his eyes are as blue and calm as the sky when he will appear. His voice will blow as a strong wind one moon and as a gentle breeze on another. His attacks will beat as heavy rain upon our foes. His glory will shine as brightly as the glowing ball in the heaven where the spirits live. His anger at those who threaten us and betray us will rumble as loud thunder. As with snow in our sacred hills, his heart and mind are pure. He will come when Grandfather says the time is here. The maiden who is chosen to battle with him will know a great destiny; her legend will speak of She-Who-Rode-With-The-Sky-Warrior."

"Who is this maiden, Wise One? Why must a female ride with a white warrior to defeat our enemies?" A third man asked the question in all their hearts.

"I do not know."

During the ensuing silence, Sun Cloud glanced at the pictorial history of his Red Heart Band that was painted upon a tanned buffalo hide that hung on the lodge's wall. It recorded the events that had taken place since the birth of his grandfather, Chief Running Wolf. It told of past conflicts with whites and with enemy tribes. Sun Cloud dreaded the scenes that would be added to it one day. His dark eyes scanned the faces of his warriors and tribal leaders. He wondered who would live to see those ominous times. The thirty-four-year-old chief wondered if he would still be their leader then. "When will this black sun come?" he asked in a grave tone, believing the shaman's medicine powerful and his counsel wise.

"I do not know," Standing Tree said once more. "But not for many, many winters." He took a seat cross-legged on a buffalo hide.

Sun Cloud did not understand the meaning of this strange and distant vision. Yet he trusted and believed the mystical shaman and the Great Spirit. His father, the legendary Gray Eagle, was with Wakantanka; as was his mother, Alisha Williams, a white captive whom his father had loved and married. Bright Arrow and his wife had joined their parents last summer. Sun Cloud felt it was good and merciful when the Great Spirit called mates to His side on the same sun, as it had been with his parents and his brother. He knew it must be hard and lonely to live without the love of your heart.

Sun Cloud heard the others leaving the meeting lodge while he was deep in thought. Except for the Crow, Shoshone, and Pawnee, peace had ruled their land since the treaty with Sturgis in 1820. That truce had followed the ambush of his father and a painful struggle with his brother over the chief's bonnet. He had won that honor and duty and won the hand of Singing Wind. Years of joy, success, and love had ensued.

Now it was nearing time to begin his son's warrior training, and he prayed the man in Standing Tree's vision was not his only child. Singing Wind, his beloved wife, would bear another child when summer came. Perhaps it would be another son. No matter, a second child at last would bring much pride and happiness to his heart. He would make certain there was no confusion or conflict over which child would follow him as chief, as there had been with his brother eleven summers ago.

The Red Heart chief of the Oglala/Teton branch of the Dakota Nation got to his feet. He flexed his muscular body and told himself that if dark moons were ahead, he must enjoy all the bright ones until then. A man's destiny could not be changed; his Life-Circle was drawn by the Great Spirit before his birth. There was no need to worry over distant threats. Grandfather would always be there to guide, protect, and love His people.

A hungry smile softened his handsome features. Sun Cloud headed for his tepee and his wife, who would chase away the night's chill with fiery passion. Until Grandfather sent Sky Warrior to them, he would forget the perilous times ahead. For the present, all the chief wanted to think about were his wife, his young son, and the child Singing Wind carried.

Chapter One

"Hello in camp! Can I join you for coffee and rest?" Joe called out before approaching the camp. It was a precaution he had quickly learned to take in this wild Dakota territory to avoid getting shot by accident.

"Come on in," a voice replied, "but take it slow and easy."

Joe dismounted and secured his reins to a bush. He didn't unsaddle the animal, since he always liked to be prepared for a quick escape. It was chilly tonight. He removed his leather riding gloves and stuffed them into his saddlebag, but kept on the thin wool jacket he had donned a mile back.

Joe headed through the wooded location toward a fire near the riverbank. As he passed two wagons, he saw a beautiful Indian girl secured to one of the wheels. Her arms were extended, her wrists tied to the spokes, and her legs were bound at the ankles. He was intrigued by her presence, but ignored her for now. He had other matters on his troubled mind.

Not far away, he noticed, eight horses for pulling the two wagons were tethered and grazing. An abundance of trees, with the river eastward, had forced the men to leave those wagons thirty feet from their waterside camp. Yet the spacings of oaks and cottonwoods and a three-fourths waxing moon made the female prisoner visible to her captors.

Joe's azure gaze studied each of the three men as he approached them, just as they were eyeing him with interest. The condition of the camp—the large amount of coals, the trampled ground, more than a few hours' smell of manure, and the many items scattered about—told him it was several days' old. When he'd found their trail, he had known the wagons were a few days beyond him. He hoped he wasn't wasting valuable time and energy on what could be an impulsive chase. "Thanks," he answered the man. "I was getting tired, sore, and hungry. This area is mighty deserted. I'm glad I happened up on you men. Mind if I share your coffee and beans? My last meal was a long way back."

"Help yourself, but ain't you out late tonight, stranger?" a barrel-chested man remarked. He gestured for the new arrival to sit on the ground.

As Joe poured himself some steaming coffee and set the tin cup on the grass beside him, he explained, "I was about to make camp earlier when several Indians chose the same clearing I had. I thought it best to let them have first choice," Joe jested with a wry grin. "It doesn't take long in this wild territory to learn you don't want to meet up with them when you're alone."

"What tribe was they?" the youngest man asked.

Joe glanced at the towhead with dark-blue eyes as he guilefully remarked, "Indians are Indians, aren't they?" He took in details: the man was just under twenty and had a long knife scar on his left cheek.

"Nope" came the reply. "Some are friendlies; others, real mean."

"Friendlies, hell. They're all blood-thirsty savages. Ain't worth the salt it'd take to cure 'em fur dog meat. Only good ones are on your payroll or dead," the third man refuted with a cold chuckle, then sipped his whiskey.

Joe didn't like these crude men. The third one was tall and slender, with a pockmarked face and dirty hands wrapped around the bottle he was nursing. He appeared to be about thirty. His brown hair was as filthy as his clothes, and his hazel eyes had an emotionless expression that put Joseph Lawrence, Jr., on guard. His father's friend Stede Gaston had told him to never trust a man whose eyes stay frozen when he smiles. He had found that warning to be accurate.

Joe stopped dishing up beans to feign surprise. "Indians work for whites?" he asked. "I thought they were independent free-roaming men who lived only to hunt and raid, and that they made their women do all the work."

"If ya give enough trinkets, they'll do most any chore fur ya."

The burly man scowled and spat on the ground. "What you work too much is your jaws, Clem. Put up that fire water; you've had enough. What are you doing in these parts?" he asked the stranger.

To be convincing, Joe used half-truths. "My father's in the shipping business, and I got tired of making voyages for him," he said. "I hated being a sailor. Sea trips aren't any fun when you spend most of your time heaving your meals over the rails. I heard it was exciting and challenging out here, so I decided to leave dull Virginia and seek a few adventures."

Joe smiled to relax the wary man with his scraggly beard and muddy brown hair that flowed over his broad shoulders. It looked as if that tangled mane hadn't seen a comb or brush in ages, and it didn't take a keen observer to realize that their clothes hadn't seen a washpot in weeks. It was apparent these rough characters cared nothing about their appearances. "A man who lacks pride in himself usually lacks morals and a conscience," his father had told him, "so sail clear of him, son. Even poor folk, if they're decent and honest, keep themselves clean and neat." That wise remembrance told him to be vigilant. "My name's Joe Lawrence," he introduced himself. "As I said, I'm glad I came upon you tonight. I'll admit I was getting a little nervous out here alone. Who are you?"

"I'm Zeke," the leader replied, watchful of the newcomer. "That's Clem." He nodded to the disobedient man who had the bottle to his lips once more. "And that's Farley." He named the youngest of the group.

No last names were supplied, and Joe wondered if there was a special reason. He also noted that Zeke had silenced Clem to prevent him from revealing any facts the leery man wanted kept secret. The wariness aroused Joe's interest as much as the contents of those wagons. Between bites he made small talk to calm them while he tried to entice slips of the tongue. "Where's the best place to look for work in this area?"

"What kind of job you got in mind?" Zeke asked, lazing against a tree.

"Haven't thought much about that, but I'm not joining the cavalry. I don't want to trade one boss for another one. If I didn't like soldiering, I wouldn't want the Army hunting me down as a deserter. Since I don't know this territory, scouting is out. Besides, I don't care to go tangling with hostiles every other day or two. When I get ready to return home, I want to take my hair with me," he said with a chuckle. "From what I've read and heard, Indians like to take scalps as trophies, especially blond ones."

"You kin bet your boots an' pants they do," Farley concurred. He stroked the lengthy knife scar on his boyish face and frowned.

Joe caught the hint. "I'm not much of a gambler, so I'll take your word, friend. Where are you men heading? Maybe I can tag along for safety, if you don't mind." Joe took a few more bites of beans, then washed them down with strong coffee. Neither tasted good; his appetite was lagging, but he pretended to enjoy the scanty meal and company.

"Sorry, Lawrence, but we're heading for a private camp."

Joe focused his attention on the leader. "No jobs available there?"

"The boss don't like to hire strangers or greenhorns."

"I learn fast and follow orders good," Joe told him, then set aside the tin plate and empty cup. "Most people say I'm easy to get along with, even on my bad days. I'd be grateful for help. I'll give you a cut of my salary for a while to get me hired on and to teach me my way around these parts."

Zeke tossed the two dishes and spoon into a pile with other dirty ones. "That's a tempting offer, Lawrence, but no. Strangers are too nosy, and greenhorns are too dangerous. Both cause too much trouble."

"Iffen he's good with fightin' and shootin', Zeke, the boss might want him. We kin always use a skilled—"

"Nope. You know the boss's orders, Farley. If I was you, Lawrence, I'd ride to Fort Tabor where the Missouri joins the White River or to Pratte's Trading Post at Pierre. Men looking for work do best there." Zeke's distrustful gaze roved Joe as he talked. "You don't appear a man to take to trapping or trading. If you don't want to join the Army or do scouting, best I can think of is guarding places or hauling goods."

Joe glanced at the two wagons thirty feet away. He knew they were loaded because of the deep ruts the wheels had made, the ones he had located and followed. He tried not to look at the female prisoner who was watching all four men with her dark eyes. The blond-haired man presumed she must be cold so far from the fire and without a blanket or long sleeves. But for now he had to ignore her plight. Later he would decide what to do about her. He looked back at Zeke and casually inquired, "That what you do, transport supplies?"

Zeke kept his gaze locked onto Joe's face. "Not exactly."

Joe sensed the man's caution and let the touchy subject drop. He noticed how Zeke's eyes stayed on him as tight as a rope on a capstan. The leader looked tense, and his dirty fingers kept drumming on one thigh.

"If you came from Virginny," Zeke asked. "Why didn't you stop at Fort Tabor or at Lookout? Or head upriver to Pierre? What kind of work you expect to find in a wilderness? This area's a long way from civilization."

To calm the still edgy leader, Joe decided to start speaking more like these men and drop the correct English that he'd been taught during his years of schooling. "I was ridin' for Benton near the headwaters of the Missouri," he fabricated. "I got a friend there who's been beggin' me to join him. He hired on with the American Fur Company in '47. Been with them ever since. I figured I'd see more of this wild territory if I rode across country, rather than take a boat the long route by water. I heard the Missouri gets mighty treacherous in places, and I ain't one to challenge crazy water much. I had my fill of that workin' for my father back East."

"Maybe I know your friend. I've traded with lots of trappers."

"Ever met Ben Murphy? About forty—short, husky, black hair."

"Nope. I thought I knew all those American Fur boys."

"Ben's quiet. He usually keeps to himself. We trapped together back South. He taught me most of what I know. When we'd take off huntin' or trappin', my father always sent somebody to fetch me home if we didn't return in a month or two. He was determined I was going to learn his shippin' business and take it over one day. I figured if I joined Ben out here, I'd be too far away for Old Joe to find me and drag me home again. I guess I got too used to being on my own at school, and I didn't take to Old Joe's runnin' my life from dawn to dusk like he did his company."

"So why you looking for a job in these parts if it's to Benton you're heading?" Zeke asked. When an owl hooted, he glanced in that direction, his nerves obviously on edge.

"I been ridin' for weeks and my tail's tryin' to grow to the saddle." Joe answered. "I need a rest. It's a long way to Benton. Frankly, I ain't lookin' forward to crossin' Crow Territory. It drained me to come this far through Sioux land."

"Don't let them hear you call 'em Sioux," Zeke warned, "or they'll lift your hair for sure. That's a chopped-off French word meaning 'treacherous snake.' They call themselves *Dakotas*, 'friends.' Best remember that."

"Are they?"

"Are they what?" Zeke asked, confused.

"Friends, friendly," Joe hinted as a reminder.

"Sioux are about the lowest and meanest savages alive." Zeke spat again, as if clearing his mouth of a foul taste.

"*You're* working this area and you still have your scalp. You got a truce with them?"

"Sioux don't make no truces with whites, but they'll leave you be if they think you're smarter and stronger than them. I've beaten some of their best warriors, so the others avoid tangling with me."

"Sounds like you're the right man to join up with in this area."

"I don't need nobody else to tend or to slow me down. Clem and Farley do more than enough of both. You'll do better to head for Crow Territory than hang around in Sioux."

"Why is that, Zeke? Don't they hate whites, too?"

"Not like the Sioux. Don't show no fear of them when you're alone, and Crow'll let you pass. One of their prophets told them his vision said not to war with whites. All Injuns are big believers in them peyote dreams they call visions, but braves will still ambush and rob you if you act scared."

"Hell, Zeke! Most of 'em are cowards and beggars. They'd rather have a trinket 'an fight a real man for his scalp," Clem said between chuckles.

Zeke glared at his companion before giving his advice to Joe. "If you ain't heading on to Benton at first light, you best ride east to one of the trading posts on the river. For a few dollars you can catch a boat to join your friend. Trappers who don't work for companies mostly come to sell their winter catches before long. They spend a month or so jawing, drinking, whoring, and gambling. Then they resupply and go back to their trapping grounds. River's the safest way to get there from here. It's eastward. We're heading southwest. You don't need to ride in that direction."

Joe knew the man was lying. The trail he'd followed for days was heading northwestward and Crow Territory and Benton were both in that direction! Zeke's careless mistake and odd behavior told Joe he'd been smart to follow his gut instinct. But it was clear that the ruffian was adamant about them parting ways at sunrise. When the others remained silent, Joe yawned and flexed his shoulders. "I wish I could change your mind, Zeke, but I understand." "I'll get my gun and help keep guard tonight," he offered. "I don't want any Indians sneaking into camp while we're asleep."

"No need," Zeke said. "We take two-hour shifts each, even when it seems safe. We've done scouted the area. The Sioux are still holed up in their winter camps south of here, and it's a good ways to Crow Territory. You can rest easy tonight, then be on your way at dawn."

Joe smiled, then asked Clem, "You got another bottle of that good whiskey I can buy? It's been a dusty and tiring ride today."

Before Clem or Zeke could reply, Farley said, "Plenty, iffen you got—"

"No!" the hefty leader interrupted and came to his feet. "The way Clem's been slopping down our supply like a bottomless pig, it's about gone, except for that bottle I got in my gear. You're welcome to a swig or two of it, Lawrence. I'll fetch it. You stay here with the boys."

Joe saw how the large man got to his feet with ease and agility, then left the smoky fire to head for the front wagon. With Zeke gone, maybe he could get answers to the beautiful mystery nearby, he thought. "One of you having trouble with your squaw?" Joe inquired in a genial tone as he nodded to the captive some thirty feet away at the second wagon. The moon's angle and tall trees now placed the confining wagon and young female in almost obscuring shadows, but Joseph Lawrence had a mental picture of her that would never vanish.

The half-inebriated Clem glanced in the beauty's direction, chuckled, and revealed, "We's taking her to the boss. Caught her whilst we wuz scouting. He likes 'em young, full of spirit and fight. She oughta last a few weeks, maybe months if he's more careful this time. He uses 'em up fast. Just 'twixt us, Joe, I'd like a bite of her flesh meself. Maybe we can talk—"

"Shut up, you drunken fool," Zeke warned, his eyes narrowing as he passed Joe the half-empty bottle. "Don't pay Clem no mind," he said. "His brain's sour mash by now. He's teasing you. But if he don't stop drinking and lying so much, I'm gonna get rid of him. He knows I traded for her in a Crow camp yesterday. You can see she didn't care much for being sold by her pappy. She'll settle down soon and make me a good squaw."

Joe noticed the bite mark on Zeke's hand that he rubbed as he lied. The woman presented Joe with a difficult decision: rescue her and lose this contact, or ignore her imminent fate so he could try to stay with these offensive men. With Zeke so mad at Clem, maybe he could persuade the leader to let him join them. If he pulled off that feat and they reached their destination, he'd never be able to free her. Yet if these men were connected to the murderous villain he was after . . . "She's beautiful, Zeke. I'm sure a strong man like you will have her tamed fast. I've always heard that a woman with fire is more fun than one who's quiet and cowardly. I'd say you got a good deal, a real challenge." He sipped whiskey and deliberated which course to sail tonight.

The Oglala maiden was awake and alert, and she tried to ignore the chill on her flesh. Morning Star hated the men who had taken her prisoner and the dark fate they had in mind for her. And now there were four to fight against. Although she pretended not to understand their words, her parents had taught her English. Years ago she had practiced that skill with any light-skinned visitor who had come to their camp. Those days were gone because of the recent trouble between the two cultures. Her father had signed a treaty with the palefaces in 1820, and peace had ensued for years. But during the past two summers, sporadic fights and false charges had marred that truce.

A new breed of encroachers seemed determined to war with them now, a breed that was to provoke even more hatred and trouble between the Crow and the Oglalas. Soon her people expected more conflicts, violence, and false accusations. Yet she could not forget that her family and tribe had befriended some lightskins. Nor could she forget that her grandmother and aunt were of white blood, or that she carried a trace of it. She had concluded long ago that not all palefaces were bad. It was unfair and wrong to judge an entire race by the evil doings of some of its members, as most whites did with Indians.

This past winter had been tranquil. In fact, she had known mostly peace since her birth and had not witnessed the new troubles, so a fierce hatred for all whites did not exist in her heart. She wanted to study them and discover why there were such hostilities and differences between them. Only by learning from a problem could it be resolved, and bloodshed be prevented. Yet her captors seemed to be proving that her brother's ominous words about most palefaces were true.

Morning Star prayed that the Indians the last man had mentioned earlier were from her travel party and not Crow warriors arriving early. The Crow were fierce enemies of her people, the Dakotas, and had been for generations. If she were recognized as the daughter of Oglala Chief Sun Cloud, the Bird People would demand to buy her as a slave. She could imagine the horrors—or even death—she would endure at their hands. Yet she must not lose hope and courage. She must not lose her wits. She had to remain ready to seize any opening. When that glorious moment came, she wanted to flee with as much information as she could. She forced herself to concentrate on the men's conversation.

The last man's words revealed he was new to her land. He seemed different from her cold and mean captors. She sensed that the big foe did not trust the handsome stranger. Morning Star decided that the sunny-haired man would be lucky to get away from the others alive.

Sun Cloud's daughter tried to ignore Joe, as she needed to concentrate on the others and their plans. She wished she knew who was the "Boss" they had mentioned several times within her hearing and wished they would reveal more. She knew there were weapons inside the wagons for the Bird People to use against her tribe. She needed to discover why these men wanted to create an inter-tribal war.

Morning Star watched them drink and talk. She knew the stranger had noticed her but was pretending she did not exist. Even if he were a good man, she could not cry out for his help. He was as outnumbered as she; he was also white, and that probably made him a foe.

She closed her eyes and leaned her weary head against a spoke of the wagon.

She was thirsty and hungry; the men were punishing her with the denial of food and water for battling them, especially the big one. Several times he had shaken her, slapped her, and shouted of horrible things he would do to her if she weren't a gift for his boss. Then he had laughed—an evil sound—and said she would soon wish he were her owner instead of the other man! Despite her fear, she had pretended not to understand his threats.

The wind's coolness and strength increased and blew over her flesh, causing her to tremble. She wished she had been given a blanket to ward off the night's chill, but told herself that her comfort wasn't the most important thing at this time, even if she *were* miserable. Her outstretched arms ached, and her tightly bound wrists caused her fingers to tingle and lose feeling. The hub of the wagon pressed into her back and made it beg for relief. Her buttocks were sore and numb from being confined to the same awkward position for hours. It was a struggle to accept such torments in silence, to resist fatigue, and to quell her fears. She prayed her party had not been misled by the false trail her captors had set for them. If so, her world could be lost forever. Once she was enslaved and used, even if she escaped, how could she return to her tribe without her honor?

"You can toss down your bedroll and sleep here," the Oglala maiden heard the big man say to Joe. "Best get an early start tomorrow; you got a ways to ride." She heard Joe excuse himself and saw him vanish into the denser trees and bushes to the right of the campfire. The other men huddled and whispered. A bad sign, she decided. No doubt they were—

Morning Star perceived someone's stealthy approach behind her under the wagon. The scent was unfamiliar. Her heart rate increased and she quivered in suspense.

Joseph Lawrence, Jr., could not allow an innocent girl to suffer the terrible fate that Clem had mentioned before Zeke had silenced him. If he could free her without getting caught, he would continue his deceitful attempt to join up with the suspicious men. If not . . .

Joe had removed his jacket to keep from putting telltale stains on it. He used his elbows and feet to wriggle to the female. He hoped the shadows and her pinioned body would conceal him. He lifted himself to his knees and leaned close to her head. "I hope you understand me, woman, because I don't have much time," he whispered. "I'm a friend, but those men over there are real bad. I'm going to cut you free, but keep still and quiet until I get back to the fire and distract them. I'll leave my knife beside you. When I have their attention, free your legs, then sneak away. If you understand what I'm saying, nod your head."

Morning Star did not know all of the words he used, but she grasped his meaning. Though she worried that the man's strange behavior was a trick to make her expose herself, something within her said to trust him. She gathered her courage and nodded.

"That's a relief," Joe murmured. With caution, he sliced through the rope at one wrist, then the other. As ordered, the female didn't move from her strained position. He slid his knife to her right side. "Make sure they aren't looking when you free your legs. Hide until they stop searching for you. I'll get back to the campfire to spy on them. Good luck."

Joe worked his way from beneath the wagon and retrieved his jacket. After brushing the debris from his shirt and trousers, he slipped on the jacket and sneaked into the concealing trees. So far his plan was a success, but he remained guarded. He began to whistle as he walked along the riverbank to camp. He entered the clearing with his shirttail hanging out, as if he had relieved himself and hadn't straightened his clothing. The other men were bedding down, their weapons nearby. Joe wondered why no guard was being posted, as Zeke had talked about earlier. He wondered if it had been a ruse to keep him rifleless. He came to full alert and decided that perhaps he should get away while he could, as soon as the girl was safe. To stall for time and conceal his wariness, he remarked, "That coffee and whiskey ran through me fast. I'd sure love a bath if that water wasn't so cold. I'll fetch my bedroll and join you. I'll be—"

Clem looked toward the lovely reason why he was in trouble tonight. His shout cut off Joe's sentence. "That Injun gal's escaping, Zeke!"

All eyes riveted to the wagon and the female, who was leaning forward and cutting the bonds on her ankles. She glanced up, then hurried back to work on the rope. Zeke and Farley tossed aside their covers and leapt to their feet to halt her. The drunken Clem moved slower. The three men hesitated only long enough to glance about for warriors, as somebody had obviously aided her escape attempt. They saw and heard none.

Morning Star almost panicked when the alarm was given, as she was so close to freedom. Her heart beat as a kettle drum. With haste and shaky fingers, she severed her ankle bonds. Keeping the knife, she jumped to her feet and dashed toward the thick treeline.

Zeke aimed his rifle in her direction. Instinctively Joe lunged at the big man and thwarted his intention, causing the weapon to discharge upward in a loud roar. "You can't shoot a woman!" he shouted. "Let her go!"

As soon as she was concealed by trees and darkness, Morning Star halted to observe the perilous scene left behind. She saw Joe arguing with Zeke and blocking another shot at her. The big man was clearly furious. As Zeke tried to fling Joe aside to fire again, Farley halted his pursuit of her and attacked Joe. With a speed and skill that impressed her, Joe struck him a stunning blow across the jaw that sent him backward.

"You'll die for that, Injun lover!" Zeke shouted. "You helped her!"

The sunny-haired man whirled to meet Zeke's assault. Zeke's blow to Joe's stomach doubled him over for a moment. Morning Star knew her rescuer was in trouble, but how could she help without a weapon? What could a knife do against powerful guns? How she wished she had a bow and arrows or a lance. Her head screamed for her to flee, but her heart and feet refused to obey that cowardly and selfish command. She lingered and watched with wide eyes.

Joe yanked his head aside before the burly man could bring down his clenched hands on his neck, then Joe rammed Zeke's stomach, sending him to the ground in a noisy fall.

Farley recovered enough to rejoin the fight. Joe knew he had to disable the youngest man fast, as Zeke, cursing, was getting to his feet and Clem was fetching his gun. Joe lifted his knee and sent it with force into Farley's groin. The towhead screamed in pain, dropped to his knees, then rolled on the grass as he cupped the injured area and groaned.

Morning Star knew she must go back and help Joe. The stranger had risked his life to free her, so she couldn't leave him to battle three wicked men. Her gentle heart and conscience spurred her into motion.

From the corner of his eye, Joe saw the Indian maiden using a sturdy limb to club Clem unconscious. He was astonished that she had returned to help him but happy she was repaying his kindness to her. Knowing he had only Zeke to conquer, Joe confronted the large man with renewed energy and resolve. He soon learned that Zeke was hard at best.

The two men struggled for the upper hand. The girl used her club to land a hard blow on Zeke's back. The big man then turned and shoved her to the earth.

"Run!" Joe yelled to her as he slammed his lowered shoulder into Zeke's stomach. He was glad to see she obeyed, but, distracted for that instant, Zeke sent him tumbling to the ground with a fisted jab to his chest that claimed his breath for a short time. When he saw the leader stalking toward him with a kill-gleam in his eyes, Joe knew he had to recover and move fast.

Morning Star raced to the first wagon and retrieved her bundle from where she had seen the large man toss it. She hurried to the men's horses and freed them. She loosened the reins to her mount, then went for Joe's.

The sunny-haired man scrambled to his feet just in time to avoid Zeke's next attack. The two men circled each other, then Zeke landed a blow to the side of Joe's head, almost stunning him. Joe fell to the earth, entangled his legs with his opponent's, and twisted his body. The movement caused Zeke to trip and fall hard.

"*U wo!*" The girl on horseback shouted for Joe to come to her.

While Zeke was down, Joe obeyed without a second thought. He leapt upon his horse and took the reins from her extended hand. Their knees urged the horses to flee, and the animals obeyed. The furious Zeke grabbed for Clem's rifle, aimed, and fired a shot before they vanished into the darkness. The ball passed through Joe's upper right arm but missed the bone. Though he grunted from the pain, it didn't stop or slow his retreat.

"When I find you, I'll kill you, you bastard!" they heard Zeke threaten as they rode out of rifle and hearing range. They galloped for over an hour before they halted to rest the horses.

Joe twisted in his saddle and looked behind them but heard and saw nothing of a pursuit. They had escaped, but what now? he mused.

"They not coming. I free horses," she told him. "They be slow to catch and follow. We rest, ride, find secret place till gone."

"You speak good English. I'm glad, because . . ." He couldn't say; he didn't want to give away the fact he knew a little Lakota from Stede Gaston. He thought it was best to keep that skill a secret for now. "Thanks for what you did back there. I couldn't have escaped without your help."

Morning Star was surprised that the man wasn't the least embarrassed or angered by a woman's assistance; most warriors would be both. She liked his warm and grateful smile. She wished she could see him better, but the moon's early ride across the heavens did not allow a clearer study. "You good white man," she told him. When rushed or flustered, she often skipped words in sentences, and she didn't get much practice in using her English these days anyhow.

"That sounds as if you haven't met many good ones," he hinted.

Her smile faded. "White men *sica*, bad," she replied in a grave tone. "They hate, fear Dakotas. They kill, steal from Dakotas."

"For no reason?" Joe prodded to learn her feelings. He needed to discover all he could from this maiden about the Indians and quickly, too, before his throbbing wound dulled his wits. He felt warm, sticky moisture easing down his arm and wetting his shirt and jacket.

Unaware of his wound, as she was positioned to his left, Morning Star mistook the meaning of his question. "They have reason; we Indian."

"That's no reason to kill anyone." Joe's voice was serious as he refuted, "I'm white and you're Indian, but we helped each other. Surely there must be more to any trouble between the two peoples."

"You not been here long. If yes, you know I speak truth."

"I wasn't calling you a liar, miss. I was stating a fact."

"A fact is truth?" she questioned for clarity.

"Yes. Who are you? Why were those men holding you captive?"

"Talk later. Story long. Must find good place to hide. They after us soon." She needed to hurry in case her group was still nearby and searching for her. She must warn them about the Crow band and, if possible, stop their enemy from receiving the powerful weapons.

"Wait a minute. I need to tie a strip around my arm to halt this bleeding. Soon I'll be leaving a trail even a child could follow."

"O-o? You wounded, shot?" she asked. Morning Star edged closer to him and peered around his body. She saw his darkened sleeve.

Joe also eyed the wet area. "I took a ball in my arm back there as we were leaving. I'll be fine. Just help me tie a bandage around it."

As Joe pulled a cloth from his saddlebag, Morning Star guided her mount to his other side. "Si. Makipazo we," she said in a firm tone. When he looked at her, she translated. "Be still. Show to me." She eased the jacket off his right shoulder and hand, then pushed up his sleeve.

Joe handed her the cloth. "Will you just bind it for me?" he asked. "We have to hurry. I don't want them to catch up with us. We'll tend it later."

Morning Star leaned toward him and bound the wound with gentleness and care, then she pulled down his sleeve and helped him put his jacket back on. "I tend with medicine when camp. Must find place to hide. They search for us soon. Crow party meeting them on new sun."

That was a clue Joe had been searching for, but it wouldn't do him any good now. Rescuing her had severed any chance of using that contact. He was back to the first step in his difficult journey to the truth. Unless this woman knew more . . . "Why meet a Crow party? What's in those wagons? Who are those men? What were you doing with them?" he questioned in a rush.

Morning Star was intrigued by his reaction. "Must go fast. Speak later." She readjusted the bundle on her lap.

"Lead the way," he said. "I don't know this territory."

"Come. You safe if be good white man. Oglalas honor words to others."

"Oglala? That's your tribe?" he asked.

Morning Star sensed curious pleasure in the man. "Han."

"That means yes?" he knowingly inquired with a grin.

"Yes. Your eyes say you heard of Oglala tribe of Teton Dakotas."

"Does anybody come to this territory and not hear of them?"

"No. This be Teton land. This always remain Teton land."

"What Oglala band are you from?" Joe pressed with undisguised eagerness. Maybe his luck hadn't run out tonight; maybe it had improved.

Morning Star became wary. She wondered why he was so pleased to learn her tribe, but lacked time to question him. She decided not to ride for her last campsite, as that would give their trackers a point to begin a search. With a Crow band helping the white men, her small party could be overtaken and slain. "Must go. Not be captured again. Come."

Joe realized she was nervous about the impending arrival of the Crow, and he knew why: they were fierce enemies of the Dakotas. "I'm ready to ride," he proclaimed.

The white man and the Indian maiden galloped for another hour until they entered the Black Hills. He followed her over grassy terrain and into a treeline. They journeyed up a hill and into a rocky section that demanded vigilant riding. By the angle of the moon, it was getting darker by the half hour. When they came to a wide stream, they guided their horses into it, and followed its course. When they reached an area where the bank was trampled into mire by numerous hooves, they left the water.

"Soon, many buffalo come to drink. They cover tracks. I know place to hide. Men and Crow search hard for me. Come, Joe."

"Why do they want you so badly?" he questioned during their slow pace, but she didn't explain or even speak again. The area was steep, and had been named accurately for the black boulders and towering pinnacles. Roots and rocks jutting from the earth forced the horses to move slowly as they picked their way over the rough terrain. It was a jarring and sluggish pace. Joe was exhausted and weakened by his wound. He had ridden since yesterday morning, and knew it must be Wednesday by now. His tension had not lessened since catching up to those men of whom the Indian woman was so afraid. He wanted to know her identity and why she was such a valuable captive.

Morning Star led him to a sheltered area that was surrounded by dew-covered spruce, pine, and ash. Joe inhaled the fresh smells that were enhanced by mountain air. He heard animals moving in the darkness, no doubt spooked by their arrival. He was relieved when she halted.

"We hide in cave. Must rest. Must tend arm." She slid off her horse and tied her reins to a bush. "Come. You need help?"

"I can make it fine," Joe said, dismounting and securing his reins. He ignored his discomfort to give his loyal steed relief by removing the saddle, then tossed it over a small boulder. He was glad to find a seep there from which the animals could drink and lush grass where they could graze. This female was smart, and familiar with the area. He saw her waiting for him clutching a small bundle against her breasts, and he joined her with his saddlebags.

"You ride with skill, woman, and fight like a warrior," he complimented her, and then he remarked on the mottled Appaloosa that she had ridden bareback with ease and agility.

She sent him a smile for his kind words. Love was in her tone as she responded, "His name Hanmani; it mean 'to walk in the night.' He clever in darkness, not step wrong. Your horse good; he strong, much wind."

Joe glanced at the roan with the white splotch on his forehead. "His name's Star. I've had him a long time, and he's been a fine mount." When he saw her grin, he asked, "Why are you smiling like that?"

"My name *Anpaowicanhpi*." She laughed as he tried to repeat it before she could explain her amusement and the meaning of the word. She then told him how to pronounce it. "Ahn'pao'we'con'hpee'. It mean 'the dawning of the morning star;' that why I laugh at horse's name."

"Morning Star," he murmured as he studied her in the remaining moonlight.

"It's beautiful." He halted himself from adding, *just as you are*. Her long ebony hair was shiny and soft, her eyes a warm brown. No one could call this golden-fleshed, smooth-complected beauty a "redskin." He guessed her height at around five feet seven-inches. Her nose was small and dainty, and her lips were full. She was the most exquisite woman he had ever seen. His stare brought a curious gaze to her eyes, so he halted it.

"Come, we go. It dark. Hold hand." She held one out to him and she noticed how he grasped it with eagerness and speed, a grip that exposed strength and trust. His hand was warm and pliant, and its inner surface revealed marks of hard work, while the back was smooth. She liked the contact with him, didn't consider Joe an enemy. And she sensed he felt the same. She entered the cave and walked into the shadows that engulfed them. Morning Star knew the center of this path was clear of obstacles, as she had played and camped there many times since birth. When she reached the area she wanted, having counted off the steps, she halted and said, "Be still. I light torch."

Joe waited in the blackness after she left him. He heard movements, then saw a spark. Soon, a glow revealed the interior and Morning Star to him. He watched her build a small fire with bush left there from another time. "How do you know your way around in the dark?" he asked.

"Come here many suns and moons since Life-Circle begin. Many times tie cloth over eyes to play games. Other times, cover eyes to test skills and make them grow larger. There not always light to guide feet when danger come. It good to be friends with darkness."

"You're right. I'd never thought of that before," Joe said. His eyes had adjusted to the amount of light from the fire, and as he looked around, he decided it was a safe hideout. There was a spot where a stream trickled down the rocky surface and formed a pool to supply them with water. There was enough brush to keep the fire going for another day or two. The floor was smooth in most places, and several areas had lengthy ledges like bunks. He didn't detect any musky or foul smell in the cave. It was a fresh, clean, and unusual chamber. With a fire and a beautiful woman, it was cozy—too cozy.

"Take off shirt. I tend wound," Morning Star said.

Even with her gentle assistance, Joe winced as he removed his jacket and shirt, but he was pleased that the snug binding had stopped most of the bleeding. He watched Morning Star open her parfleche and remove several things. He kept his gaze on hers as she examined the injury.

"White man's ball go in and out. That good." She asked if he had a bowl, but he didn't. She took the tin cup he handed to her. Morning Star knew Joe watched her as she crushed the pond lilies that would halt his bleeding completely. She pulled a small pouch suspended from a thong around her neck from beneath her top, loosened the string, and poured dried herbs into her palm, then finger-brushed them into the cup. She added enough water to blend them and prepare a mixture to prevent infection. She took care not to hurt him while smearing it onto the entrance and exit wounds. Afterward, she bound his upper arm with a clean cloth.

"What was that?" Joe inquired, pointing to her medicine pouch.

"*Pezuta wopahte*, medicine bundle," she explained.

"I meant those herbs you used."

"I not know. They halt wound from growing red with fever and stop bad yellow water from coming. Payaba gave to me. He shaman many seasons past. I seek herbs, plants, barks for him when captured. Hawk Eyes is shaman these suns. Payaba was Standing Tree in seasons past. His name Payaba these suns, 'Pushed Aside.' Hawk Eyes say his magic and skills larger, but Morning Star not believe. Payaba eighty winters. His legs and mind walk slow these suns, and many times not go where he wishes them. When he sick on mat for many suns, Hawk Eyes tell council Standing Tree soon go to join Grandfather; he say our people must vote for new medicine chief with many seasons until his Life-Circle end."

Joe realized the young woman spoke better English when she talked slower and chose her words with care. It was also apparent she did not like Hawk Eyes or the retirement of her friend Standing Tree, now Payaba. "Why do you gather medicines for him if he's no longer your shaman?"

"Many visit Payaba's tepee; his powers strong. He cannot seek herbs, plants, and barks he needs; Morning Star gathers for him."

"That means your camp can't be too far from here."

"You not know how long I captive."

"Not long enough for those plants in your pouch to die and rot."

She grinned. "You see and know much, Joe Lawrence."

"Tell me how and why you were taken prisoner," he urged, feeling more at ease with her by the minute. It was a strange but good, sensation.

"Must sleep. Morning Star tired. Joe tired, hurt. We talk later."

"You sure you won't sneak off during the night?" he asked.

"Night flees. *Wi* awakens soon to climb into sky."

"You'll be here when I wake up?" Joe asked again.

"Morning Star be at your side." She moved to a place where she could rest her head on her folded arms on a rock, then closed her eyes.

After Joe put on his shirt, he went to the woman to slip his jacket around her shoulders. When she opened her dark eyes and looked at him, he couldn't seem to break their gazes or move back to his place.

Firelight flickered on the man's face. Morning Star saw that he had sky blue eyes to go with his handsome face and sunny hair. He was tall, about half a foot taller than herself, and strong; he possessed a good spirit and could be trusted. She enjoyed his smile and voice, and felt strangely warmed when he used them on her. When he had removed his shirt, she saw that his chest was as hairless as an Indian's. She liked this stranger who made her feel safe and happy. There were not many whites like him, and that was why lasting peace was impossible. She had no urge to sneak off from him while he slept, but she didn't know what she would do with him when the time came for parting. She hated to send him back into danger, as he didn't know this territory.

"You be in our land many suns?" she inquired.

"Yes, Morning Star, for many, many suns. I'll explain everything after we sleep. You're right; I'm exhausted." He knew he had to return to his place in the cave, as this woman was more tempting than any he'd ever met.

The daughter of Chief Sun Cloud observed Joe's retreat and sensed a reluctance in him to leave her side. She asked herself if he failed to grasp the differences in them, in their cultures, in their skins. He looked at her as a man of her kind would. She found that odd but pleasing. Soon they would learn more about each other. She closed her eyes.

Joe reclined on his side to prevent staring at her. He tried to believe it was her connection to the Oglalas that held his interest, but he knew it was not; it was

Morning Star herself. He warned himself to stop thinking such crazy thoughts about her; he was here on a vital mission, not to woo a woman, especially one so different from him.

In a short time, the two fatigued people were asleep, only to dream of each other.

When he awoke, Joe yawned and stretched. He noticed that his wound was not as sore as he had expected. Perhaps it was because of the herbs Morning Star had placed on it. He glanced at the spot she had taken last night; no, early this morning. It was empty! Morning Star was gone!

Chapter Two

Joe jerked to a sitting position and looked around the cave. A small fire was burning. He listened, then caught her voice far away. He got to his feet and headed for the entrance. He saw Morning Star outside with her horse, stroking and speaking to him. His blue gaze moved over her shapely figure in the buckskin dress. He assumed the hidden part of her body was as firm and supple as her arms and legs. As if sensing his approach—or maybe she'd heard it—she turned and smiled.

"You close eyes long time, Joe Lawrence. *Wi* climb high. Morning Star see, hear no danger. We rest. Joe heal until *Wi* come again and enemies gone. Morning Star return home, and Joe ride away."

"Where is your home, Morning Star?" he asked, joining her.

"Must go in cave. If danger come, Hanmani warn. Hole in cave for escape. Hanmani, Star have water and grass. They fine."

Joe followed the Indian maiden back inside the rock shelter. "You never answer my questions, Morning Star. Why? Do you distrust me?"

"*Hiya,*" she replied with haste. "No. Story long, hard. Morning Star *yuonihansni*, shamed by evil whites' capture. Eager to scout and not hear Hanmani warning. Morning Star foolish, pride too big."

"Don't scold yourself. If it hadn't been for you, I would be dead now. You helped me better than any warrior could have. I can understand why you'd want to spy on those men. You said they were taking guns and whiskey to your enemies, the Crow."

She stared at Joe in dismay and sudden mistrust. "Morning Star not speak such words! Say they meet Crow band on this sun. Not say why they meet or what in wagons. How you know such things?"

Joe noticed that she had strapped a beaded belt with a knife sheath around her waist and that her hand had shifted to the weapon. He had let her beauty steal his wits, and he'd made a slip. He didn't know who she was, where she was from, or if the Oglalas were involved in the trouble as charged or merely being framed. "Somebody is trading guns and whiskey to the Crow, and it's going to cause big trouble. Their tracks told me those wagons were loaded heavily; that's why I trailed them. When they acted strange and didn't want me around, I added up the clues."

"Why you care if they trade with Bird People? Crow friends with whites. Crow and whites want Dakota land and lives! Do you trick Morning Star to take you to her camp, to return to destroy it?"

"I swear that isn't true. We helped each other back there because we're good people and we want peace."

To see his reaction, she told Joe, "Dakotas cannot have peace with whites. Palefaces lie, cheat, steal, kill. They forget words of truce on paper. They want all we possess."

Her eyes and tone did not agree with the evocative words she spoke. If she believed them, she would not have helped him or remained here with him, he reasoned. "Some whites do, Morning Star, but not all of us, not me. I want peace. You can trust me."

The dark-haired beauty stared at Joseph Lawrence. His blue gaze was filled with honesty, hope, and gentleness. "Tell why you here. Why track men? Why rescue Morning Star?"

Joe sat down on a rock as he decided what to tell her. "I was traveling with a friend of mine. We got separated at Pratte's Post east of here. Tanner was knifed badly. Before he died, he mentioned guns and whiskey, a boss called 'Snake-Man', and something about picking up a big load. When I came across those wagon ruts, my instinct told me to follow them. I've heard about the trouble between the Crow and Dakotas and that the Army thinks the Dakotas are going on the warpath again this year. I was going to join those men until I could find Tanner's killer. While I was getting justice and revenge, if I could stop a war between Indians and whites by getting at the truth, I'd be glad."

"People lie to you. We not want war," Morning Star said adamantly. "We not start war. We defend our lives and lands from attack. Whites are ones who not honor words. Oglalas make treaty many winters past. Have peace long time. Five winters past, white men make trails on Lakota lands. Many wagons use. Some whites stay in Lakota lands. They start new troubles. More soldiers and forts come to help them. Crow help them; they help Crow. When *Wi* hot and long last season, more trouble come. I not see, but hear of bad deeds. When cold and snow come, whites and soldiers quiet. They afraid to attack in winter camp; we too strong. Soldiers send message that we stop attacks we not make. We tell truth; they no believe. We say Crow do; Crow say no. They take Bird People's words. Bands find tracks of white man's horses at wicked sights. Not know who. Father say more trouble come when we hunt buffalo soon, when warriors gone from camp and defense low. How have peace?"

"By helping me prove your people are innocent and want peace."

"Tokel he?" She asked him how.

"Take me to your people. Let me talk with them. I have to discover who this Snake-Man is and why he's trying to start a war here."

Her eyes widened and her voice lowered. "We hear of Snake-Man. He have powerful magic. He evil. We not know his name and face. You must go, or die." Her tone and expression were filled with worry.

"Your people would kill me? But I'm trying to help them."

"Not my people. Bad whites and Crow allies."

"Not if your people help me. I need a guide and translator. If I can get proof as to who is to blame, the Army will stop the evil whites and the sly Crow."

"*Toke he?*" She asked why. This situation was befuddling her.

"They killed my best friend, and they want to stir up a war. I don't think you want a bloody war to start, either, so help me prevent one."

"Make no promises to Joe, but take to Father to talk."

"Who is your father? How far away is your camp?"

"Ride fast, two suns. Father called Mahpiya-Wi, Oancan: Sun Cloud, Chief. Great Spirit create Dakota Nation in three parts: Lakota, Nakota, and Dakota." She explained the major divisions of what the whites called the Sioux Nation. "It like three branches with many limbs on big tree called *Dakota Oceti Sakawin*: 'Seven Council Fires of the Dakota.' Tribes like limbs. Dakota/Santee branch have four limbs: Mdewakanton, Wahpekute, Wahpeton, and Sisseton. Nakota branch have two limbs: Yankton and Yanktonais. Lakota branch have one big limb: Teton. It have many small limbs: Oglala, Brule, Hunkpapa, Blackfeet, Two Kettle, Sans Arc, and Minneconjou. Small limbs have many bands like pinecones. Morning Star belong to Red Heart Band of Oglala tribe, Teton limb, Lakota branch of tree. Dakota/Santee branch not same as big Dakota tree. When Santee sign Pike's Treaty, they give whites part of their territory far away. Whites think Dakota/Santee sign for Dakota tree. That not true, not same, not one."

Joe knew about the 1805 treaty where the Santee ceded some of their territory in Minnesota to the United States for forts. That treaty confused whites who didn't know the Santee chief could not speak for the entire Dakota Nation, as the President ruled and represented America. Most whites believed there was a treaty with all Dakota Indians and they could come and go as they pleased in any Dakota area. But, in truth, the woodland tribes had no claim or control over their Plains brothers' regions. It would be like the governor of Virginia selling someone land in Georgia without Georgia's permission or knowledge. Suddenly, Joe realized who Morning Star really was. Stunned, he asked, "You're Sun Cloud's daughter? Sun Cloud, son of Gray Eagle?" And also Tanner's cousin, he added to himself.

She was pleased by the awe in his expression. "*Han*, yes, it so. You hear of Father and Grandfather."

"Many times. They're both great legends, men as tall as the sky. Thank God I didn't let those bastards harm you. It would have been a bloodbath for certain. How did Zeke and his men get you? I'm sure your father has a search party out looking for you."

"Word not reached his ears. Take friends five moons to reach camp from place Morning Star captured on past sun. Joe rest, heal. We ride on new sun. Catch friends on trail. Friends ride this sun, travel slow; have women, children, old ones. Evil whites hide capture trail; mark false one to Crow Territory. Friends not know Morning Star near; cannot ride into Bird People lands to attack, rescue. Need more warriors for big fight. They ride home, tell Father. Take many moons."

"Are you sure we shouldn't leave right now? They might travel fast with such bad news. We could catch up to them before they tell your father."

"No. Will ride fast; be close behind in two . . . days. If not stay hidden, evil whites and Crow find. Must not guide to friends; they be slain."

"You're right. We'll wait until tomorrow. Tell me about yourself and your people," Joe coaxed. "I didn't know Sun Cloud had a daughter. The more I learn before I reach your camp, the better we can all work together. First, I want to hear about your capture, and what you heard those men say."

"You strange white man. Morning Star speak, but Joe must . . ." She halted and looked toward the entrance. She touched a finger to her lips for silence, then cupped an ear with her hand: sign language for *listen*.

Joe remained quiet and alert. He heard what had captured her attention. Slowly and carefully he reached for his Sharp's '48 rifle. He must not allow anything to happen to this valuable woman, even if it cost him his life.

With caution, Joseph Lawrence and Morning Star crept toward the entrance of the cave. They heard the roan's shoes and the Appaloosa's hooves striking against rocks as the two horses shifted about in rising anxiety. Their ears caught a whinny several times as someone or something frightened their mounts. Joe motioned for his companion to stay back, but she continued to follow him. His rifle was ready for use, as was the knife in her grasp.

Joe peered outside to the right of the opening. He gave a sigh of relief and relaxed his taut body. "Look," he said, pointing to the seep where a porcupine was drinking.

The horses knew it was wise to give the prickly creature all the space it wanted. When the animal had drunk its fill, it waddled through the bushes and vanished. The horses settled down the moment the porcupine was gone and returned to their grazing.

Morning Star laughed and dismissed her own tension. "It wise not to challenge *pahin* when he thirsty."

Joe chuckled. "Or any other time. Those spines give a nasty bite."

"Hawk Eyes say quills have poison; Payaba say it not so. It hard to work with them. Pricks sting; they . . . become sore; they not kill. Hawk Eyes say they no kill Red Heart women because we bathe hands in *ska utahu can* when we done; medicine bark heal pricks."

He noticed the tone of her voice and the look on her face. He knew they held unintentional clues he might need later in camp. "You don't like or trust Hawk Eyes, do you?"

Morning Star glanced at Joe and frowned, but at herself, not him. "It wrong to think, speak bad of shaman. Hawk Eyes not always this way. His son, Knife-Slayer, desires great rank and power for his father and for Knife-Slayer. He places . . . mischief in Hawk Eyes' head. Many times wish they not Oglalas. Morning Star fear their hunger for war against bluecoats and whites will bring much suffering to our people. Think others not see bad in them."

Morning Star's dark-brown eyes scanned their green-and-black enclosure before she continued. "Hawk Eyes want Buckskin Girl as mate. He have two; one die. She say no; Morning Star tell her say no. Buckskin Girl Morning Star's friend. She granddaughter of White Arrow; before he join Great Spirit, he great warrior and friend to Gray Eagle, Morning Star's grandfather. They live, hunt, raid as brothers from birth until leave Mother Earth. Morning Star not know Gray Eagle;

he killed long before she born. Bad bluecoats slay in trap. Father become chief when Grandfather ride Ghost Trail. Bad bluecoats punished. Father make treaty with white leader to have peace. For past two summers, whites forget truce. More trouble coming."

The Indian maiden realized she was rambling to take her mind off the white man. She did not understand his potent effect on her. She wanted to caress the bruises on his face from the battle to rescue her. She longed to tease her fingers over the dark stubble that was growing along his strong jawline, cleft chin, and above his lips. She liked the way his sunny hair, slightly mussed from sleep, journeyed like low, rolling hills from his head to his collar. She could stare into his azure eyes forever. She liked the size and shape—not too large or too thin—of his nose, and the appealing fullness of his mouth. His shoulders were broad, his muscles well defined and toned to sleek hardness. She enjoyed his calming smile, his soothing voice, and his nearness. She felt at ease with him, yet tense in his presence. When his gaze met hers, her body warmed and trembled without warning. It was confusing, alarming . . . and forbidden under her tribal laws.

Joe saw how she looked at him. It was as if strong currents were pulling them into the same whirlpool and spinning them around together, drawing them closer and deeper by the hour. She was beautiful and tempting—irresistible. The sides of her lustrous black hair were braided near a flawless face; the rest flowed down her back like a silky and shiny river. He was surprised it wasn't tangled or mussed this morning. Perhaps she had a brush in the parfleche from which she had taken her knife and sheath, after she had returned his blade he had lent her during her rescue.

Entranced, he studied her from head to toe. Morning Star's eyes were wide in the center, then tapered to fetching points at the outer edges. Her lashes were thick, and her brows were thin. They traveled above her eyes in perfect harmony. A straight nose that attempted to tilt upward was above full lips that evoked a desire to kiss them many times. Her oval face had bone structure any female would delight in having, and it was the same with her figure. Without a doubt, many warriors craved this beauty.

The tawny dress she wore was a different shade than her golden-brown flesh, and it was stained in several places, probably from struggling with her captors. The sleeves and tail displayed short fringes that swayed with her movements. She wore low-cut moccasins with lovely beadwork, which he surmised she had made.

As they gazed at each other, both forgot their peril and her last words. A hawk's shrill cry overhead startled them back to reality.

Morning Star was bewildered by her lapse of attention and wayward thoughts. She could not comprehend how their spirits could touch so soon and so powerfully after meeting less than a sun ago. "We go in, be near escape hole if danger come," she suggested, suddenly feeling apprehensive.

"I'll join you in a minute. I need to . . . have privacy," he hinted.

Morning Star grasped his meaning and left him alone. After Joe relieved himself nearby, he joined her in the cave.

Morning Star had listened intently to Joe's use of English and she called to mind her past lessons. She spoke slowly in an attempt to be correct. "We must put out fire. We must not let smoke or smell show hiding place. We will hunt and eat when dark come and danger gone. Yes?"

"Yes." Joe set aside his rifle, retrieved his saddlebag, and withdrew a pouch of dried venison strips he had purchased at Fort Laramie. "We can chew on these and have water until later. You must be hungry. I didn't see Zeke give you anything to eat, and there were only three dirty dishes in the pile."

Morning Star was impressed by how little escaped his senses. She *was* hungry. She hadn't eaten since leaving her people's camp yesterday morning, and, accepting the meat, she said, *"Pilamaya."*

"You're welcome," he responded to her thanks, but neither noticed that and other slips. He used his cup to fetch water from the nature-formed basin, then shared it with her. Joe chewed off a bite of the jerky. "Not too good, but not too bad," he jested.

The sun's angle cast a bright glow into the cave's entrance and prevented them from being in total darkness, though its power diminished the farther it drifted into the interior. It was a pleasant spring afternoon that Joe decided must be the fourteenth of May. The night's chill was gone; the odor of a fire lingered in the air. Water trickled down rocks and flowed into the small pool that must have an opening beneath, because it did not pour over the sides into the cave. A hawk signaled to its mate and warned an intruder away from his domain. Crickets chirped in the darkness behind them. Birds sang in the bushes and trees and beyond the cave. The dirt floor gave off its own unique odor of earth. The strong but not offensive smell of jerky filled their noses as it was consumed. It was harder to eat than fresh game, but it removed any hunger pangs. The cool and refreshing water they shared was the best part of their meager meal.

Morning Star toyed with one braid as she reflected on their past conversations and the one she had overheard in the white men's camp. She looked at her companion and remarked, "You spoke lies to white men. Why you come to Oglala land with friend? Who is Murphy and Old Joe? To trust and help, must know more, must know truth."

Joe swallowed the water in his mouth, then coughed to clear his throat. Her first statement had caught him off guard. She had keen wits, so he needed to be as honest as possible. He didn't want her to mistrust or fear him. "I was trying to trick them with words so I could join them, but they were too nervous around a stranger and they were hiding something. I was hoping they'd lead me to Snake-Man. That seemed like the only way to track down Tanner's killer. It wasn't all lies, Morning Star. I did come here for excitement and challenges with Tanner and his father; a man needs those kinds of things sometime in his life."

Joe slid off his rock seat and moved to the ground where he could stretch out his long legs. He propped his back against the rock, then continued. "What I told them about Ben Murphy was true, except the part about him coming out here to trap for a fur company. Ben still lives back South. It seemed a good way to explain my presence in this secluded area. The other man is my father, Joseph Benjamin Lawrence, Sr. I was named after him: When you have the same name, the father is called senior and the son is called junior. He's a good man, Morning Star, but I wasn't ready to get deeper into the shipping business yet."

"What is . . . the shipping business?" she inquired.

Joe contemplated a way to clarify it for her. "Large boats are called ships. When you use them to carry supplies to other places, it's called shipping. Business is the work you do. We own many ships and we get paid money to deliver goods for other men. Some of those places can only be reached by water. To other places, it's faster, easier, and cheaper by ship."

"What is 'cheaper'?" she queried another word she did not know.

"It's like when a man asks for two horses to take your supplies to another camp to sell or trade, but a second man only asks for one horse to take them. You hire the man who asks for one because he's cheaper. A ship is very big; it can carry a lot of supplies, not a few as in a wagon. A ship can hold more supplies than six trading posts; it could hold an entire Indian village. Ships can move faster and easier over water than wagons can over land. One day, I'll go home and work with my father. But . . ."

When he halted, she pressed. "But?"

"My father forgets I'm no longer a boy. He wants me to follow orders like a hired man. I need to prove my worth to him and to myself. I want to experience more than water and ships. I want to face challenges. I want to see this wild land. So much is happening out here; the country's growing. I want to be a part of it before I settle down. My father didn't understand these hungers in me. He was disappointed when I left home."

"Morning Star understand. Father and people see only a woman. Morning Star can battle, hunt, and track as warrior. Can shoot bow with skill. Morning Star arrows, lance, and knife not miss targets. Morning Star hunger to see and do many things before . . . settle down. Others say no. Say woman must cook, fetch water and wood, wash, make garments, join, and bear children: do only woman's chores. Such work must be done, but it give no . . . excitement. We much alike."

"Yes, we are." He noticed how she worked to improve her English, and he was impressed by her quick intelligence. He moved to a topic of great interest to him. "Those men who held you prisoner, what did they say? Why do your people let them roam your lands freely?"

"Father sign truce many winters before daughter born not to kill whites or make war with bluecoats. Whites not honor their part of treaty. If they attack, we must defend lives and lands. If they not attack, we let travel on and beyond our land. They must not come and steal Oglala land. They must not slay buffalo and many creatures for hides. Buffalo give life to Oglalas and our brothers. Bad whites raid sleeping places; steal warriors' weapons, garments, all their possessions. They kill hunters; they take scalps to sell and trade. White law say no give guns and whiskey to Indians, but greedy whites trade to Crow to kill Oglalas. Whites steal horses, burn mark on hide, put shoes on feet, and claim. Warriors know all ponies in herds. Tell soldiers to make return. Soldiers say brand make Oglala ponies white man's horses. They not to build more forts if Father and tribe say no. They not to steal trees from face of Mother Earth and makes cuts in her body for . . . farms. They not to graze spotted buffaloes on grasslands."

Joe knew the Indians called cattle by that peculiar name. He listened with interest to her list of grievances against his people.

"White men not know Morning Star speak English. They not know much Oglala. They not talk much where Morning Star can hear many words. Big man say they . . . de-liv-er supplies to Crow. They go back to man called Boss. They speak no name and no call him Snake-Man, so not know if Boss is same man. He say Crow be mad soon and attack Oglalas. Not know why. He say, when Sioux gone, all be fine, Boss can do his plans. They hope Crow slay us, so we can no return to battle another su—another day," she corrected herself. "You must ride far. They search for you to slay for saving Morning Star. If you ride here to look for friend's killer, you be killed. Morning Star not want Joe Lawrence killed. You good man."

Joe was moved by her concern. "I have to stay and avenge Tanner. I promised myself and his father. Tanner was like a brother to me."

"Task of *watokicon* dangerous," she warned.

"What is that?" he asked.

"Avenger. Snake-Man is *wakansica,* a Bad Spirit. Cannot slay spirits."

"He's not a spirit, Morning Star, Just an evil white man using tricks to scare and fool the Indians. Why do you think he's a spirit?"

"Knife-Slayer and raid band see him with Crow. They hide to watch; they not have enough men to attack enemies. *Wakansica* have snakes on arms. They crawl up arms, with heads here," she said, gesturing toward her breasts, showing him how the "snakes" curled around the man's arms, over his shoulder, and downward to his breasts. "Spirit Snakes big and many colors. They have bad eyes, sharp fangs, long tongues. They no see Spirit Snakes move or strike; they sleep on *Wakansica's* body. Hawk Eyes say they powerful and evil medicine. Band see *Wakansica* do magic. He throw little balls into fire; make much noise and smoke. Make little suns glow and dance in wind. When suns and smoke gone, Snake-Man gone. His men ride away in wagons. Band no attack Crow in evil place where Bad Spirit hiding. Might return and slay Red Hearts."

Joe realized this clever Snake-Man was using Indian superstition and their lack of knowledge to frighten and delude them. "Those were only cunning tricks, Morning Star. I've seen such things before during my travels far away. The snakes are painted into his skin, they're called tattoos. They're much like the pictures painted on tepees and shields. Across the big waters, there's a place called the Orient. Wise men live there. They make the balls that shine and give off smoke. That's where Snake-Man gets his magic tricks from. I've seen how men can sneak away when the air is filled with heavy smoke; it blinds the eyes for a short time. He probably slipped to the wagon and hid there while the Indians couldn't see. He wants the Crow to believe he's a powerful shaman so they'll work for him to destroy your people. If I traveled in my ship to that land, I could buy balls like those and do the same tricks. It's not real magic. It has no power, except to fool people who don't know about them. When we reach your camp, I'll ask Knife-Slayer how Snake-Man looked. That will help find him."

"No good. His face behind ceremony mask, head of big snake."

Joe was disappointed. "Because he didn't want anyone to recognize him," he murmured. "He chose a good disguise and scheme. He's clever."

"What is disguise and scheme?"

"Disguise is when you use things like masks to hide who you are. A scheme is a wicked plan to fool people. I wonder if Zeke, the man who captured you, is smart enough to be Snake-Man."

"He no have snakes on arms. I claw and bite when captured."

It didn't surprise Joe that Zeke wasn't his man. "How did he capture you, Morning Star?"

"Small party go to Mato Paha, Bear Mountain. It sacred place where go to pray and give gifts to Great Spirit. Men go to seek visions and to think much. Holy mountain where we given Sun Dance and our beliefs by Great Spirit after he create Dakotas. We hang prayer cloths and tokens on trees that grow on sleeping bear hill. Sometimes white men steal; that bad medicine. Not even Crow steal sacred gifts from trees. Grandfather punish."

She sat down near him and crossed her legs. "Morning Star go there with brother, Night Stalker. He take wife and son. He go to pray for safety of our people when we ride for summer camp and for good hunt when we seek buffalo. Others go with us. Hawk Eyes go to seek vision, take his wife. Flaming Star and Thunder Spirit go to give thanks and to pray. They sons of White Arrow. They have many winters on their bodies; may never go to sacred mountain again. Mates go to tend chores. Buckskin Girl travel with parents, Flaming Star and Morning Light. Little Feet is wife of Thunder Spirit; she daughter of Bright Arrow, brother to Father. Bright Arrow walks Mother Earth no more. Crow war party kill before Morning Star born. Summer Rain and son go with Lone Horn; he war chief. He give thanks and seek vision to lead warriors if attack come soon."

Morning Star sighed heavily at that distressing thought. "We stay at Mato Paha five suns, days. We ride for village. Stop at Elk Creek for men to hunt game for journey in Paha Sapa, means Black Hills. This sacred place, where we make winter camps, where old ones rest on *wicagnakapi wiconte*, death scaffolds. Spirits and Thunderbirds live in black mountains. Much game here. This Oglala land and must defend to death," she said with deep feeling, then returned to her story. "Women stay in camp and make ready to ride when hunters return after *Wi* passes overhead. Morning Star finish chores and go seek medicine plants for Payaba. Touched-A-Crow, she brother's wife, go with Morning Star. She gather roots and plants. She take son. He two winters; he bad boy many moons. He bad on trail; she must return to camp. Morning Star ride on to do Payaba chore. Stay near edge of forest. Morning Star think, walk too far, hear noise and hide."

Her dark eyes grew wide and she spoke faster with excitement. "See two white men scout. Get bad feeling. Follow them on Hanmani. They go to Mato Paha. They take prayer tokens! Morning Star angry, but have only knife as weapon. Cannot attack. While thinking, man—big one—sneak up and capture. Morning Star fight. He strong, mean. He take to others. They put on horse with big man. They take Hanmani to make false trail to Crow land. They drop Crow arrows and cloth to fool Red Heart band. They know small band cannot ride into camp of many Crow. They know others must return home, cannot challenge Bird People. We ride to river. We travel water far to wagon camp. Morning Star bound and given no food, no water, no blanket. Wait all sun. Moon and Joe come. Joe help escape."

"We *are* a lot alike," Joe said, grinning. "We were both trailing them to gather clues. That was smart and brave."

"Not smart; got captured," she refuted, then frowned.

"That happens sometimes even to the best warriors," Joe reassured her. "I came along to help you, and you returned to help me. We're both good fighters and we make a good pair. After I see your father, if he'll work with me, we'll put a stop to this trouble before it leads to war."

"Joe's voice and eyes say much. You seek men who kill friend. More to Joe's ride and task. Is not so? What more you seek?"

Joe decided if he told her the truth he might win her help and trust. If so, it would be easier to obtain her father's. "Ever hear of a white man named Thomas Fitzpatrick? The Indians call him Broken-Hand." She eyed him strangely, but nodded. "He trapped in this territory for twenty years, and later worked as a wilderness guide. He became the Indian agent five years ago at Fort Laramie. Know where that is?"

Again, Morning Star nodded.

"Tom's honest and fair and smart. He knows this territory and the people here, white and Indian. He's working on a big treaty between all tribes, and between Indians and whites. Tom suspects that somebody doesn't want the Indians to make peace among themselves and keeps stirring tribes up one against the other. He knows that if intertribal warfare breaks out, whites will be caught in the middle. Besides, it's against the law to sell weapons and whiskey to Indians. There are many clues that point to the Red Hearts and other Lakota tribes as the trouble-makers. Tom thinks this Snake-Man may be behind the problems. He's talked to Crow, but they won't tell him anything. He's talked to Lakotas, too, but they claim they don't know anything. Tom wants me to find out who Snake-Man is, what he's trying to do here, if he's the guilty one, and how he can be stopped. The United States government and our chief don't want a war with your people or any other Indian tribe."

"Why bluecoats attack hunters if this be so?" she argued.

"To keep them from killing white settlers who come here and from killing white immigrants passing through your territory heading west. Many wagon trains are attacked. Boats on rivers and soldiers on patrol have been attacked. Settlers and farmers have been burned out. Trading posts have been robbed. Almost every time, Lakota arrows have been found."

"It not Oglalas, not Red Hearts. Inkpaduta and Little Thunder raid wagons on trails; they not Oglalas; they Santee and Brule. They part of Seven Council Fires, but not same tribe. Whites have land and game where Wi awakens. Must not come and steal Lakota land and creatures. They stay in their land, they be safe; we be safe. No trouble, no battle."

"That sounds simple, Morning Star, but it isn't."

"What is . . . simple?"

"Easy, not hard . . . what's right. The smart and good thing to do."

"It be simple, if whites honor truce and not come to our land."

"More settlers, trappers, traders, and others will come. This area is beautiful and exciting," he said, then thought, *like you are*. "Many whites want new or better lives, Morning Star. Things are bad for them back East, where the sun awakens. Some don't have money to buy land, and they want to make a good place for their families. They can do that here. This land is big. There's plenty of room for everyone. Sometimes I've ridden all day without seeing one Indian. If we can stop the troublemakers and become friends, everybody can live in peace in the same territory. Some of the people on the wagon trains have to stop here because they can't make it all the way to Oregon or California. They get sick, or tired, or discouraged; or they run out of money. Some just fall in love with this territory."

"They try to take land, claim it, not use it, not share it," Morning Star argued. "Grandfather owns the land. They kill His creatures for furs and hides; they waste meat. When game killed, all of creature must be used. They bring strange sickness. They scare game. They build across animal trails and confuse creatures. They want best hunting grounds. They want trees in sacred hills. They not travel as we do. They camp in one place; they destroy it. They bring whiskey to dull warriors' wits. Traders and trappers speak false; they cheat Indians. They bring trouble; they blame Indians. They use false words to get more forts and bluecoats. When whites come and we let stay, it tell more whites to come. Soon, no land and game for Indians. Crow are fools; they no see whites trick and how much hate Crow. If agent Tom want peace, he keep whites away. Simple." She used her new word.

Joe changed his position and faced her fully. "Lordy, I wish it were. I don't want to see your people or other tribes destroyed. If war comes, Morning Star, that could happen. The whites have many more people than the Indians; they have more and better weapons. To challenge them is a mistake. I hope your father will work for peace."

She did not like that scary information, but said with confidence and courage, "If peace means lose land, honor, and lives—he no make peace."

"I hope I can help him obtain peace with honor and without losses," Joe said. "That's hard when each side wants the same thing, and each side thinks they're right. The man I came here with feels and thinks the same way I do: Tanner's father. He's an observer and adviser on the situation for President Fillmore," he said, then explained the situation, after deciding how much and what to tell her about Stede Gaston.

"Tanner's father is like a scout and speaker for the Great White Chief Fillmore. He learns what's happening, then tells our chief what he thinks must be done to prevent problems and war. Our chief trusts him and will listen to him. Many of the white man's problems have been halted, so more white-eyes are on these lands. We had many enemies, like you have the Crow, Pawnee, and the Shoshone. We made peace with them. War ended with the Mexicans, people who live south. Our border conflict with the British was settled. We traded money for a large track of land that includes this territory. Indians say land can't be owned, but the French claimed this territory and sold it to us years ago. Whites do believe land can be owned and claimed. The United States now claims this territory. The path wagon trains use is called the Oregon Trail; the one near it is called the Mormon Trail. Many whites use the trails to travel west.

"There's another problem about a yellow rock called gold that white men desire. A lot of it was discovered west of here in a place called California. Many of the men passing through this territory went there and are still going there to search for gold. Trying to stop passage through your lands can't be done."

Joe stretched out his legs again. "With more whites coming here and through here, Morning Star, they demand more forts, trading posts, and roads. Roads are cleared trails for easy and fast travel." He knew she would not understand what the Topographical Bureau was and he didn't know how to explain it, so he skipped over the survey they had done near Laramie in '49. "You can't stop settlers any more than you can stop the rain. But rain and soil work together to give life and beauty to the land and people. Whites and Indians can do the same. First, peace is needed, but that can't come until evil men are caught and punished. Those working in your territory don't attack where they can be seen and caught. They trick the Crow into fighting for them. They don't do their own dirty work because they don't want the Army involved. Tanner and I were to travel around and be his father's eyes and ears. Tanner saw or heard something dangerous; he was killed so he couldn't tell others. If I'd been with him, he'd be alive. I was getting a new shoe for Star. He'd thrown one on the way to Pratte's Post."

When Joe became silent, Morning Star grasped his grief and guilt. "If you be with him, you be dead like Tanner dead."

"Maybe," he half agreed. "I'm going to find who killed him, then get justice.

After I buried him, I went to Fort Laramie to tell his father. Lordy, that was hard. He would have come back with me to find the killer, but his leg is broken and he can't ride. I was returning to Pratte's Post to search for clues when I found Zeke's wagon trail. A gut instinct told me to follow it. I'm glad I did. Meeting you was fate, Morning Star."

"What is fate?" she asked, intrigued by his tone.

"Destiny, something meant to happen, part of my Life-Circle that must cross another person's at a certain time and place."

She liked his explanation. "It so. You want peace much as you want Tanner's killer. This be good. Morning Star help you find both."

He felt there wasn't anything she could do other than help him with her father and people, but he didn't refute her words or refuse her offer. "If anything happens to me, tell your father to send word to Captain James Thomas at Fort Tabor. Make certain the soldiers know you want peace so they won't be tricked by Snake-Man and the Crow into attacking your camp."

"Captain James Thomas," she repeated. "Morning Star remember."

Joe was feeling stiff and restless. She was too close to ignore. "Are you sure your band would head for home without you? If not, we should warn them of the Crow coming today. If they stayed, they're in danger."

"They gone. When Morning Star not return to camp, Night Stalker search. He good hunter and tracker. When he see trail to Crow land, he not follow. He leave to protect others. It our way. It wrong to risk many lives to save one. If Night Stalker foolish and stay, must not lead Crow and evil whites to their camp. Most are old ones, women, and little ones."

He noticed something in her tone that told him she wasn't convinced her party was gone. "You think your brother might stay here and search for you?"

"Morning Star pray he do not trail to try rescue. Not sure," she added, being honest with him. "Night Stalker have much to learn from Father before he be chief. He hunger to drive whites from land and slay all Crow. He hunger to earn many coups and much honor. He not want to think and talk. He want to use wits and skills to defend hunting grounds, sacred lands, and people. When winter quiet, he grow restless. He not trust whites. He thirty winters, years, old. Father fifty-four years. More trouble comes. It not Night Stalker's time to be chief. Father must teach more. Morning Star pray brother listens. Knife-Slayer whispers words into ear Morning Star not think good. Morning Star pray Great Spirit opens all Oglala hearts and ears to Joe's words for peace."

"So do I, Morning Star. If a strong truce isn't made soon and your people attack the whites, the Army will retaliate." Joe fretted over the interference and resistance he suspected he would get from Knife-Slayer, Hawk Eyes, and Night Stalker. He would have to do some fast and clever talking to convince Sun Cloud, Red Hearts, and other Oglalas to cooperate with him and his cohorts, Stede Gaston and Tom Fitzpatrick. "If I only had some evidence against Snake-Man to show your people to prove I'm . . . That's it! In the morning, you ride home and I'll track Zeke to spy on his meeting with the Crow. Maybe I can get some proof. I'll come to your camp as soon as—"

"*Hiya!* Go with you. It too dangerous alone and wounded. Men bad."

Joe gazed into her defiant face. He knew it was bravery speaking, not impulsiveness. "No, Morning Star. They could capture you again. Then the Oglalas would attack the Crow, and war would surely follow."

She was touched by his concern for her safety and his desire to help Lakotas. Yet it was more her problem than Joe's, so she must assist him. "We be careful. Morning Star know land and tracks. Go with you, help."

Joe saw how determined and confident she was. He knew arguing was a waste of time and energy, and she was right. "You can come, but we won't get too close. We're not taking any risks."

"Good. Simple," she added and grinned, her eyes sparkling. Morning Star was glad he yielded. Riding together against foes sounded exciting. Her body quivered with anticipation. The chief, tribal council, and warrior societies controlled everything in Indian camps. It was thrilling to be half in charge for a change. Until they reached her village, she could use her skills and wits on something besides female chores. It was delightful not be refused and scolded because she was "only a woman." She could not help but be impressed by Joe's generosity where her help was involved.

They had talked in their hideout for hours. Dusk approached and dimmed the cave's interior. Both decided their foes must be gone by now.

Morning Star got to her feet. She was hungry, and needed privacy. "Joe stay. Morning Star hunt, track and kill with knife. It silent. Gun loud. You make fire to cook. Morning Star return soon."

Joe reasoned that any threat to them had ended, but still he protested her plan. "What if they're still looking for us? I can't let you go alone."

"Morning Star know hills, and one hunter best. Morning Star be alert, not be foolish. Be safe."

Once more, Joseph Lawrence realized he couldn't change her mind. After seeing her in action he believed she could take care of herself. She was on guard now; it was dusk; and she was familiar with the area. "Don't stay long. I'll worry until I see your face again."

After the Indian maiden left, Joe used a safety match to light a fire. As he worried over her safety, he drifted into serious thought. He knew this mission was going to be difficult. He would have foes, resisters, and dangers on both sides. Yet his tasks seemed challenging and stimulating ones. He tried to keep the loss of Tanner Gaston off his mind, as it could distract him. At a time when he was surrounded by perils, distractions could cost him his life and success. If everything worked out, he would avenge the death of his best friend, help establish peace for Stede's people and for innocent whites, and spend time with Morning Star. Once his tasks here were done, he would return to Virginia and never see her again. That thought evoked a curious ache within him.

Tanner's cousin was enchanting and unique. She stirred feelings in him that he had experienced before, but never this strong and deep. He warned himself that he could not act on those desires. She was Sun Cloud's daughter; and they were a world apart in upbringings and beliefs. If only she and her people weren't in such peril . . .

What he had told her about needing a strong treaty and no attacks or else the Army would retaliate was true. There were eight forts within a week's ride of the Dakotas' enormous territory: Atkinson and Kearny II to the south; Dodge, Ripley, and Snelling to the east; Benton to the northwest; Laramie fringed it to the southwest and within it was Fort Tabor on the Missouri River. From what Tom Fitzpatrick had told him, it wouldn't be long before Bridger, Union, Lookout, and

Pratte's posts would have forts. The Oglala's lands were almost surrounded by military sites, most of which were well armed with men and weapons.

The forts had been constructed to battle outlaws, hostile tribes, and renegades, to act as supply depots for wagon trains and other forts, to guard the immigrant trails west, and to encourage white settlement. Fort Laramie was the largest and strongest nearby, and that was where Stede Gaston, Tom Fitzpatrick, and Colonel David Twiggs were posted. Twiggs, commander of the western division of the Army, controlled the 2nd United States Dragoons, two companies of Mounted Riflemen, one company of 6th United States Infantry, and various other soldiers. The Oregon, Mormon, and California trails passed near Laramie, a major stop for wagon trains and gold seekers and an area that had become like an enormous kettle of assorted types of people.

Into a large pot were tossed disdainful soldiers, scared recruits, passing immigrants, determined settlers, prospectors, countless traders, and reckless hunters. Added to it were a batch of rival fur companies and trappers, then mistrustful Indians, warring tribes, and defiant renegades were included. Tossed in were a pinch of surveyors, scouts and explorers. That mixture had stewed for years—especially since '46—and was beginning to simmer after being spiced with greed, guile, fear, and misconceptions. To have those people and emotions provoked to the boiling point by a blackheart like Snake-Man made for a lethal meal. Worse, hotheads on both sides added new fuel weekly to the cookfire.

If the evildoers were halted and both sides made an honest attempt at getting to understand and respect each other, real peace was possible. If a southern shipper like himself could come here and grasp so much in less than a year, Joe reasoned, so could others. He had learned a great deal about the Indian. A warrior's world was his tepee, his family, his tribe, his ancestors, his hunting grounds, his enemies, his coups, and his culture. A woman's was tending to the needs of her family.

The Dakotas were a strong, proud, independent nation, born to a way of life that had existed for centuries with few changes. Their lives were simple, nomadic, and in harmony with their god and the land. They valued their allies, and they battled their foes. Intertribal feuds were passed from father to son, then kept alive with continual aggression and retaliation. They saw wars and raids as the path to glory, high rank, and livelihood. They battled to retain their ancestral, sacred, and hunting grounds. Yet most coups were earned for touching a foe or stealing his goods, not by slaying him. Scalping—taking a small lock of hair, not the whole head—was a symbol of courage, prowess, and cunning. Joe concluded that the Indians were not as he had imagined, even though Stede Gaston had told Joe many things before his arrival here.

After Stede's father—Powchutu—had been slain during the same ambush that had taken the life of Gray Eagle and made Sun Cloud the Red Heart chief, peace had ruled this area until '46, except for a few conflicts. Many events since that time had compelled more whites and soldiers into this area, which they had promised to leave in peace and privacy. The Canadian border dispute had been settled in '46. Oregon had opened up and beckoned pioneers. The Mexican War had ended in '48, giving the Union more territory to explore and settle. The gold rush to California had come in '48. More forts and posts had been constructed in '49 and '50, and more troops had come to Laramie. Some territories had become states, California just last year, making thirty-one in the Union. The whites and their states had advanced steadily: Missouri, Illinois, Iowa, and Texas. Word was Minnesota would follow suit within a year or so.

Plans for more encroachment and progress were ongoing back East. Asa Whitney had spoken to Congress in '49 about extending roads and railroads from the Great Lakes through this territory to Oregon and the Pacific. The Department of Interior, headed by Secretary Stuart, had been established in '49 to handle settlement. President Fillmore was having a difficult time over the slavery issue—which he hated but endured until he could abolish it safely—so he wanted eyes and ears on another matter. Expansion in the West offered him that solution, that reprieve. For these reasons Fillmore had sent Stede Gaston to this area to prevent any bloody confrontations borne of fear of settlement.

Joe was apprehensive over rapid advancement. He doubted the Indians realized the strength and number of whites or how impossible it would be to keep this territory to themselves. Did they, Joe mused, know how many other Indian nations and tribes—mainly eastern—had been destroyed, conquered, or moved aside for white habitation? True, he had come to be with Tanner and to share adventures with his best friend, but he had witnessed and learned enough to get him as deeply involved in this cause as was Tanner's father.

Tanner Gaston . . . Stede Gaston . . . Joe wondered if Sun Cloud and his people recalled those names from the distant past. He had not spoken them to Morning Star, for a good reason. What would happen when he mentioned Gaston to her people? By Oglala blood and tradition, Stede had more of a right to the Red Heart chief's bonnet than Sun Cloud did . . .

Morning Star's father and grandfather were legends in the worlds of the Indian and white men who had signed treaties in the past. But after each treaty, new trouble had arisen, and promises were forgotten or disregarded by the whites. Perhaps Sun Cloud and the Oglala had lost all faith in the whites. Joe couldn't blame them and he could not help but worry about what would happen if he failed in this awesome task. What if fierce war broke out between the Oglala and Crow, between the Oglala and whites? What if Sun Cloud was slain in an ambush as his father had been in 1820? From what Fitzpatrick, Stede, and others had told him—as with Gray Eagle—Sun Cloud could control and lead; he could cool hot heads or inflame restless hearts. He was loved by his people and allies but feared and hated by his enemies. He was the epitome of the perfect warrior and leader. Joe was eager to meet this great legend—son of a past legend, father of the woman with him now—to learn the truth for himself.

Joe worried what he would do if what he'd been told wasn't true or accurate and if the Oglala were at fault or partially guilty. What if they didn't want peace anymore or desire a new treaty? What if they murdered and scalped him the minute he entered their camp?

Joe had watched southern belles work their wiles on men. He knew how cunning and daring some could be, all the while looking and sounding as pure as angels. Could Morning Star have him duped by her many charms? Could she knowingly be leading him into a lethal trap? Was she fetching the white-hating warriors she had told him were gone? Was it logical for an Indian maiden to trust and help a paleface?

Chapter Three

orning Star chased the careless rabbit into an area enclosed on three sides by fallen rocks that were jammed close and tight and offered no hiding place or route to freedom. She dragged broken tree limbs into the opening to entangle her catch and prevent its escape. She eased toward the captive who was huddled in a snug ball against the rocks. She grabbed his ears, then struggled to get him under swift control as his squeals could summon a predator. She trapped the creature between her knees and cut its throat with speed, mercy, and skill. Slaying the rabbit did not evoke guilt because it was food provided by the Great Spirit, and hunting was their way of life.

Morning Star removed the head and skinned away the furry hide. She gutted it and left the entrails to feed another of the Great Spirit's creations. She took apart the barrier and went to a nearby stream to wash the meat and her hands before heading for the cave. She halted long enough to cut a sturdy limb for a skewer and two strong ones for pronged holders.

During her walk back, Morning Star thought about the white man awaiting her. Her father, uncle, grandfather, and tribe had made friends with a few whites in the past. Joseph Lawrence seemed to be the kind of man they would like and trust, as she did. His plan for peace was daring and clever. She prayed it would succeed. She knew many in her camp would speak against it and him, but hopefully the vote would go in his favor. As her rescuer, he should be safe. But his kindness would not earn him their help. If the council refused his request and he was sent away, she might never see him again. That thought displeased her.

It was strange how she wanted to watch him, to learn from him, to share more exciting and dangerous adventures with him, and to become closer. She liked the way the sun played in his golden hair and reflected its radiant glory. She lost herself in his eyes that mirrored the blue heaven and in his voice that flowed as warm honey over her. He was a good man. If she could become his guide and translator, she could help her people survive. But would Joe allow a woman to join him? If so, would her council agree? Her father?

Morning Star entered the cave as darkness settled as a cozy blanket over a chilled land. She went to the fire and sat down. "*Mastincala* to cook and eat." Her skilled hands positioned the two holders with forked ends into the ground. She skewered the rabbit with the last one and suspended it over the fire, resting the limb on the two Y-shaped ends.

"How did you get him without a trap or a bow or gun?" Joe asked.

"Buckskin Girl teach how. She," Morning Star revealed as she gestured thirty-six with her fingers, "Winters. Morning Star," she said and motioned eighteen. "We . . . best friends. How many win—years is Joe?"

"Twenty-eight," he answered, signing the number of his age as she had.

"Tell more. Where you from? When come here?"

"I'm from a place called Virginia, far away. I traveled to Fort Laramie last fall with Tanner and his father. That's the season between summer and winter. We wintered there, as your people do in these hills. When spring came, Tanner and I started riding from post to post scouting for his father." Joe didn't want to think about Tanner's death again today, so he chatted lightly. "I have one sister, Sarah Beth; she's older than I am. She's married to Andrew Reardon, who works with my father in the shipping business. They have one son, Lucas, four years old. I miss my family, especially my mother. Her name is Annabelle; you'd like her—she's a fine lady, the best."

Morning Star watched the array of expressions that came and went on Joe's face. She was glad he felt this way about his people. Families, friends, and ancestors should be important to one.

Looking at Morning Star, Joe suddenly realized that his brief doubt of her had come as a defense against his potent attraction to her and a fear that he could not resist her. Somehow he knew she could be trusted. "When we talked before, I didn't mean to sound as if my father and I aren't good friends; we are. We love each other. I guess I'm as much like him as any son could be. I just had this hunger inside that I had to feed before I settled down. I wouldn't want you to think those words I told Zeke and his men were true."

"What people see outside not always how we are inside," Morning Star commented. "Many think Morning Star too bold and act before thinking. Morning Star not try to be a warrior, but women must know skills to hunt and to defend camp when men gone. If not learn how to strike target with arrow and lance, not be able to protect and feed loved ones. A man enemy most times stronger than woman's claws and teeth. Must learn tricks to use when power is smaller than foe's. How can others say such things wrong for woman?"

"It isn't bad or wrong, Morning Star," Joe assured her. "And it doesn't make you less of a woman or a lady."

"What is lady? You say mother is lady."

Joe mused for a minute, then said, "A special woman from a good family and high birth rank, one who knows how to do the right things at the right time and place. You're from a line of great chiefs, so you have a high birth rank and a good family. You're a very special woman, so you're a lady."

The Indian maiden beamed with pleasure, and the fascinated male returned her smile. Neither realized the strength of the bond and mutual attraction between them, nor how rapidly they both were increasing. Many things had inspired their easy rapport and trust. They were sharing a heady adventure. They had depended upon and helped each other. They possessed similar dreams and goals. They were in a secluded and intimate setting where it seemed for now that only they existed.

The fire crackled and danced flames as wispy smoke rose, then vanished into the blackness. They sat on the cool earth with the fire separating them and highlighting their features. They had touched when she had tended his wound and when she had led him into the dark cave. He had shown his trust in her when he had followed her lead on the trail and into the hideout and when she had left to hunt. She had shown her trust by remaining with him. Instinct told Morning Star that Joe would not harm her, and it told Joe that she knew she was safe with him. They felt at ease, as if they had known each other for a long time.

"Are you married?" he asked.

She understood the word and replied, "No. And you? Do you have a mate?"

"No. What about a sweetheart, a special man?" he clarified.

"No. Is same for you?" she asked, and prayed it was.

"I have no special woman at home, but I'm surprised you're still free."

"I not shared a blanket with any brave or warrior." Morning Star explained the custom of romance. Privacy for courting was often hard to find. When a brave came to woo his choice of a mate, they would stand before her family's tepee and she would cover their head and shoulders with a blanket. This allowed for closeness, stolen kisses, whispers, and plans. It was the custom that everyone pretended not to notice the half-hidden couple. If a female was in great demand, she could share a blanket with many braves until she decided which one she wanted to join, marry.

"That sounds most enjoyable. I bet a brave gets jealous and scared when his choice shares a blanket with others. I would."

They laughed, then gazed at each other until Joe felt warm and tingly. "Smells good," he said, nodding at the rabbit.

Morning Star understood why he was changing the subject. Their talk had been personal. She had listened to his words carefully, and she tried to speak correctly as she said, "It is cooked. Do you have . . . dishes?"

"We'll have to share," he said, fetching a tin plate and handing it to her. He went to the pool and filled his cup, then sat beside her to feast off the shared plate and to drink from the same cup.

The rabbit was crisp, moist, and delicious. They licked their fingers after finishing each piece she carved before fetching another. The meat was nourishing and satisfying. When it was consumed, Morning Star washed the dishes and set them aside to dry. The fire had burned low. She added more wood to chase away the blend of night and cave chills.

"We must sleep. We ride when *Wi* awakens."

"We scout tomorrow," Joe reminded. "Nothing more."

"Morning Star obey. We must live to find peace for my people."

"There's something else you must understand and accept: my tasks are important. I'll do and say anything necessary to carry them out. I'm a stranger here, so I need help from your father and people. I don't want to lie to them or trick them even a little. But if I must, I will. If I don't make truce and find victory, your people and lands can be destroyed. If they're guilty of the charges against them," he added, "I'll have to report that to Fitzpatrick. No matter who's to blame, the main thing is to prevent a bloody war out here. I owe that to Tanner, and I promised his father."

She observed his expression for a moment as she mused on his words. "Morning Star understand." She claimed the same location she had used last night. She had refused Joe's polite offer of his sleeping roll, that even he had forgotten about last night. She rested her head on her parfleche and snuggled into Joe's warm jacket that held his masculine scent.

Joe felt guilty using the bedroll even though Morning Star had pointed out accurately that he was more accustomed to sleeping on one than she was. He wished she were lying beside him and curled in his arms. He scolded himself for such carnal desires about the "lady" nearby.

Joe was glad she had accepted his last words without anger or resistance; it told him that peace and survival for her people was her goal. He was cognizant of the many differences between himself and the lovely Indian maiden. Nothing serious was possible between them, yet his body ached for hers and his very soul seemed to reach out to her. He warned himself to stop thinking of her and craving her, but his heart and body refused to obey his mind's urgings.

Morning Star experienced the same longings and hesitations. She asked herself why no Oglala or ally had touched her as this sunny-haired, sky-eyed white man did. If so, she would be joined by now! She told herself she must not be drawn to him, as nothing could come of such feelings. She told herself it was wrong to want to be near him, to want to . . . She changed her position and ordered such wicked thoughts to leave her in peace. She couldn't help but wonder if the Great Spirit—Wakantanka—had guided him to her on the past moon and was using him to save her people. Wakantanka often worked in mysterious ways.

Joseph Lawrence could be one of those ways. Just as many warriors were talking of war with the encroaching whites, a special white man arrived to try to prevent new conflicts and bloodshed. Despite his skin color, she trusted Joe with all except her heart. That she must never yield to a man her people viewed as one of the enemy.

Each heard the other's restless movements. Both hoped theirs were not as noticeable. Both knew the suffering and shame any weakness would bring to themselves and their families. To allow their bond to tighten and strengthen would be like willingly leaping into a roaring fire. To even think of each other as only a man and a woman would be perilous, shameful, and destructive. Each prayed such forbidden emotions would vanish. Each knew they would not. They closed their eyes and begged for sleep to imprison them, free them. They didn't know who or what awaited them tomorrow . . .

Joseph Lawrence and Morning Star left the cozy cave and sneaked to Zeke's campsite. They found it was deserted. The age of the coals, wagon ruts, and horse droppings revealed that the three white men had left early the previous morning. Two whiskey bottles, a coffee tin, broken knife, a flattened metal cup, and an old St. Louis newspaper had been left behind.

The Indian maiden looked at the mess. "They make face of Mother Earth ugly with their leavings. Fire die after they ride away. It dangerous not to kill with water. Plenty nearby. If fire jump rocks, it run far; bad."

Joe understood her dismay. It was the same along the trails that the wagon trains took through Indian territory: various items—wagon wheels and parts, pianos, heavy furniture, broken bottles, fancy clothing, trunks—and garbage from spent supplies were strewn about from beginning to end. Skeletons of mules and horses overburdened by overloaded wagons could be seen, as well as farm animals that had died along the way. Graves and crosses caught the eye at places where fatal illness or accident had occurred. Sometimes such eyesores couldn't be helped, but used tins and such should be buried, not cast out to steal the land's beauty, Joe and Morning Star concurred.

"Let's track the wagons," Joe said. "But we have to be careful. They're probably watching for us to follow," he reminded her. As they studied the ground, Joe remarked, "Looks as if they all left together. I'm surprised they didn't come looking for us. Let's ride, but keep your eyes and ears alert. If trouble strikes, you ride for home."

"If trouble come, Joe follow Morning Star fast."

He shook his head. "No," he told her. "I'll lead them in the other direction. I want you to get away safely. Don't worry about me."

She looked into his adamant gaze. "No good to be apart. Joe must follow men. Morning Star. Safe with Joe, not safe alone."

He thought over her argument and nodded. "You're right. You're more valuable to them than I am. If we're ambushed, we make a run for it."

They followed the deep ruts and numerous hoofprints northwestward. After a few miles, they saw buzzards circling beyond them.

The hairs on Joe's body seemed to bristle in warning. "Maybe they shot an animal or one of their horses died," he remarked. "Let's move slow and easy. I'll keep a lookout for an ambush, and you keep us on their tracks."

Morning Star shared his feeling that something was wrong ahead. She watched the trail, while Joe kept his concentration on their surroundings. She didn't want either of them trapped by their enemies and tensed with apprehension and alert, summoning forth all of her skills and instincts to aid them.

When they neared the place the vultures had found their next meal, they noticed a man's body with arrows protruding from it.

Morning Star recognized the garments. "It man called Clem," she said.

Joe's gaze scanned each direction, but he didn't see or sense anyone's presence. "Stay back. He may be alive. It could be a trap."

"Death birds no come unless smell death."

"Wonder who attacked them," Joe murmured as they approached the grim site. He warned himself to stay on guard for trickery.

Anger filled Morning Star as she eyed the arrows, as each tribe had their own colors and markings. Clem was lying as if he'd been shot and had fallen from a horse, then left behind while others fled for survival. "It trick. My band gone."

"What do you mean?"

"Those Red Heart arrows. White men steal and use to make others think we attack and kill. It not true."

"You sure your band left this area? What if they did attack?"

She shook her head. "They no do. See, no pony tracks. He die or big man kill. Leave here so others blame Red Hearts."

Joe dismounted and examined the ground and Clem's body. Perhaps Clem had died from a blow to the head during the battle for their escape, Joe thought. He had taken a hard fall after Morning Star's attack with the limb, and he had been drunk, in addition. Or, from the forceful bash on Clem's skull, she could be right about Zeke getting rid of a problem. The group's leader was clearly taking advantage of the situation; he was framing Red Heart by using their arrows to mislead whoever found Clem's body. Joe couldn't allow that lie to be reported. He broke the shafts and put the feathered ends into his saddlebag. With no way or desire to bury Clem, he mounted. "Let's go," he said.

They rode to the spot where Zeke and his men had met with a large Crow party. They didn't dismount until they visually scouted the area.

"They didn't stay long. They joined up and left together. Their trail heads into Crow territory, doesn't it?"

"*Han*. We follow while, maybe catch up, spy."

"No, it's too dangerous, too many of them. I wanted to see which direction Zeke and his boys took after their trade, but that's not possible. We can't ride into a Crow camp or risk an ambush."

"You speak wise."

"We'll head for your camp so I can meet with your father. Then I have to ride to Fort Tabor to meet with Captain Thomas before I start looking around for clues. Thomas might know something helpful. I also want to give him the names of those men and their descriptions. If they come around the fort, Thomas can keep an eye on them. When I finish there, I'll return to your camp to get that guide and translator I need."

"You think white soldier help Oglalas?" she asked in a doubtful tone.

"Some of them will; this one will."

"We see. Come, camp in trees. Long ride."

They skirted the eastern side of the Black Hills. At times they had to journey slow for rest and because of hilly terrain. That change in pace allowed them to take in the beauty of the rugged peaks and towering spires in midnight black. The dark hills were a striking contrast to a deep-blue background and verdant foreground. The area was alive with green and fresh-smelling spring growth: spruce, pine, asp, cottonwood, oak, and sometimes dense underbrush. Almost every hill and meadow displayed a multitude of flowers in vivid shades. Streams were encountered frequently with sparkling water that seemed to dance and swirl around rocks with new moss. It was some of the most peaceful and inspiring scenery Joe had ever seen; he understood why Morning Star's people loved their territory so much.

They heard birds singing and calling to others as if they were the freest and happiest of God's creatures. They spooked shy deer, large elk, graceful antelope, and one coyote who looked sad to be alone. He loped away at a leisurely pace, but glanced back several times with eyes that seemed to say he wished he could join them.

They saw an enormous herd of buffalo grazing in a valley of sweet and short grasses. The beasts were massive and strong, yet they deceptively appeared to be gentle and slow. About one-third of them were lying down, but all were on alert. They hadn't shed the lighter-colored winter coats that looked like tangled curls against their dark bodies and heads. Numerous babies played near their mothers. Heavy bulls walked around as if guarding females they had selected as members of their harems. The herd evoked an impression of power, mystery, unity, and wildness. It was a stirring sight.

Wildflowers gave the valley splashes of blue, yellow, red, and white atop the green covering. Bees worked amidst countless pollen-filled offerings to gather sweet nectar. Jackrabbits, abundant in the area, darted from one hiding place to another as the couple's passing alarmed the furry creatures.

They rode until dusk, having stopped at intervals only to rest and water their mounts. They hadn't seen or heard any other travelers, but Joe had spotted and shot two quail, and the fowl were secured to his saddle. After eating cold rabbit this morning and chewing on jerky at midday, they were eager to camp and cook the birds.

When Morning Star pointed out a sheltered glen with lush grass and water for the horses and protection for them, Joe smiled and thanked her. "This is perfect. The hills and trees will hide our cooking smoke from enemy eyes. I doubt anyone could sneak up on us here, Morning Star."

"Oglala warriors can jump on the enemy before he sees or hears danger. No time to grab bow or knife. You be safe. You with me."

Joe noticed how she spoke her first sentence slowly and correctly but how the next few came swiftly and with words missing amidst her laughter and smiles. He realized how much English she knew, and how much she was either learning or remembering while riding with him. He was glad.

"You smile like cunning fox, Joe Lawrence. Why?"

"I was just thinking how smart you are. I'd better watch out or you'll show me up on the trail. Show me up—prove you're better than I am."

"Is bad for woman to show . . . better skills?"

"If you know what's best in something, you should do it and teach me. Mistakes are what's bad; they can get you killed. It's worse to hide skills."

Morning Star reasoned for a time, then smiled once more. "You teach Morning Star more English and white ways?"

"Yes, if you won't be insulted when I correct you. And I won't get mad or be insulted when you teach me something about your people and land."

"Is good trade."

He sent her a smile and a gentle correction. "*It* is a good trade."

"*It* is a good trade," she repeated. "Morning Star gather wood."

"I will gather wood. When you speak of yourself, it's I or me." Joe gave her many examples of when to use either word.

"You . . . will teach . . . me when right. No, when it is right to use."

"You're sharp, quick, and smart. I hope I will be, too."

"We make good partners."

"Good partners. *Han. Pilamaya.* You'll teach me more than *yes* and *thank you* before we reach your camp, won't you?"

"I teach Lakota; you teach English. It is a good trade."

Joe yearned to trade more than words and ways with the exquisite woman, but knew he could not. Too much was at stake to think of himself, particularly when a match between them was impossible and could hurt many people. If only—

"You look sad. What wr—What *is* wrong?"

"When my task is over, I'll have to leave your land. I'll miss you. We made friends fast and easy. With Tanner gone . . ."

"You miss him. It is bad not to have peace in death."

"He'll have peace when I find his killers and punish them."

"Revenge will not steal pain in heart. It must leave when ready."

"You're right, but at least they won't go free after taking his life."

"It is our way to punish enemies. Morn—I will help you."

Joe smiled and thanked her, but didn't comment on her offer. "Let's get wood collected so we can eat. I'm starving."

Together they gathered wood, built a fire, cleaned the quail, and put them on a spit to roast. While the fowl cooked, they tended their horses and freshened up in the stream. A full moon journeyed across the eastern sky, and shadows crept over the landscape. Except for nocturnal insects and creatures, it was quiet.

Morning Star listened to the crickets, frogs, and night birds. Their songs always relaxed her. She watched a mild breeze ruffle leaves. She saw grass and blossoms sway as if lulling themselves to sleep. She heard the distant howl of a coyote, and was glad to hear a mate's answer to the lonely wail. Water rippled around rocks and twigs in the stream. An owl hooted nearby, then again from farther away. Once in a while, the horses neighed or shifted their stances. Her world was good, safe, and happy. How she hated the thought it could be destroyed or stolen, how she and her people could be pushed out or slain.

The blond-haired male observed the Indian maiden who sat so serenely graceful as she meditated. He noticed how the moonlight shone on her midnight hair. He longed to stroke it to see if it was as soft and silky as it appeared. He wanted to caress her skin to see if it had the same feel. He had the crazy urge to nibble at her proud chin, her dainty ears, her full lips. She looked more exotic and tempting than any island or Oriental beauty he had seen during his many travels. But something had stolen the glow in her dark eyes and brought a serious expression to her face. "Now, you're the one who looks sad," Joe said, intruding on her thoughts.

Morning Star's deep-brown gaze fused with Joe's blue one. Simply hearing his voice and looking at him caused her heart to race and her body to warm. She wondered what strange and powerful magic he possessed to enchant her this way. To conceal her interest in him, she told him what she had been thinking earlier. "Oglalas must remain here forever to tend and save this land for Grandfather. If harmony is broken, the land dies; the creatures die; the people die; all is gone. The white man is not one with the land and nature; he changes and destroys. He would slay all of one creature. When one is gone, nature's Life-Cycle is broken. It changes those of all other living creatures. It is wrong, dangerous. The white man does not care; he feeds on greed and deceit. If the grass is trampled by wagons and farms, what will feed the buffalo? If the buffalo starves or is slain, what will feed the Oglalas? If trees are stolen, what will give shade and wood? If streams are changed or claimed, what will Oglalas drink? If more land is settled, where will Oglalas live and hunt? Where will Oglala dead rest?"

Joe understood what she meant. He had learned how the Indians lived, how they used all the parts of a slain animal for food, clothing, utensils, pouches, and sewing materials. Wood was gathered for tepee poles, then used in the fire, or enough trees died or shed limbs for burning. Nothing in nature was ever totally destroyed. Each creation had its purpose in nature's life-circle.

"What you say is true, Morning Star," he commented, "but some people don't understand the harmony of land and nature. Some take what they want or need without thinking about the destruction they're causing. My family has a plantation back home. It's like a big farm. We grow things, gather them to eat or to sell, then plant seeds to grow more. As long as we keep seeds, we'll have those plants. It's foolish for a man to eat all he has and not save seeds for growing more food and plants for clothing. We don't kill all of our creatures for meat and hides. We breed them, so the line will continue. We make roads for travel, so grasses won't be trampled. Many white men are this way. Many are growers, not destroyers."

Morning Star spoke slowly and carefully as she tried to explain matters to her companion while she practiced her English. She hoped she would have even more use for it soon as she wanted to become Joe's guide and translator. "We have seen and heard of such men. Those who come to our land are destroyers, not growers. They steal from our forests, streams, and prairies. They cheat and deceive when they make trade. They bring guns and disease to kill. They bring whiskey to weaken minds and bodies. They say they will be friends, but they work as enemies. They say they wish to share, but they take. They wish us to become as they are. We do not want or need white man's laws and ways."

Joe held silent as she checked the roasting quail; he didn't want to disturb her line of thought.

"Some come to say we must accept their . . . religion; but the white man has many religions. We have one, Wakantanka the Great Spirit. Those called missionaries say it wrong to kill and steal, but whites do not follow the words in their Bible and religion. Father say white men cannot be trusted. They call us savages, hostiles, wild animals. They do not try to understand Oglalas. They put words on papers to sell to others to turn all whites against us. Papers say only good about whites and evil about Indians; big lies. Father say much evil done to other tribes where the whites live. He say many tribes destroyed or driven from their homelands. Many treaties signed by other tribes with white man; they not honored. Many use treaties to say they traded goods for Indian lands. The land cannot be owned or sold. When white man say he bought land, soldiers and white leaders use paper words Indians do not understand to take away their land. My people hear and learn much about whites in past winters. They do not want more here. Your task will be hard, Joe Lawrence."

"Not all white men are bad, Morning Star."

"It is . . . different with you. Joe comes in peace, to learn, to help. You do not come to steal and kill, to stay. It is not so with others."

"There are other whites like me. They only want a good and safe place to settle and live. They want peace, too, Morning Star."

"How can peace come when they take Oglala land and insult us?"

"Both sides must change and share; they must learn about each other."

"We do not go to white lands to take them."

"There's more land here, and too many whites back East. It's the way things are, Morning Star. To refuse to change is dangerous and unwise."

"To defend our land and lives shows courage and honor."

"If the Oglalas and other tribes agree to stay in their own territories and let whites settle in lands between them, all can live nearby in peace; that's what Fitzpatrick wants for everyone. Oglala territory is big, Morning Star; there's room for others to live in areas they don't use."

"What would Joe do if Crow rode to your . . . plantation and took it? Would Joe make truce and share parts he does not use?" she asked.

Joe started to say that was different, but he stopped himself. She had a good point. "My family's land is small, Morning Star," he tried to explain. "All of it is used for growing food, plants to make clothing, and for raising animals. Many others live on our land and tend it for us."

"They are friends, not enemies. What if enemies settled there?"

"That's not the white way. White laws protect our lands from others."

"If we accept the whites and their laws, it would be the same here. They would claim land and keep Oglalas away from grass, water, and game."

She was right, but Joe hated to agree with her. White advancement and progress were heading to this area. If a compromise wasn't reached, it would mean bloodshed. It was a scary and costly predicament.

"Your eyes say you know my words are true, and that troubles you."

"Yes, it does. We can't stop the rain of whites from coming, Morning Star, but we can prevent a destructive flood from washing away your people. If I can get your father's help and stop these present conflicts, it will hold back the rains for a while. That's all I can promise you or them."

"I will help you in all ways," she promised in return.

The daughter of Sun Cloud liked the way Joe did not try to trick or deceive her with clever words or cunning lies. Even when the truth was bad, he spoke it. Her father had made treaty to earn a few years of peace for his people; it had stretched into thirty. Without Joe's help and victory, that truce would end and war would begin. With them, perhaps another stretch of peaceful years lay ahead. She had heard her father say many times that the white man could not be stopped forever but that he would resist their intrusion for as long as possible, even with his life. Chief Sun Cloud had said that Wakantanka always sent an answer to a problem, and Joseph Lawrence must be the answer this time. She had found him, saved his life, tended his wound, taught him things, and befriended him; it was her right to ride at his side to save her people from his. For now, she would not suggest that idea to him, though, for she surmised he would resist it.

After they had eaten, they doused the campfire and bedded down for the night with only a few feet separating them. Both lay there thinking for a time, then drifted off to sleep.

Their schedule was the same the next day. Neither talked much as they made camp. Both privately reflected on their meeting, their time together, and what confronted them soon. Each knew that once they reached Morning Star's village, things would change between them. Each knew that if something went wrong, tomorrow would be their last day together, and that caused them to share a strange apprehension.

They ate rabbit stew, this time simmered to tenderness with wild vegetable roots that Morning Star had found. After their meal was consumed and their horses tended, Joe spread his sleeping roll and a heavy blanket on the grass. He stretched out on the bedroll while Morning Star lay down on the thick blanket.

"We reach my village before next moon. Be strong and brave," she encouraged. "I will speak for you and peace to my father and people."

"*Pilamaya,*" he said. Joe noticed how uneasy Morning Star was tonight. Though she faced away from him, he could see the tension in her body. Was she afraid her people would harm him, or even kill him? Or, did she dread their parting, as he did? Even if he were given the chance to see her again, he knew it would be reckless and cruel to court the temptation. He couldn't stay here longer than six months; he had promised his family he'd be home by Christmas, and traveling by horseback required four or five weeks. She couldn't leave with him, *wouldn't* leave with him. Anything between them was hopeless. So, he asked himself, why did that thought hurt so much? It wasn't just physical desire gnawing at him. Morning Star was fun, witty, dependable, brave, intelligent, strong, and gentle. It was so easy to be with her. He wanted more than friendship!

Morning Star sensed Joe's eyes on her, and his thoughts seemed to reach out to her. She knew it was wrong to weaken toward an enemy, but her heart kept telling her he wasn't a foe. He had not come here to settle and live, and he would leave before the winter snows returned. She didn't want him to go. But, even if he remained in her land, she could not turn to him. She knew what people—Indians *and* whites—called Indian women who mated with or married white men: squaw. Worse, a *witkowin*: whore. Their lives and ways were so different, too different. A relationship between them was the same as one between a deer and a buffalo. It could not come to pass, and she must do nothing to encourage either of them to seek the impossible. Yet . . .

Joe dared not question the woman's restlessness, just as she dared not query his. Both knew that to talk at this moment was perilous and could cost them victories in the battles that were raging inside them. At last, the two weary people fell asleep.

When Morning Star told him they were nearing her camp, Joe halted their journey to remind her, "Remember I'll do and say whatever I must to win your people's trust and help. If nothing more, I need their promise they won't raid or attack while I'm working on peace."

Her gaze roamed his clean-shaven face, and she read urgency in his eyes. "Come. Scouts will see us. We must speak with Father first."

It was almost dusk. They had ridden fast to reach her village today. From the trail they had found of the group returning from Bear Butte, they knew they would arrive only a few hours after it. They had not encountered a rescue party yet, and concurred that one must be planning to leave the village at sunrise on Monday morning. They had spoken little today, and both were apprehensive about seeing Sun Cloud.

As they entered the edge of the large camp, people halted their tasks to stare at the strange sight. Warriors reached for weapons, then followed the riders toward their chief's tepee. Word of Morning Star's return and the white man spread rapidly. A curious crowd gathered.

Morning Star dismounted and called to her parents, "*Ata! Ina!*"

Singing Wind rushed outside when she heard her daughter's voice and the loud commotion. "*Anpaowicanhpi! Tokel oniglakin kta he?*" She asked what had happened as they embraced with deep love and relief.

"*Ina, he mi ye*," the girl replied, saying she was home safely.

Singing Wind asked how she had escaped her Crow captors.

Sun Cloud joined them, his dark gaze going back and forth between his daughter and the white man. He listened, waited, and watched.

Morning Star told her mother she'd been tricked and had much to tell her. "*Taku ota eci ciyapi kta bluha yele.*" Morning Star embraced her father, then related details of her misadventures.

While she talked, Joe stood still and silent. He had been told that Sun Cloud was the reflection of his father, Gray Eagle. He was tall, lithe, and muscular for a man of fifty-four. There were few strands of gray in a midnight mane that flowed past broad bronze shoulders and down a strong back. Sun Cloud's eyes were almost as black as his hair and thick brows. His bones were as finely chiseled as any aristocrat's. The one eagle feather secured behind his head and traveling downward was said to be worn always in honor of his slain father. He was not wearing his chief's bonnet, but had a necklace around his throat that depicted his name. He was clad in a breechcloth, leggings, and moccasins. Sun Cloud was indeed the epitome of a great leader, an awesome warrior, and a dignified man.

Joe let his observant gaze slip to the woman with the chief and his daughter, Singing Wind. At fifty-four, as well, she was still beautiful and slim. He sensed a spirited nature in her that her daughter had inherited, as well as her awesome beauty. Her eyes were as brown as rich chocolate, but her hair was not as dark and long as Morning Star's. The few wrinkles on her face did not detract from its loveliness. She carried herself as a lady, a woman of high rank and birth, a woman of importance. Joe detected no vanity or arrogance in either female, nor in Sun Cloud. That pleased him.

Joe assumed the warrior nearby was her brother, Night Stalker, who had been the leader of the pilgrimage to Bear Butte and who had returned home without her. He looked surprised at his sister's arrival and angered by Joe's presence and part in the rescue. He wasn't as tall as his father, but he was more muscular. Nor did he have Sun Cloud's handsome face and dignified carriage. A lance scar ran down his left side, and Sun Dance scars marred his broad chest. His dark hair was worn loose, but a headband held it in place. Joe knew this man would be one of his obstacles.

Joe's eyes were pulled to a warrior next to Night Stalker. The man's dark gaze was narrowed and chilled by the story he was hearing. Joe guessed his age in the early twenties and his height at five feet eleven inches. His hair hung in two thick braids, with coup feathers suspended near the bottoms of both plaits. A small knife was suspended from a thong about his neck. He, too, was wearing only a breech-cloth, leggings, and moccasins. Joe perceived a coldness and arrogance in this bronze-skinned warrior whose chest displayed Sun Dance scars that proved his prowess. The only time the Oglala's gaze altered was when it touched on Morning Star; then, open desire was apparent. Joe felt his temper rising against the warrior who craved Morning Star. He didn't have to be told this was Knife-Slayer, and an enemy.

Many others, men and women and children, gathered around the group, but Joe returned his attention to the talk in progress and tried to catch a word here and there to learn how it was going.

"Why did you bring a white foe to our camp?" Knife-Slayer demanded in Lakota. "He will learn our strength and tell others, if he is not slain."

"*Hiya! Ito kawe kin papsunpi sni ye!*" Morning Star shouted, saying not to spill Joe's blood. "He is a friend," she continued in her tongue. "He helped me. He is here to help us. Father, you must spare his life and heed his words."

"How can an enemy help us?" Night Stalker asked.

Morning Star focused on her father. "He is our friend, Father. He *can* help us. He has a plan to draw our real enemies from hiding. If he does so, the soldiers will punish them." To Joe, she said in English, "Speak the words to my father you say to me on trail."

Joe's blue gaze locked with Sun Cloud's dark one. "I know only a few of your words, though Morning Star is teaching me more, so you must forgive me for addressing you in my language. I am not your enemy, Sun Cloud. The Great White Chief and most Americans want to live in peace with your people and all other Indian Nations. I am here with a man who is seeking answers to the troubles between whites and Indians. We're here to help Agent Tom Fitzpatrick at Fort

Laramie obtain a new treaty that all peoples can accept and honor. The real enemy in your territory is called Snake-Man. He sells guns, whiskey, and supplies to the Crow and encourages them to destroy the Lakotas. We don't know why he wants war, but we must stop him before he begins a bloodbath in this area. If the Crow and Oglala go on the warpath, the Shoshone and Pawnee will side with the Crow; and the Cheyenne and Blackfoot will aid their allies, the Dakotas. Whites will be trapped between the warring tribes. More soldiers will come. Fitzpatrick has sent word to you about the new treaty, but you have not responded. Many things have happened, and your tribe has been blamed. I don't think you're guilty, but I need help proving it. I have to discover who Snake-Man is and capture him. If not, this area and all people here can have no peace."

"If he is white, why do you side against him?" Sun Cloud asked.

"He's evil. His actions cause the deaths of innocent Indians and whites. He enflames the hatred between the Oglala and Crow. It must stop."

"We have always warred with Bird People!" Night Stalker shouted.

"That time must end, Night Stalker. If both tribes honor the new treaty and remain in their territories, peace is possible. I need a guide and interpreter, someone to teach me your people's ways."

"You seek to learn our ways to use them to destroy us," Knife-Slayer accused in English. "You must die!" He reached for the blade at his waist.

Morning Star covered his hand. *"Hiya! Wicake! I'ye waste!"*

Sun Cloud noticed how the girl shouted in the white man's defense, claiming he spoke the truth and was a good man. He didn't have time at that moment to worry over the tone of her voice or the expression in her eyes.

"If we harm him, we harm ourselves!" Morning Star added in Lakota.

Knife-Slayer noticed her tone and gaze, and retorted in his tongue, "You are a woman, and his cunning rescue has blinded you. He must die."

"I want peace and survival for my people. I am no coward. I will ride, track, and fight with him. I will be his tongue, ears, and teacher," she avowed.

"No!" Knife-Slayer shouted. "He will trick you again, and slay you."

The girl glared at the warrior for his subtle insult. "If such a threat was true, why do I stand here now, alive and unharmed?"

"You are his path to our camp, sister," Night Stalker replied. "My band was riding at first light to rescue you. I could not come after you in Crow Territory. I saw many tracks. It was my duty to get others home safely."

"It was your duty, brother, and I do not blame you for leaving me behind. The false clues were cunning. I knew you would be tricked by them. You must listen to this white man; his words are wise and true."

Sun Cloud raised his hand and asked for silence. "Hold your tongues, my people. We will hear his words before his fate is decided. First, I must speak with him. We do not strike a death blow before we learn the truth."

Though Joe could not grasp the rapid flow of Lakota between Morning Star, Night Stalker, and Knife-Slayer, he surmised that the two men were speaking against him and that Morning Star was pleading his good cause. Joe knew it was unusual for a woman to argue with men, especially in public. He was glad when Sun Cloud halted the heated words and turned to address him.

"For many winters, the Red Heart Band had a treaty with your leader and people. Why has it been broken? Why does White Chief Monroe let more whites and soldiers enter our lands? Why have more forts been placed on the face of

Mother Earth? Soon they will encircle us and tighten as a rope on a wild stallion's neck to choke the life from us. Why do they make more trails through our lands? Why do they settle on our sacred and hunting grounds? Why do they give and sell supplies and weapons to our foes? Why have they set their eyes upon the buffalo, our life's blood? Why do they bring their diseases to sneak upon us in the night and slay us?"

Joe held silent and let the chief continue.

"We were foolish to allow the first white footprints on our land. Now their tracks are everywhere. They refuse to leave, and they battle us to stay. We are forced to fight them to save our land and people. The leader called Broken-Hand at Laramie asks us to sign a new treaty with the whites and our foes. It is no good. The whites and Crow would not honor it."

Joe had listened closely and respectfully and hoped he wouldn't forget any of Sun Cloud's questions, even though most had been spoken as statements of fact and feeling. "Tom Fitzpatrick, Broken-Hand, is a good man. He is fair and honest. You knew him when he trapped in this area. He respects your people, and he knows the Indian ways. He wants peace between all tribes and whites. As long as tribes war against each other, white travelers are in danger and more soldiers and forts will come to give them protection. You don't want that, so it's wise and good to make treaty so all sides can survive and be happy. Most battles are fights over hunting grounds and revenge for raids. If every tribe stays in its own territory and doesn't attack another, peace will come, Sun Cloud."

"We have warred with our enemies since long before the birth of my grandfather and his father," Night Stalker shouted. "How will marks on a paper stop a war passed from father to son for more winters than are marked on the buffalo record of our people?"

"By everyone wanting and needing peace and survival more than scalps and war prizes," Joe responded in a calm and careful tone.

"Words come easy from your mouth, White man. Honor does not come easy from the Crow or your people. Another treaty matters not."

"The first treaty never reached the hands of the White Chief Monroe," Joe revealed. "Derek Sturgis, friend to Gray Eagle and Sun Cloud, was injured in a fire that destroyed his dwelling and the paper. He did not live to return to make another one. Our new White Chief is President Fillmore. He desires a treaty. I am here as his helper to make truce."

"You speak for the new White Chief?" Sun Cloud asked.

"Yes. I speak for him through the man who brought me here."

"He lies to save his life," Knife-Slayer charged. "He will betray us."

"It is true many forts have been built in this vast territory," Joe revealed, "but they are to protect our Indian allies as well as white settlers. They defend everyone against bad whites, called outlaws, and against bad Indians, called renegades. Such men attack good Indians and good whites. Fort Tabor's soldiers do not attack the Lakotas. Neither does Fort Laramie where Broken-Hand lives and works for peace. When the soldiers battle, it's to punish and halt attacks on innocent people. It's true a trail crosses to the south of your lands. Most whites are riding far to the west to begin new lives. Some halt and settle here; they're tired and have no money to continue to their destination. They want to live in peace. They—"

"Peace!" Knife-Slayer interrupted in anger. "They—"

Sun Cloud halted the furious warrior and said, "Let him speak, Knife-Slayer. He did not break into my words. You can speak later."

"The white man who sells weapons to your enemies is bad," Joe continued. "He must be caught and punished. Your father, Gray Eagle, was a great chief. He wished for peace and survival. Long ago, you did the same. It must be that way again, Sun Cloud. Give me the help I need," he urged.

"How do we know this warrior would be safe at your side?"

Joe anticipated resistance to the suggestion he was about to make, but his plan was clever enough to work. "What I need and request is a brave and smart woman to lead me to the Crow camps and white settlements. The evil whites would not suspect a white trader or trapper with an Indian wife of being a spy. We could go anyplace together and search for clues."

"You speak of my sister, Morning Star?" Night Stalker asked.

"Another trick!" Knife-Slayer charged. "He will hold her prisoner. Think of Morning Star's value to the bluecoats."

"If I wished to take her captive, there was plenty of time on the trail," Joe pointed out.

"You did not so she would lead you to our village!"

"That isn't true. Besides, I don't want Morning Star as my helper. It's too dangerous. I don't want Sun Cloud's daughter harmed. That would cause more distrust between us. Select the woman best trained to help me."

"I best," Sun Cloud's daughter stated. "I know Oglala land. I speak English and understand Crow signs. I have warrior skills."

"No, Morning Star. I can't risk your life again. It's too perilous. Sun Cloud has lost too many of his family. It must be another female."

As Knife-Slayer, Night Stalker, and Morning Star argued amongst themselves, warriors whispered and watched. Those who knew English explained the situation to others nearby who didn't. Then they passed along the shocking news to Red Hearts distant from the center of activity.

A man with narrow, piercing eyes stepped forward. *"Wicakewala sni. Wowocake sni. Kastaka."*

"Who is he? What did he say?" Joe murmured to the stunned girl at his right. He had a dark suspicion of his words, and dread washed over him.

Morning Star felt her heart race and her mouth go dry. A chill passed over her as if she were standing barefoot and naked in the snow. She had feared this man's resistance and hatred, and, more so, his power. It was up to Joe to change her people's mind. "Hawk Eyes, our shaman, father of Knife-Slayer," she replied. "He says you lie and must be slain."

Joe knew it was a bad sign for such a powerful man to talk against him. He saw the looks on most faces that said they agreed or would follow any advice given by their medicine chief and holy man. He read mistrust and hostility in some faces. He read confusion in others. In a few stoic expressions, he could glean no clue to their thoughts and feelings. "I do not lie, Hawk Eyes. All I have said is true. I come as a friend, an ally."

"I say his mouth must be silenced by death this moon!" was the shaman's reply, this time in English and spoken as a command.

Two strong warriors seized Joe's arms. Morning Star panicked. Even if they refused to give Joe help, she could not let him be slain. But what could she say or do to save his life? Nothing came to her terrified mind.

Alarmed and desperate, a bold and cunning idea entered Joe's head. He prayed Morning Star would understand his motive and keep his secret. If he didn't attempt it, he was a dead man, and war was a certainty. If he did and she exposed him, he was a dead man. He glanced at her frightened expression and decided his ruse was worth the risk he would take.

Chapter Four

Joe shouted over affirmative "yips" of the Kit-Fox cult and murmurings for and against killing him, "Sun Cloud! I'm Tanner Gaston! The son of Stede Gaston! Son of Powchutu, son of Running Wolf, your grandfather! I only use the name Joe Lawrence to trick evil whites! I'm Tanner Gaston!"

As the warriors, who did not understand English, yanked at Joe, Sun Cloud raised his hand and ordered them to halt and release him. The chief stared at the white man as those shocking words struck home like flaming arrows. The braves unhanded Joe and looked at their leader for an explanation.

"He speaks words I must hear," Sun Cloud related in Lakota.

"Do not listen to more lies!" Knife-Slayer shouted.

Sun Cloud sent the Sacred Bow Carrier a warning glance to be silent, then returned his probing gaze to the stranger.

Joe took that as a sign to finish his startling revelation. "Stede Gaston, my father, is the man who brought me here. He's waiting for me at Fort Laramie. He works with Broken-Hand and President Fillmore for peace. My father is old and injured. I'm here as his legs, arms, eyes, ears, mouth, and heart. The Great Spirit called him to his father's lands to make peace."

While Sun Cloud and others who knew English gaped at the white stranger and Morning Star did not interrupt him, Joe hurried on to save his life and his mission. "My grandfather, Powchutu, was the firstborn son of Running Wolf. If the chief's bonnet hadn't been stolen from his head by evil when his mother married a French trapper and denied Running Wolf his son, Powchutu would have been chief in Gray Eagle's place. When my grandfather was forced from these lands he loved and his rightful rank was stolen from him, my father was born and raised as white, as was I. When danger came to these lands, the Great Spirit troubled his heart and called him here to help save his people, the Oglalas. We are of the same bloodline, Sun Cloud. Would you slay your cousin? Your friend? Your ally?"

Night Stalker found his voice and shouted a translation to his people. He dared not accuse the stranger of lying until his father decided it was or wasn't the truth. He didn't want the white man's arrival and words to intrude on his life and desires. The Oglala had been given many challenges from the whites and Crow during the last few years, but his father had continued to urge for peace. Night Stalker didn't believe peace was possible. He believed his warriors should confront their enemies in glorious battles—battles that would drive the whites and Bird People from their lands forever; battles that would bring him many coups, wealth, and prestige as in the olden days. He wanted to prove his wits and prowess, especially after failing to rescue his sister. He wanted to defend his lands and people, and to earn the chief's bonnet soon. He did not want to lie around and grow lazy and fat. He did not trust the whites, and he was restless from the long, quiet winter in camp.

Payaba made his way through the whispering crowd. Once known as Standing Tree and shaman, he declared in the Lakota tongue in a strong voice that belied his eighty years, "I say he speaks the truth. Has Sun Cloud and the council forgotten my vision of twenty winters past?" For those who didn't recall it and those who hadn't heard it, the old man repeated it. "Look at his eyes and hair. Think of his bloodline and words. As my vision warned, a season of bitter conflicts and greed have destroyed truce with the whites. Two men have come to our land to help us defeat this first trouble. He speaks the truth. He is Sky Warrior, the white helper we have awaited for twenty winters. I say we must listen and accept his words. We must help him. To do so obeys Grandfather's commands in my sacred vision."

The elderly man had spoken too fast for Joe to catch more than a few words that didn't make sense to him. All dark eyes had shifted from the past shaman to him. Joe sensed that something important about him had been revealed. An array of emotions filled the Oglalas' faces: awe, confusion, trust, anger, and apprehension. When Morning Star translated for him, astonishment, tension, and befuddlement filled Joe. He knew the Indians were believers of what they called visions, but he was amazed by the exactitude of one that had taken place twenty years ago. He wondered how the old man could have foreseen this episode. Yet Payaba had! The past shaman's insight and prophecy baffled Joe. "What does it mean?" he asked Morning Star.

Morning Star studied him closely. This was the first time she had heard of the *wowanyake*, a vision coming true before her senses. She was stirred by the news of the woman in Payaba's vision long ago, as Joe had asked for a female helper now! Her actions were justified, foretold! The vision matched Joe and the current situation perfectly! She had done nothing more than be used and guided by the Great Spirit! She was blessed and honored and proud. What did it matter who defeated their foes and won peace? She must prove her mettle to become that vision woman. Yet she replied, "*Slolwaye sni;* I do not know." She needed to learn more before she could explain things to Joe.

"Morning Star told him such things on the trail," Night Stalker charged. "He is not Sky Warrior. He does not carry Oglala blood."

"I did not tell him such things!" Morning Star retorted. "I did not know of them until this moment! I believe the vision and his words. Grandfather crossed our path so I could bring him to our camp to fulfill his destiny and ours. A vision must be obeyed, my brother."

"How do we know Payaba did not have a dream?" Knife-Slayer asked.

"If it was a sacred vision, why was I not shown it?" Hawk Eyes added.

"How can only a dream match what has come to be?" Morning Star reasoned, then reminded them, "All know Payaba was a great shaman who was taught by Mind-Who-Roams, the powerful medicine chief who led our tribe under Gray Eagle. His powers and insight have not vanished. Grandfather let Payaba live to speak to our people on this sun about the forgotten vision. Only Grandfather knows why He did not share the truth with Hawk Eyes."

Sun Cloud was shocked by the man's claims. Joe had no Indian coloring or bone structure; he bore no resemblance to Powchutu. He remembered his father's half brother. They had become close friends before Powchutu's death at the side of Gray Eagle during the white man's ambush in 1820. Afterward, he had signed a treaty with Derek Sturgis because he wanted to save his people, his family, his ways, and his lands. But troubles over the past few years had stolen his trust in the white man and their great leader. Now he must confront that same decision again: war or peace. "How do we know you are Tanner Gaston, son of Stede, grandson of Powchutu? Why did you not tell Morning Star? Or speak it sooner to me?"

"There are many charges against your band," Joe replied carefully. "I didn't want to reveal my identity until I was sure I could trust you. I thought you would speak and act differently to Joe than to Tanner. When the first whites came, you met them in peace. You did not resist settlers until they began to intrude in large numbers and to claim parts of your land. When gold—the yellow rock white man craves—was discovered in California, many prospectors and traders swarmed over your territory as countless bees. When land was purchased or claimed in Oregon Territory, white pioneers had to pass through your lands to reach it. Many stopped and remained. Troops were sent to patrol the area, to protect the whites, and to obtain peace with the Indians." He saw Sun Cloud nod.

"When the numbers of the settlers, traders, trappers, and soldiers became too large, your people and other tribes, as well, worried that they would steal all lands from you. There are many differences between the two peoples, Sun Cloud. The whites do not understand how bad it is to kill the buffalo that sustains your way of life. They cut timber to build homes, fences, forts, and barns. They don't realize that their guns scare off game. They don't understand why they can't let their stock graze on the same grasslands with buffalo, deer, and elk. They don't know that you believe they scar the face of Mother Earth when they clear land to grow food, to raise stock, and to build homes, forts, posts, churches, and schools. They clear land for roads because they're easier for wagons to travel than trails. They don't know Indian ways. The same is true of the Oglalas and other tribes; they don't understand the white man's ways. Many events in history are beyond the control of a leader and his people. What happens here is not, Sun Cloud. What you decide and do will become history—good or bad—and it will affect the lives of these people and all generations to follow."

Sun Cloud was impressed and silently concurred, but he responded, "Those are wise and good words, but they do not make you Tanner."

Joe did not comprehend how Payaba had prophesied his coming, but he could not ignore the strange truth. The mystical holy man had described him—not Tanner Gaston—accurately! Some power greater than all of them was at work and had led him—not Powchutu's grandson—to this place and problem. Yet he needed that blood connection and his lie to make the remainder of the "vision" come true.

Confident he was doing the right thing for all concerned, Joe reasoned, "There's no way I could have known about Payaba's vision to use it to deceive you.

I'm as shocked as you are to see me here today fulfilling it. I don't understand such magic and mysteries in life, but I know I'm here to help. I'll tell you what Powchutu told Stede and he told me. Powchutu lived and worked as a half-breed scout at the fort; that's where he met your mother, when she lived as Alisha Williams after she was stolen from your father by soldiers. When she was returned to your grandfather, she was proven to be Shalee, long-lost daughter of Chief Black Cloud. She didn't understand or believe such claims, and she fled Gray Eagle with Powchutu. Gray Eagle tracked her to St. Louis, told her the truth, and brought her home. Powchutu was said to be slain by the white enemy holding your mother captive, but he was only injured and had been sold into white slavery. For many years, he didn't remember his name. When the Great Spirit returned his mind, he left your grandparents in peace and married a half-white woman. But you know the truth about her," Joe hinted.

Yes, Sun Cloud knew the truth about Sarah Devane Gaston. She was the real Shalee, abducted daughter of Black Cloud, the woman whose identity his mother had used until her death the same day as Gray Eagle's. Yet only a few people knew and had known that secret because it would have been damaging to many. He also knew that Powchutu's mother was a Crow, not a Cheyenne as recorded on the family history hide. Love between enemies was torment for all involved. That was the main reason Running Wolf had been denied his firstborn son from a forbidden love for a Bird Woman and the impossible union between lovers of enemy tribes.

"When my grandfather returned to his people thirty-one years ago, he became Eagle's Arm," Joe continued. "Running Wolf had confessed the truth of his first son to Shalee, and she revealed it to Gray Eagle. All was forgiven and they became brothers. Powchutu rode to the fort with your brother Bright Arrow to spy on the soldiers; that's how he earned his way into your tribe. He became the friend of Sun Cloud, and you shared many talks. When he rode to the fort with Bright Arrow, he sent a letter to my father and told him such things. He rode at Gray Eagle's side the day both were slain. You became chief. You sent Derek Sturgis away with a treaty. Sturgis came to see my father and told him of *his* father's death. He gave my father a letter written by Powchutu before his death; it told us the truth of his birth and all that happened after his return to his homeland. It told the truth of my grandmother," he reminded the observant chief.

Joe withdrew the necklace he had taken from Tanner's pocket after his death, the one Stede had told him to keep for assistance. "You gave this *wanapin* to Sturgis that last day. It's a replica of Gray Eagle's that you used when you rode as his ghost to frighten the soldiers. Sturgis thought my father should have it. My father, Stede, gave it to me to use as a sign to you that I'm telling the truth. Oglala blood runs swift and thick in Stede Gaston's blood. As with his father when he grew old, he felt called home to his people and ancestral lands. We came to prevent war."

Sun Cloud caressed the *wanapin* of a white eagle and recalled the day he had placed it in Sturgis's hand. He remembered the days he had worn it, along with the chief's bonnet and garments, to "haunt" the soldiers who had murdered his father. "Seasons past, the whites and soldiers were afraid of the Oglalas because of my father's prowess and power, even of his ghost," he said. "That time is no more. Whites and soldiers grow too bold and greedy."

"They fear you just as much as they feared Gray Eagle. That's why Snake-Man is so eager to destroy your people. He knows he can't take over this territory as long as Oglalas remain here. He's tricking the Crow into attacking, and he supplies them with weapons and goods. He's tricking the whites and soldiers into believing your people want war and that you're raiding and killing. They see the image of Gray Eagle in you, Sun Cloud. You have his wits, courage, prowess, and power. They know you can band the Dakota tribes and your allies together, as Gray Eagle once did. The last time there was trouble, you met and worked with good white men. Together you battled evil white men. But there were and are evil Indians, too. Have you forgotten about Silver Hawk, Red Band, and renegades?"

Sun Cloud wished he hadn't mentioned the treacherous and traitorous Silver Hawk, who had been his wife's brother. "They are not Oglalas."

"Just as all Indians aren't the same, Sun Cloud, all whites aren't the same. Most whites want peace; they're looking for new lives here. Most soldiers are only obeying orders, so we have to make certain those orders are kind ones. Broken-Hand Fitzpatrick is a good white man. So is Captain Thomas at Fort Tabor. These men want to help your people."

"Soldiers provoke and attack us! If we retaliate, they say we challenge for war!" Night Stalker charged, dreading how Joe might effect his life.

"Even if you refuse to give me help with a guide and translator, at least don't attack for a while—only defend yourselves. Give me time to unmask Snake-Man and his tricks. Let me go to the Crow camps and gather clues. Let me prove your people are blameless and want peace. You don't want bloodshed; the whites don't want bloodshed. Allow me time to find this villain and then stop him. I'll ride to Fort Tabor and speak with Captain Thomas. Broken-Hand says I can trust him. I'll see if he has any clues. Then I'll return here and make plans with you."

"No!" Knife-Slayer shouted. "He will lead bluecoats to our camp."

"You have my word of honor, Sun Cloud; I will not betray my grandfather's people. When he's healed, I'll bring Stede to see you."

"A chief leads his tribe, but all warriors can speak, and the Council must vote. We must think on your words and claims, then call the Council to meeting. Morning Star, take him to my tepee to await our answer."

"Put him at the captive's post!" Knife-Slayer demanded. He did not want Joe around Morning Star any longer. He was suspicious and envious of the way the woman whom he desired, trusted and defended the stranger. He was determined to win the chief's daughter as his wife. He was furious about the days and nights she and the white man had spent together on the trail, alone.

Sun Cloud eyed the hostile warrior, and again worried over his effect on Night Stalker and others. "He will be our friend and ally until we prove he is our foe. Your chief can say and do this much without a vote."

"Thank you, Father," Morning Star said. "Come, Tanner. I give you food and tend your wound while the Council meets."

"For the sake of both sides, Sun Cloud, you must trust me and help me." Joe headed for the chief's colorful tepee with the Indian beauty. He glanced back to see Night Stalker, Knife-Slayer, and Hawk Eyes huddled together and talking. Dread washed over his weary body, because he knew the awesome power those warriors possessed. If they even suspected he'd lied, he was a dead man. If they sent for Tanner's father and Stede exposed him, he was in deep peril. Right now he wanted to learn why Morning Star had taken his side and kept his secret . . .

Morning Star guided Joe inside her home, then turned to him. "You lie," she remarked. "You not of Running Wolf bloodline."

"Why didn't you challenge me?" Joe inquired.

"I trust other words. I believe you here to help."

"I swear it. I hated to trick your father and people, but I had to save my life and get their help. You know what will happen if I fail. Tanner was my best friend. He wouldn't mind if I used his name and bloodline to save his father's people. Everything else is the truth, Morning Star."

"You seek to avenge Tanner's death," she said in slow speech.

"It's true that Stede is hurt and he's at Fort Laramie. It's true he's working for the President. Stede heard and read stories about what was happening out here. He wanted to come to learn where and how his father had lived. He wanted to meet his relatives and help them. He wanted to learn more about his ancestors. If Powchutu, his father, hadn't been denied his birthright, Powchutu would have been chief of the Oglalas, not Gray Eagle. If that were true, Stede could be chief now, not your father. But I think fate worked in the best way. No leaders could be better than Gray Eagle or your father. Fate sent Powchutu away, so his son could return at this time to offer a path to peace. It's Life-Circles touching again. When I came here with Stede and Tanner, it was to share adventures. Now that I've learned the truth and Tanner is dead, their task is mine."

"Great Spirit capture my tongue when you lie. I understand. You Sky Warrior, man in Payaba's vision long ago. Other man Stede Gaston, Grandfather's brother. I must ride with Joe. We friends; we must help each other. I wish to become warrior maiden in sacred vision."

"No, it's too dangerous. I don't want you hurt."

"I speak not with false pride, but I be best trained female. You say I ride with skill and fight as warrior. You say I save Joe's life. You say we make good pair. Great Spirit let Morning Star be captured for us to meet and work together. In Joe's mind, he know and want this. Why does Joe's heart battle what should be?"

Fatigued, hungry, and concerned with the council meeting, Joe's wits were not as sharp as usual. He didn't deny the truth that troubled his heart. "You know why, Morning Star. When peace is won and the treaty is signed, I must go far away. My family, home, and destiny are there; my Life-Circle is there."

"My family, home, and destiny here, so I must help save them."

"It's too dangerous for us to ride and work together. From the first moment I saw you in Zeke's camp, you gave me a funny feeling inside. It's best if I keep that feeling buried. With you at my side, my head wouldn't be clear. I have a hunger for you that I can't feed."

"You speak bold words to woman you know for short time," she replied as her heart raced.

Joe knew he must be honest. "I speak the truth as a warning to both of us. When I said I didn't want you hurt, I meant more than your body and more than by others. Our lives and cultures are different, Morning Star. With you as my helper, I'd be too tempted to forget that. If we did, it would be hard and painful for both of us when all this is over."

"If you not take best woman, you may fail and die. We both strong and brave. We let nothing weaken our wills and defeat our duties."

"That's also why you kept quiet; you didn't want me killed by your people. Don't you see how we've been pulled toward each other?"

"I silent because of sacred vision."

"You held silent before it was revealed. When I look into your eyes, Morning

Star, I see the same things I'm feeling inside. You would never leave here with me, and I can stay only until winter. We mustn't trap ourselves in a hopeless situation. I don't want to hurt you, and I don't want to be hurt. Please forget your desire to become this vision woman. If I lost control with you, Sun Cloud would slay me—not to mention that the mission would fail."

Before Morning Star could respond, her mother returned to the tepee with fresh water. She turned to do her chores to hide her expression.

"*Loyacin he?*" Singing Wind asked.

"English, Mother," the girl reminded in a gentle tone.

"Are you hungry?" the older woman inquired once more to Joe.

"Yes, ma'am. We rode hard and fast to get here before the rescue party was sent out."

Singing Wind dished up meat stew and served it with buffalo berry wine and bread pones that were speckled with dried fruits and nuts. She handed them to the white man, then observed him as he ate. It was the Indian custom for men to eat first, then women and children; but Joe was not Indian, so Morning Star joined him. As the couple devoured the best meal they had eaten in days, Singing Wind watched with interest. She couldn't help but wonder if her daughter was to be the woman in Payaba's vision. Despite her fears and worries, she couldn't help but hope that was true. In her younger days, her Blackfoot people had called Singing Wind—headstrong, bold, and impulsive. She had been one with deep and strong emotions, with a wish to do more than a woman's work. She had wanted adventure and excitement. She had learned the same skills that warriors possess, the same ones her daughter now possessed. How could she fault Morning Star's behavior and traits when they had been hers so long ago?

Each of them was from a long line and respected tepees of chiefs. Morning Star's maternal grandfather had been the Blackfoot chief Brave Bear, adopted son of Chief Black Cloud. Following Brave Bear's death, she herself had been raised by Chief Medicine Bear and trained by his sons.

What worried Singing Wind were the powerful currents she was perceiving between her youngest child and the stranger. If Morning Star turned to one of the enemy, she and her family would know great loss of face. A marriage between them was not possible or right. For either to seek one would cause bitterness, antagonism, and suffering.

Yet the older woman knew how willful and strong love could be, and how fast it could work. She had pursued and yielded to Sun Cloud while promised to his brother! Even knowing what anguish and shame her actions and desires could cause she had been unable to control herself; it had been the same for her husband. They had risked humiliation and banishment, perhaps death, to win each other. Everything had worked out, and they had been happy for thirty-one years.

There had been other mixed unions in her husband's bloodline. Gray Eagle had joined a white woman; Bright Arrow had joined a white woman; Alisha/Shalee's alleged father, Chief Black Cloud, had joined a white woman. Singing Wind knew that Sun Cloud and his people would fiercely resist more enemy blood weakening his Indian line. If Morning Star leaned toward a paleface, it would appear that his bloodline preferred white—enemy—mates over their own kind. It would bring great *yuonihansni*—shame, loss of face, dishonor—to their tepee. Added to that sting, mixed marriages were hard on a couple. Whose ways would they choose? Which side would they take during warfare?

Singing Wind knew how like herself Morning Star was. She prayed her daughter would not forget her traditions, family, duties, and people. She prayed her child would not yearn for what could not be. She prayed that her instincts and intuition were mistaken.

"Takucahe, Ina?" Morning Star asked her mother what was wrong.

Singing Wind remembered that Joe had said he knew a little Lakota, so she responded in English, "We talk later, Daughter. Eat. Rest."

As he ate and waited, Joe wondered what was taking place in the council meeting, as it affected more than his own fate.

Morning Star asked her mother if she could go see Buckskin Girl while the council was in progress. Singing Wind gave her permission. After telling Joe to relax and that she would return soon, Morning Star left. But she did not go to the tepee of Flaming Star to visit his daughter, her friend. She sneaked toward the meeting lodge to eavesdrop. She was glad the large and colorfully marked tepee was erected in an area near concealing trees that would aid in her bold action.

The Oglalas' camp was situated between black rock formations and a large lake, amidst fragrant pines and spruces. It offered more privacy than their nomadic summer camps on the Plains when tepees formed ever-widening circles around the chief's tepee and meeting lodge. Here, they spread out amongst trees, along the lakeside, and before hills and rocks.

Night had settled on the land, and a full moon's light was dulled by curious clouds that gave her an eerie sensation. Women were inside their conical dwellings, occupied with children and chores. Council members and other warriors were at the meeting. Any other people were in their tepees or at waterside campfires discussing the strange event that had occurred earlier. She passed rope and branch corrals at many places, as there was no need in this safe and secluded location for warriors to picket their horses beside their tepees. She was relieved they knew her scent and stayed calm.

Morning Star slipped from tree to tree, halting to look and listen at each one to make certain her forbidden behavior was not discovered. She had to hear what was being said and by whom . . .

Inside the crowded lodge, the ritual pipe smoking and prayers had taken a long time with so many participating. The meeting in 1831 where Payaba had revealed his vision had been attended by the Council. Tonight, all warriors of high-standing were present to voice opinions.

Members of the O-Zu-Ye Wicasta stood in circles around the councilmen who were seated on buffalo skins in the center of the group. There were several warrior societies represented whose jobs were to preserve order in camp and during moves and hunts. Some punished offenders of their laws. Some guarded the camp, led battles, and oversaw feasts and dances. Some were the keepers of the tribe's heritage and traditions. All were highly trained warriors with numerous coups and great prowess. Most were members of the Tall Ones or Kit-Fox cults, military societies that demanded courage and honor. A few were members of the Sacred Bow cult, to which Sun Cloud had belonged in years past. Presently, Night Stalker and Knife-Slayer were Sacred Bow carriers: two of four men who took places at the fronts of battles. It was a perilous rank and had to be earned. The Sacred Bow test was as difficult and dangerous as the Sun Dance. After proving himself, a Sacred Bow carrier could resign with honor, as Sun Cloud had done when he became chief.

Sun Cloud, other chiefs, shamen—past and present—and mature, renowned warriors were members of the Big Belly society. They were responsible for the tribe's leadership. Since they were advanced in years and their skills were not as sharp as in earlier days, ten younger warriors—"shirt wearers"—were appointed by them to carry out their orders. Night Stalker and Knife-Slayer were also "shirt wearers."

Payaba, a Big Belly, was one of the few Oglalas who was also a member of the Elk Dreamer cult. It was considered powerful and special and he took his rank seriously. He knew that if a man disobeyed a vision, he would be punished, usually by death. He prayed his people would heed his vision of long ago. He waited with patience.

Wolf Eyes, the ceremonial chief, said before taking a seat, "In the east where Wi rises, the whites are as many as the drops of rain that have fallen on our land since Grandfather created it for us. They do not come here to nourish it as rain does; they come to flood, destroy, and change it. But their weapons have as great power as the lightning. If they grow many and strong and we challenge them, they will roll over us as the mighty thunder when it roars with anger."

The man once called Standing Tree stood tall and proud after he rose to speak. Long white hair traveled his shoulders. His eyes were clouded by age, but he saw things these days with a sharp mental vision. Numerous wrinkles lined his face, but did not take away from his pleasant expression. Gnarled fingers made tasks difficult for him, but he never complained. There was a gentleness about him that men like Hawk Eyes and his son mistook for weakness. Yet his resonant voice and dignity evoked love and respect in nearly all of his people. "We cannot fight our allied foes and the white-eyes. If we go from battle to battle, how can we make enough weapons? Or hunt buffalo for food and other needs? How can we laugh and sing, with many to place upon scaffolds? How can our women have children without fathers to plant their seeds? If we ride into battle, who will protect our camps and people? If we do not make peace, there will be no time for hunts, joys, smiles, births, or ceremonies. There will be only battles, sadness, tears, deaths, and war dances. I say we fight only in defense. I say we make truce with the whites-eyes and Crow."

"Both are evil," Night Stalker said. "The Crow have slain many of our tribe. They attacked and killed my uncle, Bright Arrow and his mate. They have become friends with the whites. They are unworthy of our truce."

"Their truce with the white-eyes lets them survive and grow stronger. Have you forgotten how many Bird People we have slain for their bad deeds? How many prizes we have brought home after raiding their camps? We do not have to make them allies and blood brothers as with the Cheyenne and Blackfoot; but we can make truce with the Crow, Pawnee, and Shoshone. The white-eyes made truce with their enemies, the Mexicans and the British. If Indian nations remain separate and foes, the united white one will be strongest. One by one, they will defeat nation by nation, and take all Indian lands. The badger is fierce and cunning, but we respect his skills and territory. Can it not be the same with our white and Indian foes? If the white-eyes and Crow band together, the Oglala will be destroyed, and Crow will get our lands. The Great Spirit has sent us a path to truce and survival. We must help Sky Warrior ride it for us."

"We fight our own battles and make our own truces. We need no white man to do them for us. I say, kill him, then ride against our foes."

"That is why the Crow and white-eyes will listen to him, Knife-Slayer, because his skin is white. The Great White Chief honors Tanner's words, and all white-eyes must obey the White Chief's words and their laws."

"The White Chief's words, laws, and ways are for *his* people. They are not for Oglalas and our brothers. They have made what they call reservations in many places and confined whole tribes as captives. Have you forgotten what the trapper told us the winter after your . . . vision? He said the White Chief had made a law called the 'Indian Removal Act' so they can drive the Cherokees and other tribes toward the setting sun. If we do not resist, they will come to drive us far from our lands. We must live free or die fighting."

"The treaty will protect our lives and territory, Knife-Slayer. To give a challenge with no hope of victory is foolish and deadly."

"A new treaty will protect us only until the whites crave more land. Such a warning was in your past vision," Catch the Bear reminded.

"It is so, but that is a battle for another season. While there is peace, we can grow strong with children, weapons, and skills. If we battle every moon, we will grow small and weak; Oglalas will perish. All living things need rest, as the trees in winter. When spring comes, they are strong enough to grow taller and larger. If foes cut into their bodies and chop off their arms, they die. It is the same with the Dakota Nation."

"Payaba is wise and his words reach deep," Sun Cloud said. "We must not speak or act too quickly and rashly. What do others say?"

Flaming Star, son of White Arrow who was best friend to Gray Eagle, said, "My heart says the words of our chief and our past shaman are wise. My hatred of the Crow is great for slaying my friend Bright Arrow. I took many Crow scalps and ponies in revenge. But it is time for my sons and grandchildren to know peace. I will bury my hatred to seek it for them."

"When the Cheyenne and Blackfoot unite with the Seven Council Fires," Night Stalker said, "we will be stronger than the whites or the Crow. It is wrong to crawl as a frightened or wounded dog to our foes. We must fight."

"Do you forget Payaba's vision?" Talking Rock asked. "It commands truce. Speak it again, Wise One, for all to hear and understand. Tell all the white man said, for those who missed his words."

So for those who might not have caught everything during the excitement and loud noise, Payaba repeated his past vision. Then, Sun Cloud related what Joe had said earlier.

"We do not know whose hands claimed the messages Powchutu sent long ago," Knife-Slayer debated. "Any eyes that touched upon them would learn the secrets inside. We do not know if Stede Gaston told others what his father told him? We do not know if this white man is his son. A hunter and warrior must live by instincts. Mine say he is not Sky Warrior."

"How would he know of the vision he fulfills?" Plenty Coups asked.

"It was told to the Council and others long ago," Knife-Slayer replied. "Warriors and hunters sometimes fall prey to white captors. Perhaps the vision was forced from one's lips."

"No Red Heart would reveal our sacred secrets," Tracks Good refuted, "not even if he is tortured and slain."

"Not all Red Hearts are as strong and wise as members of our great council," Knife-Slayer retorted. "The white man has whiskey to dull wits and strange sicknesses to burn heads with fever. Some men will speak secrets when their minds are stolen by such evils. At Night Stalker's side, we ride against our foes and shoot them from their horses with our Sacred Bows. They have never failed us. We must do so again."

"You cannot make and fire enough arrows to win such a battle," Sun Cloud replied, "even with a powerful weapon of the Sacred Bow Cult. It would be hard for the same white man to steal the letters written long ago and sent far away to Stede," he pointed out, "to learn of the past vision here, and to have his face match it. I do not believe such a thing is possible. What do you say, Hawk Eyes?" he questioned the medicine chief.

"My heart and mind war over all I have seen and heard. I must seek counsel from the Great Spirit before I know what is right for our people. When I traveled to our Holy Mountain for guidance, I did not see this white man in my vision. If Payaba's vision was real, not a dream, perhaps this man is not the Sky Warrior who rode in it. Evil can work in powerful and mysterious ways. The words of my son could hold strange truth."

"The words of Grandfather that I revealed long ago are the same as the story he told to us. I say, let him live and ride to the fort. If he lies, we will slay him when he returns." Payaba said, glancing at Sun Cloud to see if he agreed.

Hawk Eyes spoke again. "After I seek my vision, if it says he is Sky Warrior, we will help him. If it says he is not, we will remove his evil tongue and heart and feed them to the death-eating birds. We have known much evil from the whites. They will not change their bad hearts."

"What of the other Dakota tribes?" Jumping Elk asked.

Long Horn, the war chief, replied, "When Sun Cloud and Lone Horn visited the camps of our brothers, some spoke for peace and some for war. Brave Bear of the Brule wars against the whites and attacks travelers on the white man's trail west. Little Thunder of another Brule tribe speaks for war. Wamdesapa's son leads his Santee as renegades; Inkpaduta's band is for war. Tashunkopipape sees the power of the soldiers and restrains his Oglala band until we choose a path, at which time he will ride the same one. Red Cloud has joined the Bad Faces Band to his mother's Old Smoke Band. He resists the white man's encroachment, and he carries much power among the Tetons; but he desires peace with honor. Sitting Bull and Gall of the Hunkpapas will join us in battle; they do not trust the whites. Jumping Buffalo will vote for peace. He has many white friends, as the white trapper who gave him his medicine symbol from the raccoon and calls him Spotted Tail. Even at ten winters, his nephew Crazy Horse rides with him. Many say he will be a great warrior and he urges his uncle to fight. Wacouta, who took Walking Buffalo's chief bonnet of the Red Wings, wants peace and will sign a new treaty. Walking Buffalo signed treaties in what the white man calls '1815' and '1825,' but he refused to sign again fourteen winters past. Most of the Santee Council Fires warred at the sides of the British against the whites when they fought their two great wars seventy-five and thirty-nine winters past. The British promised not to enter Dakota lands if the Dakotas helped them defeat their white colonists."

"The colonists were stronger and defeated the British even with the help of the Santee tribes," Payaba reminded. "The whites are more numerous and stronger now. How can Lakotas alone defeat such a force? We cannot."

"Once," Flaming Star said, "the Dakota Nation ruled more land than the whites and other tribes claim as theirs. But the woodland bands of the Santee

Council Fires to the east let the Chippawas and whites push them closer to us. They were foolish to make trade with Pike for part of their territory; Mother Earth cannot and must not be sold."

Catch the Bear repeated the story he had been told, "They know this. They tricked the whites to get money to buy guns to battle their foes. Pike's Treaty is worthless. The same is true of the Prairie de Chien Council and Treaty twenty-six winters past. The whites think their words and papers made truces and boundaries. They think they gave the Dakotas a large territory. The land belongs to Grandfather and is for the Dakotas' use. The white man says we took these lands from our foes, and they will take them from us. But Tetons have been here since before the fathers of our father's fathers. We have always been Dwellers of the Plains, as our name says, and we will always remain here."

"Our Indian brothers to the east—the Sauk, Fox, Shawneee, Ottawan, and Chippewa—where are they now?" Hawk Eyes asked. "Indians to the south—Cherokee, Seminole, and others—where are they now? What of the Nez Perce and Yakima to the west? What of the Kiowas, Apaches, and Comanches who fiercely battle the whites for three winters now? What of the Cheyenne and Arapaho whose lands the whites look upon with greed these suns? The whites want us to live and think as they do. They want us to worship their god. They say we must accept their laws. They write words in what they call newspapers to arouse all whites against us. Some chiefs did not understand the meanings of their treaties; they believed the whites gave them supplies to use their lands, not to buy them. The whites used the papers the chiefs signed to get the white government to take Indian lands when the chiefs argued and resisted leaving. Some whites are good, but they are few. The bad whites are strongest and rule all whites."

"*Hocoka* is the center of all things," Walks Tall said. "All power comes from the Sacred Hoop. As long as it is unbroken, our people will live and flourish. If we let the whites break our Circle of Life, we will die."

"We did not invade their lands to the east; they must not invade ours. Most come as settlers, not warriors," Thunder Spirit, brother of Flaming Star, stated. "Their armies are great. We do not want our sons and daughters, our parents and their children slain. We must not challenge until we are certain of victory. The whites do not understand our ways. They believe they purchased Dakota lands. One man cannot sell another's horses. The Santee cannot sell the Plains. The French cannot sell the Plains. Thunder Spirit can say Walks Tall's horses are his, but it would not be so. If Thunder Spirit steals Pawnee horses, they are his to claim and sell. The French did not conquer our territory, so they cannot sell it to the whites."

"We accepted many whites among us," Night Stalker said. "When my uncle Bright Arrow traveled with the men called Lewis and Clark, he saw and learned many things. He told my people much when he returned. That was long ago, before I was born. Since that season, many whites have followed their trail to the big waters, into the territory called Oregon. They make homesteads there and push out villages. When Indians resist, whites say they are provoked to war, so they can kill and take all. Other tribes accepted them as friends, but whites did not honor that friendship. It will be the same in our territory. We must stand against them this season."

Charging Dog, one of the oldest men in the Big Belly Society, asked, "Many have forgotten or do not know of the visit from Tecumseh, the Shawnee chief, before the last white war with the British. Tecumseh called Dakota tribes together to warn us of white danger. Many Teton bands went to the council. Many Oglalas went: Gray Eagle, White Arrow, Plenty Coups, Charging Dog, Payaba when he was Standing Tree, and others. The Shawnee chief told of eastern tribes who were massacred by white settlers. He spoke of camps and villages burned by bluecoats. Each winter, the whites journey closer to our lands, claiming all they pass. Tecumseh came to urge all Indian nations to band together against the whites. He told how they greeted the first whites in peace; whites were given food, blankets, and help. Whites grew strong; they wanted more land, from the rising to the setting suns; they killed all Indians who resisted their desires. He told of how whites hated, cheated, insulted, and abused Indians. We did not join him, and his warnings have come true. The Great Spirit gave the whites lands across the big waters and gave us these lands. The greed of the whites brought them across the big waters and into our lands. I say for Hawk Eyes to read the words spoken by Tecumseh, written on the Tribal Buffalo Record. Those words are as powerful as Payaba's old vision."

"A vision must be obeyed, Charging Dog," the elderly man urged.

"It was long ago, Payaba," Knife-Slayer said. "You should seek another vision. Perhaps Grandfather no longer wants us to obey the old one."

Payaba did not display the anger he felt toward the troublemaker. "If such is true, Knife-Slayer, why did he send Sky Warrior to us?"

"Evil is strong these suns, Old One. Perhaps Evil sent the white man to trick us. I have not heard the warnings of Tecumseh. Read them, Father. All must hear them before we vote which medicine is strongest."

All of the council members and warriors were silent as the shaman retrieved the tribal record from its place in the meeting lodge.

Hawk Eyes stood to read it, so all could hear the words clearly, as he wanted the vote to go the same way his son did. "Tecumseh told us; 'Brothers, if you do not unite with us, they will first destroy us, and then you will fall an easy prey to them. They have destroyed many nations of red men because they were not united. The white people send runners amongst us; they wish to make us enemies, that they may sweep like devastating winds. Where today is many other once powerful tribes? They have vanished before the avarice and oppression of the white man, as snow before a summer sun. Think not you can remain indifferent to the common danger. Your people, too, will soon be as fallen leaves driven before the wintry storms. Every year our white intruders become more greedy, oppressive, and overbearing. Let us defend to the last warrior our country, our homes, our liberty, and the graves of our fathers.' His words have come to be."

Everyone was silent and thoughtful for a time.

Sun Cloud reflected on words his mother had told him long ago: "You must be strong, Sun Cloud," she said, "for many dark days are ahead. Being a chief is difficult and painful, but your father has trained you well. Lasting peace is gone forever. You must defend your people; you must guide them wisely. You must seek truce if the whites will allow it; only through peace can the Oglalas survive. You must learn to share our lands, or the whites will take them by force. You must learn to accept them, or they will destroy all you know and love. They are powerful, my son. Know and accept this fact, or you will battle for a victory which can never be won. Seek peace with honor, even if you must taste it as a bitter defeat . . . Some white leaders and peoples are not evil; it is those you must seek out and work with. . . . I lived with the whites, and I know them. Truce, however bitter, is better than Mother Earth with no Oglalas. One day, the white man will realize his evil and he will halt it. Until that day, you must make certain the Oglalas survive." Sun Cloud remembered the last words she had spoken to him: "Life is often brief and hard, and you must feast on its rewards each day. . . . Do not allow the white man's hostilities to harden your heart." His mother had been a wise and kind woman, a white woman. Yet her words were as hard to accept today as they had been shortly before her death. But he was chief, and he must think of his people before himself.

Sun Cloud rose from his buffalo mat. His fingers clutched the *wanapin* Tanner Gaston had returned to him. His other fingers touched the eagle feather behind his head as if drawing strength and wisdom from the man it represented. He gazed around the circles of men of many ages and ranks. He had fought battles at the sides of most of them. He had watched some grow to manhood. Some reminded him of fathers or brothers lost during raids or wars with whites and with Indian foes.

Sun Cloud glanced at his thirty-year-old son. He knew Night Stalker was not ready to become chief, and he wondered where and how he had failed to make him the man *his* father had made *him*. If only Gray Eagle and Shalee had lived long enough to influence and guide Night Stalker along the right trail, as they had done with him. At his son's age, he had been chief for seven years. If he believed his son was ready to accept the chief's bonnet, he would yield it to the skilled warrior. At fifty-four, Sun Cloud felt soul-tired from years of bearing burdens for so many people; he wanted to enjoy the rest of his life. He was willing to complete his Life Circle as a Big Belly. But Night Stalker was too hotheaded, too impulsive, too consumed by hatred for the whites and a hunger for war, too swayed by Knife-Slayer, for him to turn leadership over to his only son. But for now there was the decision to make about Tanner Gaston and his mission. "We must vote," he said.

Morning Star's heart drummed with trepidation. After listening to everyone's words, she could not guess how the decision would go. It was getting late, and she couldn't remain hidden there much longer. Her mother might become worried and search for her. If her mischief was discovered, everyone would blame Joe for her bad conduct. With reluctance, she started to leave, then more words halted her in mid-step . . .

Chapter Five

❧   "*I*s there more to say before our sticks are tossed?" Sun Cloud asked?

"There is a glowing ring around the full moon tonight," Payaba said. "It is an omen to say this time is important. We must vote for peace."

Knife-Slayer had seen the hazy look that seemed to encircle the moon. "I say it is black magic, evil magic, to warn us to vote for war."

Hawk Eyes wanted to agree, but held silent.

"Our vote this moon must be only about the white man's life," Flaming Star suggested. "I say, let him live. We must give him time to prove his words and learn if he can win us peace with honor."

Thunder Spirit added to his brother's words. "What harm can giving him his life for saving Morning Star's do? What harm can it do to let him seek and destroy the one who sells weapons to our foes? What harm can it do to let him work for an honorable peace? If he fails, we can war later."

"His task will distract our foes while we hunt buffalo and make more weapons," Walks Tall said.

"Payaba's words carry much strong medicine," Catch the Bear said. "We must test his vision and this white man. Free him to prove himself to us."

When it was silent for a while, Wolf Eyes assumed everyone had given their feelings and opinions. He explained the voting procedure. "If you wish to free the white man and to allow him to attempt his mission, toss your white stick into the basket. If you do not, vote with your black stick."

Hawk Eyes spoke again. "If the vote is no, he must die. If he is slain, we will call another council to talk war. It is true he rescued Morning Star, but if we vote we do not trust him, he must die to protect the secrets he has learned in our camp."

"I say that the white man's story matches Payaba's vision," Sun Cloud told his people, "so we must accept both as truth, as Grandfather's message. We must let Tanner prove he is unlike other whites and will side with us. If peace lies within his grasp, we must not slay him. It is true his words are hard to accept and obey. Look at our tribal record," he said, pointing to the pictorial history of the Oglala depicted on a tanned buffalo hide. "Until these past few summers few conflicts were painted on its surface after our treaty. The 'time of great danger' Payaba spoke of has arrived, so have two men who match the vision. I speak for peace. The day for a great war will come, but this is not that season. If we do not allow Sky Warrior to defeat Snake-Man and the Crow, our lands will run fast and dark with

Oglala blood. That will be Grandfather's punishment for not obeying the sacred vision he gave to our shaman long ago."

The men who were wavering in their decisions made them after the chief's final words. Sun Cloud was loved, awed, and respected. Many older eyes still saw the image of the legendary Gray Eagle in him. Others knew what a wise and brave leader he had been for years. All eyes closed and the basket was passed from man to man. Sticks were dropped inside.

When the basket was dumped before Wolf Eyes, the ceremonial chief, for him to count the votes, all sticks were white—yes—except for three.

Sun Cloud guessed that two "no's" were from Night Stalker and Knife-Slayer; he presumed the third was from Hawk Eyes. It disappointed and worried him that his son—the future chief—and the tribe's shaman were so against peace, if won with honor. The other "no" did not surprise him.

"He is to go free," Wolf Eyes announced.

Knife-Slayer told the group, *"Puzani ni kte lo. I'ye sica yelo,"* and left.

Morning Star watched the furious man stalk away, having behaved as no honorable warrior should have. Before others left and she was exposed, she hurried to Flaming Star's tepee and called to her friend.

Buckskin Girl came out and embraced her, then started to ask rapid-fire questions.

Morning Star smiled and silenced her. "I must hurry back to my tepee. I am fine and will tell you all things tomorrow." She rushed home.

In the meeting lodge, Sun Cloud did not heed Knife-Slayer's warning: "You will see you are wrong. He is bad." He was eager to reach his tepee and speak with Tanner, the grandson of his long-dead friend. He quickly thanked his close friends for their votes, then departed.

When the chief ducked into his tepee, he glanced first at his wife, who was sewing on a new shirt for him, then looked at his daughter, who was beading a new pair of moccasins. Morning Star smiled at him, but her eyes were filled with concern over the fate of her white rescuer. Well trained in their ways and a respectful girl, she did not question him about the council meeting. Sun Cloud thought how like her mother she was in looks and personality. If only she were a son, an older son, she would be worthy of their chief's bonnet. It was sad that Night Stalker didn't have more of her good traits. Sun Cloud went to sit beside the dying fire near the man who had entered their lives to change them forever.

Joe met the chief's probing gaze. It told him nothing of their decision. He was impressed by this great man, and lying to him gnawed at his conscience. One day he would confess the truth. If his mission succeeded, hopefully Sun Cloud would understand and accept the necessity of his deceit. Although anxious, he waited for the older man to speak.

"Many whites have visited our lands and camps," he began. "The first ones mentioned on our tribal record came in my grandfather's day, Verendrye brothers who were accepted as friends. Many trappers and traders followed. One called Manuel Lisa created the Missouri Fur Company and had many posts and men. He died the year my father was slain. Pierre Chouteau claimed his territory and called his post American Fur Company. First they came for beaver, muskrat, and otter; later, for any and all hides and pelts. More posts were built: Pratte at Pierre,

Columbia at Lookout, McMichael to where the Sahiyela and Mnisose rivers join. Each season, more follow."

Joe knew he was referring to the confluence of the Cheyenne and Missouri rivers where Orin McMichael owned and ran a trading post. He and Tanner hadn't made it that far north before his friend's death, but they had been told the Scotsman was friendly with all Indians.

"Now, they seek deer, elk, and buffalo. They kill without feeling and with much waste. If the game are all taken or frightened away, the Oglalas will die. When Indians try to trade furs to them, they pay little, and they ask high for their goods. They are filled with greed and deceit."

Singing Wind handed both men buffalo berry wine to wet their throats and to calm them during the tense situation. She returned to her sitting mat and backrest to work and listen.

"We have helped the bluecoats. In what you call '1823,' we rode with Colonel Leavenworth and U.S. troops to defeat the Arikaras. We let the man called George Catlin come to our villages and paint pictures of us on strange paper. We let the one called Francis Parkman visit camps and write words about our tribes and Nation. He stayed long with Chiefs Old Smoke and Whirlwind. Lewis and Clark journeyed our lands. They drew pictures of trees, animals, and plants. They made maps of forests, streams, hills, and trails. They were not harmed. Joe Kenny, father of my brother's wife, was our friend. Soldiers like Sturgis and Ames were our friends. In the old days, few wars came between whites and Indians. Those days are gone."

Joe held silent, alert, and respectful while Sun Cloud sipped his drink. He didn't know which direction this talk was taking.

"Once the Dakotas ruled from Canada to the Platte River, from Minnesota to the Yellowstone. Many of those hunting grounds and streams have been stolen by whites. Tribes have left them or been pushed out by soldiers. When your people signed a treaty with the French called the Louisiana Purchase, it was wrong. They did not own these lands. Now your people will not confess their mistake and leave us in peace. Our ancestors live in the winds that blow over us, in the rains that refresh Mother Earth, in the trees and grasses and flowers that make her beautiful. They live in the glows of the sun and moon, and in all forces of nature that claimed their bodies from death scaffolds. Their spirits live in the hearts and memories of those left behind. They live in the legends they created, in the images of their bloodlines, in the scenes on the tribal record hide, in our songs and stories, and in all they taught us. Now your people want us to forget our dead, our ways, our world. How can a man forget all he is? Does that not make peace cost too much? If you steal all a man has, what good is survival without his spirit and dignity?"

"A good man can't forget what he is, Sun Cloud," Joe concurred. "That's why Stede Gaston came here. We don't want your lands, and we want to make certain others don't steal them. A man can't live without his dignity and honor. The Americans know Dakotas sided with the British during their war for independence and during the War of 1812; what they don't know is that it wasn't the Oglalas. The Dakota Nation is viewed as a whole, and the Americans know it's a strong and large nation. They don't want to fight you."

"They ask for treaties. When we sign, they use them to make soldiers force us from our lands. If we do not mark our names on papers, they cannot lie about us; they cannot say we sold them our lands."

"If you'll sign the new treaty with Fitzpatrick, I'll read every word to you. I'll make certain no tricks or lies are included. You can record every word in your language, then have them sign your paper. If trouble comes again, you can read the treaty to the authorities to prove you're right."

"Their words on paper are worthless."

"No, Sun Cloud," Joe answered him. "Treaties are legal. They're like laws; they can't be broken unless your side declares war on us. If one side wants changes made, a meeting must be called so differences can be discussed. A treaty isn't and can't be destroyed without a good reason. We signed treaties with the British. They're our friends now. We haven't battled in thirty-six years. We visit their countries and trade with them, and they do the same with us. Can you say that about the Crow? President Fillmore will honor the treaty."

"What if another white chief takes his place?"

"We do change leaders more than your people, but new leaders honor treaties and laws other Presidents made. It's our way, Sun Cloud. If you made a treaty with us, wouldn't Night Stalker honor it when he became chief? Wouldn't he need a good reason to break it?"

Sun Cloud watched the white man as he said, "Night Stalker does not trust whites; he voted against you. If I am slain or hand the bonnet over to him, he will speak against you and for war. Most follow the chief."

Joe was stunned by that revelation, as Morning Star had told him the voting was cast in secret, even though most men voiced their opinions aloud. Unless everyone voted against him and all sticks were black, how could Sun Cloud know which way his son voted? His concern showed.

Morning Star came to sit beside her father. She could stand the suspense no longer, as she knew how worried Joe must be. She gazed into her father's eyes with a pleading she hoped would coax exposure of his good news.

Sun Cloud grasped her unspoken request and the warring emotions within her. He was concerned over how the vote would affect his family. He prayed that she was not the female in Payaba's vision, but feared she was. He speculated that was why the two had been thrown together. He was acquainted with her skills, so he knew she could handle the task. But he didn't want her traveling with Tanner alone for so long.

"What did you vote, Sun Cloud?" Joe asked to break the silence.

"I voted to free you," the older man revealed, then explained the meeting to the other man. "If you lie, I will slay you with my own hands," he warned. "You will leave when the sun rises. Go to the fort and speak with the man you trust there. Return and meet with us. A female will be chosen to travel with you. We will give you until the end of buffalo season to seek and destroy our enemy, or until the bluecoats attack. We will not raid against whites or Crow. If you fail, you must leave our lands."

"It is agreed, Sun Cloud." Joe smiled in relief.

"It is good, Father," Morning Star concurred in excitement. Now that her father had related the events of the meeting, she wouldn't have to fear unmasking herself with careless slips.

"We shall see, Daughter."

"I will gather supplies to be ready to ride when . . . Tanner returns."

"No, Morning Star."

"I am best trained," she argued as dismay filled her.

"Your father's right, Morning Star," Joe concurred prematurely.

"There will be a contest while he is gone. All women who wish to enter may do so. The winner will ride with Tanner Gaston. It will be the female with the most skills and courage who wins. All must have the chance to become She-Who-Rode-With-The-Sky-Warrior. Grandfather did not reveal her face and name to Payaba, but he will choose her in the test."

Joe didn't like that idea, as he somehow knew Morning Star had spoken the truth when she told him she was the best trained. Still, it was a fair way to make a choice. If Sun Cloud's daughter won, it wouldn't be the same as him selecting her above the others, so it shouldn't cause jealousy and trouble. He was elated and alarmed by the prospect of being alone with her.

Morning Star beamed with joy and anticipation. She was eager for the contest to begin, as she felt confident about winning it. What other girl in their tribe could shoot, ride, hunt, and fight as she could? None.

"We must sleep. Have you tended his wound?" Sun Cloud asked.

"*Han, Ata,*" she replied.

"You sleep there," he told Joe, pointing to a mat away from the other three which were positioned close tonight on the other side.

"*Pilamaya, Mahpiya Wi,*" Joe thanked him.

"It is good you learn our tongue and ways. Knowing them, you will not offend with mistakes that can bring shame and death." Sun Cloud glanced at his radiant daughter, then returned his meaningful gaze to the newcomer.

Joe captured the hint in the chief's words and nodded understanding and acceptance, though he knew how hard it would be to keep his word.

They took their places to pass an unusual night. The small, rock-enclosed fire had died. For a time, an unoffensive odor of smoke lingered in the conical dwelling. The top flap was adjusted for the flow of fresh air, but the entry flap was closed for privacy. Except for distant sounds of nocturnal birds, insects, and frogs, it was quiet in this secluded area.

The clean, neat tepee told Joseph Lawrence that Singing Wind was an organized woman. He knew that she and Morning Star had tanned these hides, gathered these poles, and constructed this cozy surrounding. Even though it was too dim to see much, his keen eyes and alert senses had taken in many details during the evening. Six large poles—tall, straight, and debarked—made a sturdy framework, then many slender ones leaned against them to provide strength, support, and shaping. The fifteen-foot pointed cluster was covered by buffalo skins that were laced together by deft hands to stay in place, especially during brisk winds and storms.

A colorfully painted dew-cloth, an added layer of brain-tanned hides stitched together to form a lengthy roll, was suspended from a height of five feet to the ground; this strip discouraged drafts at the base and provided added warmth and beauty for the simple home. It also diverted the rain that could run down the poles to the outside, and created an air flow that forced smoke upward and out the top flap. The numerous lining ties were secured to a rope that went from post to post and was attached to each. Possessions hung from the strong rope: medicine bag, parfleches—the equal of white man's drawers and chests for clothing and such—sewing pouch, weapons—which women never handled—backrests, larger pouches for holding dishes and cookware. When not in use, sitting and sleeping mats were rolled and kept near the tepee base. Joe was amazed that all their worldly possessions could be contained in such a small abode.

Yet Joe knew that Lakotas were nomadic, and that they lived a simple and routine existence. Other than horses, acquired by trade or theft, they cared little for collecting "worldly" riches. He mused on the number and variety of items in his home and in his father's office in Virginia, when this family could hold almost all of their goods inside one Lawrence closet. He thought of the amount of clothing and jewels most women of his acquaintance owned, when Morning Star had only a few garments and modest beadwork. He reflected on the foods and treats that whites loved and demanded during a meal, particularly when dining out, when these people had a simple diet that they themselves gathered or killed.

As Joe's mind drifted before slumber claimed him, he realized again how many differences there were between himself and the daughter of the Red Heart chief. Whites worshipped in churches and learned in schools, while Indians used nature's surroundings or their tepees. Whites executed or jailed criminals, whereas Indians slew or banished theirs. Lakotas met other tribes for exchange fairs or, on a rare occasion, dealt with a post or traveling trader; there were no stores, specialty shops, and busy towns in this territory. There were no trains, ships, or coaches here—only horses and *travois* for travel and transport. There were no theaters for plays and orchestras to offer enjoyment, or casinos for gambling, or businessmen to obtain wanted items, or workers to hire for laborious tasks, or seamstresses to make clothing, or large homes for parties and dances, or servants for doing daily chores.

He had been reared by a wealthy and educated family. But he had Stede, Molly, and Tanner Gaston to thank for teaching him about down-to-earth living. He had learned much from them over the years since meeting Tanner at school. He had spent many holidays in their home and shared many trips with the family. Not that his parents had allowed him to become spoiled, self-indulgent, or lazy— but the Gastons had honed his best traits and had inspired others. To him, Stede and Molly had been like a special uncle and aunt; Tanner had been like his brother.

Tanner—his loss was terrible. Joe couldn't imagine never seeing his best friend again or sharing good times with him. It was painful to think of never hearing Tanner's voice and laughter, of never viewing his lopsided smile, of never hunting and riding side by side, of all the things they would never get to do together, of him missing this soul-stirring adventure. Anger and bitterness gnawed at Joe, and he knew he must find Tanner's murderer.

Tanner would have liked Morning Star and his other Indian relatives. He was liked by nearly everyone he met. He had possessed an instinct about people and he'd known how to deal with all types. Many times Tanner's wits and skills had gotten Joe out of a bad situation or prevented one. Tanner had been easygoing and unique.

Unique, as was his beautiful Indian cousin. Joe was aware of Morning Star's close proximity. Her essence was in the still air and it seemed to engulf him, as if her spirit was touching his flesh from head to toe. He admired and respected her and her parents. He was pleased and proud of his success today. When he left in the morning, he would miss the young woman nearby. He would hurry to return from his trip to Fort Tabor to see Captain James "Jim" Thomas. At least he was grateful that Zeke and his boys were heading in the opposite direction, unless they had used another false trail to mislead him!

Joe was fatigued from riding and worrying, but he was relaxed over the council vote and his acceptance by Sun Cloud. His heavy lids drooped and closed. Soon, he was asleep.

Morning Star was not a captive of slumber but an emotional prisoner of the white man in her home. His pattern of breathing told her his restive spirit had found release. It was wrong, but she wished she were lying on the mat with him. She had felt safe but stimulated at his side. Any distance between them now seemed to evoke a feeling of denial. Yet she must conceal those emotions, must halt and prevent such forbidden desires. Her father believed in avoiding temptations to prevent yielding to them.

Morning Star was tired, but elated. She was eager for Joe to return, and hated for him to leave even for a short period. Soon, they would share so many adventures and confront so many challenges on the trail. She glanced at the shaft of light coming through the ventilation opening at the tepee point. The full moon could not pierce the heavy hides, so the enclosed area was nearly dark. If only they were alone in this cozy . . . Morning Star warned herself again to cease such hopeless yearnings and dreams. She forced her eyes shut and told herself to go to sleep.

Neither was Singing Wind asleep. She hoped that Sun Cloud hadn't noticed the strong pull between their daughter and the grandson of her husband's uncle. She knew that her love, her chief, had enough to worry over without including their youngest child. When Sun Cloud gathered her closer to his body, Singing Wind relaxed and eased into slumber.

Sun Cloud wished he could do the same. He perceived the restlessness in everyone in his tepee. He sensed the attraction between his daughter and new-found cousin. He trusted Morning Star, but love was powerful, often irresistible, as it had been between himself and his wife long ago. He remembered the risks and chances they had taken to be together. He didn't want his child to be hurt by craving a food she must never taste. If only he could keep them apart, their temptation would be easier to control. Maybe she would not win the contest to become Tanner's helper. He would do all he could to make certain she lost. If she won, it would mean it was the will of the Great Spirit. He had made many sacrifices in the past for his people. Surely Wakantanka would not make his daughter another one . . .

As Joe saddled Star, Sun Cloud gave him directions to the fort. The chief tied a beaded band around his forearm with markings that revealed Joe as a friend of the Red Hearts. "If other Dakotas approach, point to the *isto wikan* and say, *Mahpiya Wi, mitakola, mita tahansi.* It means, Sun Cloud, my friend, my cousin. They will let you go in peace. If Crow or Whites approach, remove from your arm and hide."

"*Pilamaya.*" He thanked the chief, then secured his bedroll and rain slicker behind the cantle, and positioned his saddlebags. He suspended a canteen and supply sack over the horn and slid his Sharp's rifle into an oblong leather holster. He was wearing a Colt pistol at his waist, and a knife sheath above his ankle. Tanner had trained him to be a near expert with guns and knives. Joe turned to

Sun Cloud. "I'll tell the Army your people aren't responsible for those raids on boats, wagons, homes, and soldiers," he said.

"We raided Crow camps to look for Red Heart arrows to learn if they seek to make us look guilty," Sun Cloud said. "We found none. Many times we find tracks of shod horses, white man's shoes, but we do not know who rides them. They travel too far to follow. We will wait to learn if you can stop the war breeding this season. If you cannot, leave our land and do not get trapped between us."

Joe asked a troubling question. "One thing I don't understand, Sun Cloud; why did you allow a small party to journey to Bear Mountain when there are Crow and bad whites in the area?"

"No Crow or other enemy band will attack a sacred party at a holy place. We did not think the evil whites would be in that area this soon. We believed they would wait for us to move our camps to the plains to hunt buffalo before they cause trouble. Whites do not honor sacred lands and times. Others went because they felt the Great Spirit's call; it is our way."

Singing Wind joined them and handed supplies to Joe: *papa*, dried strips of meat similar to the white man's jerky, *aguyapi*, pones of bread of which half were plain and half were speckled with dried nuts and fruit, and *wakapanpi*, prepared meat and berries—what the white man called pemmican. Still unadjusted to speaking English at this time, she told Joe, "*Ake ecana wancinyankin kte. Wakantanka nici un.*"

Morning Star smiled and said, "Mother says, Good-bye, I see you again soon. May Great Spirit go with you and guide you."

Joe smiled and responded, "I'll return as soon as possible. Good-bye, Sun Cloud, Morning Star, Singing Wind. Thanks for everything. I'll do my best to win peace for your people."

Joe mounted his roan, glanced at the three upturned faces, smiled again, and left the camp. As he rode away, he recalled what the chief had told him was the council's orders: the vote was to spare his life, to let him seek an honorable treaty, to allow him to defeat Snake-Man, and to distract their foes during the buffalo hunt. If Joe failed, there would be another council meeting and vote for war. This morning he had noticed Knife-Slayer, Hawk Eyes, and Night Stalker watching his every move and listening to his every word. He prayed that Sun Cloud could control them while he was gone. He kneed Star into a gallop.

Morning Star stood with her father for a time, but she was careful not to stare after Joe as he departed or to expose her warring emotions. It was the first time they had been alone since her return with the white man.

Sun Cloud said in his language, "I am happy you returned home safely, Daughter. It was rash to stray so far from the others."

Morning Star accepted the gentle reprimand with love and respect. "I was distracted while gathering herbs for Payaba, Father. When I saw the two white men, I had to follow them and spy to decide if a warning to our people was needed. They could have been scouts for an attack. My father did not raise a coward, and my mother did not birth a reckless fool. I knew the risks, but chose to take them. A chief's people and his duty come first to him; I am a chief's daughter, so I feel the same. Would you have me do less than I am able because I am a female? I believe my capture was the Great Spirit's plan to allow a meeting with . . . Tanner."

"I believe it is so," he concurred. "You were wise and brave to trust him and to bring him to us, Daughter. Pride lives in my heart for your deed. You have much of your mother's wits, skills, and daring. At your age, she was this same way. But her emotions often ran too deep, like a stream hidden beneath the face of Mother Earth. When heavy rains come, the stream can burst forth from its secret place and do much damage. Too often her love of adventure made her impulsive and willful. The first time I realized how strong my feelings were for Singing Wind, she was trailing white men to spy on them. Many times she rode alone and ignored dangers."

Morning Star laughed and replied, "Those things made her a strong and brave woman, Father, a special one who captured your eye and heart. Only such a woman can be the best wife for a chief."

Sun Cloud grinned and agreed. Then he warned, "If you are to ride with Sky Warrior, Morning Star, always remember you are Oglala, daughter of the chief. Do not let his white ways enter your head and heart."

"I will remember your words and obey them, Father," she responded, then prayed she could keep that promise.

After they parted and she headed to begin her daily chores, Night Stalker approached her. "It is a good day, Brother," she greeted him.

"A good day," he scoffed, "when a white man rides from our camp to expose our strength to the soldiers so they can return and attack?"

Morning Star was dismayed by his distrust and bitterness, by his dangerous need to battle the whites at any cost. "He goes to help us, Brother," she argued, "not to betray us. He and his task were revealed to us in a sacred vision. How can you not believe, accept, and obey that?"

"I am not convinced the vision is real. If it is true, how do we know he is Sky Warrior? Even so, he is but one wolf attacking a herd of strong buffalo. He cannot slay or halt its stampede. He will cease to try and will join them. We have vowed to battle the whites to victory or our deaths. There is no white man's peace without defeat and dishonor. Every treaty has been broken or used against Indians. The whites invade our lands and seek to steal them. They challenge us, spit upon us, curse us. They desire all we have and will slay us to get it. If this is not so, why do more soldiers come and why do they build more forts? They do so to prepare to attack and take. The white man cannot be trusted. He is evil and greedy. He must be pushed back to his lands or destroyed. We wait for Tanner to seek truce while our foes get stronger. It is foolish and deadly."

"No, Brother. If we challenge the whites, we will die. If we do not seek truce with the Bird People, the wars with them will continue forever and will endanger all children to follow us. I will help Tanner seek peace."

Night Stalker's long black mane moved about as he shook his head. "It is not our way for a woman to be a warrior!"

"Our way will die if our foes are not defeated. Tanner is the one to lead us to victory. And I am best trained to become his helper."

"Prove it, Sister," he challenged. "What will you say when you lose the contest Father plans? Will you shame your family with a pride too big? The warrior who boasts loudest is usually the weakest. When the time comes for him to prove his words, his skills fail and dishonor him."

"What will Night Stalker say when his sister wins the contest, and when, at Tanner's side," she retorted, "she obtains peace for our people? You will be chief one day, Brother. The time must come when you think and seek more for survival of our people than for personal coups and honors."

As she stalked away, he murmured to himself, "The granddaughter of Chief Gray Eagle, the child of Chief Sun Cloud, and the sister of future Chief Night Stalker must not shame us or help the whites destroy us. I will make certain you do not, my sister."

Morning Star and Buckskin Girl knelt at the lake's edge and talked as they washed clothing. The chief's daughter told her best friend of her capture, treatment by the white men, and her time with Joe. Yet she withheld the secret of Joe's true identity and her mixed feelings about him.

The lovely and gentle Buckskin Girl remarked, "I was so worried when you vanished. When scouts found clues to your capture, fear shot into my heart as a flaming arrow. Night Stalker wished to track them and rescue you. If the others had not reasoned with him and changed his mind, he would have done so."

"My brother is blind to the wrongs in his heart, Buckskin Girl. I pray the Great Spirit will clear his eyes and uncloud his mind. When Tanner wins peace for us, Night Stalker will be forced to accept the truth. It will be so exciting. She-Who-Rode-With-The-Sky-Warrior is my destiny."

"What if it is not?" the daughter of Flaming Star asked as she kept her gaze on her chore. "What if it is another's destiny? What if he is not Sky Warrior?" Buckskin Girl hinted at but did not reveal her suspicions or her hopes. The hopeful woman did not want Tanner harmed, but she prayed the real Sky Warrior would arrive soon. No, she corrected, would *return* soon. It was obvious that everyone—except her—had forgotten about his existence. He had been gone for sixteen years from this territory, driven away by shame and anguish, after the war chief's bonnet was stripped from his head by evil. He had gone to the white world to seek himself. Everyone seemed to have forgotten about *Notaxe tse-amo-estse*, the Cheyenne name for Sky Warrior. His father was Cheyenne and his mother was white, but his grandmother was Oglala. Perhaps Stede Gaston was the first man in Payaba's vision, but *Notaxe tse-amo-estse* was the second! His looks and Life Circle matched the vision words perfectly! Soon, the Great Spirit would call him home to her side and to his great destiny!

She missed the blue-eyed, sunny-haired warrior, and she loved him with all her heart. The day Sky Warrior had said, "*Na-ese,*" she had understood the Cheyenne words: "I'm leaving." It had broken her heart, but she had believed he would return one day, especially after she learned of the sacred vision years ago. She had refused to join with another and had lived for the sun when he came back to take his place of honor as foretold in the sacred vision. She knew that Morning Star did not think of Sky Warrior because her friend had been only three winters old when he left. But Tanner's coming was strange. If the vision *was* about Tanner and Morning Star, Buckskin Girl worried, her dreams were over.

Morning Star shook her friend's arm with a wet hand. "You do not hear my voice and words, Buckskin Girl. Where has your mind traveled? Why do you say such things? How can you doubt Payaba's vision?"

Buckskin Girl's dark gaze met her friend's worried one. "I do not doubt it,

Morning Star. But you must not dream rashly. I do not wish you to be unhappy if you lose the contest and if Tanner is not the vision helper."

"How can such be true, my friend? I do not understand."

The older maiden chose her words carefully. "It is possible the first man is Stede Gaston, but the second is not his son. Tanner is not the only man with sky eyes and sun hair and white blood. You hunger for him to be the man and you to be the woman, but that will not make it so."

Morning Star looked toward camp as the ceremonial drum, the *can cega*, alerted men to a coming announcement. A verbal message rang out in the air: *"Omniciye ekta u wo"*—Come to the meeting. She knew the contest would be discussed and she was anxious to enter and win it. "You sound as doubtful of Tanner and the vision as my brother and Knife-Slayer. I wish this was not so, my friend."

Buckskin Girl knew how Morning Star would feel tomorrow when she became her challenger, but it was something she must do. She knew that the daughter of Sun Cloud was skilled in many areas, but so was she. She must win the contest, so she would be at her love's side when he replaced Tanner Gaston! But, until everyone was shown the truth of this mistake, it was best to withhold her secrets. If the Great Spirit had a purpose for this episode, she must not intrude. "I am sorry, my friend, but I cannot help what Grandfather places in my heart."

"That is true," Morning Star conceded with reluctance and understanding. She glanced at her friend from lowered eyes. She sensed that something was troubling Buckskin Girl, but a friend did not pry. A good friend stood close and patient until the right time arrived.

As the two females worked in silence, Morning Star wondered how Hawk Eye's vision-quest had gone this morning. She knew the shaman had purified his body in the sweat lodge, then gone into the hills to "find his way to a spiritual path to Grandfather" with the aid of a peyote button. She wondered if the medicine chief would see the truth and, if so, would he speak it? Again, she chided herself for having such wicked thoughts about him.

As Morning Star hurried from the woods with her burden at dusk, Knife-Slayer halted her and said, *"Wociciyaka wacin velo. Unkomani kte lo."*

She did not want to speak with him or to take a walk with him today or any day, and wished he would halt his pursuit of her. "I am busy, Knife-Slayer," she refused in a polite tone.

Morning Star continued on her way, with the man trailing her and urging her to spend time with him. They came to Sun Cloud, Singing Wind, and Hawk Eyes.

Singing Wind smiled and said to her daughter, "You work late. We have eaten. Your food is by the fire. Do not let it get cold."

"I was gathering wood for Payaba and Winter Woman," she responded as she adjusted the loaded carrying sling on her back. The much loved and elderly couple had no children left to help with their chores so many Red Hearts assisted them. Morning Star had deep affection and respect for the past shaman and his wife, and she often did their tasks. "I must fetch water for them from the lake before I eat. Thank you, Mother."

As Morning Star left the small group, she heard Hawk Eyes tell her father that the Great Spirit had told him in his vision today to wait, that He would reveal all soon. She didn't know if that pleased or dismayed her. She heard Knife-Slayer quickly excuse himself from the group, and she prayed he would not follow and join her. She was glad when he did not.

Later, when Morning Star entered her tepee, she sat down by the dying fire, removed the cloth from a bowl, and ate her evening meal.

Sun Cloud and Singing Wind returned an hour later. The chief explained the contest, revealed the judges, and related the rules. He said it would begin tomorrow and would require all day to complete.

Morning Star was thrilled but apprehensive. By tomorrow night she would know if she was to ride with Joe. She scolded herself for allowing her brother and best friend to shake her self-confidence. Yet what if they were right? What if she did lose? But surely it was not vain or wrong to believe in herself and her skills. Surely Grandfather had thrown her and Joe together to meet and to work as partners.

Morning Star curled into a tight ball and clutched her stomach with her arms. She was nauseous, feverish, and shaky. Beads of moisture dampened her flesh and caused her hair and garments to cling to her body. She heard her stomach rumble in protest as something evil attacked and slashed at it with an unknown knife. Pain seared through her, and she trembled. Her perspiration increased. Her head ached. Her throat warned of a violent eruption in the making. Without pulling on her moccasins, she crept from her sleeping mat and entered the woods near their tepee, thankful for its close location during winter camp.

For over twenty minutes, her body emptied itself. Her weakness increased, and the agony mounted. She shook from illness and fear. Her mouth tasted terrible. She felt awful. Dizziness swept over her, and she clutched a tree to steady herself. When she felt relief for a time, she cleaned the area as best she could.

Morning Star went to the lake to wash out her mouth and to cool her face. She knew she wasn't finished with the strange illness, but she had to lie down or risk fainting. She sought her mat once more.

It wasn't long before she was compelled to dash for the woods again. This time, Singing Wind followed her daughter and asked, *"Nikuja he?"*

When she felt a little better, Morning Star replied, "Yes, Mother, I am sick." She explained the curious illness. "What medicine do you have? I must get well before morning for the contest."

When Singing Wind asked where it hurt, Morning Star pointed to her stomach as she replied, *"Lel mayazan."*

"I will take you to your mat, then seek Payaba's help."

Morning Star's torment was too great to refuse, despite the late hour. Holding her mother's arm, she returned to her mat.

"What is wrong?" Sun Cloud asked from the shadows.

"Anpaowicanhpi li'la kujape." She replied that their child was very ill.

"Do you wish me to call Hawk Eyes to her side?" he inquired.

"Hiya," Morning Star refused in a weak voice.

"Do you wish me to call Payaba?" he offered.

Morning Star nodded and said, *"Han."*

Sun Cloud went to the past shaman's tepee and called out softly to avoid awakening others.

"Tuwa kuja hwo?" The old man asked if he knew the problem.

"It is Morning Star, Wise One." The chief related the symptoms.

Payaba gathered his medicines and followed Sun Cloud to his tepee. Singing Wind had started a fire to give light and to heat any water needed. The white-haired, slump-shouldered man went to the girl's mat and knelt. Her parents hovered nearby, waiting and watching, praying and worrying.

Morning Star and Payaba talked for a time. Then he went to work to prepare a medicinal tea from white oak, water avens, and several herbs to halt the diarrhea and vomiting.

Before it was ready to consume, Morning Star knew she was about to be sick again. "I must go, Mother."

Singing Wind assisted her child into the forest. Morning Star was hunched over with pain, and she could not suppress her groans. When she was finished, they returned to the tepee. The younger woman sank to her damp sleeping mat, exhausted and frightened.

When the tea cooled enough, Payaba handed it to the quivering girl.

When he saw how she was shaking from weakness and fever, Payaba held the cup for her. "Drink, precious one. It will make the leavings of the body firm, not as the running of water. It will stop the food from retreating on the same trail it took inside."

Morning Star drank the bitter liquid, fearing it would return before her aching stomach kept it long enough to do its task. *"I'mapuze."*

"No, you must not drink water until the medicine heals you inside."

For several hours, Morning Star continued her treks into the forest, then returned to drink more tea. She fretted that the liquid was not working and she would grow weaker. Surely she had nothing left inside her body to expel!

At last the bouts ceased and the herbs worked their magic. When she drifted off to sleep, Sun Cloud thanked Payaba and walked him to his tepee. The old shaman had warned Singing Wind not to give her daughter anything to eat or drink until he checked her, in two hours, in the morning.

Sun Cloud cuddled his weary and relieved wife in his arms. He whispered into her ear, "I do not think she can enter the contest today. She is too weak. Perhaps it is the Great Spirit's way of letting another win."

Singing Wind did not believe that was true, but held silent.

The sounds of dogs barking, horses neighing, and people talking and laughing awoke Morning Star. She ached from head to foot. Her mouth was as dry as grass burned by a scorching sun after months without rain. Her stomach was sore from emptiness. Her throat scratched its discomfort. Her chest protested breathing after its exertions last night. She felt as limp as a wet cloth. She was in trouble . . .

Tears misted her dark brown eyes and she fought to control them. She felt awful; but worse, she felt weak as a newborn. How could she participate in the events in the contest today: race, ride, battle a warrior, track, shoot? In her condition, even a strong child could beat her!

"Help me, Great Spirit," she prayed with all her soul and might.

A day's ride from the Red Heart encampment, Joe reined in his horse and stared at the scene before his wide eyes. He was in trouble . . . "God, help me," he prayed with all his soul and might.

Chapter Six

A mounted Indian party had left the trees ahead and had taken a position in Joe's path, watching him with brandished weapons.

The blond-haired man knew it was too late to remove the armband—Sun Cloud's safety token and a connection to the dreaded Sioux—and conceal it. His keen mind, which hadn't detected their presence earlier, took in fifteen warriors who were ready to pursue him if he fled. Yet they appeared content to let him make the first move; be it one of peace, aggression, or cowardice. He was glad they were not wearing warpaint and hadn't ambushed him before giving him time to speak. If he was lucky and clever, and if he made the right choice, maybe he could save his life. He ordered himself to appear unworried, as he'd heard that most Indians respected courage in a foe. He kneed Star's sides and walked his roan toward the waiting men, hoping they were only curious about him.

When he was close enough to view their clothing, Joe recognized the geometric beading design of the Lakotas. Realizing they were not Crow, relief washed over him like a calming wave. Then he remembered Morning Star telling him some bands hated whites and rode as renegades against them. If this was such a band and their hostility was deep, they might not honor Sun Cloud's message. Yet all he could do was approach them.

Joe reined in his horse and used the little sign language he knew. He greeted them by making a combination of three signals: *sunrise*, *day*, and *good*. He raised his right hand to neck level—palm out and with index and middle fingers touching and extended—then lifted his hand until his fingertips were even with his face: the sign for *friend*. Next he moved his left hand, palm up, to his waist and grasped it with his right, allowing his thumb to rest on the back of it: the sign for *peace*. So far no brave moved, spoke, or threatened him.

The only emotion the chief exposed was interest. His black hair, parted in the center, was straight, breast length, and shiny. His most prominent facial feature was a long nose with a large base. His wide mouth was full lipped; and it was relaxed, neither smiling nor frowning. Joe decided the leader's expression and mood were calm and controlled, as was expected of a man of his rank. An air of dignity exuded from the chief, who appeared to be a sailor's knot under thirty. Then Joe noticed a clue to his identity, or hoped he had.

"*Lakota kitnla ia*," telling them he spoke very little Lakota. As he waited a response before continuing, his mind drifted for a moment. The elder Tanner Gaston—Powchutu—had taught his son Stede sign language and the Lakota tongue before returning here and dying, almost as if he'd known the man would need them one day. Stede had taught his son and had tried to teach Joe during the journey here and the winter at Fort Laramie. Joe found the Indian language difficult to learn. Their words were not positioned in the same sentence order as English: time was always mentioned first; adjectives and prepositions followed nouns; direct objects went before verbs; plurality was shown with verbs, not nouns; and certain endings identified the sex of the speaker or listener. In many cases, *is* and *was* were left out of sentences, which explained why Morning Star often skipped those English verbs. Too, the Dakota, Nakota, and Lakota dialects differed in some spellings and pronunciations; all reasons why he needed a translator for his coming task.

When the Indians held silent, Joe pointed to his armband, which he was sure had been noticed, and told them he was Sun Cloud's friend and cousin as the Oglala chiefs instructed. *"Nituwe hwo?"* he asked.

"Sinte Galeska," the chief replied. "Spotted Tail of the Brules. I speak white tongue. How is man with white face family of Sun Cloud of Oglalas?"

With brevity, Joe explained his assumed identity and mission to the dark-skinned man wearing a raccoon tail as his medicine and name symbol. His guess was correct; the leader was Spotted Tail, a Brule, a tribe of the Teton branch, as was the Oglala. Tom Fitzpatrick had told him the names and tribes of the most important chiefs in the territory. Spotted Tail was said to be a clever man who was cautious and cunning in his dealings with the whites, a man who preferred truce to war.

Spotted Tail had heard stories of Powchutu and the 1820 ambush, which had occurred three years before his birth. "Evil white men like mist, hard to capture. Wet hand give clue he been there, but bad spirit gone. I trade and speak with whites many times. Since trouble come, whites no trust any Dakota. It bad to see good and bad Indians as one people to attack. It good to seek peace; it hard to find between wolf, buffalo, and bird."

"Han," Joe agreed. Indian Agent Tom Fitzpatrick had told him to use the Indian way of speaking to relax them, to reveal respect, and, of course, to be understood clearly. His comparison was, "Game does not come to a warrior's tepee; he must hunt it or starve. It is the same with truce; peace must be sought and taken into the body or it will die from war wounds."

A suppressed smile caused the chief's eyes to shine. "You speak wise and good for white man," Spotted Tail remarked. "Need more like you."

"Pilamaya." Joe expressed his gratitude.

Spotted Tail translated for his band before telling Joe, "We ride to Sun Cloud camp to speak of new trouble. War rides the wind this season. If you find victory, war not dismount to attack both sides. Go in peace, Tanner Gaston. You be safe in Dakota lands and camps."

Joe signed *good-bye*, then continued his journey. Thoughts of the two great chiefs he had met entered his mind. If all Dakotas were like Sun Cloud and Spotted Tail, he concluded, his search for truce would succeed. But he needed to work rapidly and victoriously before trouble changed their minds. If he didn't fail and it went fast, he would be gone by fall.

Morning Star wandered into his head at that possibility. He could envision her without closing his eyes. She was like stimulating rain that followed a drought; she refreshed his thirsty landscape, gave him new life, and brought beauty to his surroundings. Her aura was like the fragrances of certain flowers whose scents lingered in the air. Being with her was like riding waves in his ship: some were calm and quiet, others tempestuous and rough. He would love to take her on a voyage around the world on one of their ships, show her wonderful sights, and teach her many things. She was too brave and adventurous to be frightened by exotic lands and busy ports. She would be enthralled by all the world offered. There was so much that she didn't know existed, and her hungry spirit would feast on all of it. She was eager to confront the unknown, to overcome obstacles, to endure hardships, to battle dangers. But her challenges were here in her land, for her people, in her culture.

How could an Indian maiden with a simple rearing fit into an aristocratic setting—balls, dinners, theater, and such? He could easily sail anywhere with Morning Star, but he couldn't take her into his society. His fear wasn't that she would embarrass him, as the smart female could learn all the correct things. She would be beautiful in a walking dress with a parasol clutched in her dainty hand or in a riding habit racing over their plantation or in an expensive ball gown with her black hair piled atop her head. Yet she would be like a lost child in his world; she could be hurt, humiliated, and scorned. Too many whites feared and despised all Indians, viewing them as savages. What *she* lacked was the background and education to help her become an accepted part of the southern scene she would enter if . . .

Joe shook his head to clear it of those crazy dreams. He hadn't ridden far when he realized he might have to make camp soon and possibly lose a day's travel. He hated for this trip to take even an hour longer than necessary, but it looked as if it couldn't be helped . . .

Payaba entered Sun Cloud's tepee and went to Morning Star's side. He forced his achy body to kneel beside her mat and his gnarled-fingered hand touched her cheek with gentleness and affection. "Do not fear, precious one," he coaxed. "All goes as Grandfather plans. Does your body heal?"

The weakened maiden related her sorry condition to the wise old shaman who had been like a grandfather to her, as her natural one had died long before her birth. "I will lose, Payaba. I have not the strength to win."

Payaba sent her an encouraging smile. "Drink this soup; it will give you the strength you need. Many special herbs are inside."

Singing Wind returned with water she had fetched. *"Toniktuka he?"*

"I am fine, Mother," Morning Star replied, but knew she was not.

"She must drink the medicine soup. Take her to the water to bathe. It will bring new life to her weary body," he instructed the older woman.

"She must stay on her mat today, Payaba. She is weak and ill."

"No, Singing Wind, she must enter the contest. She will win."

"Was this in your vision, Wise One?" the mother inquired.

The past shaman felt it was not the time to reveal the whole truth. "It is in my heart and head," he replied. "They say she is the one to be chosen."

"How can she enter the contest when she cannot walk from her mat?"

"Before the kettle drum summons her challengers, she will be ready."

The two women watched the elderly man get to his feet with great difficulty and leave their abode.

"Help me to do this, Mother. We must let Grandfather choose."

Singing Wind assisted her ailing daughter to a private area at the serene lake and helped her bathe. Morning Star donned cleaned garments and her moccasins. Singing Wind brushed her hair and braided it, to prevent it from getting into her eyes during the events. When they returned to their tepee, Night Stalker was awaiting them.

"Father says you are not well, Sister. Do not enter the contest. Do not shame us with your loss. Does this illness not tell you the truth?"

Morning Star could not bear the thought of another woman riding with Joe. "It tells me there are evil forces against me, Brother, but I will win."

Before they could argue the issue the *can cega* and *wagmula*—the ceremonial drum and rattle—sent forth the message for the contestants to gather for the beginning of the ritual.

Morning Star summoned all of her strength, will, and courage to face what was before her today. The outcome was in the Great Spirit's hands. She walked to the crowded area with her mother and brother. Her father joined them, and in a quiet voice questioned her health. She told him she was fine, but both realized she was not at her best.

Ceremonial chief Wolf Eyes stepped to the center of the gathering. There was no purification rite in the sweat lodge as the men participated in before their special rituals, and for that, the weakened Morning Star was grateful.

Wolf Eyes lifted the sacred buffalo skull in his hands. It was used in all important ceremonies. Its horns were wrapped with long grass, on which the life-sustaining buffalo grazed. Its interior was stuffed with sweetgrass, herbs, sacred tokens, and spring flowers. The painted images upon its prairie-weathered surface depicted sun, rain, lightning, and hail: all forces of nature that his special vision had said to paint there.

Wolf Eyes raised the skull heavenward and used it to salute the north for life, the east for knowledge, the south for quiet meditation, and the west for danger. "Hear us, Grandfather. Your people call you to witness this great event. Judge the women who enter this contest and choose one to carry out the vision you sent to Payaba long ago."

The ceremonial chief placed the skull on a short pole. "*Whope,* sacred White Buffalo Calf Woman, who honors girls as they enter womanhood," he called out. "She who has the power to heal with her touch, whose eyes can pierce the shadows that hide the future, who helped Wakantanka with the creation of His people, watch over and guide your blessed ones this sun."

Morning Star was anxious for the contest to get underway before the little energy she had regained deserted her, but she did not view the ritual as a waste of time. She felt as if her legs were filled with water. She hoped her tremors weren't noticeable to others. Beads of moisture made her feel as if she needed a bath rather than she had just taken one. Her fever was gone, as were her other disturbing symptoms, but the illness had left her feeling powerless in body and spirit.

"Who will step forward to attempt this great task?" Wolf Eyes asked.

Flying Feather, granddaughter of Catch the Bear, was first. Gray Squirrel, granddaughter of Tracks Good, was second. Comes Running, granddaughter of Wolf Eyes, was third. The fourth competitor shocked Morning Star: Buckskin Girl, her best friend and child of Flaming Star. The daughter of Sun Cloud made the fifth and last contestant.

As this was the result of Payaba's vision and he was one of the few members of the Elk Dreamer Society, he stepped forward to do the ritual dance while the spirits gathered to observe and bless the event. A hair hoop wrapped in flattened and colored porcupine quills with a white downy eagle feather suspended from its center was in a head of white hair, coarse and dulled by age and dryness, above Payaba's left ear. A circle was painted around his body of sagging muscles to symbolize the Hoop of Life. He carried an Elk Dreamer hoop, called a rainbow, in his left hand. The hoop was made from a flexible willow limb, wrapped in furry elk hide and adorned with clusters of herbs, animal claws, and other special tokens revealed to him in his vision. The power of elk medicine was considered very strong and rare.

As the elderly man chanted and danced about the cleared circle, Morning Star's renewed strength faded like a sinking sun. She feared she would faint before he finished and the first event began. Her fingers clutched her thighs to control their quiverings. She locked her knees to halt their wobbling. Nervous perspiration broke out all over her body and heat rosed her cheeks.

Payaba ignored his body's pains to perform the beloved task. His movements were steady, measured, and self-assured. His shoulders and back were bent, and his flowing white hair concealed his lined face as his feet followed a pattern and drumbeat he knew well. When the right moment came, he lifted his head skyward and invoked, "Hear me, Grandfather; Sun Cloud and his people need your help and guidance. Speak to us. Send us a sign."

Those words echoed through the Red Heart chief's head from a distant time when he had spoken the same ones during his Sun Dance ordeal. Many images and memories of that tormenting season raced through his mind, but he tried to push them aside.

Before Payaba completed his prayful chant and sacred dance, the reason Joseph Lawrence feared the delay of his journey neared the camp.

"*Icamna lecetkiya,*" Singing Wind whispered.

Morning Star glanced eastward to see the dark clouds moving toward them fast; it was going to storm, as her mother warned. Suspense and joy filled her heart. Surely that was the answer to her desperate prayers, as a violent storm would postpone the contest and give her time to heal.

The others were so attentive to the ritual that they failed to notice the changing weather. But they couldn't ignore it when the wind suddenly gusted through the trees and clearing. Within minutes, it yanked at hair and garments, stirring up dust. Its power increased rapidly and caused trees to sway and grasses to wave. The sky darkened with speed and vivid flashes of lightning shot across the heaven, followed by a thundering boom. The storm closed in on the encampment, sending forth more streaks of light and loud roars. The sound seemed to echo off the rocks, cliffs, and earth. Large drops of rain began to fall. First the water came down slow, then fast and heavy.

In a short time, everyone was soaked. Drenched garments clung to bodies. Dripping hair stuck to skin. Many women with babies and children raced for their tepees. A dazzling bolt of lightning struck a tree near the edge of camp; it crashed to the ground, and all forces rumbled together. Falling water became as loud as the thunder and the wind.

"It rains too hard!" Wolf Eyes shouted over the combined noises of stormy nature. "The contest must wait until the new sun when it is gone!"

"No! It is bad medicine!" Knife-Slayer shouted. "Payaba used his power and magic to call the storm here to protect Morning Star! She is ill and he fears she will lose! Will it not storm when the winner must do her task at Tanner's side? This is a good test of her skills!"

The ceremonial chief, whose granddaughter was involved, reasoned, "How can they track when rain washes away trails? It must wait."

"If Grandfather has halted the test, Wolf Eyes, there is a reason," the young warrior persisted. "He tells us the test, our help, and a truce are wrong. He shows his anger and prevents it."

Payaba stepped closer to be heard. "Your words are not true. I did not call down the storm. My Elk Dreamer hoop does no evil magic. Grandfather has a reason for us to change the test until another day. It is not my doing."

Three girls shivered and huddled as the chilling rain beat down upon them. Buckskin Girl stood with her father, and Morning Star with hers. The five females, as others still present, could hardly see from the water streaming into their eyes. Mud splattered on everyone's moccasins and legs. The entrants glanced at each other, but none gave her opinion.

Nor did Sun Cloud want to give his, since his daughter was involved. He waited for council members, who would be judges, to cancel the competition. Within minutes, a verbal vote brought the decision nearly all had hoped for: postponement until the next day, if the weather improved.

"Why can we not continue when the rain stops?" Knife-Slayer reasoned. "The ceremonies are done; the spirits have been called."

"And they have spoken for another sun," Payaba responded.

The participants were excused for the day and all raced for their tepees. Sun Cloud grasped his daughter's arm and assisted her back to her home. He turned his back while Singing Wind helped Morning Star get out of her soaked clothes. She dried off the trembling girl and covered her with a warm buffalo hide after she lay down. Before she let her daughter fall into exhausted sleep, Singing Wind urged more herbal tea down her throat.

Morning Star closed her eyes and relaxed; she was rescued for now. She tried not to worry over Buckskin Girl's challenge in the contest. Yet she wondered why her best friend would go against her in this matter. Knowing Flaming Star's daughter, there must be a good reason.

She wondered where Joe was along the trail and how he was doing. She had spent only a short time with him, but she missed him, and longed for his quick and safe return. He inspired such excitement and happiness within her. He made her feel as if she could do anything she attempted. It was as if she were more than only a woman with him. He made her feel braver, smarter, more alive than anyone ever had. With him, she could be her best. She wanted to use and enjoy every moment she could have with him. If only he were truly Tanner Gaston and had Oglala blood and if only he could remain here forever, she daydreamed. No, her drifting mind told her, that would make them grandchildren of half brothers. Was that kinship too close for joining? Before she could reason on the matter, the herbs, warmth, and her fatigue carried her to slumberland.

As Morning Star napped and Singing Wind sewed, Sun Cloud sat on his mat and reflected. He heard the storm unleashing its fury outside and it brought a similar one to mind. Shortly after his father's lethal ambush, which had provoked a rivalry with Bright Arrow for the chiefs bonnet, he had submitted to the Sun

Dance. A man's body was all he truly owned and was the most important thing he could offer willingly to the Great spirit as a sacrifice. He had chosen the hanging position which Gray Eagle had endured many seasons earlier. Most warriors used the standing one that allowed their feet to push against the earth to help obtain freedom. The shaman had worried over him participating after just finishing the Sacred Bow ritual and race—which he had won—and subjecting himself to two purification rites in the sweat lodge. He had been tired and weakened, but determined.

The Sun Dance could cost a man his life if his stamina was weak. His chest was pierced with an eagle's claw and thongs were secured around the freed muscles. Then he was suspended by them in the air from a cottonwood post. Never had he known such physical agony. He had hung there for hours as his flesh refused to tear free and release him. It meant either a victory or death ordeal. His face had been painted with the markings of his name and medicine symbols. Just when he feared failure, as Morning Star had today, a violent storm had arisen. The sacred pole had swayed and his body had twirled, shooting more torment through it.

The shaman had jumped to his feet to dance and chant, and no one had left the scene. A vision for victory over their white foes had been given to him, along with personal messages. Lightning had struck the pole, as it had the spruce today, and freed him, as today's storm had rescued his daughter from certain defeat. Rain had smeared his facial paint to make it reflect that of his father's markings. The storm had ceased and the sun had peeked from behind a large white cloud: nature had created his name and symbol in the sky. Many had thought it was the Great Spirit's way of displaying His selection of Sun Cloud over his brother for chief.

"What do you think of, Husband?" Singing Wind inquired.

Sun Cloud related his thoughts. "The Great Spirit and forces of nature helped our daughter this day as they helped me long ago. All within me cries out that she not be the one, for I fear it will take her from us."

"If it is the will of Grandfather, we cannot battle it, Husband."

"That is true. But I will pray she is not His choice."

"As will I, my husband and love."

Wednesday was a glorious day. Payaba came early to check on Morning Star. He asked if she was well and if she could do the contest.

"I am better, Wise One, but my strength is less than usual. I will try to win. Is all prepared?"

"Yes. Our people gather. Come."

Morning Star accompanied Payaba to the chosen area. The ground was soft and wet, but was drying out from sun and breeze. She joined the others. Buckskin Girl did not look her way, and that saddened her. She listened as Wolf Eyes listed the thirteen events. He told how a stone would be given for each victory, and the one with the most stones would be the winner. There would be a drawing in case of a tie, he said.

Wanji, the first event, was in self-defense. Her judge was war chief Lone Horn. The warrior who would test her was Hoka Inyanke, Running Badger, grandson of Plenty Coups and a skilled fighter. It almost seemed as if this first test was meant to eliminate her quickly, as if they doubted her skills and wits following her capture by the white men! At least she would battle the twenty-three-year-old man while she was at her freshest and strongest. She saw the ceremonial chief hand each of the five warriors a strip for binding the wrists of a captured girl—the show of defeat. The females were told they could run anywhere or try anything to elude their captors. The winner was the one who remained free the longest.

A signal was given. The girls fled in different directions. Running Badger raced after his target. He was fast and surefooted on the softened terrain, but so was Morning Star. When he closed the distance between them, his arms banded her chest. Quickly she lifted her arms and slipped from his grasp like a slimy eel, causing him to hesitate in surprise. She whirled, rammed her head into his abdomen, and sent him stumbling backward—a tactic she had seen Joe use in the enemy camp. Off she ran once more.

Gaining on her, Running Badger reached the large rock behind which she took refuge to recover her wind. They circled it a few times as the warrior laughed and grinned, but Morning Star never took her eyes from his. Her father had taught her that was where a man exposed his next move if you learned how to read the signs. She didn't drop her attention or laugh when he told her she was as slippery as a wet fish in a greasy hand.

She saw Running Badger step one way, turn rapidly, then flip himself over the obstacle. She got her breathing back under control, dodging his body and eluding his grasping fingers. She ran toward a tepee, but his hand snaked out and seized one of hers. Morning Star yanked it to her lowered head and bit him! When his other hand sought to loosen the one under attack, she clawed at it and jerked free. Once again, she fled.

Running Badger caught up and lunged at the maiden, throwing her off balance. As she landed on the ground, she grabbed a handful of wet dirt and flung it into his face, but it did not have the same effect as when dry and dusty. Thinking fast, she entangled his ankles with hers and tripped him, another trick she had seen Joe use while fighting Zeke. She was up and behind a horse before the warrior could react.

Over the animal's back, the man teased, "You battle dirty."

"Only to win," she retorted. "Today you play my bad enemy, not my good friend. I must do all to defeat you." As those last words left her lips, she stooped and sent her foot upward into his groin beneath the animal's belly. It was a naughty action she hated to use, but felt it necessary.

Running Badger, who had been standing with his legs spread, dropped to his knees and moaned. He saw the sneaky girl race away and knew he must recover and pursue quickly, as his male pride was stung.

A quick glance toward the ceremonial chief told Morning Star the others were captured and bound. Still free, she ran to the war chief's side and asked, "Do I continue, Lone Horn?" To conserve energy, she hoped he would say no.

Wolf Eyes responded for the judge. "The others are bound," he said. "You run free. You fought well. You are winner. Give her a stone, Hawk Eyes."

Morning Star clutched the hard-won prize, then handed it to her father to hold. They exchanged smiles, his eyes full of pride.

The others were cut free for *nunpa*, the second test: English. Thunder Spirit, son of White Arrow, was to quiz and judge her, as he spoke the white man's tongue.

When the event was over, there was a tie between Morning Star and

Buckskin Girl, whose father was as skilled in English as his brother, her judge, and he had taught his daughter well.

Hawk Eyes held out his closed fists to the woman he had been wooing for a long time for her to choose first. When he opened the one Buckskin Girl tapped, the second stone was awarded to her.

Morning Star was upset that her best friend had denied her a second victory. Now each possessed one stone. She wondered if the medicine man had intentionally stared at the hand which held the coveted prize.

Yamni, test number three, was to play the part of a squaw, the role which would be used at Joe's side. Each girl acted out a part before the council, who voted on their performances. Each was told why she lost. Morning Star heard that she talked too much and kept her eyes up: squaw should be quiet and humble and almost grovel in fear of her owner! The stone was handed to Flying Feather, who held it up and giggled.

Topa, test number four, was with the bow and arrow. Tracks Good was Morning Star's judge. She tried not to dwell on the two losses and three-way tie, but had trouble keeping them off her mind.

Flaming Star whispered to her to take her time, as he knew she had been ill and weak. He, too, wondered why his child was competing.

When all five of her arrows struck the center of the target, Morning Star won her second stone. She took a deep breath that did not lessen her tension. She knew she was tiring again from her recent sickness. She also knew what loomed before her.

Zaptan was a knife-throwing test. Buckskin Girl won the fifth stone easily, tying her friend once more with two stones each.

Sakpe was a lance-throwing test. Morning Star ordered her arms to stop trembling. She grasped the lengthy weapon and flung it with all her might, but it did not hit the center of the circle drawn on the ground. She watched with apprehension as the other girls hurled theirs. She mopped away glistening perspiration before she handed her third stone to Sun Cloud.

Wolf Eyes announced a break for the girls to rest and to take refreshments. They were given thirty minutes until the next event.

Morning Star went to her tepee and lay down. She had to relax. She had to gain strength. She had to win. She kept recalling what her brother had said about the shame of losing after being so cocky about winning. She admitted that her pride had been too large. The contest was not the "simple" victory she had envisioned it to be.

"Toniktuka he?" Singing Wind asked how she was.

"Weak as a rabbit the moon of its birth," the maiden responded.

"Must you do this, Morning Star? There is no shame in stopping because you are weak from sickness. It is worse to continue and lose."

"As Morning Star, would you quit a task so important?" she asked.

"No, my daughter, I would continue."

"Thank you, Mother," she replied, grateful for the honesty.

Payaba arrived and gave Morning Star soup and tea laced with herbs. "They will give you strength, precious one. Do not be discouraged."

Morning Star consumed the liquids and rested until it was time to rejoin the others. She noticed Hawk Eyes speaking with Buckskin Girl, praising her and wooing her. A surge of anger, frustration, and disappointment engulfed the daughter of Sun Cloud, and she hurriedly quelled those feelings.

Sakowin was a test for reading tracks and trail signs. Catch the Bear was her judge. It included fourteen parts. She guessed the three smoke signals correctly: one puff for *danger*, two puffs for *all is safe*, and three puffs for *send help*. As each Indian nation had different moccasin prints, it was vital for a tracker to be able to recognize those he found and trailed. She guessed correctly for the Crow, Dakota, Cheyenne, and Pawnee prints. Trail signs were tested, as they gave crucial information: directions, warnings, water locations, and so forth. Most were made of grass bunches tied differently, or rocks stacked in certain patterns and numbers, or cuts made on trees. Morning Star read all seven accurately.

Pleased with herself, she waited for the others to finish. It was another tie between her and—this time—Gray Squirrel for the seventh stone. Tracks Good, her grandfather, had taught her competitor well.

The drawing did not go in her favor, and she lost another stone. It was terrible to lose an event she had done successfully! At least, she reasoned, she was still ahead by one victory. She had to try harder!

Saglogan was another tracking test, a skill vital to survival and success: locating or avoiding enemies and finding game. Each girl was shown to a different starting point and told to return with a certain object. Morning Star's was her father's *wanapin*, his name and medicine symbol. The clues and tracks had been made and the objects hidden during the break. Whoever returned with her object first was the winner.

Morning Star followed the clues into the woods and located her father's medallion. She hurried back to camp, but Gray Squirrel was there holding the eighth stone. She almost wanted to scold Tracks Good for teaching the girl such expert skills. Again, she had succeeded, but still had lost. Perhaps her renewed fatigue was slowing her down and dulling her wits. Now Flying Feather possessed one stone, Buckskin Girl and Gray Squirrel had two each, and Morning Star owned three. Ahead, she fretted, but in danger of being caught up to and passed. At least three of the remaining five events were in her strongest areas, if her lagging body didn't fail her.

The test of *napciunka* should be easy for her: sign language, vital for communicating with friends and foes of other tongues. Hawk Eyes was her judge for the fifty-six chosen signals. She cautioned herself to make no mistakes. When the shaman spoke a word, Morning Star made the motions for it. Some included: counting, tribes, greetings, responses, foods, supplies, colors, trade, gratitude, names, and farewell. Her last two were for indicating tribes. For Crow, she signaled *bird* and *Indian*; for Dakota, she signed "throat cutter," used by others over the correct meaning, *friends*.

Hawk Eyes went to meet with the other judges. Then Wolf Eyes announced a tie between Morning Star and Gray Squirrel. The two females approached the shaman, and Gray Squirrel won her third, the ninth, stone to tie Morning Star in the running for victory.

The chief's daughter was visibly dismayed and fatigued. Buckskin Girl touched her arm and smiled in empathy. At that moment, Morning Star did not feel kindly toward the woman who possessed the two stones she would have herself if Buckskin Girl weren't a challenger. She sensed something was terribly wrong, as if dark forces were trying to defeat her. If only she could draw first one time; if

there was another tie, maybe her luck would change! She chided herself for thinking the shaman was to blame for her losses.

"*Kiinyanka iyehantu.*" Wolf Eyes called out it was time to race.

Event number ten—*wikcemna*—was to prove escape skills. The course was
marked, and the council as a whole would observe and judge. The five females
lined up, readied themselves, then took off at the signal.

Morning Star gave it her all, but she was too weak by now to keep up. After a
stumble and near fall, she came in fourth. She watched with envy and discourage-
ment as Comes Running accepted the tenth stone.

"*Kuwa iyehantu.*" Wolf Eyes announced the hunt for food.

Morning Star was aware of her friend's skill with the knife, as Buckskin Girl
had taught her how to trap and slay small animals with one! This event was in two
parts—*ake wanji* and *ake numpa*: number eleven was with knife, and number
twelve was with a bow. In each, the first girl to return to camp with a kill by the
specified weapon was the winner.

After Buckskin Girl accepted her third stone for skill with a knife hunting,
there was a three-way tie between her, Morning Star, and Gray Squirrel. Hawk
Eyes praised the oldest woman highly.

At the signal, Morning Star raced into the woods, determined not to lose
another event and stone. Her pride was taking a beating, as were her body and
spirit. She urged herself to win this hunt and the last test. She saw a fawn tangled
in underbrush. She knew she must hurry. With reluctance, she lifted her bow,
placed her arrow, and drew back the string. From the corner of her eye, Morning
Star caught a glimpse of a beautiful doe. The mother deer moved about nervously,
sensing danger and refusing to leave her baby imperiled.

Morning Star knew she could not slay the panicked fawn, and knew what her
tender-hearted generosity could cost her. She put the bow aside and freed the
small creature, who hurried to its mother. She watched the two race off into
hiding. She retrieved her weapon, then heard noisy chatter overhead. She looked
up and saw a fussing squirrel. Carefully she took aim and brought down the furry
rodent. Size didn't matter, only that she used an arrow and returned to camp
before the other girls.

Morning Star succeeded, and claimed her fourth—the twelfth—stone. Again,
she was one victory ahead of her two closest competitors.

"*Akanyanka iyehantu.*" Wolf Eyes said it was time to test riding skills.

The last event—*ake yamni*—would reveal who could mount, ride, retrieve
objects astride the horse, dodge thrown objects as substitutes for arrows and lances,
and dismount the fastest.

Morning Star was an expert rider, but so were two of the other girls. To win,
she must ignore her lack of strength and energy, as she didn't want another tie or
loss. Flaming Star was her judge to see how many or if any objects struck her, and
to see if she retrieved others fairly. As she lined up with the four girls behind their
mounts, she was stunned to see that Buckskin Girl would be riding Knife-Slayer's
pinto, a well-trained animal. That told Morning Star that her friend's romantic
pursuer wanted her to lose! All she could do was hope that Hanmani did not fail
her today.

The signal was given and all ran to their horses having no trouble mounting
swiftly and agilely. After three runs of a marked course, each girl raced to her
assigned testing area. As each rode her course, warriors jumped from behind rocks,

trees, and tepees to try to hit the contestant with soft leather balls. The judge was to count how many struck the female target. Afterward, she was to ride past posts and grab various-size hoops from them, then return to her judge.

Morning Star wondered why her beloved animal faltered several times and seemed agitated. She was third to reach her assigned area. As she galloped that course, only one warrior succeeded in hitting her, and only one hoop was left behind—both results of unusual mistakes by her horse. She urged Hanmani to hurry back to Flaming Star, then dismounted and handed him the hoops. She spoke soothingly to the Appaloosa and noticed how wild-eyed he was. She must ask Payaba to check him.

Wolf Eyes met with the five judges, then announced a tie between Morning Star and Buckskin Girl.

Sun Cloud's daughter knew that if she got the stone, she would win with five of them. If she did not, it would be a four-stone tie, and a final drawing. As feared, Buckskin Girl won her fourth—the thirteenth—stone.

As the council complimented all of the girls on their skills, courage, and victories, Morning Star fretted over another drawing, as she hadn't won a tie yet. She was suspicious of several things—Hanmani's strange behavior, the three drawings to settle ties with a challenger always choosing first and right, and her curious illness the day before. If the Great Spirit rescued her yesterday and helped her save the fawn today, why was He deserting her now? It was disappointing enough to lose fairly, but infuriating to lose unfairly.

"The others also have skills, Morning Star, but that makes yours no less great," Flaming Star murmured. "You did not lose the ties because your skills were less, but from bad luck. If you had not missed one sign, you would be winner without another draw. It is my fault you missed it, as I am the one who taught you and practiced with you."

Morning Star gaped at her elder. "What do you mean? I missed none."

The sixty-eight-year-old Big Belly looked surprised. "Hawk Eyes said you missed one. That is why you tied, then lost."

At that moment, the shaman called the two women to settle the tie and the championship. "Victory is in the hands of the Great Spirit," he said, then extended both closed fists to Buckskin Girl to select one first.

"No," Morning Star refuted, pushing her friend's hand away before it touched Hawk Eyes' left fist. She worried over a loss of face by her challenge of their medicine chief. Yet she despised cheating and defeat.

Sun Cloud stepped forward and asked, "What is wrong, Daughter? It does not matter who chooses first. Grandfather is in control of victory."

Morning Star's determined gaze met her father's confused one. "Flaming Star said a strange thing," she explained. "Hawk Eyes told the others I missed a signal in the sign language test. That is why Gray Squirrel tied with me and she drew the winning stone. I say, I missed none!"

The crowd was silent and alert. Sun Cloud looked dismayed by his daughter's challenge of the shaman's honesty. Hawk Eyes looked angered by the bold insult on his honor. Morning Star locked her gaze to the shaman's.

"I missed none, Hawk Eyes," she stressed with confidence.

"She did not give the correct sign for *treaty*," he alleged. "She—"

"No!" The girl shouted at him to halt, shocking everyone. "Speak only the word, then Wolf Eyes will watch me give it to see if I was wrong."

"You say I did not speak the truth?" Hawk Eyes asked indignantly.

"I say you made the mistake, not Morning Star," she replied.

Sun Cloud was distressed by his daughter's behavior. A woman did not speak this way to a man, especially to a holy man, a council member! Even though she had chosen her words and reply carefully, she had called him a liar, a cheater. If she was wrong, she and all in her tepee would be dishonored. Yet he had never known his daughter to be rude and unkind. It was obvious she believed she was right and that this victory was important to her. Too, she was still suffering from her recent illness and was not herself.

Wolf Eyes eased a difficult situation by saying, "I will ask her."

"If you give our chief's daughter a chance to correct a mistake, to be fair, you must do the same with the others," Hawk Eyes argued.

"I made no mistake," the maiden emphasized.

Wolf Eye asked the other females if they would be troubled by his testing Morning Star's challenge.

Flying Feather, who had entered the contest for the fun of it, replied, "I lost the other stones fairly. I do not wish to repeat any test. It is her right to lose only because she was wrong. Ask the word again."

"It is the same with me, Grandfather," Comes Running added.

Gray Squirrel, who was serious in her vie for the championship, said, "Morning Star is skilled in sign language. It is strange she was wrong. If she missed before, she will miss again. Ask her, Wolf Eyes."

Buckskin Girl had no choice but to say, "I wish to win, so my feelings are confused. I will accept the ceremonial chief's decision."

Morning Star, who was well liked by the other girls, was grateful for their understanding and help and relieved that none of them protested. She sent each girl a smile of thanks. Even though she did not comprehend Buckskin Girl's motive for competing, she appreciated her honesty.

"It is agreed to test the word again," Wolf Eyes said. "Morning Star, what is the sign for *treaty* between two tribes?"

The maiden moved her hands to give the signals for *much*, *smoke*, and *handshake*. "Is that not right?" she inquired with confidence.

Hawk Eyes debated. "She is right this time, but in the test, she gave the signs for *handshake* and *white*; that is the sign for treaty with a white man, not with another tribe."

"She is right," Flaming Star announced to the whispering crowd. "She must be proclaimed winner."

"She was ill and shaky; she was wrong," Hawk Eyes protested.

"No," she argued on her own behalf, "I was not. Perhaps in the excitement, you were confused. Flaming Star taught me well. I did not confuse the two different signs. I swear on my life and honor."

Wolf Eyes, ceremonial chief, suggested, "Why do we not repeat one of the events to settle this disputed tie? This will make the victor win on her skills, not on luck or mistakes."

The council members quickly nodded agreement to the solution.

"The sun will sleep soon," Hawk Eyes said. "Tracking is too long. They are skilled at all others. Use the foot race. It is quick and fair."

Morning Star guessed why the medicine chief selected that event; he realized she had little or no strength left to run a race against Buckskin Girl. Yet, she could not demand one of the other tests, in which all knew she was strong; she could not refuse a deciding test she had risked dishonor to obtain. She nodded.

Buckskin Girl knew she had an advantage in strength over Morning Star so she held silent. She wanted to win. She truly believed the white man was not Sky Warrior in the sacred vision. When her lost love returned and claimed that rank from Tanner Gaston, all would understand her motive, especially her friend. To ride at her love's side, she must become the vision woman. Perhaps the Great Spirit had weakened Morning Star so she herself could become victor. With her friend at her best, the contest would have been won easily by the chief's daughter.

Darkness settled on the land as the talk took place. "Night blankets us," Wolf Eyes said. "They will race when the sun returns. They can rest and grow strong while *Wi* sleeps. The race will be fair to both."

Hawk Eyes disagreed, as did his son, but they were out-voted. The shaman wanted the race run immediately and for Buckskin Girl to triumph so everyone would be convinced he had not cheated to prevent Morning Star's victory. He was annoyed that Flaming Star had exposed the error, and furious that she had challenged him. He had promised his son to help defeat the chief's daughter, whom Knife-Slayer was determined to take as wife because of her beauty and rank. His son would do anything to keep Morning Star from riding away and spending time alone with a white man. If the contest had taken place yesterday while she was sick, she would have lost quickly and easily. After everyone left the clearing and there would be no tie-breaking draw, he tossed away a stone from each hand . . .

Upon rising, Morning Star pulled on her soft buckskin garment, braided her hair, and left to be excused in the nearby forest.

Knife-Slayer entered the chief's tepee when the maiden was out of sight. He greeted Singing Wind and handed her berry-and-nut speckled pones. He smiled and said, "Mother says they will help Morning Star regain her strength. She does not want Singing Wind and her daughter to believe Father thinks badly of Morning Star for her challenge."

As he talked, Knife-Slayer noticed the empty bowl that indicated Sun Cloud had eaten his early meal and left. He saw two others prepared for the women. Upon his entrance, Singing Wind had set one down from which she was about to eat. That told him the other bowl was Morning Star's. When the woman turned to put aside the gift he had brought, he dropped herbs into the bowl.

Singing Wind faced him and said, "Thank Waterlily for her kindness. Tell Hawk Eyes we have no bad feelings for the mistake on the past sun."

Knife-Slayer did not debate her choice of words. He smiled, nodded, and left. He went to prepare himself to witness Morning Star's defeat and to give her comfort in his arms.

Morning Star returned to her tepee, lifted a bowl, and ate . . .

Chapter Seven

*M*orning Star glanced up as her mother returned to their tepee. "Where did you go?" she asked. "Your food grows cold."

Singing Wind related the visit by Knife-Slayer, then said, "We have plenty, so I took the fruit pones to Winter Woman and Payaba."

"Knife-Slayer and Hawk Eyes waste words on apologies that do not come from their hearts," Morning Star contended. "Both desired me to lose." She revealed her suspicions to the shocked woman.

"You should not say or think such wicked things, Daughter."

"Should I hold silent to my mother about what is in my heart?"

"No, Morning Star. I am happy you share all things with me. I worry that the contest is too important to you and blinds you."

"Have you known me to do my skills so badly?"

"You have been ill, Daughter," Singing Wing reminded.

"What of Hanmani's strange behavior? What of losing all ties? What of letting others always choose first in the draws? What of Hawk Eyes' mistake? What of his protests and the bad feelings he showed?"

"Payaba said your horse is fine. Perhaps Hawk Eyes did not realize he made you choose last each time or did not want to show favor for his chief's daughter. You challenged him, Morning Star, and he feared trouble and dishonor. He only wished the contest to be fair for all who entered it."

"That is why he insisted upon a foot race when he knew I was too weak to win it?" she asserted skeptically.

"All agreed it was the best choice to settle the dispute."

"All did not demand it be run in darkness."

"Do you have ways to prove your claims against him?"

"No, Mother, and I will say nothing to him or to others."

"That is best. In this time of trouble and danger, we do not need more. You are well this sun. The race will be fair."

"I would be winner without trouble if Buckskin Girl had not entered the test. She is my friend. I do not understand why she challenges me."

Singing Wind saw how hurt and confused her daughter was. "It is a great honor to become the vision woman," she pointed out. "Buckskin Girl has many skills. Must friendship make her deny them and not chase after her desires?"

"But she knows how much I want this task."

"And you must see how much *she* wants it. What did she tell you?"

"She asked, 'What if it is another's destiny? What if he is not Sky Warrior?' How can she doubt the truth? He matches the vision."

"Are there clues in her words?" the mother inquired.

The younger female mused a minute, then suggested, "Perhaps she thinks it is her destiny. She told me she could not help what Grandfather places in her heart. She did not warn me she believed His message was for her to enter the contest! There is a strangeness in her gaze and spirit she will not explain. I do not know why she makes me wait for the truth. We have not kept secrets from each other before this time."

A brief moment of guilt chewed on Morning Star as she remembered she did withhold a large secret from her best friend. Her tone altered from dismay to anger as she revealed, "She does not trust Hawk Eyes, but she did not speak for fairness or defend me on the past sun. I do not wish this to come between us, but she hungers too greatly to win."

"And Morning Star does not hunger just as greatly to win?"

"I have good reasons," the girl avowed.

"How do you know she does not, if she holds silent?"

Morning Star wondered if Buckskin Girl wanted to win to keep her and Joe apart. Did Buckskin Girl sense her feelings and dangerous weakness for "Tanner" and was trying to protect her from herself and shame? Or protect her from the journey's perils? If such was true, why not reveal it? No, the maiden deduced, that was not her friend's motive.

"Accept what happens as Grandfather's will," Singing Wind urged.

The troubled girl nodded a promise, then changed that subject. "Eat, for we must do our chores before it is time for the race."

Singing Wind reached for her bowl. It was gone. "Did you take the food from here?" she asked, pointing to a sitting mat.

"Yes. Was it not for me?"

The older woman smiled and answered, "It was mine, but it does not matter. I will take the bowl I prepared for you and left by the fire."

"I go to see if Hanmani is fine this sun. I will return soon for chores."

Spotted Tail and his party arrived in Sun Cloud's camp. The Red Heart chief greeted them and talked for a while. He invited the Brule chief to his tepee for refreshment, as was their way. The other warriors made camp at the edge of the village, then spread out to visit with friends.

Morning Star saw the visitors arrive and enter her home. She went to the lake to tell her mother of their guests. Singing Wind's water bags were there, but she was not. The maiden looked around, but did not sight her. She filled the bags and joined her father and Spotted Tail. After welcoming the young chief to their camp, she served the men water and fruit pones. "While you speak, I will fetch Mother. She does chores now."

Morning Star searched for her mother, to learn Fast Hands saw her enter the trees earlier. The maiden followed the woman's directions. She called out, "Ina!" and her ears captured a faint response. When she located Singing Wind, the older woman was doubled over and violently ill. "Ina?"

She looked up at her daughter and said, "Help me to my mat."

Morning Star realized that her mother was attacked by the same strange illness she had had. Recalling how many times she had dashed to the woods for her body to empty itself, she knew her mother would not want to display such private and uncontrollable behavior before a visitor. "We have a guest. Chief Spotted Tail visits with a small band. I served pones and water, then came to seek you. I will take you to Payaba. He will make you well, as he did Morning Star. Do not worry; I will tend our guest."

As the ailing woman lay in misery on a mat in the old shaman's tepee, Winter Woman and Payaba tended her. She drank the healing tea that the old man prepared from special herbs.

"Did you eat any of the pones Knife-Slayer brought to you?" Morning Star asked in a near whisper.

"No," the woman replied, but she grasped her daughter's meaning.

"Were our bowls waiting while he was there?" Morning Star asked.

"Yes, but he was not alone with them. I looked away but a moment."

"Evil can work swiftly, Mother. Did he know which was mine?"

Singing Wind thought a moment, then admitted, "Yes. I was holding mine when he entered. He saw me place it on the mat. You ate it."

"And you ate mine, after he left. Have you forgotten I ate from another waiting bowl before I became ill? Knife-Slayer heard you tell me it was ready. He heard me say I had a task to finish before I returned."

"Do you say he put something in both to make you ill?"

"He wants for me to lose, Mother. He was with the horses before the race to fetch his for Buckskin Girl. Perhaps he gave something to Hanmani."

"That is wicked, Daughter, your thoughts and words," she chided.

"No, Mother, what he has done is wicked."

"There can be truth in her claims, Singing Wind," Payaba related. "There are plants which bring on such sickness. Hawk Eyes knows them. In my vision long ago, Grandfather warned that some would try to stop it. I have not forgotten how Hawk Eyes convinced all I was dying and took my place. He is the reason I am called Pushed Aside, not Standing Tree."

Morning Star saw how this conversation was distressing her mother. "We will speak of this later when you are well," she said.

"Until he is caught doing evil, do not accuse him, Daughter. Your father has many worries on his mind. Without proof, do not add another. After your challenge of Hawk Eyes, it will make bad trouble."

Morning Star stroked the woman's moist brow. "We will say nothing, Mother, but we will be alert to more mischief."

Payaba nodded agreement to the necessary silence. He, too, had been suspicious, but hadn't mentioned it to anyone. He was glad Morning Star had the intelligence to notice the same clues he himself had. "I will heal her. She will remain here with us. Go, tend your guest. Win the race."

"It is to be, Wise One; I feel it in my heart."

The white-haired man smiled and nodded agreement once more.

"Mother is ill, Father. Payaba tends her in his tepee. Do not worry. He says she will be fine by the new sun. When the race is over, I will prepare food for Spotted Tail, our honored guest."

"Your father told me of the vision and contest, Morning Star. If the storm had not forced us to camp all day, we would have witnessed it. I wish victory this day for the daughter of a great chief. On the trail I met the white man called Tanner Gaston, family of Sun Cloud. His task is large."

"Obtaining peace is never an easy one, our friend. Will you vote for treaty when the time comes?" she couldn't help but ask.

"Peace with honor is a greater task. If the whites offer it, I will accept. When you ride with Sky Warrior, seek rest and safety in my camp."

Morning Star smiled and thanked him. News of Joe warmed her heart and sent surges of energy through her body. She felt wonderful today, her old self again. She could tell that Joe had impressed the Brule chief, and that pleased her. She wondered if he had been delayed by the storm, too.

The ceremonial drum began its summons for the race. Morning Star left the tepee and headed for the clearing ahead of her father and guest. Her brother halted her before she reached the appointed spot.

"I have seen Mother in Payaba's tepee. She is very ill. You brought the white man's disease to our father's tepee and our camp. It attacked you and Hanmani, then our mother. Pray your evil does not slay her and others."

Morning Star resented his remarks. She was not to blame. "That is cruel, Brother. And how did you know Hanmani was sick?" she asked, wondering if she had judged the wrong man guilty of wickedness.

As he stroked the lance scar on the side of his face, inflicted by a Crow weapon, he answered, "I heard you tell Payaba to check him. Why do you do this evil thing, Sister? Your words shamed you and your family on the past sun."

She stared at him and wondered how he could be so different from their father. "If a man is wrong, does Night Stalker not challenge him?"

"I am a man. As a woman, you gave great insult to our shaman."

"Should I yield and lose so great a victory when he was mistaken?"

"Was he, Sister?" her brother scoffed.

"Yes, Night Stalker," she responded. She was tempted to reveal her suspicions, but kept her promise to keep silent about them. Besides, her brother was close friends with Knife-Slayer, and he was in favor of war. When the truth was placed in her hands, she would pass it to his!

Morning Star left Night Stalker standing there, staring at her retreating back. She encountered Buckskin Girl on her way to the clearing to compete with her. "Why do you challenge me, my friend?" she asked her friend.

"When the time comes, you will learn all things," the daughter of Flaming Star replied. "I must do this, Morning Star. I do not challenge to hurt you. When the truth is revealed, you will understand and accept why I seek to win. I cannot speak such words today, but I am happy we race when you are stronger. It is fair. Know you are my friend and I love you."

As the female walked away, Morning Star prayed, Wakantanka, omakiyi: Great Spirit, help me. This was it, her final chance for victory.

The two competitors lined up at the starting point. After her earlier words, Morning Star glanced at Buckskin Girl and smiled. No matter if she was wrong, Buckskin Girl was her friend and felt she must do this deed. Surely Grandfather had a good reason for it, one He would reveal soon.

Wolf Eyes gave the signal, and the two females raced toward a marked point. They remained even at the turning spot and down the return stretch. At the last minute, Morning Star thought of Joe and surged forward to be the first to cross the line drawn on Mother Earth. The ceremonial chief handed her the thirteenth stone and announced her as the winner.

Morning Star grinned at her father as she recovered her breath. Buckskin Girl congratulated her with a sad smile and walked away in an aura of depression, to be halted by Hawk Eyes wanting to console and woo her. Morning Star wondered why her friend was so upset, but knew she would learn the reason one day. She read pride and concern in her father's gaze. When she joined him, he spoke to her.

"This sacred event must be painted upon the tribal and our family's buffalo records. I am proud, my daughter," he said before the others, but his heart drummed in trepidation of what the victory could cost him.

Spotted Tail smiled and remarked, "It is good to know Morning Star will become the legend She-Who-Rode-With-The-Sky-Warrior."

"*Pilamaya, Sinte Geleska.*"

As Morning Star envisioned her coup upon the pictorial records, her heart raced with excitement and pride. She had known Joseph Lawrence for the passings of only seven moons, and already he had changed her life. She could not imagine exactly how traveling and working with him for many full moons would alter her and her existence. Yet she knew and accepted that he was a vital part of her destiny.

At dusk, Joseph Lawrence reached Fort Tabor. Sunday's storm had passed his location quickly, then settled over the Black Hills without delaying him. After concealing his Lakota armband, he entered the military site, a small one built in '49. He located Captain James Thomas and introduced himself. As he sat across the desk from the officer in charge, he looked into the brown eyes of the sandy-haired man with tall and lanky body and pleasant expression who immediately said to call him Jim.

Joe revealed that Tom Fitzpatrick had said James was the man to see in this area. "He has great faith in you, Jim."

"That's good to hear, but why did Tom send you to me?"

"You know about the big treaty he's working on . . ." Joe began and the officer nodded. "He thinks somebody is trying to prevent it, to stir up trouble between the Dakotas and Crow. If those two nations go on the warpath, whites will be trapped in the middle of a bloody and violent confrontation. Every wagon train passing through this area will be in danger, and so will every soldier and settler in these parts. The trappers and traders won't be any safer, either, despite how long they've been here."

Joe explained who Stede Gaston was and why he had come to this territory. The captain recognized the names Sun Cloud and Gray Eagle, and he displayed instant interest. Joe disclosed his mission with Tanner, and Tanner's subsequent murder. He told Jim about his run-in with Zeke and his boys and about his rescue of Sun Cloud's daughter and the visit to the Oglala camp, and described his meeting on the trail with the Brule chief. "From what I've seen and heard, Jim, I think somebody is trying to frame the Dakotas, make whites terrified of them so the Army will wipe them out for him. I believe the villain is Snake-Man." Joe passed along the scanty description that Morning Star had given him from Knife-Slayer's spying.

Captain James Thomas propped his arms on his desk and leaned forward.

"I've heard rumors about such a man, but I haven't talked to anyone who's willing to say he's met him. The Crow say he's a good spirit, not a real man. They claim he doesn't give or sell them weapons and whiskey. They claim the Dakotas lie to provoke soldiers into attacking Crow camps to recover arms and firewater that do not exist."

"They're wrong, or lying to cover their guilt and connection. He's real, and he's fooling them with Oriental magic," Joe insisted, then explained his suspicions. "I know Zeke and his boys were hauling guns and whiskey, probably to the Crow; that's where their trail headed."

"I've seen Zeke, Clem, and Farley around here and at trading posts. From what I know, Zeke works for himself. He hires out to any trader to haul goods. But I didn't realize he was carrying illegal supplies to the Indians. I'll question him later."

"Zeke might claim he works for himself, but he doesn't. He's hired by somebody he calls 'Boss.' I heard his boys slip up and so did Morning Star."

"I'll keep that in mind, and I won't drop any clues to him. If he knows you're on to him, he'll be more careful."

"After what happened between us on the trail, I can't get near him. What I'm certain of is that the Dakotas, most of them, want peace, and they're not making those attacks I've heard about. They're still in winter camps. Spotted Tail was traveling only to speak to Sun Cloud about the new trouble and accusations. I was impressed by both chiefs."

Jim sipped his cool coffee. "I've been here almost a year and I haven't met either one. I'm surprised you got in and out of that Oglala camp alive with your light hair. You're lucky they befriended you."

"They had good reason; I claimed to be Tanner Gaston so they'd accept me and help me. Once the treaty is signed, I'll tell Sun Cloud the truth. For now, as long as he thinks I'm his kin, I'm safe. You'll need to keep my work for Fitzpatrick and that lie to Sun Cloud secret."

Jim leaned back in his wooden chair and relaxed. "You have my word. I want peace, too, so I hope you succeed. I'll give any help I can."

"Tell me, what would Snake-Man have to gain with new trouble?"

Jim leaned forward again, his expression serious. "If he gets the Dakotas pushed out by Crow or whites, and he has enough men and money to take control of large tracks of land, he'll be rich and powerful. There are valuable furs and hides for the taking or buying. Most of the timber, certainly the best, is along the rivers and in those Black Hills. Endless miles of grasslands make for good ranching. The soil is fertile for farms, and not much clearing is necessary. There are plenty of rivers for water and for easy travel. If he gets into trading posts, supplies for settlers and wagon trains could bring in a fortune. Not to mention if he brings in women and whiskey for soldiers. Some old-timers speak of gold, but even the Crow won't tell where it is or use it for trade. That's one secret all Indians realize is dangerous. All he has to do is stop the treaty and keep gaining strongholds. To do that, he has to stir up big trouble. I hope you're wrong, but I'm afraid you aren't. How you planning to work this mission?"

Tom Fitzpatrick had told him to confide in and to work with this man, so Joe trusted Jim. "When I leave, I'm going back to Sun Cloud's camp. They're letting me borrow their smartest female to act as my guide and translator. I'll pretend to be a traveling trader and she'll be my squaw. We should be able to get into and out of most Indian camps and settled areas. If all goes well, I should pick up clues."

"Sounds clever but dangerous. Don't tangle with Zeke again. He'll be looking for you with blood in his eye. He's big and mean and strong."

"Does he work one post and area more than the others?"

"Not that I know of. Most of my time is spent on the post or close by."

"Tanner and I met some of the men at Lookout. Those Columbia Fur boys seemed all right; nothing that sparked suspicion. Simon Adams at Pratte's was busy and only talked to us a little, but we overheard some things he said to others. He didn't make any secret of how much he hates the Indians, but a lot of white men feel the same."

"If you'd been here as long as some of them and experienced what they have," Jim explained, "you'd understand their feelings, even though most are mistaken. Trouble is, all Indians get blamed for the raids and brutalities of a few bands of renegades. Overeager or confused officers order retaliations on the wrong bands. Or whites join together and attack hunters. Then the Indians blame all whites and soldiers for the actions of a few. It's a crazy circle, Joe. Biggest problem is that neither side takes the time to get to know the other. We're all too wary. I doubt that will ever change. All a new treaty will do is hold off the inevitable a while longer."

Joe feared the captain was accurate in his assessment. He returned to Simon Adams. "Men who have something to hide and protect usually aren't as verbal as Adams was about their feelings," he said to Jim. "I could be wrong; it could be an act. He was a big man and he wore long sleeves. He could be this Snake-Man. He warned me and Tanner about the Lakotas, just before my friend was killed. I'm sure Tanner saw or heard something more than he was able to tell me before he died. At least, they thought he witnessed something damaging. The owner, Bernard Pratte, wasn't around, so I don't have an impression of him. We didn't make it north to McMichael's post."

"Bernard Pratte's a last choice for Snake-Man," Jim asserted. "He's been there since '31; that's a long time to wait to cause trouble. Most Indians like him and deal with him over the other traders. Orin McMichael seems a pretty good fellow, too, a jolly Scotsman. Hasn't given us any trouble. He stays close to his post and runs it himself. I do know Zeke hauls for Pratte. Why didn't you and Tanner come to see me before roaming around?"

"I wish we had; he might still be alive. Tanner suggested we look around and get a feel of the area before seeing you. I was riding with him, so I let him do the planning and deciding."

"You don't have any idea who killed Tanner Gaston or why?"

Joe revealed what his friend had told him. "Not much to go on, but that's why I followed those ruts left by Zeke's wagons."

"Too bad you didn't find anything out. Make sure you visit me often now and keep me informed of what you learn. I won't make out a report on this. I wouldn't want someone finding that file about you. A man doesn't always know whom he can trust. Who will you be traveling as?"

"Joseph Lawrence. I don't want anyone connecting me to Stede Gaston at Fort Laramie. Besides, Simon Adams and Zeke know me by that name, and know about Tanner's murder, so it might stir up suspicions if I use his name. I'm sure Snake-Man has spies everywhere."

"Was Zeke around Pratte's that day? You said he knew about Tanner."

"I didn't see him. But if he's working for Snake-Man, he knows."

They talked a while longer. Then Jim stood, shook hands with Joe, and said, "Good luck. Be careful out there. And don't forget your reports."

"Thanks, Jim. I can use your help. I'll keep you informed."

Before Joe left Fort Tabor the next morning, he wrote and mailed two letters: one to his parents and one to his married sister. He told them all of his challenging work here with Stede for peace, of meeting Stede's Indian kin, and of how beautiful this area was. He didn't mention Tanner's death, as he didn't want to worry them. He closed by saying he would be home in six months. He asked his sister to keep an eye on their parents until he returned, as his father had been upset by Joe's decision to come here. In time, he hoped his father would understand why it was so important to him.

As he rode away, Joe's mind was on the loss of his best friend. He wished Tanner was with him, sharing this ultimately fulfilling task. He wished Tanner could have met his Indian relatives. He missed their talks and friendship. It was hard to accept they were gone forever. He vowed anew that he would not rest or quit until his friend's murderer was punished.

Joe pushed his grief into the back corner of his mind by thinking of Morning Star. He could hardly wait to see her again. Soon . . .

The daughter of Sun Cloud completed her chores and visited with Hanmani, whose curious behavior had been exhibited only during the riding event. It had been four moons since the winning race against her friend. Spotted Tail and his band had left the following day to visit with Oglala chief Red Cloud, another powerful leader. Singing Wind had healed within two days, as Morning Star herself had. Her brother was still urging her not to ride with Joe. Though her father had painted her coup upon the pictorial records of the tribe and their family, she had noticed how quiet he was; she knew he did not want her to leave but felt he must say and do nothing to stop her.

Buckskin Girl had not explained her curious challenge, but still vowed to reveal the motive soon. Her friend seemed disappointed over her loss of the contest. They continued to share chores, but something was different between them. Buckskin Girl seemed unsure of herself and a little distant. Morning Star wished she knew why.

Morning Star recalled an exciting episode that had taken place two days ago. Wind Bird's vision quest had shown him an elk and he had been taken into the Elk Dreamer Society. Payaba was teaching and training him to be a shaman. Naturally that did not please Hawk Eyes, as a tribe had only one medicine chief. She hoped something, a message or sign from the Great Spirit, would return Payaba to that rank; or He would let it pass to Wind Bird. She had been polite to Hawk Eyes, but his resentment toward her remained obvious.

Knife-Slayer, his son, was pursuing her with frequency and boldness since her victory. As if thinking of him summoned him, the Indian brave approached.

"*Wociciyaka wacin yelo.*" He said he wished to speak with her.

"*Takuwe he?*" she asked, dreading another annoying conversation.

"Ye sni yo. Hecetu sni ye. Hanke-wasicun, sunka-ska Tanner!"

She was vexed when he told her not to go with Joe. She was angered by him calling "Tanner" a half-breed and a white dog. *"Wacin nis econ akinica he?"* She asked him if he wished to argue.

"Hiya," he quickly refuted. *"Waste cedake. Nis wacin."* He vowed his love and desire for her.

Morning Star knew that desire was to marry her, and though she had rejected him many times, he kept asking? *"Okihisni Anpaowicanhpi."* She told him she could not accept.

"Micante petani niye," he vowed.

The maiden did not believe she was the fire in his heart. She replied, *"Micante wookiye wacin,"* telling him that the fire in *her* heart was a flaming desire for peace. She accused him of wanting to go on the warpath, which they both knew was true. *"Zuya iyaka nis wacin!"*

"Oyate makoce unkita kici kiza ecinsni toktuka hwo?" he contended.

His words—"How is it wrong to fight for our people and land?"—drummed through her head. He was a quick and clever debater. Yet she countered with haste, *"Wiconi wowahwa."*

He wanted to shout her foolish words—"Peace is life"—back into her beautiful face. How could someone so smart, brave, and skilled work for costly peace against such fierce enemies? he fumed. *"Wimacasa yelo! Wicasa iyecel mat'in kte yelo!"* he vowed: I am a man! I will die like a man!

Morning Star shook her head in vexation, turned, and left him.

Knife-Slayer glared at her retreat and vowed to himself, *Mitawa Anpaowicanhpe! Wicasta wanzi tohni icu kte sni!*

If Sun Cloud's daughter had overheard the ominous words of his vow—"Morning Star is mine! I will let no man take her from me!"—her troubled heart would have pounded in trepidation.

The following day, as Morning Star and Singing Wind left the forest with loaded wood slings, both sighted Joe's horse tethered near their tepee at the same time. Apprehension washed over the mother as she realized what the white man's return meant, the departure and perilous task of her daughter. But suspense and joy raced through the maiden as she comprehended that the moment to seek her true fate had arrived.

"Tanner has come," Singing Wind murmured. "Soon, you must go."

"Do not be sad, Mother. This task will bring peace for our people."

"I pray it is so, Daughter, but great fear lives in my heart."

"We will take no risks. Grandfather will guide us and protect us. Have you forgotten the sacred vision told of our victory to come?"

Singing Wind did not doubt that success would be won; she only worried over what their journey together could cost her family. Observing the expression in her child's eyes and the happiness in her spirit over the man's return warned Singing Wind of how strong her daughter's feelings were for the grandson of Powchutu/Eagle's Arm. She sent a mental prayer to the Great Spirit to keep Morning Star's mind clear. The two females entered the tepee to find "Sky Warrior" and Sun Cloud talking.

Joe glanced at the beautiful maiden who had filled his thoughts for days.

Learning she had won the contest hadn't shocked him, and his worries had become overshadowed by excitement. He had never doubted her skills and wits, as
he had witnessed them during their trek together. After greeting the mother, he
focused his attention on his impending partner. "Hello, Morning Star. I'm proud of
your victory. Your father showed me your coup painted there," he remarked, motioning to the pictorial family record suspended from the tepee-lining rope to dry.
"I told Sun Cloud about my meetings with Jim at the fort and with Spotted Tail on
the way there. I'll tell you everything after we're on the trail tomorrow. We're
riding out at first light. I want to start before more trouble arises. Can you be ready
to leave early in the morning?"

"*Han.* Yes," she switched to English for practice.

"Good. I almost made it here yesterday, but the sun gave out on me. I camped
about ten miles away because I thought it might be dangerous to ride in after dark.
I didn't want to risk getting shot as an intruder." He smiled.

"We break camp in five moons to ride for the grasslands to hunt buffalo," Sun
Cloud reminded his daughter. After the customary signal of tepee dismantling by
the chief's wife, the others would begin their tasks to journey to their first summer
camp. He told her where he would make trail signs to let her know which direction they took, which was determined by where the most buffalo grazed. As the
great herds moved, so did the Indians and their nomadic camps. They would begin
in the lush plateaus and canyons that composed or surrounded the area known as
Maka Sica, what the white men also called the Badlands.

Joe was delighted that Morning Star could read trail signs and could locate
Sun Cloud's new location after they left this one on the first of June. He noticed
how she kept her gaze controlled and off him unless he spoke to her, and he
suspected—and hoped—it was to conceal her joy at seeing him. He also tried to
keep his frequently straying mind on the business at hand. He was eager to begin
their journey and to participate in the ceremony tonight that would make him a
Tanhan-We, blood brother.

"Rest, Tanner," the chief said. "We talk more before the moon rises."

Morning Star and Singing Wind began the final preparations for their departure. They packed supplies, but Joe didn't offer help because that was "woman's
work." Sun Cloud loaned them one of his horses to carry their supplies; it would be
loaded in the morning.

Joseph Lawrence gave the women privacy as he strolled around the Indian
encampment. Dogs raced about and barked or lay in the warming sun. Horses were
held in rope and brush corrals or staked beside tepees that were positioned between
black hills and a serene lake. The pointed dwellings with many poles reaching
heavenward were colored from the use of different colored buffalo hides, varying
from light tan to almost black. Spring grass was lush and green, the sky clear and
blue. Reeds and water plants grew along the lake's edge, and assorted wildflowers
offered beauty here and there. It was a lovely and peaceful setting.

Joe encountered older women and youthful maidens doing chores. Most
halted to stare at him, with the youngest cupping their mouths to whisper and
giggle. He was relieved and delighted not to sense hatred in them; their behavior
told him that he and his task had been accepted. His keen mind took in details of
camp life.

At the lake, women washed clothes or fetched water. Others went to or
returned from gathering wood or edible plants. Some were hanging strips of meat

on racks to dry and preserve. A few were beading, sewing, or flattening quills with their teeth. Cradleboards, travois bindings, securing thongs, and saddle pads were being made or repaired in preparation for the moving of the camp soon. Small children entertained themselves nearby, girls with toys made to teach them their roles in life: miniature tepees, wooden horses, travois, and grass-stuffed dolls. Babies slept or played on buffalo mats near their mother or tender's sides, and older children—especially boys—were off enjoying themselves.

As Joe roamed the active area, teenage boys also delayed their games to eye him as he passed them. He witnessed mock hunts to hone instincts, races to acquire speed and agility, balls of tightly rolled buffalo hair tossed into distant baskets to learn accuracy for when the ball changed to a lance, and the rolling of a willow hoop with a stick for dexterity and control. Soon, many of them would go into serious training to one day ride with their fathers on hunts—or perhaps raids if the truce parley failed.

Most fathers and older brothers were occupied with important tasks. Some warriors and braves were away hunting or scouting for enemy tracks. Others sat near their conical abodes or in the forest shade to work. Joe lingered for a while at a few groups to watch them sharpen old weapons whose blades were dulled from use or repair edges that were chipped. He observed the preparation of feathers for one end of the arrow shafts, as they controlled the flight of the most frequently used weapon. He saw how they smoothed slender and sturdy limbs chosen for shafts, as any rough spot could change its speed and direction. He watched them chiseling away at certain stones to make arrowheads with sharp and jagged points, and how they attached the tips and feathers to the shafts. Joe was intrigued by the men's deftness, and how they balanced the weights of each piece to construct a lethal and accurate weapon. He observed men restringing bows, their strength and skill displayed in rippling muscles and agility. Some of the elders sat with them smoking pipes, telling stories, or gambling. Joe was impressed by their comradeship and hard work.

He liked the way they smiled or nodded at him and allowed him to spend time with them. Those who could speak English explained the details of their chores to him. Some were more genial and open than others. Most of them had ridden with Sun Cloud over the years, and a few with the legendary Gray Eagle. He wished he had gifts of gratitude and friendship for each of them, but he had made purchases for only one man: Payaba, the old shaman who had foretold his coming and aided it.

Joe went to his horse and retrieved the knife and small ax, more like a hatchet. He headed for the past medicine chief's tepee, as he'd seen the elderly man return home earlier. From the custom he had learned, he called out, asking for permission to come inside and visit.

"*U wo.*" Payaba granted it.

Joe held out the knife and hatchet. "I bring you gifts of friendship and thanks, Payaba. I don't understand visions, but yours was filled with knowledge and truth. Morning Star speaks only good and loving words of you. I'm honored to know you. If there's a chore I can do for you today, my hands and mind are willing."

"Your heart is kind and pure, Tanner Gaston. Payaba thanks you. Many others see me as a grandfather, brother, and uncle; they do chores for Payaba and Winter Woman. They fetch wood and water, and bring food. Morning Star gathers herbs and plants for my medicines. I need nothing more. My heart is warmed by your generosity and friendship."

Payaba retrieved something from a medicine pouch and wrapped it in a small piece of hide. "It is medicine to tend the cut you place on your hand in the ceremony this moon," he explained. "It will halt redness, bad water, and fever. No evil spirit must be allowed to sicken a man who has a great task before him."

Joe thanked him for the gift. "Payaba's medicine is strong. Morning Star used it to tend a bullet wound I got after I helped her escape those white men. It's almost healed now."

"Cover the cut. Let no dirt or insect enter. The evil white-eyes put many bad things into Mother Earth."

As the snowy-haired man watched Joe's departure, he reflected on the dream he had experienced following the contest. He decided it would be damaging to reveal it to his chief. Besides, if it was more than a dream—as he suspected— destinies of those involved could not be changed. There was no need to worry his leader until the time came . . .

As Morning Star went through her possessions one last time to make certain she had packed everything she would need on the trail, she lifted her flesher and gazed at it with pride and joy. At a girl's ritual introduction to womanhood, she was given a special elkhorn upon which her good deeds were recorded by whom- ever was in charge of an event. The color, shape, and number of dots revealed the reasons for those marks. Some were for tanning hides and making robes, for win- ning beading or quilling contests, for helping others construct their first tepee before a joining ceremony, and for performing a charitable or brave deed. Possible suitors often asked to view a woman's flesher before he shared a blanket with her or asked her to become his wife. For a female, counting her dots was comparable to a warrior counting his coups of prowess and generosity.

Many women had earned a new dot for helping Morning Star prepare for the great task before her. The Lakota beading was removed from all her possessions and replaced with the colors and symbols of the Arapaho, a tribe that was neither ally nor foe of either the Dakotas or the Crow. It would be a safe identity to assume as Joe's squaw. Even her new necklace and wristlets were Arapaho.

Morning Star wondered where Joe was and how he was doing in her camp. As soon as the last task was completed, she would look for him.

Knife-Slayer returned from hunting with a buck across his horse. He sighted the white man near a corral and headed to speak with the paleface before skinning his kill. As he approached, the hated rival heard him.

Joe noticed the cold glare in the warrior's narrowed eyes and the hostility in his expression. He perceived hatred and resentment in the Indian's aura. Hoping to avoid an unpleasant confrontation, he complimented the man. "Your hunt was successful; that's a fine buck. How many arrows did it take to bring him down?" he attempted to converse in a genial way.

"A skilled hunter slays his game with one shot, White man. Knife-Slayer is a skilled hunter and a skilled warrior. Can you do the same?"

Joe tried to make peace by grinning and replying, "Most of the time, but I wouldn't want to compete in hunting and shooting with a man of your prowess. I'm glad we're on the same side. You'd make a tough enemy."

The Indian avowed, "We are enemies, White-Dog. You do not trick me with your words as you blind others with them. Before many suns and moons pass across the heaven, you will prove to my people you are false, that your skills are few, and your task futile. When the whites and Crow attack us on the plains, war will come. Until my people see the truth, protect Morning Star from danger. And do not touch her," he added with a coldness that startled Joe.

"I'm not your enemy, Knife-Slayer," the blond argued. "I'm here to help your people. How can you doubt and reject a sacred vision?"

Ebony braids with coup feathers attached near their ends grazed strong shoulders as the warrior shook his head. "You cannot stop a war we have battled with the Crow since Grandfather created us. You cannot stop the whites from attacking. Yes, Half-Breed, we are enemies. Your white blood and ways are strongest. When war comes, you will side with them. On that sun, I will slay you with great joy. If you try to steal Morning Star from me and her people, I will slay you sooner."

Knife-Slayer's insults and warnings angered Joe, but he controlled his temper. Joe knew the warrior was arrogant, as no other one wore his coup feathers in camp. He glanced at two Sun Dance scars on the bronzed chest of the man who craved the same woman he did; they told him the warrior could endure as much pain as he could inflict on foes. He couldn't imagine Morning Star marrying and yielding to this fierce male. She was too gentle, kind, and smart. Yet, if Knife-Slayer stopped others from wooing Morning Star and made himself her only suitor, and if he offered many possessions to her father for her hand in marriage, would Morning Star feel compelled to accept her only proposal to avoid embarrassing her family by having no mate? The idea of her being entrapped by the wicked warrior vexed Joe. With boldness, he chided, "Your heart is filled with hatred and bitterness. Men like you are the only ones who can prevent peace with the whites and the Crow. It's wrong, Knife-Slayer, to endanger and destroy your people."

"A man fights his own battles, White-Dog."

"Your intrusion can create a battle you can't win, Knife-Slayer."

"There is no battle I cannot win! There is no foe I cannot defeat!"

"Then why didn't you attack and slay Snake-Man when you located him and spied on him?" Joe challenged, his own blue eyes narrowed now.

Although only two inches separated their heights, Knife-Slayer drew himself up tall and stiff to level their gazes. "He is an evil spirit," he responded. "They cannot be slain, except with powerful magic. I am no shaman."

"He isn't a spirit. He's only a man, a white man, a clever man."

"You have not seen him! How do you know such things?"

"In a land far away, I have seen the kind of magic he does. They're only tricks to fool Indians who haven't seen them. I'm going to defeat him. Like you, he craves war, but I'll find him and stop him."

"If he does not find and stop you first."

"At least I'm not afraid to go after him," Joe snapped unwisely.

"Knife-Slayer fears no man and no task, Piss of the Coyote!"

Provoked, Joe spoke his mind. "You fear I have the prowess to steal the woman you desire. You fear I have the prowess to gain a treaty to halt another war. You fear my victory will earn me a bigger coup than you've won. You fear that victory will put an end to the bloody raids you love. Fear is a strong and wicked power, Knife-Slayer, one you'd better defeat or learn to control for the good of your people and lands. If you change your mind about me and peace, I'll offer you my hand in friendship," Joe finished, but only to avoid more hostility. He walked away.

Morning Star was concealed behind a tree. After she saw Joe depart, she joined the warrior and warned, "Remove such fears and doubts from your mind and heart, Knife-Slayer, or they will bring much trouble and suffering to many. It is wrong to insult a man with Oglala blood, the same blood that lives within your chief and in my body. When the great task is done and peace rules our lands, I will return to my people and he will return to his. He is not what stands between us. We are too different."

"If he tries to steal you, I will challenge him to the death."

"He cannot steal from you what you do not own," she retorted. "If you intrude on the sacred vision, you will be banished or slain. We have known each other since children. I do not want such shame and torment to enter your mother's tepee. Visit the sweat lodge to purify yourself of such wickedness. Pray to Grandfather to change your heart. Endure a vision-quest to receive His warnings of wisdom. Seek another female to share your love and tepee. Only this way can you survive and be happy."

"I do not wish to survive without my love, my lands, and my honor."

"You do not love me, Knife-Slayer," Morning Star corrected, "you desire me and you crave the daughter of your chief as first wife. If you are patient, a true love will come to you. If you are patient, Joe will win truce, and your honor and our lands will not be endangered."

"Why do you call him Joe?" He pounced on her slip.

Thinking fast, she explained, "That is the name he uses to fool the whites. I practice to avoid mistakes when we travel together. No one must know he is the grandson of Powchutu who was first called Tanner Gaston."

"You are wrong, Morning Star. My love and need for you are as strong as my doubts of him. Do not shame our chief and people by not returning."

"Have you forgotten we are of the same bloodline and cannot mate? Have you forgotten we are different? Morning Star cannot go to the white lands and accept the white ways; I am Oglala; I will always be Oglala. I swear to you, he will return to his home far away when his task is done."

"Swear it to Grandfather, for you will not break your word to Him."

"Nothing I say or do will change your mind, Knife-Slayer. I am troubled by the feelings I see in you. I pray they are gone when I return."

Morning Star encountered her brother before she reached her tepee. She knew that meant another quarrel, and she dreaded it. She smiled and greeted Night Stalker, hoping he would be kind today.

"I pray you can return safely after the truth is revealed, Sister. Know, if you do not, your brother and Knife-Slayer will avenge any harm to you."

"I will be safe with Tanner, my brother."

"He was raised white. He is a half-blood. Do not trust him."

"His bloodline is as strong and true as ours. Tanner said Powchutu joined a half-white woman. Both bloodlines have Indians and whites."

Coldness entered the proud warrior's dark eyes. "No, our blood is almost pure. His has been weakened and stained many times. Enemy blood came to Tanner from his paleface mother, his half-white grandmother, and a paleface parent before her."

Seeing how upset Night Stalker was, she debated in a soft tone, "What of Shalee's mother? What of Jenny's parents? All were white, my brother. Much as you despise the truth, you cannot remove it or forget it. If Running Wolf had claimed his firstborn son, Powchutu would have become Red Heart chief, not Gray Eagle, the second born. If Powchutu had been chief, his son—Stede—would now be chief, not our father. If so, Tanner/Sky Warrior would be next in line, not Night Stalker."

He glared at her and alleged, "If Powchutu had become chief, he would not have met his half-breed woman in the white world he joined by choice. Do not forget, Powchutu loved our grandmother; if he had become chief, he would have taken Shalee as wife. All would be the same for us. I would still be chief next."

"It would not be so, Brother. Different mates bear different children. We would not exist if Gray Eagle had not won and mated with Alisha/Shalee."

"You are wrong, Morning Star. The Great Spirit and *Whope* give a maiden her seeds when she comes to season. No matter which man brings one to life, the child is the same."

"If that is true, how does a white captive bear an Indian child, as Alisha did our father and uncle?"

"Because the Great Spirit makes a warrior's water of life overpower the white woman's seed."

"If that is true," she reasoned again, "Powchutu's flow overpowered his mate's seed to make Stede an Indian, and Stede's flow overpowered his mate's to make Tanner an Indian. As Oglala, you have no fight with him. To you, Tanner must be as Indian as you are, my wise brother."

Night Stalker realized she was turning his argument against him, but he vowed to open her mind! "The Great Spirit does not live and work in the white world where Powchutu fled and mated. Stede was raised as a paleface and he joined to one. The Great Spirit did not intrude on their mating, and their son was born of her white seed. Tanner's face marks him as white, and he carries little Oglala blood."

Morning Star asked herself if her brother's explanation was right, or even partly right. She did not know how either Stede or the real Tanner looked, and she told herself to ask Joe when they had privacy. Yet every child of a mixed union that she knew looked Indian or revealed only a tiny mark of their white heritage. Except Alisha/Shalee, she reminded herself. "Does that mean the Great Spirit did not intrude on the mating of Black Cloud and Jenny Pilcher?" she questioned. "All say Shalee had hair of fire and eyes like grass when Mother Earth renews her face. Why would the Great Spirit let a white captive's seed be stronger than a Blackfoot chief's?"

"Perhaps the Great Spirit was angered when Black Cloud took his white captive as wife."

"If so, was the Great Spirit not more angered when Gray Eagle—the greatest warrior to ever live—took his white captive as wife?"

"It is not the same, Sister! Our grandmother was half Indian. That is why the Great Spirit did not mark our father and uncle as half-breeds or whites; He made them Indian to show He was not displeased."

"Perhaps the Great Spirit gave grandmother a white face to show all that some whites are good. How can you hate the son and grandson of Powchutu when our grandmother and her mother also carried white blood? The Great Spirit chose Tanner as our helper; He does not hate or reject all white blood. If you battle him, you will be punished," she warned.

To silence her, he accused, "You speak too strong for him, Sister."

"I trust him and believe he can help us. A sacred vision does not lie."

"I fear I see more than trust in your eyes."

"Do not be foolish, Brother. We are of the same bloodline: Running Wolf's. We cannot mate. Is that what troubles you about my leaving?"

"I have not seen this strange glow in your eyes before. He touches your heart, Sister, but be certain he does not touch your body."

"Your warning is not needed, for I know and accept such things."

"Do you, my sister? Remember, if you turn to him and we are betrayed, you and your family will be shamed. You will be banished."

Morning Star fretted as she watched her brother leave. He and Knife-Slayer suspected her feelings for Joe; her mother had hinted at them, and her father was too quiet and watchful. That could only mean she was not doing a good task of concealing her forbidden emotions! She cautioned herself to be more careful. She did not want anything, especially her weakness for Joe, to hinder the sacred mission before them. The fact that Joseph Lawrence was a man of pure white blood made him as taboo as if he were her blood cousin. She was vexed by the contradiction that an Indian male could take a white female but that it was a disgrace for an Indian woman to take a white man!

Morning Star scolded herself for worrying about such an impossible situation. Joe was not like Knife-Slayer, a man who would take a female he desired even if he couldn't join her! Joe had pride, honor, and goodness. Joe knew they were unmatched, and would not pursue her. Yet a curious sensation washed over her. She prayed it was too late for anything or anyone to prevent her from leaving with him in the morning.

Chapter Eight

After the evening meal in Sun Cloud's tepee, Joe, the chief, his wife, and Morning Star joined the Red Hearts who gathered in a clearing near the water for the unusual ritual to make a white man a blood brother.

Green spruces and pines, obsidian hills, and a blue lake surrounded the people with colorful beauty. A half moon floated across an indigo sky with countless silvery stars which reminded all of an artistic piece of Indian beadwork. The water's surface was as tranquil as a lazy southern evening; it reflected the partial moon rising above it as if the moon held a narcissistic spirit who wanted to view its image in nature's mirror. Frogs, crickets, and nocturnal birds sang loudly and merrily as if joining in on the special event, their tunes competing at one time and blending at another. Tepees were outlined against the firmament, their protruding poles like skinny fingers pointing to the heaven. The wind was calm, so no limb or grass blade moved. It was a pleasant night.

In the center of the large gathering was a bonfire with leaping flames of red, orange, and yellow. Soon it would die down to an almost intimate glow. The fire was a signal to draw close to share something special with the tribe; it was a unifying spirit. Near it, there was a post with the sacred Medicine Wheel and Wolf Eyes' Ceremonial Skull: vital symbols of the culture and beliefs of the Lakotas. The four eagle feathers suspended from the wheel's bottom and representing the Lakota virtues—wisdom, bravery, constancy, and generosity—did not flutter in the still air. Morning Star had told Joe they were the first coup feathers earned by the last four Red Heart chiefs. When Night Stalker, or another, became chief, his first coup feather would replace Red Hawk's, as only four could dangle there. The four intersecting bars of shiny metal glittered in the firelight. The center of life was represented at the place where they met in the middle: harmony with the Great Spirit, with oneself, and with nature. It depicted a neverending circle, the continuity of Indian life.

In the forefront of the circle of bodies, the Big Bellies sat on furry mats in the location of importance and control. Next came the cult members of proven warriors, hunters who had not been taken into a society yet, and male elders who were not members of the ruling society. The circle of Indians was completed with the women and children.

The first step of the occasion was to give thanks for past blessings and to summon the Great Spirit to witness this solemnity. Wolf Eyes then continued. "We take *Mahpiya Wicasta,* Your helper, into our hearts and band, Grandfather. You called him home from where *Wi* rises to bring peace and enlightenment to Your children. Tanner seeks harmony with himself, with his grandfather's people, and with Mother Nature. We ask You to give him these things. Tanner has shown the four virtues we honor, as with the eagle feathers on our sacred Medicine Wheel. You have joined his Life-Circle to ours once more. As we share Your breath, prepare our hearts and minds to become as one in purpose and feeling."

The second step in the ritual was pipe smoking, to share the breath of the Great Spirit and to inspire solidarity between the men. Normally the ceremonial chief was first, followed by the tribal chief, the war chief, the shaman, and other Big Bellies. Afterward, all warriors of high rank took their turns. Tonight, their honored guest was third to smoke.

Joe sat on one side of Sun Cloud, Morning Star on the other. Though she was a part of the sacred vision and mission ahead, she did not share the smoking rite. Women were never allowed to touch men's sacred objects or weapons, for it was believed they would steal their magic and strength.

Wolf Eyes packed the red stone bowl, lit the tobacco, drew deeply and reverently from its long stem, and handed it to their leader. Sun Cloud inhaled smoke, then released it. He passed the pipe to Joe, who repeated their actions while Morning Star observed.

When the pipe was passed four times, Wolf Eyes stood to pray for the safety, survival, and success of Tanner Gaston and Morning Star.

As the maiden listened to the words being sent to her god, she knew He would not punish her and Joe for their necessary deception. If the Great Spirit was angered by it, He would have exposed them or even slain them by now. She believed that Stede and Joe—not Tanner—were the vision helpers. It could not be bad or wrong to do the will of her god, even if she had to lie to her loved ones for a while. Once peace was won and the villains defeated, surely her family and tribe would understand and forgive her trickery.

The ceremonial and medicine chiefs performed a special dance and chant to the timing of stone-filled gord rattles, eagle-bone whistles, and a kettle drum that was beat upon by eight men using sturdy sticks with ends wrapped in buffalo hide. As the almost hypnotic music played and the two men moved around the fire with matching steps and words, Sun Cloud withdrew his knife and made a slice across the palm of his right hand.

Joe did as the chief had instructed earlier, and took the fire-sterilized blade and sliced across his hand. Sun Cloud had told him of his mother's warnings about cuts made with dirty weapons and left untended. Morning Star had told Joe how refusing to inflict "mourning cuts" upon his body after his parents' deaths had angered many tribe members and almost cost her father their votes for him as chief over Bright Arrow. Joe held up his bleeding hand and, when Sun Cloud lifted his, he grasped it and mingled their blood. As the red liquid eased down his arm, Joe knew he had done the right thing by claiming to be his murdered friend. Their gazes met, each exposing friendship and belief in this ceremony. "I will always be your friend and blood brother, Sun Cloud."

"Your eyes and voice say your words are true, friend and brother."

Morning Star was touched by the scene of uplifted clasped hands and stirring words between her father and the man who was stealing her heart. She couldn't help but think of the physical differences in the two men, and between Joe and Knife-Slayer whose glare exposed his ill feelings. From their positions with Sun Cloud between them, she could barely see Joe, and she dared not lean aside to peer around her father's body. As she waited, she envisioned how he must look in the sienna breechcloth, fringed leggings, and beaded moccasins that her father had loaned to him. She could almost see the adoring flames dancing on his handsome face.

With his face shaved and his chest hairless, Joe almost stole her breath! For a few wild moments, she imagined him riding across the Plains as a band leader or a hunter, dancing around a campfire in only a breechcloth with sweat glistening on his taut body, and battling their foes in warpaint. Of course he would mark his face with blue, white, and yellow to represent his new name: Mahpiya Wicasta, Sky Warrior.

The daydreaming maiden pictured how the blue paint would enhance Joe's azure eyes, and how all three colors would look against his sunbronzed flesh with a golden mane flowing past his strong neck. That sunny hair grazed the top of powerful shoulders that tapered into a sleek middle. In Indian clothing, with his sparse body hair, strong bone structure, and darkly tanned skin, if it were not for his blond hair and sky eyes, he wouldn't look so different from her people. Yet it would always be those eyes and hair which reminded her of the impassable canyon between them.

Morning Star felt proud and honored to be a special part of this period in her people's history. She was ready to challenge dangers, confront the unknown, and to learn more about Joseph Lawrence and herself. She was the only one who knew the truth about him, and that trust warmed her. He could have fooled her too, but he hadn't. He had confided in her from the start, proving her faith in him was justified. As soon as his cut was tended and night passed, they would leave. But before her departure, there was something important she had to do: make peace with Buckskin Girl. She would do so when the ceremony ended.

After the ritual, the men's cuts were tended and they chatted with others and enjoyed refreshments. When things quieted down, Sun Cloud asked "Tanner" to join him for a walk to speak privately.

The chief did not want his daughter to return home and overhear the matter that troubled him tonight. He guided his blood brother beyond the last tepee and settled himself on a large rock near even larger boulders. Sun Cloud motioned for the man to sit. "We must talk before you ride, Tanner. There is a promise you must make to me."

Joe sat down near the Indian. "What is it?" he asked warily.

"After you left nine suns ago, I remembered what you said when you first entered our camp. You know the truth of my mother and your grandmother," he ventured, more as a statement than a question.

"Yes, Sun Cloud, I know Sarah Gaston was the real Shalee, not your mother. I know Alisha Williams was a white woman, not the abducted daughter of Chief Black Cloud. Powchutu told Stede the truth about his mother, and he told me before we came here."

The Red Heart Chief exhaled audibly. "For many years I have believed all who knew that dangerous secret were dead, except for me and Singing Wind. My parents, White Arrow, Powchutu, my brother, and the old woman who placed the *akito* of Black Cloud on my mother's body when she lay near death are gone. I did not think of Powchutu telling his son. Matu meant no harm when she placed the mark of her chief on my mother; she wished to return home to die with her people. When Black Cloud came to claim my father's captive as his long-lost daughter, my parents did not know of Matu's trick. If Father had revealed his suspicion, Alisha and Matu would have been slain. Father believed it was the Great Spirit's way of giving him the woman he loved and needed, so he held silent and took her as wife. When Matu died, only Father, White Arrow—his best friend since birth—Mother, and Powchutu knew she was not the real Shalee. All held silent to save Mother's life, to protect my father's honor, and to prevent disharmony. In a time of war—unity, friendship, and trust are important. To reveal such a trick then or now would destroy them."

"You're telling me that only you, Singing Wind, Stede, and myself know the truth? Night Stalker and Morning Star don't know this secret?"

"They do not, and the secret must never leave the mouths of the four of us. Swear as my blood brother and friend you will not betray my trust. If we must war with the whites, my people must be as one in spirit and action. They cannot follow a leader whose honor and face are stained by lies. Night Stalker hates whites, and his spirit is troubled. If my son learns the truth, he will become bitter and dangerous. He will do terrible things to prove he is more Oglala than white. It must not be. If Morning Star learns the truth of her grandmother, I fear she will be pulled toward the white world; and that will destroy her. My daughter was raised Oglala and looks Oglala. You know how Indian women are treated in the white lands. It must not be."

"You have my word of honor I won't tell anyone this secret. Stede Gaston will hold silent, too. I understand why everyone who knew the truth kept quiet, and I agree with what they did. So does Stede. Powchutu only wanted his son to know who his mother was, which makes him who *he* is. Stede knows his father loved Alisha Williams, and he wouldn't do anything to stain her memory. Neither would I. We've heard the glorious legends about Gray Eagle and Shalee. They were remarkable people who let love overcome the differences between them and their cultures. That rarely happens. When it does, it's too beautiful and special and powerful to destroy. I won't ever do that, Sun Cloud. I promise."

"Does your father wish to return to our tribe?"

Joe grasped the unspoken meaning behind his question. "Only to visit. When peace is won, we'll return to our homes far away. Stede believes the Red Hearts have their rightful and best chief: you. His father believed the same thing about Gray Eagle."

"When the time comes, I'll meet with the son of my uncle. Long ago, Powchutu was a close friend when he lived and rode as Eagle's Arm with my father. He lives in my memory and in our legends."

"Your family gave him the peace of mind he needed before he died. It was good he returned to his father's land to seek it. His heart was troubled by all the problems he made for your parents. It's good they all made peace before they died."

"As it is good his son and grandson return to help us."

Joe realized he had been saying "Stede" and "Powchutu" rather than my "father" and "grandfather." If Sun Cloud had noticed that curious slip, he didn't seem suspicious. Joe surmised that the chief must assume he was using their names for clarity. "I'll do my best for peace, Sun Cloud. So will my father," he added as a safety measure, and prayed the foul taste of that lie in his mouth didn't show in his expression.

"That is all any man can do, Tanner—his best."

After the men left the secluded area, Morning Star relaxed her strained body. She had stayed motionless behind the large boulder so their keen senses would not detect her presence. She had not intended to eavesdrop, but they had arrived just as she finished excusing herself and she hadn't wanted to be caught at such a private moment. She had assumed they would talk of the impending task, then leave. The conversation had frozen her in place.

Its implication shot through her keen mind. Her grandmother was not half Indian, or any Indian! She herself, her father, her uncle, and her brother were more white than she had been told! She knew of the Blackfoot custom of a father using a sharp bone to scratch his symbol—*akito*—into the buttock flesh of his children. Ash was rubbed into it to make the mark permanent. It was used to identify children stolen during raids by enemies, especially if it was many years before their rescue and their faces had changed. Perhaps Snake-Man had used such a practice to make the symbols on his body—those Joe had called tattoos—but had rubbed colors into his scratches instead of black ash. But Snake-Man left her thoughts quickly.

This news was astonishing, but not distressing. Why should she be upset to discover she had a little more white blood than she had known, particularly when it came from an exceptional female? Alisha Williams, who had lived as Shalee, had been a strong, proud, and brave woman who had gone from white captive to wife of Gray Eagle, a chief whose legendary exploits had never been matched. Alisha had saved Gray Eagle's life when he was captured and tortured by whites. She had led her husband to a past villainous enemy so Jeffrey Gordon could be defeated. She had made Black Cloud's last days happy ones. She had saved Running Wolf's life. She had saved their tribe from a cavalry attack. She had given Gray Eagle and the Red Hearts two great leaders in Sun Cloud and Bright Arrow, and had raised them to be superior men. She had taught her sons English and white ways to help them with peace and understanding.

Alisha/Shalee had become Indian in heart and spirit. She had been a lesson in courage and strength to everyone. She had earned the love, respect, and acceptance of Gray Eagle, the Red Hearts, and other tribes; something she could not have done as a white captive. Becoming Shalee, even by deception, had given her that chance and all had learned from it. She had lived a full and rewarding life. The love she had shared with Gray Eagle was so powerful that they had even died the same day. The Great Spirit had blessed and honored the loving couple. They would never be forgotten by her band or the Dakota Nation. It would be wrong and cruel to stain their golden memories.

Morning Star understood why her father and the others had kept the truth concealed, and why it must remain buried in the past. She knew Joe would keep his word to Sun Cloud. Without their knowledge, she would help protect the truth. Yet the Great Spirit had led her to this spot tonight to discover it, so He must have a good reason for enlightening her.

Just as Buckskin Girl must have a good reason for her curious actions, which she had not revealed during their short visit. Buckskin Girl had promised to tell her everything soon. Whatever distressed the other female, it could not—must not —destroy their friendship.

Morning Star pushed what she had learned tonight into a special corner of her memory, then headed for her tepee for much needed rest. She would deal with both matters another time.

The exciting moment arrived, and many gathered around Sun Cloud's tepee. Morning Star embraced her mother, father, Payaba, and Buckskin Girl. She comprehended how anxious her parents were, how excited the old medicine man was, and how depressed her friend was not to be going. She spoke to other friends and tribe members, all of whom wished them well.

Morning Star noticed how her brother stayed in the background. His wife, Touched-A-Crow, did not approach the genial group either. The woman's action did not surprise her, as the Brule female kept mostly to herself. Touched-A-Crow was uncommonly quiet and not very smart. She had shown no interest in the stirring contest and had not visited Morning Star and Singing Wind when they were ill. Sun Cloud's daughter wondered why Night Stalker did not take a second wife, unless he didn't want a crowded tepee or to assume responsibility for another person.

As Joe conversed with others, Morning Star's gaze settled on her nephew in Touched-a-Crow's arms. Blood Arrow's lips protruded in an angry pout, as usual, and the defiant gleam in his eyes was visible at that short distance. The two-year-old squirmed to get down, but Touched-a-Crow refused to release him. When the moody boy began to whine and to slap at his mother, Night Stalker apparently ordered his wife to take their son home, no doubt to spare the warrior embarrassment at Bloody Arrow's misbehavior. Morning Star hated to imagine what kind of man her nephew would become if not disciplined soon.

Morning Star looked at her older cousin, Little Feet, who was near the age of her father. The eldest daughter of her slain uncle had well behaved and happy children, and a loving husband in Thunder Spirit. The maiden decided that was how she wanted her own family to be someday.

Joe clasped wrists with the chief and said, "I'll guard her life with my own, Sun Cloud. After we gather enough information, we'll report to you in the new camp. You won't be disappointed by your decision to make peace."

"I will trust you to do what is best for all, Tanner, nothing more."

Whether or not the chief intended to make a dual point with his words, Joe took it that way. He smiled and nodded.

The white man and maiden mounted, and Sun Cloud handed Joe the reins to the pack horse. Farewells and waves followed them from the scene. Neither Joe nor Morning Star failed to notice the icy stares of Knife-Slayer, Hawk Eyes, and Night Stalker.

As both Morning Star and Joe wondered what would happen during their trek together, they rode for a long time without talking or glancing at each other. Though their trust had not vanished, nor any uneasiness settled in, each realized the most difficult part of their task was controlling their emotions. Neither wanted to tempt or be tempted beyond their strength to refuse what both knew existed between them.

When they halted to rest themselves and the horses, Morning Star told Joe, "I worked on English while you gone. I practiced with Father, Mother, and others who speak white tongue. You teach me more."

Joe asked, "Can you read any English?"

Morning Star surprised him by replying, "Little," as she held up her hand with her index finger and thumb about an inch apart. "Grandfather, Gray Eagle, have learning book from white captive who schoolmarm. Grandmother teach him more; she teach sons, Bright Arrow and Sun Cloud. Father teach Mother more after they joined. Father teach Night Stalker and Morning Star. Many white words hard. Indians not have as many for same thing. Even same color have many white names. Words put together and confuse; whites say 'it's' and 'you'll' for it is and you will."

"Those are called contractions. Whites use them in speaking, but they aren't —are not—used in formal English, best English." Joe had noticed how she glowed when she spoke of Alisha/Shalee. "Your grandmother was a special woman. I've heard many wonderful stories about her. It's a shame you never knew her. From what I've seen, you have many of her good traits." His mind wandered back in history. Sarah/Shalee had taken after her white mother, so she had been "rescued" by soldiers, then sent to New Orleans as a small child, where she was adopted by Dr. Devane. As fate would have it, Powchutu had met and married her as Tanner Gaston, then discovered Black Cloud's *akito* that revealed her true identity.

Morning Star saw Joe's attention escape for a moment, and she knew where it had fled. She felt it was best to relate the story she had been told of her heritage. "I not know what Powchutu tell Stede and Stede tell Tanner and Joe. I tell you about Grandmother. She part white. Her father Blackfoot chief Black Cloud. He take Brave Bear, Singing Wind's father, as son after his father killed. Shalee stolen when two winters. Many summers later, Gray Eagle capture white girl. He come to love, but cannot join; she enemy blood. Soldiers steal Grandmother from camp; he attack fort and take back. She ill, and he tend. He find mark of Black Cloud on her body. He happy. It fine to join chief's daughter with white blood. She great woman; all loved her. Morning Star have little white blood," she finished, making the same motion with her fingers as before.

"It not trouble me, but Brother would make many cuts on his body if they let white blood flow out. He not know Grandmother; he born next winter. If so, he not hate all whites so much. She legend. She . . . lady," the maiden finished with a bright smile. "He not remember *Wahea*—it mean Red Flower, 'cause she have red hair. He nine winters old when she killed. She uncle's wife, white woman. She do many good deeds. Whole tribe love and accept. She lady, too. When captured by Bright Arrow, she have bad time; he have bad time. He banished many years. They do good deeds; tribe forgive and take back, but no can become chief. It good for all."

Joe couldn't blame Gray Eagle for allowing the misconception about his love to stand so he could have her. He couldn't blame Sun Cloud for letting it continue to protect his parents' lives or for both chiefs to prevent disrupting the unity of the tribe. The Red Hearts had accepted a white woman into the life of their beloved chief only because they hadn't known the truth about Alisha. His lie about being Tanner Gaston, was an example of how sometimes deception was necessary for the good of all. What if, Joe mused, he never exposed the truth about his identity? As part Indian, could he claim Morning Star as—No, his mind shouted; staying Tanner made them kin! He could pursue her only by exposing his identity. By doing so, he made a match between them just as impossible. Besides, why was he thinking this way?

"What trouble you, Joe?" she asked the quiet man.

"I was planning our strategy," he said, hating to deceive her.

Morning Star sensed he was taking a different trail to mislead her, but didn't contradict or challenge him. "What is stra—te—gy?"

"A cunning plan to surprise and trick the enemy," he explained.

"What stra-te-gy we use?"

"After your rescue, I can't join up with Zeke and his men. Maybe we can find them, trail 'em, and spy on them. First, we need to locate clues to see where to begin. We'll ride and look for tracks to follow."

"Ride to place where Zeke met Crow to see if they do so again. See if pick up trail or signs to follow," she suggested.

"That's a good idea; it could be a regular rendezvous point. Meeting place," he clarified. "That'll give us time to get to know each other before we enter any white or Crow areas. If you're my squaw, we don't want to seem like strangers to each other. That'll create suspicions."

"You right. We ride and become friends before see whites and Crow."

"We *are* friends, aren't we?"

Morning Star gazed into his hopeful eyes. She smiled and said, "Yes, we friends. Morning Star and Joe friends not same as white man and squaw friends. Is not so?"

He grinned and nodded. "That's true. We'll have to pretend . . ."

"What is pretend?" she inquired when he halted and looked uneasy.

"Like playing a game, a trick, behaving in a way that isn't true to fool others. Pretend we're . . . married, man and wife."

"Like disguise." She used one of her new words. When he grinned and nodded again, she added, "Not all squaws join to men who buy. Some join in Indian way, but not in white eyes and laws."

"Which do you want? Joined or not?" he asked.

She considered her two choices for a moment. "We pretend joined; that more fun, bigger challenge. Good disguise. Others we meet respect squaw more who claimed by white man. Not so with squaw not joined."

He grasped her meaning; she didn't want anyone—friend or foe—to view her as an unchaste mistress, or captive property. "You're right; wife it is. To make it seem real to us, we'll have a pretend joining ceremony."

"Taku?" she asked, astonished by his suggestion.

What? his mind echoed. Feeling mischievous, Joe asked, "Why not? If we pretend to join, it'll make it seem more real when we claim we are."

"We not have ceremonial chief to say words. Joe have no gifts for Father. We not shared the blanket. How can seem real?"

Joe untied a blanket from his saddle, grinned, and tossed it over their heads. "One rule covered," he jested in the dimness. "Your Great Spirit and my God are watching over us. Aren't They the highest chiefs of all before whom to say words?"

"It . . . is so," she faltered in confusion and suspense.

"My gifts to your father are my blood, friendship, and peace. Surely they're as valuable as horses. The whites say, Before God, I, Joseph Lawrence, Jr., take you, Morning Star, as my wedded wife." Her expression of pleased astonishment yanked Joe back to reality. He asked himself what in blazes he was thinking and doing! She was so close, so entrancing. To halt or to say it was a joke could offend her, so he needed to carry out the pretense he had begun. Yet he didn't think it wise to use the remaining words that leapt into his head. "Your turn."

Little space separated their bodies, something she was too aware of beneath the cozy cover. She trembled and warmed. Curious emotions surged through her. Recalling his words, she spoke slowly, "Before Great Spirit, I, Morning Star, take you, Joseph Lawrence, Jr., as my wedded . . . husband. Is that all? Are we pretend joined?"

Gazing into her dark eyes and having her so near, Joe lost his wits again. "All white weddings end with a kiss. It makes a bond between husband and wife and their vows to each other. If you'd rather not do that part—"

"It fine to do ceremony right," she interrupted before her courage deserted her. "It hot, hard to breathe; must hurry," she prompted him.

Joe's hands lifted and cupped her face. He looked deep into her dark-brown eyes. "You're my wife now, Morning Star," he murmured, then covered her lips with his.

Morning Star experienced new sensations of pleasure and heat. Running Badger and Knife-Slayer had stolen kisses before; she had been unwilling, and they hadn't felt like this one. Joe's mouth had a nice taste and a gentle pressure that was pleasing and enticing. His lips guided hers toward the correct response. When his arms banded her body, she did the same with his. The kiss became as powerful and hot as a wildfire racing across dried grasslands. It was wonderful to touch him this way.

Joe's arms tightened, and he felt his body reacting to her contact and response. He didn't want to pull away, but knew he should. His breathing altered, as did hers, and he knew she was as affected as he was. He tossed aside the stuffy blanket. The kiss continued.

Hanmani stomped one foot and whickered from a fly bite, causing the two almost to jerk apart. When the pesky insect tried to steal blood from another foreleg, the animal repeated his discouraging action, which gave the couple time to recover their wits.

"We are pretend joined?" she asked once more.

"Yes, you're my woman," he responded, and it was how he felt. "Let's ride." Joe scooped up the blanket and rolled it.

They mounted and rode on.

It was almost dusk when they halted to make their first camp near a tree-lined stream that offered shade and cover. Joe tended the horses while Morning Star unpacked their supplies and prepared their meal. The ride, skirting the Black Hills, had been an easy one with a pace that hadn't allowed much chance for talking. The maiden had led the way; Joe had followed close behind and kept his wits on alert for trouble.

Joe sat on the ground and stretched out his long legs. He watched her work with skilled hands. "Tell me about the contest," he coaxed, as the silence and serenity were sending his mind in a hazardous direction.

Morning Star continued her chores as she related the events. "It was not . . . simple as Morning Star thought. I win, but it hard. It . . . fate. It hard because I sick and weak." She explained her strange illness, her brother's cruel words, and her suspicions of Knife-Slayer and Hawk Eyes.

Joe was troubled. He ignored his romantic rival for the time being and said, "I can't blame Night Stalker for being scared of white men's diseases. We have some bad ones, but they harm Indians more than whites, because we know how to avoid them and tend them. They're strangers to Indians and they can wipe out an entire tribe."

"Long ago, white man's disease almost destroy Cheyenne camp of our allies. It Windrider's camp and tribe when he was chief and best friend to Bright Arrow. White wife of Bright Arrow and white captive of Windrider, who powerful medicine woman, save tribe. Disease steal children from both. Windrider take white shaman as wife. Windrider son, Soul of Thunder, now chief. He joined to Tashina, daughter of Bright Arrow."

"How did Bright Arrow and his wife die?"

"Crow attack camp when warriors and hunters gone. Bright Arrow return and battle. He killed. Wife killed saving children from Crow who capture for slaves. Others return and slay all Crow."

Morning Star passed Joe his wooden dish. As he devoured the meat that was softened in heated water and flavored with unfamiliar seasonings, he ate the wild vegetable roots she had cooked with it. He washed them down with fresh water from the stream, as did she.

"Agent Fitzpatrick told me how your grandfather was killed in an ambush by wicked soldiers, but when did you lose your grandmother?"

"She die same day, just go to sleep when Great Spirit call her name to come join Grandfather. Both die before I born. I know from stories and songs about them. I not know Mother's parents. Brave Bear die in battle. Chela die when Mother enter life. She made daughter of new Blackfoot chief. Father say it best for mates to leave Mother Earth on same sun."

Joe liked her poignant statement. "I agree. I'm sure it's hard on the one left behind to face life alone. How did your parents meet?" he inquired to keep up the casual conversation. Still, it was hard to keep his mind off the fetching female. He kept remembering how she had felt in his arms and how her lips had tasted upon his. He kept recalling how she seemed attracted to him, too. The playful ceremony had exposed to him how he wanted her as a wife. But how, even if he could persuade her, could she fit into his world? How could he take her away from all she knew?

When she finished chewing and swallowing the food in her mouth, she sipped water before answering. "Blackfoot and Oglala been allies many winters. Old chief was my grandmother's father. He was good friends with Running Wolf, Gray Eagle's father. When Black Cloud hear daughter returned, he come to camp and take Shalee home. Gray Eagle wish to join. She refuse, been captive and angry. Black Cloud want to join her to Brave Bear. Gray Eagle come and fight challenge for her. He win. He give promised one—Chela—to Brave Bear to join. Make good choice and truce."

Morning Star saw how intrigued Joe was by her family history, so she continued it. "Bright Arrow was good friend to Singing Wind brother, Silver Hawk. He bad; he side with evil soldiers; he slain after Gray Eagle die, and before parents join. Rebecca, she Bright Arrow mate, missing long time, stolen by white men. Father and uncle both want Singing Wind and chief's bonnet. Half tribe want one; half tribe want other. Father prove best warrior; he win Mother and chief's bonnet. Rebecca returned to uncle."

Joe put aside his empty plate. "I was wondering how the youngest son became chief while his older brother was still alive. Now I understand. I knew about the ambush and Silver Hawk's treachery from the reports by Colonel Sturgis and Major Ames. The Army let me, Stede, and Tanner read them to learn what happened here thirty-one years ago. You eat while I tell you about my meeting with Captain James Thomas. I've kept you talking until your food is probably cold."

"It fine. Tell of soldier you met," she coaxed.

Joe had promised to help her with her English, but hadn't corrected her because he didn't want to interrupt her interesting revelations. There was plenty of time for lessons along their journey. As she ate and observed him, he related his meeting with Spotted Tail and with Jim.

Finished with her meal, Morning Star set her plate on the ground. "Can Joe and Morning Star trust him?" she asked.

Joe reflected on the meeting. "I hope we can; I think so. I didn't sense any dishonesty in him."

"Joe have sharp wits, so must be good man."

"I'm glad you have so much faith in me, Morning Star. I don't want to do or say anything to hurt or mislead you. I'll always tell you everything . . . when I can," he qualified his vow.

She understood. "I think and do same. We keep riding, looking?"

"Yes, but from now on, I don't cut my hair or shave my face. If I'm going to play a trader or trapper, I have to look like one. You'll have to excuse my unkempt appearance until we finish this task."

"Part of disguise?" she used another favorite new word, then laughed.

"Yep," he concurred, then smiled at her.

"I tend hand before wash things. Not want wound to go bad."

He grinned. "English lesson time. I will tend your hand before I wash the dishes. I do not want the wound to get infected."

Morning Star ran the words through her keen mind, then repeated them twice to stress the correct order to herself.

"Good," he complimented. "You're smart and fast."

"Thank you. I . . . will work hard to be good . . . partner."

"You're more than a good partner, Morning Star." Catching his lapse, Joe added, "Let's get these dishes washed and turn in."

"We will wash these dishes and go to sleep," she jested.

"Before I know it, you'll be teaching me a thing or two," he teased in return. "I'll help with the chores." He halted her refusal by saying, "In the white man's world, sometimes we help with women's chores. This is one of those times. We're both tired and we both need sleep. If I help, you'll be done sooner. There's no need for you to work harder than I do."

"You are kind and generous, Joe Lawrence. You do as you want, but it does not hurt your pride as a man. That is good. It pleases me."

It was dark by the time they finished the task and lay on their sleeping rolls. The fire had burned low, and would be allowed to go out to guard their safety. They didn't want any flames or smoke showing at a distance to entice trouble. The location was quiet. There were not many frogs or crickets; they heard an occasional owl hoot and the running of the stream. A slight breeze stirred the leaves and grass, but it carried along very few scents from wildflowers.

"Good night, Morning Star," he murmured.

"Good night, Joe." She refused to let the bittersweet memory of what had happened between them earlier come to her mind. It would only create a troubled spirit as she reminded herself why it shouldn't happen again. She remembered she hadn't tended his hand and started to remind him, but she decided it was best if they didn't touch again today. He had used Payaba's medicine and wrapped it in a clean cloth this morning anyhow. Yes, it was best to check on it after the sun chased away the romantic shadows.

As they ate and prepared to break camp, Joe asked, "Why did Night Stalker name his son Bloody Arrow? That seems strange for a baby."

Morning Star related the custom of her people. "Child is named when born. Most come from nature or something happening when enter life. When Night Stalker born, tribe traveling to summer camp. He called Trail Son. When boy reach flap to manhood and seeks vision, he takes new name, one given to him in vision-quest. Sometimes, but few, names not changed. Sun Cloud and Bright Arrow named by Gray Eagle. In vision-quests, Grandfather not give them new names. Grandfather name sons in Gray Eagle's visions."

Her English suffered as she related a terrible raid by their enemies two years ago. "When brother's son born, camp attacked by Pawnee. They big enemy like Crow and Shoshone. Wife shot by warrior. Bloody arrow removed from her arm as son enter life. Night Stalker use sign to give son name. He say it will be as with Father and Grandfather, and Great Spirit will not change when he become man. That bad; name and sign rule man and life. No place for bloody arrows in peace." She told Joe how strange was Touched-A-Crow and how bad Bloody Arrow. "I not want mate, child, or tepee like brother have."

"One last question before we ride out," Joe said. "Why did Buckskin Girl compete with you in the contest? You told me you girls are best friends." He had perceived her distress over that episode as she told of the contest.

"I not know. It strange." She repeated what Buckskin Girl had told her, which wasn't an explanation, only a promise for a future one.

"I do have one more question. Will you teach me the bow and arrow?" Joe asked.

"You steal surprise. I bring one for you. They silent, not loud like guns. I good with bow. I teach you. I must tend hand before we ride."

"I took care of it while you were downstream bathing. It's already healing and doesn't hurt. But thanks. Let's go."

It was late that afternoon when they came upon a Crow hunting or scouting party. Every member was dead. After checking to make sure no enemies were still in the area, they approached the bloody scene and dismounted. The five Bird People had Red Heart arrows protruding from their bodies, the red stripes on the shafts assessing to her people's guilt.

"See with eyes, we no do! All in camp!" she shouted, angered by the unknown foes who were trying to provoke a war to get her people killed.

"It's clear to me your people are being framed."

"Bad men have good . . . scheme. Soldiers and others blame Red Hearts. They attack and destroy for evil man. See tracks," she said, and pointed to them. "Some shod and some not. They use Lakota moccasins. Nations have different moccasins and tracks. They steal, use to fool. See broken armband? It Red Heart." Her eyes enlarged as she retrieved it and looked closer. There was no mistaking its meaning, and she was angry.

"What's wrong?" He questioned her reaction.

"It have marks, symbols, of Man-Who-Rides-Wild-Horses; he put on *wicagnakapi wiconti*, death scaffold, in sacred hills in past winter. Warriors buried with possessions. That where enemies get weapons and possessions to use in . . . frame. It bad, evil, to steal from death scaffold. Crow would not do. It work of evil whitemen. I check tracks and trail."

Joe followed as the woman moved from place to place, bending here and there to study signs upon the ground. She tested the dryness of broken blades of grass and horse droppings. She checked to make certain the depth of the tracks revealed that all horses had heavy riders and none were pack animals or hauling raid booty. That and other clues, which she explained to him as she did her examination, told her how long the attackers had stayed in this location and when they had departed. He was impressed by her many talents.

"Seven men. Three on shod horses. Four not. Crow killed on last sun. Men ride that way," she remarked, pointing north. "They leave before sun sink into chest of Mother Earth to sleep. They not go far before camp; it soon dark. They less than one sun ahead. We follow. Must get Red Heart possessions and return to *wicag*—scaffolds. They must die."

Joe observed Morning Star's expression during her last two statements. Her eyes were squinted and her lips drawn tight. Her aura seemed as chilled as her dark gaze. "If we can capture one, Morning Star," he reasoned, "we can take him to the fort to be questioned. We need to convince others of what we've learned. If we kill all of them, we have no proof for the Army."

She protested his plan. "We get other proof. Morning Star know guilty. They must die for bad deed; Red Heart law say this. Must obey."

Joe studied her expression which exuded determination to see justice meted out under her laws. "Under white law, we arrest and jail thieves," he explained. "If the crime—deed—is very bad, the law punishes them by taking their lives. We can't gun down men just for stealing Indian possessions. That would make us as cold-blooded and wicked as they are."

"Not *just Indian possessions!* Sacred possessions. They dishonor dead and insult my people with this very bad deed. Warrior must have things on Ghost Trail, or he be naked and helpless. Evil spirits can attack before he reach Grandfather. It more . . . crime than *just stealing.*"

Joe wasn't certain how to argue against her religious beliefs without offending her, so he took a soft path. "The whites believe," he clarified, "when a man dies, he goes straight to our God. It is an insult to desecrate a grave and body, but the spirit is safe from all harm. Perhaps your Great Spirit saw the evil and He protected the warriors on the Ghost Trail. If He's kind and powerful, He won't let evil spirits attack His people. I promise we'll try to get their possessions back and return them."

Morning Star realized that part of his words were meant to appease her, and to obtain her agreement to his capture plan. "They murder Crow, and Crow friends of whites. That very bad crime. No white law here to . . . arrest and punish. We law here. We must punish."

"The Army's nearby, and they're white law."

"They far away, many suns' ride. How we carry evil men that far without trouble? If we seen or they talk, others learn our scheme and it over. They become too careful to find and punish. To do white man's law is not good trade to expose sacred vision task. It bad strategy."

Joe admitted she had a good point, a disturbing one. To take men in for questioning might expose their actions to Snake-Man. The only crimes the men had committed that he could prove were to wear moccasins, to steal burial treasures, and to kill Crow with stolen arrows. Those didn't tie them to Snake-Man, and they surely wouldn't confess to being his hirelings. Men on the payroll of such a clever and powerful villain would be more afraid of their boss than the law. Still,

Joe was too civilized to gun men down without valid reason. He must find a way to capture one of the men, make him talk, then turn him over to Captain Jim Thomas without exposing his mission. "We have to do this the legal way, the right way under white man's law, Morning Star, or we'll be in as much trouble as Snake-Men and his boys when they're captured."

"If we make mistake, Joseph Lawrence be in big trouble. If Snake-Man learn of us, he try to kill to stop task. If he no can find and kill Joe, he kill men who sent Joe. If they slay soldier, agent, and Tanner's father—they can say you side with Indians against whites. You be framed. If they killed and Snake-Man leave Red Heart clues, Army say my people guilty and they attack. If we exposed, they frame Joe. Big trouble."

Joe comprehended that her main concern was for him. "I'm safe, Morning Star. The President knows about me and this mission."

"What if they tell President lies like false words they tell soldiers? What if they say Joe killed and buried, and Tanner lives and sides with us?"

He smiled and caressed her cheek. "You worry too much."

"What is worry?" she asked, locking her gaze to his.

"To feel uneasy, shaky inside, tormented by bad thoughts and feelings, a troubled spirit. Too much worry steals your peace of mind. It makes you think the worst will happen."

Her dark-brown eyes roamed his face, and she felt herself warm. "Morning Star have reasons to worry. If we defeated, big war come. Many of my people slain. Worry keeps tracker on alert. Some worry is same as instincts. If worry, not get reckless, make mistakes. Stay alive."

To ease her tension, Joe chuckled and said, "You're right. I'll stay a little worried, too. Right now, woman, let's get rid of these Red Heart arrows and moccasin tracks. This is one crime your people won't get blamed for. Let's see how we'll do this," he murmured.

"I teach you. Come, do with me."

Morning Star and Joe pulled the falsely incriminating arrows from the Crow bodies. Together they dragged the dead men to a spot, where she cut a sturdy branch from a tree, then roughly brushed the area clear of moccasin tracks. She checked to make certain no other clues were visible to the trained eye of an Indian or Army scout.

"You walk here to make boot tracks," she instructed, motioning for him to stomp around the area. When he finished, she told him, "Do same with horse with shoes. White men do; white men take blame."

When everything was arranged to her satisfaction, they mounted and rode northward. Morning Star kept a little ahead of him to read the trail signs. Joe stayed on alert, apprehensive about catching up with seven dangerous men. They tracked until it was too dark to continue.

As they made camp, Morning Star said, "We safe. Signs say they half sun more than us. We ride fast on new sun and catch."

"We are safe. The signs say they are a half day ahead of us. We will ride fast tomorrow and catch up with them," he corrected with a smile.

"That is best English?" she queried as she worked on their meal.

"Yes. Or, you can say: We're safe. The signs say they're a half day ahead of us. We'll ride fast tomorrow and catch up with them."

"How do you know when to use best English?"

"In an important situation, in company with many people, in a formal setting."

"What is formal?" she asked.

Joe stroked his stubbled jawline and knit his brow. "That's a hard one. Let me think a minute." He did so. "Mercy, it means to be proper, and that means to be right at the right time."

Her expression was quizzical. She grasped all but one point. "How do you know when . . . it is the right time?"

Joe stretched out his legs and leaned against the tree behind him. "That's something you learn while you're growing up and going to school. Your teachers and parents tell you the right things to do."

"I did not go to school. Joe will teach me such things?"

"I'll try my best, Morning Star. It sounds easier than it is."

"It sounds . . . simple," she jested with a cheerful smile.

Joe laughed and nodded. "See, you have learned some good words. I'm not such a bad teacher after all."

She lowered her gaze to her task. "You are not bad in all ways. I change to, You are *good* in all ways. Is that right?"

"The English is right, and I'm grateful, but I'm not perfect." He laughed and quickly said, "Perfect means there's nothing wrong with me."

"Why is Joe not perfect? What is wrong with you?"

Joe couldn't take his eyes from Morning Star. Her allure was potent, nearly overpowering. To break the hold she was gaining over him, he jested, "Plenty, but I'll let you discover the truth for yourself." Joe was unaccustomed to any female other than his mother and sister being so honest. He liked that trait in Morning Star, but sometimes it caught him off-guard. He knew Annabelle Lawrence and Sarah Beth Lawrence Readon would like his Morning Star, and the Indian maiden would like his family. Joseph Sr. would take to this female easily and quickly. If—

"If Joe is not perfect, tell me one bad thing," she challenged as she broke into his reverie.

He said the first thing that came to mind, "I think like a white man."

Puzzled, she said, "You *are* white man. You must think white."

Joe crossed his legs at the ankles and drew them close to his buttocks. He leaned forward to rest his elbows on his thighs, letting his hands dangle toward the ground. "To me that's bad, because I have to do things the way I was raised, the way I believe. The same for you, Morning Star; you'll want to do things the way you were raised and believe. At times, we'll think the other is wrong or stubborn. We'll have to compromise; that's do it your way sometimes, and do it my way sometimes."

"Compromise," she echoed. "That is fair."

"Another thing—I lied to your father; that was wrong."

She shook her head. "It was . . ."

When she faltered in search of the right word, Joe said, "Necessary."

"Neces-sa-sary. Yes, it was necessary to get help."

"But it was still wrong, and I feel badly about it."

"Grandfather understand and forgive us. He knows all things."

"But I made you lie to them, too. I'm sorry."

"How is true?" she asked, looking dismayed.

"You knew the truth and you didn't expose me. By holding silent, you lied, too. We're in this together, partners. Until this danger is conquered, we can be honest only with each other, no one else. Understand?"

In a serious tone, she replied, "I understand and will obey."

He abruptly changed the subject, "When we're in your camp, be careful of Hawk Eyes and Knife-Slayer. I don't like them cheating—doing wrong—at something that's supposed to be sacred to them. If a man can betray himself, his people, and especially his God, he's dangerous."

Morning Star handed Joe his evening meal. As if revealing a crucial secret, her voice was a near whisper as she related, "Hawk Eyes may not be shaman long. Running Water went on vision-quest and saw elk. He member of Elk Dreamers. Payaba teaches him. Payaba say his vision powerful medicine. Big bird ride wind, then land on elk's head. They speak; they tell Running Water he to become Wind Bird and shaman. It good, yes?"

Joe realized she was excited by that possibility because of the change in her speech. "Yes, that will be very good."

Her food waited as she rushed on. "Night Stalker sides with his friend, Knife-Slayer. When truth comes soon, his eyes will clear. It make me happy. Brother cannot become chief until he is better man. He make Father sad with bad ways. I will make Father happy and proud with victory."

Darkness had closed in on them. Flickers from the fire danced wild and seductive patterns on their faces. They finished their meal in silence, as each felt the strong currents pulling them closer and tighter together. The area they were in was secluded, intimate, and intimidating. Each was thinking too much about the other, and trying to discourage such forbidden emotions.

Reacting to the strain and wanting it to lessen, Joe suggested, "Why don't we get to sleep? We had a long day, and it's late."

"That is best," she murmured in agreement.

The dishes were washed hurriedly and put away. Their sleeping mats were unrolled and placed at a safe distance apart. The fire was doused. They lay down, both breathing deeply in an attempt to relax.

"Good night, Morning Star."

"Good night, Joseph Lawrence."

Fatigued and well fed, they finally drifted off to sleep.

It was nearing dusk when the Oglala maiden lifted her hand to halt their progress. "Not far ahead. We leave horses and walk."

They dismounted and secured their animals' reins to bushes. Sneaking from tree to tree, they made their way forward to the enemy camp. Only three men were present, all palefaces, who were drinking, talking, and playing cards. Their horses were tethered by a stream.

Joe cupped his mouth to her ear and whispered, "Where are the others? We've been trailing seven. See or hear anything of them?"

Morning Star leaned close and replied, "Tracks of seven enter camp. If four leave another way, I not see from here."

Joe strained his eyes and ears to pick up any clues as to the location of the other men. He didn't like this. He prayed they hadn't been exposed and they weren't walking into a trap. "They could be farther ahead in another clearing. Maybe they're Indians, and they don't camp together. If we make too much noise, they'll come running to help. I wish I knew how to use a bow for silence. I can't risk using my guns. We'll have to wait until dark to attack. What is it?" Joe asked as he saw Morning Star's eyes suddenly widen, then just as suddenly narrow.

Morning Star glared at the sight of a white man laughing and holding up an Oglala religious object. She watched him pour whiskey into one opening while drunkenly asking if the buffalo wanted a drink of firewater. The more the man laughed and jested, the angrier she became. When the men began playing toss with the sacred item, she was consumed by ire. They had no respect or understanding of her people and their ways. It was the same as if an Indian dishonored one of their holy Bibles! "They have sacred buffalo skull whose spirit guards burial ground. Spirits angry, restless. Must get it back. That very bad sign. They much evil."

Joe knew they were in for another disagreement as to the men's fates. He could read it in her grave expression and deadly tone. If there were only three left in the area, they had a good chance of capturing at least one to question. "Don't worry; we'll get everything back. Just stay calm until dark. Two against three aren't bad odds. I just hope those others are gone permanently. They could be off hunting or scouting. No risks, Morning Star; I promised your father."

She looked him in the eye and said, "They must die. Die this moon."

Chapter Nine

usk closed in on them at a slow pace, but time for action would arrive soon. Morning Star's words to Joe kept echoing through her head. She realized she had sounded cold and hostile. When she had battled Clem, she had not tried to slay him, despite the white men's wicked treatment of her. Presently, she was facing another test of her ways and beliefs: foes were to be killed for such evil deeds. But, she asked herself, could she obey the laws of her people?

Morning Star had been given time to settle down and to think. Unless their lives were threatened, could she slay those scaffold robbers in cold blood? she fretted. The Indians those men had killed were enemies of her people, so their murders should not trouble her, yet they did. Added to that, the men had tried to blame her tribe and get them massacred. The most important tasks to her were to retrieve the sacred objects and falsely incriminating clues and to prevent the men from doing such a thing again. Did they have to die? Could they be frightened into not repeating that foul deed or into leaving Oglala territory? She doubted her last thought.

Together she and Joe had battled three-to-two odds in Zeke's camp. They could do the same here. These men were not on guard and might be weakened by whiskey. Perhaps it was best not to sneak up and slay them as animals during a hunt. Too, she didn't want to appear a bloodthirsty, wild savage to Joseph Lawrence. As his past words traveled through her mind, she knew it was compromise time.

Morning Star glanced at her handsome companion from the corners of her eyes. His azure gaze was locked on the enemy camp, and his expression was one of intense concentration. The events of the last few weeks filled her mind. Joe was so unlike any man she had known. He was kind and gentle, yet so strong and self-assured. He possessed a fox's cunning, a wolf's daring, and a hawk's speed during a strike at its prey. The color of heaven lived in his eyes; the golden sun reflected on his head; the shade of a tanned doe hide spread over his muscled body. He had all the traits and skills of a highly trained warrior, ones that would require a great force to defeat. His voice could be as soothing to a troubled spirit as rippling water in a stream or as powerful as a strong wind that blew where it willed. It was as if many forces of nature touched, honed, and controlled him. As one who lived in a world of nature, that pulled her closer to him.

So why, Morning Star mused, was it so terrible to desire such a special man, a man chosen and sent to them by the Great Spirit? Her wits responded that desire wasn't the main problem; yielding to it was. They warned her she must retain the strength to avoid dishonoring her family by surrendering to a forbidden situation. They demanded she be true to her parents, traditions, and people. If only, she worried, that task didn't become harder by the day! Resisting Joe was difficult, particularly when she didn't view it as wrong, as her people and laws did. Her grandfather and uncle had met, loved, and joined white women. If warriors could capture and bond with female enemies, why was it so wicked and shameful for an Indian maiden to do the same with a white man? It was unfair! With more and more whites entering their territory, the two cultures could not remain separate long.

A breeze from the north picked up in pace and strength. It ruffled Joe's tawny hair, but lacked enough power to have any effect on the maiden's heavy braids. It brought the campfire smell to them. It enticed tranquil nature to life. Grass bent southward, as if too lazy or weak to stand tall against such a force. Leaves moved as if trembling with cold. Fragrances of wildflowers drifted on the air currents. The breeze felt refreshing on their skin. It was a peaceful time of day. If only they did not have the dangerous chore awaiting them, they could relax and enjoy it.

Joe inhaled the mingled odors of simmering beans and perked coffee that wafted in the wind. He was glad his hungry stomach did not growl aloud. It was almost dark, and the less-than-half-moon would help conceal them. The men had eaten, then settled down to more cards and whiskey. To Joe, they seemed in no hurry to turn in, as if they had no tiring ride ahead tomorrow. He speculated that they were waiting for somebody or something. He'd like to spy until he learned the answer to that puzzle, but it was too risky. Their prey could be awaiting a Crow party to spread lies about the Oglalas, or Snake-Man's hirelings and a delivery, or the return of their four friends. He couldn't stay and chance overwhelming odds; nor could he retreat, because he needed some questions answered and a starting point to solve this task.

Joe sensed Morning Star watching him, and it played havoc with his concentration on the camp. He sensed she had mastered her fiery emotions. Being near her was like sailing into the tropics, sultry and invigorating. It inspired suspense about what one would discover in that paradise. She was so alive and full of energetic fire that he could almost warm himself in her glowing essence. Morning Star was sensual, earthy, an innocent child of nature, a woman of provocative and entrancing spirit.

As she lay on the grassy incline beside him, Joe glimpsed lovely legs that were exposed from the way her buckskin dress had hiked up itself from wriggling movements during her observations. The well-fitting garment did more than hint at her shapely and taut figure. The short fringe at elbow-length sleeves grazed coppery skin on her arms; longer fringe at the tail caressed matching flesh on her legs. The beadwork—red, light and dark blue, and yellow—was in the Arapaho design, in line with her alleged identity. It was the same with her matching moccasins with their red mountain symbols rising into blue sky and the double-pointed yellow arrow to indicate the span of Arapaho territory. Her ebony hair, parted down the center, was braided, the ends decorated with colorful rosettes of skilled beadwork on small circles of buckskin. Her features were soft yet defined, giving her a unique beauty. He wanted to stroke her silky flesh, but dared not.

When Morning Star teased her lower lip with her top teeth, Joe had the urge to pull her into his arms so he could do the same. He yearned to feel her mouth against his once more, to taste her sweetness, to coax her response. His loins came to life, and his breathing quickened. He scolded himself for his lapse in attention to their peril and for his carnal cravings for Sun Cloud's daughter. He must keep reminding himself of that truth, of that and all the other many obstacles which stood between them, including his implied promise to Sun Cloud.

Joe focused on the still-active camp and frowned. His tension increased by the hour. He wanted this hazardous matter settled soon. It wasn't good to let anxiety build, as it stole alertness and it dulled wits. He studied the location again. It was impossible to sneak over safely without a cover of darkness, which was slow in arriving. He waited.

Morning Star perceived Joe's attraction to her; it made her happy and worried. She needed his strength of denial to help her retain hers. If he leaned her way, how could she ever resist him? A fierce longing for him mounted within her each day, and she did not know how long she could control it. His warning about the emotional peril of them riding together was accurate. Yet she wanted to be no other place except in his arms. He was so close that she could reach over and touch him, and was tempted to do so. *No*, she ordered. *Always hold your distance or all is lost.*

At last, night blanketed the area, but the men added wood to the already dancing flames to brighten their campsite. Joe and Morning Star lingered on the embankment for the right moment to attack and prepared themselves. They removed anything that would make noise and prevent stealth. They covered anything light or shiny that might reflect the moon's glow or firelight, including Joe's blond hair. They also discarded anything cumbersome that might slow their pace. When all was ready, they observed with heightened alertness, eager to make their move.

When one man stood, stretched, and told his friends he was going to be excused, Joe reacted with haste. "Stay down and be quiet," he whispered into the woman's ear. "I'll work my way over and get rid of one of them. Don't move until I return or signal you," he ordered in a tone of protectiveness.

After he vanished into the shadows, Morning Star smiled, delighted by his concern. She listened and watched. Joe moved in complete silence, and she was proud of his prowess. She nocked her weapon to be ready to fire an arrow when needed. She almost held her breath in suspense. This was the first test of their skills during the sacred mission. She prayed that everything would go right.

Time passed. All she heard were muffled voices from the two men near the fire, a pair of owls calling to each other, and the thudding of her heart within her ears. The large fire illuminated the clearing and provided a perfect view of the site. She wondered why they wanted such a big one, when only a slight chill was in the air tonight. Besides, it revealed their number and positions to any foe who happened by. It wasn't a smart action for men who had gotten away with so many clever deeds! Why were they so reckless—or so confident? Surely it wasn't a trick to lure them into that trap Joe had feared. If the other four were still nearby, wouldn't her keen senses detect them? She concentrated on the scene. Her ears strained to catch any warning sound and her eyes searched the shadows for a sign of trouble lurking in them. Nothing. She cautioned herself not to allow her worry over Joe to cloud her judgment and skills.

A man in camp stood and called to the one who had left the lighted area, "Hey, Coop! Wot's takin' so long?" When no response came, he called louder, "Coop! Anythin' wrong?" Nothing, so he yelled again, "Coop, where are ya, man?" then retrieved his rifle.

Morning Star saw the missing man appear at the edge of the campsite, and she froze in panic. There had been plenty of time for Joe to reach and conquer him. What had gone wrong? Where was Sky Warrior? If he'd been unable to attack, why hadn't he returned to her side?

Joe, disguised in the first man's jacket and floppy hat, walked closer to his target with a lowered head. He ignored their questions, as his voice would expose him. He hoped to get near enough to clobber the one with the rifle hanging loosely in his grasp and get some answers as to why he and the others had slain that Crow band and framed the Red Hearts. He wasn't sure how far he would go to force out information; only time would answer that for him. Joe did not reach and overpower the armed man before the other one became suspicious of his behavior and shouted a warning.

"Sompin's wrong! He ain't got Coop's limp! An' his beard's too short!"

The man's friend turned fast for someone who had been drinking for hours and stared. He comprehended the trick, especially when Joe didn't refute the warning and identify himself. He yanked up his rifle to shoot.

Joe had no choice but to shove open the jacket, grab his Colt Walker, and fire it. He did so with speed, agility, and accuracy, his lethal bullet striking the shocked man. Before he could turn the nine-inch barrel of his .44 caliber on the last man, who also had lunged for his weapon, it was over. His astonished gaze traced the path of the deadly arrow that struck home with a thud, but it was too dark to see her. He knocked off the hat and shouted, "It's me, Morning Star! Don't shoot!"

Guessing the clever ruse unfolding in camp, Morning Star had jumped to her feet and hurried forward to level ground. She had braced herself, aimed, and sent an arrow into the last man's heart to save Joe's life.

She rushed forward to his side as he discarded the jacket. "I know is Joe. I see trick. Very cunning. When take long time, I worry." Her gaze raced over him from head to foot to make certain he was all right. She gave a loud exhale of relief, then watched him check the men.

His blue gaze met her brown one as he reported, "All dead. Thanks for saving my neck again. I'm glad you didn't panic and that you jumped in when I needed help. That was a good shot. Don't forget to teach it to me later." Impressed by her quick reflexes, he smiled and explained, "I stepped on a branch in the dark and exposed myself to that land pirate. He pulled a knife and came at me. Thank goodness he didn't shout a warning. I knew I had to silence him fast before he did. When I heard another one call to him, I was afraid they might have heard our struggle. I still thought it was worth the chance to get the drop on them with that disguise."

"Disguise cunning. We make good partners, yes?"

"Yes, we do. I just wish I'd noticed Coop's limp, but I was talking to you and didn't see it. He was easy to find in the dark; he wasn't trying to be quiet. I figured I could get close enough to take them before I gave myself away. I'll have to work on my sneaky skills. In the cave you said that is was good to be friends with the dark, but I guess I haven't learned enough yet. I'm happy you're here with me, Morning Star."

"You not angry we kill them?" she asked, looking concerned.

His hand lifted to caress her flushed cheek. "We had no choice this time. Let's get what we came for and move out fast. I'm still worried about those other four returning. That big campfire makes me suspicious. If they're still around, that gunfire could bring them running." Joe didn't want to risk a shootout with four men who knew of their presence and probably were well armed. During such a battle, it was doubtful he could capture one of the villains to question, and he didn't want to get pinned down until more culprits arrived. Even if an ambush worked in their favor, leaving too many bodies around would create suspicions in the wrong man—their boss.

"It's too dark to locate and follow their trail," he murmured, "and we can't hang around to see if they come back at first light. They might not be alone. Hopefully they're long gone and didn't hear those shots." Joe glanced at the grim sight they would leave behind. "It's time to put my other plan in motion," he told her. "Let's return these relics to their scaffolds, then ride for Orin McMichael's trading post to see what we can learn. Don't forget your arrow; we don't want innocent Arapahoes blamed for this."

Morning Star agreed with Joe. Together they collected the stolen Oglala possessions and sacred skull. Joe searched the men's saddlebags, but found nothing that could aid his mission. While Morning Star packed up the things she wanted returned to the tribal gravesite and recovered her arrow, Joe freed the men's horses. They returned to their mounts and rode five miles southwestward before making camp.

Exhausted, they ate the dried meat called *wasna* and bread pones called *aguyapi* and washed them down with fresh water. They did not build a campfire, as the area had not been scouted for enemy presence. Morning Star put away their supplies, and Joe prepared their bedrolls. He placed only a short distance between them tonight. Both lay down.

Since their lethal task in the white men's camp, they had spoken little. Each seemed to be adjusting to the gravity of the episode. Killing men, even in self-defense, did not come easy for either one. The incident had stressed how serious their mission was and what it would require of them. Many things would be difficult to do, but surely peace was worth that price. Each knew it was wrong to view the situation as a pretense, and each knew they had to do their best not to kill more than necessary.

They lay in silence and gazed at the stars overhead. The night seemed too peaceful to hold a deadly confrontation so that reality moved to the backs of their minds. Soon, both drifted off to sleep.

Morning Star and Joe entered the Black Hills by late afternoon. The path that she took was not an arduous one, so their ride was easy and steady. Joe had no problem keeping up with his beautiful guide. As they traveled to the area she sought, his gaze took in the wonder of the setting, as hers had done many times in the past. They journeyed through color-splashed meadows, between towering pinnacles of obsidian rocks in many shapes and sizes, into and out of cool forests of spruce and pine and hardwoods, and beside running streams whose water played around stones and twigs. Everything was green and alive and fragrant. A refreshing breeze and frequent shade prevented the sun's heat from affecting them too severely. Though the sky was a deep blue, snowy clouds were turning gray in the distance. Several times they spooked deer, elk, antelope, and smaller creatures and a few times they encountered small herds of buffalo who were grazing on lush grass or lazing upon the verdant surface.

Joe understood why this area was so valued. Timber was abundant and sturdy, when much of the adjoining territory lacked a wood supply. Water was fresh and plentiful, as was lush grass for grazing. Lovely valleys offered sheltered surroundings from the harsh northern winters. The Plains could feed numerous cattle or other stock, and no clearing was needed for farms. It was perfect for civilization and exploitation.

They reached a clearing that was enclosed on three sides by tall rock formations. Bushes and trees grew at the edges and the center was filled with scaffolds that looked like beds of wood on lofty stilts. The flow of wind and tightly wrapped bodies prevented the heavy odor of death that Joe had expected to find there; that was also the reason why no scavengers were drawn to the sacred site to feast.

Joe experienced a sensation of awe, as if he were in a holy place or church. He heard and saw no animal or bird to rend the tranquility, but it did not give him an eerie feeling. It almost felt as if he were on hallowed ground, as the Indians believed of their burial sites. If the Great Spirit existed, or was God in another form and He did watch over a special location, this had to be one. It sent home the Indian's belief in the sacred Circle of Life, from Great Spirit and Mother Earth at birth to their return in death. Morning Star had told him the bodies and possessions remained on the scaffolds until the forces of nature reclaimed them. Sturdy and built with love, the eternal sleeping beds lasted as long as they were needed.

Joe and Morning Star dismounted and secured the reins of the three horses to bushes at the natural entrance of the clearing. A tall cottonwood post was in the middle of the path. Eagle feathers and rawhide pouches were attached to the top. A large stub at head height caught his attention, and he watched the maiden slip the weather-bleached buffalo skull onto it, then he saw her retrieve items from the ground and replace them: religious tokens and special grasses and herbs that the white thieves had snatched out and discarded.

Morning Star glanced at her companion and said, "Natahu Wakan guards fallen warriors until journey to Grandfather is done. It warns enemies not to enter this sacred place. Most do not. Grandfather guided us to evil whites to take back Natahu Wakan. It is good. Come, I return warriors' possessions. Their spirits will be happy with our great deed."

As Joe followed her around the area, he carried the bundle and helped her replace the stolen property. Morning Star was tall, but many of the scaffolds were beyond her easy reach. He watched her use markings on the eastern posts to identify from which ones the items had been taken, as the belongings were also marked with ownership. While they worked, he kept glancing at the signs of a storm heading their way.

Morning Star noticed nature's warnings, too. The sky displayed puffy white clouds whose faces were quickly turning a dark gray, as if anger were building inside them. The rapid change in colors told her the weather's temper would explode soon in a violent storm. The wind's force increased steadily, tugging at feathers on lances, shields, and bows. It teased across her flesh, and it raced through leaves and grass. Her skin detected moisture in the air; her keen nose smelled it.

The maiden studied the heaven once more and said, "Must hurry. Bad storm come soon. *Wakinyan*, Thunder Birds, live inside *tipi* clouds. When Grandfather say Mother Earth need water, He tell *Wakinyan* to leave *tipi*, to flap wings and make thunder, to open and close eyes to make lightning, to spill water from big lakes on backs. Eyes not see Thunder Birds. They fly fast and high, and hide in sky mist. Thunder warn people to seek shelter."

Joe was amused by her explanation of thunder, rain, and lightning, yet, he did not smile or chuckle and offend her for those erroneous beliefs and superstitions. It was the way she had been reared. Even if he explained science and weather to her, she might not understand it or believe him. He could not tell her she was mistaken or ignorant about so many things. But, as time passed, he would educate her with respect. For now, he continued his task.

As they moved through the burial site, they collected Crow beads, bits of red trade cloth that the Bird People favored, a tribal exposing arrow here and there, and a few other falsely incriminating clues dropped around to inflame the Oglala against the Crow. Just as the slain Crow party would appear the work of the Red Heart Band, this "evidence" was meant to frame the Oglalas' foes. Since Joe and Morning Star knew who was responsible for both incidents, both comprehended they were right in presuming someone wanted to provoke an intertribal war.

"We need to make certain the Crow and your people learn about these two tricks, Morning Star. There's no telling how many frames we won't find and halt, or how many old ones weren't genuine. I know they're enemies of your people and have been for generations, but these tricks can cause a bloody war. I hate to think of how many innocent people have died in retalitory raids for crimes their tribe didn't commit. When warriors go into battle, they aren't the only ones at risk. Their camps and families are in danger of attacks—children, women, and old people who can't defend themselves. If we don't open everyone's eyes to the truth, this entire area will become a blood-soaked battlefield." His mind wouldn't let him forget that Morning Star and her family—Tanner's kin—would be trapped in the middle, as would blameless white settlers and soldiers.

"Grandfather will guide us and help us, Joe," she encouraged. "He works with us for peace. Can you not see this truth in all that has been?"

"We'll keep talking to our gods, and pray they listen."

She tugged at his arm. "Come, I know place to hide from storm."

Joe lifted the bundle, this time filled with enemy items, and followed her to the horses. At the burial site entrance, he waited for her to pray to her god, then mount. Joe closed his eyes and sent a prayer to his, then pulled himself into his saddle. "You're the leader, Morning Star; guide on."

The maiden returned his smile and kneed her Appaloosa. Joe's gaze sent warm tingles over her body. She pushed that thought and the desecrated burial ground out of her mind. She must reach cover before bad weather overtook them.

The storm was approaching fast, but Morning Star knew her way around these hills. She headed for a place she remembered where the lower part of a black cliffside suddenly jutted outward near the base. The outthrust was sufficient to create an overhang with enough height, depth, and width for them to obtain protection from rain and lightning. It wasn't large enough for the horses, too, but animals were used to being out in the weather and would be safe in a copse of hardwoods.

Joe eyed the spot she chose. Beneath the ledge was a space of five feet by five feet, with a ceiling of four feet. The smooth rock seemed to form a slate roof to cover the inviting location. By then, thunder rumbled and lightning slashed overhead. "Let's get our supplies and bedrolls under cover," Joe shouted. "You grab some wood and I'll tend the horses. That rain'll be coming down in barrels soon."

They worked with haste, and had everything prepared within a short time. A small campfire heated the beans that Joe had taken from the dead men's supplies. Along with the dried meat and bread pones from Singing Wind, the couple ate a quick and satisfying meal. Joe set their empty dishes on a ring of inky stones around a cheery blaze. Drops of water struck his body and the surroundings, then rapidly became larger and heavier.

"Hurry, it's here. Leave the dishes. The rain will wash 'em."

Sounds of wind and thunder were joined by a noisy deluge of water. The campfire just beyond the rock overhang was doused within seconds. Joe and Morning Star laughed as they wriggled to the back of the snug area to keep dry and warm. They sat on Joe's bedroll to watch nature's drama unfold. Supplies, stored at one side and covered by his slicker, compelled them to sit close in the gradually darkening hideout.

Brilliant flashes of lightning frequently illuminated the cozy area. A few times, both jumped as startling thunderbolts boomed nearby. After each reaction, they exchanged glances and shared laughter. Heavy rain flowed down the cliff face that rose upward to a towering spire with a rounded top. It poured over the extended ledge, but there was enough of an incline to send the flood of liquid the other way. Except for earth-dampening splatters, their area stayed dry. They kept their feet tucked close to their bodies so they wouldn't get wet. They leaned their heads against an inky wall and gazed at the partition of water that obscured the outside world.

Trapped between the downpour and rocks, they were enclosed in a setting that reeked of intimacy. When vivid streaks of lightning blazed across the sky, it sparkled on the watery flap to their romantic tepee. During one lengthy bout of lightning that split into many branches and seemed to hang in the sky a long time,

Joe looked over at his companion. She was so beautiful and desirable, so close, so out of reach.

Morning Star returned Joe's lingering gaze. The whiskers on his face had grown during their days together, and, for a man with golden hair, the short beard looked dark against his tanned face. In the dimness with only nature's flashes of light, she saw how blue his eyes were. Her shoulder touched his, and the contact was pleasing and arousing. She was glad the space was tight and forced them to sit close. The shadows of their present world and the sounds from beyond it created an aura of mystery and anticipation. She realized she was apprehensive about their impending journey into the white settlement, but felt safe and strong knowing Joe would be at her side. With him, she felt as if she could do almost anything. She watched him remove his boots and set them aside; she did the same with her moccasins. They shared a sleeping roll, keeping their weapons within reach. When a burst of dazzling light came again, Joe was still watching her with that bittersweet look.

Joe observed Morning Star as she unbraided her ebony hair and withdrew a brush to work on it. Soon, it lay silky and sensual around her shoulders. When she started to replait it, his hand stayed hers and he coaxed, "Don't. Leave it free. It's as shiny and black as a raven's wing. It's beautiful, like you are, Morning Star."

When she trembled at his stirring words, he assumed she was chilled, as the temperature had dropped. He retrieved a blanket and tossed it over their legs, then drew it up to their shoulders. He put his arm around her to settle the cover into place on her distant shoulder, then left his arm there. It felt warm and strong to Morning Star and she could not resist snuggling against him. Joe responded by moving his arm across her chest, near her throat, and clasping her nearest shoulder with his fingers. Morning Star leaned her head back to rest it against his cheek and neck. Her hand lifted to cover his. She felt Joe lean his head into hers. It was delightful to be snuggled together in the serene setting.

Joe told himself to enjoy this brief moment of weakness and contact but to go no further with his yearnings. Yet a fierce longing to kiss her galloped through his body at breakneck speed. He seemed unable to restrain that runaway sensation. "I've never met a woman like you, Morning Star," he murmured. "You make me feel so good inside. I missed you when I rode to the fort. I couldn't get back fast enough. I was afraid you'd become my helper—but more afraid you wouldn't. I want to be with you all the time. I want to hold you and kiss you. I'm sorry you think I'm stronger and more trustworthy than I deserve."

Sun Cloud's daughter rashly turned her head and body until their faces were within inches of each other. She raised her hand and stroked his cheek. As dusk had dimmed the light inside their rock dwelling, she could barely see him. She wished each burst of brightness was longer, as she couldn't look at him enough. "It is same with me, Joe. I am weak and cannot be trusted. What we do?"

The desire in her voice was evident to him. He seemed to tremble with yearning as much as she did; that was unusual for him, as he had learned self-control. He had to kiss her, he had to! Joe's head bent downward and his mouth sought hers. With her assistance, he had no difficulty finding her sweet lips.

Morning Star was staggered by the potency of the lengthy kiss. She thrilled to the way his mouth explored hers, and was surprised by the instinctive way hers responded. She heard him moan at the same time she did. She felt him tense and shudder at the same time she did. Her heart told her that a little kissing and hugging wouldn't do any harm. If her mind argued, she didn't hear it. She twisted her body until she was lying in his arms and facing the back of the shelter. She nestled closer. She felt his embrace tighten and his kisses deepen. Her arms clung to his body, wanting no space between them for a short time.

Joe had the same good intentions of only enjoying a few kisses, hugs, and caresses. His fingers wandered into her silky hair, then trailed over her satiny skin. She was so soft and sleek. He ached to have her completely, just once. It would give him a beautiful memory that he would never forget and probably never find again. His body burned with flames of desire. His spirit hungered to feast on her.

Morning Star was lost in a rapturous world of spinning desires. As her lips teased over his face and nibbled at his mouth, she murmured, "We fit like pair of moccasins. We match like petals on flower." She had been told that most men were not good with romantic words, that most used actions to show their feelings. Joe was different; he did both.

Soon they were inflamed beyond clear reason. Her hands traveled under his loosened shirt for her eager fingers to feel the hardness of his supple frame. She wore a two-piece buckskin outfit today, and Joe's hand slipped beneath her top and closed over one breast. Surges of pleasure stormed their bodies as fiercely as the weather was storming the world outside their secluded dwelling.

"I want you so much, Morning Star," Joe almost growled against her responsive mouth. "I know I shouldn't, but I can't help myself."

Before she could tell him she felt the same, his lips captured her and sent her mind to reeling. She loved him and wanted him. How could such powerful feelings be wrong? So many forces had tried to keep Gray Eagle and Alisha, Bright Arrow and Rebecca, apart; they had all failed, because the Great Spirit had brought both mixed couples together and given them a love too strong and tight to be broken or denied. It was as if she had waited for this tender ecstasy all of her life. A savage and bittersweet longing swept through her. Her mind and heart were too ensnared to resist this stolen moment. Her grandfather and uncle had surrendered to mixed love, so it could not be so terribly wrong for her to do so. They were honored legends, as she hoped she would be when this sacred task was done. She could not summon the will to refuse what she wanted with all her soul. Tonight, she and Joe could not help themselves; their match was irresistible, was fated, at least this much of it was, no matter what happened later.

Joe was lost in a whirlwind of emotions and sensation. He drew her to him with possessiveness. His breathing was ragged, his heart drummed within his chest. He seemed to quiver like a feather in a strong breeze. The storm outside ravaging the land was nothing compared to the one assailing him. He had no choice but to submit to whatever fate had in store for them tonight. He shifted his weight, which allowed them to sink to his bedroll.

Morning Star went along with him, willing and eager. His masculine scent filled her nostrils. His touch was tantalizing. Her deft fingers freed the buttons on his shirt and her fingers traced the smooth and hard surface of his chest where no hair grew but where muscles rippled like water over rocks. She explored the wonders of his compelling physique. Her head rolled to one side as his tongue trailed down her throat, then with titillating leisure returned to her mouth.

Their lips meshed with fierceness and urgency. The emotions they had tried to deny and restrain for so long burst free and galloped away. There was no way to recapture the innocence they were leaving behind.

Morning Star savored the way Joe's hands felt on her pliant body. Her breasts did not want him to leave them. Yet she longed for so much more, and she had a suspicion where their new trail would lead.

Joe was as spellbound by the blissful moment as she was. His lips brushed over her face, halting at each feature to explore it in detail. His experiences with women had never prepared him for this rare one. He didn't want this to end. He wanted to keep her forever.

They continued their discoveries of each other, and reveled in the joys of them. Each knew their destinies were being forged into one, and they must find some way to help fate along. Each burned with desire. Each knew there was no turning back.

As their mouths clung together, Joe, with her help, wriggled out of his shirt. Morning Star, with Joe's assistance, removed her top, their lips parting only long enough for the garment to pass between them. When their bare chests touched, they seemed to cling to each other with wills of their own. While Joe caressed a breast with one hand and showered the other with ecstatic kisses, Morning Star loosened the ties of her breechcloth, as her skirttail had raised itself long ago during her writhings. She did not pull away to remove her skirt, and was only half conscious of it being between them. After Joe's seeking hand covered the distance between her breasts and abdomen, she arched and moaned when it made contact where she had never been caressed before.

Joe stroked and caressed his love until both could no longer stand the denial. His hand halted only long enough for him to work the fasteners of his pants. He moved atop Morning Star and slipped between her parted thighs, lowering his pants as he did so. He did not have to ask her if she was sure about continuing, her actions told him she was as willing to proceed as he was. With caution, he lowered his body to hers and entered the paradise he had dreamed of for weeks. Her response told him he had not hurt her.

Morning Star was consumed by the wonder of becoming a woman, Joe's woman, of surrendering to love completely. She had been right; they fit as perfectly as the best matched pair of moccasins. It did not feel strange to have him within her; it felt right, wonderful, as if it should be.

Joe experienced those same thoughts and feelings. They were joined as one, as it was destined to be. Perhaps he had sensed that truth the first night they met. He accepted the fact that he loved her. In all ways but one— under white law—she was his wife. He vowed to keep her for as long as possible. She was his, so that had to be forever.

Morning Star's fingers halted their trek at the wound Joe had gotten while rescuing her. Even when they were strangers, he had been willing to die for her. Whatever it took, they had to find a way to stay together during and after this sacred mission. Surely Grandfather would not put such love in their hearts only to force them apart later.

As the most glorious moment of this new and rapturous experience burst upon them, they kissed and clung together as if promising nothing and no one would ever come between them. There was no retreat, no restraint. They savored the final destination they had reached together. For a time they were aswirl in a glowing mist that shut out all reality except for this blissful ending to something both had craved. Pleasure melted into contentment as they snuggled together, sated for now.

The thunder and lightning had ceased, but heavy rain continued to fall. It was music to their ears and relaxing to their spirits. Both sighed deeply as they rested after their lovemaking. Without meaning to do so, each allowed the reality of the world outside to enter their minds. Perhaps it was the darkness of their surroundings which denied sight of each other's face that reminded them of their grim situation.

"Morning Star—"

She covered his mouth with her quivering hand. "Do not speak bad words. We joined in hearts and spirits. We have much this moon. We can have nothing more. Do not bring sadness and pain to our hearts."

Joe understood what she was saying and feeling. This was her world and her culture. His were far away; they could not join or overlap. He agonized over that truth, as neither could give up who they were. Her world would not accept him, and his would not accept her. They were too smart to say that nothing mattered except their love. And he knew he did love her. Those words were hard for a man to confess the first time he truly meant them. Surely she guessed it from his mood and actions, as he knew she must love him to surrender tonight. If he spoke his innermost feelings aloud, it could frighten her and cause her to withdraw from him. People could not survive by love alone. Having everyone and everything against a union could damage it severely. But he was not ready to face that challenge yet. For as long as he could, he had to hold on to her. He embraced her tightly as he tried to accept what his heart refused to believe: that he would lose her.

Morning Star tried to halt any dream of a future with Joe from forming. It was futile, hopeless, and forbidden.

When she started to tense, he asked, "What is it?"

"I wash while rain still comes." She freed herself from his arms and, finding her way with her fingers against the stone roof, she crawled to the front of their shelter. She moved outside and stood in the pouring rain, naked, chilled, and heartbroken. The rain flowed over her slender, shapely body and washed away the traces of their lovemaking.

Joe finished removing his pants, then joined her and did the same. He lifted his face skyward and allowed the cold water to cool his hot body and remove his sweat. His heart felt heavy inside his chest. He raged at the obstacles that stood between him and the only woman he had ever loved. More so, he raged at his helplessness, his inability to overcome them. Despite his father's strength and Joe's respect for him, Joe had left home against the elder Joseph Lawrence's wishes. Something within him had demanded he seek the man he was inside, the man hidden by his father's shadow. He had been compelled to do something on his own, not just take over a business handed to him through an inheritance. He had hungered for adventure and excitement, and couldn't be blamed for seeing shipping as unfulfilling. He loved his parents and had obeyed them until his restlessness had forced him to walk away from home. One day he would return and take the place expected of him. By then, he would be mature and his wild thirst would be quenched. He would be confident and content, a man of his own. At least he had felt that way until meeting the woman beside him. Now, what would his life be without her?

As they stood there in anguish and silence, the rain slowed and halted. Clouds drifted westward, and the partial moon offered scant light. Joe gave a loud sigh then fetched a blanket. He handed it to Morning Star and watched her dry her flesh. Neither could see much of the other's unclad body, but neither shielded themselves. She returned the cover, and he did the same. Joe hung it over the ledge to dry if the sun came out in the morning. They ducked and returned to the bedroll, but they did not redress in the cramped darkness.

Joe took another blanket and lay down on it. "Let's get some sleep. We'll talk tomorrow," he suggested, and tossed the cover over them.

Morning Star snuggled into his beckoning arms and her chill left. For now she would enjoy his embrace but, she cautioned herself, there was no way to remove the stone wall separating them. When morning came, she must concentrate only on the dangerous task looming before them. "Sleep, Joe. A hard task rides before us."

The white man's arms pulled her more closely against him. He smiled when she nestled into his embrace. She fit perfectly in his arms. If only, he agonized, she could fit as perfectly into his life in Virginia. Even if she studied and worked hard for years, she could not change herself into an aristocratic southern belle. And even if by some miracle she did, she would no longer be Morning Star. He could not alter her into something she wasn't just so he could have her forever.

Nor, Joseph Lawrence the younger realized, could he remain here in Lakota Territory for the rest of his life. His family, work, friends, and life were back in Virginia. He had responsibilities and duties to his family and to his father's shipping business. He loved this wild and carefree existence but, he admitted, he would miss civilization eventually. It was just as cruel to let Morning Star think he would remain here after their task. A world and breed apart—that said it all and he must accept it.

Morning Star was not sorry she had yielded to Joe. Her problem was forcing wild thoughts and dreams from her head. She had heard many tales of how life was in the white world: eating at big tables, having wooden tepees with furniture, dressing in long gowns, behaving in strange ways, working away from your home to earn money, having slaves—servants—to tend your chores, getting food and supplies in stores. To think of going there was intimidating. She could imagine how the whites would treat her, and how they would treat Joe for bringing her into their "society." No, she could not be happy in the white world, just as Joe could not be happy here. She must not hope for more from him than he had given tonight. She could no more expect him to live in her strange world than he could expect her to do so in his.

After an hour of each telling themselves a permanent bond between them could never come to pass, their troubled hearts found appeasement in sleep.

Joe eased from her side and grabbed his clothes. He slipped away to excuse himself and dress. He knew he had awakened her, so he gave her time to do the same while he checked on the horses. When he returned to the shelter, Morning Star had the sleeping mats rolled and tied. She was clad in the same buckskin outfit she had worn yesterday, and she looked as fresh as the spring day in progress. She glanced at him and smiled. Relieved, he returned the gesture.

She focused on her chore. "Wood is wet and no burn. We eat little and ride. We eat more when stop to rest and wood is dry for fire."

"Morning Star . . ." he began in a hesitant voice, kneeling near her.

Her chocolate gaze met his blue one. She caressed his bearded cheek. "No need to speak of last moon. Let it sleep in our hearts until best time to speak of it. That not today. We friends. We partners."

"When the time comes for both of us, we'll have to talk about it."

She gazed deeply into his eyes. "That is so," she said, grasping how dismayed he was. She believed he loved her as she loved him, but it was too soon to expose such strong feelings. They needed more time together. If their Life Circles were meant to cross or to mingle, they would discover that wonderful truth when the Great Spirit willed it.

"Thanks," he said, his gaze softening and glowing.

She knew what he meant. "Eat, and we ride."

It was midafternoon and they were out of the Black Hills. The sun was radiant and the sky was clear. Everything smelled fresh and was vivid green following the drenching rain. In four days they should reach Orin McMichael's trading post on the Missouri River, about forty miles north of the settlement that had come to be known as Pierre, pronounced Peer.

Joe lifted himself in his saddle and stared beyond them. He locked his eyes on a rider he recognized and studied him. His mind went to work quickly. He related his daring plan to Morning Star, who nodded her agreement with apprehension. "Let's ride. There's our chance to put a good plan into motion. Remember, you're my squaw, so behave like one," he jested and grinned. "We don't want to get ourselves shot."

Morning Star summoned her courage to face this challenge.

Chapter Ten

Joe and Morning Star realized they were about twenty miles from the site where they had met weeks ago. They had just crossed Elk Creek and left a treeline, after watering their mounts and pack animal. The man Joe had spied was approaching their location slightly to their left, coming from the northwest and heading southeast. As they were riding from the southwest to northeast, their paths would intersect soon. The stranger had seen them leave the trees and was continuing his course, obviously unafraid of them.

As the two traveling parties neared each other, the sunny-haired man and Oglala maiden noticed that the man with two loaded mules was dressed in a buckskin shirt and pants with lengthy fringes. The closer they rode, the more Joe and Morning Star took in details about him. The stranger's appearance and possessions told the couple he was a mountain man who was coming out of the wilderness to sell furs and pelts.

Joe told Morning Star to rein up and await the man's arrival, to see what they could learn from him. When he reminded her of her deceitful role, the maiden lowered her head and began her part as a submissive squaw to fool their company. She recalled how she had lost that part of the vision contest and how she was expected to behave. She cautioned herself to do and say nothing to endanger their task.

The trapper joined them. He removed a pelt hat and used one hand to mop perspiration from his brow. "Whar you headin'?" he asked Joe.

The blue-eyed man leaned forward and propped his arms on his saddle horn. Smiling, Joe replied, "For McMichael's post on the Missouri. You're the first person I've seen in days. Name's Joe Lawrence. This is my Arapaho squaw, Little Flower. Where you heading?"

After sending a spit of tobacco-filled liquid to the ground, he replied, "To Lookout. First trip since last fall." He rested a Hawken rifle across his thighs and adjusted the bullet pouch hanging around his neck that had shifted positions during his ride. A powder horn dangled from his pommel, and a large knife was secured around his waist in a decorative sheath. A man in this territory and in his occupation never went anywhere without being heavily armed.

"Have any trouble on the trail? Any of those Indians acting up?"

The man replaced his hat on a head of long and wavy hair that was thick at the base and thin on top. "Nope. Ain't seen narry a soul since I left my trappin' grounds, 'ceptin' a few Crow huntin' parties from a distance. I know whar they camp, so I avoids 'em. Ain't no need to tempt 'em to steal my winter's catch," he jested.

"I know what you mean. I keep a sharp eye out for them, too. Aren't you coming in a mite early?" Joe inquired, knowing there were two trapping seasons. One was in late autumn after furs and pelts had thickened for protection during the impending winter and the other was in the early spring after the snow and ice had cleared enough and before the quality of a trapper's targets had lessened when the animals shed their excess hair for comfort during the coming summer.

"Pete—he's my partner—Pete and me take turns gettin' our catch to Columbia Fur. I comes down firs' and sells our prime batch; then, he comes down second and sells our last batch. One of us always stays behind to guard and work our trap lines. This late of year, we're in need of supplies, and I git there afore the others. Columbia pays the best price to private trappers, but all them tradin' posts are too high on supplies. I leaves there and rides over to the suttler at Fort Laramie to stock up and visit friends. I git back sometime in late June; then Pete takes off to do the same. He gits back sometime in August. That leaves us time to work on our traps and cut firewood and git dryin' frames built. This year we need to repair our cabin. Mighty cold this past winter."

Joe caught the clues in the man's words. "Why don't we sit and talk a spell? Little Flower can prepare us some supper."

"That sounds temptin' to me. My name's John Howard, but most folks calls me Big John. I'll tend my critters firs'." He dismounted and headed for the creek to water his horse and two mules.

From beneath her lashes, Morning Star noticed how large the man was; his name suited him. His hair was dark on top, then steadily lightened to medium brown as it flowed from its roots. He looked to be about forty years of age. His jawline was thick with whiskers and they surrounded his mouth as thirsty grass did a pond. His eyes were small and squinty, but the expression in them was gentle and trustworthy. She was relieved by that, as she didn't want any trouble from the stranger.

Joe and Morning Star dismounted. She took their reins, as an obedient squaw, and secured them to bushes. She whispered to her man that she would gather roots and wood then prepare their meal while the two men talked. She left to carry out those chores.

Big John hobbled his horse and mules where they could drink and graze. He didn't seem to pay much attention to the beautiful Indian maiden with the genial stranger. He sat down to converse with Joe, unmindful of the earth still damp from yesterday's rain.

"Where do you trap, Big John?"

Following another stream of brown spittle over his left shoulder, John replied, "Along the Yellowstone and Powder rivers. It's a prime area most years. This past winter weren't so good, though. Too many com'ny boys encroachin' on the Stony and Missouri these days, tryin' to get rich fast. Last year, Pete and me made nine hunnard dollars. We'll be lucky to git five to six hunnard this season. That don't sit well with either of us. We came here from Kintucky to trap for five year; two of 'em's gone. I tol' Pete I was comin' in early to beat them Crow and Sioux afore theys go on the warpath. We don't want them furs and our hard work to rot 'cause we cain't git out."

"What makes you think new trouble is brewing, John?"

"It's been comin' nigh unto two year. Ever' time we git a visitor, that's all we hear, that a big war's a comin' soon."

"You and Pete ever have trouble with the Crow or Blackfoot?"

John spat again. "Nope, they leave us be. We respect 'em and stays outta their way, and they do the same with us. Me and Pete shares a Crow squaw; she's a good worker, right purty, too. Injuns ain't bad if you treat 'em right. Trouble is, they don't give some men time to treat 'em any way afore they kill 'em. I don't want to be 'twixt warring Injuns. When trouble comes, you best ride clear of them Plains," he warned.

"I will. Tell me, John, isn't it a long ride to Lookout, then to Laramie and home? That's a lot of days in the saddle."

"Yep, but, like I said, Columbia Fur Com'ny pays the best price for prime furs, and I git the cheapest supplies at Laramie. Laramie's where I have my fun. Them tradin' posts got too many men lazin' around, drunk and overusin' them pleasure women. They cheat you at cards, nearly charge you for the air you breathe, rob you while you're drunk or asleep, and fight all the time. I don't like to spend my relaxin' time at them crazy posts."

"That makes it sound worth the time and saddle sores," Joe jested.

The sun was low on the horizon, so John's gaze, as he faced west, was narrower than usual. The big man stroked his scraggly beard and mustache as he eyed the younger male.

"What you doin' way out here?" he questioned.

Joe pulled out a bottle of whiskey that he had taken from the burial-site robbers; he offered the man a drink to loosen his tongue even more. Big John beamed with pleasure, thanked him, and took a long swig. As the bottle was held out in return, Joe smiled and said, "Keep it, I have one more." John thanked him again, then took another long drink. Afterward the big man licked his lips to catch every drop.

As the trapper drank, Joe pondered asking him to take word to Tanner's father. He decided, since John would be a long way from there soon, his message wouldn't enter the wrong ears. He took a chance and asked, "Would you mind delivering a message to a friend of mine at Fort Laramie? I'd be much obliged. His name is Stede Gaston. I want to let him know I'm safe and heading to McMichael's post."

"No trouble," the other man agreed. "What work you do?"

Morning Star had tensed when her companion exposed a connection to Stede. Yet she assumed he must know what he was doing. She continued with her preparation of the evening meal and listened to the conversation.

Joe invented an explanation. "I've been a trader between here and Texas for years. A few months ago, I decided it was time to try a new area, see something different, learn some new things. I sent word to Stede and he checked out this territory for me. He said McMichael's is the biggest and busiest post. I'm heading there to try to make a deal with Orin McMichael. I think I can convince him he can sell more supplies if he hires me to travel around the territory taking and delivering orders to white and Indian camps. You know how people hate to leave their settlements and cabins to shop, even when supplies run low or give out. They also buy more things if you make it easy for them. Orin can make more money, and I can make a nice share. It's a perfect partnership. I sold all my goods last month and headed this way. I'll be there in five or six days."

"Sounds like a good deal to me," John remarked. "You can sell plenty of salt, sugar, coffee, ammunition, and flour. Folks will be happy to have stuff brought to 'em. Save 'em lots of time and ridin'."

"That's what I'm counting on to make my plan work. If Orin doesn't accept, I'll try at Pierre or Lookout. If none of them agrees, I'll just have to go into business alone. I'll do that later. For now, I need to be connected with someone who has supplies and knows this area."

Morning Star, with lowered head, served the two men their evening meal. She was careful not to look at either one and to assume an air of subservience. She would eat later. She busied herself about the fire and paid close attention to the conversation.

The men feasted on stewed meat with wild roots, heated beans, and johnny-cakes and washed the food down with coffee and whiskey.

Joe halted a moment to suggest, "If you want to head on to Laramie, John, I'll be glad to buy your furs, then sell them at McMichael's. I hear the price this season is two to three dollars a pound. Looks like you have about a hundred pounds," he guessed, from years of weighing cotton and goods for shipping. "I have that much from the sale of my goods. I'd just as soon travel with money in pelts as in my saddlebag. Showing Orin I can make a good deal before I reach him should be impressive."

"You got a sharp eye, Joe. I figured it at a hunnard pounds, too. I been gittin' three dollar a pound for prime grade at Lookout. I plan to sell my mules for twenty dollar each, and buy new ones at Laramie."

Joe added up the price of that response and compared it to the money he possessed. "I can pay you two-fifty per pound, John, and forty for the mules; that makes two hundred and ninety dollars. I only have three hundred with me. That would cost you fifty to trade with me, if Columbia is paying three this year. I could," Joe murmured aloud, "give you the whole three hundred and some supplies. I'll reach Orin's in a few days, so I won't need much. That way you'll be out less than forty dollars, and you'll save lots of aching bones and two to three weeks of travel. Then I'll sell the furs and mules for three-forty, so I'll make forty. Less replacement supplies."

The weary mountain man contemplated Joe's offer. He didn't care about visiting Lookout and having to face the many aggravations there. In all honesty, his mules weren't worth twenty dollars each. He could save two bone-jarring weeks in the saddle; he could be back to his trapping grounds two weeks early or spend that extra time in Laramie having fun and be out of this potentially dangerous area in a few days. Avoiding enemy bands as they moved to the Plains, which he'd have to cross twice, and all the other reasons compelled him to say, "You got a deal, Joe."

"It'll be a good one for both of us, John."

Morning Star was pleased with her partner's cunning. Now, they could head to the trading post as a trapper and his squaw; the furs and mules would make their pretense look real. When he had suggested the plan to the man to obtain pelts, she hadn't been sure it would work. She was relieved he had enough white man's money to make it come true. Surely the Great Spirit was guiding them. She experienced anxiety again when the conversation continued.

"You know a big man named Zeke?" Joe asked in a casual tone. He described the villain's hireling, then added, "He travels with two fellows called Clem and Farley. Clem's a drunk, and Farley has a knife scar."

"I seen 'em together last season at Lookout. Don't know 'em good."

"I learned that Zeke and his boys haul goods for some of the posts. I figure he'll be my biggest competition for a deal with McMichael. I know they travel around out here, so I thought you might have run into them."

"Nope, and hope I don't. I didn't take to 'em. Bad, if you ask me."

"From what I've heard about them, I can't blame you. If you do cross trails with them, don't mention our deal. I don't want them hurrying to McMichael's to save their jobs and cost me mine."

When the men finished eating and took a walk in opposite directions to excuse themselves, Sun Cloud's daughter ate a quick meal. She washed the dishes in the stream and straightened the campsite. Taking a hatchet, she chopped off leafy branches to place on the ground, over which she laid the bedrolls to keep away the earth's dampness. The men returned to find everything ready for turning in for the night. She was surprised when the visitor spoke to her.

"Thank you for a wonderful meal, Little Flower. You do a good job."

Morning Star nodded gratitude, but did not lift her head and lashes. She excused herself in the woods, then went to her mat and lay down.

To avoid raising John's suspicions, Joe said nothing more than "Good-night, woman." He curled on his mat and closed his eyes, congratulating himself.

Shortly after sunrise, the happy couple watched Big John Howard head southwestward with the message for Stede Gaston.

When the also happy trapper was out of sight, Joe scooped Morning Star up in his arms and swung her around while laughing in merriment. "We did it, woman," he bragged. "You were perfect."

As her feet touched the ground again, Morning Star smiled and said, "We have good disguise now. Joe plenty smart and clever." Her hands rested on his broad chest and she gazed into his blue eyes.

They talked about the deal Joe had made before he said, "We make a good pair, woman. I'm proud of you. I almost hated to fool him," he admitted. "He seemed like a good man."

"Not too good," she refuted with a grin. "Mules not worth much. You say you pay too much."

He chuckled and stroked her cheek. "That's right, but it wasn't worth arguing over, because we both knew he was losing money by trading with me. I'll probably get about ten dollars each for them. I won't lose any money, and I wasn't looking to make any off him, but I'll get twenty more than I spent. I might even do better. I've heard some of the posts are paying four dollars a pound this year. In a way, I tricked and cheated him, but it couldn't be helped. We need those furs, but I only had three hundred dollars. All the supplies I gave him are the ones we took off those grave robbers. I just hope he doesn't find out about the better price, and come looking for me."

"If mad, he tell others Joe's name. He tell about message to Stede."

"I had to take that risk, Morning Star, to let him know I'm all right."

"Tanner's father be happy you safe. If man called John tell him you with squaw, he catch clue and know plan working."

"I hope so. After what happened to Tanner, I know he's worried."

"What Tanner and Stede look like?" she inquired.

Surprised and curious, Joe responded, "Why?"

"They family. Want to know how look."

Joe sensed there was more to her question. "They both had black hair, brown eyes, and dark skin," he answered. "They both looked Indian, if that's what you mean, but everyone thought they were of Spanish blood. Stede's hair has some white now. I was told he favors Powchutu. Those who knew his father will recognize him as the son." He wanted to explain that Stede looked Indian because he carried little white blood, but he had promised Sun Cloud to withhold that secret. As for Tanner, his mother had possessed brown eyes and hair, so her coloring hadn't affected his. Tanner . . .

"You look sad. What wrong?"

"I was thinking about Tanner. God, I miss him," he confessed with deep emotion. "How can he be gone forever, Morning Star? He was like a brother to me, and I'll never see him again. Damn those bastards! I'm going to find them and kill them," he swore. "Just like they killed Tanner!"

She caressed his cheek. "I understand and help. I sorry ask about him. Pain still great." She explained why the answer was important to her and related her confusing conversation with her brother.

"He's wrong, Morning Star. Babies come from both parents. I do believe that God decides when to give you one, but the child is part of the mother and father. As I said, Stede and Tanner look Indian. Some blood is stronger and affects a child's looks more, but neither parent is ever totally overpowered. He's wrong, too, about it not mattering who the father is. If Powchutu and Alisha had married, they would have had their own child, not Bright Arrow and Sun Cloud. The two of them are part of Gray Eagle and Alisha. You and Night Stalker would not come from a child by Powchutu and Alisha. Gray Eagle's blood flows in you, and you would not be the same without it."

"It is how I believed, but Brother make good points and confuse."

"That's only natural. That's how people learn and grow. They search for answers and ask questions, then fit all the pieces together to make their own picture of understanding."

"You plenty smart. You teach me all you know."

Joe smiled and said, "I'll do my best, but I'm not very skilled in that area. We'll do lessons every night in camp. Right now, let's get those mules packed and head out. It's adventure time, Little Flower," he teased.

Together they loaded the bundles of pelts onto the scrawny mules. Joe saddled their horses while she secured their supplies onto their packhorse. The fire was doused, the campsite cleaned. They mounted and rode toward the Missouri and Cheyenne rivers conflux.

At the next campsite, Joe answered her questions about his life and family in Virginia. He related his years growing up between the plantation near Richmond and a townhouse in Alexandria. He told her about his years at school and about going to work with his father in the shipping business. At first he sailed with his father, and later he sailed alone, unless Joseph Senior had a reason for going along. "I guess I can captain a ship as good as the next man," he admitted. "Father did business with Stede; that's how I met him and Tanner. When I took over most of the important runs, Tanner was my first mate, meaning he was my best helper. Stede didn't mind; he had his brother-in-law, his sister's husband, to run his firm. She was named Alisha after your grandmother. When Powchutu came here years ago, Stede ran his firm. When Stede came, he put Wesley—that's Alisha's husband —in control of his company. Alisha and Wesley have four children. She hasn't been told about her nephew's death yet. Stede won't do that until we return home. I haven't sent word about it to my family, either; I don't want them to worry I'll get killed, too."

Joe took a deep breath. He waited a moment, but Morning Star didn't make any comments. "Tanner and I shared a lot of adventures. We visited many exciting and strange places. Then Wesley got sick, and Tanner had to help his father in their shipping business. Trips weren't any fun with Tanner gone. It was all work and too much dull time on water. I received a letter from Tanner last July, telling me about his father's plans to come here. He invited me to ride along. Father was upset, but I had to accept. Before winter arrived, we were at Fort Laramie."

"You have sister. Tell about her," she encouraged a happy subject.

"Her name is Sarah Beth. She's older than I am and is married to Andrew Reardon. He works for Father, and loves the shipping business. They have one child, a son, age four, named Lucas, a boy I'd be proud to have. He's a wonderful child, Morning Star; you'd love him."

"What if Great Spirit give Joe girls?"

As Joe envisioned a tiny replica of the woman beside him, he smiled. "I'd love them and raise them the best I could."

"When return home, you go back to shipping business?"

"I'd prefer to run our plantation, or the business office. I wouldn't mind a few trips a year, but I don't want to be sailing every week." He gazed into her eyes as the reality of his eventual departure struck him. "I'll miss you."

"Morning Star will miss Joe, too."

He drew her into his arms and pressed his lips to hers. She responded. The kiss was sweet and mellow. Their spirits soared with the pleasurable contact. The ensuing kiss was more ardent. Their emotions were so powerful that they were alarming, and caused them to seize control before it was too late to prevent what would take place if they continued to kiss in this heated manner. Their talk of babies had warned them of the consequences of fusing their fiery bodies once more. They knew they must not allow those feelings to take command and run wild. As if passing an unspoken and necessary message between them, they kissed lightly, then cuddled until self-control returned.

The next morning, Joe set a pattern he would continue daily during their months together. He related facts about America and the world: geography, history, laws, customs, religion, and more. He worked with her English, verbs and pronouns in particular. He helped her practice numbers, times—hours, days, weeks, months, years—and seasons. When he came to training her in the use of his weapons, she was reluctant, telling him it stole their magic and power for a woman to touch them. Joe finally convinced her that was part of her tribal customs and laws, but it didn't apply to his rifle and pistol, and there might be times when their lives depended upon such knowledge and skill. He was delighted when she learned quickly. Each lesson was enjoyable, yet, somewhere deep inside his mind, he knew what he was trying to prepare her for, even if he couldn't admit it to himself or suggest it to her.

In return, Morning Star taught Joe how to use a bow and arrows, how to become more skilled at reading tracks and trail signs, how to find his way around the territory in case they became separated, and how to speak more Lakota. She pointed out which plants were edible. Later she planned to teach him use of the lance and more. She daydreamed that perhaps there was a way to keep him here, keep him in her life and arms.

Their work together was challenging and fun. It drew them closer and tighter each hour. Their friendship, respect, and trust increased; and their love became stronger and deeper.

In camp that evening, after he scouted the east and north and she scouted the west, they knew it was safe to practice with his weapons. Aware of how the echo of gunfire traveled across the land, they were assured no one was close enough to hear it.

Having acquainted her earlier with his Colt Walker .44 pistol, Joe felt it was time to educate her about his other powerful weapon. He showed Morning Star how to handle and fire his Sharp's rifle, a '48 breech model that used a self-contained paper cartridge. He kept his ammunition in a leather ammo pouch that was faster to get to, rather than in an awkward cartridge box which could cause a man to fumble for bullets in a rush.

As the sunny-haired man helped her hold and aim the rifle, Morning Star remarked, "It easier to use than heavy pistol. I need stronger hand."

Joe knew the nine-inch barrel and over four-pound weight of his six-shot cylinder Colt was more difficult to control and master than a long rifle that distributed its weight in two hands and was supported by one shoulder. "The thing is, you'll know how to use either one if trouble arises."

The white man stood slightly to her left and rear with their bodies touching. One hand steadied her left arm and his other supported her right. Both became overly conscious of the contact and heat between them.

Morning Star turned her head to look at Joe, who was staring at her. "I please Joe with my new skills?" she hinted.

"You please me in every way," he heard himself respond.

Their gazes met. They gazed at each other as if mesmerized, captive in an enrapt world neither wanted to flee. They felt the emotions rising between and within them. Their hearts pounded.

With Joe's assistance, Morning Star finished turning to face him. The rifle butt slid to the ground, and she unknowingly released her loosened grasp on the barrel; the weapon fell harmlessly to the grass. They caressed each other's faces and bodies as their mouths joined in sheer delight. The smoldering embers between them burned brighter and hotter until they felt engulfed by a roaring blaze. Swept away by a surge of hungers, they were helpless to do anything except be carried along in the swift currents.

Soon, the enticement of heady passion prevented any thought of the consequences of their joining. They wanted and needed each other; for the present, nothing else mattered. Their kisses were greedy and stimulating. Their arousing caresses took and gave exquisite delight. Discarding garments and shoes, they sank into the bed of grass beneath their shaky legs. The past and future did not exist, only this moment and themselves.

Their appetites for each other did not need whetting, but nature seemed to guide them in that direction. They embraced and nibbled and savored each other.

Joe's lips roamed her features, and his hands journeyed her supple flesh. His fingers trekked down her neck and teased over her breasts. As if a lost traveler, they wandered everywhere, searching for hidden treasures instead of a path of escape. They did not worry about finding their way home, only about making this trip a blissful one.

Morning Star adored the feel of Joe's sleek frame against her skin. She loved the way he held her, touched her, kissed her, and tantalized her beyond resistance. She was thrilled by the way he shuddered with need for her and the way sensuous groans came from deep within his brawny chest. It seemed as if his feelings came from the depths of his soul, as did hers. The maiden's hands reveled in the ripplings of his muscles. His body was perfect, hard beneath a surface of soft skin. His hands were strong, but more than gentle. He was so special, so unique, and he was hers.

Joe was drawn to everything about the maiden with him. She possessed so many strengths yet none detracted from her femininity. She was beautiful. She was exciting. She was fulfilling. She was perfect for him. She belonged to him, tonight and forever.

They pressed closer together, their hands roving wild and free. Their mouths met and their tongues danced the ritual of desire. Their bodies worked as one, laboring with joy and eagerness. As they explored each other and their still budding love, passion burst into vivid bloom, unfolding one petal of pleasure after another until a rosy blossom filled their senses with fragrance and beauty. Sweet, fierce ecstasy washed over them, first as powerful waves which they rode urgently, later as ebbing ones which lapped gently at them. Ever so slowly, love's flower closed its petals like a morning glory going to sleep, to await its next burst into bloom.

Both sighed peacefully and nestled together as their contented bodies returned to normal. Each realized their actions had been unstoppable; their oneness on the trail was fated. It was dishonest to say it meant nothing, or was only physical lust; it was foolish to ignore their emotional attraction; it was futile to resist it. Whatever the future held, they could not change what was between them.

As they lay cuddled together, Joe realized this was only the second time in his life he had made love, not just enjoyed sex. The key part in lovemaking was *love*, and he knew beyond a shadow of doubt that he loved the woman in his embrace.

He had seen many females in the past; he had had fun with most of them. Some had been sweet and nice, some smart and polished, and some pretentious. He had known he would marry one day when the right woman came along. He had been told that real love grabbed you and never let go; or that was the way it should be. He had taken women to bed around the world, but none compared with Morning Star. She was the woman he had waited for and craved. He wasn't certain yet if he could win her, or how to do so.

Morning Star nestled closer to Joe. She recalled what her cousin—her uncle's youngest child—had told her last summer: "When spring arrives, all eyes and hearts think of love and mating; It is the way of nature to inspire hungers to renew old life and to birth new life. Warm and scented nights cause stirrings in young bodies. Such fevers are as old as Wakantanka and will continue forever." Tashina had been told that by their grandmother long ago, and it was still true today. Alisha/Shalee had also said, "Life is not easy, and neither is love." That was true during Alisha and Tashina's battles for true love. It was true of her own situation.

During visits to her father's band, Tashina had told her many things about their grandmother and about life. Sometimes she wished her cousin were closer for more talks, but Tashina was the Cheyenne chief's wife. Yet, Morning Star reminded herself she had her mother, and they were close. If only this matter was something she could discuss with Singing Wind. But it was not.

Morning Star reflected on their customs. When a girl joined, it was usually arranged by her father, and hopefully she approved of the choice. The man or his family mentioned the subject first, so it was best for a girl to let an interested pursuer learn her feelings before that happened. Even if she didn't approve of him, a well-raised maiden normally accepted her father's wishes. Morning Star knew she was lucky her father had not chosen a man for her or shown interest in Knife-Slayer's pursuit of her. Fortunately the offensive warrior hadn't made an offer for her. Not that a brave purchased a woman for a wife, but he offered many gifts to the girl's family to prove his depth of love and his prowess as a hunter and provider.

Thankfully it was rare for a warrior to pursue or ask for a female who made her dislike for him known publicly. It was just as natural for a husband not to hold on to a wife who wanted to leave him. What the white man called divorce was simple in Indian life for a woman: as the tepee was hers, either she tossed out a husband's belongings or she packed hers and left. No man with any pride would return to her or beg her to take him back. For a man, all he had to do was announce his intentions, then leave the tepee.

One thing of which Morning Star was certain was that her husband would have one mate, not several as was acceptable in her society. Many from her bloodline felt and behaved that way. It was not mocking the white custom of one wife to one husband but *love* that prevented a need for others. She could not accept sharing her love, her husband, with another woman or women.

Among her people, a girl's purity was guarded carefully by her family and herself and was honored by her tribe. A girl was taught she must not give away her future husband's treasure.

But was it not hers alone to give to the man of her choice? Morning Star asked. When she was with Joe, she forgot the importance placed on virtue. He stirred feelings to life within her which she knew must be love. Even if it were wicked of her to feel and behave as she had with him, she could not help herself. She could not convince herself such beautiful emotions and actions were wrong. She loved him, and surely that made it all right. In the eyes of their gods, they were mates. True, they had performed the joining ceremony as a pretense, but both accepted it as real and meaningful, as a commitment to each other.

Having been raised with little privacy in a tepee by two parents who were much in love and who shared fiery passion for each other, lovemaking was no secret to her. It was a part of love, the sharing of all you are with your chosen one. It was obvious Joe felt the same. She also knew that a baby did not come from every mating. Joe had said one came when God said it was the right time. Since the all-knowing and generous Great Spirit knew this was not the time to bless them with one, she would not become heavy with child while riding this sacred mission.

Morning Star recalled that three days ago her people broke camp to journey to their first camp on the Great Plains to hunt buffalo. She prayed their hunt would be safe and successful, as would her impending task.

For four days, the terrain was a mixture of flat lands and low, rolling hills. Tall bluestem grass added color to that of gray-green needle and buffalo, as did the purplish hue of scattered bunches of switch. Pasque, the harbinger of spring, decorated areas with blue, lavender, and white faces. A few clumps of prickly pear displayed buds and unripened cactus fruits. Morning Star told Joe that Indians used the red fruits for food, as they did with the bulb of the creamy white segolily. An array of other wildflowers snuggled amidst the mixed grasses to dot the solid blanket of green.

The landscape altered to higher hills with lengthy plateaus—up a steep incline, across a pancake surface, and down into a valley with lumpy waves. The cycle was repeated over and over. Visibility was excellent, and a good safety factor. When they saw trees—usually cottonwoods—that indicated a water source was nearby: a sign any greenhorn had better learn fast, and Joe had done so under Morning Star's skilled tutorship.

About four o'clock, the couple neared the trading post of Orin McMichael. Noticeable apprehension chewed at both.

"What if Zeke and other man here?" she asked.

Joe didn't hesitate before replying, "We hit the trail fast. If anything looks or sounds strange, flee. If we get separated, head for our last campsite. I'll join you there. We can't take any chances of both of us getting captured. If anything happens to me, get word to Captain Thomas. If you get caught, stay calm and I'll find a way to rescue you. Keep your eyes and ears open. Don't trust anybody. Anybody," he stressed.

Morning Star did not insist for them to stay together at all times. It might not be possible. Confident that Joe was clever and careful, she would follow his orders, whether or not she agreed with them.

Joe spoke his thoughts aloud. "It's been three weeks since our run-in with Zeke. He's had time to get here, if he was heading this way. This is a big territory; he could be anywhere. I don't see his wagons—that's a good sign. If he's been here, I doubt he told anyone about his trouble with us; it would be humiliating to expose his defeat."

"You right. I try not to . . . worry much."

The sunny-haired man reminded, "Remember, we don't want to do any private talking here. I don't want us overheard in case somebody decides to spy on us. We will play our parts as if they're real."

"I obey, do my best to play good squaw."

The alert couple studied the settled area as they entered it. Everything faced south, instead of the Missouri River and rising sun as one might expect. The Cheyenne River was behind, its many watery fingers pointing northwest, which created an excellent rear defense to prevent being flanked by attackers. The surging "Big Muddy" did the same eastward. Joe told Morning Star the purpose and power of two cannons—one aimed west and the other south—that asserted this settlement had little vulnerability and that the owner was determined to be safe. The undamaged landscape told them the weapons had not been used.

Orin's trading post was large, well-constructed, and rustic. A porch ran the full length of the front, with wooden poles supporting the roof. There was a small house to its right, probably the owner's home. It, too, looked strong and well suited to the wilderness that surrounded it. To the left was an oblong building with a door at each end. Joe suggested to his companion that it was half for storage and half for guest quarters, as he'd seen elsewhere. Between the two structures, they saw a stable and corral and through one open door, they sighted a flat-bed wagon for hauling goods from the nearby river. The corral held six horses and seven mules. They noticed a worn trail snaking eastward, which indicated in which direction the boat landing was located. There were scattered copses of hardwoods around the clean settlement, and a dense tree line along most of the grassy bank of "The Misery" that joined the Cheyenne not far away.

They rode to the trading post, dismounted, and secured their horses' reins to hitching poles with metal loops. Joe did the same with the mules' reins. It was late afternoon on the seventh of June. Sunset would arrive in a few hours. It was time for serious work.

A tall, burly man with red hair and matching burnsides left the post and joined them. His brows were wiry, with hairs growing in all directions over hazel eyes. His complexion was flushed, but from natural coloring rather than results from any kind of exertion. The sparkle in his eyes and the broad smile on his face alleged him to be good-natured and friendly.

"Good tae see ye, friend," he greeted the stranger, barely glancing at the woman. "I'm Orin McMichael, tha proud proprietor of this fine establishment. I see ye've come tae sell 'r trade furs. Ye made ae wise choice." He rubbed his clean-shaven chin, finger-flicked his whiskered jawline, then stroked his thick mustache.

Joe grasped the large, strong hand extended to him and shook it. He noticed Orin's voice was deep and mellow with a Scottish burr. "The name's Joe Lawrence. Glad to meet you. It's been a long, hard ride." If Orin recognized his name, it didn't show. He had seen only one other man with a similar facial haircut, who had said he shaved his chin to keep food bits and grease out of his beard. From his attire and manner, Orin seemed to be a man inclined toward neatness. The redhead was dressed in a dark coat with matching trousers, a white shirt, patterned vest, and a bowtie. Orin looked as if he belonged more in an office in a large city than in a wild area like this one.

The Scotsman smiled. "Time for drinking, talking, and having fun, Joe Lawrence," Orin said, as if stressing the man's name to brand it into memory. "I have e'er'thing ye need 'r want here. Ye can set up camp o'er there in tha trees," he suggested, pointing to a shady area that faced his home. "Ye can stay with yer woman 'r stay in me fine lodgins. Either way, she'll be safe in Orin's shadow. She speak English?"

Joe removed his hat and held it by the brim at his left leg. "A little. I bought her last year. She's been a good helper. She's Arapaho."

Orin looked her over as he replied, "I recognized her markings. If ye don't learn tae do that fast out here, ye don't survive long."

"With so many forts within a few days' or weeks' ride, this area should be settled soon. That'll make it safer."

Orin chuckled. "Not soon enough tae suit most folks. Come inside. Meet tha others. Have ae drink, loosen ye jaws, and rest. Me woman will be serving ae good meal in about an hour. Ye be welcome tae buy ae plateful for twenty-five cent. If she likes white food," he added, nodding at the woman, "ye can buy her ae plateful, too. I don't mistreat Indians."

"Little Flower likes to eat her own cooking, but thanks." He looked at the Indian beauty, whose head and lashes remained lowered. "Woman, set up camp there," he ordered in a pleasant tone, motioning to the copse Orin had pointed out. "Tend the horses, then stay there. Don't leave camp. You eat. Don't cook for me. I'll return after dark."

Without lifting her head, Sun Cloud's daughter nodded in understanding and obeyed swiftly. She loosened the reins of his roan and her Appaloosa, and guided their animals to the river to drink. When they finished, she led them to the wooded area and tethered them there. She began her chores of setting up camp.

"Will these mules and furs be all right here for a spell?" Joe asked.

Orin pulled his attention from the beautiful maiden back to Joe. "Naebody bothers anything around here, Joe. She's ae pretty one. Ye best keep yere eyes on her, 'r she'll be stolen by some hot-blooded buck. Follow me. I have some friends for ye tae meet."

Joe hoped his tension didn't show, but he was nervous about entering the confined space before him. He prayed Zeke and Farley weren't inside. He had left his rifle on his saddle, but was wearing his pistol. He flexed his fingers to be ready for action, and he summoned all his senses to full alert.

During the previous two days, Morning Star had experienced her woman's flow. She had come prepared with trade cloth for it. Whenever necessary, she had excused herself behind knolls to tend the task. Now she wanted a cleansing bath.

Watching Joe from a distance, Morning Star whispered the same prayer he had. From their assigned location, she could see the fronts of all structures and she was in plain view of anyone inside of them, so a bath had to wait. Although she looked to be busy with chores, she remained ready to spring into action if Joe needed her help. Her eyes and ears had never been more focused on something than the door through which Joe vanished.

Protect him, Great Spirit, she prayed again. *I do not like this white man's world. Help us to find what we seek and to leave here soon.*

Chapter Eleven

Joe glanced around the interior of the trading post; it was stocked heavily with anything a man or woman could need in these parts.

"It was rowdy here two days ago," Orin said, "but it's quieted down now. Had ae boat stop by tae unload supplies. It was heading upriver tae Union and Benton —American Fur Company posts. Had several company fur buyers along and ae few men seeking thrills in tha wilds. Only have three guests now; I'll introduce them tae ye soon. They're in tha back room, drinking and gambling and running their mouths. I sell good aged rye whiskey, not that rot-gut 'r watered-down stuff. I don't sell it tae Indians because it makes them crazy; that's why tha boys drink in the back room. If ye tell them ye don't have any, ye best not show it around and cause trouble. Where're ye from, Joe?"

"I've been trapping northeast of here for the past nine months," he alleged. "That area wasn't too good for me, so I decided to try my luck farther west this next season, along the upper Yellowstone and Missouri. If I don't decide to do something else before then," he amended with a grin to set his strategy into motion. "I've been a sailor and a soldier, and I didn't like either job. Too many rules and demands. You could say I haven't found the right opportunity to suit me yet."

"I doubt ye want tae be heading up that way. I hear trouble is coming this year between tha Crow and Dakotas."

Joe sent the observer a displeased frown. "If that's true, it could mess up my other plan," he muttered, then scowled in feigned displeasure.

"What is that?" Orin questioned as he leaned against the counter.

"I thought about starting a traveling trader business. I figured if I could join up with someone who owns an established post, I could travel around taking orders and delivering them for a nice profit for both of us. I think people—Indians and whites—would buy more goods if they're brought to their doors. I thought I'd try it out until fall; if I found I didn't like it, I'd go back to trapping. You interested in such a proposition?"

The red-haired man didn't take time to think before answering, "That idea sounds as dangerous as yer first one."

"A man don't make much money playing it safe. Since you're sitting in the middle of Indian country, you know you have to take risks to get rich."

Orin grinned as he fingered his smooth chin. "Ye be right, tae ae point. It's an interesting idea, but I don't think this is the season for it. Yere plan will be safer in ae year or two."

Joe decided to be bold, especially before he entered that back room. "You know a big man named Zeke? Hauls goods in these parts."

"E'er'body knows Zeke. Why ask about him?"

"I hear he transports most of the supplies in this territory, so I figured I'd better not infringe on his territory without checking him out first. Maybe he'd be interested in having a partner. From what I've been told, he knows this area and these people better than anyone."

"I haven't seen him in weeks." He glanced to his left at the closed door before saying, "I'll warn ye about Zeke: he's ae loner. He can get mean and odd on ye. I doubt he'll want tae share earnings with ye 'r anyone. He's high-priced, but I've used him many times because he is dependable. Zeke isn't scared of anything 'r anyone. I can't blame him for charging so much; his job is dangerous, especially with those Indians acting up."

"You have much trouble with them? I noticed your cannons."

"None sae far. Ne'er had to fire ae shot. They're tae scare off thieves and renegades. Robbery is ae big threat in ae wilderness. No big problems with the Indians. Tae be honest, I don't like or dislike them. They're paying customers like anybody else, sae I'd be foolish tae offend them. And stupid taw rile them. Sometimes they'll try tae cheat ye, 'r intimidate ye into giving them ae cheaper price 'r goods for free. They know they're welcome here and I treat them fair. Best way tae get along with one is tae treat him like any other man, if he'll let ye. That's why I don't let them know about tae whiskey; they don't take kindly ta being lied tae 'r cheated. 'Course, it's against tha law tae sell whiskey tae Indians, e'en though it's done all tha time." Orin changed the subject. "Let's get our business settled, then ye can join tha others for cards. I pay three dollars ae pound. That suit ye?"

Joe smiled and said, "That's fair. You want to buy those two mules?"

"I'll have tae take ae look at them." He headed for the door.

Joe followed, then watched Orin examine the furs and animals. He glanced at Morning Star, who appeared busy with camp tasks. Yet he sensed her eyes on them, and had to suppress flashing a smile in her direction.

"I can pay ye seven dollars ae piece, and three hundred for tha furs."

Joe looked at the laden beasts, pretended to think a minute, smiled again, and said, "It's a deal." At least he would recover his investment.

"I'll make ye another offer: if ye decide tae buy ae wagon and supplies tae trade on tha trail, I'll make ye ae good price on both. If ye live tae see September and ye make good money, we'll talk about ae partnership then."

"After I leave, I'll look around and check out the area and any brewing trouble. If it suits me and appears safe, I'll return and deal with you. If I'm not back in four weeks, you'll know it didn't look good and I moved on."

"Ye be ae smart man, Joe Lawrence. Let me introduce ye ta tha boys before I unload these furs and corral these mules."

Joe followed Orin back inside the trading post. The big man halted at the counter; he took some money from a metal box and paid Joe the amount due. Joe pocketed his earnings and took a deep breath as the older man opened the door to the other room. As soon as Orin's large frame was out of the way, Joe's gaze rushed around the area. He was relieved to find that none of the three men present was familiar.

"Tha Army scout is George," Orin said. "He likes ta take his leave here with tha best women and whiskey." The soldier nodded, then returned his gaze to his cards. "George doesn't talk much. I suppose he doesn't want civilians getting worried about this trouble brewing." The scout didn't look up or respond to Orin's genial remarks. The red-haired man moved on, "That's Ben; he's ae prospector. He's been searching this territory for several years for ae lucky strike."

"Gonna find me one, too, you'll see," the gold seeker declared, then smiled through several missing teeth.

"Not if ye head into them Black Hills like ye're planning."

"Don't be worryin', Orin. Them Injuns are headin' fur the Plains as we jaw. Soon as they git outta them hills, I'm takin' me a look-see. You kin bet yore britches they's gold in there somewheres. I'm gonna find it."

"What ye're going ta find is yer hair missing," Orin jested.

Ben chuckled and stroked the thinning strands that needed a good washing and brushing, as much as his body and garments needed scrubbing. "Hell's bullets, them Injuns think I'm crazy! Theys don't bother no crazy folk. I'll be back here, rich as a king, afore the leaves are fallin'."

"I wish ye luck, Ben, but ye best be careful of those Lakotas. They're real protective and selfish with their territory. Ask George; he'll tell ye tha straight of it." Getting back to the last introduction, Orin said, "That's Ephraim; he's ae trapper like ye, Joe. He's down early this year. He might know more about tha western area than any of us."

"You 'tending to trap over my way?" the buckskin-clad man asked, squinting his already beady eyes to examine Joe from head to foot.

"Haven't decided yet. Trapping sure isn't good east of here. I came by to sell my furs to Orin, then take a look around. I may get into trading."

"You wuz smart to come here. Orin's got the best prices. Them American Fur boys at Benton and Union don't pay as good as him. I has to haul my pelts further, but Orin makes it worth me while."

Orin smiled and thanked Ephraim. He motioned to the last person in the room, a woman with blond hair and green eyes. "She's Mattie Lou. I only have one girl at present. Three more 'r coming by tha fifteenth. Most of tha boys don't come in until tha end of June or first of July. Mattie Lou is ten dollars for one service, twenty-five dollars for all night. She's tha best trained pleaser I've e'er hired. She can give ye any treat ye want. Right?"

The pretty prostitute sent Joe a seductive smile and agreed with her boss, "Anything you like or want, I'm best at it."

"I'll get ye ae drink, Joe; first one's on tha house. I'm sure tha boys would like ae fourth hand in their card game. Relax. I'll finish me chores and join ye boys later." Orin made eye contact with the woman before he served the newcomer a glass of aged rye whiskey. He asked the other customers if they needed anything, and everyone shook their heads no. He left the room and closed the door.

Joe caught the interaction between Orin and Mattie Lou, but did not comprehend its meaning. He sat in the empty chair at the square wooden table.

"Good to meet you boys. Don't get to see many faces when you're trapping. Right, Ephraim?"

"Nope, but it don't trouble me none when I'm working. How much pelts did you bring in?"

Evening shadows were dimming the three-window room, and Joe saw the prostitute light two lanterns. "A hundred pounds of beaver, otter, and muskrat. Prime quality, but not enough critters in that area. How is it over your way?"

"Not as good this year as most. Thick and healthy, but slim takin's. Too much work to keep going. Figured I'd come on in and have some fun."

Joe noticed how Ephraim eyed the pretty woman nearby and assumed the trapper was whetting his appetite to enjoy her later. He sipped his free drink as he studied the men.

"Any trouble over your way this spring?" George asked.

Joe wondered why the Army scout didn't look up at him, but just kept staring at his card hand. "Nothing that I saw or heard about. Did my trapping on the upper Minnesota and James rivers. Those woodland tribes are pretty friendly, if they come around at all. What's the trouble between the Lakotas and Crow that Orin mentioned?"

"Same as always: old enemies, and too many whites settling in."

"What about that rumored treaty the Indian agent is working on?"

George didn't look up to respond, "It'll be summer here all year long before those two nations make peace. Longer before whites are accepted."

"Sounds as if you don't care much for Indians or treaties," Joe hinted.

The scout looked him in the eye. "I don't care for anybody who ain't a friend of mine or anything that makes my life harder," he revealed. "Out here, it's risky to accept strangers fast. Too many men who'll put a bullet in your back or slit your throat while you sleep just to get your horse and supplies, or to empty your pockets, or to take your winter's catch. If you stay here, you've got to keep your eyes and ears open to survive. Don't trust anybody until you know for sure he's worth your time. You playing?" he asked, his tone gruff.

Joe was surprised by the amount of words George spit out. He nodded. "If you boys don't mind, I'll join in on the next hand."

"Be happy to take your money," Ephraim said with a lopsided grin.

Joe waited patiently while the three men finished the game in progress. Mattie Lou came up behind him and rested her ivory hands on his shoulders. She pressed her body against the chair and him. He felt the heat radiating from her like a blazing sun. Her open overture made him uncomfortable.

She bent forward and murmured into Joe's ear, "You've been in the wilderness a long time. I'm sure I can help you relax between supper and bedtime. Ephraim has me later."

"I got her all night, Joe," the trapper boasted.

"She'll wear you out in an hour," the crusty prospector jested.

"Ain't seen the day or night any female could tire me, Ben."

"He ain't had a go at you, has he, Mattie Lou?" the prospector refuted as he leaned over and playfully patted the woman's buttocks.

She laughed throatily and tickled Joe's ear. "I've never left any man awake, hungry, or without his money's worth. I promise you'll never forget me, Joe. You'll be hanging around for days just to get stocked up on me before leaving."

"You don't git no free sample of her, Joe, like whiskey."

Joe felt the woman rub her ample breasts against the back of his head. Her skilled fingers drifted over his shoulders to his chest where they caressed the flesh through his shirt. He smelled her cloying perfume in the air. He was repulsed by the provocative invitation to hire her.

Ben nudged the scout and jested, "Only person who gits it free is George there for keepin' Orin up on news around this ter'tory."

"That's not true," she refuted with a giggle. "George has to pay like everyone. Isn't that so, George?"

The scout spread out a winning hand as he muttered, "If I'm in the mood for a woman, I pay for her, if she ain't for the taking."

Joe was unconvinced that Orin didn't give Mattie Lou to George anytime he desired in exchange for scouting information. That didn't strike Joe as being too suspicious, as Orin had a profitable business and his life to protect. But Corporal George Whatever, he was a man to check out with Jim. Joe grasped that the scout didn't like attention and questions, so it was best to avoid both until tomorrow after they had gotten friendly.

The prostitute's forefingers began to make erotic circles around Joe's nipples. He jerked in surprise at her vexing boldness, and captured her invading hands and pushed them away. With a genial chuckle, he discouraged, "Sorry, Mattie Lou, but I have my own woman with me. I won't be needing your fine skills." When the female made a noise of displeasure, Joe assumed it was because few men had refused her charms.

"You have a wife with you?" she questioned.

"Nope," Joe replied, picking up the cards passed to him.

"A squaw?"

"Yep, perfect in obedience, and skills. I'm sure you are, too, but one woman is plenty for me," he added to soften his rejection.

"Men need variety. Wouldn't you enjoy bedding me for a change?"

"Thanks, but no. Little Flower provides everything I need. You open?" Joe asked Ephraim, displeased with the personal topic. It was common for men to talk and joke about conquests, but it left a foul taste in his mouth for his beloved Morning Star to be discussed openly this way.

Mattie Lou left the handsome newcomer and stood at one window to watch the dark-haired beauty in Joe's camp while she sulked.

The four men played cards for a time and talked only when betting. Joe pretended to concentrate on the game, but he was closely observing each man. More drinks were ordered, and the quiet female served them. One game drifted into another and another, with Joe winning two of them. Small talk ensued by all except George, who remained distant, sullen. Even Mattie Lou calmed down and joked with the men, particularly her customer for later.

When Joe felt confident enough to query the men, he asked, "Any of you know a man named Zeke?"

Ephraim and Ben nodded, George shrugged, and the woman grinned.

Joe tried again. "Where I can find him? I have a deal to discuss."

"What kind of deal?" George asked. "Zeke don't like strangers."

With a smile and in a genial tone, Joe related the traveling-trader story he had told to Orin. "Zeke and I could make good partners."

"Zeke works alone. He's real strange," George remarked.

"If he isn't interested, at least I won't get him mad at me by working his territory. I'd be obliged if you can tell me where to find him."

"Don't know. Zeke's all over the place all the time. If I run into him while scouting, I'll give him your message. Just hang around any of the trading posts, he'll ride up soon. Zeke stays on the move this time of year. Everybody knows him, so he won't be hard to locate."

Ephraim finally got to speak. "He's gitting furs from them Crow west of here. Ever' spring he travels around buying up all he can, real cheap. He takes 'em to a boat at Lookout to send downriver to St. Louis. Gits a better price than anybody here, 'cluding Orin. Costs him a mite to boat 'em out." He asked for two cards, then continued. "I saw him in the Powder River country when I wuz coming down. Said he wuz joining some friends at Rake's Hollow; they wuz to ride as guards across them Plains. Redskins are on the move this time of year. Been . . ." He thought a moment, then said, "Two weeks past, so he ain't had enough time to git back. Don't know where he's heading after that. He was in a bad mood, wors'en usual."

"Probably ridin' to Lookout on the 'Souri," Ben guessed. "If you head downriver, you should run in to him along the way."

"Maybe, but it could be a waste of my time. Zeke might head in any direction from Lookout," Joe surmised. He assumed the reason for Zeke's bad mood was his recent deceit and Morning Star's escape. He could envision an even worse mood after he discovered his cohorts slain.

From the trapper's words, Joe deduced that the men he and Morning Star had attacked must have been the escort Zeke was to meet. It was a good thing they hadn't waited around that area! The news told him that Zeke was trading ammo, weapons, and whiskey for furs. But, Joe speculated, for whom? Surely buying Indian pelts was only a cover to get arms and supplies to the Crow with which to battle the Lakotas. He also wondered if Zeke had ordered his hirelings to rob the Oglala burial ground for possessions to use as falsely incriminating clues, and if Zeke had been using those men to rile each side against the other. There was no doubt in Joe's mind now that Zeke was working for Snake-Man.

From then on, Joe had trouble keeping his mind on poker and lost two games. He finished his second whiskey to the other men's fifth drink. He was about to dig for details on the Indians and brewing conflict when Orin McMichael returned.

"If ye boys're ready tae eat, clear tha table. I have ae fine meal acoming. Good timing; yer game just ended."

It was dark outside, so only lanternlight brightened the room, adorned only with several tables and two sideboards. Through open windows, crickets, frogs, and nocturnal birds made music in the darkness they loved. George collected and stowed the cards. Mattie Lou cleared away empty glasses. The men stretched and sighed.

A hefty Indian woman entered the room carrying bowls of food. The prostitute fetched plates and utensils, then set two tables. Each man, including George, reached into his pocket for money to pay for the meal.

Joe saw the silent Indian woman go back and forth as she brought in more platters and bowls whose delictible odors filled the room. He wondered how his love was doing, but he must eat before joining her. He was past ready to leave this tension-inspiring chore for a night's rest.

"I call her Lucy," Orin told Joe, " 'cause her Indian name is ae foot long. She does me cooking, cleaning, and washing. She's Pawnee. I traded ae horse-load of goods for her. She's tight-tongued, but she's a good worker. If this isn't tha best meal tae pass yer lips, ye don't have tae pay."

Joe tasted the roasted meat and vegetables. He took a bite of a cat's-head biscuit with butter and honey. Orin had not exaggerated. He licked his lips and complimented, "Delicious."

"Lucy is tha best cook anywhere. I have vegetables and fruits sent up from downriver. My guests eat better than at any trading post. She's made apple pie for dessert. Mattie Lou, pour tha coffee, woman, afore tha men choke tae death and I lose good customers. Help yeself tae all ye want."

The men feasted on the wonderful meal. Orin and Mattie Lou sat at another table. The Pawnee servant came and went from a kitchen in the other house to replace empty bowls and platters with full ones. Another pot of steaming and aromatic coffee arrived, along with the apple pie. Joe had to admit to himself that it was the best food he had tasted since leaving Fort Laramie, and he wished Morning Star could enjoy it with him.

Joe finished eating. He bid the men good night and headed to his camp. A gentle breeze gave the air a soothing freshness that was effective medicine for settling his taut nerves. A new moon was overhead, so it was dark outside. With the aid of a lantern, Joe strolled toward the dying glow of a small fire. In the shadows beneath several hardwoods, he saw Morning Star on her bedroll. As he removed his boots and pistol, Joe whispered, "We'll talk tomorrow when we can see our surroundings."

To let him know she heard and understood his precaution, Sun Cloud's daughter gave a soft, "Hum." She wished they could talk, as she had things to tell Joe, but they must wait. She had worried about his safety all evening and was relieved to have him nearby again. She was eager to hear what he had learned, and was eager to leave this intimidating place.

Morning Star watched three visiting men leave the post with lanterns lighting their path and faces. A golden-haired female clutched the arm of one white man and she pressed against his body in a way that needed no explanation. The maiden observed them until they entered the west end of the oblong building. Laughter and voices came her way, but their words were not clear. She saw Orin and the Pawnee squaw go into his home. Light flickered against curtains for a short time, then was gone. Yet she sensed a powerful gaze in her direction. She heard occasional noises from the horses and mules, and heard the rushing of the adjacent river. Soon, she calmed her anxieties enough to go to sleep.

When Joe awoke, he saw Morning Star sitting beside a fire. He hadn't heard her rise, so he knew he had been in a deep sleep. It was unusual for him to drop his guard so low, even during slumber. He smiled when she turned her lovely face to him. No matter how many times or how long he watched, he never tired of seeing her and having her close. He wished they were closer, but embraces had to wait until they were alone. That time could not come soon enough to please him.

Morning Star noticed how Joe looked at her and realized what trail his thoughts rode—the same one hers traveled. Every day she came to love and want him more; every day she had to remind herself it was impossible. Being around whites and in one of their settlements impressed that reality deeper into her mind. Even though these men were nothing like Joseph Lawrence, other whites were like them. There was no place for her in his hostile world. If only he could—

"Don't think sad thoughts, love," he murmured after witnessing the glow in her eyes fade. "No matter how bad things look, there's always a path to escape."

Morning Star did not disagree with him at this time. But later, they must speak the truth and accept it. For now, being and working together, and having each other was all that mattered, all they could ever have.

Dawn lightened the landscape and their campsite. Birds sang or took flight to begin their daily chores. Horses neighed and mules brayed in the corral to signal it was feeding time. Smoke rose from the chimney on Orin McMichael's home.

Morning Star glanced at Joe. She was afraid to look too long in case anyone was watching them, but found it difficult to pull away her gaze. She loved how the early light played on his sunny locks. His hair was longer and thicker than at their first meeting. She yearned to stroke the wavy golden mane. The increasing light seemed to darken his blue eyes. Sometimes she believed she could stare into those sky-colored depths forever. She wasn't sure if she liked his short beard, as weeks of growth caused it to conceal too much of his tanned, handsome face. She wanted to spread kisses over it. She craved to flee to a place where their differences didn't matter, where peace and love ruled.

"If you keep looking at me like that, woman, I'm going to burst into flames. You have me kindled good already," he teased in a husky whisper.

Morning Star lowered her head to hide her amused grin from any watchful gaze. "I cannot kiss and hold fire," she whispered back. "Jump into the cold water to save and cool yourself."

"I'd love to share a bath with you, but not here," he responded.

"As a good squaw, I will scrub you clean in our next camp."

Joe caught how well she spoke. Their many lessons on the trail were working. He was delighted and proud. "Your English improves, grows better, my love. Your victory warms my heart and enlarges my pride."

Morning Star grinned once more. He always made her feel so happy. "I make a good squaw?"

"You make a good anything. I wish you did belong to me. Then, when this task here ended, I'd take you home with me. We'd—" Her head had lifted and she was staring at him, dismay written in her gaze. He inhaled deeply and apologized, "I'm sorry, Morning Star, but you make me forget myself."

"You make me forget myself. That is bad, wrong, Joe. We have nothing more than many days on the trail together. And many nights."

He grasped her meaning, and it pained him. He almost declared his love for her, but restrained himself. Yet it was something he—they—must deal with sooner or later.

"I must go into the forest," she hinted, her look clarifying her words.

Joe explained about the outhouse behind the oblong building. "It gives privacy. I'll walk to the edge of the building with you. I need it, too."

He guided her in that direction, then waited while she excused herself. She lingered while he did the same. They returned to their camp.

Just as they reached that area, Orin came out of his home. He stretched his healthy body. "Good morning tae ye!" he shouted.

Joe returned the cheerful greeting, but Morning Star remained quiet.

"Breakfast in one hour, if ye be eating with us. I bet it's been ae long time since ye had ae real breakfast," he said as he joined Joe near the trees. "Scrambled eggs stirred just right, crisp fried pork strips, biscuits with butter and jelly, steaming coffee, grits that slide down yer throat like honey," he tempted. "Join me while I hay tha stock?" Orin invited.

As they walked toward the corral, the proprietor disclosed, "I get me eggs and milk from farmers downriver, some vegetables and meats, too. I don't like grubbing in tha dirt, 'r like hearing chickens cluck and leave their droppings all o'er. Ye want some sweet feed for yer horses?"

"I think they'd like a treat," Joe replied. He took the bucket Orin handed to him. He lingered to inquire, "You do all your chores? Surely you don't work and live here alone when you don't have guests."

Orin lifted a board in a slanting trench to allow water to flow from the river into a sunken trough for the animals. He tossed hay from the barn into a corner of the corral. As he worked, he related, "I have two men who do me work. They're delivering supplies, tools, and furniture tae local farmers and homesteaders that came on tha boat. They rarely leave me alone, but tha money was tae good tae refuse." He brushed off his suit and smiled.

"It's ae good thing they don't venture far and wide, or you wouldn't need to consider my proposal. If thunder is in the wind like you said, I don't blame you for keeping them close."

"They'll be back later. They know Mattie Lou is here. She keeps me boys happy when they aren't busy. She be a good piece of property. She would have worked ye good last night, Joe, but I understand ye didn't want tae offend yer woman. If ye get tired of her, bring her here. She can help Lucy with me cooking and cleaning. Sometimes it gets very busy. I'll make ye ae good offer for her, and she'll have ae good home here."

"Thanks, Orin, but I doubt I'll ever sell or trade Little Flower."

"When it comes time for ae good-looking lad like ye ta marry and settle down, remember me offer. Just don't bring no babies with ye."

Joe laughed, because he couldn't think of a clever or guileful retort to terminate the vexing talk. "I best feed my horses and get washed up for that tempting breakfast. I'll see you later, Orin."

He barely finished treating the three horses when Ephraim, Ben, and Mattie Lou left the oblong building. The two men sent greetings his way, which Joe returned in a genial manner. The blond prostitute headed toward him. Joe warned his love about the bold woman.

Mattie Lou eyed the Indian beauty from her glossy black hair to moccasined feet. "This your woman?" she asked the obvious.

Joe didn't give the nosy female a smile. "Her name is Little Flower. She's Arapaho. She's kind of shy, but she's the best worker I've seen."

Mattie Lou ruffled her curly hair and placed her hands on rounded hips. With pouty lips, she asked, "She speak English? Understand it?"

"A little of both." Joe was careful with his words, knowing they would no doubt be repeated to her boss. He didn't like this intrusion, but there was little he could do at the moment. He wanted things to stay calm here.

"Don't you get bored without talk?" the whore asked in an almost hateful tone. "You need a woman with fire and spirit."

Joe had to suppress his irritation to reply in a passive tone, "Little Flower has everything I need. She never gives me a hard time."

"All men need a hard time in some areas." She licked her mouth in lewdness.

"I can give you an unforgettable one today. These hands and lips have skills to take you to heaven. Why not give me a try, Joe?"

"A beautiful and talented woman doesn't need to rustle up reluctant business, Mattie Lou. I'm just not the kind of man who needs more than one woman. Why don't you work your magic on George this morning?"

"George left before sunup. He stayed here a day longer than he should. He had to ride fast and hard to make up lost time."

Joe controlled his reaction to that news. He wondered if Mattie Lou was telling the truth or if she even knew it. He didn't like hearing that the strange scout had left so early, especially since George knew Zeke. "I have to get finished here, so I won't be late for breakfast. See you inside."

"I'm leaving," she snapped, his words more than a subtle hint.

Joe watched the annoyed woman stalk toward the post. He compared her to his love. Mattie Lou was tough, deceitful, and worn. Morning Star was gentle, honest, and fresh. One was a fake; the other was genuine. Both were strong; both were survivors.

"Lordy, Morning Star, she's worse than fleas. I'm sorry she came over," he apologized.

Joe's interaction with the white woman had not caused any jealousy in Sun Cloud's daughter, but she was angry with the wanton creature who lusted for her man. She would never suggest he act receptive to her just to glean clues for their mission! As a distraction, she asked, "What are fleas?"

Joe grinned and explained, "Those little blood-sucking bugs on dogs."

Morning Star laughed and nodded agreement, then added, "She is bad. I do not like her."

"I don't, either, but I was trying not to cause trouble here."

"I understand."

"I'm going to get us something to eat so we won't have to make a fire and cook. I'm uneasy about that scout leaving before dawn. After breakfast, I'll buy our supplies, and we'll ride soon."

"Scout wake me when leave," Morning Star revealed. "He ride west."

Her manner of speech told Joe she was anxious. "The same direction Zeke is in. Don't look in a hurry, but let's get moving as fast as possible."

"I work while you get food. To hurry, I eat white man's this day."

He chuckled at her amusing frown. "It isn't bad, I promise."

When Joe returned with two filled plates, they sat down and ate the tasty meal. Morning Star smiled and licked her lips in enjoyment.

"Good, right?"

"Plenty good. I surprised," she admitted.

They finished in silence, then, Joe returned the plates to Lucy.

Morning Star packed their belongings while Joe was gone. Having enjoyed the paleface meal, she didn't dread future ones during their journey. She realized she had much to learn about his ways.

Inside the trading post, Joe selected their trail supplies: flour, meal, sugar, salt, cured meat, canned goods, and ammunition. As he and Orin gathered his choices, Joe told the three men, "I'm not much on gambling and drinking, and we rode in slow and easy, so we don't need to laze around or catch up on rest. I like to stay on the move. I'm eager to check out this area before any trouble starts."

"Keep your eyes and ears open, Joe," the trapper cautioned. "Them redskins are on the move. They can be sneaky devils."

"Thanks, Ephraim, I will," he replied as he paid the owner.

"I'll be leavin' in a few days meself. Maybe I'll see you on the trail."

"That would be nice, Ben; I'll watch for you. I plan to head west today. I'll stop at those homesteads and farms you mentioned, Orin, to see if they're interested in my plan. I'll probably camp near one of them tonight. If things look promising, I'll be back for trade goods soon."

"Ride along tha Cheyenne and ye'll find them easy."

Joe and Morning Star mounted and headed west from the post. As he turned and waved, he saw Orin and Mattie Lou observing their departure from the porch. Ephraim and Ben weren't in sight.

The couple rode for miles until they were out of sight and were certain they weren't being followed. They did not talk until they halted for their first water and rest break.

Morning Star listened as Joe explained the new plan.

"We'll ride about fifteen miles toward the setting sun before we turn southeast to Pierre. We'll make a few stops at homesteads and farms, just in case Orin checks on us. Once I'm sure he—or anyone—will be fooled, we'll enter the water and set a false trail. That'll give us about sixty miles to Pratte's. I want us to travel easy, Morning Star, so we and the animals won't get there too tired to make an escape if necessary. With this terrain and taking time to establish our cover, it'll take three days."

"Plan is good. I am glad we ride from Orin's. I do not like him."

"Tell me what happened while we were there," he coaxed.

"When you gone, he put furs in big tepee, building. He put mules in fence. He look at me many times. When task finished, he stand at post and watch me. I worry. Afraid I not being good squaw. Other times, he stand in door and watch our camp. I not like to be afraid. I see Pawnee squaw take food from house to post many times. She not visit me. That strange."

Joe noticed how her English suffered during the retelling of her uneasiness at McMichael's post. "Orin called her Lucy. She didn't speak any, but she's a great cook. Maybe he told her to leave you alone."

"Lucy strange. She walk as if not see me. Maybe she afraid of man with fiery hair. He come to camp and bring me food. I not like his eyes. I not speak to him. Take food and nod thank you. He ask questions, but I no answer. He look at our supplies. He go inside where you are."

Joe was displeased to learn of Orin's visit. "What kind of questions did he ask you, Morning Star?"

"If I speak English. If I be happy with you. Where I come from? How you buy me? Where we going? If I need help or goods. When I no talk and no look at him, he go. I think he mad at Morning Star. I no like, no trust."

Joe assumed Orin was annoyed because she refused to talk with him while he was practically wooing her. Now he understood why Orin wanted Mattie Lou to enchant him—to help effectuate a sale of his woman! Such transactions were common out here, and he understood Orin's lust for this beauty. "You're a beautiful woman, Morning Star. He asked about buying you. He said to help Lucy with cooking and cleaning, but I doubt that's why he wanted you. I can't blame him for craving you. His desire was what you sensed and made you nervous. He seemed all right to me."

"When he go home at night, I feel eyes watching our camp. Strange."

"He was wishing he was in my place with you. I didn't see or hear anything to make me suspicious of him. We can't let his lust confuse us."

"What is lust?"

"Strong desire, a big craving, usually the bad kind. It's when you see someone you want badly, even without knowing or wanting to know her. All you want to do is take her or him to your mat and join your bodies. You don't care about having more than sex. Understand?"

Morning Star knew it was not like that between her and Joe. They shared desire. "I understand; lust can be good or bad, but most times bad."

Joe grinned and nodded. He wanted to pull her into his arms, kiss her, and sink to the grass with her beneath him. He dared not make a single move toward the enchanting creature or his control would vanish.

He knew this was not a safe time and place to make love. "Let's ride."

When dusk arrived, Joe and Morning Star halted their journey. As a precaution, they had stopped at two homesteads where Joe talked with the husband and wife. They had eaten a noon meal at one, with Joe inside and her—a squaw—outside. They had traveled fifteen miles westward along the wide and muddy Cheyenne. They had weaved around cottonwoods, bushes, and underbrush, and had crossed many creek and stream offshoots. Tomorrow, after setting a fake trail, they would head southeast for Pierre.

As they prepared the evening meal together, Joe said, "We need to take turns sleeping while the other stands guard. We don't know who's in this area, Indians or whites. We can't take any risks of being surprised."

"That is good." She glanced at him and asked, "What about big guns at post? Will Orin fire against my people?"

"Don't worry; he can't risk using those cannons against any tribe. The Army would know where they came from; they'd be furious."

Recalling their power as Joe had explained it, she was relieved.

They completed their meal and ate it. Both knew they could not make love in this area, so neither made romantic overtures to the other.

It was dark; the tiny sliver of moon gave off only dim light. "We'll let the fire die so we can't be seen," Joe said, "I'll put the safety matches and a torch here. If any noise sounds threatening, it can be lit fast."

Morning Star liked his keen wits. She smiled.

Joe took the first guard shift. He watched Morning Star settle herself on her sleeping mat. He did not get to observe her long before the firelight was gone, and darkness soon engulfed them like an impenetrable black fog at sea. He listened to various sounds and guessed what made them. He remembered what Morning Star had told him about being friends with the night. He practiced that skill until it was time to awaken her.

Morning Star awoke quickly. She and Joe exchanged places by using their hands to feel their way. His touch was warm and encouraging. She wanted to kiss him and to talk with him, but did neither. She wished she could see him, watch him sleep. The moment she imagined his tanned and chiseled features, she scolded herself for her lack of attention to her task. She returned to full alert, listened to noises and absorbing scents. She detected nothing unusual, but she kept herself on guard against another lapse. Hours passed, and she awoke Joe for his turn.

They followed the same routine for two days and nights. As they traveled, they continued their lessons. Morning Star's English improved, as did Joe's use of the bow. She did not practice firing his weapons, as they didn't know who was within hearing range. At one location, they had to journey close to a wide bend in the river to avoid adding numerous extra miles. As they rode, they skirted homesteads, farms, Indian camps, and "woodhawks"—men, Indian, white or mixed—who cut and sold wood along the bank to passing boats. A perilous and hard job, the men charged high prices and received them. When they did approach the Missouri River to water their animals, they were careful. Once they saw a keelboat heading northward. Another time they almost rode into a woodhawk camp where two men were resting, their axes silent.

Tuesday, following Joe's advice about entering Pierre in a rested state, they halted early. They camped behind a cluster of dirt-topped hills between them and the post. Many trees near the river also helped obscure their presence.

Morning Star was nervous about visiting another white area, but she promised herself she would remain brave and helpful.

Joe was anxious, too, for other reasons. Tanner had been murdered in Pierre, and was buried in the graveyard there. It was where his best suspect to date worked and lived: Simon Adams. On the last visit, Simon had been too busy to talk and reveal much. Joe knew he would have to work harder this time to withdraw information.

Pierre was a large and busy settlement, one of the oldest posts in the territory. It was situated at the mouth of the Bad River where steamboats and keel boats docked and traded. Joe recalled a large stable, small boardinghouse that served meals, several cabins, the trading post, and a house used as a saloon for drinking and gambling, with rooms in the back for prostitutes to ply their trade. Unlike Fort Laramie and other western posts, none of the three posts along "The Misery" had Indian tepees around them.

The only good thing Joe could think of was that there had not been enough time for Zeke to reach Pierre, if Ephraim had his timing right . . .

Chapter Twelve

*M*orning Star stayed close to Joe as they entered the settlement. She longed to hold his hand, as she needed his comforting touch. If she were alone or still Zeke's captive, she would be terrified surrounded by so many whites who mostly hated her kind. With head lowered in a servile manner, she glanced at the setting from the corners of her dark brown eyes. She realized that Joe had described it with accuracy and had prepared her well for this intimidating adventure. She recalled that he had admitted he was tense about this place where her cousin had been slain. She wished she could have met Tanner, and presumed he had been like Joe, as most best friends were a great deal alike. That belief was one thing that alarmed her about her brother's close and long friendship with Knife-Slayer.

They reached the stable and dismounted. Both tried to behave naturally. Without being obvious, both studied the busy area. Each noticed that Zeke's wagons were not in sight and were relieved.

Joe asked the liveryman if he could leave his horses tethered at the corral while he took care of business. If he decided to stay longer than a few hours, he said, he would return later to make arrangements for the feed and care of the animals. Joe wanted them ready to depart if they had to move fast. He didn't hesitate to leave the three horses and supplies there, as few robberies occurred in daylight and in an occupied area.

Morning Star followed Joe inside the trading post in a meek manner. She was glad Joe wore his pistol and was skilled with the weapon. They had arranged two signals—*danger* and *move fast*—before entering Pierre, as they could use neither English nor Lakota as a warning if a perilous situation arose. Her heart pounded, her mouth was dry, and her hands were cold and damp. A strange sensation gripped her stomach. She wondered if her apprehension showed, as she seemed aquiver all over. If anyone guessed she was the daughter of Sun Cloud and granddaughter of Gray Eagle, she would be in deep trouble. So would Joe! She worried over his safety more than her own. Coming here was a big risk, but one that must be taken. The lives of her band and other tribes were at stake, as was peace with the whites. She was relieved Joe had been more afraid of hiding her somewhere to wait rather than of bringing her along. She wanted to be here to help him if the bold plan failed.

Morning Star felt eyes on her, many eyes. She dared not lift hers to look around or to return gazes, as that was considered brazen and offensive conduct for a lowly squaw. Joe had told her not to worry about stares, that her beauty was the reason for them. She knew she was pretty, and knew it was not vain to admit it. Denying the truth, even about oneself, was the same as lying or being a coward.

Morning Star waited nearby while Joe chatted with the men and picked up a few items. She was careful not to get caught studying the man who worked for Bernard Pratte, the post's owner. Simon Adams was tall, the same height as Joe. His hair was as dark as a moonless night, and his eyes were as green as spring leaves. He looked strong, and appeared about ten years older than Joe. Her companion had told her this man hated Indians, especially her nation. She tried to envision him in the costume Knife-Slayer had described. She paid close attention to details so she could question the warrior about them when she returned home. She saw Simon leave by the back door.

Joe approached the short man behind the long wooden counter. "Simon returning soon? I need to speak with him?"

As he continued his work, the man replied, "Outside resting and smoking. Been busy this morning with that keelboat in."

"Can I go out the back door?"

Without looking up, he replied, "Sure, just close it."

Morning Star followed Joe outside. She went to stand near the corner of the building. She didn't want her presence to hold the man's tongue, but still she listened to their words.

"Hello, Mr. Adams. Joe Lawrence, remember?"

Simon released a curl of smoke from his cigar. "You were in a few months ago with your friend who was robbed and killed. You report it to the Army at Fort Tabor?"

Tanner had not been robbed, but Joe didn't correct him. "Didn't think it would do much good. Anything like that happen here again?"

Simon lazed against the wall with his back to the Indian woman. He took another drag on his cigar before replying, "Not that I know of. If anyone's been attacked, no body was left behind to alert us. Such things rarely happen in Pierre. Pratte doesn't like trouble and a bad reputation."

Joe watched the man flick ashes off his long sleeve. He noticed the sizable brown birthmark on his right hand. "That's good news for everybody except Tanner! If we'd arrived a day later, he'd still be alive. I was the one in a stupid hurry to get off the trail," he invented with hopes Simon would respond to a guilt-riddled man. "We were like family, like brothers. We always took care of each other. I should have been more alert in a strange place. I figured we'd be safe here and get some needed rest; I was fatigued from keeping on alert day and night for renegades. I'm alone now, and I miss him. All our dreams were slain with Tanner. It twists my gut for him to die like that and for me to be powerless to avenge his death. That's no way for a man to die; it's as bad as Indian slaughter. If you've ever lost a best friend and nobody was punished for it, you know how I feel."

Simon stood straight and stiff, with a scowl on his face. "I do. I've lost people to those infernal Sioux who got away with murder. Riles me. They sneak around doing their dirty business without getting caught and punished, but they leave enough behind to show who's guilty. I'm surprised the Army hasn't shoved them into hell where they belong. They won't have much choice soon but to retaliate."

Joe witnessed the coldness in Simon's voice and eyes and how the man's body was now taut with pent-up rage and hate. "What do you mean?"

Simon leaned back once more. "The soldiers know who's to blame; they'll have to chase them down—and soon, with more incidents happening all the time. I don't understand what's taking them so long to react. They're supposed to be here to protect us."

"And to keep the peace," Joe amended, keeping his tone genial.

Simon tensed and straightened. He shot back, "Peace, hell! Whites can't have peace with bloodthirsty savages. Truces, either. They forget we own this territory. Our government purchased it, with *our* taxes. We have a right to settle and work here, and to be protected while we do. Let those savages fight. We'll wipe them out and conquer this area like we did the eastern half." He settled back again, drawing deep on a cigar. "The Crow ain't no better, but at least they know their place and don't attack their betters. I wish they'd wipe out those Sioux for us. Then the Army could get rid of them. Indians are nothing but a pack of wild animals. All they know is raiding and killing. White or red targets, it doesn't matter to them. This territory would be a wonderful place without them."

Joe also leaned against the wall to appear relaxed. He didn't refute Simon's opinions of Indians or argue over who had a rightful claim to this territory. "I haven't been here long enough to know much about either tribe," he alleged. "They were still holed up in winter camps when Tanner and I rode through. They as bad as you say?"

"Worse. I wish we could sell them rot-gut whiskey to eat up their minds and spirits. They love firewater, but the law stops us. A man could make a fortune in a territory like this if those Sioux were pushed out or cowered. Never trust an Indian, Joe; they'll turn on you in a minute and slit your throat without feeling a thing."

Joe saw Simon glance at Morning Star and frown. He headed off trouble by explaining, "She's Arapaho. I bought her off a trapper heading south. He said he couldn't take his squaw home because his wife wouldn't like that at all. Little Flower's shy, but she's been a good worker."

"Bedding and doing chores are all they're good for, if you don't mind Injun smell on you."

"I make sure she bathes every day and doesn't use any fat on her skin. I'm inclined to cleanliness myself. That trapper told me lots of men in these parts have Indian servants. She was real cheap, and he was in a hurry. Gave me a good deal, so I figured, what the heck? Let her take care of me and my chores." He chuckled, then continued. "I didn't realize my having her would offend some folks. Maybe I shouldn't keep her. What do you think, Simon?" he asked. Joe knew how powerful giving advice made some people feel. He knew he'd guessed right about Simon when the man grinned and leaned close to respond.

"Most men around here don't care if you have a squaw, Joe. I'd keep her and use her good, unless she's trouble. Those savages have certainly stolen and used plenty of white women. It drives bucks crazy when we take their woman, particularly the pretty ones." He glanced at the raven-haired woman again. "She is a good looker, and seems to know her place. Since those bastards are greedy and cruel enough to sell or trade us their females, why should they care what we do with them? If I had the money, I'd build fancy brothels along the river and stuff them full of young beauties like her. I'd be rich in a month, because I'd train the little creatures myself on how to please a white man." He chewed the cigar butt a minute while his eyes glittered strangely. His attention returned and he asked, "Where you been since your last visit? Where you heading from here?"

Joe used the same traveling trader story he had told Orin McMichael. He noticed that Simon's interest was captured by it. "Since my friend is dead and I want to stay here a while longer, it seems a good way to earn money and see this territory. Of course, I didn't know the Indians would be acting up soon. That could mess up my plan."

"Don't worry; the Army will slap them down before summer's over."

"This territory has promise, Simon, if trouble can be averted. A man could carve out a nice ranch here. Plenty of water and grass. I'm sure more forts will be coming soon to provide more protection. All I need is some money for building and for buying stock. I think I can earn it by selling goods on the trail—if those hostiles don't start a war and interfere," he muttered, trying to sound as if his opinion of the Indians matched Simon's.

"It'll come to a fight, Joe, but we'll win. The Army will be like a boa constrictor; it'll wrap around those Sioux and squeeze the life from them. Nobody will be happier than me to witness that glorious day." Simon grinned as if envisioning the heartless massacre he admitted he craved. "Those Crow are like coyotes; they run when wolves appear. I'd like to see their nasty dens cleaned out, too. It's a shame we can't put them all in cages and train them like the wild beasts they are. We'd make a fortune displaying such intriguing specimens around the world. Yes, sir, Joe, we'd make a fortune if this territory was conquered and real settlement began."

"Speaking of displays, I saw a war shield and headdress on the wall inside. They for sale? I'd love to mount a souvenir collection in my ranch. I was almost hoping for a run-in with a highly decorated warrior so I could snatch a few treasures when the Army and his band weren't watching. No such luck yet. Haven't caught or seen one alone in his finery."

Simon's eyes gleamed. "Those were gifts to Pratte," he whispered, "but I can get you some, for a good price. You can't say how or where you bought them, though. Pratte would have my scalp for sure if he heard about it."

Joe feigned a look of delight and complicity. "Don't worry, Simon; I'll stay quiet. I'll be back through in a few weeks. I'll see what you have then and ship them to my family back South to hold for me until I get that ranch house built." Joe grinned as an idea came to mind. "I bet Papa would like a set, too. We'd want Sioux artifacts, fierce warriors, with plenty of symbols exposing their prowess. As you said, Crow aren't that brave. That makes Sioux souvenirs more valuable."

"I know the different colors and markings of tribes, so don't worry about getting the wrong ones. I buy them off a man who comes across plenty. He roams all over this area. Isn't scared of anything or anyone."

"Sounds like Zeke," Joe remarked.

Simon looked at him. "You know Zeke Randall?"

Joe shook his head as he replied, "No, but I've heard plenty of tales about him. Seems he's becoming quite a legend."

Simon laughed heartily. "Zeke will love hearing that news. He deals with Indians, mostly Crow, but he hates all of them."

"Why?"

"Like me, he has his reasons. Nothing a man likes to discuss."

When Simon didn't explain, Joe let it pass. "I'm sure he does. I'd like to meet him one day. I bet he could teach me plenty about Indians and this territory. He probably knows the perfect spot to place a ranch. I might hire him to help me claim it."

"Zeke's here every month. Maybe he'll be around when you return." Simon stretched his tall frame. "I'd better get to the privy and back inside. We're busier than a lion in mating season. Too many orders to hump."

Joe shared laughter with the other man, and made a mental note to remember Simon's constant references to animals. Simon dropped his cigar and mashed it beneath his boot, but Joe had already registered that he was right-handed; that and the birthmark could be valuable identification clues.

"You guard your hide out there, Joe. I'll mention you to Zeke. Maybe he can use a partner and help you with your idea. It's a clever one. Could make a lot of money if handled right. Wish I'd thought of it. If I had the money to finance it, I would be tempted to steal it from you, or even join you."

"I bet we'd make good partners if we could afford to join up."

"You might consider hauling around a wagonload of delicious white whores. You'd tempt starving white men to empty their pockets faster than they could drop their pants. And some of those Injuns would love a little taste of creamy white meat. If you do, better get blondes and redheads; braves hunger for women different from theirs."

Joe was astonished by Simon's crude suggestion. He wondered how a man who hated Indians so much could want an Indian to have sex with *any* white woman, including soiled doves. "Thanks, Simon. I'll—"

Morning Star caught Joe's eye and gave both the signals they had arranged. She looked frightened. His hesitation caused Simon to turn and look her way. Quick-witted, his love lowered her head.

"Something wrong, Joe?"

"For a minute I thought she was about to run off. Must have been a bug bite. I haven't had her long, but she might not like me or being a piece of property. Or maybe she needs to use the privy, too. I'm a stranger to traveling with a female, so I don't know their curious ways."

Simon chuckled. "There's a public privy behind the boardinghouse," he said, implying she was not to use his.

"Thanks. I'll be going now, but we'll talk again soon."

Simon went into the outhouse, and Joe joined Morning Star. She was peeking around the wall she had jumped behind moments ago.

"What's up?"

"Zeke and other man come!" she reported. "They go in that building! They no see me."

Joe looked around the corner and saw a wagon in front of the structure used as a saloon. "Let's get out of here before he spots us or our horses. Hurry, before Simon finishes and stalls us."

They walked around the other way, careful not to use a suspicious run. He casually checked for safety, then they went to their horses. They mounted and rode out of the settlement in the other direction—north.

Later, they skirted Pierre and headed south. They didn't talk, as their pace was fast to put distance between them and peril. They crossed rising and falling slopes, avoided gulches, and galloped over grassland.

When they finally halted to rest, Joe gave a loud exhalation of air and said, "Damn, I didn't expect to run into Zeke this soon. I was hoping he was still a long way from here. Once Simon tells him about us, that will get him to thinking. He'll know I'm not anxious to meet him and that you're still with me. Simon will realize I lied to him, so that'll put Pratte's post off bounds. Worse, when Zeke goes to Orin's and they talk, Orin will know I tricked him, too. That makes another visit to his post risky. Damn!" he swore again in frustration, as it was evident Zeke's return would lock them out of much of this area that held clues to the mystery.

Morning Star touched Joe's arm and smiled to calm him. "Not worry so much. What if Zeke think you ask questions to . . . avoid him?" she asked. "What if he think he captured your woman and you tricked him to rescue me? He learn by now we here, so he must wonder if we cannot be ones who killed friends far away. Maybe he believe Oglala warriors attack friends to punish, to take back stolen possessions. Why he think, on many moons later, we do that deed? What if he believe you trapper and believe clever story you tell Orin? What if Zeke think you travel here only to seek friend's killer? Why he think you think he . . . villain and you seek to defeat him with only a woman helper? He think he smart and careful, so give others no reason to be . . . suspicious." She finished her reasoning with, "Why he worry over one man and his squaw?"

Joe was impressed. She was perceptive and intelligent. He didn't point out the loopholes in her speculations, such as his being here earlier with Tanner, without her, and not as a trapper, but he sent her a broad smile and caressed her cheek. He fused his gaze to hers and wanted to fuse their lips. Her expression exposed matching emotions. But danger was too close for them to halt for loving play. He sailed to another island of concern. "I wish we hadn't had to leave so suddenly. I wanted to get a look inside Simon's place for evidence, and maybe get a look at his arms for tattoos. He raises my suspicions; I'd like to know if I'm riding the wrong trail and wasting time." He drew in a deep breath, then added, "I wish we'd had time to visit Tanner's grave. I don't like leaving his body there."

Morning Star knew his friend—her cousin—had been on Joe's mind since yesterday. "Do not worry; he is safe," she comforted.

He knew she was right. "You have a kind heart and gentle spirit. You and Tanner would have liked each other." To prevent renewed grief from distracting him, Joe returned to their task.

They went over what they had learned from and about Simon Adams.

"Smart . . . villain would not say so many bad words to stranger. He talked much. Is not smart enough to be Snake-Man," she concluded.

"Maybe that's a trick, a disguise, a cunning scheme. He might figure no one would suspect a man like him who's so open about his ill feelings."

"He . . . pretend to hate Indians?" she asked, misunderstanding him.

"No, he hates them all right, especially the Dakota Nation. What I meant was, he could be making sure everybody—especially strangers—knows he hates Indians, and he could be assuming nobody would become a loudmouth and make himself a suspect. If I were Snake-Man, would I pretend to like or hate Indians?" he reasoned aloud. "I think leaning too far in either direction isn't smart. Whatever, that villain is very smart and very dangerous."

"It confusing, Joe. If I have enemy, I not hide it. But I not trying to start war between sides. I say, smart man not hide it or show it."

"I agree, but sometimes desperate or greedy men don't act smart. They make mistakes, and that's what finally defeats them."

Morning Star thought of how her brother and Knife-Slayer behaved sometimes. Soon, they would make mistakes and be entrapped by them.

"With Zeke around, we can't do much in this area," Joe said. "By the time he learns we've been to Pierre and Orin's, he'll be searching for us, probably with more hired men. If his boss doesn't suspect us by now, he will as soon as he and Zeke add up the facts, then suspect we're up to something. They'll be out to stop us any way they can."

Morning Star grasped that he didn't accept her speculations and still believed they were in great peril. She had to concede to his thoughts, because Joe knew whites better than she did. "We be careful and alert."

"Since we don't know who or where this boss is," Joe decided aloud, "we should get out of sight and reach for a while. Let's try to get information from the Indians, the Crow. We'll need trade goods. Let's risk going on to Lookout to buy them."

"Zeke come from Lookout," she reminded.

His blue gaze locked with her brown one. "I know, but we have no choice. We can't go back to Pratte or Orin's and we need trade goods. We can't give up, Morning Star. But we have to get out of this boiling kettle for a while; I just hope we aren't jumping out of it into a roaring fire out there." He caressed her cheek and urged, "Don't worry, love, we'll be careful." His tone altered as he said, "I want you to lead me to the first Crow camp, then hide until I finish my business and return to you."

Her sunny smile vanished. "I go with you!"

Joe shook his blond head. "Crow won't harm a white trader with gifts. I've put you in too much danger already."

Determination filled her eyes. "I go, too, or I not lead you there."

Joe eyed her raven hair spilling over her shoulders and how it swayed when she tossed her head in defiance. He had to keep her safe! He decided there would be time on the trail to persuade her to stay behind at the last minute, so he didn't argue. "Let's ride, woman."

"I see fox sneak into Joe's body. Eyes expose you. You not fool me or leave me behind. I part of sacred vision, too. Must go and help."

"You know me too well, Morning Star. I yield, but I don't like it. I couldn't stand for anything to happen to you. We take no risks, woman."

Sun Cloud's daughter smiled. She was happy Joe possessed the self-confidence to concede when necessary. She loved looking at him. His hair grazed his broad shoulders like a golden mane. It waved like rolling hills and gleamed when the sun kissed it. And she could lose sight of reality when she stared into his blue gaze, as beautiful as the sky above them. The sienna buckskin garments enhanced his dark tan and clung to his muscled frame. His features were bold, perfect. Joe was irresistible in looks and character, though she did not care for the white man's beard that grew thicker and darker each day. She adored being with him; she loved him beyond control.

When Joe sent her a quizzical look for her long and silent study, she grinned and teased, "Very good decision. You plenty smart, Joe Lawrence."

They traveled as fast as possible for two days. At night, they took guard shifts once more. Early Saturday morning, the apprehensive couple rode to Lookout, a trading post owned by the Columbia Fur Company. It was not busy, as the keel-boat had stopped here first and trappers hadn't arrived yet.

This time, Morning Star remained with the horses while Joe went to purchase "gifts" for the Crow. She was tense the entire time he was gone, and strove to keep herself on full alert. This was their last stop in a white settlement, at least for a while. She was glad. She wanted to return to the Plains and forests and hills where she felt at home and safe. She struggled not to think of the people who were depending upon her to guide their destinies in the right direction and who were depending upon her to remain true to her heritage and customs.

Morning Star confessed she had tried but failed to keep to the last part. By now, being with Joseph Lawrence was as natural and vital as breathing. Their love was the food upon which her spirit survived and grew. Her life would never be the same after his inevitable departure. She could never yield to another man after being with Joe. Without that part of life, she would bear no children. Perhaps, she ventured, the loss of a true love was why Buckskin Girl had never joined another! But her friend had never mentioned a lost loved one.

Lost . . . Forever . . . Those words cut into her soul with a white-hot knife that seared her from head to toe with burning wounds. It was a fact she could not leave with Joe. It was a fact he could not remain with her. But it was possible to have him and love him until this sacred mission ended, one way or another. Payaba's vision had claimed that would be in glorious victory, so she must not be so afraid. Yet, her faith lagged on occasion. She felt that surely the Great Spirit understood and forgave human frailty. Surely He would not allow her weakness to endanger—

A mule brayed loudly in the corral, jerking Morning Star back to reality. She scolded herself for such a terrible loss of attention. Her dulled wits could get them killed. She commanded herself back to full alert.

Inside the trading post, Joe chatted with Harvey Meade. He had met the perky fellow on his visit with Tanner. So far, nothing looked or sounded suspicious. Joe used the same strategy as at the other posts; it appeared to work again. He was told Zeke headed for Pierre on Monday.

"I must have missed him on the trail. I think I'll do some looking around before I try to catch up with him again." Noticing the manager's reaction, he took a risk by adding, "Or maybe I won't try to herd up with Zeke. From what I hear about him, that could be a mistake. I just thought I shouldn't work this territory without checking him out first, as most folks act like he runs it. I'm not a coward, but he sounds like the kind who'd be riled and dangerous if pushed." Joe was delighted when Harvey responded favorably to his deceit.

"You'd be smart to avoid him, Joe. He's trouble, the kind we don't need here. You mentioned ranching and settling down," the post manager began. "Didn't Simon tell you about the Pre-Emption Homestead Law?" When Joe shook his head, the short man explained, "It's been in effect since '41. You can purchase up to one hundred sixty acres of land at a dollar-twenty-five per acre in many locations of this territory. Best place to check which areas are for sale is at Fort Laramie. That's where most territorial business is carried out and where the Indian agent stays. I know Simon's purchased a tract and bought a couple off other fellows. If you asked me, he used them as go-betweens to get his hands on more land. After this area opens up, they'll be worth a lot more money. Others have bought up tracts, too. Me included."

"Our government claims they own it," Harvey continued, "bought it from the French, so I guess they have the right to sell parcels. They've even paid more dollars to some tribes to avoid conflicts. I guess I shouldn't feel guilty over the Dakotas' claims they still own it. If I hadn't bought my parcel, some other man would. It's on the James River, east of here. As soon as I'm sure of a real treaty, I plan to build on it and farm the land."

"Sounds like a good opportunity to me. I'm surprised that Simon didn't tell me about the Pre-Emption Law. I'm also surprised he's buying up land. It's odd he would stay here since he makes no secret of his hatred for Indians. Must have been something real bad to cause such feelings."

Harvey glanced around to make sure no one was coming inside the post. "It was," he confided. "When Simon first came here a few years back, his keelboat was attacked by marauding Indians; his wife was killed and he was robbed clean by Oglalas. He intended to open a trading post, but lost everything. He survived by slipping over the rail, swimming underwater, and hiding in bank brush. Everybody aboard was killed; even three women were raped and murdered. That was strange, because Indians usually take them captive. Law figured they were in a hurry and didn't want to be slowed by prisoners. Evidence said they were Red Heart warriors. I don't have to tell you that Simon was consumed by hatred and a hunger for revenge; but there was nothing he could do to find and punish the guilty ones. I was sure they were only renegades, but he wasn't. Still isn't. He had to go to work for Pratte for survival money. Believe me, he didn't take to being a hired hand instead of an owner and boss. Sticks in his craw; so does running away and leaving his wife to suffer and die. I can't fault him there; wasn't anything he could do to save her or the others. I think he's only working Pratte's until he earns enough to get out on his own again. I bet that land he bought is for a post. Sad how cruel fate changes a man. 'Course, I don't know what he was like before coming here. But now—"

Harvey listened and looked for arrivals once more. "I hear he sells bloody souvenirs behind his boss's back. Bernard Pratte would be furious; he's a good and honest man. It's the worst thing any man could do to cause more trouble. All it does is provoke scoundrels to rob scaffolds and ambush Indians for goods to sell him. I hear he sells Indians guns and whiskey, too, but I've never witnessed it with my own eyes, just overheard trappers whispering. It's wrong, and it's against the law. If everybody would take it slow and easy, we could have peace here. If we give the Indians time to get used to us, expand real slow and careful, they'd accept us."

"You ever mentioned this to your company or the Army?" Joe asked.

An expression akin to sheer terror filled Harvey's face and enlarged his eyes. In a quavering voice, he vowed, "I don't interfere because I don't want Simon riled at me. He's the kind of man who would make a bad enemy if you crossed him. He's tight with that Zeke Randall."

"Don't worry, Harvey, my mouth won't open to the wrong ears. I don't want Simon and Zeke gunning for me, either. It'll be our secret. I'm going to skip looking up Zeke and head on to the Plains. I'll need plenty of gifts to make friends with the Indians. I want to see for myself if trouble's brewing. If it is, I bet Zeke has his hands in it."

"You can win that bet, Joe. I'll get the usual trinket sack ready. You can check it over and pay me."

"Thanks, I'm sure you know what the Indians like." As Joe waited and looked around, he sighted an interesting object. He questioned Harvey Meade about it, then purchased the enchanting item.

It was dark, as they had ridden as long as possible before stopping to camp. Without wasting time and energy, they tended the three horses, prepared a hot meal, and settled down to rest.

"You think Meade say—said—those things about Zeke and Simon to point eyes to them?" Morning Star asked. "Take eyes from him?"

Joe mused on her question. "I don't think so. He's too short. In all honesty, I'm not sure whom I trust. For all I know, Zeke could be doing a side business with Simon on those souvenirs. In view of what happened to Simon years ago, it's not unusual for him to be filled with bitterness and hatred."

"My people do not slay women and children."

He smiled at her and said, "I know. I'm just wondering if Snake-Man was here and working before Simon's arrival or if it was only renegades. It could be that our villain has no connection to any of the trading posts."

"Where would villain live?"

"Could be on a farm or homestead. Could be a camp along the river."

"Could be at fort," she amended, looking worried.

"Perhaps, but I doubt it. I think it's too big a plan for a soldier."

"You look good at fort when arrive . . . tomorrow," she cautioned.

"I think it's best if we stop by Tabor and see Captain Thomas. We're close, and it's been a while since I reported my finds to him. I can send a message to Stede and the Indian agent at Laramie. I'll write it up at first light. I'll send my family a letter, too. Let them know I'm all right."

"Our families worry about us."

"At least you'll get to see yours soon. It's been a long time since I saw mine. I miss them, more than I realized I would. I hope my father's settled down by now. He was against my coming here. I'm sure Mother's done plenty of talking to him; she has a special way with him. With luck, he'll listen to her this time; she understood why I had to leave. So did my sister. You'd like my mother and Sarah Beth." He smiled. "I bet Lucas is growing like a spring weed. Little boys change fast at four."

Morning Star didn't want to discuss or think about the strong family ties that would soon take Joseph Lawrence from her side and life. Nor did she want to ponder her own. She wished she and Joe were a family and had a future together. That could never be, and it tormented her.

Joe sensed her warring emotions and let the melancholy topic die. "We'd best get to sleep. Tomorrow is a busy day."

Joe's report and letter home were finished. Breakfast was over, all chores were done, and the horses were saddled. Their weapons and supplies were loaded and their canteens were full. They would reach Fort Tabor by midmorning, if they left within a short time. By noon, they could be on the trail toward the first Crow camp.

Joe went to Morning Star and held out the gift he had purchased at the last trading post. "Remember when I told you white men can do tricks to fool people who don't know about them?" he reminded. "This is one of them. Hold it up like this and look into that hole," he instructed, assisting her. "See, magic can be created with tricks and skills. Keep it pointed toward bright light and turn it slowly."

Morning Star did as he said. Her breath caught in wonder. Her hands trembled as she clasped the gift.

"It's called a kaleidoscope. The first one was invented, created, by Sir David Brewster about thirty-five years ago. My mother loves them and collects them. Every time I sailed someplace, she'd ask me to look for a new one. She has them with beads, colored glass, pebbles, dried flowers, shells, insects, all kinds of things. Every time you move it, the pattern and colors change. It's amazing, isn't it?"

Each rotation offered a different design and hues from the tiny specks of glass inside it. "How does it do such magic?" she asked. When she stopped turning the long tube, her eyes filled with awe.

"I'm not sure I can explain in words you'll understand, but I'll try. It's an optical—that means anything to do with eyes and seeing—optical instrument. An instrument is something like a tool that does a certain task." He motioned to areas as he explained, "There are two small mirrors at each end of the tube. Glass or whatever is used is put into a space at one end. The mirrors reflect them like water does your face when you look into a pond or river. This is the peephole, because you peep—that means, look—into it. I wish you could see my mother's collection. The one with flowers is breathtaking, and the one with insects is almost unbelievable."

"You give this one to me?"

"Yes."

"What of your mother?"

"She would be happy for you to have such a special treasure." As she held it up again, closed one eye, and peered inside, Joe watched her with joy. She was as excited as a child at Christmas. She twisted the tube many times, almost squealing with delight at each new design it made. When she lowered it, she gazed at him with gratitude and joy.

Joe saw how the tears in her eyes sparkled like dewdrops under the morning sun. Their shade of brown reminded him of the darkest band of the stripes in the carnelian and onyx he had shipped from Brazil. Her skin was as soft as the cotton raised on his family's plantation, the color of a newborn fawn. Her hair was as black and shiny as the coal from mines back East. He recalled how, when they galloped across plains and meadows, her ebony mane spread out behind her in glorious splendor. She could not possibly know how beautiful she was, or how deeply she affected him. Being near her was paradise, and sometimes hell when he could not touch her. How, he fretted, could he return to an existence without this woman who had become a vital part of his life?

"I will protect it and love it always," she said in her best English.

When she leaned against Joe and kissed him, his body shuddered with longing for hers. He was relieved but dismayed when they parted. If he knew they would not be distur— He warned himself not to lose control. They were too near the fort for privacy. "Let's go," he urged tenderly.

Morning Star comprehended his reaction, and knew how she felt, too. It was unwise to remain here any longer. "I am ready."

Captain James Thomas was standing on the porch of his office when Joe and

Morning Star rode to the hitching post before it. He looked surprised to see them, and eyed the beauty with undisguised curiosity.

The couple dismounted and secured their reins. When Joe greeted the soldier, Jim returned it, but looked rather hesitant.

"We need to talk. I have plenty to report," Joe hinted.

"You best leave her here. It might look odd to anyone watching if she goes inside with us. No offense intended, just a precaution."

Joe explained to his companion, who nodded. He followed Jim inside. He was a little intrigued when the officer closed the door, as the June day was warm. "What's up?" he asked.

Jim took his seat and told Joe to do the same with the chair before his desk. "So that's the legendary Sun Cloud's daughter," he remarked. "She's beautiful. She understood you, so that means she speaks English."

"She spoke some when I met her, and I've been teaching her more on the trail. This is the first chance I've had to report to you what I've learned."

"What have you learned?" Jim propped his elbows on the desk.

"I wrote out a full report to Stede Gaston and Tom Fitzpatrick and asked them to check on a few things for me. I'd be obliged if you'd send one of your fastest and most dependable men to deliver it to Fort Laramie."

"I have the perfect man for the job. He's never failed me. What's in here?" he inquired as he accepted the sealed packet Joe passed to him.

Joe told about the slaughtered Crow hunting party, with Red Heart arrows in the bodies. He revealed how they had tracked the men responsible and attacked three at Rake's Hollow and how four others had escaped before they arrived. He explained about recovering the sacred possessions and returning them to the Oglala burial ground, and of how Crow arrows had been left there to incriminate the wrong people. He told Jim about meeting the trapper, buying his furs, then visiting Orin McMichael's trading post. He halted his report to ask who George was.

"I don't recall an Army scout named George with that description. Maybe he's from Fort Laramie or Ripley or Snelling. He's a long way from wherever he's posted. I'll check on him. I wonder why I wasn't informed of his mission in my area and why he hasn't contacted me. That's strange, unless he's on leave. You sure Fort Laramie or Tom didn't put someone else on this investigation besides you?" Joe shook his head. "A corporal, you say?" Jim murmured. "No doubt he's military?"

Joe found Jim's lack of knowledge dismaying. "That's what the others told me, and the stripes he was wearing verified it. The men at Orin's seemed to know him. Said he visits there frequently. Implied he shares his scouting reports with McMichael. But if Orin was our man and that scout's one of his hirelings, he and George wouldn't be so open about his visits. George knows Zeke, but so do plenty of people. Simon said Zeke is there every month, so they have a connection. That scout puzzles and worries me; but if somebody else was on this case, I'm sure they would have told me. George didn't seem to guess who I was, but he left fast and early the next morning. I was afraid he was hooked up with Zeke and was going to warn him of me." Joe was puzzled as to why the scout, said to be in this area often, was unknown to the officer before him.

Jim's thoughts seemed to stray a moment as he commented, "I knew about Orin's cannons; they're a scare tactic. He'd never fire them. You sure those men Ephraim mentioned were the ones waiting for Zeke's arrival?"

"I don't know, but it made sense."

"You best not mention them to anyone," Jim warned. "It could appear an unprovoked attack. You only have your word about their foul deeds, which no white law considers a punishable crime. You don't want to get into legal trouble. If I were you, I'd do my best to prevent any more attacks and killings; murder's a serious matter."

Joe thought Jim's choice of words and reaction were strange. "It was all self-defense, but I can't prove it." He related how they visited Pierre and what was said by Simon Adams; that brought a scowl to the officer's face. He revealed how Zeke had arrived and they had fled.

"I've heard rumors about Adams' dirty dealings, but have no proof against him. I can't act without evidence or a witness. I sure wish one or the other would step forward. That kind of thing is dangerous. If I questioned them, they'd deny it. All they'd do is be careful for a while. If you buy that stuff from Adams, you'll be partly responsible for how he got it."

Joe finished his report by telling Jim about his visit to the Columbia Fur post with Harvey Meade. On gut instinct, he decided to keep Harvey's confidence about Simon and Zeke, as he'd already told Jim about his "souvenir" talk with Simon. "That report to Stede and Tom has a few questions I need answers to. After I spend a few weeks with the Crow and Dakotas, I'll be back for them. Get your man to wait for their replies. I'd like to know more about the Pre-Emption Homestead Law and who's buying up land. That issue can make for trouble and provide clues. I'll be playing the white trader for a while. I might luck out on an Indian who drops clues about Snake-Man or Zeke. So what have you learned so far?"

"To be honest with you, Joe, I haven't done much investigating. I was afraid I'd endanger you if the wrong person discovered I was nosing around. We don't actually have a formal case yet, just suspicions and rumors. If we can just get some proof documented, I'll open one, secret, of course. Then you'll be protected from any recriminating charges. Until this is official, our necks are stretched out for chopping off. Frankly, I need a letter of authorization from Tom, and from the President on behalf of Mr. Gaston. I'll request them when I send this over. I like my rank, Joe, and I don't want to risk losing it and my hide if you're on your own."

"I understand, Jim. Get the papers you need. No problem."

"You realize that once you and I are connected, your cover is destroyed. That could be today. That beautiful girl outside won't go unnoticed. It wasn't smart to bring her along. She'll draw attention to your visit."

"Sorry, Jim, but I couldn't leave her alone out there. I figured she'd pass for a squaw. Plenty of men have them."

"But not men who keep visiting my office regularly."

"How else can I report information?"

"There's a hollow tree about two miles from here. From now on, I think we should leave our messages there. I'll draw you a map. That's where I'll put the answer to this," he said, tapping the missive to Fort Laramie, "when it arrives." He sketched a map and explained it.

"You're right, Jim. We have to be careful from here on. Zeke is no doubt searching for me. He's probably reported to his boss by now. We could be in big trouble if they come after us."

"You already are in big trouble, Joe. I haven't told you what's been happening while you were out of touch. It's bad, for you and your Indians. For one thing, Zeke

Randall has accused you of the murder of Clement Harris, made formal charges. He turned in evidence—a scrap of your shirt—and listed witnesses against you, and he demanded I use a patrol to hunt you down for arrest and trial. Then, there was a payroll theft by Red Heart warriors last Wednesday. The entire unit was wiped out." Jim took two items from his drawer as he talked and placed them on the desk between him and Joe. "From what my best scout tells me, these possessions belong to Knife-Slayer and Night Stalker. Know them? The last one is the brother of the girl outside, right? The Red Heart chief's son?"

Chapter Thirteen

Joe's mind whirled. Jim hadn't done anything to help him this time. The officer alluded to the storm ahead of recriminating charges, murder, evidence, witnesses! During their May meeting, Jim hadn't mentioned the 1841 Pre-Emption Law, needing letters of authorization, or Simon and Harvey. Jim had said only that Bernard Pratte and Orin McMichael were good men and doubtful suspects. Joe worried over why Jim had waited until after receiving a full report before putting him in a vulnerable position.

Joe couldn't allow this important task to blow up in his face. He had known such a mission would be perilous, but he had expected more help than he was receiving. He recalled Morning Star telling him that Payaba's sacred vision prophesied both whites and Indians would work against him. Joe didn't want to believe that James Thomas, Fitzpatrick's friend, also a man who knew their every move, was his nemesis. He couldn't help but glance at the captain's long sleeves as he thought furiously.

The evidence against his Morning Star's brother and her people was mounting. He must decide if Jim was trying only to protect himself from problems over this explosive matter and protect the mission or if the officer had other motives . . .

Joe prayed that Morning Star hadn't overheard the two shocking charges. "Zeke Randall has the gall to accuse me of crimes!" he scoffed. "He's the one hauling illegal goods to the Indians. He's the one who captured an innocent girl and planned to have her abused by his evil boss. Can you imagine what Sun Cloud and his band, and probably all his allies, would have done if anything like that had happened to his daughter? If nothing more than preventing their retaliation, it justifies Clem's death. But I told you, we didn't kill him. Zeke did because he was becoming too much trouble. By now the vultures haven't left me any proof."

"Don't get heated up, Joe. Of course I didn't believe him. I didn't even make out a report and haven't investigated his so-called evidence. Frankly, I'm baffled by why he came to see me about it. If he's working for Snake-Man, it seems as if he'd want to avoid drawing attention to himself and his boss. And I doubt Zeke would take such a step without asking his boss first. He said he'd be checking back with me soon, so I'll have to tell him something. If I refuse to act on his accusation, he'll get suspicious of me, too. Once he thinks the Army's involved, he'll alert his boss and they'll probably halt their crimes for a while."

Jim locked his gaze with Joe's. "But if you don't come around again, I'll have a reason to not pursue you. I could say I've checked and that you're gone. That's why I suggested exchanging information through that hollow tree, and why I'm dismayed about having you here today. I have to cover myself, Joe. Whatever happens with this matter can either get me promoted or court-martialed. It can get you hanged, if you can't prove you're acting under legal orders. You've killed several men without evidence to back those slayings. You're riding with Sun Cloud's daughter and working for the Oglalas, the very Indians incriminated in so many foul deeds. This can get out of hand fast if we aren't more careful."

Joe realized the officer was making valid points. "I do have the authority to work on this mission, Jim—from Tom, Stede, and from the President himself."

"Authority to kill suspects? By your own admission, you entered camps and attacked men without proof in your favor."

"They're guilty!"

"You know it, and I believe you, but what about the law if their friends push for justification? What if this Snake-Man is rich and powerful? What if Zeke and his boys aren't working for him? Zeke said he was hauling weapons and supplies to trappers and customers in Powder River country. He has receipts to back those sales. Can you prove he did otherwise?"

"He met with a Crow party. Morning Star overheard him say he was carrying them guns and whiskey."

"Did you actually see the goods exchange hands? No. It's your word against theirs. You're the blood brother of the infamous Sun Cloud, son of the infamous Gray Eagle. You're traveling with the chief's beautiful daughter. Your best friend was Sun Cloud's cousin, whose death you want to avenge. The Indian girl as a witness, Joe? She's from the same band accused of most of the attacks."

Joe grasped the full seriousness of Jim's words.

The officer continued. "You could be asking men who think they have good reasons to hate Indians, particularly the Red Hearts, to judge you innocent of slaying white men while aiding and befriending their enemies. You know how Zeke is either feared or revered. Would you want a jury of those men to decide your fate? If I allow you to carry on without approval and at least a few shreds of proof that you're riding in the right direction, I'm in trouble."

"If I get Snake-Man and Zeke, neither of us will have to worry."

"*If*, Joe, that's the hazardous word."

"After you receive word from Tom and President Fillmore, will we be safe from backlash?"

"Yes. If you remain within the law," Jim amended. "*Nobody* can break it, Joe, for *any* reason."

Joe nodded his understanding. "What's this about a payroll theft by Red Hearts?"

"A unit was coming from Fort Laramie with it. Fifty miles south of what's called the Badlands, the unit was attacked, robbed and slaughtered. There was one survivor. He exposed the Red Hearts."

Joe remembered that Jim had said the entire unit had been killed. At full attention he asked, "When?"

"Last Wednesday. The wounded man got here yesterday. Isn't the Red Heart band camped on Sunday in or near the Badlands, hunting buffalo?"

"Yes, but they're not responsible for the slaughter. Sun Cloud promised no attacks, only self-defense. I trust him. You would, too, if you knew him. What made this soldier think it was Red Hearts?"

"The matching symbols on their chests. You probably haven't seen them prepared for a raid. They paint a red shape like a human heart on their upper left shoulders to show unity or to boast of who they are."

"Can I question him? Or can you do it for me?"

"As I said, they're all dead. Dawes, the soldier who made it here, died last night. It took him four grueling days to get here. He might have survived if he'd made it sooner. He lost too much blood along the way. He lived long enough to give a detailed account of the raid and to hand me those items. I had to file a report, Joe. It was a military defeat and other soldiers heard it."

Joe motioned to the headband and necklace. "How did he get those?"

Jim lifted the knife charm and explained. "This was torn off an attacker's neck while he was killing a soldier. Dawes pulled the headband off his killer during their struggle. He was left for dead. When he came to, he and the others were missing small scalp locks. I guess you know by now," he interrupted his answer to say, "Indians don't cut off the whole head of hair; they just carve out a button size piece to use for decoration. Anyway, Dawes still had Night Stalker's headband when he awoke. He noticed that *wanapin*, as those charms are called, and figured it could help identify the warriors responsible. I don't have to tell you how bad this looks for Sun Cloud's band. That dying soldier had no reason to lie or to aid Snake-Man's plot."

Joe glanced at the talisman, so like one he'd seen on a thong around Knife-Slayer's neck. He fingered the headband with a brown stick figure holding a bow in one hand and a knife in the other on a black background of artistic beadwork, also so like one he'd seen on his love's brother. "This leaky boat has bailers, Jim; it isn't holding the poisoned water Snake-Man tossed in to sink it. Those two warriors wouldn't be so careless, and they'd never leave behind something so valuable to them; *wanapins* are sacred objects. The band wasn't under attack from a rescue party and didn't have to get away fast, so they had time to recover them. It's part of the frame."

"Let me take these along," Joe suggested. "Maybe the Indians can tell me who made them. From what I've learned, they each have their own colors and patterns and use certain specific kinds of beads."

"I can't give you the evidence, Joe."

"Just let me borrow them. I'll return them in that hollow tree soon. I need to see if the Red Hearts recognize these imitations—and they need to see how cleverly they're being framed, in addition. This way they'll understand what we're up against, let them know why the Army has reason to doubt them."

Jim mused a moment. "All right, but make it quick," he agreed.

"I can assure you the Red Hearts aren't involved, and I'll prove it."

"I hope so, Joe. I agree that so-called evidence was left there on purpose to make them look guilty. But what if it was other Indians, another Lakota band? Not many white men can pass for Indians. Getting that many who can fool a soldier is doubtful. Timing proves it wasn't Zeke or George."

"Maybe they were Crow; they're siding with Snake-Man. After we leave, we're checking some Crow camps and we'll visit Sun Cloud. If the Red Hearts were involved this time, I'll be honest with you."

"What about her?" Jim asked, motioning toward the closed door.

"Whoever is to blame, we'll report it. She wants peace, too. If her brother and other warriors secretly attacked soldiers, she won't agree with those actions and she'll make sure they're punished."

Jim watched him. "Sounds like you trust her completely."

Joe strained to keep his real feelings from showing. "I've gotten to know her well, Jim, so I do. She's taught me all she could, and she hasn't led me on any wild chases. What about this Corporal George Whatever?" Joe ventured, wanting to change the subject. "If he's from Fort Laramie, maybe he knew about the payroll. Maybe he was over here to report it to his boss. The timing is perfect for his treachery. We need to learn who he is."

"I'll handle that when I send this report to Tom. Check the tree in a few weeks. I know Simon Adams is from New Orleans. I plan to send a trusted man downriver on the next boat to do some checking on him."

"New Orleans?" Joe echoed, and Jim nodded. "We might have answers sooner than that. Stede Gaston lives in New Orleans. He might know something about him. If he does, he'll put it in his response to my questions. I strongly implied Adams is our man."

Jim leaned back in his chair and kept his gaze on Joe. "You told me everything you've learned about him, didn't you?"

"One point I didn't stress to you is his feelings about women." Joe went over Simon's words again, then related what Clem had said concerning Morning Star's fate at the hands of their boss. "Those two patterns match, Jim. See if you can find out if he keeps Indian girls around and how they're treated."

Jim stroked his smooth face. "That'll be tricky, but I'll try."

Joe glanced at the missive to Tanner's father that revealed all the facts and clues he had gathered. It listed questions about Simon, George, and land buys. In a few weeks, he would have more pieces to this puzzle, hopefully enough to begin solving it. Then, he would be going home soon. That thought reminded Joe to ask Jim to mail a letter to Joseph and Annabelle Lawrence in Virginia.

"That's all for now, Jim. Thanks," he said as he concealed the borrowed items.

"Ride carefully, Joe," the officer said, then walked him outside.

Both men looked at Morning Star, whose expression was impassive. Jim nodded to her, and Joe joined her. The captain watched as the couple mounted and headed for the gate, then he returned to his desk.

"Hide fast!" Morning Star warned, pulling her mount's reins to the right. She walked Hanmani around a stable, Joe and the packhorse behind her.

When they were out of sight, she explained her behavior. "I look out big door. See Zeke coming. He not have time to see us."

They hid until Zeke and Farley halted their wagon at the sutler's store and went inside, then at a pace that wouldn't attract unwanted attention, they left the fort at the mouth of the White River and rode north. Within a mile, they had to conceal themselves again when they spotted the suspicious scout named George heading for Fort Tabor.

"That's strange. Zeke and George arriving at the same time," Joe observed. "As soon as that snake learned we'd been in Pierre, he headed straight here; probably came to see if we're reporting to the Army. Then, that dubious scout shows up flying in his tailwind. Could be they're in this area to collect that stolen payroll from those hired renegades. Damn. This eliminates Orin McMichael as our villain; Snake-Man is too smart to be connected so easily to his hirelings."

Morning Star asked Joe to explain the words she did not understand, then advised, "Too soon to e-lim-min-nate Orin. He give me bad feelings."

Joe knew why the man's undisguised lust made her uneasy, but he took her suggestion to heart. "We can't go back; it's too dangerous. And if we hang around to spy on them, it'd be our luck they'd stay for days or leave by boat." Joe didn't tell her that if he were alone, he'd do just that. Knowing the open range they would have to cover while trailing those bastards, she would be in too much danger of exposure and capture. Besides, those men might do nothing more than visit, then leave and he'd have wasted days, energy, and supplies. He was eager to get moving to find hard evidence. "I'll have to depend on Jim to observe them. At least he'll finally get to meet that baffling scout. Let's put some miles between us and this place. I'll tell you everything when we camp tonight."

They camped before darkness would cover the land, choosing a shady grove on a calm river.

Joe noticed how silent Morning Star had been along their journey; yet, he hadn't talked much, either. He was deciding if he should tell her everything and, if so, how. If she didn't know about the homesteading law, it was best not to mention it this soon. Her people felt that the Great Spirit owned the land and it was created for their use. To reveal that his government believed they owned her territory and was selling off parcels would only anger and distress her.

Only their chores drew forth words. Soon, a fire and hot meal were underway. As they ate, Joe asked, "Did you have any problems at the fort?"

"No. I watch soldiers, but they no come near me."

"Did you overhear anything we said?"

"No. I stay with horses. I did not want men to think I listen. I know you tell me all when we camp."

Suppressing a pang of guilt, Joe began his revelations. He explained about Jim's worries and precautions and related he had told the officer everything they had done and discovered. He knew his tone altered when he talked of Jim's not knowing George and of the captain's speculations. He saw concern fill her brown eyes when he exposed his and Jim's peril if they didn't get written approval for their actions and eventual proof to back them up. He realized she was as shocked and confused by Zeke's murder charge as he had been.

"You warned me of danger in killing men we chase. I not want you hurt for helping my people."

"Don't worry about me, love. I won't get into any trouble. But we'll be more careful from now on. I suspect Zeke was either trying to learn if the Army's on our side or wants to get the law after us to slow down our tracking. It won't matter, because Jim believes us. I was suspicious of Jim for a time back there," he admitted. "But I understand his points."

When Morning Star queried his talk of arrests, trials, courtmartials, judges, and juries, Joe explained them to her.

"You sure you trust soldier? He say not know scout, but scout come to see him. Zeke come same day. That plenty strange, Joe."

"Maybe just a coincidence, love."

"What is co-in-ci-dence?"

"Something that happens at the same time and at the same place—but one isn't a part of the other. If they were there to see Jim, it was about Zeke's wild charges and George's mission or his sneaky work for Snake-Man. He must realize he can't keep his presence in this area a secret, so he's covering his tracks. I'm sure he isn't working for Tom or the Army."

Morning Star observed Joe as his mood became hesitant. She sensed there was more to his meeting with Jim, something bad. His blue gaze exposed an inner conflict that she waited for him to reveal. He scratched his beard and took a few bites of his food as he seemingly stalled the remainder of his talk. "What is so hard to tell me?" she asked, dread chewing at her.

"Jim asked me if we would expose whoever was guilty, Morning Star, even if it's your brother or anyone from your band. I told him we would, because we both want peace. I was right, wasn't I?"

"You know you do not have to ask. Yes, I will do it for peace."

Joe let out a loud sigh of relief and smiled, his gaze filling with love and gratitude. "I was sure, Morning Star, but I had to ask. I had to make you realize what this mission can demand from you and your people. If anybody from your band commits a crime, we can't protect them."

"Father gave his word for no attacks. Did you not believe him?"

"I trust Sun Cloud. I trust most of your people. But I worry over what men like Knife-Slayer, Hawk Eyes . . . and your brother might do."

Morning Star grasped how difficult the last name was to mention, but she understood why Joe had that feeling. "They will obey Father and the council. It is our way, our . . . law."

Joe pulled the two items from inside his shirt. "This is why I asked and why I'm worried." He related the payroll robbery and massacre of the soldiers and told her how Jim and he had gotten these possessions.

Morning Star put aside her plate and took them in her hands. The tiny knife seemed identical to her pursuer's. "When we reach my camp, we will learn if he has lost his." She examined the headband, closed her eyes, and breathed her own sigh of great relief. Smiling, she looked at Joe and said, "This not my brother's. I help Mother make Night Stalker's headband. Touched-A-Crow cannot bead good. Bow and knife in wrong hands. It not long enough for brother's head. Thongs not same as we use."

"I didn't think they would be so reckless with sacred possessions."

"But you think they be so reckless to raid in secret?"

Joe glanced at the ground, then returned his gaze to hers. "Yes. Sometimes men do what they want, not what they should do. Sometimes they think that once a glorious and daring deed is done, others won't be angry with them for defying orders. Sometimes they just do as they please and keep it a secret to avoid trouble and punishment. I'm sorry, Morning Star, but I think Knife-Slayer is that kind of man; and I'm not sure he couldn't talk your brother into helping him. You know Night Stalker's feelings about whites and war, truce and the Crow. With Knife-Slayer pushing and pulling at him to prove his prowess . . ."

"I sad to say, you right. But brother stop bad journey when he see wrong trail for people. Knife-Slayer talk and push much, but brother not jump on wild horse without much thinking. He not want to get hurt so cannot become chief after Father. I not believe brother do raids now. But if trouble grows, he talk to council for war."

"With luck, he'll realize peace is best for everyone."

They finished their meal and clean-up task in silence. Each took a turn being excused in the shadows, then each did the same for a quick bath to remove the day's grime. By then, night surrounded the site. Crickets chirped, frogs croaked, owls hooted, water babbled its way around obstacles, a coyote howled in the distance and received no answer, and nocturnal birds called back and forth: all giving sounds that relaxed the couple. A cooling breeze wafted over the Indian beauty and the sunny-haired white man. The sky was clear above them, with only twinkling stars and a crescent moon to adorn it. They breathed deeply of the scents of grass, wildflowers, and burning wood. They felt far removed from civilization, basking in the glow of the campfire.

As Morning Star used a brush of blunted porcupine quills on her unbound hair, she said, "We ride on grasslands for many days. Not many trees or water. I know where to find and make camp each day. We see many bands and tribes hunting buffalo. Many be Dakotas; some be Oglalas. In five suns we reach Bird People. Most tribes use same hunting grounds every season. We be safe with Dakotas, but Crow . . . It be dangerous to enter enemy camps. We be brave and do sacred mission."

Both realized that peril and possible death lay before them. Both wanted and needed each other before confronting either one.

Joe watched the raven tresses shine more and more from her brushing; the firelight seemed to sparkle off the glossy hairs. She looked so feminine and delicate with ebony hair flowing around her shoulders and framing her exquisite face. He was too aware of the fact she had not removed the damp blanket around her freshly scrubbed body and put on clean garments, just as he was sitting opposite her with only the dying flames separating them wearing nothing but a doubled blanket around his hips.

Morning Star felt Joe's gaze and thoughts upon her, as if they gave sensuous caresses to her tingly flesh. The tenderness in his eyes gradually waxed to smoldering desire. It was evident he wanted her as much as she craved him. So much stood between them and would forever keep them apart. For them to have a life together they must prevent a war, expose the true villains, overcome the hatred and suspicions each side had for the other, understand and accept each other's people, and compromise on their beliefs and customs. Yet, if they solved or lessened any of those obstacles, more would arise and others increase. Surely there could never be more for them than what they could steal along their journey, for neither side could be changed very much. And as long as things remained the same, he could not live in her endangered world and she could not enter his hostile one.

Joe stood and went to her. "Let me do this," he entreated, urging the brush from her hand. He stepped over the cottonwood trunk she was sitting on, which had fallen from age. As he passed the bristles through her silky strands, he murmured, "Your hair is beautiful, Morning Star, like you are. I love the way it feels around my fingers; it's as smooth as water."

She closed her eyes and savored the unique pleasure. "Only Mother do this task before you. I like. I make your task every night."

Joe felt her warm laughter flow over his body. "Fine with me," he replied, and heard how husky his voice sounded.

After a time, she said, "I do Joe now," and sent forth giggles.

He was about to decline, but didn't. He exchanged places with her. She stood behind him, as he had done with her. With gentleness and care, she brushed his wheat-colored mane. He was surprised it felt so relaxing.

"You like, too?" she asked, her tone merry.

"Yep," he murmured. Her body touched his and the shape of it filled his mind. The blanket tickled his bare flesh, but he would never tell her to step away.

Morning Star delighted in the various sensations that teased through her body. The way her breasts rubbed against the blanket and then against his body tantalized her. She thought of soft rabbit fur as her fingers traveled behind her brush strokes. She felt as if this were a new and exciting adventure. Her heart raced fast and seemed as if it filled to a bursting point. The power of her feelings washed over her like a raging river that carried her away, beyond the bank of retreat.

Joe experienced contradictory sensations of tension and serenity. It was as if tiny, invisible flames from the fire before him licked at his tanned flesh. Mercy, how he yearned to turn around, pull her into his arms, cover her mouth with kisses, then make blissful love to her! *Why not?* his heart demanded. They were in a safe and private location, and soon, the open Plains would take away both. Soon, their life together would be broken apart, as his heart surely would be, too. How could he face life without her?

Morning Star perceived the change in Joe as his calmed and happy body became taut and troubled. She decided his thoughts matched hers. If only they could remain tranquil and together forever, but he knew, as well as she did, that was forbidden. Her warring heart warned, *You have only the passings of a few full moons with him, seize all of them. Store them in your heart.*

All day, each had fantasized about the other and their next joining. They had daydreamed of being in each other's embrace with emotions unleashed and passions unrestrained. They had imagined their hands traveling over each other's body—stimulating, pleasuring, sating.

Before Joe could act on his impulse to yank her into his arms, the brave Morning Star dropped her brush, stepped over the large log, and stood before him. She gazed into his eyes with obvious longing. When she saw him return that look, she maneuvered into his lap. Without boldness, she rested her legs over the cottonwood and shifted close to him, her knees hugging his hips on either side and her hands wrapped over his broad shoulders. Still, his lips were out of reach, until her fingers journeyed into his hair and pulled his head downward to mesh their mouths.

Joe's arms encircled her blanket-clad body, and he held her against him. His astonishment quickly faded, replaced by urgent desire. His lips worked ravenously at hers. He felt intoxicated by the nectar his mouth gathered from hers. His mind reeled from her nearness.

When their lips parted, Joe's trailed over her face and down her throat.

Morning Star leaned her head back and let him do as he pleased. She was his willing captive, his prisoner of delight. She thrilled to the way she felt as his mouth tasted the pulse at her neck. Her mind was awhirl in a mixture of sensations, as she let herself go completely.

Her long raven hair teased over Joe's hands at her waist. He felt the heat radiating from her womanhood to his groin. His tongue played in the hollows of her throat and trekked over her collarbone. Her flesh was like Oriental silk; no Parisian perfume could smell sweeter than she did. His teeth gripped the blanket, tugged at the thin covering that kept him from this hidden treasure, and loosened it to explore the depths of her surrender. He stroked her breasts with his cheek, then tasted the sweet flesh. He didn't know who moaned with delight, he or she, or both.

Morning Star was glad when Joe eased them downward to the grass but didn't change their position. It was bliss that he had freed the blanket around his hips as he did so. Nothing was between them now. Her knees rested on the ground at his sides. While he kissed her with greediness, she eased him inside her. As they shared endless, countless kisses, she rocked upon his lap.

The campfire was dying, but the entwined couple seemed to give off more heat than a hundred flames could. Their passions burned brighter and hotter until the greatest blaze of all ignited and consumed them. It melted their wills, then forged the molten liquid into one bond.

"I love you, Morning Star; I love you," Joe confessed.

Her heart flooded with overwhelming emotion. *"Waste cedake*, Joe; *waste cedake."* She murmured the same words in her language.

Joe understood them, or prayed he did. "We belong to each other forever," he vowed, and it was not the result of the rapture he experienced. It was true, and time to act on his feelings.

Morning Star rested her head against Joe's shoulder. She felt limp and content in his possessive embrace. She liked the way his fingers teased up and down her spine and the way his head nestled against her hair. She was at home in his arms, more at peace there than anywhere. But when he spoke, his words dissolved the golden aura that encompassed them.

Joe said in an emotion-strained voice, "We have to talk, love."

Morning Star heard the seriousness in his voice. She lifted her head and read it in his gaze. She sensed what was coming, and wondered if she were ready to confront that awesome truth. "I must bathe and dress. We talk when I return." Joe did not try to stop her as she rose. She retrieved her blanket, gathered her garments, and headed for the river. *Medicine* it was called, but could it heal what wounded her heart and diseased her life? Could anything or anyone, even her beloved Joe? She dreaded testing its powers when she left its water.

Joe bathed not far away, deep in thought. If he couldn't persuade her they belonged together and must find a way to share one life, his future existence would be as dark as the night closing in on them. To chase away those depressing shadows, he tossed more wood onto the glowing coals when he finished rinsing off and had donned his garments. Too, he wanted to be able to see her face when they talked.

Morning Star returned, dressed in a buckskin top and skirt with swaying fringes. Her feet were bare, and her flowing mane was braided.

Joe tensed. He feared the plait was symbolic of her restraining her emotions.

He spread their bedrolls, took a seat on his, and motioned for her to join him. Instead, she sat on hers. "I love you, Morning Star. I need you," he vowed in earnest.

Never had anything been harder than to not fling herself into his arms, cover him with kisses, and repeat those beautiful words. It took more strength than Sun Cloud's daughter knew she had to reply, "We do not know what Grandfather will bring on the new . . . tomorrow. We must eat the joys of today which He allows. Tomorrow or another sun, they may not be."

"I want you every day, Morning Star, for the rest of my life."

"It cannot be," she responded, her gaze exposing anguish.

"We'll find a way to stay together. I love you. I want you to become my wife. I can't lose you, woman. I can't get enough of you during the next few months to last me a lifetime. We've tried to love day to day. I want more. I want to marry you. I want to have children with you. I want to grow old with you at my side. I want to share every day with you."

"It cannot be. The path between us is filled with brush; it stops us from riding together. My trail is here. Your trail is . . ."

"I love you and must have you, Morning Star. I'll burn any brush tossed in our way. I'll fight for you, woman, any way necessary."

No matter what happened, Joe loved her and wanted her, Morning Star knew. She was no redskin, no savage, no wild animal to him. He considered her worthy to become his wife. But it required sacrificing her life here and her loved ones and entering the enemy world. She tried to halt the painful talk. "Some forests are too large and thick to burn, and some rivers are too deep and swift to cross."

Undaunted now that his decision was made, Joe argued, "I'm a good swimmer. I'll keep moving through the water to remove any obstacle between us. While we're finishing this mission, I'll teach you everything I know. When we reach my home in Virginia, my mother and sister will teach you all I don't know. My family and I will make certain you don't have any trouble adjusting to our world. My family will love you and accept you as I do."

Anxiety attacked her so forcefully that she trembled. "It cannot be! Do not hurt us with such words," she entreated.

Joe crawled to her, took her quivering hands, and refuted. "It can be."

Morning Star worried over his persistence. In her dilemma, she rushed her arguments and her English suffered. "We not the same. I die in your world. If I change to live, I not be Morning Star. If I choose Joe, I betray family, people, ways, and Great Spirit. I break law! I be banished, dishonored. Never see family and lands again. You ask Morning Star to go to enemy land where Indians hated. Where I not know how to survive. That destroy Morning Star, destroy love we share. It not . . . simple as to speak words. For Joe, perhaps it sound simple. For Morning Star, it mean denying all she is and possesses; it mean shame and separation for me and family. It mean banishment, dishonor," she stressed.

Joe realized what he was asking her to give up, or thought he did. In his culture, women always left their homes and families to go with their husbands. He would keep her safe in his world. She was too intelligent not to learn everything necessary in order to fit in perfectly. He would find a way to persuade Sun Cloud and the Red Hearts that he loved her and would treasure her always. Both the sacred vision putting them together and his success at earning peace should work in his favor. He would make certain she got to visit her people and lands. Love wasn't something that caused anguish and shame; fighting it was. Joe explained his thoughts to Morning Star. "We can make it work, love."

"No, it not possible. Whites hate Indians. They insult and push away. Whites laugh at Morning Star, laugh at Joe. You not stay here. My people not accept you. Joe family need him. Work there. Friends there. When time come, you go, Morning Star stay. We be one until that moon."

Joe used the Colonial and British wars as another argument. "We battled long and hard two times, but we're friends and allies now. One day, it'll be that way between your people and mine. My grandparents were from different sides, but they found love and happiness. So did Gray Eagle and Alisha. So did Bright Arrow and Rebecca. It can be the same for us, Morning Star. Let it happen. You know how we'll feel when we're separated. We'll both be miserable. I need you in my life. I love you. Why do we have to suffer because our peoples can't accept each other?"

Morning Star could not endure any more pressure tonight. She told him, "If it meant to be, it happen. Must not force it to happen. You like breath to me, beating of my heart, food for my body. I pray you be my destiny. If Grandfather say you not, Morning Star cannot have you."

"How will you know His answer?" Joe inquired. He was thrilled by some of her words but disappointed that he could not convince her entirely.

"When it come, I will know," she replied with careful words.

Joe studied her for a while. He hoped he had time to weaken her will, time to convince her they were matched by fate, time to teach her so much about his world that she would be eager for them to face it together. The challenge confronting him was exciting and hopefully would be rewarding. "That doesn't mean I can't do my best to convince Him to say yes. I'll prove I'm worthy of you, woman. I'm going to fight for your love and acceptance."

Morning Star comprehended how hard this rejection was for both of them. In tonight's dreamy shadows, he was snared by love's magic. Tomorrow's bright sun would dispel it and he would realize she was right. There was no need to sting him more, so she attempted to soothe his emotional wounds. "You have my love," she said softly. "You have acceptance in my heart."

"I know. That's why not winning you because of other people's feelings makes me angry. Love like ours is too rare and precious to lose. It's meant to grow, to create happiness, to birth children. If Alisha and Rebecca could live with Oglalas, why can't you live with whites? It worked for them; it can work for us. It wasn't any harder for those white women to join your Indian world than it will be for you to join my white one."

Morning Star concurred with most of what he said, but that didn't change their predicament. "Women do as men say," she murmured. "Father is boss until marry. Husband is boss after joining. That much is same in both worlds. Grandfather and uncle take captive white women they want; is way of raids and wars. Whites have slaves, too. Whites steal, trade, and sell people with brown skin. I am Indian woman and must obey Father. It different for warrior to take white captive than for Indian woman to reject people and go with paleface enemy. It bad, forbidden. Hurt many. You must understand and accept our ways and laws."

Joe caressed her cheek and whispered a mischievous threat. "Then I'll just have to steal you as my captive when I'm ready to leave."

She didn't realize he was trying to joke to lighten the situation. Her gaze widened with distress. "That worse than bad! Father and warriors come after me to rescue. They slay you!"

Joe was enthralled for a time by the idea. Why not do as the Indians—as her legendary grandfather and uncle—and seize the woman he wanted? "We'll be too far away. They'll never find us."

"Gray Eagle tracked Shalee to place called St. Louis and take her back after Powchutu steal her," Morning Star refuted. "He follow trail many weeks old. We cannot escape Oglala warrior skills. They best trackers."

"You're as skilled as they are," Joe pointed out. "If you hide our tracks, they'd never find us."

In a sad tone, she responded, "If I betray, I never return to family and lands again. Do not ask me to choose between you and my people."

"But you *are* choosing, Morning Star—them over me. Why can't you share the rest of your life with me? Think of all you've done for your people and what you're doing now for them. How could they dishonor and be cruel to She-Who-Rode-With-The-Sky-Warrior? How could they refuse to let you follow your heart and seek your true destiny?"

"Joe part right, but what can Morning Star do but duty teached her since birth? You not know how hard it was for Alisha and Rebecca, even if worked in time. You forget they not have families in white world to return to. Grandmother and Wahea not have to worry over dishonor and rejection by their people. Wahea not chief's daughter. I yield little; perhaps love strong enough to conquer enemies. We must wait, see if that powerful."

"That's the best thing I've heard you say. It gives me hope."

"I want hope. It hard. You not lived in my land long enough to know how big is the battle we face. We must pray for strength and courage."

"We will, because the battle for you is as important to me as our task."

"Sacred mission must come first. If we do good—"

"Our prayers may be answered," he finished for her.

They gazed at each other a long time, then exchanged smiles.

After breaking camp on Tuesday at the White Clay River, Morning Star gazed beyond them at the seemingly endless Great Plains. The rangy land they crossed was almost treeless and scrubless, except for a few cottonwoods and chokecherries near a water source. The ground was covered with a mixture of thick grasses in shades of green: short, tall, sweet, tender. Cactus and wildflowers were sighted at some points. Antelope, deer, and buffalo were abundant, so, too, jackrabbits and prairie dogs. Every now and then, gusts of strong wind yanked at their clothes and hair.

A few times, at a distance, she noticed what whites called sod houses, or rock homes, or dugouts. She knew sod helped defeat the summer's heat and keep out the winter's chill and winds. They were strong dwellings, with most having a combination raid-root cellar nearby. Soon, only grassland stretched before them once more; white encroachment was left behind.

Morning Star guided Joe and the animals at a steady pace. It seemed as if the land went on forever, then vanished into the blue sky far beyond any distance they could ever ride. She led Joe across a few streams and creeks and past the Bad River that flowed toward where Simon Adams's lived in Pierre.

As the day moved on, so did the hot sun across the sky. Any clouds above them were small and white. Morning Star kept on constant alert, as did Joe. She was amused by his astonishment at the number of buffalo in her territory and the size of their gatherings.

He was amazed by the size of the herds which often traveled for miles in several directions. At some points, the earth was covered by a dark blanket as far as he could see even with his fieldglasses. Antelope and deer intermingled with the buffalo. Though the huge beasts grazed contentedly and appeared sluggish, Joe knew they were dangerous and unpredictable, and anything but slow. The sizes of their horns and bodies exposed an accurate warning of how deadly the animal could be.

Joe scanned their surroundings. He had not imagined the Plains to be so immense. After a while, he realized the scenery was repetitious, with every five miles repeating the last five and the many miles before it. At least, he thought, they didn't have to use a tiring jog trot as much today.

Before dusk, she pointed to an Indian camp at the end of Plum Creek. She took Joe's fieldglasses, as he had taught her how to use them, and focused them on an area outside the encampment of numerous tepees. She checked symbols on the lance and markings on a large buffalo skull surrounded by a circle of smaller skulls. "*Mahpialuta wicoti.*"

"What?" Joe asked, staring at the nomadic village of countless tepees outlined against the gradually darkening horizon.

"Red Cloud camp," she translated. "His father Brule; that one of Lakota tribes. His mother Oglala. He become Oglala. Lead mother's people; they called Old Smoke Band. He plenty smart and brave. He tell Father he want peace, but he hate white takeover of lands. If whites push, Red Cloud fight. It important he speak and vote for new treaty. Come."

Morning Star perceived the many stares given to she and Joe. From years of celebrations, Sun Dances, trading, joint raids, and talks, she knew the Oglalas recognized the daughter of Sun Cloud. She halted at the largest, most beautiful tepee in camp. A rainbow was painted on each side. She remembered red circles on the back that represented *Wi*, the sun, and the figure of a buffalo. Yellow rings encircled the tepee with a black top for the night sky and a green bottom for the earth. The colors and markings symbolized Red Cloud's medicine and vision signs and were evocations to the Great Spirit. Morning Star related those meanings to Joe and told him the chief was a member of the White-Marked Society.

Joe comprehended how important this chief was to his mission and to Tom Fitzpatrick's new treaty. He observed the man who left the artistic home and greeted Morning Star with a smile and obvious affection. He listened to them talk a while in their tongue, but he hadn't worked on his grasp of Lakota as much as they had on hers of English.

Morning Star told Joe to dismount, then introduced him to the chief. She was relieved when her love was offered friendship and hospitality. Red Cloud invited them inside his home to eat and to spend the night.

Joe quickly learned from the sage Indian that he wanted peace, but doubted it was possible. Joe explained the treaty, his mission, and his problems so far. He told Red Cloud of his plans to spy on the Crow, and promised to warn the Oglalas of any threatening intents. He sensed that the chief believed him, even liked him.

Morning Star drew the same conclusions. She related Payaba's sacred vision, the contest, Joe's alleged identity, and their task to him.

"It is good. Sun Cloud will know great honor and pride."

After a restful night and a successful visit, Morning Star guided Joe from Red Cloud's encampment on a journey across more prairie land to the lovely location of Sinte Geleska and his band on the tree-lined Cheyenne River.

Spotted Tail greeted them with a genial and courteous manner. He said it was good to see Mahpiya Wicasta and the daughter of Sun Cloud again.

Joe liked being accepted as Sky Warrior, and the Indian name, with all it represented, made him feel proud.

Morning Star was elated by their reception and honored treatment. She was glad Joe was learning that the Lakotas wanted peace. She listened as the two men talked, and was impressed by both.

The evening passed in a pleasant way with Chief Spotted Tail and his friendly band. Then the couple enjoyed another restful and safe night.

At dawn, they mounted, bid the Brules good-bye, and rode for their next camp on an offshoot of the murky Cheyenne River.

As they traveled, even sounds—what few they heard—were repetitious: the hooffalls and breathing of the three horses, the sound of their own breathing, the squeaking of leather saddles and reins, the movement of canteens and rifle sheaths, and the shifting of trade goods on the pack animal. They couldn't talk all the time to divert their attention from the almost eerie quietness, for that dried their throats and encouraged drinking too much water that had to last from water source to water source.

Joe came to look forward to the areas where hawks soared overhead, their shrill cries renting the silence. He missed the music of songbirds, singing of crickets, and croakings of frogs. The rocking pace and unvaried scenery made it hard to stay alert. He couldn't imagine any white man choosing to spend a lifetime homesteading in a barren and lonely place like this when there was so much good land elsewhere for farming.

"I wish you could see where I live," he told Morning Star. "It's so different here. We have lots of trees. They change colors between summer and winter. Some years it looks as if the forest is on fire with reds, purples, oranges, and yellows. And in the spring after winter, flowers grow everywhere in every size, color, and shape you can imagine. We don't have places like this that are so barren. Empty," he clarified. "Our winter isn't as cold and long as yours. Our summer isn't as hot and dry. Friends live around us, not miles and days away like here. We don't have people separated into bands who attack and kill each other. It's peaceful and beautiful."

She was so attentive and interested that he went on. "During the day, men do their tasks, then spend the evening with their families. Life isn't as hard there. Men work for money, then hire others to do certain chores for them. Women don't have to work as hard, either; they have easier ways to cook and do dishes in stoves and sinks in big kitchens. They don't have to sew clothes if they don't want to or don't know how; they can buy them ready-made or hire a seamstress. Anybody who doesn't want to grow food or have the ground to grow it on can buy it in stores or at open markets. It's safe there. It's . . . I'm rambling," he said with a chuckle.

"What is rambling?"

He grinned. "To talk on and on about anything, everything, nothing."

"I like to hear you talk on and on. I learn much about you and your land. Rambling more," she coaxed. Before she let him begin again, she queried unknown words he had used during his talk, such as kitchens, seamstresses, and markets. She listened and learned.

They shared laughter and journeyed onward, chatting frequently.

Another night of safety passed as they took turns standing guard at Cherry Creek. Both were in good moods following their visits with two Dakota chiefs but fatigued by their long and tiring ride. Yet, each avoided the bittersweet subject of their forbidden love and uncertain destiny.

The vast range continued to spread before them. It was hotter and drier in this area. The ground covering was now a blend of green and tan. Winds blew in from the west at regular intervals, waving grasses to and fro in a mesmerizing motion. The sky was a mixture of pale blue and white, with few clouds having real definition. Soon, unusual formations intermittently loomed from the earth: buttes, mesas, hillocks, and rocks. Trees called attention to any waterline present. They crossed the shallow Moreau River. Ecru ground showed a pebbly surface more frequently. Then, at last, the familiar terrain returned.

Joe and Morning Star made their last camp on Rabbit Creek before entering the Grand River area where many Crow bands were doing their seasonal hunts. The couple did their chores in silence as each pondered the great peril they would confront on the next day. Both realized that before the sun was high or set on that day, they could be dead . . .

Chapter Fourteen

"Will you wait here for my return?" Joe asked. "I don't want to put you into more danger."

Morning Star caressed his cheek, smiled, and said, "The danger we face is not following Grandfather's vision. I am part of it, so I must ride with you. To change it brings trouble. You do not know much sign language." She reminded Joe of one of the main reasons she was with him.

He knew it was futile to argue. He'd probably need her assistance, and besides, he couldn't leave her alone in enemy land. "I'll hide those things I got from Jim and retrieve them after we leave the Crow camp. They would be hard to explain if we're searched. I'll also leave most of our trade goods here, so the chief won't insist on taking all of them."

They covered the last miles at a slow pace to keep themselves and the animals rested in case a speedy flight was necessary. As they looked ahead, it was as if odd formations suddenly leapt from the grasslands and rolling hills to expose the biggest change in landscape they had seen for days. The beautiful terrain had bushes and trees—cedar, spruce, pine, and hardwoods—and water and countless rocks. They almost rode into a distant semicircle of mesas and buttes. Various-colored grasses encompassed the lovely site. Most of the formations looked like castles and pinnacles grouped around an enormous one that reminded Joe of a giant fortress. Animals and birds were abundant.

The first camp, like an evil spirit in a nightmare, loomed before Joe and Morning Star. She read the markings and told him it was the camp of Black Moon; the once feared leader normally used Slim Buttes for his big camp and had again this season. She explained how small groups of hunters and women went in several directions to shoot and slaughter for days. Then, those weary groups returned with loaded travois to this location where some waited to cure the meat and others to take over the task while they rested.

Again her apprehension took a toll on her speech. "He sly, mean, and greedy. In moons past, he kill many Oglalas and steal many horses. Men who own many horses best warriors and most honored. They called Bird People because hands and feet small like birds. They have many groups; some for honor and some for battle," she told him, then explained the social and military societies. "They call best warriors Big Dogs. They not have shirt-wearers to do council's work; Big Dogs in command. They most important, like Sacred Bows in our tribe. Careful of all words you speak. They . . . pretend not to listen, but ears open big. They use tricky words to fool. Believe nothing you hear and see." After those final cautions, Morning Star fell in behind Joe in a squaw's humble position and they rode into the camp. She sent up one last prayer for their safety.

Joe observed the warriors who gathered around them, and was relieved no weapon was brandished. As if by order, the women and children moved out of sight behind or into tepees. Dogs barked, ran forward, and sniffed at the newcomers. This camp did not seem as active as Red Cloud and Spotted Tail's had been. Of course, the Crow traded with the whites for many goods that the others made.

Joe took in all the details he could while he reined in and dismounted. The Crow were indeed a people who loved finery. He knew they were hunting buffalo as all Plains Indians did this time of year, because he saw countless meat-drying racks, fresh hides, and unhitched travois. He noticed they favored beading onto red trade cloth or blanket cloth. Morning Star had told him lavender was the most valuable bead color, and he saw few of them in that color. The Crow seemed to lean toward pastels of pale blue, yellow, and green; they rarely used dark shades, particularly blue and red—colors favored by the Lakotas. He noticed tufts of horse-hair attached to coup feathers, which she had explained meant added prowess during the earning deed. He also noted how many warriors had coup feathers. Some wore highly decorated cuffs with a fringed side, similar to cavalry gauntlets. He wondered if that had become popular after the Army's arrival. Headdresses were numerous; several were made from owl feathers that were fanned out like a Tom turkey's tail. Intricate breastplates were wore by most men, and eagle-bone whistles by a few. They used more elaborate necklaces and armlets than the Dakotas. Their regalia was striking, and Joe wondered if they were clad for a special ceremony or if they did this every day.

Joe hoped it was true that an Absaroke prophet had warned them not to battle the whites and that all tribes believed that vision. He also hoped his ruse would be effective and that his enemies had not sent warnings about him to this place. He watched the chief come forward, scowling. As taught by his love, he gave the sign for *peace* and *friend*.

"What you want?" the Indian asked in a belligerent tone.

"I come with gifts for Black Moon and his chosen warriors." Joe saw suspicion gleam in the older man's dark eyes. "They are gifts from Snake-Man and Zeke Randall." That announcement got a reaction of more suspicion. Joe went to the packhorse and removed the bundles he had purchased from Harvey. He spread a blanket on the ground and emptied the cloth sacks. He watched the chief join him and eye the tobacco, pastel beads, knives, hatchets, mirrors, bells, fancy buttons, and trade cloth.

He glared at Joe and said, "This not what Black Moon want."

Joe smiled and pulled a smaller sack from the packhorse Sun Cloud had loaned him. "These are special gifts for Chief Black Moon."

The leader withdrew two cigars, a decorative can of safety matches, a pocket knife, a packet of lavender beads, and a bottle of whiskey.

Joe motioned to the other goods and said, "Those are gifts for Black Moon to give to his best warriors and wives. These," he said, tapping the woven sack in the man's grasp, "are for you." He learned why the chief was annoyed when the leader glared at him and spoke again.

"Where guns, bullets, whiskey? How we kill Sioux with trinkets? They coyote droppings. They kill, raid like rabbits. No more great warriors. No more good battles. They want white-eyes to not trust Crow and slay. They speak lies. They must die. Snake-Man say he help. Zeke his warrior. Why they break promise to bring guns in . . ." He halted to hold up ten fingers, ball his fists, then lift one finger. "Moons from one in sky."

Joe leapt on the clue that revealed a July second rendezvous in eleven days. "They don't break promises, Black Moon. The weapons and whiskey will come on the day Zeke said. I was sent to bring these gifts. You still want to meet him in the same place?"

"Yes, same place, mountain like sleeping bear."

Joe knew the site. As he repeated the numerical signals the chief had used, he stressed, "You'll be there after eleven moons cross the sky?"

"We come. No tricks," he warned with a scowl meant to frighten.

"Snake-Man said he would supply you. Don't you trust him?" Joe asked, seeking a weak spot.

"He have powerful magic. We must trust. We help kill Sioux as he wants, but need guns and bullets."

"What do you tell the soldiers who come to ask about him?"

"We say no words to bluecoats. We say Sioux lie. That Spirit's order."

Joe sensed the chief hated but feared the masquerading villain. He took a risk to say, "Don't fear him, Black Moon; spirits have weaknesses like men do. If you want to meet him, look inside his wagons while the magic smoke burns and he leaves to rest. If you find him and remove his mask, the mask and his magic will belong to you. It takes a brave man to challenge a spirit; that's how you win his strong medicine."

Black Moon pondered those astonishing words. His eyes glittered with curiosity and envy. "How man find and defeat spirit?"

Joe sensed he had the man almost ensnared and pushed to get him all the way into a cunning trap. "By being as clever and brave as the white spirit. Snake-Man would be happy to share his secrets and magic with the great Black Moon. But you must be sure to face him while his magic is weak, after he has used it and while he rests in the wagon. He must roam Mother Earth until a glorious warrior earns his medicine symbols. When he passes them to that warrior, he can join the Great White Spirit and live forever in the heavens. That is what all white spirits want."

"He white spirit?" the chief asked, looking shocked.

"Yes. Didn't you see his hands and hair?"

"Hands hidden. Hair like night."

"I've seen them; they're white, like mine," Joe claimed, extending his hands before the chief to drive his point home. "That's why he uses Zeke and white men as his helpers. But only an Indian warrior of prowess can challenge and conquer him. Think what you can do with such power."

"I ride brave trail, become great leader."

"When you become that great leader, I will bring you all the supplies you need. I must warn you, bad white men ride in this territory. They kill Oglalas, rob their burial grounds, and leave Crow arrows to make the Sioux and Army think Bird People seek war. They try to trick Crow by doing the same. I saw seven men attack a Crow hunting party and kill them. They dropped Sioux arrows and beads to anger and fool the Crow. A bad white leader provokes you against each other before it is the best time to fight. I removed the arrows and beads, tracked them, and killed them. In their camp was Oglala possessions to do the same in your territory. That's bad."

Black Moon was furious. "What man do bad tricks?"

"I don't know, but he wants the Crow and Sioux to kill each other so he can take this land for himself." Joe hoped that got the chief to thinking in the right direction. "When I defeated them and asked questions, they said Snake-Man was their boss. Surely that cannot be true."

"We not raid Sioux burial grounds. They not raid Crow. Spirits, fallen warriors be angry. Plenty bad medicine to wake them from death sleep. Always been this way. Bad to change, plenty bad."

"You speak good English, Black Moon," Joe complimented.

"Learn tongue to stop lies, to trade with white brothers."

Joe put in one last word to cause trouble. "If Black Moon takes the power and magic of spirit man, Zeke and all white traders will bring you all the weapons and whiskey you want. Even the Sioux will fear Black Moon."

"Why you not defeat spirit man and steal power?"

Joe reminded him of his earlier fabrication, "I'm not an Indian warrior, and I'm not allowed to get near him or his wagons. If you can sneak up on him in his wagon while the magic smoke fills the air, you can conquer his power. Then, no white man or Indian can defeat Black Moon."

The chief went silent in thought. "If Black Moon come near spirit man, he bring snakes to life." He motioned to his arms. "They strike, kill."

Joe did not laugh or mock the superstitious man, but played on those irrational notions. "Not if Black Moon holds a knife in each hand and puts them into the snakes' heads before they move. This territory will belong to Black Moon with such power and magic in his possession."

"Why you tell Black Moon?"

Joe hoped his answer sounded truthful. "Snake-Man punishes me when I do not do all he says. He orders me and others to steal Sioux possessions to leave where we attack whites so the Army will blame Sioux. He tells us to take tokens off trees on sleeping bear mountain. He wants the Sioux destroyed. I don't want to cause a war between the whites and the Sioux. If Black Moon becomes leader of this territory, he will honor peace with whites as your shaman saw in the vision. The Sioux will flee your magic. All will be good."

"Bad to rob Great Spirit at sacred mountain," he scolded.

Joe feigned a contrite expression. "I believe you," he said, "but I have to follow Snake-Man's orders or die. When you meet Zeke for the guns, don't tell him what I've told you about the spirit's weakness. If they learn you know the truth, they'll guard him close, and you won't be able to get near him or his wagons to steal his power and magic." Joe hoped those seeds would sprout mistrust and desire and would entice Black Moon to double cross Zeke and his boss. If so, his task would be over soon and his beloved would be safe, hopefully back home with him in Virginia. From the chief's expression and next query, Joe assumed his clever ruse was working.

"Why spirit tell you to kill whites and blame Sioux?"

Joe shrugged and faked ignorance. "I don't know. Do you know why he tells you to kill Sioux? Why does he hate them so much? Why does he want them all killed or driven out of this territory? Does he want it for himself? Is that why he supplies you with weapons to do the job for him?"

Black Moon pondered those discoveries, but said, "We enemies with Sioux more winters than Black Moon lived. You fear white spirit?"

Joe faked his discomfort. "He has lots of men and can have me killed if I don't obey him. But he's not all powerful, not really a spirit like Indian spirits. He's more like your shaman, a clever medicine man. He makes that smoke with balls of powder from far away, like the powder inside bullets. Snakes are his medicine sign like the black moons on your possessions. They're painted on his arms like you paint your symbols on your shield and tepee. Painted snakes can't come alive and strike, if he can't use his magic. That takes time. He wants people to think he can bring them to life fast only to scare them into not challenging him."

"Black Moon think on words. Come, we eat. We have Sacred Arrow Ceremony. You see bravest warriors in land."

Joe wanted to get them out of camp fast, so he smiled and alleged, "I was ordered to bring these gifts, then return quickly for another task."

"You sleep in Black Moon's camp. You friend. You leave on next sun."

Joe dared not refuse the chief's hospitality, so he was trapped into accepting. "Thank you, Black Moon."

"Woman stay with you?"

"Yes, she's my wife," Joe laced his arm around his cherished love in a possessive manner.

Black Moon eyed the beauty, particularly the tribal symbols on her garments and accessories that said she was Arapaho—neither enemy nor ally. He shrugged and motioned for them to follow him.

While they ate a hearty meal of rabbit stew, roasted antelope, boiled roots, and fry bread, Black Moon showed Joe a pocket watch and told him that Snake-Man had given it to him as a gift. He opened it to let Joe hear the "magic" music it made, something that amazed Morning Star.

Later, Joe and Morning Star sat with the chief on buffalo mats to observe the Sacred Arrow Ceremony. It was a test of bravery and skills, the rite to select which warrior was to lead in the next battle, with the winner achieving the highest rank of honor and power next to chief in the band.

The couple watched as three warriors took positions in a row, in a clearing for the safety of observers. At a signal, they rapidly fired seven arrows each overhead, then did not move as the deadly shafts fell downward with sharp tips coming straight at them. Any man who moved to avoid a wound or death was a coward and was banished. Any warrior who chose to enter the contest would rather be slain than dishonored and exiled. If he was a skilled shot, his arrows would pierce the earth around him to form a fence of great prowess. By the time the ritual ended, one participant was dead, one was injured, and one was unscathed: a warrior named Matohota in her tongue.

Morning Star hoped she appeared calm, but she was apprehensive in the midst of a tribe who had warred with her people for generations. She did not want to imagine what the Bird People would do to her if they discovered her secret or Joe's cunning tricks. She presumed the winner spoke and understood English, as he had listened with great interest to Joe's words about Snake-Man. As the fierce warrior returned to the chief for acknowledgment, she prayed the victor's name wasn't a bad omen. She knew few creatures or medicine signs were stronger than the Grizzly Bear.

After spending a restive night in the chief's tepee, Joseph Lawrence and Morning Star left Black Moon's camp after the early meal. They retrieved the hidden goods and clues to the payroll attack, then headed for the next Crow camp of Talking Wolf at South Folk River. Along the trail, they discussed what they had learned in Black Moon's camp.

Joe related seeing a half-burned crate with letters *PR* still readable, and he speculated it had come from where Simon worked. "Since he runs the post and Bernard Pratte isn't around to catch him doing mischief, he could be having guns and ammunition sent to him to pass along to Zeke. Simon does have black hair. If Simon isn't Snake-Man, he probably works for him. He's in an excellent position to receive illegal goods without anyone catching him. I wish I could have taken that board as evidence, but I couldn't figure a way to do it without Black Moon getting too curious. With luck, they'll be more when we reach Zeke's rendezvous point."

After questioning the unfamiliar words, Morning Star said, "I hope Black Moon or Grizzly Bear kills them for us."

"And does it fast, before Zeke exposes us. I just hope Snake-Man doesn't have more so-called magic up his sleeve. If he fools Black Moon again, that sneaky bastard will spill his guts about us. That means to tell all he knows. Then we'd have Zeke, his boys, and Crow chasing us."

A rush of anxiety charged through her and tainted her English words. "Why you think Black Moon believe you and attack spirit man?"

"Men like him live in both worlds, love. They're sly, greedy, and evil. They want power, and they'll do almost anything to get it."

"It not matter if you not catch Snake-Man and kill?"

Joe caught the clue to her apprehension. "All that matters is getting rid of him and his plot," he soothed. "Once he's out of the way, things will settle down. Then Tom can make his treaty work. That will stop Black Moon from attacking your people again."

She glanced at him in concern. "You wish to hurry this task?"

"Yes, to prevent more people from getting hurt and killed."

His answer delighted her, but it made their separation even more imminent unless something powerful intruded and helped them. She didn't know if it was right to pray for such divine intervention. Perhaps it was best to wait and see what happened during and after the sacred mission.

On Sunday, they visited with Talking Wolf and his band, who were much less showy and aggressive than Black Moon's. Joe used his same ruse, and it worked again. That chief also had met Snake-Man and believed in the villain's magic. He, too, wanted more guns, bullets, and whiskey, and to kill Lakotas. Yet Talking Wolf did not have an impending appointment with Zeke for additional illegal supplies; they didn't know how to take that information. But, unlike Black Moon, Talking Wolf was afraid to attack "the spirit who come and go in smoke." Wisely, Joe didn't entice him to do so.

They spent the night in the chief's tepee. It rained hard until dawn, a heavy deluge accompanied by awesome thunder and lightning. Yet the sturdy conical dwelling protected the inhabitants from the fierce powers of nature and barely disturbed their slumber.

Shortly after sunrise and a hot meal, the couple departed.

On Monday, they camped on the Grand River beneath a full moon with Two-Bulls. As he spoke little English, Morning Star used her skill with sign language to interpret for the men. Two-Bulls said he would accept the gifts, but he had told Snake-Man and Zeke he did not want war with the Lakotas. He explained he did not want guns, bullets, and whiskey found in his camp by the Army, their friends, but revealed he had accepted one load long ago for his warriors to use while hunting buffalo. He said he had told Zeke and the spirit man he would not take guns with which to attack and slay Lakotas and asked why they had sent Joe to him with another plea.

Joe explained how he didn't want war or trouble, and how both would come if those evil white men were not slain. He alleged he was leaving the area and not working for them anymore. That seemed to please the chief.

Two-Bulls vowed that he did not fear the spirit man and his white warriors. He related he would kill them if they caused him trouble.

Joe was thrilled, as Two-Bulls was the most influential and powerful Crow leader in the territory. He took great delight in telling the chief how to defeat and expose the villains. That news seemed to interest Two-Bulls, but he didn't say whether or not he would attempt to destroy them.

Joe was caught off guard and worried when the chief asked if he could buy Morning Star, who still called herself Little Flower. He had her sign that she was his wife and he loved her very much so he couldn't part with her.

When Morning Star translated, "You good white man to love, accept Indians. She have good man," Joe smiled and thanked him.

Through her, Joe asked why Two-Bulls didn't report Snake-Man and his mischief to the Army, as they were "friends." He was surprised and dismayed when the chief responded that he wasn't sure he could trust soldiers and the white laws completely, so he always denied knowing anything to prevent trouble. Two-Bulls didn't want the Army to think he knew the villains so they wouldn't suspect him of lying about receiving illegal goods.

Joe and the daughter of Sun Cloud were impressed by the good and wise leader. It relieved her to learn not all Bird People were bad or hated her people. Both made certain the renowned chief knew they respected and liked him, as Two-Bulls could be a big help with the peace treaty.

Tuesday morning, they rode to locate Zeke and his wagons at Bear Butte. They prayed he had panicked at their intrusion and come early with his delivery and to warn the Crow. They hoped he didn't have many men with him and they could accomplish the crucial task of destroying the weapons before they fell into the hands of the wicked Black Moon. If they rode fast and hard, they could be in position to wait and work in two days.

Joe told Morning Star that Stede and Fitzpatrick should have his and Jim's reports by now. He was eager to discover who George was, if the scout had a military reason for being in this territory, if Stede knew anything about Simon Adams, and to learn who was buying land here.

The last mention drew a question from Morning Star. She listened as Joe explained the Pre-Emption Law but did not argue its power.

To get her mind off the alarming matter, Joe asked, "How do you know your way around such a big territory? Women don't leave camp much."

Morning Star related the joint meetings at many times, places, and seasons that took her across this land. "Long ago," she added, "Bird People lived and hunted far away. Lakotas lived and hunted in these lands. When summer grows too hot, buffalo travel longer." She pointed to the cooler north. "We go after, must ride where they go to hunt. Crow come, and we must fight to hunt over the Cheyenne River. To save lives, Red Hearts come here no more if plenty of buffalo where we live. There is more ways."

"Are more ways," Joe gently corrected, then asked, "Like what?"

"Trail signs. I see, read. Marks everywhere if you know how to find and read. Black Moon, he come to same place; easy to find him. I use where Wi in sky for that season, where stars glow and how they move."

Ex-Captain Joseph Lawrence knew about using the sun, moon, and stars for charting courses, and he knew they were in different positions in the sky during each season.

Weeks ago, he had shown her his compass and explained how it worked. He had laughed and told her it was useful only when you knew which direction to follow, and it was particularly helpful on a cloudy day and moonless night. He had made notes, measurements, and drawn a map. He had told her it would be informative later about their journey for the authorities, but both knew it was also for a time when or if he had to travel alone.

When they neared the Belle Fourche River on Thursday, Joe sighted two men heading north. Using his fieldglasses to watch for approaching peril, he made out Zeke and Farley. At that distance, he knew they had not been seen. The couple hid themselves behind the nearest knoll. They rested and chatted until the villains were gone.

"Why he not take guns to Black Moon camp?" Morning Star asked.

"He's too clever and cautious. He doesn't want to get caught near an Indian camp with illegal goods. He has to go fetch them because he's six days early, and I doubt he wants to hang around here longer than need be. His little trip should give us about five days to do our task and be far away when he and those Crow return and find the damage we'll inflict. This time, we'll get some undeniable proof to unmask him and to protect us."

At over four thousand feet, Bear Butte—Mato Paha to the Lakotas—was highly visible long before they reached the sacred mountain as it rose in majestic splendor from the surrounding plains. Fortunate for the couple, treelines, ravines, and the Bear River were nearby to help with concealment and stealth.

With hopes Zeke had chosen the same spot, they left their horses near the water, at a distance where their noises couldn't be heard by the wrong ears. They discarded anything that might make sounds, and carried only knives for weapons. Morning Star took the initiative to check the wind direction to make certain their scents would not be detected by a guard's keen nose. They stepped with caution to avoid crunching twigs or anything that might create a telltale noise. They kept watch for animals and birds that could give away their approach and location if disturbed. They heard the "to whitcha, whitcha, whitcha" cry of one bird and the sound of another that reminded Joe of a gosling. They halted to let a deer move along so they wouldn't spook it. Another time, they stopped to allow a skunk to amble on during his forage for food.

Joe was wearing moccasins to aid his silence on the ground and to avoid boot tracks that would cut or break grass blades rather than bend them as the soft leather shoe did.

More acquainted with the signs of her land, Morning Star led the way. Abruptly she halted Joe once more. When he leaned close, she pointed to a bear trap someone had attempted to conceal. Joe smiled, impressed with her sharp eyes. After they came upon the third one, she warned Joe the traps were set to snare anyone coming close to Zeke's campsite. Joe realized he may have missed the deadly traps if he was alone or leading them, so he was even happier she was present and in control. As dusk was nearing, she told him they should slip into the river and spy on the area from it. She told him to remove his moccasins, as bare feet were quieter in water.

They neared a place where they could see and smell smoke from a campfire. Morning Star warned Joe about swatting at insects, about mastering control over his breathing, and about jerking his bare foot if a fish, weed, or rock made contact with him. In the fading light, Joe nodded understanding.

Suddenly, a trap sprang and a snared creature thrashed wildly to obtain freedom. Morning Star grabbed Joe's wrist and yanked him toward the bank, having already planned this strategy if trouble struck. She covered her mouth and nose with one hand to indicate for him to hold his breath. The wet beauty pushed Joe's head underwater, ducked, and pulled him beneath tangled debris. She pushed his face to the surface where there was only enough space in the bunched branches for catching air.

Joe was careful not to gulp air or to move a muscle. She did the same. They heard two men rush over and talk.

"What is it, Billy?"

"Justa muskrat or otta. We'll git him out in the morning."

"Zeke put out them traps along the bank to catch two nosey people. Think we best reset it?"

"I ain't sticking my hand in that water. He'll bite it off. Ain't nobody coming around herebouts tonight. Iffen they do, it'll be in the woods. Zeke's got traps all over. Come on, Murray, let's go take a drink and play cards."

The two men left, but the couple remained motionless for a time.

When they believed it was safe, they returned to their camp downriver.

"We can't make another move until daylight, woman," Joe said worriedly. "I don't want either of us stumbling into a trap in the dark. We've got time; it'll take Zeke five to six days to get back with the Crow. Let's get dried off and change clothes, then eat and rest. We're safe for now. The men won't come looking around in the dark with those traps everywhere. At least we know we have two guards to defeat. We want to capture witnesses and take evidence this time."

Morning Star concurred, even knowing that action would bring them closer to the end of their task—and separation from each other.

After they had changed their clothes and eaten, they lay on the same bedroll and snuggled together to sleep. The meal had been eaten cold, as they couldn't risk a campfire. Both savored the warm contact with each other, but knew this wasn't the time or place to make love.

As she lay curled in Joe's embrace, Morning Star's mind roamed for a time. The longer she was with him, the harder it was to imagine a life without him. She had watched him with Indians and whites. Each day her respect, trust, and admiration increased, and she had come to love and want him even more. Everything he had told her that night at Medicine River seemed right and possible. How could she give him up for any reason?

Joe's white world, from how he had described it, was different, much better than the one here that conflicted with the Indian's. Her grandmother and aunt had adapted to the Indian way and, with the help of Joe and his family, surely she could adjust to theirs. She had proven she was not a coward. Surely she possessed enough courage and wits to conquer his world to live at his side. Didn't she? her heart asked.

Qualms troubled her. Maybe she had been with Joe so long that she was blinded by love and desire, and was sleeping in the Dream World. Could she risk her family's love and respect by choosing a white man over them?

As soon as enough light permitted inspection of the ground for perils, they left camp. Morning Star had a knife in her sheath and a nocked bow in her hands. Joe had a rifle cocked, a knife at his waist, and two holstered pistols. They sneaked to the small clearing where the wagons were located. Two men sat near a cozy fire, eating and talking.

Joe had hoped the villains would sleep late so his attack party could get the drop on them without endangering anyone's life. This morning, he was attired in unbeaded Indian garments: moccasins, breechcloth, leggings, and vest. An unmarked leather band was around his head to keep his long blond hair from interfering with his vision. He asked God to help and protect them.

Morning Star implored her Great Spirit to do the same. And she implored herself to keep her eyes and thoughts off Joe. Her heart had raced with love and her body had burned with desire as she watched him dress earlier. He was indeed a well-honed and skilled warrior, the most tempting and irresistible one she had met.

Joe gave the signal to attack, bringing both of them to full alert. He focused on the man to the left, she on the one to the right. They stepped into the edge of the clearing. "Put up your hands and don't move, or we'll shoot!" Joe shouted.

The men, with cocked rifles at hand, seized them as they jumped up and turned to defend themselves against what they feared was certain death.

Joe wounded his target in the shoulder; Morning Star placed her arrow in almost the same place on hers. They dodged simultaneous fire, but the injured men, as hoped, didn't surrender after being spared. The hirelings yelped in pain and surprise, but drew pistols to save their lives.

"Give it up! You don't have a chance to escape!" Joe shouted.

They were the ones with no chance to survive if they didn't take the culprits' lives. The reluctant couple did what they must.

Afterward, they approached the campfire and dead men. "Damn," Joe swore under his breath. "I wanted a witness. To protect our cover with Jim, we could have taken him to Fort Laramie."

"They fear capture more than dying," she remarked.

He exhaled audibly, then suggested, "Let's get our work done and get out of here. We can't do anything for them."

Joe collected weapons and ammunition as gifts to Sun Cloud for hunting. He yanked off a board with *PRATTE AND COMPANY* stamped on it. "Here's proof this load either came from or through Simon Adams. One way or another, this will help trace it. When Zeke and the Crow find this mess, all they'll see are moccasin tracks. Hopefully that'll confuse them for a while."

"I have Crow possessions in pack. We put some here to fool them?"

"That won't work, love. If Crow attacked, they'd take the supplies, not destroy them as we're going to do."

"But we take some," she reminded, "many as small band can carry. They will think others destroyed so Lakotas and Army not find and take."

"You're right. As usual," he amended with a broad grin. "It's worth trying. I'll start here while you fetch them. Be careful of those traps."

* * *

By early afternoon, Joe and Morning Star had used hatchet butts to ruin the rifles. With broken or bent hammers, breechloading covers, or crushed barrels, the weapons were useless. Gunpowder was spread over a wide area and kicked into dirt and grass; it was too perilous to fish and animals to dump it into the water. It was also too hazardous to set aflame and risk igniting the forest and prairie with an explosive blaze. The whiskey was poured out for the earth to drink. Identifying boards for company and contents were taken from the ammunition and whiskey barrels. Everything possible was completed, including the false clues.

At twilight, Morning Star and Joe made camp miles away from the site of their daring ploy. After the horses were tended and they had eaten a hot meal, they settled down to talk before bedtime.

"I can't figure why Simon would incriminate himself by not removing the marked boards before giving Zeke those shipments," Joe wondered aloud. "I keep thinking that he might be Snake-Man or that he's working for him. Then I get a gut feeling that says he isn't involved."

"He is a bad man, but I do not think he is the man we seek."

Joe glanced at her and smiled, noticing how good her English was these days. "I'm proud of you, Morning Star; your parents and band will be, too. I couldn't have done all I have without your help and friendship. I hate putting you in danger, but you've proven over and over how much I need you with me."

Her expression revealed her joy at those words. "Thank you."

Just looking at her aroused Joe, but he knew they were both too tired to enjoy lovemaking to the fullest. He didn't want a fast joining only to release his pent-up tension. It was best to wait until tomorrow night when they were rested and farther away from Zeke's camp. "I think I'll shave. I don't need this beard any more, and it scratches like wool on a summer day."

Morning Star observed as Joe heated water in a shallow basin and placed soap nearby. She watched him sit near the fire with a mirror resting on his knees and a sharp razor in his grasp. "I will help," she offered, knowing the job would be difficult at night. "I cut shorter first," she suggested, then used the scissors he gave to her. When she finished, she held the mirror up for him to take over the chore.

Cognizant of her tender gaze witnessing his every expression and stroke, Joe felt lucky not to have cut himself.

"Shaving is like small Sun Dance," Morning Star remarked. "All a man owns is his body to offer pieces to the Great Spirit. You grow and cut off hair for sacred mission; that is part of Joe's body. Great Spirit is happy." She didn't include that a clear face made his appearance seem more Indian. He was shirtless, and she looked at the scar on his arm where Zeke's bullet had passed through it when he rescued her. Yes, that night had been destined between them.

Morning Star prayed there was also a bright future destined for them. She hated to think of their imminent separation. She had agreed to part with Joe for a short time for three reasons: first, two tasks needed tending before they could journey again together, and she wanted to accomplish them soon. Second, she wanted to see her parents and friends. Third, she wanted to have her "woman's flow" in the privacy of her tepee. She had completed one just before her capture by

Zeke, another just before reaching Orin McMichael's, and the next was due in three or four suns. She thought she had been able to conceal her female condition from Joe last time, but a man reared around a sister knew about such things. When he had purchased supplies at Lookout, he had bought her a length of white cloth and only said, "This is for you when you need it." His expression had made his meaning clear.

Joe finished and put away his things. "Better?" he hinted.

"It is bad to hide face like yours" was her merry response. She wanted to caress the hairless surface, but something halted her. She suddenly realized what it was, that the skin was white against the rest of a face that had been darkly tanned by the prairie sun. It was as if the recently concealed flesh beside the dark flesh pointed out the differences in them.

"Something wrong?" he queried her altered expression.

"No, just tired," she had to reply.

Joe didn't question her. "Me, too. Let's get to sleep."

After a steady ride, they halted on Elk Creek. They tended their chores and ate, then bathed in the refreshing water.

While Joe made more notes and marked his map, Morning Star did some serious thinking. Tomorrow they would separate, and she dreaded not being with him. She was so confused and tormented, and she feared that visiting her people would increase her dilemma. She knew what she wanted, but deciding to take that path would cost her much. Yet, by nightfall on the next sun or at any time, either or both of them could be dead, out of the other's reach forever. Life was often short and dangerous. It should not be spent in misery. Was there a way for them to remain together after this sacred task? Could she convince the Great Spirit, her parents, and her people that she belonged with Sky Warrior? And if she did, what would it be like for her, for them, in Joe's world?

Surely there are many whites like Joe, she reasoned—Alisha Williams, Rebecca Kenny and her parents, Bonnie Thorne, wife of the past Cheyenne chief Windrider—Stede and Tanner Gaston, and the friends her ancestors and band had made in the past. As with the other women from her bloodline, to have her man surely she could adjust to another type of life. There must be so many wonders she didn't know about, added to the ones her lover had related during their long journey. There were so many things to experience with him. More, she admitted, than she could do here where her life was simple and often hard, where death stalked with each new and closer encroachment by whites or raids by Crow. To live in a place surrounded by safety sounded wonderful. Could she—dare she—choose Joe and his world over hers?

The sunny-haired man wrapped his arms around the beauty with such a serious expression on her face. "Stop worrying, woman; I'm not going to chase you down and carry you off like I teased. I'll let you make your decision about us when you're ready. I realize how hard it is for you, and a future for us might indeed not be possible. From now on, we live and love day to day. We'll expect nothing more than that from each other. Agreed?"

Morning Star tensed in Joe's embrace and wished she could see the expression in his eyes. He had been so loving and tender, so compassionate and understanding of her feelings. She prayed her last rejection had not stung him so deeply that he had lost hope for them, had changed his mind about pursuing her. Perhaps she should discuss the matter with him this moment. Yet she did not want to give him false hopes they could overcome all the obstacles between them. He could be wrong about his family and friends. His father had not wanted him to come here. They might not be happy about him taking an Indian as wife.

Joe knew, as well as she, there were good and bad whites and good and bad Indians. Surely he understood her trapped position by now. Surely he had been telling her so much about his world and teaching her so many things to persuade her she could fit in there. Every day he whet her appetite for what was beyond her territory—that had to be an intentional ploy. She had witnessed how quickly and easily the Dakotas accepted and believed Joe. His arguments held much truth not long ago. Once this great mission succeeded and he was honored by her people, the Red Hearts couldn't think too badly of her for wanting to remain with the glorious Sky Warrior. Surely they would realize the Great Spirit had put them together and wanted them to remain together. Joe had worked for peace in her world; perhaps she was destined to work for peace and understanding in his.

Morning Star asked herself how Sun Cloud could say it was wrong to marry a white-eye when his father and brother had done so and had been very happy with their choice of mates. She wondered if her people could resist this union when the Red Hearts knew what Alisha/Shalee and Rebecca/Wahea had done for their band. When peace was within their grasps, how could anyone call Joe an enemy? How could her family and people not want her to return for visits to relate all she learned about the whites? Even if she left in banishment and dishonor, how long could it last? Surely time would bring understanding and forgiveness.

For all her dreamy hopes and desperate prayers, Morning Star knew it would not be that easy to leave with Joe or to enter his world. It troubled her that he was having doubts, was retreating from her. No, she decided, it was a clever and necessary move for their safety and peace of mind.

She turned and gazed into his eyes. "My choice is made, Joe. I—"

"You don't have to explain," he interrupted in a sad tone.

She realized he anticipated the worst from her strange mood. She smiled, caressed his cheek, and said, "I love you. If possible, we will find a way to be together when our task is done."

Joe stared into her softened gaze. He was afraid to trust what he was hearing. "Are you saying . . . Do you mean . . ."

Morning Star grinned, then laughed. "I will marry you after our mission is completed."

"You aren't teasing me? You aren't saying this to clear my head?"

She realized that her own was as clear as it could ever be. No matter what anybody said or did, they were destined to live as one. "It will not be simple," she said slowly, trying her best to speak correct English, to show him how much she had learned about fitting into his world. She related to him all she had been thinking and feeling. "I love you," she finally concluded.

Joe scooped her up and swung her around, laughing with joy as he did so. "You just made me the happiest man alive. I promise, Morning Star, I'll make you happy and I'll protect you from any harm."

She believed him, but cautioned, "We must say nothing to others before our sacred task is done. It will be hard to win acceptance of our joining . . . and my leaving."

Enchanted by her, Joe suggested, "Would it be best to start dropping hints about our feelings when we visit your family?"

She shook her head. "You forget you are Tanner Gaston, of our bloodline. To reveal the lie now will bring much harm to us and our task."

"You're right," he conceded. As he held her in his arms, he confessed, "The hardest thing I've ever done will be to pretend our love and bond don't exist when we're in your camp."

"If we reveal it," she warned, "how can Father, Mother, and others believe any words we speak after lies and tricks are exposed?"

"You're one of the smartest women I've known. No, *the* smartest. And the bravest," he added with a wide smile.

"Some will cause trouble for us," she alluded.

"Knife-Slayer. Does Knife-Slayer mean anything special to you?"

Morning Star traced his lips with her finger. "You are the only man I have loved. He desires me and chases me. I do not like him or trust him. But he will battle us with all his skills. So will Night Stalker. I do not know what Mother and Father will . . ."

Joe tightened his embrace a moment. "We'll find a way to make everyone understand and agree. After our victory and the new treaty, they'll see why I had to trick them. They can't deny I'm Sky Warrior. I look and behave like the man in Payaba's vision; it's sacred. It's meant to be."

She smiled. "I pray you are right. We must not fail in our mission. If we do, my people will say it is punishment for our deceit, and they will not allow me to leave with you." *Even if I must die to be halted or punished . . .*

"We won't fail, love; I swear it."

Morning Star decided there was no better time than *anpetu tonpi*, her birthday, to make her choice and to receive the gift of a future with Joe.

The happy white man and nineteen-year-old beauty sank to his bedroll and made passionate love before sleeping entwined in each other's arms.

Joe watched Morning Star head south while he continued east. He was glad she was going home for a visit. He knew she could make the half-day trip alone. He hated being apart from her, but he felt he would be safe stopping near the fort to retrieve the messages from Stede, Fitzpatrick, and Jim. If anything went wrong, he could always expose his identity as a government agent. As soon as he had answers from them about troubling questions, he would head for Sun Cloud's camp and his love. He wanted this mission completed so he could marry the woman of his heart.

Morning Star followed the trail signs to her people's second location of this nomadic season and rode into the Red Heart camp. It didn't take her long to make several shocking discoveries. She was relieved Joe wasn't with her or he might be slain before she could reveal the good news and clear up one particular and dangerous mistake.

Chapter Fifteen

orning Star gaped at her best friend, who had left her tasks and rushed to meet her. Her dark-brown eyes were wide and her mouth agape as she took in the thirty-six-year-old woman's shocking words.

As if she hadn't heard them, Buckskin Girl repeated, "He has come, the true vision warrior. Did Tanner learn this news and flee for his life?"

Confused, Morning Star replied, "Tanner has gone to the fort to speak with the soldier who helps us. I returned to tell Father and the council all we have learned and done. *He* is the true Sky Warrior. I do not understand your strange words."

With glowing eyes, Buckskin Girl caught her breath and explained, "Sky Warrior returned two suns' past to help us defeat the evil whites. Sky Warrior, Notaxe tse-amo-estse, son of Windrider and his white mate, Bonnie Thorne. I can tell you all that lives in my heart now, Morning Star. When you won the contest, I feared I was wrong. I was not. Tanner Gaston is not the Sky Warrior in Payaba's vision. The son of Windrider is. All forgot about him, for he has been gone sixteen winters. He was driven from his band by dishonor and anguish. He was stripped of his chief's bonnet by evil. He—"

"Soul-of-Thunder followed Windrider as chief, not his half-blooded brother; Morning Star interrupted. "Your mind is confused. I will seek Payaba to tend you." Before she could leave, the woman's grasp halted her.

"No, you must hear my words. Sky Warrior was war chief. The sacred vision did not say what chief's bonnet was lost. He has been in the white world. He is half white and half Cheyenne. His grandmother was Oglala, Red Heart. He is of our band." She stressed the connection. "I do not doubt Stede Gaston is the first vision man, but my love is the second. His looks and Life Circle match the vision words. I believed the Great Spirit would call him home to find his true destiny. He has done so. I tried to warn you Tanner is not the vision warrior," she reminded. "There is another bond to our band, to Gray Eagle's bloodline: his brother, the chief, is mate to Bright Arrow's daughter, Tashina."

All of this was news to Morning Star, but it didn't change what she and Joe had done and must continue doing. But now she knew what had driven her friend. "Such things do not make him the Sky Warrior in the sacred vision."

"Do not be blind, my friend," Buckskin Girl urged.

The kind-hearted daughter of Sun Cloud did not toss those words back into the woman's face. Suddenly she thought of how her brother and Knife-Slayer might try to use this unexpected event to cause trouble for her and Joe. To learn everything about the past episode, she entreated, "Tell me why he was banished."

The daughter of Flaming Star assumed her friend accepted her words, so she complied with eagerness. "Sky Warrior's mate and children were slain during a Shoshone raid. Before his heart was healed, he sought another mate. He chose the shaman's daughter, a beautiful girl. But she was evil. She let no one see her entice him. She sneaked into the forest and lay upon his sleeping mat many times. She desired him as a man, but did not want a half-breed as a mate. She did not want her children stained by his blood." Buckskin Girl's eyes filled with anger and hatred.

"He did not know she tricked him, as his mind was clouded with pain. When a warrior lay claim to her, Sky Warrior saw another woman being taken away, so he challenged for her and fought to the death of the other man. The slain warrior was a Dog Man, the highest-ranking sash wearer. Many were troubled by his death over a woman. She refused to join him. She lied to her father and people."

Buckskin Girl's tone became colder as she related the tale. "She told them Sky Warrior wanted her so much he threatened her and her family if she did not join him. Her father, the shaman, was fooled and he spoke for her. He spoke against Sky Warrior, the half-breed. He claimed his daughter had not shared a blanket with my love or listened to his flute music. He demanded my love be banished. The tribe was aroused against him. The words of Windrider, Bonnie, and Soul-of-Thunder were not heard above the shouts to dishonor him. Shamed and hurt, he left the Cheyenne camp and he entered our camp to stay with us, his grandmother's people. Many offered him a place in their tepee. I came to love him and desire him, but he feared such feelings because he was in great pain. He went into his mother's white world to learn if that was his destiny."

Morning Star was touched by the tragic story and listened to more.

"I have longed for his return. I love him. That is why I have not joined another. I believed the Great Spirit would answer my prayers, and He has. When Sky Warrior came to us sixteen winters past, no one thought of the vision of four winters before it. There was no war, and he was not returning after a long absence, as he is this season. His hair is the color of the sun and moon, and his eyes match the blue in the sky. My heart was knifed when I challenged you in the contest, but I wished to ride with Sky Warrior. I believed he would come soon to take Tanner's place. I do not care if his blood is mixed. I love him and want to join to him. I loved him long before I even knew of those feelings. Our fathers were best friends. You were three winters old when he rode away, so you did not remember him. Tanner's coming was strange. I feared I was mistaken; I had waited for nothing. Something in my heart and mind said that was untrue. Do you understand now why I challenged you and why Tanner is not the true Sky Warrior? Others believe my love is the vision warrior. They wait for Tanner to return to be challenged on his claim."

"Only those who wish to cause trouble, my friend," Morning Star contended. "Open your heart to the truth: I am riding with the true Sky Warrior."

"Here comes your father and mother returning from the hunt. My love is with them. He rides next to Knife-Slayer."

There was no need for Buckskin Girl to point out the handsome half-breed in the party. Morning Star eyed him with intrigue and dismay: his appearance did match the vision words! She prayed the son of Windrider would not become trouble for her and Joe, but she feared he would, especially if he believed he was Sky Warrior more than in Cheyenne name.

Knife-Slayer leapt off his pinto and hurried to the woman he desired. "Where is Tanner?" he asked, glancing about for his rival.

Eyes on her parents, she replied, "He has gone to the fort to share our news. He will return soon for me. We ride again in a few suns."

"No! It cannot be. He lies. Stede Gaston and the son of Windrider are the vision men. Only one true medicine warrior; Tanner is false! He heard of Sky Warrior's return and is gone to betray us."

She protested the accusation, "Your words are foolish! You speak as a man who knows and feels nothing. You seek to cause trouble again."

"Silence!" Sun Cloud ordered as he joined them. "You fight as children," the chief scolded. "Morning Star, a woman does not speak to a man and warrior this way."

Before he could be reprimanded in public, Knife-Slayer charged, "It is the evil white man's doing. He teaches her to behave as a woman of his kind. He steals her heart from us and her eyes from me. He is bad."

Morning Star was angered. "He steals nothing! He—"

"Silence! We will hear my daughter's words when the council meets after we rest and eat. Say no more harsh words," Sun Cloud told both.

Singing Wind had joined them. She embraced her child and whispered, "Hold your words until we are in our tepee."

Morning Star nodded. She saw Knife-Slayer, who was wearing his *wanapin*, join his father. She noticed how Buckskin Girl edged her way to the stranger's side. Before she followed her parents home, Morning Star quickly studied the newcomer. He was almost as tall as Joe, but was many winters older: forty-six, Buckskin Girl had told her. His skin was the same color as her own. The hard and toned muscles of his body were as defined as those on a skinned deer. His bare chest exposed Sun Dance scars, marks attesting to his great prowess. Another scar ran along his left jawline; as if following her line of vision, the man stroked it. His stormy blue eyes had not left her face since dismounting. A breeze swept through his hair and lifted strands of moonglow and sunlight. Notaxe tse-amo-estse was a man, a warrior, to steal a woman's eye and heart—as he had done with her friend.

"Do not worry over him," Singing Wind whispered. "Come."

Sun Cloud walked with his wife and child past the meat-laden travois that would be unloaded and cured tomorrow. Covered by hides to protect the hunks from insects and spoilage, they would be fine tonight. He was anxious to hear of his daughter's adventures and to prevent dissension.

Inside the dwelling, Morning Star pointed to the rifles and ammunition. "They are gifts to you and Night Stalker from Tanner. We defeated men hauling them to the Bird People. We destroyed all others."

As the chief lifted one to study it, Singing Wind said, "Our fear was great for your safety. It is good to see you home."

"It is good to be home, Mother, but we must leave when he returns. Father, do you wish me to speak all things to you, or wait until council?"

"There is no need to weary you with speaking two times."

* * *

The council began with Knife-Slayer charging that "Tanner" was not the vision man, that Notaxe tse-amo-estse must replace him in the mission.

Morning Star had been given time to think and plan during the meal and rest period. Having been given permission to speak freely, she pointed out that "the sacred vision said *two* men, different men. It did not say the vision warrior with Oglala blood *lost* his chief's bonnet or *returned*. It said he was *denied* his rank, land, and people. The man with sky eyes, white blood, and sun hair is not the same as the man with Oglala blood who was *denied* such things. It cannot be Windrider's son."

Hawk Eyes, shaman and father of Knife-Slayer suggested, "It may be only one vision man. Two may be a symbol: the man before leaving and the man after returning. Payaba saw no faces. All words match Notaxe tse-amo-estse. He was a great warrior, a cunning chief, and will be so again."

"No, it is two men," Payaba refuted, "not the same man."

Wind Bird, who was training under the old shaman, ventured, "What if there are two Sky Warriors? What if the Great Spirit called the son of Windrider home to help him with the sacred mission?"

"The vision did not show three men," Hawk Eyes argued.

Morning Star leapt on his words. "If two can be a symbol for one warrior as you believe and reasoned, Hawk Eyes," she contended, "why do you say one cannot be a symbol for two? Is it not strange two men come who match the vision? I say one does not come to prove the other false. I say let both work to help us. We must halt the trouble before buffalo season ends and the Bird People raid with guns from the evil white man. We have traveled far and much and our faces are known to enemies and those we doubt. His is not. He can do tasks at white posts we cannot enter. He was sent to join us, not to take Tanner's place. The vision said our helper would have hair that blazes like the sun. Tanner's hair is of the sun, but Sky Warrior's has the light of the sun *and* moon. Tanner's eyes are as blue and calm as the day he came to us; Sky Warrior's are dark as a sky before a storm. We have ridden the vision trail. How can you say what we have done was not meant to be? Many bad things would be past if Sky Warrior came this late to help us."

"Tell us what *great* things he has done" came Knife-Slayer's words in a sarcastic tone.

Morning Star used patience and self-control as she related their adventures for the past thirty-two suns. She observed the men as she talked, to interpret their feelings and reactions to her news. As was their way, none interrupted. She noted worried looks when she exposed the incriminating Red Heart arrows at the massacre of Crow hunters. Smiles and nods greeted news of their tracking of the attackers, their slayings, and the return of sacred possessions to the burial ground. Dismay was obvious when she told them of the Crow false clues left there and suggested the evil whites were provoking the tribes against each other. More smiles and nods came her way when she spoke of the fur-trapper ruse. She saw the men listen intently to information about Orin McMichael, the strange scout, Simon Adams, and Harvey Meade. She explained about the murder charge against "Tanner" and their visit to the fort to see Captain James Thomas. She told them how much they trusted this white soldier and how eager he was for peace with them.

Morning Star watched Knife-Slayer almost jump up to argue, but his father's hand stayed the scowling warrior. She revealed how Zeke and George had arrived as they were leaving and explained that matter. She related their pleasant visits with Red Cloud and Spotted Tail and saw her pursuer's scowl deepen and his eyes chill to hear of how her love was accepted by those two respected chiefs. Knife-Slayer's envy, anger, and doubts increased as she spoke of their daring visits to three Crow camps as a trader, hireling of Snake-Man, and Arapaho squaw. When she asserted that Chief Two-Bulls was a good man who wanted peace, the tense warrior could not contain his fury.

"He was sly and tricked you! We cannot have peace with Bird People! He trails you this sun to attack our camp to slay all Red Hearts."

"If so, he and his warriors would be here by now. There has been time for such a dark deed, Knife-Slayer, but it has not and will not come to pass." She saw Hawk Eyes prevent another outburst from his son.

Morning Star continued her revelations with a detailed description of the destruction of the wagons with guns, ammunition, and whiskey.

Once more, Knife-Slayer interrupted. "Why did you destroy the supplies? We need them to protect our lives and camp."

Her patience was tried and strained, but she replied calmly. "I brought some to Father and Night Stalker and others, but it was all I could carry. We could not steal the wagons and reach camp before the evil ones caught up and slayed us; heavy wagons travel slow and leave a big track. We destroyed them so Black Moon's band could not use them against us."

"It was a brave and wise decision," Sun Cloud remarked. He hoped his words would quiet the intrusive and belligerent warrior before he was compelled to scold him in front of the council. He was relieved when others concurred and Knife-Slayer silenced himself.

"Tanner goes to the fort to speak with our helper there. He carries proof of where the crates came from. He tells the soldier of the treachery of Black Moon and Talking Wolf. He goes to retrieve a message from Stede Gaston who gathered answers elsewhere for us. He will return in nine suns to ride the trail again. There is other trouble," she alluded and withdrew the *wanapin* charm and headband from a parfleche. She told them about the payroll theft, massacre, and clues found.

"It is not mine!" Knife-Slayer shouted.

Morning Star smiled knowingly, "That is true," she replied. "We told the soldier these are not Red Heart possessions; he believes what we tell him. But things like these and the false attacks on Crow and whites point to our band. We told the soldier how possessions are stolen from burial grounds and slain warriors, or made by others like these I hold. We do not know who leads the bad whites, but we are tracking him. We defeat many of their evil deeds. We have the Crow doubting them. We have the Army alert and suspicious."

Proud and impressed, Sun Cloud asked, "What do you do now?"

"We will see what the messages say and what the soldier has learned since our visit there. That will tell us what trail to take."

"The Crow do not raid yet. All are busy hunting for winter food. When it is done, they will come with guns from the men you track to defeat."

"The soldier will warn them and prevent war. Soon we will have the proof needed to bring Stede and the agent here to make treaty."

Sun Cloud looked forward to the visit of Powchutu's son and said so.

"Knife-Slayer," Morning Star asked, "will you tell me what you saw when you spied on the one called Snake-Man? Did you see his hair and hands? Was his voice strange from other whites?"

The warrior liked the way she spoke to him this time. He smiled as he responded, "He is tall like Tanner. Hair is like night. I could not see his hands and eyes. His voice was the same as other whites. Why do you ask?"

"A man we suspect has a strange voice, but his hair blazes as a fire. It cannot be Orin McMichael. Another we suspect has black hair, is tall, and has a mark on his hand the color of a buffalo hide. He is Simon Adams. He works and lives in the post called Pratte's at Pierre. Many clues point to him, but something tells us he is not Snake-Man. The one called Harvey Meade is at Lookout; he gave us no reason to doubt him. The soldier has our trust, but there could be another in the fort we have not seen."

"You have worked hard and done much, Daughter."

"Thank you, Father. Is there more you wish to hear?" she inquired, glancing around the many faces who nodded agreement with Sun Cloud.

As no one had more questions at that moment, the council ended.

"The journey has been long," Morning Star told her father. "I will bathe and rest. Tomorrow I will help the women with their chores."

Buckskin Girl joined her at a stream near camp. It was almost dark with the moon waning to half, so they had to hurry their task and talk.

As she washed away trail dust and perspiration from her body, Morning Star coaxed, "Tell me more about your love."

Flaming Star had related news of the council meeting to his daughter, so she said first, "They did not vote who was Sky Warrior in the vision. Father says both men could be the vision helper; that would be good."

Morning Star smiled and agreed, glad her friend was happy.

"My heart is filled with joy at his return. He has not found another mate. His looks say his past feelings for me still live. I let him see I love him and want him. I do not care about his bloodline and white looks. If I must be dishonored and banished to join a half-breed, I do not care. Great love is rare. Some Life-Circles are small. I must win him this time."

"I hope he loves and wants you, too, my friend. It is smart to show your feelings. Men cannot read women's heads and hearts as they read tracks. I do not believe his bloodline matters. It is the man who matters. You would not be shamed and sent away for joining to your true love. I will pray for Grandfather to help you win him."

"I must hurry before he returns to his tribe."

"Why that, when he was dishonored and banished?"

"The shaman's daughter bore his son. She killed it, for he favored his father. She became ill. Her head burned with fever; she revealed many things. Before she died, the truth was learned: my love was innocent. But he was gone and did not know they wanted his return. I have told him that news from Tashina, but he is not ready to return home. He wishes to help us because we did not scorn and reject him. We did not think him guilty. He wants to be a great warrior again, to ride home in honor and victory. He must be a part of the vision-quest to do this."

"What does he say and think of the vision? Of you?"

"He says he will help with the task, but he is not the vision warrior," the older woman admitted. "I do not know how he feels for me."

* * *

Before Morning Star could begin her chores with the other women, the stranger approached her near her father's tepee. She watched his self-assured gait and looked straight into his secretive eyes. He was attired as an Indian, with a leather band around his sunny head of shoulder-grazing hair. His features were strong, his hairless chest broad, and his abdomen flat.

"I figured we should get something settled up front, Morning Star. I know about the vision, the contest, and your work with Tanner Gaston. I told them I wasn't the man in Payaba's words, but I do want to help you two. I think I can; and you do, too. Let me explain why I'm here."

Morning Star didn't halt him as she listened to him.

"I've been all over the place since I left here years ago. I already knew English from my mother, so it wasn't hard fitting in with my white looks. Stop me if I talk too fast or say something you don't understand. Buckskin Girl told me you speak English." After she nodded, he went on. "I use the name Clay Thorne, after my mother. My last job was in St. Louis, loading and unloading boats. I kept hearing bad tales of what was happening here and what was expected to happen soon. I saw Red Heart and other Lakota possessions sold as souvenirs. I realized crates were bringing too many guns and too much ammunition to these parts. I knew the charges I was hearing about had to be wrong. When one trapper joked that the Army was going to 'whip Sun Cloud and his redskins all over the place,' I knew I had to come help."

Morning Star watched the play of emotions in those secretive eyes. His tone and conduct were under his control, a result of his Indian upbringing and years of practice in the white world. He was strong and healthy, hard and sleek. He had a habit of stroking the scar on his jawline every so often, as if reminding himself it was there and why.

Aware of her gaze, Thorne/Sky Warrior disclosed, "Got it in that fight before I was banished. He was going for my throat, but I wasn't ready to die."

"I am sorry you knew such pain for many years. Buckskin Girl told me your story; I had not heard it before. You are welcome here always."

"You speak excellent English," he noted with undisguised surprise. To win her confidence, he sent her a lopsided grin and softened his gaze.

Morning Star was intentionally careful with her speech. She grinned before explaining, "My parents taught me. Tanner taught me more on the trail. We practice much. I teach him skills and things I know. It is a good trade. Where do the crates of weapons come from? Who sends them?"

He shrugged powerful shoulders as he replied, "I don't know. They ship to Lookout, Pratte's, and McMichael's in this area. A few go farther upriver, but not enough to draw suspicion. I do know the man's name on the slip to pick up the suspicious crates is always Zeke Randall. From what Buckskin Girl told me, you've already had run-ins with him."

Morning Star went over those episodes quickly. She liked this man and felt he could be trusted. "You are much like your father and brother," she observed. "They are good men, great warriors."

Clay thumbed his scar. "You're right. I've missed them."

"Will you go home after you help us with the mission?"

"At least for a long visit, probably stay the winter. After that, I don't know.

I'll have to see how much I've changed, and them, too. It was a bad time for everyone before I left home. When you've been done wrong by your own people, sometimes it's hard to switch from resentment to forgiveness and understanding," he confessed with a wry smile. "I didn't know what happened in my camp after I left until Buckskin Girl told me. That was sixteen years ago to them, but only a few days for me to deal with it."

"Buckskin Girl will be happy if you live with your grandmother's band."

The blue-eyed blond looked uneasy with that subject. Obviously, Morning Star deduced, he was one of those men who had trouble expressing feelings, or had trouble trusting women. She was glad it was not that way between her and Joe.

Finally, Clay replied, "She's a fine woman. We were close before I left. I guess I'll have to wait and see what changes there are in that area, too."

"I will not speak of it again." She changed the topic back to the vision. "Tanner will return in nine suns. He will like you; you will like him. We will speak and make plans for your help." Morning Star realized that meant she would no longer be alone with Joe, and prayed that coupled with Clay's arrival were not signs from the great Spirit about their forbidden relationship. Yet she grasped that she could learn more about white existence from this half-Indian who had spent sixteen years among Joe's kind. With Clay's help, they could finish this task sooner, then work on their personal challenge.

Morning Star had to get to her chores. "We will talk more later," she said. "I want to hear about your life in the white world."

"We'll have plenty of talking time on the trail."

"Do you wish to be called by your white or Cheyenne name?"

"Here, by my Indian name. Out there, by my white name."

"On the trail I am called Little Flower, Arapaho squaw."

"That's smart. The Crow would die to get their hands on Morning Star, daughter of Sun Cloud. Tanner's protected you well so far."

"He is a good man. I must go."

As she worked, Morning Star knew she could not expose her true feelings for Joe or drop any hints he was not Tanner Gaston. That shocking discovery would give Knife-Slayer and others the right to challenge her love as Sky Warrior. They would say it proved the Cheyenne warrior was the vision man. She prayed Joe would return fast so they could depart soon.

She watched Clay leave to join the hunters miles beyond and above camp on the prairie land. The tepees were situated in a safe canyon with no fear of frightened buffalo racing headlong over people and dwellings. Most whites thought the area wild and forbidding, but it was beautiful to her. It was a location of oddly shaped and colored rocks, ridges, ravines, spires, buttes, gorges, lush grass, and streams.

As Morning Star scraped a hide to remove fat and bits of flesh, she recalled past hunts she had witnessed and worked. Brave and skilled men rode around and into a large herd and shot the number that could be handled that day. Women in the small group skinned and gutted the animals where they fell and loaded meat onto a travois. After the needed number was brought down, the men traveled back and forth to the site as they hauled their kill to camp to be divided and prepared by all families. Beneath the hot summer sun it was a long, hard, and bloody task. Exhausted workers returned near dusk, to be replaced the next day.

In camp, countless wooden meat racks held strips while they dried beneath the sun: *pa-pa* to the Oglalas, and jerky to the whites. Some meat was packed in parfleches, to be eaten as was. Other portions were pounded almost to a powder, mixed with berries and hot fat and sometimes nuts, allowed to cool, then formed into rolls of *wakapanpi*: pemmican. The rolls did not spoil for years, and they could be transported easily.

Other women labored on preparing hides, as Morning Star and her mother did today. Once they were free of all unwanted specks, they were stretched on a frame to dry. Their final use determined the remaining treatment. Some would remain furry, while others would be stripped of all hair. The ones Morning Star and Singing Wind prepared were for warm winter robes.

When the seasonal hunt was completed, tribes met for a great feast and to observe the Sun Dance before heading for their winter camps in the sheltered valleys, canyons, and meadows of the Black Hills. Morning Star wondered if this would be her last buffalo hunt and Sun Dance.

As they worked in silence, Singing Wind wondered almost the same. Though her daughter had said nothing alarming about Tanner, she suspected the girl's feelings. At least, the worried mother concluded, her daughter was being virtuous, as her woman's flow revealed this morning. For that much, the wife of Sun Cloud was grateful, as she recalled how hot and dangerous desires could burn for the man you loved and wanted.

When the women took a break to eat and chat, Morning Star showed them the kaleidoscope Joe had given to her. The gift passed from one eager hand to the other for the tube to be turned and enjoyed.

While she strolled about camp to loosen her back and neck muscles, Morning Star visited Waterlily. The young woman felt the older one was too good and kind to be the wife and mother of two men as awful as Hawk Eyes and Knife-Slayer. She noticed what the woman was working on and questioned, "Where did you get this hide?"

Waterlily looked up. "Knife-Slayer and Night Stalker found a herd of spotted buffaloes. They brought one to me. They wished me to see how it cures and the meat tastes. If it is good, they will slaughter the others."

Morning Star was alarmed. "They are white man's cattle. We will be accused of stealing them. Kill no more, Waterlily. They must be returned."

The woman was upset by those remarks, but she nodded in compliance.

Morning Star knew she must discuss this discovery with her father. How, she scoffed, could a herd of steers get lost from its paleface owner? Doubts about the two men shot through her panicked mind. If they could steal cattle, could they steal an Army payroll and massacre soldiers? Could they be doing other things without her father and the council's knowing? If so, they could bring down the Army's and white man's wrath.

The July days in camp seemed hotter and longer for Morning Star. She busied herself with preserving meat, scraping hides, gathering buffalo chips and scrubwood for the fire, cooking, sewing garments, and washing clothes in the stream. She missed Joe and worried over his safety. The markers were out for him to find his way along the White River to their second seasonal camp. She was eager to share news of the events here. Her brother and his untrustworthy friend had sworn to the chief and council they had found the herd on the Plains, but the cattle had not been returned yet. She fretted over the steers being found in the Red Heart camp, but she had said and done all she could to warn them.

The time she spent with Clay Thorne was enjoyable and enlightening. He had revealed many exciting things about his years far away, and she related details of the sacred mission and recent council meeting. If he suspected the reason behind her many questions, he said nothing. She was happy to see him taking up time with a glowing Buckskin Girl who had blossomed like a spring flower under his gaze and attention. She also noticed the longer Clay stayed, the more he relaxed. But as with her, he was waiting for Joe's arrival and the continuation of the great task.

Soon, Joe would return and their search for peace would resume. If all was fine, he had reached the message tree and retrieved helpful clues. Surely he was on his way back to her this very sun. Also by now, Zeke and the Crow had found their destruction. She wondered, though she had used all her skills and knowledge to conceal their tracks, could those villains be heading for her people's camp, and some be trailing Joe? Her love was to leave a note telling Jim where he had hidden the gun/board evidence nearby. She must not doubt that proof would aid their cause. She prayed for his protection and a painless solution to their personal predicament.

On the afternoon Clay calculated the white man's return, he suggested to Morning Star that they ride to intercept Joe to chat privately. As her chores were done, she eagerly accepted. A few miles away, they halted to wait for him. They would remain there until dusk left only enough light for returning to camp.

When "Tanner Gaston" was sighted, Clay said, "I'll wait here. You ride to meet him. You'd probably want to speak with him alone first."

"Does it show?" she asked, dismayed.

"You hid it well, but I know the truth now," he responded.

To win his confidence, she said, "You are of two bloods and worlds. You understand why I must say nothing to others until the task is done."

"I understand, but waiting won't make any difference. If you were of my tribe or not of the chief's bloodline, it wouldn't matter. It will, Morning Star. Be ready to face dishonor and banishment. It's your law."

"It is not fair or right, Clay. I did not choose to love him."

In a bitter tone, he murmured, "Not much in life is fair or easy."

"You will not speak to others?" She pressed for secrecy.

"No, it isn't my place. Just be careful how you act around him."

Morning Star rode to meet Joe, who was watching her with a quizzical gaze. She smiled, allowing her eyes to roam him.

"Who is that?" he asked, nodding toward the lingering male.

"Much has happened. We must talk fast." She dismounted and Joe followed her lead, but glanced at the stranger once more. When she asked him to report first, he obliged. "I didn't see Jim, but I left him a report and that evidence we gathered. He'll know that Black Moon and Talking Wolf are getting illegal supplies from Zeke. I told him what you said about those clues found at the payroll massacre not being Red Heart. I left him answers to his questions, and sent another letter home to my family. Jim said Harvey Meade has been acting strangely, but he doesn't thinks he's involved in this mess. I don't, either."

He took a breath. "George visited him and claimed he was following a marauding band of renegades into this area, said he was headed back to Fort Laramie. But Jim suspects another officer of working with them, Sergeant Bartholomew Carnes. This Bart hates Indians; he's mean and tough, and Jim doesn't trust him. He said Bart didn't meet with George and Zeke because Bart was recovering bodies from that attack; that means he didn't see us visit Jim, either. He said Zeke wanted to know if he was pursuing me to arrest me. Jim told him he'd made a search, but couldn't locate me and couldn't venture farther from the fort. He warned us to be more careful."

Joe glanced at the stranger again who didn't seem to be paying them any attention. "Stede's letter has some interesting information. It seems that Simon Adams talks about animals so much because he collected them around the world and exhibited them in cages. I've already told you why he hates Indians, especially Dakotas, so much. Stede said his zoo—that's where animals are kept—included snakes from many places. Simon's traveled as much and as far away as I have. He's been to the Orient, where those magic balls are from. The last Stede heard of him was when he sold his property and business in New Orleans and left town after trouble with another man over stealing his wife. Jim said Simon didn't have anything to do with Indian girls like we heard Clem say his boss did. I just can't decide what Simon's role is. So many clues point to him, but I keep thinking they're coincidence or intentional false clues."

Joe sipped water from his canteen and mopped sweat from his brow. "Stede said they'd question George when he returns to the fort; he's supposed to be scouting in the Powder River area. They also want to know what he's doing over here. Tom sent a list of names for land buyers. It includes Zeke, George, Farley, Orin, Harvey, Simon, Bart, and some trappers who trade with all three posts. That ties a lot of names together, but doesn't give us too much more to use."

Joe looked at the other man again, but didn't stop his report to question her further. "Things are getting worse along the Missouri River, love. Homesteaders and farmers have been attacked. They left Red Heart and other Lakota stuff again. Jim isn't falling for those tricks, but he can't keep holding off his men and the complaints much longer. He needs something done fast. One of the worst things is another attack on soldiers. They were bringing cattle to the fort, and they were massacred and the herd stolen. A patrol couldn't trail them because their tracks were covered by a buffalo stampede. I can't guess why those villains have changed their strategy, but they must be killing whites now to provoke the Army into attacking the Lakotas. They must think the Crow aren't doing much to push the Oglalas out fast enough. Jim suspects they're enticing an Indian against white war now, not just an intertribal war. Jim's doing all he can to stall things to keep from exposing us and our mission, but the settlers are demanding protection and retaliation. You realize what this means, love: Snake-Man wants Lakotas out badly enough to use the Army and innocent whites to do his dirty work. The last thing is, Zeke is spreading lies about us. We can't be found in your father's camp, love, and neither can those cattle."

Morning Star was distressed by Joe's news, and concurred with his precautions. "We must leave at dawn. We cannot let them win."

"You want to tell me about him?" Joe hinted, eyeing the stranger who was toying with his reins while he watched the couple.

Morning Star told Joe all she had done and learned since returning home. He reacted strongest to Clay's arrival and to the news of the stolen cattle being near their camp.

"We have to move those cattle tomorrow. If this was a deadly plan, soldiers could be here any day. They'd never believe us with all that's been happening. I'm not sure Jim could control hot-headed men; if this Bart comes, he won't even try. This incident could begin the war, love."

"Sky Warrior will help us; they do not know him."

"*You* know him?" Joe probed, still uneasy about the development.

"Only since I returned. He left when I was three," she reminded. "Others know him. He can be trusted. My people accepted him and helped him long ago. He would not betray us or harm us."

Joe wanted to test that for himself. "Let's talk to him." As they walked to join Clay, Joe asked, "How much have you told him?"

Just above a whisper, she responded, "I told Father, the council, and Sky Warrior all things. He is the only one to see my heart is weak for you. He will tell no one. I did not tell him you are not Tanner."

Joe saw how the man, whose description matched his, observed their approach. He prayed Clay Thorne didn't feel bitter and vindictive toward his Indian blood, as he knew all their secrets.

Clay half-smiled and extended his hand in the white custom to shake Joe's. The two men quickly sized up each other.

"Morning Star said she filled you in. We can sure use your help, Clay. We're too known in Crow camp and at posts. We have to move around carefully. If you can spy for us in settlements, we'll do the field work. First, I'd like to get that herd near Fort Tabor before soldiers come looking for it."

"You think you can prevent a war and help make a treaty?"

"We're doing our best," Joe answered to the unusual query. "I hope so."

Clay's hand casually drifted to his pistol and he had the weapon leveled on the other man before Joe could blink. The startled couple gaped at the half-breed with a narrowed gaze and a cocked gun on Joe.

Sun Cloud's daughter inched closer to her love, and Clay frowned. "You tricked me," she accused. "Why do you do this bad thing?"

Clay didn't smile as he told her, "Sorry, Morning Star, but I have no choice. He has to be stopped. I have to kill him."

Fear consumed her. Her heart raced with panic. Her gaze widened. She felt betrayed. "You must kill me, too," she vowed in honesty.

Clay shook his head. "No, you're coming with me."

Morning Star was near him, but Joe knew he couldn't draw and fire his weapon before Clay's bullet struck home. He was angered by his helplessness and his love's peril. This traitor would defeat their mission and take their lives! He would help provoke a bloody war. No doubt Jim, Stede, and Tom would be in danger, too. He raged at himself for letting down his guard and for dismissing any suspicions about this man.

To stall Clay's attack while he attempted to think of a way to rescue them, Joe scoffed, "Don't tell me the famous Sky Warrior, ex-Cheyenne war chief, is working for Zeke Randall and Snake-Man."

Chapter Sixteen

"*I*'m not," Clay replied in a cold tone, "but you probably are." He glanced at the frightened woman and said, "I told you I wasn't the vision warrior, but I guess I am. He surely isn't. I have to kill him."

"Do not do this, Sky Warrior," she pleaded.

"He has you and your people fooled, Morning Star. He isn't Tanner Gaston; I've met Stede and his son. This man isn't him."

Joe exhaled in relief. "That's all? You know I'm not Tanner?"

Clay ignored the man's question to ask, "Did you know the truth, Morning Star? You hesitated over his name like you weren't used to calling him Tanner. I know love can blind you, but don't let this liar trick you into betraying yourself and your people."

"Tanner was my best friend, Clay," Joe hurried to explain, "I came to this territory with him and his father. He was murdered at Pierre by the gang I'm after. We were scouting for Stede and Tom Fitzpatrick, the Indian agent at Fort Laramie, when Tanner overheard something they didn't want him to. One of the men killed him. He gave me a clue before he died. I was tracking Zeke when I met Morning Star, but she's probably already told you that part of our story. When I learned she was Tanner's cousin, I told her everything. Of course the Red Hearts didn't trust a white stranger and things were going badly for me. I had to use Tanner's name to win Sun Cloud's confidence and help, and to save my hide. Morning Star knows the whole truth, and she agreed it was necessary to keep my identity a secret. They've let her travel with me as a translator and guide because they believe we're blood kin and nothing physical can happen between us. As for that sacred vision I matched, I don't know about mystical things. All I know is it seemed to be a prophecy coming true and it won them over."

He extended his hand again, this time in an offer of friendship. "I'm Joe, Joseph Lawrence, Junior, from Virginia. My family owns a shipping firm like Stede's. That's how we met and became friends. I've been honest with Sun Cloud about everything else. How do you know Stede and Tanner?"

Clay studied Joe a minute, holstered his weapon, and accepted the man's amiable offer and explanation. "I was fifteen when Gray Eagle's half brother returned home to make peace. I rode with my father's warriors when the Cheyenne helped retaliate after their ambush. When I was banished, I remembered how Powchutu had survived in the white world. I figured, with my looks, I could, too. My father had told me many things about Bright Arrow's uncle. Windrider was best friends with Gray Eagle's oldest son, so he knew many stories about Gray Eagle's bloodline. When I left this territory, I worked many jobs and places. Three years ago, I worked for Stede Gaston in New Orleans. I met his son twice."

Joe was curious, not suspicious, when he asked, "Stede and Tanner have never mentioned you to me. Why not?"

"I never told them who I was. I was still denying my Indian blood, and I wasn't sure how much they knew about Powchutu's history. From what Morning Star's explained, they pretty much know it all."

"You guessed the truth," she ventured, "when they told you Sky Warrior was Tanner Gaston. You knew he did not have sun hair and blue eyes. To slay him is why you rode to meet him."

"That's true," Clay admitted with his wry grin. "I'm glad you're an honest man, Joe. I would have hated to kill the man Morning Star loves, and I would have hated to tell the Red Hearts how they'd been deceived. I was also worried about exposing you and taking your rank in the sacred vision. It's been a long time since I was war chief."

"You're mighty handy with a gun," Joe remarked with a grin. "Thank goodness you listen before you gun down a man."

"I've had to be good with guns and fists over the years moving around so much. Some men are determined to be dangerous."

"You planning to stay here after this trouble is cleared up?"

"Don't know yet. I've missed my family, people, and the way I was raised. I guess my Indian blood's the strongest. We'd better get back to camp before a search party comes looking for us."

They rode into camp as dusk approached. Sun Cloud and Singing Wind came to meet them, both looking worried about their daughter's lengthy absence. The chief and his wife greeted "Tanner" and queried his success.

Joe briefly went over his journey alone. Then, Sun Cloud called for a council meeting of the Big Bellies and any warriors available.

As soon as everyone had eaten, the Red Hearts gathered to hear Joe's words. The meeting was interrupted by a late-arriving Knife-Slayer and Night Stalker. The shaman's son challenged Joe's rank once more and demanded Joe and Clay battle to the death to decide which one was the true Sky Warrior. Most Indians were dismayed by the man's wicked behavior.

Joe and Clay refused to fight and insisted on working together on the mission. The chief and council agreed that was wise.

Joe handed Sun Cloud two flags from Jim—white truce and striped American —to fly over the camp to ward off Crow and white attacks until the trouble ended and peace ruled the territory.

"We are not weaklings who need enemy cloth to protect us! We are warriors!" Knife Slayer proclaimed. "We will battle and slay any man who attacks us!"

"A good and wise warrior knows when to fight, when to retreat, and when to compromise, Knife-Slayer," Clay told him.

"Your mind has been captured by whites!" the angry man accused.

"Your mind and heart live in the past," Clay retorted. "It is a new time. To survive, you must forget old days and make peace. If you care little for your life and safety, think of those of your people."

Hawk Eyes caught Knife-Slayer's arm and pulled him back to his sitting mat. "Forgive my son," he said. "His blood burns hot to punish those who threaten us. It is hard for a warrior to sit while others ride against his foes. Is there not a task he can do for his people?"

Joe leapt at the chance to appease the medicine man and his son. "Yes, Shaman, there is an important and daring task for Knife-Slayer, if he wants it. He can ride with Running Badger to the camps of Red Cloud and Spotted Tail to tell them all we have learned."

"How is that important and daring?" the warrior scoffed.

"The Army, Crow, and evil men are searching for me and Morning Star in that area. You'll have to use great prowess to sneak by them to visit and then to return. I know you're skilled at tracking and raiding. Are you also skilled at crossing open land without being seen and captured?"

Knife-Slayer took the challenge. "I will go."

"Why do you send Running Badger, not me?" Night Stalker asked. "Do you not trust us together?"

"The son of the chief is needed here, Night Stalker. If your father is slain or injured, you must lead your people and defend them."

Morning Star grasped Joe's ruses to keep the two warriors separated. She hoped the men would be too busy to get into trouble while the matter was being settled. The third—her opponent in one of the contests—was an excellent choice to accompany and control the headstrong Knife-Slayer.

Clay comprehended the ruse, too, and was impressed by Joe's wits. He looked forward to getting to know Joseph Lawrence better.

Joe, Morning Star, and Clay departed with the cattle at dawn. They followed the White River toward Fort Tabor at a good pace. They used all of the daylight hours, then camped at dusk. But at night, the new moon offered no help with security and the three took shifts doing guard duty, allowing each more sleep and providing all with protection.

As they traveled, the three became close friends. Morning Star was taught more about the white world, her next challenge. She enjoyed the easy rapport and Clay's lessons. She thought he was an excellent choice as Joe's best friend, though no one could replace Tanner. She was happy that Sky Warrior agreed that she and Joe were perfect for each other, but he continued to warn them of serious obstacles they would confront soon.

Seven days later, they made their last camp of this trek, a third of a day's travel, with the herd from the fort.

Before darkness shadowed the land, Joe left them to fetch Jim's latest message. He was delighted to find a letter from home in the hiding spot, as he had told his mother in May to contact him through the officer. As instructed, she had addressed it to Lucas Reardon, his nephew's name, for secrecy and protection.

Joe thought that his family might not have received his mid-June letter yet, and surely not the one he had written in early July. Nor had there been enough time for a response to either one to reach him. Joe recalled he had related news in June about meeting Morning Star and her people and told a little about the work he planned in this area. Two weeks ago, he had revealed his love for the woman and his proposal to her. He knew his parents would be surprised by this, and would realize the task before all of them would not be an easy one. Yet he was certain they would be happy about his impending marriage and the thought of having grandchildren by their only son to carry on the family name. He wished he could have told them about his love in person, but he didn't want to arrive home with a fiancée about whom they had heard nothing.

Joe ripped open the letter from his mother. He knew he must hurry, but he wanted to read it in private. He covered the business, political, and social news, grinning at the way Annabelle Lawrence related some of it. His mother always tried to find something good or amusing in every situation. She possessed a special knack for lightening burdens, lessening tension, and getting to the truth of a matter.

Joe chuckled at humorous remarks about his nephew's recent antics. She said everyone was doing fine and missed him. She was praying for his safe return by Christmas. He halted a moment as he caught a change of tone in the letter that caused love and a smidgen of homesickness to swell in his chest and constrict his throat. He had been gone almost a year, but it suddenly seemed longer. He loved and missed his parents, and his sister and her family. He was eager for them to meet Morning Star, and for her to meet them. He was positive all of them would get along splendidly. Such thoughts called the Indian beauty to mind, and he galloped back to her.

Morning Star had their meal ready when Joe returned. The steers grazed near the water, as did the horses. Clay was standing lookout. As soon as his mount was unsaddled and tended, Joe approached the fire. They ate, then went over Jim's news.

Joe summarized the information as he read Jim's words. "Says Stede and Tom are checking on Orin McMichael, Simon Adams, and Harvey Meade. They've sent men to question the local authorities. I hadn't thought of suggesting that kind of investigation; it could be helpful," Joe commented, then went back to reading. "Jim's happy about that last message I left two weeks ago telling him about Red Cloud, Spotted Tail, and Two-Bulls' agreement for truce. He's upset that Black Moon and Talking Wolf have had illegal dealings with Zeke. Says he won't investigate that part yet and risk endangering us. He doesn't want the Crow coming after us, too. Says he hasn't seen Zeke since his last message. He's visited Simon and Harvey, but nothing new there. He is keeping a tight eye on Sergeant Bartholomew Carnes. He's real pleased with the evidence I left for him and with our destruction of those weapons and whiskey. What's this?" Joe murmured, rereading the last few lines.

"Damn," he muttered. "It says Stede warned us that Corporal George Hollis shot a soldier and fled when he was questioned about being here. Says for us to be on alert for the deserter. They chased him northwest, but he got away. Stede and Tom think he'll make his way here to his boss."

"At least we know he's guilty," Clay surmised for all three. "If we could get our hands on him, we could *persuade* him to talk."

"Or get our grips on Zeke or Farley. We know they're in on this mess. We can't beat information out of Simon or Bart since we haven't fully connected them to the case." He related Jim's warnings concerning the necessity of acting within the legal framework.

"Tell me, Joe, if there are as many attacks and they're as bad as this Jim says, why isn't the Army over here doing more to check them out? With Red Heart and Oglala clues left at the scenes, why haven't white men banded together and retaliated? How is this Jim keeping the homesteaders and his soldiers under control?"

"I don't doubt the raids, Clay, but nobody can prove who did them. Even if they're tempted, I don't think there are enough men to mount an attack on a strong Indian camp. As for the Army, besides hanging back to let us work on this trouble, they don't usually intrude on Indian conflicts with each other unless it gets big and nasty. From the way it looks, those boys at Fort Tabor are happy not to ride out and challenge the mighty Lakotas. If it's Jim you don't trust, see what you think about him when you two meet. You'll need to return that evidence from the payroll massacre that I borrowed, explain again how it was faked. Give him Knife-Slayer's scanty description of Snake-Man, be sure to tell him what you learned in St. Louis, and let him know you're joining us. The return of the cattle should convince any hotheads there the Red Hearts don't want any trouble."

"What are you planning to do?"

"Morning Star and I will ride back to Bear Butte and see if we can pick up Zeke's trail. With luck, he's so mad that he'll head straight for his boss and leave us clear tracks to follow. While we're gone, you nose around those posts. If you see any of our suspects, watch them closely. We should be back near Pierre in . . ." He calculated the distance and timing. "Ten to twelve days. Meet us two miles upriver and two miles westward."

The couple and Clay Thorne parted at dawn. The half-breed herded the steers toward the fort and to meet with Captain Thomas. Morning Star and Joe headed northwest toward the site of their last victory.

Clay would reach his destination by noon. Morning Star and Joe would reach theirs after four days of long and hard riding across relatively flat prairieland.

Joe and Morning Star scouted the location, found it unoccupied, and camped in the trees near the sacred mountain. They planned to follow the wagon ruts tomorrow. They tended the horses, ate, and bathed.

The full moon and a glowing campfire brightened the clearing where the couple shared a bedroll and snuggled in each other's arms. As they kissed and caressed, the blankets around their bodies slipped away. Their love was so pure and real, that neither was embarrassed by their nakedness.

"You're so beautiful, and I love you so much," he murmured.

"We are mates in our hearts. One day we will join under your law. If my people do not battle us, we will become mates under my law before we leave. I love you. I must remain with you."

Joe stroked the raven hair that flowed like a river of ebony silk around her shoulders and spilled forth upon his bedroll. It framed the most exquisite face he had seen anywhere. He gazed into the warm chocolate eyes that expressed her deep feelings. Besides his mother and sister, she was the most gentle and loving person he had known. If he made love to her every day, it would not be enough to feed his insatiable craving for her. She intoxicated him more than any liquor, and bewitched him as no other could. She was a part of him, a part he must not live without. He could not voyage through the rest of his existence without her as the gentle wind behind his sails, caressing him and being the source of his power. The months with her had proven he had made a wise choice in loving her and proposing to her.

Morning Star trailed her fingers over Joe's face. She enjoyed any contact with him, whether it was emotional or physical. She traced the strong jawline where two tiny nicks exposed his haste while shaving earlier. There was such joy in touching him and watching him. She guided her fingers down his throat, aware of the rapid pulse there. One hand halted for a time to feel the pounding of his heart, knowing she and their contact were the reasons for it. This was what Singing Wind felt with Sun Cloud, what Alisha Williams had experienced with Gray Eagle long ago. It was real, special, rare. It was the tight bond and true love that all couples should find and keep. It was wrong and cruel to deny such emotions, for others to prevent them. Yes, her heart concurred with what Joe was thinking, she had made a wise choice in loving him and agreeing to marry him, no matter what that decision demanded of her.

Joe's hands savored the tautness of her breasts, the flatness of her abdomen, the ridges of her rounded hips, the lithe length of her sleek legs, and those secret places only he had visited. For a time he wanted and needed only Morning Star to be his reality, to control his feelings, to engulf his heart.

Their bare flesh met and clung as they explored each other's body with leisure and skill. They had learned from experience what pleased the other, but found it difficult to prolong this wondrous foreplay. Their lips met and traveled on for a while to sample other delights. Their fingers roamed every area within reach until both writhed with heightened need. Each knew when the time came to join their bodies.

At first, they moved slowly, seductively. As their hungers increased, they embraced fiercely, tightly, possessively, seizing rapturous ecstasy, reveling in every moment it consumed them. Even when contentment and relaxation came, they did not separate. They held on to the satisfaction of this long-awaited joining. They never knew when another total sharing was possible, so they must drink every drop of nourishment from this one to sustain them to the next.

The couple examined the wagon ruts and horse droppings at the site. Joe arrived at the same conclusion as Morning Star. The Crow rode north; Zeke rode east; and one man on an unshod horse followed their trail.

"A big storm came. Zeke could not leave for two suns," she deduced from the amount of manure and ashes. "Mother Earth will not let him travel easy. She will pull at the wagon to slow him for us. Streams will slow and fight him. He left *ake zaptan* days ago." She held up that number of fingers.

"Fifteen," Joe reminded her.

She smiled and continued. "He travels . . . east. Much rain on Mother Earth does not hide his trail; it becomes deep."

"Deeper," he grinned as he corrected, knowing that's what she wanted him to do. "Let's ride to see how fast he's going and to where."

* * *

Before nightfall, Morning Star said, "More rain came. Hard. Zeke camped . . . one day. I cannot tell what day. Horse chips are wet and—"

"Scattered," he filled in as they looked at the disintegrating clue.

"I read how dry they are and how they fall apart to learn time."

"That's all right, love. At least we know he was slowed a little. Wherever he was heading, he should be there by now. We'll stay on his trail. We don't have to worry about that warrior; he rode southeast."

"It is Grizzly Bear," she speculated with instinctive accuracy.

Tuesday afternoon, Morning Star halted to study the ground and concluded, "Zeke moved faster, but he lost time. Streams were full, they were hard to cross in wagon. He is only . . . six days ahead."

"Yep, and riding straight for Pierre and Simon Adams."

"Or to get more guns and whiskey. Crow must be plenty mad."

"I suppose his direction doesn't tell us much, does it?"

"Yep," she said with a laugh. "If he is not gone, we can see what he does and where he goes. We can follow and spy, perhaps capture."

"If we get near him, we will. Clay and I can make him talk."

At six, they halted on the Cheyenne River. Before camping, they split up to scout the area and arranged to meet back there when done. Leaving their pack-horse concealed in the cottonwoods, Joe headed to check north and east while Morning Star rode south.

She completed her part in thirty minutes, finding nothing and no one in that direction. While she awaited Joe's return, she made camp. She gathered scrubwood and arranged it, but would not light a fire until he said it was safe. She readied the supplies to cook their meal, filled canteens, and spread out their bedrolls. If he arrived and said the location wasn't a good spot, she could quickly repack everything. He would make certain that he would not let whatever threat he saw follow him here.

More time passed. The waning full moon appeared low in the eastern sky, a pale white ball against a still-blue backdrop. Morning Star scanned the horizon, straining her eyes and ears for Joe's approach. She paced as she waited and watched, and became anxious. She knew something was wrong; Joe should have returned by now. With dusk now blanketing the land, she realized daylight would be gone in half an hour, and tracking would be difficult by moonglow. It was vital to begin a prompt search for him and see what the problem was. She worried that he had been injured or had encountered enemies. As he was to ride only a few miles in both directions, she leapt on Hanmani's bare back with her weapons and fieldglasses. With wariness and vigilance, she trailed Star's hoofprints to find Joe.

It did not take long to locate the alarming spot where two men on unshod horses had apparently intercepted him: Crow, she fretted. It appeared they had been concealed in trees at the riverbank, then sprung upon her love. The condition of the attackers' tracks exposed the fast movement of a surprise attack, as did Star's prints indicating an abrupt halt and nervous prancing.

Morning Star sighed in relief at not sighting Joe's body or blood, which indicated he had been captured. She dismounted and walked to where the Bird

People had recovered hidden horses, also unshod and probably stolen. She knew the other animals carried no riders, as their tracks were not deep enough to be bearing weight. Using her fieldglasses in the fading light, she moved with caution. As darkness arrived, she saw smoke rising from trees along the river. She left her Appaloosa and sneaked closer. When she could study the enemy camp without continuing farther, she halted, as she must not allow her scent or sounds to reach her foes. She had to prevent her capture in order to rescue Joe.

Two enemy warriors sat at a small campfire close to the water. They laughed, talked, drank whiskey, and went through Joe's saddlebags. Her love was bound to a tree, twenty feet from the men and blaze, edging the grassland. There were no other trees or bushes close to him to provide concealing assistance to carry out her rescue. He did not appear to be harmed. His horse was with the other five, to the right of the villains.

Morning Star studied the site. She couldn't approach from the water; with the river wide and the bank low and beneath a full moon, she would be seen swimming across or surfacing for air or coming ashore. She could not sneak in on the right, as the horses would catch her smell and expose her. To the left, there was nothing close enough to use for cover to begin a successful attack. Around Joe, there was nothing to use for freeing him, and his tree was too slender to hide her forward movement. She needed more feet to obtain an accurate shot at the warriors with either bow or gun. Under a bright full moon, she could not even crawl closer in the open on her belly. The braves had selected this location and Joe's confining post with great skill and caution.

She tensed as one man stood on liquor-shaky legs and staggered to Joe. The warrior looked the prisoner up and down. He laughed and pointed and poked while he made insults for his friend's enjoyment. She moved two trees closer to the scene, unable to get nearer without risking being noticed and captured or slain. She could hear one villain's words.

"You bad white man. You in big trouble. We capture for Zeke. He want you plenty bad. He give many horses, goods for trade. Zeke talk, kill."

Morning Star realized they were holding Joe for Zeke Randall to question— and inevitably, slay. But that meant he was safe for now. She could leave to prepare herself for his rescue, using the only desperate plan that came to mind. She retraced the path to her camp.

Morning Star lay on her stomach under a blanket covered with grass. She had captured several fireflies and secured them with blades to the disguise over her. Their flickers of light would imply to her foes that any movement they glimpsed was only grass swaying in the breeze; those brief flashes would say nothing could be near or under the insects, or they would take flight. Every few minutes, she inched herself and her weapons closer to Joe. The Crow were at their campfire, drinking and snooping through her love's possessions. It took a long time and great patience to cover the open distance from where she began the belly trek to her destination.

Finally she reached the confining tree. Using Joe's larger body as a shield, she eased from beneath the blanket and stood behind him. "I am here," she whispered to prevent startling him, then touched his bound hands. "Do not move or speak. It is like my rescue long ago." She sliced through the rope, careful not to cut him, then placed his pistol in his freed grasp. "When I say *now*, kill the one on the right. I will shoot the one on the left," she instructed, glad she recalled the direction words.

After he cocked the hammer and she placed her arrow, she saw the warriors stand to be excused before taking to their sleeping mats. "Now!" She gave the signal, stepped from behind her love, and fired at her target.

Joe swung his armed hand around and fired at his. Both braves were slain. He whirled to sweep her into his embrace, kiss her, and praise her courage and wits. He listened to her explanation of how she had planned and carried out the rescue. "Thanks, love. I was so worried about you. I was afraid they'd retrace my trail and take you by surprise, too."

"Come, we must hurry. We will take your possessions and return to our camp. It is ready. We must eat and sleep, and go from here fast."

"It's almost like Zeke expected us to track him, so he planted these men here to stop us. He doesn't want us to know where he's going. That could mean it's straight to his boss, and he's riding for Pierre."

"We will know soon. We must stay alert. More Crow may be chasing us." Morning Star realized that caution meant no more nights of sharing a bedroll, of nights spent separated by guard duty. She dreaded the perilous suns and moons ahead. She craved a quick and successful victory that would allow them to be together again as lovers.

Thursday, they neared Pierre. Zeke's wagon ruts continued on into the settlement. They hadn't encountered any more Crow ambushers, nor had they found Red Cloud still camped on Plum Creek. They rode for the location where Clay was to meet them, but they were a day early from their swift pace and sunrise-to-sunset schedule. Two miles upriver and two miles west of water from Pierre, they reached the meeting spot.

Clay Thorne was waiting for them. "You're back early," he said.

As they dismounted, Joe remarked, "You, too. Learn anything?"

"I reported to Jim like you said. We got along fine. No trouble over returning those cattle. We told everybody I found them grazing on the river and herded them in. He's sending another report to Fort Laramie. Jim was worried about you two going back to Bear Butte and tracking Zeke. I told him you two would be fine."

"We almost didn't make it," Joe revealed, then related the events and findings of their journey.

Clay was amazed by Morning Star's skills and courage, and he praised her for them. "You're right about him coming to Pierre. Before I get to that part, I'll tell you about Farley. He was at Fort Tabor when I arrived."

"What was he doing there? Spying? Reporting to Bart?"

Clay shrugged as he replied, "Don't know. I followed him to Lookout. He talked with Meade, then left."

Joe was surprised by that news. "He visited Harvey Meade? Why?"

"Don't know, couldn't get close enough to hear anything. Looked to be just a friendly conversation and rest stop."

Joe didn't like this unexpected twist, as he trusted Harvey. "But Meade is out of the way between Fort Tabor and Pierre."

"Yep, but that's all I saw. I trailed him to Pierre. He met Zeke there."

Joe caught what he thought was a contradiction. "Wait a minute, Clay. Farley was with Zeke at Bear Butte. It must have been someone else."

"That was four weeks past, Joe," the half-breed pointed out. "He had plenty of time to get to Fort Tabor after he split up with Zeke. It was him."

"Zeke must have sent him ahead to report the trouble with us," Joe surmised. "But why would Farley ride to Bart instead of to Snake-Man? Unless Zeke's the only one who knows who their boss is." The blond argued against his own speculation. "But if that were true, Zeke wouldn't need to report our mischief so fast to Bart. That's real strange. I didn't get to meet Sergeant Carnes and size him up. Did you see Farley talk with anyone else?" Clay shook his head, and Joe added, "Did you meet Bart Carnes?"

"No time." Clay responded. "I took care of business with Jim fast because Farley was getting ready to pull out when I arrived. Jim pointed him out to me, but he didn't know who Farley met or if he met with *anyone*. I hurried because I wanted to make sure I didn't lose sight of him."

"That was smart, but I wish one of us knew something about Bart."

"What does Jim say about him?"

"Not much more than he's mean, tough, tight-lipped, and hates Indians. His name on that land-buying list doesn't mean much if we can't tie him to the trouble. Talking with Zeke and Farley isn't a crime and can't be used as evidence. My gut instinct says there's an important reason why Bart was contacted so fast. Maybe he's the leader we're after. He's certainly in a position to know the movements of the Army and the Indians. He's also sitting in the right saddle to use hired soldiers to frame Red Hearts for raids he's investigating. Besides, who would suspect an Army officer of instigating an Indian uprising? Or of being Snake-Man? Damn," Joe muttered, "just what we don't need, another suspect as boss."

"What if Farley only went to fort to see if we go there to tell Army about the guns and our attack?" Morning Star speculated, and Joe nodded.

"Makes sense," Clay remarked. "Anyhow, Zeke and Farley took a keelboat upriver. I rode along the bank to make sure they didn't get off anyplace. When I reached Orin McMichael's, they were there. So was a man called George, but he wasn't in uniform. He stayed hidden except to sneak out at night to catch air, take a smoke, and use the little house. I watched the post for two days. It's real busy this time of year; lots of men were around. Those three were staying in Orin's house. They looked pretty settled in for a while, so I left yesterday to ride here to leave you a message. I was planning on heading back in the morning to watch them. Seems to me they're meeting with their boss, Orin McMichael."

Joe pondered those facts. "But Orin has red hair," he told Clay, "Knife-Slayer said Snake-Man's is black. But if Orin isn't working with those villains, why would they be meeting there and staying in his home?"

"He looked at me as the boss Clem . . ." Morning Star reminded.

"Described," Joe filled in for her. "If Snake-Man has a craving for young Indian girls like Clem said, Orin would fit that. Simon Adams certainly doesn't keep any around."

"If Orin has magic balls to use," Morning Star suggested, "maybe he has a way to make his hair black to fool everyone. Snake-Man has many tricks."

"You're right," Joe said, excited and pleased. "It fits together perfectly. All three suspects are there with their boss. It has to be Orin. Zeke and Farley thought they'd throw any pursuer off their trail by using a boat to leave Pierre. They know we can't come around without being recognized. They think they're safe to come and go as they please now. As for George Hollis, that deserter has to stay hidden a while."

"It does fit, Joe. It must be McMichael. That means he knows you two from your visit there. But he doesn't know me. I'll head back in the morning and see what more I can learn."

"That's good, Clay. We'll ride to Fort Tabor and share our conclusions with Jim. As soon as we leave him a message, we'll sneak back to meet you." Joe described the safest location to join up near Orin's post.

As the three headed out for their separate tasks, they did not know that the men they sought were in Pierre and plotting worse mischief . . .

Saturday, Clay reached Orin's, to discover all three suspects were gone. He surmised they had taken a boat downriver. He headed back to warn the couple of approaching peril.

By Sunday evening, Joe and Morning Star found a concealed location on the White River near the fort and made camp. At dawn, they would head for Orin's trading post to rejoin Clay Thorne in a few days.

Joe rode to the message tree, where he found a missive from Captain Thomas and another letter from home. Knowing Morning Star was safe in the dense tree-line and on alert, he decided to open both there, in case either related bad news. Morning Star was sensitive to his moods and expressions, and he didn't want to worry her. He focused on the note first and smiled as he learned that Stede, Tom, and troops were coming from Fort Laramie. As the date for the proposed treaty council was approaching, they wanted to help settle the problem here as quickly as possible. They were expected to arrive in two weeks. Joe frowned as he read that Bart was acting strange and might suspect Jim of working with Joe. Jim warned the couple to be on guard until help arrived.

Joe hoped Jim would visit the exchange spot either tonight or early tomorrow so they could talk. If not, Jim would find his message soon and would mail the concealed letter to his parents.

After Joe ripped open the letter from his mother, he realized it was a response to his mid-June one about more news of Morning Star and his work here. When Annabelle wrote her letter, she hadn't known about his early July revelation of love and marriage. By now, his family knew everything, and probably another letter was on the way to congratulate him.

Joe was glad his mother understood the hunger in him, his search for something he hadn't quite been able to comprehend or explain. She grasped how exciting and fulfilling his mission was. Best of all, she had convinced his father of those truths. That made Joe happy, as he deeply loved and respected both his parents. He laughed aloud when his mother teased him about soon losing his heart to the Indian beauty who obviously had stolen his eye, especially since he had guarded them so well for twenty-eight years. It no longer amazed Joe that Annabelle was so perceptive and intuitive, as was Morning Star. He knew the two women, along with his sister, would become fast friends.

Yet Joe detected a subtle coaxing for him to return home as soon as possible, and he pondered if something was wrong there. He was eager to see them all again.

Those yearnings increased as he envisioned his parents. Their mental images revealed they were older than Joe had realized before this reflective moment.

Suddenly he was anxious to spend time with them before it was too late. Perhaps advancing age and declining health were the real reasons his father had urged him not to make this journey and to take control of the shipping business this year. Joe had not considered those possibilities before, and his proud father would never admit them. Yes, he needed to go home as soon as he settled matters here.

Those worries evoked a need to be near the woman he loved, who would share his life as the first Joseph had Annabelle's. He pocketed the letter and note, then mounted to get back to her.

Morning Star sensed her love's serious mood. When she questioned him, Joe told her about the letter from home and its effect on him. "It is good they understand why you came here and why you must stay until the sacred mission is done. It is good to love and miss family, to have a strong bond. It is good they do not warn you to not love me. I will learn fast and make them proud of me. I will not dishonor you or your family."

Joe pulled her into his arms to hug and kiss her. "I love you, woman."

"I love you," she responded before their lips meshed. Morning Star was relieved by the news from Joe's mother. She could relax now, knowing they would accept and help her. She prayed her family would be as kind and understanding, and feared they would not.

Joe and Morning Star did not break camp before they heard a loud noise—the sound of many horses galloping northward from the fort on a worn trail. He told her to stay hidden while he investigated. With his fieldglasses, Joe saw that Captain James Thomas was not with the troop; rather the man leading it was burly, brown-haired, and wearing sergeant's stripes.

A homesteader in a wagon came along, obviously leaving the sutler's store after spending the night at the fort. Joe halted him and queried the commotion so early in the day.

"Captain Thomas and a deserter were killed yesterday. Sergeant Carnes said it was the work of an outlaw named Joseph Lawrence and his renegade squaw. Woodhawks saw 'em canoeing upriver toward Pierre. He's gone to pursue 'em and capture 'em. I hope he catches 'em fast. We don't need no murderers and savages causing more trouble in these parts."

Joe concealed his shock. "Thanks, friend. Did Bart say what this Lawrence looks like? I don't want to run in to him by mistake."

"Nope, but he knows him. He's heading upriver, so this area's safe."

"Much obliged," Joe said, and watched the men leave.

He rejoined Morning Star and gave her the distressing news about Jim's murder, George's death, and the stunning accusation against them. He saw the panic in her eyes and cuddled her close to him. "I love you, woman. I promise I won't let anyone harm you."

"It is bad, Joe. What will we do?" she asked, worried.

"I bet anything Bart killed both of them, and he's using the Army and that fake charge to kill us. That's probably what Farley came to tell him. Nobody saw us going upriver, so that was a lie. But what's behind it? Bart has to be going to join up with Zeke and Farley in Pierre. George must have come downriver by boat after Clay left Orin's. I bet Zeke and Farley are on the move, too. That means Clay should be back near Pierre. Something's bad wrong, love. I have to follow that patrol to see who Bart meets. You'll go home while Clay and I settle this. I don't want you in any more danger."

Morning Star embraced Joe and refused. "No, I stay with you. If soldiers, Crow, and bad men are looking for us, I am safe with you."

Joe held her in his arms as they drew comfort and courage from each other. This mission was more dangerous than he ever imagined it could be when he started it with Tanner. The villains were determined to stop them any way possible. Joe wondered if they would be called upon to sacrifice their lives for peace. He asked himself if it was *his* duty to continue, if it was *his* war, *his* fate, a reason for both of them to lose their lives. They had given this task their best efforts. Why couldn't they just accept they were battling overwhelming odds and retreat? Why couldn't they just leave the perils and sacrifices behind and ride away to Virginia? He knew why not. Morning Star would never give up this sacred task and ride away at this point in time; she would never desert her family, tribe, and vision orders. That meant he could not leave her in danger or risk losing her. Besides, so much was at stake, and he had made himself a part of this situation. They couldn't quit now; they had come too far in solving this mystery. "All right, love, you come with me; it's safer. We'll free the packhorse here and get rid of any extra supplies. We can't be slowed down if we're sighted and have to run for our lives. First, we need to retrieve my message to Jim and my letter to Mother."

Joe and Morning Star hid the horses behind a hillock and lay on their stomachs at its crest. From their distant and lofty position, they had time to flee to safety and had a view of the trail to the post. They could see who came and went from Pierre after Bart and his patrol entered the settlement, if the men came by land. Suddenly, they were using the river for speed and for secrecy in movement. That worried him, because they could not track men in boats or keep up with crafts from horseback.

They waited and watched for hours. The late-July sun seared down on them. So vital was their task that they ignored their discomforts. At last, dusk appeared with its darkening and cooling shadows.

Joe continuously scanned the landscape with his fieldglasses. He sighted their new partner coming from Pierre. "It's Clay. Too far for shouting. I don't want to ride out and meet him. If anyone comes by, I don't want us seen together. How can I signal him?" he wondered aloud.

"Flaming arrow," Morning Star suggested.

"Let me see if anyone else will sight it," he murmured, searching the terrain through the fieldglasses. "Looks all right. Let's do it."

Joe used a safety match to light the cloth wrapped around the arrowhead. Morning Star fired it into the air at a southeast angle. Joe saw Clay's head follow the fiery shaft's flight, then retrace its path. He watched the man think a moment, then ride to where the arrow landed.

Clay poured water from his canteen onto the burning rag to prevent a prairie fire. He studied his surroundings and figured it was safe to check out the unusual message. He hoped he was right about who sent it.

When the half-Cheyenne warrior dismounted behind the hillock, he didn't smile. "Big trouble, you two."

"We know. We trailed Bart's patrol from Fort Tabor. The bastard murdered Jim and George and framed us. Did you see who he met?"

"Yep, Zeke and Farley. But you've got more trouble than that; Simon Adams is dead. Those snakes must have left Orin's while I was camped with you. Somehow they lured Adams away from the post and into an ambush. He was found shot not far away in a wagon with guns and whiskey—not many, just enough to make their point. Charge is, you came here after killing Jim and George at Tabor to silence your partner in crime."

"That's crazy! They can't prove I was anywhere near Pierre."

"Problem is," Clay informed them, "he had a letter on him to you, Joe, about how good your plan to provoke the Sioux against the Crow and whites was going. They were smart; they had Simon write it. They checked his script against the post's books. I don't know if they forced him or he worked with them or if he just joined up with them. Those are some powerful charges against you two. With Jim gone, you don't have any protection now. With Bart in control and working with the villains, you two should hide for a while, but not in your camp, Morning Star. If the Army finds you there, your people will be in great danger."

Joe told his new friend about Jim's message saying help was on the way. "All we have to do is stay out of their sights until it arrives. Now that we know who Snake-Man is and who's working for him, I have a scheme for entrapping that bastard and his gang. While we fetch something we need to make it work, you watch for Stede and the soldiers near Fort Tabor. Try to catch them before Bart and the others know they're in the territory. We need secrecy for my plan to work." He explained it to Clay and Morning Star. She smiled and nodded agreement.

But Clay ventured, "What if Jim never got his message sent? What if the soldier he assigned to deliver it is one of Snake-Man's boys? Or what if he never reaches Fort Laramie? Lots of dangers between here and there. Besides, what you've got in mind is risky. Crazy," he added.

Before dawn, Joe gave Clay a letter to mail home, addressed to his sister to pass through Pierre, changing his contact to Stede. He told his family he would finish his mission and leave here in six to eight weeks. The couple headed west to fetch an item needed to carry out their daring plan.

Clay, who would leave soon, watched them ride away. He shook his head. If Joe's plan didn't get them killed, the forces after them might. All they could all do was hope that help was on the way.

Chapter Seventeen

A week later at Slim Buttes, Joe and Morning Star spied on Black Moon's camp from a rock formation near the site. The invisible new moon allowed them to get close without being seen. Many campfires illuminated the Crow area enough to see what was taking place.

They had ridden fast and hard to carry out their hazardous task, the August days providing long hours of needed daylight. They had stayed on full alert, but confronted no peril during the arduous journey.

They were glad sunset had released them from the demands of the summer heat. The area needed rain, and they would welcome its cooling effect. The ground was dry and hard. Prairie grasses had changed to shades of yellow, tan, and gold. Some had withered, but most were of hearty varieties well suited to this climate. Animals were still abundant, as if no tribe had slaughtered many for winter rations.

The camp beyond them was busy and noisy. Two wagons stood to its right with four white strangers. Women and children rummaged contents of crates and cloth sacks. Indian men were in a section of trees to the left, guzzling the recently arrived whiskey and examining the trinkets.

"Must be those four men who escaped our attack at Rake's Hollow," Joe whispered. "Looks as if Orin has sent plenty of firewater and gifts to settle them down until more guns and ammunition arrive."

Morning Star concurred with his conclusions. She listened to the drumming that provided music for the drunken warriors to dance to. The braves moved about as they laughed, shared tall tales of past exploits, and boasted of future raids on the Lakotas. Such bloody plans had to be prevented, even at the cost of her life. She didn't know how either or both of them could get to the chief to steal the watch Orin had given to him, the bait needed to lure their foe into Joe's clever trap. She invoked the Great Spirit's help, guidance, and protection.

After two hours of drinking and merrymaking, Black Moon staggered to a fallen tree, sank to the ground, and rested his head against it. He appeared to be dazed or asleep. Every so often, a few women brought over food, delivered more whiskey in buffalo paunches, and obeyed other orders.

Morning Star recognized the opportunity the Great Spirit had placed before her eyes. As was common on such an occasion, where food and drink were in such wild abundance, the men paid little attention to the females serving their needs. "I will cover my hair and shoulders with a blanket to hide my face and Arapaho markings," she told Joe. "I can sneak to Black Moon, pretend to help him, and take the possession we need."

"It's too dangerous. You'll be in the middle of those crazy warriors."

Morning Star knew the risk she would be taking. She was scared, but confident. "I will be careful. He is away from the others. Women come and go. It is the only path to victory. I must walk it, fast and alone."

Joe studied the area as he recalled how cunningly she had rescued him and all she had done at his side. It was a big risk, but she could do it. Too, it was the only way to get their hands on that bait. If they could pull off his trap, war would be averted and their future could begin. He agreed.

Morning Star tossed a blanket over her head and positioned it around her face and shoulders. With the assistance of the dark moon, she crept toward the site. She lowered her head and casually went to where the chief lay, snoring and sprawled on the ground. She knelt and straightened his limbs, placed another folded blanket beneath his head, and lifted an empty water pouch that reeked of whiskey. As Joe had instructed, she unfastened the musical watch from the cut in Black Moon's vest where he wore it. She secreted it into her garments, then did the same with his knife as a raid gift for her father. She rose, with lowered head, and left the trees. She was quickly encompassed by dark shadows and ran with skill and caution to Joe's side.

"You did it," he praised her success, then kissed her.

Morning Star allowed herself to relax for the first time since leaving him. She returned the kiss, elated by her daring coup.

When they parted, he said, "Let's make tracks, woman."

"No, we must not. We do not wish them to follow us."

Joe chuckled softly. "That means, let's leave fast," he explained.

They rode ten miles in the darkness, traveling at a walk to prevent accidents. They camped on Antelope Creek, too weary to do more than take turns standing guard and sleeping.

Friday around five-thirty, they reached Spearfish Canyon. Morning Star told him the direction to take while she rode to the rear, concealing their trail to the lovely location. The valley near the northern boundary of the Black Hills was lush and green, smelling of spruce and pine and fresh air. It was sheltered from the outside world, but unused this time of year when the Plains beckoned nomadic hunters. Ebony peaks, spires, and rocks loomed beyond their gazes. Timber and grass were abundant. Deer, elk, and birds favored the enclosed area. A towering waterfall cascaded over a line of ivory limestone cliffs, its roar loud. The rush of liquid was so white that it almost looked like running ice or snow. The clear blue creek it created journeyed for miles through the area, playing around rocks or twigs in its path.

Joe looked around and smiled. It was the perfect spot to spend what would probably be their last time together until victory was won and their love revealed. They could remain here only tonight and a short time tomorrow. It would require three to four days to reach Sun Cloud's third camp of the season, which Morning Star said he would be at by now. Their rest in this canyon would provide safety while Clay guided help to Sun Cloud at Buffalo Gap. If all went as planned, they would be in her father's tepee only one or two days—hopefully not long enough to endanger the Red Hearts.

Joe tended the horses while she unpacked their supplies. As the two animals grazed, he went with her to collect firewood. As they foraged for fuel to feed the fire, Joe felt a thump on his back. He turned as Morning Star tossed another pinecone at him, then giggled as her eyes sparkled.

"A big coup to strike great warrior without slaying him," she jested.

"Is that so?" he replied with a broad grin. "I thought you had to touch the enemy without slaying him. Let's see if Sky Warrior can earn a coup."

When Joe came after her, Morning Star squealed, dropped the wood, and raced behind a spruce. She darted from side to side as Joe attempted to round the tree and capture her. They both laughed as they romped like children in the idyllic location, perils forgotten for a while.

"You're fast and clever, woman, but I'll get you," he playfully warned.

Morning Star dashed for the stream, thinking Joe would halt. She hurried to the waterfall. As she was splattered, she shrieked, "It is cold!"

Joe reached her, grasped her wrist, and pulled her toward him. "Let me warm you," he murmured as his mouth closed over hers.

They kissed with great need. Soon, the chilly water soaking them went unnoticed in the heat of rising passion. They removed their garments and flung the drenched items to the bank. They splashed and bathed themselves and each other. The water's temperature enlivened them as their bodies burned hotter with raging desires. They explored each other's flesh with hands and lips, removing clear drops in their paths.

Soon, Joe scooped her up in his arms and carried her to the lush grass. They rolled upon the soft surface as they tantalized and tempted each other beyond self-control. Grass tickled their skin, as did mischievous fingers and daring lips. Both were enthralled by the other and neither wanted to wait much longer.

Joe entered her body to join them together as one force striving for unity of hearts and spirits. He felt as if everything he was and knew was bound to this moment in time, to the love in his embrace. This woman tempted, sated, and completed him as no other ever could. He was eager for the day when everyone would know that truth, accept it, and abide by it.

Morning Star thrilled to the way Joe made her feel. He loved her fully, honestly, and thoroughly. She enjoyed giving him pleasure, and savored how his responses affected her. Just to touch him brought rapture. To gaze into his adoring eyes warmed her soul. To kiss him drove her wild. To feel his hands and mouth upon her evoked ecstasy. To mate with him was beauty and delight beyond measure and words.

They lay nestled as their bodies returned to normal. The grass made a soft bed. They gazed at the sky above and felt its tranquility within themselves. They listened to the rush of water over the cascade and to birds singing. They smelled clean air, evergreens, wildflowers, and the erotic scent of love. They were at peace in their verdant and romantic haven.

Finally, Joe teased, "If we don't get moving, love, we'll both be asleep. I'll wash off, then help you cook."

"I will join you, but it will be more cold. The sun goes to sleep. How do you say this?" she asked, knowing she had spoken wrong.

"I will join you, but the water will be colder. The sun is setting, or going down," he corrected, then he shifted to gaze to her eyes. As his fingers pushed aside stray hair from her lovely face, he murmured, "I love you, Morning Star. You've learned so much; I'm proud of you." His fingers caressed delicate features. "I want you and need you more than I realized. This will be over soon, then we'll leave to begin our life together. I can't wait to marry you and know you're mine forever."

Morning Star drew his mouth to hers and kissed him. She looked into his serene gaze and cautioned, "When we reach my camp, we must not reveal our feelings. We must wait until the sacred victory is ours."

A troubled look filled his blue eyes as a streak of panic ran through him. "Promise you won't change your mind about me," he urged.

Morning Star smiled and vowed, "I will not. I love you. We must be mates for life. But we must take no risk with victory."

"I understand and agree. We're too close to success to endanger it."

They made love again the following morning before they dressed. It was time to go home, to put their cunning plan into motion. They would camp tonight on Elk Creek; tomorrow night, on the southern branch of the Cheyenne. Late the next day, they would reach Buffalo Gap.

Monday nearing dusk, Joe and Morning Star walked their horses into Sun Cloud's last camp of the hunting season. Her parents and people halted their shared tasks to greet them. Both smiled and dismounted. Young braves took their mounts to tend them.

"Come, sit, rest," the chief invited the weary travelers. Sun Cloud's keen glance scanned both, but nothing seemed amiss. He did detect friendship and closeness, but that was not unusual for cousins and partners. He was glad they seemed to trust, like, and respect each other. The Great Spirit had brought them together and sent them on the sacred quest. Sun Cloud thanked his god for protecting his child and the son of Stede.

As they took places on the buffalo mats that Singing Wind spread for them, Buckskin Girl hurried forward to offer the couple refreshments. Morning Star knew her friend was anxious to hear news of her missing love, but both women realized that personal talk would have to wait until later.

"Tell us of your adventures," the chief encouraged.

People gathered around the seated group to hear news of their daring exploits. Elderly Red Heart males threw down mats for relaxation during the talk. Children pressed close to parents' legs. Warriors were on alert, eager to learn of any impending threat to their band. Women studied the handsome paleface with their leader's daughter. Night Stalker, his timid wife, and contrary son stood nearby, both parents grasping a hand of the unruly boy.

Joe related the events since their last report. He witnessed the awe and approval for Morning Star's participation, particularly her daring rescue of him from the Crow. He went over it in detail to give her all the credit she deserved. "She's out of danger now. Stede and Indian Agent Tom Fitzpatrick will arrive soon with help to finish the task. She will not need to leave camp again. You," he said to Sun

Cloud, "will lead your band of warriors in the final battle, if there is one. I pray we can end the matter without a bloody conflict. We're certain Orin McMichael is Snake-Man. After we send a brave warrior to him with the watch from Black Moon, he'll be forced to come and meet with the Crow chief and will be snared."

When Joe revealed how they had gotten hold of the token to be used in the trap, more praise was spoken for Morning Star. He watched her give her father Black Moon's knife as a raid prize. Joe saw the chief examine it, smile, then lean over to embrace her with pride.

"You have done as the sacred vision claimed, my daughter. Your coups are many and your legend will be great; they will shine as brightly as those of Gray Eagle. Songs will be sung and stories told of She-Who-Rode-With-The-Sky-Warrior. My heart feels much joy at your victories and safe return. I am glad you are home and your task is finished. Sky Warrior," he addressed Joe. "You have done well, my brother and friend. Bring me the gift I made for him to carry in the final battle," he instructed Wind Bird.

Wind Bird fetched the shield he had worked on for days.

Singing Wind was thrilled by her child's deeds and prowess, but was happy the girl was home to stay, out of peril's reach and away from the white man's temptation. Morning Star deserved a matching shield, but that was not their way. Yet, the girl's daring deeds would be painted on the tribe's and family's pictorial histories—buffalo hides that hung in the meeting lodge and their tepee.

Sun Cloud handed the gift to Joe and said, "It is the Shooting Star shield. It has big medicine. Few men have carried one. Only those whose signs are of the heavens—as are *Mahpiya Wicasta*—and who have earned the right to carry one may do so. My father was the last of our band to earn and carry such a powerful shield; Gray Eagle's was destroyed after his death to keep it from enemy hands. This one is yours, Tanner, for you have earned it."

Joe felt a twinge of guilt over deceiving the man who trusted and admired him, who rewarded him with their highest honor. He wished Tanner were here to share this moment, the past months, and the future. He handled and looked upon the object with gratitude and sacred reverence. It symbolized the essence of the powers of nature and their god. The sunburst that filled the center in blue, white, and yellow was of the colors of the heavens, the brown hide representing the earth. It was believed to protect its bearer from all dangers, physical and supernatural. A weasel pelt was suspended from the center, sign of the Great Spirit's messenger. Coup feathers, one for each of Joe's previous deeds, and good-luck tokens hung from the lower points between each peak of the sunburst. An eagle feather was attached with the weasel pelt, one from Sun Cloud's chief's bonnet. The shield was of tautly stretched buffalo hide on a willow frame. It would withstand arrows, lances, and even bullets.

Joe listened as the chief told him about such meanings and powers. "Thank you, Sun Cloud. I shall treasure it always, my brother and friend."

The chief noticed an emotional catch in the white man's throat that controlled his voice, and he was glad to find Joe so moved by the gesture, of which the Red Heart Council—with the exception of Knife-Slayer—approved.

The antagonistic warrior was so vexed by Joe's acceptance and great honor that he shouted, "We must not wait for bluecoats! We must ride to the post on the Big River and slay the one called Orin, as I killed Grizzly Bear who tracked Sky Warrior and Morning Star from Bear Mountain."

Night Stalker explained his friend's words to his confused sister and the white man. "He wears the scalp of Matohota on his war lance. He tracked you from the sacred mountain to slay you. Knife-slayer found the camp where the Crow waited for you, and he attacked."

Joe thanked him, as did Morning Star, then praised his skills. But he refuted the brave's suggestion, "We must ride with the Army and do this last deed by white law to stop the evil men."

"We cannot trust the whites and the white laws! We must not let soldiers ride into our camp. They will spy, return, and attack."

"Jim, Captain James Thomas at Fort Tabor, died helping your people, Knife-Slayer. He was a bluecoat, a white, a man of the white laws. If we do not trap Orin and his men with Black Moon's token, we have no proof he is guilty. Without proof, an attack will appear an act of war against whites. The Army will be forced to come here for retaliation instead of friendship. Surely Indians and whites can work together for truce this time. If Red Hearts lead the way at Bear Butte, all will know they want peace, not war. Everybody will know the charges against them are false, that they were Snake-Man's work. This is the great day all have awaited; do not spoil it now."

Sun Cloud and other council members spoke up before the warrior could argue. They agreed with Joe's clever plan. Blood rushed with excitement and suspense. Hearts pounded with eagerness. Mouths tasted sweet victory in the making. Eyes envisioned it upon the horizon. Hands knew all they had to do was reach out and seize it.

"Crow are sly, but we will fool them," the chief said with a chuckle. "It is a big laugh. A good victory. It will stop the trouble and prevent danger. We will ride with Sky Warrior and the bluecoats. We will follow the words of my uncle's son and the agent from Fort Laramie. We will have peace again. Men will hunt in safety. Women will work in safety. Children will play in safety. Old ones will sit beneath a safe sun to rest in their last days. This is what Grandfather promised in Payaba's vision. It will be so."

After a day and a half of rest and talk, a lookout galloped into camp to reveal that a unit of bluecoats was approaching. Joe seized his fieldglasses, mounted, and rode out with the warrior to see if it was the Fort Laramie troops or Sergeant Bart Carnes with his men. He breathed easy when he sighted Clay Thorne, Stede Gaston, and Tom Fitzpatrick in the lead.

Joe rode to meet them. "Glad you finally made it. Sun Cloud and the Red Hearts are willing to work for peace and help with our trap." He reiterated what Clay had explained earlier, and the soldiers agreed. "Let's go work out the details. I want this settled before more incidents occur."

Sun Cloud and Stede Gaston eyed each other as the latter dismounted with difficulty after the long ride. They shook hands as Stede said, "It's an honor to finally meet you, Sun Cloud, and to be among my people. My father told me many great stories about his brother and kin. I'm only sorry it took me so long to visit you, particularly under such grim circumstances."

The chief liked his cousin's words and the sincerity of Stede's tone and gaze.

He smiled in pleasure. "It is good to meet the son of Powchutu, Eagle's Arm, half brother to my father. We have many words to speak, many seasons to cover. First, there are other matters to discuss."

The white man was impressed by the chief's wits and command of English taught to him by his white mother. Stede liked this man, and he knew they would get along fine. "I'm eager to hear everything," Stede replied as he massaged his aching leg. "We've gotten excellent reports from him," he said, nodding to Joe. "He and your daughter have done a brave and fine thing for everyone concerned. You must be proud."

"I am proud of Morning Star and Tanner. Peace will come from their great deeds. Again, I will ride with a great warrior as I once did with your father. He died a brave man at the side of my father. When the war moon rises next, their sons will ride together and will survive the evil of their enemies. It will be a glorious day. Come, sit, rest, and eat. We will talk of past days and families after we have spoken of traps and peace with others."

Stede moved on a leg stiff from the past break that had prevented him from accompanying Joe after his son's murder. He was glad Joe had taken Tanner's place, but hated deceiving the great leader—his kin. He hoped the truth could be revealed soon, and that Sun Cloud would not feel used and betrayed by the deception. He sat down beside his cousin, awed by the dignity of the chief.

Morning Star and Joe took places nearby, each apprehensive about a slip from Stede Gaston or from one of the others with him. They knew the damage careless words could do, and both prayed to their gods to hold a tight rein on tongues. The moment of final victory and a treaty loomed before them, and nothing must prevent that.

Sun Cloud asked Thomas Fitzpatrick to join them. The ex-mountain man sat down, crossed his legs at the ankles, and cupped his knees with his hands. One hand—the reason for his Indian name, was missing three fingers from a gun accident. White hair, straight and thin, barely grazed his collar, as he favored a neat appearance. Deep-set eyes beneath protruding brow bones revealed a serious nature. He was still a hearty man at fifty-two.

Sun Cloud had met the past explorer, renowned wilderness guide, and ex-trapper several times in the past. Tom had worked most of the streams in the Dakota Territory, beginning in 1822. Tom was considered smart, brave, skilled, and self-reliant. He got along with most Indians because of his good character and pleasant personality. Sun Cloud believed Tom was an excellent choice for peacemaker between whites and Indians. He said to the agent, "It is good Broken-Hand visits the Red Hearts to prove the words he speaks on paper are wise and true."

Tom had talked with Indians many times during his thirty years here, so he knew the most effective words to use. He had sent messages to all the big tribes, but he stressed the important points again. "It is an honor to sit and speak with the noble chief Sun Cloud. I have asked the Great White Father in Washington to reward the Lakotas for allowing his people to cross your lands, to trap your streams, and to take animals for food; he has agreed. He desires all men—Indian and white —to live in peace. If the Great Plains are divided into hunting territories for each Indian nation and the Great White Father gives each many supplies, no tribe will need to invade another's land for survival. Your people will be safe from enemy raids and their needs will be filled. The chief of each tribe will sign the joint treaty; he will be responsible for honoring their part of it and for punishing any warrior who breaks it. Many nations are sending their leaders and warriors to Fort Laramie to discuss peace and to sign the big treaty. Some are your allies; some have been your enemies for generations."

Tom kept his gaze locked with Sun Cloud's, a sign to show he was being open and honest. "It is time to put aside raids, wars, and bloodshed. It is time to live in truce. Too many warriors, women, children, and old ones have died over hunting-ground disputes. Too many have died attacking white immigrants who cross your lands heading west, or from conflicts with soldiers over those raids. There have been too many fights between soldiers and warriors because each side feared and misunderstood the other. It is time for peace between Indian nations, time for peace between Indians and whites. It is time for learning, healing, and accepting each other. To obtain these goals, everyone must compromise; everyone must think of the good of their people. I have lived and worked in this territory for many years, so I know many wrongs have been done to Indians out of fear, ignorance, carelessness, or greed. The Great White Father wants them stopped. He wants our Red Brothers compensated for their losses and for their future generosity in allowing whites to travel through your lands and permitting some to settle on them. He wants peace now and forever."

"Broken-Hand's words are hard to accept, but they are wise and just. We know you to be a fair and honorable man. We have heard many tales of Broken-Hand's exploits and daring; your coups and prowess have made you a legend among Indians and whites. After we defeat the evil paleface who provokes the Crow and bluecoats against us, we will ride to Fort Laramie to make treaty. We do this because of Broken-Hand's promises and because of the sacred vision Grandfather gave to Payaba twenty years ago. The coming of Stede and Tanner Gaston have proved its magic and power. First we war against evil, then, we ride for good. We must share the pipe of friendship to bond our words to our hearts."

While the smoking ritual was in progress and no one spoke, Tom's mind drifted over the situation. It was known that whichever way Sun Cloud leaned—so did most Oglalas: the most powerful and largest branch of the Lakota Indians. In addition, most allies followed Sun Cloud's lead in crucial episodes. Tom was relieved and grateful Joseph Lawrence and Stede Gaston had helped bring about the chief's receptive mood.

Tom did not betray Joe's secret identity. His deceit could damage the treaty he and Colonel/Superintendent David Mitchell had worked so hard to achieve. He felt compassion and empathy for the Indians' plight—one he knew could only worsen in time—but he was not unduly emotional about it. He was not a glory-seeker in this historic mission.

Tom did not believe this truce would last, but it would be a life-saving reprieve for both sides for a few years. He had warned his superiors in Washington of "the consequences should twenty thousand Indians well armed, well mounted, and experts in war turn out in hostile array against all American travelers." He had suggested the annuity of fifty thousand dollars worth of supplies to be given every year for fifty years, and his government had agreed. In less than a month, redmen from most Plains nations would gather at Horse Creek to establish intertribal peace, and would unknowingly open the door for more whites to walk into the territory. That inevitable reality did not escape Tom's keen mind, nor did the grim consequences of it. He was certain Sun Cloud knew and felt the same way, and that increased Tom's respect for the Red Heart chief.

As Morning Star observed her father among the whites, she gained hope that their joint efforts for peace would inspire friendship and acceptance with their new allies. She noticed her father's rapport with the white agent and with Stede Gaston. Surely a shared pipe and battle and a treaty would mellow his feelings toward palefaces. While he was soaring on the wings of victory and peace and while her and Joe's great coups were fresh in his mind, surely her father would not stand between her and her love. As her gaze met Stede's, his gentle brown eyes seemed to read her thoughts. She returned his encouraging smile. She dared not look at Joe, as her expression could expose her forbidden feelings for him.

Morning Star glanced at Lone Wolf and hoped their war chief's rank would become only an honorary one. She looked at Hawk Eyes and prayed the deceitful shaman's influence over her people would rapidly diminish until it ceased. Her gaze sought Payaba, and love filled her heart for him. She studied her silent brother and wondered why Night Stalker did nothing more than watch and listen. Her roaming eyes jumped over the sullen Knife-Slayer, but she refused to worry about him tonight. They returned to her father as pride, love, and respect washed over her body. Her gaze met Singing Wind's, and they exchanged smiles. Morning Star grasped the meaning of her mother's nod and rose to help serve food.

Following the meal and a discussion in the meeting lodge where plans were made, Sun Cloud and Stede Gaston entered the chief's tepee to speak of the past, present, future, and their blood connection. Singing Wind served buffalo berry wine and listened to the genial conversation.

Soldiers camped outside the village, feeling at ease after their cordial reception. Most were surprised to find the Red Hearts so friendly, honest, and intelligent. When curious braves visited the area, they chatted amiably.

Knife-Slayer and Night Stalker went to the chief's son's tepee to talk privately of the disagreeable events controlling their lives. When the contrary Bloody Arrow became naughty, the men left to speak elsewhere.

Morning Star and Buckskin Girl took a walk with Joe and Clay near the river. The two couples laughed and talked. The women, best friends for years, had confided in each other about their loves for men of white blood. Both had decided to pursue their choices and to follow them wherever they led, no matter the consequences.

Joe and Morning Star noticed how Buckskin Girl and Clay Thorne glanced at each other, and knew a romance had been revived. Both were glad for their friends, and were eager for all to begin bright futures.

When Clay asked Joe what his future plans were, Joe grinned before answering, as the half-Cheyenne already knew the answer. Joe guessed his motive with accuracy, to give Clay a chance to speak his. "I'll be heading back to Virginia to help my family. My parents are getting old and need me to take over the business. I won't stay long after we're done here. What about you, Clay? What are your plans?"

Clay ruffled his blond hair and stroked his smooth jawline as he pretended to consider the query. "I'll stay here." he divulged. "This is where I was born and raised, where I belong. If I've learned one thing during my long absence and journey, it's that I have more of my father's blood and feelings than my mother's. I'll make certain the whites and Indians live up to their impending agreement. Your people have agents and soldiers to protect them; mine need me to do the same. I'll work closely with Tom Fitzpatrick to keep things fair and safe."

Joe smiled. "That sounds good to me. But where will you settle?"

"I plan to visit my family and people first to settle what happened years ago. Then I'm going to accept Sun Cloud's offer to live with my grandmother's people, here with the Red Hearts."

Buckskin Girl glowed with happiness at that news. "You will be welcome here, Sky Warrior. I will make a tepee for you."

Clay faced her and asked, "Will you make it for me and my wife?"

Buckskin Girl did not catch the humor in his tone and eyes, and she missed the meaning of his words. Her smile faded, but she replied, "Yes."

"Good, because I wouldn't want you to be displeased with your home."

Confusion was evident in the older woman's gaze. She glanced at Morning Star as the younger female giggled and covered her mouth.

"You will join to me, won't you?" Clay asked, caressing her cheek.

Buckskin Girl gaped at the half-white man who was grinning at her. She stuttered, "You ask m-me to be-come your . . . m-mate?"

Clay chuckled. "Yes. You loved me and wanted me years ago. I hope you haven't changed your mind. It just took me a long time to realize that what I was seeking elsewhere was waiting for me here."

Those words flowed through Buckskin Girl as warm honey in her veins. Tears glistened in her dark eyes. Her cheeks rosed with joy. Without modesty, she confessed, "I love you and will join you."

Clay let out a loud sigh of relief. Only because Morning Star had assured him of the woman's love had he found the courage to take another chance with love and marriage. "I'll make you a good husband," he vowed.

Buckskin Girl forgot her friends' presence for a time. She gazed into Clay's dark-blue eyes and handsome face. She loved him with all her heart and soul, as Morning Star did Joseph Lawrence. At last, both of them would share true love. "I will make you a good wife," she murmured, "I have waited many years for your return. In my dreams, Grandfather said he would bring you home to me. It is so, but I feared it would not happen when Tanner appeared as the vision man."

"Morning Star, why don't we leave them alone to talk?" Joe suggested, "I think they have a lot to discuss."

The chief's daughter was filled with joy for her best friend. "That is a good idea. But we must not be alone together," she reminded. She hated to sacrifice any of the little time remaining with him. She was worried about the danger he would face soon without her help. She prayed the soldiers and Clay would guard him well when he challenged Orin alone.

Buckskin Girl and Clay/Sky Warrior looked at them with empathy. Their union would be easy to achieve, but it was not so with their friends.

"Don't worry, love," Joe said, "this won't be for much longer."

"He is your destiny; you are his," Buckskin Girl remarked. "Many will resist your mating, but let nothing and no one halt it."

"We won't," Joe responded for them, and Morning Star nodded.

He sent her an encouraging smile and whispered, "Soon, love."

As she left his side, Morning Star was plagued by Buckskin Girl's words. For a short time, she had deluded herself by thinking anything—including peace and her many coups—could change the laws and customs of her people or influence her father's mind about her intention. She must not allow herself to get wishful again, as it clouded the mind.

How she longed to be a part of the exciting final victory over Snake-Man, to be at Joe's side when the obstacle to their departure was removed. She wanted to ride to Bear Butte and participate, but her father and Joe had refused her request. She would not defy their order or display recklessness by sneaking there; that was the act of a foolish woman. She must not be disrespectful or dishonorable. She would obey them, even if she didn't agree with being left behind during this triumphant episode.

Later, Joe and Stede took a walk as dusk was yielding to night. The older man said, "I received a letter from your mother just before I left Fort Laramie. She's worried about you. She asked me to make sure you stay safe and return home soon. She also wanted to know all about Morning Star."

Joe related what he had written to his parents and when. "Did you write her back?" he inquired, a strange sensation gnawing at him.

Stede clasped Joe's shoulder with a strong hand. His gaze was filled with kindness and affection. Wind played through his graying deep-brown hair and ruffled the lashes around dark eyes: signs of his Indian heritage. At sixty-five, he knew his years were numbered, but he had accomplished his last wish. He had met his kin, found the missing part of his roots, and would help win peace for them as his father would have wanted. He felt complete, even thought a vital part of him was gone forever. But soon he would join his brave son, whose death had not been in vain. He would be with his beloved wife again, leaving only his sister and her family behind. It was the way of life. "Yes, but she'll worry anyway. Mothers are like that."

Joe had noticed the brief, faraway look in Stede's eyes, and suspected where the man's thoughts had fled. He loved and missed Tanner, too. Nothing could bring him back, but the memories of their years together would always live in his mind. As a distraction, he asked, "You don't think she and Father will reject Morning Star, do you?"

"No. They're fine people, Son. Besides, they know I'm part Indian and they like me. They have no prejudice against our kind."

"That's good, because I can't give her up for anybody."

"Tanner would be happy you're marrying his cousin. He would be proud of all you've done to help our kin. I am."

"Lordy, how I miss him. He was closer than a brother to me. Sometimes I think this is all a bad dream; I'll wake up, and he'll be there. His killer will be punished soon." He met Stede's gaze. "I'm sorry you're caught in this deceit of mine, sir, but it was the only way to help them."

"I understand, Joe. But I'll be glad when we can tell the truth."

"You think it will turn Sun Cloud against me?"

"Frankly, Son, I don't know. From what my father told me, Indians are taught to keep their bloodlines pure, and they're reared to honor their customs and laws. It's even more restrictive for chiefs and their families. You'll be asking Sun Cloud to send his only daughter into a world where some people want to conquer or destroy his culture. Worse, from some points of view, his bloodline is already tainted with enemy blood, and I'm sure he wants to get it back to its purest state. I'm sure he has no idea of your feelings and intentions for his daughter, nor hers for you. He knows what you've done for his people, and he likes you. But I can't venture a guess how he'll react to such news."

"I appreciate your honesty and candor, sir. Somehow we'll have to convince him of my love and persuade him I can protect her in my land. It will help, when the time comes, if you speak in our favor."

"I'll do what I can, Son, but I'm a half-breed and visitor, too."

Early the following morning, Wind Bird, who was being trained by Payaba to become a shaman one day, departed for Orin McMichael's trading post with Black Moon's musical watch and alleged message. A man with small hands and feet, he could pass more easily for a Crow than any other Red Heart. He was instructed how to use his wits, English expressions, and a white truce flag. If Orin wondered how a Crow knew to come to his place, Wind Bird was to say he was seeking Zeke Randall. That culprit had no doubt rejoined his boss while they awaited news from Bart of their blond intruder's death.

Joe was sure Sergeant Carnes would not search too far into the vast grasslands for him and risk confronting an Oglala war party. Bart was probably back at Fort Tabor, enjoying his stolen command. No matter, the traitorous officer would be arrested soon and be kept out of their way.

If things went as planned, Zeke would talk with Wind Bird, then report the message to Orin. The crafty Scotsman should respond without delay. While at Orin's long ago, Joe had glimpsed a wagon in the barn, but had not thought to check it for a false bottom and "magic" balls. Nor had he thought to ask Clay to examine it during one of his spying trips. Yet Joe was positive it was there and Orin was guilty.

Wind Bird was ordered to ride slowly to give the others time to reach Bear Butte to prepare for the impending trap and for Joe's party to carry out their additional task. The Red Heart brave was to tell Zeke the Crow would no longer follow, trust, or obey Snake-Man's words unless the spirit met them at the sacred mountain and commanded it. Snake-Man must again prove his magic and powers to them, or their truce was over. Wind Bird was to dangle another piece of bait before the heartless villain: Joseph Lawrence, whom they had captured for him as a gift. The meeting was set for six suns after the message was delivered. It would require that long for Orin to travel there by wagon, as he would need his special one for Snake-Man's vanishing trick. It would be good for Black Moon to see him unmasked and to be taught the error of his ways.

Joe and Morning Star were certain Orin and his gang would fall for the ruse. The villains needed to retain control of the Bird People for their vicious scheme to work, and the blackhearts were eager to get their hands on Joe to question and torture him. The couple was sure Wind Bird could entice the culprits there for defeat.

That same day, Joe, Stede, Tom, Clay, Sun Cloud, Red Heart warriors, and half of the troop departed to set their part of the plan in motion. The other soldiers left for the fort, to arrest Sergeant Bart Carnes and to take command of the post to prevent any trouble during the final episode.

Miles northwestward, the forces would separate, with most journeying on to Bear Butte to make preparations there, while Joe and a few others continued northward to carry out Tom Fitzpatrick's added order.

Joe admitted it was a clever but risky scheme, and he wished he had thought of it. He envisioned Black Moon's reaction when he was issued such an ultimatum.

It was a cunning coup de grace to the Crow chief's final treachery. Over the years, Tom had learned about good and bad Indians, and Joe was glad the agent had suggested this ploy.

Joe's only regret about this final confrontation was Morning Star's exclusion from it, as she deserved to be included, but it was best not to have a beautiful Oglala woman around so many men. Every mind had to be focused on their joint task. He wished he could take her in his embrace and kiss her goodbye. But soon she would be in his arms and life forever, and he eagerly anticipated that day.

As the large group rode away, women and children watched them take their leave, as did the warriors left behind to guard the camp.

Morning Star, Singing Wind, and Buckskin Girl watched until their loved ones were out of sight. Concern filled each woman.

"Come, we have chores," the oldest woman told the younger two.

"What if this plan fails?" Buckskin Girl worried aloud.

Morning Star murmured with undisguised trepidation, "It must not. But I fear the change the Indian agent made in it. Broken-Hand does not want Orin to know he walks into a trap. It is clever," she admitted, "to have Black Moon waiting for him to destroy any suspicions. It will be good if Sky Warrior can learn why Orin does this evil thing. But this deed has many dangers. Sky Warrior will be bound and helpless among many foes. He could be slain before soldiers or our warriors can help him. When Snake-Man sees he is trapped, he will strike at Sky Warrior before his capture or death. Broken-Hand wishes to prove enemy tribes can work together, but it is dangerous to let the Bird People share in this great moment. Black Moon has proven he is our foe and Orin's friend. Why must they ride to his camp to seek his help? It may defeat the sacred vision."

"No, my daughter, it is a good plan," Singing Wind refuted in a gentle tone, trying to conceal her own fears. "It will draw us together for future peace. It will force Black Moon to give up his bad ways. He does not wish to anger the soldiers and whites. He fears them more than he fears the false spirit. He will obey and help. When the evil white man and his men see Black Moon, they will approach and be trapped by forces working together."

"I understand such hopes, my mother, but I do not trust him, and it was not in Payaba's vision. Evil is strong this season and seeks to defeat all that is good. I should be there, for all know Sky Warrior rides with a squaw."

Singing Wind patted her shoulder. "Your tasks are over, my child. Women do not ride into battle with men. There is no need to risk your life again. Your presence would worry and distract others and it could anger Black Moon to learn the daughter of Sun Cloud tricked him many times. It is dangerous to walk on a man's pride; it make him behave bad."

"What if Black Moon slays them when they reach his camp? Do you not fear for Father's life? Do you not know what a great coup Black Moon will earn if he slays Sun Cloud and Sky Warrior? All he must tell other whites is they did not reach his camp. If he buries their bodies, Mother, who can prove he lies? If the agent is slain, there will be no peace. Snake-Man will pay many guns and supplies to stop the treaty. Black Moon's heart is filled with greed and evil. What is to stop him?"

Singing Wind had thought of such grim possibilities, but cast them aside. "Grandfather will not allow such evil to win over good. You must believe the sacred vision, my daughter. You must learn to trust and accept past foes. It is the new way. What is more important than peace and survival?"

"Can you accept and trust past foes, Mother?" the girl probed.

"I must, for the sake of our people. But your words and eyes carry a different question. Speak it, Morning Star. What worries you more?"

Payaba had joined them during Morning Star's list of worries. "Do not fear, my child," he coaxed. "Victory will be ours. What you must say to your mother must be spoken to her alone; it is not for the ears of others on this sun. Go with her, Singing Wind. Listen with your heart and mind. Know what she says is the will of the Great Spirit, for I saw it in a vision. I did not speak of it because Grandfather held my tongue. Go, Morning Star, and tell the words in your heart and mind; this is the sun for them."

"You know what I must say and do, Wise One?" she queried with torment in her gaze and voice.

His eyes filled with wisdom, his mind controlled by insight, and his tone tinged with grief at her impending loss and sufferings, Payaba nodded. "Yes. It will be hard and much pain will come from it, but it must be done. It is your destiny, your sacrifice, your Life-Circle."

"Is there no way to make it easy, Wise One?" she fretted.

The gentle and tender-hearted old man shook his head of white hair. "No, little one. The path you must soon walk will destroy your old one. Do not lose courage and faith. It is the will of Grandfather."

"No," Singing Wind murmured in alarm and anguish, guessing what the two meant, what she had feared since the white man's arrival. "It cannot be. It must not be. It is wrong. Bad. Shame and dishonor. He is of your blood, Morning Star. Turn away before it is too late."

"No, Mother, he is not—"

"In your tepee," Payaba interrupted. "Nothing must destroy peace."

Singing Wind and Morning Star obeyed Payaba's soft order, both noticing the way this matter affected their elderly friend.

Inside, Singing Wind faced her only daughter and urged, "Tell me what I fear is not so. Tell me you do not challenge a loss of face and dishonor."

Morning Star dreaded this confession, but it was time to make it. Now that Payaba had revealed it was part of the sacred vision, she had the courage to expose her feelings and intended departure. "I love him, Mother. I will go with him to his land and join to him when the mission is over. When Father returns, I will tell him of my choice."

Singing Wind's eyes enlarged with panic and disbelief. She had feared her child would come to love the paleface, but had believed she would remain true to her heritage. She imagined the effect of this news on Sun Cloud. "How can this be so, my daughter? He is of Sun Cloud's bloodline."

"He is not. His name is Joseph Lawrence, not Tanner Gaston." While her mother gaped at her in astonishment, Morning Star explained the ruse and the reason for it. She related Joe's true identity. "I am sorry I tricked my parents and people, but Grandfather commanded it. You said nothing was more important than peace and survival. Can you deny words you spoke from your heart?"

Singing Wind was distressed, but she tried to remain calm. She had to reach her daughter and change her mind. Her voice quavered as she reasoned, "That was before I knew of such lies and tricks, my daughter. You will be banished forever.

The whites will not accept you among them. They will see and treat you as a wild savage; they will make fun of you, for joining with Joe. Have you not thought of such torments? You must be true to your blood and your people, to your ways and laws. We did not teach our child to shame herself and her family. How can you accept white laws, enemy ways, their god? How can you leave our land forever? How can you eat, dress, live, and behave as white? How can you raise the grand-children of Sun Cloud, bloodline of Gray Eagle and Brave Bear, as palefaces, half-breeds? You will destroy a great bloodline; you will hurt and shame your father deeply. You will never see us again. Whites will insult you, hate you, reject you. How will you feel when the new treaty is broken, as Payaba warned long ago? Which side will you choose then, my daughter—his or ours? You cannot take both."

"I have thought of such things, Mother. They trouble me, but I will face those challenges when they appear. Joe is the sacred warrior, Mother; he has done all the vision said. Did you not hear Payaba? This is part of the vision; it is my destiny. The Great Spirit put us together many moons ago when I was a captive of the evil whites. He would not do so if it was wrong to love and marry Joe, for He knows all things. He gave us special time together to work for peace and to yield to our love for each other. He has not separated us or slain us for such feelings. He has not punished us, so how can our love be wrong?"

"He allowed your weakness to continue for the good of our people." Singing Wind realized how much her daughter had learned from the white man. Morning Star was stronger and more confident now. "What if Grandfather proves to you this joining must not be? If He says you cannot go and the white man cannot stay, will you obey Him?"

"Yes, but that will not happen," she replied with certainty. "You say the whites will not accept Indians, but they did not reject Powchutu and Stede. They did not scorn Bright Arrow and Clay Thorne when they lived among them. The Great White Father, their President, commanded acceptance and friendship. We must do the same."

"Powchutu, Stede, Bright Arrow, and Clay were accepted because they all passed for white and none revealed their Indian blood in words or deed. Your face cannot fool the whites."

"Joe says they will think I am from a land far away. They will think I am a . . . bride he found while riding his ship over the big water. The ocean," she corrected. "You say I must be true to my Oglala blood. How will that be so if I defy Grandfather's sacred command? The treaty will be broken one day, if I go or if I stay; my actions do not control that bad deed."

Singing Wind knew she was losing the battle to save her child and to spare Morning Star from terrible wounds. If only she and her husband could have talked to Joe first, they could have made him realize he would destroy the woman he loved if he took her to his enemy land. Perhaps when Joe returned, she and Sun Cloud could convince him to sacrifice Morning Star and leave her here where she belonged. "How can you love and join a paleface, my daughter?"

"How could Grandfather love and join a white woman? How could Bright Arrow love and join a white woman? How could Black Cloud love and join a white woman? If it was not wrong for them, why is it wrong for me? Life can be strange, Mother; Life-Circles sometimes join with enemy ones. Your mother was to join Gray Eagle, but Grandfather chose a white mate for him. Your father loved her, too. If Chela and Gray Eagle had wed, you would not be here. That was His will. Grandfather sent Powchutu into the white world to find and marry the real Shalee, to have a son who could return to bring peace. That was His will. Bright Arrow desired you and the chief's bonnet, but Father won both. That was His will. The Great Spirit gave my uncle a white woman to love, to bear his children, to give one to the Cheyenne chief, son of a chief who joined a white woman. All of these Life-Circles have touched on some moon. Yet both sides said they were forbidden, wicked, shameful. How can that be when they were powerful and victorious? All found happiness with true loves that could not be denied, that were destined. It is the same with me and Joe."

Singing Wind felt her heart drumming in alarm at one sentence. "What do you mean, Powchutu joined the *real* Shalee?"

"I know the truth, Mother. Joe did not tell me. I heard Father speak it to him and ask him to tell no one about my grandmother. I do not care she was white; Alisha/Shalee was a great woman, an honored legend. I have told no one I know the truth; I did not tell Joe I heard those words. I only speak them now to you in secret to prove our union will work. You scolded me for using lies and tricks, but my grandfather and father did the same to win their loves and to keep peace. I cannot hate half-breeds; Sun Cloud, Bright Arrow, Night Stalker, and Morning Star are mix-bloods. Can you hate my child who will carry two bloods, as your husband does? Did the truth about Alisha change your feelings for her? Do you scorn Gray Eagle for joining a white? No, no, no, Mother," she answered the three questions with accuracy. "Powchutu was full-blooded, son of a great chief, but he was forced to suffer the life of a half-breed. We must learn to feel with our hearts, not judge with our eyes against those who look different from us."

"Your words touch my heart, Morning Star, and make me proud," Singing Wind declared. "But change takes time. Love controls you, so you are blinded to many things. You think your choice will work because you want it to do so. Powchutu was raised half white, my daughter; Shalee/Sarah was raised all white, so they were accepted by the palefaces who did not know their secrets. Rebecca earned her way into our tribe by risking her life for Oglalas and Cheyenne, as did Bonnie Thorne. Your grandmother was believed to be half Indian, daughter of Chief Black Cloud, so she was accepted. Such is not true with you, my daughter. You are Oglala; you were raised Oglala. You cannot become and live as white."

"Alisha was born white and raised white," Morning Star countered, "but she became Blackfoot and Red Heart. She was worthy of Gray Eagle. The same is true of Rebecca Kenny with Bright Arrow. Why can I not do the same with their people? Why is it not bad for Sun Cloud's father and brother to have forbidden loves, but is bad for his daughter to love and join Sky Warrior from a sacred vision? Joe risked his life for Red Hearts, and he is blood brother of Sun Cloud."

"They accepted our ways and joined us. For you to join him, you must accept his world. How can a maiden with the bloods of Gray Eagle, Black Cloud, Running Wolf, and Sun Cloud deny her bloodline, people, and ways to love an enemy, to sacrifice all she is and knows?"

"He is not our enemy," Morning Star protested softly in dismay.

"But his people are, and a wife must go with her husband and accept his band as hers. Yes, there are many good whites, and we will make peace with them soon. But it will not last; they will not change. What then?"

"Can I deny what Grandfather places in my heart? Can I refuse to walk the path He has planned for me?"

"If it is His will, my daughter. I do not understand it. If such is true, I will not stand in your path. But it will be different with your father. He is chief. All watch what he and his family do. He will not believe or accept this until the Great Spirit proves it to him."

"How will He do this, Mother?"

"I do not know. If it is, he must obey it; but he will never accept it, for it means the loss of his daughter. He will be forced to turn his back, to deny you, to banish you, as is our law. The Red Hearts yielded for Gray Eagle and Bright Arrow, but not until much suffering was endured. It will cause worse trouble to ask them to do so again for the bloodline of their chiefs. That will say Gray Eagle's line wants white mates."

"But Father married you, an Indian." Morning Star contended, "Night Stalker, the next chief, is joined to an Indian. Bloody Arrow, chief after him, has no mark of the white man on him; the bloodline is strong and pure again in my brother's son. I am a woman and cannot become chief. My sons are not in line for the chief's bonnet. Why must our people care if mine is broken? Why must they order me to stay here and to join an Indian, a man I cannot love? It is not fair or good, Mother."

"You are Oglala and it is our way. If you defy our law, your father will be forced to never speak your name again, to never look upon your face again. Can you shame and hurt him this way, our child? Many suns from now, will it not harm your feelings and marriage when your husband's people attack and slay Oglalas? When they steal our beloved lands? When they try to put us on reservations after our strength and will are broken, as they have done with other Red nations? When the people you have chosen kill or rule all you loved, what will you feel? That moon will come, my child, for Payaba has seen it. Do you love Joe this much?"

Tears ran down Morning Star's cheeks, but she did not brush them away. They dropped to her buckskin garment and made dark spots there. Her heart ached, and a heaviness burdened her chest. Despite what her mother had said about her being too blinded by love to see this matter clearly, such was not the case. She realized how hard a break with her life would be. She realized how difficult and intimidating—and perhaps painful—her new challenge would be. She had agonized over her decision; she had not rushed carelessly and selfishly into it, as she knew it affected many people.

Yet the full reality of her choice had just hit her. Hearing the things she had feared spoken aloud was different than when her mind gave those warnings in silence or gave them while Joe was near with his love and assurances. She considered the many challenges and sacrifices: a mysterious world far away, filled with strangers who might reject her, unfamiliar customs she must learn, an unknown religion she would be expected to embrace, the necessary demand of hiding her race and upbringing, the strain of behaving as a paleface every day, accepting the fact she was dead to her family and this life. Banished forever. Live as white until she died. Never see her family. Hurt her loved ones. Never come—

Singing Wind intruded on her concerns. "Can you become white, Morning Star, *forever?*" she asked. "What will happen to you there if Joe dies before your training is complete? You will be alone in an enemy land. What if his parents do not accept you and they reject him for joining you? What if his friends leave his side? Will he remain happy with you? Is his love enough to receive in return for so many sacrifices? Does his love have the strength to help you win the many battles you will face? Think on this more. Once you choose, my daughter, your path leads but one way."

Chapter Eighteen

t Bear Butte, the lookout rode into the clearing to report that a wagon and seven men were sighted: six white-eyes and Wind Bird. The party had halted an hour away while two of the men rode toward them to scout the area. It appeared that Orin McMichael was taking no chances this time, though the red-haired man with an unusual half-beard had not been seen. It was presumed the trader was staying concealed in the "white tepee."

Everything was ready, every precaution had been taken. Black Moon and a few Crow were camped at the regular meeting site. Soldiers and Red Hearts were concealed behind trees, rolling hills, and bushes that encircled the location, but at a safe distance to avoid discovery by the approaching scouts. Horses, except for the Crow's, were tethered a mile away to prevent their sounds from alerting the prey to a cunningly baited trap. The signals were arranged—one by Joe and/or one by Tom Fitzpatrick. No one was to fire a weapon or make any movement until either or both was given. Then they were to fire only in self-defense, as they wanted all villains captured alive.

Joe's hands were bound behind his back and he sat on the earth before a tree. Clay's rifle was aimed on his spot for quick rescue if things went badly. Other sharpshooters had weapons trained on the scene to make certain no lawbreaker escaped, particularly the boss. Joe and the others would bide their time until Orin's motive was uncovered, if possible. Then the trap would close around him and his gang.

The scouts arrived: Zeke Randall and Farley. The husky man eyed his surroundings before he dismounted, and the towhead followed his lead. Zeke glanced at the blond captive, grinned, and turned to the Crow chief.

"What's the problem, Black Moon? Ain't we treated you fair?"

"Bad feelings come, Hair Face. We capture man you want. He say Snake-Man no spirit. He say use tricks on Crow. When Spirit come to prove white man wrong, prove great magic and power?"

"Farley's going after him now. We had to be sure this place is safe. Get him," Zeke ordered his companion, who obeyed without speaking.

"Why man with big medicine afraid? What can hurt spirit?"

"I meant, safe for his men; we ain't spirits. Nothing can hurt Snake-Man. You'll see. He'll reward you big for that gift." He pointed to Joe.

Zeke walked to the prisoner, but the others stayed behind. He looked down at the helpless man and chuckled. "I told you I'd get you, boy. You're gonna suffer good before you're dead."

"You didn't get me, Zeke; the Crow did. I've led you a merry chase for a long time. We both underestimated Black Moon; he's a sly devil. You and Orin won't fool him much longer."

Zeke stared at him, then snarled, "Shut up."

Joe read the threatening glare, but asked, "Why? Afraid Orin's tricks won't be strong enough to protect you when Black Moon learns the truth? When he does, he'll skin the lot of you. He'll feed—"

Zeke silenced him with a backhanded blow to the cheek as the bearish male growled, "Shut up. Talk again, and I'll take out your tongue."

Joe didn't provoke the enraged man to lose his temper. If he had to be rescued from a beating, the trap would be sprung too early. He was glad Clay and the others hadn't panicked when he was struck and come to his aid. Joe looked at his enemy with what appeared a contempt for danger.

"Where's the woman you took from me? She's been riding with you."

Joe didn't answer, just stared with an insulting sneer.

Zeke used his booted toe to kick the bottom of Joe's foot, several times and hard. "Answer me, dead man," he ordered.

"First you say to keep quiet, then you ask questions and demand answers. Which do you want, Randall, silence or talk?"

Zeke stroked his beard as he sneered, "Think you're real brave and smart, don't you?"

"I haven't done badly until now, and my trouble didn't come from you."

More fury glistened in Zeke's shiny eyes, so Joe cautioned himself to settle down. He couldn't be too cocky or Zeke would get suspicious. He was attempting to keep the burly man distracted from the Crow until Orin joined them; he didn't want any slips from the Bird People. "She's with Black Moon's wives. He decided to keep her and to trade me. I tried to bargain with him, but he thought I was more valuable to you than what I had to offer. I tried to convince him he's being a fool, but you two have him duped good. As to your question, you've got it wrong; you stole her from me; I just took back my property. If you'd harmed my wife, you'd be dead by now instead of just mad."

"Your wife?" Zeke echoed in surprise.

"That's right. Little Flower was gathering herbs while I hunted. She was to meet me nearby at noon. You snatched her. You did a pretty good job of hiding your trail back to camp, but I'm an Apache trained ex-Texas Ranger, so I'm not fooled easy. If you'd let her be, we'd have been out of this territory the next day. Then you went and put a ball in my arm and roughed her up. That made me real mad."

Joe saw that he'd captured Zeke's attention with his tale, so he continued it. "I guessed what you had in your wagons and what you were up to. Being an ex-lawman and plenty riled, I figured I'd hang around a while and take a little revenge. Trouble is, Randall, you and your boys kept pulling me deeper into your business. I don't like being accused of murder—Clem, remember? I had a tough time convincing Captain Thomas at Fort Tabor I was innocent, but my Ranger badge carried more persuasion than your claims. Your lie riled me more. I told Thomas what I suspected was going on, but he believed this Snake-Man stuff was Indian superstition. I could see you boys were going to get away with your crimes. It wouldn't have drawn me in if you'd left us alone. You didn't, so I destroyed your guns. We were heading out of this sorry area when the Army came after us for two more murders. That made me mad again. I had you, soldiers, and your Crow friends chasing us with blood in the eye. With Thomas dead and framed good, I figured it was smarter to ride west and forget about you and your dealings, but we ran in to some of Black Moon's braves."

"You saying all this trouble was over that woman, a squaw?"

"My woman, Zeke; that's a big difference to a man."

"Why didn't you ride into my camp and lay claim to her?"

"Texans aren't fools. You'd have killed me and kept her."

"Damn right," he admitted. "I shoulda hired you that night. You're good, Lawrence. You've been a wound in the gut to us."

Joe glanced at his bonds, chuckled, and said, "But I ain't perfect, or I'd be free and long gone. Standing too much guard and getting too little sleep dulled my wits." He realized Zeke was falling for his story and relaxing. The evildoer even seemed to expose a begrudging respect for his prowess.

"You'll get plenty of rest soon," Zeke jested.

"In a permanent bed six feet underground?" Joe retorted.

"Yep, so why you so calm?" he asked, glancing around again.

"A man has to die sometime. A Ranger stares it in the face every day; I got used to living on the edge of a grave. Once you accept the fact it's coming for you and you can't stop it, you learn not to fear it as much. In your line of work and surrounded by hostiles, I'm surprised you haven't learned that lesson, too; or maybe you have. Tell me, Randall, why do you boys want to provoke an Indian uprising?"

Zeke looked at Black Moon and his braves at the campfire. He turned to frown at Joe. "You're talking too much again," he warned.

"When a man's gonna die, he needs a reason for it. It isn't because I riled you boys a few times. It's because of why you thought I was challenging you. I've guessed that much, but not the why behind it."

"Who are you? Who you working for?" Zeke demanded.

"Joe Lawrence, like I told you that first night. I've been drifting with my wife for about two years. Ever since the Apaches burned our ranch, killed our son, and captured our daughter," he said in an icy tone, with a frozen glare in his blue eyes. "They didn't like me using the skills they'd taught me against them. Trouble is, only an Apache can track an Apache, and even I'm not that good. Never could find where they took my little girl. Finally had to give up searching for her to make a fresh start. So, we've been drifting around and looking for a new place to settle. We want to stay in the West, we don't like crowded areas, but we've found Indian trouble everywhere we've looked, and we don't want that risk again. You boys stirring up Indians to go on the warpath was part of why I was so riled against you. Too many innocent whites get hurt and killed. Ever seen a real massacre, Zeke? Probably not or you'd think twice about what you're doing. I bet you don't have any family to worry about losing to hostile attacks."

"Nope, just have me. Why's an Injun hater married to a squaw?"

"Married her before all the trouble. Except for her skin color, she's as white as you and me. Speaks good English, so she heard all you said. Little Flower figured it was safer and smarter to stay silent."

"She was a real looker. Be glad she'll last longer with Black Moon than Snake-Man. He likes to use a strong hand with his women."

Joe scowled for effect. "I guessed that much from Clem's slips. You were smart to silence him; a man with a loose tongue and a weakness for whiskey is dangerous. Any chance we can make a deal? You get me back my wife and we'll clear out of your territory?"

"You ain't in no seat to deal. It's too late, Joe."

"I figured that, but can't you tell me why I'm dying?"

"So you can yell it to them Injuns?" Zeke jested.

Joe chuckled. "In my place, wouldn't you use just about any trick to save your hide?" He laughed again as if resigned to his predicament.

"Wagon come!" Black Moon shouted and stood.

"Your last card's been played, Joe. Game's over and lost."

"Yep, I guess it will be over soon. Leastwise, I'll meet your boss. I'm real curious about a man with so much power and money. Clever, too."

Joe watched Zeke join the Bird People, who watched the wagon pull into place. He assumed the other four cutthroats, whom he'd seen at Black Moon's camp recently, were survivors from his Rake's Hollow attack. Their employer wasn't in sight yet, and Joe prayed he was with them. The riders dismounted and tethered their reins. Farley went to Zeke like a moth to a flame. Wind Bird made his way toward Joe, but they didn't speak or look at each other. Joe was relieved by the brave's safe return and success.

The tailgate was unbolted and lowered. The string closing the cloth-bowed top was loosened and flared, creating a large opening. A big man stood under the white canvas arch with hands on hips. His lower body was clad in fringed buckskin pants and moccasins. His chest was bare and hairless. Colorful tattoos of fierce snakes began above his wrists, coiled round and round his strong arms, and seemingly crawled over his broad shoulders. Their triangular heads were depicted over each breast with forked tongues, bared fangs, glassy black eyes, and flared pits. The vipers were drawn with effective skill, to entice fear and superstition.

Joe's alert gaze examined the disguise that covered the leader's face and half of his head, reaching to behind his ears and to the base of his neck. The painted metal mask that hid his identity was in the shape of a snake's head. The holes in it —eye, pit, and mouth—were small or shaped to prevent clues. The hair Joe glimpsed was black, dark, and silky. But shoulder length! Even if Orin's hair was sooted or dyed, Joe reasoned, he knew it wasn't long! He noticed the shade of the man's skin, which was much too dark for Orin's! In fact, Joe decided, the devil hinted at being . . . an Indian! He was baffled. He recalled Zeke's curious expression when he mentioned Orin's name earlier. Was it possible, Joe wondered, that Orin wasn't the captain of these land pirates? Either way, he'd know the truth soon.

Zeke whispered a report, then fetched him. As they approached, Snake-Man spoke to the Indians. Despite new facts, Joe was surprised at not hearing a Scottish accent! He didn't recognize the deep voice, but listened carefully. He knew there had to be clues to glean.

"My friends, why do you doubt me? Have I not proven myself to you? I have given you guns, bullets, whiskey, and many gifts of friendship. Have I not sent word where the Lakotas hunt and camp so you can raid your enemies? Have I not shown you my big medicine? Have I not provoked the soldiers against your enemies? Have I not kept the bluecoats away from your camps? Did I not give Black Moon a magic present?" He tossed the musical watch that Wind Bird had delivered to him back to the Crow chief.

"You promise more rifles, but they no come," Black Moon replied. "Crow cannot fight enemies with whiskey and trinkets. You say, kill all Sioux. How we kill with no weapons?"

"More will come soon, my friend. You have captured the white man who destroyed your supply and who stopped more wagons."

The last part was a crafty lie. Joe caught how slowly and carefully the head of the gang spoke. He studied the man's physique, and culled his memory.

"I will speak with him. Then he will die. He will stop no more wagons from reaching Black Moon. Bring the captive to me, Hair Face. Rest, my friends, while we speak. I must learn if others work with him who will take his place to steal your supplies."

The Crow returned to the campfire in the center of the clearing, as the wagon was on its edge. Everyone except Zeke and his master joined the Indians there. The husky hireling yanked Joe closer to the lowered tailgate.

"You want me to stay?" he asked.

The man studied Joe a moment, then replied, "No, he will not run. Keep your gun ready. If he does, shoot him down. Strike only his legs."

Zeke checked Joe's bonds, then left him alone with Snake-Man.

"You have much to tell me, Joseph Lawrence. Who sent you on this mission? What are your orders? Are you Army or Special Agent?"

Joe used a desperate ploy. "You can stop the ruse with me, Orin. That ochre dust on your skin and that fake accent don't fool me. Did you scalp an Indian for that hair or order Zeke to get it for you? Just tell me why you're instigating an Indian war before you have me killed."

Convinced he was safe by the length of time his men had been there and from fieldglass study, Snake-Man laughed and relaxed, basking in his power and success. "Sly tae tha end 'r' ye?" he jested near a whisper. "Good, nae need tae work sae hard tae talk like ye. Ne'er have I met ae man who's been such ae trouble tae me. Why, Joe?" he asked in a pleasant tone.

Joe was delighted the blackheart was incriminating himself before concealed witnesses. "I've already told Zeke and I'm sure he reported it all to you, so why repeat it? Let's get on with my dying and the why of it."

"Blarney, me lad, pure blarney. Ye're nae speaking with ae man who can be duped easy. Talk tha truth, and I'll make yer death easy and swift. Hold yer tongue, and I'll make ye beg for it all night."

"How about you tell me first why I have to die? I figured out what you're doing here, but your motive escapes me. I don't like holes in things, and I can't seem to fill the one to this situation, and that riles me as much as being defeated. Why would any man go to such lengths to take control of a vast wasteland? What's so valuable here?"

"If ye're stalling for help tae come, it won't. Me boys scouted tha area before we rode in; naebody for miles. If ye don't tell me what I want tae know, I'll send Zeke after yer woman. Ye'll be sure tae beg tae speak plenty when ye see what I can do with her. But it would be tae late then. Once I start me pleasures, it's nigh impossible tae stop until she's used up. Understand me, Joseph Lawrence?"

"Clear as a mountain stream," he responded between gritted teeth. He hesitated as he pretended to consider his predicament and decide his course. The kind of man this enemy assumed him to be would not yield easily or quickly. Orin waited patiently in confidence of victory. Joe shrugged and quipped, "Why not? No need to risk Little Flower's death or my torture for a job I've failed. I'm certain you'd carry out such vile threats. If there was any other thing to do, you can bet I wouldn't tell you a single word."

Joe perceived a begrudging respect for him in Orin similar to the one he had witnessed in Zeke. "To protect my wife, I'll do it your way," he said. "I'm a scout for a private company that plans to build a railroad from the Great Lakes to the Pacific, using Asa Whitney's route. They want this matter kept secret to prevent competition. President Fillmore has promised them federal land grants for surveys next spring. They hope to begin laying tracks in the East by late May. I was sent here to check out the terrain and climate, availability of supplies and protection, any Indian trouble, and possible opposition from landowners."

Joe took a breath and went on. "It didn't take me long to realize somebody was provoking the Indians and trying to prevent that treaty Agent Fitzpatrick promised my employers. They need that truce, Orin. They need the roads and forts it'll bring about; they need peace with the Indians to obtain water and timber and game to feed the workers. My run-in with Zeke helped get me started. That story about my wife is true, so is most of what I told Zeke. What you called 'blarney' is what happened before I took this job. It shouldn't surprise you that neither easterners nor southerners would accept my Indian wife. Taking this job served our needs. I nosed around until tracks led to you."

"Ye may be telling tha truth on most part, but ye're lying about ae trail tae me. I've been too careful tae conceal it."

Joe laughed. "Yep, until today." When Orin's head jerked around as if to search for trouble, he rushed on with, "Or rather until Zeke went to you after I destroyed those guns. Shipping those illegal crates through Pierre didn't fool me; a smart man would never be so careless. And you have to be one of the cleverest I've met to get this far with your bloody scheme. I realized Simon was an ignorant go-between. I figured Zeke would head there after he discovered my mischief. He did, after he joined up with Farley. That kid isn't alert and skilled like Zeke; no problem dogging him. I trailed him to his meeting with Carnes at Tabor, then on to Pierre to meet Zeke. They steamed straight to your trading post—and you."

Joe rolled his shoulders to loosen their tautness. "I figured I had enough facts to get Captain Thomas interested in the case, so I left to convince him. Trouble was, Carnes had killed him, taken command, and declared me an outlaw. I knew by then he was in your pocket and trying to kill me, so explanations or threats were useless. The odds here were too uneven, so I decided to continue westward. It seemed best to report what I'd learned to my bosses and let them decide how to deal with you and your hirelings. But we rode straight into Black Moon's arms; the Crow should have been farther north that day," he muttered.

Joe exhaled in fake annoyance. "Anyway, I suspected you were the ringleader, but I didn't know for certain until today. You just fell for my last trick, for all the good it does me. Besides, I couldn't find another man clever enough to be pulling off your scheme. The railroad is important, Orin, so I'll be replaced. Better tell

Zeke to be more careful with him. And next time, find a better man than Simon Adams to cast suspicions on."

Orin continued to make sure they weren't overheard. "Tae bad we work opposite sides, Joe. I could have used ae skilled man like ye."

"Pay me more than the East-West Railroad and I'll jump into your pocket. Survival is a big incentive to change jobs."

Orin chuckled in amusement. "I don't think sae. Ye strike me as ae man who's loyal tae who hires him first. I could ne'er trust ye."

Joe shrugged his shoulders. "Can't fault a man for trying to save his hide. But I'd still like to know why I'm losing it. You owe me the truth for the information I just supplied; it'll probably save your hide one day."

Orin's confidence was at a peak now. "Ye'll be dead before dark, sae I'll tell ye. I want tha Black Hills, and tha Sioux owns them."

"The Black Hills? Why are they so important to you?"

"They have e'erthing I need: timber, finest grazeland, plenty of game, abundant water, sheltered valleys for winter protection, strongholds against enemies, and gold."

Joe's astonishment was genuine. "Gold?"

"Plenty, maybe even more than California has. One of me men found some when he was raiding death scaffolds; he didn't tell tha others. He thought he'd become partners with me because I could help him get out more than he could do alone. He needed me backing and protection, but I didn't need him. He's dead, sae I'm tha only one who knows where it is."

Joe was relieved they were talking low and in a secluded location. Gold was one motive that no one must learn of! But if he allowed Orin to live, be arrested, and be questioned . . .

"Of course, timber is like gold in this territory. I know about tha push for ae railroad; it has tae come one day. With the Black Hills and her treasures in me possession, I can be their main and only supplier in these parts. I'll be rich and famous, ruler of this area."

"Except the Lakotas stand in the way of your plans."

"Ye're right. But not for long. I made ae deal with Black Moon tae supply him with guns and goods if he'd use them first tae kill off'r run out tha Sioux. Then he'd control the rest of the territory."

"Until you provoked the Army to get rid of him for you."

Orin chuckled. "Yer wits impress me, Joe."

"Thanks," he scoffed.

"If ye hadn't of destroyed me last shipment tae Black Moon, with two more in ae few weeks, me war would have begun in a month. Now, it'll have tae be in October. When yer surveyors come next spring, I'll be the man they negotiate with o'er land, water, game, and timber rights."

Joe had one last thing to learn before he gave the attack signal. "Aren't you forgetting about the treaty council at Laramie in a few weeks?"

"Treaties 'r' made tae be broken. I'll be sure it fails before winter settles in. I'll give tha Sioux and Crow plenty of cause tae battle again."

Joe leaned against the wooden hull. "What if—"

Several incidents suddenly happened simultaneously: Joe yelped and jerked aside as a bee stung his cheek; Orin, who had seen the insect land and poise to strike, leaned forward without thinking to brush it away; a startling war hoop sounded across the quiet clearing; and an arrow caught Orin in his left shoulder.

The Scotsman groaned and fell backward from the hit.

"What in blazes!" Joe yelled. If they hadn't moved at the same time, he would have been a lethal target! He jerked around to look for trouble.

Orin seized the shaft and yanked out the arrowhead. He held one hand over the bleeding wound as his gaze scanned the scene.

Another arrow thudded into wood too close to the bound Joe. His keen gaze retraced its flight path to Knife-Slayer. The warrior was trying to kill *him!* He needed cover fast in his vulnerable state. Joe saw the masked leader grab a nearby pistol and heard him murmur something about "ae war party attack." Joe knew he'd best get out of Orin's line of fire before the man realized his assumption was wrong. He ducked beside the wagon, hoping Clay Thorne could cover him with rifle fire and would come to untie him fast.

The trap prematurely exposed caught confusion on both sides, especially when Tom held off the signal long enough to give Joe time to roll under the wagon and no soldier showed himself. Melee ensued.

Orin's men backed toward their boss to defend him while firing at moving shadows in the woods. Crow dashed for cover, having been ordered to capture, not slay, the culprits. The sound and smell of gunfire filled the clearing, as did shouts back and forth between both sides.

As soldiers and warriors revealed themselves and called for the evildoers to surrender, Orin reached for his best weapons. He smashed the Oriental balls against the hard ground, creating an impenetrable veil. When the twinkling smoke vanished, Snake-Man was gone.

Clay rushed forward to free Joe. The two men joined their forces in a brief battle. When it was over, Zeke was wounded; two cohorts were dead; Farley and the last two were prisoners. On the other side, only four soldiers had minor injuries; three Indians were wounded and two were slain: Hawk Eyes and Knife-Slayer.

It was revealed that the sullen Red Heart warrior had been the one to act before either signal was given. The shaman had caught one of Zeke's first bullets as he witnessed his son's treacherous behavior and apparently sacrificed his protection in an attempt to halt it. Knife-Slayer had been slain by Wind Bird while trying to kill Joe. No doubt the antagonistic warrior had intended to allege that Joe had given the attack signal and was aiming for Snake-Man to protect Sky Warrior.

Joe surmised the shaman had tried to perform the good deed to hide his and his son's past misdeeds, or to make up for them before his god. Surely Hawk Eyes had realized no one would believe the action was an accident, as Knife-Slayer was an expert shot. Justice, often strange and swift, had claimed both men.

Night Stalker was angered by his friend's deceit and his dishonorable conduct. During the past week, it had become clear to the chief's son that peace was the best trail to ride; working with whites, especially soldiers, had shown him most were not bad men and most wanted truce. He now knew that his father and others were right to seek peace, and he would obey the sacred vision. He pleased Sun Cloud with his change of heart and behavior.

Joe walked around the wagon and examined it. Near the front, he kicked the wooden hull and shouted, "Come on out, Orin, the game's over. We know about your hiding place." There was no response. "You want us to chop through your fake bottom or burn you out?" Joe threatened.

Everyone gathered around the white-topped wagon as Joe issued his warnings and kicks again. The clearing had been surrounded by their forces, so they knew Orin couldn't have escaped.

"Bring the hatchets, boys; we'll chop our way to him."

A shot rang out, and everyone jumped back as they assumed Orin was firing at them. Nothing happened for a while.

Then, Joe spotted blood dripping to the ground beneath the wagon. He climbed inside, and Clay followed. They searched for an entrance to the secret compartment and found it. They were not surprised by the grim sight that greeted them.

Orin's body was hauled outside—dead from a self-inflicted wound to the head, preferring that to arrest and execution or prison. Joe removed his metal mask to show Black Moon and the others the truth. The flowing black hair was attached, so the mane left with the disguise. He watched Black Moon, his braves, and Red Heart warriors touch the tattooed snakes. He heard them laugh in relief to discover the man was human and the vipers unreal.

Joe recovered some of the "magic" balls and demonstrated how they worked. He passed out the remaining ones from Orin's supply. Despite the fact that the Indians knew the balls were tricks, they were amazed by them and continued to call them "big magic." Since Orin's target was the Oglalas, Sun Cloud was presented with the snake mask. To prevent jealousy, Black Moon was given the wagon, horses, and supplies. Both chiefs were pleased with their presents.

Tom and Stede were overjoyed by the removal of the final obstacle to peace in the territory. A burial detail tended to the chore of interring the remains of Orin McMichael, along with his two men, near the sacred location McMichael had craved. Joe related the motive behind the Scotsman's scheme, excluding one part: gold in the Black Hills. He would keep that fact a secret, except to warn Sun Cloud at a later date to make certain whites were kept out of the rich hills. Once gold was discovered, Joe was certain encroachment and a bitter war would take place.

When Black Moon comprehended how he had been duped, the Crow chief was silent in his shame. It helped matters when Sun Cloud told him they, too, had been falsely provoked against the Bird People by Orin's tricks. It made everyone happy to see the two leaders make truce. It was hoped that when news of their joint attack reached the ears of other Crow and Lakota tribes, it would entice them to lessen their hatreds.

Three camps were made as dusk appeared: Crow, Red Heart, and white. Yet men from each visited others and chatted with new friends and allies. The prisoners were held in the white camp by soldiers, to be taken to Fort Tabor the next day. It was decided to hold them there until after the treaty council to prevent any distractions from its importance. Men were assigned to take charge of Orin's trading post until a decision was made concerning it. They were ordered to search for the stolen payroll shipment from June eleventh, if the money wasn't already spent on illegal guns and whiskey.

Horses were fetched and tended. Wounded were treated. Meals were cooked and eaten. Chores were completed. Groups gathered to talk about this shared coup, the impending treaty, and future plans.

They were to split up in the morning. Sun Cloud and his band would ride home to prepare for their journey to Fort Laramie, to place the two warriors on death scaffolds, to send his people on the way to their winter camp, and to make Wind Bird their next shaman. Clay Thorne was to travel with them to speak with Buckskin Girl and Morning Star. He would journey to the meeting with his grandmother's tribe, with whom he would live. Then he would visit his family and people—the Cheyenne. Black Moon and his party would ride home to make their preparations to attend the joint council far away. Troops would ride to Fort Tabor with the prisoners, most to remain there until they were relieved in a month. The agent, Stede, Joe, and three soldiers would head for Laramie.

While Tom wrote out a report on this episode, Stede and Joe visited Sun Cloud's campsite. The three chatted genially for a time, with Sun Cloud praising the work of "Tanner" and his daughter. Neither white man revealed the truth of Joe's identity. That was something that needed to be handled in private and after the treaty was signed. Once the big council was over, Joe would go after Morning Star and expose the truth.

The treaty talk was scheduled to begin on September seventh, so each group had to hurry with their camp tasks and get to Laramie. Joe wanted to be present, and wished his love could be there. He wanted to witness the termination of their mission. He wanted to view the historic event so he could tell their children about it one day. It would enable Morning Star to leave home knowing peace ruled her land and protected her family and people.

Joe was eager to see her, hold her, kiss her. He dreaded the revelations they must make to Sun Cloud of their love and deceit. He had come to like and respect the chief more and more during his stay here. He prayed that time would soften the crushing blow. He grasped that what they must do would hurt the noble chief deeply. Joe hoped understanding and forgiveness would not be long in coming.

As the sun rose on a glorious day, Sun Cloud bid Stede and "Tanner" farewell until he saw them again at Horse Creek. He rode homeward with his band, a changed son, a new medicine chief, and two dead Oglalas. He carried his coup prize with him: Orin's mask. Elation surged through him as he imagined his parents —Gray Eagle and Alisha/Shalee—and his brother, Bright Arrow, witnessing this event from the Great Spirit's side. He knew how happy his beloved wife would be to see his safe return and to hear of their victory. There would be much celebrating in his camp when they reached home. He never suspected what grim news awaited him . . .

One of the main reasons Clay—Sky Warrior—Thorne accompanied the Red Hearts was to tell Morning Star not to expose anything about the couple's scandalous plan until Joe returned home with her father. Joe had asked him to warn her that if Sun Cloud learned they'd all tricked him, he might think he'd be tricked again at the peace council. "He mustn't have any doubts about the treaty or refuse to attend the meeting," Joe commanded. "Don't do or say anything to stop your father from coming." If Morning Star let their secret slip, he would be there to defend Joe's motives and character. Clay knew Morning Star might need his support and encouragement. He also wanted to ask Flaming Star for his daughter in joining, even though Buckskin Girl had already accepted him. By the time he returned from Laramie, the woman would have their tepee ready and their joining ceremony could take place. At last, his heart and mind were at peace. He felt he belonged here living as an Indian in the Dakota territory with a fine woman. He wished Joe and Morning Star the same happiness, but felt it would be long in coming.

Joe waved to Clay and Sun Cloud and watched them ride out of sight. He walked to the spot Zeke Randall was bound to force out of him the final piece of information he needed. Before he began, he had one of the soldiers take Farley to another area. "There's something I have to know, Zeke. Who—"

"You sorry bastard, I ain't telling you nothing!"

"I think you will. I know a few more things you've done here that I haven't mentioned in my reports yet. Be stubborn, and I'll gladly add them to the list of charges against you. That information should make certain you're hanged, or put a lot more years on your prison sentence. Tell me what I want to know, and I'll keep it to myself."

"What's so damn important to you?" Zeke sneered.

"I came here in early spring with a friend, Tanner Gaston, son of that man over there," Joe explained. "While we were in Pierre, somebody put a knife in him and murdered him. I want to know who's responsible. If you did it, I'll still honor my deal with you. I have to know who killed him before my mind can rest. His death is one of the main reasons I was so determined to defeat all of you. I'm offering you a good deal, Zeke, one you don't deserve. I advise you to accept it and not rile me again. I think you've witnessed how dangerous I can be when crossed."

"He a dark-haired man about your age, looked half-breed?"

"Yes," Joe answered. He was angered by Zeke's insulting tone and surprised the miscreant complied. "Tanner overheard something by accident, and one of you made certain he couldn't repeat it. Fact is, he lived long enough to give me a few clues that put me on your trail. It was probably about that wagon trip you took when we met. Talk. We don't have much time left."

"Ain't nothing you can do about it now; Clem gutted your friend. He's dead. It was his loose tongue that Gaston overheard, so the boys told him he had to clean up his mess. Me and Farley wasn't in Pierre that night, but they told me about killing a spy. Guess that was him. Too bad the boys didn't know about you that night and slit your miserable neck."

"Yep, it's a real shame they didn't commit two murders!" Joe growled. "If you've told the truth, our deal stands. If you lied, I'll let you hang for his death, guilty or not." Joe had Zeke gagged to make certain the big man didn't shout any warnings to his buddy. He went to the spot where Farley was captive, out of hearing range from his companion.

Joe intimidated Farley into talking. He was relieved in a strange way to hear the same account from him. Maybe it was because he knew he finally had the truth about Tanner's murder, and the killer was dead. Justice had been carried out without his participation. He had Farley returned to the others and Zeke's gag removed. While he waited for his party to move out, he completed his own report for Tom and the authorities. He left nothing out, and felt no remorse over duping Zeke. When Stede joined him, he related what he had learned about Tanner's death, and both grieved the heavy loss in silence for a time.

The detail mounted and departed with the prisoners, riding east to Fort Tabor. Joe was glad to have them out of his life forever. He was also glad the officer in charge was taking care of those false accusations against him and Morning Star. With Sergeant Bart Carnes in custody, the man would stand trial for the murder of

Captain James Thomas and the deserter, George Hollis. Joe had liked Jim, and was sorry he had been slain while helping to solve this case.

Black Moon had left about the same time the Oglalas had, so the clearing was rather quiet, with only six men and horses present. Everything was packed and ready. The smallest group mounted and rode southwest. They entered the northwest section of the Black Hills to journey to the grasslands beyond it and on to Fort Laramie. The trek would require six or seven days.

As they traveled, Joe thought about Morning Star and his family. He wondered what she was doing as she spent her last few weeks with her family. He knew she must be experiencing an array of emotions. He was anxious to get finished here and head home. He wanted to see his parents, sister, and her family. He wanted to make certain everything and everyone there was all right. He wanted to roam the plantation, and enjoy life and peace to the fullest. He had experienced enough excitement and adventure to last him a long time. He was ready to get married, to settle down, to build his own home, and to have children. He knew the perfect spot on the Lawrence property for them to live. Soon, he kept telling himself, his dreams and goals would be realized.

The men made camp an hour before dusk. They were exhausted from yesterday's tense episode and their journey today. The weary horses, dusty and sweaty, were eager to rest and graze after being unsaddled. Joe and one of the soldiers cooked the evening meal. Tom and Stede conversed and relaxed. As they ate, another scout from Fort Laramie arrived, an extra horse in tow.

He dismounted, and one of the men tended his fatigued animals. He walked to the campfire and asked, "Which one of you is Stede Gaston?"

"I am," Stede replied, a curious sensation attacking his gut.

"Urgent message, sir." As he unfastened his pouch and withdrew the letter, he explained, "Colonel Mitchell ordered me to bring it to you at Fort Tabor. The boys there sent me to find you at Bear Butte. Before I reached it, I met the detail heading in with prisoners. They told me which route you were taking back to Fort Laramie. I rode across country to intercept you. This is it, sir," he finished his report and handed over the missive that was marked URGENT across the front in two places.

Stede tore open the envelope with shaky hands, fearing it was bad news about his older sister or her family. He had lost his only son here, and he prayed he wasn't about to learn he had lost another loved one during his long absence. He was shocked by the contents of the letter.

"What is it, sir?" Joe asked, concerned by his friend's reaction.

Stede's dark gaze, filled with sadness, met the younger man's. His voice was hoarsened by emotion as he revealed, "Bad news, Joe, about your father. It's from Annabelle. She thought I could locate you and get you home quickly. Joseph's very ill, Son, dying."

Joe paled, and a shudder raced over his body. He tossed his plate aside, intense apprehension flooding him. *Father, dying,* his mind echoed.

Stede had no choice but to continue with the terrible news. "The doctor says he can't linger more than six or seven weeks. Annabelle wants you to get home as soon as possible. She hired a man to deliver this to me, so it was written only a few weeks ago. If you hurry, there should still be time to reach home before . . ."

Joe was glad Stede didn't finish that awful sentence. His mind was dazed with many thoughts about getting home swiftly and about Morning Star. Retrieving his love and perhaps battling to win her from Sun Cloud would require precious time his father might not have. *Only weeks more to live . . .* and it took that many to reach home without any delays. *Any delays . . .*

Stede grasped how upset the man was, so he offered some suggestions. "If you leave in the morning for Tabor, you can catch a steamer there. At St. Louis, you can get a horse and cut across country to Richmond to the plantation. That's the quickest route. You can leave Star at Tabor. I'll see to him after the treaty. When Sun Cloud gets to Laramie, I'll explain everything to him. I'll visit his camp and tell Morning Star what happened. If you want, Son, I'll bring her to Virginia. You have to get home fast to spend any last days with him. You lost your best friend here, and I'll be losing a good one there. Life makes these demands on us."

Joe stood, paced, and protested, "I can't just leave for . . . I don't know how long without seeing her, sir. She'll be upset and afraid. She might not come with you, and I don't know when I can return. Sun Cloud may not let her leave home if I'm not there to persuade him I love her."

Stede understood his dilemma, but stressed that if he took the time to visit her or fight for her, he could reach home too late. "I haven't gotten over the fact I wasn't with Molly or Tanner when they died," he confided. "You need to speak with Joseph, Son; you didn't leave home with his blessing. And your mother needs you. Love is strong; it can wait a while."

"If you start trouble with Sun Cloud in your state of mind and rush him," Tom added, "you could stop him from attending the peace conference. We've all worked hard for this treaty to succeed, Joe. Don't ruin it now. I'm sure she'll either wait for your return or go with Stede. Will you be able to forgive yourself if you get there too late because of romantic notions? You have years ahead with her, but not with your father, from how it sounds."

Stede withdrew money from his pocket, handed it to Joe, and said, "You'll need this for passage and to buy a horse in St. Louis. Don't worry about anything here. I'll make sure the treaty is fair to Sun Cloud and his tribe. I'll tell you everything when I bring Morning Star to you in Virginia."

"You can use my other horse," the scout offered. "You can travel faster by changing mounts every few hours. Just leave him at Tabor, and the boys there will bring him to me when they return to Laramie. Both of them are fast and sure-footed."

Those kindnesses touched Joe deeply. "Thanks, you two. I'll leave right now," he decided, but Stede halted him with a grip on one wrist.

"No, Son. You and those horses are exhausted. You wouldn't get far before both of you collapse. Clear your head and don't be rash. It's a long and hard journey facing you. The trail is fraught with perils. Get a good night's sleep and ride out fresh and alert at dawn. We'll have your horses and supplies ready at first light. I'll see to Morning Star, I promise. Go straight home, Joe," he urged.

"I will, sir. Right now, I need to be alone for a while." Joe headed into a copse of hardwoods to get his emotions under control.

Chapter Nineteen

un Cloud and his party reached Buffalo Gap at midmorning. Red Hearts gathered around to hear the glorious tale of victory at Bear Butte and reports of Joe's perilous role in it. The ecstatic group was given food and water, and boys guided their horses away to be tended. Wives embraced husbands, mothers hugged sons, and children clasped the necks and legs of fathers. It was a time of celebration and happiness, a time of looking to the future, a moment of relief for safe returns.

The elated chief explained how they had worked with Crow, enemies for generations. He talked of the soldiers' friendliness and acceptance of him. He related the motive behind Snake-Man's greed and wickedness, and everyone comprehended why their Great Spirit had been eager to stop it. His party was praised and congratulated.

Sun Cloud held up his souvenir, then hung Orin's mask on a pole near the meeting lodge for all to see and study. He exposed the grim news about Hawk Eyes and Knife-Slayer, and the good news about Wind Bird becoming shaman. He called the man forward to demonstrate the "magic balls" Joe had given to him. The display drew sounds of amazement and approval of such "big medicine."

Morning Star was not happy about the two deaths, but she was relieved the bad influence of both men had been removed. She was glad when War Chief Lone Horn invited the grieving Waterlily into his tepee for protection and support until she recovered from her two losses and took another husband. She was relieved that her love was safe somewhere.

Sun Cloud spoke of his impending journey to Fort Laramie. He planned to leave at sunrise with chosen warriors to sign a joint treaty with allies and past foes. He gave the command to break summer camp the next day to head for the Black Hills to set up their winter one. Men were assigned their duties during the seasonal trek.

As the people returned to their chores and families, Sun Cloud said to his wife and daughter, "It is a good day. The bloodline of my father has gathered many coups. My pride is large for you, Morning Star, and for Sky Warrior, grandson of my uncle. When Tanner returns with me after the treaty council, we will have a great feast to honor my daughter and blood brother. Truce, my loved ones, has been long and hard in coming. Until it is gone, we will enjoy peace and happiness. My heart is filled to bursting."

Singing Wind cast Morning Star a look of regret at having to spoil this glorious moment, but Sun Cloud was leaving tomorrow. She wanted to be the one to reveal the shocking truth to her husband, not risk his learning it from someone else while he was gone.

Morning Star's eyes pled for silence, but her mother did not catch the signal to postpone the revelation until another day. She wanted Joe here with her when their dark secret came to light; she had not thought of him riding on to Fort Laramie with Stede and the others. She prayed her actions would not delay the search for peace.

Sun Cloud noticed the curious behavior. "What fox walks in the heads of my loved ones?" he teased the two women.

"Come, my husband, and I will tell you."

While glancing at his nervous daughter, the intrigued chief let his wife guide him into their tepee. He watched her seal the flap, the signal for privacy. When she grasped his hand, pulled him to their sleeping mat, and drew him down to sit beside her, Sun Cloud misunderstood, and his desires flamed. He grinned and jested, "You grow brave, Singing Wind, to let others see your great hunger for me. It is good our hearts and bodies still burn for each other, and we have the strength to feed them at our ages."

"Love and hunger are not what burns in me this sun. I am sorry."

Morning Star stared at the closed flap of the tepee, then sought refuge away from camp. She sat beside a rushing stream and wished time would pass as swiftly. She wished Joe had returned with Sun Cloud. She needed him at her side when she faced her father soon. She had spoken with her mother many times in the last thirteen days. She had obeyed Singing Wind's urgent request to give the important decision more study, but nothing had changed her mind. She loved Joseph Lawrence, she wanted to marry him, she wanted to spend her life with him, and she wanted to bear his children. Whatever challenges confronted them, they would meet them together.

She looked up as Clay joined her to pass along her love's messages and warning. When he discovered the secret had been revealed to her mother who was presently telling Sun Cloud, he looked worried. As Buckskin Girl arrived, Clay offered her his help if there was trouble. Feeling there was nothing he could do, she smiled and told him to spend his short time with Buckskin Girl. The two walked away, hand in hand, to speak with Flaming Star about a joining ceremony.

Time passed too slowly for Morning Star in her state of dismay. Singing Wind had insisted on being the one to break the news to her husband. She had told Morning Star it was best for everyone involved if she related the decision and the reasons behind it. She had disagreed with her mother, but relented when it seemed so important to Singing Wind.

Her mother had spoken with her and had considered the matter at length. At last Singing Wind had said she understood and accepted that choice and realized how difficult and painful it had been for her daughter to make it. That and assurance of her mother's love eased her anxieties for a while, but they had returned with her father's arrival and the talk in progress.

Singing Wind was sad about her child's leaving. The older woman feared they would never see each other again. Her final words before Sun Cloud arrived were,

"Go in peace, my daughter, and walk the path Grandfather makes for you. It will be long and hard, but do it bravely."

Morning Star dreaded the upcoming talk with her father, but knew the matter must be settled. She could not stay here and lose Joe. She could not marry another and bear his children. Joe was her heart, her future. Her life here was over. With Joe, once the anguish of her decision passed and she eased into his world, she would be happy and free. Whatever the sacrifice to follow her true destiny, her true love, she would make it.

The nervous woman glanced toward camp and wondered what was being said between her parents. If only she did not have to shame and hurt them to make her dreams come true . . .

The exuberance of victory left Sun Cloud's heart and mind; now they were consumed by disbelief, anguish, turmoil, and anger. He listened to his beloved wife's stunning revelation about their daughter and Joseph Lawrence. He felt betrayed by them, their deceit, their weakness, their cowardice. He was hurt by their lack of trust in him, and their surrender to a forbidden union, as he knew they must have yielded to temptation while on the trail alone and in love. He wondered how his beautiful, gentle, sweet Morning Star could do this awful thing.

As promised before Singing Wind began this talk, he listened and held silent until she finished. Then Sun Cloud agonized aloud. "Does she not realize this cannot be? She and her family will be dishonored and attacked by pain. Has she forgotten our laws? It is wrong, shameful. I cannot break them or bend them for my child; that is unfair to all others. If I do not banish her, my people will see me as a weakling, unworthy to be their chief. If she is sent away, never can my eyes gaze upon the proof of her betrayal. She will no longer be my daughter. She will be cut from our lives, the story of our family, from our bloodline."

"Nothing can remove your blood from her, my love," Singing Wind refuted. "It can only be denied. She did not plan to trick us; Joe did not plan to trick us. Sometimes such actions must be taken. Remember what happened the night he came to us and understand why they did this. When Morning Star learned of the sacred vision and believed Joe was Sky Warrior, she acted swiftly to save his life. The Great Spirit silenced her tongue, my husband, not evil and defiance."

In his torment and shock, Sun Cloud disagreed, "There have been many times since that moon to reveal the truth; they have not. I trusted Sky Warrior; I made him blood brother and thought him a man of honor, a man of Running Wolf's bloodline. In secret, as the sly raccoon sneaks about in the night, he stole precious food from my tepee. Others know he is not Tanner—Stede, Broken-Hand, Clay, the soldiers—but none revealed his deceit. How do I know they will not keep other secrets from me? How do I know they will not make deceit for me and all Indians with the treaty?"

"Truce tricks are not in Payaba's vision, my love."

"My daughter's betrayal was not in Payaba's vision, but it is done."

"You are wrong, my husband. Their love is there, so, too, their leaving, but Wakantanka held Payaba's tongue silent until the right time to reveal them. That is now, my love."

Sun Cloud gaped at his wife. "Why have so many secrets been kept from me and Red Hearts? Why must she do this? It was selfish, defiant, and blind to jump on a wild horse she cannot ride."

Singing Wind caressed his cheek and reminded, "As we did long ago, my husband? Have you forgotten how we broke the laws of our peoples when we surrendered to love while I was promised to your brother? We risked banishment, dishonor, and death to have each other. I teased you that it would take more than an Eagle's fledgling to tame Singing Wind or to give her sweet pleasure, but you did both. Perhaps it will take more than an Indian warrior to do the same for our daughter. She is different from others, my love. She is strong, proud, brave, smart; but she is gentle and caring. She does not do this to be selfish. She does not wish to hurt us or to punish us. She is now as we were long ago—young, passionate, and in love."

"It is different, my wife; no one knew of our secret, our weakness."

"Does that make it any less true, or us any less guilty? We were not forced to choose between love and banishment, as she must do. We were not forced to choose between our loves and our families, as she must do. We were not forced to choose between joy and sadness, as she must do. We did not choose each other to love and join; Wakantanka put such feelings in our hearts and bodies, and He removed all obstacles from our union path. It is the same with Morning Star and Joe."

"How will the obstacle of our laws be removed, my wife? More whites and wars will come. If I change our laws, it will bring more palefaces into our tribe. If our bloods are weakened, we will know great defeats when the new battles come. When sides go to war, it will split the mixed families. My people listened to the words of Gray Eagle and obeyed them. They listen to mine and obey me. If I speak to change the law, it will bring trouble, sadness, and dissension. My people accepted whites in the lives of my father and brother. For my daughter to choose a white man sets a bad example. It will appear that the bloodline of Gray Eagle prefers white mates over ones of their own kind. I am chief and must think of my duty."

"Morning Star knows the truth about Alisha, my love," she revealed, then explained how the girl had learned the news. "How can we say it was good for Gray Eagle to love and join a white woman but it is bad for our daughter to do the same with a white man, one who has risked his life to save our people and to bring peace to our land? What of our child's coups and risks, my love? She faced as many dangers. She tried to obey our laws; she tried to remain strong. When fate seemed against us long ago, we battled our feelings, but could not stay strong and loyal to our ways. We knew what was right and wrong, but love swayed and ruled us."

"We are the same; they are not."

"Morning Star is half like him, my love, and she knows this."

"But he was raised white, and she was raised Indian. You take their side when you must fight it. You make excuses for them."

"As we did for ourselves long ago?" she asked in a gentle tone.

"It is not the same," he contended without raising his voice in anger.

"How is it different?"

"You think as a woman, with the heart."

"You think as a man and a chief, with the head. But Morning Star is a woman, and she has been a warrior. Her head battled fiercely with her heart. Only because she truly believes this is Grandfather's will did she have the courage to follow her heart. Remember what you said to me when we were entrapped by our laws?' If evil has separated us, we must destroy it to be joined.' Hatred is evil, my love; war is evil, my love; they are destructive forces. They must be defeated. That was done at the sacred mountain."

"But only for a time, my wife," the chief reminded. "They will return, even stronger and deadlier the next time."

"Is that not a good reason to have our child far away, safe and happy? Do not let a man's pride be stronger than a father's love in this matter. Do not make us lose her heart along with her body. Do not make her suffer more than she must. Remember how Gray Eagle could not battle his love and destiny. Remember how we could not battle them. Accept it is the same for Morning Star and Joe," she urged.

Sun Cloud fused his troubled gaze with Singing Wind's imploring one. He had no more answers, only torment and sadness—and grief over the impending loss of his cherished daughter. He was glad Singing Wind had disclosed this news to him. If his daughter had done so, he might have said terrible things to her in his anger and dismay, and provoked a vicious quarrel. It was too late to change the situation, so he must deal with it in the only way left open to him. "I will speak with her."

Morning Star rose as her father approached. His gaze and expression revealed nothing of his turbulent feelings, a skill he used well when necessary. Her heart drummed in her tight chest, her mouth was dry, and her body trembled. She did not fear her father, but she feared the demands of this matter. "Mother told you?" she asked, her voice quavering, her eyes filled with anguish.

Sun Cloud did not speak for a time. His impenetrable gaze roamed her from head to toe, then settled on her face, which was lined with worry and tension. "Singing Wind told me of your secret. You have spoken with her many times and you know what sacrifices you must make. They are not yours alone, my daughter; we must share your dishonor and banishment. After the words are given to our people, I cannot speak your name or see your face again."

That news was expected, but still it was a crushing blow to hear him deliver it. "That is not my choice, Father. I love you. I do not want to hurt you or shame you before others. It cuts into my heart to lose you and Mother. I do not want to leave in banishment and dishonor, but that is our law."

"You know I cannot change it for you."

"Yes, Father, and I am sorry it must be so. I pray you to seek and find understanding and forgiveness as I take the true path of my Life-Circle. If it is wrong to love and join Joe, the Great Spirit would not allow it. I will learn the white ways, seek to understand their hatred and greed, and will send that knowledge to help my people."

"It will not stop what is to be, my child. When Joe's people come to destroy us, what then? Your heart will war with your mind once more. You must become white to live among them; you must deny your Indian heritage and blood to be accepted."

"War must end forever some day, Father."

"It will not until one side is destroyed or conquered. You rode Payaba's vision. Do not forget the rest of it—more war, a great and bloody war. Can you deny all and who you are, Morning Star? What of honor, duty, blood? What of love for your family, your people, your land? The line of Gray Eagle must continue; it must become strong and pure once more. Do not stain it with more white blood. Bright Arrow has only daughters, no son to carry on the chief's line. You must bear an Indian child, my daughter."

"The line will pass through Night Stalker and Bloody Arrow."

"What if they do not survive the next white man's attack? If you have no Indian son to take their place, the chief's line will pass from ours. When it has done so, we will be defeated, almost destroyed. That warning was in the sacred vision of Mind-Who-Roams when he was shaman to Gray Eagle."

"Bright Arrow has many grandsons from Little Feet and Tashina," Morning Star pointed out, "They are sons of chiefs. Little Feet has more sons with Thunder Spirit, child of White Arrow, best friend to Gray Eagle when they lived. If those sons are too old to ride as chief when the new war comes, there is the son of Soaring Hawk, child of Tashina. The Cheyenne shaman says he is marked for greatness; and he is of Gray Eagle's bloodline. Have you forgotten how Red Cloud's father was a Brule, but he leads his mother's Oglala band? The Cheyenne are our allies and friends. Why could the grandson of Tashina not become Red Heart chief —if Night Stalker, Bloody Arrow, and all others are taken from his path?"

She caught his hand in hers. "What I do, Father, will not change the destinies of others. It will not halt or bring war. If I stay and join an Indian, that does not mean I will bear sons. Bright Arrow had no sons, and many others have no sons. All lives and fates are in the Great Spirit's hands. I must go to Virginia with Joe and become his wife. He helped rid our lands of evil ones. The Great White Chief has commanded peace, and all nations and tribes have agreed to sign the treaty. You must let nothing halt Sun Cloud from signing it. Joe needed my skills to win this great victory for our people. You, Father, are the one who gave them to me. You taught me the white man's tongue. You taught me warrior skills. You trained me to be clever and daring. You showed me how to be strong, how to do what must be done for the good of our tribe. Do you not see—Grandfather was leading you to prepare me for the sacred vision?"

"I do not deny such words and truths."

Before he could continue, she contended, "You said not to forget the rest of the sacred vision. I have not, but there is more Payaba must tell you about it. My love and leaving are parts of it, Father; they are His will, my destiny. Obeying is painful and hard, but I must and will do so. You are a great chief, a good father; you can expect nothing less of me. When Joe returns, you must not harm him. You must let me ride away with him."

Sun Cloud turned away to think and to master his warring emotions. His mind roamed to days long past, and to days beyond his birth that his parents had revealed to him.

Morning Star gazed at her father's back, still muscled and strong. She looked at the flowing ebony mane with its few streaks of white. Sun Cloud was still sleek and honed. He was still handsome and virile. He was loved, respected, and obeyed by the Red Hearts, and by most allies. Like his father, he was a legend awed and feared by their enemies.

She wanted to make his task easier for him, so she said in English, "I know how this pre-dic-ament must distress and torment you, Father. I know, as chief, you can not make ex-ceptions for me. I understand your duty and why you must stand taller and stronger than other Indians. Do what you must, Father, for I will love you and respect you forever, even more now because I know it is harder for you this time. I understand our laws, and we must both honor them."

At last, Sun Cloud made his heartrending decision and faced her. Despite his enormous strength of mind and will, his dark eyes glistened with deep and warring emotions. "I will say this but once, Morning Star, for the last time. I love you; I am proud of you; I will miss you. Go to live in peace, happiness, and safety. Have children where they will not be forced to live as half-breeds and where they will not endure wars and death. You have helped your people to survive many more years. I will sign the treaty, and I will honor it as long as I can. Your people love you and praise your brave coups, but they cannot disobey our laws for their chief's daughter. I must not coax them to change those laws, for they mean the survival of our bloodlines and race. I will tell them the truth this night. I will banish you before them. I will forbid the speaking of your name again. Only the legend of She-Who-Rode-With-The-Sky-Warrior will be upon our lips and on our tribal records. It pains my heart to deny you, but it must be this way for the good of our people. You must not return home, ever. It will do much harm for others to see you joined to a white man. He will not be safe in our land when the treaty is broken, and it *will* be broken." He drew her into his arms and embraced her. "Good-bye, my daughter. We will never touch or see each other again. What I must do this moon is hard, but it is for the good of our people."

"I know, Father. I love you. Come, end the pain of this matter."

Nearing four o'clock, Sun Cloud asked Wolf Eyes to summon the people to a clearing, and the ceremonial chief obeyed.

Morning Star stood beside her father with her head held high. She concealed her anxiety, and displayed courage and pride. She must not allow anyone to think she was ashamed of what the chief was revealing. Her gaze roamed the large group: Sun Cloud, Singing Wind, Night Stalker, Buckskin Girl, Clay Thorne, Payaba, her kin, and her people. She saw Touched-A-Crow leave with a surly Bloody Arrow, and she prayed her brother could eventually change the boy's behavior. If the child continued to walk his rebellious path, he would become more like a son of Knife-Slayer than her brother. It was bad and alarming for Bloody Arrow to be in line for the chief's bonnet. Surely Grandfather would alter or remove him . . .

Morning Star saw girls whispering amongst themselves as they speculated on the reason of the tribal meeting and their friend's involvement in it. She knew from Buckskin Girl that unmarried braves wondered if the meeting was being called to announce her joining. She could not help but be relieved that Hawk Eyes and Knife-Slayer were not present to cause trouble. Her father lifted his hand for silence and attention. The moment arrived.

"Hear me, my people. Morning Star told me Sky Warrior is not Tanner Gaston; his name is Joseph Lawrence. Payaba said of his vision: 'The Great Mystery showed me two men. One's face was hidden from my eyes, but Grandfather said he carried Oglala blood . . . He will call the lost warrior back to the land of his people to share our destiny.' That man is Stede Gaston, son of Powchutu, Eagle's Arm. Payaba said of the second man: 'Trouble will be reborn, but its life will be cut short by the warrior Grandfather sends to us. A long peace will follow . . . He is a white-eye who will come to help us defeat our enemies . . . Peace lies within the grasp of the white-eye whose hair blazes as the sun and in whose eyes the blue of sky lives. His heart will side with us. Many foes, Indian and white, will try to defeat him.' This is all true of Joseph Lawrence and what has taken place. The vision did not say Sky Warrior carried Indian blood; Joe does not. It did not say Sky Warrior is the son of the man with Oglala blood; Joe is not."

Sun Cloud witnessed the shocked and baffled reactions to his words, but his people held silent, as was their custom. He saw how some looked at his daughter with suspicion and curiosity. "When Joe came to us to seek our help and friendship, many resisted him and some tried to have him slain. Joe came to our land with Stede and Tanner Gaston to work for peace. When Tanner was killed by the evil ones and we scorned Joe, he claimed to be Tanner to win our acceptance. The Great Spirit works in mysterious ways. Grandfather allowed this trick to happen and to remain hidden until now, because Grandfather needed Joe to work for our peace and survival. When many resisted Joe's words, he believed the only way to win our trust, acceptance, and help was to claim he was Tanner Gaston of Running Wolf's bloodline. Joe did not want to trick us; he did not plan to trick us. It came to him as he was attacked and threatened with death. He did this to save his life to work on the sacred vision. His deceit was wrong, and our behavior that night was wrong. We are all living creatures and make such mistakes. It is true he wanted to save us and to get peace; he wished to do this for Tanner and Stede, who are as father and brother to him. When he came to know us, he came to like, respect, and accept us as worthy to save. One weakness in him does not take away his honor and many coups."

Many heads nodded in understanding. Sun Cloud awaited their reaction to his imminent disclosure. "When the treaty council ends, Morning Star will leave our land with Sky Warrior, to live in the white world and to become his mate." As people looked confused, Sun Cloud reminded, "They are not of the same bloodline, for Joe is not Tanner, not the grandson of Eagle's Arm, son of Running Wolf. Morning Star's destiny is not here with us. Payaba saw this in his vision, but Grandfather commanded him not to speak of it until peace ruled our land and the sacred mission was victorious. Payaba revealed it to me this sun; I believe and accept it as the will of the Great Spirit. Morning Star's destiny is in the land where her grandmother was raised. Perhaps our two Gods have made truce, as we make truce with our enemies. The white God sent Alisha/Shalee to my father, and the Great Spirit must send Morning Star to Joe. Gray Eagle claimed Shalee as wife. Now, Joe claims their granddaughter as wife. This is our great sacrifice for peace and survival; it is Morning Star's Sun Dance ritual to surrender herself to destiny and Wakantanka's will."

The hard part of Sun Cloud's task arrived. "But Payaba's vision also said: 'More white-eyes will journey here in great numbers. Their hungers will bring even darker and bloodier suns' than we have known for these past seasons. We must sign the treaty, though it will be broken one day, so we can enjoy many winters of peace, happiness, and survival. But, as Payaba warned: 'The white-eyes will come to fear and battle the Dakota Nation as they do with no other. The Tetons will lead all tribes of the Seven Council Fires and our allies in the last battle for survival.' It is our law not to join with our enemies, the whites. We must not change this law. We must keep our bloodlines pure and strong; they must stay Indian. If this law is broken, the guilty one is pushed from our camp and lives. This is what I must do with my daughter, for even a chief's family is not above tribal law."

As Sun Cloud took a few breaths, he saw people stare at Morning Star. Some reactions said his words were right; some said cruel; some said they felt empathy, but agreed with the law.

"No Red Heart, not even the chief and his family, must speak her name again. She must be banished. Our laws must not be changed. Morning Star understands and agrees. From this moon until our days cease, we must speak only of She-Who-Rode-With-The-Sky-Warrior, and she must never return to us. When my people break camp on the new sun to move into the Black Hills, she must remain here to wait for Joseph Lawrence."

Singing Wind, standing beside her daughter, started to protest the cruelty of leaving their child alone and in possible peril from renegades and wicked whites and from the forces of Mother Nature. But Morning Star grasped her hand and squeezed it to tell her to hold silent. It was one of the hardest things she had ever done, but she obeyed the message.

Morning Star locked her gaze with her brother's. Disbelief, anger, and disappointment filled Night Stalker's eyes. She smiled at him to let him know she was all right. As her father reminded everyone, her departure and mixed marriage were in the sacred vision and wills of the Great Spirit, Night Stalker returned the smile and nodded understanding.

To let those who resisted this decision know he wasn't being cruel and unfair or sacrificing an unwilling child, Sun Cloud added, "Morning Star loves this white man and chooses to go with him. From this time on to forever, Morning Star is dead to us, to her family and to her people; and we are dead to her. She must gather her possessions and make camp away from us until she leaves our land. She must be avoided; she must not be spoken to or looked at; she must not be helped with chores or visited. Morning Star is no more. Only the legend of She-Who-Rode-With-The-Sky-Warrior can be spoken, remembered, and honored."

Again, Morning Star squeezed her mother's quivering hand to halt the protest she perceived. Neither she nor her mother had thought of this part of banishment. Both had forgotten, once the words were spoken publicly, the deed was done and the punishment began. Her heart was breaking, and she wished Joe were here to give her courage. She prayed the peace council and his return would not be long in coming. Her father would tell him what had happened when he reached Fort Laramie and surely Joe would hurry to her side, here where she must camp alone and wait for him.

Sun Cloud commanded as chief, not her grieving father, "Turn your eyes and backs to her, my people. She is dead to us." To his lost child, he ordered, "Go, fetch your possessions and leave camp. Do not approach it again. This is our law. Live nearby until the white man comes for you."

Morning Star was consumed by anguish. She was cut off from her family and friends. They could not exchange goodbyes. To them, she must be as the wind—invisible, ignored. She must be as the flower—silent. She must be as the cactus spines—untouched. She was banished, forever. It was done.

The band, many with broken hearts, obeyed the chief and their law. They turned away from the beautiful creature with misty eyes. No one spoke, though many wished to do so, as it was their way and was necessary. Many said a mute farewell to the exquisite female, the brave vision woman.

Singing Wind did not care who witnessed her defiance. She embraced her·

child and whispered, "I love you, Morning Star. I will miss you and never forget you. You will always be my daughter. Be safe and happy."

She hugged the woman and whispered in her ear, "Be strong, Mother. I love you and will miss you. I will never forget all you have taught me. Help Father through this hard time. Soon I will be fine."

Night Stalker also embraced her and whispered, "Forever you are my sister and I will love you, no matter our law. I will be a good chief. Do not worry about our parents and people. I will take care of them."

Morning Star gazed into his dark eyes and smiled, as she knew he spoke the truth. Tears blurred her vision. She could not speak again, so she answered by caressing his cheek. She watched her mother and brother slowly turn away from her. She captured Sun Cloud's hand, squeezed it, and whispered, "I love you, Father. Never be sorry for obeying our law." It gave her strength when the man clasped her hand tightly for a moment.

Morning Star weaved her way through the silent crowd with lowered head. She went to her parents' tepee and packed her belongings, then walked to Hanmani, took his reins, and guided him out of camp. She did not look back, or halt until she was a mile from her people. She released the faithful animal's reins, dropped her possessions, and sat down to weep over her losses. Her decision was much harder than she had imagined, and it could never be changed or taken back. Tomorrow, her father and his band would leave for Fort Laramie; her people would depart for the sacred hills. She would be alone. "Come quickly to me, my love," she prayed.

Chapter Twenty

Joseph Lawrence reached his destination and dismounted. It was dark and quiet, and no one seemed disturbed by his late arrival. To make certain, he left Star at the edge of the camp and moved quietly to obtain the privacy he needed for what he must do. He realized his father did not have long to live. Yet, he was doing the best he could for everyone involved. He also realized that no matter how fast he traveled his father already might be dead, but he fervently hoped not.

Joe could not bring himself to leave without Morning Star. He would lose only half a day—a day at most if there was trouble—by veering off the route to fetch her. He knew Stede's urgings had come from a heart filled with remorse over missing last moments with his wife and son; the older man had not stopped to think how close to Sun Cloud's summer camp the route from their campsite to

Fort Tabor would bring Joe. As best he could judge, the chief and his band should have reached home earlier today. That meant there had not been enough time to begin moving to the Black Hills.

Joe felt it was his responsibility as a man and a suitor to face Sun Cloud with the truth. He comprehended Tom's concern over damaging all their work with the confession, but he knew he must take that risk. He had to have faith in the chief's character and honor, in himself, and in God.

He approached Sun Cloud's tepee, knelt at the open flap, and called his blood brother's name. It was only moments before the chief responded and called him inside. Joe ducked and entered. His gaze widened and showed confusion when he did not see his love inside so late at night. He sensed a strange and alarming tension in the air. In the fire's small glow, he read expressions on the Indian couple's faces that worried him. Astute, Joe asked, "What's wrong, Sun Cloud? Where is Morning Star?"

"She is gone," Mahpiya Wi replied to the white man his child loved and had sacrificed all to have, the sacred vision warrior, the trickster, the power taking away his beloved daughter, his blood brother. Which—if any or all—of those things should rule his emotions and behavior tonight?

"Gone? Did she follow us to Bear Butte and get into danger?" *Please, God, don't let her be hurt. Don't let her be somewhere else. I don't have more time to spare. Help us get out of here quickly and painlessly.*

"No, she was banished this sun. She camps alone nearby. She is dead to us. We cannot speak her name or look upon her face again. It is our law."

Joe did not have to be told why the action was taken, but it shocked him. His gentle love was alone and in anguish. "My people will not banish me for choosing her. How could you do this to your own child?"

"It is our law. I could not break it for her." As the angry white man stared at him, Sun Cloud related all that had happened. "She is downstream waiting for your return. Why have you come tonight? Why did you halt your ride to the peace council?"

"A scout from Fort Laramie caught up with us that first night. He delivered an urgent letter from my mother. My father is dying. I must hurry home. Even now, I may be too late to see him. I have to ride fast and hard, Sun Cloud, but I had to come for Morning Star first. I wanted to be the one to explain everything to you. I wanted you to hear from me how sorry I am for having to deceive you about being Tanner. From what you told me, I can tell you think it was wrong, but that you understand my motives. I'm glad, because I don't want you of all men to think badly of me. Tanner was my best friend, like a brother to me. How I miss him. He wanted to help his father; they both wanted to help their Indian kin. At first, I took over his place to find his killer, but I became attached to Morning Star and her people. I really care what happens you and the Red Hearts; you must believe that. In all honesty, I took those risks more for your people than to keep the whites out of a war. This is Indian territory, and I wish it could remain that way forever. We both know it won't, and I'm sorry."

Joe related the talk that had taken place in his camp after the urgent message reached him and Stede's offer to escort his love to Virginia. "It wasn't right to let him be the one to face you about our secret. Stede and Tom, Broken-Hand, told me not to come here because they were afraid you'd be angry about my deceit and it would stop you from attending the treaty talk. I don't believe that, not of a man like the son of Gray Eagle. You might hate me and distrust me, but from what I've seen and learned about the Red Heart chief, you have too much honor to sacrifice peace for your people. You know this treaty is genuine, and signing it is vital to years of peace. What I've done wrong can't stop you from signing."

Joe was relieved when the chief allowed him to have his say before taking his turn. "I love Morning Star, Sun Cloud; I need her. She's a part of me now. I want to marry her. I want to share the rest of my life with her. I want her children. God knows we tried to prevent this from happening. We battled our attraction to each other as long and as hard as we could. It didn't work. We realized how difficult a mixed marriage would be. We knew what trouble and pain it would cause many people, especially her family. She's the most wonderful woman I've ever met. You raised her to be strong and skilled. She's my friend, my helper, all I want and need in a woman. I swear to you I'll make her happy. She'll be safe and free at my home. I won't let anyone mistreat her or harm her. You have my word."

Sun Cloud was pleased by Joe's confession, though he couldn't let it show. Yet his voice was not harsh when he informed the man, "I do not need your word, and you do not need my permission. She has chosen you; she has been banished. All you must do is go after her and leave. And you must never return to our land and camp."

"I know it's your law and I understand why you have to keep it, but I want you to understand our feelings. I want you to forgive us for tricking you. I want you to be happy about our love and marriage. I don't want to lose your respect and friendship. And I don't want the woman I love to suffer because of me. She doesn't deserve cruel treatment like this; she was the vision woman. She only obeyed it. Banish her if you must, but don't deny her; don't say she's dead to you and that her family is dead to her."

Sun Cloud studied the white man with blue eyes and blond hair. Joe's tone said he was sincere and honest. "It must be this way; laws are for every person. You must understand why we cannot change them. I believe your words, but they change nothing for her."

Joe took a deep breath, then released it. "You're right, but your decision hurts many people. I guess it was foolish, but I was hoping this wouldn't happen to Sky Warrior and the vision woman. Maybe I never believed it would, not even when Morning Star kept warning me of the grim consequences. What I don't understand is why you banished her before I spoke to you and made a claim on her. Until we exposed the truth, why was she sent off alone? What if I'd done as Stede urged and left for home? She could have been in great danger until Stede saw you at Laramie, then rode here for her."

Sun Cloud looked at the insect bite that had saved Joe's life from Knife-Slayer's treachery and the bruise from Zeke Randall's blow to his cheek. "She revealed the truth and forced me to act on it. By choosing you, she is your wife in our eyes. The Great Spirit brought you here tonight to rescue her and to take her home with you. She is a skilled warrior; I knew she would be safe until you came for her. I did not want you to come to our winter camp to claim her. I did not want my people to see my daughter—bloodline of Gray Eagle—ride away with a white man. I wanted them to remember you as Sky Warrior, not as the sly paleface who tricked us and took her from us. You have done much for me and my people. I thank you and honor you for this. But you have stolen my daughter from me; understanding and forgiveness will take time to fill my heart. But when they come, it will change nothing. You must understand this and not battle for what can never be again. You have been my friend and blood brother; never return as my enemy with my enemies. Keep her from harm and give her much joy, but never return," he stressed.

Joe perceived clues in the chief's speech: love and concern between the lines of it, the anguish Sun Cloud was experiencing, and the strength of this great leader to carry out his heartbreaking duty. "It will be as you say. We'll be gone at first light. But I'll contact you in the future to see if your feelings have changed. I won't tell Morning Star about my message until they do. If things are ever different, I'll bring her home to visit."

Sun Cloud used all his willpower not to reply in the way his heart begged him to do so. As chief he must not weaken. He did not.

Joe grasped the turmoil in his love's father. "I understand, and we'll obey," he murmured. "There's one last thing, Sun Cloud. I didn't reveal all of Orin's motives at Bear Butte." He related the last one, probably the most important to the greedy villain. He cautioned the chief to keep whites out of the sacred hills as long as possible. "I won't tell anybody about the gold, not even Stede. I don't want him to mention it by accident."

Sun Cloud clasped wrists with Joe. "You are a good and honorable man, Joseph Lawrence. I will long remember you and your coups. When you hear that the treaty is broken and war has come, do not return. It cannot be stopped next time; the sacred vision warned of this. Do not risk your life to challenge what is our tribal destiny; it cannot be defeated as you defeated Snake-Man. Do not bring her here to witness the sufferings and deaths of her family and people. If you love her, keep her there forever."

Joe noticed how Sun Cloud obeyed his law by not once speaking his lost daughter's name. How he wished it didn't have to be this way for all of them. Maybe things would change in the future; he hoped so, for his wife's sake. "I love Morning Star, sir. We'll obey your words and laws. If you ever need to reach us, contact the President, our Great White Chief; he can tell you where we live." Joe glanced at the older woman who looked in great pain. "Good-bye, Singing Wind. I'm sorry we've hurt you. Don't worry about Morning Star. I promise to take good care of her." He turned to the chief and said, "Good-bye, Sun Cloud. I'll never forget you and my time here. And I won't forget all I've learned." Joe looked at his love's parents one last time, and left the tepee.

After a time, Sun Cloud joined his wife on their sleeping mat. He pulled Singing Wind into his arms. "He is right; do not worry. Payaba says she walks the path Grandfather planned for her. We must accept this."

"I will be strong, my husband, but it will be hard for a time."

"I love you, Singing Wind," he murmured against her lips.

"I love you," she replied, then kissed him to ease her torment.

Sun Cloud did not relate the rest of Payaba's vision for it would hurt and frighten his wife. What the past shaman had revealed in private about his daughter had given him the strength to banish her: "Let her go with Sky Warrior or she will die in the dark days ahead, as will many others."

The old man had spoken of a time when another great warrior—a legend larger than himself and Gray Eagle—would ride the Plains and war against the interloping whites. Payaba had spoken of another child in their tepee, a boy who would become a great warrior, whose prowess would blaze as a bright star in the darkened sky. But the old shaman did not know if the two men were the same. Payaba had warned of an arrow, dripping in blood and firing over the land, that must be watched closely over the years; and Sun Cloud suspected his identity—his unruly grandson.

"When dark shadows blanket our land once more, the bloodline of Gray Eagle and Sun Cloud will become strong again," Payaba had said. "Do not resist what must be, or the vision will be defeated and all will perish."

Sun Cloud wondered if those parts of the prophecy—told only to him— meant they would have another son and the chief's line would not pass through Night Stalker and Bloody Arrow. They were no longer young, but the Great Spirit had the power to do anything. Until he was shown the meaning of those parts, he would keep them to himself.

The Red Heart chief accepted the Great Spirit's words and warnings. He closed his eyes and thought, *Good-bye, my beloved Morning Star . . .*

"Morning Star, it's me, Joe!" he called out to prevent startling her and getting shot in the process. "I've come to get you, love."

The overjoyed woman tossed down the bow and arrow. "Joe!" she squealed and raced into his arms.

He covered her face with kisses and held her tightly. His mouth covered hers, feasting in delight as she responded and clung to him.

When their lips parted and he nestled her head against his chest, he murmured, "I'm here now, love. Everything will be all right."

Morning Star leaned her head back, straining to see his handsome face in the light of a half-moon. "Why did you return early?"

In a hoarse tone, he related the grim news about his father and his decision to come for her before leaving the territory. "We have to get home fast, love. We ride at first light. I've seen your father; he told me what happened today. I'm sorry you had to face this alone. That won't ever happen again, I promise you."

"What did Father say? How was he?" she asked, worried.

Joe told her everything they had said to each other and his impressions of her parents' feelings. "What about Clay, love? Why didn't he help you? Why isn't he here to protect you?"

"I told him not to speak or act. There is nothing he can do about our laws, except cause trouble for himself and Buckskin Girl. No one must look at me, speak to me, or help me. If he disobeys, he must be banished. That is how the law makes all obey it. He did as I asked, what was best."

"Sometimes a person has to do what he feels is right, not obey unfair laws. I'm disappointed he would leave you in danger."

"Do not be angry with him, my love. He seeks a new life with a mate and with our people. This is our decision, our problem, not theirs. Soon, we will be far away forever; they will not."

"You're right, but I can't help feeling a little angry." He changed the subject. "We'll take a big boat, called a steamer, at Fort Tabor. We'll travel down the Missouri River to St. Louis. We'll buy horses and ride overland to my home. It'll take a few weeks."

"What will happen when we reach your home and family?"

"We'll take care of my father until . . . For as long as he's with us. I hope we make it in time. I want you two to meet each other. You'll like him, Morning Star, and he'll like you. We'll get married as soon as possible; I hope we can do it at Fort Tabor before we sail. We'll buy you some clothes there, so you won't feel different from other women we meet along the trail." The talk distracted and soothed them, so he continued with it for a while. "We'll live at the plantation. It's beautiful and quiet, and away from town. Mother and I will teach you all you need to know before we visit Alexandria; that's where our shipping business is. With Father ill, you might have to stay with Mother at the plantation while I check on things at the firm. You'll love her, Morning Star. She's a wonderful lady. She'll be so happy about our marriage. She'll enjoy her lessons with you; it'll take her mind off . . . Father's loss. Then, there's Sarah Beth, my sister, her husband, Andrew, who works with Father, and their little boy, Lucas. They'll all love you and accept you. With me gone so much, at least Father had Andrew to run the business for him. If we're lucky, we'll give Lucas some friends to play with real soon."

Morning Star smiled, but knew from her woman's flow last week that she carried no child at this time. Perhaps children, grandchildren, would be the path back to her family. How could anyone not want to see the continuation of their bloodline? Joe's words about her laws changing one day gave her hope to pray for that occurrence.

As they snuggled on the buffalo mat and shared endearments, Joe murmured, "Do you want to be called Morning Star, or do you want to take a white name after we're married?"

"I will live in a white land with whites, so I will follow your customs."

Joe had pondered this several times and was ready with a suggestion. "What about Marie Lawrence? Marie was my grandmother's name."

Morning Star tested it upon her lips, "Ma-rie. Marie Lawrence. Marie Lawrence. Yes, it is a good name. I will take it."

Joe embraced her. "I love you, woman. Don't worry; everything will work out fine. Let's get some sleep. We have a long hard trip ahead."

They cuddled and closed their eyes, imagining what lay before them.

Light and the horses' movements awakened Joe and Morning Star. Both instantly noticed the man sitting at the meandering stream: Clay. Joe tossed aside their cover, and joined him.

"I didn't expect to find you here, Joe," Clay remarked. "I brought supplies and extra horses. I was planning to bring Morning Star to you at Fort Laramie. I figured by changing mounts back and forth, we could beat Sun Cloud's party there and let you know what's happened."

"Sun Cloud told me last night; I reached camp late." Joe explained why he had come, and he thanked Clay—Sky Warrior—Thorne for his help.

"I'm sorry about your father. I'll help you two get to Tabor fast."

"You're a good friend, Clay; thanks," Joe said again. "But you'll be in big trouble. I understand what an awkward position you're in. If nobody knows you're here, get back before anyone finds out about your action."

"It doesn't matter now. I can't leave friends in trouble. I'm afraid I had to change my mind about joining the Red Heart Band. I don't agree with their law that banished Morning Star, not after all you two have done for them and for peace. Since I look more white than Indian, it could give me trouble down the trail. I don't want that to happen. I decided it was best to return to my family and people; the Cheyenne don't have that law. Buckskin Girl is helping her parents move to the winter campground. When I return, I'll take her home with me. She's agreed it's for the best."

Morning Star was relieved his change of heart didn't include giving up her best friend. She did not defend or speak against the law in question that demanded so much from her. Though it seemed cruel, it protected her people against diluting their Indian blood. That was important and good.

"Sun Cloud is riding in an hour. The others are breaking camp today. Don't worry about the treaty; it'll be signed. You two did a good job, and I'm glad I got to help out a little. Be proud of yourselves. Don't suffer over what it cost Morning Star. Get married, have a good life, and be happy."

"That's good advice, my friend. I hope you do the same. Let's eat and get moving. We've got a long ride ahead."

Five days later, the three entered Fort Tabor, having camped outside the previous night after a late arrival. Joe and Morning Star went to the sutler's store to purchase her several white woman's garments for their impending voyage and new life. Clay left them to check on the next steamer heading down the Missouri River. All three knew they must hurry, so tensions were high.

Fortunately the sutler's wife, a kind and plump woman, was present. Joe explained their needs. The gentle-spirited female walked around Morning Star and eyed her up and down to decide what sizes were best. She searched through stacks of ready-made dresses, undergarments, and shoes, then guided the Indian beauty into the back room to find her judgments were accurate. The two females exchanged smiles. Morning Star kept on the prettiest cotton dress and went to show it to Joe who was pacing nervously.

Joe's eyes brightened as he gazed at the lovely sight. He noticed that Morning Star had released her braids and brushed her ebony hair to shiny free-flowing tresses. Her dark eyes glowed with excitement. Joe thanked the sutler's beaming wife and paid the man. He lifted the three packages, wrapped in brown paper, and guided his love toward the door.

Before they could depart to look for Clay, their friend rushed to them and urged, "You two have to get moving pronto! The ship leaves in less than an hour. Here are your tickets. Your gear is already loaded."

"We have to see the chaplain first," Joe reminded. He hoped there was enough time to locate the man and persuade him to marry them.

"I just saw him leaving the jail. Guess he's been ministering to those prisoners we sent here. Lot of good it'll do them now!" Clay scoffed.

"I need a long bath and a shave before I see a preacher, but I'll have to do in this mess," Joe remarked with a wry grin as he rubbed the rough stubble on his face. "Let's find him."

They located the post chaplain in the small structure, the front of which was used for services, the rear, for his personal quarters. Joe explained his request and the rush for the ceremony.

The sympathetic man eyed both, then asked, "You two sure you know what you're doing? A mixed marriage has lots of problems. You love each other enough to confront whatever comes your way?"

"Yes, sir, we love each other, and we've given our future together a lot of serious thought. We know what we're doing. We'll be fine."

"What about you, young lady?" the chaplain inquired.

Morning Star glanced at Joe, then looked at the other man. "Yes, sir," she responded in her best English, "I love him and will be a good wife. If trouble rides after us, we will flee it or defeat it."

The chaplain studied their pleading gazes, glanced at their clasped hands, and nodded. "I believe you. I just like to make sure couples don't rush into something as serious as marriage without lots of thinking. You two stand here," he instructed, placing them in front of him and opening his Bible. He found the place he wanted, then read two scriptural passages on love and marriage. He knew they didn't have much time, but a religious service had to be done proper even in a rush.

"Do you Joseph Lawrence, Junior, take this woman to be your lawful wife in the eyes of God and man?" the chaplain asked Joe.

Joe gazed into Morning Star's lovely eyes and replied, "I do."

"Do you Marie Morning Star take this man to be your lawful husband in the eyes of God and man?"

"I do," she responded, following Joe's lead.

"Do you both promise to love, help, protect, and keep only unto each other all the days of your lives?" he asked.

"I do," the couple answered at the same time.

"God being our witness in this holy place, I pronounce you man and wife. Let no man, other God, or trouble come between you or part you," he advised in a grave tone. "I'll fill out a paper to say you're legally wed. You'll both have to sign it, and your witness there, Mr. Thorne."

Everyone remained silent as the chaplain wrote out a makeshift license, but Joe's mind raced with thoughts. He wished his parents, sister and her family, Tanner, Stede, Sun Cloud, and Singing Wind could be present. He wished the ceremony hadn't needed to be performed so quickly and with such a lack of romance. He wished he had a ring to slip on his love's finger. He vowed again to himself to protect, love, and make this woman happy, as he had sworn to her parents a few days ago.

Morning Star's mind roamed, too. She was bidding one life farewell and greeting a new one. She wished some things could be different, but she had no regrets. She loved Joe and wanted to spend her life with him. It was as it should be.

The religious man turned the page toward Joe for his signature first, then to Morning Star, and finally to Clay Thorne. When all three had marked their names on the paper, the chaplain signed and dated it. He recorded the ceremony in his Bible, then passed the binding page to Joe.

It was obvious the couple loved each other. He smiled and said, "Good luck, Mr. and Mrs. Lawrence. God go with you and protect you."

"Thank you, sir." Joe shook the man's hand. He clutched the license in one of his hands and held his wife's hand with the other. "Let's go, Mrs. Lawrence."

Morning Star smiled, and her fingers tightened around his. She thanked the chaplain and left with her husband and Clay.

At the ship, they bade farewell to Clay Thorne. Both knew they would miss their half-Cheyenne friend. Clay shook hands with Joe and embraced Morning

Star, knowing, too, how much he would miss them. She and Joe sent messages to her family and friends.

The horse Joe had borrowed from the scout had been left with an officer at Tabor, who promised to return it to its owner at Laramie.

Joe asked Clay to take his roan and her Appaloosa back to Sun Cloud as gifts to Morning Star's father, a small exchange for the treasure at his side. They waved good-bye and boarded the vessel. They watched Clay mount, gather the reins of their horses, the ones to the pack animal, then ride toward the Red Heart winter camp to claim Buckskin Girl as his wife.

A crew member showed the newly wed couple to their cabin, then left them alone. Their saddles and gear were stored beside the bed, as were their other possessions, including the new clothes Joe had purchased for her from the sutler at Tabor.

The cabin was small, so there was little room for settling in comfortably. But the voyage wouldn't take long. Their eyes met as a whistle blasted the time for departure had arrived. When the ship moved into the swift current of the Missouri River their new life would be underway.

Joe left his bride to rest and adjust to the new experience before her while he went on deck to calm himself and to view the beginning of their voyage.

After many questions to passing crewmen and the revelation that he was an ex-sea captain, Joe was invited to join the *Lucy Mae*'s captain in the pilot house. He learned that the first steamship, the *Yellowstone*, had been brought up the river to this area in the early thirties by Pierre Chouteau.

The captain of the *Lucy Mae* chatted about how buying and trading had increased over the years until steamboats worked this area frequently when the climate allowed. He told Joe that most captains quickly learned how difficult the "Big Muddy" was to navigate with her shifting, changing, and twisting channels and with her perils of snags, logs, sandbars, and mercurial currents. Even in the best boat and with the most skilled captain, it was a hazardous journey.

Joe smiled, observed, and complimented the genial captain on his skills, courage, and wits.

An hour later, Joe headed for his cabin, to be with his new bride.

Most of the day, Joe remained in the cabin, cramped and barren though it was. He didn't want his love to become frightened by this sometimes scary voyage. The swirling water around the steamer was as dark as the coffee he had transported to his country from tropical ones far away. The winter thaw and summer rains were long gone, so the water level was lower than Joe or the pilot wanted for a safe and easy voyage. Joe knew there was plenty of time during the trip for Morning Star to witness the passing sites and learn about boats.

Joe could hardly wait to reach home where his mother would help Morning Star buy pretty clothes or have a skilled seamstress make them. He envisioned her begowned and bejeweled, and him the envy of every man present. The first thing he wanted to purchase was a wedding band to slide on her finger. He used such thoughts to keep his mind off what awaited him there: his dying father.

Joe was ecstatic about a few things. His dreams were coming true: they were married, man and wife, thanks to the chaplain at Tabor. They were sailing—steaming—toward their bright future.

They ate their evening meal in a small dining area, part of the ticket price. The other three passengers—trappers going downriver who were accustomed to seeing men with Indian wives—paid little attention them. Twice during the day, Joe had gone outside to catch a breath of fresh air when they halted to take on more wood for fuel. At last it was night, and they felt relaxed enough in the strange surroundings to share intimacy.

Joe bolted the cabin door and turned to gaze at his wife. He didn't know he felt a little shy about being alone and getting ready for bed. They had made love many times and had shared a sleeping mat even more times. They were married now, committed to each other for life.

Morning Star experienced the same curious feelings and thoughts. She could not understand why it seemed so different with him tonight. She was happy and excited, and she knew he was, too. Yet . . .

"Maybe it's because we know we aren't alone in this place," Joe suggested. "Out on the Plains or in the forest, we were away from other people. It was quiet and romantic. This room is small and ugly. We had fresh air and stars around us, we weren't closed in by brown walls. We'll be on this boat for a while, so I guess we'll get used to it."

"You read my mind as I read trail signs," she teased. "I miss the open places. But if we did not have this bed, the room would be like a tepee. I will get . . . used to walls and beds."

Joe sat on the bed and removed his boots. "At our plantation, the rooms are big. We have plenty of doors and windows to let in fresh air and sunshine. The walls are painted pretty colors, light colors. The floors have rugs with flowers, as do the chairs and couches. Nice pictures are on the walls and the furniture is comfortable. It's nothing like this drab cabin, Morning Star."

"I am sure it is beautiful," she said, working with difficulty on the small buttons of her new dress.

"Let me help you," Joe offered. "These can be devils until you get used to them. I never understood why women have such little buttons on their garments. Men's are bigger and easier to manage."

As her husband did the task for her, Morning Star reminded, "You must call me Marie, my love. You must . . . get used to my new name."

"Marie Lawrence . . . Mrs. Joseph Lawrence, Junior. . . . Very nice."

"I have two new names?" she asked.

Joe explained the custom of a wife taking a husband's name and told her when she should use each of them.

"It is like the custom of marking spotted buffaloes, cattle," Morning Star teased. "You white men brand your women with your name."

"Yep," he replied, grinning as he slipped the dress off her shoulders. He placed a kiss on each one. "That's so other men will know they're private property. I wouldn't take kindly to any man trying to steal my woman. I want everybody to know you're mine: Joe's wife, Joe's love."

Both began to relax as their tensions melted and their surroundings were forgotten or ignored. They had been through a harrowing time, but now at last their future had begun.

"We're safe now, my love, and together forever," Joe said gently. "No more standing guard at night, at least not on this boat. No more dangers and hardships. I hope we reach my father in time, but if we don't, we did our best to get to him. He understands what I'm doing out here, and he must know I'm on my way home as fast as possible. I'm proud of what we've accomplished, and we should never be ashamed of falling in love. In a week, the peace council will begin. When Stede returns home, he'll tell us all about it. But until we reach St. Louis and take off on horseback, we can rest and enjoy ourselves. For a while, Marie Lawrence, we will think only of us."

"I like your words and plans, my husband. It has been a long and lonely time since we joined." Morning Star lifted her hand to caress his strong jawline, hairless after his shave. Her fingertips rubbed over his full lips and she could not resist the impulse to stroke his powerful torso and to feel his sleek flesh. She gazed into his eyes, a summer sky of inviting blue, and toyed with his sunny hair. She adored its texture and how it framed his face, how its color made his eyes look bluer and his skin darker. "I love you so much it causes me to feel strange inside," she said passionately. "I see and hear nothing except you. I want nothing but you."

"That's how I feel, too, Morning Star. It used to be scary to want you so much, to feel your effect on me. Not any more. I love you."

Morning Star unfastened the buttons on his shirt and peeled it off his muscled torso. She dropped it to the floor. His body was as sleek and toned as the best trained warrior's. He was a splendid man, and he was hers. With Joe nearby and touching her, nothing mattered except him and their love. There was no shame and no regrets. Their bond was pure and right. She was ready to face the challenges before her. As she unlaced the ribbons on her chemise, she remarked, "White garments are strange."

"But they're fun to remove," he teased, slipping it over her head. He pulled her back into his arms, their bare skin making blissful contact. Her nearness caused his heart to race with desire. He captured her hands and lifted them to his mouth to place kisses on her fingers, her knuckles, and her wrists. He turned one over and let his tongue play in its palm, which evoked soft laughter from her. Slowly, his lips journeyed up one arm to her shoulder, her throat, and then her face. His hands drifted up and down her back a few times, then sent his fingers into her cascading hair. He loved the way the ebony mane felt wound around them. His lips went to hers.

Their tongues played a seductive game of seek and find, then mated in a heady ritual. Their bodies trembled with passion, building to a frenzied level. Their flesh clung together, sharing warmth and pleasure. Their hands and lips teased and tempted. They were spellbound in a world of love and magic, and nothing could destroy it or break it.

Morning Star quivered and tingled. Her legs felt weak and her body heavy. It had been weeks since they had come together at Spearfish Canyon. Her heart was filled with longing. Her breath came in shallow, quick gasps; then it was stolen by his kiss. Her entire body experienced a rush of heat and tingling, a blend of wild sensations.

Joe's hands slipped around her sides and closed over her firm breasts. With gentleness, he kneaded them. His mouth roved her face and his nose inhaled her sweet fragrance. His manhood ached to be within her; it burned with a need only she could satisfy. Her tongue danced with his, and he savored the taste of her. He moaned in bittersweet need.

Joe paused to remove the rest of their constricting garments. He pushed the dress over her hips and followed it with her bloomers. He lifted Morning Star in his arms and placed her on the bed. Without delay, he was out of his clothes, naked, aroused, and lying beside his wife.

For a while, he made love to her with his eyes, caressing, tantalizing. To him, she was exquisite, perfect, beautiful, irresistible. He nibbled at her ears, and caused her to laugh once more. His mouth claimed hers again to explore and to heighten their desires. His hands were bold, determined, skilled.

Joe's hot breath on her made Morning Star's yearning for him flame brighter. She trailed her fingers over his honed frame, savored his manly scent. His body was hard, smooth, and golden. Her fingers wanted to trace every inch. She stroked the injuries he had received at Bear Butte and she felt the scar he had gotten from her rescue. Yet, nothing detracted from his beauty. She felt aglow with love, afire with passion, and fortunate to have him. No man could compare with Joe, in appearance or in character. He was more important to her than her life and honor, something she had proven with more than words. She was alive, elated, and fulfilled in his arms. For once she did not care if a man, but only this man, took control of her will and her body, of her entire being. She surrendered with eagerness. She responded and reacted to every touch, every kiss, every action, then she mutely begged for more. She had known great rapture in his arms, but tonight she found ecstasy.

Joe's hands trekked over her silky skin. She was so close, so intoxicating, so responsive. Her lithe body evoked him to stimulate it. As lightly as a butterfly, his lips brushed over her breasts. His tongue swirled round and round one bud to sample its nectar. His teeth teased at the taut nubs that revealed the intensity of her desire and his effect upon her. Their contact and her reactions played havoc with his mastery over his raging loins. He had never felt more alive or inflamed than he did now. He was almost mindless with hunger for her.

Morning Star trembled when his hand drifted down her flat stomach. Her entire being was enthralled by him. Reality had fled long ago. He and his actions were her only awareness. She wanted to relax and enjoy the sweet pleasures, but she was too ravenous with need. Each kiss and touch pleased her, but they whet her appetite for much more. She seemed swept away in a flood of bliss. Her hands grasped his shoulders and clutched them tightly. She wanted, she needed, she must have Joseph Lawrence or be dazed with starvation. Soon, there was no place upon her that did not cry out for his attention. As with him, muffled moans escaped her lips between feverish kisses.

Joe fingered the petal-soft flesh between her thighs until she urged him to end the sweet madness. He entered her body with a groan of delight. His breathing became labored and swift with his excitement and the strain of his self-control. He kissed her over and over as he murmured words of love and pleasure. "You're like a fierce desire burning within me. I need you and love you, woman." He felt her work with him, matching his rhythm.

Morning Star's legs wrapped around his and her arms clung to him. Her mouth meshed with his as her heart pounded and her blood raced hot and fast. She saw and felt the muscles of his arms and back as they rippled with his movements. "You are my air, my heart, my life. I want no one but you."

Joe tossed restraint aside and hurried after her. Higher and higher Sky Warrior soared with her on his wings. He grasped the star in his heaven and let it shine on him.

Morning Star held on to the all-consuming man and let her body yield completely to his touch, thrilling to the ecstasy they reached together.

Joe lay half atop Morning Star as he held her tightly in love's aftermath. His gaze roamed her flushed face. Her dark eyes glistened with joy. His heart, filled with love for her, pounded in his chest. He had never, even with her, experienced anything like this, a total joining of all they were. His fingers traced her lips, nose, and cheeks.

"Lordy, how I love you, woman. Every time I think my heart is so full it can't hold more, somehow it stretches and does. Every time I make love to you, it's better than the last time, better than all the other times put together. I don't know how it happens, but I surely do like it."

"I understand. It is the same with me. Perhaps it is the way of love, to grow larger and stronger each day, with each union. It is not the joining of bodies that does this alone; it is all the things that travel with it. I have made the right choice —you, my love, my husband."

Joe gazed into her serene eyes and smiled. They had faced thunder in the wind together, and they had found sweet ecstasy during that fierce battle. "We both made the right choice, my beautiful Morning Star, my sweet Marie, my wife, my woman, the true love of my heart and soul."

She laughed, a glow in her eyes. "I am many things to you, as you are many things to me. It is best of all things you are my love, my husband, my destiny."

Joe rolled to his back, and his wife curled against him. Her right leg slipped between his. Joe's left hand pillowed his head; the other one twirled ebony hair around playful fingers. Morning Star nestled her cheek to her husband's broad chest. The backs of her fingers stroked his damp flesh. For an hour, they remained quiet as each reflected on their lives before and since they met. They had experienced many dangers, tests, and adventures together. They had suffered and sacrificed for others. It was time for them, time for their own happiness. *Time for receiving life's rewards.*

Morning Star pondered the challenges behind her, and those still before her. She had Joe to make her strong and brave. Whatever tomorrow brought, she was ready and willing to face. She was Morning Star, daughter of Sun Cloud and Singing Wind; she was the granddaughter of Gray Eagle and Alisha/Shalee; she was Marie Lawrence, wife and love of Mahpiya Wicasta, the greatest white warrior to ever ride the open Plains. Each of them was controlled by fate, and she accepted that reality.

Thank you, Mother and Father, for your love and understanding, for all you taught me, she silently prayed. *Thank you, Payaba, for your vision long ago and for many years of friendship. Thank you, Great Spirit, for giving me this man.*

Morning Star bid a final farewell to the past and welcomed the bright future before her. In the days ahead, she would draw courage, strength, and comfort from all she had been, from all she was, and from all she would become. Peace of mind filled the daughter of the Red Heart chief.

Joe also said his mental farewell to Tanner Gaston, and prayed that his best friend knew he hadn't lost his life in vain. He prayed for Stede's success at the treaty council and for the man's safe return home. He prayed for his father's survival until he reached him, and for strength to help his mother through the difficult days after her husband's death. He prayed for a future reconciliation between his love and her parents and people.

He realized how much he had learned about himself, about whites and Indians, and about life. He had changed and matured by coming here, by meeting Morning Star and the Red Hearts, and by giving so much of himself to others. Yet he had received far more in return. He had made friends, such as Sun Cloud and Clay Thorne. He had helped prevent a bloody conflict. He had helped establish a vital treaty.

Joe heard his wife sigh dreamily as she cuddled more snugly against him. He caressed her cheek and murmured, "We have each other, my love, so we'll be all right. More than all right, absolutely wonderful."

Morning Star lifted her head to look deeply into her love's blue eyes. "Yes," the daughter of Sun Cloud replied, "I know we will."

Epilogue

Virginia, 1856

Marie Lawrence gazed at her sleeping children. She bent over to straighten the covers and to kiss their cheeks. They were beautiful girls, born two years ago. One had golden curls and sky-blue eyes like her father; the other had dark-brown hair and eyes like her. It seemed as if they proclaimed how the Indian and white cultures had fused into a lovely and precious reality.

Joe tiptoed into the nursery and joined his wife. He wrapped his arms around her from behind and looked over her shoulder at their twin daughters, who favored each other heavily but were not identical. He was proud of them, and of his wife and her numerous accomplishments.

After a moment, Joe released Marie, grasped her hand, and led her into their bedroom. He closed the door, then turned to smile at her. Her gown was stunning. The V neckline was trimmed in overlapping rows of narrow lace. The snug midriff exposed Marie's small waist before it, too, dipped into a V onto a full skirt with three tiers. Each layer was edged in delicate embroidery and wide lace. Marie's hair was dressed in a large bun near the back crown of her head, and several ringlets dangled near her ears. His love was a vision of genteel beauty. "You looked beautiful tonight. Every man present envied me," he said proudly.

"Thank you, my adoring husband. But you looked too handsome tonight and too many women tried to steal your eye from me."

He knew she was jesting, but he responded, "No woman could ever entice me away from you. They're only friends and wives of friends. I'm fortunate to have so many of them. They're yours, too."

"Yes, I have made many good friends here. I had a wonderful time at your sister's; Sarah Beth knows how to give a marvelous party." She removed his bowtie and placed it on the dresser. She helped him off with his frock coat with its contrasting revers and hung it in his wardrobe. She did the same with his vest.

As she worked, Joe grinned and said, "That's because everyone adores and enjoys my exquisite and intelligent wife."

Marie turned to him and he unfastened the diamond-and-emerald necklace and undid the buttons of her green satin gown. She slipped out of the rustling garment and hung it in her armoire as she responded to her husband's last remark. "That is because most whites are good people, my love. I wish—" Marie halted and took a deep breath. She removed her petticoat, chemise, and bloomers, all trimmed in ribbons and lace.

When his wife did not finish her statement, Joe ventured, "Your family and tribe could make that same discovery?"

Marie nodded, then listened to him as she continued her tasks. She took off her slippers and stockings, and put them away in their places.

"The problem is, too many whites who go west are evil and greedy, then soldiers have to play devils cleaning up their sorry messes. It sets bad examples and makes the Indians think all whites are that way. If your tribe and others could live around people such as the ones we know, they would learn the same truth you have. They will someday, my love; I'm sure of it. We made truce first with the British and other past enemies, then lasting peace and friendship resulted. It'll be the same between Indians and whites."

Marie recalled Payaba's vision about no lasting peace, but she said, "I hope so, my husband. The treaty is still in effect, and we have heard of nothing terrible happening in that area. I pray it is not broken soon."

"Both sides worked too hard to establish peace and truce, my love, to let minor differences destroy the treaty," he comforted. "Both sides will be slow to instigate another war. Everybody realizes how destructive war is."

She prayed he was right. "I hope my family and friends are safe and happy. I only wish Father and Mother could see our girls."

"They will someday, Marie, even if we have to sneak them there and meet in secret to avoid trouble with your band. What grandparents could refuse to see their grandchildren when they're nearby? I've tried to keep an ear in their direction, but accurate news is hard to come by." Joe hoped that wasn't because the government wanted to keep bad news quiet. He was so settled and contented that he didn't want to receive alarming news, and he knew what his wife would want to do if it came. "When it seems the right time, I'll send someone to check on things for us. Srede's seventy now, so he can't make such a hard journey again. I'll find the right man."

"Thank you, my love." Marie mentally packed up her past once more and stored it in the back of her mind. She did not want to spoil this romantic evening. She put away her undergarments. White clothing no longer felt strange and uncomfortable to her. Over the past years, she had become accustomed to expensive jewels and splendid gowns. She had become accustomed to living in a house and had adapted to his culture with skill and enjoyment, thanks to her husband and Joe's mother and the tutors they had hired to assist her. "I miss Stede's visits," she remarked. "He took such trouble to bring us news of the peace council long ago, then checked on us several times. When the girls are a little older, we must go to see him in New Orleans. Perhaps next spring."

"I'm not sure that'll be possible; he's not in good health. You remember how quickly my father went—only a week after Mother wrote me to hurry home." To think of Stede's short time left on earth and of his deceased parents made Joe mournful for a moment. He placed the heel of his dress boot against a jack and wiggled it off his foot, then did the same with the other one. As he removed his shirt and evening trousers, he murmured, "At least Father left that special letter for me."

"Do not be sad, my love. Joseph loved you and was proud of you. He told you he understood why you left. He was no longer angry with you."

Joe finished undressing as he admitted, "That made it easier to get over not seeing him again. I just wish they weren't both gone. I wish Mother were here to help raise the girls."

"Father said long ago, 'It is good when mates leave the land at the same time or not long after the other. It is hard to live without your heart.' Annabelle was strong and brave. She hid her pain well, but it never went away. She was ready and eager to join her lost love. They were not young when you were born, and their Life-Circles were large and full. Be happy she was with us for several years. She taught me much. I shall never forget Annabelle and her kindness. Our pasts are gone; they must not trouble us."

Joe gazed at the nude beauty before him. Yes, his mother had helped him help Morning Star become a fine lady. Few would guess she hadn't been born and reared in her current social position. Her mind was quick and responsive. She never stopped learning and trying new things. She was a constant amazement, a rare treasure. In spite of all the forces against their marriage and their many cultural differences, their union had worked. Their love for each other was so strong that it had made it easy to brush aside problems and to compromise on important points. Love had conquered all.

Joe lifted her left hand and kissed the gold ring upon her third finger. "As soon as I finish my business here in town, we'll go to the plantation to relax. The girls enjoy the animals, open space, and fresh air. Especially Miranda. She's a bundle of energy." Joe removed the pins from Marie's hair, loosened the bun, and spread the ebony mane around her bare shoulders. He gazed into her eyes, which sparkled with seductive mischief.

"Amanda is quiet and calm like you, my love, but Miranda's heart and body burn from the fires of nature as mine. She will be more of a challenge to raise."

"What you mean is, it looks as if she's inherited her mother's wild and willful streak," he teased, then nibbled at her chin.

"If you do not behave and be kind, my husband, I will send Captain Joseph Lawrence off on one of his ships until he learns how," she quipped.

Joe scooped up the laughing female in his arms, chuckled, and carried her to their bed. "You know I don't go to sea anymore, wife. I'm content to run the shipping business from shore, with Andrew's help." His voice lowered to a husky tone when he hinted, "What I'd like to do is spend time trying to get Lucas a boy cousin to play with; he loves those two girls, but he needs a Tanner like I had."

Marie rubbed her nude body against his naked frame. She caressed his cheek and trailed fingers over his lips. "If you do not remember how to make babies, my husband, I will refresh your memory tonight."

Joe laughed. He captured her wandering hands, brought them to his mouth, and kissed them. "From many nights shared with you, my beautiful wife, I know we've learned those delightful lessons well."

"Then, we must practice them," she murmured against his lips.

As Marie and Joseph Lawrence sailed away on an intimate sea of rapture, Morning Star and Sky Warrior soared the heavens in each other's arms and flew to the land of wild, sweet ecstasy—this time, forever . . .

Author's Notes

For those of you who want to know what happens to the characters in this book, their story continues in *Savage Conquest*. For those of you who missed any of the previous seven sagas in this series—*Savage Ecstasy*, *Defiant Ecstasy*, *Forbidden Ecstasy*, *Brazen Ecstasy*, *Tender Ecstasy*, *Stolen Ecstasy*, and *Bittersweet Ecstasy*—they are available from your local bookstore or from Zebra Books.

Each book in the "Ecstasy Saga" features a story based on the lives and loves of Lakota warrior Gray Eagle, his white wife Alisha Williams, or their heirs. The series covers a time span from 1776 to 1873. Although *Savage Conquest* was not written originally as part of this series it fits in perfectly as Saga #9. It continues the story of Joseph and Marie Lawrence, their twin daughters, Sun Cloud, Bloody Arrow, and Blazing Star and it's one of the most suspenseful books of the series.

As *Savage Conquest* was published in February 1985 and was written before the intervening books, certain people and events do not appear in *Savage Conquest* or its genealogy chart; and that book controls part of the plot of this one. It is for this reason that the sacred vision, the adventures of Joe and Morning Star, the peace treaty, Stede and Tanner Gaston, Clay Thorne, and a few other events and characters are not mentioned in *Savage Conquest*. *Savage Conquest* reveals only that Morning Star was banished and Joe was called home because of his father's death, so I had to include those painful episodes here, and I tried to write them as sensitively as possible.

I hope you will enjoy the last book on these special characters. Having "lived" on pages with the Oglalas for thirteen years, I cannot bring myself to write another, as *Savage Conquest* takes my loved ones up to Custer's arrival and intrusion. I want to say good-bye to my people while they are free and happy, not carry them through agony and near annihilation. But if I do think of a spin-off story, you'll be sure to see it one day in the bookstores.

For those of you interested in what happened historically after this novel, the first of two Fort Laramie peace councils began with talks on September eighth of 1851 and ended on September seventeenth with the tribes signing to pledge eternal peace among themselves and with the whites. It was called the Treaty of Fort Laramie. At the invitation of the United States government, Thomas Fitzpatrick, and Colonel David Mitchell, more than ten thousand Plains Indians from many nations and tribes gathered at Horse Creek near Fort Laramie to parley. The terms and payments mentioned earlier in this novel are factual. The problem with the treaty was that many Indians did not grasp what they were signing away and initiating. Whites were granted permission to build roads and to travel through their territories and the Army was given the right to build forts to protect settlers and immigrants. These two provisions created a disastrously permanent and larger white presence in the territory.

Oglala Chief Red Cloud attended the powwow, signed the joint treaty, and tried to keep his word. Tragically, the whites did not keep theirs. Annuities were needed to replace the growing shortage of game and other supplies, but the American government reneged on the reparation terms of the treaty. What few supplies and cattle were delivered were of low quality or unusable. Added to the growing list of complaints or wrongdoings were corrupt Indian agents who carried out criminal and immoral deeds. As whites flooded the territory, buffalo, beaver, and other animals were hunted to near extinction or driven far from agreed upon intertribal boundaries. These problems led to conflicts between Indian nations and between greedy whites and near-starving Indians, who depended upon nature— particularly the buffalo—for survival. As hunters were compelled to forage other tribes' assigned grounds, the invasions provoked new outbreaks of intertribal wars.

In 1853, Thomas Fitzpatrick wrote that the Indians "are in abject want of food half the year. . . . Their women are pinched with want, and their children are constantly crying with hunger." His letters had no effect.

Hard feelings smoldered until a minor incident fanned the embers into a roaring blaze. In 1854, a Lakota brave was accused of stealing and slaughtering a pioneer's cow. A scornful, militant lieutenant named John Grattan rode into the Brule camp. Gratten became infuriated by what he considered hostile behavior, opened fire, and killed Chief Brave Bear. The outraged warriors attacked and slew the entire unit. General William Harney—"By God, I'm for battle, no peace"— was ordered to retaliate. Among other reprisals, he led the infamous Ash Hollow Massacre and earned the name "The Butcher" for his bloody tactics.

Oglala Chief Red Cloud could not bear the sufferings and abuses any longer. He later said, "The white men have crowded the Indians back year by year . . . and now our last hunting grounds . . . [are] to be taken from us. Our women and children will starve. . . . I prefer to die fighting than by starvation." At Horse Creek in 1851, "The Great Father made a treaty with us . . . We kept our word . . . but only once did [the promised goods] reach us, and soon the Great Father took away the only good man he had sent to us, Colonel [sic] Fitzpatrick. . . . When I reach [sic] Washington, the Great Father . . . showed me that the inter-preters had deceived me. . . . All I want is right and justice. I represent the whole Sioux nation, and they will be bound by what I say. . . . We do not want riches, we want peace and love."

During years of conflicts and impending warfare, Tom Fitzpatrick urged the government to correct its mistakes of treatment and broken promises. His pleas and warnings were ignored and aggressive actions were taken against the Indians with whom they had signed a treaty.

It was the opening of the Bozeman Trail in '62 and the building of four forts between 1865 and 1867 to guard it that took their best hunting grounds, increased their miseries and fears, and provoked between 1866 and 1868 "Red Cloud's War." Until Crazy Horse, Red Cloud was the most feared and skilled Lakota chief. His daring and costly exploits eventually led to the Army abandoning the forts along the 967-mile trail and to new negotiations.

The second peace conference in 1868 concluded with the Laramie Treaty, which formed a "permanent" Dakota reservation. That parley ended the warpath of Red Cloud, who believed the United States government was being honest with him. He accepted that there would be no more encroachment of their lands and that the whites would honor their new promises. It was the breaking of the second, better known, treaty that led to the series of events and clashes that finally allowed the invasion of the sacred Black Hills for gold, provoked the massacre of Custer and his men at the Little Big Horn, and caused the near destruction of the Dakotas and many of their allies.

In this novel, the Oglala rituals, societies, laws, and customs are factual to the best of the knowledge gleaned from thirteen years of research during the writing of the series. However, the Red Heart banishment law for interracial marriage is part fact and part fiction. I did not find authentication of such an actual law, but it *was* forbidden and scorned to intermarry, which was thought to weaken the Indian bloodline. The Oglala language—dialogue and sign—is genuine. Some words in past books, however, were translated incorrectly for the Lakota tongue due to dialect and spelling differences, but are correct for the Dakota. All forts, except Tabor, and all trading posts and fur companies, except for Orin McMichael's, are historically accurate. Throughout the series, all treaties used are authentic, except for the 1782 and 1820 ones used in previous sagas.

The mentions of Colonel Leavenworth, Francis Parkman, George Catlin, Asa Whitney, and the Topographical Bureau Survey are accurate. Events leading to the Indian/white conflicts portrayed in this book are true, as are the trails, states, and Indian chiefs mentioned. Sitting Bull, Crazy Horse, Gall, Red Cloud, Inkpaduta, Jumping Buffalo/Spotted Tail, Tashunkopipape (Man Afraid of His Horses), Little Thunder, Wacouta (The Shooter), Wamdesapa, and Tecumseh were real men.

The lives and fates of the most legendary chiefs were similar to one another. The great Sitting Bull, Tatanka Yotanka, battled at the Little Big Horn, was later arrested, confined to a reservation, resigned himself to his fate, but was slain there in 1890. Crazy Horse, Tashunka Witco, also battled Custer, warred many more years, surrendered in spring of 1877, lived on a reservation, but was slain there in autumn of the same year. Heirs of sculptor Korczak Ziolkowski continue working on a monument at Custer on Thunderhead Mountain to honor the legendary spirit of the Lakotas, whom he represents as an heroic leader who always rode before his bands.

Gall, Pizi, battled Custer, later surrendered and lived on a reservation, where he worked for peace, and died at home in 1896. Besides the mentions in the story and earlier in this section, ultimately Red Cloud, Mahpiya Luta, settled on a reservation, where he resigned himself to his fate. He had an agency named after him, and lived there until his death in 1909. The American government built a home for Spotted Tail, Sinte Geleska, his wives and children but he left it to return to life in a tepee. He was honored and respected by white leaders, had an agency named after him in 1873, but was murdered by a jealous rival in 1881. Today, there is a college named after him: Sinte Geleska in Rosebud. Tashunkopipape (incorrectly translated through history and should be "Man Of Whose Horses We Are Afraid") worked for peace until his death. Little Thunder, following the Ash Hollow massacre by General Harney, settled on a reservation, where he died in 1879. Inkpaduta fought at the Little Big Horn, then fled across the Canadian border; he never made peace with the whites or returned, and died there in 1882.

Some of the most enlightening and poignant speeches and letters in history were written by Lakota chiefs Sitting Bull and Red Cloud. Also, the Oglala chief and prophet Black Elk, cousin to Crazy Horse, is noted for his physical, mental, and literary prowess.

The Crow chiefs, warriors, and their roles in this story are fictional. My novel is about a Lakota maiden, her band, and their hereditary enemies, as told from an Oglala point of view. I read many non-fiction, including Indian, sources to understand the emotions and motivations of these two nations, who warred for many generations. I do not want to mislead or offend with the products of my imagination. It is my wish that the good traits in Two-Bulls counterbalance the evil ones in Black Moon. In all Indian nations there have been bands and warriors who resemble my characterizations. It was necessary to my fictional plot to use the Oglalas' strongest enemy and the Crow's weakest facet.

Historically, between these two nations existed "a rancorous hatred, transmitted from father to son, and inflamed by constant aggression and retaliation," wrote Francis Parkman in 1846. Sitting Bull's limp resulted from a Crow bullet. The Crow accepted and sided with whites during the Indian wars between 1850 and 1870. This was an action the Dakotas themselves could not do or understand—any Indian perpetrating against his Red brothers, foe or not. In 1876, the Crow aided General Crook in tracking and battling the forces of Sitting Bull and Crazy Horse; the whites would have lost the Battle of the Rosebud if not for Crow prowess, courage, and tenacity. In 1877, the Crow aided Colonel Sturgis in tracking and defeating the famous Chief Joseph and his Nez Perces at Canyon Creek. Custer used Crow scouts and allies.

It is implied that the Crow recognized and feared the power and intelligence of the white man, particularly the soldiers and their weapons, and that was why they allied themselves with whites against Indians. The Crow served as scouts, guides, hunters, and couriers, some of the best skilled history has recorded. The Crow saw the alliance as a path to retaliation, safe raids, and vengeance against their hereditary foes. Added to the traditional warfare and enmity between the two Red nations, the Lakotas and their allies disdained and hated the Crow even more for such traitorous treachery.

I based Orin McMichael's and Black Moon's motivations on those of real men such as Absaroke chiefs Plenty Coops and Old Crow, and soldiers such as General Crook, Colonel Gibbon, Custer, and others. Many officers took advantage of the generational animosities as Gibbon did: "I have come down here to make war on the Sioux. The Sioux are your enemy and ours. For a long time they have been killing white men and killing Crow. I am going down to punish them. If the Crow want to make war upon the Sioux . . . [and] get revenge for Crows . . . now is their time." The Absaroke believed that "these are our lands, but the Sioux stole them from us. . . . the Sioux . . . heart is black. But the heart of the pale face . . . is red to the Crow. . . . Where the white warrior goes there shall we be also."

The historical quotations and facts featured in this story were found in too many sources to list for credit and are facts of public record. However, six non-fiction books were helpful in clarifying people and events. I list for acknowledgment: *Forts Of The West,* by Robert Frazer, University of Oklahoma Press, 1965; *They Led A Nation,* by Virginia Driving Hawk Sneve, Brevet Press, 1975; *The Indian Wars,* by Robert Utley and Wilcomb Washburn, Bonanza Books, 1977; *Story of the Great American West,* edited by Edward Barnard, Reader's Digest Association, Inc., 1977; *Let Me Be A Free Man,* compiled and edited by Jane Katz, Lerner Publications, 1975; and *South Dakota, Land of Shining Gold,* by Francie Berg, Flying Diamond Books, 1982, for information on the 1841 Pre-Emption Law. Thank you all—authors and publishers—for historical data and for written permission to use your research to enlighten and entertain readers. One last book I found useful is *Everyday Lakota,* collected and edited by Joseph Karol, Rosebud Educational Society, in 1971. It filled in translations missing due to the death of my Dakota friend and interpreter, Hiram Owen.

In South Dakota, there are two locations called Slim Buttes; I used the one near Reva, where the 1876 battle between General Crook and Lakotas took place. For reader recognition, I took the liberty of using the name Crazy Horse before this great legend received it in his vision-quest.

Many people in South Dakota were helpful with my extensive research and my attempts to be accurate, but the list in the beginning of the book acknowledges those who went to extra effort and cost to send me material and pictures. I want to thank each of you generous people again. Lawrence Blazek, aged seventy-five, *hand*-wrote me numerous pages of facts. He even entertained me with humorous tales of his boyhood days in Marcus.

To readers who enjoyed and supported this series over the years, thank you. Your letters, recommendations to friends, and kindnesses during tours and research trips have touched me deeply. In particular, I express my gratitude to: Eileen Wilson, who gifted me with ceramic busts she made of Gray Eagle and Alisha; Laverne Heiter, who made a beautiful and authentic white buckskin garment for me and had it beaded by One Sun with the symbols of Gray Eagle, Bright Arrow, and Sun Cloud. She also gifted me with a Lakota Medicine Wheel hair ornament (the female equivalent of the warrior's coup feather); Christy Johnson, who presented me with a Cheyenne Red-Tailed Hawk coup feather on a beaded rosette; and Debbie Keffer, for the many pieces of Indian beadwork she has made and given to me over the years. I want to thank bookstore managers and their staffs for keeping the series available for their customers, and thank distributors and their employees for their support and hard work over the years by keeping the series in stock and by promoting it to stores. No author is more grateful and moved by reader and bookseller loyalties than I am.

Your satisfaction and appreciation make my work meaningful and worthwhile.

I tried to the best of my abilities to give you a story, a series, and characters you will never forget and will love as much as I do. Of the twenty-three novels I've written, this series brought me special friends among Indians and whites and has been emotionally rewarding. To tell me you have learned about history and the two cultures involved thrills me. To tell me it inspires you to learn more about them warms my heart.

Until our next visit on the pages of my new book, keep reading, and learning, and loving!

Savage Conquest

FOR:

Michael, Angela, and Melanie, whose help
and support prevent "warring winds"
from destroying my deadlines
and creative flow.

And for my good friend Elaine Raco Chase,
whose letters, calls, and wit
help me retain my sanity.

And lastly for my good friend
and helper, Hiram C. Owen.

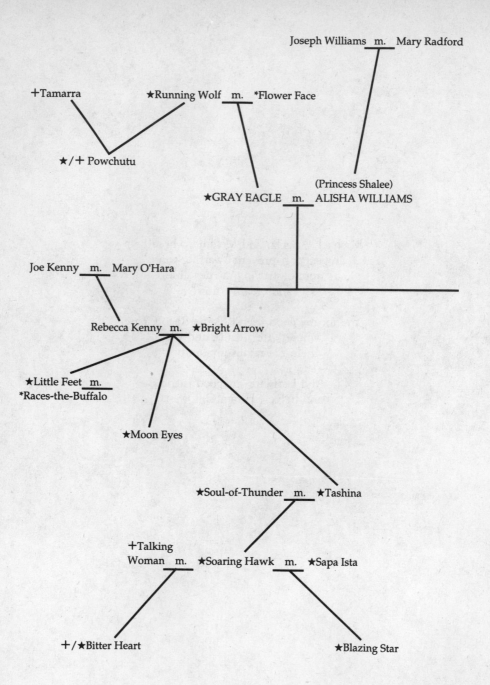

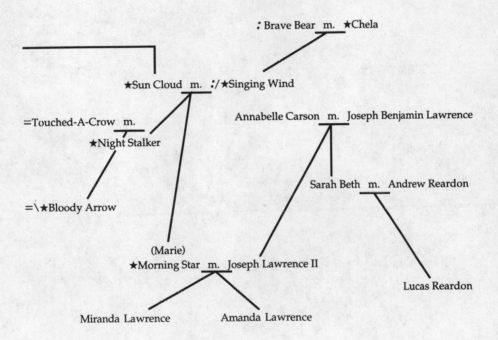

: Brave Bear m. ★Chela

★Sun Cloud m. :/★Singing Wind

Annabelle Carson m. Joseph Benjamin Lawrence

=Touched-A-Crow m.
★Night Stalker

Sarah Beth m. Andrew Reardon

=\★Bloody Arrow

(Marie)
★Morning Star m. Joseph Lawrence II

Lucas Reardon

Miranda Lawrence   Amanda Lawrence

Chapter One

Alexandria, Virginia
May, 1873

❦ *T*he past nine weeks had been difficult for the two young women sitting on the floral sofa in their brightly decorated parlor. Their mother had loved bold color schemes, but the lively shades didn't match the girls' solemn moods. Both were trapped in painful silence as they struggled to come to grips with a horrible truth—Lawyer McVane had just told them that their parents must be assumed dead, at least legally. Joe and Marie Lawrence had gone sailing in early March; only debris of their shattered craft had returned. Even if the girls did not want to accept this agonizing fact, they knew it was time to make some decisions about their current situation. They couldn't spend their lives feeding on grief and false hopes.

Amanda Lawrence shifted to glance at her fraternal twin sister, Miranda. Amanda's light blue eyes were filled with uncommon doubt and sadness as she met Miranda's somber brown gaze. Amanda felt as though she were looking in a mirror. Despite their different coloring—Amanda's flowing curls were light and dark blond, her complexion fair, and her eyes bright blue, while Miranda bore sleek chestnut locks, an olive complexion, and tawny eyes—they could have passed for identical twins. But the two eighteen-year-olds were completely unlike in personality.

They had always been very close. Amanda knew her sister was more beautiful, but it had never been a source of jealousy or trouble between them. Most men viewed Miranda as a sensual, enticing creature with an aura of mystery and a provocative innocence. Miranda was more than exquisite; she was warm, gentle, and unselfish. She was direct and honest but always tactful, carrying out her social obligations with grace and charm, but preferring close friends and simple events to crowds and soirées. Miranda seemed to be waiting, planning, dreaming of something vital to her existence, her destiny, her happiness.

A well-bred young lady from a wealthy and prominent family, Miranda concealed her "unfeminine" yearnings for adventure. In truth, she and Amanda could ride and shoot better than most men. Miranda could even fight better than most men, having been taught the "ancient arts" of self-defense by Ling, their Chinese cook's son. The last thing Miranda Lawrence wanted to be was a refined lady condemned to household chores and a "proper marriage," or so she had proclaimed at every available chance.

Miranda had never loved the parties, dances, theaters, dashing suitors, elegant clothes, and jewels as the outgoing Amanda did. Amanda would be the first to admit she enjoyed being coy and flirtatious. Why not? After all, Amanda Lawrence was wealthy, a Southern "blue blood," a valuable "catch." And men didn't have to tell Amanda that she was ravishing; the mirror did that. Even so, Amanda Lawrence accepted her beauty and acquired charms as blessings, gifts from Fate to be treasured and used to her best advantage.

Amanda knew what she wanted from life and was determined to have it. But how she wished the war hadn't destroyed that enviable Old South life style of belles and balls, of romantic duels, of grace and beauty, before she could taste and enjoy them. Dreams of such days had filled her youthful head until the nightmare of war with kin against kin had awakened her to their passing. Amanda felt she had been denied something essential—some loss of history, of ancestry, of heritage. She would never know such times, such daring and romantic men, such elegant evenings, for the Old South was gone forever.

Perhaps, Amanda mused, it was time for her to mature. She was no longer a child but a woman responsible for her own fate. In these past weeks, Amanda had come to realize life was more than looking and behaving the irresistible lady, more than having fun. Her parents had tried to teach her to be independent and brave, to be basically honest and caring. Suddenly her carefree search for the perfect storybook marriage had lost its magic.

Amanda had never known real fear before this dire period, and the taste of it was sour. Her parents had always been there as a defense between her and the cruel world. She didn't like feeling vulnerable and, in a brief moment of fear and panic, she had almost surrendered to a protective marriage. But now the initial shock had passed; the intense agony had dulled. Amanda's thinking was clearer and braver; she was ready and willing to challenge her future. She had spent a great deal of time with her father at his shipping firm, and she recognized that the first step toward her new life was obviously there . . .

"I don't care what Lawyer McVane says, Randy. I'm not going to sell Papa's business," Amanda stated calmly. "I'm going to run it myself," she announced.

"But, Mandy, you're a woman," Miranda argued. Her beloved sister had always believed she could do whatever she wanted, and she did understand and love the business, but what smug businessman would deal with a female owner? Their only source of livelihood could be crushed.

Amanda looked down at her shapely body clad in a lovely gown of sapphire, grinned, and playfully jested, "From my point of view, Randy, I do believe you're right. However, our competitors and customers will soon learn that brains can also be encased in a nicely rounded package." They laughed musically, feeling happy for the first time since they had heard about their parents' accident. Yes, it felt good to laugh and smile again.

Miranda gazed at the renewed life in her sister's eyes, thankful it had returned. She asked, "Mandy, are you going to marry Web?"

Disturbed by the nearly inaudible question, Amanda hesitated before candidly replying, "I don't know, Randy."

"It isn't like you to be so indecisive. You're not seeing anyone except Weber Richardson. Do you love him?"

"Do you remember what Mama told us on our eighteenth birthday? She said we would know the right man for us when we met him. She said she knew Papa was to be in her life-circle the moment she looked into his eyes. They loved each other so deeply. Do you really think it happens that way?" Amanda inquired seriously, for no suitor had made her feel and think the way her beloved mother had described.

"Yes," Miranda responded quickly. "That's why they wouldn't arrange any marriages for us. We must choose for ourselves. What do you think about when you look at Web? Does he make you feel warm and tingly inside?"

"I've sampled lots of stolen kisses, Randy, but none as good as Web's. He can be so romantic and dashing. Every single girl in town is after him, including many widows and even a few married tarts. It's exciting to know he's chosen me. I'll soon be nineteen, and if I wish to marry well, who's better than Web? Yet . . ."

Miranda's heart had been racing with panic until her sister wavered. "If you have any doubts, wait until after our birthday," she coaxed.

"First, I must learn if Web loves and wants me more than he wants Papa's firm. That should come to light when I take over."

A knock sounded loudly on the Lawrences' door. Their housekeeper/cook had been given the day off to allow them total privacy for the meeting with Lawyer McVane, so Amanda rose to answer the summons. She was both pleased and annoyed to find their first cousin, Lucas Reardon, lazing against the portal. As much as she adored this kinsman standing before her, she was eager to continue her conversation with her sister.

A broad grin claimed Lucas's mouth, creating little wrinkles near the corners of his dark green eyes and full lips. "A bad time to call, Mandy?" he astutely surmised, his grin widening and eyes sparkling.

"No, and yes," Amanda replied, stepping aside to allow him to enter. "Lawyer McVane just left. Randy and I were discussing the implications of his advice. A glass of sherry, Luke?" she offered.

Lucas sat in a plush chair, watching both girls with intense interest. Sometimes he wished he weren't related to the radiant beauties but, between the war and the recent accident, they were the only family he had left.

At one time, Lucas's father had been in business with Joseph Lawrence. But when Joe sided with the North and his father with the South, all bonds had been severed. Joe had always claimed that he remained neutral, not having the heart to battle either side. But there had been times when Joe's decisions had greatly affected one side or the other. The North hadn't fully trusted him because he was Southern, but Southerners despised any kinsman who didn't aid their cause. Now, Joe was dead and the twins were all alone, except for their cousin.

Lucas understood how his cousins must be feeling at this moment. It had been only nine years ago when his parents, Sarah Beth Lawrence and Andrew Reardon, had been slain during a battle near their home. Time would dull the anguish, but it would never completely vanish.

Amanda passed the sherry to Lucas then sat near her sister. "What brings you here today, Luke?" she asked, observing a curious strain in his expression and voice.

Lucas's smile faded, a worried scowl replacing it. "It's been weeks, my loves.

What are you two planning to do with the business? Any offers?" he inquired, sinking back into the cushiony chair, crossing one booted foot over his sturdy thigh.

"Plenty of offers, but we'll accept none," Amanda announced. "We're keeping Papa's business, and I'm going to manage it. Right, Randy?"

Lucas's mouth fell open and his leafy eyes became large circles. "You can't be serious, Mandy! A woman in shipping? You'll lose every account within a month. They'll laugh you off the docks."

Amanda puffed up with pride, jutting out her dainty chin. "I know that business inside and out, Luke," she declared smugly.

"From the books and your father's mouth, Mandy love. What about the warehouses, the workmen, the ships? You planning to do the rounds on them? The first sailor or loader who caught you alone would toss you on your fanny and take liberties. It isn't safe or smart. I can't allow you to take such foolish chances," he stated firmly.

"Don't be such a pessimist, Luke. You should know I can take care of myself. According to McVane, Randy and I own the business now. What I don't know, I'll learn, or I'll find someone who does know. Perhaps I'll hire a strong man who can do the rounds for me," she teased, eyes twinkling with merriment.

"Make sure he's an honest one, or he'll steal you blind while your nose is in those books," he warned seriously.

"If you're referring to Web, drop it, Luke. He's only taking care of things until Randy and I get matters settled. He made us an excellent offer, but we're not selling. For now, I can use Web's assistance. One day you'll have to tell me why you two dislike each other," she insisted, probing for a response which he refused to give.

Lucas and Amanda discussed and debated this topic for a long time as Miranda quietly listened and watched. She was amused by the verbal battle, for she already knew what the outcome would be.

Miranda studied Lucas as he conversed with her sister. Miranda and Lucas were very close; he was a friend, a teacher, a companion, a confidant, a partner in daring adventures. At twenty-seven, her handsome cousin still possessed a boyish mien and boundless energy. His dark green eyes glowed with a vitality she envied; they almost seemed to burn brightly from some inner fire. Lucas was strong and agile, which discouraged other men from provoking him. But her cousin rarely fought, for he was intelligent and perceptive. He could talk himself out of most troubles.

Lucas had a combination of traits which made him very attractive to women. He had a most enchanting and winning grin—when Lucas Reardon smiled, it was with his entire face, his entire being. His sable hair fell into a natural part down the middle then winged backward as the feathers near a hawk's throat. Just above his collar, his thick hair curled upward, almost impishly. Yes, Miranda decided to herself, Lucas Reardon was a man to stir a woman's heart, body, and soul—if she weren't his blood kin. Next to Amanda, Lucas was the most special person in her world; there wasn't anyone she admired or trusted more than Lucas.

In a humorous display of defeat, Lucas threw up his hands and shrieked, "I yield, love. Just remember I'm around if you need me."

All three joined in shared laughter. Miranda asked, "Luke, what are you writing now? I haven't noticed any articles in the paper recently."

Lucas sighed heavily. "I quit the paper, Randy. I wasn't doing any good there. It'll be years before the North listens to our side of the war. With that damn cartoonist, Nast, and his other jaundice-eyed cohorts, still portraying us as barbarians in *Harper's Weekly*, the South might never be vindicated or understood. You'd think he did enough damage to us during the war. Did you know that even their school books now carry the Northern bias against the South? Sometimes I think those journalists and newspapers did more to continue the war and hostilities than the soldier. How do they sleep at night after writing and publishing such injurious trash? What about truth and honor?"

"What can you do about it, Lucas?" Amanda questioned, knowing how much it meant to Lucas to set the records straight.

"I just wish there were some way to get reports or books to the Northern people. All they hear and read is how bad it still is down here. They're led to believe we're savages ready for another uprising. They take minor events and exploit them. The only path to lasting peace is for both sides to learn the truth about each other. And I want to be the pathlighter," he eagerly announced.

"But how?" Miranda asked, listening intently.

"I've worked and waited a long time to get into a position to be of use to the South. As Richelieu said, 'The pen is mightier than the sword.' I have a plan to strike a heavy blow at our Yankee conquerors. When it's in motion, I'll tell you two all about it," he revealed conspiratorially then winked at Miranda.

Miranda witnessed the mischievous look on Lucas's face, one she had come to know well. "Give, Luke; what's so funny?"

Cuffing her chin, he would only whisper, "You'll be the first to know, Randy. I just might have a vital role for you."

Following a light dinner, the three carried their desserts into the parlor to sit before a warm fire. The weather had turned slightly chilly, and the three sat on the floor near the fireplace as they chatted and enjoyed the treats prepared earlier by the housekeeper. Amanda still insisted on formal evening meals in the dining room, including proper clothing, silver, crystal, china, and candles, but tonight they also enjoyed the serene atmosphere of the sitting room.

"I'm glad to see you two smiling again. I've been plenty worried," Lucas confessed. "I wish there were something I could do."

"Just standing by us is enough, Luke," Amanda remarked softly. "We'll take care of everything until . . ." She went silent.

Lucas's head jerked upward. He stared at the golden-haired girl, and then at Miranda. Both their expressions shouted "trouble." His heart thudded heavily. "Until what?"

"Randy and I won't believe they're dead until we view the bodies. Maybe a passing ship found them. They might be alive somewhere. Papa was a skilled sailor; the *Merry Wind* was in excellent shape. And the weather wasn't bad. It doesn't make sense, Luke."

"The *Merry Wind* was found shattered on the coast, Mandy. You're dreaming, loves. If they survived, we would know by now. Don't build up for a crushing fall. They're dead," he stated with finality.

Miranda looked at him and shook her chestnut head of hair. "Hope is a free commodity, Luke. It isn't impossible."

"Don't do this," he pleaded, distressed by this unexpected defiance of reality, wishing he could alter it. Their gazes battled for a time. Lucas argued reluctantly, "You're denying the evidence."

"Evidence of a broken ship but not our parents' certain deaths," Miranda retorted.

Lucas looked from one girl to the other. "What if the bodies are never found? What if they're never recovered?"

"Then Randy and I have each other. At least Mama and Papa had a happy life together, and they have us to carry on for them. But as long as we can retain a glimmer of hope, it will see us through this dreadful period. When the time comes to accept the 'evidence,' we'll be strong enough to do so. But not yet, Luke, not yet. You must admit, we've survived the roughest part and we're getting on with our lives. Don't fret. We're going to be just fine."

Another knock sounded on their door. This time, Lucas went to answer it. "What do you want, Richardson?" he asked, not bothering to mask his dislike for this man who was hotly pursuing his cousin.

"I came to speak with Amanda, if you don't object, Reardon. Isn't it time for you to get over Marissa's loss?" Web hinted tauntingly.

"You never cared about her, so why did you ruin her?" he flared angrily. With luck, his investigative work on Web would pay off soon. With proof, Amanda would be compelled to see it was more than male pride and rivalry between them.

"If you care so much, why not take her back?" Web scoffed.

Before Lucas could reply, Amanda joined them. She was puzzled by the endless hostility between these two vital men. As they stood facing each other in the entrance hall, the currents of antagonism were so strong they were almost a tangible force. Amanda was piqued by their childish behavior. She was weary of trying not to take sides and of trying to settle their mysterious dispute.

"May I come in, Amanda?" Weber asked in a thick southern accent. If his secret plans worked out, Weber thought to himself, Lucas would soon be long gone, putting a halt to his nosing around. Luke always provoked him into acting badly before Amanda, and those reporter's instincts could soon get them both into trouble.

"Of course," Amanda responded, hoping they would conduct themselves like gentlemen tonight. She almost stomped her foot in irritation when they exchanged surly grins. It was evident they were going to be as nasty as the rainy weather outside.

Lucas stalked into the sitting room, leaving them in the hallway. He sat beside Miranda this time, flashing her a frown. Amanda and Weber joined them, each taking a chair before the sofa. Amanda served Weber coffee and listened to his business report.

Although Weber was courting Amanda, Lucas never missed that flicker of desire for Miranda in Weber's dark eyes. Positively, this ex-Rebel craved both the Lawrence Shipping Firm and one of the Lawrence girls. Weber had leveled his sights on Amanda, but Lucas felt Web would just as soon have either sister if the firm was included in her dowry. Lucas was alarmed by Amanda's blind spot where Web was concerned, but as much as he hated to admit it, he knew Web could be a real charmer. If only Amanda knew the real Web . . .

Weber Richardson was a die-hard Southerner to the soul. During and after the war, there had been rumors of his cruelties to Yankee prisoners, even female ones. Web despised the North and what she had done to the South, to his family, to him. The Richardsons had lost everything: power, riches, property, and family. And Lucas was very eager to learn how Web had come back into money and property so quickly. Web owned a smaller shipping business near Joe's. Unknown to the girls, Web had once approached Joe about merging the two firms and marrying Amanda. But Joe had refused both requests. Undoubtedly Joe had recognized those same bad traits which dismayed Lucas: Web was conniving, greedy, vindictive, and cold-blooded. Now that Joe was gone, Lucas felt he must protect the girls from Web. But to attack the man verbally without proof would place Mandy on Web's side. Too, Web was dangerous and wily. If only some suitor would come along to distract Mandy and save her from Web, Lucas wished silently.

Lucas wondered what women saw in a man like Weber. Sure, he was nice looking, wealthy, and influential. At thirty-four, Weber was what the Northerners called a "typical Southern aristocrat." His features were prominent, strong, and arrogant, but Lucas knew all that to be a facade.

Miranda's thoughts were similar to Lucas's. There was something about Web Richardson that unsettled her. How she wished Amanda would never see him again.

Miranda admitted that Weber Richardson was imposing. He was educated and well traveled, and he could be witty and romantic. It was obvious women found him immensely attractive, but she wondered if Amanda had any real affection for Weber. So far, Miranda had carefully concealed her reservations about Weber. For now, she would allow Amanda to make her own decisions about him. But Miranda had glimpsed flickers in Web's eyes which chilled her heart. Just thinking of him sent shivers of dread through her body.

"Cold, love?" Lucas inquired, pulling her from her dark thoughts.

"Let's get some brandy to warm me," she replied, sending Lucas a look which said it had been her thoughts and not the weather which had inspired her tremors. Lucas smiled and nodded.

When Miranda and Lucas left the room, Weber quickly arose and went to Amanda, pulling her to her feet. Before Amanda knew what he had in mind, his arms were holding her tightly and his mouth was settling over hers. He murmured huskily, "I've been waiting all day for that. You're driving me wild, Amanda. Why must you resist me? No man is more suited to you than me," he whispered confidently.

"Behave yourself, Weber Richardson," she scolded playfully. "It's too soon to think of such matters."

"If you won't agree to marry me or become affianced, at least don't see anyone besides me," he entreated.

"I've seen no man but you in over three months. Still, only by comparing you to other men can I judge if you are truly the right one for me," she jested coyly, grinning at him.

"But you've dated every man within fifty miles," he argued. "I have to be away on business for a few days. When I return, we need to be alone and talk. I have something important to ask you."

His tone revealed what he had in mind—sex and marriage, in any order. Uncertainty washed over her. Web's kisses were nice, but they didn't stir her desires. And she didn't know if she was ready for a permanent relationship. Right now, Amanda didn't want any complications in her life, including marriage. Maybe Weber was the ideal choice for a husband, or at least a business partner.

Each day he was becoming more amorous and persistent even though Amanda had not encouraged him. What would he do, she wondered, if she refused him?

"Please, Web, not here. Randy and Luke will return any moment. We'll have dinner and talk when you come back."

"At my home?" he suggested, eyes glowing with interest.

"At the Duke House," she refused laughingly, wondering what was missing between her and Web—or, perhaps, only in her.

He shrugged. "One day soon I hope you'll tire of leading me a merry chase, Amanda. Be mine. I promise you won't be sorry."

Amanda pulled away as she heard voices nearing the room. She realized that if she kept refusing to make any commitment to Web, he would demand one or leave her and her business. But did she care? When he discovered she was taking over the firm, his reaction would tell her a great deal. She decided not to tell him her news until his return. Since her parents' deaths, she had acted both spineless and brainless, but that was going to change. Web could take it or leave it!

As Miranda was pouring four brandies, another knock sounded at the door. "This is certainly our day for company," Amanda declared, her voice unnaturally high with tension. To escape Web's mocking gaze and to recover her wits and poise, she went to answer the summons. It was raining hard, and the night air was nippy and brisk.

"Yes?" she asked shakily of the man whose back was to the open door. Even though he was wearing a rain slicker, Amanda could tell he was several inches over six feet and powerfully built. She thought it odd he was wearing a western hat over his coal black hair.

He spoke in a stirring tone as he turned to face her. "Would you please tell Joseph Lawrence that Reis Harrison is here to see him?" he stated politely, sweeping off his hat and running strong fingers through his hat-ruffled hair.

In the darkness, neither could make out the features of the other. As the damp breeze teased at her clothes and hair, Amanda invited the stranger inside to deliver her depressing news. There was nothing menacing in his stance or voice, and there were two strong men inside the house who could offer their protection. She closed the door and leaned her forehead against it, summoning the strength to utter words which ripped at her heart. She inhaled then slowly released her breath.

Reis sensed something was terribly wrong. He waited patiently for the young woman to speak. As he removed his rain slicker and tossed it over his right arm, his eyes slipped from her silky head of blond curls down her slender body, to return to where her eyes would be once she faced him. When she did, her words, "Joseph Lawrence is dead," temporarily went unnoticed as his entranced senses hastily absorbed every detail about her.

Reis had heard the silly phrases "breath-taking" and "heart-stopping," but in his thirty-two years no woman had ever made his breath catch or his heart race. Now, without warning or preparation, he was assailed by both sensations. The instant her pale blue eyes fused with his rich blue ones, all wits and words were lost to him. Like some foolish lad, he gaped at her.

Once Amanda's gaze met his, she was unaware of anything except this vital man. Amanda had been wooed by countless suitors, and she knew instinctively this man was special. What could be more pleasurable, she imagined, than losing herself in his arms?

Amanda had not closed the door securely, and a sudden gust of wind flung it against her back. She jumped and gasped. Reis's hand shot over her shoulder to press the door shut, bringing their bodies into close contact, making each aware of the nearness of the other. Reis's palm flattened against the door and his arm rested lightly on her shoulder.

Amanda could feel the warmth of his breath upon her forehead. Never had she seen such handsome features. He had startlingly blue, mesmeric eyes, which flaunted a softness and sparkle that tugged at her thudding heart. His lips were full and inviting; his jawline was wide and his chin squared. If a man's nose could be beautiful, his was. Such strength of character was stamped upon his tanned face, and when he smiled, his whole face lit up like a candle in the darkness. His eyes and mouth had tiny creases near their corners—the kinds of lines which implied he was a man who loved life and was pleased with his role in it.

Without realizing she was inspecting him from head to foot, she noted his clothes. Surely his garments were specially tailored for that well-developed and well-toned physique. But why was he wearing western attire? His snug shirt, black leather vest, dark blue Levi jeans and black knee boots were not the usual dress for men in this area.

When Amanda realized she was leaning sideways and examining him from ebony head to black boot, she blushed in embarrassment, an uncommon reaction for her. What was wrong with her? To cover her lapse, she asked, "Who are you, sir?"

Reis straightened, placing his wayward hand on his hip. "Reis Harrison, Miss . . . ," he replied entreatingly. Reis was bemused by his novel loss of self-control. Surely she was an angel sent to Earth to warm his heart and soul. Her hair coloring was a mixture of lemonade and aged brandy. Her eyes were as striking as a peaceful summer sky.

"I caught your name, sir. What business do you have with Joseph Lawrence? As I said, he—he was killed in a recent accident," she told him hoarsely, eyes dewy.

Reis could tell she was upset by her words and her previous behavior. Then again, he was also unnerved by this vision of beauty. He quickly detected her spark of courage and pride. Reis Harrison, an ex-Yankee officer presently employed by President Grant as a special agent, was accustomed to getting his wishes, one way or another. Right now, Reis found this female more intriguing than his case . . .

Killed? Reis mentally echoed. "May I extend my condolences, Miss . . ." He tried to obtain her identity once more.

"Amanda Lawrence, Mister Harrison." She took his cue.

"Wife or sister or daughter?" he inquired anxiously, praying her answer wouldn't be his first query.

"Joseph Lawrence was my father, Mister Harrison. I'm the new owner and manager of Lawrence Shipping. So if your business concerns the firm, you'll have to deal with me now," she informed him crisply, anticipating a mocking attitude.

Reis read her emotions accurately and smiled. "I have no qualms about dealing with a woman, even if she is extremely beautiful. I do hope you don't use your distracting charms to take advantage of a client. Shall we get acquainted and discuss our business over lunch tomorrow? I just arrived and wanted to introduce myself. Shall we say noon at the Windsor?"

At his bold flattery, surprise registered on Amanda's face. When she read no trace of guile in him, she smiled. "If all male customers and clients take my news as well as you did, Mister Harrison, I shall consider myself a believer in miracles. Thank you. I would prefer to discuss these matters tomorrow, as I have guests tonight."

"At your convenience, Miss Lawrence. It is Miss?" he pressed.

Amanda laughed softly and parried, "It is Mister, isn't it?"

"If there's anything better than a breath of fresh air, it's a charming and witty lady," he teased. He boldly reached for her left hand and held it up to view the third finger. "Why that finger's naked I'll never understand, but I am most grateful," he murmured.

Not to be outdone, Amanda audaciously repeated the action on his hand. "Since many men don't wear gold bands, is there a Mrs. Harrison?" she brazenly inquired, refusing to break their locked gaze.

"Not yet. Would you care to apply for that position?" he asked mirthfully, eyes glittering with appreciation. His cheery mood was contagious and his easy smile was infectious.

"Shouldn't we get acquainted first?" Amanda fenced deftly, warming and tingling all over.

Reis's glowing eyes eased over Amanda, then he chuckled. "Is there some dark secret about you which might change my mind? A nasty temper? Some hideous scar? Perhaps you're a witch?"

The smoldering fire in his gaze ignited her very soul. Amanda laughed at his comical look. The conversation was ridiculous, but so much fun. "The truth is out, sir; alas, a witch."

As Reis trailed a finger over her lips, he murmured, "What but truth could pass such sweet lips. A bewitcher indeed." Neither had kissed a total stranger before, but both were sorely tempted.

"Is there some problem, Amanda?" a frigid voice asked from down the hallway as Weber noisily approached them, having missed Reis's words but not his interest in Amanda.

Amanda quickly stepped aside, as if guilty of some offense. Weber joined them and Amanda eased her inexplicable tension by introducing the two men. "Weber Richardson, meet Reis Harrison. Reis and my father were friends, Web. He came to pay his respects and to discuss some family business. As I said, we'll chat tomorrow," she stated to an astute Reis. "Web is also a friend of the family," she added nonsensically.

"Haven't we met before, Harrison?" Weber asked suspiciously. His eyes chilled and narrowed as he scanned the vaguely familiar taut frame and handsome face near Amanda.

"Where?" Reis cautiously speculated, implying no recollection. He wondered why Amanda had insinuated that they had met before, but he went along with her deception. Apparently she didn't want Richardson to know he was here on business. Answers could come later.

Weber stepped closer, slipping his arm around Amanda's waist and smiling down into her baffled expression. As Amanda watched and listened, there it was again, that brief flash of intimidating coldness which warned her to keep Weber at arm's length. "Why don't you invite Harrison inside for a brandy? Since I'm handling your affairs, he can discuss his business with me," he stated boldly, wanting to study this man who caused ripples of warning and fury in him.

As if Reis wanted to do the same, he didn't decline or speak. As both men waited for Amanda's reaction, she grasped intangible sensations which didn't sit well with her. With unsuccessfully disguised annoyance, she chided, "You don't handle family or personal matters, Web, only business ones," trying to sound playfully casual. She looked up at Reis and said, "I'm sorry, Reis. I hope you don't think me rude, but it is late. Web and my cousin Luke were just about to leave." Somehow she wanted Reis to know she and Weber weren't alone. How dare Web act as if she were his property! "My sister and I have family matters to discuss in private." To Weber, she said, "I'll see you later. It's been a long and tiring day for me and Miranda."

Weber knew he had angered her and was being dismissed. Before he could contrive an excuse to stay, Miranda and Lucas joined them. Lucas asked, "Is there some problem, Mandy?"

"Web was just leaving," Amanda answered. Turning to Reis, she said, "This is my cousin, Lucas Reardon, and my sister, Miranda. Luke, Randy, this is Reis Harrison, one of Papa's friends. Goodnight, Web," she added to make her dismissal and vexation clear.

Miranda accepted Reis's handshake and smiled warmly. "It's a pleasure to meet you, sir. Shall I take your coat?"

Reis's eyes went from one beauty to the next. "You're almost twins," he muttered in surprise. "With different coloring."

The girls looked at each other and smiled. Miranda hugged Lucas and said good night, her eyes motioning for him to usher the despicable Weber out with him. Lucas grinned, only too delighted to comply. Weber couldn't refuse without acting a fool, so he left.

When the door closed behind the two men—one frowning and one smiling—Amanda invited Reis to have a brandy. She smiled sheepishly as she told him, "I'm sorry about that little lie, Mister Harrison. Sometimes Web is a bit presumptuous. He has a bad habit of trying to be too helpful," she jested.

Knowing Weber Richardson was probably lurking outside to see how long he remained, Reis was sorely tempted to accept the invitation. He would have, if Amanda had been alone. But he politely refused the offer, giving the late hour as his excuse. He slipped on his rain slicker and said good night, sending Amanda a smoldering smile which could have melted an entire snowdrift.

As he walked away from the house with a fluid and confident stride, Amanda stood in the open doorway, oblivious to the cool, damp air, watching him until the shadows devoured him. She closed the door and leaned against it, sighing peacefully.

Miranda giggled and commented, "He's quite a man."

Amanda sighed again, eyes dreamy. "Yes, he is, Randy. We're meeting for lunch tomorrow," she divulged happily, then revealed who Reis was and why he had appeared at their door tonight.

"Aren't you spoken for, Mandy? What about Web?" Miranda asked softly, observing her sister's interest in Reis.

"Who?" Amanda teased playfully, winking at Miranda. "Besides, Reis is only business, my first client."

Their gazes fused; they burst into mirthful laughter.

* * *

Reis stood before his hotel window watching the gentle rainfall and sipping a tepid brandy. He hadn't expected to find Joseph Lawrence dead under mysterious circumstances. Reis flung himself across his bed without bothering to undress. This case was suddenly very complex and perilous. He hadn't imagined he would meet a dream like Amanda Lawrence and positively not on this crucial trip. More so, he hadn't envisioned confronting Lieutenant Weber Richardson here! Perhaps that sadistic ex-Rebel officer had forgotten the awesome day when they had met, but Major Reis Harrison never would.

Reis had tried to accept his losses during a vicious war. He had tried to repair his torn life, to master his bitterness, to govern the urge to track that one foe and justifiably slay him. After all, if every person gave in to vengeful impulses, the conflict between the two sides would never end.

Somehow all these facts and people were intertwined, and he dreaded untangling them. Only President Grant knew why Reis had been sent here. With so much greed and corruption surrounding him, Grant didn't know who to trust. It was up to Reis to find some answers for him, answers to halt some explosive problems, answers to who was involved and why.

He cursed the heavens for putting Amanda in the center of this new crisis, for there could be no middle ground . . .

Chapter Two

hen Miranda entered the sitting room the following morning, she found her sister pacing the floor, a look of annoyance wrinkling her forehead. Miranda watched from the doorway for a few moments before asking, "What's wrong, Mandy?"

Amanda halted her movements and glanced at her discerning sister. Waving a paper in her tight grasp, she replied, "See this? It says Mister Reis Harrison doesn't want to meet with me today. He could have sent his refusal before I was dressed and ready to leave," she declared angrily, unaccustomed to being put off by a man.

Miranda was quick to notice how lovely her sister looked this gloomy morning. Clearly Amanda had taken extra pains with her clothes and hair. She had been so excited about this appointment. Now, she looked distressed. Obviously, Amanda was suffering more from disappointment at not seeing Reis than from singed pride. "What does the letter say? Why did he cancel the meeting?" Miranda probed curiously.

Amanda stated skeptically, "He claims the weather is too bad for me to leave home. He wants to postpone our talk for a few days. He says he has other business he can settle first. Damn him!" she muttered, jerking the ribbons loose from her stylish hat and tossing it on the sofa with her cape. This action revealed the extent of her edginess, as Amanda was always careful with her clothes and belongings.

"Amanda Lawrence! You shouldn't speak so crudely. You recall how often Papa had to change plans at the last minute. The weather's awful. I think he's most considerate."

"You believe this excuse about the weather and other business? He probably thinks I don't have the brains to run Lawrence Shipping!" she declared, wanting her sister to convince her otherwise.

"Mandy, you stop this! You shouldn't judge him guilty of deception until you have proof. He didn't strike me as a dishonest or calculating man. If you hadn't found Mister Harrison so handsome and charming, you wouldn't be so vexed by this note. I saw the way you two looked at each other," she teased knowingly. "Mandy, don't spoil things before giving him a chance to explain," she entreated, praying this vital man could pull Amanda's attention from Weber.

"Spoil things?" Amanda echoed. "There's nothing to spoil. We only met last night, and we've nothing in common but business."

Miranda gayly challenged, "That isn't the way it looked to me, nor to Weber. Did you see the look on his face when you dismissed him like an errant child? I'd bet he wanted to choke you and Mister Harrison." Miranda's voice waxed serious as she asked, "Mandy, isn't Weber getting awfully possessive of you? You two aren't betrothed. Why did Weber act so rude and hostile last night?"

"Probably jealousy. You met Reis; can you blame Web? Reis was being flirtatious when Web joined us. Actually, I was rude to Web first, but he made me so mad!" she confessed.

"Web was definitely trying to show Mister Harrison he has a prior claim on you. From the way you two acted, maybe Mister Harrison thought he had interrupted a lover's spat. Maybe that's why he canceled; perhaps he's waiting to see if you're available," Miranda hinted slyly.

"Don't be silly, Randy. Reis was just playing a game with me. He probably thinks he can enchant every female he meets. I bet he had no intention of doing business with us. I could flog myself for acting like a fool! That damn Yankee probably thinks Southern girls don't know how to do anything but look pretty! Just wait until I see Mister Reis Harrison again; I'll straighten out his thinking," she threatened. She would not be an amusing game for any man.

"Don't do anything you'll be sorry for, Mandy. Mister Harrison doesn't appear the designing type, like some of your other suitors. He probably knows you're flooded with offers, and he's afraid of the competition. After all, he is a stranger and a Yankee."

"Reis Harrison didn't strike me as a man afraid of anything. But if he thinks to entice me by seeming disinterested, he's wrong!" Suddenly Amanda's expression grew thoughtful.

"What is it?" Miranda inquired, coming to stand by her sister.

"Before you and Luke joined us, something odd happened. Web asked Reis if they had met before. Reis didn't say yes or no. But the way they looked and acted . . . It was like—"

"Like what?" Miranda asked anxiously.

"Fierce enemies meeting again. Worse than the situation between Web and Luke. I wonder why," Amanda murmured worriedly.

"Are you forgetting Web was a Confederate officer and Reis was a Yankee less than eight years ago? Some men can't forgive or forget those times. From what I've seen, Web hates all Yankees. And if Reis thinks you and Web are close, that might cause resentment toward you. You did tell white lies to both men. If you'll remember, the trouble started last night when Web confronted you two in the hallway and acted as if he owned you," Miranda speculated.

Amanda wondered if Weber was the real reason for Reis's change of plans. Or was Reis merely used to having his way where women were concerned? She wanted to learn more about both men, especially that magnetic stranger who was affecting her emotionally. "I think I'll go down to the office," Amanda announced.

"But the weather is too bad to go out," Miranda debated. "If you run into that dashing Reis, he might think you're chasing him. I wonder what Weber will have to say about Reis dropping your meeting?"

The cunning hints struck home. Amanda didn't want either man to speculate wildly on her actions. Web would be gone by midafternoon, and Reis was out there somewhere. She was being childish and impulsive. Postponing a business meeting with her was not a crime, an insult, or a rejection.

"You're right as usual, Randy. I'll go to the office tomorrow. I want a good look at our books while Web is away. If Reis's business is near our firm, it wouldn't be wise to run into him *accidentally.*"

Miranda stared at her mercurial sister. "If he merely put off your talk until the weather clears, why are you acting this way?"

"Because he could have delivered the message himself. It was storming last night when he came here. So why does he suddenly use the weather as an excuse to avoid me? If he truly thinks it's too bad to go meet him, he could come here," she rationalized.

"What privacy could you have if Web called again? He could have learned Weber is handling the firm for you. Since Reis doesn't know how often you see each other, it might be Web he wants to avoid."

Amanda met her sister's mischievous smile. "You think so?"

"You know more than I about men and romance. He's different, Mandy. I've never seen you act like this about a man. I think something happened between you two the moment you met, just like Mama said. Reis Harrison is a rare find, and I think you're a fool if you mess it up before you see that fact too," her sister blurted out.

Before Amanda could tell her how silly or absurd that was, Miranda danced toward the door, humming to herself. Just before closing it, Miranda warned devilishly, "Watch out, Mandy; you might be falling in love with Reis." Amanda stared at the closed door, allowing those startling seeds to take root in her fertile mind.

That's ridiculous! she mentally rationalized. *How could I fall in love with a perfect stranger? Perfect. Perhaps you're too perfect, Reis Harrison. Of all the men I've ever known or seen, none have compared to you. Can Randy be right? Did you cast some magical spell over me last night? If not, why can I think of nothing but you? Why did I go to sleep thinking of you? Awake thinking of you? Why am I so afraid you won't come around again? Why does the thought we've met for the first and last time cause me such sadness and anguish? Is this a cruel joke by Fate? Have you done to me what I've done to so many men? I must see you again, Reis. I must understand these crazy feelings.*

Around eight that evening, the housekeeper answered the door and delivered a note to Amanda. Her anger returned twofold when she read it. "How dare he!"

she shrieked aloud. "Listen to this, Randy: 'Miss Amanda Lawrence, I have reserved a private table at the Windsor for our lunch and to discuss a possible business deal. I shall expect you at noon.' It's signed by Reis Harrison. Not, 'will you meet me'; or, 'is it convenient'; just an order!"

Miranda wanted to tell her sister she was overreacting, but she knew Amanda wouldn't listen. A masterful man was a new thing to Amanda. Men had always pursued her, falling over themselves and each other to gain her eye or to carry out her wishes. Suddenly, here was a man whom she couldn't control or bewitch, one who made her the huntress and not the prey for a delightful change. Obviously this Reis wasn't overly impressed with her beauty, wealth, and station. Miranda wondered how her sister would deal with this unspoken challenge, a challenge poor Reis might not realize he had issued. Apparently her sister had much to learn about a real man.

"I'm not going," Amanda stated defiantly. "If Mister Harrison wants to see me, he can ask, not summon! He should pick me up in a carriage. Him and his stupid notes! When I don't appear, that should teach him a thing or two about ladies and manners!"

"You're being spiteful, Amanda Lawrence. He's arranged a business meeting, not a date," Miranda reminded her stubborn sister.

"Then perhaps I should think twice about doing business with an ill-mannered rake. How does he know I'm not busy tomorrow? He could have asked," she reasoned petulantly.

"First, you're angry because he cancels; now, you're angry when he sets a new appointment. What's wrong with you, Mandy? Do you or do you not wish to see him? You could lose his business by behaving like a spurned woman or a spoiled brat. Go and meet with him," Miranda encouraged.

"I can't," she vowed willfully. "If I rush to meet him, he'll think he can treat me in this despicable and rude manner. Mister Reis Harrison needs to learn a valuable lesson about women. If I had been a man, he wouldn't have canceled the first meeting; and he surely wouldn't set up a new one in such an offensive way. If we're to do business, he must treat me equally and respectfully."

"Be honest with yourself, Mandy," her sister advised gravely. "You're really upset because he's ignoring you as a woman. If he's stung your pride, don't let it show. You can't bedazzle every male. Are you afraid of him?" she conjectured seriously.

"Afraid of him? He didn't appear to be dangerous," she replied.

"That's not what I meant. He frightens you in some way."

Amanda flushed guiltily. "There is something about him which confuses me. He made a fool of me last night. He flirted outrageously with me, and I responded likewise. Now, he feels he can treat me as he pleases. I won't chase any man, and certainly not a total stranger. I don't like losing control of such a situation," she admitted.

"What's so terrible about giving the reins to such a stimulating man? How many times have you complained about suitors who lack courage and brains? You don't want someone you can lead around by a ring through his nose. If he intrigues you, Mandy, discover why."

"For one who claims to know little about men and romance, you offer a great deal of advice," Amanda teased her sister. "What about you, Randy? Have you ever met anyone intriguing?"

"Not yet, but I will one day," Miranda replied confidently.

"How so, when you stay home all the time? You think some irresistible stranger is going to appear at your door one stormy night to sweep you off your feet?" she continued merrily.

"Why not? It happened with you," she ventured boldly.

"Miranda Lawrence, you never give up, do you?" she wailed.

"Not when I see that same look in your eyes as I saw in Mama's. Have you ever met a man like Reis? No," she answered her own question.

Still, Miranda couldn't persuade her sister to accept the appointment with Reis the next day. Instead, Amanda went to visit friends, just to be unavailable if Reis called. Actually, Amanda was disturbed by the way she had behaved with Reis. She had never met a commanding and imposing man, and she didn't know how to deal with one or the sensations which he aroused. She had acted like an infatuated and foolish young girl, and knew she had to be wary of his powerful effect. She refused even to send a note of regret or refusal.

When Reis came by in midafternoon to see why Amanda hadn't arrived for their meeting, Miranda was too embarrassed to speak with him. Knowing she couldn't lie with a clear conscience or straight face, she ordered their housekeeper to tell Reis that Amanda was out for the day. She was bemused by the message Reis left for Amanda: "If Miss Lawrence decides to meet with me, tell her to contact me at the hotel before I leave Friday."

Amanda was given the cool message upon her arrival home. "First, a command appearance; now, an ultimatum. Just who does he think he is, Randy? Mrs. Reed said he looked terribly angry."

"He should be. You insult his manners then behave just as rudely. The least you could have done was send a note to say you weren't coming," Miranda scolded her. "Is this any way to handle business? If you don't want to be treated like a spoiled woman, then don't behave like one. If you want him to pursue you, Mandy, then you'd best give him the opportunity before he leaves Friday."

"Why are you speaking so hatefully, Randy?" she quizzed.

"Because I'm mad. You rant about how all males are alike; then when someone different comes along, you're furious because he doesn't behave like all the rest. I don't understand you, Mandy. You haven't chosen a sweetheart because not one man you've dated has stood out from the others. Suddenly a strong and virile male magically appears on your doorstep, and you're chasing him away because you can't wrap him around your finger like all the rest who aren't worth having."

"That isn't true, Randy. I'm just . . ." She fell silent, turning her back to her sister. How could she explain her feelings?

"Just what?" the dark-haired girl demanded.

"You asked me if I was afraid of Reis. Maybe I am. Oh, Randy, he makes me feel and think such puzzling things. I'm at such a loss when he's near. I'd probably act like an idiot at our meeting. Can I risk falling for the only man who doesn't seem interested in me?" Tears glimmered on her lashes.

"From what I observed, Reis is most impressed by you."

"But in what way, Randy? I won't argue that he found me charming or desirable. What if that's all he sees and wants from me? He's dangerous, Randy, for he has the power to hurt me." With that fear spoken aloud, she knew she must deal with it, with the source of it.

"You're serious, aren't you?" When Amanda nodded, Miranda smiled and suggested, "Why don't you find out how you affect him? It isn't like you to be a coward or to be so insecure."

"That's the problem," Amanda sighed. "I haven't been me since I met Reis."

Reis sat at the table in his room, making notes and planning. He had done some checking on Richardson, Amanda Lawrence, and both shipping firms. He didn't like what his search had revealed or the implications. He couldn't figure out why Amanda didn't want Weber to know he was here on business, not after discovering that Weber was in control of her firm. More confusing and plaguing was the fact that Weber and Amanda were rumored to be heading for the altar. Very strange . . .

He pondered Amanda's reasons for deceiving her sweetheart and temporary partner. But if Amanda was in love with Weber, why had she flirted with him? Who had killed Joseph Lawrence, and why? Reis couldn't believe his convenient death was an accident. Had Joseph found out too much? Amanda had wanted their meeting kept a secret from Weber, but why conceal it and why refuse to set up another one? What was Richardson's involvement in this mystery? Reis cautioned himself to forget vengeful justice against Weber until this mission was completed. The situation was getting more complicated and suspicious every minute. Amanda couldn't know who and what he was, so why was she avoiding him? Or was it merely a feminine ploy to entice and to baffle him?

The answers he needed were concealed in the Lawrence firm. Like it or not, Reis would have to use Amanda to get them. She was a proud and stubborn beauty. He couldn't wait around and hope for her to make the next move. Doubtlessly she was used to getting her way with men. If he had the time, he would spark her interest by showing a resistance to her charms and beauty, giving her a much-needed lesson. Then again, maybe he had been overly confident in his approach to her, for he was also accustomed to getting his way with the opposite sex. Frankly, her rebuffs were a shock to him. If Amanda Lawrence expected and needed romantic wooing, then she would receive it, and receive it from a master . . .

The following day was clear and warm. Miranda lifted the basket of fresh flowers and turned to enter the house. She was surprised to find Reis leaning negligently against the gatepost behind her. "Mister Harrison, I didn't hear you arrive. Have you been standing there long?"

"Only a few moments. I didn't want to startle you, Miss Miranda. You looked so deep in thought. It's a lovely day, isn't it?"

Miranda glanced skyward and smiled. "Yes, it is. Spring is one of my favorite seasons. But I fear the recent rains nearly destroyed the flowers." She waited for him to reveal his reason for being there.

As if reading her thought, he said, "I came by to see if Miss Amanda could join me for lunch or dinner, if she isn't occupied today. I would like to get our business settled as quickly as possible."

"My sister isn't home, Mister Harrison. And I don't know when she'll be returning. Would you care to leave her a message?"

"Please call me Reis. If I've offended your sister in some way, Miss Miranda, I would appreciate your passing along my apology." When Miranda lowered her lashes and didn't immediately respond, Reis had his answer. "Is there some reason why she doesn't wish to meet with me?"

Miranda looked up at him. "I don't discuss my sister with strangers, sir. You'll have to speak with her yourself," she told him politely. "However, it would be wise to invite rather than to summon her," she added slyly.

A broad grin captured Reis's mouth and eyes. "Thank you, Miss Miranda. I thought that might be the crux of the matter. I fear I've had little dealings with ladies. I'll call again later, if that's agreeable?"

"You may call me Miranda or Randy," she offered. Her hesitation was noticeable before she added, "Mandy went to Papa's office to work on the books. Perhaps you could drop by and see her there."

"I was under the impression Weber Richardson handled the business for her," he probed.

Miranda didn't realize her distaste for Weber was revealed in her eyes and voice when she replied, "After the accident, Weber was to take care of matters only until Mandy could do so. Weber is away for a few days," she informed him, hoping he would catch her hint.

"May I ask a rather personal question, Miranda?"

"Such as?" she inquired curiously.

"Rumor has it that Amanda and Weber are to be married. Is that true?" he asked.

Miranda knew she shouldn't answer such a loaded question, but she couldn't stop herself. To remain silent would imply a positive answer and discourage a possible pursuit by Reis. Even if nothing happened between Amanda and Reis, perhaps he could destroy any relationship between Mandy and Weber. She knew it was wrong to interfere, but she felt compelled by Reis's intent gaze. "Only if Weber has his way, which he hasn't to date."

"You don't like him, do you?" he inquired.

"I don't think he's right for my sister," she parried.

"Neither do I, Miranda," he readily concurred. "I hope this doesn't sound too forward, but I hope to sever that relationship."

Miranda gasped in astonishment at the confession, then smiled. "I hope it doesn't sound too forward to wish you luck, Reis."

Reis was in high spirits as he left Miranda. If Amanda was anything like her twin sister, he was in for a delightful adventure. He whistled as he strolled down the street, plotting the surrender of a golden-haired minx. He halted by the hotel to set his plans in motion.

Amanda had been reading for hours. She had gone over all reports and books available. But there was one book missing, and she wondered why. The only explanation was that Weber had taken it to work on while he was away. Weary from her labor and recent loss of sleep, she dozed lightly. She didn't hear the key as it turned in the lock, sealing her in this private world with a determined Reis Harrison.

He came forward to halt at her side, eyes passing over her from head to lap. He bent forward, his lips pressing against hers ever so lightly, then firmly and passionately as hers parted and responded.

He held her face gently between his hands, as his lips refused to end the long-awaited kiss which was more intoxicating than he had expected. Amanda's arms eased around Reis's body as she arched upward. When Reis's lips pressed light kisses to her eyes, she murmured dreamily, "Why did you wait so long to come, Reis?"

Reis realized she was half-asleep, but her words exposed her hidden thoughts and thrilled his heart. She had called his name, not Weber's.

Reis sat on the edge of the desk, Amanda's chair between his spread thighs. He placed his hands on either side of her shoulders, knowing she would bolt the moment her senses cleared.

Amanda opened her eyes then froze briefly in confusion. "What are you doing here? How did you get in?" she exclaimed.

"You shouldn't leave the door unlocked when you're alone, Amanda. Sorry, but I couldn't resist kissing you," he declared huskily.

Her cheeks flushed a deep crimson. "How dare you take such liberties when I'm senseless," she chided him. "What do you want?" she asked nervously, warming to his quick and easy smile.

"To talk, after we have lunch," he calmly announced to the befuddled Amanda, pointing to the picnic basket on her desk.

"Lunch?" she repeated as she stalled to clear her wits, which was nearly impossible while gazing into those expressive sapphire eyes.

"At your service, ma'am." As Amanda watched, Reis withdrew fried chicken, baked bread, and wine from the basket. As he spread a cloth over the desk and arranged the items, he remarked, "It isn't much or fancy, but it'll fill our stomachs while we talk."

Struck speechless, Amanda remained silent. Reis poured two glasses of wine and handed one to her. Amanda accepted it with a shaky hand. He set a plate and utensils before her, then lay a rose across her plate. "That's to say I'm sorry."

Bewilderment filled her blue eyes. "For what?" she questioned.

"I'm not quite sure, but I seem to have offended you into avoiding me. Could we make a fresh start?" he beseeched her.

"Just what are you trying to pull, Mister Harrison?" she asked suspiciously, touched by his romantic gestures.

"The wool over those entrancing eyes so I can think clearly," he murmured roguishly, grinning at her.

Amanda couldn't suppress her laughter. "I will say one thing for you, Mister Harrison, you are a most persistent and surprising man."

"I hope that's a compliment," he retorted hastily. "Shall we eat, then discuss future business?"

"Why not? I am ravenous, and this looks delicious."

To her further delight, Reis prepared her plate. As he worked, she eyed him intently as she sniffed the fragrant rose.

They ate in silence, but for his offer of more food and wine. When they finished, he promptly cleared the desk. He pulled a chair up before it, then sat down and met her amused gaze. "Well?"

"Well what, Mister Harrison?" she replied.

"Do we do business together?" he ventured.

"What did you have in mind?" she asked, leaning back in her chair as she teased her nose with the flower.

Their eyes met and danced with desire. "Business this afternoon and dinner tonight?" he suggested warmly.

Temporarily ignoring his last invitation, she asked, "What kind of business? Have you dealt with my father before?"

"I haven't, but the men I represent have. They've been doing business with another firm for months, but they've decided to deal with yours again, if you'll agree. They asked me to handle it for them."

"Why did they change to another firm?" she asked astutely.

"Businessmen always look for faster and cheaper service. They've decided it's to their advantage to return to Lawrence Shipping," he explained without actually lying to her. When this matter was settled, he would reveal the truth, that he and Grant had coaxed the clients to aid in this investigation. Reis had already uncovered certain facts in this case. A theft or switch in products was being done by this firm and on a ship employed by this firm. It was Reis's job to find out how the switch was carried out, by whom, and for what purpose. There was more to this intricate plot than ruining Northern-owned companies or destroying "traitorous" Southern sympathizers and carpetbaggers. He suspected that Joseph Lawrence had been innocent in this illegal and cunning deception. Perhaps he had been killed after discovering his firm was being used. Reis needed to find out the connection between Amanda and Weber, which didn't seem romantic on her part. But many aristocratic marriages had nothing to do with love.

Reis and Grant had discovered some of these evil profits were being used to finance the activities of the despicable Ku-Klux-Klan and to purchase black votes to put certain Southern whites in influential positions in national, state, and local governments. When money failed to produce the desired results, the Klan used other means to get their wishes. During a preliminary investigation, Reis had uncovered several interrelated plots which dismayed him and the President.

Reis had unmasked Northerners who were still victimizing Southern planters or exploiting them. He had found traces of dangerous hostilities still lingering in certain areas. He had discovered diehard ex-Rebs who were causing trouble disguised as antagonistic ex-Yankees. He had learned of unfair tariffs which were favorable to the North but devastating to the South. There were Northern interests which were preventing progress in the Southern railroads and mills, which would lessen the proceeds in the North. There were Southerners seeking any means to recover power and property confiscated during and after the war. Most discouraging and perilous were the hints at an attempt to one day revive the Confederacy—gold, weapons, and supplies were being purchased and shipped to the South and concealed. It troubled Reis that most of his clues pointed to involvement by this firm.

Damn! he swore mentally. Hadn't this war done enough damage to the North and South? Why couldn't it be over once and for all? Sometimes Reis didn't know who to blame. If the damn newspapers and embittered writers would stop stirring up trouble with those poisonous pens, matters might settle down. Reis warned himself not to be vindictively blind where Weber was concerned. It bothered him to realize that he hoped that bastard was responsible so he could arrest him. No matter how much he despised Weber, he couldn't let the guilty parties escape while trying to pin something on his enemy. He had never allowed personal feelings to color his duty, but it was difficult where Amanda and Weber were concerned.

He sighed heavily then noticed that Amanda was staring at him. He reprimanded himself when she commented, "If you're tired or bored, Mister Harrison, we can discuss this tomorrow."

"I'm sorry, Amanda; it's hard to concentrate with you before me. How about we take a walk and get some fresh air to clear my head?"

Chapter Three

As he requested, Amanda gave Reis a tour of her office, docking area, warehouses, and a ship which was in port. At first, she had been subdued. But Reis watched the suspense and excitement which flashed over her eyes as she took in the sights. He could tell she was just as curious about these areas as he was, just as pleased to inspect them. He observed her as she laughed and chatted with workers whom she had known for years, or accepted words of sympathy and encouragement about her parents. As if he inspired feelings of confidence and safety, if he lagged behind she would glance around to locate him. An almost timid smile would brighten her face when her blue eyes touched upon him, a smile which he always returned.

Once as they discussed the differences in local and foreign markets, their gazes had locked and they had fallen silent for a time. A noisy loader had broken the magical spell. As they continued their tour, Reis knew she had spoken truthfully; she knew all about this business, but not from experience. Even though she took this business seriously, she was like a child with a new toy.

As the sun moved closer to the horizon, Amanda obviously began finding things to discuss or examine. Reis wondered if she were reluctant to leave him or the docks. No matter, for it was getting late and cool.

As they watched a flatboat pull anchor and glide down the river, Reis inquired, "Is this your first visit here?"

"I've been here many times with my father, but never alone. I mostly helped with the books. I hope that doesn't change your opinion, Reis. I'm sure I can learn anything I don't know." She was eager to prove herself, and she needed Reis's three accounts to begin.

To her relief, he smiled and agreed. "Is safety the reason why you hired Weber Richardson? The docks aren't any place for a lady, even a brave one. In fact, we're inviting trouble to remain after dark."

"Believe it or not, Reis, I can take care of myself. But I'm not stupid, so I wouldn't come down here alone. I didn't exactly hire Web; he was kind enough to take control and run things after . . . the accident. I'm grateful to him, but I'm ready to take over now. This business has been part of my life for as long as I can remember; I've even gone on trips with Papa to make deliveries, to entice new accounts, or to check out problems, so I can handle those matters when they come up. To sell it seems like cutting all ties with my past. If I didn't have the business, I wouldn't have anything to do. A woman can't read and sew all the time. It's important to me, Reis. This isn't some childish whim. I promise you I won't disappoint your friends."

As they returned to her office to lock up for the day, Reis offered, "I'll make you a deal, Amanda. If I can hang around for protection and advice while you adjust to your new position as owner, you can have these three accounts. That way, everyone's interest will be safeguarded. I'll even work for free." He winked at her.

Amanda looked up into his handsome face. "You want to help me get started? But I thought you were leaving Friday," she hinted.

"That was just a sneaky trick to make you see me sooner," he told her. "For the next few months, my job is to see to my friends' business. That appears to include assisting their shipper, if she agrees."

Her heart fluttered at the idea of working side-by-side with this intoxicating man. How would she keep her mind on business! Suddenly she remembered Weber and, before she could stop herself, she blurted out her worry. "Web won't like this at all."

"Does that matter to you? You are the owner," he teased.

Amanda tried to cover her mistake and to keep Reis off balance. "It just seems kind of traitorous to fire him and to hire you. The firm might be out of business right now if he hadn't taken care of it. I was planning to take over completely when he returns, but I don't want him to think it's because of you," she rationalized aloud.

"Are you in love with him? Going to marry him?" He caught her off guard with those blunt and jarring questions.

"That's none of your business, Reis," she informed him curtly.

"But it is, Amanda," he refuted, backing her against the wall and pinning her to it with his steely body. "If you're another man's woman, I can't do this," he whispered, nibbling at her right ear. "Or this," he added, closing her lids with kisses. "Or this," he murmured again, sealing their lips. When she didn't resist him, he pulled her into his embrace, fusing his mouth to hers.

Amanda's arms were caught between them and her lips were helpless to do anything but yield to his masterful assault. She moaned softly as she pressed closer to him. Sensing a thrilling innocence in her response, Reis knew he must halt this madness or risk seducing her on the wooden floor. He had just enough presence of mind to realize the damage that could do to their budding relationship. If he didn't cease this tempting game, all would be lost. He ached from the flames which were licking painfully at his loins, flames which didn't want to be doused by words or self-control. He stared into her passion-glazed eyes. At least he knew she desired him as much as he desired her.

He stepped backward and inhaled raggedly. Amanda sank weakly against the wall, staring at him. "My God, Amanda, do you know what you do to a man? How you tempt him beyond control? If I thought for one moment you knew what you were doing . . ."

Amanda's hand came up to touch her lips, lips which throbbed with hunger for his. She had never been kissed like this or had any man cause such bittersweet sensations to attack her mind and body. "Why did you do that?" she asked hoarsely. She had been so mesmerized that he could have taken anything he desired from her. Why had Reis halted? Web wouldn't have!

"I've been wanting to since the first moment I met you, but I was trying to control myself until we got to know each other better. I'm sorry if I offended you." He stepped to the desk and sat on its edge.

"Do you go around stealing kisses from any female who catches your eye?" she inquired, moistening her dry lips. She wanted to ask why he hadn't seduced her, but she dared not. Still, she found it odd that she felt no shame or embarrassment at her unbridled response.

"No, but you're not just any female. Will you have dinner with me tonight?" Reis changed the subject but kept his distance.

"If you promise to control such wild impulses," she jested, regaining a measure of poise. She must keep his power over her a secret. Maybe it was her imagination or wishful thinking, but Reis also appeared unnerved and puzzled by her effect on him.

"Ouch," he winced playfully. "You wouldn't want me to lie, would you?" he tested her as the passion faded in her blue eyes.

"Of course not," she stated too quickly.

"Then I can't make such a promise. But I will try to behave." He tensed as he awaited her response. Damn, but he wanted her!

"You, sir, are a rake," she declared, then laughed.

"It's one of my dark secrets. I hope it doesn't change your mind. However, I don't have a nasty temper or any hideous scars."

Both recalled their first conversation on which he was playing at that moment. "Do you have other dark secrets, Mister Harrison?"

Hearty laughter filled the quiet room. "Why don't we let you decide?" he murmured in a stirring tone.

"All right, Mister Rake. Do I meet you somewhere, or will you pick me up at home?" She accepted his stimulating challenge. She had to learn why this man was so unique, so irresistible, so unsettling.

Reis noted the softened eyes which watched him. He should warn her not to look at him like that, but he couldn't deny himself. "I'll pick you up at seven, if that's agreeable. First, I'll see you home safely." He lifted the borrowed basket and turned to face her. "Ready?" he asked, his tone sensually provocative.

Amanda grinned but didn't make the naughty comment which was teasing her tongue. He certainly had a way of making her feel like freshly churned butter beneath a blazing sun. She couldn't decide why she felt so carefree and daring around Reis, so happy and alive. She nodded and followed him out, locking the door.

As they approached a busy street, Reis took her hand and guided her across. At the other side he didn't release it, and Amanda couldn't break this pleasing contact. Even if she had thought about someone seeing them, it wouldn't have worried her today. His hand was so warm and strong but his grip so gentle. Nothing felt more natural than strolling with Reis, or more serene than being in his company, or more enticing than his touch. Amanda was glad she wasn't wearing gloves, for his flesh was delightful.

Reis left her at her front door, saying he would return later. The moment he was out of sight, she raced inside and up the stairs to decide which gown to wear.

Miranda had been watching from her window. She sighed happily and smiled, heading for Amanda's room.

When she knocked, Amanda sang out for her to enter. "Did you get much work done?" she asked innocently.

Amanda whirled and laughed. "I saw Reis this afternoon. He's taking me to dinner tonight. That should please you, dear sister."

"It obviously pleases you, dear sister," she teased, witnessing Amanda's exuberance and starry eyes. Amanda had never pursued a man; but from the way she was acting, it appeared she intended to start with this one. Miranda was happy for her, as Reis seemed a perfect match.

"Yes, it does," Amanda stated honestly. She told Miranda about their deal and visit. "Need I say you were right?"

"It's just like Mama said, isn't it, Mandy?" she asked hopefully as she observed her ecstatic sister.

Amanda giggled as she vowed, "Even better."

When Reis came for her that night, he couldn't believe his senses. She was even more beautiful, if possible. "The way you look, you're not planning to help me keep my word, are you?" he chided her, remembering that she hadn't pulled her hand from his or spurned his touch at her office. Did she think he was made of iron? Did she think he could govern the situation between them without her help? Where was the arrogant ice maiden she was alleged to be? Doubtlessly, spurned males considered her such because she had refused their advances. He realized that only a rare and lucky man could win Amanda's love and stir her passions. Fortunately, he thrived on challenge.

She laughed merrily. "If that was a veiled compliment, Reis, thank you. You look quite handsome yourself."

"A woman who isn't afraid to speak her mind. Excellent."

As they dined in a candle-lit corner of the restaurant in the Windsor Hotel, she asked, "Where are you from, Reis?"

"Texas, but I live in Washington," he replied casually.

"That explains your western attire, but I thought you were a Yankee," she remarked, her mind spinning at his nearness.

"You say that as if it's a nasty word, Amanda. If it makes a difference to you, I was in the Union army," he informed her, knowing Weber would tell her, if he hadn't already.

"Why?" she probed inquisitively, lowering her fork and focusing her full attention on him. Something different about him tugged at her mind, but she was too enchanted to comprehend it.

"Do you really want to discuss my past politics? Do you hold some grudge against the Union?" he inquired anxiously, dismayed that she had broached this particular subject tonight. After dropping his pretense, he should have expected it, as Amanda was smart and alert.

"Of course not. Papa remained neutral because he didn't feel either side was totally right. We never had slaves on our plantation, but we are Southerners. When Virginia sided with the Confederacy, we were included in the hostilities whether we wanted to be or not."

"But your father held on to his plantation and shipping firm," he asserted genially, hoping she would explain how and why. He had to make certain he could trust this winsome beauty.

"Yes, but it was difficult. We made enemies on both sides," she answered sadly as she recalled unpleasant memories.

Comprehending this point, he stated, "But the war has been over for years, Amanda. Are you having problems with someone?"

"I know it's over, but many don't accept it. There are Northerners and Southerners who still won't do business with us. Sometimes I think the conflicts will never end. Is it over for you, Reis?"

"Any man who battles his brother gets scars from it, Amanda, wounds which heal slowly or not at all," he answered candidly. "Each man must find his own cure or method of treating such injuries."

"Do you have any family?" she asked abruptly.

"No," he stated sullenly. "Would you like some dessert?"

"What happened to them?" She persisted despite his chilling mood.

He met her gaze and replied evenly, "Rebs killed them while I was off fighting other Rebs. Afterward, they burned our ranch to the ground. I still own the property, but I've never gone back."

"I'm sorry," she murmured, wishing she hadn't pressed him.

"Dessert?" he asked again, seeming to look right through her. He was suddenly tense and distant. Could he trust this woman who had ties to a snake like Richardson? If he was wrong about Amanda, she could destroy him and crush this vital mission. Until he was sure of her, he dared not get too close.

"No thanks," she replied, witnessing a withdrawal in him.

As if anxious to end their evening, the moment they finished he remarked, "It's late. I'd best get you home. I'll see you tomorrow."

Reis paid for their meal then escorted her home, all in moody silence. At the steps, he bid her good night and turned to leave.

"Reis," she called to him in panic. He halted and turned, his expression concealed by shadows. He seemed so remote. "Nothing," she murmured, scolding herself for spoiling a lovely evening, pondering how she had done so.

In the moonlight playing upon her face, Reis saw the effects of his rash behavior. Tears glittered on her lashes; her expression exposed hurt and confusion. From what he had learned about her, this was unusual behavior for haughty and coy Amanda Lawrence. Reis knew he had upset her and he didn't want to push her away, but he couldn't explain matters to her for a long time. This case was forcing him to relive some painful times, times he hadn't allowed himself to think of in years. He surged forward, caught her in his arms, kissed her soundly, then hurried away before she could respond or speak. Whatever her part in this messy and hazardous affair—innocent or intentional—Reis felt he must find a way to protect her, to save her from danger.

Amanda stood there, utterly bewildered. If any other man had treated her this way, she would have berated him furiously and refused to see him again. Oddly, she wanted to comfort Reis, to go after him. She concluded Reis must have some hidden scars, if not on that firm and virile body, then surely on his soul. She must never mention the war or his family again, if he returned. That had to have been the source of his abrupt change.

Change, she mused to herself. She slipped her arms around the porch pillar and rested her cheek against it, concentrating on this mysterious and arresting man. All at once, she knew what had been bothering her all evening. Until he had kissed her this afternoon, Reis had spoken with a northern accent; since then, his voice had altered to a stirring blend of western and southern drawls!

Amanda was puzzled. That's why she had assumed he was a Northerner. The change had registered in her mind; that's why thoughts of Yankees and Rebs had come forth. But why would a man use a phony northern accent then switch to a southern one? Was it intentional or accidental? Did he think her so dense she wouldn't notice?

But he had confessed to being from Texas, to being a Southerner! Was this some kind of game she didn't understand? She couldn't help but feel duped, and she needed to know why he had deceived her. What was he doing to her? What did he want here? She tried to recall every word he had spoken and every expression since their meeting. No explanation came to mind. Amanda was very adept at playing wily games with people, and she felt that Reis was up to some mischief. Before he gained too much influence over her, she vowed to uncover his sport and its rules.

Amanda left the house early the next morning, anxious to get to the office and complete her study of the books before Weber's return. After opening the safe, she was astonished to find the missing book behind the others. Her eyes widened in confusion. Weber had not returned to Alexandria, so how had this book found its way back into a locked safe and office? How could she have overlooked an item of its size and importance? She sighed in frustration and scolded herself for her carelessness.

Clearly the book must have been there yesterday. She ordered herself to clear her wits. This book contained the most recent business dealings of her father's firm, with some personal entries at the rear. Perhaps the names of Reis's clients would offer her a clue to his sudden appearance and curious conduct.

Reis had told her that his friends had changed firms months ago. Perhaps her father had made helpful notations about those dissatisfied customers. Sure enough, Amanda located the three names which had halted business with Lawrence Shipping, all at the same time—their three largest accounts! She was shocked to learn that all three had switched to Richardson's Shipping.

She carefully went over those three records. There were old notes about shipments and cargoes, coded messages which only her father could understand. Was it possible those clients had created phony complaints just to cancel with him?

Amanda wondered how Weber's firm was handling that much business. If Weber had pulled some trick to gain those accounts, he would have destroyed this enlightening evidence, knowing she would eventually see it. After all, Weber had been in control of her firm and its books for two months. Was it true that Reis's friends weren't receiving the cheaper and faster service they had sought from Richardson's? Did Web know he was losing these accounts back to her? Had he gone to see these men, to try to hold them? She knew Weber wanted to expand his business, needed to do so. Was Weber afraid of losing everything a second time? Reis or no Reis, if these men were trouble, she didn't want to have them back.

Amanda returned her attention to the critical book at hand. She went over every fact and figure listed there. When she doubted her conclusions, she went over them again, and again.

When she couldn't deny the implications of those pages, she lay the book aside and closed her eyes to rest them. Amanda was alarmed by the shocking discovery that the firm was in terrible financial condition, the plantation had been sold, and the townhouse was mortgaged. How was that possible? Her father had said nothing to them. If business didn't pick up, the company wouldn't survive through June. What would happen to her and Miranda? Even if they sold their possessions and jewels, the money wouldn't last long.

Was this why Weber was pressing her about marriage? Not to gain a lucrative company and a wealthy business, but to spare her from humiliating bankruptcy? Was this why he didn't want her to take over, to keep her from learning the grim truth? She recalled him saying something about choosing him for himself and not for his position. She had taken the remark as a joke. Weber was so proud; he didn't want anyone to think she was marrying him for his money. He wanted them affianced before this news could be revealed. Did he hope to save her company by absorbing it into his? One thing appeared certain. Weber wasn't after her for the business; he couldn't be, for he knew its condition.

Amanda felt awful that she had had such wicked thoughts about Weber. One particular item plagued her; Weber had loaned her company a large amount of money to pay the bills for the past month . . .

What a selfish fool she was! While dear Weber was trying to help her, she was romancing another man. How could she take over and run a business that was losing money every day? How blind she had been. So much for Luke's suspicions and contempt. If not for Weber, she and Miranda would have lost everything.

How could she accept the accounts Reis was offering to her? From her father's past notations, they had switched to Web's company. They had to be his three largest accounts, and to take them away might ruin him, alienate him. Could she do such a cruel thing after all Weber had done for her and her sister? Far worse, how deeply would it hurt Weber if she put Reis Harrison in his place, in the firm and in her life? Did Web truly love her and want her for herself?

Why hadn't Weber told her how things really stood? He must think her ungrateful and insensitive. From the way it looked, Weber had supported her and Miranda for the past two months and never claimed any credit or repayment. Now that she was indebted to Web, what would he expect or demand in return? Did Web want her totally dependent upon him before telling her about the sorry state of her business and personal finances? Were his actions selfish or lovingly generous? This situation was painful and complex.

Amanda realized that Weber would know she had discovered the truth when he returned to find her in the office with her nose in the books. She should get out of here quickly and not return until she decided what to do with this dreadful information. She quickly put things as they had been left before his departure. She could only pray that he wouldn't discover her probing actions and force a talk before she was ready.

But what about Reis? her heart screamed. She told herself she couldn't think about the mysterious Reis at present. Her way of life was on the verge of collapse; her future survival and happiness were at stake. Until she searched her heart and conscience about both men, she shouldn't see Reis again.

Amanda didn't like what she was thinking and feeling. Only a few months ago, her conscience wouldn't have troubled her at all, but today it did. If she had known Reis longer, or knew him better . . . Reis was a cunning stranger, and she couldn't expect anything from him. There were strong hints of genteel breeding and wealth exuding from Reis. If she confided in him or if he learned the truth, he might think her interest in him was selfish and greedy. Could she marry Weber when she wanted Reis? Could she refuse to accept Web's proposal if her and Miranda's livelihood depended upon her submission to Web? Her decision would have been simple and quick if Reis Harrison hadn't entered her life one stormy night.

Weber would return in a few days; he would insist upon that talk he had mentioned. Could she risk losing Web by seeing Reis? Yet, if she didn't see Reis, how could she uncover his true feelings? Even if she accepted Reis and his clients, her firm couldn't be saved. If Reis left as mysteriously as he had appeared, where would she be then?

Such thoughts and plots made her feel cheap and heartless. Yet, what choice did a woman have but a profitable marriage? So many times she had toyed with men, tempted them with a treasure they could never have. Now vengeful Fate was dangling a tempting treat before her hungry eyes and bound hands, teasing and tormenting her. Reis was a dream; Weber was reality. Fury and frustration overwhelmed Amanda.

"Hell's bells!" she shrieked, flinging a book at the wall to reduce her tension and anger. "It's too late," she murmured.

"Are you all right, Amanda?" Reis's compelling voice asked from the doorway. "You shouldn't leave that door unlocked," he chided for the second time, wondering at the meaning of her last words.

Startled, Amanda whirled, drilling her fiery blue eyes into his tanned face and worried expression. "What do you want, Mister Harrison, besides the opportunity to scold me like a child?" she panted coldly, her ire directed at the forbidden object of her desire.

"I know I was rude last night, Amanda, but aren't you overreacting?" he reasoned tenderly. "I'm sorry," he stated simply.

She had to get rid of him, to halt this temptation, to cease this punishment! Her pride demanded she make him think his deception was behind her rejection of him and his accounts. "You traitor, I wonder what I find different about you," she scoffed, daring to stroll around the towering man as he remained stiff and alert. She halted before him, placing her hands on her hips and glaring up into his inquisitive gaze, her eyes exposing more anguish than anger.

Reis's hands snaked out and seized her gently but firmly. "What's gotten into you, woman?" he demanded. If he didn't know any better, he might think her hysterical. What did she mean by "too late" and "traitor"? Was she pledged to Weber? Was she in trouble?

"What happened to your Yankee accent, Reis?" she blurted out. "It took a while to comprehend the change, but I did. Get out!"

"That was a naughty trick, but I had my reasons," he began.

"I'll just bet you did," she injected acidly before he could finish.

"Since two of my friends are Yankees and the other is what you called a 'sympathizer,' I wanted to know how you felt about Northerners. To pass as one usually extracts such vital information. I should have explained when I realized the test wasn't necessary with you."

Amanda continued to glare at him. "What other games are you playing with me, Mister Harrison?" she sneered accusingly. "Is romancing your female partner a new approach to crafty business?"

"I've never mixed business and pleasure before. Do you want the accounts,

Amanda?" He evaded an answer which could have been damaging. "Are you in the mood to settle it now, or shall we wait until later?"

Amanda swallowed the lump in her throat. She knew what had to be done and did it bravely. "Since Weber Richardson handles such matters for me, I suggest you discuss it with him when he returns," she bluntly informed him.

Reis couldn't help but show disbelief and anger at those words. "I was given the authority to assign them to you, not him. Are you refusing them because I go along with the deal? Or you're afraid to annoy dear Weber? Have you suddenly lost your courage and confidence?"

Amanda couldn't say anything more without giving away her motives for this behavior. "If you don't mind, Mister Harrison, I would prefer that you forget our previous talk and meeting. Any business you have for Lawrence Shipping must be approved by Web. I'm really tired, so I'm going home. Goodbye."

Reis was alarmed by the way she spoke her last word. He was confused by this change of heart, this loss of spirit. Richardson hadn't returned, so he couldn't have threatened or misled her. "Would you have dinner with me?" he coaxed, smiling at her.

"I can't," she declined unhappily. She retrieved the book and completed her task. She knew he was watching her intently, disturbingly.

"Mandy, what did I do to earn this frosty treatment?" he asked from behind her as he slipped his arms around her waist.

Amanda stiffened and tried to pull free, but he wouldn't allow it. There was only one way to make Reis leave her alone, to stop tormenting her and tempting her. "I shouldn't be seeing you alone; it's wrong. Web has asked me to marry him, and I've . . ."

When she faltered, Reis's heart skipped a beat as he feared the rest of her statement. His embrace tightened, as if he could halt the words from coming forth. He could feel her tremors, sense her turmoil, and detect her withdrawal from him. Despite their closeness, Weber was between them. How? Why? "Don't say it, Mandy, please," he beseeched her. "If you loved him, you wouldn't be suffering. Damnit, you can't marry him! You want me!" he stormed at her.

If only having was as simple as wanting, she thought. "I didn't say I had agreed to his proposal yet. But I can't think seriously about it while I'm seeing another man," she deliberated aloud. "It isn't fair to Weber, or me, or to you. I owe Weber so much," she murmured.

"No matter what he's done for you, Mandy, you aren't obligated to marry him to repay a debt," he argued frantically. "Hell woman, you can't buy or trade love!"

Amanda remained silent, praying he would say the words which could change her mind, which could halt her necessary decision. But Reis kept quiet about his personal feelings and wishes. She debated sadly, "Why not? Women have done so for centuries, either by choice or compulsion. There are things about me and Weber which you don't know."

Reis turned her to face him, but she lowered her head. He gripped her chin and lifted it. "Then explain them to me," he coaxed.

"I can't. Please don't try to see me again," she told him. She waited to see if he would force answers from her. He didn't.

Reis's brain was working fast and hard on this mystery. She was frightened by something. She might become defensive if he pressed her. She couldn't love Weber Richardson, but she felt compelled to marry him. What hold did that devil have over her? Whatever it was, she had discovered it this morning. Before he made demands on her, he needed to investigate this problem. He would never allow her to marry Weber. Not when she wanted him instead.

"Are you afraid of me, Mandy?" he asked softly. At her baffled look, he clarified, "Afraid I'll change your mind about Weber?"

"What could you possibly say or do to influence my decisions?" she inquired, eager for his explanation.

Since he had no proof that Weber was part of the crimes he was investigating, he would have to keep his opinions secret for now. Also, he wasn't in a position at present to force a battle over Amanda. His only course of action seemed to be in showing Amanda her own feelings.

"You said it was wrong to see me. But isn't it worse to marry one man when you have such strong feelings of desire for another?" The moment he made his rash statement, he regretted it.

"And who might I desire more than Weber, my conceited rake?" she questioned.

He chuckled. "I see you know whom I was referring to, but not from conceit, Mandy." As his thumb gently rubbed over her quivering lips, he vowed tenderly, "No woman has ever kissed me as you did."

"If I misled you, Reis, I'm sorry. You do have a cunning way of clouding a woman's senses. I've been under a great strain lately, and I wasn't myself. If you'll excuse me, I'll be leaving."

"You're misleading yourself, Mandy, not me. As to clouding senses, you're the expert there. Before you make your decision, just realize that marriage is forever," he warned gravely.

"Forever," she echoed the word as if it were a death sentence which she couldn't avoid.

"Look at me, Mandy, and tell me you love him," he insisted.

"Why else would I marry a man?" she eluded his trap.

"I damn well intend to discover that answer," he stated boldly. Reis caught her face between his hands and lowered his head to fuse their lips. When she tried to prevent this stirring assault on her warring senses, he skillfully parted her lips, probing the sweetness of her mouth. His arms entrapped her as he invaded her heart and mind.

Amanda didn't know how many times Reis kissed her, but she knew she didn't want him to stop. Her arms encircled his body as she feverishly responded to his rapturous invitation. Reis's hands wandered up and down her back, causing tingles to sweep over her entire body. An age-old craving grew at her core, spreading its need over her quivering and fiery flesh.

Amanda snuggled up to Reis as he nestled his face into her fragrant hair. Such yearning filled her, a yearning to explore this fierce aching which plagued her very soul. A soft groan escaped her parted lips as Reis's hand drifted over a firm breast, his palm stroking the taut point through her dress. When his tongue danced merrily around her ear, she shuddered with intense need. Soon, his mouth fastened onto hers, taking her beyond the limits of reality.

She swayed in his embrace as his hands and lips worked magical wonders over her face and body. The tension built within her until she ardently meshed her mouth with his and unknowingly dug her nails into his back as she tried to pull him even closer to her. She desperately wanted him; nothing and no one else mattered now. She instinctively knew the only way to appease such an awesome hunger, and she was willing to feed it then and there. Whatever might happen after this blissful moment of wild passion, she knew she must have Reis Harrison this one time.

Reis was snared by his own trap, too enflamed to think or care about anything but making love to Amanda. He trembled with the urgency which raced through his smoldering frame. He wanted her, needed her completely.

"Yield to me, love," he urged hoarsely. "You're driving me wild. I hurt all over with wanting you. You can't marry Web, Mandy; he's no good for you. He can't make you feel the way I do. If you loved him, you wouldn't be in my arms. Forget that heartless Reb," he pleaded earnestly, unaware of his rash error which struck Amanda forcefully.

It took Reis a while to realize Amanda was pushing him away from her, that she was suddenly resisting him with all her might. "Let go of me, Reis. Stop or I'll scream," she threatened wildly.

Reis leaned away from her. "Mandy?" he whispered huskily.

"I'm not some harlot to be rolled on the floor," she panted at him. "Stop doing this to me. You don't want me; you only want to hurt Weber. I don't know why, but I won't let you use me like this! Get out of my life and stay out," she demanded weakly, hardly aware of what she was saying but aware of how she was hurting without really knowing why or how to stop the knifing pains in her heart.

"Doing this to you!" he thundered in return. "You can't tease a man with surrender, then go cold on him! I need you, Mandy. If you don't need me, then why entice me? You're a witch, Amanda Lawrence. You enchant a fellow then punish him for his weakness. If it's only games with you, then stay clear of me, woman. I don't respect the rules. The next time you get me this hot, you'd best plan to cool me down," he warned, anger flashing in his deep blue eyes. "A man does crazy things when he's pushed beyond control or reason. If you want me to steer clear, I will. But first you'll have to convince me that's what you want."

Amanda was afraid she couldn't convince him with desperate lies, so she didn't try. Instead, she snatched her cape and raced out before he could stop her panicky flight. The office keys were lying on her desk; the safe was still open. Reis locked up hurriedly, then followed her to make sure she reached home safely.

He forcefully cooled his anger and his passion. He secretively returned to her office to search for the motive behind her vexing mood. He scanned the contents of her desk and the safe, then went through her files. He put everything back in its place, then locked the safe. He made sure all lights were out and the door was secured. He stuffed her drawstring purse into his pocket and headed for her house.

He would leave her purse with Miranda, hopefully without an explanation. Then he would head to the privacy of his hotel room. He had some thinking and planning to do. It all made perfect sense to him, even if Amanda was mistaken and impulsive . . .

A mischievous grin tugged at the corners of his mouth. Devilish lights twinkled in his eyes. If he planned this scheme just right, he could obtain all his wishes. He would take Weber's rope and tie up that menacing Rebel and that fetching tart, one victim on each end with a cunning and victorious Reis in the middle!

"When I finish with you, you'll never forget the first and last time we clashed,

Weber Richardson, you bloody son of a bitch. As for you, my exquisite butterfly, you'll never escape me. You were mine from the moment we met. You just try to fly away before paying me what you owe me. That Reb's debt is nothing compared to mine!"

Chapter Four

Again, Amanda refused to come downstairs for dinner, this time pleading a headache which Miranda knew came from some emotional upheaval. Each time she approached Amanda's door, she could hear muffled sobs which rent her tender heart. She and her sister had always been close, sharing even their innermost feelings. What was so terrible that Amanda felt she couldn't share it? Miranda knew her sister would confide in her when she was ready. Until then, Miranda silently suffered with her.

Since Reis was the only person Amanda had spent time with today, it evidently had something to do with him. What had he said or done to cause Amanda such anguish? It had to be something important because Amanda was always so calm and controlled. It pained Miranda to think she might be to blame for assisting Reis's torment of her sister. Miranda couldn't understand her sister's drastic swings in mood and behavior. But somewhere behind them was a charmingly handsome rogue.

The night was long for both girls. When Reis had delivered Amanda's purse last night, that told Miranda her sister had raced from Reis's company. This morning, lovely flowers and an invitation to dinner and the theater arrived, but Amanda declined both. She told Miranda and the housekeeper to refuse all gifts and messages from Reis Harrison. She made it bluntly clear she didn't wish to see or hear from him, that he was not to be allowed in her home.

It was midafternoon before Amanda ventured downstairs to sip hot chocolate and to nibble some cake. She looked so pale and weary, as if she hadn't slept all night. Before the housekeeper left to do shopping, Amanda convinced her she simply wasn't feeling well. She sat on the floral sofa and gazed off into empty space.

"Randy," she spoke faintly, "I know you're concerned about me, but I'm not ready to discuss this yet. I just need a little time to sort out some feelings and make a decision." Amanda couldn't bring herself to tell Miranda how critical their situation was, not until she decided how to resolve it. Amanda wasn't blind, so she was aware of Miranda's feelings for Weber. She knew Miranda would battle an enforced marriage to Weber as fiercely as the South had battled the North. But would marriage to Weber be so terrible in light of her scant options? Until she fully comprehended this dire episode herself, she could neither defend Weber nor praise him. She berated herself for suspecting some ulterior motive in Weber. But her dear sister had suffered enough lately, and she couldn't add this additional burden to Miranda's slender back. Until settled, it would be her problem.

"Did you and Reis quarrel?" Miranda asked helplessly.

To prevent any further mention of Reis, Amanda edged into lying when she replied, "I won't be seeing him again, Randy. He's even worse than the others; he's tried to seduce me twice in two days. Every time he's near me, he can't keep his hands off me. I'm not some cheap slut to be pawed or ravished. The accounts he was dangling before me as bait are nothing more than troublemakers. Papa got rid of them months ago; now Reis thinks I'm too stupid to refuse them. He even claimed he goes along with the deal. I don't trust him, Randy. He acts like the only thing he wants is to get into my bloomers! He's a smooth charmer, and I should have known better."

Miranda gaped at her, eyes and mouth wide open with shock. "But he seemed so nice, Mandy. I don't understand." Had she misjudged Reis? Or was her beloved sister fibbing to her for the first time? Miranda knew that change was often for the better, but Amanda was being forced to change too much too rapidly. Miranda was alarmed by the pain in her sister's ice-blue eyes. Perhaps the key word in Amanda's tale was "seduce," not ravish.

"You have a lot to learn about wily males, dear Randy. All men are nice while they're trying to get you under the sheets with them. I've never been fooled like this before, and it angers me. And yes, it hurts, too. I thought Reis was so special, so different. You asked if we quarreled. I suppose we did have a one-sided dispute. When he kept pressing me, I thought the best way to cool his passion was to tell him Weber had proposed, which he has many times. Instead of cooling his ardor, I inflamed his temper. He was furious; can you imagine that? Then he proceeded to prove I don't love or want to marry Weber by assailing me with embraces and kisses! And he excused his lewd actions by claiming that I am besotted by him!"

Miranda had a gut feeling that Amanda was defensively exaggerating. Reis didn't seem like a man who would force his attentions on a woman. Surely Amanda hadn't tried to play coy games with the masterful Mister Harrison. Didn't Amanda realize that her looks and actions toward Reis were sensually provocative? Besides, if Reis was enchanted by Amanda, that would explain why he was so bold and persistent. Perhaps he was trying to prove something to Amanda. "Is that why you ran out on him so quickly that you forgot your purse?"

"Please, drop it for now. I'm too upset to discuss it further."

"Did you tell him just that Weber had asked, or did you also tell him you had accepted?" Miranda boldly continued the conversation with a point which worried her. To Miranda, it seemed the quarrel had been over Reis's passion and jealousy—two emotions which hinted at affection.

"I told him the truth, that I was seriously considering Web's proposal," Amanda announced incredibly. Before her sister could speak, Amanda added, "I know you don't like Web, Randy, but you won't be the one marrying him; I will. There's a lot you don't know about Weber, but I'll tell you everything one day soon. I must decide how important Reis is to me before I mess it up between us. Please, Randy, trust me to make the right decision."

"By 'mess it up,' you mean with Reis?" Miranda inquired softly, fearing to silence Amanda if she wasn't careful with her words and mood. Miranda's heart thudded heavily, for it sounded as if Amanda had already made her decision in favor of Weber. Had she been this assured with Reis? It didn't make any sense; why was Amanda viewing Web in a new light? There had to be much more to this turn of events!

"I'll admit I was infatuated by Reis's good looks and charm." She inhaled loudly, then used her previous thought as her last argument. "Reis is a playful dream, but Weber is reality. A fantasy fades with time, Randy; reality is always there."

That comparison revealed much about Amanda's feelings and fears. Miranda entreated, "Just make certain Reis is only a dream before you say yes to Weber."

"I did, Randy, last night," Amanda confessed sadly.

When Miranda held out a note for her sister the next morning, Amanda sullenly reminded her, "I told you, no more messages."

"It's from Weber," Miranda stated crisply.

"From Weber?" she inquired suspiciously. "He's back?"

"Evidently," came the reluctant response as she handed the missive to her wary sister.

Amanda read it and frowned. "He wants me to come down to the office to meet him for lunch," she stated in visible dread.

"Are you going to yield to this summons, this command performance?" Miranda inquired almost belligerently.

"Please don't treat me this way, Randy," her sister pleaded.

"What way?" Miranda innocently asked. "You're going to marry him, aren't you? Out of spite to Reis over a disagreement?"

"Don't be silly. I haven't decided yet, but I am leaning toward yes. Randy . . . Never mind," Amanda responded, dropping the topic.

"You'd better dress quickly; it's eleven now." Miranda was dismayed by the resignation she was detecting in her sister. But why were those normally bright eyes so somber?

"I'm not going," Amanda stated surprisingly.

"You're not?" Miranda asked in gleeful disbelief.

"I don't feel like rushing. I'll send Weber a note of regret. He can come over tonight if he wishes," she told her sister casually. "Randy, don't mention anything to Weber before I do."

The note never reached Weber as he hurried around checking out matters. When he called later that day, nettled with Amanda for ignoring his message, Miranda hoped her sister would refuse to see him. But, to Miranda's distress, Amanda appeared eager to see him. She had donned one of her loveliest gowns, matching slippers, and most appealing perfume as if she were setting the stage for a drama.

When Amanda realized the reason for Web's black mood, she apologized sweetly, then explained the mix-up. "I've had so much on my mind since McVane's visit. And the weather's turned so damp and chilly again. I thought spring was in full bloom." She pouted prettily to distract him. It might be wrong, but she needed to hang on to Web until she made her final decision. As she had done so often in the past, Amanda used all her charms. Yet, this time she didn't enjoy the coyness.

"I saw your new friend today," Web stated caustically.

"My new friend?" she echoed in confusion.

"Reis Harrison," he replied tersely, as if that told all. "You've been seeing him while I was gone. Why, Mandy? He's not a family friend. Why did you two go down to the docks and warehouse?"

"We had dinner one night at the Windsor, and I gave him a tour of my property. He wanted to meet the new owner of Lawrence Shipping. He represents three clients who want to sign with my company. Did I commit some crime?" she asked playfully to reduce his anger. She wondered just how much Weber had discovered.

"Since I'm handling the firm, why didn't you refer him to me?" he questioned, his gaze and voice accusing as he stared at the exquisite beauty who was sitting so gracefully before him.

Amanda knew this was the perfect time to clarify some points, while keeping other facts a secret. She didn't want Web to discover what she had learned. She had to mislead him carefully. She smiled and responded cheerfully, "Because I wanted to surprise you with the new accounts. Don't be so cross with me, Web. While you were gone, I wanted to see if I was capable of handling the business, to see if a customer would actually deal with a female owner. I only talked and listened, Web; I didn't make any deals. When he pressed me for an answer, I told him the matter would have to be settled with you."

"You did?" he asked in astonishment. "Then why meet with him?"

"Ego. And because he sent a message he was leaving by Friday if I didn't meet with him. We talked over dinner, then he asked to see how we run things. He seemed pleased and agreed to assign the accounts to me." She refilled his coffee cup with a steady hand.

"If everything worked out, then why didn't you complete the deal? Did he say why he was so anxious to sign and leave so quickly?" he asked, trying to appear and sound as poised as she was.

"He didn't say, and I wouldn't ask. I wanted to hand you the contracts when you returned, but that seemed rash. I was afraid of making mistakes. He asked questions which I couldn't answer. I realized there was much I didn't know. I thought I could run Papa's business, but now I'm not so sure. It's more complicated and risky than I realized," she confessed cunningly beginning to drop her desperate hints.

"What kinds of questions did he ask, Mandy?" he quizzed, feeling a mixture of elation and wariness. Was she truly backing out?

Amanda didn't ask about Web's emphasis on "questions" or his strange expression, but she noticed them. She hastily contrived a logical reply. "About laws, and tariffs, and schedules, and such. I couldn't even give him prices for shipments. He must have thought I was awfully dumb."

"If that were true, why would he offer you the accounts?" He needed to know what Reis had told Amanda without arousing her suspicion. Just what was this Yankee trying to pull?

A reason escaped her keen mind. "I don't know."

"He's been deceiving you, Mandy. Perhaps his interest is in you, not the accounts. He claimed he was here to do business with the Lawrence firm, and you said he verbally agreed to a deal. So why is he visiting all the others and asking so many questions about your company, you, and your father?"

"Is it uncommon to check out a firm and its owner?" she asked.

"Not before a deal is made. But it seems suspicious to do it afterward. From what I've been told, Harrison was nosing around yesterday and today. Don't trust him, Mandy," he stated firmly.

Amanda quickly concealed her surprise and pain—she wouldn't think about Reis right now. She laughed saucily. "You can hardly blame him for checking out my firm's stability. He certainly didn't expect to deal with a female. As I told you, I didn't agree to a contract. Wouldn't that explain his checking around? Why are you so mistrustful? Do you know him, Web?" she inquired.

"Yep, I know who he is," he informed her, hatred flaming in his eyes. "It took a while to recall when and where we met. I guess I was trying to forget the bloody bastard. Fact is, I thought he was dead; I wish he were. I'm warning you, Mandy; stay away from him. He's sly and dangerous. He's a vengeful Yank."

Amanda was startled by the vehemence in Weber. She hadn't been mistaken; they had met before. "He didn't mention knowing you. Why did you think he was dead?" she questioned curiously.

"Because I shot him during the war," he stated casually. "Evidently my aim was bad."

"You what?" she exclaimed incredulously. Weber was clearly furious to find Reis still alive. Had Reis also recognized Weber that first night? If so . . .

"If you see him again, Mandy, ask him about his friend Sherman and their grisly escapades through the South. Make sure you don't carry a gun to your meeting with him. If he tells you the truth about his war ventures, you might finish where I left off. I can see from your shock that he didn't tell you about our meeting years ago."

Amanda paled and trembled. Web must be lying! Reis wasn't like that. But Web knew her well enough to realize she would check out such a grim accusation if Reis mattered to her. Web stood up and looked down at her. "The next time you see him, Mandy, it will be the last time you see me. I love you and I want to marry you; I want to protect you and take care of you. The firm's yours and you can do as you please, but not with my help and not with our enemy."

Suddenly Amanda realized that for the first time since their meeting, Weber was calling her by her nickname and she wondered if that meant something special. In an effort to comprehend Web's feelings, she answered softly, "The war has been over for years, Web. Both sides did wicked things to the other. The hatred and bitterness must end. Let them go, Web. Evidently Mister Harrison doesn't hold a grudge against ex-Rebs; he came to do business with my father. Perhaps he doesn't know you shot him. After he learned you handled matters for me, he was still willing to sign with me. To stay in business, I need all the clients I can find. If I decide to work in the firm, I'll have to prove myself, Web."

"Forgive and forget?" he sneered sarcastically, as if those words were evil, those emotions impossible. "You're too naïve and trusting. You don't know what the war was like, Mandy, but you know what Sherman's outfit did in the South. Every man who rode with him is just as guilty. Picture the blood of friends and family spattered all over you. Imagine showing up after a battle to see arms, legs, entrails, and brains all over the ground. You've never had someone die in your arms, Mandy, die with his blood soaking into your clothes, and then have to wear them for weeks or months. Do you know what it's like to have enemies chasing you day and night? No rest. No sleep. No food. Freezing your ass off while you hide like a coward to stay alive one more day to do it all again. Damnit, Mandy! They stole everything from me, from us! You say let it go? How? At least twice a week I wake up seeing and hearing those gory sights and sounds again, sweating and squirming like a beaten animal."

When Weber felt his vividly crafted words had had the desired effect, he became silent. He sighed dramatically, as if fatigued by a tale which had been cut from his very soul. That should give Amanda some sympathy for him and some contempt for Reis! That should keep her away from Harrison and his damaging secrets! "Marry me, Mandy. We can merge the two firms. If you want to work there, no man will refuse to deal with my wife," he coaxed. "This Harrison is trouble, Mandy. He's deadly and cunning. I have a bad feeling he didn't come here for the reason he told you. Watch out for him, or you'll live to regret it. I told you I shot him during the war. If he didn't know I was connected to the Lawrences before his arrival, he knows now. My feelings for you are no secret. Don't let my foe use my love against me. He could be after revenge, Mandy."

"Revenge?" she echoed the wicked word.

"What better vengeance than stealing my woman and destroying my business? Did he tell you the three accounts he offered you belong to me? Did he tell you it could ruin me to lose them? There are many ways to kill a man. What could be worse for a man than losing everything precious to him, all of his reasons for living? It's me he's after, Mandy. Don't be a pawn in his vindictive game."

Amanda was horrified by Weber's speculations. She wished they didn't sound so diabolically logical. "Surely both of you shot many men during the war. Why would he single you out for revenge?" she questioned sadly.

"Because he thinks my outfit was the one which burned his home and killed his family. He started tracking us, killing off my men one at a time. The only reason I survived was because I ambushed him before he could murder me too," he informed her, his gaze never leaving hers.

Amanda was afraid to ask if Reis was correct, but her eyes exposed her alarm and turmoil. He shook his head and asked, "Do I seem like a Sherman to you, a devil who could slay innocent people?"

Amanda couldn't imagine any man being so evil, so she was compelled to shake her head. Weber grinned and hugged her tightly. Just before leaving, he asked, "Will you consider my proposal, Mandy?"

"That's exactly what I've been doing for days, Web. I promise to give you an answer very soon," she told him, then smiled.

After Weber left, Amanda was trapped by deep and grave thoughts. After all this time, had she been given a glimpse into what had made Web the way he was now? Had the war taken a cruel toll on him?

Web had been born to and trained for a genteel life. After all was lost, he had changed. Web glorified the Old South, the Confederacy, the Rebel soldiers. Web had been compelled to find a new role in life, even as he yearned for the one lost forever. He believed that wealth and power would make things right again. It saddened Amanda to see the wasted energy and emotions that churned inside Weber Richardson. Should she try to help him, to change him? And at what cost to herself?

Amanda sought the privacy of her room for some necessary soul-searching. There was so much she didn't understand, didn't know, didn't want to accept. She pondered how she could investigate Reis Harrison and Weber's story. Weber was so full of hatred and bitterness; could she trust him to be honest with her? If only she didn't know what was inside that book!

When she closed her lids, Reis's image appeared before her mind's eye. Could a man with such gentle eyes and sensitivity have done such evil things? Was there any man worse than Sherman, or the men who had ridden with him without halting his devastation? If Reis had trailed and slain Weber's men, had it been a mistake brought on by grief? She recalled what Reis had told her about men doing crazy things when pushed beyond control and reason. Did these facts explain why he didn't want to discuss the war, why he had reacted so strangely and coldly? Had he been pressing her because he knew Weber would expose his secrets? She remembered the way he had looked at her, the way he had kissed her. It couldn't be true. It couldn't . . .

Amanda realized her time was running out. Considering everything she knew, there was only one answer to her mingled dilemmas. But when she thought of what would follow her surrender to Weber's proposal, she shuddered. Could she be a wife to him? Could she forget Reis?

Miranda was in her room reading in bed. She knew the hour was late and her sister was still pacing her floor. Amanda had been extremely quiet and melancholy after Weber's visit this afternoon. She had even refused dinner and sought privacy. This abnormal behavior panicked Miranda. It was time to unravel the mystery.

When she heard Amanda go downstairs, she tossed the covers aside and followed. She found her sister sitting on the rug before a cheery blaze, knees propped up and feet crossed at the ankles. Amanda's chin was resting on one knee as she tightly hugged her legs. The flickering flames seemed to perform a wild dance upon Amanda's pale face and in her blank eyes. What pained Miranda the most were the sparkles off the teardrops which were silently flowing down Amanda's cheeks and dropping to her gown. What was causing Amanda such anguish?

"Mandy?" she called softly. "Can I help? You need to talk?"

Amanda fused her solemn gaze to Miranda's entreating one. Amanda burst into uncontrollable sobs. Only once before had Miranda seen her sister weep this way, the night the news came about their parents. Distraught, Amanda blurted out Web's charges against Reis. She told Miranda everything, except the reason why she was going to marry Weber Richardson.

"But, Mandy, you can't marry Weber because Reis hurt you," she argued. "Even if what Web said about Reis were true, it happened years ago, during the war. Reis didn't strike me as a vengeful and cruel man. You just can't marry Web to hide from Reis. You're in love with Reis, aren't you?"

"If that were true, it still wouldn't make any difference," she replied tearfully. "Web is the man I must marry."

"Must? Why must you marry a man you don't love? See Reis, Mandy, and let him explain," she begged her irrational sister.

"I can't. There's nothing he can say or do to change matters. Oh, Randy, there's so much you don't understand," she wailed.

"Then make me understand," she pleaded fiercely. How could level-headed, proud Amanda Lawrence do such a reckless thing?

"If you ever get trapped between two men, you'll learn that love can't always be the deciding factor in choosing between them. I must do what is right for me, Randy. In time, I'll forget about Reis. Weber loves me and needs me," she vowed, as if that were a curse.

There were no words to ease such agony. All Miranda could do was listen,

listen and be there for solace. For the first time, Amanda had met a man who touched her deeply. How tragic that she believed Reis wasn't what he appeared. Yet, Miranda sensed some unspoken motive for her sister's drastic decision, one she must discover. Amanda had never been a coward or a quitter, so why had she become both at this late date? Just above a whisper, Miranda asked, "But whom do you love and need, Mandy? What if Reis didn't come here for revenge on Weber? What if you discover the truth after you're wed to the wrong man? It's wrong to marry Weber when you're in love with Reis."

When Amanda gained control of her emotions, she murmured sadly, "Web did kill him, Randy, at least for me. How can I possibly have anything to do with a devil like that? Why did Reis come here? Why? I despise the things men do in the name of honor! I hate revenge! The war's been over for years; when will a Southern daughter no longer have to ask her love the color of his uniform?"

Chapter Five

For a week Amanda refused all visits and messages from Reis Harrison, but it was one of the hardest things she had done in her life. When Reis appeared to halt his siege upon her, Amanda didn't know which emotion was greater, relief or disappointment. Once she had admitted to being in love with him, she realized it was too risky to see him even briefly or to read his urgent requests for an explanation. She feared Reis would mesmerize her again, deceitfully convince her she was mistaken about him. She couldn't allow it, if she were going to marry Weber; and that seemed her only path to survival. She was exhausted from battling her warring emotions.

Wasn't love supposed to be simple and serene? she wondered. Wasn't it supposed to bring happiness, not sadness and pain? Shouldn't it be the most natural thing in the world to marry the man you love? How could such dark clouds hover over the flames of love and cruelly douse them before they could burst into a roaring blaze of passion and commitment?

Amanda knew she had to regain a measure of joy and confidence or pretend she had, or else many people would become curious about her mood. She couldn't go on suffering and wavering. She would find the courage to carry out her decision before anyone discovered her motive. Yet, she knew she was stalling, stalling Weber and the inevitable. Soon Weber would force the issue. It was only a matter of time before he exposed his actions and her obligation. She kept waiting for Weber to reveal her dire straits, to learn how he was going to use them as a persuasive tactic.

Amanda hadn't mentioned her father's books to Weber or shown any desire to take over from him. She wondered if he found that suspicious, considering how anxious she had been not long ago. She had used lingering grief and self-doubts as excuses, but they were wearing thin and tasting foul upon her lips.

Knowing the reason for Amanda's behavior, Reis avoided any embarrassing contact when she was with Weber. Although he watched them furtively, he was assailed by doubts and fears himself. Somehow he had to uncover Weber's game. He had to prevent her marriage, to win her for himself. But she needed time, time to relax and time to become wary of her close friend. He needed to come up with a ploy of his own, one to get her alone with him . . .

But Reis's subtle strategy had one drawback, one he didn't recognize: as he stayed away, it became easier for Amanda to convince herself that he should remain out of her life . . .

Weber continued to give Amanda business reports, reports she felt were false, designed only to keep her happy and naïve. Feeling she must begin to show some interest in the firm, she began asking simple questions. Weber was evasive about certain information, as if reluctant to give up this hold over Amanda until he was ready to use her dependence on him to his advantage. Not a day had passed since his vilification of Reis that he had not tried to convince Amanda to marry him. Unfortunately, Reis had shown Amanda what was missing in other men, in Weber, and in her emotions.

Amanda threw herself into chores at home, trying to shut out the emotional demands of both Reis and Weber. She told herself Reis was just another man, a past enemy, a treacherous beguiler. But Reis wasn't just a man. He was unique. Amanda was torn between wanting him and rejecting him. Why did Reis have to be the one to bring her emotions to life? Why did thoughts of him torment her day and night? How could she punish him for her misery? Had Reis lied to her or misled her? If she questioned him, would he? Amanda finally realized she was being a coward. She was too frightened to seek the truth, fearing the revelation could hurt her more than she was hurting now.

Miranda witnessed the rising turmoil in her sister—the desire to see Reis and to hear his side was fiercely battling the fear of how to handle what he would tell her. She wondered how her sister could agree to marry Weber when her thoughts were filled with Reis.

Needing a distraction, Miranda met Lucas Reardon for lunch and a stimulating conversation. As she was strolling home, she bumped into Reis Harrison as she rounded a corner. Miranda wondered if Reis had arranged the meeting. They smiled genially at each other and exchanged greetings. As Miranda brushed past him, Reis gently caught her arm.

"Miss Lawrence, could you tell me why your sister is avoiding me? Did I say or do something to offend her?" he inquired, setting his plan into motion, a plan which could use an understanding partner.

"It seems we've had this conversation before, Mister Harrison. Why don't you ask Amanda, not me?" she suggested softly.

Reis sighed in frustration. "I've tried countless times. Amanda is a very special lady. I thought we were getting close. Then something happened which I need to understand. Is it because of Weber or me? How can I solve a problem which she refuses to clarify?"

Miranda looked up at him. Unless she was mistaken, he was distressed by

Amanda's behavior. Did she have the right to interfere? "May I ask you a question first, sir?" she countered.

"Of course," Reis responded curiously.

"Why did you really come to Alexandria, Mister Harrison?" she questioned candidly, her eyes clear and her tone direct.

"I'm here on business, Miss Lawrence. But I sense that isn't the meaning behind your question," he astutely remarked.

"What kind of business, sir?" she pressed boldly.

"Private," he replied, watching for any clue to her scheme.

"When is revenge a private business, sir?" Miranda asked softly, stunning him and confusing him.

It wasn't what Reis had expected to hear. "Revenge? I don't follow your meaning. I came here to clear up some shipping problems with your father. That first night at your home, Amanda said she had taken control, and I would deal with her. I must confess I was wary about dealing with a woman, but Amanda is a most unusual one," he remarked mischievously, then grinned at some pleasant thought.

His voice waxed grave as he continued. "Everything was going fine, then she backed away from our deal the morning after we'd had dinner together. She seemed nervous, almost frightened of something. I'll be honest with you, Miranda; I did steal a few kisses, but it's not just a romantic rebuff I'm getting. She's rejecting me on all levels. She told me to discuss my deal with Richardson. That's a little tricky since he's the one who holds those accounts at present. We spent a lot of time together while Richardson was away; we toured the docks and discussed business. I'm positive she's capable of running that firm herself, so why hand it over to him? Why refuse to take back accounts which he enticed from your father months ago?"

He looked into Miranda's troubled gaze as he inquired, "Is it a matter of loyalty to him? I found her crying in the office one afternoon. When I tried to comfort and question her, she raced out as if terrified of me, or something else. Suddenly she won't have anything to do with me. Why is she refusing to see me? I must know, Miranda; she means a lot to me. Maybe I was dreaming, but I thought she was feeling the same about me."

Seeking her own clues to this riddle, Miranda bravely asked, "What happened that last morning in the office before she raced home? Why doesn't she want Weber to know you two met and talked there?"

Reis made no attempt to hide his astonishment at those words. To see how much, if anything, Miranda knew about their situation, he told her that Amanda had been going over the books, when he arrived. He disclosed her behavior, her refusal of his contracts, and her odd request to keep their talks and visits a secret from Weber. "She didn't want him to know she'd been in the office or seen the books. Since both are hers, I thought her request strange, but I honored it."

Miranda became pensively silent. What was going on with Amanda? She had been enchanted by Reis Harrison; she had been ready to take control of their firm; she had seemed prepared to drop Weber from her life. Then suddenly it all changed. She was rejecting Reis and the firm, and accepting Weber. Why? What had she seen in those books? Positively, Amanda was keeping something alarming and critical from her . . .

"Miranda, is something wrong? Do you know what the problem is?" he inquired gently, although Reis was positive Miranda didn't know the dismaying situation which Weber and McVane had cleverly arranged with their false entries.

"No, but I intend to learn what's troubling my sister. You're right about one thing; it started that morning. It's gotten worse during the last week since Weber's return. Did you ride with Sherman during the war? Did Weber really shoot you?" she asked bluntly.

Reis stiffened. "So that's it," he murmured coldly. "Just what did Richardson tell your sister about me?"

Instead of answering, Miranda asked more questions. "Did he tell Mandy the truth about you? Do you think he burned your ranch and killed your family? Did you track his troops and kill all except him? Did you come here to take revenge on him? Is Mandy a cruel part of it?" she probed, barely stopping to take a breath.

"I must know everything he said about me. Is Amanda going to marry this Richardson to punish me, to spite me?" He clenched his fists in frustration.

Before Miranda could help herself, she blurted out, "I hope not!"

"So do I, Miranda, so do I," he quickly agreed.

Miranda's piercing gaze traveled over Reis's face. "You didn't answer my questions, Mister Harrison. Tell me how you know Weber."

"If you don't mind, I'd rather explain all of this to your sister and let her explain it to you. It's a long, painful story. I will tell you this much, Miranda; it wasn't like he said. About the only truth he told was that he shot me. Weber Richardson is a sly and dangerous man. It might help if you remind Amanda that he has been in full control of her books for months; whatever's recorded there, he entered it. Perhaps she shouldn't trust everything she reads in them. And she certainly shouldn't feel obligated to marry him because of what she thinks he's doing for her," he stated mysteriously.

Miranda gazed inquisitively at him. "You know what's in those books, don't you? You know why she feels she must marry him."

"If I told Amanda what I suspect, she wouldn't believe me. Besides, I can't explain to either of you how I know such things. Weber has set a cunning trap for Amanda, but she's so confused she doesn't see it. Try to inspire some suspicion about those books and Weber's claims. You might also let her know that Lawyer McVane is a close friend of Weber's. If I were you two, I wouldn't trust him so completely. Weber has Amanda convinced I'm the enemy, but I'm not, Miranda. I'm going to save her from that devil, even if I have to kidnap her!"

Miranda smiled warmly. "I don't know why, sir, but I believe you. If it matters what my sister thinks and feels about you, I would explain things to her as quickly as possible," she suggested.

"How? I can't get near her," he stated in exasperation.

Miranda grinned as she offered a solution. Reis chuckled. "What happens when Amanda discovers you've helped me?"

"If I haven't misjudged you, sir, she'll be delighted—after she flogs us all for pulling such a trick! If I'm wrong about you, you'd best fear me and Luke more than Weber." They joined in mirthful laughter, then shook hands before going their separate ways to dress and prepare for their impending charade.

It was nearing midnight when Miranda returned home from dinner with Lucas and Reis. She was apprehensive but excited about putting her daring scheme into motion. She was grateful Lucas had agreed to play a role in this delightful drama. Reis had met them at a small and quiet restaurant near the edge of town.

After talking for hours, Miranda and Lucas were both eager to assist the bold Mister Harrison.

Lucas was willing to help just to get even with Weber for stealing his sweetheart, then casting the unfortunate and tarnished girl into the street to work as a cheap prostitute. What made the sore fester rather than heal was Weber's constant reminders of his foul deed, his tauntings about Luke's taking Marissa back into his arms. For all of Lucas's previous affection, he couldn't bring himself to love or touch Marissa again, not after Web's use and abuse. But since Marissa's betrayal, Lucas hadn't fully trusted another female, except for his twin cousins. Both girls hoped Lucas would find someone very special one day.

"You're late, Randy. I was beginning to worry," Amanda chided her sister. "Where have you been? It's midnight. No lady should be out this late, even with her cousin. Why didn't Luke come in?"

Miranda prayed she could carry off this act, as she was always so honest. "I'm sorry, Mandy; time took wings tonight. But I don't think you want to know where I was or with whom. Luke isn't the one who brought me home. It's late and I'm tired. Good night."

When she headed past Amanda for the steps, Amanda seized her arm and shrieked, "Just a minute, Miranda Lawrence! Don't you dare leave this room until you explain yourself."

Miranda looked indecisive and tense. "You won't like it," she warned before adding, "I had dinner with Luke and . . . Reis Harrison. Luke was busy making notes, so Reis saw me home. You said you didn't want to hear his name mentioned, so I wasn't going to tell you."

Amanda's mouth fell open and she gaped at her sister in disbelief. "Why on earth would you do such a thing?" she demanded.

Miranda gazed at her innocently. "Have dinner with Luke? Or stay out so late?"

Her eyes filling with outrage, Amanda shouted, "How dare you be seen with that damn Yankee! And to allow him to escort you home? I told you what Weber said about him."

"I know what Weber said, and how he feels about Yankees. Frankly, I don't care. As you put it the other day, you'll be marrying Web, not me. I can see whom I please," she stated sullenly to stun Amanda into a confession of some kind. "The war is over for me. I like Reis. So I'll see him again if I wish," she announced saucily. She anxiously waited to see how that news would affect her sister.

"You can't be serious!" Amanda stormed in dismay. "What about me and my feelings?" she panted.

"What about your feelings?" Miranda probed nonchalantly, perceiving the fury and tension building within her distraught sister.

"You know I was seeing Reis! How could you do this?" Amanda inquired sadly. Had Miranda been impressed with Reis from the beginning? Did she think he was free for the taking now? How could her own sister be so traitorous? If Randy and Reis became close, that would put Reis in her life once more! How could she bear to see him with another woman, especially her sister? If Randy knew what Web had done for them, she wouldn't despise him so much.

"I believe you've told me many times this week that you're going to marry Weber. Surely you can't have serious feelings about Reis, then marry Weber?"

"I told you how I felt about Reis, and why I had to stop seeing him! You can't bring him into my life again. Please, Randy," she beseeched her sister. "It's just a mean trick to get back at me."

"For what? Besides, once you marry Weber, you won't be living with me any more. So I won't be forcing Reis's company on you. If you told me the truth about loving Reis, you would never marry Web. I can't believe my own sister would be so conniving and cruel. Even if you can't marry Reis, there's no reason to marry just anyone! I'm shocked by your behavior, Amanda Lawrence, and hurt."

"But you'll be living with me and Web," Amanda informed her.

Before Miranda could stop herself, she shouted, "Never!"

Amanda stared at her twin. Should she reveal their financial situation? Should she expose Weber's rescue from humiliation and poverty? Without money and with their property lost, Miranda would be forced to live with them. "You're thinking only of yourself, Randy. What about me? Must you be so hateful to Web?"

"No, Mandy, you're the one being selfish and dishonest. If I didn't love you above everyone else, I wouldn't try to prevent this terrible mistake. I can't pretend I like Weber; I don't. What about Reis, Mandy? How can you hurt him this way? And how will Web act if he learns the truth about your feelings? It's wrong to play with other's lives and emotions."

"Hurt Reis? If he cared about me, he wouldn't be chasing after my sister! Don't you see, Randy? He's after revenge on Weber."

Miranda scoffed sarcastically, "According to Weber, you mean. You're hurting Reis by acting this way. I've seen the look in his eyes when he asks about you; it isn't spite or treachery. Why did you lead him on, Mandy? He seems bewildered by your stinging rejection. If revenge is a part of things, it's Weber's revenge on Reis. Web's keeping you and the business from Reis. You spent time with Reis; do you honestly believe he's so evil and cruel? I just can't accept Web's allegations. I can't understand why you won't give Reis a chance to explain. It's absurd to refuse a simple talk which could settle everything. What makes you so positive you can trust Weber implicitly?" she challenged coldly. "You're a fool if you discard Reis Harrison!"

"How do you know so much about me and Reis?" Amanda asked.

"You always said I was uncannily intuitive," she retorted slyly.

Amanda knew her sister would try to talk her out of her self-sacrifice if she revealed the truth. She couldn't make such a risky confession. Miranda was too taken with Reis; she might disclose the truth to him. This situation was becoming more and more complex. If only her sacrifice didn't include Reis.

Amanda quietly asked, "Are you going after Reis?"

Miranda came back with a question of her own, "Are you really going to marry Web?" Each girl studied the expression of the other.

"Is this some game to make me jealous?" Amanda inquired warily.

Miranda realized her sister wasn't going to tell her anything vital. To prevent trouble between them, Miranda ceased the ruse. "To put your mind at ease, dear sister, it's nothing more than friendship. If I'm not mistaken, Reis was falling in love with you until you messed it up between you two. Reis is giving Luke some information for a book about the war. You'd be surprised how Reis's version of it differs from Weber's," she hinted casually. "It's a shame you're tied to Weber. Reis is quite a catch. The more I see him, the more I'm convinced you two are perfect for each other. No, Mandy, I'm not romantically interested in Reis," she sighed. "Goodnight, Mrs. Richardson; you should get used to that name. As you wish, I won't mention Reis again. But it pains me to realize how much you've changed lately; you don't even trust me enough to tell me why you're forcing yourself into a despicable marriage. What hold does Web have over you?"

Appalled, Amanda questioned, "What do you mean, Randy?"

"I'm not blind or dim-witted, Mandy. I just wish you could talk to me like before. If you haven't given Web your answer yet, please search your heart again. If I were you, I would ask both men lots of questions and very soon. If you can't turn to Reis or Luke for help, then confide in me. We can work out whatever's bothering you."

"Why do you insist something's wrong? Why would I need help? With what?" She tested to see if Miranda knew about their circumstances.

"I'll make a pact with you, Mandy. I promise not to say another word and I'll stop worrying about you, if you can look me in the eye and swear things are fine with you. Swear you love and want Weber."

Amanda paled slightly. "How can things be fine when you badger me all the time? You constantly insult Web, even knowing how close we are. You go out with Reis, then expect me not to be upset." She tried to distract her sister with defensive questions.

Tears formed in Miranda's tawny eyes and her lips quivered. "I never thought the day would come when you would build a wall between us. I want to help, but I don't know how to reach you, Mandy. I wish Mama were here," she murmured dejectedly, then burst into racking sobs and fled to her room.

Amanda seemed glued to the floor. Anguish and guilt attacked her viciously. She wanted to go after Miranda and explain, but she was too emotional to carry on a conversation. She needed to think and relax. Tomorrow, she would find a way to confide in Miranda, to make her understand.

Neither girl slept well that night. Miranda made a desperate decision to visit the plantation, leaving Amanda alone to think. When Amanda awakened, Miranda was already packed and gone. Before taking the train to Richmond and hiring a buggy to Morning Star Plantation, Miranda stopped off to see Reis. She told him of her failure to reach Amanda and of her travel plans and asked him to send word to Lucas. When Reis asked about the servants with Amanda, Miranda told him there was only their housekeeper and cook, Alice Reed; tomorrow was her day off, so Amanda would be alone for two nights and a day.

After putting Miranda on the train, Reis hurried to make preparations for a brazen move . . . He had decided it was past time for Amanda to learn some facts about herself, Reis Harrison, and Weber Richardson!

After Amanda arose and dressed, she headed for Miranda's room, finding it empty. She went downstairs, but Miranda couldn't be found there either. Odd, she thought, since it was only ten o'clock. Amanda worried over her sister's absence until four that afternoon, then panicked when Lucas dropped by to explain Miranda's departure.

"I would have come by sooner, but I was busy with an interview. Miranda said she didn't leave you a note, but she had to go away for a while. She seemed upset, Mandy. What's going on between you two?" Lucas questioned, as if he didn't know about Miranda's plans.

Amanda was frantic. *Morning Star isn't ours anymore. When she arrives, she'll be confused and distressed. She'll wonder why I didn't tell her. If she starts getting suspi-*

cious, she might learn everything. "Luke, can you go after her?" she entreated anxiously.

"Go after her? Why? It isn't strange for her to visit there, but it's awfully strange that she wouldn't leave you a note to tell you herself. Did you two quarrel?" he asked, watching Amanda's reaction closely.

"She's angry because of me and Web," Amanda told him.

"Then it's true, you're actually going to marry him?"

"I know you don't like Web, but Randy has no reason to be so spiteful. Are you planning to desert me too?" she asked sarcastically.

"If you marry Web, I won't come around again, if that's what you mean. But I have a strong feeling that Randy didn't leave because of you and Web. Why are you sitting home instead of working? And why are you being so nasty to Reis Harrison?" he asked sternly.

"Since when do you have the right to interfere in my private life, Lucas Reardon?" she snapped at him.

"Since you seem to have lost your senses and appear determined to ruin it! Since you choose Web over Randy, me, and Reis! I don't know what you're trying to pull, but you'll regret it. I'm not going after Randy; she said she'd be home in three days. You don't have to worry about me intruding again. I'll be moving west soon."

"Moving west? But what about me and Randy? You're the only family we have left," she shrieked, dreading his loss.

"Soon, dear cuz, you'll have a whole new family. Weber and all the tiny Webers," he said coldly.

"If you don't care about me, then what about Randy? You know she'll never come to live with us."

"As soon as she returns, I plan to ask her to go west with me. You know how she feels about your mother's people, and I need her help."

Amanda was staggered by that news. "You can't take Randy on such a dangerous journey! I won't allow it!"

Lucas's voice became soft and compelling as he protested, "If she wants to go with me, you can't stop her, Mandy. Once you marry Web, there's nothing to keep her here. She wants to meet her grandfather and uncle. She wants to see what Indian life is all about, how your mother and her people lived. I'll protect her; you needn't worry. Besides, the Indian hostilities are under control. Nearly all the tribes are on reservations now; they can't even own guns. They've got soldiers and forts everywhere for protection. It's easy to get there—there are trains, riverboats, stages. It's been a dream of hers for years. Your parents were planning a visit this summer, remember?"

"But why are you going out there?" Amanda asked.

"It concerns that book I'm writing. Would you believe three of the most notorious Yankee leaders—Custer, Sherman, and Sheridan—are assigned to the Missouri Division which includes the Dakota Territory? How's that for research luck? They'll be more willing to talk out there, little suspecting I'm an ex-Reb out to extract the truth about them. This is a chance of a lifetime, Mandy. I'm not sure how I was selected for this assignment, but I'll be damned if I refuse it! Randy could use the diversion. Don't try to stop her," he coaxed gently. "Who knows, she might find her own true love out there, hopefully a Reis Harrison."

"Why are you two shoving Reis down my throat! I have to marry Web!" she rashly screamed at him.

"Why?" Lucas snarled.

Cornered, she declared heatedly, "Because I love him!"

"Like hell you do," Lucas debated, then stalked out of the house.

Weber came by to visit briefly around six, just before the housekeeper was to leave. Amanda tried to act cheerful, but she was exhausted from chores. When Weber chided her for not leaving such menial labor to the servant, she smiled and told him it was good exercise and a distraction from her sadness. Then Weber asked about Miranda. Amanda claimed she was visiting friends in Boston. If Weber suspected she was lying, he didn't let on to her. He told her to get some rest and he would see her in two days.

She looked surprised, so he explained he would be away on business. "If you have any problems while I'm away, contact McVane. I've hired him to manage both our firms while I'm gone. He'll be working out of your father's office. You rest, my dear; you're looking pale. See you in a few days." He stood up to leave. "Oh, yes." He turned back to add, "You don't have to worry about Harrison bothering you again. He checked out of the hotel and left town."

"Did you two settle any business?" she asked, trying to sound calm. No wonder Weber felt it was safe for him to go away for days. *Gone*, her heart sighed painfully. And with McVane in her father's office, there was no way she could sneak in to go over the books again.

"I guess he decided to leave the accounts with my firm, for now. Since his vindictive plot failed, he's probably gone off somewhere to sulk or to make new plans. I'm glad you didn't see him again, Mandy. The men on the docks and in the warehouse have been teasing me about seeing you there with him. Give Randy my regards."

Amanda suffered through a lingering kiss, then waved farewell from the front porch. Had Weber been trying to tell her he knew about her times with Reis? Did Web truly think Reis would show up here again? Sometimes Weber could be so damn cocky! Suddenly Amanda wiped her lips. How could she ever make love to Web when a simple kiss turned her stomach?

Her heart ached. Her parents were lost to her forever. Reis was gone. Luke was leaving soon, perhaps taking Randy with him. By now, Randy was learning of their loss of Morning Star, the plantation that bore their mother's Indian name. When Randy returned, she would demand more answers. Was it too late to tell the truth? Reis was gone, and she didn't know where to locate him. And even if she found him, would he care or listen?

If they lost the townhouse and business too, could she find some way to survive without selling her soul to Weber? If she sold her jewels and anything not mortgaged, would there be enough money to live on after she repaid Weber? Besides Luke, there was no family or home to run to for help. Pride would demand they seek another place for a new beginning. What kind of decent work could she and Randy do? What would happen to them? She had read and heard so many wicked things about working women, about their vulnerability and abuse . . .

Amanda paced the carpet in her bedroom until she could have screamed from tension. As if to drive herself into mindless slumber, she downed two glasses of Irish whiskey taken from her father's private stock. Clad in a silky nightgown of azure blue, she threw herself upon the bed to ease her spinning head. She hazily scolded herself for drinking on an empty stomach.

As her mind drifted like a cloud, she had the strangest sensation that hands were binding her arms and legs. She felt as if she were being wrapped in a blanket then carried from her room. From a distance, she heard the clicking of boots as they descended the steps. Cool air wafted across her cheeks, then warmth covered them. She tried to force her lids open, but she was too tired to expend the energy. She was clasped against some firm object, and strong arms were protectively encircling her body. Comfortable and limp, she snuggled against the warmth of the object, then inhaled his manly odor and murmured peacefully, "Reis . . ."

The man looked down into her sleeping face, asking himself why she had called that name as he gagged her tempting lips. Soon her little game would be over!

Chapter Six

Miranda sat in the swing which hung from a towering tree, swaying back and forth as she sank into deep thought. The trip to Morning Star had been uneventful, but her visit was anything but dull and tranquilizing. Now that she was here and making odd discoveries, she didn't regret coming. But without her parents and Amanda, it was lonely and cold. The longtime servants couldn't seem to relieve the melancholy mood of their deceased employer's child. They had tried to clear up her somber mood and calm her anxiety, but instead they unknowingly increased them. They told her how much the plantation had prospered, which pleased her immensely. They asked what would happen now that her parents were gone, but Miranda couldn't tell them. She revealed that her sister was considering marriage; if it took place, Miranda would come to live here.

Tomorrow, the overseer had promised to take her on a tour of the entire plantation. He wanted her to inspect the replanked barns, to meet the new workers and speak with old ones, and to see how he was rotating the crops. Miranda didn't know anything about crops, but she could meet the workers and view what she and her sister owned. Clearly, this plantation was beautiful and valuable. Her father had always made certain the majestic ante-bellum mansion was in excellent repair. Without her family, the house seemed enormous and formal. Perhaps she could persuade Amanda to sell the shipping firm, refuse Weber, and move here to begin a new life.

Earlier in the day, Miranda had made several disturbing discoveries. The overseer had told her he had been instructed by Daniel McVane to send the monthly reports to Weber Richardson, and Weber had made two visits out here. Worse, Weber had been hinting to him about a probable sale of Morning Star.

Miranda tried to recall the overseer's words. Weber had Mister Farley making full reports on each area of the profitable plantation. The money was being transferred to Daniel McVane, their lawyer. Why had McVane failed to mention these enormous profits during their recent conference? He had made it sound as if the plantation had been steadily losing money since her family's last visit a year ago! Had McVane been misinformed or had he deceived them?

Since Weber had made two visits, why hadn't he corrected McVane's errors? Something funny was going on, and she was determined to discover what it was. It was a wild idea, but what if Amanda had uncovered some crime against them when she checked the books? And what if she was being threatened into marrying Weber? No, Amanda wouldn't agree to such evil even to save her life! But what if Weber and his unknown cohorts had threatened those Amanda loved: herself, Luke, and Reis! Amanda would do anything to protect them, even sacrifice herself to a demon like Weber.

Luke and Reis kept hinting that Weber was sly and dangerous. Blackmail would explain Amanda's irrational moods and her reluctance to confide in her sister. That would clarify why she was refusing to talk to Reis. And her sudden surrender to Weber's proposal! Why else would she take Weber, a man who couldn't even walk in the shadow of Reis Harrison! A bright and daring female like Amanda wouldn't lose the man of her dreams over a silly dispute; she would fight for him and demand an explanation for his behavior. She must have found something in those books to terrify her, to entrap her!

Miranda decided to send Lucas a telegram the next day, using the code which they had worked out long ago as a childhood game. Reis and Luke could do some snooping on their end while she remained here a few more days to see what worms she could unearth.

Amanda dozed for two hours in the warm embrace of her abductor until a violent storm began to pelt her face with raindrops and to saturate the blanket and her gown. She shivered and stirred, confused by her surroundings and predicament. She was bound and gagged! Held securely by powerful arms, she was being taken away on horseback by a black-clad villain! She assumed she was having a nightmare and struggled to awaken. Finally, she was forced to comprehend she was being kidnapped, wrapped in a sopping blanket and a flimsy nightgown!

She squirmed to sit up in the man's arms, but he wouldn't allow it. The wet blanket clung to her body. She moaned and thrashed her head, unable to speak. She was helpless and nearly naked! Wet curls clung to her cheeks and forehead. Who was doing this to her? Why? Terror filled her and she shuddered.

Aware she was coming around, the man slowed the horse to a walk. He pushed back the hood to his rainslicker and his black hair was soaked instantly. Beads of water dripped off his chin and nose. When lightning flashed across the heavens, her eyes became large circles as she viewed his face and the implication of this scene. Her breath caught in her throat, and her heart started thudding heavily.

White teeth gleamed in the next flash of lightning as he grinned down at her. Reis roguishly vowed, "I said you can't marry him, love."

Amanda simply stared at him. She wondered what he was planning to do with her. Web said that Reis had left. Obviously, he had been lurking in the shadows until he was given a chance to abduct her. If Reis wanted revenge on Weber, would he kill her before letting Weber marry her? His cunning seduction had failed; now what?

When she ceased her futile struggles, Reis grasped her around the waist and set her up straight across his lap. He tenderly brushed the wet curls from her face then smiled and caressed her cheek. When she tried to turn away from his piercing gaze, he held her chin firmly.

As Reis observed her ever-changing emotions, he told her softly, "There's no reason for you to be afraid, Mandy love. I only want to talk with you. Since you refused to see me and hear me out, you left me no choice but to force you. If it takes all day and night, we're going to settle this matter. If you refuse to explain yourself by then, I'll hold you here until you relent. No tricks, no lies, and no silence, woman. Right now, I don't care about Weber's war crimes, only about you. I can promise you won't be harmed by me, and I'll take you home as soon as you tell me why you suddenly rejected me and agreed to marry him. Hellfire, I won't lose you without knowing why."

As her eyes narrowed and her teeth clenched beneath the gag, defiance and fury glittered brightly in her lovely blue eyes. Reis knew this wasn't going to be easy, but he did have some tricks up his sleeve. "We'll be at the cabin before dawn; then I'll untie you and remove that gag. But if you try anything, I'm not adverse to giving you a good spanking. In fact, you need one," he warned playfully.

The look in her glittering blue eyes shouted, you wouldn't dare! He chuckled and replied, "Oh, yes, I would, love. You are the most exasperating and infuriating female alive. It's about time you started using those brains and wits again. If it takes a good spanking to bring you back to life, then I'll be most willing to provide it," he declared arrogantly.

Amanda's chest vibrated in heavy respiration. She glared at the smug devil, wanting to claw his handsome face. She wiggled frantically in his arms until he warned, "Be still, or I'll drop you in the mud."

That threat called an immediate halt to her thrashing. "That's more like it. It's nearly morning; get some sleep. You'll soon have the privacy and opportunity to severely tongue-lash me." He laughed mirthfully as they rode away into the stormy streaks of predawn.

Within an hour, he reined in the animal at a grove of trees. He slid her bound feet to the mushy ground, then agilely dismounted. He tied the reins to a tree, then scooped her up in his arms. Amanda kicked wildly, wanting to walk. Clutching her tightly, Reis laughed again, heading for a cabin in a small clearing. Although it was raining noisily, she could hear the rush of a nearby stream. She didn't know where they were, but it was secluded, and intimidating.

Reis placed her bare feet on the wet dirt while he unlocked the door. He carried her inside, kicking the door closed behind them, and deposited her at the entrance. After lighting a lantern, he turned and eyed her intently. She almost appeared comical, entrapped in the blanket with silvery blond curls dripping water. If this situation weren't so serious, he knew he could easily burst into hearty chuckles.

Unable to move, Amanda stood there, shaking from cold and suspense. Removing his rain gear and tossing it over a chair, Reis pulled a knife from a sheath at his waist. He came toward her. Amanda wanted to back away in fear but couldn't.

When he witnessed her reaction, he sighed in frustration. "I'm just going to cut the ropes, Mandy. Be still. We need to get you dry and warm before you take a chill."

It wasn't the knife which alarmed her; it was the beguiling grin on his face. When he removed the confining blanket, she felt naked in the wet gown which clung revealingly to her curves. He squatted to cut the rope around her ankles, then stood to sever those on her wrists behind her back. The moment her feet and hands were mobile she struck at him with both, wishing she knew how to fight like Miranda and those skilled Chinese. How dare he bring her here alone, bound and barely covered! What if someone saw them? Not having removed her gag yet, she berated him with muffled curses.

Reis captured her hands, then flung her to the bunk and pinned her beneath him. "I do believe you're aching for some discipline, love. Behave, or I might forget you're a lady and I'm—" He didn't finish that statement. It was too soon to say, I'm the man who loves you. "Settle down, and I'll build a fire and fix coffee. Deal?"

When she didn't nod, he slipped the gag down to her neck and insisted upon her answer. "Is it a deal, love? A truce?" His rain gear had been of little service; he was just as soaked as Amanda. His wet garments molded to his hard frame; that view and their contact made her too conscious of his virility and appeal.

Distressed by her attraction to him and her helpless position, Amanda screamed at him, "You sorry son of a—"

Reis's hand clamped over her mouth, denying the crude word to come forth. "Instead of a spanking, I might wash that mouth out with strong soap. Better still, I might do both! As soon as you get warm and dry, you're going to do plenty of talking. You owe me, love."

When he removed his hand, she shouted, "Owe you! I owe you nothing, Yankee! Get off of me! Take me home this instant! Are you too dense to know kidnapping is a crime? Or too wicked and arrogant to care?"

"You're a bright girl, Mandy. That means you should hear all the evidence before taking sides on a vital issue. Stop acting like a spoiled brat and listen to me!"

"Listen to your lies again? You claimed to be here on business; that isn't true. Why are you trying to hurt me?" she inquired angrily. She struggled once more, causing their bodies to mesh provocatively. When her strap slipped precariously from one shoulder and the tail of the ice blue gown wadded between her exposed thighs, she wisely halted.

"The business offer was true, Mandy. Tonight, the only thing which concerns me is your dark image of me. Hell, we're not strangers! How could you believe Web, Mandy?" he asked accusingly, acutely aware of every inch of her rain-kissed body.

Unlike her tanned sister, Amanda was as white and smooth as fresh cream. When she was calm or happy, she looked like a siren who should be perched on a rock in the ocean, luring sailors to blissful enslavement. Lord, how he wanted to lean over and spread kisses over that slender throat and those satiny shoulders. He wanted to capture that mouth with his. He yearned to turn that defiant sparkle in those blue eyes into a blaze of smoldering desire for him. He craved to have those arms and legs hungrily entwined about him. There wasn't an inch of her he didn't long to taste or explore!

"Look who's talking about washing out my mouth! You curse and lie worse than I do," she scoffed cynically, as his flaming gaze sent warm tremors down her spine. She feared the power of his hypnotic gaze and enchanting facade. If only he didn't have that roguish smile, those remarkably blue eyes, that sun-kissed flesh, that ebony hair, that . . . that everything disarming!

"Ah, so you have been lying," he baited her, attempting to keep his mind off her body. The light color, clingy material, and nearly translucent condition of her gown left little to his imagination. Despite his efforts at self-control, his traitorous body had reacted to those taut points which had appeared when her body had thrashed against his. His eyes darkened with passion at the memory.

"I didn't mean it like that!" she protested quickly as inexplicable sensations washed over her body and clouded her reason. "I'm cold and wet! My feet are freezing!" she panted, changing the subject. Truthfully, she didn't care if she was soaked, and the heat of his body was tormenting bliss. Her breathing became labored.

"Then behave while I make a fire and coffee." He stood up and smiled down at her, his gaze leisurely traveling from her straggly hair to her bare feet. Her gown had slid upward, offering him a pleasing view of shapely legs.

Amanda seized the wayward material and covered herself. "Did you think to bring along my clothes?" she sneered uneasily.

"Nope," he mischievously quipped. "But you'd better get out of that wet gown. Wrap a dry blanket around you," he suggested, chuckling at her embarrassment and outrage.

"You're insane if you think I'll wear nothing but a blanket around you, you lecherous fiend!" she shouted, sticking out her tongue at him.

"That wet gown's gonna get awfully uncomfortable. It doesn't hide your many charms anyway," he announced devilishly, grinning.

"You!" she cried in rising distress. "You'll be sorry for this!"

"If you explain and I explain, then neither of us will be sorry or miserable. That is, if you're the woman I think and pray you are. If not, I'll be signing my life away," he vowed mysteriously, his expression suddenly grave.

He stripped off his shirt and boots, then warned her to turn her head while he exchanged his saturated pants for a blanket. "You can't be serious, Reis Harrison! No gentleman would subject a lady to such indignities! Surely you don't expect us to talk while undressed?"

"I didn't plan on the storm, Mandy. If we don't get dry and warm, we'll be too sick to settle matters. I should have brought us both some clothes; I honestly didn't think about it. You needn't worry; I've never raped a woman, and I won't start with you."

Amanda's cheeks flamed a bright red as she presented her back to him. He eased out of his pants and wrapped the blanket around his slim hips, tucking the edges in at his narrow waist. He hung his pants and shirt on rickety chairs, then set his boots near the hearth. He told her she could change while he made a fire.

As he knelt before the fireplace, Amanda turned and stared at his muscled back. There was nothing between them but a thin blanket and a scanty nightgown; soon, just two blankets. Except for the noise of building a fire and a gentle rain falling outside, they were sealed in a perilously sensual world of provocative solitude. Her heart began to pound so forcefully that she imagined it could be heard in the stillness.

Her eyes scanned the room which was dimly lit by one lantern and the approaching dawn. She noticed a gun and the knife, but both were near him. She feared this was some cunning trap, to show Weber that Reis could have her if he so desired. Damn, how she wanted him! But what would happen afterward? Was a beguiling seduction part of his vengeful scheme? Could she trust him? He claimed he only wanted to talk, but this romantic setting made her doubt his intentions. Could she trust herself alone with him, alone without clothes before a cozy fire?

Panic flooded her. Before Reis realized her intention, she raced to the door, flung it open, and fled outside into the light rain. She ran as if demons were pursuing her. She didn't get far before Reis was close behind. He shouted for her to halt, but she rashly fled toward a boggy area. The squashy surface tugged at her feet, impeding her progress. She dodged low-hanging tree limbs and moisture-laden bushes, then tripped on a fallen branch, plunging full force into a mushy area of yielding earth.

When Reis made the clearing, he grabbed her arm and tried to pull her from the muddy quagmire. She fought him wildly, causing him to stumble and fall into the shallow and slushy pit. As they struggled and argued in the morass, both were covered with sticky and clingy mud. Even so, Amanda continued desperately to struggle for freedom.

Reis shouted for her to stop fighting him and get back inside the cabin, but Amanda was terrified of being alone with him. At last he had her pinned to the ground, sinking into oozing mud. The dark mixture clung to her body, matted her hair, and stained her gown. She could feel it squeezing between her fingers and thighs. Realizing at last that she could not escape him, she ceased her movements and reluctantly went limp.

"Why the hell did you run like that?" he thundered at her, sounding angered and baffled. "I told you you're safe with me!"

"I don't want to hear any more lies!" she scoffed cynically.

"Just where can you go dressed like this?" he reminded her. "Sometimes I don't think you have a brain in that beautiful head!"

"Let me up, you brute! My gown is ruined. Look at my hair! My God, I'm covered in mud! You'll pay for this, Reis Harrison! You just wait until Web comes after me!" she threatened.

"I wish to hell he would! Then I'd force him to tell you the truth! I think you're in for a big shock when Randy comes home; you'll learn you still own Morning Star and it's very prosperous. And your townhouse isn't mortgaged, and your firm is making more money than you could count in weeks! It's all a ruse, Mandy love," he snarled at her.

"What are you talking about?" she asked in puzzlement, halting all struggles and staring up into his scowling face. How did he know such things? What was he trying to pull?

"That ledger is pure fantasy—lies recorded by Weber and McVane. Every month you grow richer, Mandy. It's a cunning plot to get you to marry him. If I didn't know how sly and convincing he was, I'd think you were the dumbest female alive," he declared sullenly.

"How do you know so much about my affairs? And how can you make such ridiculous charges?" she demanded.

He replied with shocking words. "I'm an agent for President Grant. I know plenty of things. I took extra care to investigate you, Miss Amanda Lawrence. It seems I studied you too closely. I'm not here for revenge; I was sent by Grant on a secret mission. I never expected to find Richardson here. And I sure as hell didn't expect to meet someone like you. There couldn't be a worse time for romance, but I'll be damned if I allow that bastard to entrap you with lies!"

"You're the one who's lying! I've known Web for years. You're a total stranger. Why should I trust you?" she sneered. *A presidential spy? Investigate her? What in heaven's name was going on!*

"Because you'll make the biggest mistake of your life if you don't hear me out," he replied. His voice softened as he continued, "Listen to me, Mandy. You won't face poverty if you reject Weber. You're a very wealthy lady, despite what that phony book claims. Would I lie about such an easy matter to check out? Don't ask Weber or McVane; go ask the bankers and check with your accounts," he challenged. "Since I'm investigating Lawrence Shipping, I know how much business you've been doing. So why aren't those clients and shipments listed in your books? Why are only bills listed and no profits, profits which I know your firm's earned recently?"

"You keep talking about my books; how do you know what's in them? And how do you know where Randy is?" she inquired skeptically.

"That night you ran out on me, you left the safe open. I checked to see why you had panicked and turned on me. Knowing the state of your firm, I knew you were being tricked. I didn't have to guess by whom. He's taking money from your firm, Mandy, not making loans to it. And he isn't supporting you and Miranda, as you've been led to believe. I couldn't steal evidence to prove my claims to you without exposing my investigation to Weber and McVane; and without proof, I feared you wouldn't believe me. I saw Miranda before she left. I wonder how Weber planned to explain your ownership of Morning Star after your wedding. And why the townhouse is still yours."

She wondered if he was daft, or staggeringly accurate. "But Web said you were after revenge," she protested.

"I swear he deceived you, Mandy. I didn't ride with Sherman. I was in his camp briefly while on a mission for President Lincoln. Weber was a captive then; that's where he saw me first. Later I learned he was the one in charge of the troop which burned my home and killed my family. As soon as Luke completes his work, he'll show you the facts; Weber and his troop were infamous killers and destroyers. Weber would make Sherman look like an angel. I did track his men, trying to capture them. I underestimated Weber. He betrayed two of his own men in order to ambush me. I hate him, Mandy, but not enough to use you or any innocent person to gain justice. He knows how much time we spent together while he was gone. He told those war lies to keep us apart. He might even suspect who I am and why I came to Alexandria. I've been trying to find a way to protect you and my mission. But if I don't take you into my confidence, you'll marry this snake and ruin both our lives."

"How would my marriage ruin your life?" she asked sarcastically.

"It won't, if it's to me," he nonchalantly informed her.

"To you?" she murmured incredulously.

"That's right, my love. When this is over, I want you to marry me. Will you?"

"But we're strangers!"

"Does that alter your feelings, or mine?" he speculated. "Marry me, Mandy. Give us a chance to be happy and safe. Besides, we were never strangers. From the moment we met, we knew it was fated between us. You also sensed it that first night, didn't you?"

Amanda was speechless with surprise and confusion. Reis took advantage of her silence and questioned, "You spurned me because of what you saw in that book, didn't you? You felt obligated to marry him, to trust him, obligated to reject me. You don't love him, Mandy."

"Who are you, Reis? What's this about a secret mission for the President?" she probed.

Reis outlined his mission for her and his assumptions, then finished by saying, "I think your father was innocent. I told those clients if they would resign with Lawrence, I would follow the next few shipments to see how and where the changes were made and by whom. I realized there was more to this mission when I met you and Richardson. I think Richardson's behind this deception. He needs Lawrence Shipping and your plantation to carry on his covert activities, and he needs you as a respectable cover."

"Do you realize what you're saying, Reis? You're implying he's a traitor, a criminal, and a scoundrel. I know Web has his bad traits, but to think he's . . ." Amanda sighed heavily, forgetting she was lying in a mud hole beneath the man she loved but feared to trust.

Yet Amanda had a terrible sensation that Reis might be right. Crazy thoughts flashed through her mind. She recalled curious questions Weber had asked right after her father's death about these same three accounts. Could she totally trust either man? Was she the pawn in some monstrous game? Amanda tried to push aside her wild imagination. Coincidence? A deadly game?

Her quizzical gaze fused with his entreating one. "Why should I believe you, Reis? How do I know this isn't some trick to get me on your side, to use me against him? How can I accept such treachery on the word of a stranger? I'm so confused," she confessed.

"All I ask is that you go and talk with your banker. See if you're really on the verge of bankruptcy and see if you've lost the plantation. When Miranda returns, you'll know that isn't true. Don't tell Weber where she is, or she might not get back alive. You haven't told him, have you?" he asked, alarm racing through him.

"No," she replied, sensing his fear for her sister. "But Web wouldn't hurt Randy," she argued.

"She wouldn't be the first female he's injured or killed," he told her. "He has a lot at stake here. I know you find that impossible to accept, but you must. Luke's been investigating him a long time. He hopes to get proof of Weber's crimes then split you two with it."

Amanda didn't know why she was listening to such tales. "If what you say has even a grain of truth, then why would Web do such things? How can I accept this monstrous charge without proof?"

"Greed, Mandy love. He wants all and more than he lost during the war. He wants money, power, and fame. He can't risk involving his company, so he was using your father's. When I first arrived, I didn't know if you could be trusted since you and Weber were so close."

"But you just said my father was innocent," she shrieked.

"That might explain his accident, Mandy. Perhaps he discovered what was taking place and tried to stop it," he speculated softly.

Amanda went white and shuddered. "Are you saying you think my parents were murdered? You think Weber . . ." That was too much evil to accept, and she resisted that horrible accusation.

"I don't know yet, Mandy. But I suspect it wasn't an accident. You've got to realize how dangerous and desperate Weber and his men are." As soon as Reis made those statements, he grimaced. "Listen to me, Mandy. You and Miranda have to be careful until I solve this mystery. If they think you two are suspicious of them, they could harm you. Damnit! I should never have involved you! I must be a fool! What the hell could I be thinking!" he berated himself.

"You forget everything I said, Mandy. Don't you dare see those bankers! And keep this pretty nose out of your office and books. If Weber or his men think you are on to them, they could get rid of you and Miranda just like your parents. Besides money and power, their lives are in peril; they've committed treason, a hanging offense. Luke's in danger too if Weber learns of his investigation. Just remember: you aren't indebted to Weber, and I love you. Just keep quiet and safe at home until I arrest them. Don't give them any reason to harm you and your sister. Will you do that for me?" he pleaded earnestly.

"This is another trick, isn't it?" she asked painfully. Was he afraid if she did some snooping she would discover his lies? Could she be so mistaken about Weber, so blind and gullible?

Reis captured her face between his hands and shouted at her, "Tarnation, woman! All I need is a little time to prove it. Just don't marry him before Luke and I can save you. If you think you need money, I'll give you any amount. If you think I'm lying, then marry me. I have everything you want or need," he vowed.

"Marry you?" she repeated, eying him strangely. "Why?"

"Secretly, Mandy," he added a curious stipulation, then explained his reason. "If Weber thinks you're siding with me, that means you're against him. I won't put your life in danger, love. If you marry me, we'll have to keep it a secret from everyone but Randy and Luke. You'll have to pretend to remain friends with Weber. Otherwise, you'll have to go to my home and wait for me there." Reis didn't have a home anywhere, but he would buy one if she would live in it! This was a dangerous ploy, but one he couldn't resist.

"But why marry me secretly?" she probed, still doubtful.

"Marriage is legal and binding. Would I go so far just to hurt another man? Surely you would trust me then?" he tested.

"If what you say is true, then Web had me fooled completely. Who's to say you don't have similar motives?" she fenced nervously.

"Right now, you have only my word," he stated candidly.

Reis slowly bent forward, his lips coming into contact with hers when she didn't move aside. He kissed her tenderly and leisurely, then leaned away. "I swear I've spoken the truth, love, all of it."

Amanda gazed into his eyes and felt she could trust him. Suddenly she realized she was finally free of the pain of the last few weeks. She didn't have to marry Web! Reis loved her and wanted to marry her! She had nothing to fear! In spite of the gloomy weather, her heart was full of sunshine and joy. Despite her slushy surroundings, she had never been more comfortable.

She smiled at him and teased, "You're a mess, Reis. So am I." She took handfuls of mud and smeared them over his bare chest, shoulders, and back. "You forgot to tell me you like to play in mud."

"It seems I'm not the only one," he responded, covering her arms and chest with it. "Now, you'll really have to remove that gown; it's ruined, love. But we have a problem; there's only one blanket left."

"Surely your clothes will be dry soon," she retorted playfully.

"Not if I can help it," he jested merrily, kissing the tip of her nose. "Can you believe this, us playing in the rain and mud?"

"And dressed like this?" she added laughingly.

"Or undressed like this?" he parried devilishly.

"I might be sorry, Reis, but I believe you," she murmured.

Reis's mouth came down on hers, this time passionately. He parted her lips and invaded her mouth. His arms went around her neck and shoulders, lifting her head out of the mire. Almost simultaneously, her arms encircled his steely body. Suddenly the mucky hole seemed sensual and cozy.

His desire mounting, he unwillingly pulled away. "Are you brave enough to wash this off in a chilly stream?" he inquired roguishly.

She laughed and retorted, "Do we have any choice? Any chance there's some soap in that cabin?"

He chuckled and said, "I doubt it. We'll have to make do with just water. At least we can wash each other's back," he teased.

Amanda grinned. This was as wild and wonderful as their first meeting. He had a way of relaxing and enchanting her. She was no longer afraid of him, of herself, or events surrounding them. Reis said he was hers, and that was all that mattered now.

As if reading her thoughts, he chuckled and noted, "We do have a crazy way of bewitching each other, don't we? You make me feel so alive, so carefree, Mandy. It's like being a kid again, having fun and doing silly things. You realize we're perfectly suited to each other?" Reis helped her to sit up near him, yet he didn't extract them from the mud.

Amanda glanced down at her condition, then giggled as she curled her legs behind her and looked up into his amused expression. "Evidently, Reis Richardson. Maybe I'm just exhausted from fleeing your persistent chase," she jested, wiping off clumps of mud from his chest and arms. She nestled into his embrace, murmuring, "Since you're so handsome and strong, I suppose my defeat isn't that bad. I yield to your superior strength, my dashing Yankee conqueror. How could I possibly reject a suitor who captures me in such an . . . unusual manner?"

Reis hugged her tightly, then scooped her up in his arms and struggled to free his feet from the engulfing mire. She laughed as they swayed precariously. She taunted playfully, "You did threaten to drop me in the mud, but I didn't think you were serious. From now on, Mister Harrison, I shall have to respect your words."

Chuckles came from deep within that muscular chest. "Let's get you bathed, dried, and warmed. We still have some matters to discuss, Miss Lawrence."

"Such as?" she hinted curiously.

"Such as what will happen with us," he replied, tightening his grip on her as he stepped from the delightful quagmire. He headed for the stream, carrying her effortlessly. He gingerly waded into the rain-swollen stream to an area just above his knees. Suddenly he halted and stiffened, but not from the biting liquid nipping at his bare legs and feet.

"I think we have a problem," he stated nervously, comically, as his soggy blanket, heavy with mud and water, pulled from his lithe body, leaving him stark naked with Amanda clutched in his arms while the capricious covering was swept away by the strong and impish currents.

Chapter Seven

*A*manda burst into uncontrollable giggles.

"It isn't funny, Miss Lawrence. How do you propose I protect our modesty now?"

She thought but a moment before merrily suggesting, "Of course, it serves you right for being so improper in the first place, but I could close my eyes while you sit down or chase your naughty garment."

"Then what?" he pressed in rising humor, relieved that she didn't seem overly concerned or embarrassed by their predicament.

"We can wash off this mud. Then I'll return to the cabin and hide in my blanket," she offered a seemingly simple solution.

"There's only one dry blanket left. What about me?" he wailed.

"Since you're responsible for this episode, you can either use my wet blanket or your slicker. Once you build a fire, you'll be warm enough," she blithely mocked his helpless position.

"How about you use my shirt and I use the blanket?" he hinted.

"But your shirt is wet; I'll freeze," she shrieked. "Surely a man who vows love for a distressed lady can be unselfish and gallant?"

"You wouldn't be cold in my arms," he debated, grinning down at her. "I'll tell you what; let's bathe and then decide how to handle this new business."

Amanda closed her eyes tightly as she suppressed more giggles. He lowered her to the ground and nudged her into the murky water as he sank beneath its protective surface.

Amanda instantly bolted to her feet and squealed as the biting water nipped at her bare flesh. She whirled and stared down at him. "You lied, Harrison; this water is like ice!" Her teeth chattered and she wrapped her hands around her arms and rubbed them frantically, unintentionally shoving her breasts together and causing them to bulge from her low neckline. "Surely you don't expect me to sit down?"

Reis laughed heartily. "It's not so bad once you get used to it. You certainly can't remain a little piglet. That mud will eventually dry and become most scratchy," he argued, beginning to wash the mud off his body with gentle movements. "You know something? With your hair dark with mud, you almost look like Randy."

Amanda stood there indecisively. Reis caught her hand and pulled upon it, encouraging, "Get it over with, love. The water won't get any warmer."

She gritted her teeth and stiffened as she sank into the stream before him, grimacing in discomfort. Before she could begin her own cleansing, Reis tenderly captured an arm and scrubbed it, then the other one. He told her to turn around and he would wash her back, which she did. With a rakish grin, he remarked, "You'd best wash the front, or I might become excited and break my promise."

Amanda shrieked again as she splashed water on her chest time after time until the mud was gone and then did the same with her face. "This water is almost as dirty as us," she complained, trembling. "What about my hair; it's filthy and full of tangles," she fretted.

"Duck under the water and swish it around," he replied.

"That's easy for you to say; this water isn't that cold to you. Let's see if I can make you just as miserable," she threatened, splashing water on his chest and in his face.

"Two can play at that game, love," he taunted.

"Not if I escape first. Are you forgetting you can't get up?" She wickedly reminded him of his state of nudity.

He grinned sensually and huskily murmured, "I can chase you, love; and if you turn around, you've only yourself to scold. Lay your head across my arm and I'll scrub that hair for you," he offered sweetly.

She eyed him suspiciously. "Another trick, my daring rogue?"

"Since I'm to blame for getting you dirty, shouldn't I repair the damage?" he deliberated aloud, winking at her. "Surely you don't expect me to get inflamed while sitting in freezing water?"

"Reis Harrison! You crude brute," she chided his bold remark.

"If you want help with that golden mane, you'd best hurry; I'm getting numb —everywhere," he added wantonly.

Amanda gasped in astonishment, then scolded, "You're awful! But if what you say is true, then I should be perfectly safe."

She moved to sit at his left leg as directed, since he was left-handed. She slowly leaned back over his right arm which was propped on a slightly raised knee to prevent any intimate contact between them. He quickly worked with the cascade of hair which was dangling in the water until it was as mud-free as possible. "That's better. But what about that muck under your gown?" he asked mirthfully.

Their gazes met in amusement, then became serious as they fused. Unable to stop himself, he pulled her to him and kissed her intensely. One kiss led to another until the chilly water swirling around their locked bodies couldn't cool the heat of fiery passion.

"Amanda, love, I want you," he whispered against her lips, his hands moving up and down her arms as if to rub away the chill of her flesh. It was a brief, simple statement, but it said everything.

"I want you too, Reis," she responded feverishly, twisting her lips against his as she pressed closer to his taut frame. "Make love to me," she entreated him, enslaved by unbridled desire. This was the third time he had tempted her to mindless frenzy; this time she yielded.

He lifted her and carried her to the bank where they sank entwined in the wet grass, unable to wait until they reached the cabin to sate their mutual hungers. He removed her gown without removing his mouth from hers, then trailed a damp hand over the curves and planes he had dreamed about since meeting her. Reis tried to caution himself to teach her about love gently and slowly, but she was too eager and inflamed to be mastered, too impassioned to be restrained.

Amanda had wanted him for so long that she couldn't wait a moment longer. Her body was like an ember near a blazing fire, one which would die slowly if it didn't become a part of that potent blaze. As his lips teased her breasts to firm suspense, their taut peaks burned from the warmth of his mouth. Her hands moved over tanned skin which she hadn't dared to touch until now. When she was aquiver and breathless, he tenderly moved over her and gently joined his eager flesh to hers. She arched toward him in wild abandon, lost in the ecstasy of their union. There was no pain—only joy.

His deft hands and lips worked as skillfully and ardently as his throbbing manhood, until he brought her to the pinnacle of exquisite pleasure. Together, they passed through rapture's gates. Blissful serenity engulfed them, their lips still touching as they descended from the heights.

Here in this private hideaway with her body stained with obstinate mud, lying on the saturated earth beside a rain-swollen stream, Amanda had given herself freely to the man who owned her heart.

Reis propped himself on an elbow and gazed down at her, such tenderness emblazoned upon his handsome features, such love shining softly in his eyes. "You all right, love?" he inquired apprehensively.

She smiled, her entire face brightening. "Never better," she vowed, caressing his pleasing jawline. "You?"

"Never better," he happily concurred. "I love you, Amanda Lawrence, more than I could imagine possible. You cast your spell over me one stormy night, and I can never again be whole without you."

She laughed and teased, "Then I suppose it's only natural to prove it on a stormy morning. I love you, Reis Harrison. I've been so lonely and miserable without you," she confessed, her mood a curious blend of shyness and boldness.

"I've never been so afraid in my life as when I nearly lost you. I know it was crazy to kidnap you, but I had to do it. The state you were in—I didn't know what you would do next. I don't want you to be angry with Luke and Randy, but—" He hesitated briefly before confessing their daring ploy. "I don't want any more secrets between us, love. I must finish this mission, my beloved angel. We have a decision to make: do we marry later, or do we marry now in secret?"

She smiled. "I'm greedy and selfish, Reis; I want you as quickly as I can have you. But I'll comply with your orders from Grant."

"I think it would be best for both of us if we find a way to marry soon. I want to make sure you're mine, and it will be easier to spend time together. You'll be happier as my wife, not a mistress."

His meaning was clear. She had surrendered to passion today, but marriage would prevent her from feeling guilty over a pre-planned affair. "You know me too well, Mister Harrison," she teased mirthfully.

"I plan to know you even better. Say, inch by inch?" he murmured, a finger intoxicatingly encircling each nipple in turn. "Your greed is nothing compared to mine, woman," he declared, leaning forward to torment each faint, brown point with his tongue.

"I must need a lesson or two—I thought you said you were numb?"

"A fire such as you ignite could thaw any frozen object," he told her, taking her hand and clasping it around the proof of his claim.

"Then why not share your flames, my dashing Yankee; I'm chilled to the bone," she coaxed, stroking him boldly.

"All I have and am belongs to you, my love. You have but to ask or take what you will," he stated softly and truthfully.

"For now, all I need or want is for us to be one again," she told him shamelessly, her eyes never leaving his penetrating gaze.

His lips covered hers before making torturously slow and sweet love to her. Afterward, they lay together for a time until it began to mist once more. He splashed off in the stream and coaxed her to do the same, then tossed her the gown which he had rinsed for her. Ignoring its iciness, she wiggled into it. Hand in hand, they returned to the cabin.

Soon Reis had a cheery fire going and coffee warming. The aroma filled the small cabin and teased their noses. Amanda sat on a cured cowhide before the fire, clad in Reis's shirt which was nearly dry. Wrapped in the last blanket, Reis poured two cups of coffee and joined her. They didn't talk for a time, simply enjoying each other's nearness and company.

Amanda's voice broke the peaceful silence. "Reis, how do you plan to get me home dressed like this?"

"Like I stole you, in the middle of the night," he teased. When she asked if he had known her housekeeper would be off, he grinned and nodded. "If someone asks why you didn't answer the door, say you were bathing or sleeping, which you were—just somewhere else," he playfully rambled on.

"You mean Weber, don't you?" she asked gravely. "How do you plan to unmask him?" She wondered how she could pretend with Web.

"Just leave that to me. No playing the detective to end this matter sooner. Just be patient and cautious. He's dangerous, Mandy. Just carry on as usual," he instructed for her safety.

"Are you sure? You don't mind if he takes me out, and hugs me or kisses me?" she inquired behind giggles.

"If he lays a finger on you, I'll break it off," he vowed possessively. "Just as soon as I locate a minister out of town, I'll arrange our wedding. You and I can sneak off, get married, then sneak back. You'll be safe as long as Weber doesn't know you're in cahoots with me. That is, if I can't convince you to leave town for a while?"

"It sounds so exciting," she murmured dreamily.

"There's one other thing, Mandy; confide in Miranda. At times, we might need her help to . . . get together secretly. She's worried about you," he added at her coy grin.

"You like Randy, don't you?" she inquired happily.

"Yep. She's a lot like you; and yet she's very different. I think I've discovered a wonderful family for myself," he sighed contentedly.

As they consumed the food which Reis had wisely brought along, he expounded on his mission and Weber's treacherous deceptions. They passed the day talking about their lives and families or discussing their future. Once more they made love, this time on the narrow bunk in the warm cabin. Around eleven that night, Reis couldn't stall the inevitable any longer; it was time to take Amanda home before Friday's dawn exposed their rendezvous.

Snuggled in a blanket in his arms, Amanda was quiet on the return trip. Once inside her home, Reis kissed her good night and cautioned her again about Weber before leaving. To keep Weber from getting suspicious about them, Reis promised to contact her through Lucas, and she was to do the same with him. She was surprised to learn he was staying with her calculating cousin. Under such precarious circumstances, she realized it would make things easier for herself and Reis.

During the day, Amanda managed to avoid Weber by visiting friends. Later, Lucas came over for dinner and a leisurely conversation. When Weber came by around eight, he was vividly displeased to find Lucas there and more displeased when Lucas wouldn't leave them alone. Weber and Lucas exchanged surly jibes, which Amanda pretended not to notice. Soon Weber announced that he had to leave and rose to do so. Lucas smiled and remained seated.

Amanda felt she must see Weber to the door. When he tried to kiss her good night, she turned away, informing him she had the sniffles and he might catch them. In preparation for such an awkward moment, she had been sneezing and sniffling during his visit. Giving Amanda one final, searing glare, Weber left sullenly.

She rejoined Lucas in the sitting room. He grinned and stated, "That was quick thinking, Mandy, pretending to have a cold. Reis will be delighted when I tell him," he teased fondly. "Did you see the funny look on Web's face when you mentioned a possible visit to Morning Star? Where did you tell him Randy is?" It was apparent that Lucas was thoroughly enjoying this charade.

They both laughed. "Web thinks Randy is visiting friends in Boston. Once she returns and we tell her everything, we can all relax. I did find it odd that Web didn't say anything when I mentioned the plantation. I wonder when he's planning to use that little ruse."

"When I'm not around to make trouble," Lucas declared.

"How could he keep it a secret from you? Surely he knows I would mention such a shocking matter to you during one of our visits," she reasoned. "Why alter the books, then not use them?"

"I'm leaving soon, remember?" he responded, not venturing a speculation on her last question. Who could understand Web Richardson!

"But Reis is staying with you," she replied in bewilderment.

"I've told him he can use my place as long as he wishes. I have to leave within two weeks. Until then, I can be your messenger."

"Are you really going to invite Randy to go along?" she fretted.

"Why not? That would give you and Reis lots of privacy," he hinted roguishly. "He told me you two are getting married soon. Just be careful, Mandy. He's right; Weber is a devil. You leave the investigation to Reis, you hear me?"

Amanda grinned and jested, "Yes, cuz; I'll be good."

"I know you, Amanda Lawrence. Don't go sneaking around just to help Reis. You could stumble onto something which might endanger his life as well as your own. I hope he works fast and hard; you can't tell Web you have a cold for very long," he stated between chuckles.

"I would ask you to come over every night, but that would look suspicious. Besides, he would only start visiting during the day. Oh, Luke, how will I ever carry this off?" she worried aloud. Just the thought of Weber touching or kissing her was repulsive.

He mockingly lessened her tension. "Do these ears deceive me? Is Amanda Lawrence doubting her feminine wiles? You'll be great. You have Reis, so now I can stop worrying about leaving. I'll be back before winter." With comical animation, he suggested, "There is one thing you can do to roughen the waters with Weber; pick an argument with him. Then while you're pouting and reconsidering his proposal, that will give you and Reis extra time."

Amanda brightened in elation. "Over what?"

"How about over Randy?" he proposed astonishingly, then explained himself.

"You really think he has a fever for her?" she questioned, alarmed and surprised that she hadn't noticed such undercurrents.

When Lucas expounded on his observations and opinions, Amanda concurred. "Damn, I must be blind! He hasn't bothered her, has he? That explains why she's always so tense and remote when he's around. Why didn't she tell me, Luke?"

"Because you're always so defensive of him. Like me, she was probably afraid you would think she was only trying to separate you two. Don't forget, she doesn't know why you felt you must marry him. Nothing against you, my lovely cousin, but he merely wants a Lawrence. You fit his plans better than Randy, but he would settle for her. I bet Randy will be delighted to unmask that scum. And after your violent quarrel, it will seem natural for Randy to go away with me. Ah, yes, it's ingenious," he bragged, not realizing the repercussions of such a reckless charade.

"I must confess, I agree, Luke," she complimented him. "Then by the time you and Randy return, Reis and I will be settled down. You will take good care of her?"

"If she tags along. I haven't asked her yet. In fact, she doesn't know anything about this trip. I was saving the news as a surprise. I'm not sure how I landed this enviable assignment, but I'm taking it before they change their minds. Fact is, now that I've heard their proposal, I think I would even go at my own expense." Lucas didn't tell Amanda that taking her sister along with him would solve another problem: it would keep Weber from getting rid of Amanda and pursuing Miranda, now that Reis was in the picture.

"I know her, Luke; she would give anything to go to the Dakota Territory. Why shouldn't she have her dream? I am getting mine," she announced gleefully, dancing around the room.

"I'll drop around tomorrow afternoon with a note from Reis," he tempted her. "Would you like to send him a message tonight? Your housekeeper won't be off again until Sunday. Can you wait another day?"

Amanda hastily wrote three words on a page: "I love you." When Lucas accepted the missive and departed, she sighed restlessly as she headed for bed. Last night she had been with Reis; tonight, she must be content to dream of him. Two days ago, she had been utterly miserable; today, her heart sang with ecstasy.

Fortunately, Weber didn't come by to see her Saturday. Unbeknown to her, he was biding his time until the interfering Lucas Reardon left town, just as he had arranged. It was late in the day before Weber learned that Reis Harrison was not only still around but was living with that sly cousin of Amanda's. He would do some checking around before confronting her on Sunday afternoon . . .

Amanda wanted to send a telegram to her sister, encouraging her to hurry home but she dared not for fear of revealing Miranda's location. If Weber was as crafty and deadly as Lucas and Reis believed—which she no longer doubted—surely Weber was watching each of them. She desperately wanted to help solve this mystery but obeyed the wishes of Reis and her cousin. Now that she was acquainted with the facts of the situation, she didn't want to hinder her love's work.

Amanda remained in the house, continuing her illness ruse. She couldn't help but be disappointed, even slightly miffed, when Reis neither sent her a message nor made a stealthy visit on either day. This solitary game was becoming boring.

The sun came out bright and warm on Sunday morning. Amanda wanted to go outside, to go riding or picnicking with Reis. She warned herself to be patient and careful until Miranda's presence supplied a good reason to quarrel with Weber.

Oddly, Lucas didn't visit on Saturday or Sunday; Amanda worried over his absence. She fretted over Reis's behavior when he had made no contact with her since his daring escapade of Thursday. If he were as lonely and anxious as she was, he would have found a way to see her, or at least send word by Lucas! After their intimacy, did he think he could take her for granted? Did he think he owed her no explanation?

By late afternoon, she was tense and moody. She had spent the night listening for Reis's footsteps. Her hair was mussed, her face pale, and her cheeks flushed when Weber called. Thankfully, her appearance and mood added credence to her charade.

When she opened the door, Weber verbally assailed her before she could speak. "What in hell's name is going on, Amanda?" he snarled.

She looked at him in bewilderment. Lines of fury etched his forehead, and his teeth were clenched tightly. His dark eyes were cold, their gaze intimidating and accusatory. "I beg your pardon?" she murmured curiously.

"Why is that Yankee staying with your bloody cousin?" he snapped, his body stiff with rage.

"What Yankee, Web? Luke lives alone," she argued innocently.

"Reis Harrison!" he thundered, refusing to calm down and speak politely.

"Reis Harrison?" she echoed. "But you told me he had left town. Why would he be at Luke's? Did you decide to do business with him?" she asked, hoping her questions sounded logical.

"You haven't seen Harrison in the last few days?" he demanded.

"Certainly not!" she threw at him as if insulted by his tone. Actually, she was angry that it was the truth. "As for Luke, he was here the same night you were. I haven't seen him since then. Why are you attacking me like this? You know I haven't been well," she scolded him petulantly.

"When is Lucas leaving for Dakota?" Web inquired coldly.

"How did you know he was? He only told me Friday night; that's why he came over. He said it was a secret," she stated beguilingly.

"Is that Yankee going with him?" Weber went on, ignoring her question.

Puzzlement filled her eyes. "Why would they travel together? And how would I know such things? Your hateful questions are confusing," she informed him brusquely. "Luke isn't in the habit of explaining himself to me or anyone. If you don't mind, I need to go lie down again; I'm weak and shaky," she stated peevishly.

"Have you seen a doctor?" He suddenly became solicitous, actually smiling at her. Right before her eyes, he reversed his mood.

"If I'm not feeling better by tomorrow, I plan to see Doctor Ramsey. What I need is rest and quiet," she stated pointedly.

He grinned in false remorse. "I'm sorry, my dear. I shouldn't take my anger out on you."

"No, you shouldn't," she frostily concurred. "You know something? I see new facets to you each week. Sometimes I don't think I know you at all, Weber, and that troubles me. You are far too bossy at times. If you behave in this hateful way with a woman you're wooing, I wonder how you would treat a wife."

Weber tensed, then forced himself to relax. He chuckled and wheedled, "That's not true, my sweet. Besides, you'll have plenty of time to know me better once we're married. Have you made a decision yet?"

"How can I make any decisions when I feel terrible and you act so mean?" she replied, leaning against the door.

"You've had lots of time and privacy," he insisted.

"Do you realize how much has happened to me these past few months? I need time to adjust, Weber. If that seems selfish to you, then I'm sorry," she purred sarcastically.

"When is Miranda coming home? You need someone to take care of you," he remarked, tempering his vexation with feigned worry.

"She planned to be away for a week, but she could stay longer. I've been so irritable lately that I'm awful to be around. And you make it worse with your meanness. Once I feel better and get things settled with the business, I'll be fine."

"What about the business?" he pressed curiously.

"You don't mind handling it a while longer, do you? I'm just not ready to deal with it. I can't decide whether to sell it or run it." She sighed dramatically as if utterly fatigued.

"Don't worry your pretty head, my sweet. I'll take care of everything for you. Just concentrate on getting well, and on me," he added, cuffing her chin, then bid her farewell.

That night Amanda couldn't get to sleep. It was after midnight when she stood before her bedroom window looking out over the garden. Moonlight filtered through the gauzy drapes and outlined her body against them. But for stirrings and singing of nocturnal insects and birds, all was quiet and serene.

Suddenly a mellow voice teased from behind her, "How can you daydream at night, my love? A sick lady should be in bed."

She whirled, his name escaping her lips as she rushed into his beckoning arms and hugged him tightly. "It's about time you remembered I'm alive," she scolded Reis playfully. "Besides, I dream of you all the time. Where have you been? What's happening out there?"

"One question at a time, love. We've got to be more careful than I imagined. Richardson's having your house watched and he's having me and Luke followed. I had a time losing my shadow and sneaking in here. I found a minister not far away who can marry us, but getting to him in secret will be difficult. I sent Miranda a telegram; she should be coming home tomorrow. One thing that'll help distract Weber is a trip I need to take."

"A trip?" she wailed apprehensively. "Where? Why?"

"I have to follow the shipment that's leaving at dawn Wednesday. I'm staying hidden until then. Hopefully Weber will think I'm gone for good and lower his guard. When I get back, we'll see that minister first thing. You haven't changed your mind?" he asked.

"Never," she happily responded. "Do you have to leave?"

"It will speed up solving this case, and we both want that."

"But I'll be alone here, Reis. Luke is taking Randy with him," she said frantically.

"But you can refuse to see Weber for a long time after Randy finishes with him. Luke told me your little scheme. What could make a woman more angry than her suitor getting too friendly with her sister? If Luke's right about Weber, it'll work. Perfect timing is the key, love. Just don't make him think you're spurning him for keeps. I don't want him to think you're contriving an excuse to be rid of him. If Randy leaves with Luke, Weber will know she's out of his reach. He'll then work on regaining your trust and earning forgiveness. I've also come up with another scheme to confuse him. In your state of spiteful rage, you can pretend to sell your firm to someone else."

"Sell the firm?" she questioned, listening intently.

"I can have a friend of mine, a northern shipper, come down and pretend to purchase your company. You can claim you wanted to be rid of the company and its problems. Say you want to live on the plantation or in Washington. Once Weber thinks all's lost to him, he would be foolish to retaliate against you. He wouldn't be able to carry on any of his deceptions because you'll know the true facts. We'll have to wait to use this ploy until he leaves town and we can work out any tangles. The main thing is to protect the woman I love."

"Say it again," she coaxed warmly.

"I love you, Mandy. Soon you'll be mine forever," he vowed confidently, drawing her into the circle of his embrace.

Amanda's hands flattened against his hard chest, then traveled up his muscled shoulders. She snuggled close to him, wantonly rubbing her body against his without realizing how deeply she was arousing both of them. Her fingers pushed aside his shirt so she could place kisses near his heart, then drifted upward to tease at his collarbone. Her arms went around his waist and she pulled him tightly to her.

Reis was trapped in a heady conflict of wanting to remain perfectly still to enjoy this blissful torment and of needing to urgently lay siege to her body and make savagely sweet love to her. Her nearness, touch, and smell drove him wild, and her stimulating actions sent him beyond control. Yet, her movements revealed her inexperience. He flamed with passion just imagining how it would be months from now when her skills were honed and her modesty discarded.

He glanced down at her, eyes dark with desire. "If you have any intention of our honeymoon coming after our wedding, you'd best halt your tempting game, love. I feel like steel in a forging furnace."

Amanda bravely met his seeking gaze and smiled. "If you planned to deny me anything, then you shouldn't have come tonight when I'm weak from illness and cannot think clearly. Surely love is the best medicine for what ails me?" she hinted vividly.

She didn't protest when he removed her gown, or when he eased out of his garments. He lifted her and carried her to the bed. They stretched out, their naked bodies touching from head to foot. When she started to roll toward him, he gently caught her shoulder and pressed her to her back. Bending forward, he warmed the cool peaks on her chest with a moist and fiery tongue.

His lips played upward until they fastened on hers. His kisses tantalized her, sending her soaring above a high mountain of passion. Her head spun madly as his hands danced over her flesh, embracing each breast and enticing each point to readiness. One hand started a titillating journey down her tingling body. It wandered over a flat stomach which tightened with anticipation, then roved over nicely rounded hips to end its thrilling trek in a tawny forest which pleaded for his intrusion. There, he explored gently and leisurely until she was trembling with urgent need.

Passions soared; hearts and bodies united. The sensations which he inspired were achingly blissful. He slipped between creamy thighs which entreated his invasion. With tenderness and caution, he eased into a moist paradise that was his for the taking. He wanted her so much that he feared his control would be lost if he didn't concentrate fiercely on retaining it.

They soared together, higher and higher, until Amanda reached ecstasy's summit. The moment Reis was certain of her rapture, he too surrendered to the all-consuming pleasure.

Rolling to his side, he held her in his arms. Curled against his lithe frame, she lay her cheek against his steadily slowing heart. He cast a possessive leg and arm over her contented body, then trailed his fingers up and down her back. Together they savored this dreamy time so devoid of thoughts or cares.

Amanda closed her eyes and inhaled softly. Reis smiled into the darkness and briefly tightened his embrace. Whatever lay in their paths, they had each other and a powerful love. He felt so lucky to have found this special woman and to have won her heart. Amanda sighed again, thinking how glad she was that she had found love and passion with this extraordinary man.

Chapter Eight

*A*manda was relaxing in a steamy bath Monday morning when her sister burst into the private closet in a flurry of surprise and delight. For the first time in her life, Amanda revealed modesty at being naked before her own sister. Miranda giggled in amusement when Amanda shrieked and tried to cover her ample bosom with delicate hands. Her shyness vanished quickly in the elation of Miranda's return. "You're home!" she declared happily.

"Whatever are you doing bathing so late, Amanda Lawrence? It's almost noon," she teased. "I could hardly wait to get here. You'll never believe what I've learned," she hinted eagerly. "Hurry and we'll talk. I'll make us some tea and a snack while you get dressed."

Amanda finally got a word between her sister's commands and queries. "I'm so glad you're back. Just wait until I tell you my news," she further piqued her sister's curiosity. "I'll be down shortly. Send Mrs. Reed on some errand so we can have total privacy," she hastily suggested. "On second thought, give the dear woman the day off."

Within an hour, Amanda and Miranda Lawrence were sitting side-by-side in the parlor, sipping tea and preparing to exchange facts. Miranda opened the conversation. "Tell me about you and Reis."

"First, there's something I must explain before I start on Reis, for I doubt I would stop any time soon," she mirthfully confessed, bringing a smile to Miranda's face. "Oh, my, where to begin?" she muttered.

"What's been going on here, Mandy?" Miranda interrupted. "That telegram from Reis was perplexing. He said I was to hurry home but to tell everyone I had been visiting friends in Boston. What did he mean: 'W. is dangerous. A. is mine now. L. is helping me. All being watched. Can't meet you at train. Be careful'?"

While Miranda listened with disbelief and horror, Amanda revealed all the events which had taken place. She explained how she had been cunningly deceived by Weber and why she had been acting so terrible lately. She told about Reis's mission for the President and his charges against Weber. Then Miranda told her sister what she had discovered at Morning Star. They discussed this perilous situation, analyzing and speculating about Weber's motives and actions.

"What about you and Reis?" Miranda pressed once more.

Unwilling to keep secrets from her sister, Amanda exposed Reis's kidnapping ploy and its results. Miranda was thrilled by their imminent wedding plans. Clearly they loved each other, and she vowed to do all she could to help and protect them and to thwart Weber's evil plots.

"Don't be so hasty to make such rash promises," Amanda teased her, then told Miranda of Lucas's daring idea to use jealousy between the sisters to inhibit Weber's amorous demands and to foil his wicked schemes.

As Miranda pondered the ruse, Amanda warned, "If Weber discovers we're working against him, he'll be dangerous, Randy."

"More so than he is now?" Miranda debated. "Nothing would please me more than to unmask that vile devil. I think it'll work," she stated smugly, then told her sister how and why . . .

"You're a genius, Randy," she declared, hugging her sister with love and appreciation.

"There's only one thing more, Mandy. Once I encourage Weber, we'll have to find a way to protect me from him," she ventured, half in jest and half in seriousness.

"That's simple," Amanda announced. "But I'd rather let Luke give you his surprise. He's coming over this afternoon. After you and I finish with Weber tonight, we'll both be free and safe," she alleged mysteriously, grinning at her sister.

"What does Luke have to do with this? What surprise?" she eagerly persisted.

Amanda smiled mischievously and refused to say more. "You think we can pull off this adventure?" she inquired softly.

"Positively, and it will be fun," Miranda concluded gleefully. "Now, let's get this stimulating charade planned."

Miranda went upstairs to unpack from her journey. When Amanda came to tell her Lucas had arrived, Miranda was standing before a long mirror, staring dreamily at her reflection. Amanda knew where her sister's thoughts were and smiled in resignation. Lucas was right; Miranda needed to follow her dream and to settle it.

Miranda was wearing a dress of their mother's, an exquisitely beaded buckskin dress which had been made from an albino deer. The dress had been given to Marie Lawrence by her father, Sun Cloud, chief of the Oglala Sioux in the Dakota Territory. The dress brought forth images of their mother as a young girl, a Sioux princess named Morning Star who had sacrificed everything to marry a handsome adventurer named Joseph Lawrence.

Miranda turned and looked at her teary-eyed sister. "She was very beautiful. How she must have loved Papa to marry him and move here. It must have pained her deeply to forsake her family and people to accept Papa's. She once told me she could never return home because she had dishonored her people by choosing a white man. Can you imagine how hard it was to change from a carefree Indian maiden to a Southern lady? Papa taught her well, Mandy; no one would have guessed her heritage. She loved Papa and was happy with him. But many nights I found her in the garden staring at the moon, as if wondering about her family and all she'd lost. Perhaps she sensed danger closing in; perhaps that's why she wanted to go home one last time. Now it's too late. She's gone, and her family doesn't know. Do you suppose grandfather could sense her . . . death?"

"I don't know, Randy. In that dress with your hair braided, you look like she did the last time I saw her wearing it. Where did you find it? Why put it on and torment yourself?" she inquired sadly.

"It was at Morning Star. I went through many of their things, but I didn't move or discard an item. I was going to pack their belongings and store them in the attic, but something stopped me. It was the strangest feeling, Mandy, like they are still alive somewhere. When I found this dress and headband, I could almost hear Mama telling me to take them with me. She was whispering so softly that I couldn't make out where I should take them."

Amanda paled slightly and trembled. "After you talk with Luke, Randy, perhaps you'll understand Mama's message. Yes, it was meant to be," she told herself aloud.

Miranda gazed at her. "What are you talking about, Mandy?"

"Let Luke explain. But I'll agree with your decision."

"What decision? Explain what?" Miranda questioned, baffled.

"A quest for your destiny, dear sister. You must find yours as I've found mine with Reis. Come and listen to Luke," she coaxed, taking Miranda's hand and pulling her downstairs.

When they entered the sitting room, Lucas jumped to his feet and gaped at Miranda. "My God, Randy, you look just like Aunt Marie!" he cried in astonishment. "I knew you favored her, but not this much. Did you tell her, Mandy?"

"No, it's your surprise and her choice. I'll leave you two alone," she stated, closing the door behind her.

It had never been more apparent to Lucas that Amanda had taken after her father in looks and personality, while Miranda was the image of Marie. Marie had gone so far as to teach Miranda the Sioux language and history and customs, inspiring in her daughter a hunger to experience and witness that vanishing way of life. Now, Lucas was in a position to grant his cousin her lifelong fantasy.

"I'm leaving Alexandria Friday, Randy, leaving Virginia and the South," he began slowly, bringing a look of shock to Miranda's face and a staggering jolt to her senses. "I've been given an irresistible assignment, to write an historical account of the exploits of three men: Custer, Sherman, and Sheridan. The publisher is paying my expenses and a salary of ten thousand dollars. I've accepted the deal."

"You're writing the story of three Yankee destroyers? Why?"

"Because I want the truth published for once, for all time," he declared earnestly, witnessing her distress which would be shortlived.

"But where are you going? What about me and Mandy?"

"All three men are on duty in the same western area, the Dakota Territory. Would you come along as my assistant?" He dropped his news without warning. "I've discussed this with Mandy. She was reluctant at first; now she thinks it's a good idea. She knows what it would mean to you, and this is the perfect opportunity—in many ways," he added, winking at her. "After your charade with Weber, it will get you out of his path with a logical excuse. You and Mandy can have a big quarrel and you can leave home. It should take about three months; then we'll come home to find Weber arrested."

Miranda stood up and paced the room as this information was digested. "But what about Mandy, Luke? We can't leave her alone here with that demon," she fretted nervously. "Reis is leaving too."

"Reis won't be gone but a week or ten days. By the time we leave, she'll have plenty of excuses to refuse his attentions, to play the injured female, to stall for time until Reis can arrest him. In fact, it will be easier for her to fool Web if you're gone. So what do you say?" he asked.

"You aren't teasing me?" she probed before accepting. He shook his head, smiling at her. "When do we leave?"

"Friday, so get packed and ready. I'll get Mandy so we can tell her our plans." When Lucas left the room, Miranda danced around the furniture, humming and dreaming until they returned to join her.

Miranda and Amanda talked and planned far into the night. After two months of anguish, their lives were changing drastically and happily. Knowing that Reis was aware of Miranda's return, Amanda knew he would not make a nocturnal call on her tonight. Not since they were twelve had the twins curled up in the same bed and chatted the night away until slumber captured them.

To aid their plans, the twins told Alice Reed she could be off until Friday. They told her to rest, to work at her home, and to spend time with her husband. The older woman was appreciative of their generosity, but the girls had always been kind and sweet to her. Mrs. Thomas Reed left their home praying that the bright Miranda could talk some sense into her confused sister, for she felt Amanda had to be foolish to marry that rake, Weber Richardson. Many times lately Alice had bitten her tongue to keep it from running loose to her young mistress. If only Amanda learned a few of the earcurling tales about that cruel and malicious man, she would flee in terror!

At four o'clock, Lucas delivered a huge crate to the back door and told Miranda to answer the front door and seat the man standing there in the parlor. Miranda did as he instructed, studying the suit-clad gentleman inquisitively. He smiled warmly but didn't state his business. Miranda left him to question Lucas's weird behavior.

Lucas was forcing open the crate when she returned to his side. He chuckled as he told her to inform Miss Amanda Lawrence that the minister and her sweetheart were here and preparing for their marriage! Speechless, Miranda watched as Reis Harrison stepped from the crate and dusted off his clothes. "Fetch the bride, cousin," Luke commanded, filling the room with hearty laughter.

Miranda raced upstairs. "Mandy, you're not going to believe this, but you're getting married in a few minutes. Reis, Luke, and the minister are waiting for you downstairs."

"What—what did you say?" she stammered.

Miranda laughingly revealed the crafty preparations going on downstairs. "Well? Do you want to become Mrs. Reis Harrison today?"

"But I don't have a wedding gown! Look at me," she panted. "I'm a mess. I can't get married like this. What will people say?"

"Nothing, dear sister; it's a secret ceremony, remember? How about that azure-blue satin gown? I'll get it while you undress."

"How do I look?" Amanda inquired nervously when she was finished dressing. Miranda laid aside the hairbrush and hugged her tightly.

When they entered the parlor together, Reis's blue eyes were for Amanda alone. A look of pride and love flamed upon his handsome face, bringing a flush of passion and pleasure to his cheeks. He looked so elegant in his tailored, wine-colored garments. Amanda's heart fluttered wildly as she stared at him. Never had he looked more handsome.

Her gown rustled softly as she walked into his embrace. "I take it your answer is yes?" he teased her.

"You might have given me some warning, Mister Harrison. I didn't think this ceremony would be such a deep, dark secret," she replied merrily.

"It is," he casually responded. "During the night, the groom can sneak out and none will be the wiser. As for the Reverend Simons here, he knows of our dilemma and will protect our secrets. He is also a doctor and you're supposedly ill; so he has kindly visited his patient today. I'm afraid I couldn't leave on that trip until you were mine, love," he confessed roguishly. "Well?"

"What are we waiting for, my love?" she teased.

With Miranda beside her sister and Lucas beside Reis as witnesses, Reis Harrison and Amanda Lawrence became husband and wife within ten minutes on a lovely Tuesday in mid-May of 1873. The documents were signed and given to Amanda for safekeeping. After Simons's departure, a celebration began.

Lucas teased the couple, "I would take Randy out for the evening, but that would look strange to our observer. After all, if Amanda's sick in bed, she shouldn't be left alone."

Miranda giggled as she watched her sister blush from hairline to the bodice of her gown. Although Amanda hadn't confessed the prior intimacy between her and her love, Miranda sensed it was there. But Lucas was right. She couldn't leave the house this evening.

The four drank champagne which Lucas had thoughtfully furnished for this joyous occasion. Miranda said, "I'm afraid the best Luke and I can do for you two is for him to leave and for me to get lost in my room. You can have dinner and . . . talk privately. I do have to pack."

Neither Amanda nor Reis protested Miranda's suggestion. Lucas congratulated them again, shaking Reis's hand and hugging Amanda. He told Miranda he would come by tomorrow afternoon to finalize their departure plans. Just before opening the door, an outside sound halted his action. He cautiously peered through a slit in the curtains near the doorway. He stiffened as he watched Weber get out of his carriage and unlatch the gate to head up the long walkway.

He rushed into the parlor and warned Reis and Amanda to flee to her bedroom. Lucas and Miranda quickly concealed the evidence of their party, then she rushed to her own room. Lucas abruptly opened the door just as Weber raised his hand to knock, startling him.

"What the hell!" he shouted, glaring at Lucas.

"What are you doing here?" Lucas asked in vivid annoyance.

"Get out of my way, Reardon. I'm here to see my fiancée," he boldly announced, ready to brush past Lucas.

"Hold on, Richardson. The doctor just left. Amanda's in bed. You can't disturb her today," he informed the surly man, amusing himself by telling the truth in such a beguiling manner.

The man whom his spy, Jim, had reported seeing entering and leaving was a doctor? "How is she feeling?" Weber asked, pretending to calm down at the distressing news.

"How do you think since the doctor had to visit?" Lucas scoffed, implying she was very ill.

"Where's Miranda?" Weber inquired, eager to take advantage of Amanda's indisposition to have a pleasant reunion with her sister.

"She's upstairs. Where else would she be?" he sneered sarcastically. "I was just leaving. This isn't a place for visitors today."

"If you don't mind, I'd like Amanda to know I came by," Weber snapped at the infuriating man who was provoking him.

"Wait here," Lucas ordered tersely then went to the base of the steps and called out for Miranda. When she leaned over the railing and responded, he passed along Weber's message, then told her good-by. At the door, he insisted that Weber leave with him.

Convinced of Amanda's illness, Weber left hurriedly. He chided himself for being so skeptical of Amanda, since she really wasn't smart enough to deceive him. But he had feared the stranger was a messenger from that devious and calculating Reis Harrison. At least his foe hadn't made any attempt to get to Amanda! And Lucas was leaving this week.

As Weber drove away in his carriage, he congratulated himself for his cunning and wits. He admitted that Lucas was a good writer, perfect to do the exposé on his despised enemies, the exposé he was supporting financially. But it was a stroke of genius to use that mutual dream to be rid of him! Weber wasn't sure if he was mistaken about Reis's purpose for being in Alexandria, but it wouldn't matter soon. He had picked up hints around the docks that Harrison was leaving town this very day. Weber conceitedly believed that nobody was as smart as he was, for he had covered his tracks skillfully. Before anyone was the wiser, Amanda and her properties would be in his control.

Amanda Lawrence, he sneered to himself, was one bag of trouble, perhaps more than she was worth. But Amanda had things he wanted, needed. It would be a pleasure to conquer that haughty bitch. She would pay for stalling him for two months. He would take and use everything she possessed, including her delicious body. Whe he tired of her, he would arrange a neat accident. Then perhaps he would have a taste of sweet Miranda . . . Miranda . . . yes, she would be vulnerable and pliable with Amanda and Lucas out of the way. She was mysterious and exotic, but so wary and timid. Doubtlessly she possessed more fiery passion in one finger than the arrogant Amanda had in her entire body! The idea of dining greedily on Amanda's treats, then feasting ravenously on Miranda's was wildly intoxicating. It was too bad he couldn't have both at once! Both were beautiful and different. How wickedly erotic to savor two ravishing women. Weber had no way of knowing that the wily twins would use his wanton lust against him . . .

That night, Miranda awakened several times to the sound of soft laughter from her sister's room. How she longed to find a love such as her lucky sister had discovered. But Amanda and Reis's relationship was special, more than physical. The looks which had passed between them almost made her envious. How sad to never experience such wonderful and wild feelings. No one deserved such happiness more than Amanda.

Each time Amanda couldn't suppress her joyful laughter, Reis would cover her lips with his to muffle it, then mischievously seek another sensitive or ticklish spot. Their first union had been swift and savage, their passions starving to be fed. Later, they had made love slowly and tenderly, savoring each touch and movement. But, inevitably, the new day signaled its approach.

"I'll return as quickly as I can, my love," Reis promised between kisses and playful fondles.

"Just be careful, Reis," she urged anxiously.

"You, too," he murmured in her ear before initiating one last joining of their bodies and spirits.

At the back door, Amanda hugged him a final time and vowed, "I do love you something fierce, Mister Harrison, you sly Yankee. If you don't come back safe and sound, you'll answer to me."

Reis trapped her slender and shapely frame next to his hard and smooth body. "If I don't find you safe and sound upon my return home, Mrs. Harrison, you shall do more than answer to me. I love you, woman."

With a parting kiss, they released each other. Reis grinned and winked, then slipped into the gloomy, predawn light. Amanda sighed heavily then returned to her room to sleep until nine.

All morning the twins anticipated and plotted Weber's downfall. According to Weber's habits, they felt he would appear in the afternoon or early evening. Just in case Weber varied his schedule, the girls had an alternative plan.

While they ate a midday snack, Amanda and her sister talked about Reis. Neither mentioned that Reis had slipped out before dawn to catch a ship which was leaving with the morning tide carrying cargo which should unravel Web's evil operation. Nor did the twins discuss Miranda's and Lucas's impending trek west. But both were very much aware of the fleeting time before Friday morning. They had decided to pack Miranda's clothes and possessions for the summer-long journey on Thursday. Lucas came over around three to play his part in their reckless scheme.

If any male besides Lucas had been present, Miranda would have been crimson-faced with embarrassment at the sensual kimono she was wearing. Her courage would be greatly tested when it was Weber standing in this room alone with her! But these trying times called for daring measures. The silky garment in sultry red had two daring slits—one from throat to waist and one from hem to thigh—and provocatively enhanced Miranda's exotic aura. The appealing garment had been sent to Joe Lawrence from Japan by a mischievous friend who was a retired sea captain as a gift for his wife.

Suddenly at four, Lucas warned, "Get ready, cousins; he just arrived. Good luck!" he stated quickly before rushing out, leaving the door ajar as planned. Halfway down the walkway, he halted Weber to exchange taunts and to allow the girls time to settle their nerves.

When Weber approached the front door, he didn't knock when he found it unlocked. He grinned as he decided to surprise either or both girls; he could always say Lucas let him inside before leaving. He eased the door open, sneaked inside, and cautiously closed it. Hearing muffled voices from the sitting room, he furtively made his way to the half-opened door, flattening himself against the wall to listen.

Miranda had been spying on Weber's movements from the narrow slit between the door hinges. As he made his stealthy way toward the parlor, Miranda signaled her sister to begin their charade, one in which she would speak only the truth. She had to be convincing, or else Weber could come after her!

"Tell me the truth, Randy! That's why you ran off to Boston, isn't it! Did you want to hide and sulk or make some plan to get your way? My own sister . . . How could you be so cruel and wicked?" Amanda shrieked at her, wringing her hands as if nervous. "And at a time like this when I'm at death's door," she added pathetically.

"Stop this foolishness, Mandy. I told you I went to see friends and to give you some privacy to think. I'm sorry if you're ill, but you mustn't be so irritable. Whatever's wrong with you lately?"

"You're saying it's only my imagination?" Amanda sneered sarcastically. "I'm neither blind nor a fool, dear sister. I've seen how you watch him—actually drool over him. Always asking questions about my Web, pretending you don't like him. You ran off because I told you I was going to accept his proposal soon. You want to break us apart, don't you? Look me in the eye, Miranda Lawrence, and swear you aren't hanging around like some vulture waiting for Weber's love for me to die!"

"You shouldn't accuse me of such awful things, Mandy. When have I ever flirted with Web or tried to cause trouble between you two? You shouldn't be marrying him if you don't trust him; and if you do trust him, you wouldn't be insinuating I could win him from you."

"How crafty you are, dear sister. I don't hear you denying my charges, only covering your guilt with wily questions. Weber loves me. He wouldn't even look at another woman if she didn't try to wantonly bewitch him. As soon as I'm looking and feeling better, I shall make plans for us to become affianced," she curtly announced.

"I shan't stay in Alexandria after your wedding. I shall go live at Morning Star," Miranda declared soberly.

Weber almost missed part of the devious conversation as visions of having Amanda here in the townhouse and Miranda there on the plantation filled his head. Soon everything would be in his control, and possibly both women. Now he knew why Miranda was so remote and quiet around him; she was resisting her cravings for him! So, the dark beauty with her tightly controlled wildness burned with desire for him . . .

"That sounds like an excellent idea. Then I won't have to worry about you chasing and tempting Weber after we're married," she panted.

"Mandy, please don't say such things. I meant I would leave you two alone for privacy. You're being irrational. I am not trying to steal Weber from you. It's probably the illness talking. Perhaps I should ask the doctor to come over again."

"I don't need to see the doctor again. I'm just tired. I'm going upstairs and take his vile drug. I don't want to be disturbed; the medicine makes me sleep for hours. If Weber comes over before I'm awake, you had best remember he's mine," Amanda warned frostily.

"Don't you want some soup first? I'll get it for you. I gave Mrs. Reed some time off this week." Her back to the door, Miranda winked at her sister.

"I'll eat later, if I'm hungry. I can't remember if Web told me he was or wasn't coming over tonight at eight. That medicine is playing havoc with my memory," she mumbled absently. "Wake me at seven so I can dress before he arrives."

"I'll see you to your room, Mandy; you're drowsy now. I promise to wake you if Weber comes over," she told her sister.

"I'm not a baby; I can make it," Amanda responded.

Miranda stood in the doorway, watching her sister ascend the stairs and vanish from sight. She returned to the parlor and sipped a French brandy as though she needed it to calm her nerves. Miranda withdrew a flower from a nearby vase and smelled its sweet fragrance, whispering, "If only you knew the truth, Mandy . . ."

From behind her, Weber murmured huskily, "And what is the truth, my beautiful Miranda?"

She whirled and gasped in partially feigned surprise. "Weber? Where did you come from? I didn't hear you knock." Miranda observed the way Weber's dark eyes engulfed her body, especially the bare area on her throat and between her breasts. She tried to calm her anxiety as his respiration increased in speed and volume. If lust could become a tangible object, his would encase her thickly at that moment.

He licked his suddenly dry lips and struggled to conceal her staggering effect on him. His mind was wildly intoxicated by the misconception that she fiercely wanted him as he craved her. "Someone left the door open. You should be more careful, Randy. An intruder could lose his head over a matchless beauty like you."

Miranda flushed a deep red. Weber thought it was from shyness or guilt, but it was from anger. He hadn't even asked about Amanda or her health! While his love lay ill above them, he was trying to beguile her sister! The lecherous rake! Her fury inspired strength and resolve.

"I'm glad to find you home today. I've been wanting to speak to you alone. Isn't it about time we became friends, Randy?" he asked, pulling the flower from her grasp and teasing her bare flesh with it. He watched the astonishment in her eyes as he trailed the flower up her throat and across her lips. "Such pleasures shouldn't belong to a mere flower," he remarked, leaning forward to kiss her.

Miranda tried to twist away, but Weber dropped the flower to embrace her tightly. His lips forced hers apart. When his mouth left hers to wander down her neck, she scolded him, "Weber Richardson! Behave yourself. You're Mandy's beau. She'll be furious if she learns of this."

Weber leaned backward and gazed at her. "You don't care what Mandy thinks.

You want me as much as I want you," he boasted. "Perhaps I've asked the wrong twin to marry me. What do you think?"

Not having expected Weber to work so hastily or boldly, Miranda was stunned. Weber pressed her against the wall, molding his enflamed body against her rigid one. As his mouth covered hers, he ground his hips against her. He moved his chest over hers, almost dislodging the kimono from her shoulders. Miranda didn't respond to Weber, but neither did she urgently battle him as she awaited Amanda's interruption.

When Weber's hands drifted to her bosom, Miranda couldn't wait for Amanda to burst in on them. She shoved his brazen hands from her body and tried to push him away. "You stop this, Weber!" she ordered him brusquely. "How dare you insult me!" Miranda didn't want to scream for help, as that would bring about a drastic change in plans. If he were completely alienated, both girls could become dispensable. She prayed her sister would enter soon.

Weber's gaze was dark with combined passion and anger. He was too enflamed to stop now. After he had possessed her fully, Miranda wouldn't say anything to Luke or Amanda. He wasn't about to let her deny him—now or ever again! Amanda had supplied him with the perfect explanation. She was actually jealous of her sister, mistrusted her, had accused her of chasing him. If Miranda revealed what was about to take place, he would have no trouble convincing Amanda she was lying out of jealousy. He could even tell Amanda that her sister had tried to seduce him while she lay ill upstairs. But it shouldn't be necessary to travel that sacrificial path. He could easily blackmail Miranda into compliance, or sensually enslave her with his magical lips and hands. Once he gave her such exquisite pleasures tonight, she would eagerly be shoving Amanda out of her way; then, he could make Amanda's absence permanent . . . Surely gentle Miranda would be easier to master? Surely exotic Miranda would be more enjoyable in bed? Amanda was a proud and stubborn know-it-all; but Miranda was a thirsty, repressed spirit who wanted to break free, to run wild, to taste life.

Weber seized her around the waist and had her pinned beneath him on the sofa before she could think clearly. His mouth was searing hers, preventing any protests. Miranda was terrified. She couldn't control him! Where was Amanda? What about the timely rescue? It wasn't supposed to go this far! Something was wrong! Something was keeping her away! Surely Amanda wouldn't fail her . . .

Chapter Nine

With a burst of strength borne of fear and desperation, Miranda arched upward and flung Weber to the carpeted floor. She bounded off the sofa and scurried behind it. "If you touch me again, Weber Richardson, I'll scream," she warned him icily. "This isn't any way to behave with your future sister-in-law!"

Weber refused to recognize the fury in her voice. He chuckled and teased, "Come on, Randy, don't play around. We both know you want me," he smugly declared, a lewd grin curling his lips into a devilish sneer.

Miranda saw the peril she was in and the evil which filled this man. Suddenly, she was afraid for both herself and her sister. "You're wrong, Weber. I did want to be friends, for Mandy's sake, but not any more. If you truly loved my sister, you wouldn't be trying to seduce me right beneath her nose. If you don't get out and leave me alone, I'll tell Mandy what you tried to do tonight."

Weber crossed his legs and remained sitting on the floor. He laughed mirthfully, intimidatingly, vengefully—the sound chilled her soul. "She wouldn't believe you," he alleged confidently. "Come here, woman."

"No," she refused flatly. "Leave now, and we'll forget this ever happened."

Weber slowly and purposefully got to his feet. He began to stalk her around the sofa, but Miranda eluded him. "Give it up, Randy; you can't get away. From tonight on, you'll belong to me."

Miranda shook her head, chestnut locks flowing about her shoulders. Her tawny eyes were shaded with rising hatred. Her expression was lined with contempt. Yet Weber saw none of it—he was blinded by lust. He bounded over the sofa and captured her in his arms, her back to his chest. Miranda twisted and fought, but Weber's grip tightened. She stomped his booted foot and elbowed his ribs.

She panted, "Let go of me, you brute!" She jerked her head forward to throw it backward with force into his nose and chin.

Anticipating her impending action, he moved his face aside as her head landed against his shoulder. Before she could lift it, her left ear was imprisoned between his teeth and he gritted out this ominous threat: "Move, and I'll rip it off. No woman teases me like you did. Hold still while I see what you have to offer. You owe me, Randy."

Tears of panic and pain sprung to her eyes as she remained motionless, ready to savagely attack him the instant he released her ear. Before his hands could cover her breasts, the door opened and Amanda walked inside. She came to an abrupt stop and glared at them, shock and fury flooding her features. "I heard Weber's voice, so I dressed to come down. What's going on here?" she demanded.

Weber released Miranda and laughed merrily as he went to her sister. Miranda turned hastily to straighten her clothes and hair. "Randy and I were just having some fun, tussling and playing like two kids. I haven't had so much fun in years. Sorry if we disturbed you, my sweet. We're going to be good friends, a happy family, just like you want. How are you feeling? Randy said the doctor came by, but you weren't doing too well. She said you were napping, so I told her not to bother you," he chatted lightly.

Amanda's frosty eyes went from the grinning Weber to the rigid and silent Miranda who was refusing to turn and look at her. Her skeptical gaze wandered over Miranda's disheveled state and then over Weber's mussed hair and clothes. Her eyes focused briefly on Weber's flushed cheeks and still-cloudy gaze. She noted the misplaced cushions, a rumpled throw rug, and the discarded flower. "Something tells me I should be glad I didn't take that medicine and go to bed," she announced sarcastically. "I asked what's going on in here?" she repeated suspiciously, knocking Weber's hand away from her arm.

"I told you, my sweet, we were teasing around," Weber replied.

"It didn't look or sound that way to me," Amanda refuted hotly.

"Don't be silly. You're just tired and feeling poorly. You go back to bed and I'll come by to see you tomorrow," he cajoled.

"Miranda, what's wrong with you?" Amanda persisted.

"I—Nothing, Mandy. Weber and I were just . . . horsing around. Trying to make friends like you asked," she responded, edging noticeable tension and hesitation into her words.

"Dressed like that?" Amanda scoffed.

"Weber came over right after you went upstairs. I'll go change," she murmured contritely.

"Then why didn't you fetch me instead of entertaining him in that cheap attire? As for you, Weber Richardson, you and Randy are too old to be 'teasing' around," she scolded them both in a scathing tone.

"Don't be such a stick-in-the-mud," he retorted in annoyance. How dare she reprimand him like a child!

His reference to mud reminded her of Reis. She eyed Weber intently. He could actually stand here playing the innocent after trying to attack Randy only moments ago! He was worse than she had imagined! "I suppose you two think I'm gullible. I've seen enough passion to recognize its after-effects. Look at you two. Eyes glazed. Mouths red and puffy. Clothes and hair mussed. You both have guilt stamped all over you! How could you do this to me? Especially you, dear sister! Tell me, were you going to make love right here on the floor like rutting animals? Or perhaps sneak up to Randy's room?"

"Amanda!" her sister shrieked in distress. "It isn't like that!"

"She's right, Mandy," Weber injected hastily.

"Be quiet, Weber! How long have you two been scheming behind my back?"

"Don't be ridiculous!" Weber snarled. "Randy and I have never been intimate. I suggest you get off that mind-weakening drug!"

Amanda let her tears flow freely. Weber glanced at Miranda and motioned for her to keep silent. "Randy, why don't you leave us alone so I can explain to Amanda," he suggested softly.

"But . . . ," she started to protest.

Weber had pushed Amanda to the sofa. He caught Miranda's arm and led her to the door, saying, "I'll get her settled down." He winked at Miranda, then grinned conspiratorially. "I'll see you later," he promised, licking his lips and winking at her.

Miranda looked over his shoulder at the superb actress on the sofa. She nodded and left, eager to learn how Weber would extricate himself. She poured a sherry to calm her distraught nerves, then concealed herself behind the archway into the dining room to make certain Weber left after his devious talk with Amanda.

Miranda didn't have to wait long. Soon, the double doors opened and Weber headed for the front exit. After opening it, he cast a longing glance at the stairway before disappearing outside. Miranda rushed to the door and bolted it. She hurried to the parlor.

Amanda looked up and grinned. "Did you lock up?" she asked.

Miranda nodded and sat down. "Well? What did he say? What took you so long to come down? He was about to rip off my clothes! He's more dangerous than we imagined, Mandy. I was terrified."

"I'm sorry, sis. I didn't think he would pounce on you so fast! I thought you two would talk, get cozy, then he would make his play for you. After I was dressed and came down, I couldn't believe what I was hearing. I had a time controlling my temper! I wanted to tear him apart! But it would spoil things. Our plan's in motion and we know what he's really like. Heavens, Randy, I'm glad you're leaving," she blurted out in panic. "His kind of lust is scary. Are you all right?" she inquired worriedly.

"Fine now, but I was petrified," she confessed then revealed what had been between them. "Maybe we got him too worked up; he was all over me before I could think. What did he tell you?"

Amanda laughed. "He tried to cajole me and prove I was deluding myself. He wanted me to feel remorse for my suspicions. He told me how much my mistrust pained him. He wanted to convince me I was acting out of jealousy. He even scolded me for embarrassing you two. He said I should be ashamed of myself for being so ugly to you. What enormous gall and ego!"

"He just implied you were mistaken? He didn't try to insinuate I had tempted him?" Miranda asked in surprise.

"I have a feeling he'll use that ploy when he sees I didn't fall for his charm and lies. The moment you're gone, he'll fall at my feet and beg forgiveness. He'll blame you for everything. If it weren't so grave, it would be hilarious. You know what truly alarms me? If this weren't a ruse, he could take advantage of both of us," she speculated.

Miranda hugged her sister affectionately. "No, Mandy, you would never believe me capable of such betrayal. But you're right; I can't imagine trying to explain tonight if it truly took place. It's so incredible; he would have ravished me right here!"

"Make sure you avoid him until you leave," she warned.

"What about you, Mandy? Luke and I will be gone in less than two days. And Reis won't be back until the end of next week. I'm afraid for you. Weber's so strong and persistent when he's aroused. What if he tries to . . . seduce you?" Miranda fretted anxiously.

"I can handle Web's passions. It's you I'm worried about. He finds you more desirable than we realized. He might go after you and Luke. He could hurt Luke to force you to come home! I feel so duped. It's you he wants, not me. He only settled for me because he couldn't get to you. I could kill him!"

"Don't say such things, Mandy. It isn't me or you he wants; it's all we own. He just wants to enjoy us while he's stealing everything we have. I'm not sure if he's crazy or just greedy and desperate. Maybe I should stay here and help you stop him."

"No, you must go with Luke. We'd both be in peril if you remained here. If Weber believes he could have you and put me out of the way . . ." She faltered at that staggering reality and shuddered. She prayed Reis would return soon. This drama wasn't so simple; it was petrifying. She instantly berated her cowardice, reminding herself she was smart enough to outwit and foil Weber.

"Then I'll persuade him I despise him before I leave. He'll be convinced you're his only hope for success," Miranda vowed with fierce determination. "I know!" she shrieked in elation. "I'll catch the train tomorrow above Alexandria. Luke can leave from here Friday, then join me in Baltimore. That's where we take the train to St. Louis. You can tell everyone I left for Charleston for the summer. That should throw him off our path. Even if he searches for me, he'll come up empty-handed, except for you."

"That should work," Amanda concurred. "If he goes after you, that will supply me with another excuse to rebuff him. He won't risk hurting me until he's positive he can have you. I'll ask Mrs. Reed to stay over the weekend. Then, next week, I just won't open the door unless she's here to protect me."

"Perfect. When Reis gets back, you drop this game. If you can't announce your marriage, then go to his home like he suggested. Or go visit friends where you'll be safe. You can always tell Weber that I exposed his attempted assault. Or, better still, that I confessed to his forcing me to carry on a secret affair. I was so humiliated by your discovery of our torrid rendezvous that I ran away," she jested. "That should give him plenty to fret over! I can see it now; ailing Amanda trying to decide who's honest and what's the truth."

They joined in nervous laughter. "I think I'll wait to see how he reacts to your absence. He might just ignore tonight. Naturally I won't let him. I shall play the offended, betrayed maiden," she stated in a thick Southern drawl. "I shall waver back and forth, tormented by doubts, harassed by suspicions."

"Just promise me you'll be careful," Miranda entreated.

"We shall both be wary and alert," Amanda concluded.

When Lucas came over the following morning, he found the girls packing frantically. They quickly related the events of the night before. Lucas was furious; he wanted to beat Weber senseless. The twins had a difficult time pacifying him, telling him to be satisfied that his contempt and hatred had been justified. They had to be content with the knowledge Weber would eventually get his due.

They went over their new scheme to get Miranda away before Weber realized she was gone. "We need you to find some way to lure that guard from his post for an hour," Amanda said. "I can take Randy and her luggage to the station outside town. When you catch the train to Baltimore tomorrow, everyone will see you leave alone. After disguising myself as Miranda, I can purchase a ticket to Charleston, board the train, then sneak off and come home."

"That sounds very clever," he complimented them. "Now, all we have to do is pull it off. Let's see . . ." He lapsed into deep thought, then grinned as an idea came to mind. "I can disguise myself as a widow, sneak up on the guard, club and rob him, and escape. Old Weber won't think we had anything to do with the daring robbery of a spy we didn't know existed. While the devil is out cold, you two can sneak out with my help. Considering the train schedule, we have to be ready to act at two. Think we can make it?"

Amanda continued to pack Miranda's possessions while her sister took a carriage to the bank just before noon. It was Weber's custom to eat lunch at noon in the Telford Inn, near the bank. After withdrawing money for her trip, Miranda lingered near the doorway until she saw Weber round the corner to head her way. She gritted her teeth, inhaled and exhaled slowly, then stepped outside into the bright sunlight.

Weber saw her immediately and hurried to intercept her. "And whom do we have here? Are you alone?" he inquired, glancing around to see for himself. "Join me for lunch, Randy; we need to talk about last night. What did Mandy say after I left?"

Miranda jerked her arm free of his light grasp. She glared at him. "Touch me again, Mister Richardson, and I'll cut off your hand. I loathe you. How my sister has stomached you this long, I'll never know. I've tried to avoid you; I've tried to endure you. Then, I even tried to make a truce with you. You sicken me with your lewd mind and repulsive groping. As far as I'm concerned, last night was only a nightmare, and I'm fully awake now. You stay away from me."

Weber actually looked stunned by her harsh tone and cutting words. "What game is this?" he asked skeptically. "I know when a woman entices me, and you did last night. If you're worried about upsetting Mandy, I'll handle her gently. I can make her happy to spurn me. If I frightened you with my overwhelming desire, I'm sorry. I lost my head when I realized you felt the same way about me. It won't happen again, love. Just let me prove it's you I want to marry."

"You're insane, Weber. You're the last man alive I would love or marry. I have never found you desirable, and I despise you. If I hadn't been worried about my sister's health and happiness last night, I would have clawed out your eyes. But you needn't fret over my tattling to Mandy; she'll eventually see you for what you are. I must have been a fool to think we could become friends."

"You didn't act like a friend last night. Not the way you were responding to me," he sullenly protested.

"Think again, Weber. I tried to get away from you, remember? You trapped me against the wall, then chased me around, then pinned me to the sofa. I was not yielding; I was battling you. What is a helpless woman's strength compared to a violent man's? I would have reacted immediately if I hadn't been so shocked by your words and conduct. Remove your egotistic blinders and take another look at what truly happened between us."

"If you have no romantic feelings for me, then why does Mandy think you do? Why do I believe you do?" he debated wickedly.

"Perhaps she's hoping someone will come along to take you away from her. She's been confused lately, perhaps realizing her true feelings for you. There are plenty of rumors about you and women. Also, she's on a medication which clouds her reason. She doesn't honestly think I would pursue you, and I wouldn't. Bother me again, and I'll tell all."

"It won't matter. After I finish telling my side, she'll trust me, not you. She isn't as bright as you, Randy. She's vain and foolish. Of course you won't repeat that because you're too sensitive to hurt her feelings. You're a prize, Randy, one I intend to have," he boldly stated.

"You're a fool, Weber! There's no way you can have me," she declared angrily.

"I wouldn't be too confident, love. By next week, you'll be coming to me and begging me to forgive your nasty rejection. In fact, I'm willing to bet you'll become Mrs. Weber Richardson by May 30."

Miranda stared at him. He looked utterly serious. "Just how do you plan to blackmail me into such a position? What about Mandy?" she probed as if intrigued.

"When a huge debt is made and owed, Randy, someone has to repay it. I've simply decided I want you to clear the ledger, not her. As for Miss Amanda, she'll be taken care of; you needn't worry."

"What kind of debt could I possibly owe you?" she inquired.

"You'll see" was all he would say. He grinned satanically.

Weber didn't realize that Miranda knew exactly to what he was referring with his threats. She had thought he might fall for their ploy, but not this quickly. "What would people say if you suddenly dropped Mandy to marry me? What about the gossip, the scandal?"

Weber laughed in amusement. "Since you vowed you'd never marry me, why speculate?" he teased her.

"You just said I wouldn't have any choice. Why not?" she pressed.

"For one reason, you love your sister and you wouldn't want to see her troubled in any way. I have the feeling you would do anything to make her happy," he hinted between chuckles.

"Why should I be responsible for her happiness? I have my own life to consider. Since you're her sweetheart, how will she be happy if you marry another woman, especially her own sister?"

"Oh, she might rant and rave for a while because of bruised pride, but she'll come around to our way of thinking. We both know Amanda isn't in love with me; I doubt she could love anyone besides herself. I'm just the best suitor she's ever had. Since she has to marry, it might as well be to the superior choice. I was marrying her for the same reasons. But I'd rather have you. And I will," he vowed nonchalantly. "You're a beautiful, sensual creature, Randy. And you don't have any other suitors."

"Only because I don't want any at present. And you're wrong about Mandy; she has plenty of love to give, to the right man. You don't bring out her best qualities. Marriage isn't a business deal, Weber."

"Sometimes, it's the most important deal a man can make. Think it over, Randy. Don't be too hasty to spurn me."

When Weber turned to leave, Miranda called his name. He halted and turned. "Weber, why do you really want to marry me, knowing how I feel about you?"

He came to stop within inches of her. For her ears alone, he murmured, "In spite of what you think, Randy, I love you. And despite how it will anger you, I will force you to marry me. In time you'll forgive me for doing so. I won't frighten you or hurt you again. Once we're wed, I'm looking forward to finishing what we started last night. I will be the man to unleash those passions I sensed in you last night. I want you as I've never wanted any other woman. I can make you happy, Randy; I can make you feel emotions and sensations you never dreamed existed. No matter how much you try to deny it, you want me. Go home and consider my words. I want an answer Sunday afternoon. When I come over, I'll explain everything to you and Amanda. Both of you will agree to my demands, or, shall we say, my wishes."

He left her standing there staring after him. Alarm raced through her as she decided he was insane, cunningly insane. He was convinced she secretly wanted him. He even believed he felt the same way! That was the most terrifying realization of all. If she had any doubts about leaving town, they were gone now.

Miranda hurried home, anxious to get away from that lust-crazed madman. But the more she saw and learned about him, the more fear she had for her sister's safety.

At home, Miranda told her sister about the shocking meeting with Weber. Amanda's fury rose by the minute. "That despicable vermin! Just wait until I—"

Miranda grabbed her by the arms and shook her. "Listen to me, Mandy!" she shrieked in panic. "Don't you say or do anything to antagonize him until Reis gets back. If you push Weber into a corner, he'll strike out at you. Your safety lies in feigned ignorance, and don't you forget it! You can let him know he didn't fool you after he's arrested. When he realizes I'm gone, he'll be furious. But if you let him discover you know the truth and he realizes he has lost everything, there's no telling what he'll do. Promise me you'll be silent," she pleaded.

"He thinks he is so damn clever! How dare he use me like this! I can't stand the thought of him getting away with this a day longer! Maybe he isn't as dangerous as we think. Maybe he will turn tail and flee if he thinks we're on to him. I'm not afraid of him!"

"Just who's going to protect you with all of us gone? My God, Mandy, he *is* that dangerous; he's crazy! Even if you file charges against him, you have no proof. He's a powerful and wealthy man. He would be released the same day. And aren't you forgetting something else? What about Reis? If you issue a challenge, Reis will be the one to fight it for you. Weber would think nothing of having him murdered. Pride and revenge are costly, sister."

Amanda grew silent. She paced the floor then relented. "You're right. I'll behave myself. It just makes me so angry. I should have listened to you long ago and dropped Weber. I'm sorry I got you into this mess, Randy. We'd best get the carriage loaded before Luke comes," she suggested, forcing a strained smile.

"Are you sure you don't want me to stay?" Randy asked gravely.

"No. This plan is best for everyone. Just make sure you write every day. I'm going to miss you terribly. Three months is such a long time." She suddenly hugged her sister.

"When I return, Weber will be in prison, and you and Reis will be sharing a happy marriage. Just be extra careful," Randy coaxed again.

"I will. I promise you Weber won't suspect a thing."

They loaded the carriage which was waiting in the enclosed yard to the rear of their townhouse. Just before two Lucas arrived grinning and chuckling. He told them his plot had worked beautifully and Weber's spy was snoozing behind bushes across the street, his pockets emptied by a daring old widow in black. All was ready. The three mounted the carriage and drove away.

There was no time to waste in reaching the small depot outside of town. Miranda and Amanda hugged each other and cried. The whistle blew and Miranda boarded the train, pondering how long it would be before she saw her cherished sister again, wondering what would happen to each of them before that day arrived. From her window, she waved until she lost sight of Lucas and her sister. It was done. She would ride to Baltimore, then wait for Lucas to join her. They would take another train through Cincinnati to St. Louis where they would switch to a river steamer for the remainder of their journey.

Miranda settled back in her seat, dreamy thoughts filling her mind. She felt a mixture of nervousness and exhilaration. She was on her way to the Dakota Territory. Amanda was married to a wonderful man who would protect and love her. She couldn't believe this was really happening—that she was going to see her mother's family and experience her lost way of life . . .

Lucas drove Amanda to the Alexandria station. With a veiled hat covering her face and concealing the color of her hair and eyes, she purchased a ticket to Charleston under her sister's name. She boarded the waiting train and spoke to the conductor as he claimed part of her ticket. She went to her private compartment, leaving the hat on the bench there to insinuate her presence. When the man was busy with other passengers, she sneaked off the train and joined Lucas. By five, Amanda was home again; this time alone.

That night, Amanda wandered around her room in the shadowy moonlight. Never had she felt so alone or so lonely. Miranda was gone, gone for at least three months and so far away. She didn't want to think about her parents, further away than her sister, who could never return. Lucas would be leaving before noon tomorrow. And Reis was somewhere for another week. At least Mrs. Reed would be returning to work in the morning . . .

Weber was propped lazily against a post at the train depot by nine-thirty on Friday morning. He was speaking with one of his henchmen. "Just make sure Thomas Reed has a nasty accident today, one which forces his wife to stay home with him for a good spell. I need a little privacy over at the Lawrence's. Don't kill the poor fellow; just drop a heavy crate on his leg or foot."

The man nodded and left to carry out Weber's orders. Weber observed Lucas Reardon when he arrived with his belongings. He was curious as to why Miranda hadn't come to say good-by. Weber had anticipated escorting Miranda home after Lucas's train departed. Perhaps Lucas had bid them farewell yesterday afternoon while his careless guard had been unconscious. Once Lucas was gone, all of his worries would vanish. By Sunday, the twins and their properties would be in his control.

Lucas noticed Weber watching him and strolled over to where he stood. "Making sure I leave town, Richardson?" he taunted.

"Yep," Weber readily admitted. "Is it true you'll be gone until fall? Can Fate shine so brightly upon a poor Southern Reb?"

"I'll be back in a flicker if you hurt Amanda in any way," he warned icily to mislead Weber. "I love her like a sister, and she deserves better than you. I hope she changes her mind about you before my return. If not, then you'd best take real good care of her."

"No concern for Miranda?" Weber mocked him.

"No need. She hates your guts. Besides, Miranda's in Charleston until September. She left yesterday at four. I should beat her home."

"Why would she leave when Amanda's so ill?" Weber questioned, vexation starting to grow like a vicious disease within him.

"I'm not sure, but she was acting mighty strange, anxious to leave town. You two didn't have a quarrel, did you? She was a mite edgy yesterday when I drove her here. What did you do? Tell her you were moving in so she had to move out? When is the lucky wedding day, Richardson?" When Weber remained silent, Lucas frowned at him. "It sure is gonna be great to miss your face for months. See you around," he stated flippantly then turned to board the train.

Weber waited until the train had left the station, making certain Lucas Reardon didn't change his mind. He breathed a sigh of relief then tensed. He made several inquiries with the ticket agent and station manager, then headed for the Lawrence townhouse to check out this disastrous mystery.

From her bedroom window, Amanda mastered her irritation when she saw Weber arrive out front as expected. Alice Reed had been given orders to admit no one, even friends. First, Weber asked to speak with Amanda, then Miranda. Alice convincingly gave the false story she had been told—Amanda was still recovering from illness and Miranda had left on an extended holiday. When pressed for Miranda's location, Alice told him she only knew her final destination was somewhere in Charleston. As Weber scoffed at her ignorance, she indignantly vowed she was telling the truth.

When Weber demanded to see Amanda, Alice politely and firmly refused. She explained that Amanda could not be disturbed. When Weber persisted and even threatened to go upstairs, Alice told him Amanda had taken a sleeping medicine to calm her distraught nerves because Miranda had left suddenly without revealing her plans. She tried to appease him by confiding. "She's terribly worried about Miss Randy. It just isn't like her to do such a rash thing. She did promise to write Miss Mandy as soon as she's settled."

"Did they quarrel, Mrs. Reed?" he inquired, softening his tone, observing her for the slightest hint of deception.

In spite of the unspoken betrothal between her lovely mistress and this imposing man, Alice demurred with, "I don't tell about the goings on here, Mr. Richardson. All I can say is she packed and left yesterday. You'll have to ask Miss Mandy when she's feeling better."

Weber scowled at her then suggested, "If you wish to continue working here after our marriage, Mrs. Reed, you'd best hide your dislike of me a little better else I'll hire Mandy another housekeeper. In fact, I might hire someone to take your husband's place at work. I'm sure it will be hard to survive with both of you out of work. If she's distressed over something that happened between her and Randy, I have the right to know. They will be my family and my responsibilities soon. Now, I'll ask again. Did they quarrel before Randy left?"

Alice grew pale as she realized the power this man had over her. If Weber had her husband fired, he would be devastated. Good jobs at his age were difficult to find. She loved the twins. She had been loyal to the Lawrences for years and would never hurt them. Still, she was forced to yield to the demands of her future employer. "I suppose it's all right to tell you what happened this morning."

When she frowned and faltered, Weber pressed eagerly, "What happened this morning? I thought Randy left yesterday. Get on with it, woman. I have to return to work."

"When I came in this morning, Miss Mandy told me her sister had gone to Charleston for a holiday with friends. Miss Mandy said she tried to get her to go to Morning Star, but Miss Randy refused. Miss Mandy said her sister didn't want anyone to know where she was. But when I was cleaning her room, I made a terrible find. She—Miss Randy—left a note saying she had moved to Charleston and wasn't coming back." Alice's eyes lowered in sadness as she repeated her discovery. She had no way of knowing it was all a pre-arranged charade.

"Moved? What are you babbling about, woman?" he shouted. "You're daffy! She wouldn't dare leave here. What did the note say?"

Panicked by his fury, Alice said, "Miss Randy said she wanted to move far away from here to start a new life. Since you and her sister are marrying soon, she said she didn't belong here any more. She wanted to go somewhere and forget the past. She said it was best for all if she left and never came back. Miss Mandy's upset because she thinks her sister might be angry with her about something. She's hurt because she thinks she forced Miss Randy out of her home . . . by marrying you," she stated carefully, unsure of his reaction to that statement.

"Why would our marriage force her to leave home? We wouldn't leave here. That's silly, Mrs. Reed. Where's the note? Show it to me, or I'll have to get Mandy out of bed to question her."

Alice eyed him curiously, then boldly asked, "Why are you so mad about Miss Randy moving? She's a grown woman with no boss."

From her tone, Weber realized he was acting too possessive. "I thought the note might give a clue as to why she left mysteriously. If so, I can find her for Mandy. I can try to get her to come home so we can help her if she's in some kind of trouble."

Alice's heart thudded with uncertainty. Suddenly she was afraid for Miranda; why, she didn't know. "I told you all the note said. Miss Mandy read it to me, then crumpled it and burned it in the kitchen stove. If you rush upstairs and prod her with questions, she'll be more upset. You know she isn't well. She didn't know Miss Randy wasn't coming home. And she doesn't know why Miss Randy left."

Weber couldn't force answers from an ailing Amanda without arousing suspicion. He smiled at Alice and turned on his charm. "Randy's a special lady. She loves Mandy; I'm sure she'll come home."

"I don't think so, Mr. Richardson. She took most all her clothes and belongings. That's why Miss Mandy knows she's gone for good."

"What did Lucas have to say this morning?" he probed warily. "Did he help Randy run away? Didn't he know this would hurt Mandy? Surely he didn't leave without revealing Randy's location?"

"He didn't come over this morning. He said good-by yesterday. When I found the note, I asked Miss Mandy to let me go fetch him, but she said no. Miss Mandy knows how much this trip means to him, so she kept mum. She didn't want him running off to Charleston. Now Mr. Luke is gone and that poor child is alone. It isn't right for them to leave her when she's bedridden and still suffering about her parents. Now don't you go adding to her troubles today. You let that child sleep and get stronger."

"I won't disturb her this morning. You tell Mandy I came by to see her. If she needs anything, you send for me, understand?" he told her sternly.

"I'll take care of her. When she wakes, I'll give her your message," she agreed reluctantly, watching him hurry out the door.

Outside the gate, Weber motioned for his furtive cohort to join him, unaware of the piercing blue eyes which were observing him through the translucent material of the lacy drapes. Amanda couldn't hear their words, but she could see Weber's fury. From where she stood, it appeared Weber was calling off the spy and giving him new orders. Why not? Everyone was gone but her.

Weber was indeed issuing new orders. He had wanted to make sure Lucas didn't get off the train outside town and sneak back to Amanda's, and he had wisely put a man on Lucas's tail early this morning. When the man reported to him later, he would know all Lucas had done before leaving town. He would hire a man to pursue Miranda, and bring her to his home as quickly and secretively as possible. He was determined Miranda wouldn't escape him. Weber was positive Miranda hadn't confided in her sister or cousin, and he concluded she was merely running from her emotions. Just to be on the safe side, he wouldn't deal with Amanda until her sister was locked in a room at his home . . .

Chapter Ten

*I*n Baltimore Friday afternoon, Miranda was bewildered when a telegram was delivered to her hotel room under the phony name only she and Lucas knew: Marie Starr. She nervously read its contents which stated, "Not to worry. Have brief tail. Use Cin ticket. Meet in Louis. Coming via Chicago. No contact home."

Miranda comprehended the message between the lines. Obviously Weber was having Lucas followed which wasn't unexpected. As prearranged, she would take one train through Cincinnati to St. Louis and wait there. Lucas would take a decoy train to Chicago, then travel down to meet her when he lost his shadow. From St. Louis, they would journey to Omaha on the Missouri River where a steamboat would be the next step in their trip. If Amanda were in danger, Lucas would have come directly to her here. Both knew it was folly to send word home from her secret location. She wondered if Weber or his men were seeking her in Charleston. She wasn't afraid to travel alone; she would have a private compartment all the way. Still, she couldn't help but wonder what was taking place at home. She could hardly wait for Lucas to join her and to relate the news. She was glad that Lucas had a friend in Charleston who was going to mail letters from there to Amanda.

While Weber awaited his men's reports, he continued with his plot to take control of the twin's properties and to locate Miranda. He sent flowers and notes to Amanda, who shredded the papers and tossed out the flowers. When Alice questioned Amanda's curious actions, she told the woman she was annoyed with Weber and herself for inspiring her sister's departure. She went so far as to hint that Weber might have driven Miranda away and that she might reconsider her relationship with him. She pretended to get stronger and better each day.

Weber canceled the ordered accident for Thomas Reed, as it would be unnecessary until he had Miranda under his roof. When Weber hadn't called on Amanda by Monday, she fretted at his inexplicable absence. Since Miranda was lost to him, shouldn't he be wooing her again? The notes and flowers were nothing but wily deceptions. Tuesday, a message arrived telling Amanda he had left on a business trip and would see her when he returned Thursday. Amanda prayed he was heading south, not west.

The weekend had passed without trouble but now odd things were happening. Weber had left town. On Tuesday a telegram arrived from Lucas, from St. Louis. Thomas Reed broke his leg in an accident on Wednesday, and Alice had to stay home with him for a while. A letter arrived from Miranda on Thursday, posted in Charleston. No message, coded or otherwise, came from Reis.

For two nights, Amanda slept restlessly, worrying about Weber's strange actions and praying for Reis's safety. But at least she knew Lucas and Miranda were safe. She had destroyed Miranda's lengthy letter but kept the false one to use on Weber when and if he ever came around. She also kept Lucas's telegram lying on the parlor table. She wished Reis would write or return. She needed to know he was all right. She needed to see him, to touch him, to love him.

Friday afternoon, Amanda paid the Reeds a brief visit. Upon returning home, she found Weber waiting for her on the porch. As she approached him, he stared at her oddly.

"I thought you were too ill to be up and around," he stated sullenly. "I come home to find you traipsing all over town. Would you mind explaining yourself, Miss Lawrence?"

Amanda stiffened with outrage and resentment, then reminded herself to proceed with caution. "I beg your pardon, Mr. Richardson," she retorted in a similar tone of peevishness. "How would you know my state of health, seeing as you haven't called since last Friday—a week past? How long does it require for one to get well? To get jittery lying abed or confined to one's home? And since when must I explain myself to you or anyone? But to answer your insulting and nosy question, I went to visit the Reeds. I take it you're unaware of his terrible accident?"

"What accident?" he queried in confusion, wondering if his man had misinterpreted his order. He had seen Amanda Lawrence in many moods, but never one laced with such anger and rudeness.

Amanda briefly informed him of Thomas Reed's situation. "If that's all, sir, good day to you," she added snippily, unlocking her door. At that moment, she was too mad to be afraid of him.

"That isn't all, Mandy," he hastily informed her, seizing her arm and turning her around. "I came over to check on you as soon as I returned. Why are you being so hateful? Have you heard from Miranda?" he inquired, trying to sound casual.

He didn't fool Amanda in the least. Apparently he hadn't found a trace of Miranda and was seeking clues from her. "As you can see, I'm doing fine now. As to my behavior, I give as I receive. It would have been more pleasant if you had merely sent another note or bouquet of flowers. As you can also see, I'm not in the proper mood for company, thanks to you."

"I'm not company, Mandy," he playfully corrected her. "What inspired this disagreeable mood? Surely I can help change it?" he offered, his tone a mellow and husky sound.

"I doubt anyone possesses such magic, Weber. You can't change what ails me. Everything seems to be going awry these days," she murmured sadly.

"Things can't be that bad, my sweet. Tell me what has you so down, and maybe I can help," he coaxed beguilingly.

Amanda studied him for a moment, then said, "Perhaps we should have a serious talk, Weber. I'll prepare some refreshments."

She entered the house and walked into the parlor. She tossed her cape on one end of the sofa, then invited him to be seated while she made the tea. Unless he sat on her cape, he would have to sit nearest the table which held the telegram and letter. Although a book was partially concealing them, Amanda felt certain Weber would notice and read them.

Weber dropped to the sofa and sighed heavily in fatigue and annoyance. As he plotted his strategy, his gaze touched on the edge of a telegram. He moved the book aside to read the signature and found the letter beneath it. He went to the door and glanced down the hallway. He could hear Amanda moving around in the kitchen. He returned to the table and snatched up the two papers, reading them swiftly and closely. He promptly replaced them and went to stand before the front window.

He mentally went over his dilemma. His men hadn't been able to find a single track leading to Miranda, yet she was definitely hiding in Charleston. He would send word to them to search harder; she must be located with all haste. His aggravation with both females was increasing, and his lust for Miranda was rapidly turning to a desire for vengeance. She would pay for leading him this merry chase! He was beginning to think she was playing him for a fool, that she was only trying to cause a split between him and Amanda. On the other hand, perhaps she was afraid of him.

The riddle lay in Miranda's silence about the episodes between them. She hadn't mentioned either battle to Amanda. She had offered no explanation or excuses in her note or letter. She had begged Amanda to forgive her for running away and encouraged her not to worry about her. She had written she was safe and happy, staying with friends. Yet she refused to give her current address and she repeated her vow never to return to Alexandria. Was she afraid Amanda would pass the address on to him? Did she suspect he would come after her? Whatever Miranda's motives, she didn't seem to want Amanda to know about them. The question was why.

But there was a perilous hitch to this matter—what if Miranda decided to reveal the truth in a future letter? How long should he hold out for Miranda without jeopardizing his chances with Amanda? If he was forced to settle for

Amanda, it wouldn't matter what Miranda exposed after their marriage. If Miranda didn't feel guilty, she wouldn't be holding her tongue.

He recalled Lucas's telegram; his foe was leaving St. Louis for Omaha. The telegram had asked Amanda to forward Miranda's new address when she was settled for the summer, implying Lucas was alone and uninformed. His man had followed Lucas to Baltimore where Lucas had taken another train west. His man had reported nothing suspicious. From the telegram Web knew Lucas would take a boat into the Dakota Territory. At last, Lucas Reardon was out of his hair, far away.

A wary man, Weber was not often taken off guard. Tonight, Amanda surprised him when she returned to the room. He seemed to be engulfed in pensive thought, lost in some dreamy world of dark schemes. Before he came back to reality, she risked a glance at the table to find that he had taken her bait. She suppressed a smile as she placed the tray on an oblong table behind one of the matching sofas in the center of the room.

Weber actually jumped and balled his fist when she offered, "Tea, Weber?" She couldn't contain her laughter at his guilty reaction. "You're awfully jumpy," she teased mockingly.

Weber's cold glare was quickly replaced with a merry grin. "I was just about asleep on my feet. I didn't realize I was so exhausted. Maybe that tea will enliven me."

"Perhaps you should go home and rest. We can talk another time," she stated flippantly as if it didn't matter if they ever talked.

"I've been worried about you, Mandy. You're looking marvelous, but you sound dejected. Surely Miranda's contacted you by now?"

"What are you talking about, Weber? Miranda's away on a holiday. She's having too much fun to write," she jested, acting as if nothing were wrong.

"You don't fool me, Mandy. Mrs. Reed told me what happened last week with Miranda. I know you're worried about her." He strolled forward to accept the cup of hot tea then casually took a seat.

Amanda gaped at him. "Just what did Mrs. Reed tell you?" she asked angrily.

Weber told her of their conversation. "I see," Amanda muttered frostily when he finished his confession. "In the future, you will kindly refrain from discussing me and my sister with the hired help. I'm sorry she was the one to find Miranda's note, since she obviously can't be trusted. When Mrs. Reed returns to work—if I allow her to do so—she will be severely reprimanded for such disloyalty. Why Miranda left home is no one's business except hers and mine."

"Why did she leave, Mandy?" he questioned brazenly.

"I was hoping you could answer that question for me," she stated sarcastically, fusing her challenging gaze to his guarded one.

"I'm just as shocked and confused as you are, perhaps more so. Why would you think she might confide in me?"

"What happened between you and Randy last week while I was ill? Since that night I found you two 'horsing around' in this very room, she's acted strangely. Then, she came home from the bank the next day in a mood I can't even explain, much less understand. She packed and left home that same afternoon. Oh, she tried to convince me this trip had been planned for quite some time, but I knew she was lying. You know how, Weber? Because she lies badly. Just like she lied that night I caught you two in here. Then I found a note saying she'd moved and wouldn't tell me where! What is going on between you two? Something happened to make her leave. And you're involved!"

"Listen to yourself, Mandy. You sure you're off that medicine? Just what are you trying to suggest?" he demanded glacially.

"My head has never been clearer, Web. You know how close Randy and I have been since birth. But after you came around, things never were the same. It isn't my imagination! Both of you have been acting strange for weeks now. Were you two having a fight in here, or what?"

"Are you blaming me for her departure?" he snarled. "What could I possibly say or do to make her disappear?"

"Tell me what happened in here that night. Then tell me what happened the day she left town. You did see her while she was out?" she inquired, sounding as if it were a statement more than a leading question.

"I don't believe what I'm seeing and hearing. If I'm right, you're accusing me and Randy of having an affair behind your back. Is that what you think, Mandy?" he probed, placing the cup on a table.

Amanda jumped up from her chair and paced the room. Pretending to search her heart and mind for an honest answer, she deliberated her next move. She could not go too far too soon.

Weber used her confusion and hesitation to further her doubts. "I swear to you, Mandy, I've never made love to your sister. How can you hurt me with such charges?"

Amanda ceased her aimless wanderings and looked at him. "Can you also swear you haven't wanted to? Can you also swear you haven't tried to get her into your bed? Can you swear you have never held her in your arms, never kissed her? Swear those things, Weber; prove I have no reason to doubt your love and fidelity. Prove you have nothing to do with Randy's actions."

"You actually expect me to respond to such accusations!" he thundered at her, infuriated by her astute perceptions and the fact that she would dare to interrogate him. "I do believe your fever seared your brain, Amanda Lawrence! It's bad enough you charge me with such vile conduct, but to vilify your own sister like this . . ." He cunningly left the statement unfinished. "By damn, woman, what's gotten into you? I think you'd best call that doctor over to check your head. I'm not going to sit here and defend myself against such crude and foolish insinuations. Why would I court you if I wanted Miranda? Do you realize how crazy that sounds?"

"You're awfully tense and defensive, Weber. It's really rather simple to end this matter; just tell me the truth."

Weber rushed to her and grabbed her, shaking her as he shouted, "Damnation, Mandy! That's why she left! You've been badgering her with such trash, haven't you? No wonder she ran off! You've been accusing her of these same things. Did you call her filthy names and accuse her of such lewd behavior? Mandy, Mandy, what have you done? Randy and I are innocent. You've deluded yourself about some secret love affair between us. You drove her away with your cruel accusations and wild jealousy," he informed her angrily.

Amanda jerked free and glared at him. "All I want to know is who's at fault, you or she or both of you. Damn you, Weber Richardson! I'm not a blind fool. I saw the way you two acted that night. If nothing happened, then why did she leave?"

"I wish to hell I knew!" he rashly stormed at her.

To his consternation, she stated softly and firmly, "I think you and I should end this, Weber. Things haven't been right between us for some time. I've been trying to ignore it, even deny it, but I can't. A marriage between us wouldn't work."

For the first time, Weber panicked. Miranda might be lost to him, and now he was losing Amanda and all she represented. He couldn't permit that. He would deal with Miranda when she was found. Right now, he would have to persuade Amanda she was his one and only love. "I love you, Mandy; I want to marry you. Now or whenever you say."

Amanda shook her head. "You love what I have to offer, Weber, not me. I doubt you ever loved me or ever will. If Randy were here and willing, you would take her in my place. Why pretend?"

Weber felt secure in his schemes and used them. "You have nothing to offer but yourself, Mandy. Your father made some terrible business decisions. Everything you have is mortgaged past keeping. I've been supporting you and your sister for the past two months. If not for me, you and Randy would be in the streets today. I've been slaving to hold things together until we were married. I didn't want you to feel obligated to marry me. You have nothing but me, Mandy."

Now that he was heading blindly into her trap, she encouraged him to go further. "What nonsense is this?" she scoffed.

"If I hadn't made the payments on this house for the past two months, the bank would own it right now. As to Morning Star, I couldn't save it. It was losing too much money and too heavily indebted. And your firm has been on the verge of bankruptcy for months. If you doubt me, check your father's books and ask Daniel McVane. Maybe these burdens troubled your father so deeply that he was reckless that day at sea," he speculated maliciously.

Tears blurred her eyes as she comprehended the extent of Weber's cruelty. How could she have been so wrong about this man? To think she almost married him. What menacing plans he must have had for her . . . "Are you saying you own me?" she murmured.

"Don't be silly, woman. I'm trying to spare you hurt and humiliation. But I can't stall the inevitable much longer. Too many of your clients are demanding payment. I can't allow my company to sink by keeping yours afloat. Think of the embarrassment, Mandy. Do you want people saying you married me for survival? We've got to do something quick. After we're married, I'll hire a detective to locate Miranda, if you wish. I don't want either of you hurt, Mandy. And both of you must be suffering from this misunderstanding."

"I wish I could believe you, Web," she murmured quietly.

Weber tensed. "Then go to your office and check the books."

"I don't mean about my finances. I mean about Randy. I'm sorry, but you'll never convince me nothing happened. Randy was asking too many questions about you and us. She wanted me to break it off with you. She kept telling me she didn't like you or trust you. Then I find her in your arms."

"I told you, Mandy, we were calling a truce. We were talking and got carried away. We started teasing each other. She's like a child, Mandy," he lied unconvincingly.

"Then why did she act so funny when I caught you two? And why did she spout scorn and mistrust for you the next day before leaving?"

Stunned by that revelation, he shrieked helplessly, "What?"

"I find that your story and hers contradict each other. That makes me skeptical of both tales, Weber. She runs away, then you vanish on business," she stated sarcastically. "Did you go after her, Web? Did she refuse to come home with you? Did you decide to settle for me since you can't have her? Randy isn't for you, Web. She's a wild creature, a creature of the land like my mother was."

"All right, Mandy," Weber muttered as if to himself. "If you want the truth, then you'll have it. I was hoping to spare you such pain. But I can't remain silent if it's going to destroy us." Weber knew he had to make an irrevocable decision to regain Amanda and punish her sister.

Amanda sensed what was coming and mentally prepared for it. Weber was exceedingly smart and daring, but he was greedy and desperate. Such traits inspired rashness.

"I think you should sit down, Mandy. I wish I could avoid delivering so much bad news in one night." Weber took a seat, but Amanda remained standing by the front window.

Those stubborn lines on her face caused ripples of spite to wash over him. He would fix her—her and her treacherous sister! "I've been a bloody fool, Mandy. I'm sorry. I haven't outright lied to you, but I have misguided you. I thought it would be best for everyone if I forgot about the other night. I've tried to accept it as a misunderstanding. I was so excited and pleased by her change of heart about me that I didn't realize what she was doing. Frankly, I'm still not sure about her motives, but they couldn't be honorable."

Amanda didn't take her eyes off his face and she didn't debate his allegations. "Continue," she coaxed impassively when he hesitated.

"I let myself be flattered by Miranda's attention. It's rare to have one beautiful woman after you, but to have two . . . She caught me by surprise, Mandy. I've never seen Miranda like she was the other night. Laughing, teasing, smiling, dancing around the room. We were just talking and making peace—at least I thought so. From nowhere she flung herself into my arms and kissed me. At first I didn't think anything about it; I mean, it was just a little kiss. But she didn't move away; she started caressing my chest and sending me a look which was so much more than friendly. Tarnation, Mandy, she's your sister; I was bewildered. Then she rubbed against me and kissed me again. I'm not a saint, Mandy; so I won't deny I had flames nipping at me. There I stood, nailed to the floor, mindless with astonishment, and she was dancing around me. Her hands were tickling me and her mouth was all pouted up, sort of inviting. I didn't know what to do or think."

Weber paced nervously and lowered his gaze contritely. Still, Amanda didn't move or protest. "I don't know what got into her that night, Mandy, but she was a powerful witch. I can't explain what I was thinking, if anything. Lordy, a man can't control his body under trying times like that! I asked her what she was doing, and she just smiled at me. I patted her on the cheek roughly and asked her if she was drunk. She took my hand and moved it down her chest. When I tried to pull it away, she put it inside that nothing dress she was wearing. Lord's my witness, Mandy, she didn't have anything under it, and she clamped my hand over one of her breasts. By then, I was half crazy with worry. I was trying not to tear her dress but get my hand out of it. It was hard not to be affected by what she was doing."

Weber did more pacing and hand-wringing. "By then, I was trembling and sweating. Lord, I was afraid you'd walk in before I could control her. I grabbed her hands and pinned them behind her back. I started scolding her something fierce. I don't know if she wanted me, or if she was doing it to split us apart. I think she was hoping you'd find us like that. But I'm still not sure why. She wasn't herself, Mandy; she was like some wild and hungry vixen on the prowl."

He flopped to the sofa, groaning as if exhausted from the exertion of this confession. "I talked my mouth dry to your sister, Mandy. She seemed to relax. Then when you came downstairs unexpectedly, she went pale and funny. She could have changed her mind about making me look bad. When I didn't respond, maybe she realized she was wrong. Or maybe she thought you wouldn't believe her lies about me. Who knows, Mandy, maybe she was looking for a good reason to leave home. You said yourself she's different; she has a wild and mysterious streak. You can't ever tell what she's thinking or feeling; it's frightening."

Finally Amanda spoke. "You're telling me that my sister enticed you to seduce her that night? Miranda Lawrence acted like a harlot to the man who belongs to her own sister?"

"I've been flirted with plenty of times, Mandy, and invited to share passion. Randy wasn't being an innocent flirt, and she wasn't trying to become friends. She was tempting me, trying to bewitch me. If there's one thing I'm positive about, Randy was trying to coax me into her bed. As to why, only Randy knows. Maybe she did think I was bad for you; maybe she hoped to prove it that night."

"You think she left because she was embarrassed? She was afraid you'd tell me everything? Or do you think she left because her seduction failed and she couldn't bear to watch us together?"

Something about Amanda's surly undertone piqued Weber. "When I saw her Thursday, I told her we would forget it ever happened. She acted as if she didn't know what I was talking about; she looked at me like I was crazy. When I kept talking, she accused me of being insane. I don't know if it was an act or not, but she behaved as if the whole episode never happened. Has that ever happened to her before?"

"If you're wondering about her sanity, it was fine until last week. I'm not convinced you're innocent in this matter. Randy wouldn't play the slut to prove a point to me. And if she has secret longings for you, they must be buried deep from the way she talks. Perhaps you got a bit too friendly and scared her. Randy is very sensitive, very giving. Maybe she left because she didn't want to hurt me with the truth—that my future fiancé was chasing her. She dislikes you, Weber, and she doesn't want to live with us if we marry. Maybe she thought I was too enchanted by you to believe her version. Right now, I'm confused; I'm hurt and I'm worried. Until I'm convinced it was an innocent mistake I think we should spend time apart. I'm not accusing you of lying; I'm not charging you're wholly to blame. I need time to sort out my feelings. I've been through so much these past months; I can't take more pressure. I hope Randy will write or come home soon; then we can calmly discuss this mysterious misunderstanding."

"Why are you punishing me, punishing us for Randy's strange behavior? I was afraid you'd react like this if I told you about that night. By damn, I should have lied! What about the firm, Mandy? I can't support two homes and businesses much longer. Marry me tomorrow, and we'll work out everything. We'll find Randy and bring her home with us. Whatever the problem—real or imaginary—we'll help her, I promise."

When Amanda didn't seem moved or touched by his pleas, he beseeched her,

"If we stop seeing each other, you'll brood over this and maybe paint me guilty of something I didn't do. Please, Mandy, you must understand and forgive me. I love you. I need you."

Amanda felt she was pushing too far, too hard. She sighed wearily and relented to a mild degree. "I want to believe you, Weber, but my whole world is coming apart. My parents vanish and I'm told they're dead. You, my family, and property were all I had left. Now Randy and Luke are gone. You say I'm nearing a penniless state. I just recovered from an illness. It's too much at once. Can't you see how I feel? I'm drained and I'm frightened. If you truly love me, give me some time to adjust."

When Weber attempted to embrace and comfort her, she moved away. "Please don't. Not now, not today. Come to see me Sunday afternoon; we'll talk then. Bring Papa's books and we'll decide what's to be done. Just allow me breathing space to recover from these setbacks."

Weber failed to notice his reflection in a mirror on the opposite wall, one which exposed his satanic grin of satisfaction which Amanda was observing intently from the corner of her eye. Her ruse had worked; Weber believed she was utterly confused, vulnerable to his lies. The bastard actually thought he was winning this game!

"You're right, my sweet. I am being selfish and thoughtless. You've had too much dropped on you lately. Rest and think, Mandy. By Sunday when we talk, you'll know I only want what's best for you and us. Don't worry about anything. I'd never let you be hurt by a scandal. If you need anything, send for me."

"You're very kind, Weber. I'm sorry about this mess. You probably think I'm the most ungrateful woman alive. Considering all that's happened, you can't blame me for having doubts. I've just never felt so alone, so insecure, so helpless! Maybe I'm not myself yet. Can you imagine Amanda Lawrence without money; the topic of idle gossip; the butt of amusing or cruel jokes?" she murmured as if horrified by such visions, planting the seeds for her next entangling vine.

"Don't forget you have me and all I own, my sweet. I would never allow anyone to laugh at you," he claimed smugly. Weber relaxed, fooled completely. He might as well purchase a wedding ring, he thought, for we will be wed by next Friday! Amanda Lawrence would never risk poverty and ridicule. She could be his adoring and grateful wife until he found Miranda . . .

After Weber left, Amanda fumed and paced with the tension and bitterness which engulfed her. Did the bastard think her so stupid? Did he think her so dazzled by him that she would believe every word that left his lying lips? Did he think her so desperate that she would obey him without question or protest? Her fury mounted.

As she returned the dishes and tray to the kitchen, she burst into ecstatic laughter. "I wonder if you're as dangerous as you are evil and greedy? I shall enjoy my revenge on you, Weber Richardson. No one makes a fool of me. No one uses me. You thief! You liar! You traitor! You've met your match, dear Weber. Now that I have you trapped like the vermin you are, I shall torture you and tease you before you're arrested. I shall come to the jail and laugh in your face when this is over. You'll regret the day you set your sights on me and my sister," she vowed confidently.

About ten, on Saturday night, Amanda tossed aside the book she had been trying to read. She checked the lights and doors and slowly made her way upstairs to her lonely bedroom. She closed her door and leaned against it, sighing dejectedly. Suddenly her gaze widened with astonishment, then she burst into gleeful laughter.

Lying upon her bed was her irresistible love. His chest and feet were bare, his lower body clad in snug jeans. His ebony head was resting upon two pillows as his virile frame reclined seductively. His expression said "come here." But he didn't speak or move. He just grinned.

She ran to her bed squealing. "Reis! You're back. God, how I've missed you. I was so worried," she confessed, spreading kisses over his face between words.

Reis captured her in his arms and pulled her down atop him. "Not half as much as I missed you, love," he murmured huskily then kissed her with such intensity that it took her breath away. He rolled her over him and covered her body with his as his mouth savored hers.

She hugged him fiercely as she responded to his lips, her hands gently kneeding the supple flesh upon his back. After several heady kisses, he leaned back and visually devoured her beauty and smoldering gaze. "You have a potent hold over me, woman. I couldn't wait to come home to you," he stated thickly.

"Is it over, Reis? Did you get the evidence against him? I've been so lonely and miserable without you. Don't ever leave me again. I've been crazy with fear," she told him, snuggling into his arms.

"I learned plenty, but I need a few more facts. I should be able to wrap up this case in a week or two. First, I need to get inside your warehouse and his. Late at night, if you catch my drift."

"But that's dangerous!" she protested instantly. "Surely he has both guarded. What if he sees you?"

"I'm good at my job, love. Did you see or hear anything tonight? Yet, here I am," he jested playfully, tugging on a blond curl.

"But I'm not surrounded by guards," she refuted his smugness.

"But you are, love. There's one out front across the street and one out back at the rear gate," he disclosed to her shock.

"I don't understand. Weber called off his spy last week. Why would he replace him, then add another one?" she fretted nervously.

"Why don't you tell me what's been happening here while I was gone? Are you all right, love?" he inquired tenderly, possessively.

Amanda gradually revealed the events which had taken place during his absence. Although he didn't interrupt her detailed explanation, she watched the ever-changing emotions which swept over his face. When she finished, he remarked gravely, "Don't you think you went a mite far? You were supposed to act suspicious, not come right out and say it. Now that he's laid his cards on the table, he'll be more dangerous than ever. I'll have to move faster. He'll be working to get you two married quickly. There's a lot at stake here, love. I wouldn't put anything past him to get his wishes. I know him, Mandy; I witnessed his cruelty during the war. He would die or kill before losing again. Why didn't you stall him until I returned?" he asked.

She lowered her gaze when she replied honestly and remorsefully, "Pride and vengeance. I'm sorry, Reis. It was foolish."

He smiled and hugged her gently. "I know it's hard to play a simpleton when you're not. But retribution has to wait a while, love."

"Are you angry with me?" she asked quietly.

"Yes, and no," he teased, tightening his embrace and kissing her forehead. He sat up on the bed, pulling her along with him. He lifted the chain from beneath her dress and removed the gold band from it, slipping it on her finger. He smiled and whispered, "But right now, I'm too distracted to think about anything but my wife. Can we skip the talking for tonight?" he inquired roguishly, cupping her chin between his hands, then passing his left thumb over her parted lips.

An enticing smile flickered over her face as she nodded yes. He rolled off the bed to strip off his jeans, leaving himself naked before her intoxicated senses. He reached for her hand, pulling her to her feet. He removed her clothing then rested his quivering hands on her shoulders. She was so soft and sleek. In the dim light, her hair seemed a blaze of golden shades. Her eyes sparkled like rare blue diamonds.

He shifted his dark head to scan her entire body. She lifted her chin to meet the appreciative gaze of those deep blue eyes. His hand deserted her shoulder to trace lightly over her cheeks and parted lips, causing them both to tremble. His finger leisurely trailed over her nose, around her alluring eyes, and poised on her dainty chin. His hand was like an explorer, one who not only mapped out territory, but also claimed it as his.

Amanda was content to stand mesmerized by him, to allow him free rein over her body and will. She felt like a rose petal floating peacefully on an azure sea. Finally, her hands went upward to caress his chest. As her flattened palms moved over the tanned, muscled flesh, she was aware of the thudding of his heart.

Reis's head lowered ever so slowly and his mouth deftly covered hers, their tongues touching and teasing. Amanda was ecstatic that she didn't have to worry about where this unbridled behavior would lead. Never had she felt freer or more confident; she could do or say whatever she pleased. Reis was what she wanted and needed; and he was here with her. She felt so comfortable with him. She felt alive and happy again. She felt wild and wonderful.

His hands eased to her breasts, each capturing and tantalizing a firm mound. There was no need for embarrassment or shyness or resistance. They were married; they were in love; they could do anything which pleased them.

Her body accepted his tormentingly sweet invasion and her hand slid down to encircle his erect manhood, which felt so silky and hot. Recalling the wonders this firm flesh could work within her body, she yearned to feel it driving wildly and urgently into her womanhood.

Reis lifted her and pressed her to the cushiony bed. As if he had forever, he made unhurried love to her. It didn't take long for his lips and hands to have her writhing beside him. He worked skillfully and eagerly, increasing her feverish desire for him. He gently drove his aching shaft into that moist paradise which greeted him ardently.

He didn't move for a few moments, mastering the urge to ride her fast and hard to end his own painful hunger. He was sorely pressed to drive into her body again and again, having dreamed of this night for days. And she was just as ravenous and greedy. He thrilled to the wanton way she responded to him, the way she encouraged and tempted him to devour her, body and soul.

As he set his rhythmic pattern, her legs engulfed his lower body and locked around him. She worked in unison with him, arching to meet his delightful entries and sighing breathlessly each time he slightly withdrew. She struggled against the sweet tension which possessed her, attacked her, taunted her. Her nerves tingled with fierce cravings; her body burned with scorching desire.

Spasm after spasm attacked and shook the very core of her being. For an instant, colorful lights danced before her darkened vision. Reis dashed aside his restraint and raced along with her as she fought and found a blissful path to rapture. When all was spent, they relaxed into each other's arms. Still he kissed her and caressed her. Then he rolled to his side, carrying her along with him and she snuggled against him as their pounding hearts and ragged respirations returned to normal. Tenderly and lovingly his hands trailed lightly over her silky body as if memorizing this enchanting moment.

As they lay entwined and calmed, Reis realized the depth of his love for this woman. He couldn't imagine a life without her, but he surely could envision future days and nights with her at his side.

As Amanda's hand teased over the damp hair on his firm chest, she wondered how this vital and masterful man had remained single so long. He was arrestingly handsome, enormously virile, and skillful in bed. He was fearless, intelligent, confident, and roguish. He was gallant and charming; he was witty and genial. He was a treasure above price and she loved him beyond words.

Just before drifting off to sleep, Amanda murmured softly, "Reis, do you think Luke and Randy are all right?"

"Without a doubt, my love. I think this trip will be good for both of them. Don't worry. We'll be seeing them again before you know it," he replied, nuzzling her ear.

Laughter trickled from her parted lips as she nestled closer to him. "Now that I think about it, I'm glad we're alone. If anyone can take care of herself, it's Miranda Lawrence."

Reis's mouth seized possession of hers, and sleep was forgotten for the next hour . . .

Chapter Eleven

Miranda Lawrence and Lucas Reardon stood at the railing of the steamboat which was carrying them along the Missouri River from Omaha to the next stop which would be Fort Randall. From there, they would visit several military posts including Fort Sully and Fort Pierre. After Pierre, they would take an overland route north to Fort Rice and Fort Lincoln; Fort Abraham Lincoln was reputed to be the new location of George Custer, one of the objects of Lucas's journey.

Miranda had anticipated a leisurely, perhaps boring, trip by water. But she quickly discovered there was little time for personal worries; there was always something to hold her spellbound. She hoped Amanda had received their messages so she wouldn't fret over their safety. By now, Reis should be at her side, insuring her happiness. Lucas had mailed another letter from Omaha, but Miranda couldn't risk writing home yet. In a few weeks, she would send a detailed account of the trip.

Along this awesome stretch of water, Miranda viewed many sights. Huge cottonwoods grew beside the water's edge, standing tall and proud as if guarding this wild land from intruders. Joining them in beauty were lovely chokecherries and wild plum trees in full bloom. Along the banks, bushes with heavy foliage frequently concealed the inland from eager eyes and offered protection for the birds and animals. She heard tales of how pioneers had dreaded challenging this mighty river. Many days and nights the ship's passengers and crew recounted suspenseful sagas of crossings, some victorious and some disastrous. The river was said to have devoured boats of all sizes as well as the banks which tried to contain its force.

She noticed many trading posts and small settlements along the way, each supplying an exciting tale of its own. At sunset, everything appeared gold except the dark outline of trees in the distance. The tawny heavens reflected upon the water and cast a golden aura. Sometimes the air was so still and quiet it seemed eerie, but on moonless nights a mixture of sounds could be heard above the singing and laughter of the passengers, as the steamer halted its trek to avoid unseen dangers in the darkness. On such nights, Miranda enjoyed the throaty croaking of frogs, the soothing calls of bobwhite quail, and the gentle murmuring of the water as it moved along peacefully.

Miranda was relieved to have missed the most terrifying event of all: the breaking up of the frozen river in the spring. She learned that settlers along the river made bets on when "she would go." Cattle were moved to high ground when the intimidating snapping and cracking began sending warning signals from the ice-locked river. It was said the Missouri could go "raving mad" two times each year, and the people sighed with relief and offered prayers of gratitude when March and June passed uneventfully.

That news didn't sit comfortably with Miranda. She had missed the March floods after the melting snows dumped their contents into the river. But the June rains which brought the threat of more flooding were knocking on the calendar's door. Yet the heavens were clear and blue; they even seemed larger than back home. Miranda prayed they would reach their destination before Mother Nature loosened her powers upon the land.

The Missouri was tricky, often hazardous to navigate with its shifting channels, and pilots and captains cursed her yet respected her. Due to the perils of this river and the importance of its location, the riverboat pilots or keelboat captains were highly paid, and their cargo reaped large rewards. Furs, gold, foods, military ammunition and supplies, and Indian annuities were the main cargoes. Sometimes, passengers were just as important: miners, farmers, soldiers, and traders. But with the railroads closing in, steamers were not as crowded as they had once been.

Sadly, the day of the steamer and keelboat was vanishing. By the time Miranda and Lucas were ready to go home, the railroad would be finished to Yankton at Fort Randall. Before long, supply crafts would only be necessary between settlements or into areas where the railroad hadn't yet come.

For a while longer, these crafts and their adventures would continue. Many of their perils and hardships lay in submerged or floating trees or shifting sandbars. Others lay in striking sunken vessels which rested on the shallow bottom with snagged hulls or burned shells. At present, the greatest danger was low water. The spring rush from melting snows had passed and the rise from June rains hadn't come yet.

Miranda watched the river in fascination and tried not to think about her run-ins with Weber. She concentrated on envisioning her sister smiling and walking beside Reis Harrison. Miranda was confident that Reis was more than capable of protecting Amanda, solving the case surrounding Weber, and making Amanda extremely happy. Having seen Reis and Amanda together, Miranda longed for a love that powerful and unique. But she would not avidly search for love and passion, not even among the numerous males on the steamer who had vied for her attention in vain. She would let love and passion find her when the time and man were right.

Halfway between Omaha and Fort Randall, the steamer ran aground on a sandbar. The *Martha Lane* had previously had contests with smaller sandbars, which had been won quickly and almost easily. But the heavy spars used to free steamers seemed of little use this time. With a full moon to guide them, they had continued long past dusk. The sandbar seemed to have "appeared from nowhere" as the pilot claimed when they were brought to an abrupt stop, one which flung the supper dishes and several passengers to the wooden floor. As if Fate was against the voyage, the moon then vanished behind ominous clouds, preventing the crew from dislodging the boat until morning.

The following day dawned cloudy and dim. When the damage was assessed, the pilot cursed under his breath. Clearly they were too heavy to "grasshopper" off the bar without unloading the passengers, animals, and heaviest cargo. To make matters worse, the rudder had been cracked, and had to be repaired on the spot. It required over an hour to empty the craft.

Lucas was chatting amiably with some of the passengers, in particular two intriguing soldiers from Fort Rice. Miranda was allowed to stroll along the riverbank, taking in the sights and sounds. She admired the wild beauty around her and plucked several colors of pasqueflowers to put in her cabin. She watched squirrels playing in the trees and listened to birds singing joyfully.

As if to seek solitude of its own, a narrow stream departed the banks of the "Misery"—as Miranda had heard the river being called this morning by a harried pilot—and made a winding path inland, which she followed. She wasn't far from the river and the other passengers, but she felt encased in a private world, concealed from their view by leafy trees and bushes. Growing beside a fallen tree was a lovely patch of wildflowers, seemingly anxious to be the first land decorations this spring. She headed toward it to gather a few to add to those in her grasp.

As she bent forward to reach for the first one, an arrow swished past her outstretched arm. With a thud, it buried its sharp tip in the head of a rattlesnake which had been about to strike Miranda. The serpent thrashed wildly in the verdant grass and fallen leaves as it struggled against inevitable death, its ominous tail sending forth a belated rattle. Finally it was still and silent.

Miranda stared at the arrow with red-and-black-tipped feathers on one end, recalling that her mother had told her long ago that each warrior or tribe used certain feathers and colors for identification. She didn't know who was standing behind her; but there was only one way to find out if it was a white man or an Indian, a rescuer or an enemy. She turned and opened her mouth to speak, but couldn't. He was standing so close to her that she wondered how she failed to make contact with that powerful bronze body while turning. He was an Indian, doubtlessly a warrior, judging from his stance and painted face. In less than an instant, she knew she was in no danger from the virile and handsome man who entranced her with his magnetic gaze.

They merely stared at each other, both surprised and held spellbound by the other. Even though Blazing Star had been watching her since last night when the boat he was shadowing had run aground, he now saw she was even more beautiful than he had imagined. He had been trailing her since she had left the steamer and had defended her without a second thought.

Her hair was like smoldering wood, dark with shining flames. Her eyes were as golden brown as a doe's, and their expression as gentle. Her skin was shaded like a baby otter's, and he knew that it would be just as soft to his touch. He was astonished to read no fear or hatred within those expressive eyes, and more astonished to detect her attraction to him. He wasn't sure if she was white, for if dressed properly, she could pass for Indian. He couldn't seem to move or speak, as if he were in a vision trance.

Miranda warmed all over. Never had she seen such a tempting male. What a superior vision of power, self-assurance, and potent masculinity! Tingles traveled over her body as she took in his appearance. His hair was ebony, falling free down his back, but for two braids on either side of his arresting face. The braids were secured by rawhide thongs with small feathers dangling from them, again tinged with red and black. He wasn't wearing a headband as in the political cartoons by Nast in *Harper's Weekly*; nor was he savage or ugly in appearance or manner as were the Indians in Nast's works.

Other than her mother, Miranda had never seen or met an Indian. But Marie Morning Star Lawrence had told her daughter much about them, especially about her people, the Sioux. Miranda wanted to know to what tribe this man belonged. His coppery flesh was smooth, firm, and hairless. His muscular chest was bare, except for the silver star which hung from a leather strip around his neck. His lower body was clad in buckskin pants and moccasins, and around his biceps and wrists were leather, beaded bands, the loose ends of which dangled from his powerful arms. A quiver of arrows and a bow were slung over one shoulder and rested at his hip.

But it was his face which mesmerized her. Although the upper portion of his face was painted with red from hairline to below his eyes, then banded from side to side with black and white strips to the end of his nose, the design could not distract from his handsome looks, and the paints couldn't conceal them. Again, the color scheme of red and black registered in her spinning mind. His dark eyes shone like polished black jet; their expression was probing and compelling. His nose wasn't large or small, but fit his face perfectly, and his lips were wide and full, inviting Miranda's gaze to linger over them. His jaw was squared, with a slight indention in the middle of his chin which Miranda yearned to touch with her fingertip.

Blazing Star was the one to end their hypnotic drama. He shook his head as if to regain mastery of it. He hunkered down and severed the rattler tail from its body, handing the row of noisy rings to her. The smile he gave her came from his eyes, not his lips. She accepted the unusual gift and smiled up into his controlled features, causing his intense gaze to shift to her mouth. He watched it for a time, then lifted his dark eyes to fuse with hers. Miranda thought he was going to kiss her and was disappointed when he didn't.

Miranda was confused when he used his sharp knife to cut off the lower end of one of her curls. He looked at it as it wound around his finger. He grinned, then placed it inside a pouch at his waist. He couldn't decide if he should be annoyed or relieved he couldn't take a captive on this manhunt, for she appeared too special for such a life. If only his body didn't urge him to take her, or suffer denial's agony . . .

"That isn't how you take scalp locks. What does it mean?" she inquired softly in puzzlement and pleasure.

For an answer, he squeezed her hand which was holding the rattler rings, then patted his pouch, as if indicating a swap of some kind. When he heard Lucas calling her name, the warrior came to instant alertness. She could almost envision those keen instincts and skills coming to full readiness. Lucas's intrusion was unwanted, ill-timed.

"Coming," she responded to Lucas's call. She looked up at the warrior and smiled again. "Thanks for saving my life and for this gift. I shall never forget you or today. Good-by," she murmured sadly.

Blazing Star sensed her reluctance to leave him, her powerful pull toward him. He grinned, for he knew they would meet again. They were both heading in the same direction.

Lucas called her name louder. She turned toward the sound and replied, "I'm coming, Luke. Just a minute." When she turned to ask the warrior's name and to give hers, he was gone. She looked around, but she could find no trace of him. He had vanished as soundlessly and mysteriously as he had appeared. If not for the object in her grasp, she might believe the episode never had happened. To make certain, she shook the object and listened to the musical rattle. She concealed it in her pocket; why, she didn't know. When she joined Lucas, she didn't mention the warrior.

Miranda remained close to Lucas as the repairs were completed and the steamer was freed from the sandbank. But she paid little attention to Lucas's conversation, for her thoughts were of the nearby woods and the fascinating warrior.

The steamer was reloaded. Until they were out of sight, she remained at the railing, staring at the area where they had gone ashore. Her spirits were heavy, for she felt no returning gaze. But as the journey continued, Miranda couldn't forget the imposing Indian. She felt denied of something vital to her life, to her heart. The feelings she was experiencing were tormenting. It might be wrong, but she would pray for their paths to cross again.

As the days passed, Blazing Star had a difficult time pushing the girl called Miranda from his thoughts. He berated himself for dreaming of her, for desiring her above all women he had met, for allowing her to ride with him each day and to sleep with him each night. He berated himself because she was white and he was

Oglala Sioux, and the two bloods should never join again. For two such blendings in his distant past had cost him much honor. If two of his ancestors hadn't mated with white captives, he would be chief of the most awesome and powerful Indian tribe ever to rule the open Plains. Because of the love of Gray Eagle for a half-white captive and that of his son, Bright Arrow, for a white slave, the line of chiefs had passed to Bright Arrow's brother, Sun Cloud, who had wisely joined with a Blackfoot princess, Singing Wind, daughter of Chief Brave Bear and Sioux maiden, Chela, herself a daughter of a medicine chief. To make matters worse for the line of Gray Eagle, Night Stalker—son of Chief Sun Cloud—had been slain in a massacre when his only son, Bloody Arrow, was only five winters old, too young for the chief's bonnet. Now, the joint chiefs of their tribe were Sitting Bull and Crazy Horse, leaders with fame and skills to challenge those of the legendary Gray Eagle.

After having made certain the two enemies he had been assigned to kill were aboard this boat, the warrior traveled rapidly toward the steamer's next mandatory stop, the next lengthy stop which would entice the girl to leave the boat once more. He was glad he was on this raid alone; he didn't want the girl injured or slain during a battle, and certainly not captured by another warrior. After he sated his curiosity, he would seek a lofty bank in an area where the river narrowed to send two arrows toward the boat, one aimed for each enemy's heart. Then the matter would be over, for Blazing Star never missed a target.

In spite of the impossibility of the situation, he wanted to see the girl again. He would have one last chance to study her up close when the boat halted to cut wood just below Yankton, the only spot where fuel couldn't be purchased from "woodhawks," where the crew would have to cut and load it themselves. At such times, passengers left the boat to stretch their legs and relieve their boredom and tension. Riding alone and not requiring the numerous fuel stops of the steamer, the warrior could make better time. His fatal attack would come between Yankton and Pierre, on the last leg of this craft's journey.

In his stealthful trek northward, Blazing Star did not bother to slay anyone along his path. There was so much killing and fighting these days, but not for honor as in olden times. He hated the scars he observed upon the face of Mother Earth, the nakedness of cleared land for farms and settlements, the cutting of all trees in some areas, the signs of careless fires, the fences which blocked trails, the many offenses of the whiteman. These intruders had grown strong and numerous, while sentencing Indians of all tribes and nations to prison camps the white man called "reservations." Many tribes had yielded to the white man's superior weapons and ample numbers, yielded because they had grown weak and dispirited from losses, yielded because continued fighting seemed futile and costly, yielded because of the whiteman's promises and treaties which were broken before the ink dried upon the meaningless papers. But the Sioux had not and never would be conquered. The Sioux would fight against the evil and greed which were destroying their lands and peoples to the last warrior.

Miranda didn't confide her brief adventure to her cousin Lucas, but she included every detail in her letter to Amanda which couldn't be mailed for two weeks. That momentous day and the next day, she was content to remain in her cabin, dreaming of the warrior left far behind, pining for a man she would never meet again. She couldn't forget him, for he invaded her thoughts during every hour. Why had he made such an impression on her? Why did knowing she would never see him again cause such grief and loneliness?

On the fourth morning after leaving Omaha and two days after Miranda had encountered the unforgettable warrior, the *Martha Lane* halted her engines for the crew to chop wood. At first, Miranda was tempted to stay aboard, but Lucas coaxed her ashore for a leisurely walk and invigorating exercise.

Some of the men who were playing cards remained on the boat. The two soldiers were locked in a cabin having a critical conversation which Lucas would have traded a month's pay to have heard. Other men helped the crew cut or haul wood. When the few males who had come ashore and didn't offer to help ogled Miranda, she asked Lucas to stroll with her at the edge of the woods. Out of sight, they sat down to relax and talk.

Time passed as they chatted about Amanda, Reis, Weber, and their destination. When it was nearing noon, Lucas grinned as he said he was going to fetch food and wine for a picnic. Miranda laughed gaily and agreed, waiting there for his return.

She leaned against the gray boulder at her back and closed her eyes briefly. She inhaled and exhaled deeply, capturing the fragrant odor of flowers and the spicy odor of woods. When her eyes opened, she couldn't believe the sight before them. She instantly sat straight, then curled her folded legs behind her. "How did you get here?" she asked ecstatically, gazing into the dark eyes of the unknown warrior who was squatting beside her. A surge of joy rushed over her body.

From her tone of voice and expression, Blazing Star knew she was glad to see him again, as delighted as he was to see her. He stood, then extended his hand to her in invitation, which she accepted without hesitation or fear. He helped her up, then nodded toward the forest, implying he wanted her to go with him.

Miranda glanced over her shoulder toward the river. When her cousin returned, he would worry if she wasn't here. Was it rash to take a walk with a stranger who wore war paint? Her consternation was evident to him. He smiled again, holding out his hand enticingly. She longingly stared at it, perceiving no threat from him. If he wanted to abduct her or injure her, he could easily have done either. He wanted to see her alone. Should she go along with him? It seemed safe, but was it wise?

Blazing Star removed the decorative wristlet which displayed none of his *coups*, just lovely and colorful designs. He handed it to her as a sign of friendship. Miranda accepted it, noting its beauty and artistry. He motioned for her to take his hand and follow him. When she remained rigid, he smiled as if comprehending her reason for refusal, then turned to walk away into the forest.

Miranda panicked. She rushed forward, whispering, "Wait. Who are you? Why do you keep appearing to me in secret?"

He turned and looked at her anxious expression. He smiled once more to relax her tension, then reached for her hand. He led her only a short distance into the forest, just enough for privacy. When he halted and turned, Miranda nervously backed against a tree, suddenly wondering if this were a mistake.

In a voice which touched her very soul, he murmured, "*Kokipa ikopa*, Miranda." His hand came up to caress her flushed cheek, his touch as gentle as if she were a newborn infant. He was amazed and pleased by her show of trust in him, by her total lack of fear.

Surprise brightened her eyes when he told her not to be afraid, but the warrior didn't know she understood his language. Before Miranda could respond in the Sioux tongue which her mother had taught her, his mouth closed over hers, then she was a captive of his steely embrace. If Miranda had been the sweat of his own body, she could not have been closer to his flesh. He was astonished, and yet not shocked, when she responded to his kiss and embrace. Knowing this would be the last time they met, Blazing Star had the overwhelming need to hold her, to kiss her just once, to test her feelings for him.

Their thirsty lips joined, and his strong arms banded her so tightly she skipped several breaths; yet she clung to him fiercely. It was crazy! He hadn't meant to kiss her, even to touch her. It was as if he had no power over his emotions or actions. He felt he would die of hunger if he didn't feast on her lips. But the more sweetness he devoured from her lips, the more ravenous his starving body became, until it begged to feed upon hers. His weakness and her power stunned him, for such feelings should not exist. Yet, she shared this fire which burned within him.

When Lucas returned to where he had left Miranda, he called her name in concern. Miranda never heard him; she feverishly kissed the warrior before her, mindless of all else. But the warrior's senses were keen, and he heard the summons. He knew the man would come looking for her. For a wild moment, he was tempted to slay the man and to capture the girl who inspired such passion within him. But the time was wrong; he had something vital to do for his people.

He ceased his intoxicating assault upon her lips and emotions. "Miranda *ya.*" He informed her that she must leave his side, nodding toward the direction from which Lucas was calling her. He cupped her face between his hands and seemed to memorize it. Such uncommon indecision filled him. Surely it was wrong to desire an enemy so much.

Assuming Blazing Star couldn't speak or understand English, she responded to Lucas, "Just a moment, Luke, I needed privacy."

If she had known he caught each word, she would have flushed a bright scarlet. "Will I see you again?" she asked eagerly. Unfortunately, she asked in English, not Sioux.

"Miranda *wilhanmna wincinyanna,*" he stated huskily. "*Ya.*"

Before she could question his order to leave or why he was calling her a "dream girl," he kissed her urgently and clamped his hand over her mouth afterward, fearing her words might influence him.

When Lucas's voice called out loudly to her, the warrior turned her body toward it. Determined he wouldn't get away without giving his name this time, she whirled to ask it in Sioux. He was gone! Just before shouting in Sioux for him to return, she mastered the impulse. How could she explain sneaking off with a warrior, a stranger, a dreaded and feared Sioux? How could she excuse her wanton behavior, even understand it herself? Most whites despised Indians; the passengers would hold her in contempt for her actions. What a tangled web! Who was he? To which Sioux tribe did he belong? She knew there were seven tribes with many bands. Would they meet again? she mused dreamily.

She called out to Lucas, saying she was coming to join him. She wondered about the warrior's appearance here. Was he following her? Or was it merely coincidence? Was he watching her this very moment? There was only one way to find out for sure. She would leave something behind for him and see if he had it the next time they met, if they ever did. She stuffed the beaded wristlet in her pocket, then removed the lacy scarf at her throat. She pressed it to her lips, then draped it over a bush before leaving.

Three days later, the *Martha Lane* made a two-day stop at Yankton, near Fort Randall. Little did Lucas and Miranda suspect what peril was in store for them, just as Amanda and Reis little suspected what evil was confronting them in Alexandria . . .

Chapter Twelve

*A*fter his much-awaited return to Alexandria, Reis spent all day Sunday with his wife. They talked, planned, joked, and made love. Later in the day, Amanda watched in disbelief as her dark, handsome husband transformed himself into a blond sailor in grimy clothes. Checking his new image in the mirror, he smiled and complimented himself on his crafty disguise.

"Now, if old Weber or his scum see me, they'll never guess who lurks beneath this golden hair and these dirty clothes," he remarked between chuckles. "All I have to do is sneak in both warehouses this week, make some notes for Grant, then close this case."

To conceal her apprehension, she asked, "What's Grant like?"

As if exposing a national secret, he whispered softly, "He likes to dress in old, baggy clothes—he would love this outfit. He smokes big black cigars that stink up a whole house. After you leave him, you smell awful for days. But he sure knows how to win a fight. If he hadn't captured Richmond, the war might have gone on and on."

"Do you like working for him more than you did for Lincoln?"

"Both are good men, love, but Lincoln was special. It was a dark day in our history when he was slain. He could have done so much for both sides. Did you know Lincoln offered your Lee the head of the Union Army, but he refused it? If not for Lee, the war wouldn't have lasted two years. A shame all good men can't be on the same side—war wouldn't have a chance of getting started. But one always leads to another, it seems."

"What do you mean, Reis?" Mandy asked.

As he put away his supplies, he talked with ease and intelligence. "The last one we fought started with the one in '12. The New England area got real nervous when we made the Louisiana Purchase; they threatened to secede and rejoin the British Empire. The President was smart; he prevented trouble with those *New Intercourse Laws*. You know what the Northern concession did? Riled up the Southern shipping interests. Lord, you just can't please everybody at once. The

South was really suffering from lack of trade; they took heavy losses in cotton and tobacco markets. It was the Southern states that voted to go to war with the British Crown. The Northerners voted not to protect their ships and supplies. From then on, every little cut festered into one big sore until the wound burst open and spilled its vile contents. It's tragically ironic: the North threatens to secede to get her way, then goes to war when the South carries out her same threat."

The topic was depressing and Amanda changed it with a question. "How did you get in last night? You said Weber has guards out front and back."

"I sneaked into your neighbor's garden, climbed a tree near the wall, and flipped over. Considering the height of the wall around your yard, no one could see me. Whoever built this house certainly loved privacy."

"Now that you've accomplished the easy part, how do you plan to get out? I don't have a tree near the wall. Of course, you could remain prisoner here with me," she hinted, smiling provocatively as she eased up on tiptoe to kiss him.

That night, Amanda snuggled into her husband's arms and inquired, "Reis, where will we live when this is all over? What will we do about Morning Star and Lawrence Shipping?"

"I think it should be a mutual decision, love, that we make after my tour of duty is finished. Until October first I am still under orders from President Grant. Our next decision will be whether or not you go on my next assignment with me or remain here until it's done."

Amanda sat up in bed and stared at him. "There is no decision; I'm going with you, husband dear. Even if you do look like a stranger," she teased him about his blond hair. "I'm glad it's dark, or I would have trouble making love to the man in my bed."

Reis chuckled as he propped himself up on two pillows. "I should tell you, love; I have no idea where or what my final assignment will be. When I get the news, you might change your mind."

"No," she vowed confidently. "You go; I go. You could get lonesome and forget you have a wife."

"Only if I lost my memory," he retorted playfully. "I'm glad Randy and Luke got away safely. And I know I shouldn't say this, but I'm glad your housekeeper won't be around for the next week or so."

"Does that mean I shall enjoy my wily husband's company every night?" she asked seductively, twirling her tongue on his chest.

"Every one possible. I'm suspicious about Reed's accident and those new guards outside. Weber's plotting something. There's no way I'll leave you alone at night unless I can't avoid it."

"You worry about me too much, Reis. I'm fine now that you're home. Besides, I know how to shoot and fight. I'm not as good as Randy, but I can defend myself," she declared proudly.

For a while they spoke of Miranda and Lucas. When she fretted over the safety of her sister and cousin, Reis reminded her of the letter of protection they were carrying from President Grant, one he had personally acquired and given to Lucas. Then Reis told her to go to sleep, that he would be stealing out before dawn. He added he would be late tomorrow night, if he came at all. He was planning to check out her warehouse, then Weber's the next night. She teased him about his recent vow to stay with her at night. He laughed and tickled her until she was squirming and breathless. He became serious when he warned her not to speak to him or show any recognition if they met on the street during the day. He took her office keys so he would be able to study any new and false information which Weber might be putting into her books.

Amanda tensed in fear when he told her he would also be analyzing the books of Daniel McVane and the ones in Weber's private office. He even hinted at breaking into Weber's home to see if there were any records of importance there.

"I'll be careful, love," he tried to calm her. "The sooner I solve this case, the sooner you can be Mrs. Reis Harrison in public," he tempted beguilingly, then pressed her to her back as he began a leisurely and stirring bout of passion.

Monday night was one of the longest nights for Amanda, for Reis never came home. She dozed little and paced until she was exhausted, but still she couldn't sleep. Tuesday passed as sluggishly as the day and night before, and her tension increased. By two in the morning, Amanda was beside herself with anxiety. Not only had Reis been gone since dawn on Monday, but Weber had not appeared as he had warned.

She wondered if the two absences were connected. After witnessing such evil in Weber Richardson, she feared for her husband's life. She could not tell Reis, but she was now willing to lose everything and leave with him this very night! She knew how deeply he despised Weber for his cruelties during the war. She refused to press him about those times because of the unusual coldness which froze his expression and the fires of revenge which burned in his eyes. Perhaps she feared that powerful hatred in him as much as she feared for him.

Shortly after noon on Wednesday, Weber paid her a call. She was dozing when he dropped by and it took a while for his knocking to arouse her from her heavy slumber on the sofa. She felt groggy and wanted to ignore the persistent summons, knowing it could not be her husband and finding any company undesirable at the moment.

The caller pounded loudly on the door. Weber called out, "Open this door, Mandy, or I'll break it down!"

When she unlocked the door, he shoved it open, almost snagging her toes beneath it. "What took so long?" he demanded angrily.

Amanda rubbed her sleepy eyes and moistened her dry lips. She fluffed her tousled hair and straightened her rumpled clothes. Then she looked at him and snapped, "I was asleep. I'm exhausted. I haven't been sleeping well with Randy and Mrs. Reed gone. Don't start on me, Weber! I'm not in the mood for a scolding." She sighed wearily then rubbed her eyes once more. "What do you want?"

"I was called away on an emergency. I just returned. When you didn't answer the door, I was worried. I thought you'd taken ill again, perhaps passed out," he declared petulantly when she didn't appear glad to see him.

"I surely am glad you didn't break down my front door. I could have been out visiting for the day," she informed him sassily, knowing how he knew she was home. "If you don't mind, Web, could we visit another day? I'm truly fainting from fatigue. I've gone for days without sleep or rest; the moment I finally slipped off, you came barging in, screaming at me. Was the emergency with my firm or yours?" she inquired, failing to offer him entrance.

"I was checking out a lead to Randy," he announced casually.

"What!" she blurted out in fear which passed for disbelief.

"I thought we could settle our problems quicker if I located your sister and brought her home. One of my hired men thought he recognized her on the street and followed her home. When I got there, it wasn't Randy. We searched all over. I'm sorry, Mandy, but we couldn't find her. Would you like me to hire a detective?" he inquired.

"No!" she yelled at him then explained heatedly, "I don't want my sister hunted down like some animal. Randy will come home when she's ready. If not, we'll both have to accept her decision, for whatever reason."

He studied her oddly. "Mandy, are you sure you're all right? You're awfully nervous, even a bit evasive."

"What the hell are you talking about?" she scoffed crudely. "How would you feel after days and nights without sleep? My sister's run off. I have a million worries. Then my best friend attacks my every word. Damnit, Weber, I'm a wreck!"

"Then marry me and let me take care of you," he offered.

"This is no way to begin a marriage, attacking each other every time we meet. Besides, I want the biggest and finest wedding this state's ever had. When I get things settled with the company, then I can decide what to do about you and your terrible moods."

"Another excuse to stall me?" he accused sullenly. "I can handle any problem while you plan our historical wedding."

"I promise to give you an answer this coming Sunday," she stated.

"There can be only one answer, Mandy. Your choice is me or the streets. Surely you don't need to weigh one against the other?"

"But you aren't my only choice, Weber," she told him rashly.

"You have another proposal? Who?" he snarled furiously.

"I meant work, not a man," she teased him.

"Just what kind of work can you do? I can't imagine Amanda Lawrence slaving anywhere," he playfully mocked her.

"Is that a fact, Mister Richardson?" she sneered as if insulted. "I daresay I can do many things to earn a living. I'm honest and loyal, and normally full of energy. And, no doubt, I could have five marriage proposals by next week, if I put my mind to it."

"I don't wish to sound cruel, my sweet, but how long would they remain extended if your loss of wealth and station were revealed?"

"You sound as if that's the only reason a man would court me!" she panted at him. "Since you know the truth, why not withdraw your offer?"

"Because I love you and want you, not what you have," he lied.

"Well, you certainly don't sound like it or behave like it of late! All you do is harass me, or scold me, or insult me. You act as if you enjoy demeaning me," she charged peevishly.

"Then why not get dressed and I'll take you out to dinner and the theater? We could ride to Washington and make a holiday of it. Why not elope?" he suggested eagerly. "That would be exciting and romantic. Just imagine the envy of your suitors."

"Elope!" she shrieked. "Don't be absurd, Weber. You know what people think of couples who elope. I won't have people thinking me pregnant. They would stare at me for nine months!"

"Amanda Lawrence, my patience is wearing thin. I demand an answer this minute," he declared stunningly, attempting to panic her.

Amanda's mind raced wildly toward a scheme to extract her from this precarious situation. "Unless your proclaimed love is also wearing thin, you will not mind having your answer Sunday. If such is the case, there is no need to consider your proposal. Love and marriage are not contests where points must be made to prove one's feelings. If you have no respect for my suffering, you are not the man to share my life. Shall it be Sunday, or never?" she presented her own ultimatum.

"You're serious, aren't you?" he inquired in surprise.

"I have never been more so in my life," she told him smugly. "I will not discuss such a vital matter as marriage in this distraught state. I cannot make critical choices which will affect the rest of my life when I am torn by troubles and doubts and I am assailed by fatigue! If you find that unacceptable, then I bid you a permanent farewell."

"Then I shall wait until Sunday for your decision. But I must know you still want me."

"Your conduct and my numerous worries make it impossible for me to assess the depth of my feelings. I can only say they have not changed of late. Perhaps a trip would be a good diversion—give me time to relax and think. Perhaps the new owner of Morning Star wouldn't mind if I made a last visit. I do so regret losing it," she baited him.

"I don't think that's wise, Mandy. It would remind you of the days spent there with Randy and your parents. I don't want you to go so far alone," he gently protested her alarming suggestion. "If you wish to visit later, then I will escort you there."

"I suppose you're right. It would be too painful to go there again. But someday soon, I'll need to retrieve our personal belongings. Surely the new owner has packed and stored them for us. Perhaps I only need sleep," she hinted innocently.

Delighted he had changed her mind, he smiled and agreed. "To prove I'm not pushing you, I'll stay away until Sunday afternoon. If you promise to send for me if you need anything," he added jovially.

His words were like sweet music to her ears. She smiled to show her gratitude. "I promise. I don't know why you fret so, Weber; whoever could I choose over you?" she teased coyly. "Thanks for being so understanding and kind; I shan't forget it. Until Sunday," she hinted.

"Until Sunday, my sweet," he replied. He kissed her hand, then left whistling.

Amanda knew why he was so elated. He was glad he wouldn't have to see her for days and relieved not to have to play this game where he might make a wrong move. He was so cocky! Without a doubt, he believed she would say yes on Sunday. If only he knew she was already legally wed, and to a man she loved above life itself.

Relief flooded her. Surely he didn't know about Reis. Else, he would have tried to entrap her with enticing hints or blunt statements. Surely Reis would come home tonight. With that conclusion, she rushed upstairs for a nap. "I'll be wide awake and full of energy tonight," she said aloud with a happy giggle.

When she awoke, she warmed water for a bath in the private closet near the kitchen. After a leisurely soaking, she was about to don a lovely dress but decided upon a sensual nightgown instead. Just as she was brushing her golden tresses, she sniffed several times. She shook her head, telling herself she couldn't smell food cooking. How could she? She was alone, and Mrs. Reed didn't have a key. Except for coffee and water, she hadn't used the stove today. When the fragrant aromas increased, she went to investigate, her bare feet treading soundlessly on the floor.

As she peered around the doorframe, she was astonished and delighted to see her husband standing near the stove working contentedly. Deep in thought, he didn't seem aware of her. She watched his profile for a brief time, pondering his intense concentration.

She wondered over his odd behavior. He had come home and started cooking without even saying hello! "Reis Harrison, whatever are you doing?" she questioned as she entered the room.

He jumped and whirled around, his hand automatically going for his concealed weapon. He swiftly mastered his poise and expression. "Making us some supper. I'm starved. It's about time you joined me, wife. I've been exceptionally good to let you nap and bathe before showing you my splendid face. I fully expect to be rewarded for such generosity," he jested mirthfully, confusing her.

He focused his gaze on his cooking, rather than showering her with kisses and hugs. He seemed reserved, distant. Yet, she watched him cover that inexplicable mood with contrived gaiety. "I don't understand," she murmured, coming to stand beside him at the stove. She wanted to fling herself into his arms and to kiss him feverishly, but something about his manner prevented it. He seemed so different.

"While old Weber was trying to beat down the front door, I was sneaking in the back. You certainly did some mighty persuasive acting, love. I surely am glad you're on my side. I would hate to imagine those charms, wits, and courage working against me," he jested roguishly, removing the fried salt pork from the skillet.

"You've been here since noon? Why didn't you show yourself after Weber left?" she asked in confusion, hurt by his actions. That statement meant he had overheard her talk with Weber. It also meant he had been hiding from her since his furtive arrival. Why?

He excused his actions by saying, "You sounded as exhausted as you looked. I knew that part of your colorful tale was true. If you hadn't gone right to sleep, I would have joined you in bed," he stated huskily, slipping an arm around her waist as he worked with the other hand. "I took a short nap in Randy's room; I was dead tired too. I straightened the covers, but you might want to peek in there before Mrs. Reed returns to work. We don't want her discovering our little secret. How do you like your eggs cooked?" he inquired casually.

Amanda simply stared at him as he began cracking eggs and dropping their contents into a bowl. "What's wrong with you?" she asked.

He looked up from his task and questioned, "What do you mean?"

"You vanish for days, then appear without bothering to explain. Do you know how worried and frightened I've been? When you do come home, you're more interested in sleep and food than your wife!" she charged, provoked by his indifferent mood and lack of affectionate greeting.

"Can't business wait until later? I'd prefer to spend a quiet evening with my wife. Have supper and . . . turn in early," he hinted seductively. "These last few days and nights have been terrible, Mandy. Am I being selfish to want you as my only thought for tonight? Isn't it better this way? I only wanted to surprise you."

"Well, you certainly did," she informed him crisply. "I can see why you would let me take a nap, but why wait so long afterward?" She wanted to demand he tell her why he was being so remote, but she didn't. She fretted mutely over this new side of him.

Passion danced within his dark blue eyes. His mood mellowed, and he smiled contritely. "To enjoy what I'm seeing right this minute." His appreciative gaze moved over her shiny hair and enticing nightgown; then, he inhaled the freshness of her skin and the sweetness of her cologne. "I'll confess I heard what you planned for me as you raced upstairs, and I controlled myself to wait for my surprise."

He chuckled when her cheeks flushed crimson. "It isn't often a husband gets seduced by such beauty and eagerness."

"How would you know? You are new at this role, aren't you?" she responded coyly as she noted a half-grin tugging at his sensual lips.

"Yep, but I've heard plenty of tales which could inspire any male to avoid marriage. Evidently I made a wise choice," he told her, pulling her into his arms. He didn't kiss her immediately. He just held her tenderly, caressing her back and inhaling her fragrance.

Her dreamy gaze touched on a small leather case on the floor near a chair. She was puzzled when he stiffened at her question, "Were you working? Does that satchel contain evidence against Weber?"

He released her and returned to his task. "I thought we agreed business could wait until later. Let's eat and relax."

"You agreed; I didn't. Did something happen you don't want to tell me?" she asked suspiciously.

"All right, have it your way," he stated a little brusquely. "I was making out my report. I obtained some evidence, but not enough. I couldn't get home or send word without tipping my hand. I did warn you our relationship was secret and my mission might require my absence on occasion," he reminded her moodily.

"You don't have to sound so hateful," she chided him. "What evidence did you get? How much longer will it take? Weber is pressing me again, as you heard," she added snippily when he scowled.

"I told you I wanted our discussion to wait because I knew you'd get angry and upset by it. That was a foolish thing to tell him, Mandy. What if I can't solve this case by Sunday; what then? He's going to get suspicious. As to the evidence, I can't tell you. That way, you can't drop clues when you play your reckless games with Weber."

"What was I supposed to do?" she flared back at him, rankled.

"For starters, agree to his idea about Randy. That should keep him occupied for a while, maybe distracted from what I'm doing and from wooing my wife. What new excuse do you plan to use Sunday?"

She was shocked by his suggestion. "You want him to search for her? Heavens, Reis, what if he found her? I would be in danger!"

"I doubt he or his hired thugs could find any trace of her. And even so, you could always play dumb; you could act tricked by her and Luke. There's no way Weber could prove you were involved in their scheme, even if he suspected it. Aren't you forgetting he knows why she left, but he thinks you don't? He can't harm Randy. I'll know if he leaves town and heads that way. I can warn Luke. If he thinks there's the slightest chance of finding her, he won't be pushing you so hard."

"You sound as if I'm his last choice!" she pouted petulantly.

"Stow that pride, Mandy, or it'll get you into trouble. He wants her because he thinks he can manage her more easily than you and because she's unobtainable, the irresistible temptation."

"What do you mean, she's more manageable?" she probed.

"You are one bullheaded, outspoken female. You're smart and willful. Randy's quiet and reserved, and gives Weber the impression she isn't as intelligent as you. Also, you know the business and like it; she doesn't. Her lack of knowledge and interest in the firm would protect his schemes. And you don't seem easily intimidated or misled; Randy's shyness implies she can be. Weber has vastly underestimated her, and you should use that ignorance and conceit against him. Don't be so damn friendly with him," he declared possessively, his jealousy and vexation born of worry over her.

Amanda wanted to argue against his statements, but she couldn't. She sullenly acquiesced. "I'll correct my errors tomorrow."

"While we're at it, we might as well cover all points. I want you to stop taking such rash chances. I can handle the case against Weber, so stop trying to assist me. How can I concentrate on success if I'm worried about you and what you're doing? I can't promise to be around every night, and I can't risk sending a message. And I can't confide my plans to you. There are others involved now, and I won't risk endangering more lives. I don't think you realize the importance of this mission. You're being childish and selfish, Mandy. This isn't the time to prove you can outwit Weber or gain revenge on him. I take chances every time I come here. Hellfire, I risked death and defeat by confiding in you and marrying you so I wouldn't lose you! What more do you want from me?" he thundered.

Amanda determined she wouldn't cry, but it was a battle to control her tears. Why was he being so mean, so defensive, so secretive? It wasn't jealousy. "You know where I am, but I have no idea where you go or what perils you confront! For all I knew, you could have been lying dead somewhere! You're my husband, Reis. I love you. I was so frightened I almost contacted President Grant."

"You what!" he stormed at her, his eyes chilling at the vision of what her loose tongue could inspire. "Don't you ever contact him or anyone about me! You want to get me killed? Or in deep trouble? If anyone knew about us . . ." He fell silent, then struck the table forcefully in unleashed fury. "It was a mistake to marry during a critical mission. Damn, I gave you credit for more sense. All you want to do is play amateur detective, and damn the rules and consequences! Why can't you stay out of trouble and mischief? What have I gotten myself into? You could ruin everything, Mandy. Lives and national security are at stake. If you loved me and trusted me, you'd do as I asked."

She was devastated by his insults. Her chin and lips quivered and tears blurred her vision. A lump came to her throat. He had dropped into a chair and was staring blankly at his clasped hands, musing over how to handle this complex female. When she could force words from her throat, she said in a trembly voice, "If this is any indication of what marriage to a spy is like, then it was a mistake for us to wed. Perhaps we shouldn't see each other again until this 'critical' mission is over, or else we might ruin our relationship all together. I wouldn't want to jeopardize it or any lives, especially yours and mine. Don't feel obligated to check on me; I'll be just fine. As to Weber, I'll follow your orders, sir. After you feed your starving body, feel free to sneak out at your leisure. If you think you've made a terrible mistake by marrying me, then by all means correct it as quickly as possible," she stated, then fled the tormenting room, slamming and locking her bedroom door.

Reis propped his elbows on the table and rested his forehead on his palms, berating himself for taking his frustrations and fears out on his innocent wife. It wasn't fair; he had been cruel. He couldn't tell her he was distressed because one of his agents had been killed last night, for she would worry over his survival too much. Now, he must write a letter of condolence to Bill Hayes's family.

He couldn't blame her because Weber had tightened the security around both warehouses before he could complete his investigations. He was further disturbed because he and George Findley hadn't been given the time to sabotage the illegal weapons they had located in Weber's crates. And he had discovered that a Ku Klux Klan meeting had been arranged for next week, a meeting to plan violence to black voters and several carpetbaggers, and to discuss the possible assassination of Jefferson Davis to rile up the South.

He had taken an oath of silence and loyalty to America for the President. He shouldn't have become so angered by her fear for him, but he couldn't allow any contact with Washington. Grant had many enemies in his administration. Grant had made some terrible errors in judgment, in special-interest legislation, and in patronage. There was much corruption and scandal surrounding the President, and he was trying to correct it and redeem himself with Reis's help. Only Grant knew of his missions. If Amanda dropped clues into the wrong ears, all could be ruined. But if he couldn't trust her, he couldn't trust anyone! Why hadn't he simply explained that no one but Grant knew of this mission?

He couldn't admit to irrational jealousy this afternoon. It wasn't her fault her life was in danger. It wasn't her fault that he had almost been caught by Weber because he had been distracted by thoughts of her! She hadn't seduced him or tricked him into a wedding. She hadn't married him for fear of poverty. It wasn't her fault he wanted this mission over so they could be together and she could be safe.

She had become like an obsession to him, a perilous weakness, a deadly distraction. Yet, those were his problems, not hers. How could he have said such hateful things to her? Hellfire, he hadn't even shown or told her how much he had missed her! What was he doing to her, to them?

Weber Richardson—he was the evil force in this matter. God, how he wanted to kill that man barehanded! Each time he saw Weber or overheard him plotting, it became more difficult to restrain his hatred and desire for revenge. But if he killed Weber, the trail to the others involved in these crimes would be lost. This case was so complicated and demanding. He stood and stretched to relax his taut muscles, then headed for Amanda's room to beg her forgiveness and understanding.

As Reis mounted the steps wondering how to explain his mercurial moods, he knew the only way to show his love and trust was to tell her everything. He had never been this edgy or indecisive. But he had never had someone more precious than life to fret over, to protect. Amanda was right; if he died while carrying out this mission, she wouldn't even know why she had lost him. No one would even know to contact her with such grim news! He sighed heavily, thinking how glad he was that Miranda and Lucas were safe and happy . . .

Chapter Thirteen

It didn't take long for Lucas to realize that wild Yankton wasn't the place for him and Miranda, and neither was their second stop, Fort Randall. They would continue toward Pierre on the *Martha Lane* tomorrow morning.

With two railroads joining in Yankton soon, the town was overflowing with workmen, "ladies of pleasure," and a variety of opportunists. Two mills were being built near town: a flour mill and a lumber mill. A packing plant and foundry were under discussion for imminent construction. Several rowdy saloons were ready for use, with numerous others under construction or planning. Headquarters for freight companies and stagelines had blossomed in and around Yankton. The town was full of crime and violence and Lucas felt they should move on, as the area offered nothing but trouble.

But their brief stay at Fort Randall provided some grim and interesting insights. Miranda and Lucas were both surprised by the boredom and hardships which filled the average soldier's life. They had been led to believe the soldiers and settlers in this area led exciting, profitable, and pleasant lives. But the colorful adventures printed in newspapers and books were fantasies or fictionalized accounts.

Lucas was fascinated by all he saw and learned, and made careful notes for future stories or articles. He questioned almost everyone he met about three men in particular. His pouch grew fat with information, facts and figures which he was only too eager to share with Miranda.

True, the Army did protect the trails and railroads, the miners and settlers, the cattlemen and shepherders, and the traders. The Army did do surveys for railroad lines and telegraph lines or protect the crews which carried out such necessary jobs. The Army did battle "hostiles," as the Indians were labeled. Sometimes, the Army did the work for companies, such as building roads or clearing land. Yet, the majority of time was spent with arduous chores in or around the fort.

One thing which Miranda found intriguing was the Army's contradictory views on marriage amongst its enlisted men. The men were lonely and miserable; yet families were discouraged. The men's carnal needs were met in several ways. At some forts, whores were permitted to live and ply their trades. At others, women who served as cooks and laundresses also served as whores for the men who could afford such luxuries. At still others, wagons arrived every few weeks with prostitutes, games, and whiskey for sale; at such times, some men spent their entire month's wages in one day. Sadly, in some cases, widows or daughters were forced into such professions when left alone and penniless. Many soldiers used Indian women from the nearby reservations to sate their lusts. At those forts which existed near settlements, saloons offered the soldiers their three desires: drink, women, and gambling.

It seemed to Miranda that a happily married man would make a better soldier. Clearly the US Army disagreed. But those men who were fortunate enough to have wives had private homes and relief from boredom and sacrifice; they were in better health and were better fed. Miranda quickly learned that a female, especially a pretty one, was flooded with proposals of all kinds. After a few days in this territory, she was beginning to wonder if she should pretend to be Lucas's wife rather than his sister to dissuade so many men from pursuing her, including the men on the ship!

Before leaving on the steamer, Lucas sent Amanda another telegram, revealing their next destination. He asked her to contact him at Pierre, for he intended to be there for quite some time and needed to hear how she was. To continue their charade, he told Amanda to pass along his greetings to Miranda in Charleston. He stated he would write a lengthy letter from Pierre to relate his adventures there.

Lucas gradually uncovered facts which deeply distressed him. General William T. Sherman, who had terrorized and destroyed much of the South and boasted loudly of his atrocities, was the commanding general of the Army and was in charge of this territory. Lucas discovered he was operating out of Fort Richardson in Texas. President Grant had given Division of Missouri command to Philip Sheridan, who was working the middle area near Fort Dodge in Kansas.

The Division of Missouri was an immense tract, an area which included the Dakota Territory, stretching from Canada to the coast of Texas and from the Rockies to the Mississippi River, and comprising over a million frontier miles, including sacred and hunting grounds of nearly one hundred tribes. Several tribes which were causing major problems for the Army were the Sioux, Cheyenne, Apache, Comanche, and Kiowas—all known for fiercely defending their homes, lands, and people.

Added to those powerful forces was George Custer, known to have executed seven Rebels during the Civil War without a trial, and now assigned to the Seventh Cavalry at Fort Lincoln. During the Civil War, Custer had risen to the rank of general; here in the Cavalry, he was ranked a lieutenant colonel. But from all Lucas had heard, Custer was rapidly working on improving his rank to general once more. As Sheridan told Custer, "Kill or hang all warriors." This statement appeared to epitomize the thoughts and actions of all three men. Lucas had learned so much about Indians from Marie Lawrence, and it alarmed him to realize the Army's strategy was the annihilation of all Indians, male and female, old and young, especially the awesome and influential Sioux, Marie's family and people, and Miranda's relatives.

After mutually devastating the South during the war, all three leaders were now here trying to do the same with the Indian in the West. No success could be had until they realized this terrain, these battles, and this enemy were vastly dissimilar to those of the Civil War. Lucas's blood raced with elation at the thought of not only exposing the vile war deeds of these three men, but of revealing their grisly actions here in the West. Surely the combined revelations would be detrimental to their careers.

As the steamer made its way toward Pierre, Lucas spent as much time as possible with the two soldiers aboard who had been transferred from Sherman's troop to Custer's. Having a weakness for whiskey and suffering from boredom, the two men accepted the drinks purchased by Lucas, in exchange for colorful tales and intriguing facts about both men and their campaigns. Led to believe Lucas Reardon was a famous writer, the men boasted of exploits in which they had participated, hoping to become as well known as Custer and Sherman.

A wily reporter, Lucas found it easy to extract information from these men. His only problem was in separating fact from fiction. Lucas's genial personality and boyish mien aided his quest for truth. Lucas learned about the notorious "Indian Ring" of corruption and fraud. He discovered that Sherman was on the rampage once more, now that Satanta of the fierce Kiowa Indians had been released from prison. He listened to grisly tales of massacres which sickened, repulsed, and saddened him.

Both soldiers had shown a strong interest in Miranda, and Lucas cautioned her to watch her step around them. But she had to walk a fine line between silencing them with haughty rejection and inspiring a steady flow of confessions with cordial behavior. The day before they were to join their new troop, the two soldiers ceased their heavy drinking. It was time to sober up minds and clean up appearances. But clearer heads offered trouble for Lucas and Miranda. When the two soldiers began to compare mental notes on the cunning pair, they realized the couple had been asking too many questions about their leaders and exploits. Suddenly they feared Lucas might be a government agent investigating war crimes.

Ignorant of the danger they faced, Lucas went over his impending strategy with Miranda. "One of those soldiers told me our old friend, Thomas Baylor from Virginia, is assigned to Sherman. If we can catch up to him before going home, with luck Tom can get me a personal interview with the beast."

"And what if Sherman guesses what you're trying to pull?" she speculated fearfully, imagining what that man alone could do to her cousin, not daring to envision all three villains at his back.

"He won't; I'll be careful. With the egos of those three, they'll think I'm glorifying their famous names. Or should I say infamous. Besides, the way things are going out here, the settlers are starting to hate the soldiers more than the Indians. I heard a group of them bragging at Fort Randall about foraging on settlers between pay periods. They made it sound like a common practice for the entire territory."

"What's our next stop?" she inquired anxiously.

"After we load fuel once more, we're supposed to halt at the Lower Brule Reservation to drop off supplies—Indian annuities they called them. We'll only be there a few hours, then head on to Pierre. Good thing we're staying there because that's the termination point for this steamer. The pilot said we could either take another steamer or go north by stage. From the hints I've been gathering, Pierre sounds like a good place to linger," he stated, piquing her curiosity.

"Why?" she quickly probed, eyes bright and wide.

"You'll see," he teased mysteriously, playfully. "You get your letter finished to Mandy and we'll mail it in Pierre. I surely hope we have word waiting for us from her and Reis. It surely would help my mood knowing Weber had been put away for keeps."

"Me too," she concurred.

When the steamer halted its engine, Lucas wondered why Miranda was so eager to go for a walk. She looked as excited as a child on a birthday. She was even more elated when she learned there was no "woodhawk" here and the crew must cut wood—it would be a lengthy stop.

Once ashore, the two soldiers joined them for a talk and stroll, vexing Miranda for more than one reason. She didn't like these two males or trust them. She preferred to be alone or with Lucas. Still, she couldn't keep sneaking off without arousing suspicion. She was anxious to learn if the handsome warrior was still trailing her. And she didn't want to spend time with the two soldiers who made her uneasy, especially today. She sensed something different in their moods, their expressions, their tones.

Anson Miller and Jim Rhodes chatted with Lucas for five or ten minutes, but Miranda paid little attention. A provocative word here and there brought her to alertness. She listened as Jim told Lucas about an old reservation within walking distance. Since Lucas and Miranda had shown such an interest in the Indians, Jim suggested they walk there, hinting they might find arrowheads or such for souvenirs.

Anson remarked, "Surely you've heard of Spotted Tail, the famous Sioux chief? They even named the agency after him, Spotted Tail-Whetstone. The old chief went to Washington in '70 to see Grant himself. Told him the area was trouble 'cause of whiskey traders. Had to have somebody to blame when his warriors got falling-down drunk," he stated between chuckles. "Old Spotted Tail was powerful and Grant didn't want him on the warpath again, so he let them move near White River close to them sacred Black Hills. Didja know Spotted Tail's sister is Crazy Horse's mother? You do know who Crazy Horse is?" he teased.

Before Lucas or Miranda could reply either way, Jim quickly inserted, "They probably don't want to see no remains of savages—you know there's still bones in some of them trees from that crazy burial practice afore it was outlawed—just old fires and raggedy teepees."

"Luke here's a writer, Jim; he needs to see things like that. Don't you, Luke?" Anson argued as they set their trap for an unsuspecting Luke and Miranda.

"Well, I'm sure Miss Miranda don't care to gaze upon such ugly sights," Jim remarked. He grinned and muttered, " 'Course she does seem the brave, adventurous type. You got a good helper, Luke."

Lucas glanced at Miranda and asked, "You want to see it?"

Miranda didn't know which she wanted to see more, the old campsite or . . . Suppose this was that mysterious warrior's old campground; he had spoken Sioux, and the soldier had stated that Spotted Tail was Sioux. Suppose he had returned to his old territory or ancestral grounds for a special reason. She mentally chided herself for centering her plans around a man who might be days away from here. If the warrior wanted to see her again, he would find a way, as he had twice before. She smiled amiably and nodded trustingly, taking Lucas's hand to walk near him.

Anson and Jim talked freely as they guided the two out of earshot of the steamer. Finally, Lucas asked, "This seems a mite far, Jim. Maybe we should head back. We don't want to get lost."

Anson stopped and informed them, "Let me check the marker back there.

Maybe we took a wrong path. We should be there by now." He walked past them, then suddenly turned and struck Lucas on the head with its pistol butt, rendering him unconscious.

Miranda screamed, dropping to her knees to check on her cousin. Lucas was out cold and blood was wetting his hair. Alarmed and stunned, her head jerked upward as she shrieked, "Why did you do that?"

Anson leaned over and seized her around the waist. He flung her to the grass and straddled her. He stated ominously, "So I could do this," then kissed her.

Miranda struggled in his tight grasp as his slobbery lips refused to leave hers. From above their tangled bodies, she could hear Jim's laughter and jests, encouraging Anson to hurry and to give him a turn with her. As Jim verbally planned his coming actions ahead, she cringed in terror as she comprehended their plan—rape!

Miranda knew it was useless to plead, and she didn't. It would only be amusing to them. Considering the distance they had walked, she also knew it was futile to yell for help. Lucas was injured, and she had no weapon. She was at their mercy. If only she were standing, she could use the Chinese defense movements taught to her. She thrashed wildly on the ground, but Anson was strong and heavy. When she tried to claw at his face, he told Jim to tie her wrists.

The other soldier delighted in tearing a strip from her dress then binding her hands tightly. "You want me to tie her feet?" Jim asked when she continued to kick at Anson.

"Hell, no!" Anson shrieked. "How would I get twixt her legs, fool? You just hold her still while I shuck these pants."

With Anson standing between her parted thighs, Jim straddled Miranda's middle. Anson wiggled his pants down to his boots. Jim laughed when she beat at his leg with tightly bound hands and tried to twist free. "You ain't gonna git undressed?" he asked when Anson merely lowered his pants and unfastened the crotch of his longjohns to free a thick shaft which was taut and drooling with hunger.

"Ain't got time. I'm hurting as it is. This big stud needs a fast mating," Anson replied crudely, fondly caressing his aching manhood. He knelt, seizing her imprisoned hands and throwing his confining body on hers as Jim lifted his weight.

By that time, Lucas was stirring and groaning. Anson laughed satanically as Jim struck him again, this time harder. "I'll tie that sly fox whilst you have your turn with her. You ain't gonna spoil our fun, boy. You just lie still 'til we git some relief."

Miranda prayed Lucas was alive, but she feared he wasn't. He was so still and his chest didn't appear to rise and fall. There was so much blood running down into his brown curls. For a time, she had more concern and attention for Lucas than for herself. But with his groin exposed and hardened, Anson's forceful and lewd grinding against her private region refreshed her peril.

When she screamed and fought with renewed energy from fear and fury, Jim asked if Anson wanted her silenced. Anson laughed coldly and said, "No need. Can't nobody hear her. 'Sides, she'll be sighing in pleasure real soon. You know how them women from Newman's wagons fight over who's gonna take care of this boy. Hell, most of the time they don't even charge me!" he boasted falsely. "You tie that youngster, then git ready to follow me. Let's get some relief, then we'll have some slow fun. These two'll pay for tricking us. Luke there won't make no reports to nobody. As for this little filly, we might find somebody willing to pay hefty for 'er, if they's anything left."

There wasn't time for Miranda to ponder his odd words or ominous threat. While she tried to resist the demands of Anson, Jim bound Lucas with his belt and rolled him into the bushes, saying he didn't want no kin staring at him while he enjoyed a "good balling."

Jim started undressing, hopping around on one foot as he removed the boot from the other. Unable to pull his eyes from Anson as he fumbled to find the waistband of her bloomers, Jim pulled off the other boot and his pants, tossing his clothes and gun in a pile. He unbuttoned his longjohns and was attempting to yank them off.

The air was silent but for the heavy breathing from three people and Miranda's grunts as she attempted to keep Anson from removing her bloomers. Unable to stop herself, she yelled at him, "You bastard! You'll pay for this! Get off of me! Touch me and I'll kill you!"

Suddenly, loud and ferocious growls offered more noise and threat than a violent thunderstorm. Anson ceased his attack to shout, "What was that, Jim?" Both men stiffened as small trees to their left moved violently as something awesome headed in their direction.

"I hope it ain't what I think," Jim replied hastily, frantically trying to free his arms from his last garment. He lunged for his discarded weapon, wishing he had his Springfield rifle from the boat.

Jim tossed clothes and boots in all directions and located his Army-issue revolver, but it jammed during the panic of the moment as he fired wildly into the trees. He cursed as he fumbled feverishly to get it working. If only he had that new Colt he had been promised.

Anson made a rolling dive for his weapon, but it was too late. A large, dark blur had surged from the concealing trees, heading for Anson who had tripped on the pants around his ankles. Still fully clothed, Miranda scrambled to lower her skirt and to avoid attracting the bear's attention. She hastily pressed herself against a large rock and attempted to control her noisy respiration.

Miranda had never seen a bear so large. His head and body were massive. When he growled, she could see long, sharp teeth, as well as the saliva which drooled from his mouth. Although his eyes appeared very small, he seemed to have no trouble locating his prey. He moved swiftly and formidably, not at all like the clumsy performing bears back east. His furry coat was a thick yellowy brown. As he agilely ambled toward the two men, Miranda froze in terror.

The creature suddenly raised himself to his full height of over seven feet, seven feet of powerful muscle without fear. She realized his arms nearly reached his groin. At the ends of those forelegs were two sets of claws longer than her fingers!

During the initial flurry of action, the two soldiers had shouted back and forth. "Forget the gun and clothes, Jim! Let's run, run. It's a grizzly." But Anson had fallen forward as his trembling hands couldn't pull his pants from around his shaky ankles. The grizzly was on him in a flicker of an eye. Those gaping jaws ripped flesh and clothes, sending bits of both flying in all directions as the beast viciously mauled him.

When Jim tossed the useless gun aside and was about to leave all behind to flee to safety, the monstrous animal left the severely wounded Anson to pursue him. The man didn't get far before the grizzly came to full height again, waving his paws and growling. Jim made a fatal error when he turned to see how close behind the bear was. With a lightning flash of one paw, the bear made a lethal slash across Jim's throat. Jim was dead before the silence returned after his agonizing scream.

When the groggy and pain-riddled Anson began to moan, the bear's attention became focused on him again. The smell of blood overwhelmed the fresh air, and the stench of slaughter gradually joined it. Miranda's brain was too dazed to order her to flee this ghastly sight. With a rolling gait, the bear nonchalantly returned to Anson's scarlet-covered frame. Anson screamed and sobbed, rolling to his stomach to protect his face and vulnerable belly, forgetting to play dead until the bear lost interest and left. As Anson shuddered and wept, fear permeated the air, an emotion which encouraged and pleased the enormous animal.

The grizzly rolled Anson to his back with one forceful swipe, tearing flesh and clothes with those sharp instruments of death and destruction. Miranda was grateful the fuzzy body prevented her view, as she seemed unable to look away.

How she wished she couldn't hear the sounds of torture and death. Her heart pounded so forcefully that her chest and throat ached. Nausea churned her stomach and assailed her throat. Her gaze seemed to go out of focus, and lightness filled her head. Her mouth was dry. She was so cold, her body felt like stone. She feared she would faint, yet she couldn't scream in terror, or cry in fear, or even babble in hysteria. All she could do was sit petrified, unable to move. She, or Lucas, would be the next victim.

A warm hand clamped over her mouth and shifted her head. Her eyes enlarged and misted as they took in the most beautiful and encouraging sight she had ever viewed. Blazing Star pressed his finger to his lips, commanding silence. His keen eyes glanced at the bear whose attention was on the dead soldier. Without making a sound, he took his knife and severed her bonds.

Uncontrollably and ecstatically, she flung herself against his coppery chest and burst into alerting sobs as her arms encircled his waist. For a moment, the warrior's arms embraced and comforted her. Instantly the bear's attention was seized and the massive head turned in their direction. Blazing Star stiffened, coming to full alert. As the animal slowly lumbered their way, the warrior gently shoved Miranda aside and shifted his knife in his grip.

The bear was considered a warrior of the forest by the Indians, a symbol of wisdom. A bear was never killed lightly. When necessary, it had to be done with skill and daring, in hand-to-paw combat. Only a warrior who had slain a bear could wear the claws around his neck. The warrior didn't wish to slay his brother of the forest, but he had no choice. He could easily flee danger, but the girl couldn't.

To draw attention from Miranda, Blazing Star jumped to his feet and rushed to a small clearing, sending forth Indian whoops. The warrior crouched and awaited the answer to his challenge, one which was sure to come. The grizzly headed for the warrior, ignoring the girl who was gaping in sheer terror.

Miranda knew she was to blame for endangering their lives. But no power could enable her to take back her rash mistake. She prayed as she had never prayed before. But what could a knife do against such imposing strength and ten lethal claws? Should she run? Was the warrior only distracting the beast for her to escape? But what about Lucas? What if her escape movements attracted the bear's attention? What about the man who was risking his life for her?

She watched the intrepid warrior and the large creature as each sized up the other. She couldn't suppress a scream when the bear swiped at the warrior with those deadly paws. But the warrior was agile and quick, and the bear's attack was unsuccessful. As they moved and slashed at each other, it became a deadly dance of death. She wondered how long the warrior could avoid those destructive weapons. Surely his six-foot frame was no match for such height and weight.

If possible, Miranda's terror had increased with the warrior's involvement in this drama. She saw blood on the knife; yet the warrior's virile body revealed no cuts. She witnessed confidence and determination in the warrior's expression and movements. He exuded physical prowess. Was it possible he could win such a fierce battle?

Weapon . . . She recalled the soldier's guns. She forced her wobbly legs to crawl toward them, desperately trying to keep her gaze off two grim sights. Her eyes darted around as she failed to locate either pistol. It was as if they had vanished. But Miranda hadn't seen the bear's paw fling them into the bushes during his two attacks.

She hurried to Lucas's prone body, placing her ear on his chest to find his heart still beating. She struggled to free him, finally succeeding. But she couldn't arouse him. With luck and prayers, the bear might overlook him, so she left Lucas where he was.

When she entered the open area once more, screams of horror were torn from her throat as the warrior fell backward to the ground and the grizzly charged at him with claws curled ominously. Miranda shouted and stomped the hard ground, trying to pull the bear's attention from the warrior until he could regain his footing and balance. She avidly sought items to seize the menacing foe's eye, tossing rocks and small limbs at the huge body of dark fur. The bear ignored her and continued his charge on the fallen and weaponless Indian. Unable to witness this man's death, she screamed an echoing "no" and slipped to the ground as protective and merciful blackness engulfed her.

Blazing Star was given the split second needed for victory when the bear whirled toward the loud noise. The bear was fatigued from his previous killings and the battle with the warrior. He was distracted and sluggish. Already weakening from a speedy loss of blood from the wounds in his chest and throat, the animal was doomed as Blazing Star sent his lethal blade home. The bear staggered and slowly sank to the blood-spattered ground.

Blazing Star rushed to Miranda's side, dropping to his knees to pull her into his arms. Clearly she had tried to draw the creature's attention and attack to her, to save his life. She had been willing to die for him. That reality stunned his senses but thrilled his heart. She was so pale and cool. Blazing Star sat down and cuddled her in his embrace. He placed kisses on her face and lips. He thanked the Great Spirit for bringing him here to save her life. His mission was over; the two soldiers were dead. For some inexplicable reason, he was glad he hadn't been compelled to kill them before her lovely eyes. It was time to return to his people. He fretted over the feelings he was experiencing: loneliness, desire, and indecision.

Miranda's eyes fluttered and opened. She was bewildered. She was lying on her back in the forest, gazing at the movement of leaves overhead as the wind slipped through them. But for the singing of birds and the soft rustle of leaves, it was so quiet and peaceful. She sighed tranquilly and stretched her limp body.

Abruptly she bolted to a sitting position and looked around her. Lucas was lying near her, his head bandaged with strips from his shirt. They were alone, in a different spot!

Voices caught her attention in the distance. She realized they were near the river, near the anchored steamer, near help. But who had brought them here? Where was the warrior?

Her heart thudded with suspense and hope. Did this mean he wasn't dead? She tried to awaken Lucas but couldn't. She had to go back to see if the warrior lived! Whatever the danger, she had to know his fate!

Breathing raggedly, she burst into the small clearing where the rank odor of violent death stung her nostrils. Her hand flew upward to cover her nose and mouth. She inched past the mutilated Jim and Anson, then halted in disbelief. The bear lay dead, without his furry coat and lethal paws and massive head. There was no sign of the warrior who had saved her life and removed her from this grim setting.

Clamping her hand over her mouth to keep from retching, she commanded her feet to take her back to Lucas. She had her answer; he had survived, survived with the strength to take a bloody trophy. As she fought against fainting again, she leaned against a tree to regain her control and wits. She murmured softly, "Thank God, you're alive. I couldn't live with your death on my hands. Will we ever meet again? I don't even know your name. I didn't even get to thank you."

She cried for a long time, releasing her anguish and tension. When she walked away, she was unaware of the somber black eyes which followed her. He mastered the impulse to capture her, for she offered great danger to his emotions and pride. It was wrong for him to take a white woman, so why was he tormented by such desire for her? Why did her sadness and tears pain him more than a knife wound? Why did it take all of his control to keep himself hidden from her, denying both a farewell? Who was this girl with such potent magic that she could have such stirring and forbidden effects on him? Why did he want her at his side under the sun as much as he wanted her beneath him at night? These were new and baffling feelings, feelings he must conquer and forget.

Forget, he scoffed to himself as she vanished from sight. How he wished he had never seen or touched her, for he could never forget her now. But it would be worse if he had shown himself, if he had joined her body to his. Would he be as stirring and haunting to her? If only she weren't so rare, he would take her prisoner and sate his lust for her! But she was, and such treatment would destroy her. For a few moments beneath the sun, they had touched and kissed. He could allow nothing more, for she was more dangerous than any peril or foe or beast he had ever confronted.

At Lucas's side, Miranda tried to arouse him once more. When she failed, she cried out for help, which came swiftly. When Lucas was carried aboard the steamer to a doctor who was heading for Fort Sully, Miranda told him they had been attacked by a grizzly and that she and Lucas had been rescued by a strange trapper dressed in buckskins. After slaying the bear which had killed the two soldiers, the man had helped them get this far and then returned to skin the bear before someone else found it. She added that the trapper said he would see to burying the two soldiers. She didn't know what she would do if they checked out her story and found the two soldiers nearly nude. What if there was evidence it was an Indian warrior? They would force the humiliating truth about the foiled rape from her. They might even suspect she knew the warrior.

One man shook his head and informed the others, "Them grizzlies are known to travel in pairs. I ain't going in there after no mauled bodies. Let that trapper bury 'em like she said."

One of the crew members said the wood was cut and nearly loaded, and they needed to get underway. Several others agreed there was no need to fetch the bodies or to waste more time. Before noon, the steamer was moving again, with one last stop before Pierre.

Miranda was sitting beside Lucas's bunk when he came around, his head freshly bandaged. When he groaned and touched the sensitive area, Miranda caught his hand and warned him to leave it alone. When he was fully alert, she revealed the events which had taken place, confessing her other meetings with the Indian warrior to him, all except the kisses and embraces which they had shared at that second stop. She also related the false tale she had told their fellow passengers.

Lucas was astonished by her behavior. "You mean he's been following the steamer to meet with you?" he asked incredulously.

Miranda replied honestly, "I don't know, Luke. He just appeared each time. If he hadn't, we'd be dead now," she reminded him.

"Considering the tales I've been told about these warriors, it sounds crazy. You don't know his name or tribe?" he probed.

"Neither. He always came and went so quickly and secretly. As I said, I fainted before the fight with the bear was over. I assume he wasn't injured because he brought us near the river to be found." She explained the precarious riddle as best she could.

"But why did you go back?" he demanded.

"I had to know if he survived. He could have been wounded. He could have used his remaining energy to help us. He saved our lives, Luke. He was kind and gentle. He never harmed me and I wasn't afraid of him."

Lucas couldn't debate her statements. But he fretted over the identity and motives of the warrior. Still, the man had spared her innocence and saved her life. He cautioned himself to watch her more closely. He had almost gotten her raped and killed.

"I'll be fine, Randy. Why don't you get some rest or write Mandy and Reis," he suggested to distract her from her thoughts of the warrior.

"I wonder what they're doing right now," she murmured aloud. She would have cringed in renewed fear if she had known the answer to that question, for matters were just as complex and dangerous back in Alexandria . . .

Chapter Fourteen

🌸 *A*fter Rëis persuaded Amanda to unlock the door, he poured out his soul to her, telling her nearly everything he knew or felt. Comprehending how important she was to him and how much he loved her, Amanda's anguish and doubts fled. He ended his confession with a declaration of love. "I love you and need you as no other person in my life, Mandy. What would I be without you? My life would have no joy or meaning. Please forgive me for hurting you. I promise to do my best never to hurt you again."

Tears sparkled in her light blue eyes. "I love you too, Reis. I suppose this situation is difficult for both of us, a new marriage and a critical mission at the same time. I'll try to be more understanding and patient," she vowed softly, smiling into his expression of relief.

"That's a good suggestion for both of us. But I don't want to mislead you. Until this case is over, there will be times like this week when I can't get to you, love, and times when I can't explain what's happening. But I will be as open with you as possible."

"Now that I know more about this case and your duties, I'll accept your rules. I don't have to like them, but I will try to follow them," she added with joyful laughter. "You were right, my darling; there was so much I didn't know. But I love you and trust you."

Reis's mouth closed over hers in a tender kiss of love and commitment. When his lips brushed back and forth across hers, she murmured hoarsely, "Make love to me. I've missed you so."

Reis discarded his boots and clothes, then slipped the gown straps from her shoulders and let the garment slide down her silky flesh to the floor. His smoldering eyes flickered over her tawny curls and touched each feature upon her face. His gaze became as a warm liquid flowing down her trembling frame, from face to bare feet, over curves and planes that ached to be sensuously invaded. He placed his hands on her shoulders, then leisurely moved them down her arms to grasp her quivering hands. He pulled her toward him, their nude bodies melting together before they sank to the bed behind them.

As they fell entwined into the arms of love, they were oblivious to all but each other and their cravings. Their love and passion were rich and deep, given and returned. He murmured words of endearment into her ears, inspiring feverish responses to him. Her hands caressed his firm, smooth body, and she touched him gently, then almost savagely as her hunger increased. He pulled her closer and tighter to him.

He nibbled at her lips, favoring the fuller lower one. He fondled her in daring new ways, touches which enflamed her to a matching boldness. He seemed to explore and conquer each part of her body, as she did his. He teased and tantalized her with lips and hands until she was tensed and warmed all over, begging to be sated.

She moaned in desire. She was certain she could climb no higher on love's spiral, but she did. Fires leaped and burned within both as they meshed together upon the soft bed. Her head rolled from side to side and she breathed erratically as his mouth feasted upon breasts which were swollen and firm with passion. For a time, she lay mesmerized by his actions and the sensations they aroused.

She discovered the stimulating thrill of bringing him intense pleasure with her bold caresses. Shamelessly and greedily, she gave and took with unbridled desire and new courage. When he entered her, she arched and engulfed his manhood with an urgency which surprised and pleased him, crying out in blissful rapture at that first inner contact.

They moved in unison, Reis whispering instructions into her ears, all of which she eagerly followed. Although each thrust and response inspired ecstasy in both, their needs flamed into one roaring blaze which demanded to be extinguished before they were consumed.

They soared toward passion's peak together, the heights they were reaching bringing a lightness to their heads. They touched, kissed, and mingled bodies and spirits until they could no longer restrain themselves. Fulfillment burst upon them and shook them with an intensity unknown before. Scaling the peak, they gradually eased down into a tranquil valley. They lay locked together, relishing the power and pleasure of this joining. They kissed and embraced tenderly as slumber claimed their exhausted bodies.

On Thursday and Friday, Reis remained with Amanda during the daylight but ventured out both nights to meet with George Findley and carry out his investigation. Amanda could sense his dismay over the accumulating evidence, but she didn't pry. Before dawn on Saturday, Reis slipped out of the house to head for Washington—eighteen miles from Alexandria—to discuss his findings with Grant.

When Reis returned home late that night, he told Amanda the decision had been made to entrap Weber and his men the following week. He didn't tell her that the arrests would come during a meeting of the illegal Ku Klux Klan, or while he was confiscating revealing pages from the books in both firms, in McVane's office, and from letters hidden in Weber's home. Timing was essential to success and survival. To prevent discovery or suspicion, Reis couldn't steal those pages and letters until the last minute. It would be a perilous climax to weeks of work and determination, and it would be a beginning to his new life with Amanda Lawrence Harrison.

Reis was concealed from view when the unsuspecting Weber called on Amanda Sunday afternoon. Reis had warned Amanda he would attack Weber on the spot if that villain offered any threat to her safety, no matter the cost to the mission. Amanda had cautioned him not to react too hastily or rashly or show himself unless Weber physically assailed her and she screamed for help. They agreed on their signals and actions, then waited for Weber to appear.

Wanting this foul matter settled quickly and without trouble, she immediately came to the point the moment Weber was seated. "I have made a decision, Weber. I told you I would respond to your proposal today, but I cannot." When he started to protest, she hastily silenced him. "Wait! Hear me out first. I think you'll agree with my conclusions."

Weber sullenly leaned back against the sofa but remained attentive. She informed him calmly, "I want you to hire someone to find Randy. That distressing and puzzling matter needs to be resolved before you and I can make plans for us. I don't mean to imply I don't trust you, but I must make certain you had nothing to do with her departure. I'm sorry, but I feel there is something I don't know. I want you to locate her and bring her home. If there's nothing between you two, then I'll marry you on any day you choose. If there is love between you two, then I will step aside for Randy to marry you. If the feelings are on her side alone, it should be settled before we wed. If you have even the slightest desire for her, it should be faced and dealt with before you make a mistake by marrying the wrong woman. I hope you agree this is a fair solution for all concerned. Well, what do you think? Can you find my sister?"

She inhaled and exhaled to release her tension. Stunned by this unexpected proposition, Weber couldn't speak and had difficulty thinking clearly. In his hesitation, she added, "I won't lie to you, Weber. I am not madly in love with you and I won't pretend I am. I'll even admit to being selfish and conceited. I will do whatever necessary for survival. Is that honest enough for you? I shall set a time limit of two weeks."

Weber probed her incredible suggestion. "I told you I couldn't find her when I went there. What if she can't be found, ever?"

"Perhaps this will help your detective," she stated, handing him a brass oval frame with Miranda's miniature portrait inside. "She can't simply vanish without a trace. Tell your man to work harder, or hire a better one. Someone in Charleston must have seen her by now. If I get another telegram or a letter from her, I will make it available to you." She went on to tell him about the first one, knowing it was unnecessary. "I'm warning you now, Weber; don't marry me with any desire in your heart for my sister. I don't demand love, but I will demand fidelity. If you have any doubts at all, end them in the next two weeks. If Randy is suffering from unrequited love for you, then she will never return home after we wed. Surely it is best for all of us to make peace first. Do you agree?"

Weber rose and faced her. He needed privacy to study this turn of events and time to make some plans. Whatever happened now, he would come out the winner. He smiled and nodded. "I'll locate Randy for you, then you can vanquish any doubts you have about me. If she has any fantasy where I'm concerned, we shall deal with it."

Amanda came to her feet and smiled faintly in return. "Unless there is some pressing business to discuss, I would appreciate your getting to this matter as quickly as possible. I feel it would be best to settle our private lives before we discuss our business affiliation."

Weber concurred and left without even attempting to kiss or embrace her, which suited Amanda perfectly. He was too busy thinking that now that he didn't have to be so furtive with his search, he could pull out all stops in order to locate Miranda and finally decide whom to marry and whom to slay.

Amanda turned to smile at her husband as he entered the room clapping in admiration for her performance. "Excellent, love, excellent," he complimented her, then swept her into his arms and danced her around the sofa as she giggled happily.

When he halted and gazed down into her upturned face which shone with such love and joy, he kissed the tip of her nose. "All we have to do now is pray Weber doesn't come across any clues to Randy's whereabouts," she remarked, slightly worried about this brazen ruse. "You did mail my letter to Luke and Randy from Washington yesterday?"

"It's on the way to Pierre right this moment, love," he replied. "But I'd be willing to bet my boots, comfortable as they are, the case will be over before Randy has it in her hand," he alleged smugly.

But at that moment in the Dakota Territory, Miranda had her hands full with another matter, an injured and stubborn cousin. The steamer was lingering at its last stop, unloading supplies at the Lower Brule Indian Agency, before heading for its termination point.

Determined to carry out his own investigation, Lucas insisted they visit the agency to see what they could learn. He assured Randy he felt fine as they left the steamer for a few hours on land. But they observed and discovered things that shocked them. Life on the reservation was not what it was reported or promised to be . . .

The once proud and energetic Indians appeared spiritless, weary, and poor. Many were in rags, small children naked. Most looked hungry and unhealthy. It was a pathetic and depressing sight.

Wagons of supplies from the steamer were being unloaded at the wooden structure which housed the agency. Indians in tattered clothing dejectedly waited for their meager portions to be doled out. She could hear complaints about the moldy flour, the spoiled meat, the flimsy materials for clothing, the injustice of this beggarly practice, the humiliations they were helplessly subjected to by corrupt white men, and the despair all felt at being unable to change their new destiny—a destiny which demanded either an acceptance of degradation or the total destruction of their families.

As Lucas questioned several traders and workers, Miranda learned of the children being forced into schools where they were forced to wear the white man's clothes, where they spoke only the white tongue, where they had to accept the white man's customs and ways over those of their own people. The young boys were required to cut their braids to show obedience to the white man's rules, an act which robbed them of what little pride remained. She discovered that many places used boarding schools to keep the Indian children away from the influences of their parents and tribes. There was a look of bewilderment and sadness in those small faces and somber eyes and it pained Miranda to view such cruelty.

The entire Indian culture was being destroyed. Indians were stripped of their customs, their religion, their language, their pride and dignity, their very reason for existence and happiness. Tree and scaffold burials were outlawed. Leaders and chiefs were often slain or imprisoned to subjugate the remaining members of their tribes. The males were refused guns or horses for hunting and were forced to depend solely on the whites for food, clothing, and shelter. Unable to seek medicinal herbs, many Indians grew sick and died. It was almost as if the sadistic plan was to starve, freeze, or sicken the remaining Indians until they died or were compelled to escape, only to be tracked down and killed as dangerous renegades.

She learned of the demoralizing action of constantly moving reservations from one place to another. The Indians had difficulty settling down, for they were whisked away before teepees were barely in place. They were commanded to become farmers, when they knew nothing but hunting and when the reservation lands were unfertile.

Treaties and promises had been broken or changed as frequently as the white men wished. Randy caught hints of the "Indian Ring," in which dishonest agents or suppliers to government contracts stole part of the goods or shipped inferior ones. Although whiskey was outlawed on reservations, traders were allowed to camp nearby and entice the spirit-broken and restless braves to drink themselves into stupors. It was heartbreaking to witness and hear of such evil and cruelty, to see a proud race trampled and destroyed.

Now she understood why so many tribes and leaders refused to make peace with the white men. She could see why the Indians didn't trust them, why they continued to make war. The whites didn't want peaceful coexistence; they wanted to take and have everything here. They wanted to subjugate these noble people into demeaning slavery. Where was their Lincoln? Who would bravely sign their "Emancipation Proclamation"? Who would battle to free them?

When Lucas and Miranda returned to the *Martha Lane*, both were too gloomy to discuss what they had encountered here. Lucas was also dizzy and lay down to rest, falling asleep quickly. Miranda paced the floor of her small cabin, trying to forget the sights and sounds of this day. If her father hadn't come here years before and eloped with Princess Morning Star, her mother could have been one of those miserable people she had seen today. It stunned and alarmed Miranda to realize her mother's old tribe was now imprisoned and slowly dying near the Red Cloud Agency. Miranda was relieved her mother had not returned here to view such anguish and devastation. All she could do was pray her grandfather and other relatives were alive and safe. She tried to push such haunting knowledge from her troubled mind, but found it impossible to do so.

Nor could she forget the warrior who had saved her life. She knew he must be one of those "renegades" who refused to stop fighting and settle down on one of those despicable reservations. She couldn't imagine that fearless and strong male confined to those conditions. Why had he defended her and followed her? Why didn't he hate her and all she represented? Apparently, fierce warriors made no distinctions between male and female enemies. If that were true, how could she explain their relationship? She couldn't.

Upon arrival in Pierre, Lucas discovered this settlement was worse than Yankton, if that were possible. He refused to remain there a single night, gaining passage on a keelboat heading for Fort Sully. He could only hope the conditions there were better and he was beginning to regret bringing Miranda along. If not for the danger in Alexandria and along the way, he would have been tempted to send her home or somewhere safe. He had not imagined any place could be worse or more perilous than being near Weber. But it was too late to stop this journey, and he was too driven to change his plans. At least Miranda was holding up excellently under these arduous circumstances.

Lucas was delighted to find that Fort Sully was indeed better. What fences existed were low stone ones to separate the officers' quarters or homes from other sections of the fort; there was no tall outer wall to protect the inhabitants from enemies. Lucas and Miranda found this strange in light of the continuing skirmishes between whites and "hostiles." The only barrier of any height surrounded the ammunition and supply sheds and yards, for soldiers were rumored to be as prone to thieving as renegades or white drifters.

The structures were made of varying materials from wood to adobe. There were barracks, stables, a guard house, trader shops, sutler stores, an infirmary, a chow hall, assorted privies, private homes, small cabins, and supply sheds. There was one oblong building which they learned was a recreation hall, complete with tables and chairs for games and reading. Fortunately, Fort Sully boasted of a library of nearly a thousand books and several periodicals.

The fort structures were in close proximity to each other, with officers' private homes nearby. The military compound was designed like the hub of a wagonwheel, with businesses radiating like its spokes and settlers encircling it as an outer rim. From there in three directions, other cabins and structures were built haphazardly. Some brave and solitary types had put up their homes and barns at a farther distance away, toward the Missouri River east from Fort Sully. It appeared few people found the western area desirable, for it edged on proclaimed Sioux Territory. In the military surroundings, trees and bushes were scant, grass even sparser. But as the semicircle increased, so did the amount of greenery. There was an abundance of trees, bushes, grasses, and wildflowers. North of the civilian and military encampments was a small Indian village where workers and scouts lived.

Wanting to keep his real assignment a secret, Lucas decided not to use the letter of protection and introduction from President Grant unless necessary. With so much corruption and fraud in this area, some men might be suspicious of him and his job. After all, those two soldiers had behaved as if there was something important to conceal.

Lucas found a sturdy log cabin to rent near the fort, one recently vacated when the fort sutler's brother had died from a snakebite. Unknown to Lucas and Miranda, it was uninhabited because it lay west of the fort and was one of the most distant structures.

Aware that Lucas Reardon's sister was a real lady, the sutler was glad he had cleaned and repaired the cabin, completing his tasks just that morning in hope of renting it to an incoming and ignorant officer from the fort. When the sutler escorted them to the cabin, Miranda was relieved to find it freshly scrubbed and in excellent condition. She thanked the man who in turn offered any assistance she needed. While she remained behind, the man helped Lucas fetch their belongings from his store, where they were under strict guard.

Before dusk, they were unpacked and settled into their new home. Lucas had assisted Miranda with the sweeping and dusting, and he had opened the windows to allow fresh air to flow through the cabin. Miranda had scrubbed all the dishes, even though they had appeared clean when she began her mandatory task. Lucas had purchased enough wood from the sutler to last until he could join a woodcutting crew and furnish their own. As they dined on the meal which she had prepared, they relaxed and chatted about their new home. The cabin had two rooms: one was a combination kitchen and living area; the other was a small bedroom. It was agreed she would have the private room and Lucas would sleep on a cot purchased from the sutler.

The next week passed swiftly in a blur of excitement. Lucas's injury healed nicely and ceased to trouble him. He spent his days making friends with the soldiers and settlers, observing and questioning everything he saw or heard. It was a simple task for someone with Lucas's jovial personality and good looks. The people in this rugged area admired artists and writers, people who could put life into words or capture it in oils or photographs. Each person was eager to play a part in the making and recording of history. Every time Lucas lazed around the sutler's shop, men lingered to "talk off his ears." As for those from the fort, the bored soldiers were eager for any source of diversion and talked freely and rashly with the cheerful young man.

Miranda was full of questions when Lucas returned from a visit to the whiskey wagons which were camped nearby in a grove of cottonwoods for one week, pay week. He described what he had seen in colorful details for her, including the prostitutes and two musicians who traveled with the group. Miranda jestingly inquired if Lucas had partaken of either trade. He grinned and shook his head.

Miranda spent most of her time with Lucas; she hadn't made many female friends. The upper officers' wives seemed to be waiting until they were assured of her social station before offering their company or inviting hers. The lower officers' and enlisted men's wives, what few there were, felt it was improper to approach her and kept their distances. On fear of penalty from the commander, the lowly "laundresses" made it a point to avoid her completely, as was required of them where all "proper" females were concerned. The social system was rigid here, and Miranda didn't know where she belonged. She concluded that she, as the stranger and newcomer, should be approached first by whoever wished to become her friend or acquaintance.

There was one female who Miranda and Lucas found fascinating and colorful, Calamity Jane. Martha Jane Canary was a large, strapping woman who was widely known for her foul language, hard drinking, expert horsemanship, skilled shooting, and men's attire. She was reputed to be the most famous female in the entire Dakota Territory, and often teased about being continually drunk and broke, even though she worked at several jobs normally held by males. She rotated between being a driver for supply wagons and stagecoaches, and a scout for the cavalry. Of course most people said she spent her money buying drinks for all present when she entered a new town or saloon, for that was her way of making friends and gaining attention. She boasted of knowing every legendary male in the West, good or bad. But most of them denied knowing her.

Miranda and Lucas met this rustic character in the sutler's shop one afternoon. Despite her mannish appearance in looks and clothing, both were taken with her vivacity and genial nature. Jane had been many places and had faced countless dangers, or so she claimed. Her independent and obstinate nature caused many people to avoid her or to gossip about her. It was sad and unfair, for Jane simply wanted freedom and adventure, things which the present age didn't allow even a strong and smart female. Jane was so interesting and charming that Lucas and Miranda didn't care if her tales were true or not. After that day, Jane became a welcome visitor in their cabin whenever she was at Fort Sully. It did not take long for Lucas and Miranda to realize that being Jane's friend meant she would defend them with her life if need be.

But there was a sadness about Jane, for she knew that the present society would never permit her to reach her potential and to carry out her dreams. Miranda decided that Jane used her boistrous and comical manner to conceal her disappointments and bitterness. At twenty-one, the Missouri born Jane Canary could probably outshoot and outride most scouts, soldiers, Indians, and outlaws. Yet, few were willing to let her prove it. Only Custer and Miles were appreciative of her skills and courage; they had discovered she was an excellent scout, when sober.

Most women here viewed life as dull and arduous, but Miranda thrived on the excitement which surrounded her. Due to the confiscation of Indian horses, animals were in abundance at the fort. Lucas would frequently rent two and they would go riding, never straying far alone unless in the company of the soldiers until they could learn their way around the rugged terrain.

Each night, Lucas would record the day's events and store his notes in a leather pouch. He hid the precious packet under a loosened board beneath the table. Miranda also started a journal about her own adventures. She wrote Amanda several long letters but held them until news arrived saying it was safe to contact her sister.

One morning, Lucas rushed to the cabin to tell Miranda he was riding out on patrol with a small troop from the fort. Later, Calamity Jane came by for a visit. Miranda's chores were done, so she was sitting at the table, writing another letter to her sister to pass the time. Jane asked her to go for a ride, but Miranda was reluctant. When Jane convinced her there was no danger, for Indians believed her "touched by the evil spirits" and left her alone, Miranda promptly accepted and quickly changed into her riding habit.

They rode for a time with Jane pointing out sights and telling Miranda tales about the area's turbulent past. When Jane spotted smoke curling up in the distance, she ordered Miranda to wait while she checked it out, for the cavalry paid her high prices for valuable information. Miranda pleaded with her not to go or to allow her to tag along. Jane blatantly refused, saying she could escape swiftly if there was any trouble. She told Miranda to ride hard and fast for the fort if she fired shots into the air.

Miranda watched Jane gallop off toward the hills. She tied her reins to a small bush and walked to a large boulder. She climbed upon it and sat down to wait, tucking her flowing hems beneath her legs. She was apprehensive about the possible dangers Jane might face out there, but she wasn't terrified of being left alone. Yet as time passed and solitude closed in on her, Miranda had the strangest feeling she was being watched. She scanned her surroundings in all directions, seeing nothing and no one. But the sensation persisted.

She waited about twenty minutes before she saw Jane coming her way at a steady pace. She sighed in relief and headed for her horse. As she mounted, she glanced around, finding and hearing nothing. The warrior's image flickered before her mind's eye and she studied the harsh landscape, wondering where he was at that moment.

At home alone, Miranda reflected on the strange episode, scolding herself for not checking out the mystery. She had not felt peril or evil but she had sensed a sadness and longing. She had actually warmed and tingled! Was she fantasizing, dreaming, hoping? Had it actually been the unknown warrior's powerful gaze on her, his forceful magnetism, his heady allure? Her heart soared with pleasure and her mind raced in confusion. Who was he and where? Recalling her cousin's reaction to her last confession, Miranda couldn't tell Lucas about this intriguing event and she couldn't ask anyone about the warrior, but inwardly she felt elated by this delightful mystery. Miranda danced around the cabin, then caressed the white buckskin dress which had belonged to her mother. She had brought it along to wear the first time she met her grandfather and uncle. If she braided her hair and dressed in her mother's Indian garments, she would appear more Indian than white. Surely that would inspire him to accept her.

Days passed as the June weather grew warmer. A letter arrived from Amanda, posted in Washington. When Lucas and Miranda read it together at supper, he grimaced and she paled. Their gazes met as Lucas exploded, "Are they crazy! Of all people, Reis should know a good detective can uncover clues and track us down! Doesn't he realize Weber will go to any expense for revenge?"

"Do you think he knows yet?" she asked shakily, the emphasis on "he" telling to whom she referred. She panicked at the thought of being thwarted in her quest when so close to victory. "Help me, Luke; I must get to grandfather before it's too late. Find us a guide," she coaxed, eyes tearing and voice quavering.

"I know how much this means to you, Randy. You've been patient while I rushed around chasing my dream. Don't worry; I'll find some way to get you to Sun Cloud this very week." He checked the postmark and chuckled, then commented, "This letter got here quickly. I doubt Weber has discovered any tracks yet. I'll bet Reis has him arrested and imprisoned before he can sniff out the right trail. At least Mandy and Reis are safe and happy."

But things had gone awry in Virginia, perilously awry. The night before the climactic raid, Reis had overheard something which he couldn't share with his wife. The accident involving her parents had been ordered by none other than Weber Richardson. As Weber spouted off to Daniel McVane, neither was aware of the man who hid outside McVane's office door, listening to Weber smugly discuss his many schemes. But Weber made one statement about Joe and Marie which sent surges of hope through Reis; he would hire a search party in the morning then pray with all his might.

That following evening, Reis and George made their rounds, collecting all the books and letters relating to the case. Not far out of town, the men assigned by Grant converged on the meeting of the Ku-Klux-Klan and arrested all present. Because a business meeting between all partners was to have been held afterward, every man involved was present and apprehended with the exception of Weber Richardson.

A tense week passed as Reis failed to locate and arrest the leader of this menacing group. A friend of Reis arrived to manage Amanda's shipping firm and to appropriate Weber's property for the American government.

Reis fretted over Weber's disappearance and his inability to find his enemy. Grant had already decided on Reis's next assignment, but they couldn't discuss it until Weber was apprehended and this case was closed. Reis had turned the evidence over to Grant, who locked it in his safe until the trials could commence. The case was in limbo as long as Weber remained free. Reis was infuriated by the man's actions; it seemed as if the Devil himself was guarding his servant!

Amanda cried in fear and tension, speculating that Weber was probably on his way west to harm Lucas and Miranda or lurking nearby with the hope of slaying Reis. To ease her worries, Reis sent Lucas a telegram to warn him of Weber's disappearance and the results of the case so far. Reis told them to be careful and alert, to notify him if Weber appeared there, and to have the Army arrest and hold Weber for the U.S. government and President Grant.

It wasn't Weber's cunning or a warning from anyone which had kept him from that meeting; it was lust for Miranda and for vengeance, and a quirk of fate. His escape had nothing to do with a premonition of danger or capture. Word had arrived that afternoon that Miranda had been located and was being held prisoner by his detective. Weber had placed McVane in charge of both meetings to rush to Charleston by train. But, ironically, McVane had been robbed and killed by a common thief as he left his office that evening, preventing him from canceling the pernicious meetings, exposing Weber's location, or contacting and warning Weber after the raid.

Upon arriving in Charleston, Weber went wild with rage and frustration, for it was the wrong girl again. He was in such a frenzy by then that he yanked his gun, a small knuckle-duster .32, from its belt holster and shot the innocent female in the heart. It happened so swiftly and unexpectedly that the girl never had time to suspect her fate. Petrified, the queasy and frantic detective fled the scene when Weber laughed satanically and hysterically as he watched the blood saturate the front of her yellow gown.

When he was settled, Weber calmly strolled over to the girl. He seized her auburn hair and jerked her head backward. She did favor Miranda greatly. As his wintry gaze eased over her body, he decided he had slain her too quickly, for pleasure should always precede pain. He left her as she was, laughing sardonically as he mused on the authorities puzzling over this brutal and mysterious crime.

Before Weber could catch the next train home, one of his men met him with the dire news from Alexandria. His fury was limitless; his hunger for revenge boundless. He sent his man back to Alexandria to spy for him, and each following report increased his hatred and madness. Miranda had better pray to every known god that he wouldn't find her. If he did, he vowed he would do unspeakable things to her before mutilating her lovely body and face! As for Amanda and Reis, their punishments and deaths would be far worse, for he had heard the announcement of their secret marriage. Clearly he had been duped, and they would pay in blood!

Chapter Fifteen

While Lucas was trying to figure out how to get into the Sioux camp without arousing suspicion, an eye-catching officer arrived at Fort Sully from Custer's Seventh Cavalry Regiment. He was there to escort ten recruits to Fort Lincoln, as Custer liked a full report on his new men before they arrived in camp. Major Brody Sheen was Custer's most trusted officer.

Although cavalrymen rarely wore their sabers except for ceremonies, Brody

Sheen was in full dress upon arrival. He cut a most impressive figure in his dark blue and sunny yellow uniform, an outfit which looked custom tailored for his well-muscled body. His brown hair was shorter than most men's and very curly. He had hazel eyes which concealed his thoughts and feelings, unless he chose to expose them, and he wore a neat mustache. Six feet tall and twenty-nine years old, Brody was well toned and darkly tanned from his active, outdoor lifestyle. He was dashing in looks and immaculate in dress. Among such rough men who gave little care to their appearance and to amenities, Brody's conduct and charm shone. But while outwardly he was considered handsome and virile, Miranda Lawrence was to find him less than perfect.

Once he learned that Brody was Custer's right arm, Lucas promptly made his acquaintance, thinking that when they eventually headed to Fort Lincoln, Brody's friendship would be a valuable asset. Brody seemed to take an instant liking to Lucas, who was as jovial and bright as he was and of similar breeding and education. Brody was from a wealthy and prestigious Northern family, and he had served loyally with Custer during the Civil War. For that reason, Custer had personally requested him as an officer in his regiment. A hard man to admire and like, Custer needed someone with him who held him in high esteem and affection.

Major Sheen introduced Lucas to the officers at Fort Sully, strengthening the writer's position there. While waiting for the recruits to arrive by keelboat, Brody had time to spend with Lucas and Miranda. The second evening of their meeting, Lucas brought him to their cabin for supper. Brody made no effort to hide his strong attraction to Miranda, entertaining her with tales of bravery and daring, pleasing her with his wit and charm. At first, Miranda found him appealing and stimulating company, a delightful conversationalist. If Miranda's mind and heart had not been already claimed by a mysterious warrior, she might have fallen under the disarming spell of this dashing soldier. And, after that night, Brody spent as much time with Miranda as with Lucas.

They would take walks together, alone, or with Lucas. They went riding and shared several meals, including a picnic on a pond near the river. One night, there was a dance in the yard around the flagpole. Hardly three songs had been played before the men there realized Brody had staked a claim on this beautiful stranger. Knowing of Major Brody Sheen's reputed prowess with the ladies, no one dared challenge him.

If Miranda and Lucas had not been present to occupy his time and attention, Brody would have been furious with the delay in the recruits' arrival. The June rains had failed to come as yet, and the Missouri River was treacherously low. The recruits had been compelled to leave their stranded craft before Yankton and come overland to Fort Randall to take a keelboat, requiring ten days more than anticipated. The men were fortunate that Major Sheen was too busy with a delightful and enchanting Miranda Lawrence to notice the lost time.

The day before Brody was to leave Fort Sully, he made a terrible error in judgment. Feeling Miranda was as enamored of him as he was of her, he showered his romantic attention on her. He tricked her into a private stroll, then attempted to kiss and embrace her. When she tried to reject him without embarrassing either of them, he didn't realize she was serious. When he playfully tripped her, then caught her and rolled upon the grass with her in his tight grasp, she was angered by his boldness and persistence. Still, the arrogant Brody believed her to be coy and timid. He couldn't imagine any female would spurn him. After all, he had given her plenty of time, more than any other woman who had caught his eye. He continued his roguish siege, until she frostily scolded him and made her refusal very clear. Although Brody apologized for his misconception and behavior, Miranda noticed a glow of insincerity and impatience in his eyes. Clearly, Brody found her desirable and was resolved to have her!

As Brody left, he encouraged Lucas to hasten his trip to Fort Lincoln, telling him there was much more going on in that area for the reporter to record. Lucas told him they would be along in about three weeks and politely refused Brody's escort this trip. Brody responded with courtesy but felt annoyance. He told Lucas he would notify him if a mission called him back this way.

Miranda had learned many facts about her mother's people and other Indian tribes from Brody. He had made no secret of his hatred for several warriors, chiefs, and leaders: Sitting Bull, Crazy Horse, Gall, Red Hawk, Bloody Arrow, and Blazing Star of varying Sioux tribes, and Two Moons of the Cheyenne. She listened intently, learning all she could about these men.

Two names in particular had brought fiery lights of rivalry and antagonism to Brody's hazel eyes: Crazy Horse and Blazing Star. Several times Brody had made comments about the feud between those two men. Brody had seemed to think that if Crazy Horse did not exist, Blazing Star would be war chief under the direction and influence of the imposing and powerful medicine and spiritual chief, Sitting Bull. Brody had laughingly remarked one night that he hoped they killed off each other over the chief's bonnet. Brody had not seemed to fear those powerful warriors, but he clearly respected and envied their skills and ranks.

After Brody departed, Miranda gave him a good deal of mental study. Now that he was no longer present to use his charms and good looks to sway her, she mused on his personality and disarming appeal. He was unlike most men she knew. But she realized something she hadn't noticed before; Brody had a beguiling way of making a person feel a particular way about him—his way. It was as if he possessed a magical power of suggestion. Now that he was gone, she could see certain things more clearly.

She thought about the way Brody had handled himself, and treated others, and she was astonished to conclude that Brody was arrogant and obsessive but covered such traits when it suited his purpose. Visibly, he was a man used to giving orders, to having his way or else. Qualms filled Miranda as she decided Brody could be pleasant when he gained his way or was after something, but she sensed he could be dangerous if crossed or denied. She felt sure Brody had shown his real self that last day and she shuddered as she found herself comparing Brody Sheen to Weber Richardson.

Miranda didn't mention her concern to her cousin, but she was glad Brody was gone. She didn't trust that contradictory man. Besides, her thoughts were claimed by another, as were her dreams. A strange loneliness and hunger chewed at her, and a feeling of loss assailed her warring senses. Slowly the truth dawned on Miranda, and she chided her foolish behavior. Perhaps she had given Brody the wrong impression—that she truly cared for him. Had she unknowingly been using Brody as a needed diversion? Had he perceived her loneliness and genial overtures as romantic signals?

Again, she pressed Lucas to help her reach her grandfather. Lucas was working on a safe solution to that problem with Calamity Jane, as she knew this territory, its people, and its dangers.

Three days had passed when word arrived by special messenger from Brody. Two days from Fort Sully, near the Cheyenne River Agency, his troop had joined his notorious leader who was waiting there before heading west to Fort Phil Kearny. There, a meeting was to take place of the commanding officers from this immense area. The entreating letter informed Lucas of the possible historic importance of this talk, for General Terry, Colonel Gibbon, and General Crook would be present—three of the most successful and destructive officers in the cavalry. Colonel Custer had left Captain Benteen behind to guard his fort and had ordered Major Reno to ride with him. But the name which irresistibly drew Lucas was Philip Sheridan—he, too, was alleged to be heading for this parlay.

Lucas read the message over and over, his excitement mounting each time. He was so eager that his hands shook, causing the paper to crackle noisily, and his green eyes danced with elation. Unable to restrain himself, he gave a whoop of victory and joy. He was mentally applauding his good fortune when Miranda entered from the other room to question his merry behavior.

He revealed his incredible and exhilarating news, but it did not have the same effect on her. Her smile faded and her heart skipped several beats, for she knew he would accept the invitation to ride along and her dream would be forced to yield to his. Miranda could not share his exuberance and zeal, but she comprehended what a priceless opportunity had been dropped into her cousin's lap. She was too dejected to care about his work, too nettled to consider its importance for history or the South. For weeks, everything had gone her cousin's way; was it selfish to demand time for her dream, to obtain her desires? They were so close to her mother's people; the new fort would put them hundreds of miles from her goal.

Miranda also realized that if she tagged along as invited, she would be in the company of untrustworthy, cunning Brody Sheen and many squadrons of rowdy men. Evidently there was no peril in this trek, or she would not have been invited. She wondered how Brody had gained approval for her presence from Custer.

Caught up in his own world, Lucas did not notice the staggering effect this "golden opportunity" had on his cousin. A resentful shadow dulled Miranda's brown gaze; anger enticed little creases around her mouth and near her eyes. Defiance began boiling within her.

Lucas turned to ask, "How soon can you be packed and ready to leave, Randy? Brody sent a written order for an escort to take us to meet him. There won't be any danger," he stated smugly.

With a clear and calm voice, Miranda replied nonchalantly, "I know, because I'm not going. I'm staying here. If at all possible, I'll find a way to get to my grandfather. You go along with Major Sheen. I'm sure you'll obtain enough material for several books."

Shocked by her icy demeanor and incredible announcement, he shrieked frantically, "You can't go into a Sioux camp alone! Be patient until this trip is over, then I'll take you there. I promise, Randy."

"I have been patient, Luke, patient and unselfish," she declared accusingly. "Do you realize how far away this parlay is? Afterward, we'll be forced to remain with those troops for safety. They could ride in any direction and for any length of time. It could be months before we return here. By then, my people could be gone to their winter grounds, out of my reach. Besides, with all of those infamous killers joining forces, it could be a conference to plot a new war against the remaining Indians. If so, the Sioux won't let a white within ten miles of their camp, or they'll go into hiding until spring. I can't risk losing this chance, Luke. I'm sorry, but I'm not going with you. If I can't find a path to grandfather, I'll be fine here in our cabin."

"I can't let you stay here alone," Luke stated obstinately, believing he could change her mind. "This is the moment I've been waiting and working for, Randy; please don't take it from me," he beseeched her.

"I can say the same thing, Luke," she told him sadly. "Please don't ask me to leave when I'm so close to my people. I wouldn't ask you to sacrifice your one path to victory. I have plenty of company and protection here, and I promise I won't leave the fort unless I know it's safe. At least by remaining here, I might have the chance to send word to grandfather. If I leave and trouble begins, my dream could be lost forever. Jane told me sometimes Indian chiefs or leaders come to forts for talks. If I leave, I could miss a visit. Don't you see I have to stay?"

"This is dangerous and crazy, Randy. I could be gone for weeks or months."

"I know; that's the problem. Time could be against me, Luke. Besides, why would I want to tag along with countless men. Surely you realize what kind of harsh conditions I would face on such a lengthy journey? In some barren spots, there would be no privacy at all. It's no place for a woman—a lady. I should wait for you here where I'll be comfortable and happy."

Lucas noted that defiant glimmer in her eyes, that fierce determination which told him he could not change her mind. Either he had to leave her here alone or remain himself. Neither choice was pleasing. After all, he could not force her to ride with him. And in a way, she was right about being safe here in the rented cabin. But he tried one other approach. "Brody Sheen would be your protector."

"That's another reason to stay behind," she answered. "Perhaps the best one," she added sullenly.

"What do you mean? He's loco about you, Randy. I'd bet he's asked me just so he can see you again. I thought you liked him," he stated probingly, eyes and ears alert.

"He's your friend, not mine. I don't like him or trust him. And I can think of nothing more disagreeable than enduring his company and pawings for weeks on end," she brusquely announced. Wisely, she didn't say he reminded her of Weber; for she didn't want to refresh that threat in Luke's mind.

"You mean you were just pretending to be friends?" he asked, that revelation coming as a complete surprise.

"I was merely being polite to your company. You made it clear he could be important to your work, so I did nothing to offend him. I was delighted when he left and I prayed he wouldn't return. In case you didn't know it, I had to scold him severely that last day when he practically forced his intentions on me. I'm surprised he's asking for another chance to be rejected. If he issued his invitation because of me, then he is out of luck. I see you failed to notice that streak of ruthlessness in him. Didn't you see the look in his eyes or hear the coldness in his voice when he boasted of bloody victories, when he vowed to tack the scalps of Crazy Horse and Blazing Star on his wall? He's dangerous and conniving, Luke. If I were you, I would guard my back around him. Most assuredly I would guard my journals. If he or Custer even slightly suspected what you were after, you would find them more of a threat than . . . Sherman was to Georgia," she panted breathlessly, having the wits to alter her comparison from the grizzly. She didn't want Lucas recalling the warrior who might have trailed her for days; after all, he was long gone.

They debated their dilemma until both were weary and depressed. Neither would give in to the other. Realizing he might never have another chance such as this one, Lucas could not bring himself to refuse it. And knowing each of Miranda's arguments was valid, he still encouraged her to go with him but with less conviction. The matter was settled when Calamity Jane came over with some news of her own, news which would displease Lucas and delight Miranda.

Jane revealed she was "unrollin' my bedroll in the rear of the sutler's shed," and she would be staying around for several weeks. She told them she would be working with a friend and fellow scout, Tom Two-Feathers Fletcher. The two had been assigned to check on the camps of Indians who had refused to sign treaties or live on reservations, several of which were Sioux and Jane thought might be of interest to Lucas and Miranda.

Before Lucas could relate his new plans, Jane told them about the other scout. Tom was half white and half Cheyenne. He had scouted for the cavalry for years but refused to join any troop. He came and went as it suited him, or when he needed money for supplies and weapons.

When Jane settled her roughly dressed and ample figure in a chair, Lucas told her about his plans and Miranda's refusal to accept them. Jane, who was in her early twenties but looked forty-five, glanced from one person to the other as she mused on their conflict of interests. She felt she could protect and assist Miranda while Lucas was away, and, besides, Miranda appeared a woman of mettle.

Jane removed her floppy hat and dropped it to the table, shoulder-length dark hair tumbling from its confinement. "Don't you be worryin' none, Luke. I'll watch'er like a mother hawk. She won't git three feet without me tailing her backside," Jane vowed fondly. "Me and ole Pete will guard'er," she added, affectionately patting the butt of her pistol in the holster swinging from her thick waist.

"You don't know her like I do, Jane. She could talk a bandit out of his weapon if she had the mind to. She's willful and stubborn. I'm not sure I should leave her here to get into mischief," he protested.

"Watcha gonna do, Luke? Hogtie'er and throw'er cross yore saddle," Jane teased mirthfully, winking at Miranda. "She don't wanna ride with them ruffians. Ain't narry a good man 'mongst'em; at least, ain't a one who can outride er outshoot Calamity Jane. Miss Miranda's a lady, Luke, my boy. You git'er out there where they ain't no trees and rocks fur miles; how's she gonna shuck her bloomers and have privicy? And ya knows she cain't go fur days with no bath like us'en."

Lucas threw up his hands in a gesture of surrender. "All right, you two. Randy can stay here," he acquiesced reluctantly. "But I'll warn you now; one speck of trouble and I'll hightail it back and redden two behinds. Savvy?"

That was Lucas's last warning before packing and riding off under the escort of five men from Fort Sully. It would require several days for the small group to catch up with Custer's regiment and for Brody to learn of Miranda's startling rebuff. Once there, Lucas would be in for many surprises and perils.

Jane and Tom ate supper with Miranda that night. They planned their outing for the next day, telling Miranda they needed to ride out at dawn to avoid being noticed by the commander of the fort. He would not have approved of her spending time with the scouts.

Miranda was so ecstatic about her quest the next morning that she could hardly sleep that night. Miranda felt that both Jane and Tom were trustworthy; both had been told of her goal. Jane had teased that the North Pole would melt before either of them betrayed her to a single soul. Both found her secret intriguing and stimulating. It was rare to have a daughter of an Indian princess and grand-daughter of a famous chief as a friend. Miranda recalled how Tom's dark eyes had glittered with excitement, and she was very aware of his rugged good looks and powerfully built frame. Finding Tom charming and bright, Miranda wondered why he was called "that half-breed trash," and why the soldiers found Tom repulsive. If Tom was such offensive and undesirable company, why had the Army hired him? As she lay in bed, Miranda's mind wandered back to tales her mother had told her . . .

Joseph Lawrence had come to this wild and rugged territory in 1850 to seek adventure before taking control of his family's shipping firm on the Potomac River. Soon after his arrival, Joe met and fell in love with a Sioux princess named Morning Star. She was the daughter of Chief Sun Cloud, second son of the legend-ary and powerful Gray Eagle. Joe won the heart of Morning Star, a beautiful girl with doe eyes and ebony braids. When neither side would accept their love and Joe was called home because of his father's death, Joe convinced Morning Star to elope with him to Virginia.

Those first years in "civilization" were made easier for Morning Star by Joe's mother, who adored the young girl from the first. Joe gave his new wife his mother's middle name, Marie. Before Annabelle Marie Carson Lawrence died, she taught Marie all she could about her new role in the white society. While Joe traveled between the Alexandria townhouse, the shipping firm, and the plantation which he considered his home, the two women stayed on the plantation—later renamed Morning Star—to complete Marie's cultural training.

Marie learned how to converse and to conduct herself as a lady. She fooled everyone she met; most thought her of Spanish descent, for they never would have accepted an Indian. Her broken English flowed correctly after the months of An-nabelle's gentle tutoring. Secretly Marie was taught to read. She was taught geogra-phy and history, and she was trained in manners and customs. She learned about theaters, plays, literature, and politics. She was shown how to dress properly and how to wear her flowing dark hair. She was trained in household tasks and in-structing servants. Marie Morning Star Lawrence was bright and quick; she learned enough to join her husband in Alexandria after Annabelle's death in '53, sliding smoothly and unsuspected into the elite society there.

And now, if all went as planned, Miranda would finally be meeting her mother's people and observing their way of life in a matter of days. She tried to recall all her mother had told her about her Indian family. Marie had had one brother when she left her people; his name was Night Stalker. He had married a Brule Sioux called Touched-a-Crow and they had had a male child. As far as Miranda knew, she had a cousin here whose name she could not recall. But since the time for his "vision quest" must have already passed, he doubtlessly had taken another name. Her grandfather, Sun Cloud, had had a brother named Bright Arrow who had wed Rebecca Kenny, a white girl; both had died before Morning Star's birth. For that reason, Sun Cloud had assumed the chief's bonnet after Gray Eagle.

Gray Eagle—that name stirred memories for Miranda of tales of immense bravery and cunning. He had wed Alisha Williams, a girl he believed to be white and his captive. But the Oglalas discovered her to be the missing Blackfoot princess, Shalee. Their love story was beautiful and bittersweet, and it thrilled and warmed Miranda's heart when she reflected upon it.

She wondered if the Oglalas would accept her, for her mother had dishonored herself and her people by choosing a white man over a Sioux or other Indian warrior. She had been banned from the tribe. As the hostilities between whites and Indians increased over the years, she had realized her people would never forgive her.

Miranda could not imagine what she would confront within the next few days. But as she drifted off to sleep, visions of a tall, lithe warrior with a silver star around his neck stayed with her.

Miranda was dressed and waiting eagerly when Jane and Tom appeared before dawn. Beneath its shadowy protection, the three rode away from Fort Sully toward the Sioux camp, galloping swiftly across the terrain. Their stops were brief, merely to rest and water the animals. To avoid trouble, they wanted their trip to be as short as possible.

It was the end of June and the days were longer and warmer. Miranda did not know she was entering the Sioux territory during the same month Alisha Williams had in 1776. Neither could she know what tragedy had struck her mother's people in the year of her birth. Nor could she imagine what horrors this same month would bring in 1876 . . .

At dusk, Jane and Miranda hid while Tom rode into the Sioux encampment under a white flag of truce. They were to wait two hours for him, then ride for the fort if he had not returned. Jane attempted to draw Miranda from her silent and apprehensive state, but she failed to do so because Miranda was feverishly praying her grandfather would not refuse to see her. To prove her identity, she had sent a locket to him, one which contained a miniature painting of Morning Star in the white doeskin dress, matching moccasins, and headband which Miranda was now wearing. For years, Joe had kept the locket hidden, fearing someone would find it and guess his wife's secret.

Miranda paced back and forth in the coulee while Jane reclined on the grass. Scattered thoughts floated across Miranda's mind. She tried to imagine her mother living in this vast and arduous territory. She tried to picture her parents riding across the Plains. She could not help but recall the mysterious warrior had spoken Sioux. Yet, there were seven divisions and numerous tribes and bands. The unknown warrior could belong to any of them . . . Miranda forced herself to concentrate on meeting her relatives.

It seemed hours before Tom returned alone, but it was actually less than one. His solemn expression and lax stance said everything. Miranda cupped her face and cried. She had known this could happen but had refused to consider it. Her weeping ceased abruptly and her head jerked upward as she questioned Tom. "You explained who I am and why I must see him? You showed him the locket? He refuses to see me?" Tom nodded after each question, then shook his head at her next two. "Can I disobey? Can I ride into the camp as you did?"

"It is not done. When you make a request under a truce flag, you must honor the answer. To defy it would make you look foolish and arrogant, not brave. It would stain your honor in their eyes. Let him think on this matter for a time, then we'll try again. You must accept his refusal, at least for now," Tom replied.

Miranda inhaled raggedly. It was her moment of truth. Did she leave without meeting Sun Cloud, or did she dare to defy his wishes? She fused her gaze on Tom's face and asked seriously, "Will they shoot me if I go there and demand he speak with me?"

"He forbids you to come. He says his eyes must not touch upon the evidence of his child's betrayal. He says he no longer has a daughter; he denies you are of his blood. If you go, others will prevent you from seeing him. They will be angry with you for forcing yourself upon their old chief. They might order you from the camp or ignore you until you leave. But I don't think they will harm you. I could be wrong."

His meaning was clear to her. Anger and courage flooded her. She had come so far and faced many dangers; he was cruel to reject her without an explanation. Could he do so if she personally presented her request? Without thinking twice, Miranda willfully declared, "Let's go. I will make the selfish coward disown me to my face. After I've come so far, let him reject me himself."

Before Jane or Tom could protest her actions, she was racing toward the village, muttering to herself, "Mandy wouldn't yield to such a crushing blow, and I won't either!" But if she had known what was happening in Virginia, she would not have made that statement.

Chapter Sixteen

Two weeks had passed since Weber's band of daring and misguided traitors had been arrested. When it appeared their leader was long gone, Grant called off the extensive search for Weber Richardson, assuming someone had warned the villain to flee the country. Reis was positive a vengeful Weber would return, and he was furious to think that Weber was still free after committing so many crimes. But he had received his new assignment and would soon have to leave.

When Reis told Amanda where his next mission was, she could hardly believe her ears. They were going to the Dakota Territory where Grant's civilian son, Frederick, was working under George Custer, a man who was rapidly becoming another thorn in Grant's tender side. If Grant had merely suspected what menacing role his own son would play in the tragic history of this territory, he would have summoned Frederick home as hastily as possible. Reis explained that this investigatory mission was also secret, so Amanda did not question her husband further.

Actually she was delighted to be heading for a reunion with her sister and cousin, as they were in the same area. That very night, she wrote a letter to them, telling of their plans. All they needed to do was make arrangements for the Alexandria townhouse, the plantation, and the packing. Amanda Lawrence had learned that social status, wealth, and beauty did not compare with love and happiness. She knew she would sacrifice all she owned and would challenge any danger to be at Reis's side, for he was the only man to stir her heart to overwhelming love and her body to fiery passion.

Reis's friend was already managing her firm, so she felt content with the plans to leave home and Virginia. Since Weber was still on the loose, she was thrilled to be traveling so far away.

During the next week, Reis completed his reports and took care of business matters for his wife. Amanda kept busy preparing for their exciting trip. When Reis was not home by seven one night, Amanda fretted. It was not like him to be late without sending word. When the meal was beyond saving and serving, she placed the pots on the sink, biting her lower lip in mounting worry. She was alarmed when a note arrived from George Findley at eight-thirty which stated her husband had been injured and she was to come with the messenger at once. She left everything as it was to accompany the man to her warehouse.

Upon entering the large structure, she was seized from behind and held tightly. Her captor laughed satanically as he whispered, "I bet you're glad to see me, my sweet. Did you think I'd forgotten about my fiancée? It was wrong of me to leave you in that Yankee's grip."

At the sound of that familiar voice, Amanda nearly fainted in paralyzing fear. After her hands were bound, Weber flung her aside where she tumbled over cotton sacks and landed on the hard floor, bruising and scratching herself. She hurriedly came to a sitting position and leaned against another pile of sacks, gazing at him through shock-filled eyes. Her hair was in wild disarray and her clothes were mussed and soiled.

"Weber? Whatever are you doing in Alexandria? Don't you know there's a warrant out for your arrest, for treason? Where have you been all this time? Why did you send that note? Where is Reis?" she asked fearfully.

"Your beloved husband is fine for the moment. You could say he's a bit tied up, but fine," he joked devilishly. "I didn't know your blood was so hot that you needed two men to cool it. You amaze me, woman; romancing two men at once. Before I decide what to do with you two, I might show you what you've been missing."

Comprehending his lewd meaning, she warned carefully, "You're in terrible trouble, Weber. Surrender before they kill you on sight. McVane's dead, but you could find another smart lawyer to help you." *Let your mind work faster than your mouth*, she told herself.

"I never surrender, my sweet. Ask your husband. After I killed his family and burned his stinking ranch to the ground, he chased me for months, but I was too fast and clever. Too bad my aim wasn't truer. As to them killing me, you needn't fret about my safety, my sly vixen. I've managed to avoid them thus far. And if I still wanted you, I could take anything I please. In fact, you'd be begging to comply to spare your love from torture. Might be educating to that Yank to watch how a Reb pleasures a woman."

"You wouldn't," she murmured hoarsely.

His sardonic grin sent shivers over her. Weber thrilled to her terror and fed ravenously on it. He sought to increase it by saying, "I can promise you'll have a man to compare with old Reis, but I haven't decided if it's to be me or one of my men. I'm not sure if you're worthy of my touch. Of course, afterward, you'll have plenty of comparisons. I'm selling you for a pleasure slave. I don't really have the stomach to murder you, so I'll find other ways to enjoy revenge."

He strolled around her, nudging her with his boot when her attention seemed to stray. "I thought about killing Reis, but I changed my mind. Death would be too quick, too merciful. Months and years of suffering will be much better punishment. He'll blame himself for your sorry fate. He'll search the world for you, but he won't find you. As for our firms, nobody will profit from them. I'm burning them down before I start my search for Randy. Don't look so surprised," he jested cruelly when she paled. "That damn Union won't steal anything more from me! After I'm rid of Luke, I plan to enjoy Miranda for a long time."

"So, I was right to suspect you craved her more than me. She hates you, Web. She'll kill you first," Amanda spat at him before she could prevent the rash words from spilling forth.

"She won't have the strength, my sweet. No woman can resist me for long."

"My God, you're mad," she cried.

"Mad, yes; but crazy, no," he argued between chuckles which chilled her flesh. "I'm afraid you'll have to pay for siding with our enemy, the Yankees."

"The war is over, Weber!" she shouted at him.

"Far from it, my sweet. When we assassinate Jeff Davis, the South will rise in defiance and beat the North this time. They caught us unprepared last time but not this time. I've seen to it myself."

"Davis is a Southerner, the ex-Confederate President, you fool!" she shrieked incisively to pierce his veil of madness.

"Then he won't mind being a martyr for his cause. Life isn't the most important asset, unless you have the best," he debated nonsensically, his dark eyes rolling wildly.

Amanda was becoming frantic trying to find a way to reach him. She tried a different approach. She asked softly, "You mean the South will become powerful and free again? Is it truly possible, Web? How can you do it without your money and men? They were all arrested. Surely anyone else involved will be too frightened to help?"

At her softened tone and curious questions, he eyed her strangely. "Why'd you marry that damn Yankee spy?" he snarled. "Only a whore would choose a Yank over a Reb!"

"What was I supposed to do? You disappeared, and everything went crazy here. You left me at their mercy. You don't understand, Web; I had no choice. He was blackmailing me. He threatened to kill Luke and Randy if I didn't do as he demanded. I was stalling until Luke could get away. Reis was having me and Randy watched; he was even spying on the men you had watching me! Every time you came over, he was hiding in the house and listening to everything I told you. That's why I acted so crazy! Damn you, why didn't you help me!"

When he stiffened and squatted to pay closer attention, she continued her cunning tale. "Until I received a letter from Randy last week, I thought he was holding her captive somewhere. I knew why she ran away; she left because of the way I was treating you. She knew I was seeing Reis, but she didn't know why. And I dared not tell her or refuse to follow his strange orders. When I called his bluff with her letter, he told me if I hired anyone to warn her he would have one of his men slay her that very day—that he knew where she was."

When she halted to catch a breath while thinking what to say next, he snarled coldly, "What kind of lies are you feeding me?"

"Reis was gone that day I asked you to search for her, but his men were lurking outside. I was afraid your actions would warn them had I confided in you. Reis told me they had orders to shoot both of us if I betrayed him to you. I thought if I dropped some crafty hints, you would track her down and rescue her. But I was trying to get you to search secretly to protect all of us. He said he was a government agent. How could I refuse to cooperate? He told me he was after some notorious ring of ex-Rebels who were buying and stocking arms for another war. He said they were using your firm and mine, but he didn't talk like he thought either of us were involved. When he said you were the leader, I couldn't believe you were guilty of treason. Heavens, Web, how could you do something foolish like that?" she asked angrily.

When the befuddled Weber did not respond, she wearily continued. "If I didn't obey his orders or if I warned you, he said I would be arrested as your accomplice. Me—Amanda Lawrence—arrested and imprisoned for treason! Do you have any idea how female prisoners are treated inside those stone walls? I do; Reis vividly described it. I was so confused and frightened, I didn't know what to do. He told me everything would be over in two weeks. But everything went crazy. He said you would be arrested and hung for treason, that he possessed positive proof. I couldn't understand why he forced me to marry him then kept it a secret. During the raid on your meeting that night, he explained why. He was using your fiancée to punish you, to gain something for what you took from him. He wanted your woman and a wealthy position and business, in exchange for that family and ranch you boasted of destroying. Like you just did, he threatened to take whatever pleased him; if I resisted or defied him, he vowed to find a way to implicate me in your traitorous schemes. I didn't want to go to prison, Web. When you escaped, he was furious. When I told him it served him right for all he'd done to me, he said you would kill me when you came back because you would never believe me innocent of helping him trap you. Look what you've done to me, to my life. How can you say you loved me after hurting me so much? Oh, Weber, are you really going to kill me?"

Weber watched the fragile creature as she focused those innocent and entreating eyes on him. He listened to her pitiful voice and he was consumed by confusion. "Surely you don't expect me to believe all this?" he debated, his eyes exhibiting his doubts. "You tricked me, woman. You nearly got me killed. You lied to me," he declared, opening the door for some valid charges from her.

"I *tricked* you? I nearly got *you* killed? I *lied* to you?" she sneered, stressing his ridiculous accusations. "Reis showed me the books and letters he confiscated from the firms as evidence. He was boasting about how much he owned now, compliments of his wife and you. You lied to me about the firm, Weber! You lied about the townhouse and Morning Star! I wasn't going broke; I'm a wealthy woman. Or I was until that spiteful Yankee took control of everything! You were using me, duping me all along! It was a cruel game to steal all I owned. Oh, he enjoyed showing me how you had been deceiving me. Now you accuse me of betrayal? What a stupid, blind fool I was. I thought you were my gallant knight, saving me from all of life's dragons, when all along, you were the fire from their nostrils; you were the enemy trying to consume me. You were even spying on me! Why? You know what's so ironic and tragic? You didn't have to trick me at all. If not for your crimes bringing that Yankee here to ruin both our lives, we would be married now and our mutual firm would be thriving. And Randy would be safe at home. She's in Dakota with Luke," she added desperately to win his trust. "All this time she's been safe. If only she or Luke had told me . . ."

Weber was staggered by her vast knowledge and accusations. She seemed to know everything and she was blaming him for this defeat and danger. She had seen the evidence, so he could not deny it. She appeared bitter and angry, vulnerable and sad. He had planned to kill them both and burn the businesses, then vanish. Did it change things if she were innocent? It was too late to correct his mistakes, too late for Reis's death to alter his dire situation.

In a way, his revenge on Reis could still take place. Reis wanted Amanda and her lucrative firm and holdings. He could make certain Reis gained nothing and he could burn the townhouse and the plantation. Once again, all the Yankee would have would be a scorched parcel of dirt and charred trees. The kink in his plans was Amanda. Reis had been using her like he had. It would not matter to Reis if he killed or sold the haughty bitch. In fact, as her husband, Reis would gain everything without having to endure Amanda. It irked Weber to realize his plans were being usurped by his enemy. Even with a few fires here and there, Reis would win.

"You never loved me, did you, Web?" she asked somberly, as if that realization pained her deeply.

"I wanted you because you were wealthy and beautiful—and because you were desired by so many men," he replied calmly. He went on to confess his lust for Miranda and what had happened between them.

"You mean she left because of you, not Reis?" she shrieked as if surprised by that statement. "I was only using that jealousy argument to stall your proposal. I never suspected you actually wanted her. I honestly thought I was hurting you, insulting you. You tried to attack her in our home! You tried to force her to marry you in my place! She despises you. My God, Web . . ."

Suddenly Amanda jerked her head toward him. She seemed to brighten with a new thought. "Reis knew! Randy must have told him and Luke. Of course— that's why they helped her get away. That's why she wouldn't confide in me. You tried to ravish her, so naturally she turned to chivalrous Reis! Reis probably told him you were the one blackmailing and threatening me. They were all three in on that plot. How could Luke and Randy side with him?" she wailed. "Don't tell me he's in love with her, too. I wonder if Reis is planning to get rid of me before she comes home! That devil! I hate them all! There's no telling what that Yankee said to them. You don't think Reis convinced them I was working with you, that I'm a traitor? Merciful heavens, Randy doesn't know it was Reis making me so jittery and secretive, not you. Your lust tossed her right into Reis's lap and plans!"

Weber did not realize Amanda was filling his head with doubts and suspicions, hoping to drive a wedge between his madness and his desire for vengeance. If she could persuade him she was on his side, that she also wanted revenge . . . If only she could disarm him . . . If she could entice him to trust her, to untie her . . .

Amanda sensed he was wavering as he gave this matter new study. She murmured, "My own sister and cousin . . . How could they do such evil to me? Is there no one I can trust? Am I so terrible that everyone hates me? If only Mama and Papa were here—they wouldn't let this happen to me." She began to cry.

Her last statement reminded Weber of what he had done to Joe and Marie. Their missing bodies did not matter now, for all was lost. Just before cruelly breaking her heart by disclosing that final secret, he changed his mind. "You do have a way of bringing out the worst in people," he informed her sullenly.

"Besides everything else, must I take the blame for the wickedness and greed . of others?" she scoffed tearfully. "That isn't fair." One last and desperate plan to save her beloved entered her mind. "There is one way to spite them, Web," she hinted.

"How, Miss Lawrence?" he sneered sarcastically, yet his curiosity was piqued. She looked so tantalizing, all tied up like that. She probably still wanted him, the foolish tart.

"How could a jury convict you without evidence?" she asked. When he perked up with interest, she went on, "Why not force Reis to steal it for you? If you destroy it, they can't touch you legally."

"How do I accomplish such a feat?" he scoffed, eying the soft swell of her breasts.

Amanda tried to ignore the dreadful reason for the flush on Weber's face, the passion glaze over his dark eyes, his harsh breathing. As consternation flooded her, she pretended to think of a plan. "I doubt using me as bait would work. He doesn't care what happens to me. He would probably thank you for removing me for him. And you can't threaten to burn down all he owns; he would merely place guards around the buildings. Besides, with my money under his control, he can rebuild everything with no problem. Luke and Randy are out of your reach, so you can't use . . . That's it!" she squealed. "Randy! That's how to get to him. Sweet Randy will lure him into our trap."

"What?" he growled in befuddlement. "She's in Dakota."

"You know how much we favor each other. What if we use soot or something to darken my hair? Perhaps use a blindfold to hide my blue eyes. If he glanced at me at a distance in the shadows, he would think you had Randy captive. He would steal the evidence to save her. You could dress one of your men to pass as Luke. If you keep us in dim light and at a distance, with mouths gagged, he would be fooled. I can hire a lawyer to prove he blackmailed me, then I'll be free of this repulsive marriage. We'll make certain we obey every American law and give them no new evidence or suspicions for a new case; agreed? After he lowers his guard, you can get rid of the beast."

"And just how did I capture Randy and Luke?" he queried.

"You've been missing for weeks, Web. You've had time to locate them and bring them back as prisoners," she snapped in frustration, as if irritated by his lack of intelligence.

"And what if he asks to see you?" he added, finding another inconsistency.

"Must I think of everything!" she exploded in fury. "You were clever enough to trick me for months and to almost pull off a second civil war! The least you can do is help me figure out how to defeat them and save both our lives and fortunes! In case you're not thinking clearly, I've just as much to lose as you have! I don't want to be Harrison's showpiece! I don't want him commanding me! I want to come and go as I please. As long as he's in control of me and my wealth, I'm helpless; I'm like a prisoner! You can show me bound in one area of the warehouse. Then surely you can find some way to taunt and delay him while I disguise myself and sneak to where you're supposedly holding Randy and Luke for exhibition," she suggested.

"Why would you help me?" he questioned skeptically.

"As I said, for a price," she replied hastily, glaring at him.

"What price?" he inquired, piqued.

"Everything I just told you and my escape. After the ruse is over, you destroy the evidence against you. Then you must help me get free of Reis, either by his death or an annulment. In exchange for my help, I'll sign Lawrence Shipping over to you. I'll sell everything else, move to another state, and begin a new life—perhaps in New Orleans or New York. When my traitorous sister returns, she'll be at your whim because I won't be around. And neither will our property and money for her protection and support. Since you find her so pleasing and desirable, you can rescue her from poverty. But I don't want her beaten or killed; is that understood? You can make her your mistress or wife, whatever suits you and her. As for Reis, you can do as you please with him. That way, we'll both have what we want."

Just as Amanda suspected and prayed, Weber agreed to go along with this scheme to obtain the crucial file. But she knew he would attempt to delude her into believing he would free her and help her afterward, which he would never do. Despite his hazy madness, Amanda was reading him clearly. Yes, Weber would try to use her one last time, but he would fail!

The plans were made. Weber untied her but placed a guard on her. She frowned at him, mocking his mistrust. "Prove yourself, my sweet, then I'll trust you with my life," he teased her. "In fact, I might do all I can to persuade you to marry me. We would make a fine team, Mandy. We could both come and go as we pleased, discreetly, of course. I would enjoy having your sister as my mistress for a while, if you didn't mind." She shrugged nonchalantly as if agreeing.

When all was prepared, Amanda was nervous. All she could do was go along with her scheme as she awaited a moment to attack him. She hoped Reis would see through this farce. If he did not, he would be offered a chance for escape and to summon help. For the first time, she knew what it meant to be willing to sacrifice her life for that of someone she loved. But to think this could be the last time she saw her love was staggering and tormenting.

Amanda was bound and gagged, then placed in a corner. Her guard concealed himself and she was ordered to feign unconsciousness. Weber went to get Reis. He brought her beloved to the center of the immense room, then had another guard come and stand near her. A flaming torch illuminated her limp figure, revealing her disheveled and dirtied state. She remained still and silent.

Weber warned Reis she would be killed instantly if he made any moves or called for help. As they headed for the office, she could hear Reis threatening to slay Weber with his bare hands if she were harmed in any way. It ripped at her heart to note the anguish in his voice, the pain and fury which she prayed Weber would ignore or think false. His hands bound, Reis could help no one, including himself. And with her as a prisoner, her love feared to escape or resist.

The guard untied her the moment Weber and Reis were out of sight. He was already dressed to resemble Lucas. Amanda sealed herself in a closet to change dresses, then the two of them sooted her blond hair until it appeared dark. They hurried to an adjoining warehouse to take their places. When the guard leaned over to move a crate to partially shield them, she furtively seized a crowbar. Refusing to feel any remorse, she slammed it across his head, then quickly bound and gagged him. She grabbed his knife and stuck it into a cotton sack near where Weber would stand while pointing them out. She took the guard's gun and her assigned place, calculating that there would be Weber and another armed guard against a bound Reis and herself. All she could do was wait with her stolen gun, and pray Reis noticed the shiny knife.

She went rigid when she heard the door open then close. She ordered herself to relax yet remain alert. She could hear Weber's voice, but could not make out his words. He halted near the center of the structure, telling the guard to show Reis "their little surprises."

Amanda knew their lives were at stake but wondered if she could actually pull the trigger and shoot a man. Her arms were in a position to indicate she was bound, and she had remembered to gag herself. The other man moved the torch back and forth over the couple as Weber referred to them as Miranda and Lucas. Reis was unprepared for the sly ruse and was briefly deceived at that distance.

As Weber issued his demands, Reis snarled, "How do I know the three of them are still alive? All I've seen are limp bodies. I want to talk to them."

As pre-planned without Amanda's knowledge, Weber signaled the guard who instantly shot the man playing Lucas. It did not surprise the other guard or Weber when the unsuspecting man did not move or scream, or when Amanda jumped in astonishment. Weber casually informed the stunned Reis that he could only bargain for the two twins now. If he refused Weber's orders, both girls would be murdered tonight.

"You son-of-a-bitch!" Reis stormed at him, causing Weber to shove him backward. Miraculously, Reis's hands made contact with the knife, and he hastily closed his fingers around the handle.

Then everything went wild. Amanda panicked and shot the guard, the thunderous roar of her gunfire drawing Weber's attention from Reis. The wounded guard tried to get his gun out of his holster, but she closed her eyes and fired once more. This time he stopped permanently.

It was evident to Weber that he had been duped by her again, and that both of his guards were now dead or seriously injured. With a loud yell of hatred, he jerked out his concealed weapon to kill her. Reis yanked the knife from its place and whirled around. There was no time to sever his hands. He slammed himself into Weber's back, driving the knife into his demented body. Both men fell to the floor. With speed and agility, Reis pulled the bloody knife free and rolled away. He instantly came to his feet and raced to where Miranda was hiding.

When he turned to ask if she was all right, he was shocked; the woman beside him was his wife. She ripped off the gag and smiled at him, then hugged him tightly. Weber's agonized voice returned her anxiety. Reis told her to cut him free, which she did with some effort. She handed him the guard's gun, then he smiled at her, and stole a brief kiss of encouragement.

"I'll kill you, you bitch!" Weber shouted in pain and fury.

"It's over, Richardson," Reis announced confidently, shoving Amanda's head down when she tried to peer over the crate.

She understood the precaution when Weber fired shots at them. Reis attempted to talk Weber into surrendering, but he adamantly refused. Spouting how he was going to "roast them alive," Weber staggered toward the only unsealed exit. From his wild rantings, it appeared he was planning to barricade the door and set fire to the building. Reis could not allow him to escape or give him a chance to trap them. He fired at Weber's legs, one bullet shattering a knee. As Weber screamed in pain and clutched at a stack of crates for balance, the heavy pile tumbled down crushing him. Weber Richardson would threaten them no more.

Finding the guards dead as well, Reis left the bodies while he took the trembling Amanda home. Later, in each other's arms, they compared stories. At last their ordeal was over, the anguish of the past and present. They nestled together, sharing comfort and joy.

Before leaving Alexandria, Reis hired a crew for the desperate search which Weber's boastful words had inspired. Only in the event that his men were successful, would he tell his wife anything about it. Soon they would be in Dakota to challenge new adventures. But they would also confront perils as yet unknown, perils more numerous and lethal than any devised by the late Weber Richardson . . .

Chapter Seventeen

Calamity Jane and Tom Two-Feathers Fletcher had no choice but to mount hastily and follow the impulsive and courageous girl toward the Oglala camp. Tom caught up with Miranda and cautioned her to conduct herself with patience and respect. He warned her not to make trouble if Sun Cloud refused a second time to meet her.

Tom witnessed the look of fierce determination and resentment which were visible in her tawny eyes and upon her lovely face. This audacious and exquisite creature would be a sensuously wild vixen to tame, an assignment he would relish. What more could a man who survived in the wilderness desire than a woman who was beautiful, brave, sturdy, and keen witted? He could easily envision the type of wife and mother this half-girl, half-woman would make in some lucky family. And luck was something a clever man created for himself in this barren, onerous territory. With her half-blooded heritage, Miranda was a perfect match for him.

They reined in before the colorfully painted teepee of the famed war chief, Crazy Horse. Tom and Jane gingerly dismounted and Tom assisted Miranda down to the ground. Miranda stood poised and guarded as Tom spoke with the leader who had left his teepee at the commotion outside.

"*Tashunka Witco*," Tom addressed the chief by name in Sioux, then related that the girl with him wished to know why her grandfather refused to see her after she had come so far and faced many dangers.

Crazy Horse eyed the beauty at the scout's side, a female who looked as Indian as the women nearby. His sweeping gaze surveyed her manner of dress: she was wearing the garment and headband of an Oglala princess! Did the proud creature think she had the right by birth to commit such an offense? She was *hanke-wasichun*, half blooded!

No one approached the small group or dared to speak without their leader's permission. But all observed the strange sight. Miranda remained alert and silent while Tom reasoned with the chief. From the expression and tone of Crazy Horse's voice, she knew he did not realize she spoke his tongue and understood his cutting words. Forewarned by Tom, she held her anxious tongue as her anger increased.

Miranda observed the masterful warrior who was rumored to be dauntless—a powerful man who challenged any force or obstacle, an intelligent man whose cunning was feared and respected, an heroic man whose influence and prowess were held in awe and dread. *Tashunka Witco* was said to be a seasoned leader who rode before his band, always putting himself in the first line of danger. And he was known also for his military tactics and expertise, a "Plains soldier" unsurpassed. He was a proficient warrior of such enormous mettle and skill that others envied him but feared to challenge his rank. So immense was his valiance that he had become a member of the *O-zu-ye Wicasta*, the Warrior Society, before reaching his sixteenth birthday. It was as if Crazy Horse had been trained from birth for his rank in history, as if no person or nothing could prevent him from being thrust into the role of the Sioux's most powerful warrior. It was true that he trusted no white man, and with just cause. Believing himself protected and blessed by the Great Spirit, he could endure intense pain without flinching. It was alleged that the intrepid warrior "dreamed" himself into an aura of invincibility and matchless valor before every battle, seeing a vision in which his horse pranced eagerly and crazily, and from this dream the illustrious warrior took his name. Just over thirty, Crazy Horse was a growing legend amongst both whites and Indians.

One thing which surprised Miranda was the lightness of his hair and skin. He possessed bold features and piercing eyes on a face which could be called ruggedly handsome. He was the son of the sister of Spotted Tail, the noted Brule chief confined to a reservation. The defeat and humiliation of his once-great uncle inspired and encouraged Crazy Horse to make certain he and his people never shared such a despicable and degrading fate.

Another curiosity for Miranda was the physical size of Crazy Horse. She had expected this legend to be tall and muscular, as was the unknown warrior she had met several times. But Crazy Horse was of medium height and lean, with the lithe build of a swordsman. Yet, strength of body and character were emblazoned upon his face and frame. As the two men talked, Miranda admired both the mental and physical attributes of the war chief.

The warrior chief speaking with the half-blooded scout knew the story behind this girl's birth and the shame and betrayal of her mother. Although he had been only ten years old at the time, Crazy Horse could recall the day when Princess Morning Star deserted her father and people to marry a white man. He respected the past skills and prowess of Sun Cloud, now seventy-five and growing more eager each day to seek the Great Spirit, and he could understand why Sun Cloud refused to meet this woman. He was keenly aware of her intense study of him, and her conclusions. But perhaps, he silently reasoned, he should change the old warrior's mind; perhaps she offered solutions to several problems.

Miranda thought it was best to keep her knowledge of the Sioux tongue a secret in order to discover all she could, unaware that her great-grandfather, Gray

Eagle, had used this same ploy to learn the white man's secrets. She asked the scout to translate her words. "Tell my grandfather that his daughter, Morning Star, and my father were killed; they now live with the Great Spirit. Tell him I have come a great distance alone to meet him. Ask him to forgive the pain and sadness which my mother brought to him. If she had not been taken from my life-circle, she would be here this sun speaking these words. She longed to see her father once more and hungered for peace in her heart and mind."

She waited while Tom interpreted her statements. "Tell him I am not my mother; tell him I should not pay for her acts which brought shame and sadness to the teepee of Sun Cloud. Is it not the Sioux way for each man to earn his own honor and to pay for his own evil? Why must I pay and suffer for the deeds of my mother? If he will not speak with me, I will never return. Will he deny himself my love? Can his bitterness and hatred of my mother and her child be so great that he denies I carry his blood? Will such a denial remove that blood from my body? He was a great warrior, a worthy chief. Where is the wisdom and logic in rejecting me?" she reasoned candidly in a tremulous voice.

Those words were translated for the Sioux chief, even though he comprehended most of her English words. Miranda selected her next words carefully and brazenly. "Surely such a great man has no reason to fear a mere woman? Have I denied that an Oglala Indian is my grandfather? Have I rejected him because he is Indian? Have I refused to travel through great distance and danger to see him only one sun? Does this mean I hold more courage, generosity, and wisdom than your former chief? If a man or woman cannot steal another's good or bad shadow, then how can he use my mother's dark shadow as the reason to deny me sight of his face and the sound of his voice? What man of honor and bravery cannot speak for himself? Can he not find the courage and generosity to share but one hour with me?" She knew she had cleverly used two of the most respected Indian arguments, tempering her tone with appealing frankness and honesty.

Crazy Horse's expression softened with appreciation, but he did not smile. To her surprise, Crazy Horse told them to wait while he spoke with Sun Cloud. Miranda's gaze trailed him to a teepee in the second ring. He ducked and entered. Tension increased within her as she waited. When he finally returned, she was prepared to hear another refusal. She could not hide her astonishment and pleasure when Crazy Horse related the summons of her grandfather, to share "one hour" as requested.

Miranda's hands were trembling and her heart raced as she followed the chief into her grandfather's presence. Complying with the instructions from Crazy Horse to Tom, Miranda seated herself on a buffalo skin before the older man, three feet away. Jane had been ordered to wait with the horses, which she reluctantly did.

Sun Cloud's hair was mostly gray with only traces of ebony. His stoic face was lined from the passage of time and exposure to the elements. Even after so many years, Sun Cloud still radiated courage and greatness. Such wisdom, pride, and intelligence flickered in those age-glazed eyes. His once strong body was now slim, having lost its firmness and power. He was sitting cross-legged on another buffalo hide, erect and silent, watchful and wary.

The unnecessary translations began. Her grandfather asked why she had come to him, his voice vital and clear despite his age and increasing weakness. A twinge of sadness and disappointment assailed her, for he did not inquire about his deceased daughter or even hint he was glad she had come. He appeared untouched by her arrival and identity. She struggled to contain the tears which threatened to expose her turmoil. Whatever happened today, she would show great courage and control.

Before replying, she quietly asked permission to begin her tale where it started, here in 1850. She waited for Sun Cloud to object. His response was for her to choose her own words. If either warrior was moved by her narrative, it did not show on their impassive faces. Fearing her time was limited, Miranda revealed only the major points of her and her mother's pasts. Sun Cloud did not react to the news of her twin sister or to the perils they had faced recently. Only Crazy Horse perked up when she exposed her cousin's assignment here. Knowing Tom hated the blond-haired Custer, she felt no qualms in revealing it.

When she finished telling of her history and motives, her grandfather asked if she had spoken all the words she wished him to hear. Miranda wondered if her heart truly stopped for a moment, for it sounded like a dismissal. When she nodded, Sun Cloud asked if she had completed her quest and was ready to leave. Miranda stared at him, for she could not respond in the way she felt he wanted her to. She wondered if Sun Cloud possessed any feelings of affection or loyalty or respect for her. She was disheartened by what she did not see in his eyes or perceive from his mien. At least she had made the effort.

Miranda rose slowly and stood proudly before Sun Cloud, sealing her fathomless gaze on her grandfather's face, ignoring the others present. She stated with false calm, "My hour has passed, Grandfather, and I will leave as promised. I pray you will seek and find understanding and forgiveness before you join my mother with the Great Spirit. Do not blame her for loving and choosing my father, for she answered the call of her own destiny. If joining with my father was wrong for her, the Great Spirit would have prevented it. Perhaps it was not the wish of the Great Spirit for Morning Star to marry a white man, but He allowed her to follow her heart. I will not trouble you with the telling of their love story and happiness. It is not for you or me to judge her actions; only the Great Spirit has that right. Goodbye, Grandfather. Until you look into the face of the Great Spirit and learn all things, I wish you health and happiness." With that, she turned to leave, unable to bear the weighty anguish of this moment any longer.

Just before she ducked to exit the teepee, Sun Cloud stated she had not answered his last question. Miranda inhaled and exhaled several times before turning to face him. In a clear and compelling tone, she replied, *"Hiya. Cante ceya,"* saying no and that her heart was weeping in sadness. She went on to tell of her desire for peace with him. *"Wookiye wocin."* Both warriors stared at her as she spoke fluent Sioux with ease.

The elderly man told her to come and sit once more. Miranda hesitated. Sun Cloud's expression warmed and relaxed as he coaxed again. *"Ku-wa, cinstinna,"* calling her "little one."

When she did as he had requested, he stated evocatively, "You speak my tongue. How is this so? Why do you leave without fighting words?"

"My mother taught me to speak Oglala. She loved you deeply, Grandfather. It pained her heart to leave you and her people; it pained her more never to return. She missed you and longed to visit you. She spoke of the Sioux history and her life here. She spoke of you, telling me what a great warrior and chief you were. She told me why her love and marriage were wrong in the eyes of her people. For many years I have hungered to come here, to know you, to know this life. When she was taken from me, the hunger increased. It was as if I had no power or wish to resist the summons of the Great Spirit, as if He were calling me home. I belong here, Grandfather; I am more Indian than white. She taught me your customs and ways and that is why I knew it was wrong to beg or resist," she explained.

"But you resisted my command not to come," he refuted astutely.

Miranda lowered her gaze in guilt. "Yes," she admitted. "But I did not feel it was right for you to reject me from a distance, to reject me for another's deeds. I was drawn here by a force too powerful to resist."

Sun Cloud observed the girl who returned his daughter's image to life. Morning Star had always been different from other Oglala maidens. She had been willful and daring, yet gentle and unselfish. This girl was much like his own. Seeing her made him feel younger and his spirit freer. Morning Star had left of her own will; Miranda returned in that same way. After the death of Night Stalker, his loneliness for his only child had increased. He had feared and prayed for her safety, though he never mentioned her name after her departure. His body had survived many winters and hardships, his heart had known many emotions, and his eyes had seen many changes in his life and lands. His children had reached the Great Spirit before him. All he had left were memories of past glorious days, and two grandchildren who differed as much as day and night. He mentally corrected himself—three grandchildren.

"To speak the truth takes great courage, little one. You will stay in my teepee for five suns then return to your sister," he calmly informed her, then asked Tom to return for her on the sixth day.

Tom gazed at Miranda. "What if someone learns your secret?" he asked.

"I want to stay, Tom; I need to stay. Please help me. If the truth leaks out, I'll face that problem when it arises. Jane can say she took me to visit friends downriver while Luke's away. Who could doubt us?" she reasoned aloud. "Please," she urged him.

"That sounds good," Tom agreed, smiling at her.

Miranda told her grandfather she would stay with him. She said she must bid her friend, Jane, farewell, and she left the teepee. Jane agreed to live in the cabin while she was in the Sioux camp, then return with Tom for her.

While Miranda and Jane were exchanging their stories, Sun Cloud was asking Crazy Horse, "Has she earned a *coup* feather, for she stole this old warrior's heart? Did I speak and act like a foolish old man?"

"You spoke as a wise, unselfish man. She carries much of the blood and spirit of Sun Cloud. She will make no trouble. She will bring you peace and smiles," the youthful leader concluded. He added mischievously, "Perhaps she will remind Bloody Arrow why he does not wear the chief's bonnet. Perhaps she will soften his anger and bitterness."

Sun Cloud nodded gravely. "Each moon I pray the Great Spirit will remove his pride and greed. It was the will of the Great Spirit for you to guide us. In time, my grandson must see and accept this."

Sun Cloud was relieved when Crazy Horse did not mention another warrior in the distant line of Gray Eagle, the great-grandson of Bright Arrow. If the white man's evil took the life of Crazy Horse, there was only one warrior to take his place, Blazing Star. But Sun Cloud and others knew that Blazing Star would not challenge Crazy Horse for the chief's bonnet, or vainly try to rival their leader's *coups*. Surely a smart and intuitive man like Crazy Horse realized as well that

Blazing Star posed no threat to him. In many ways, Blazing Star was more like a son or grandson to Sun Cloud, and he was anxious for Blazing Star to return to him and his people. Sun Cloud was determined not to permit Bloody Arrow to plant any more seeds of doubt in his mind about the absent warrior, and he trampled his grandson's malicious suspicions within his heart. He hoped Crazy Horse had not ordered Blazing Star on so many dangerous raids just to be rid of him.

Crazy Horse left Sun Cloud and Miranda alone to talk, which they did for a short time as it was nearing the hour of the evening meal. Although Miranda had not noticed her, there was an Indian slave preparing their meal beside the teepee to allow them privacy. Miranda learned about a ghastly massacre during 1854, the year her mother had given birth to twins. Besides many people in the tribe, others in Gray Eagle's bloodline had lost their lives to the bullets and sabers of treacherous bluecoats. She learned of the slaughter of her grandmother, Singing Wind, daughter of Oglala maiden, Chela, and Blackfoot chief, Brave Bear, and of her uncle, Chief Night Stalker and his Brule wife, Touched-A-Crow, from Sun Cloud's line. From Bright Arrow's bloodline Tashina was lost, youngest daughter of Bright Arrow, along with her husband, Soul-of-Thunder, and their son, Soaring Hawk, both his wives, Talking Woman and Sapa Ista, and one granddaughter called Bitter Heart, who was the twelve-year-old half-sister of Blazing Star. She listened as Sun Cloud revealed that Blazing Star was the only survivor in Bright Arrow's bloodline, and that Bloody Arrow—her first cousin—and she and Amanda were the only ones to carry on Sun Cloud's line.

Having heard the name of Blazing Star so often from the whites and now the Indians, Miranda inquired about him as their food was served by the sullen girl. Because men, especially Indian men, did not consider physical appearances, Sun Cloud talked only of the immense prowess and accomplishments of the awesome warrior. As she listened, she realized that Crazy Horse and this mysterious Blazing Star were very much alike in strength and courage. In the days to come, Miranda would hear a great deal more about this warrior.

After the meal, Sun Cloud left her to attend a council meeting. Miranda relaxed on her assigned pallet to ponder this momentous day which had gone extremely well. Her drowsy thoughts were of her eagerness to meet her cousin, Bloody Arrow, and the legendary Sitting Bull tomorrow. She was disappointed that the intrepid Blazing Star would not return to camp before her departure. She snuggled against the fuzzy hide, inhaled deeply, and totally relaxed as a pleasing odor assailed her hazy senses. She smiled and pressed her face closer to the hide, inhaling again. Her mind floated toward a warrior whose face and body she knew, but not his name. Perhaps she would describe him and seek his identity after she had been here a few days, she mused dreamily. Contented and fatigued, she was soon sleeping peacefully.

When Miranda awoke the next morning, she felt wonderful. She ate with her grandfather, again served by the unfriendly girl of about twenty. Afterward, Sun Cloud guided Miranda around the camp, introducing her to everyone who caught his eye or ear. She smiled each time he called her his granddaughter, *Tamaha*, which meant "Rising Moon." When she asked him why he had selected that name, he said it had been Sitting Bull's suggestion. When she probed deeper, he told her that Morning Star was the name for the moon rising during the day to cast a faint white image upon the blue sky, just as she had arisen in her mother's image.

She was touched and moved by the significance behind the lovely Sioux name which sounded like she was saying, "Ta-my-ya." Sioux was a difficult and guttural tongue, but her name sounded soft and flowing like a gentle stream, as warming as the spring sun. She thanked him.

Later, she met the man who had chosen her Indian name. Sitting Bull, *Tatanka Yotanka*, was a medicine man and spiritual leader. She wondered why the soldiers thought he was a chief. Said to have great mystical powers and immense courage, Sitting Bull was very perceptive and intuitive, a prophetic man to rival the Biblical Isaiah. His silvery tongue had reached the minds and hearts of Indians and whites. Little did Sitting Bull or Miranda realize that many of his letters and speeches would become historical readings, revelations of the dark blot upon humanity and American history.

Around forty, Sitting Bull was a tall and powerfully built man. His broad shoulders seemed capable of taking on the burdens of his tribe, or the entire seven-tribe Sioux Nation. Only the skills and prowess of Crazy Horse or Blazing Star could rival those of Sitting Bull. He possessed piercing eyes which seemed to cut through one's body and view the very soul. Upon his chest were the marks of courage and sacrifice, the scars of the Sun Dance. If ever a man embodied and exemplified stoic greatness, fierce courage, keen intelligence, and stamina of mind and body, here was that man—Sitting Bull.

All Indian tribes knew of him and respected him. His words could be trusted. Sitting Bull, like Crazy Horse, had no respect and feeling for those who condemned themselves to reservations. Sitting Bull called them fools who would enslave their souls for rotten food and ragged blankets. As long as he had breath, he determined to remain free on the lands given to his people by the Great Spirit, *Wakantanka*.

Miranda was greatly impressed by this unique man. How she prayed he could keep his people free and alive. Having seen how they lived off the land in such harmony and tranquility, it pained her to envision their defeat. She could not imagine these proud and vital people lazing around a reservation. The Indians were the epitome of courage and strength. Why couldn't they be left in peace? Hadn't the whites taken enough land and lives?

Sun Cloud had told Miranda how the bloodline of Gray Eagle had lost the chief's bonnet when Sun Cloud was wounded badly at fifty-five and could not lead his people. The chief's bonnet was passed to Night Stalker, Sun Cloud's firstborn, who wore it with glory and honor for two years until his death during the grim 1854 massacre. That tragic event had returned the chief's bonnet to Sun Cloud's head, as Bloody Arrow at five and Blazing Star at eight were too young to become the tribe's leader. After Sun Cloud reached an age too advanced for the leadership needed in dangerous times, Crazy Horse was asked to step into those legendary moccasins. Following Crazy Horse's successful and daring victory over Captain William Fetterman and his troop, Sun Cloud had agreed with his people's choice and decision. Seventeen at that selection time, Bloody Arrow had been too young and rash to become war chief, too inexperienced, too distracted by shameful pride, and too hot tempered. Since that day, her grandfather had confided in worry, Bloody Arrow had been unable or unwilling to accept his loss.

Sun Cloud had just been served his evening meal when Bloody Arrow swept into the teepee like a conquering hero returning home after a victorious raid. As was the Indian custom, Miranda had been waiting for her grandfather to finish eating before she was served. Bloody Arrow's audacity shone like a bright beacon on the darkest of stygian nights. At first glimpse, he seemed intense, moody, and rebellious; such traits were unusual for a warrior. Clearly, here was a force she would have to reckon with before this day was over. The warrior halted instantly when his eyes touched the beautiful Indian girl sitting near his placid grandfather. His gaze took in her features quickly, then shifted to his grandfather as he decided he would enjoy this new slave.

Bloody Arrow took a seat near Sun Cloud and was served by the Crow captive. His gaze was cold and his demeanor forbidding as he ordered the slave to see to the freshly slain deer outside. His dark eyes settled on Miranda as he commanded her to help the other woman, warning her of punishment if she disobeyed or made any mistakes.

Startled by his wintry stare and mood, she did not know how to respond. Was she supposed to help with chores in the teepee? Could she skin and cure a lovely deer? She swallowed with difficulty. Was she subject to her cousin's orders and whims? Wasn't she a guest?

Sun Cloud suppressed laughter as he revealed her identity to the astonished warrior. Bloody Arrow's gaze narrowed and clouded as he gaped at his cousin. "You are Tamaha, my cousin?" he asked in disbelief.

"*Sha,*" she cheerfully replied yes in Oglala, although he had spoken in English.

He came to full alert at her use of his language. "Tell me why you came to the teepee of Sun Cloud and Bloody Arrow?" he inquired oddly.

Miranda allowed Sun Cloud to relate her story and his invitation. She noticed the increasing coolness in the younger warrior as he watched and heard the warmth and pleasure in their grandfather's eyes and voice. Surely a blind person could detect the jealousy and bitterness in Bloody Arrow at her arrival and treatment, Miranda thought to herself.

Bloody Arrow asked question after question until he felt he knew everything about this girl and her visit. Miranda sensed there was something peculiar about his interest; it certainly appeared to be more than curiosity about a new relative. He seemed particularly interested in how she had been received by Sitting Bull and Crazy Horse. At the end of their talk, he asked if she had met Blazing Star. Sun Cloud told him that Blazing Star had not returned from his scouting mission and probably would not return before she left. That statement caught his attention, and he looked pleased to learn she would be leaving soon.

At bedtime, Bloody Arrow did not attempt to hide his irritation when he was told to go outside while she changed for sleep. He was more vexed to discover he would have to sleep in his breechclout while she was there. He teased her about not knowing the ways of their people, telling her if she remained here long she must cast aside her modesty and accept them. Miranda could not imagine sleeping nude even with family!

As she lay on her pallet listening to the heavy breathing of both men, she comprehended several dismaying realities. She had recognized the antagonism in her cousin's voice and eyes when three names had been mentioned: Crazy Horse, Sitting Bull, and Blazing Star. Having met two of the three men, she could not understand this leashed hatred and envy. Clearly her cousin did not want her around, and it would be difficult, if not impossible, to win his friendship and acceptance. She pondered how much contention or unhappiness he could bring to her. But she had discovered another fact which Sun Cloud had not mentioned, a fact which would force her to end her visit as planned, for she now knew that she could never take up permanent residence in this abode. Blazing Star also lived in this teepee and would be home soon.

Now she understood why there were three prayer pipes and so many weapons, items she knew females were forbidden to touch. Certainly she could not live with three men. And she and Blazing Star were so far apart on Gray Eagle's ancestral chart that they could hardly be called relatives. If they had been children, living together would not have made a difference; but they were adults.

And there was another factor. Since Bloody Arrow's return, the atmosphere in the teepee had changed drastically. It seemed intimidating and unfriendly now, and that plagued her. Did her grandfather feel this chilling atmosphere? She admitted that hearing about Indian life and living it were vastly dissimilar. Having Indian blood did not necessarily make her suitable for this existence. No matter how much she wanted to fit in, she wondered if she could, or if her cousin would permit it.

Miranda asked herself why her cousin disliked her and why he was anxious for her to leave. He had seemed delighted by her presence when he thought her a helpless captive. There were many conflicts and ill feelings in that skilled warrior. Why could he not accept his role in life and in this camp and be happy? He had accused her of being ignorant of Indian ways and customs, but his attitude and behavior were wrong for a warrior—despicable! Her first impression had been accurate; he was trouble and anguish for her. But did it matter when she had only three days left here? She had fulfilled her dream, but now she was so confused. Did she belong to this world? Was she more Indian or white, or neither? She drifted off to sleep with these poignant questions haunting her.

When she awoke the morning of the third day, Sun Cloud was gone; Bloody Arrow was sitting cross-legged on his mat, watching her intently. She rubbed her eyes and sat up, holding the light blanket before her. She smiled faintly and told him good morning. His stare unnerved her, as he no doubt intended.

He suddenly grinned and teased, "Do you enjoy sleeping on the mat of Blazing Star? Be glad he has not returned and joined you. His prowess upon the sleeping mats is known by many females."

Miranda paled then flushed a deep red at his crude insinuations. "The lust of Blazing Star does not interest me, dear cousin. Nor does your childish dislike of my visit," she told him brazenly, hoping her chilling displeasure and brave words would prevent more insults.

He scolded her mischievously. "It is not the way of Indian women to speak so rudely to a great warrior."

She promptly retorted, "Is it the way of a great warrior to insult his relatives? Is it acceptable for a warrior to be rude and hateful to the granddaughter of Sun Cloud?"

"Your wit is keen and your tongue is quick, Tamaha. But they are scornful. Perhaps it is because you have more white blood than Oglala," he mocked.

"Your wit is black and your tongue sharp, Bloody Arrow. Perhaps you have more hatred and envy in your body than pride and intelligence."

"You possess great courage or stupidity to speak so boldly to me. I will think more on you before we talk again," he declared sullenly, then quickly left.

"And I will think more on you, too, cousin," she scoffed softly.

Later that morning, Bloody Arrow watched his cousin as she walked and talked with Crazy Horse, unaware the chief was probing her about the defenses at Fort Sully and things she had perhaps overheard which might inform him of the soldiers' plans. He observed the easy and genial manner of the envied war chief, then noticed the sullen way the Cheyenne wife of Crazy Horse was furtively observing the two. Bloody Arrow grinned as he envisioned the warring teepee of their leader if Crazy Horse revealed too much interest in this beautiful girl.

Bloody Arrow needed time to think and plan, things he did best while hunting. He called several braves together for a hunt for the widows of slain warriors or the families of those warriors who were away from camp. This was a common practice but not usually suggested by him. He rode out of camp with rising pleasure at the game he was plotting, a sport to defeat more than one rival.

Before leaving, Bloody Arrow commanded the Crow slave to loan Miranda one of her best dresses, the one she kept folded inside a leather parfleche for the day of her escape and return home. The girl was filled with anger and defiance at this cruel order. Her feelings altered, however, when Bloody Arrow told her he wanted his cousin looking her best until she left their camp, and he promised to bring her a beautiful doeskin for a new dress in return for her services to Tamaha. The prisoner sensed spite in her captor, spite toward the chief he had been secretly watching all morning and spite against the half-white girl who now shared his grandfather's affections. She also wanted revenge on the Sioux, and agreed to do as commanded. Her captor's scheme would come to light, and she would enjoy his punishment.

Miranda was surprised and pleased when the captive offered her a clean buckskin dress and undergarment to wear. Her astonishment grew when the girl suggested a bath and hairwashing with her assistance. The slave smiled shyly, craftily, as she said it was to please Tamaha's family, to perhaps inspire her release for kindness. Of a gentle and trusting nature, Miranda smiled and accepted the captive's devious words. She followed the girl to the stream where she bathed and scrubbed her hair. After the sun dried it, the Crow woman brushed and braided it, then secured Miranda's headband around her forehead. Donning the fringed and beaded dress, Miranda looked exquisite. The girl told her to return to camp while she washed her dress for tomorrow.

The Indian custom was to rest after lunch, but Miranda was too excited to take a nap. Her grandfather was in a council meeting, discussing the reports of two scouts who had returned during her bath. She decided to stroll around the camp to study the artistic adventures painted on the teepees while the village was still and quiet. Within an hour, she was at the edge of camp. She strolled to a large tree and leaned against it, her contented gaze sweeping over the sight of her grandfather's immense village.

The thunderous sound of many hoofbeats seized her rambling attention. Panic filled her as she recalled tales of surprise raids on Indian camps. She rashly jumped from behind the tree, stepping into the path of a band of returning warriors. She screamed as she was knocked face down to the hard and dusty ground by the leader's horse.

In their elated and distracted mood, the leader and his band almost raced over the reckless and inquisitive girl who had stepped from behind the tree. He was relieved to see she had been thrown aside before being trampled by the pounding hooves of seven horses. The startled warrior agilely bounded off his horse to check on her. He was scolding her furiously as she lifted her head to present his stunned senses with the same beautiful face which filled his dreams!

Both were silent as they stared at each other. His astute gaze flashed over her tawny eyes and sun-kissed skin, and the unmarred flesh which had been soiled by her fall. Her hair was as soft and dark as a bearskin, braided neatly. Having been about to speak, her lips were parted, displaying a mouth which was provocative and whose taste and softness he recalled too well. Her wide gaze revealed her astonishment at seeing him again. Yet, there was another emotion emblazoned there, an emotion which caused his loins to flame with desire, a response which made him forget where he was or who he was!

Miranda could not pull her captive gaze from the magnetic attraction of this man who had haunted her dreams for many weeks. Here he was before her once more, here with his arresting features and strong, virile body. He was like an intoxicating blend of stormy black and molten bronze. Her mouth was suddenly dry and she could not speak. Her heart was racing madly and she could not think. Her eyes were glued to him and she could not free them. Intense desire flooded her as she stared at this embodiment of manhood, this savage and powerful warlord of the Plains, this captor of her heart and inspiration of her fantasies. In her wildest imagination, she had not thought of finding him again, and surely not here in her grandfather's camp! How fortunate he had come to visit before her departure.

The mutual trance which seemed to hold them was broken when the other warriors dismounted and surged forward to demand the identity of the beautiful Indian maiden. Miranda watched the mood of the handsome warrior as it changed rapidly, confusingly. His face was unpainted today, giving her a clear view of his mounting fury and resentment, reactions she could not understand. With feet planted apart in an arrogant and forbidding stance, he glared at her, refusing to offer her assistance in rising. He merely gaped at the hand she extended entreatingly for his help, gaped as if it were leprous.

For a brief time, she had presumed he was glad to see her. Now, he was acting as if they were strangers, foes. She had watched coldness cover the warmth on his face and freeze his eyes. Why? She slowly and gracefully stood up and dusted off her clothes and bare arms. The other males were laughing, teasing, and ribbing each other as they watched her closely, watched her and the curious behavior of their leader. Miranda did not know what to say.

He stood tall and erect, recalling the day he had secretly watched her riding with the female scout from Fort Sully. He berated himself for not capturing her that day or one of the other times they had met. He knew where she lived, in that small wooden teepee near the fort. He knew a white man shared that teepee, the one who had traveled with her to his land. Now she was the captive of another warrior, out of his reach forever. He cursed his pride which had prevented her capture, his ego which had wanted to be spared the teasing and taunting of other warriors at his taking a white slave. In the back of his mind, he had known he would fall prey to his desires one day. He had known he would attack that cabin during the night and ride away with her bound to his body, to become his slave. Now that was impossible; he could never take her after another man!

The instant that thought left his tormented mind, he knew it was a lie. She could not be blamed for her capture, or any treatment afterward. He had seen the way her eyes lit up with joy and relief when they touched upon him. Whatever price her captor asked, he would pay it. He had to pay it and have her. Yet, his honor had to remain intact. He could not reveal love and desire for this white girl. He silently prayed she had not been injured, then realized how exceptionally clean and healthy she appeared. Surely she wasn't Indian or half-blooded? Surely she wasn't some warrior's wife or willing whore!

Miranda and the others were stunned and baffled when he sarcastically demanded to know whose captive whore she was. Before she could recover from the staggering insult to respond, others questioned his words to her. He coldly revealed she was a white girl from Fort Sully who had come to this land recently. He told them she had been on the boat he had trailed while stalking the two soldiers he had been ordered to slay. He related how they had been killed by a forest warrior while trying to rape this very girl.

Unaware she understood his words and the degrading meaning behind them, she was speechless in disbelief and anguish. She did not realize the warrior was infuriated by his stupefied reaction to her, angered in his belief that she was out of his reach, nettled by his weakness toward her before his band. Miranda's watchful and wary gaze shifted from warrior to warrior as they stared at her differently now, disdainfully.

When he cruelly asked again in English whose whore she was her wits and words returned in a fury of her own. "No man's! Get away from me, you savage beast!" She whirled to leave.

The warrior's hand snaked out and grabbed her wrist painfully, yanking her against his hard chest and rigid body. "Whose teepee holds such a sharp tongue and brazen whore?" he pressed boldly as the others watched his curious actions, for one warrior did not touch another's slave.

Through clenched teeth, she snapped in vexation, "I am no man's whore. I sleep in the teepee of Bloody Arrow and Sun Cloud."

She was determined to yank free of this insolent, smug, and cruel master of her heart. She owed him no explanation! "Release me before I cut off your offensive hand! Don't ever touch me or come near me again," she threatened.

Her previous statements had enticed a strange reaction. "You live in the teepee of Sun Cloud and Bloody Arrow?" he pressed skeptically.

Since he was speaking in English, so did she. "Yes. Sun Cloud will slay you if you harm me," she warned icily.

"You do not belong to Bloody Arrow?" He needed clarification but wondered what he would do if she said yes.

"Of course not!" she sneered as if insulted. "I belong to Sun Cloud," she added vaguely, wanting to flee this painful scene. His grip was as firm and confining as a band of steel.

Sun Cloud was told of the quarrel outside camp involving Tamaha and the warriors. He arrived and demanded her release. Miranda fled into the protective and affectionate embrace of her grandfather, trying not to sob. Sun Cloud smiled at her and patted her shoulder, his gaze settling angrily on the man who had dared such an offense.

One of the younger warriors rashly teased, "Surely our old chief does not take a white whore to his mats at his great age? If she is for trade, speak her price," he coaxed, as others added their bids.

Outrage filled the older man. He drilled his snow-clouded, ebony eyes into the oddly furious leader of this group. With a distinct voice, he informed them, "This is Tamaha, my granddaughter, child of Morning Star, my daughter. Do not ever touch or insult her again, or I will forget I am an old man. I will paint for a challenge with the warrior who dares to dishonor or hurt her, including you, Blazing Star."

At that name, Miranda's head jerked upward and she stared at the man whom her grandfather had called Blazing Star. As if no one else were present, she asked in a trembling voice, "You're Blazing Star?" He had shown astonishment at her identity, but he blinked in disbelief when she spoke fluent Oglala. When he nodded, she paled, suddenly realizing what distinctive and dream-inspiring odor had assailed her each night, each night upon this man's sleeping mat.

Miranda told Sun Cloud she was fine. She left her grandfather's embrace to flee as if demons were chasing her. When Sun Cloud questioned their strange behavior, Blazing Star asked the others to leave for privacy. He explained how he knew Miranda. Sun Cloud asked him why she had fled in fear; Blazing Star honestly replied he did not know. The old chief asked what had taken place between them today. Blazing Star ruefully repeated his words, abruptly comprehending that she had known what he said. Sun Cloud related her arrival and story.

"She did not know about me?" he inquired anxiously.

"She has heard many tales of the great warrior called Blazing Star, from Indians and whites. She has not asked about a warrior who saved her from the grizzly, who paints his face as you do. She has not asked who shoots arrows tipped with red and black. She sleeps upon your mat each moon. You return before enough suns pass. She is to leave soon. I did not tell her you lived in my teepee," he replied.

He was dismayed she had not inquired about him, since she had understood his Sioux words at each meeting. Her identity explained her previous lack of fear or scorn toward him. Blazing Star was intrigued by where she was sleeping and her reaction at seeing him. She had not expected the man who met her secretly to be the famed Blazing Star. "Did Bloody Arrow tell her I live in your teepee?" he pressed oddly.

"I do not know. Why do you ask such a question?"

Blazing Star deceived the old man by saying defensively, "She will be eager to leave now that I am home and she uses my mat."

"We can borrow a mat for her for two moons," he announced.

"Two moons?" Blazing Star echoed in bewilderment.

"She was to stay for five suns; three have passed. She will return to her people soon," Sun Cloud explained.

"Why must she go?" the warrior asked quietly.

"You know why, Blazing Star. Soon the white waters will try to roll over us and drown us. I do not wish her to find pain and death. She has been raised white; she must return to that world."

"She does not wish to live here with her grandfather?" he pried.

"She has not asked. If she does, I will refuse. I must," he stated sadly, sounding as old and weary as he looked at that moment.

"What of the white man who traveled with her?" he questioned.

Sun Cloud looked at him. "He is as Bloody Arrow to her. Luke puts words on papers for others to read. He comes secretly and cunningly as the fox, seeking to record the soldiers' evil. His eyes are on butchers and Yellowhair. And your eyes speak words I have not seen written there before. Do I see love and desire? Do I read pain and anger? Do I read jealousy and shame? Tell me if these eyes are too old and clouded."

Blazing Star fused his gaze to Sun Cloud's. He replied truthfully, "I cannot explain feelings I do not understand. There is a pull from her as strong and mysterious as the one to our sacred hills. I have resisted its power and magic, for I believed her white. But . . ."

When he wavered in confusion, Sun Cloud smiled and remarked, "But she is not. She is the granddaughter of a chief, the daughter of a princess, from the blood of Gray Eagle."

"Such truth makes trouble for us, Grandfather," he concluded aloud, using the endearing name he called this beloved man. He chuckled as he said, "I hurt her with cruel words, yet she fought as a wildcat, Grandfather. Can she be tamed?"

"The answer is, who should be the man to try?" he jested slyly.

"Has another warrior cast hungry eyes upon her?" he asked worriedly, wondering if he must battle for her.

"Many," Sun Cloud replied mirthfully. "But none have brought the lights to her eyes as you did," he whispered devilishly.

Blazing Star recalled their past meetings and smiled happily. The smile quickly faded as he recalled his behavior today. "I must speak with her," he declared, dreading her reaction.

A lone rider approached with a message from Bloody Arrow, telling Sun Cloud the band had joined with one from the Cheyenne camp. They were heading into the Black Hills to make raids upon the camps of white trappers who had intruded upon their sacred ground. The message stated they would be gone for one or two moons. The rider mounted up again and headed to join his friends on their blood-thirsty trek.

Blazing Star smiled and remarked roguishly, "We have no need now to borrow a sleeping mat, Grandfather."

The two exchanged smiles and matching thoughts. At Blazing Star's request, Sun Cloud headed for the special council meeting. Blazing Star returned to their teepee to find Miranda sitting on the ground near the stone pit used for cooking. Lost in thought, she failed to hear his approach. It was a stirring voice which had become familiar to her that broke her intense concentration.

"I spoke too hastily and cruelly, Tamaha," he told her.

Miranda battled to keep her gaze from him as he spoke a sort of apology. She wanted to scream at him, to refuse it. He had hurt her, embarrassed her. She did not want to behave childishly or reveal her turmoil, so she let him know of her anger by ignoring him completely. How she wished she had something to occupy her hands and attention! It was alarming to be alone with him, to know his name and rank.

He saw she was not ready to listen or forgive. "So be it," he informed her calmly. "When your temper cools, we will talk."

Her head jerked upward and she glared at him. "I have no words for you, now or later. I will leave in the morning."

"Do you run from me or yourself, Tamaha?" he inquired in a husky tone. "A girl who challenged the eye and claws of the grizzly to save another's life showed more courage than I see in you this sun."

"I was not the one who came and went in secrecy, Blazing Star. I'm leaving because there is no room in my grandfather's teepee," she explained, trying to excuse her hasty flight from his closeness.

"I am glad you are here, Tamaha. Bloody Arrow will not return for two moons. You will sleep on his mat, unless you wish to stay on mine," he murmured seductively. "I wish—"

"I wish to share nothing of yours, you arrogant beast!" she panted at him as he teased her playfully, cutting off his tender words.

"I did not say share, Tamaha. Sleep where you will; it matters not to me," he stated flippantly to goad her.

"It matters to me," she vowed sullenly.

"And to me," he contradicted himself, grinning at her. "It matters, if it is not alone, or with me."

She was about to take his beguiling bait when his grin alerted her to his ruse. "I have heard you rarely sleep alone," she sneered before thinking, then blushed at her shameful boldness.

He warmed to the spark of jealousy in her. "The speaker of such words is a liar. For many moons, I have craved but one female, one female I have denied myself," he stated suggestively, meaningfully.

Miranda did not know how to respond to such a statement, so she remained silent. She dared not ask the name of the woman, fearing she was wrong to think it was she.

He hunkered down before her and said, "Grandfather has gone to council. I must join him. We will talk later," he stated firmly.

Their gazes locked; neither moved. His hand reached out to run the back of it over her flushed cheek. "You are beautiful, Tamaha. I feared you were another's captive. You should not put such conflict in me," he murmured mysteriously, his dark eyes glowing strangely.

"Conflict?" she echoed hoarsely, her anger a thing of the past.

His thumb rubbed over her lips very gently, noting her erratic breathing. "You have caused my mind to war with my body."

"I do not understand," she responded naïvely.

He was disappointed by her words. "If you do not, a battle does not rage within you. We will return after the moon passes overhead."

He was gone before she could ask for a clearer explanation. How she wished he had embraced and kissed her! Was she a wanton creature? Her mind was spinning in confusion and her body ached with a strange . . . Conflict? Battle? Did he mean what she was thinking?

Chapter Eighteen

lazing Star had spoken accurately; it was long past midnight when the two men returned from the meeting. She had tossed and turned for hours, trying to understand this complex man and this new situation. Their reunion had been most unexpected; his reaction, most disturbing and distressing. Try as she did, she could not get this afternoon off her mind. She was deeply concerned over his chilly and almost brutal conduct at first sighting her today. Before, he had not seemed to care that she was white. But in front of his people, particularly the other warriors, it had made a vivid difference. Was it so essential, so significant that she was proven Indian or half Indian? From what she had heard and witnessed, it was worse to be half-blooded! She fretted over his treatment when he had viewed her as white, a slave. She could not help but wonder how he would feel and act if she had appeared in his life again as another's "captive whore," white or Indian. If he had seen her being abused by a cruel master, would he have done anything to help her? It was the contradictions in his behavior which plagued her. His affection and desire had been shown only in secret, and the complete change in him when he understood her relationship to Sun Cloud confused Miranda even more. She reflected, too, on his seductive behavior and stirring words when they had been alone in this teepee. She cautioned herself to be still after they entered quietly, hoping they would not realize she was still awake.

But the moment Blazing Star lay upon his mat, he smiled into the darkness. Her fragrance still clung to it, a scent which aroused his body to sensual hunger. He should have known she would change mats after learning whose she had been sleeping on for nights. He could not stop thinking about how close she was to him; yet she was so far out of his reach.

What he did not know was that she had absently claimed his mat at bedtime, then quickly gone to her cousin's. She sighed heavily and rolled to her back, staring up into darkness. How would she ever get to sleep knowing Blazing Star was within a few feet of her!

His senses keen, he knew she was awake and restless. What was worse was the fact that he also knew Sun Cloud was deeply entrapped by slumber. He did not even stir when a violent thunderstorm attacked the lands. But Miranda jumped and gasped at several bolts of lightning which struck too close to camp, then shook the earth with rumbling echoes.

"Do not be afraid, Tamaha," he whispered tenderly across the dark span which separated them, telling her he was also awake.

She was too unsettled by the turbulent weather to recall how angry she was with him. And it was easier to be annoyed when he was not so near. Perhaps he had responded from jealousy and pride this afternoon. Surely he would be furious to find her the captive of another, if he truly cared about her. And surely under those circumstances, he would be embarrassed by their reaction to each other in public? When the winds whipped at the teepee and heavy rain poured upon it, she asked softly, "Are the storms always this bad?"

"When they come so late," he replied. "The rivers and lands are thirsty; they require much rain to refresh them."

Miranda hid her face as another streak of lightning seemed to invade the teepee itself. Blazing Star went to her side and pulled her into his arms. "It will be this way for a long time. Sleep, Tamaha. I will guard you from all harm."

When he made no romantic overtures, but simply offered her the comfort of his arms, she relaxed and nestled against him. He stretched out on Bloody Arrow's mat and curled her against his side. He did not move or talk again. He felt her body going limp and her respiration becoming steady. Soon she was asleep in his arms. As if feeling completely safe, nothing more troubled her.

Just before dawn, he eased from her side and returned to his mat. He was baffled by the fact that he had slept next to the most beautiful and desirable woman he had ever known without making love to her. There was a strange contentment and great pleasure in being near her. He had not felt such emotions before. How could a smile warm him? How could a touch make him happy? How could a voice stir his soul? How could a gaze steal his thoughts? If such was true, what would it be like to make love to her? How could he lose her? Yet, how could he keep her here in the face of such death and destruction?

Agony chewed at him. Sun Cloud was right. She must not remain here. If he enticed her to fall in love with him, each of them would be hurt. It would be easier for both to forget if nothing happened between them. She was so trusting and innocent, so vulnerable to the feelings he inspired within her. To reject her would be the fiercest battle he had ever fought, but he knew it would be wrong to take her to his mat and to love her wildly and freely, then force her to leave him. It would be cruel to encourage her love and desire when there could be no more between them. She must be sent away.

He slipped from the teepee. He would have to find the strength and courage to resist her. If he were right, why did this unselfish act torment him? The white man was like a mighty eagle, its talons ever closing around his people, preparing to rip them to bloody pieces. So many battles and lives had been lost. The white man's forces and weapons were many and powerful. One by one, they were destroying or conquering each tribe. No matter how smart or brave the Indians were, they could not last forever against such an enemy.

He had never thought to see the sun when his lands were owned by foes. He had never envisioned such crushing defeats, such wanton slaughter of his kind. Never had he dreamed the sun would come when he doubted the survival of a single Indian. But the white butchers were slaying women and children to annihilate the entire race. Why was the Great Spirit allowing such evil to breed, to grow larger? Why must he find his true love when it was too late and dangerous to claim her?

It rained all morning, forcing Miranda to remain inside the teepee. To pass the time, her grandfather taught her a game played with small pebbles. Sun Cloud napped for several hours during the afternoon, and Miranda stood at the teepee entrance, gazing out at the teepees in the first circle. She wondered where Blazing Star had gone; she wondered why he had not returned for their talk.

He had confessed he was glad she was here. If she inspired such "conflict" in him, why didn't he confront her and discuss his feelings, feelings she shared? He had not gone hunting, and there was no council meeting. She remembered again how he had held her and comforted her. She glanced in all directions but could find no trace of him. She instinctively knew he was avoiding her. But why?

The evening meal came and went without Blazing Star's return. She wanted to question his absence but was too proud to do so. What was he trying to prove? Was this some joke or test? Why waste such precious moments? It took her a long time to fall asleep that night. She realized, as she knew he must, there was only one day left of her visit.

When he was certain she was asleep, Blazing Star sneaked into the teepee and slept restlessly. He was up and slipping out at dawn when she saw him. She sat up and cleared her throat, the noise drawing his attention. When he turned, she motioned for him to come over to her. Concealing his love and turmoil, he scowled as if annoyed by her and her request, then shook his head and left.

Miranda stared at the waving flap. Why was he doing this to her? He was making it clear he did not want to speak with her or see her. Sadness gripped her heart, and panic tugged at her mind. She would be leaving in the morning. Was that why he did not want to start anything between them? That speculation warmed her.

At rest time that afternoon, Blazing Star was still keeping his distance. Once when he sighted her watching him, he began flirting with a lovely Indian maiden. From her tortured expression, he knew she understood his message. He could not allow her to linger here, not after learning of the white war council.

While her grandfather slept, Miranda left the teepee to walk near the stream. She found a lovely spot and sat on a rock studying the newly green foliage. She was about to continue her stroll when Blazing Star came into sight. She called his name. He glanced her way then headed in the opposite direction.

Miranda jumped up and raced after him. They needed to have a talk. He owed her an explanation. There was no time for modesty or manners. She caught up with him, but he quickened his pace to prevent their confrontation. She ran forward again, grabbing his arm. She panted breathlessly, "Why don't you talk to me? I'll be leaving tomorrow, and we have so much to say to each other. Why are you avoiding me? Why are you being so distant?"

"There is nothing to say. Return to your people, Miranda. You do not belong here. You are more white than Indian," he stated coldly.

"But, why?" she beseeched him. "I thought we were friends," she murmured in a quavering voice. He had called her Miranda. He was clearly rejecting her. He was trying to hurt her. She must know why.

"If you wish to be my friend, do not chase me as a she-dog with mating lust. When a woman steals my eye, I will chase her. Why do you trap a man who wishes to escape?" he asked insultingly, hoping to encourage her to leave, for this necessary game was hurting both of them.

His words were as physical blows. Tears welled in her golden brown eyes, and her face became the color of fire. "You need not be cruel, Blazing Star. I've never chased any man, and I surely won't start with one who despises me and deceives me. I didn't mean to give you the impression I was the whore you called me. But I can understand why you would think such evil of me after the way I behaved when we first met. I don't need or want you as my friend. I won't inflict my repulsive company on you again or trouble you further," she told him then fled.

Before Miranda reached the teepee, Tom Fletcher met her, saying he needed to escort her back today as he was leaving on a scouting mission tomorrow at noon. This timely rescue was welcomed, and she told him she was ready to leave and would fetch her belongings. When she entered the teepee, her grandfather was still asleep. She decided it would be better to leave without awakening him, for he might read her turmoil, and she wanted the painful matter between her and her tormenting love kept private. She took the small bundle of her possessions. She wondered who could give her farewell message to her grandfather. She could not ask Sitting Bull or Crazy Horse, as both had left camp. Whom could she trust to be kind and gentle?

Yellow Bird, wife of Fox Eyes, was the perfect choice. She took one last look at her grandfather, love and sadness filling her. It was best to avoid a painful good-bye, and it was vital to avoid Blazing Star. Perhaps Fate had kindly provided this gentle departure. She left the teepee, clutching the little burden under her arm. She explained to Yellow Bird why she wished to leave secretly, to spare her grandfather's feelings and hers. The woman did not concur, but agreed to pass along the message when it was too late to follow or stop her. Yellow Bird sensed there was more to her hasty and furtive departure, but she did not feel she had the right to pry.

Miranda and Tom walked to the edge of camp to mount their horses and ride away. She suppressed the anguish which plagued her. She told herself she was doing the right thing for everyone. She wished Blazing Star had remained a mystery, a lovely fantasy. They set out in the direction of the tree-lined gully where she had awaited the response from her grandfather a few days past. She would never regret riding brazenly into his camp. It was done; her quest was over and her dreams had vanished. Perhaps she would visit her grandfather briefly again before returning to Virginia.

For two hours, Yellow Bird fretted over the girl's departure. Finally, she could restrain herself no longer. She went to find Blazing Star, as she dreaded to tell Sun Cloud of her part in this matter. When the warrior heard her tale, he told her not to repeat it to Sun Cloud, that he would explain Tamaha's actions. It was too late to catch up with her, to change her mind.

After repeating the astonishing tale to Sun Cloud, Blazing Star revealed that he was going after her. He said he would sneak to her cabin during the night and speak with her, to make sure she was home safely and nothing was troubling her. Sun Cloud could tell that the warrior was concerned for his granddaughter. It almost seemed as if Blazing Star suspected another motive behind her secret departure.

He did. Blazing Star could not forget the look on her face or the sound of her voice when he had scolded her. He had not meant to make it sound as if he despised her, scorned her. He had to see that she was all right. He quickly mounted his horse, knowing he could not allow her to leave this way. He must have hurt her deeply.

To prevent the discovery of their trip, Tom and Miranda rode hard and fast until they neared the outskirts of the fort shortly after midnight. They dismounted and spoke for a few minutes, as talk had been impossible along the trail. Miranda did not realize the effect she had on Tom when she caught his hand and thanked him as she smiled genially and gratefully. It had been an innocent and friendly gesture for her, but one which stirred Tom's blood and passion. As she sneaked to her cabin, Tom guarded her. He had sensed a sadness, a conflict within her, and he wanted to comfort her, but he was afraid of alarming or offending her. At that moment Tom knew he must have her, and knew a path to such a victory was near.

When Miranda was inside, he left with no one the wiser about their actions. Miranda was relieved that Jane had left yesterday for a scouting trek southward and would be gone for several weeks. Once Tom left tomorrow, she would be alone for a time. Frankly, she didn't care; she was glad to have solitude. She secured the door, went into the small bedroom, and began to unpack her belongings.

As she lifted her nightgown, she felt something hard and heard a strange noise. She opened the bundle to find a tormenting and baffling gift. It was a *wanapin*, a special necklace. There was a long, sharp bear claw suspended on a leather thong, and there were five rattler-rings separated by six sets of blue beads between twelve white beads, strung on either side of the unforgettable weapon of the grizzly. It was evident who had made the necklace and hidden it in her bundle. It was also evident who had taken her first souvenir, though she had presumed she had lost the rattler-ring from her dress pocket that awesome day.

But why had he made it, and why had he concealed it so she would find it after their separation? Did he want her to have a remembrance of their meetings, of him? She began to cry softly. If he cared about her, why had he been so cruel and cold?

Miranda placed the haunting necklace on the table near the bed. She changed into her nightgown and flung the covers aside. Before she could get into bed, she heard a soft tapping at her door. At first she tensed in panic then decided it must be Tom with a message. She went to the door and called softly, "Who's there?"

Knowing she would not open the door to him, Blazing Star muffled his voice and said, "Tom," in an undistinguishable whisper.

When she asked what he wanted, he muffled his voice so that she was compelled to open the door to hear his words. She stood behind the thick door and peered around it as she said, "I couldn't hear you."

"Tamaha," he called her Indian name as he pushed the door aside and entered. "I must speak with you."

Miranda turned and stared at him. "What are you doing here? Get out before I scream for help. As I recall, we have nothing to say."

He stepped forward, pinning her between his iron-muscled arms and the door, which he closed and locked. "Why did you sneak away like a cunning fox in the night? Sun Cloud worries over this behavior."

She looked up at him through tear-soaked lashes. This time, she did not want to see him or talk with him. She did not want him maliciously toying with her emotions again. She should not have trusted Yellow Bird. How dare he come here to torment her! She pushed his confining arm away and walked into her bedroom to retrieve something. He followed her to the doorway. She snatched up the necklace and flung it at him, sneering, "I don't want your gifts! I don't want anything to remind me of you! Just stay away from me, you beast!"

He had ducked to avoid the forcefully thrown necklace. He came toward her, closing the short span which separated them. When she attempted to flee past him, he lunged at her and reached for one wrist. She fought him wildly, cursing and berating him in a quiet tone. When he attempted to imprison her arms, she shocked him by seizing his arm and whirling and flipping him to the floor with a thud. As he scrambled to his feet, she kicked him in the abdomen. Unprepared for such a blow and action, he was knocked backward to his seat in the middle of the doorway. He stared at her as she assumed a crouched position, ready to ward off his next attack. As he grabbed the doorframe to rise, he observed her stance and hand positions.

"Where did you learn to fight this way?" he asked warily. No one had ever thrown him, not in a contest or battle! How could this fragile girl do what no warrior had done? "You are a trained warrior in skills many men cannot master. But if you continue this battle or scream, others will know of my presence here. You will be trapped by danger and shame, and I will be captured and killed," he advised her, hoping to settle her down so they could talk.

"I know skills which can bring a quick death or a slow one. Come near me, and I will show you," she warned. "Return to your camp. Don't waste time on a white girl with whorish ways," she sneered coldly. "And thank Yellow Bird for her betrayal."

She was full of anguish and fury. He had to deal with her carefully. "Your grandfather is sad you left this way. Will you return?" he asked, trying to distract her from their personal battle.

"It was not wrong to refuse to say farewell to his face. Perhaps I will try to visit him before I return home. But I will never return while you are there," she vowed, relaxing when he did not retaliate.

"Then I will go away to allow your grandfather this time with you," he offered seriously, for the white war council meeting to the west might prevent it later. "I accept your terms. Let us go swiftly."

"No. I haven't decided if I will go back to his camp. When and if I do, I won't need your escort! You were right; I should not have come or remained. It is better for both of us that I left this way."

"I will tell him why you left. I will speak the truth, Tamaha," he informed her. "He will be hurt that I drove you from his side. I spoke falsely and cruelly," he confessed contritely.

"To you, my name is Miranda Lawrence. But if you're really concerned about him, you'll lie to spare his feelings. You've certainly had plenty of practice at deception! Explain how the scout came for me. I didn't run away. He doesn't have to worry about me. I can defend myself, and I have a gun."

"I will tell him all that happened between us," he declared.

"No! I want you out of my sight," she told him. "And take your gift with you. I don't want anything you've touched and nothing to remind me of you. I wish you'd never come home while I was there. I would rather have remembered you as . . ." She halted the confession and cried, "Go away! I hate you, you bloody savage!"

Her icy tone and expression alarmed him. Had his game succeeded beyond his wishes? How could he tell her that his words had been meant to free them from this trap they faced? How could he say there could be no love between them, when they both felt such an emotion now? How could he claim their lives could not mingle, when they already had many times? "My words were harsh, Tamaha. I was angry when I heard you pulled the eyes of Crazy Horse to you many times. Why so after you showed desire for me? It is dangerous to desire you when you have offered your heart to our chief. Return to camp. I will not hurt you more, but I cannot remove the pain I have inflicted."

"That's ridiculous! Crazy Horse is a stranger; he's married. We've only talked a few times. I would never flirt with him. And I didn't go there searching for you. I never expected to see you again, and I wish I hadn't!" she vowed angrily, but her revealing gaze belied her words. She scoffed, "What makes you think I have such feelings for you, you conceited rogue? And the only reason you caught and held my brief interest was because you enticed it! What female wouldn't be curious about a handsome and mysterious stranger who saved her life two times? But I'm not a she-bitch in heat! I never asked you to desire me! I never asked you to do anything for me!"

Her voice altered as she confessed, "Yes, you did hurt me. You hurt me because I thought we . . . were friends. First you said we must talk; then, you claimed there was nothing to say! You offered friendship and comfort; then you behaved as my enemy and tormented me. I don't understand you! Play your games on someone else, Blazing Star. You're a wicked devil; I'll never . . . like you again."

When he did not respond, she asked sarcastically, "Would you explain a few things? Who told you I was chasing after your chief? And why would you believe such lies? I'm not in love with him and never could be. You sound as if it's a crime or a sin to find me desirable. Even so, why punish me for your feelings? I didn't try to entrap you. I only wanted to know why you were avoiding me and being so cold after behaving so differently the other times we met."

He inhaled deeply. "The wife of Crazy Horse and others think you desire him and he desires you. To become his second wife would cause much trouble in his teepee and much trouble in camp. Perhaps envy blinded their eyes to the truth. When I said I must not desire you, it was for your happiness and safety, and mine. You were to leave on the new sun. If you desired me as I believed, it would be wrong to take you to my mat knowing our union would make you think I was claiming you as my woman, my mate. If you yielded to me, it would change nothing between us. When you learned this, you would hate me; you would think I used your desire to trick you to my mat. You are beautiful and rare, Tamaha. You strip a warrior's mind of reason and place wild thoughts in his head. You cause a man's blood to run swiftly and his body to hunger. I cannot help wanting you. I thought it wiser to cool the heat which burns within us."

"You think I'm a whore, Blazing Star? You think I would sleep on the mat of a stranger? That you and I would . . . Even so, when does a man unselfishly reject a woman he finds desirable? Besides, I would never sleep with a man I didn't love," she told him bluntly.

"I have not and do not see you as a whore, Tamaha. Desire is a powerful force, one which can defeat or control the strongest person. It would be wrong to let you believe love and desire are mates."

Something in his tone of voice during his last statement snared her attention. "I do not understand the difference between love and desire, Blazing Star. How can a person desire someone they don't love?"

"You are much too pure in mind and body, Tamaha, or you could answer your question. For you, they are the same. For me and others, it is not so. It does not take love for a hungry body to feed on another's. If you were not the granddaughter of Sun Cloud, I would take you this moon, or I would try. Each time I saw you, I craved you. I did not take you because I thought you white. When I learned of your Oglala blood, I could not take you and hurt Sun Cloud or you. A body that burns with such a fire is dangerous and hard to master. But to master two wildfires would be impossible. My cruel words and actions were to put out your fire for me. If I could anger you, you would not let me near and your temptation would be removed. But though I did not wish to hurt you so deeply, I could not lead you to think there could be love after such a union. Do you understand, Tamaha? Your dream does not match mine," he lied desperately.

She lacked experience and knowledge about men, but his meaning was clear; he felt passion for her but not love. Even so, he cared enough to spare her anguish and shame by spurning her. Could she leave forever without knowing him, without having him? "You hurt me and angered me, Blazing Star, but you did not put out the fire within me. I have never known such feelings for a man. I swear there is nothing between me and your chief. I cannot return with you, for the temptation you present is too great. I would make your words true, for I would coax you to my mat. I know a real lady wouldn't say such things, probably not even feel such things; if she did, she would never confess them aloud. I have been so confused since I met you. Even that first day, I felt a powerful pull toward you. Whether it's wrong or not, I can't help how I feel. But I wouldn't want you to think badly of me after I left. So I must remain here and never see you again. If I had known you were beyond my life-circle and you were in Grandfather's camp and teepee, I would never have gone there. Please find some way to comfort Grandfather; I love him very much. Would it be too difficult to hold me and kiss me good-by?"

He was as taken by surprise at her request as she was to hear herself issue it. She flushed but did not back down. "I could not promise to stop with a kiss, Tamaha. I have wanted no female since my eyes touched upon you. I hunger for you like a starving man. To touch would cause smoldering embers to burst into a roaring fire. Such flames could consume us. You must not tempt me; you must free us from this forbidden spell. You cannot be my woman."

"Why do you speak of what cannot be? Why can't you admit to what is there between us? I need to feel your arms around me, our spirits touching. I need to sense you share my feelings. I need to understand why it cannot be for us. I need you, Blazing Star." She showed all her feelings in those few words. She loved this man, and she was about to lose him. She had told Amanda to pursue Reis boldly and brazenly. Should she not take her own advice? Time was fleeing, and so was he.

She earnestly offered, "For a short time before we must part forever, can't we forget everything but us? Can't we be man and woman, Tamaha and Blazing Star, for a short span? Must we part as white and Indian, as Miranda and a Sioux warrior? I swear I will let you leave when the time comes, but must you go away like this? Surely no pain can be greater than never having you?"

"I fear you would not let me leave after we joined, Tamaha. Once you have known me and our union, the fires would burn brighter and higher. You do not know the powers of passion. I do not speak from pride. I speak from the lights I see in your eyes and the defiance which I have seen in you. You should not love me, Tamaha; you cannot have me. I will take you to Sun Cloud, then ride away."

"Are you so weak and cowardly that you cannot control your body and mind long enough to give me a single kiss?"

Blazing Star was aware of her coaxing ploy and took no offense at her clever taunt. Despite his expertise at concealing his inner emotions, turmoil was exposed in his gaze. "It takes all my strength and courage to master my hunger for you. Do not sway me, Tamaha. Do not ask for the forbidden."

Miranda knew she was flirting with emotional peril, challenging Fate. "You say I should not love you; but I do. You say I cannot have you; yet I want you more than life itself. You say I cannot be your woman; yet, in heart and soul, I belong to you forever. You say I must free us, but I have no strength or will to do so. You say I should not tempt you; yet you have tempted me many times. Even when you aren't standing before me in temptation, you visit my dreams and encourage my surrender. You say it cannot be; yet it is and always will be," she murmured raggedly as tears slipped down her cheeks.

"Go, Blazing Star. I'm not holding you prisoner. Take the *wanapin* with you; its memories are too painful to bear. Why did you enter my life-cycle if you can't become part of it? Why did you keep appearing to me, imprisoning my heart and soul? There is no other man to compare with you. I could never desire and love another after knowing you. You shouldn't have come after me. It was less cruel to let me leave in anger. It was so much easier when I thought you despised me. But knowing you want me as I . . . ." She could not finish, for tears choked off her words. She turned and walked to the bed and flung herself face down upon it. She had never imagined the day when she would be enticing a man to seduce her! The sacrifice of Blazing Star was too much to endure, and she wept at her loss.

He watched her for a time, then went to sit beside her. He stroked her silky hair as he pondered what to do. He stretched out beside her, moving his hand up and down her back as his dilemma increased. He encircled her body with his arms and pulled her against him. "Do not weep, Tamaha. It is as a sharp lance into my body to see you suffer this way."

She turned her head and locked her gaze with his. There was no need for words; her eyes said it all. She rolled to her back, her hand caressing his tanned cheek. His head came down to seal their lips, to fuse their destinies into one. Her arms went around his neck, and they sank entwined to the bed where their bodies would join in rapture in a dreamy world shared only by lovers.

When his lips left hers and he leaned away, both read the passion blazing brightly within the other's eyes. Right or wrong, dangerous or wise, this moment could take no other course. When she smiled up at him, it drove every doubt or restraint from his mind and body. His mouth returned to hers, exploring and tasting the sweetness of her response. He crushed her so tightly in his arms that she could hardly breathe, but she did not care.

For a long time he held her tenderly, and his gentle kiss became more savage. He knew this time could not be rushed, for it would exist only once for them. His lips touched every inch of her face and throat, then each hand. His body surged with new life and joy. He could as easily stop the seasons as this joining.

Never had Miranda known such excitement and happiness as here in his arms. His warm breath caused tremors to sweep over her tingly flesh. As his tongue swirled about in her palm, she shivered with delight. When he removed her gown, she made no attempt to halt him. Nor was she embarrassed when he removed his own garments, dropping them to the floor upon hers.

His gaze was so loving as he murmured huskily, "If you wish to say no, Tamaha, now is the last moment."

She smiled and replied, "There is no such word for you."

As it should be between lovers, there were no reservations, no inhibitions; it was right and natural between them. There was no modesty or shame, only pure love and its mate, desire. His hands were careful as they claimed her flesh, roaming her sensitive body as each area responded instantly to his contact. His touch was skilled and masterful. Soon, there was no spot upon her that did not cry out for him to conquer it and to claim it as his own. Flames licked greedily at their bodies, enticing him to hasten his leisurely conquest of her body.

When he bent forward and captured a compelling breast with his lips, she groaned in pleasure. As his tongue circled the taut point, she watched with fascination, wondering how such an action caused her body to quiver and warm. Wildly wonderful emotions played havoc with her thinking; it seemed she could do nothing but surrender to pure sensation. One hand slipped down her flat stomach to claim another peak, and he teased both simultaneously.

Her hand wandered up his powerful back into the ebony mane. Each time his mouth left one breast to feast upon the other, it would protest the loss of warmth and stimulation. His mouth drifted upward to fuse with hers. Between kisses, moans escaped her lips, moans which spoke of her rising passion, moans which proved all she had said was true.

His own passion straining to be freed, he moved over her to feel her warm moistness against his throbbing flesh. Assured she was prepared for his entrance, he cautiously pushed past the barrier which eagerly gave way to his loving. Her demanding womanhood surrounded his aching shaft with exquisite bliss. He was so consumed by desire that he nearly lost all control, something that had never happened to him before. He halted all movement to cool his molten blood. Dazed by heady passion, he urged her to lie still until his control returned, but she did not.

She was feverish by now, thrashing her body against his. As he began to move within her, the contact was staggering and she cried out softly in mounting need. Her face was imprisoned between his hands as he deftly savored it with his lips. His hips worked swiftly and skillfully as he increased her great need. She heatedly yielded her body to his loving assault, seeking the pleasures and contentment only he could provide.

He dared not free her mouth as he felt her body tense and shudder with her release, muffling the cry of ecstasy which would have alerted anyone nearby. A sense of intoxicating power surged through him just before his own stunning release came forth. He was so shaken by their potent joining and enchanted by her magic, that he almost shouted his victory aloud. He moved rhythmically until the urgency had fled and they were curled together peacefully.

He held her in his arms as he lay on his side. When his respiration returned to normal, he twisted his head to gaze over at her. Sensing his movement, she shifted her eyes to meet his probing gaze. They exchanged smiles, then hugged tightly. There was such an immense sharing of love and joy. She lay her face on his damp chest and snuggled closer to him. He kissed her forehead and sighed tranquilly. It was not the time for speaking; it was a time for touching and feeling, which they did until she was fast asleep with her arm lying across his chest.

Blazing Star knew his time was gone and he must leave. How he longed to stay at her side, laughing and talking and making love for hours. He looked at her, memorizing each feature. He whispered too quietly to disturb her, "If it is the will of the Great Spirit, we will meet again. If we do not, love for you will live forever in my heart and desire in my body, Tamaha."

The valiant warrior recalled what she had said about painful farewells. She was right. It was easier to leave while she slept, while those lovely eyes of golden brown could not tempt him to stay or to take her along, while those sweet lips as soft as the petals of a pasqueflower could not tease him so he would forget to leave before dawn, while her clever tongue could not plead or argue against their necessary parting.

He arose carefully so as not to awaken her. He slipped into his clothes, cursing the war which was tearing them apart, which would always separate them. She snuggled into the warm spot he had left beside her, inhaling the musky odor from his sated body, stirring his soul to joyful song. He watched a serene smile which flickered briefly on those lips. His dark eyes traveled over her bare flesh, sparking new fires within him, fires which had no time to burn. He must leave quickly!

His gaze fell on the *wanapin*, and he vividly envisioned those two episodes which had supplied the rattler-rings and the grizzly claw. He placed it on her pillow, for she was resting on his. He hunkered down beside the bed, staring into her face. There was so much he wanted to share with her, so much to tell her and so much to hear, so much to enjoy; but he could not. Where she was concerned, there was no difference between love and desire within him. But he dared not confess that to her. More than anything, he wanted to lie down beside her, to make love to her again, to hear her laughter, to see her smile, to hold her tightly, to run his hands over her skin, to spew his seed within her and to let it grow into proof of their love. He wanted to walk beside her beneath the sun in the cool forest, holding her hand, listening to her giggles as the grass tickled her bare feet. He wanted her pressed against his body every moon. It was too late to linger, too late for her to become his wife, but not too late to dream and to suffer for what could not be.

When he recalled how one of the most awesome and grisly massacres of an Indian village had taken place under a white flag of truce and an American flag of submission, he grieved for what this despicable war was costing him. He would rather give up his life than his love! But memories and warnings could not be denied or forgotten. He had been an impressionable eighteen winters on that frosty day at Sand Creek. He would never forget the white butcher named Chivington, that white killer who did not care what Indians he slew, friendly or hostile, armed or weaponless. Blazing Star could not understand the hatred behind a man who could instigate and plan the slaughter of babies and women, declaring, "Nits make lice!" It had not mattered that the Cheyenne Indians at Sand Creek had been friendly, had been camped there under orders of the soldiers at Fort Lyon! It had not mattered that they had surrendered immediately! It had not mattered that the truce and American flags had been raised to reveal their friendship! It had not mattered to the other whites that the soldiers at the Sand Creek Massacre had slaughtered innocent women and children, nor that they had mutilated the slain males, nor that they had scalped any Indian of any age and sex!

Yet, the whites accused the Indians of being savages! They claimed the Indians started the wars and refused to cease the conflicts! *Refused?* he mentally scoffed. All they refused were defeat, death, reservations, and annihilation!

Chief Black Kettle and his wife survived and escaped the Sand Creek Massacre in 1864, only to be slaughtered by a yellow-haired man called Custer four winters later, in 1868, at the Washita bloodbath! It was between those two bloodlettings, in 1866, that the white-eyes called Sherman said on paper to the Great White Father in Washington that the Sioux "must be exterminated." Sherman— said to have tried to destroy half of the white lands in a war not long past—told the white leader that the soldiers would act quickly and harshly to complete the "extermination of men, women, and children" of the Sioux! Now, here in the Indian ancestral grounds and nearby hunting grounds, there were three powerful white warriors with hatred burning in their hearts: Sherman, Custer, and Sheridan. They had joined once before to battle an enemy larger and more powerful than the Sioux Nation, defeating what they called the Confederacy, the South, the Rebels. Now they were joining forces against the Indians, mainly the Sioux. He could not place his beloved in such danger, danger which even a flag of truce or surrender could not halt!

He reached for the locket with her mother's picture, placing it in his medicine pouch. It was Tamaha's image he saw in the picture, an image he would forever hold. Taking one look at his beloved, he turned and left, using a string to close the latch behind him. *"Waste cedake, Tamaha."* He murmured his love for her, then vanished into the shadows.

Chapter Nineteen

The moment her tawny eyes opened, Miranda sensed he was gone, and pangs of loneliness and loss filled her along with a twinge of anger. She did not have to turn over to look around the cabin. She felt an emotional chill in the air. Blazing Star's warmth and vitality had been taken away, and his special scent had vanished. His spiritual aura was missing. She suddenly felt very alone and sad. Why was he determined to prevent their love?

She could not go after him; she could not even visit the camp under the guise of seeing her grandfather. She had promised to part after one night with him. How rashly that vow had been spoken! But she prayed he would miss her, miss her enough to send for her or to sneak back to see her. If not, perhaps she would be compelled to find him once more.

It thrilled her heart when she discovered her locket gone and found the *wanapin* on her pillow. She smiled, then danced around the table. Her heart surged with life and joy, for they had touched in many ways. How could he deny or ignore what had passed between them?

She recalled his warnings: "Once you have known me and our union, the fires would burn brighter and higher . . . You do not know the powers of passion . . . I have wanted no female since my eyes touched upon you." Were those warnings as painful for him as for her, and as truthful?

In the throes of ecstasy, he had said, *"Ni-ye mitawa,* Tamaha," which meant "you are mine, Tamaha." Had he forgotten she could speak Sioux and had understood those words?

She bathed and dressed, then prepared a small meal for herself. Around three, there was a knock at her door. Her heart did not lurch with excitement; she knew her love would not return in the daylight. She opened the door and gaped at the two grinning people standing there: Amanda and Reis. Miranda squealed with surprise and hugged both as she bubbled with delight, spilling forth countless questions.

"Slow down, Randy," Reis teased her. "It's been a long trip and Mandy is tired. Let's catch our breath, and we'll tell you everything. Where's Luke?" he inquired, having much to tell his friend.

When Miranda answered, Amanda could not believe their cousin had been so careless with her sister. "He left you here alone?" she blurted incredulously. "Just wait until I get my hands on Lucas Reardon! He promised he would take care of you and protect you, yet he ran off and left you at the mercy and lust of these crude soldiers!"

Miranda giggled, then replied mirthfully, "I've been perfectly safe, Mandy. Surely you know I can take care of myself. Remember how many times I had you or Luke pinned helpless to the floor or ground? Remember how many suitors I sent scurrying in fear? I'm so glad you're here; I've so much to tell you," she murmured, mystery and joy shining brightly in her dark eyes. "I'll prepare some coffee and shortbread, then we'll talk for hours."

Reis noticed the same mysterious lights which Amanda observed, sensually dreamy lights which matched the softened tone of her voice, all of which hinted at a change in Miranda's life, a masculine change. Reis grinned and winked at his adoring wife. He excused himself under the guise of looking around the fort, leaving the two sisters to talk privately. Evidently both females had plenty to relate.

Miranda insisted her sister give her news first. She was stunned to learn of the danger they had faced in Alexandria but was relieved it was over. She could not grieve for Weber Richardson, for he had brought about his own fate. She smiled at Amanda, thrilled by her sister's happiness. Clearly her sister loved Reis Harrison deeply.

Miranda did think it slightly odd that her sister knew so little of her husband's current mission. Then again, men could be such mysterious, complex, and mercurial creatures! But Amanda would be safe with him and surely more happy at his side. Miranda was glad to discover this was Reis's last duty and they would be establishing a home afterward. It was easy to picture them with children, herself as a loving aunt. Her heart warmed at such pleasing thoughts. Amanda had found her destiny and followed it.

When Miranda heard they would be traveling around the territory while Reis did whatever it was he had come to do, she warned her sister about the continual hostilities and perils in this rugged area. She revealed all she had learned about the whites and Indians nearby. She told about her episodes with Lieutenant Brody Sheen and Lucas's subsequent journey with him and Custer's regiment. It was evident to Amanda that her sister disliked Brody; she had even compared him to Weber! Miranda talked about Calamity Jane and Tom Two-feathers Fletcher and related how Lucas had found and rented this cabin. When she halted briefly, Miranda had told about everything except her visit to the Sioux camp and her love for an Oglala warrior.

Amanda watched her sister closely, knowing something vital was about to spill forth from those parted lips. Amanda sat rigid and silent as Miranda divulged her exciting trek to see their grandfather, describing him and the camp and her adventures. Amanda was so staggered by this unimaginable and frightening tale that she could not speak. Having heard horrifying tales about certain warriors and events, she could not believe her sister would calmly ride into an enemy camp! Yet, she also could not deny that her sister had returned safe and happy.

Again, Miranda hesitated noticeably, for there was only one drama left to unfold. She realized Amanda was shocked by her conduct, and she could not envision Amanda's reaction to her imminent confession. She waited for her sister to regain her clear head and tongue.

"How could you do such a reckless and dangerous thing, Randy? You could have been killed! Or taken prisoner! Or worse! I should never have allowed you to come here with Luke. Whatever were you two thinking? You just told me both sides are preparing for war."

"I was never in any danger, Mandy. What white would harm a woman with a letter of protection from President Grant? And what Indian would harm the granddaughter of Chief Sun Cloud?" she asserted.

Amanda threw her hands into the air and shrieked in exasperation, "I don't believe what I'm hearing! After all we've been through lately, you think you're safe from all evil? There are Webers everywhere, Randy! If you were captured and slain out in the wilderness, who would know who did it or why? Don't you realize how few females live out here? Haven't you noticed how crude and rough these men are?" she rebutted.

"No one has tried to attack me, Mandy. I carry a gun, and I can fight like Ling taught me. You worry too much," she teased.

"It seems I didn't worry enough. If we leave before Luke returns, you're coming with us. But if he does show his roguish face, he'll have to promise not to leave you alone again. I doubt he will after I finish with him," Amanda determined aloud.

"I'm not leaving here just yet," Miranda announced defiantly.

"If Luke isn't back when Reis and I depart, you're going with us, young lady," Amanda argued just as stubbornly and firmly. "I mean it, Randy; we're not leaving you in this hellish place alone."

Miranda stared her straight in the eye and stated, "I'm in love with someone who lives nearby. I'm not leaving until I learn if he feels the same. Now that you have Reis, can't you understand my feelings? I love him. I need him and I want him," she vowed earnestly.

"Who?" Amanda probed. "You haven't mentioned anyone to me."

"Yes, I have. He's the Indian warrior I wrote you about, the one I met on the way here by steamer," Miranda informed her softly.

"The Indian warrior? He lives around here? Have you seen him again?" she pressed, a curious qualm chewing at her racing heart.

Slowly and carefully, Miranda related much of what she knew about the warrior, except their intimate night together here in this cabin. She told her sister about their meetings and how she felt. "I can't help it, Mandy; I'm in love with Blazing Star."

Amanda went white and trembled. "Who . . . did you say?" she stammered, that name terrifyingly familiar to her.

"I see you've heard of him," Miranda scoffed as she witnessed her sister's alarm. "He isn't like that, Mandy," she protested, then revealed more facts about him and this racial conflict.

"How could you fall in love with a barbarian, an enemy? Oh, Randy, what's gotten into you? What have you done?" Amanda fretted in a near whisper, recognizing a vast change in her gentle sister.

"During the war, Yankees were considered bloody barbarians, our fiercest enemies. Have you forgotten the horrible atrocities they committed against the South? Even so, you fell in love with one and married him," she retorted cleverly.

"That's different!" Amanda shouted at her.

"How so?" Miranda debated. "If we make peace with the Sioux, our differences will be the same as yours and your Yankee husband's."

"From the way things appear, there will never be peace," Amanda remarked, her opinions colored by false information.

"I believe that same statement was made about the North and South only a few years ago," Miranda reminded her astonished sister.

"But Reis's life isn't vastly different from mine, Randy. You and Blazing Star have nothing in common," she contended.

"Love," Miranda slyly announced, smiling dreamily.

"I doubt even powerful love is sufficient to overcome such complicated differences, Randy." Her sister softened her argument.

"Until I know beyond a single doubt that I can't have him, I'm not leaving here."

"You don't know him, Randy. You've only spent a few days with him. Love takes time; it takes working and being together. You can't love at a distance. You can't love through war."

"Tell me something, Mandy; how long did it take for you to fall in love with Reis? How long before you knew you wanted him beyond caution or wisdom? How long before you knew you couldn't live without him? How long after meeting him did you two marry?" When Amanda sighed heavily at her inability to argue those points, Miranda asked quietly, "Did you make love to him before you wed?"

Amanda went scarlet with modesty more than guilt. She gasped in shock at her sister's bold query. "Miranda Lawrence!" she panted reproachfully. "How could you ask such a question?"

Miranda had gotten her answer. She glued her gaze to Amanda's and made her confession of love and passion. "After experiencing such emotions for Reis, Mandy, can't you see how I feel? He is my destiny, my one true love. Like you did with Reis, I must pursue him, whatever the price or danger. Don't you understand that one day with him is worth any price?"

"But Reis loves me in return, Randy. Sharing passion isn't enough. What about your future, your happiness? What if you can't have him? You can't force this man to love you," she explained sadly.

Miranda considered those words, then replied, "I believe he does love me and need me. I just have to make him realize it."

"How do you plan to do that?" Amanda asked seriously.

"I don't know, Mandy. I wish I did," she admitted hoarsely. "When I think of never seeing him or touching him again, it's like fiery arrows are being shot into my body. It's such an awful feeling of loneliness and pain, worse than when Mama and Papa died," she confessed. "Do you remember how you felt when you thought you couldn't have Reis? Imagine how you would feel if you lost him this very day."

Amanda stood up and went to her sister. She hugged her affectionately and comfortingly. "I wish there was something I could say or do to help, Randy. I'll just have to trust you to do the right thing, as you did with me where Weber was concerned. Will you promise me to act slowly and carefully?" she entreated.

Miranda smiled and hugged her tightly. She had never loved or needed her sister more than she did this very moment. "I promise. Just stand by me, and I know everything will work out fine."

That night, Miranda slept on the cot in the living area while Reis and Amanda used the small bedroom. She could hear them whispering far into the night. She knew Amanda was revealing their conversations to her beloved husband, but that did not matter to Miranda. Later, she ached for Blazing Star while her sister made passionate love to Reis, their muffled cries escaping beneath the closed door. Finally, all was quiet; still, Miranda found it difficult to get to sleep.

Two days passed while Miranda and Amanda shared each other's company. After announcing himself as the liaison from President Grant to the commanding officers in this area, Reis was busy asking questions, making observations, and writing reports, reports which he concealed in the same hiding place which Lucas used for his critical and secret papers.

Each time Miranda remarked on Reis's assignment and curious actions, Amanda would shrug and say it was a covert mission and they should not discuss it. But Miranda caught her sister's longing gazes over the area beneath the eating table several times. When Miranda laughingly suggested they sneak and read the reports, Amanda was horrified. She warned Miranda never to attempt such an unforgivable act. When Miranda asked if Reis's work was dangerous, Amanda grimaced and said she did not know but suspected it was from his dealings with Weber. Even more confusing and intriguing was the second set of papers which he wrote upon, then intentionally left on the table near the bed.

Reis sent a telegram to Lucas, relating their arrival at his cabin. Again, he stated he was here as a liaison for Grant. He asked Lucas to send word of the impending locations of several important officers. When an answer came the next day, Reis informed the two women that Lucas was on his way home. Arriving with their cousin would be Brody Sheen and Custer. Apparently, Custer was piqued with curiosity about Reis and his business.

Miranda did not know what to think when Reis sat her down at the table and began probing her for answers or speculations about the Sioux Indians, especially the Oglala tribe. He seemed particularly interested in learning all he could about Crazy Horse, Sitting Bull, and Blazing Star. He even exhibited a keen interest in the Indian agencies which she had seen, and anything she had overheard about them. She wondered why he did not ask any questions about her grandfather or her Indian cousin, Bloody Arrow. Oddest of all was the fact that he had sent Amanda to the sutler's shop to prevent her from hearing their talk!

Miranda started asking questions of her own, wanting and needing to understand Reis's desire for facts and figures. Obviously, these questions and facts had something to do with his mission. Yet he evaded her probes and went on with his interrogation.

"No more, Reis, until you tell me why you need such information," she eventually declared, eying him intently, oddly.

"Just tell me all you know, Randy, then I'll explain. First, I need a clearer and larger picture to study. This area's like a volcano ready to explode, and Grant wants to know why and who's furnishing the molten lava," he hedged.

"No. Not until I'm assured of your intentions. I can't betray or endanger my grandfather and his people, or . . ." She did not finish.

"Or Blazing Star," he completed the name which worried her the most. "If I'm to help your mother's people, Randy, and possibly avert more bloodshed, I need facts for President Grant. I have to be careful who supplies such information; too many people are profiting from lies and greed. What's so unique about this area? The land isn't that good for ranching or farming. The game is as good anywhere else. There has to be something else to inspire the whites to crave it at any cost. Do you think it's possible to speak with the Sioux chiefs? Would Tom Fletcher take us there without any questions?" he asked shockingly.

"You want to see Crazy Horse and Sitting Bull? Why?" she pried.

"I can't explain my mission right now, Randy. You've got to trust me and help me. Can you get me into the Oglala camp? Naturally it has to be in total secrecy," he urged her.

"You want to spy out their strengths and defenses for Custer!" she surmised coldly. "You expect me to help defeat them?" she sneered.

"I expect you to help save their lives and lands. You know the kind of men in charge out here, the ones Luke is writing about. Custer and Grant aren't friends. You've seen what's taking place at those agencies. There's corruption and fraud here, Randy, and Grant wants to know who's behind it and how to stop it. Evidently there are plenty of reasons behind the continual hostilities. That's all I can say. Will you help me?" he coaxed gravely. "You could see Blazing Star," he tempted in order to sway her. "And I don't work with the cavalry or army," he declared honestly.

"I hope I'm understanding you correctly, Reis. If you're lying to me or misleading me . . ." she hinted ominously. She abruptly asked, "Did you know about this mission before you married my sister? Did you know we were Sun Cloud's granddaughters?"

A frown lined his handsome features. "Please don't even think such things, Randy. But to answer you, no and no. I swear to you I'm no threat to the Oglalas. My investigation isn't for military purposes. Anything I learn is for the ears of Grant alone."

"All right," she finally acquiesced after studying him intently. "Tom seems completely trustworthy. But just in case, I'll take you to my grandfather's camp; I know the way. If anyone sees us, you can say we were out riding and got lost. I can get you in and out, but don't betray us. What about Mandy? She would increase the danger of getting caught. Besides, she sounds afraid of them; she might accidentally insult one of them. Then, we'd be in big trouble."

"This mission could be very dangerous for both of us, Randy. I've already explained matters to her; she knows she can't tag along. She's going to remain here and cover for us. If it appears safe, I'll take her back to visit Sun Cloud later. She's a little miffed, but she understands why we have to leave her behind. I'm glad you agree."

Miranda guessed from her sister's gaze and voice that this idea did not suit her at all, but she would follow her husband's wishes. Just after midnight, Miranda and Reis walked their horses a safe distance from the settlement, then mounted and rode away at a swift gallop. All went as planned until dawn when they halted to water and rest their animals. Miranda had brought along her Indian dress but had not changed into it yet. To avoid being noticed as a woman, she was wearing jeans, a blue cotton shirt, and a floppy hat to conceal her chestnut locks.

Reis and Miranda were strolling around, loosening stiff muscles, when they were suddenly surrounded by ten painted braves. Reis did not have time to draw his weapon, fortunately. It required three men to hold Reis under control as he fought to save Miranda. A fourth brave was standing before Reis with his lance pointing directly at Reis's heart, yet, Reis showed no fear of him or death, gaining the brave's respect.

Miranda was seized and imprisoned between two strong males and lost her hat during her brief struggle. When the leader spoke, Miranda recognized his voice. In Oglala, she shouted, "Bloody Arrow, it's me, Tamaha. We're heading to speak with Grandfather and Crazy Horse."

Her cousin whirled and glared at her. He asked why she was here and who the white dog was with her. She explained Reis's identity and asked her cousin to take them to camp. A quiver of alarm raced over her, for she read contempt and reluctance in Bloody Arrow. Yet there were others around to witness his actions, to control them and his hatred.

Reis stayed quiet and alert. He assumed Miranda knew this brave and was reasoning with him. Although taken by surprise that she could speak Sioux, Reis waited until she could explain. The leader appeared to recognize her and to listen to her words. He wondered if it was Blazing Star, then hastily concluded it could not be.

Suddenly Bloody Arrow nodded and agreed to take them to the Oglala camp. Everyone was ordered to mount up and follow him. Miranda hastily explained the circumstances to Reis, her eyes hinting at more news to come later. Riding in the midst of the group, they were escorted to the entrance of Crazy Horse's teepee.

The noted chief observed this curious sight as Bloody Arrow informed him of Miranda's words and actions. The imposing chief looked at her and asked why she had brought a white man into their camp. Miranda asked if he would speak with Reis alone, as his words were important and private. She gave her word of honor Reis could be trusted. When the stoic leader did not respond, she actually pleaded, saying Reis was from the white chief far away.

"If he speaks false or his words are not important to the ears of Crazy Horse and the council, you may kill me where I stand. For the lives of all we love, hear him," she urged.

Crazy Horse agreed to see Reis, in the company of Sitting Bull. The three men went into his teepee and the flap was sealed. Bloody Arrow was furious when she refused to reveal the meaning of Reis's visit. Miranda apologized but held silent. She headed to see her grandfather while the critical meeting took place.

Bloody Arrow followed her, to see what she would tell Sun Cloud. When she asked about Blazing Star, Bloody Arrow lied to her, claiming he was off chasing a wife. Her startled reaction confirmed his suspicions.

"So it is true you seek the eye of Blazing Star. It is foolish, Tamaha. He loves honor and battle, not a woman. He takes a wife to give him his teepee and a son. He would not stain the blood and skin of his child by mating with a girl with white blood. Seek your kind, Tamaha; the blood of your mother's dishonor and shame runs within you. Do not come again," he warned coldly. "What does the white man want?"

"I don't know. But if I did, I wouldn't tell you. Don't you think I know you would have killed both of us if you'd been alone today? Why do you hate me, Bloody Arrow?" she asked bluntly.

"Your eyes are clouded with lust for Blazing Star, Tamaha. He joined with Black Buffalo Woman of the Cheyenne. He lies upon her mat this moon. His neck carries the joining necklace to match hers. The white man can do nothing to win Blazing Star for you," he baited her.

"I didn't come here to capture Blazing Star's heart or eyes. Stay away from me; your heart is cold and evil," she murmured softly, to avoid being overheard. Her heart was aching at his news. Could it be true? Or was it a cruel and malicious joke? Dare she ask her grandfather and risk having her very soul lacerated? If it were not true, why would her cousin speak a lie so easy to unmask? Blazing Star had made no promises to her, no commitments, no vows of love and loyalty. He had done all he could to prevent any contact between them. Perhaps that hurt the most; he had not lied or tricked her. She had surrendered willingly, eagerly, wantonly, helplessly . . .

Sun Cloud was ecstatic to see her. He hugged her and kissed her cheek. He scolded her for leaving him without a good-by, but understood her generous motive. She told him that Amanda and her husband had arrived at Fort Sully. She told him Reis had come to parlay with the chiefs and he would learn of the meaning in council later. After promising to visit again if possible, she asked about Blazing Star. It was silly to be a coward; it was silly to allow hazy words or a simple misunderstanding to come between them.

Her grandfather suspected her reason for inquiring. His heart soared with happiness at the thought of his father's bloodline joining and strengthening in Blazing Star and Miranda. But he could not interfere. It must be the will of the Great Spirit. It warmed his aging heart to recall how both looked at each other and how each asked about the other, as it had been with his beloved Singing Wind before the white dogs attacked their village and wantonly slaughtered her and many others. He had lived with sadness, bitterness, and hatred for many winters, but this fresh and gentle creature enlivened him once more. She was the essence of life and joy.

He smiled and stated innocently, "He visits the camp of our brothers, the Cheyenne. He brings a surprise to my teepee," he added mischievously, thinking of the horse which was to be a gift for her from her grandfather, a swift and agile pinto.

Miranda misconstrued his words and excitement, assuming he did not know of her love for Blazing Star. When her smile faded, her eyes teared, and she trembled, he asked if she were ill or distressed. She forced a smile and told him she was simply fatigued.

Sun Cloud was still alert enough to notice the sarcastic and mocking sneer which flickered over Bloody Arrow's face when Miranda glanced at him. The old man did not realize he had aided Bloody Arrow's spite, but he sensed a chilling aura which he did not like. As Miranda was encased in pensive silence, Sun Cloud furtively observed the way Bloody Arrow watched her.

Sun Cloud knew his days were short. He wondered if his granddaughter might choose to remain with his people. She knew a great deal about them, but there was more to learn. Did he have the days to teach her? Would she be accepted? Would she be safe and happy here? If only the bluecoats would leave them in peace.

The unexpected appearance of the beautiful descendent of Gray Eagle and Sun Cloud had sparked great interest and mixed feelings amongst his people, a blend of rejection and acceptance, affection and dislike. The rumors of jealousy in the wife of Crazy Horse had not avoided his keen ears. How sad for such lies to be born, to be allowed to grow. What would happen to his granddaughter after his death, if anything happened to Blazing Star? She would be alone, and jealousy and envy were powerful destroyers.

She was such an uncommon creature, half woman and half vixen. She was as eager for adventure as any brave. She possessed such energy, such daring, such courage. Here, she could be as free and wild as the winds. If only they were not warring winds.

As all three came to attention at the sound of drumming, the call went forth, "Ominiciye kte lo," summoning the leaders to council. Sun Cloud and Bloody Arrow reached for their prayer pipes to leave.

Miranda tensed but did not ask questions. But her heart lurched and beat wildly as Bloody Arrow returned briefly to say, "Pray to your Great Spirit, Tamaha, if they vote to slay the white dog and hold you captive for your offense. If you have helped our enemy, no man can save you, even Sun Cloud. I will vote for your punishment."

Tremors raced over her body, as her malevolent cousin laughed satanically. She mastered her rampant emotions and stated clearly and evenly, "I will pray, Bloody Arrow, but for you. I will ask the Great Spirit to burn the hatred and evil from your body. I will pray He sears away your hatred for me, for there is no reason for it. I will pray for Him to open your eyes to the truth, to honor."

Miranda paced the confines of the teepee until she thought she would scream from anxiety. To pass the time, she removed her soiled riding clothes and donned her Indian dress. The meeting went on for hours while each man had his say in a matter which was unknown to her. Never had she prayed so intensely or swiftly in her life. No matter how Blazing Star felt about her, she wished he were here. He was so intelligent, so influential. His words and power might be needed.

When she felt as if she could not breathe from the tension which was attacking her chest, she left the teepee to stroll along the stream bank. She walked back and forth until she made a path upon the lush grass. She halted and leaned against a towering tree, the evening breeze playing softly through its leaves and small branches. She inhaled deeply, then sighed. She closed her eyes and murmured, "Please let everything be all right."

"What could be wrong, Tamaha?" a stirring voice questioned.

Her eyes flew open and she stared into the arresting face of Blazing Star. A smile captured her features and brightened them. Joyful tears of relief threatened to spill forth. She was about to fling herself into his arms when she recalled Bloody

Arrow's words. She clasped her raised hands and lowered them, the beaming smile vanishing before his baffled eyes. She moistened her suddenly dry lips and pulled her tormented gaze from his, trying vainly to mask her warring emotions. "I didn't know you were home," she murmured, turning slightly to lean against the tree as if needing its support while avoiding his piercing gaze. "I was waiting for Reis to finish his meeting so we could leave," she informed him to explain her unwanted presence.

"The meeting is over. He waits for you in Sun Cloud's teepee," he responded, unintentionally giving her the impression he was telling her it was time to go. He witnessed a shadow of anguish and turmoil which dulled her somber eyes. When her chin and lower lip quivered, she caught it between her teeth. He wondered at her strange behavior.

Without looking at him again, she straightened and tried to move past him toward camp. To think of him with another woman seared her heart. She was afraid she would burst into racking sobs at any moment. When he imprisoned her left arm and refused to allow her to leave, she shuddered at the contact. "Please let me go, Blazing Star," she beseeched him in a choked voice, shivering as if cold.

He studied her lowered head and behavior. "Do you hate me so that you cannot face me? You can share no words with me?" he asked worriedly, dreading the reason for her strange conduct.

Stunned by his words, she looked up into his solemn expression. "I don't hate you; I could never hate you," she vowed sadly. "I didn't want you to think I had broken my promise to you by returning here."

Still he did not relax or free her. "I have been in council; I know why you are here. But why do you wish to run from me? Why are your eyes so full of pain? I do not understand, Tamaha. Did the moon which passed between us change your feelings for me?"

She stared at him in disbelief. Was he being cruel without meaning to be? Did he not understand how the news of his marriage would affect her? Did he not know how much she loved and wanted him? Did he not realize she could not accept the Indian custom of having more than one woman or wife? Did he not realize she could never share him with anyone! "I have not changed, Blazing Star; you have," she responded mysteriously. "If my feelings have changed, they have grown stronger, just as you warned me. Please don't torment me."

His bewilderment increased. "Why does it torment you to be with me? Why do you draw away in such coldness?" he probed tensely.

Tears wet her lashes, then slipped down her cheeks. "Because you belong to another. Because you think I am unworthy of your love and teepee. Because I can never forget you or what we shared. I must go," she stated frantically, yanking on her arm.

His grip tightened, then he encircled her body with his powerful embrace. She struggled wildly for freedom from this agonizing embrace. He would not let her go. When she accepted her helpless and vulnerable position, she rested her forehead upon his chest and cried. He found this action stunning. "I belong to no other woman, Tamaha. What woman is more precious than you? If it could be, I would take you to my heart and mat this very moon. You fill my thoughts each sun and my dreams each moon. Why do you speak this way?"

Miranda lifted her head and stared at him. "I know the white customs differ from yours, Blazing Star, but you can't have me and her, too. How can you take a wife, then speak such words to me? It's wrong for us to be together now that you're married. I can't. And I hate myself for wanting you so much."

Blazing Star shook his head, trying to clear his steadily rising confusion. "I have taken no wife, Tamaha. Explain your words."

Shocked and baffled herself, she asked warily, "You didn't marry Black Buffalo Woman in the Cheyenne camp?"

Blazing Star threw back his head and laughed in amusement. When she punched him in the stomach and demanded he stop his laughter, he did. Grinning broadly, he grasped her chin and kissed her nose. "I have taken no wife, Tamaha, nor any woman to my mat since knowing you. Black Buffalo Woman has enough winters to be my grandmother. I can think of no woman when my people are at war, when my life is in danger each sun and moon. Your jealousy pleases me, but your head mixes another's words," he jested playfully.

Miranda realized what Bloody Arrow had done. Her eyes narrowed and frosted; she grit her teeth as she planned her revenge.

Observing her anger, he demanded sternly, "Explain the fires of revenge which flame within your eyes, Tamaha."

"I didn't understand about you and her. I was told clearly that you married her," she stated, then revealed the source.

"Bloody Arrow wishes to hurt us, Tamaha. I will watch him closely. Has he been cruel to you another time?" he probed oddly.

Miranda related their capture this afternoon and all other events involving her and her cousin. "Do not turn your back to him," he warned after she finished. "I will settle this matter later. Reveal no sadness or anger when we return to the teepee. Let him believe his words never harmed you or played in your mind. You must trust me, Tamaha. Do not believe such lies. I could take no woman while you fill my senses. When the moon of peace comes, then we will talk of our love and desires." He wisely did not add, if I still live.

She hugged him and spread kisses over his chest. "Then I shall pray with all my might for the moon of peace to come quickly, my love," she whispered against his thudding heart. "Can I stay and visit?"

"No, Tamaha, it is too dangerous," he blatantly refused.

"But I've missed you so much," she protested urgently, snuggling provocatively against his hard and taut frame.

His voice was strained as he confessed, "As I miss you. We must remain apart until a final truce," he asserted unflinchingly, stubbornly, protectively. "Do not beg, for my mind is as stone."

They were standing so close that she noticed his hunger for her. She smiled enticingly and murmured, "But your body is not."

He glanced at her and shook his head roguishly. "Your tongue speaks too quickly and freely, Tamaha," he jested seductively. "I can control all, except my desire for you. Return to the teepee while I cool this fire you have started." He knew he should send her away immediately. He knew he should not touch or kiss her. He knew he should not be saying such encouraging words to her. But her nearness dazed his senses and inflamed his body.

Her senses were also spinning wildly at his nearness. Their foreheads were touching; his breath warmed her flushed face as he spoke. Their gazes were locked and their needs exposed. He shuddered with loosely leashed control; she trembled with unbridled passion. "You must go, Tamaha; they wait for you." He tried one last time to deny what they both wanted and needed.

"I can't," she murmured simply, those words saying much. "I feel no shame or modesty with you, Blazing Star. Our time is too short and precious for such feelings. Is there no place we can . . . be alone?" she asked boldly, revealingly.

"Do you know what you say, Tamaha?" he asked huskily, his manhood throbbing with painful craving.

She needed to prove to him how much he loved and desired her. She needed to show him they belonged together. She needed to break down all barriers between them, all forces against them. He was on the verge of giving in to his emotions, and she needed to assist that blissful defeat. Once he accepted his love and need for her, then he would keep her with him.

There was so much love and desire emblazoned in her eyes when she smiled and murmured, "Yes, I want you. I love you."

Those words rang warnings in his mind, warnings he refused to hear or follow. "What if they come looking for us?" he argued weakly.

She grinned. "I know you can go and come in secret. If you wish to hide us, you will find a way," she replied trustingly.

He debated once more, "There is little time before they seek us. Passion should not run as swiftly as the river after a rain. Such moments should not be rushed."

"Are you saying a treat eaten quickly is not as filling or enjoyable as one eaten slowly?" she teased brazenly, sensuously.

For an answer, he scooped her up in his sturdy arms and headed into the forest. She suppressed her giggles by sealing her lips to his shoulder. When he felt he had put a sufficient distance between them and the camp, he lowered her feet to the grassy earth. The only sounds present were from the birds, a gentle wind, and their erratic breathing. "You are sure?" he asked one final time.

She nodded as she smiled happily. His fingers shook as they unlaced the ties at her throat and removed her dress. His smoldering gaze slipped from her passion-glazed eyes down her throat to heat her breasts with its flames. His hands upon her shoulders eased down her arms with snaillike leisure, halting at her wrists and capturing them gently as he leaned forward to tantalize those firm points with his tongue. She moaned and swayed at the intensity of that pleasure.

He caught the ties of her breechclout and untangled them, to allow the triangular garment to drift to her ankles. He straightened, then leaned away to gain a full view of her. She was so beautiful. His hands cupped her breasts, his thumbs caressing the hardened peaks. When she fused her lips to his mouth, his hands traveled down her sides and encircled her body, grasping her buttocks and drawing her naked body against his shuddering one.

Their tongues touched and explored the taste of the other. The peaks of her breasts were like two coals burning into his chest. He groaned in achingly sweet desire. He unlaced the ties of his breechclout, allowing it to fall to the earth at his feet. They sank together upon the forest floor, their lips and bodies meshed tightly.

As his lips worked between her mouth, ears, and breasts, his skilled, aggressive hands stimulated her womanhood to quivering need. Her hand drifted over his shoulders and hips until it made a discovery which enticed him to feverish pleasure. As if by instinct, her hand encircled the swollen, fiery object which could grant such delight. It felt so smooth and sensual. When her hand moved up and down its length several times, he groaned and writhed his hips, his mouth increasing its feasting upon her breasts and his hand working swiftly at a lower point. An urgency to fuse their bodies assailed them.

They moved together gracefully. Her thighs parted as he slid between them. As his shaft sank into her moist, dark warmth, her legs encased his body. They kissed savagely, greedily as their bodies surged in unison toward a mutual goal. There was no time for leisurely lovemaking; their starving senses were ravenous.

There was no restraint or caution. Their bodies blended time and time again until they were rewarded with rapturous ecstasy. When every drop of passion's nectar had been released, they lay exhausted in a serene bed of love and contentment. Both wished they could remain here like this for a long time, but it was getting dark.

Reluctantly he lifted his head and smiled at her. "We must go, Tamaha," he murmured against her lips, then kissed her thoroughly, wishing he meant they could go to their teepee for more lovemaking.

She hugged him desperately. "I know, my love."

She blushed when he suggested they splash off in the stream to remove the musky odors of sated passion. He cuffed her chin and laughed merrily. "There is some shyness left in you," he teased.

"Perhaps in time you can conquer all of it," she retorted coyly.

"Change nothing in you, Tamaha. I desire you as you are," he stated honestly, kissing her palm. She quivered. "Do not look at me so, Tamaha," he playfully warned when renewed passion glowed within her golden brown eyes.

"You have a strange and powerful effect over me, Blazing Star. When I am with you, you are the only person alive. You've cast a magical spell over me, and I am powerless to resist you or to refuse you anything. What will happen to us if there is no truce?" She spoke her inner fears aloud. "How long must we live separate lives? How long must we steal such golden moments?"

"You will not refuse or resist my wishes; you will stay apart from me and the war which controls my life and destiny."

"Please don't ask such a sacrifice of me," she begged him.

"I must, Tamaha. As long as there is war between our people, we cannot share a life or a teepee," he vowed.

"You want me to return home with Reis?" she asked somberly.

"Yes," he replied almost tersely, fearing her defiance.

She sighed heavily, knowing it was foolish to argue. "Let's go," she conceded, feeling she had improved her chances of winning him sooner. Now, she merely had to wait patiently. It would not be wise to reveal she was not as submissive and manageable as Indian women were alleged to be.

He seemed surprised, even suspicious, at her willingness to obey his commands. He watched her slip away to the stream to wash off and dress. He lay there for a time, thinking of her. When he finally joined her, she was ready and waiting for him. She sat meekly while he tossed water upon his body, then dressed.

When he extended his hand to help her rise, she smiled and declined it, saying, "Someone might think we're too close if we hold hands. We wouldn't want anyone to imagine I was your woman." She laughed merrily and raced away toward the camp, wondering if a man was more tempted by a seemingly elusive prize.

Her mood was odd, and he mused on it. Would he ever understand this playful creature? Would he be able to capture her, when she was as carefree and quick as a wild wind? Her mother had left her home during times of war; the conflicts had increased with the passing winters. Tamaha had been born a daughter of two enemy bloods, a daughter who had returned to confront those warring winds.

Chapter Twenty

In Sun Cloud's teepee, Miranda questioned her brother-in-law about the council meeting. Reis told her it was better if she did not know anything; that way she could not drop any clues by mistake. Miranda did not want to imagine Reis betraying her or her people, but she was alarmed by his refusal to discuss his mission. She persisted in asking what was going on between him and the Oglalas. How else could she judge his honesty and sincerity?

Sun Cloud recognized her fears and their reasons. He smiled and consoled her, telling her to trust Reis and to follow his orders. Blazing Star added his encouragement and prodding. Only Bloody Arrow remained silent and watchful.

Miranda's gaze went from one man to the next, sensing all were in total agreement except her cousin. How could she argue against such odds? She relented and kept silent.

When Blazing Star smiled raffishly at her, no one missed the warmth or power behind it. Nor did they miss the way Miranda's eyes softened and glowed when she returned the smile. Reis had to shake her arm to catch her attention. She blushed and listened as he said it was time to go.

She hugged and kissed her grandfather, telling him she would come again if possible. The old man's eyes were moist as he smiled. She glanced at her cousin and politely said good-by. When she turned to Blazing Star, thankfully her back was to the others. Her eyes wandered over his arresting form, mutely asking how long it would be until they were together again. She smiled and caught his hand in a sort of genial gesture, needing that final contact. She told him good-by, hoping her voice did not betray her excitement and turmoil as his thumb caressed the back of her hand.

Outside, Sun Cloud presented her with his "surprise" from the Cheyenne camp. "He's beautiful, Grandfather," she cried, nuzzling the pinto's nose. "But I can't take him with me. How would I explain him?" she fretted in disappointment. "Will you keep him a while longer?"

Reis solved the dilemma by suggesting that he say he purchased the horse downriver. All agreed. After her saddle was switched to the pinto, Miranda was helped to mount. She bid them all farewell, her gaze lingering on Blazing Star. Just before they were out of sight, she glanced over her shoulder and waved.

Blazing Star turned to find Bloody Arrow's wintry gaze on him. "Why did you lie to her about Black Buffalo Woman?" he demanded.

Even amidst the knowledge of Bloody Arrow's envy and spite, no one realized the extent of his hunger for power and revenge. No one could imagine the heights to which he would reach to obtain his wishes, or the depths to which he would sink if denied. He deceitfully said, "Because you trick her. Because you pull her into your arms when she cannot remain there. What of her feelings, Blazing Star? What of the moon when she learns the truth? What of Sun Cloud when he learns of your deed? Who will kill you for taking her body when you will not share her life-circle, Sun Cloud or Miranda Lawrence? Your lust for her blinds you to your cruelty and evil. Do you forget she carries the same blood as Sun Cloud and Bloody Arrow? Do not force us to protect her from you. I wished to end her feelings before she was harmed by them."

Blazing Star knew he was lying but rashly allowed it to pass. This was not the time or place for a private battle between kin. There was a greater matter at hand. "I will end it when the time is right, Bloody Arrow. I would not harm Tamaha. I have spoken words of truth to her. Do not interfere," he warned ominously.

Miranda and Reis repeated their arduous journey, arriving home near three in the morning. Reis unsaddled their horses and placed them inside the small corral which he had constructed and attached to the side wall of the cabin. He tossed hay into one corner and carried in two buckets of fresh water from the well. Then they went to the cabin door.

When Amanda answered their summons, she hugged each one tightly, telling them how relieved she was to have them back. She wanted to hear everything, but Reis and Miranda were exhausted. Miranda collapsed upon the cot and fell asleep without undressing. Amanda was nettled when Reis gave her a light peck on the cheek and did the same in the bedroom.

Amanda struggled to remove his boots and pants. He mumbled his thanks, then rolled to his side and went limp. Amanda was very quiet that morning, not even building a fire for coffee. She knew they needed to sleep as long as possible. She sat in a chair reading or sewing to pass the time. But as noon came and went, she became anxious to hear about the daring trek. And she was getting hungry.

She went into the bedroom and sat down on the edge of the bed. She watched her husband sleep for a long time, relieved he was home safe. She wondered why his mission had to be kept secret from her. Had he confided in Miranda? A note of discord struck her at that insensitive thought. But how could Miranda help Reis if she did not know what was going on out here? If this case were as dangerous and time-consuming as the previous one, he would damn well confess matters soon!

When would Reis realize that ignorance did not provide safety or prevent worry? Why could others know facts or assist Reis, but she could not? It was almost as if being his wife was nothing but a cover for his assignments! After all, she only had Reis's word that he was a government agent! For all she knew, he could be a sly criminal!

Amanda scolded herself for being so silly and dramatic, but she was tired of secrecy. She wanted to meet her grandfather, too. She wanted to join in the excitement and suspense. She longed to be a part of this mission, and she yearned for Reis to trust her implicitly.

He stirred and opened his eyes, his keen senses detecting a presence. He smiled faintly as he rubbed his eyes, yawning and stretching. He sat on the side of the bed opposite her. He stretched his body several times and massaged his sore neck. "Any coffee left?"

"I haven't made any. I was afraid of disturbing you two. Do you think it's all right to awaken Randy?" she inquired hesitantly.

"What time is it?" Reis asked before replying.

"A little past one," Amanda responded. "I missed you."

He flashed her a smile, then stood up to flex once more. "We could both use more sleep. But I think it should come later. Why don't we fix some coffee and food, and talk? Your grandfather's quite a man. And so is Randy's warrior," he added playfully.

"You met them? You liked them?" she pressed eagerly.

He stretched and yawned a final time, then splashed his face with tepid water. While drying it, he nodded and grunted affirmatively. "What's Grandfather like Reis?" she probed, coming to stand near him.

He fluffed her golden hair and remarked, "A real chief. Let's get that coffee, then I'll tell you all about him." As she turned to obey, he reached for her, pulling her into his arms. "Don't I get a welcome kiss and hug first?" he jested, grinning beguilingly.

As the kiss lengthened and deepened, Reis drew away and murmured, "I think we should close the door for a while."

His implication was clear, and the feeling shared. But before he could do so, Miranda sat up and caught sight of him, telling him good morning. He responded, then turned to Amanda and stated ruefully, "Randy's awake. We can prepare that coffee and breakfast."

When Amanda came to his side and embraced him, she teased, "I do believe my husband has acquired modesty from some place. The more I lose, the more you find."

Arm in arm, they entered the front room. While Miranda freshened up, Reis helped his wife with their meal, and as they consumed it, Miranda and Reis went over their trip. Both women were perturbed when Reis withheld the motive for his visit. Amanda questioned her sister about this secrecy.

Miranda shrugged and contended, "He wouldn't tell me either, Mandy. Even Grandfather took a vow of silence. I think we're merely decorations for your husband's work. Who would suspect a sinister villain lurking behind two delicate ladies?" she jested mirthfully. "Could it be your love doesn't trust women to have brains and courage?"

Reis chuckled, shaking his head. "I'll never survive this mission with two females picking at me all the time," he speculated jovially.

"We wouldn't have to if you didn't keep us under a basket of secrecy," Amanda teased him, and they laughed. Amanda snickered when she asked her sister, "Did you see your handsome warrior?"

Miranda's expression was a blend of joy and sadness. "For a short time. Too short," she added petulantly. "You should teach your husband about love and romance. From the way he ardently courted you, I believed he was familiar with both. He insisted we leave as soon as the council meeting ended. We were barely given any time alone."

Reis felt it unwise and insensitive to jest about the length of time it took the warrior to retrieve her before they could depart, or to remark suggestively on the telltale signs of the cause of their delay. In fact, he was worried and concerned about Miranda and her choice of sweethearts. What could come of such an impossible match? With Blazing Star's rank and the continual conflicts, he would be lucky to live out this month! Reis feared he could not change the situation quickly enough to spare two lives so precious and vital to his sister-in-law. There was so much greed, corruption, lust for power, and hatred here; and he was only one man with limited time.

After their meal, the sisters helped Reis move aside the table and chairs to conceal a packet of papers, unaware of its critical nature. The packet contained the power to alter history and many destinies if it were used properly. But even as Reis thought about the council meeting which Crazy Horse had agreed to schedule among all chiefs off and on the reservations, the forces and powers of evil were plotting rapidly against him . . .

Reis was so ensnared by his mental musings that Amanda had to call his name twice and shake his arm to gain his attention. "Reis! Whatever are you thinking about?" she asked.

He forced a beguiling smile to his lips and stated unconvincingly, "Nothing to worry that pretty head, love. I think I'll take another look around." With that, he left the two women looking at each other.

"Randy, did something happen to worry Reis so much?" she inquired anxiously. "That's the same look and mood I saw when things started getting complicated with Weber. This entire matter frightens me."

"I know what you mean. But he wouldn't tell me. Do you think we should take a look at those papers? What if he's in danger or trouble? We can't help him if we don't know anything."

Amanda fretted over such a desperate action. She was trapped between concern and loyalty. Reis loved her. How would he deal with such a traitorous act? Would her motives matter to him? She could not understand why this part of his life must remain a black void to her. Yet, he felt it must and was most adamant about it.

"We can't do such a thing, Randy. Reis would be hurt and angry if he felt I didn't trust him completely," she asserted faintly.

"And you aren't 'hurt and angry' because he doesn't fully trust you?" Miranda asked bluntly. When she saw her sister's stricken look, she relented. "I'm sorry, Mandy; I shouldn't have said that. I don't know what's gotten into me lately. Why does everything have to be so complex and difficult?"

"Did you get to see Blazing Star alone?" Amanda inquired carefully. Miranda nodded. "Did he say something to hurt you?"

"He says we can't think about us until this war is over. What if it's never over, Mandy? What if something happens to him?"

Amanda slipped her arm around her sister's trembling shoulders and advised, "Don't worry, sis. You did tell me how strong and brave he is. I'm sure he can protect himself."

"You don't understand, Mandy. There are so many soldiers in this area, so many of them determined to kill him. There's no comparison in their weapons.

The Indians don't have someone to provide their ammunition and supplies! They have to make them or hunt them. And while the braves are doing so, the soldiers wipe out villages and tribes! As long as the whites press closer and tighter to Indian lands, the warriors will go forth to battle them. It can't stop unless one side yields. And the Oglalas will never do so as long as they live and breathe. You haven't been to their camp and listened to them. You haven't seen the terrible things the whites and soldiers do. He'll die, Mandy; he'll die before accepting defeat and dishonor."

Miranda locked her gaze with her sister's and explained, "Don't you see? That's why I have to spend every moment I can with him. When the time comes that we're parted forever, I'll have these days and memories. Am I so awful to want all I can have of him before it's too late? Do you see why he keeps pushing me away, back to so-called safety? If he didn't love me, my life and happiness wouldn't be so important to him. He loves me enough to unselfishly sacrifice me. And I love him so much that no danger is sufficient to obey him."

Suddenly Miranda laughed reproachfully. "He's a lot like your Reis. He thinks ignorance provides safety and prevents worry. Do you realize how lucky we are? We both have loves who will do anything to protect us. I'm glad Reis is working with Blazing Star. If any two men can make a difference in this conflict, they can."

Amanda had not comprehended how much suffering and turmoil her sister was enduring until now. Nor had she guessed that her husband was being pulled into a situation which was deadly and uncontrollable, a situation which would alter and destroy many lives. She tried to encourage and comfort her sister. As their destinies overlapped, they were being drawn ever closer.

Around four that afternoon, Fort Sully was assailed by commotion and excitement as the Seventh Cavalry set up camp in a clearing nearby, under the command of George Armstrong Custer and his favored officer, Major Brody Sheen. Lucas hurried to the cabin to relate this news to Amanda, Reis, and Miranda.

At nearly the same time, in a smaller clearing miles from the fort, another meeting was taking place. A vindictive and menacing Oglala warrior was passing detrimental information to a half-blooded scout whose cunning, vengeance, and hatred far exceeded that of the Indian's. So blinded by his own greed and bitterness, the warrior failed to recognize the traitorous enemy he was supposedly using to gain his own wishes. The aggressive and sinister scout was cleverly plotting revenge on both sides, white and Indian. Once the opposing leaders killed each other, he would take over this area, for he possessed the intelligence and daring to fool both sides. Who better to rule than a man who carried both bloods, who knew the strengths and weaknesses of each. As he watched the treacherous warrior ride off, he sneered at the man's stupidity. For the warrior had just given him the means to accomplish his ends.

When Lucas finished telling of his journey, he told Reis that Colonel Custer wanted to meet him tonight at dinner. Lucas then told Miranda that Brody was eager to visit with her. When she scowled, Lucas added that he had tried to discourage Brody's interest but could not.

"How long do they plan to stay around here?" Miranda inquired.

"It looks as if they'll set up camp and headquarters here. Custer's been ordered to check out the Sioux hostilities and get them under control. He said it would be easier to work out of Fort Sully for a while," he explained to her dismay.

When Reis and Miranda related their eventful tales, Lucas realized why

Custer's presence might present a problem. With Brody dogging Miranda, it would be difficult for her to leave home for another visit to her grandfather and Blazing Star. She feared for her love's life and safety with two of his worst foes so near. Perhaps she should find some way to warn him and his people, for she knew Custer was not here for a truce.

When Brody came to call later, Amanda was forced to lie to him. She claimed her sister was not feeling well. After disarming Amanda with compliments and his dashing manner, Brody said he would call again tomorrow afternoon and left.

"Are you sure you have him pegged right? You were enchanted by Blazing Star when you met Major Sheen. Perhaps you've misjudged him. He's quite handsome and charming," Amanda remarked as she watched Brody swagger back toward their makeshift camp of tents.

"Brody is devious, clever, and sinister, just like Weber Richardson was," Miranda sneered sarcastically. "Take another study."

The subject was dropped instantly. The two waited nervously until Lucas and Reis returned from their meal and conversation. Each woman was full of questions for the men who tried to answer them amidst laughter and amusement.

"The President's son, Frederick, wasn't with Custer tonight?" Amanda asked, knowing that was one cover Reis was using.

"Custer says Frederick's planning to join him when he's ready to ride into the Black Hills for that survey," Lucas responded before Reis.

"They're riding into the Black Hills?" Miranda echoed in shock.

"Yep. They claim it's just a mapping expedition, but it's going to cause trouble. I think the military is asking for it, just seeking an excuse to wipe out those renegade tribes," Lucas spoke out again.

"But what about the Laramie Treaty of '68? It makes trespassing on their sacred grounds forbidden. That's the last and most crucial promise to the Indians, to stay out! From the Missouri River past the Black Hills, the land has been declared the Great Sioux Reservation. They've broken all the treaties and promises except that one. They establish reservations until they find a reason to move them another place, but this time it's a lethal mistake. If they ride into that territory, no Indian—Sioux or otherwise—will back down from that challenge," Miranda stated fearfully. "You've got to contact President Grant, Reis. You've got to convince him to stop Custer."

"I plan to do my best, Randy. But you have to trust me and keep silent. If anyone suspects what I'm up to or who I really am, it's all over for us and the Indians. Just as soon as I get my facts collected and recorded, Grant will know all about the crux of this matter," Reis promised them, revealing more today than he had to date.

"You realize there are people in Washington involved in some of this fraud and corruption, people in high places, people in the Indian Bureau, people close to the President? What's he planning to do about his kin?" Lucas questioned gravely.

"He promised to punish whoever is involved," Reis replied.

"You think he will?" Amanda asked skeptically.

"If Custer's connected to it, yes. There's no love lost between those two. As to his blood, I can't say for sure," he answered candidly.

"But if it's brought into public light, even his kin would be forced to halt such vile and criminal behavior," Miranda surmised.

"That's what I'm working and hoping for," Reis declared.

"When Custer asked why you were here, what did you tell him, Reis?" Miranda probed apprehensively.

"I said Grant sent me out here to look around and see how things were progressing. I made it sound more like a pleasure trip than business. I told him I was recently married and this was a sort of honeymoon. If he mentions that we're looking at ranchland to settle in these parts, don't act surprised," he said with a smile.

"Did he believe you?" Miranda asked merrily.

"Partly. But he did make a joking comment about first a writer showing up with a Lawrence girl, then a liaison from the President with another Lawrence girl. He remarked on what a potent and curious pair a government ex-agent and a writer made. I hadn't considered him associating me and Luke as some undercover team. We'll all have to be careful what we say and do. It's going to appear strange for me and Luke to be asking questions and making observations. We could be hindering each other's progress."

"Right now, yours seems more important, Reis. You're working on history in the making," Lucas said.

"That's real generous of you, Luke. I know how important this trip and book are to you." Reis acknowledged.

"Not quite so meaningful since I discovered Weber Richardson arranged and financed it—no doubt to get me away from Alexandria and my cousins," Luke ventured in lingering annoyance.

That disclosure gave way to talk of the past. After coffee and pie, Lucas went to sleep on a bedroll and Miranda used the cot while Reis and Amanda were given the bedroom. They tried to protest, but neither Miranda nor Lucas would budge from their positions.

In the camp nearby, Brody was asking Custer, "Do you believe Harrison is just wandering around for no special reason?"

Yellowy blond curls tossed around blue-clad shoulders as his commander shook his head. "Grant doesn't do anything without a purpose. You keep a close eye on our four friends. See what you can learn about the writer and see if you can get some of his work to me. Let's see which side of the fence he landed on, and how long ago. As for Harrison, get me all the information your contacts can locate. He's a troubleshooter if I ever saw one. I want to know just what he and Grant are pulling," he remarked, then began whistling an aria.

While he clipped his mustache and evened his curls, he told his aide to roll the locks of hair in strips of cloth and give them to his female admirers. After receiving orders to check his horse, Vic, once again before bedtime, the aide left muttering about how glad he was that Custer had not brought along any of his numerous dogs on this journey.

Custer was a strange man, a man either fiercely hated or genuinely admired. He cut a dashing figure as the epitome of a professional soldier, a man obsessed with fame and power, a man who believed he could conquer any force. When the Civil War ended, Custer needed excitement and danger as others needed nourishment for survival. He started his new career with the Seventh Cavalry Regiment in Kansas in 1867. Only recently had he been ordered to take command of the Dakota Territory, operating out of Fort Lincoln.

Considered a proud or vain man, depending on the source, Custer appeared fearless, often charging headlong into the heat of battle. Some called him reckless and vainglorious, but above all, Custer was a military man. He followed orders, even if he resented or disagreed with them. He was often called a brilliant strategist, but others claimed it was merely luck. Custer never drank alcoholic spirits and rarely used profanity. He believed in the total authority of a commanding officer. Although he loved his wife Libby deeply, it was rumored he had a Cheyenne mistress. As much as he was alleged to despise Indians, he felt it his duty to try and uphold the treaties and promises made to them.

Custer was now being thrust into historical events beyond his control. He saw many wrongs but felt his first loyalty was to his country and his men. Often overzealous in his conduct, he was determined to go down in history as a brave and intelligent leader, but Fate was swiftly coloring the pages upon which his personal drama was being recorded.

When Miranda told her sister of her intentions to sneak to the Oglala camp and warn them of Custer's arrival, Amanda was petrified. Miranda angrily declared that her sister could cover her absence by sticking to the story of her illness. They argued for a long time, until Lucas finally intervened and told Miranda she could not go.

"You can't order me about, Lucas Reardon," she snapped.

"If you're caught, Randy, it would spoil everything," Luke retorted, his own eyes glittering frostily. "This time you listen and obey!"

"That's Custer out there, Luke!" she panted frantically. "And Sherman and Sheridan aren't far away. I'm going!" she announced.

"You don't have to! Reis is . . . Just wait awhile and things will settle down," he finished, trying to cover his slip.

When she questioned his half-statement, he passed it off nonchalantly. But Miranda guessed what he had been about to say; she relaxed, assuming Reis and Lucas were going to warn her people.

When Brody called again, Miranda could not refuse to see him, for he caught her outside getting fresh air with Amanda and Reis. They chatted for a time, then Brody asked her to go for a walk or allow him to step inside for some coffee. Recalling that Reis's reports were lying on the table, Miranda had no choice but to accept his invitation. Reis smiled at her, knowing why she had agreed, sensing why she disliked this man. He resolved to find a way to keep them apart, even though he could have used her to distract Brody.

As Brody and Miranda strolled along, he asked how she had been occupying her time and why she had not joined Lucas for the trek. Miranda passed off his questions with light remarks and sunny smiles. She tensed when Brody said he wanted to get to know her and her family better. He asked if she would join him for a picnic the next day.

Miranda was not caught unprepared for his romantic siege, but she had not expected the rapidity of his onslaught. Her mind was elsewhere and she was not thinking clearly or calmly. She stammered and fidgeted. "I think . . . we should get . . . to know each other better."

"That's what I just said, Miranda," he teased devilishly. "Do I make you nervous?" he asked, reaching out to take her hand.

She jerked it away and flushed. She tried to recall every feminine wile she had seen Amanda use, every coquettish gesture, every shy expression. "I fear you press too quickly, sir," she hinted in a thick Southern drawl, fluttering her lashes demurely. "I'm unaccustomed to men being so bold and persistent as you Westerners. Now that my parents are . . . dead, I find it strange to choose my own companions and activities. I thought perhaps this trip with cousin Luke would make me a bit more daring and confident, but alas . . ." She sighed dramatically as if disappointed with her progress and modesty.

Brody grinned mischievously and hinted, "No one could doubt your courage or mettle, Miranda. You remained here alone while Luke was with us. Surely you have become less fainthearted," he teased her.

"That was different, sir. I was locked in my cabin each night, and there were soldiers to guard me during the day. A lady could not travel in the company of so many men and under such deplorable conditions. I was greatly shocked that your invitation included me. Surely you would not wish me to face such dangers and deprivations?"

He huskily declared, "I would confront whatever necessary to be with you. In my eagerness to have you at my side, I overlooked such matters. You are an exquisite treasure, Miranda. I never dreamed of meeting such a divine creature, and surely not in this hellish place."

Miranda's face grew redder with each compliment. "Sir, you should not speak so boldly. But thank you. If you are to be at Fort Sully for an extended period, perhaps we shall have time to become properly acquainted. I should return home now," she stated uneasily.

"Please don't go," he coaxed. "I've thought of nothing but you since we parted. I persuaded Custer to set up command here just so I could be near you. You have me utterly bewitched, and my duties have suffered greatly from lack of attention. Join me for a picnic tomorrow? We can be alone and . . . we can share Cupid's potent spell."

She stared in amazement. "You should not suggest such a thing, sir. It seems our morals and breeding differ immensely. I think it best if you do not call on me again. I fear you misconstrued our relationship and my feelings." Her scheme to discourage him had failed miserably.

Witnessing her reaction, he hastily declared, "I didn't mean to offend or alarm you. Perhaps my manners have dulled in this uncivil land. When a man faces death every day, he comes to live for each hour and to speak frankly. We wouldn't be totally alone, Miranda."

"We wouldn't?" she questioned his meaning, imagining what she could learn from this man about Custer's plans.

"Not if it made you uncomfortable. I could have an aide serve us and remain as your guardian. I would prefer to have privacy to talk, but I don't want to panic you with my eagerness."

Miranda eyed him skeptically. Something in his inflection told her he was being dishonest. But she could take care of herself. Perhaps it would do Brody Sheen a world of good to be tossed on his ear by a refined and delicate lady! "All right, Major Sheen," she acquiesced. "But only if your aide accompanies us," she added.

He grinned roguishly and agreed to her terms, even as he plotted how to outmaneuver her. "I'll pick you up at noon," he suggested.

She smiled genially and nodded in agreement. Afterward, Brody escorted her back to the cabin. Confident of his sexual prowess, he felt there was no need to rush this delicate flower. No doubt she was confused and dismayed by her wanton attraction to him. He must attack her virtuous, naïve shell with skill and caution. She had been taught to keep those legs tightly locked until marriage. But his fiery passion could melt the moral clamp which prevented his possession.

Once she became his mistress and he observed her closely, then he would judge her appeal and value as a wife. His tour of duty would end next spring; perhaps Miranda Lawrence was the ideal choice for him. If a man had to be shackled to a wife, who better than a beautiful and genteel woman? On the surface she seemed an angel; but her sensuality was earthy and powerful. With a little training, he could have her right where he wanted her. He was a master of seduction and guile; and they would be alone in a romantic setting tomorrow afternoon . . .

When Miranda told Reis of the picnic plans, he was both delighted and dismayed. He revealed that he had vital plans tomorrow afternoon which she could aid by distracting Brody Sheen while Lucas commanded Custer's attention with an interview for his phony book. Reis said he would take Amanda with him to meet her grandfather; his wife's presence would make their journey from the settlement appear a romantic outing for the honeymooners. But Reis warned Miranda to be alert and wary of Brody.

When Miranda pleaded to go see Blazing Star, Reis protested. If she went along, Sheen would be encouraged to ride after them and attempt to join their party. He forced her to realize the importance of misleading Brody Sheen and Custer. He promised to give a message to her love, to try to set up a secret meeting between them. She unhappily agreed before retiring to dream of her intrepid warrior.

While Reis and Amanda made passionate love and Lucas envisioned literary accolades and Miranda dreamed of her copper-skinned lover, Brody Sheen was staring coldly and sardonically at the odious scout who had told him of the upcoming parlay and Reis's covert mission. It did not matter that the scout declared Miranda ignorant and innocent of Reis's mischief; Brody painted her guilty of deceit. That night, Brody dreamed of punishing a girl who had made a complete fool of him, of capturing a savage chief whose name sent shivers of fear through most whites, and of helping his friend and commander by destroying all of his enemies!

Chapter Twenty-One

🌿 *D*espite the vitality of the landscape, death whispered upon the gentle breezes which swayed the verdant grasses and supple leaves, played through colorful wildflowers, and teased the wings of the brilliantly shaped butterflies that danced with the currents. Suspense hung heavy over the settlement that next morning as each person planned his or her day's events.

A pleased Tom Fletcher rode off early to watch his plot unfold from a distance through his field glasses. The drama was in motion, but the naïve actors did not as yet know their roles. The final act had begun on this warm morning, and nothing could save the white and red players from destruction.

Lucas Reardon obtained permission from Custer to ride along with part of his troop to the Cheyenne River Agency to check on rumors of trouble on the reservation. The larger part of his regiment was to remain camped near Fort Sully, under the command of Brody Sheen. Practically ordered to mount up and accompany the departing squad, Lucas was dismayed by the fact that he was not given time to return to his cabin to warn Reis of their destination, where Chief Red Cloud would be found missing if Custer requested to see and speak with him.

Reis and Amanda Lawrence Harrison rode off with a picnic basket, laughing and chatting as if on the way to a romantic tryst. Reis cleverly headed in the opposite direction from the council meeting, planning to skirt the settlement to prevent discovery. He hoped his wife was in excellent condition, as they would be forced to ride strenuously to arrive on schedule after this diversionary tactic. Reis felt no qualms about taking his wife along on this trip. Crazy Horse had promised they would be observed and protected from a distance.

Amanda was glowing with exuberance, delighted to be a part of this monumental conference and thrilled about meeting Sun Cloud and her sister's love.

From surrounding areas, imposing and illustrious chiefs and spiritual leaders headed for the meeting which Reis Harrison had arranged with Crazy Horse and Sitting Bull. Soon to convene were: Two Moons of the Cheyenne; Lame Deer and Hump of the Minniconjous; Sitting Bull, Gall, Black Moon, and Crow King of the Hunkpapas; Crazy Horse, Big Road, and He Dog of the Oglalas; and Red Hawk of another Sioux tribe. The Brule chief, Spotted Tail, and another Oglala chief, Red Cloud, slipped away from the agencies named for them to attend this crucial parlay. Along with these historic leaders came their most legendary warriors, a group which included Blazing Star.

Reis had convinced Crazy Horse, Sitting Bull, and their council that the

"Great White Father" did not know of the evil taking place on their lands. He asked that each tribe list their grievances and sign the paper; then he would personally carry the papers to the "chief of the whites and bluecoats." He told them Chief Grant would halt the bloodshed and punish the whites and bluecoats consumed by greed and evil. He tried to convince them that Chief Grant wanted peace, that he had sent Reis here to unmask the evil and correct it. Reis also warned that the meeting and papers must be kept secret, as those evil whites would try to prevent him and the evidence from reaching the "Great White Father."

Crazy Horse, Sitting Bull, and the members of the council had sensed courage and honesty in the white man. The conflicts were increasing. Each time they slew a "white butcher," another would take his place with better weapons, endless supplies, and further aggression. If there could be peace without dishonor or defeat, this was the last chance to attain it. They agreed to trust Reis, to help prevent more war. They wanted to live in freedom and happiness upon their ancestral grounds; they would agree to allow the whites and bluecoats to settle on lands not included in the Laramie Treaty. They wanted to hunt and enjoy their existence close to Mother Earth. They wanted safety and honor for their families and homes.

"Mahpialuta, Sinte Galeska, ku-wa," Crazy Horse greeted Red Cloud and Spotted Tail and invited them to join his campfire as they awaited the arrival of others.

"Tashunka Witco," both greeted Crazy Horse in return, then gave the sign for peace. *"Pizi,"* Red Cloud nodded at Gall and addressed him in friendship.

At Fort Sully, Brody Sheen and his aide called on Miranda Lawrence to commence their scheduled picnic. Although Brody was attempting to be outwardly charming and genial, Miranda perceived an intimidating remoteness in him. She wondered why he was beginning their afternoon so sullenly. A shiver of alarm ran over her body, and she wished she could cancel the outing.

As they mounted their horses, Miranda asked about the squads which were riding east and north from Fort Sully. Brody glanced in their directions, then shrugged noncommittally. He said the men were heading for a military exercise. She prayed she was not acting too curious or nervous. She watched the swallow-tailed cavalry guidon as it waved rapidly with the flag carrier's movements and dismissed her fears and doubts. If he were suspicious of Reis's conduct, Brody would not have remained behind.

Brody and Miranda rode to a serene and lovely spot near the river. As Brody helped Miranda dismount, the look in his hazel eyes caused her twinges of forbod-ing to return. Yet she felt there was nothing she could do but carry out this charade. After all, they were not alone. And, she was not helpless. She could fight like a trained wildcat, and she had the small derringer from Reis strapped to her thigh.

"We should have invited your sister and her husband to join us. I noticed they had the same idea when they rode off this morning," Brody commented casually as he spread the blanket for sitting.

"They're newlyweds, Major Sheen. I think they preferred to be alone," she conversed lightly, returning his amiable smile. "Shall we eat?"

Miranda tensed apprehensively when Brody signaled to the aide, who mounted and rode off instead of serving them. She looked at the man beside her whose expression was cryptic. "If this is a joke or trick, sir, I do not find it amusing or pleasing. I shall leave now," she announced haughtily, sending him a frown of reproach.

"No, Miranda, you shall not leave," Brody informed her icily.

"Sir, you are an officer in the United States Cavalry! This is most distressing and repulsive behavior," she criticized sharply.

"And you, Miss Miranda Lawrence, are a half-breed slut," he stated calmly and insultingly. "You're an enemy to whites—you and your heathen family. I believe the infamous Chief Sun Cloud is your grandpa. Here I was courting Injun royalty. But not for long. Before nightfall, your family and those savage leaders will be dead or captured."

Miranda went ashen beneath her olive complexion. Tremors swept over her body. For a time, she thought her heart had ceased beating, until it began to race frantically. Horror filled her as his words settled into her distraught mind. She decided to call his bluff first, then physically battle him if she had to. "Whatever are you saying, Major Sheen? Surely this is some malicious ruse to spite or frighten me? I shan't deny my mother was Indian, but that gives you no right to verbally degrade or harass me. I am not ashamed of my heritage. Colonel Custer will be told of your despicable and rude conduct when he returns. My family shall demand your apology and punishment. I will listen to no more of this offensive talk, nor shall I see you again. You, sir, are no gentleman!"

"And you, ma'am, are no lady," he satanically sneered, placing his hand upon her chest and shoving her backward to the blanket.

Miranda alertly and agilely rolled aside, landing on all fours, then jumping to her feet. "How dare you touch me, you vile beast!"

As Brody scrambled to his feet, she struggled to withdraw the tiny pistol. Before she could grip it properly, Brody slapped her across the wrist and sent the weapon flying into the bushes. To her rising terror, when she tried to battle him as Ling had taught her, she discovered Brody knew the same tactics and movements but was far superior in skill and strength. And he was not reluctant to physically battle or beat her!

Miranda tumbled backward and landed roughly on her seat when he kicked her in the abdomen. This was the first time a male had returned her attack. But he had wisely controlled the force of his blow, only wishing to stun her. Miranda gasped for breath as he approached her like a stalking beast. When he came within reach, she tripped him with her leg before he realized she retained the strength and courage to do so. His fall sprained his left wrist and enraged him.

As he pushed himself up from the hard ground, he laughed bitterly and sneered, "So, you like to play rough, do you?"

When Miranda continued to battle him with every skill she possessed, his anger mounted to a dangerous level. She had just enough talent and nimbleness to keep him at bay for a time, but he inflicted many bruises. Twice, he struck her across the face, bringing a darkening bruise to one cheek and a steady flow of blood from the corner of her mouth. She started to retreat while panting breathlessly.

For each step she took backward, Brody took two forward, his eyes glittering with lustful intention. He savored relating where Custer and his men were heading after joining forces away from the settlement. He mockingly revealed the fates of

Reis and Amanda but claimed that hers was in his hands. As his arm snaked out to seize her, his gaze never left hers, watching for any sign of attack or defeat. But all he saw was the feigned look of terror and vulnerability which Miranda desperately displayed.

She had to escape and warn them. Her booted foot lifted with such quickness that it landed accurately and rackingly in his private region before he could dodge it. Just as instinctively and rapidly, his fist shot out and made contact with the side of her head instead of her jaw as she shifted with her movement. Rather than breaking her jaw or cheekbone, the blow dazed and staggered her. She fell sideways, injuring the other temple when it struck a large rock.

Muffled curses and groans filtered into her hazy mind as she attempted to clear her head and flee. As she pushed upward to a wobbly sitting position, she saw Brody in a crouched stance, his face a mask of grimacing agony and his hands cupping his throbbing groin. She shook her head and blinked her eyes to regain her senses. It was useless; her vision blurred as pains and drowsiness assailed her. She crumbled to the ground, chestnut curls falling over her bloody face. She was weary and groggy; she could no longer defend herself.

Brody mastered his pain and started toward her, drawing his Colt from its holster. Suddenly, a red-and-black-tipped arrow sang ominously through the still air and slammed into Brody's back. He wavered for a moment, then fell dead near Miranda. She could not react, but she roused herself slightly. In the tiny opening between two fiery curls, she could make out two masculine figures heading toward her. Her confused gaze returned to the arrow whose colors and markings did not match the identity of either male. Perhaps she was dreaming. The arrow was her lover's, but it was her Indian cousin and the fort scout who were approaching her prone and limp body. She could not summon the strength to speak or move, but she listened to their words.

"Why did you shoot the bluecoat with Blazing Star's arrow? Why did you not let him slay her?" Bloody Arrow sneered maliciously.

"She is mine. I claim her as reward for helping you defeat your rivals." As Tom kicked Brody in the ribs, he scoffed, "I wondered why he didn't ride out with Custer to attack the parlay. When I gave him your words about the council meeting, he looked strange. What real man would choose vengeful rape over a glorious battle? When they are all dead, Bloody Arrow, you will rule the Indians and I will rule the whites as we planned. If you try to trick or slay me, I will call down more soldiers upon you than I sent to slay those at the meeting," he threatened malevolently. After today's victory, he would slay Bloody Arrow in his own time and in his own way.

"You wish to have this half-breed whore as your woman? I will sell her and her sister to the Apaches as slaves. No white female can survive such torment. She must die. After this sun, only Bloody Arrow will carry the blood of Gray Eagle," the warrior vowed. "Such matchless blood will flow only in my sons."

"You forget, Bloody Arrow, I also carry two bloods within me. Do not insult the man who helps you earn your dream. She will be my mate and slave. Do as you wish with her sister, but Tamaha is mine. You must go and prepare to call the warriors from all tribes together to avenge the slaughter of their chiefs," he suggested coldly.

"In death, they will do more to free and avenge our many tribes than they did in life and battle. Their deaths will spark hatred and unity in all tribes. I will lead the final battle to slay the killers of our chiefs. At last, the chief's bonnet will be mine. Take her; she is yours. But do not let her escape you," he warned.

When Bloody Arrow rode away to observe the results of his careful and daring plans, Tom threw back his head and laughed heartily. "You are a fool, Bloody Arrow. Once all white and Indian leaders are killed, you will join them in death and I will be chief of all Indians and whites. When you and your family are slain today, only Miranda will carry the blood of Gray Eagle and Sun Cloud within her. My sons will carry the blood of the two great chiefs which flows in Tamaha's body; she will pass such honor to our sons." Chilling laughter filled Miranda's humming ears as she lost consciousness.

Tom gathered Miranda into his arms, his rage boundless when he saw her injuries. He laid her down, then scalped the dead soldier. He had told Sheen that Miranda was not involved in this matter. The fool should have listened! He held the bloody trophy high and issued a Sioux war cry, then tossed it into the bushes. When this deed was discovered and reported, all evidence would point to the deceased Blazing Star.

He lifted Miranda in his arms and headed for his horse. He had previously decided where to conceal her until this matter was settled. Once her family and people were all dead, she would turn to him for love and protection; she would be grateful for his rescue and solace.

At the council meeting, another drama was unfolding. Several Oglala scouts had arrived with dismaying news; bands of soldiers were converging on the area from three directions. Crazy Horse retained his self-control and concealed his infuriating suspicions as he ordered the chiefs to disperse quickly and furtively; he told them soldiers were scouting the area and the parlay must be cancelled. He said he would send word when the next meeting would take place. He scolded himself for having been fooled by this white foe.

Reis failed to perceive the danger he now faced. When the others were gone, Crazy Horse and his small band of warriors lingered to capture the white dog who had arranged this trap. Crazy Horse turned to Blazing Star and ordered him to seize Reis and Amanda, to bind them and bring them to their camp for questioning and punishment.

Reis was grabbed by several warriors and bound securely. Initially he was alarmed and bewildered by their actions, since he could not understand the Sioux tongue. The two small pistols in his suspender holster beneath his jacket were taken; then the Barns .50 boot pistol with its lengthy butt and barrel was yanked from its concealed position.

Amanda screamed in fright as she was bound and handled roughly. Sun Cloud inwardly doubted their guilt and asked to take control of his treacherous granddaughter until this affair was clarified. Reis wished he had brought Miranda along to translate for him. When he appealed for mercy and gentleness for his wife, Blazing Star glared at him coldly and declared that she would be executed along with him!

The situation was extremely perilous. Reis was worried about Amanda, who had fainted in shock. He tried to convince the Indian chiefs that he had not betrayed them, that he knew nothing of the cavalry's plans. He protested against their harsh treatment, arguing that he would not have brought his beloved wife along if this was a trap, reminding them of her Indian heritage. Reis beseeched Sun Cloud to take their side, to protect Amanda; but the old man hung his head in renewed shame and refused. As a last resort, Reis entreated them to wait until they discovered the truth before harming his wife. Clearly, they did not believe him.

Blazing Star took control of the female prisoner, wondering if his beloved Tamaha knew of their treachery and had been unable to warn them. Either way, the Oglalas would never accept her into their village and hearts after this betrayal. As surely as *Wi* arose each morning, these two would die for their evil. But as they rode for camp with Reis and Amanda as prisoners, Blazing Star prayed that Miranda was not involved and prayed that she would not risk showing her face in his camp to defend her family. She had encouraged this situation; she had brought the white dog to camp. She would be slain on sight!

By the time they reached camp, Blazing Star's anger and anguish had been mastered. He was skeptical of Reis's guilt. Obviously the white man felt no fear for himself, no fear of death or torture; his only concern was for the safety and survival of his wife. The white man would not intentionally have endangered his woman's life. The warrior noted lines of anger in the white man's face, anger which indicated he was being falsely accused and bitterly resented it. The look in Reis's dark blue eyes shouted he had trusted the Indians rashly, that he was disappointed by their treachery.

Amanda was held captive in Sun Cloud's teepee. She cried and trembled in fear of her beloved's fate. What did she care about her own death if she lost her love? How could they be so cruel to people trying to help them? She glared at her grandfather and Blazing Star. She had seen her husband bound to a thick post in the center of camp. The signal had been given for the leaders to meet in council to decide their fates. Poor Miranda had been so mistaken about these barbarians!

Before the two men could leave her secured to the center pole, she scoffed at Sun Cloud, "No wonder my mother ran away from you and this vile life! You're cruel and evil! I'll never understand why she longed to visit you! I wish I had never laid eyes on you. You're not my grandfather; Gray Eagle's son and Morning Star's father could not be a savage coward!"

To Blazing Star, she sneered, "I'm glad my sister didn't come along with us. How could she love an animal like you? She'll hate you both and never come here again. I pray she never learns her cherished grandfather and her beloved killed her sister. I despise you both! If you harm Reis, you'd best kill me too."

Then she murmured sadly, "You two really fooled her, didn't you?" Tears eased down her pale cheeks as she whispered in disbelief, "You're killing the only man who can help you stop this war. He's telling the truth. I don't know how the soldiers learned of the meeting, but it wasn't from me or Reis. At least try to uncover the truth!" she panted angrily.

Blazing Star related her words to Sun Cloud, then disclosed his own misgivings about this situation. Sun Cloud spoke to the younger warrior, then left for council. Blazing Star knelt before Amanda and told her, "Your grandfather is saddened by your cruel words and hatred. He says to tell you he will speak for mercy. He does not believe you and your mate betrayed us. He believes you because, Sky Eyes, you are the sister of Rising Moon and the daughter of Morning Star."

She exhibited utter shock at her grandfather's understanding. "And what do you think, Blazing Star? What vote will you cast in council?" she asked.

Shiny jet eyes fused with misty blue ones. "I will vote for your release," he stated simply, evading a full explanation.

In a quavering voice, she pressed, "My release? Or mine and Reis's freedom? If you slay him, I don't wish to live. He is my life."

"I will vote to free you and your mate," he responded warily.

"Why?" Amanda questioned incredulously. "Because of my sister? Do you believe we're innocent?" Suddenly she was no longer afraid.

"I vote with my head, not my heart, Sky Eyes. You said I have fooled Tamaha. I have not. I have told her she cannot be my woman. I have told her we cannot love each other. I have told her to stay where she is safe and happy. She cannot live here. These things I have told her. When you go free, you must also tell her. Do not allow her to dream of what cannot be. Our people are enemies, and we battle to the death. She must not be forced to choose between her bloods, for she must be white or Indian. Do you understand, Sky Eyes?"

"Yes, Blazing Star. You love her enough to spare her from death. I will do as you ask, if I am freed. You are a very generous and unselfish man. I'm sorry you can't share a life with her."

The look of yearning in his eyes exposed his feelings. As he turned to go, Amanda added, "She loves you very much, Blazing Star. Now, I understand why. If —if the council doesn't vote to free us, will you . . . go to her and tell her . . . what happened? If you don't, she will come to you for answers and comfort. If they kill us, they will kill her too. The truth will be softer coming from your lips."

He did not turn. He simply inhaled loudly and responded, "Yes. But if you do not go free, she will hate Blazing Star and Sun Cloud. She will blame us for your deaths. I cannot go against the council vote."

"Blazing Star!" she called out to him as he ducked to exit. "I have a plan! Wait!" When he came back to her, she entreated, "Will you go to our cabin and speak with my sister and cousin? Perhaps they can tell you what really happened today!"

"If Crazy Horse agrees, I will go seek the truth," he replied. "I will tell Reis you are safe and unafraid," he added, then smiled.

She smiled in response and thanked him. Their fates were probably in Blazing Star's kind, strong hands. Surely he would help free them. But what if he failed? No, she could not think that way!

When Bloody Arrow returned to camp, no one suspected his thwarted plot, or comprehended the true reason for his fury over the near massacre. Fortunately for him, but tragically for others, he had been assigned to scout the only direction from which soldiers did not arrive. He had sat alone, dreaming of fame, while he presumed the attack was taking place. When he went to view his victory, he found the same thing Custer had: nothing! Not a trace!

When Custer checked with the Indian agencies, all chiefs were present and no hints of trouble were sighted or reported. Custer had no choice but to accept this mission as a wild goose chase, somebody's mistake or clever ruse. He planned to question Brody the moment he returned to camp. He wished now that he had not sent Lucas Reardon back to the fort under guard. Even if that writer had gotten away from his two men, he could not have warned the Indians in time for so many to vanish completely. Perhaps he should interrogate both Reis Harrison and Lucas Reardon, and perhaps the two women with them. Or perhaps that arrogant scout was playing games with him; that was where the information had originated! He would have his answers by tonight, and someone's head! He ordered the regiment back to Fort Sully.

Not expecting Custer to return so early, Tom Fletcher pretended to have found Sheen's bloody body and brought it to the commanding officer just before Custer's stormy arrival. Tom had just identified the arrow and charged Blazing Star with the crime when Custer swaggered into the room. When Tom was asked to repeat his tale about the council meeting once more, he lied again, claiming he had overheard several warriors who had been talking around a campfire. No matter how Custer debated or challenged his words, Tom stuck to his false claims.

Tom was furious when Custer placed him under arrest. He knew he had to find some way to escape, for he was holding the unconscious Miranda prisoner in a place no one could find. If he did not return in a few days, she would die! Yet if he had to, he would sacrifice her life rather than expose his guilt by revealing her location. He was taken to the blockhouse and imprisoned.

Custer headed for the cabin. Lucas was pacing anxiously, awaiting word of Miranda and the others. Custer could not deny the man's shock at the news of Brody's death and Miranda's abduction. Custer related the events of the day, which further stunned Lucas. He told Custer he did not know anything about such a meeting. He asked Custer to send out a search party for Reis, Amanda, and Miranda, for Lucas knew something was terribly wrong.

"You have no idea where they are?" Custer demanded sternly.

"Reis and Amanda went for a picnic; they're just married, you know. The last time I saw Miranda, she was waiting for your Major Sheen to take her riding and picnicking. What's going on here? That scout said Sheen was murdered and scalped, and Miranda is missing. Here it is nearly dark, and Reis and Mandy haven't come home. I'm worried, sir. Something awful is going on out there. You've got to do something; you've got to locate them. Is that scout trustworthy?"

"Frankly, I doubt it, but he's sticking to his story. I'm beginning to think there wasn't any parlay. But you're right about one thing; there's a stench in the air I don't like. If any of them return home tonight, you wake me at any hour. If not, we'll take us a look around tomorrow. A man should know his enemies, Reardon; I do. Blazing Star doesn't take full scalp, only a small lock. That was his arrow in Sheen's back, but not his handiwork. When you come over in the morning, bring Harrison's papers with you. They could give us a clue."

Lucas did not fall into his baited trap. He suggested slyly, "Why don't you take them tonight and study them? If there's a clue in them to help find my cousins and Reis, you can have 'em now. I'll fetch 'em." He went into the bedroom and retrieved the false set of papers, then handed them to Custer. "Just make sure you return them undamaged."

To the west of the Missouri River, there was a small and narrow cave which had been dug into the side of a hill by miners as a hiding place from the Indians. At one time, large boulders had been used to conceal the entrance. Later, they were left aside and trees were propped before the opening to hide it, being replaced as they wilted. It was in this cave that Miranda regained consciousness.

When Miranda stirred, her entire body ached. Any movement sent pains washing over her. Her head throbbed and her mouth was cottony dry, but she endured the anguish to sit up and look around her.

She was groggy and disoriented but managed to lean against the damp surface at her back. She appeared to be inside a dirt chamber, the oblong entrance to which was sealed by a barrier of crisscrossed ropes. She stood on rubbery legs and struggled with the unusual fence which refused to yield. The confining door was covered with numerous branches, no doubt to prevent anyone from locating her. She pressed her sensitive face against the ropes to discover why they refused to give way. Obviously they were secured around heavy rocks, and all covered by leafy branches. The square openings were too small to allow escape, even for someone as slender as herself. Trying to unsnag the ropes, she yanked until she had rope burns on her palms. She finally ceased the futile waste of energy. Without a knife, the ropes were as strong as iron. Someone had used plenty of skill and time with this confining doorway!

She returned to her former place and collapsed to the makeshift pallet of two blankets over supple branches. Nearby, she discovered a canteen of fresh water and a leather pouch with dried beef strips and cornpones. Inside a square cloth, she found wild berries. She sipped the water but did not eat. There was no knife inside the pouch or any other weapon for defense, but she had expected none.

As she leaned weakly against the moist wall, she surveyed her sepulchral surroundings once more. The cave was seven feet from back wall to sealed entrance; from side to side, it was almost three feet; and from floor to ceiling the walls were between eight and ten feet high. Due to the recent rains, it was musky and damp but oddly clean.

Around five in the afternoon, there was still light inside the dirt prison. She stared longingly at an opening far above her, frustratingly beyond her reach. She tried to suppress the visions of snakes and crawly things that assailed her. Normally such creatures did not frighten her, but she was vulnerable here. She shuddered as she prayed her captor would free her before darkness, or at least come to guard her.

Her captor . . . Why was Tom doing this to her? She had had no idea he was so obsessed with her. He and Bloody Arrow made such an implausible pair of villains. Had they spoken truthfully? Could everyone she loved be dead or imprisoned right now? If not, were they searching for her? How long would Tom keep her here? How long before she had any news about her family and her love?

She had underestimated the hatred and evil in her Indian cousin. Would he get away with this satanic deed? Until Tom killed him? Until he killed Tom? Even if the Indians were warned in time to prevent or respond to Custer's attack, they would hold Reis and Amanda responsible. What if an awesome battle was raging somewhere this very moment? What if Tom and Bloody Arrow were slain? No one would find her; she would die here in this cave alone. What if her love thought she had betrayed him? No, he would never think such evil of her!

All she could do was wait and pray. If they were all dead, she would make no attempt to dupe Tom. If they were only captured, she would do anything to gain her freedom to help them, even kill him. She lay down on the blanket and wept at her helplessness.

In the Oglala camp, a fierce debate was in progress. Bloody Arrow demanded the torture and deaths of Reis and Amanda as strongly as Blazing Star and Sun Cloud demanded a chance to prove their innocence. Bloody Arrow listed the crimes of all whites during his verbal condemnation. When Sun Cloud used

Amanda's heritage as a favorable point, Bloody Arrow disputed it by saying there was no proof that either woman was the daughter of Morning Star. And even if it were true, they would have learned treachery from their mother, who had brought shame and sadness to her family and people.

As the meeting went on, it became clear to all that Bloody Arrow despised his female cousins and wanted them dead. Yet no one could deny the accuracy of many of his arguments. Bloody Arrow asserted that only Reis or Miranda could have betrayed them to the soldiers. How else could the bluecoats have known exactly where to attack? The cavalry had not merely been out scouting; it had been sighted heading straight for the location of the council meeting!

When Blazing Star suggested Reis would not have knowingly brought his wife into danger, Bloody Arrow contended that the two white-eyes had assumed they would be safe because of Amanda's claim to be the granddaughter of Sun Cloud. He declared that Amanda probably had been ordered to sneak away during the talks but had not been given the chance before her capture.

When Bloody Arrow feared his vengeful arguments were failing, he sneered, "Sun Cloud's eyes are blinded by love for the child of his child. The eyes of Blazing Star are clouded by lust for the white girl's sister who came here as Tamaha. I tell them to think and vote with the head, not loin or heart."

Blazing Star stiffened and glared at the insolent warrior. "I do not deny I have love and desire for Tamaha, but it would not prevent me from voting against this white man and woman if I believed them guilty. I do not. Let me go to the wooden teepee of Tamaha and speak with her. Let me see who lies and who speaks truth. A man can die on any sun or moon, but he should die in guilt, not innocence."

"How can we trust Blazing Star to return with the truth he finds? I will go," Bloody Arrow announced. "I claim the right to prove the guilt or innocence of my family. Tamaha and her sister are of Sun Cloud's bloodline, as I am. It is my right."

"Do you think us fools, Bloody Arrow?" Sun Cloud shrieked in unnatural anger and agitation. "Your hatred of Tamaha shines as brightly as Wi. I feel shame that you are of my blood. I choose Blazing Star to seek the truth. Who challenges me? Who votes for the child of my blood to be slain and for the death of her mate?"

The ceremonial lodge was deathly silent after Bloody Arrow stated coldly, "I do. I will prove the three white-eyes are guilty."

Crazy Horse's unfathomable gaze went from one man to the next. In a resolute tone, he stated, "We will take the vote. All warriors will accept it or leave our camp and tribe. Do you wish them to go free? Do you say they are innocent? Do we seek the truth?"

In each man's hand were two painted sticks, one black and one white. The pure white was an affirmative vote; the deathly black was negative. As it came to each man's turn, he tossed in the stick which revealed his vote. Blazing Star and Sun Cloud could not watch as the pile grew larger . . .

Chapter Twenty-Two

The Oglala Sioux warrior keenly observed the cabin near the edge of the bluecoat settlement. Soon, the fates of many would be sealed; soon, he would be free of the past. There was no sign of the half-blooded scout or Tamaha, but there was one dark-haired witness who knew the truth! The warrior waited impatiently until all signs of movement ceased. Then, he daringly headed for the cabin to see what the white cousin knew . . .

In the Oglala camp, Amanda nestled as closely as possible to the powerful frame of her husband, whose chest and feet were bare. After the council meeting, Reis had been cut free and imprisoned in Sun Cloud's teepee with his wife. Though this could be their last night together, there was no way they could have a loving farewell, for the hands and ankles of both were bound securely to prevent escape. All they could do was snuggle close to each other and share intoxicating kisses.

Suddenly Reis rolled to his back and lifted his bent knees. He wiggled and struggled, grunting and breathing heavily with his exertions. Amanda watched silently, as it was obvious what he was trying to do. At last, he was successful and knelt before her with extended arms beckoning her into his confining embrace. She worked her way to her knees and slid between those muscular bands of warm flesh. He smiled radiantly at her, lowering his bound arms to encircle her in them.

He sealed his mouth over hers, and as his fingers interlocked with hers behind her back, they savored this contact of bodies and spirits. Reis guided her carefully to the buffalo mat. They lay on their sides, kissing and nuzzling each other.

He murmured earnestly and tenderly, "I love you, Mandy, and I would give everything I own to have you one last time."

She leaned her tawny head away from his hard, smooth shoulders, and smiling at him, she replied, "So would I, Reis. I love you so much. Don't blame yourself for this. I'd rather be here with you, even if it's to die together. I couldn't live without you."

Reis's dark blue eyes sparkled with moisture, and he cleared his lumpy throat to speak. "I could never watch you die, my love. If we must end this way, I pray they show mercy with you but take me first. You see, I'm a selfish coward after all."

A gaze as soft and light as baby blue cotton fused with his. "I wish I could slip my arms around you, but I doubt I'm that limber," she teased, both attempting to lighten the dismal mood and ease the anguish of the other.

"One day, I'll teach you," he promised with a playful grin.

"I hope so," she responded, forcing a cheerful smile. "Reis, do you think he will tell the truth when he returns? What will he do with Randy? What if he captures her and brings her back to die with us?"

"He was ordered to seek the truth, Mandy. Warriors are famous for their obedience and honor," he reminded her.

"But are honor and honesty the same in this affair?" she deliberated worriedly, rubbing her lips over his furry chest. "What if the truth doesn't suit his purposes? How do you suppose Custer found out about the meeting?" she inquired gravely.

"I wish I knew, love. Even if Randy dropped a clue with Sheen today, the timing would be wrong. Custer knew last night or early this morning. But who told him, and why? There's something else, love," he hinted ominously, dreading to mention it.

"What?" she asked, sensing his alarm and reluctance.

"Why didn't Sheen ride out with the others? Blazing Star said the man who rode at Custer's side was missing today," Reis revealed.

"I don't follow your insinuation," she murmured. "Maybe he was left in charge of the fort or other men."

"If Custer knows you and I are involved in this parlay, I wonder what he's done with Randy and Luke. On a patrol this important, something urgent kept Brody at the camp. By now, Custer knows we're missing, but does he suspect why? I'd bet my scalp he's reading those false reports right this minute," he surmised astutely.

"If they arrested Luke and Randy, they wouldn't harm them without proof, would they?" she fretted at this distressing news. "And they couldn't possibly have any firm evidence against any of us. Besides, you're working for the President. He'll protect us, if we get out of this."

In the vanishing light, Reis observed the unfamiliar shadows in her eyes. He questioned them. Tears began to ease down into her tawny curls. "Randy and I have always been close, Reis. There's some kind of mystical bond between us. She's in terrible danger. I sense such a chill and blackness. It's like she's . . ." Amanda shuddered violently, unable to say, in a grave.

Tom Fletcher angrily paced the dirt floor of his cell. He had demanded his release; he had demanded to go scouting for the facts to exonerate him. He had demanded to be shown any evidence against him. None of his demands had a favorable effect on Custer. It was past midnight, and he was still imprisoned. But he had left food and water with Miranda and she was not severely injured. There was no danger of her dying within two or three days. Surely he would be free by then. Besides Miranda, only Bloody Arrow knew the truth about their daring plot; and neither would ever reveal it. Tom intended to slay the antagonistic Indian as soon as he was free. Then he would take Miranda to another place and begin a new life. At least he had earned one reward from this devastated plot! No one would locate her, for the cave was in an area no one ever visited.

Tom exhaled in vexation as he leaned the back of his head against the window bars. He could not even trick a sentry into giving him freedom, for Custer had not placed one at the stone brig. It seemed Custer had felt no Indian would dare sneak into this settlement with him in command, certainly not to free a half-breed scout!

In the flicker of an eye, a bronze hand closed over Tom's mouth and forced his head backward. A sharp blade slid smoothly and swiftly across his neck. As if to make certain the scout was dead, the intruder forcefully drove the shiny weapon directly into the scout's heart, then twisted it viciously. Before releasing the body to let it sink into the dust of the cell, Bloody Arrow wiped his knife clean upon his victim's clothes and hair. He grinned satanically as he tossed a red and black feather into the brig, then sneaked away. There was one other person to silence tonight . . .

In the cabin not far away, Lucas was pacing frantically, unable to sleep. When he responded to the light tapping at the door, he was astonished to find a warrior standing there. The man introduced himself as Blazing Star and asked to enter and speak with him. Assuming the warrior had either news of or a message from Amanda and Reis, Lucas stepped aside and motioned for him to enter. Lucas hurriedly locked the door and turned to speak with the Indian who had once saved his life, whose face now exhibited a pattern of color designs, as if he were painted for war . . .

Far away, Miranda pushed herself to her feet, her buttocks aching from her last attempt to reach the hole at the top of the cave. It looked just large enough for her to wiggle through to the outside. But her first attempt had failed, sending her crashing to the hard ground, straining one wrist and bruising her bottom.

Her hands and arms were scratched, and her dress was muddy. But she did not curse the mud, for it made the surface she was trying to overcome sticky, sticky enough to aid her treacherous climb. She caught her breath and sipped more water. Tears rolled down her grimy face, for her escape might come too late for those she loved.

She had recalled two occasions at the plantation when a similar situation had existed. Once, a worker had fallen into an abandoned well whose wooden covering had rotted and given way. Another time, a worker had fallen into a well containing several feet of water. Both times, the men had not used ropes or help to climb out; they had eased up the sides by pressing their backs to one side and their feet on the other. Inch by inch, they had wiggled to the top and climbed out. She had heard both tales. But could she do the same?

Concluding she would have more agility and control if her feet were bare, she removed her stiff boots and cast them aside. She had previously removed her petticoats; now, she twisted her skirt hem and tucked it into her bloomers to free her legs. She pressed her back to one wall and lifted one foot against the opposite side then cautiously placed the other foot just below the first one. Seesawing her shoulder blades, she flattened her palms to the semi-hard surface near her buttocks. She warned herself not to rush her movements this time.

She worked upward a short distance, then rested. She held her body stiff, bracing herself between the two surfaces. As she neared the top, she feared she would not succeed this time either. Her injured wrist was throbbing as much as her head. Her thigh and calf muscles were cramping; her knees and ankles were quivering. If she fell from this height, she could be hurt badly. She had to make it! She had to get out before Tom returned, or before he never returned.

Her feet were growing numb from the damp chill and lack of circulation. Miranda was positive her shoulders were getting raw. Her hands were bleeding from tiny cuts and broken nails. She knew she was weakening. She wanted to sob hysterically from exhaustion, pain, and fear. She fiercely overcame that rash urge.

The chestnut haired beauty prayed for one final burst of energy as she prepared to seize the edges of the hole above her. As she gripped them, she cautioned herself not to become careless. She struggled frantically to pull her upper torso into the night air. Her vision began to blur precariously, and her arms trembled ominously. She was so close to victory. But if she passed out now, she could drop back into the entombing chamber. Sobbing, she pushed and shoved desperately to free herself. Gradually everything went black as Miranda went limp . . .

Near Fort Sully in a quiet cabin filled with rising tension, Lucas questioned the warrior with penetrating eyes. "Where are Mandy and Reis? What happened out there? Why haven't they come home? Why the hell did you kill Major Sheen and kidnap Randy this afternoon? Where'd you take her, and why didn't you bring her back tonight?"

"You ask many questions; your words make no sense," Blazing Star ventured curiously. "Why do you ask if I killed the bluecoat and took this Randy captive?" His ebony eyes glanced around for his love. He was bewildered when she did not appear. "Where is Tamaha, Miranda?"

"Miranda is called Randy by her family. What have you done with her? Why'd you kill Major Sheen?" Lucas demanded tersely.

"I have not seen Tamaha since she came to our camp with the man called Reis. Why do you say I captured her? I have not slain the white-eyes called Sheen. What do your words say?" he probed, an uneasy feeling assailing his keen senses.

"Where are Reis and Amanda?" Lucas insisted.

"They are in our camp. They are safe. Tell me what happened this sun," Blazing Star pressed. "How did Yellowhair learn of the parlay? Where is Tamaha?"

The two men compared tales and facts until a curious picture formed, one which puzzled and alarmed them. Lucas vowed his cousins and Reis were innocent. He related all he knew, and the more they talked, the darker the mystery became.

Lucas muttered fearfully, "If you didn't kill Sheen and abduct Randy, then who did? And why? Where is she now? They said it was your arrow, one with a black-and-red-tipped feather." Lucas then told the warrior why Custer doubted Blazing Star had killed Brody.

"Yellowhair has the mind of a fox and the eyes of an eagle, for he sees the truth in my enemy's cunning. We must return to my camp. I must get warriors to help search for Tamaha. I do not like the cold winds which blow over my heart. I must seek the face of my enemy, one who dares to steal my woman, one who slays a foe in my name. I will protect you with my life if you return with me and speak to the council. There is great evil playing in our lands. We must stop it."

Lucas and Blazing Star headed for the Oglala camp just before the first streaks of dawn tickled the horizon with pink and gray fingers. At that same moment, Bloody Arrow was scouring the countryside, seeking the place where Tom had concealed Miranda . . .

*   *   *

Dazed and injured, the bloody and dirty Miranda urged herself to keep walking on her sore, bare feet. Often, she staggered and fell to the ground, but stopped only briefly before forcing her body to move forward again. She had no idea where she was, so she followed the angle of the sun, knowing the Oglala camp was in the southwest. But that was from the fort, and that was if she was not already beyond the camp.

She was so thirsty and groggy, yet she had to go on. Time was of the essence, if it was not too late. She tried to control her tears and sobs, for they pained her throat and chest. She was so tired and her body hurt all over. Soon, she was so exhausted that she dreamily wondered if this mental and physical anguish was worth it. When she knew she could walk no further, she sank to her knees and cursed cruel fate with her fleeting consciousness.

Three Oglala warriors hovered over the pitiful body lying on the grass. One nudged the other and asked, "She is Tamaha?"

The second warrior knelt, pushing her tangled hair from her injured face for a closer inspection. "*Sha,*" he replied uneasily.

The three warriors who had been scouting the area for signs of Custer's return discussed this problem. They wondered how she had gotten here, who had injured her so badly, and what they should do with her. Her family was being held captive, but these warriors were friends of Blazing Star's; they knew of his love and desire for this half-white girl. What if the council voted for her death? Should they try to warn their friend? Should they conceal her until his return? That was wrong, and she was hurt. It was decided to return to camp with her.

When Miranda was taken to Sun Cloud's teepee, Amanda screamed in disbelief. "My God, Reis, what have they done to her?"

Both Reis and Amanda battled for freedom to help Miranda. Sun Cloud ordered one of the warriors to fetch the medicine man. Crazy Horse entered the teepee and ordered Miranda taken to the medicine lodge. Her strange wounds would have to be treated before she could be questioned. There was a disturbing mystery here. Had the whites tried to beat the truth of the parlay from Tamaha? Somehow, the war chief doubted she would talk even under torture. It was no secret to him that Blazing Star and Tamaha were in love. Had she escaped too late to warn the Sioux?

The warriors and Sun Cloud departed with the limp Miranda. Crazy Horse glanced at the terrified and worried Amanda. He stated clearly, "We have not harmed your sister. She was found injured by the warriors. We will care for her wounds. Then we will have answers."

Shortly, Blazing Star and Lucas entered the teepee. Reis shouted at them, "They have Miranda! I don't know what they've done to her, but she's hurt badly. Help her, Blazing Star," Reis pleaded urgently.

When Lucas tried to go with him, Blazing Star ordered him to remain here where he was safe. He promised to send news after he saw her. The moment he left, Lucas seized a knife to cut Reis and Amanda free. Before he could do so, two of the warriors returned to guard them, but they did not bind Lucas or free Reis and Amanda.

When Blazing Star raced into the medicine lodge, he discovered Crazy Horse and the others staring at Miranda oddly. As his dark eyes moved over her face and body, pain and fury attacked him. He dropped to his knees and pulled her into his arms. He held her gently and protectively. "Who did this?" he asked in icy contempt, his temper and control unleashed. "There will be no vote for her life. I will take her and leave. No one will slay her. I will battle any man who steps into my path to stop me. She is my heart."

Blazing Star lowered her carefully, aware of her numerous injuries. Suddenly he realized some were bandaged. "Why do you treat the wounds you have inflicted? She is as innocent as her sister and the white man."

Crazy Horse locked his gaze on Miranda's face, recalling the look in her eyes when she had awakened briefly and told her incredible tale. Crazy Horse temporarily ignored Blazing Star to ask Sun Cloud, "Do you think she spoke the truth? Is her mind trapped by dreams or pain?"

The old man sighed wearily. "She did not lie. But I feel shame at his great evil, for I did not see it with these old eyes and weak heart. How could he hurt my little Tamaha? How could he wish us dead?"

"What words do you speak?" Blazing Star demanded angrily.

"Tamaha said Bloody Arrow betrayed us to the scout who betrayed us to Yellowhair," the chief informed him then repeated Miranda's shocking story of treachery.

Blazing Star revealed all he had learned from Lucas. They realized Bloody Arrow had not been present that awesome afternoon. They also knew he had left camp right after Blazing Star rode away.

"Where is Bloody Arrow now?" Sun Cloud wondered aloud, his old heart suffering with this dishonor and distress. "Did he do such injury to her? May *Wakantanka* forgive me for allowing such evil in my teepee."

Sitting Bull, the medicine chief of great power and wisdom, said, "She is weak, Blazing Star. She used all of her fighting spirit to come here. She is very brave. I will try to save her. But she is in the hands of the Great Spirit; He will decide her fate."

Shivers ran over the warrior's bronze frame. "Are you saying Tamaha . . . could die?" His heart thudded painfully when Sitting Bull nodded, his steely gaze exposing his sympathy and respect for the girl.

"She is only tired from her journey and her wounds," Blazing Star protested in panic.

"She has many injuries, Blazing Star. Beneath her garments, there is a blackness here," he explained, touching her left rib area. "Her back bleeds and flames red. She has many bad wounds, my son. We do not know how long she has been without food or water. Look at her feet," he instructed. "Look at her hands. It is as if she dug herself from a grave. The scout did this to her. Bloody Arrow wished to sell her and Sky Eyes to the Apaches, but the scout wanted her for himself. We will prepare for Bloody Arrow's return."

Crazy Horse and Sitting Bull exchanged meaningful looks. The younger chief told Blazing Star to free the prisoners and bring them to Tamaha's side. When Reis, Amanda, and Lucas were shown into the large teepee, Reis spoke first. He told Sun Cloud and Blazing Star that Miranda must be taken back to Fort Sully where the doctor knew how to treat such injuries and had powerful medicines to use.

It was noon before Blazing Star and Sun Cloud convinced Crazy Horse that the whites must leave. If they did not leave, Miranda could die, and Custer would surely start a search for them. They decided to use the story that Tom had captured Reis and Amanda when they happened upon him abducting Miranda. Lucas came searching for them early this morning, but they had been rescued by friendly Indians. They would say Miranda had been injured defending herself after Brody was murdered and increased her injuries while trying to escape the vicious scout. They would blame everything on Fletcher.

It was settled. A travois was constructed to carry Miranda to the fort. Lucas, Reis, and Amanda were given horses. A band of warriors would follow them to the fort, to make certain they arrived safely. But the warriors would also make certain they were not seen escorting the white party home.

When all was prepared, Blazing Star knelt by the travois to say farewell to his love. Soon, Reis and Lucas would leave this land and take both women home to safety before Reis delivered words to the white leader. This would be the last time his hungry eyes fed upon his Tamaha. She had come so close to death, was still challenging it; he could not allow her to remain where it lived each sun and moon. Death and danger could not be averted, for Yellowhair had been ordered to control this region and the Sioux at all costs.

Amanda came to Blazing Star's side. "I'll make sure she gets well. Is there anything you want me to tell her when she awakes?"

Blazing Star did not care who was watching or what they said or thought. He leaned over and lightly kissed Miranda's lips, then her forehead. "There is nothing to say, Sky Eyes. Our lives must take separate paths. You must never let her return to our camp. Take her far away from this death and evil. She must forget Blazing Star and the Oglalas."

"She will never forget you, no matter how much distance there is between you. I'm sorry, Blazing Star," she murmured sadly, her meaning understood. "She will never love another as she loves you."

"You are kind, Sky Eyes. For as long as I breathe the air of the Great Spirit, she will live in my heart and mind," he vowed.

Reis helped Amanda to mount, then clasped wrists with Blazing Star and Sun Cloud. Reis looked at Crazy Horse and stated, "I will tell Chief Grant what I have learned and seen here. Try to avoid as much bloodshed as you can; that will please him. No matter what happens, Crazy Horse, I will do my best to bring peace to your lands."

Crazy Horse gave the sign of peace and friendship to Reis. But his words were, "It is too late for such dreams. You leave in friendship, but do not come again. I do not wish your blood to stain our lands. You have warmed the heart of our old chief Sun Cloud. It was good you came to us before his death. Go in peace," he dismissed them.

When the dust settled and the small group was gone, Crazy Horse looked at the courageous warrior at his side. "I am sorry you cannot take Tamaha as your mate. You have chosen the right path, Blazing Star, but walking it will be hard for a long time. You will ride as my chosen band leader, at my side. Come, we must decide the fate of Bloody Arrow; he was captured by Gall's band."

Blazing Star's gaze chilled. He declared, "Let me battle him, Crazy Horse; it is my right."

"*Ki-ci-e-conape?*" Crazy Horse inquired knowingly.

"Yes, I will fight him to the death in challenge."

"Bloody Arrow is a skilled warrior, Blazing Star. He is strong and cunning. He battles for his life, with the power of evil behind him. If I allow the challenge, the winner goes free," the chief argued.

"He must die at my hand. If he slays me, then evil is greater than good, then evil is more powerful than the Great Spirit. If such is true, we are all fools to worship Him. He will guide my hand in battle, or I will die as the fool I have been since birth."

"So be it," Crazy Horse agreed. "But if he goes free, Blazing Star, I will be the next fool to challenge him."

As they walked toward the teepee where Bloody Arrow was being held captive, Crazy Horse said, "We must move our camp closer to the sacred hills. Soon the bluecoat with yellow hair rides there. We must go and prepare to stop him. We must defend our sacred grounds. Do you wish to send a message telling her of our new location?"

Blazing Star caught his hint. Shaking his ebony head of hair, he replied sadly, "It is best if she does not know where to find me."

"What if she returns to this place when she is healed?" Crazy Horse speculated.

"She will find nothing. She will not know where to seek us, and she will go home. This is best," Blazing Star remarked dejectedly.

Crazy Horse watched him from the corner of his eye and wondered, Best for whom?

Chapter Twenty-Three

When the small group arrived at the rented cabin, Lucas went to fetch the doctor while Miranda was taken inside by Reis and her sister. She had not regained consciousness. Unaware the sleep had been induced by Sitting Bull's healing herbs, Amanda was terribly worried. They placed her on the bed and waited for Doctor Starns to come.

Amanda assisted the doctor with her sister's examination and treatment. Colonel Custer arrived to question Reis about their curious adventure. Reis gave him the colorful story which had been agreed upon by all concerned. Reis was surprised, but not shocked, to hear of Tom Fletcher's gory murder. He shrewdly guessed it was the foul deed of Bloody Arrow to cover his guilt. But naturally Reis could not reveal his accurate conclusion.

Custer insisted on seeing Miranda and speaking to her sister. When pressed for answers, Amanda corroborated her husband's story. Then Lucas was briefly interrogated. Custer could not be sure they were telling the truth, but they certainly told the same wild tale.

While he awaited his final orders to ride into the Black Hills for an extensive survey, Custer directed his troops to break camp and head for Fort Lincoln. It was said that Custer often raced off to visit with his wife just before a new mission was undertaken, and this new mission would prove to be his ultimate challenge.

The countryside was curiously peaceful. Custer was far away with his regiment, the Oglalas had moved secretly toward the Black Hills, their sacred *Paha Sapa*; Reis was completing his final reports; Amanda was enjoying the serenity of her love, and the new life growing within her.

Lucas wrote several articles and sent them back East. He also slaved over two manuscripts, one he had planned before coming here and one which had been inspired by recent experiences and lessons learned.

Miranda was nearly healed after two weeks of enforced rest and treatment. Only occasionally did a fading bruise or sensitive area remind her of her ordeal. But the more her body healed, the sicker her heart became, until she was in a fever to return to her love.

Miranda argued and cajoled to no avail. Reis and Lucas refused to take her back to the camp, and Amanda protested the idea fervently, relating Blazing Star's parting words to her. When Miranda reached the point of rebellion, Reis told her the Oglalas had moved west, far from this hazardous area.

"He's gone?" she shrieked. "No! He wouldn't leave without telling me good-by!" She desperately refuted the tormenting words. "He wouldn't leave until he was sure I was all right."

Reis calmly and patiently went over the circumstances and events of these past weeks. Amanda told her sister what Blazing Star had said that last day about the impossibility of a shared life. "I swear he's gone, Randy. I'm sorry," Reis said and Amanda concurred.

"Then I'll find him!" Miranda declared stubbornly.

"Do you realize how large this territory is? Do you realize what dangers await you out there?" Lucas reasoned. "I know."

Miranda fled in tears to the bedroom. Amanda looked at Reis, tears in her eyes. Reis shook his head, indicating there was nothing they could do to comfort or help her sister. This was one problem Miranda would have to solve for herself.

A telegram came for Lucas that week from a noted Boston publisher who wanted to meet with him and discuss his articles and the two works in progress. Lucas packed and was gone that same day, promising to contact them with any news, vowing he would become either an illustrious novelist or famed historian.

Another week passed. Reis told Miranda they should begin packing for the trip home to Alexandria. He then told her that after he filed his reports with President Grant, he and Amanda would be traveling to Texas to decide where they wanted to settle and build their home. He said they would sell the shipping firm and townhouse unless she wanted either or both. Miranda told them she did not want anything except Blazing Star.

Even the news of Amanda's pregnancy failed to lighten Miranda's gloomy spirits. What was there for her in Virginia? Or anywhere? She did not want to work. She did not want to amuse herself frivolously. She certainly could not marry. Her heart was here with this land and the love who had deserted her.

Still another week passed. Miranda finally agreed she would leave with Reis and Amanda if she could see Blazing Star and be certain he did not want her. "If he says he doesn't love me, whether it's true or not, I will return to the plantation. You and Reis can have everything else."

Miranda left the cabin for some fresh air and serious thought. She could not force Blazing Star to love her. She could not deny the perils here. But there had been just as much danger back in Virginia, in so-called civilization. She could not intrude on Amanda's and Reis's lives. But no matter what decision Blazing Star might make, she would hear it face to face!

When Miranda returned to the cabin, the sight which greeted her was so totally astonishing that she fainted in shock. When she recovered, she found herself face to face with her parents! After an abundance of joyful embraces, Joe and Marie told the incredible tale of how they had been found and rescued by Reis's search party.

Amanda and Miranda stared at Reis Harrison. He explained how he had learned of their attempted abduction on the sloop and the disappearance of the "bodies" after the shipwreck in the South Seas. He revealed a conversation he had overheard in which Weber worried over the sinking of the vessel which had been taking them to the Far East where they were to be sold as slaves. Weber had ranted at McVane that he had not wanted to kill them mercifully but had wanted them to be tormented as slaves. Knowing how much they loved their daughters, Weber had known they would endure more anguish alive than dead.

McVane had declared that no survivors had been found, and he gave Weber the location of the sinking. On the chance Joe and Marie had survived and made it to an island, Reis had hired men to search the entire area. Joe and Marie had been located and returned to Alexandria where they learned of the recent events concerning Weber Richardson, Amanda's marriage, and these two trips west. They immediately followed their daughters, hoping to find them in order to deliver their joyous news in person.

The five talked for hours, exchanging tales. Every so often, the girls would jump up to hug their parents. It was a happy occasion despite the problems and dangers all had faced. But Marie Morning Star Lawrence was particularly intrigued by the dramas involving them and her people. Again and again, she insisted on hearing them.

Marie tried to envision the warrior whom she had not seen since he was four, the man who caused a mixture of joy and sadness in her daughter's eyes. There had been so many changes since she had left her father's teepee to marry Joseph Lawrence. She was pained by the deaths of her mother, brother, and so many relatives during the 1854 massacre. She asked Miranda countless questions.

Miranda's heart fluttered wildly when Marie asked Joe if she could see her father and her people before their return home. Marie cast her dark eyes upon her daughter's face and smiled. "There are those Randy and I must bid farewell one last time."

Miranda went to her mother and hugged her, for perhaps only Marie could truly understand her inner conflict. There were no words to express her love and appreciation. Marie looked down into the face which so closely resembled her own and teased, "You do wish to go with me? Since my father has smiled upon you, perhaps it will lessen his anger and bitterness toward me. He will be shocked to hear I am alive."

For everyone's protection, Reis suggested that he go to the new camp and bring Sun Cloud and Blazing Star to the old one to visit with them, if the two warriors agreed. Miranda glared at Reis when she realized her brother-in-law had known their location all along. He confessed contritely that he had promised not to reveal it to anyone, including and especially her.

Marie witnessed the devastating effect of Reis's enlightening words and unexpected admission on her chestnut-haired daughter. The tawny gaze which focused on Reis was filled with accusation, anger, sadness, and disbelief. Miranda hurriedly excused herself before she could verbally or physically attack her brother-in-law. When she left, Marie demanded to know the extent of the relationship and the problems existing between the warrior and her child. When Amanda and Reis completed their stories, she knew how Miranda must be suffering.

"Perhaps I shouldn't have suggested she go along to see him. I did not think of the impossibility of the situation." Marie looked at her husband, who smiled at her with love and tenderness. "We know her suffering and confusion, don't we, my love?" she whispered.

Joe nodded, recalling that complicated and arduous path too clearly. "This is different, Marie. You must understand that. War is costly and bloody. We can't allow her to remain here."

"I know," Marie concurred sadly. "It won't be easy for her. Perhaps we should return home in the morning," she generously suggested, her tone exposing her turmoil.

"It wouldn't help her if you sacrificed your desire to see your father," Joe answered. "Should we let her go with us? Won't it hurt too much to see him? You think he'll return to see her?" He addressed this last question to Reis.

"I honestly don't know, sir. He is in love with her. But he loves her too much, too unselfishly. He would lose her rather than risk her life," Reis confided to them. "He wants her to leave as much as he wants her to stay. He could be afraid to see her, afraid of weakening in his decision."

"I can understand the pain of that dilemma," Marie stated softly. "I will speak with her. Perhaps I can persuade her not to go."

The mother-daughter talk failed to deter Miranda from making the journey. How could Marie convince Miranda a mixed marriage would not work when she and Joe were living proof that it could? But times had changed; antagonism had increased. Life was precarious here. But love did not see such obstacles. That night, the women shared the bedroom and more conversation, while Reis and Joe bunked in the living area.

Two weeks later, four people rode from the cabin to the campsite deserted by the Oglalas after the death of Bloody Arrow. Marie and Reis had insisted the pregnant Amanda remain behind at the cabin in safety and comfort. Reis had contacted Sun Cloud and set up this crucial and emotional meeting. When they arrived at the assigned location, there were four men waiting for them. Three braves were sitting around a campfire as protection for the elderly ex-chief, and Sun Cloud was sitting alone not far away. When Marie dismounted, she hesitated only moments before racing toward her father. After embracing affectionately and filling the quiet air with joyful laughter, they sat down upon buffalo hides to talk. Sometime later Reis, Joe, and Miranda joined the reunited father and daughter. After Miranda had had a chance to speak with her grandfather, she insisted on taking a walk alone. Knowing their daughter needed privacy to master her warring emotions, Marie and Joe did not try to stop her. Obviously, Blazing Star had not come; his painful decision was evident to all.

When Reis tried to comfort Miranda, she pulled away from him. "You're the last person who should try to console me. You lied to me, Reis; you used me and betrayed my trust and friendship. It wasn't your right to withhold the truth from me. My destiny isn't in your hands. You can't make my decisions or control my life. I'll never forgive you for duping me. I need time alone, away from traitors. Please don't follow me. I'll return before Mama's ready to leave."

"Please listen to me, Randy," he entreated earnestly. "I promised Blazing Star I would hold silent. What kind of man would I be if I betrayed a promise? I had no right to interfere either way."

"Aren't you forgetting how I assisted your romance and conquest of my sister? When you pleaded for my help and interference, I didn't hold silent or keep my promise to her. You know why, Reis? Because I knew you two loved and needed each other. I doubt you two would be happily wed right now if I had retained my *honorable silence*," she sneered sarcastically. "After all I've done to help you with my people and my sister, you damn well owed me your help! Whether you agree or not, you have interfered in my destiny! You're selfish and insensitive."

When Reis made no attempt to justify his behavior, Miranda fled into the forest to the stream and followed its winding bank until she was assured of privacy. She halted, staring into the swirling water just below a small cascade. He was not coming. Did he even know or care if she was alive; she had left this camp injured and unconscious. He had not checked on her. He had not sent word to her. He had simply ridden out of her life as if she meant little or nothing to him.

Anguish assailed her. Tears silently rolled down her cheeks. She removed the *wanapin* and stared at it. "What a stupid, blind fool you are, Miranda Lawrence. Blazing Star never loved me. He never cared about me. I could have died by now for all he knew or cared. It was all lies to trick me to his mat. How he must laugh at me now. Why did he have to be so cruel? Why did he want to hurt me and punish me? How he must hate me to do this to me. Oh, God, it hurts so much," she cried out, flinging the necklace into the stream.

"Damn you, you traitor! You could have the decency and courage to tell me the truth! You never loved me! You were only using me. You didn't even care enough to say good-by," she sneered sarcastically. "Why, Blazing Star? Why must you punish me for loving you? You owe me the truth. *Damn you, you owe me the truth!*"

She sank to her knees and cried. When the tender word "Tamaha" was spoken, she did not know it was real. Her heart was aching; her world seemed to be ending. "Why did you betray me? I can't live without you," she sobbed raggedly into her palms.

Two strong hands imprisoned her head and lifted it, and ebony eyes gazed into her tormented expression. "Do not weep, Tamaha. Your words are untrue. I told you it could not be between us. Why do you come here to torment us this way? Return home with your family."

"You've been hiding?" she asked angrily as the stunning reality settled into her warring mind. He had come to protect Sun Cloud, but he was not going to tell her good-by! Did she mean nothing to him?

"I thought it best if we did not see each other again. You must go, Tamaha. I did not lie. I told you it was impossible," he stated sadly.

"You did lie! Your lips said no, but your eyes said yes. Your words said it could not be, but your heart shouted yes each time we touched! I thought you loved me, but I was a fool. I don't need your pity! Go back to your wars and hatred! Make love to your pride and *coups!* Just leave me alone. You were right—is that what you want to hear? Will it soothe your conscience? End all guilt? I did chase you like a she-dog; isn't that what you called me? I pursued you because I loved you. Because I thought you loved me too. What a fool I am not to have realized what you've been telling me all along; you don't love me or want me. The least you can do, great warrior, is tell the truth. You owe me an explanation. Say it, Blazing Star! Tell me you don't love me and free me from these golden dreams which you helped create."

Her anguish pierced his soul like sharp lances. How could he end it without pain? "I did not mean to hurt you, Tamaha. I tried to speak in truth to you. I said our life-circles could not join," he reminded her gently.

"But you did hurt me. Was I supposed to believe your words when your loving touch proved them false? How could I have been so wrong about you, Blazing Star? I promised I would go, but for once, tell me the truth. Is it difficult to say you don't love me?"

"I cannot, Tamaha. It would be a lie," he informed her bluntly. "You promised to go, but you have not. Why did you come again? Must you cut my heart with the knifing words of farewell?"

"I don't understand your game, Blazing Star. If you loved me, you would not treat me this way. Love isn't selfish or cruel. If you loved me, nothing and no one could keep us apart." She stood up and turned to leave. "If I could not have your love, why did you tempt me with it each time we met? If you loved me, how could you take all I had to give, then force me to leave with nothing left? If you wished to protect my life, then why have you destroyed it? How can you be the center of my life-circle, then claim it is not . . ."

She could not finish. She just started walking slowly along the stream bank. Finally she stopped and sat down, propping her chin on a large rock. "No, Blazing Star, you are wrong. Love is not cruel. Love does not punish or destroy. Love isn't sad or painful. Love doesn't betray or desert. Not when it's shared. Not when it's real. No, my deceitful warrior, you do not love me. But I love you with all my being."

"Have you learned nothing here? Do you refuse to see the hatred and dangers around you, refuse to see why we must part? You wish the truth, Tamaha? Then I will tell you, and it will hurt. But it will change nothing. I will make you leave," he declared stubbornly.

He sat down beside her, fusing his gaze to hers. "You are white, Miranda; I am Oglala. I am Indian," he began.

"I am half Oglala, half Indian," she corrected him, noticing which name he was calling her. But something in his tone and expression compelled her to listen, to delve deeper into his meaning.

"You were born white and raised white. You cannot change," he replied. "Even so, it is too late to become Indian. We are at war."

"I am not your enemy, Blazing Star, nor any Indian's. Must I be viewed as one because my father is white?" she implored him. "Must you punish me for what I cannot change? Must you reject me?"

"If you become more Indian than white, you are your own worst enemy, Miranda." He observed her increasing confusion. He tried to explain. "White and Indian are at war, a war for the destruction of one side. You are half of each. What happens when one side fiercely battles the other? Or your heart wars against your mind? To become Oglala, you must become all Indian in thought and action. Ask Morning Star about such a life between two separate people. Ask Morning Star of the pain of such a choice," he challenged gravely. "Ask how her Indian blood felt when she learned her brother and mother were slain by her husband's kind? Ask how she felt knowing whites were slain in retaliation? Ask how she feels when she knows she can never return here, for she has chosen the white world. If you chose my world and love, you could never return to your father's kind. If your white friends come to slay us, I will battle them. How can you endure this?"

"The war must end someday, Blazing Star," she asserted.

"It will not, Tamaha. It will not until all Indians are wiped out or conquered. The whites and bluecoats will not allow it," he refuted.

"But Reis will help, Blazing Star," she argued hopefully.

"What is one drop of rain upon such a roaring fire?" He caressed her cheek as he entreated, "What of your white friends and family? What of their deaths at Indian hands during this endless war? What of losing all you have and have ever known to become Oglala? To choose me and the Oglalas, you must do such things, for we have vowed to battle to the death against the white man's evil and greed. You speak of knowing such troubles; you speak of understanding such a choice. But you do not, Tamaha. When you realize what you have done, what you have lost, it will be too late. You have not seen torture and slaughter. You have not witnessed the draining of pride and strength. We are weary of the fighting and killing, but they give us no choice. They will not accept peace without defeat and dishonor. They demand the surrender of our land, our freedom, our dignity, our spirit, our way of life! Is any peace or survival worth such a price, Tamaha?"

Miranda gazed into midnight eyes which shone with frustration and anger. "Can either side win?" she asked dejectedly. "No, so why must the fighting continue?"

"The whites started this war, Tamaha. They invaded our lands. They spit upon us and curse us. They take and destroy. They attack peaceful villages under a flag of truce, under the colors of the Great White Father. They kill all Indians, even women and children. They call us savages, animals. But they force us to fight this way. They make us live and battle as the wild creatures of these lands. And the soldiers keep coming. The more we slay, the more the White Chief sends. But we have no warriors to take the place of those murdered, for the white-eyes kill the young braves and children who would follow in our tracks. The White Chief sends more weapons, but we are harassed and have no time to make new weapons or trade for them. They burn villages and supplies during the winter when such things cannot be replaced, and many of our people freeze and starve. And you ask me to bring you into such a life-circle?" he scoffed bitterly.

Blazing Star's voice trembled with emotion. "They speak of their honor; they do not understand the word. When your grandfather goes to join the Great Spirit, I will be last in the line of Gray Eagle. Look at me, Tamaha. I was a great warrior; now I must flee like a coward to save my life so that I may fight another sun for a peace which will never be born. They offer truces and the fighting halts for a few moons. But the whites always find another reason to take more land and lives."

He sat down with his back against the rock. He murmured tenderly. "It is wrong for me to ask you to make such a choice, such a sacrifice. It is wrong and selfish to keep you here in danger. It is wrong to make such a decision more painful by showing you my love and need for you. You only see me and our love, Tamaha.

You refuse to see beyond that. If I allow you to fall into such a powerful trap, you will suffer greatly. I cannot permit it. You must return to your family and forget the Oglalas. You must forget me. You must not be caught between two warring peoples. This is why it cannot be between us. I cannot endanger your life to have you at my side. I love you too much to watch you suffer or die. Do not ask such of me."

"It's too late, Blazing Star. I'm in love with you. Since the first time we met, you've stayed in my heart day and night. I've wanted and needed you more than anything in my life. There's nothing you can say or do to change those feelings. I don't care about the dangers. I can adapt to your way of life. I will live as an Indian. Please don't ask me to leave you," she pleaded urgently.

"I must. If you refuse, I will force you to go," he vowed.

"You seek to run from the truth, Blazing Star, and cowardice is not within you. Must two hearts bleed from such unnecessary wounds? Why must our hearts and lives be divided? Everyone must die sometime. Isn't it better to do so together? Don't you see it's the will of the Great Spirit for us to share a life-circle? Surely that's why He guided my feet back to the lands of my true people, to the warrior who now rules my heart. With all my being, I love and desire only you among all men of any race. What good is safety if we're both unhappy? I cannot say good-by. And I will depart only if you do not love me and want me. Say it, and I will leave with my family," she dared him desperately.

Blazing Star was fighting his most difficult adversary—himself. Could he risk her life by keeping her? Could he bind her to the cruel lifestyle of the vanishing Sioux? Could she become Indian and side against her father's people when that awesome time arrived, as he knew it would? If he but weakened his stand for a moment, she would remain.

As he wavered, Miranda moved closer to him on her knees, placing her hand on his chest over his heart, detecting its fierce drumming. Tears silently flowed down her cheeks as she challenged, "Say I am unworthy of your love and touch. Say you do not love me or desire me. Say you wish another woman to share your life, your mat, your pain, your happiness. Say you wish another woman to bear your children. Say you can forget me and what we share. Say you would feel no pain in your heart if you lost me forever. Say the war between our peoples has greater power and meaning than our love. Say these things, Blazing Star, and I will walk away this moment. Even if you lie, say them, and I will go. I swear it."

Blazing Star could not think clearly with her so near. He jumped to his feet and put some distance between them. His arm extended, he placed one hand upon a tree and propped himself wearily against it. He gazed into the forest, unseeing. His next words would seal their futures. Could he lie?

Miranda came to stand behind him. She watched and waited, her fears and anxieties mounting. His motives were unselfish but so misguided. He was so proud, so stubborn, so caring. If he said no, could she keep her promise?

His voice seemed distant when he spoke. "The white man's greed, hatred, and weapons are stronger than love, Miranda. Their numbers and powers sprout and grow stronger each moon; with each sun they spread as wild grass over our lands. Ours wither and die beneath their evil and force. I cannot deny your words. But my love cannot protect you from such powerful evil. If I selfishly claim your love, I risk finding your innocent blood upon my hands. You know my rank, Tamaha. Many soldiers are eager for my scalp and life. What will happen if I am slain and you are left alone in our teepee? What will happen if you bear our child, and he is slaughtered by your whites?"

"Then come away where we can live in peace, Blazing Star. Come and speak with our leader; make him see and hear the wrongs our people endure. Reis will help you. If not, we can buy land here, near our people and sacred grounds. I have money. I have a paper of protection from the White Chief. You say the Sioux are not farmers. We can ranch; we can raise horses or cattle or sheep. Or we can pay men to do it for us. You can hunt and fish on your lands, lands which cannot be taken from us. We can have a home and children. We can find peace and happiness. You say the war is futile, a lost cause. Must you die to prove some point which will be forgotten before your blood soaks into the ground? Isn't there pride and honor in the wisdom of change? To begin a new life when the old one is destroyed doesn't show weakness or dishonor, Blazing Star. Amanda has married a white man and weakened the bloodline of Gray Eagle. Only in us can the Great Spirit renew its power. Surely that is why I am here?"

Miranda moved between his stalwart body and the sturdy tree, clasping his chiseled jawline between her hands. "If you were right, Blazing Star, the Great Spirit would not trouble your heart and head this way. Open your senses to understand his wishes. He wants you to live; He wants the line of Gray Eagle to be reborn. Come away with me, my love; come away until we can return here in peace. You said Reis was only one man, a tiny drop of water. So are you, my love. Will your prowess win this war? Will your death change anything? Soon there could be no one to chant your *coups*. I need you—more than your people. The line of Gray Eagle must continue."

"You ask a warrior to flee as a coward to save his life, to exchange honor for love? You ask a warrior to desert his people when they are at war? You ask a warrior to deny all he is and has learned? You ask a warrior to live and die in a white teepee, in white clothes, living as a white? You ask a warrior to deny his heritage, his duty, his honor?" he inquired sadly.

"I did not say to flee as a coward, but to walk away proudly and wisely. Your people have warred since the sun was born. If you wait until there is no battle to fight, it will be too late. I want you to protect your heritage, to record it, to make certain it survives this monstrous devastation. Who will be left to lead those who aren't slain? Who will there be to remind them of their customs and history? I'm not asking you to pretend you're white. If I wanted a white man, I would not be standing here imploring you. I am willing to challenge any danger for us. Is it so hard for you to do the same? Isn't a compromise the answer? We can have it all, Blazing Star, if you will reach out and take it with me."

"You should not have come, Tamaha. You make it harder for me to see my duty and to follow it. You try to blind me with love, as you are blinded. Is it not enough to know I love you, to know the truth?"

Miranda dropped her hands to her sides. It was no use to debate with him, to plead or to reason. She clenched her teeth to control the trembling of her chin and lips as her golden brown eyes filled with tears. His thoughts and feelings were so ingrained that she could not alter them. Her line of vision was directed at his defiant heart, for she could not meet his gaze and do what must be done.

"No, Blazing Star, it is not enough for me. If words are enough for you, then your love is small and unworthy of return. But I will accept your words of rejection and go as I promised. May the Great Spirit protect you in battle. Perhaps you will find another who can share your life this way. I will always love you and remember you. Always," she murmured, then slipped under his arm to leave.

"Will you not kiss me and say farewell?" he asked, needing to hold her one last time. He knew she was telling the truth, that she would leave because he was demanding it. But he wanted her and needed her. Could he let her go? Could he pay the price to keep her?

"I cannot. The pain in me is too great now. You have cut out my heart and spirit, and I can take no more agony. I would rather be tortured than touch you for a last time. If a farewell is spoken between us, it must come from you. I will never say such cruel words," she whispered faintly without looking back at him.

"Tamaha, I love—"

He tried to speak his heart one last time, but she sharply injected, "Say no more! It is over, as you demand."

Miranda turned and fled. Blazing Star's attention was drawn to Reis when he said, "You are a fool, Blazing Star. There are some things more precious than dying heroically in battle. I thought I'd find you lurking around somewhere. Why did you do that to her? Why didn't you show some mercy and tell her lies? Why didn't you say you only felt lust for her? Why didn't you tell her you don't love her? No, you had to play the long-suffering, unselfish hero. Honor—you call what you did just now honor? You're selfish and vindictive. You can't have her, so you made sure she'd never want another man. You wanted her to believe no man alive could compare to you, could match you, could love her so much he would spare her suffering and death!"

"Why do you spy on us? Why do you speak such words?" the warrior snarled angrily at the white man with fiery blue eyes.

"I came to fetch her to leave. Do you hear me, Blazing Star? We are leaving this area at first light, and she will be out of your life forever." Reis realized it was time he gave Randy the help she deserved.

"You do not understand. I cannot have her," Blazing Star argued, then gave Reis all his reasons.

When he finished, Reis explained about the Civil War, his own battle for honor. He told how his family had been killed. He revealed that he and Amanda had been on different sides, enemies. He compared the two conflicts, the two love affairs. Reis told him how he and Amanda had overcome their differences, because of love. "My wife was a daughter of the warring winds, Blazing Star. But that war ended. Many on both sides are still enemies; many say the battle will begin anew someday. But we cannot live for future battles. Life is short and hard. We must take what love and happiness we find, for both are rare and precious. Your life will accomplish far more than your death. Your blood should run in your children, not on the dry earth. Miranda will never be happy again, for she will never be free of your hold."

Observing the warrior's turmoil and anguish, Reis was relieved that he had not met Amanda during the war. He could not imagine how their lives and love would be different if that Southern belle had first looked upon him as a Yankee officer.

Reis clasped Blazing Star's wrist and murmured what Miranda had taught him. *"Wookiye wocin, koda."*

Blazing Star glanced at the white man who had called him friend and wished for peace between them. He said the same, then watched Reis vanish. He slowly and helplessly walked to the edge of the forest to observe their departure. He watched the two women embrace Sun Cloud affectionately, bidding him a last farewell. He watched the two men speak their last words to the old chief. He watched the four mount. He watched Sun Cloud exchange smiles and waves with his child and granddaughter. He witnessed the look which passed between Joe and Marie, a look which spoke of powerful love and total acceptance.

Miranda did not glance toward the forest; she sat alert and poised in her saddle. But Reis and Marie watched the intrepid warrior who was observing them. The white friend waved and turned, but the Indian princess stared for a moment. Then Marie looked at her rigid and somber daughter, so full of pride and resolve, so full of anguish and disappointment. Marie's gaze returned to the warrior, so rigid and somber, so full of pride and resolve, so full of anguish and disappointment. She shook her head sadly and joined her retreating family. Love and acceptance had to come freely, and they had to be felt by both. She could not interfere.

As the love story of Morning Star and Joseph Lawrence echoed in his keen mind, Sun Cloud caught the younger warrior's eye. The days of greatness were past for his people. He had spoken with his granddaughter, the mate of Sky Eyes, the mate of Morning Star, and his own daughter. The old man knew of the raging battle with Blazing Star, one he now understood. Sky Eye's mate was right; such a noble warrior should not die in defeat. His voice rang across the distance like sweet music as he fervently called, "If you are to catch her, Blazing Star, you must ride swiftly. Tamaha belongs here with us until the war's end sends you both to safety. My father's spirit is restless this sun, for he fears his line will die in you. There is no warrior greater than Gray Eagle, and he refused to let white blood and battles take his woman from his life. How can this love and match be wrong when Tamaha carries more Oglala and Indian blood than Princess Shalee?"

Blazing Star hurried over to Sun Cloud. "You think I should go after her? I should join with her? I should endanger her life?"

"Only you know the feelings within your heart. Each moment of life holds some unknown danger, my son. But love and happiness are found rarely. If she goes away, she will take the heart of Blazing Star with her; what good is a fierce warrior without a heart? Unless you love Tamaha more than life itself, do not go after her. But if your love is such a love, you are a fool to lose her."

Blazing Star's gaze shifted from the retreating group to Sun Cloud, time and again. His decision would be irrevocable. Finally his gaze settled on Miranda's back as it became smaller. Soon, his love and heart would be out of his reach. He raced to his horse and mounted determinedly. He galloped after her, shouting her name.

In her pensive state, Miranda heard nothing, and Marie was compelled to shake her daughter's arm to gain her attention. "He pursues his true love," she teased, pointing toward the warrior racing their way. "Go and speak with him. We will wait nearby. Whatever you decide, little one, I love you."

Miranda smiled and hugged her joyfully. She kneed her pinto and pulled on the reins to turn him around. With a radiant smile, she raced toward Blazing Star as swiftly as he was moving toward her, his splendid features lit with love.

When they met, he scooped her off her horse and sat her before him. He held her tightly in his arms. "I love you, Tamaha. Stay and be my wife, the mother of my children. When the time comes, we will ranch if peace is refused my people. You must not leave me. All you said was true. It will be hard and dangerous for many suns. But you must share those suns and moons with me. I was the one blinded by love and fear for your safety. It was meant to be between us; I cannot deny it or resist it. You are my life and breath, the beating of my heart." Their eyes met, their gazes misty and rapturous.

He had spoken in English, but she vowed her love in Sioux. *"Waste cedake. Ni-ye mitawa."*

Exuberant laughter filled the air. "Yes, my love, I am yours, as you are mine." His mouth closed over hers as they hugged each other fiercely.

Joe and Marie Lawrence watched the romantic scene, then exchanged knowing smiles. The road to happiness would be rough but the lovers would travel it happily.

Reis was consumed with relief and pleasure at the sight before him, only wishing that Amanda were beside him to witness this delightful scene. He knew that he and Amanda shared a love as powerful as that of Blazing Star and Miranda Tamaha Lawrence. He was eager to complete this last mission and more than ready to settle down with his beloved wife and their eagerly awaited child. He had not decided yet if they would live in Virginia or Texas; that was a choice to be made with his wife. Perhaps a large ranch run by brothers-in-law was an idea to ponder . . . Yes, the twins would be close to each other. And Reis could think of no better partner and friend than the proud warrior. Perhaps he would speak with Blazing Star before he left the Dakota Territory . . .

As Miranda snuggled into her lover's bronze embrace and returned his passionate kisses, Joseph Lawrence grinned and sighed tranquilly. Each of his daughters had faced warring winds from within and without. Each had discovered love and happiness with the one man who could fulfill her destiny and dreams. Watching the compelling scene before him, Joe concluded that his two daughters had chosen exceedingly well. He was proud of them and he loved them deeply.

Joe knew the conflicts between North and South, Indian and white, were far from over. But the raging winds of Fate had swirled into gentle breezes for his two daughters, and for his cherished love, his Morning Star . . .

Historical Epilogue

As many readers are eager to learn more about the lives and fates of real characters used in novels, and often such information is difficult or impossible to locate, the author of this tale will discuss the major historical characters and their roles in history following the end of this story in the autumn of 1873.

In mid 1874, Custer was sent on an exploratory expedition into the sacred

Black Hills of South Dakota. In 1875, Philip Sheridan planned and initiated the Plains campaign to finalize the white conquest and the United States Government ordered that all Indians be confined to reservations by January of 1876. Lieutenant Frederick Grant, son of the current President, became a party to the "gold craze" exploitation of the Black Hills; thus, the crucial Laramie Treaty of 1868 was broken when countless prospectors, miners, settlers, and opportunists poured into that area and defiled the sacred and burial grounds.

The Indian/White conflicts and hostilities mounted rapidly and ominously during 1875 and early 1876. In June of 1876, Custer and his regiment rode to the Little Bighorn Mountains in Montana to attack the Sioux encampment there, little suspecting the awesome force awaiting them. Custer's regiment of approximately six hundred men was rashly and fatally divided into three units—units commanded by Captain Benteen, Major Reno, and Colonel Custer. Custer did not wait for the regiments of Crook, Terry, and Gibbon to assist in what was to be his final battle. Tragically, Custer rode with only several hundred men into the waiting arms of thousands of Indians, mainly Sioux and Cheyenne. In less than one hour, Custer and his unit were slain.

This monumental battle was led by Crazy Horse and many other chiefs. Sitting Bull, Gall, Two Moons, and Hump were a few of the illustrious warriors present. After the stunning Indian victory which would be recorded in history as "Custer's Last Stand," Crazy Horse and Sitting Bull were hunted with a vengeance. These two leaders held the power to choose continual warfare or peace, but it would be peace without honor.

At that historical battle, four of Custer's relatives were slain: two brothers, one nephew, and a brother-in-law. Later, Major Reno was court-martialed, and while he was eventually exonerated for his conduct, he lived the next ten years under the stigma of betrayal and cowardice.

Crazy Horse and his Oglala band hunted and camped until the next spring when the famed warrior was compelled to surrender to the Cavalry to save the lives of his remaining people. His camp had been attacked by Col. Nelson A. Miles, but Crazy Horse and his band had escaped. Crook had then offered the warrior chief a favored reservation, among other promises. Without food and weapons and with his people dying, Crazy Horse gave himself up to the Cavalry at Fort Robinson in May of 1877. When the Army feared the warrior was going to escape and instigate new uprisings, they took it upon themselves to arrest and imprison the influential chief. During a scuffle to avoid imprisonment, Crazy Horse was bayoneted. He died in September of 1877 at age 37.

The cry had gone forth to "avenge" Custer. The Black Hills were taken from the Sioux and other Indian tribes. Any Indian survivor had to be confined to a reservation or be slain. Any leader or chief with influence was hunted down and either killed or imprisoned. Indian language, customs, religion, ceremonies, dances, dress, and burial practices were outlawed as a means of control and punishment.

After the Little Bighorn battle, Sitting Bull was harassed and pursued until he fled with his band into Canada. There they faced starvation and cold. The wily General Terry offered Sitting Bull a pardon if he would surrender to him. Knowing that Crazy Horse had been slain, and other bands were being wiped out or conquered, in 1881, Sitting Bull was compelled to surrender in order to save his remaining people from certain death in the Canadian wilds. He was held prisoner at Fort Randall, then moved frequently to guard his location. At the Standing

Rock Reservation, Sitting Bull was allowed some peace for a time. He wrote, spoke, and visited Washington and the "White Chief." His poignant letters and speeches reveal the depth of the Indian suffering.

In 1888 Wovoka began the "Ghost Dance" religion. The whites and military dreaded and respected the power and influence of medicine chiefs and skilled warriors such as Sitting Bull, and they were distressed over this new religion which united and encouraged the spirit of the warriors. Fearing Sitting Bull would escape and stir up new conflicts, he was ordered arrested. His people rebelled against this new humiliation of their chief. On December 15, 1890, a ruckus broke out over the alleged "liberation" of Tatanka Yotanka, and he was declared shot during a confrontation with Indian police.

The death of Sitting Bull convinced many of his followers to flee to the Pine Ridge Reservation near the Black Hills. Miles and Gibbon were ordered to pursue and recapture them. On December 29, 1890, the massacre of Wounded Knee took place, with the slaying of over 300 unarmed Indians of both sexes and all ages. (The second battle at Wounded Knee occurred on February 27, 1973.) Ironically, Custer's Seventh Cavalry was almost annihilated at the Little Bighorn battle; yet it was the Seventh Cavalry who was responsible for the Wounded Knee Massacre fourteen days after the death of Sitting Bull.

Other great chiefs mentioned in this story experienced similar fates. The two major chiefs who signed the Laramie Treaty in 1868 and had agencies and reservations named after them were Red Cloud (Mahpialuta) and Spotted Tail (Sinte Galeska). Red Cloud, whose son was with Crazy Horse at the Little Bighorn, is also known for his poignant speeches and letters to Washington. His remaining spirit was broken after the death of Sitting Bull and the Wounded Knee Massacre. Oglala Chief Red Cloud lived sadly and quietly until his death in 1909. Brule Sioux Chief Spotted Tail, whose sister was the mother of Crazy Horse, was most influential in peace efforts. While living on the Rosebud Reservation, he was shot and killed in 1881. Hunkpapa Sioux Chief Gall (Pizi), adopted brother of Sitting Bull, fled with Sitting Bull into Canada but returned to his old hunting grounds in 1881. Without food and weapons, he was compelled to surrender to Miles. Once one of the fiercest warriors, he became known for his peace efforts which he continued until his death in 1896.

Martha Jane Canary Burke (Calamity Jane) lived and worked in the manner described in this novel. Later she performed in Wild West shows. She died in 1903.

The soldiers included in this story were responsible for the conquest and subjugation of other tribes in addition to the powerful and noble Sioux. Crook and his troops overcame the Apache. With the aid of Miles, the famed Geronimo was captured in 1886. Miles had already defeated the prestigious Nez Perce Chief Joseph in 1877 with the assistance of Gibbon. Sherman had previously ordered the "utter extermination" of the Modocs in 1872, and had suppressed the powerful Kiowa Chief Satanta, whose prison release in 1873 sent Sherman on another rampage. Either by action or order, these soldiers were responsible for the conquest and defeat of most major Western tribes. Oddly, among these white soldiers, Crook and Custer had the most favorable images in the eyes of the Indians.

This author has made every attempt to portray the historical events and characters, Indian and white, as accurately as possible. I extend my appreciation for the assistance and Sioux translations furnished by my friend, Hiram Owen, of the Sisseton-Wahpeton Sioux Tribes.

About the Author

*J*anelle Taylor has won many awards for her writing, and has had seven *New York Times* bestsellers: *First Love, Wild Love; Savage Conquest; Stolen Ecstasy; Moondust and Madness; Kiss of the Night Wind; Whispered Kisses;* and *Follow the Wind.*

The University of Georgia's library houses a collection of her books, manuscripts, and papers. She is the author of thirty novels, with more than twenty-six million copies in print.

For a Janelle Taylor Newsletter and bookmark, please send a self-addressed, stamped envelope (long size) to Janelle Taylor; P.O. Box 211646; Martinez, GA., 30917-1646. Please print clearly.